Pamela Evans was born and brought up in Hanwell in the borough of Ealing, London. She has two grown-up sons and now lives in Wales with her husband.

Always There

Pamela Evans

headline

First published in 2002
by HEADLINE BOOK PUBLISHING

First published in paperback in 2002
by HEADLINE BOOK PUBLISHING

A HEADLINE paperback

4

ISBN 978 0 7472 6514 6

Typeset in Times by
Letterpart Limited, Reigate, Surrey

Printed and bound in Great Britain by
CPI Antony Rowe, Chippenham, Wiltshire

HEADLINE BOOK PUBLISHING
A division of Hodder Headline
338 Euston Road
LONDON NW1 3BH

www.headline.co.uk
www.hodderheadline.com

To Fred and the family, with love.

To Tom and the family, with love

Chapter One

Undesirables were no rarity on the streets of Notting Hill Gate after dark in 1954, and Daisy Rivers ran into a crowd of them one night as she walked home from the station.

A gang of Teddy boys, gathered outside a late-night café, were amusing themselves by hurling abuse across the street to a group of West Indian youths, whose wide-brimmed fedoras were visible in the neon glare of the street lighting, as characteristic of them as the DA haircuts were of the Teds. The balmy summer night was fraught with obscenities.

'Excuse me, please,' requested Daisy, a petite woman of twenty-five, unfashionably dressed in a cotton dress that was thin and faded from the wear of many summers. 'Can I get by?'

The Teds, who were blocking the pavement and some of the road, ignored her.

'Excuse me,' she repeated more assertively, 'can I get through here . . . *please*?'

Heads turned towards her but none of the gang moved; they just eyed her with a kind of lazy disdain. The Teds around here had a proprietorial attitude towards the streets, almost to the point where the other residents felt they should ask their permission to use them. It was impossible for Daisy not to feel intimidated by these lads, whose drainpipe trousers, crepe-soled shoes and drape jackets were synonymous for many people with the coshes, razors and flick knives some of them were known to carry beneath their Edwardian finery, and which gave the entire youth cult a bad name. Not every boy who belonged to this minority group was a thug – some just liked the clothes – but rebellion against authority and antisocial behaviour were common among the big gangs.

Daisy daren't allow herself to be too unnerved by these or any other dodgy characters because her evening job as a waitress at a Bayswater hotel meant she had no choice but to be out at night on her own. She needed the money to support her two little daughters.

'So, you wanna get by, do yer . . .? Well, we're not sure about that, are we, lads?' one of the youths finally responded in a slow, mocking voice. He had a heavily greased quiff and a frightening earnestness about him.

In the luminous glow from the streetlamps Daisy could see the malevolence in his eyes; could feel it emanating from him, a tangible thing. The implied violence in his manner stirred a feeling of panic within her which wasn't entirely related to this situation, and her nerves jangled even more. Desperate to get home, she tried to break through the wall of aggression by pushing past into the road, only to have a youth with protruding teeth and elongated sideburns place himself deliberately in her way. He was wearing the uniform of his kind – a long jacket, plain white shirt with a bootlace tie, a silver chain jangling on his wrist.

It had been a long day and Daisy was tired. 'Oh, for goodness' sake, can't you stop behaving like morons just for long enough to let me get by?' she snapped.

'Ooh, hark at her,' sneered someone.

'Dunno who she thinks she is,' said another.

'Look,' she began through gritted teeth, 'you lot might have nothing better to do than roam the streets making a nuisance of yourselves but I've been working and I want to get home.'

2

'Don't waste your time on 'er,' one of the others suggested. 'Let 'er pass.'

Daisy had neither the time nor the money to look glamorous, as such, but she was easy on the eye with her big tawny eyes, dainty features and luxuriant light brown hair that fell loosely around her face when it wasn't tucked into her waitress's cap. Her looks didn't go unnoticed by the Teds.

'Fancy her, do yer?' taunted his mate, sizing Daisy up.

'I wouldn't say no,' came the boastful reply. 'She's not smart or nothin'. But she's not bad-looking, and older women are more experienced.' He paused, grinning. 'If you know what I mean.'

'Get out of my way,' demanded Daisy, trying to push past.

'Don't waste your energy trying to stop 'er,' said one of the gang. 'She ain't worth botherin' with. We've more important things to do.'

'Like stirring up trouble with the boys across the street, I suppose,' blurted out the indomitable Daisy.

'So what if we are? They shouldn't be here, stealing our homes and our jobs. They ought to go back to the jungle,' was the youth's ignorant reply.

'That's just the sort of stupid comment I'd expect from a bunch of goons like you,' Daisy said bravely. But she was frighteningly aware that the Teds weren't the only promoters of racial tension around here, which was growing along with the increasing number of immigrants. The Government didn't seem to do much to ease the inevitable culture clash, and the housing shortage didn't help.

'Nigger lover,' the ignorant one accused.

'Black man's trollop,' said another.

'Don't you dare talk to me like that,' Daisy objected.

'Why are you sticking up for 'em if you're not going with 'em?' the first one wanted to know.

'Because of something you wouldn't understand,' was her answer. 'It's called decency.'

One of their number stepped forward and stood so close to her she wanted to retch from a pungent mixture of nicotine breath and Brylcreem. 'We've had enough of you. We don't want black sympathisers polluting the air near us, so sling your hook before we catch something off you,' he said to a roar of support from the rest, and they all moved back to let her through, pushing and jeering.

Angry, but realising that further argument would serve no useful purpose and probably fire them up even more on the subject, she went on her way, eventually turning into Portobello Road. This narrow, winding thoroughfare – which was flanked by terraces of small shops and drew crowds to its famous market by day – seemed dismal and sinister at this hour, the heady sounds of jazz music and drunken laughter drifting from the basement windows of a drinking club. There were still some people about, despite the late hour: men talking and shouting outside a pub, some of them staggering; a noisy crowd coming out of a grill-room restaurant; a gathering of youths leaning against a wall and wolf-whistling at some girls, who shrieked expletives in return. It was no wonder this area had a bad reputation, Daisy thought, even more so since the Christie murders at Rillington Place had given it worldwide notoriety.

Turning into a side street, she headed past bomb sites, tumbledown crescents and cavities where the bulldozers had been. Despite the much-needed slum clearance programme in the area, more slums had been created than cleared as the bomb-damaged properties deteriorated further and the housing shortage continued despite some of the slum-dwellers being rehoused in the new towns and suburbs.

This was a contrasting corner of London where occasional gentrified areas thrived alongside poor but cosy

4

neighbourhoods, the latter mostly tenanted by members of the indigenous population, where a sense of community and true neighbourliness still existed. Different again were the large, multi-tenanted houses that were filled with outsiders like Daisy, who lived there because they had nowhere else to go and the accommodation was cheap.

Benly Square came into this category. Huge terraced houses, split into bedsits and flatlets, stood around a small area of balding grassland scattered with broken milk bottles and household litter. Despite the general air of degradation, Daisy felt a warm feeling inside as she hurried up the crumbling steps of number twenty to the dilapidated front door with peeling paint and a rusty knocker.

This neighbourhood was a residential sewer and her tiny part of this house just a couple of shabby furnished rooms in the attic. But they were her home, hers and her daughters'. Rented accommodation was extremely scarce in central London, and unfurnished rooms almost nonexistent so she was grateful to have a roof over her head. Anyway, living in an area like this did have its advantages: there was a kind of freedom here because no one asked you who you were or where you came from or where your children's father was. She could hardly bear to imagine the persecution she would have had to endure in a respectable leafy suburb.

Refusing to dwell on the fact that the new landlord was making the future at the house uncertain for all of his statutory tenants lately, she put her key in the lock, heaving a sigh of relief to be indoors. She made her way up the stairs, careful not to trip on the craters in the lino.

'I'll make us some cocoa, shall I, dear?' offered Nora Dove, Daisy's friend, neighbour and baby-sitter, a middle-aged spinster who lived in the attic rooms across the landing. She was a tall, angular woman with strong arms, large hands and feet and a little round face that seemed out of proportion with the rest of her. Her poker-straight ginger hair was heavily peppered with grey and clipped to the side with kirby grips. Intelligent, vivid blue eyes beamed out from a sea of freckles, sometimes from behind the spectacles that she strung around her neck because she was always losing them.

'Yes, please,' approved Daisy, emerging from the adjoining bedroom where she'd been checking on her sleeping daughters. She and Nora usually had a companionable bedtime drink together when Daisy got home from work. It was almost a ritual.

'You look dead on your feet,' remarked the older woman, sniffing the milk bottle before pouring some of its contents into a saucepan and putting it on the gas to heat. She and Daisy were quite at home in each other's places and never stood on ceremony.

'We were busy at the hotel tonight so I do feel a bit whacked. But I shall sleep the sleep of the shattered and be fine in the morning,' she said, making light of her tiredness. 'You know me, I'm as strong as a horse.'

Nora nodded but they both knew that wasn't quite true. Daisy's strict upbringing in a Catholic orphanage had given her immense strength of character but her physical health wasn't so robust. Although she didn't make much of it, she was quite delicate and suffered dreadfully from bronchitis in the winter.

'Any problems with the girls while I was out?' Daisy enquired, taking a packet of digestive biscuits out of the cupboard and arranging some on a plate carefully. Poor living conditions hadn't robbed her of the will to maintain certain standards.

'None at all, dear. They're never any trouble to me, as you know.' Nora's beautiful diction was incongruous with her humble surroundings but natural to her, and her deep husky

6

voice somehow reflected her warm personality even though it made her sound like a chain smoker. 'They love that Enid Blyton book I got from the library to read to them.'

'I guessed they would,' smiled Daisy.

'They were really tired tonight, though,' Nora went on. 'Neither of them could keep their eyes open beyond the first few pages.'

'That'll be the effect of the warm weather and the fresh air, I expect,' Daisy suggested. 'I took them to Avondale Park this afternoon as a change from playing in the street. At least it's grass under their feet. They certainly got rid of some of their excess energy.'

'They told me all about it,' said Nora, smiling at the memory. 'They had a whale of a time.'

'I try to take them to the park as often as I can in the summer.' The tiny backyard was full of potholes and smelly dustbins so she couldn't let her children play there. 'They're happy enough playing in the street with their skipping ropes and whips and tops but I don't want them to become complete street urchins like some of the poor little devils who play barefoot out there while their mums are in the pub. Once they start school it won't matter so much because they'll be out during the day.'

'Life will be easier for you altogether when they start school,' her friend suggested.

'Yeah, it will but I'm not wishing the time onwards because I enjoy having them at home so much.'

'Enjoy it while you can, dear, they'll grow up fast enough,' nodded Nora. 'Anyway, I'll take them over the park on Sunday for a breather while you're doing your lunchtime shift at the hotel, if the weather's fine.'

Daisy's heart warmed at Nora's endless supply of kindness, all the more genuine because she refused to take payment for looking after Shirley and Belinda, who were just coming up to five and four respectively. Because Daisy couldn't bear the idea of having them minded by a stranger, she worked weekday evenings, when Nora was around to look after them, and the lunchtime shift on Sundays because Nora was at home then too.

'That'll please them,' said Daisy, as the two women settled down with their cocoa in matching ancient and torn brown leatherette armchairs by the open sash window through which a light breeze was wafting, bringing with it foul fumes from the gasworks. 'What would we do without you?'

'You'd manage,' said Nora, settling back. 'But you won't have to because I'll be here for you for as long as you need me.'

While they were talking Daisy glanced idly round the room. Even the most ardently self-deluded couldn't call it smart. But with a little ingenuity and minimum expense, Daisy had managed to create an air of cosiness, despite the landlord's ugly furnishings and the smell of damp that lingered even in summer. New curtains with a bright contemporary pattern added colour to the room and a few cheap ornaments and vases gave it a homely touch. She had even, with the previous landlord's permission, repapered the walls during the six years she'd been here, and bought a second-hand wireless set, which sat on top of the sideboard, from the market.

The kitchen corner was small and basic, with a cooker, a table and a free-standing food cupboard. The cold water sink, which she shared with Nora, was on the landing. There was a leaky, smelly communal bathroom and lavatory for all the tenants on the ground floor.

'You're so good to us,' said Daisy.

'No more than you are to me,' Nora was quick to point out. 'What sort of a life would it be if we didn't help each other?'

'You always seem to be the one doing the helping, though,'

8

observed Daisy, who was deeply indebted to this dear person, 'looking after the girls while I go out to work at night and giving me so much back-up support with them. I only wish there was more I could do for you.'

'You let me be part of your life and I don't need anything more,' Nora assured her. 'Besides, you've got the kiddies to bring up on your own, and I've only got myself to look out for. It's good for me to have someone else to think about. Anyway, I like to think I'm one of the family.'

'And you are.'

Daisy and Nora had become friends almost as soon as Daisy had moved in here. They were mutually supportive but the only practical way Daisy knew of to repay Nora, since she wouldn't take money, was to invite her to share meals with her and the girls on a regular basis and bring her a bottle of stout from the off-licence every so often.

'That means a lot to me,' said Nora.

Of a different generation, they were none the less two of a kind: both outcasts from society's norm, Daisy because she was an unmarried mother, Nora because she was a spinster. Nora, well-spoken and with such lovely manners, was an educated woman from a good family. Daisy had been told her friend's story and found it heartbreaking . . .

Having been an exceptionally bright pupil at school, Nora had gone on to train as a teacher. But while on the training course she'd fallen in love with a fellow student, a young man of a frail constitution. When she'd got pregnant, her outraged parents had banished her from the family in disgust but her lover had stood by her and promised to marry her. But the consumption that had taken so many lives back in the nineteen twenties had already got a hold on him and he'd become sick and died before the two had had a chance to marry.

The shock of his death had resulted in a miscarriage, the

strain and grief eventually culminating in a nervous break-down. Although she'd recovered, her loss of confidence was such that she didn't feel able to do anything other than menial kitchen work, which was why she now worked in a factory canteen instead of a library or a school, and lived in a shabby tenement house instead of a home of her own.

She found great pleasure in books, though. Daisy thought Nora must be one of the library's most regular borrowers, which accounted for her huge store of general knowledge. She was also an avid reader of newspapers so was always well informed about what was going on in the world. She was wise, sensitive and funny – some might say a little eccentric with her idealistic views – but Daisy admired her intelligence; it gave her such dignity.

Sadly, Nora was entirely alone in the world for there had never been a reconciliation with her family, or another man in her life. Once she'd reached an age to be labelled a spinster, men steered clear. Since Daisy had no family either, and had been motherless since she was five, they found strength and encouragement in each other. Nora was the most loving surrogate grannie her daughters could have wished for and the closest friend Daisy had ever had.

Now Daisy told Nora about the Teddy boys she had encountered on the way home.

'Young buggers. They're attention-seeking, that's all,' announced Nora. 'There was an article in the paper the other day about these Teddy boy gangs we've been seeing on the streets just lately. They're just working-class boys looking for some sort of an identity by wearing outrageous clothes and behaving badly.'

'Some of them can get quite violent, though,' declared Daisy, 'pursuing vandalism in the streets and dance halls. They smashed up a café the other week, according to the local paper.'

'Their violence is usually directed at other gangs, though, I think,' Nora pointed out in an effort to reassure Daisy. 'They might give you a lot of cheek but I don't think they'd actually harm you physically.'

'They were spoiling for a fight with the West Indian lads tonight,' Daisy told her.

'Because they're a rival group and the Teds see them as a threat,' surmised Nora. 'I don't think people like us are in any danger from them.'

'I don't either, but it doesn't feel like that when you come up against a crowd of them,' Daisy told her. 'I tried not to show it but they scared the pants off me.'

'Who wouldn't be scared?' Nora sympathised. 'Anyway, it's not nice for you to be out on the streets at that time of night on your own.'

'I don't have any choice, unless I put the girls into a nursery and go to work during the day,' Daisy reminded her. 'Working evenings suits me for the moment.'

Nora loved Daisy as her own, and her heart ached to see her struggling to raise her daughters with no contribution from their father, Nat Barker, who scrounged off her and used her. He hadn't actually deserted her when she fell pregnant but he hadn't helped her either. In Nora's opinion he was a thoroughly bad lot who didn't give a damn about Daisy or his beautiful daughters and didn't deserve her loyalty.

'Yes, I realise that, dear. So you'll just have to try not to let all this talk of Teddy boy violence in the papers frighten you on the way home. After all, we haven't yet reached a stage where a woman isn't safe to walk the streets at night, not even around here.'

Daisy cradled her cocoa mug in her hands, hesitant about her next words because she knew Nora didn't approve of the subject of her enquiry. 'Did anyone call while I was out?' she asked.

11

The other woman knew exactly who she meant but just said, 'No, dear. Nobody called.'

'Oh.' Her obvious disappointment twisted Nora's heart. 'I just thought Nat might have popped in to see the girls, if he happened to be passing. He knows I'd be at work so he wouldn't have called to see me.' She paused. 'Still, I suppose he guessed that the girls would be in bed.'

Nora believed that the main reason Nat Barker was likely to call on Daisy was to get his thieving hands on her pay packet. Either that or something of a carnal nature. It certainly wouldn't be out of genuine concern for her. Nora had been there to pick up the pieces on too many occasions to think well of him. He'd let Daisy down, broken promises and even stolen money from her purse. Her loveless childhood had made her strong and independent but it had also made her hungry for love, and she was a naturally warm and giving woman with a weak spot when it came to Nat.

'You're better off when he stays away,' she blurted out.

'Nat's all right,' defended Daisy, who had a tigerish need to stand by her man.

'He breaks your heart on a regular basis,' Nora couldn't help pointing out, though she did try not to make her feelings known too often because Daisy was so defensive of him. 'You should value yourself more than to let him go on doing it.'

'I never was attracted to gentlemanly types.' Daisy kept her tone light to avoid a serious argument. 'Anyway, he's the father of my kids, and we are sort of engaged. I know I don't have a ring but we do have an understanding.'

'If he had any sense of responsibility, you wouldn't have to go out waiting on tables at night to feed the girls because he'd be doing what he should and looking after you all,' was Nora's impulsive response.

In common with many women, marriage was the ultimate to Daisy. She didn't want a career or a good job or

12

independence, just marriage to Nat and a family life for her children. 'He'll make an honest woman of me one of these days, you'll see,' she said.

The older woman frowned. Nat had been promising to do that ever since Nora had known Daisy. 'You're worth better than him,' she burst out. 'The best thing you can do is get rid of him.'

'If only it was that simple,' sighed Daisy, and the troubled expression in her eyes pierced Nora's heart. 'You're an intelligent woman, Nora. You were in love once. You must know that we don't have a choice in these things, and you can't stop loving someone just because they don't treat you right. Maybe it's the bad boy in him that attracts me to him – women have fallen for rogues since time began. I don't know why, but I do know that I can't change the way I feel about him.'

Nora regretted having let her affection for Daisy cause her to speak from the heart. It was bad enough falling for someone like Nat. Daisy didn't need to have it rubbed in. 'I shouldn't have spoken out like that. You've enough problems. You don't need me going on at you.'

'That's all right,' said Daisy with a shrug. 'I know it's because you care about me.'

Nora nodded.

'In romantic stories the orphan girl usually claws her way out of poverty and finds herself a rich husband and lives happily ever after,' Daisy went on. 'Unfortunately, it doesn't work like that in real life. I didn't plan to get involved with someone like Nat, a ducker and diver who's never had a proper job in his life and who ignores me and the girls for weeks at a time. But I have done, and that's all there is to it.' She paused, thinking back to the time when Nat had asked her to marry him and how wonderful and romantic that had been. After he'd persuaded her to sleep with him, however,

13

he'd said the wedding would have to wait until he had enough money to give her the sort of wedding she deserved; then the delay had been because he didn't have a decent home to offer her. By the time she'd realised he was just making excuses she'd been too hopelessly besotted to end the relationship, and also pregnant with Shirley as a result of Daisy's idealistic Catholic views on contraception that she'd been later forced to revise for practical reasons after Belinda's birth. 'I have to go on believing that he'll marry me one day because I so much want us to be together.'

Lowering her eyes, Nora tightened her jaw with the effort of holding back. She'd already said too much on the subject. It was obvious to her that Nat Barker had no intention of marrying Daisy and she believed that the young woman knew that in her heart too. Nora had seen her reviled and abused because of her status as an unmarried mother; she'd even been refused help with the pain during labour when she was having the girls because she wasn't married. Nat could have spared her all that but he'd chosen not to because he was too damned selfish.

Nora's dearest wish was to see Daisy married to a decent man who would treat her with the love and respect she deserved. But what chance did a single woman with two kids and a ruined reputation have of finding someone like that?

'I can't pretend to like Nat or think he's right for you, dear,' she said kindly. 'But if he really is the one you want, I hope it works out for you, and I'll try not to go on at you about him.'

'Thanks, Nora.'

'And on a lighter note,' said Nora, hoping to defuse the tension with a swift change of subject, 'are you coming down the Porto tomorrow?'

'You bet,' replied Daisy. They always went to Portobello market together on a Saturday afternoon.

Nora had a sudden idea to remove any lingering awkwardness between them. 'How about us having a ceremonial tearing up of ration books as we won't be needing them any more after today?' she suggested.

'What a smashing idea.'

Daisy went to the sideboard drawer to get hers while Nora popped across the landing for her own. Together they ripped the ration books into little pieces and threw them in the air to celebrate the end of all rationing after fourteen years, with meat the last thing to go. As the books turned to confetti, Daisy began to laugh, filling the room with the infectious giggle that was so much a part of her. They had come to the end of a punishing era and it felt so good they both went into paroxysms of laughter at the sheer joy of it.

The streetlights shining through the attic window was sufficient for Daisy to see to get undressed without switching on the bedroom light and possibly disturbing the girls. Slipping her nightdress over her head, she looked at them in the double bed they shared, two heads close together, brown hair spread over the pillow. They were very much alike to look at and had their mother's colouring as well as her eyes. Studying them now in repose, Daisy found their innocence and childish beauty bringing tears to her eyes. Her relationship with her children was the most important and sustaining thing in her life.

Daisy had had a sister once a long time ago; the age difference between them had been about the same as it was between her own daughters. Before the orphanage, they'd shared a bed too, just like Shirley and Belinda did now. She remembered less about her sister than the indescribable pain of losing her when she'd been taken away for adoption. Daisy had cried herself to sleep every night for ages after that. She still couldn't think of it without wanting to weep.

It was as though her sister had never existed after that. Daisy had been told by the nuns that she'd gone away to a new life, and was ordered to forget her. She'd done her best because the nuns were strict disciplinarians and she'd been terrified to defy them, even in thought. Looking back at her childhood from the perspective of a parent, she could see that some of the nuns' treatment of the children had been harsh to the point of cruelty, and their methods were not what she'd use on any child of hers. But although she'd never felt loved, and had truly hated some of the nuns at the time, she'd always felt secure in their care. As an adult, considering her upbringing she'd come to the conclusion that the nuns must have believed their rigid regime to be in the children's best interests. The kids had certainly known what to expect – even if it was a good hiding.

There had been happiness of a kind at the home too, a camaraderie with the other children which meant she'd never felt alone. She'd been bereft of this security and companionship when she left there at fifteen to make her own way in the world.

At some point she must have been told that her father had abandoned her and her sister because that's what she'd grown up to believe. You learned not to ask questions when you lived in an orphanage in the nineteen thirties and forties because it wasn't considered right to give a child personal information.

She'd often wondered what sort of a life her sister was having and longed to see her again. But since Daisy had left St Clare's she'd been too busy surviving from day to day to do anything about finding her. She'd had a variety of jobs: she'd worked in a factory, been a café counterhand, and had got into hotel waitressing after the girls were born.

The very last thing she'd planned was to bring up two children outside of marriage. But having got pregnant, her

16

strict Catholic upbringing had ruled out an illegal abortion and she hadn't been able to bring herself to put her babies up for adoption, or to do what her father had done to her and her sister, just abandon them. She was very glad she hadn't been driven by desperation to take any of these steps because the girls were her *raison d'être*. Her religious faith had been a great strength and comfort to her through it all, in spite of the guilt that came with it.

Gently she covered them up, placed a kiss on each brow and got into the single bed beside them, saying a silent prayer for all the people she cared about, including one of the gentler nuns at St Clare's with whom Daisy had stayed in touch by letter.

In reflective mood as she closed her eyes, she found herself troubled again by the same uneasy feeling she'd had earlier that had been triggered off by the Teddy boys' threatening attitude. Her eyes snapped open as she tried to banish tormenting thoughts. When she was feeling calmer, she turned over on to her side and curled up into her favourite sleeping position.

She was just dozing off when she was woken with a start by a loud din from downstairs: jazz music filling the house and booming voices, shrill laughter, drunken singing. The unmistakable sound of a riotous party.

'Oh, no, not again,' she groaned, because this sort of thing was getting to be a regular occurrence since the musicians had moved into the basement. Nobody minded a party but these shindigs didn't start until decent people had gone to bed and went on until all hours. It was generally believed among the statutory tenants here that the rowdy parties were being encouraged by the landlord as part of his plot to harass and drive them out so that he could relet the rooms at higher rents.

Judging by the fact that all complaints had fallen on deaf ears, the speculation would seem to be correct. Rent restrictions meant nothing to the unscrupulous man who had recently taken over the house. He knew his tenants weren't likely to report him because they were of the disadvantaged classes who felt powerless against the likes of him and his strong-arm tactics.

Rumour had it that he wanted to emulate other landlords in the area by removing white tenants so that he could exploit West Indian immigrants by charging them per head rather than for the room with as many as six to a room. The newcomers were particularly vulnerable because many property owners refused to rent to them. Some of the tenants here believed that the landlord also wanted to relet some of the rooms to prostitutes on a daily basis.

'Mummy,' murmured Shirley sleepily, 'what's happening? What's that noise?'

'It's all right, darling,' soothed Daisy, gently brushing the child's hair from her brow with her hand. 'It's only someone having a party. Go back to sleep, love, or you'll wake Belinda.'

In the attic, the noise from below wasn't as distressing as it would be for the tenants on the lower floors, and the children usually managed to sleep through most of it, albeit restlessly. Waiting until Shirley had gone back to sleep, Daisy went across the landing and tapped on Nora's door. She could hear people downstairs shouting at the basement tenants for the noise to stop and banging on the door of the offenders.

'Just popped across to see if you're OK with all the racket going on downstairs,' she said when Nora opened the door.

'I'm all right, dear,' Nora assured her. 'It's just a question of sticking our fingers in our ears and trying to sleep through it. As we know from past experience, if we try to make them stop they'll do it all the more. The tenants who are down there objecting ought to realise that by now.'

Daisy nodded in agreement. Previous confrontations with

18

the basement tenants had resulted only in foul language and even louder music. 'I think I'd better pay our landlord a visit in the morning,' she decided. 'Something's got to be done about this. Can the girls come in with you while I'm out?'

'Course they can.' Nora looked worried. 'But you be careful. He's a nasty piece of work and can be dangerous to those who cross him, so I've heard. He isn't much of a muscleman himself but the blokes who work for him are real heavyweights.'

'Mm, I know,' said Daisy. 'But I can't just sit back and take it.'

'I'll come with you?' offered Nora.

'No. I'd rather you stayed here to look after the girls, if you don't mind.'

'Right you are, dear,' Nora agreed. 'Good luck. And mind how you go.'

'Don't worry about me,' said Daisy, moving back to her own door. 'I'll see you in the morning.'

Roland Ellwood lived in a ground-floor flat in a tenement house he owned a few minutes' walk from Benly Square. He didn't try to hide away from his tenants so Daisy didn't anticipate trouble in getting to see him. For the moment it suited him to be seen to be a caring landlord who was accessible to anyone with a problem, something she guessed would change as soon as he got rich enough to conceal himself in a mansion somewhere away from the area.

'So . . . what can I do for you?' he asked, showing her into a sitting room-cum-office where easy chairs were intermingled with a desk and a filing cabinet.

'It's about the people in the basement flat at number twenty Benly Square and the noise they make at nights with their parties,' she explained.

A small dapper man of about forty-five with heavily

19

greased grey hair worn flat to his head and thin features, Ellwood was well turned out in a suit, but flashy with a bow tie and purple waistcoat. He leaned back in his chair, smoking a cigar and looking bored with Daisy's comments.

'People are entitled to let their hair down now and again, you know,' he pointed out.

'Of course they are. And nobody minds it now and again but this is a lot more often than that,' she told him. 'It's two or three times a week and it goes on for most of the night. The tenants on the lower floors are being driven mad.' She paused, giving him a knowing look. 'But you already know that, don't you?'

'It has been mentioned to me, yes,' he confirmed, his manner studiously congenial.

'Well, I'm mentioning it again.'

'With the idea that I'll have a few words with the offenders, I assume?'

'As long as you don't tell them to carry on with the good work,' she blurted out.

His dark, deep-set eyes hardened. 'What exactly are you implying?' he asked.

'I think you know.'

'Do I?' His gaze didn't falter.

'You're trying to drive us statutory tenants out so that you can let the flats at a higher rent and make a fortune,' she informed him briskly. 'Well, you won't get away with it as far as I'm concerned because I have a proper rent agreement from the previous owner and I'm staying put. So please get the noise at nights stopped. I've got two little girls and they need their sleep.'

Ellwood puffed on his cigar and exhaled a cloud of smoke. 'I'm not trying to drive you out but neither am I forcing you to stay,' he said after some consideration. 'Maybe you'd be happier living somewhere quieter.'

'And play right into your hands?' she replied, puffing her lips out in disgust. 'Not likely.'

His manner changed completely, the urbane attitude replaced by brutal honesty. 'You'd do well to realise, you stupid woman, that all my money is tied up in the houses I own and I've every right to get as much as I can in rent. I'm the one who has to pay for all the repairs and maintenance.'

'Repairs! Maintenance!' Daisy exploded. 'When do you ever do either? You've done nothing since you bought the house. The banisters are broken, the paint's peeling and the bathroom basin started leaking soon after you took over, and you've done nothing about any of it.'

'If you're so dissatisfied I'm sure you'd be better suited living somewhere else,' he suggested again.

'Oh, no. As I've just told you, you won't get rid of me that easily,' she made it clear. 'I'm not going anywhere.'

'In that case you'll have to put up with any . . .' he paused; she waited, 'with any little inconveniences that might arise, won't you?'

She knew he was threatening her. 'I'm not going to just sit back and take it, if that's what you think,' she declared.

Ellwood gave her a contemptuous look and dropped all pretence of civility. 'You're taking up space in my house that I could fill more profitably and, yes, I do want you out,' he informed her gruffly. 'People are crying out for accommodation in this area and I don't have any petty restrictions in my properties. I'm not prejudiced like some landlords around here. You won't see a "No Blacks, No Irish, No Dogs" sign on any of my houses.'

'I should think not,' said the outraged Daisy.

'There are plenty who aren't so easy-going as I am.' He paused, fixing her with a vicious look. 'I must be broad-minded. I even let unmarried mothers in,' he said pointedly.

She should have been immune to this sort of insult but it

21

still hurt. She was suddenly painfully aware of what she had known all along: that he had all the power in this argument and she had none. But she wouldn't give in. 'You're all heart. You'll have me in tears in a minute,' she said sarcastically.

'The fact of the matter is, I want you and the rest of the statutory tenants out of my house,' he continued. 'And you'll go, I can promise you that. As you've told me, I can't throw you out because of your agreement but you'll go of your own accord, I can guarantee it. It might take a bit of time but you'll leave and be glad to.'

Put like that, it was frightening. 'This is harassment,' she retaliated. 'I've a good mind to report you.'

'Who to?' he challenged, his thin lips curling into a triumphant smile. 'The authorities won't be interested because this is private rented accommodation, not council housing. With the housing shortage in this area being so serious, I'm sure they've got better things to do with their time than bother about some moaning mother of two who got herself knocked up.' He paused for a moment, looking at her with malice. 'And not just once either, but twice, and probably doesn't even know who the father of her kids is.'

'That isn't true.' Daisy was shaking with rage now.

'There are no witnesses to this conversation so it would just be your word against mine, if you were foolish enough to go to the authorities,' Ellwood went on as though she hadn't spoken. 'And no one is going to take any notice of you. No one cares about scum like you and your kind – no-hopers who don't have two ha'pennies to rub together and no place in decent society.'

It was as much as Daisy could do to keep her hands off him but she managed to restrain herself, only because she didn't want to give him even more of an upper hand. 'You really are an evil little man,' she told him.

'If you say so,' he said indifferently. 'Though I see myself

22

more as a good businessman. So why don't you go and get the local paper and see if you can find yourself somewhere else to live because you don't have a future in any of my houses.'

'You won't force me out.'

'Just watch me.' He drew on his cigar. 'In the meantime, I'd like you to leave. I'm a very busy man.' His tone was vicious. 'So get out.'

'I'll be glad to,' she said. 'Just being in the same room as you makes me want to throw up.'

And with that she hurried from the house. For all her ostensible courage, her legs felt like jelly and the stress had made her feel sick. Nora was right: he was a dangerous man. She wouldn't be beaten by him but his threats were scary, mostly because she had the girls to think of.

Unfortunately, she couldn't afford to pay more rent than she paid now, even if she could manage to find somewhere else to live, which was doubtful. But Roland Ellwood obviously intended to make life wretched for her and the others if they stayed on. Terrorising tenants was his speciality, so she'd heard. What made it even harder to take was knowing that some of what he said was true. People like her and Nora and the other tenants just didn't have a voice against someone like him.

All she could do was deal with whatever came as best as she could and not be driven out, she told herself, as she hurried through the grimy, run-down streets. There was always the faint hope that Nat would come to the rescue by keeping his long-term promise to marry her. But it was such a remote possibility, the thought didn't linger.

Shirley and Belinda were very taken with some glass beads on a stall in the Portobello market that afternoon. Amber and emerald winked in the sunlight among strings of simulated pearls and flashy cameo brooches.

'Ten bob,' announced the female stallholder, a bottle blonde with a shelf-like bosom and a multitude of chins.

'You do mean for two necklaces, don't you?' queried Daisy meaningfully.

'Don't try and rob me,' objected the woman. 'These are quality gear, the genuine article. Ten bob each.'

'Oh, do me a favour,' bartered Daisy. 'They're too expensive at half that price.'

'Daylight robbery,' put in Nora.

'OK, two for ten bob, one each for the little girls and that's my last offer,' said the woman.

'Five bob each for junk like that?' was Daisy's sparky response. 'A shilling is the most I'd pay.'

'Four bob each,' the woman offered.

'Three,' countered Daisy.

'Now you're just taking the mick.'

The stallholder was obviously not prepared to haggle further so Daisy and the others moved on. Her daughters looked somewhat downcast but not for long because they weren't used to expensive treats. Anyway, they still had the highlight of the week to look forward to – a visit to the sweet shop where they could choose what they wanted. The narrow street was heaving with noisy humanity and fringed by stalls displaying everything from cucumbers to Chippendale chairs.

Saturday was the big day here, especially recently since the antique trade had begun to arrive and the market was expanded by a few antique and junk stalls. Daisy and co. wandered from stall to stall, seeing silver trays and meat platters, antique clocks and Victorian china. Even rusty old lamps found a buyer here.

Being out among the crowds, with good-humoured bargaining all around her, cheered Daisy up after the traumatic meeting with Roland Ellwood. Nora had been a tower of strength too. Nothing was ever quite so bad when she'd talked to her about it.

Having rummaged through the entire stock at a second-hand clothes stall, they wandered on to the food barrows where Daisy bought fresh fruit and vegetables, giving the girls an apple each to eat right away.

'Wotcha, Daisy,' said a deep male voice, a hand simultaneously clamped on her shoulder. 'I guessed I'd find you around here somewhere.'

'Nat,' said Daisy, smiling at a stockily built man in a navy-blue pinstripe suit and a garish, multicoloured tie. Every inch a spiv, he had rich dark eyes, a dazzling smile and black hair with long sideburns. He wasn't handsome as such – his features were too uneven for that – but his rough charm was magnetic. 'We haven't seen you for ages.'

'Sorry about that, love, but I've been busy,' he said, spreading his hands apologetically.

'Doing what?' she enquired lightly.

With a nonchalant shrug, he cocked his head and told her uninformatively, 'Oh, a bit o' this, a bit o' that. You know me, I've always got something on the go.'

He dealt in anything with a potential market and carried out his business anywhere he could find customers: in pubs and clubs, even from a suitcase in the street.

'Surely you could have found the time to call round to see us?' she said in a tone of mild admonition.

'Don't give me a hard time,' he said with boyish persuasion.

'Well, you could have made an effort.'

'You know I'd have been round if I'd had the time,' he went on. 'Anyway, there's no point in my coming round in the evening, is there, as you're out working?'

'You could have popped in to see the girls.'

'OK, I should have but I didn't and I'm wrong and I'm sorry,' he reeled off. 'But don't have a go at me.'

Shirley had cuddled closer to her mother, Belinda was clutching Nora's hand. They were shy of their father, who rarely took any notice of them. When he came to the flat it was usually after they were in bed. Daisy drew comfort from the fact that he hadn't deserted her when she fell pregnant like many men would in that situation. But she wished most ardently that he would take more of a fatherly role, and constantly strived to encourage some sort of a rapport between him and his daughters, for their sake.

'Hey, you two,' she said, smiling down at them reassuringly, 'aren't you going to say hello to your dad?'

''Ello,' they chorused obediently, unusually subdued.

'Wotcha, girls,' Nat said awkwardly. He wasn't at ease with children; never knew what to say to them so said the first thing that came into his mind. 'How's school?'

'We don't go to school yet,' informed Shirley, staring at him accusingly. 'We can't start until we're five.'

'Whoops. Sorry.' He grinned, unbothered by the mistake. 'Trust me to get it wrong.'

Nora made a timely intervention. 'Come on, girls,' she said kindly. 'Let's walk on to the sweet shop while your mum and dad have a chat, and you can start choosing what you want. I know how long it takes you to make up your mind sometimes.'

'I'll meet you there in about ten minutes,' said Daisy, and they trotted off holding Nora's hand, two endearing little figures in summer frocks, each with light brown hair tied with a bow of blue ribbon on the side.

'I'll see to it that she doesn't keep you waiting, Nora,' Nat called after them.

'Sweet, aren't they?' she said to him, yearning for some sign of affection for them from him.

But all he said was, 'Yeah, they're nice kids, a real credit to you, Daisy.'

26

'Thanks.'

'So, how's it going?' he asked.

'I've had better days,' she told him.

'Why, what's happened?'

'I had a run-in with the landlord this morning.' She went on to tell him more about it.

'Blimey, that's a bit rough,' said Nat, who had furnished rooms in Paddington which he never offered to share with Daisy or invited her to visit. He said the place was barely big enough for one and was far too small to accommodate visitors.

'You can say that again.'

'There's a lot of that sort of thing going on around here.'

'Of course, if we were to get married,' Daisy began in a persuasive tone, 'that would solve my problem.'

She knew she was being pushy but Nat was the sort of man who needed a shove to get him to make any sort of a commitment beyond the next half-hour. He wasn't the marrying kind but she had an unwavering belief that she was the only woman in his life and if he married anyone it would be her; she also believed that if she waited long enough it would happen.

In Daisy's opinion love wasn't about owning someone and she would never try to do that. But at the same time she had been involved with him since she was nineteen and felt she knew him well enough to exert a little gentle pressure from time to time.

'All in good time, babe,' he said predictably, putting his head to one side and tapping it. 'I've got it in mind. It's all up here.'

'Fibber,' she joshed, keeping the mood light because if she came on too strong he'd just find an excuse to leave.

'Don't be like that,' he coaxed, putting his hand on her arm. 'You know you're the only woman for me, and that I'll marry you, eventually.'

'I hope you manage it before the girls make grandparents of us,' she quipped.

'Oh, Daisy, you are a case,' he laughed.

'And you're a dead loss as a boyfriend.'

'You don't mean that.'

'I do,' she said, but there was a smile in her voice. 'I don't know what I see in you.'

'It must be my good looks.' He was teasing her.

'It certainly isn't your modesty.'

'Being humble never got anyone anywhere.'

'You might be right at that,' she agreed, becoming deadly serious as she remembered the meeting with the landlord.

Seeing the change in Daisy's expression and suspecting that things might begin to get heavy, Nat effected a swift change of subject. 'You and me ought to have a night out together soon, when you get an evening off. What do you say?'

She threw him a shrewd look. 'You wouldn't be trying to change the subject so that I won't mention the M word again, would you?' she suggested.

'As if I would . . .'

'You do it all the time.'

He made a face. 'You know how allergic I am to it.'

'Oh, Nat,' she rebuked.

'I thought you'd like a night out.'

'I would.'

'Well then, let's go out and enjoy ourselves,' he grinned. 'Plenty of time to talk marriage, later on.'

She should have been angry but suddenly it didn't matter because he gave her one of his most melting smiles and took her in his arms. All she could think of was how good it felt to be close to him; even after all this time the magic was still there. As they stood there hugging each other with the crowds milling about all around them, she remembered why she had fallen in love with him all those years ago when they'd met in a café in Paddington where she'd been working. They'd had such fun in those early days. He could be loving and tender now too, when he was in the mood.

Nora only saw Nat's worst side, the side of him that caused him to let Daisy down and refuse to give her the respectability of marriage. She didn't see the tenderness he showed to her when they were on their own, or experience the sweet intensity of feeling that filled her whenever he was near. Daisy realised that a lot of women wouldn't put up with his offhand ways. The truth was she would sooner have him this way than not at all.

When, in the next instant, he tried to cadge money from her, she despaired of him. Her common sense told her she would be better off without him. But there was no logic to her feelings and she knew with absolute certainty that she could never give him up.

Chapter Two

Later that same day June Masters was dressed in a sun top and shorts, and sprawled out in a deck chair on the top-floor balcony of the Cliff Head Hotel on the outskirts of Torquay. The view of the bay was stunning from here. Elegant white hotels sat high above thickly wooded slopes that swept down to golden sands, the entire scene washed with early evening sunlight that turned the sea turquoise. The beaches and promenade were beginning to empty as holidaymakers headed back to hotels and guesthouses for their evening meals.

Glancing at her watch, June finished her tea and hurried inside to the flat, which was cool and luxuriously appointed, as might be expected of the private accommodation of the proprietors' son and his wife.

'Ah, there you are. I was just about to give you a call,' said her husband, Alan, appearing from the bedroom, fastening a black bow tie around the neck of a starched white shirt. 'Thought you might have forgotten the time.'

'No. I was just enjoying a few extra minutes in the sunshine. It's lovely out there,' she told him, taking her teacup to the kitchen, then joining him in the bedroom. 'But I'll start getting ready to go on duty now.'

Because they worked such late hours in the hotel, they needed to rest for an hour or two in the afternoons. He usually went to bed; she just sat on the balcony if the weather was nice, or relaxed in an armchair inside if it wasn't.

'Did you get some sleep?' she enquired.

'Yeah, I managed an hour and feel all the better for it,' he replied, slipping into a black tuxedo. 'I'll be glad later on as we're in for a busy night. There's nothing worse than feeling shattered on duty. I don't know how you keep going without a nap.'

'Plenty of staying power, I suppose,' she suggested. 'I never feel tired enough to sleep during the day.'

'You should come to bed with me,' he suggested waggishly. 'You'd sleep then . . . eventually.'

'Animal,' she accused jokingly.

'I try,' he laughed.

She smiled, slipping out of her clothes and into a housecoat ready for a bath. 'So . . . you reckon we're going to have a busy night, then?'

'Very,' he nodded, brushing his hair in front of the wardrobe mirror. 'Saturday nights in high season are hectic enough anyway, but it'll be especially mad tonight as we have a couple of parties of nonresidents booked into the restaurant as well. We're stretching our numbers to the limit.'

'But we'd be worried if we weren't rushed off our feet at the height of the season,' she commented.

'Exactly,' he agreed. 'It isn't good business practice to turn people away if we can possibly accommodate them.'

Alan was front-of-house manager in his parents' hotel and also a partner in the business. June worked in reception but would turn her hand to anything. Having worked here for nine years, she'd learned to be versatile.

But now Alan turned to her, looking magnificent, his brown curly hair brushed back from a tanned countenance blessed with shandy-coloured eyes and fine-cut features. At twenty-eight he was gorgeous and she was proud to be married to him, even after seven years together.

'I'll head off downstairs then.' His voice was deep and rich, a boarding school education having eliminated any tendency towards a Devonshire accent. 'I'll see you down there when you're ready.'

'You don't need to go on duty yet,' she pointed out, purely with his interests at heart. 'You could stay up here for another half-hour at least.'

'I'd sooner go down,' was his predictable response. 'You know me, I'm never happier than when I'm in the thick of it down in the hotel.'

'I just thought you could relax for a while longer, love, as it's going to be a long night.'

'As I'm ready I might as well go.'

She shrugged. 'If it's what you want,' she said amiably.

Alan had been brought up at the hotel and, apart from a spell in the army, had worked here since he left school. He was totally absorbed in the affairs of the Cliff Head, and dedicated to his job. Although it carried some weight in theory, he was very much subject to his parents, especially when it came to decisions. They lived off-site now but were still active in the running of the hotel, albeit that they worked fewer hours than they had in their younger days. They had a variety of duties behind the scenes, and June couldn't imagine them ever letting go of the reins, especially Alan's mother.

'See you later then,' he said, kissing her lightly on the cheek and striding purposefully from the room.

June had a quick bath and got dressed in a crisp white blouse and black skirt deemed suitable by Alan's mother for the receptionist of this prestigious hotel, which was traditional and run on formal lines.

Applying her make-up at the dressing-table mirror, June saw an attractive face with fine bone structure, striking dark eyes and glossy black hair worn in a sleek shoulder-length bob, which was looked after regularly by one of the town's leading hairdressers.

She was well aware of the fact that she was extremely fortunate. At twenty-six she had more than most women could reasonably hope for: a husband she adored, a comfortable home, nice clothes and no shortage of money. People probably said she'd done very well for herself, and they would be right.

Following a miserable childhood she'd left home in a London suburb at fifteen, found cheap lodgings and worked in a factory until the war ended two years later. One day she'd spotted an advertisement in the *Evening News* which had changed her life. It was for a kitchen worker at a Torquay hotel. Attracted by the thought of living on the coast and the fact that accommodation was provided, she'd applied.

Determined to make something of herself, she'd worked hard in the kitchens here, while at the same time finding out everything she could about hotel administration so that when a vacancy for a receptionist had arisen, she'd got the job, assisted by the refined demeanour she'd had drummed into her as a child. Two years after her arrival here, when she was nineteen, she'd married the boss's son.

But now this woman of beauty and good fortune was suddenly overcome by the despair she'd been stifling all afternoon. She wept uncontrollably, rivers of mascara streaking her cheeks, make-up turning to blotches. She put her head on her hands on the dressing table and sobbed with the misery of knowing that she wasn't worthy of her husband's love.

Managing eventually to pull herself together, she washed her face and reapplied her make-up, combed her hair, straightened her clothes and left the flat, heading for the ground floor in the rattly old-fashioned lift.

To the casual observer she was a sophisticated and

composed woman in control of her life. Because she was so skilled in projecting this image, nobody would suspect the depth of her emotional problems.

'If you'd just like to sign the register, I'll have someone take your luggage up to your room for you,' June said to a couple of late arrivals, handing them the key to their room across the reception desk. 'You're on the third floor but the lift is just down the passage on the left.' She paused, smiling from one to the other. 'May I take this opportunity to welcome you to the Cliff Head Hotel. All of us here wish you a very happy . holiday and hope you'll enjoy your stay with us.'

'I'm sure we will,' said the man, glancing around. 'It seems very nice.'

'We think so,' said June truthfully.

Purpose-built as a hotel in the early part of the century, but tastefully modernised internally, the hotel was white-rendered, had balconies to all the front rooms and was set in extensive grounds. Here in the foyer, the walls were wood-panelled and a wide staircase rose to the gallery in a wealth of polished mahogany. On the ground floor there were various public rooms including a bar and restaurant that were open to nonresidents.

With expert timing, Alan appeared with the teenage boy they employed as a porter and general runaround. Alan introduced himself to the new arrivals and the boy led them to the lift, carrying their luggage.

'Are we expecting any more new arrivals tonight?' Alan enquired.

'No, they're the last,' June told him, glancing at the reservations book. 'A few are expected tomorrow but apart from them the guests for this week are all present and correct, and every room booked.'

'That's the way we like it, eh?' he smiled.

'It certainly is.'

It was turned ten o'clock and people were milling about in the foyer, some going out for after-dinner strolls, others asking at the desk for their keys so that they could turn in for the night. People tended to speak in hushed tones because this was a select hotel catering for a refined clientele. A mausoleum, June had been known to call it when she and Alan were alone. They both thought it needed an injection of new life and had discussed the possibility of making the place more child-friendly and attractive to families. They'd even talked about introducing some sort of evening entertainment such as weekly dances and cabaret nights. One of the lounges could easily be adapted to accommodate such functions.

But Alan's parents were fiercely opposed to any such changes, which they believed would lower the tone of the hotel. Apart from a period during the war, when it was requisitioned by the Government as a convalescent home for wounded soldiers, the hotel had been run on the same traditional lines for two generations. People came here for peace and tranquillity, was the Masters' argument. With characteristic hauteur they claimed that there were places like Butlins for people who needed entertainment and didn't mind dance music blaring out at all hours, or children shouting and screaming about the place.

June had no say in such matters, and it annoyed her that Alan had so little power. She wished he would be more assertive towards his parents, and told him so from time to time. But his easy-going nature and love of the hotel made him malleable.

Now a youngish man, with blond hair and blue eyes, and wearing a tuxedo, came up to the reception desk – Jack Saunders, the restaurant manager. 'Could you order a taxi, please, June?'

'Sure. Who's it for?'

'A Mr and Mrs Taylor from one of the nonresident parties.'

'Is the party breaking up already?' She was surprised. 'They looked in fine form and set to stay until we chuck them out when I passed the restaurant a little while ago.'

'The others in the party probably are,' he told her. 'But Mrs Taylor isn't feeling well so they're leaving early.'

'Oh dear,' she frowned. 'Nothing she's eaten, I hope.'

'In our restaurant, *never*,' Jack grinned. 'I suspect the answer lies in a few too many gins.'

June and Alan both chuckled. The same age as Alan, Jack was a pal of his, and June liked him too. Born and raised in London's East End, Jack had gone to Australia with his family in the post-war emigration craze. The rest of the family had settled there but Jack hadn't been happy so had come back to England after a couple of years. He'd gained hotel experience as a waiter, then head waiter in one of the big London hotels before coming to the Cliff Head three years ago.

'I'll do it right away,' said June, picking up the phone.

'Fancy a drink after work, you two?' Jack suggested. His voice was deep and husky with an attractive hint of his East End roots.

'Love to,' smiled June. They usually needed to wind down when they came off duty after a busy night or it was difficult to sleep.

'Suits me,' added Alan.

'I'll need to relax a bit after the night I'm having,' said Jack. 'What with Chef going into a mood and throwing his weight about, and a table for six being double-booked, I'll be glad when this shift is over.'

'Double-booked?' queried June in concern, putting the phone down for a moment.

'That's right,' he confirmed. 'Table number twenty. We had to set up another table sharpish since we couldn't turn the customers away as they'd made a booking, even though we were fully stretched. It's crowded in the restaurant, to say the very least.'

'Whoever took the first booking must have forgotten to write it down,' she said.

He shrugged. 'Exactly.'

A look passed between June and Jack. The culprit was probably Alan's mother, Irene, who liked to be seen front of house and sometimes covered in reception when June wasn't on duty if there was no other member of staff available. In her work behind the scenes Irene was reasonably competent, but efficiency took second place to vanity when she was out front. June's guess was that she'd been busy trying to impress someone in the foyer when the restaurant booking had come in, so had failed to enter it.

Jack was also thinking this but was far too diplomatic to say anything to Alan – partly because he was merely an employee, but also because Alan was fond of his mother, who would rather die than admit to any sort of error.

'Not guilty.' June met her husband's questioning look. 'You know me better than that.'

'It must have been one of the staff then,' tutted Alan, becoming noticeably tense. 'People really should be more careful about that sort of thing.'

'No real harm done,' intervened Jack speedily. 'We soon got the problem sorted, and if Chef can't cope with a few extra covers at short notice he doesn't deserve to be in the job.'

'True,' agreed June.

Spotting the arrival of Irene and Gerald Masters, Jack prepared to make a hasty retreat, arranging to see Alan and June in the bar after work.

Alan greeted his parents in a jovial manner. 'Can't you two keep away from the place?' He was teasing them because they weren't on duty at night, on grounds of seniority. 'Talk about gluttons for punishment.'

'We're not here to work,' explained Gerald, who was quintessentially English, in a blazer and flannels and smoking a pipe. 'We've just called in for a nightcap.'

'Looking for some company, eh?' suggested Alan. His father was the gregarious type and liked to sit in the bar of an evening, chatting to the guests.

Alan's parents had used to live in the flat that June and Alan now occupied. These days Gerald and Irene had a house within walking distance and most nights they turned up here, probably because they'd always been too wrapped up in the hotel to have much of a social life outside of it, June guessed. She got on better with Gerald than his wife, but couldn't claim to be fond of either. He wasn't openly hostile towards her but neither did he go out of his way to make her feel like one of the family. He went along with the views of his wife because it was easier, she suspected, and Irene never left June in any doubt as to how disappointed she was in her son's choice of wife.

'That's right, son,' confirmed Gerald. 'It doesn't do any harm to be sociable to the guests . . . it creates goodwill.'

'I can't argue with that,' agreed Alan.

'Is everything all right here?' enquired Irene, a short, plump woman with cold grey eyes and honey-rinsed grey hair which was tightly permed and immaculate. She was wearing a royal-blue crêpe-de-Chine cocktail dress with sequins around the neckline.

'Everything's fine,' her son assured her, 'apart from someone double-booking a table in the restaurant.'

Irene's brow furrowed. 'You ought to watch that, June,' she said, with her usual propensity to blame her daughter-in-law.

'It wasn't me,' denied June.

'You're our head receptionist,' Irene reminded her coolly.

39

'Bookings are your responsibility.'

'Not when I'm off duty.'

'You're not being fair, Mother,' Alan was swift to defend. 'If June says it wasn't her, then it wasn't. And she can't be held responsible for what other people do when she isn't on duty.'

'No, no, of course she can't,' conceded Irene quickly; she normally kept her hostility towards June out of her son's hearing and had slipped up on this occasion. 'It must have been one of the staff filling in on the desk. You need to deal with that, Alan. That sort of inefficiency is bad for business.'

'I'll look into it,' he told her.

Alan could hardly be unaware of the fact that his wife and mother didn't get on, given the tension that was always present between them. But he didn't know the extent of Irene's enmity towards June because she was so sly about it. June was only human and had mentioned some of what went on to Alan. But she wasn't heartless enough to shatter all his illusions about his mother by telling him everything.

'You've been on the desk a few times during the week, haven't you, Irene?' June didn't see why the older woman should get off scot-free when she was so eager to pass the buck.

Irene was full of affront. 'I hope you're not implying that I'm at fault,' she objected. 'I'm hardly likely to make such a careless mistake after all my experience in the hotel trade.'

'Anyone can make a mistake,' June pointed out. 'We're all only human.'

'I could run the reception desk in my sleep,' was her sharp answer to that.

A sudden flurry of guests needing attention ended any further discussion, and Irene and Gerald headed for the bar. People were checking breakfast times and ordering

40

newspapers and early morning tea, asking for keys and making general enquiries.

Although June managed to conceal it, she was inwardly quivering. Irene usually managed to unnerve her, even after all these years. Her contempt was an ever-present force even when she was pretending to be friendly for Alan's benefit. From the instant he had shown a serious interest in June, Irene had systematically tried to break them up. It would have suited her if Alan had married Paula Bright, the daughter of one of the Masters' few friends, a couple who were Torquay hoteliers.

June had hoped that Irene's hate campaign would lessen once their marriage was an established fact. But, if anything, it had become more intense. When Alan was out of earshot, she didn't try to hide her venom and had told June often and in a variety of ways how she wasn't good enough for Alan. June sometimes wondered how much more she could take, especially as she had reason to agree with her mother-in-law.

'Jack's a really good bloke, don't you think?' remarked Alan later that same night when he and June were getting ready for bed, having spent an enjoyable hour in the company of the restaurant manager.

'Yeah, he is good company,' she agreed. 'I enjoy his down-to-earth sense of humour.'

Alan tutted in an affectionate manner as he unbuttoned his shirt. 'Him and that damned motorbike of his,' he said, smiling. 'Talk about besotted.'

She laughed. 'I don't think any woman will ever come close to that thing in his priorities.'

Jack Saunders was a motorbike fanatic and devoted to the Harley-Davidson he'd bought second-hand and done up. It looked like new but he was always tinkering with it.

41

'It would have to be someone really special, that's for sure,' Alan agreed.

'He doesn't have any trouble getting women, though, does he?' June mentioned casually.

'He's a good-looking bloke, that's why,' said Alan. 'He's had a few girlfriends since he's been here.'

'Mm. There was that woman from Exeter he was going out with,' she remembered. 'I thought that might come to something but it went the same way as all the others.'

'I suppose he just hasn't met anyone he wants to settle down with yet,' observed Alan. 'He's happy as he is. What with the motorbike and his old cottage miles from anywhere, he's a one-off.'

'A good restaurant manager, though,' she pointed out. 'That's the main thing as far as we're concerned.'

'He's very good,' he agreed. 'He has a way with the guests, and he knows how to get the best out of the staff.' He paused thoughtfully, taking off his shirt. 'Yet I took a chance in giving him the job because he hadn't managed a restaurant, as such, before he came to work for us. It's just as well I interviewed him. I don't think Mum or Dad would have taken him on.'

'Which just goes to show what good judgement you have,' June praised him.

'A lucky guess more like it. I just knew he was right for the job, somehow.'

'You spotted something special in him,' she insisted, sitting on the edge of the bed in her slip to take off her stockings, 'which makes you a brilliant judge of character in my book.'

'Nice of you to say so.'

June was sitting with her back to Alan and she felt the bed shake as he got into it. She tensed as the moment she was dreading drew near. But for the time being he seemed content

42

to chat about the hotel. 'It was a good night, wasn't it?' he said.

'It was busy, certainly,' she replied.

'Busy and good are the same thing to me,' he responded with enthusiasm. 'There's nothing like the feeling I get when we've got a full house. Even apart from the business side of it, it gives me a real buzz. When Mum and Dad retire and I'm running the place, I'll have this hotel humming with life. There'll be a feeling here . . . an atmosphere so cheerful and warm, people won't be able to wait to come back.'

'Why wait until they retire before doing it?'

'You know why, June,' he reminded her. 'They want things to stay as they are.'

'So . . . persuade them otherwise,' she challenged.

He paused before answering. 'My time will come,' he said in a tone of resignation.

Because she didn't want to pressurise him into something he didn't feel right about, she just said encouragingly, 'Yeah, course it will.'

She had often wondered if they should break away from his parents' business altogether, partly because she feared that Irene would eventually come between them, but mainly because she believed Alan needed to succeed at something in his own right, away from their control, to find true fulfilment. But she couldn't seriously expect him to leave this place. It was in his blood, was his birthright, and would be his eventually.

'Anyway,' he said, yawning and sliding his hand over her back, 'that's enough shop talk. Come to bed before I get too tired to make love to you.'

'I won't be a minute.' Maybe if he fell asleep she wouldn't have to tell him.

But no such luck. He sat up, caressing her shoulders. She moved away quickly and stood up, facing him.

'What's the matter?' He frowned at her.

'I can't.'

'Why not?'

She bit her lip, hating to utter the words she knew would distress him. 'I . . . I got my period this afternoon,' she explained through dry lips.

'Oh, oh, I see.' He rolled over and lay on his back, unable to hide his disappointment.

'I'm sorry there's not going to be a baby, Alan,' she told him miserably, slipping into her nightdress.

'Yeah, so am I.' He paused and she could feel tension draw tight between them as he struggled to compose himself. 'But we mustn't lose heart. It'll happen one day.'

'I hope so,' she said with feeling. 'I really do.'

He lay still, staring at the ceiling for a while, then turned his head towards her. 'Look, June, I know how upset you must be feeling but you mustn't let it get to you,' he said.

'How can I not? I feel terrible, not only for myself but for you. I know how much you want kids.'

'We both do, don't we? But there's plenty of time.' She knew he was forcing himself to stay positive with great difficulty. 'We're still quite young. Maybe next month your period will oblige us and stay away.'

They'd been saying that for seven years and still a pregnancy eluded them. 'We'll just have to keep hoping,' she said.

'We will indeed.' He patted the bed beside him. 'Come on,' he urged her. 'I think we both need a cuddle.'

She slipped in beside him, only partly reassured to have him close to her. 'I feel as though I'm failing you, Alan,' she confessed.

'Don't be daft, of course you're not. It takes two to make a baby, remember.' He slipped his arm around her and she snuggled against him.

'I suppose so.'

'But for both our sakes, perhaps it's time we thought about getting some medical advice, as nothing seems to be happening in that direction,' he suggested. 'I was reading something about it the other day. Apparently, quite often just a minor adjustment is needed.'

June froze and he felt her trembling.

'Hey, why so tense?'

'It must be the thought of an operation,' she fibbed.

'Surgery probably won't even be necessary,' he was quick to reassure her. 'There might not be anything wrong at all. But if we see a doctor, at least we'll have more of an idea of what we're up against.'

'It's probably just a question of time,' she suggested, as though she really believed it. 'Unexplained infertility, they call it.'

'Exactly,' he agreed. 'But it won't do any harm to get some professional advice, will it?'

'It might be worth looking into ... at some point,' she hedged.

'I think we should do it sooner rather than later. I know we're still young but we have been trying for quite a long time.'

'I'll think about it.'

'Promise?'

'I promise.'

'Good,' he said sleepily.

How hurt he would be to know what a fraud she was, she thought. She had no intention of going to see any doctor *ever* about her inability to conceive because she knew exactly why it wasn't happening. But she couldn't tell him the reason. God, what a mess this was.

'Oh well, tomorrow's another day,' he yawned, kissing the top of her head. 'Good night, darling.'

'Good night, Alan.'

Just as she had settled to go to sleep the memory came, bringing her to with a start. She was trembling, her heart palpitating horribly. It always seemed to resurface when she was worried or upset about something and was always so vivid she could almost taste the fear as though it had happened yesterday instead of twenty years ago at least. Why it continued to bother her, she didn't know. But every so often back it came, unfaded by the passing of time.

Far too tense now to sleep, she slipped out of bed and went to the kitchen to make some tea, which she took into the living room, still feeling shaky. Her memory of her early childhood was somewhat sketchy, probably because she'd been told to forget everything before adoption. She knew she'd been six when she was adopted and that she hadn't been at the orphanage very long. She knew that her birth mother was dead and that she and her sister had been abandoned by their father. The rest was a mystery. She'd learned never to ask questions of her new parents, especially about her original background.

As always the flashback evoked memories of her sister, a small child with pigtails and a giggle, as far as she could remember. The pain of their parting had been awful. She'd never forget it. She'd often thought about her and wondered how life had treated her, particularly as she'd grown into adulthood. She'd wanted to see her again but, having been brought up to believe that she must leave her alone to get on with her own life, she'd never made a move in that direction.

Drinking her tea, she came back to the present and her current problems, of which there seemed no way out. She couldn't give Alan the child he wanted, and didn't know for how much longer she could go on fooling him into believing that she could. If her reproductive apparatus was in good working order, it would have happened by now.

46

She finished her tea and went back to bed, careful not to disturb Alan. Listening to his even breathing beside her, she was imbued with love for him. There had been tension between them lately because she couldn't get pregnant. How long would it be before it destroyed their marriage altogether?

One afternoon a few weeks later, June found herself alone in the office with her mother-in-law, having gone there to collect some of the forms she used to make up the guests' bills. The office was behind the reception area and it was here that all the major hotel administration happened: the ordering of food and drink, the organisation of staff and wages, everything apart from the receptionist's work, which included hotel and restaurant bookings, making up guests' bills, answering the telephone and dealing with all enquiries.

It was a quiet time between lunch and tea. The guests were either out or resting. Gerald and Alan were taking a break and the secretary had gone to the kitchen to get some tea.

'Oh, hello, Irene,' said June. 'I didn't realise you were still here. I thought you'd have gone home by now.'

'I bet you did,' snapped Irene, who was seated at a desk, holding her spectacles between thumb and forefinger and idly swinging them to and fro. 'You wouldn't have come in if you'd known I was in here on my own.'

'Too true, I wouldn't.' June and Irene didn't pretend to like each other when they were alone. 'I'm not a masochist.'

'Sorry to disappoint you.'

June said nothing; just went to the store cupboard and took out a batch of the forms she needed. 'I'll take plenty of these,' she told her. 'I'm right out of them.'

'Fine.'

June walked to the door.

'While we're on our own,' began Irene, making June's

heart sink because those words always heralded criticism of some sort, 'I'd like a word.'

June turned to face her, clutching the pile of forms. 'What about?'

'I'd like to know how much longer I'm going to have to wait for a grandchild.'

It wasn't the first time Irene had asked such an impertinent question but the subject was so raw and at the forefront of June's mind at the moment, it had more of an impact than usual. She turned scarlet, the forms slipping from her grasp and falling with a thud into an untidy heap on the floor. 'I think that's a personal matter between Alan and myself, don't you?' she replied, unable to conceal the quiver in her voice.

'Alan is our only child,' the other woman pointed out, her grey eyes resting coldly on June. 'Naturally Gerald and I are keen to have a grandchild. We want the family line to continue and not end with Alan. Surely you can understand that.'

'Of course.'

'As you know, this hotel has been in Gerald's family for a long time and we want to know that it will pass on through the generations after our time and Alan's,' she went on as though June had said nothing. 'And that can't happen if there are no succeeding generations, can it?'

'Obviously not.'

'Anyway, it's the natural thing to want grandchildren, and I don't want to be deprived of them or be too old to enjoy them if they do come along.'

'There's plenty of time,' June said steadily. 'Alan and I are both still in our twenties, and you're not exactly in your dotage.'

'Even so, you've been married long enough.' She was like a dog with a bone.

June felt her temper rising at this blatant intrusion of

privacy. 'It's a personal matter,' she told her again. 'I can understand your wanting a grandchild but that doesn't give you the right to pry into our private life. Alan's a grown man now. He doesn't have to account to you and neither do I.'

'Maybe not. But Alan makes no secret of the fact that he wants a child,' Irene reminded her. 'You can't deny that.'

'I wouldn't dream of denying it,' June protested. 'All I can say is, that when we have any news on that subject, you and Gerald will be the first to know.'

'You've no reason to put it off,' the other woman persisted, as though trying to drive June into a corner. 'I mean, it isn't as though there's any shortage of money. You do well out of this business and could afford to move out of the flat and into accommodation more suited to a family.'

June went down on her haunches to gather the forms that were all over the floor. 'Drop the subject, for goodness' sake,' she said, standing up. 'It's none of your business.'

'I think it is,' the other woman disagreed. 'Alan is my son and when he isn't happy, I don't like it.'

Smarting from the impact of her words, June asked, 'What makes you think he isn't happy?'

'It's obvious. How can he be happy when he hasn't got the child he wants so badly?' she declared. 'He can't be properly fulfilled without that.'

June was so shocked to have her own fears spelled out so clearly, her head spun and she felt sick. She offloaded the forms on to the secretary's desk and held the edge for a moment to steady herself. But she was determined not to give Irene the satisfaction of knowing how rattled she was. 'He's contented enough as things are, with just the two of us,' she told her mother-in-law.

'He might pretend to be—'

'He isn't just pretending.'

'You don't believe that any more than I do.'

49

June was forced to stare at the floor so that Irene couldn't see the pain in her eyes.

'Is there a problem?' asked Irene, her eyes narrowing on June in a questioning manner. 'Is that it? Is all not well in that department?'

Choking back the tears, June was unable to answer and Irene took this to be a confirmation. 'Have you taken medical advice?' she enquired.

'No,' June managed to utter.

'Why not?'

'Because I've been hoping it would happen and there would be no need,' she said, and it wasn't a lie. 'Not that it's anything to do with you.'

'You can't leave something as important as that to chance,' Irene nagged.

'Give it a rest, Irene, please.'

'That's typical of you to let something as vital as that go on unchecked.'

June brushed a tired hand across her brow. 'How do you know what is typical of me?' she asked. 'You've never taken the trouble to get to know me.'

'You and I are poles apart so I couldn't see the point.'

'Do you hate me so much, you find it impossible to leave me alone?' June wanted to know.

'I don't hate you,' Irene corrected, 'I just don't think you're the right woman for my son.'

'I'd never have guessed,' June said with bitter irony. 'But apart from the fact that I'm not Paula Bright, what else have you got against me? I'm a good wife to him. I love him. He's my life and I'd do anything for him.'

'You hold him back,' Irene stated categorically. 'You always have done in other ways and now you're doing it in the worst way possible – by depriving him of a child.'

'I've never held Alan back,' June disagreed. 'If I've held

50

anyone back, it's you and Gerald by getting in the way of your plans for him and Paula Bright, which would have made things nice and cosy, all good friends together.'

'And what's wrong with that?' Irene wanted to know. 'At least he'd have been with someone of his own type.'

'Instead of a jumped-up kitchen hand?'

'You said it,' returned Irene. 'If the cap fits . . .'

'You really are vicious.'

'I've never pretended to be a saint.'

'Except in front of Alan.'

Irene gave her a sharp look. 'Look, I'm just a mother who wants the best for her son. I've never made any secret of the fact that I wanted him to marry Paula,' she responded. 'Those two would have been perfect for each other.'

'Alan obviously didn't think so or he'd have married her.'

'And he would have done if you hadn't got your claws into him.'

'That just isn't true. I worked and lived at this hotel for a long time before I married him, remember?' June pointed out. 'And I know that nothing was ever going to happen between him and Paula Bright. Not on his part, anyway. He never felt anything of a romantic nature for her.'

'Only because you stood in the way of it,' Irene persisted. 'Once you'd set your sights on him no one else stood a chance. You were absolutely determined to have him from the minute you set foot inside this hotel.'

June couldn't deny that she'd been smitten with him the moment she'd set eyes on him. She'd been seventeen, he nineteen, a soldier home on leave. The war was over but he'd still had some service left to do. She had wanted him desperately but she certainly hadn't entered into a callous campaign to get him in the way that Irene was suggesting. It had been a mutual thing. 'I fell for him at the start, I won't deny that,' she admitted. 'The feeling was reciprocated or we'd never have got together. Alan's very much his own man.' She paused before adding pointedly, 'Except, of course, in his dealings with you and Gerald.'

Irene chose to ignore this last remark. 'All men are susceptible to a flirtatious woman,' she declared, 'and Alan is no exception.'

'We fell in love. It wouldn't have gone beyond a flirtation if we hadn't.'

'Yes, well, that's all water under the bridge,' Irene said impatiently. 'As you did get your hooks into him, the least you can do is give him a child.' She hesitated for a moment, looking at June. 'If you have a medical problem, you must get it seen to without delay. You owe him that much.'

All the fight went out of June, just drained away with the awful truth of Irene's words. 'I'm fully aware of what I owe your son and I have his best interests at heart always, you have my word on that,' she said dully. 'I don't need you to tell me what I have to do.' She was ashen-faced and longing to get away from this woman's cruel tongue. 'Anyway, it's time I took a break from duty until this evening so I'll get some cover in reception and go upstairs to the flat for a couple of hours.'

And with that she left the office.

Alan was sitting in a deck chair on the balcony reading the *Hoteliers' Chronicle* when June got back to the flat.

'Not doing any serious sleeping this afternoon, then?' she said with false levity.

'I will have a snooze in a minute,' he told her. 'I was just glancing through this to keep up to date with what's going on in the trade.'

'We might as well make the most of the nice weather,' she remarked, sitting in the chair beside him and glancing out across the sunlit bay. 'It'll be winter soon enough.'

'You look as though you could do with some sun,' he mentioned, giving her a close look.

'Do I?'

'I'll say you do. You're very pale.' He looked concerned. 'You feeling all right?'

'I'm fine,' she assured him quickly, avoiding his eyes. 'I'll make a cup of tea and join you out here.'

'No tea for me, thanks. I'm going for a kip.' He put the magazine on the table and got up. 'See you later.'

'OK.'

She didn't bother to make tea for herself but sat alone on the balcony, browsing absently through the *Chronicle*. But thoughts of the encounter with Irene lingered, making concentration impossible. The advertisements were about all she could take in so she put the magazine down on the small table beside her and gave her thoughts full rein.

Alan was a good and loving husband. Irene was right when she said June owed it to him to give him the child he wanted. She had been nothing when she'd met him, just a seventeen-year-old kitchen worker who'd run away from home at fifteen. As his wife she'd enjoyed status and a good standard of living. All she'd had to give him in return was her love and loyalty. She didn't have Paula Bright's family background or connections in the hotel trade. And now it seemed she didn't even have the capacity to fulfil that most basic of all human needs.

Even worse was the fact that she couldn't be honest with him about it. Although he was supportive and reassuring to her, the lack of a baby was beginning to put a strain on their relationship. She could feel tension simmering below the surface with ever increasing frequency. That would get worse as it became obvious that a pregnancy wasn't going to happen. Alan was much too good-natured to admit it, but a barren wife would become a burden to him eventually.

53

She couldn't allow that to happen. She loved him too much. So she must leave. Disappear from his life and give him the freedom to make a new start with someone who could make his life complete. She must do it in such a way that he wouldn't be able to talk her out of it. Irene's lethal tongue had accelerated this decision but it wasn't the cause. Sooner or later, June knew, she would have realised that this was the only solution.

Remembering something that had only half registered a few minutes ago, she reached across to the table and picked up the *Chronicle*, searching for an advertisement that had caught her eye and now seemed vital.

'Receptionist/bookings clerk wanted for busy London hotel. Marble Arch area. Experience essential – accommodation available if required.'

There was a telephone number and a box number.

Hesitating for only a moment, she went inside and found a pencil with which she ringed the advert. Then she took the magazine and went to the telephone in the hall, closing the door carefully behind her.

Early the next morning while the hotel was still silent she slipped out of bed, packed a small bag, put an envelope containing a short letter on the kitchen table, planted a kiss on her sleeping husband's brow, took one last long look at him and stepped quietly from the room.

She left the Cliff Head and headed for the station to get an early train. There was hardly anyone about to see this sad figure walking through the streets carrying a holdall, tears streaming down her cheeks.

Later that morning, Alan stood with his finger on the doorbell of his parents' house near the seafront. When his mother came to the door, he stormed inside, waving a letter at her.

'What have you said to her?' he demanded. 'What have you done?'

'What have I said and done to whom, dear?' She was genuinely puzzled.

'To June, of course,' he blasted. 'She's gone. Left me. Just like that.'

Irene's eyes widened with surprise. 'Oh,' was all she could manage. She was careful to conceal her delight. 'How dreadful for you.'

'That must be the biggest understatement in the history of the world.' He was distraught. 'She wouldn't have just gone unless something had really upset her. So, Mother, I'll ask you again, what have you said to her?'

'Your wife's departure has nothing to do with me,' insisted Irene, secretly wondering if her conversation with June yesterday had had anything to do with it. 'Does she mention me in that letter you're flapping about?'

'No.'

'Why blame me then?'

'Because it's obvious that you don't like her.'

'I never have liked her but it doesn't follow that she left because of me,' she pointed out.

'What else could it be?'

'I've no idea,' she told him. 'What reason does she give in the letter?'

'She doesn't give one,' he explained distractedly. 'She just says she can't stay and it's better for us both if she goes, and I have to trust that she's made the right decision. No forwarding address or clue as to where she's going – nothing.'

'You're better off without her,' his mother couldn't help blurting out. 'I've always thought you were too good for her.'

They were ill-chosen words which served only to fuel his anger even more. 'You've never given her a chance or made any effort to like her,' he accused. 'I bet you've said things to her that I don't know about. It's sure to be something you've said that's finally driven her away. June wouldn't just go off and hurt me like this for no reason.'

Gerald appeared from another room and wanted to know what all the noise was about.

'His wife's gone,' Irene informed him. 'Walked out on him, just like that.'

'No!' gasped Gerald.

'Yes,' Irene confirmed triumphantly.

'I'm not letting her go,' mumbled Alan, holding his head in despair.

'She's already gone, son,' his father said gently.

'I'll find her,' Alan told them. 'I'm not leaving it at this. She loves me, I know that.'

'She's got a funny way of showing it,' was his mother's cynical reaction.

'Has she got another man, do you think?' suggested Gerald tactlessly.

'Definitely not,' was Alan's categorical reply. 'I would have known if anything like that had been going on. Anyway, she never goes anywhere to meet anyone. She could hardly have an affair when she's always at the hotel with me.'

'The best thing you can do is forget all about her, son,' his father advised.

'No!' roared Alan.

'You'll be a fool if you don't,' Gerald went on. 'Anyone who's capable of doing something like that isn't worth bothering with.'

'Your father's right.' Irene was in her element.

'She was never really one of us, anyway,' Gerald opined.

'Of course she was one of us,' Alan disagreed, his voice rising. 'She's my wife, which automatically makes her one of us, despite the fact that you two didn't accept her.'

'Yes, of course it does, dear,' conceded Irene, changing

56

tack for fear of losing too much favour with her son. 'Your father and I are just upset on your behalf.'

'I've got to get her back but I don't know where to start looking.' He combed his hair back with his fingers in agitation. 'She could have gone anywhere.'

'Her mother's perhaps?' suggested Irene.

'She definitely wouldn't have gone there.' That much he did know. 'They don't get on. She hasn't lived at home since she was fifteen.'

'She'll have to let her mother know where she is at some point, though, won't she?' Irene pointed out, deeming it beneficial to her own relationship with her son to seem to be helpful and reassuring and not too damning about June at this point. 'She's still her daughter even if they hate the sight of each other. You can get her new address from her.'

'I can't because I don't have an address or phone number for her mother,' he muttered absently. 'All I know about her is that she lives in London somewhere. June has never said much about her family.'

'Oh, well,' sighed Irene. 'Perhaps June will get in touch with you to let you know where she is, eventually. As you said, she wouldn't just walk out for no reason at all. Perhaps it's just a temporary thing. She might have got into a mood about something and wants some extra attention.'

He shook his head. 'That's the last thing June would ever do. She isn't the type to seek attention.' He was adamant. 'No, she means it. She won't come back of her own accord, which is why I have to find her.'

'I don't see how you can, son, as you've got nothing to go on,' said his mother.

'Me neither,' added his father.

'Did she say anything at all or give any indication to either of you that she wasn't happy lately?' enquired Alan, looking from one of them to the other.

Irene wondered if it would be a good or bad move to mention the childlessness. She decided it wouldn't do any harm to remind him of his wife's flaws. 'I think perhaps she might have been fretting because a baby is a long time in coming,' she told him.

Alan scratched his head, pondering. 'Mm, there is that,' he said. 'I told her not to worry about it.'

'I said much the same thing,' lied Irene. 'These things happen in their own good time, that's what I told her.'

'She wouldn't have walked out on me just because of that, though, surely,' he said, becoming more frantic with every passing moment. 'There must be more to it than that. I have to find her; find out what all this is about.'

'Calm down,' advised his mother.

'How can I when I feel so powerless?' he snapped. 'How could she do this to me? How could she?'

'Come and sit down and have a cup of tea, dear,' suggested his mother. 'Have you had breakfast?'

'Breakfast!' he exploded. 'My world's just fallen apart and you ask me if I've had breakfast?'

'You must eat, son,' said Gerald.

'Of course you must.' Irene put her hand on Alan's arm. 'Just some tea and toast then.'

'No. I don't want any bloody toast, Mother, thank you very much,' he shouted at her. 'And will you please stop treating me like a five-year-old child?'

'Just trying to help.'

He sighed. 'I know you are and I'm sorry. I must go. There's no point in my staying here upsetting you.'

'I'd better come with you,' she said.

'Whatever for?' he thundered, misunderstanding her motive.

'To replace June in reception, of course,' she explained. 'Someone will have to do it until we get a new receptionist.'

'Oh, yes, of course,' he muttered. 'But that's the least of my worries at this precise moment. The way I feel, the hotel can grind to a halt for all I care.'

'That's an extremely selfish and irresponsible attitude,' admonished his father.

'I know it is,' Alan agreed, 'but I think I can be forgiven for a little selfishness when my wife's just left me. I'm hardly likely to be full of the joys of spring, am I?'

'No. But business must go on, whatever your personal problems,' preached his father.

'Yeah, yeah,' sighed Alan. 'I know all about that so you can spare me the lecture.'

But Gerald wasn't that easily silenced when it came to the subject of his hotel. 'The guests have paid good money to be well looked after and it's our job to see that they are, no matter what's going on in our personal lives,' he went on. 'They come to us to have a good holiday and if they don't have it, it must be through no fault of ours. A reputation can take years to build but it can be ruined much quicker.'

'Don't worry, I won't drive them all away with my bad temper. I'm too well trained for that,' Alan told him. 'To the guests, I'll be my charming self, as usual.'

'You can take the morning off if you don't feel up to it,' offered his father. 'Your mother and I will stand in for you.'

'No, no,' said Alan. 'As you say, the show must go on and I intend to see that it does.'

'That's the spirit,' approved Gerald.

'I'll be over in a few minutes,' Irene told him. 'I'll just wash the dishes and make myself look decent.'

'I'll come with her,' said Gerald.

Alan softened towards them. They meant well and it wasn't their fault that he hadn't been able to hang on to his wife. 'Thanks for the support,' he said.

'The least we can do,' said his mother.

Alan left and walked back to the Cliff Head. He couldn't ever remember feeling this desolate. There had been bad times when he'd been in action during the war, but at least he'd been able to fight back then. How could he fight back now when he didn't know what he was up against? Even worse was the thought that if he did find her, June might not want to come back. How could he reverse the process if she'd fallen out of love with him?

No, he couldn't accept that that's what had happened. He and June had had their ups and downs and things had been a bit strained between them lately because she couldn't get pregnant. But they still loved each other, despite everything. He was convinced of that. Why then had she left him?

His head was throbbing with tension as he made his way up the wide stone steps and into the hotel foyer.

Chapter Three

During a prolonged spell of wet weather in August that confined two lively little girls to two small rooms for longer than their ability to amuse themselves, Daisy saved the sanity of them all by teaching them how to play snap.

Being about right for their age group, the game quickly became a favourite, producing fun and sibling rivalry in equal measures. Shrieks of excitement and laughter were punctuated with howls of disagreement after simultaneous cries of 'snap'. They kept themselves amused for ages and Daisy congratulated herself on finding such a gem.

One rainy Saturday evening, when Daisy had a rare night off from waitressing, the girls persuaded her and Nora to join them in a game, and a companionable atmosphere settled over Daisy's flat as the four of them entered into this childish activity with gusto. To make her night off into a special occasion for them all, Daisy had bought crisps, pop, and a bottle of stout for Nora.

'Snap!' yelled Shirley, eyes gleaming victoriously.

'It was me, I said it first,' disputed Belinda heatedly.

'You did *not*, I did,' argued her sister.

'Liar,' came the vehement accusation.

'You're the liar,' Shirley returned hotly. 'Tell her, Mum. Go on, tell her.'

'That's quite enough squabbling, both of you,' admonished their mother. 'So pack it in.'

'It's her fault.' Belinda was very put out, her lips turned down at the corners and trembling slightly. 'She's cheating.'

'No she is *not*,' intervened the fair-minded Daisy. 'Shirley called snap first so don't spoil the game by being a bad sport.'

'She's the bad sport,' huffed Belinda, glaring at her sister. 'It's not fair.'

'Shirley was first to say it,' Daisy told her youngest daughter again and with emphasis.

'Your mother's right,' came back-up support from Nora.

'I said it first.' Belinda was really digging her heels in on this one.

But her mother could be equally as determined. 'I was listening carefully and I heard you both,' she said firmly to Belinda. 'She beat you to it by a fraction of a second but she *was* first. You'll probably do it next time, love.'

'I did it this time,' the child insisted, eyes brimming with angry tears at this conspiracy against her.

'Right, that's it.' Daisy decided it was time to get tough. 'You, Belinda, are behaving like a spoiled little brat and you'll go to bed if you don't give up . . . and you can stop smirking, Shirley, or you'll go with her. If the two of you can't play together without practically coming to blows, I shall confiscate the cards so that you can't play at all. I've never heard such a carry-on. You don't usually behave like this, do they, Nora?'

'Not normally, no,' supported the other woman, switching her gaze to the girls and adding, 'but you're like a couple of spiteful cats tonight.'

Belinda pouted a bit but finally decided to swallow her pride and they continued the game with noisy hilarity. Amid the gales of laughter there was an assertive knock at the door.

'You play my cards for me, Nora,' requested Daisy, smiling

as she went to answer it. 'I won't be a minute.'

Opening the door to find herself confronted by two men she hadn't seen before, Daisy felt a chill settle over her at the air of menace about them. Tall and muscular, they both had their hair slicked back with grease and were wearing open-necked shirts with the sleeves rolled up to reveal big, solid arms. Each man was holding an Alsatian dog on a leash, one of which strained towards Daisy, barking and baring its teeth.

Its keeper pulled at the lead. 'Heel, boy,' he ordered gruffly, and the animal quietened down, though a growl continued to rumble in the back of its throat.

'Yes?' she said enquiringly, struggling to quell her rising panic.

'Rent,' was the brief reply.

'Oh? But it isn't due until Monday,' she explained. 'Someone usually comes to collect it on a Monday morning.'

'The boss wants it today,' she was informed by the man who seemed to be the spokesman.

As it happened she did have the rent money put aside so early payment wasn't a problem. But she was curious as to the reason for this premature demand. 'Does this mean you'll always be collecting on Saturdays in future?' she asked.

The man shrugged indifferently. 'Dunno,' he told her. 'We're just carrying out orders.'

She went inside to get the money from one of a series of empty jam jars in which she kept the cash for various bills, and handed it over with the rent book in which he entered the amount.

Giving her the book back, he spoke to her in a gruff monotone. 'We've got a message for you from the boss.'

'Oh?'

'Mr Ellwood said to tell you that he hopes your kids ain't afraid of dogs,' he informed her, looking towards the animals. 'He said to tell you that these two can get very vicious.'

'He ought to be ashamed of himself, threatening the safety of little children,' declared an outraged Nora, who had come up behind Daisy, leaving the girls sitting at the table waiting for the game to continue.

'Nothing to do with us, missus.' The second man spoke at last. 'We're just messengers.'

'You ought to be ashamed of yourselves too, working for a man like Ellwood,' Nora continued, 'someone who goes about threatening decent people with dangerous dogs.'

The man just shrugged.

While Nora went to her rooms to get her rent money, muttering furiously under her breath, Daisy stepped outside and pulled the door to behind her so that the children were out of earshot. 'You tell Mr Ellwood that if those dogs go anywhere near my children, I'll have him done for threatening behaviour.' The protective instinct towards her children was so strong as to make her fearless, despite her obvious vulnerability. 'I'll have the law on to him so fast he'll wonder what's hit him.'

The thug's manner was completely insouciant. 'We'll tell him,' he said lazily, and they turned and went towards Nora's front door, collected her rent, then made their way downstairs.

'That Ellwood is really stepping up his campaign to get us out, isn't he?' observed Nora, as the men's footsteps receded down the stairs. 'He's putting pressure on from all sides now.'

'Yeah, it's a real worry.'

Over the past month or so, since Daisy's confrontation with the landlord, the annoyance factor in the house had worsened. There were more frequent and louder all-night parties in the basement, radiograms playing at all hours and drunken brawls. Several of the other statutory tenants had left.

'Are we still agreed that we won't be moved, though?' asked Nora.

'I'm not prepared to be driven out of my home by a thug like Ellwood, are you?'

'Not likely,' Nora confirmed. 'The way I see it, it's a war of attrition. He'll try to wear us down and frighten us, but he wouldn't dare to cause us or the kids actual physical harm because then we really would have grounds to involve the law and he wouldn't want the police sniffing around.' She shook her head, puffing out her lips to emphasise the point. 'Oh, no. He's far too dodgy to let that happen.'

'Exactly,' agreed Daisy. 'So we have to stand firm and make sure that we keep that in mind when he makes things difficult for us. We mustn't be panicked into leaving and making ourselves homeless. It's a question of keeping our nerve no matter what he comes up with to scare us.'

'And in the meantime, we have a game of snap awaiting our attention.'

Daisy grinned. 'That's right. It'll take more than a couple of heavies and their snarling mutts to spoil our evening, eh, Nora?'

'Not half,' was her hearty agreement, and they went back inside together.

Within minutes the game was back underway, a warm, enveloping buzz of conversation and laughter filling the room as though they hadn't had visitors with a sinister message. Even the sound of the rain beating against the creaky old windows was barely noticeable alongside the merry din. But Daisy was far more worried than she was letting on. She could be brave when facing thugs, and positive in front of Nora and the children, but what chance did she and Nora really stand against someone like Roland Ellwood, who had money behind him and an army of strong men on his payroll? For how much longer could the women hold out against him if he was determined to get them out of here? And what lengths was he prepared to go to, to destat his property?

Although she hated to admit it, the prospect of homelessness was beginning to loom with sickening intensity. If that were to happen and the authorities got to know about it, they would try to take the girls away from her.

She was recalled to the present by Belinda telling her it was her turn. 'If you don't pay attention, Mum, you'll have to stop playing because we don't want daydreamers in our game,' she said in an amusing parody of her mother.

'Don't push your luck, my girl.' But Daisy was smiling as she put her card down and shouted, 'Snap.'

Imbued by a strong feeling of wellbeing generated by the company, she felt cheered by a surge of new resolve. She had a huge incentive to fight back against the landlord: two little girls who were reliant on her to put a roof over their heads, and a neighbour she'd grown to love as a mother. They might all be society's cast-offs but they were a unit in themselves, a caring little sisterhood making the best of life at the bottom of the pile. This attic was cold, damp and hopelessly inadequate but it was their home and she was damned if she'd let a skunk like Roland Ellwood drive them out because of greed. If they ever did move from here it would be from choice and because they had somewhere better to go, she was determined about that.

It was raining heavily in Torquay that Saturday night, too.

'Bloody weather,' Alan complained to Jack Saunders, with whom he was having a drink at the bar after work. 'It's more like November than August.'

'That's the British summer for you,' said Jack. 'Unreliable to say the least.'

'You must have been mad to leave all that lovely Australian sunshine behind to come back to our miserable weather,' commented Alan, who had been in the blackest of moods since June's departure a week ago.

'There's more to a place than good weather, mate,' he pointed out. 'It's a completely different way of life out there.'

'That's why people go abroad to live, surely.'

'And why some of them come back,' was Jack's answer to that. 'You've got to actually experience a country to know if you're going to take to it. Australia's a beautiful place with wonderful scenery and bags of opportunity – I can't speak highly enough of the country – but it just wasn't for me. It wasn't easy leaving my folks out there, but the longing to come home was just too strong in the end.'

'I suppose there was no point in your staying if you felt like that.' Alan sipped his beer, gloomily looking at the rain running down the windows. 'The way I feel at the moment I'd go there tomorrow if I could.'

'It isn't just the weather that's making you feel like that, though, is it?'

'No, of course not,' he confirmed. 'But the weather doesn't help when you're feeling down – not when you're running a seaside hotel, anyway.'

'Our line of business does make us more susceptible to the rain, I must admit,' agreed Jack.

'It isn't much fun for the guests when the weather does the dirty on them,' Alan went on. 'All year they look forward to a holiday by the sea and the last thing they want is to spend the whole time sitting about the hotel lounge playing cards and waiting for the rain to stop.'

'Still, at least we've had a television installed for them,' Jack reminded him. 'That helps to keep them entertained.'

Alan nodded. 'Mm. There is that. But people don't go on holiday to watch the telly. It's the kids I feel sorry for. I know we don't have many children staying at the Cliff Head but you see them trailing around the town with their mums and dads, hoping it will stop raining. All they want is for the sun to come out so they can go on the beach with their buckets and spades.'

'They're better off at home when it's like this.'

'They are,' agreed Alan. 'If I had my way I'd turn this place into a family hotel with an indoor pool and entertainment laid on for the bad weather.' He sighed resignedly. 'Still, I'm not likely to get my way about that, so there's no point my going on about it.'

'I gather from your mood that there's still no news of June, then,' Jack surmised.

'Not a word, mate,' Alan told him. 'What the hell possessed her to go off like that?'

'Don't ask me,' said Jack. 'I'm just a single bloke, and the last person to know what goes on in a woman's mind.'

Alan cast a studious eye over his handsome pal. 'You must know a thing or two about them, though,' he suggested. 'I mean, you're not exactly a novice in that direction, are you?'

'There have been women in my life, naturally,' Jack confirmed. 'I'm a normal, healthy twenty-eight-year-old.'

'But you haven't got married . . .'

'I've come close to it,' he confessed. 'But never actually did the deed.'

'Wouldn't you like someone to share your life with?' asked Alan, who'd loathed the single life this past week.

'Wouldn't we all? But not just anyone to save me from being alone,' he explained. 'I'm still soft enough to believe that there's someone specially for me out there somewhere. And if I meet her – wonderful. But until that happens my bachelor life suits me down to the ground. I've got my motorbike, my cottage and my freedom – that'll do me.'

'You can't seriously compare those things to a woman in your life?' said Alan.

'I'm not that weird,' Jack protested, 'but I'd never get married just because it's the thing to do. Anyway, I've got a bit set in my ways now. I come and go as I please. It would take someone really special to make me want to change my way of life.'

'Don't you get lonely living at the cottage on your own?' Alan asked. 'With it being a bit off the beaten track.'

Jack had an old stone cottage on the seashore at Gullscombe Bay, a small village a few miles outside Torquay. It was a beautiful spot but very remote, with a long sandy beach, rugged red cliffs and large expanses of open grassland.

'No, not at all,' he said without hesitation. 'I'm here at the hotel surrounded by people most of the time, anyway. And when I'm off duty I've got a friendly local pub where I can go at any time and find someone I know to talk to.' He shrugged. 'If I feel in need of something a bit more sophisticated, I just get on the bike and come in to town. It only takes about ten minutes. And Exeter's no distance on the bike if I fancy something livelier.'

'Sounds as though you've got yourself sorted.'

'I've no complaints.'

'Was it just the price that made you buy a place in such an out-of-the-way spot?' Alan enquired chattily.

'The fact that it was dirt cheap was the deciding factor, yeah,' he confirmed. 'But I've got to love it there and I wouldn't want to live anywhere else, especially now that I've renovated the cottage and got it how I want it. The location's great for me. I enjoy all that open space and rolling surf on my doorstep.' He grinned, raising his brows. 'And I don't live like a recluse. I do have the occasional female visitor.'

'Footloose and fancy-free, eh?' Alan was staring moodily into his beer glass.

'Exactly.'

'Technically that's what I am now, I suppose, now that my wife's left me,' Alan pondered. 'But I don't feel free. I just feel lonely and miserable.'

'Yeah, well, you're bound to feel like that at this early

stage. Anyone would.' Jack was thoughtful. 'I still can't help thinking that there's more to June going off than you know about.'

'Another man is odds-on favourite among the staff, I bet,' assumed Alan. 'The gossips must be having a field day. It's wives who usually get deserted, not the other way round. She's made a right fool of me.'

'I expect there is gossip, but not in front of me,' Jack was quick to assure him. 'They wouldn't dare because they know we're friendly, and I would give them a mouthful. June was devoted to you, anyone could see that. And she certainly isn't the type to play around. You'd have spotted the signs if anything like that had been going on.'

'Yeah, I think so too – and being made a fool of is the least of my worries, to be honest.' He paused, looking at Jack in a questioning manner. 'You knew her quite well. Had she seemed to be worried or unhappy to you just lately?'

'No,' was Jack's considered reply. 'She didn't get on with your folks, that's common knowledge. But I don't think she'd have left over that at this stage because it's been going on for so long. You never know what someone's feeling inside, of course, but I got the impression she was used to the way things were between them and her, and didn't let it get her down.'

'It always seemed like that. And my mother swears blind she hadn't said anything to upset her.' Alan raised his eyes, tutting. 'God, I feel so powerless. If only I knew where she was.'

'You can't force her to come back, though.'

'No. But if I knew where she was, at least I could try to find out what it's all about.'

'Maybe she just needs some time on her own,' suggested Jack.

'Mm.' Alan pondered the idea. 'I've been assuming that she

left on the spur of the moment, but when you think about it, she must have had somewhere to go. She wouldn't just walk out of here with nowhere to stay, would she? So she must have planned it.'

'Not necessarily,' Jack disagreed. 'If she'd gone to a relative she'd have felt she could just turn up without warning.'

'As far as I know she doesn't have any relatives apart from her mother,' Alan said. 'And she'd sooner sleep on a park bench than go to her.'

'Really?'

Alan nodded. 'That's the impression she gave me, anyway, though she never said what the trouble was. She never talked about her parents and I didn't press her to do so as it was obvious she didn't want to. I've never even met them. They didn't come to the wedding and she didn't want me to go with her to her father's funeral.'

Suddenly this seemed hugely significant to Alan. Surely it was unusual for a wife not to talk to her husband about her family background. Glancing back on their life together, in the light of what had now happened, he could see that there had always been an air of mystery about June.

'I can't imagine June doing anything underhand,' said Jack, 'so I don't think she would have planned it in advance.'

'No, I suppose not,' agreed Alan. 'But where the hell is she?'

'Search me, mate,' was all Jack could say. 'All you can do is hope for a lead.'

'One of those isn't going to drop into my lap, is it?'

'Something will turn up, eventually,' Jack suggested hopefully. 'And in the meantime, you'll just have to try and stop tearing your hair out and carry on as best as you can without her. You know where I am if you need a mate.'

'Thanks, Jack.'

It was well after hours. The bar was closed, the customers all departed and the bar staff gone off duty. Alan went behind the counter and got them each another drink – just a small glass of beer for Jack as he had to go home on the motorbike.

'Did you see that article in the *Hoteliers' Chronicle* about private bathrooms?' Jack asked, deliberately changing the subject to take Alan's mind off things.

'No, I only flicked through this month's issue,' Alan told him. 'Why? Is it interesting?'

'It's worth a look,' replied Jack. 'They reckon that en suite bathrooms will eventually become standard in all decent class hotels, rather than just a luxury that people pay extra for.'

'They must be talking a long time into the future then,' frowned Alan.

'They're not expecting it to happen tomorrow or next week,' Jack agreed. 'But whoever wrote the article seems to think that private facilities are going to be more in demand in the not-too-distant future. Some of the new hotels being built will have them to every room as a matter of course.'

'Seems a bit far-fetched to me,' said Alan.

'That's what I thought.'

'If it does happen, though, it'll create pressure for the rest of us to do the same or lose out to the opposition,' Alan observed darkly. 'And something like that is right out of our league here at the Cliff Head. It would cost an absolute fortune to get all our rooms upgraded.'

'Mm.'

'So whatever the trend is we'll have to manage with the few rooms with private bathrooms we already have,' Alan went on. 'It isn't as though we don't have hot and cold running water in every room.'

'They're taking the view that hotel proprietors will make the changes gradually over a long period, a room at a time,' Jack explained. 'Anyway, the article's worth a few minutes of

72

your time. It might take your mind off your problems.'

'I'll have a look if the *Chronicle* hasn't been chucked out by mistake in all the upheaval of June going. I've been that distracted this week.'

'I've still got my copy if you can't find yours.' Jack finished his beer. 'Anyway, I must be off. If I have any more to drink I won't be in a fit state to go at all.'

'I'm a bad influence on you, keeping you out so late,' Alan apologised. 'I dread going to bed, that's why. Too many thoughts and too much emptiness upstairs in the flat.' He finished his drink and slipped off the bar stool with a purposeful air. 'But it has to be done and I must be man enough to do it. I mustn't keep you from your bed just because I don't want to face mine.'

'See you tomorrow.'

'Sure.'

Jack departed and Alan went behind the bar and rinsed their glasses. Then he turned off the lights and made his lonely way up to the flat in the lift.

The place felt like a morgue without her, Alan thought, as he stood in the living room staring out of the rain-soaked windows across the bay, the lights of Torquay hazed by the wet.

Still unable to face the prospect of the empty bed, he turned away from the window and rummaged through the untidy heap of newspapers and magazines on the coffee table until he found the *Hoteliers' Chronicle*. Settling into an armchair, he flicked through the pages until he found the article Jack had mentioned, which he read with interest.

The journalist predicted that hotels would thrive in the current affluent climate, which was expected to last for a while yet. People had more money to spend on leisure, which meant more of them could afford to go away on holiday, which in turn meant hoteliers would increase their profits, which would pay for them to improve their accommodation. The bit about the large increase in people taking their holidays abroad was rather worrying but the rest was fairly positive.

Alan leaned back in the chair, feeling slightly more relaxed for the diversion. He turned the pages in search of something to hold his attention until he was sleepy enough to face the lonely bedroom. Something caught his eye in the advertisement section. It wasn't the advertisement, as such, that interested him but the fact that it had a pencil ring around it. June was the only other person who would have looked at this copy of the *Chronicle* so she must have circled it. Why had she been interested in an advert?

When he read the advertisement – particularly the bit about accommodation being available – he understood why, and his heart leaped with new hope of finding her. There was no address and the name of the hotel wasn't given, but there was a phone number. It was a bit of a long shot but this just might be the lead he thought would never come. With optimism boosted considerably, he hurried to the telephone in the hall and asked the operator for a long-distance call to London.

'Central Hotel,' said a male voice he presumed to be that of the night porter.

'Sorry to bother you so late,' said Alan, pulses racing at this unexpected clue.

'No trouble at all, sir,' said the voice. 'That's what I'm here for.'

'The thing is,' began Alan, 'I have to meet someone at your hotel tomorrow and I'm not sure of your exact location. Can you help me with this, please?'

'Certainly, sir,' replied the man, and proceeded to give Alan the full address and directions to get there.

74

'Why did you do it, June?' Alan felt sad and puzzled rather than angry now that he'd actually found her. 'In heaven's name, why did you walk out on me?'

It was the evening of the next day and they were sitting drinking coffee in June's tiny room at the back of the hotel on the top floor. She'd moved in right away, having been given the job at the interview. She'd been very shaken on duty earlier when Alan had walked into reception with an overnight bag and booked a room for the night. When he'd explained how he'd tracked her down she'd cursed her carelessness. After she'd dealt with his booking, as though he was just any other guest, he'd asked for the chance to speak to her. She'd met him in the foyer when she came off duty and brought him up here because it was private.

'As I said in my letter, it's for the best.' She hadn't expected to have to confront him personally at this stage and was somewhat lost for words, as the truth wasn't an option. 'Believe me when I tell you that you're better off without me.'

'What's that supposed to mean?' he demanded, temper rising again. 'You're talking in riddles.'

'It hasn't been working for a while between us,' she stated categorically.

'That just isn't true.'

'You won't deny there's been tension between us lately,' she said.

'A little maybe, over this baby business,' he was forced to admit. 'But no marriage is a bed of roses all the time, and we shouldn't expect ours to be.'

'I realise that but—'

'Stop fobbing me off with excuses and tell me what's going on, June.' He was becoming aggressive now. 'I want to know why you walked out and I'm not leaving here until you tell me.'

75

She couldn't tell him the real reason without hurting him even more so she said rather feebly, 'I've never really fitted in at the Cliff Head.'

'You've always fitted in as far as I'm concerned. Surely that's what matters,' he was quick to point out. 'OK, so you never hit it off with my parents, but it's me you're married to, me you shared your life with, not them.' He fixed her with a stare. 'Anyway, if they were getting you down, you should have told me and I've have done something about it.' He paused again, squinting at her in a questioning manner. 'I don't believe that's why you left. We've been married for seven years and you've taken all that stuff with my parents in your stride. So let's have the real reason you walked out.'

His eyes were so full of hurt, she longed to hold him in her arms and soothe it away. But to do so would give him false hope because there was no possibility of her going back to him. She hadn't left on a whim. The decision to go had been a sudden one but she'd always known deep in her heart that she should never have married him.

Because she couldn't be honest with him, she just said, 'It wasn't any one thing—'

'It's got something to do with your not getting pregnant, hasn't it?' he guessed.

She reeled from his words but managed to answer in an even tone. 'No,' she lied to avoid any possibility of persuasion or suggestion of medical advice.

'I want a child. I'd be lying if I said otherwise,' he admitted. 'But if it isn't meant to be, I'll have to cope with that and so will you. But we will face it together. There's no point in your running away from it, June.'

'I'm sorry, Alan, but I'm not coming back.' She knew she must be strong, for his sake. 'I know it was a terrible thing for me to walk out without any warning. But I knew you'd try and stop me if I told you, and I really did have to go.'

76

He ran a critical eye around the room, which was sparsely furnished and so small as to be more of a cupboard than a room. There were no facilities beyond a bed, a wardrobe and the chairs they were sitting on. She had to go down the corridor to the bathroom, staff kitchen and sitting room.

'Look what you've come down to,' he told her. 'This is little more than a rabbit hutch.' He went to the window and stared out at the dreary view of the windows of buildings opposite and a yard far below. 'You must really be desperate to get away from me to have given up a comfortable home with a seaview for a miserable little gaff like this.' He turned to look into her face. 'We had a good life, didn't we? What more did you want from me?'

'Nothing at all, Alan,' she assured him. 'My leaving had nothing to do with any fault in you, or the way we lived.'

'All right, so we had to work bloody hard in the season,' he went on, as though trying to make sense of it. 'But things are not so bad in the winter. I was even going to suggest that we think about going abroad for a holiday this winter. Somewhere warm. I thought you'd like that.'

'I would, of course—' she began.

'Our future is assured, June,' he continued as though she hadn't spoken, too distressed for rational conversation. 'The Cliff Head will be ours one day.'

'Yours,' she corrected.

'Same thing. What's mine is yours.'

'It's irrelevant anyway because I'm not coming back.'

'I can't understand it.' He looked bewildered. 'Instead of staying to work with me and reap the rewards of our hard work, you choose to turn your back on it all, for this.'

'It's a job and a roof over my head,' she pointed out dully. 'It'll do for now.'

'But you don't need to make do in a place like this.' He

spread his hands expressively. 'Your home is with me at the Cliff Head.'

'Not any more, Alan,' she said sadly.

He was silent for a while. Then: 'In all the years we've been together, I've never thought of you as a selfish person.' His voice was distorted with anguish and frustration. 'But that's the only conclusion I can come to now. You're being downright selfish, June. Have you any idea what you're doing to me?'

'Of course I have.' She was struggling not to break down.

'So why put me through it, then?'

'It's something I have to do, Alan.' She was very subdued. 'I really am very sorry.'

'You're *sorry*? You walk out on me after seven years and all you can say is sorry?'

She bit her lip. 'It's awful, I know.'

'That's an understatement, if ever I heard one.' Really distressed now, he paced around the small room, head down, hands in pockets. 'OK, you say you weren't discontented with the way we lived. You say it isn't my parents who have driven you out and it isn't our apparent lack of ability to procreate. So the only explanation left is that you don't love me any more.'

'Leave it, Alan—'

'So tell me, when exactly did you fall out of love with me?'

She winced. Nothing could be further from the truth, but if his believing that would help him to accept the fact that she wasn't going back to Devon with him and that he must make a life without her, she would go along with it. 'It was a gradual thing,' she lied, staring at the floor.

'So . . . you don't even fancy me now, then?'

She forced herself to look up and face the torture in his eyes. 'I'm so sorry,' she said.

'Did I suddenly become repulsive to you? Did you have to

78

shut your eyes and think of other things or pretend that I was someone else?' He wasn't going to let this go. 'Is that how it was?'

'Alan, stop it.'

'I want to know.'

'I don't know exactly,' she said through dry lips. 'I didn't keep a record of my emotions.'

He grabbed her by the arms. 'Of course you don't know because it isn't true.' He was shouting now. 'I refuse to believe that you don't love me or fancy me. I just won't have it.'

'Go home, Alan,' she urged him, exhausted by the trauma. 'It's busy at this time of the year at the Cliff Head. You'll have made things very awkward for the others by rushing off and leaving them to it.'

'They'll just have to manage without me,' he said. 'This is more important.'

'Nothing you say will make me change my mind.' She was adamant. 'So there's no point in continuing with this conversation. All you're doing is upsetting us both.'

'Oh, so it's all my fault, is it?'

'Of course not.'

He moved forward and took her face in his hands, forcing her to look at him. 'Look me in the eyes and tell me you don't love me. Go on, say it.'

She tried to avoid his probing gaze but failed completely. The depth and richness of his eyes drew her to him, making tears swell beneath her lids.

'Go on,' he ordered. 'Let me hear you say it.'

'All right.' She took a deep breath and forced the words out. 'I don't love you, Alan. And I'm not coming back to Devon with you – *not ever*.'

He stared at her in silence, then: 'I still don't believe that you don't love me,' he challenged her.

'You might not want to believe it, Alan,' she told him. 'But it's true.'

He looked so utterly stricken, for a moment she thought she was going to weaken and pour her heart out to him. She had to restrain herself physically from abandoning this whole thing and taking him in her arms. But she was saved from temptation when he flew into a sudden rage, fuelled by his powerlessness over the situation.

'You selfish cow,' he said with vehemence. 'My mother was right all the time. You're not worth bothering about.'

'I wondered how long it would be before she came into it,' June blurted out.

'Any woman who can do what you've done to me can't be worth bothering with,' he ground out. 'I don't need my mother to tell me that.'

'You're right. I'm not going to argue with you about it,' she told him wearily. 'So go home to Torquay and forget about me. You can divorce me if you wish. I won't put up any opposition.'

'You speak about divorce as though it's of no more importance than what's on at the cinema,' he exploded.

'I didn't mean to give that impression.'

'I don't believe I'm hearing any of this.' He shook his head. 'I really thought I knew you. I thought we were soul mates.'

'We were for a while,' she said. 'Everything has its time, and the time for us has gone.'

'I thought you women were red hot about remembering your marriage vows but you seem to have forgotten yours completely,' he said bitterly. 'Marriage doesn't have its time. It's a forever thing . . . in good times and bad.'

'Things aren't always that neat and tidy.'

'Apparently not. After all we've been to each other, I thought I knew you,' he said through tight lips, as though she hadn't spoken. 'But you're like a stranger now.'

'No one ever really knows anyone else, Alan,' June pointed out. 'We're all on our own when it comes down to it.'

'I can do without the psychology, thank you very much.' His voice was tight with controlled rage. 'I'm just an ordinary bloke who thought he had a decent marriage. I don't need a lecture on the deeper side of human nature.'

'This isn't getting us anywhere so I think you'd better leave.' She stood up. 'If I were you, I'd get some sleep and take an early train back to Torquay in the morning.'

'I will, don't worry.' His attitude was harsh now, with a new edge of determination as he accepted the fact that she wasn't going to change her mind. 'But I can tell you one thing: you'll be sorry you did this, *very sorry.*'

He couldn't know how bitterly she regretted it already. 'Perhaps,' she sighed.

'No perhaps about it.' He was hitting out and saying things he didn't mean in the heat of the moment. 'Even if you don't miss me personally, when the novelty of freedom wears off and you're stuck in this miserable hole with no home comforts, you'll realise what you've turned your back on.'

She nodded.

'You could have had it all, June – a good life with a secure future – and you've just thrown it all away.'

'Which proves how serious I am about not coming back.' Her mouth was so parched she could hardly speak. 'No one chooses to live in accommodation like this.'

'If I'd treated you badly, what you've done would be justifiable.' It was as though he was thinking aloud. 'But I've never been unfaithful, never laid a finger on you.'

'I've told you that none of this is your fault.'

'Right, that's enough begging and pleading,' he said, his tone ice-hard. 'You've just blown your last chance with me. I wouldn't have you back now if you got down on your knees and begged me.'

She didn't say anything.

'So don't come crawling back when you've had enough of being on your own because my door will be closed to you,' he roared. 'Understand?'

Still she didn't put up a fight or try to explain the real reason for her behaviour. There was no point as she had no defence she could tell him about. There hadn't been a word of truth in what she'd said. Her brutal callousness was the best thing for him in the long term and she must stand by her decision. 'I understand,' she said in a subdued tone.

'What shall I do with your stuff?' he asked bitterly. 'You only took the basic essentials.'

'Perhaps you could give it to a charity, or if that's too much bother just throw it out,' she suggested sadly.

He gave her a long hard look, the fury in his eyes softening momentarily into a look of pleading. She almost weakened but managed to stand firm.

Without another word, he marched to the door and opened it, turning towards her. 'I hope you rot in hell,' he said, and left, slamming the door behind him.

She couldn't move; just stood where she was, frozen to the spot. She had experienced terrible things in her life, things most people couldn't even imagine: indescribable pain and humiliation almost beyond human endurance. But she couldn't remember ever feeling this desolate before.

Forcing her limbs to work, she walked slowly over to the bed in the corner and lay face down, burying her head in the pillow, unable even to relieve herself in tears. She thought this must surely be her darkest moment.

Chapter Four

It was a big day in the Rivers household because Shirley was starting school. Despite her mother's most ardent reassurance, the little girl was beset with doubts about the 'new adventure' on account of something she'd heard from an authority on the subject, a seasoned schoolgirl of several months' standing whom she played with in the street.

'She said the teachers are all horrid old witches who shout at you and make you stand in the corner if you do anything wrong,' she said while Daisy was brushing her daughter's hair and putting an Alice band on it.

'The teachers aren't all horrid old witches at all,' Daisy assured her. 'They're good people who'll teach you to do lots of new things.'

'They're horrid.' Shirley was convinced. 'Jane said if you're really bad you get the cane, though I think that mostly happens to the boys.'

'Whoever's been filling your head with these stories obviously doesn't behave herself.' Daisy chose her words carefully, wanting to be honest without frightening her. 'If you're naughty, of course the teacher will get cross with you, the same as I do. But I'm sure you won't give her any cause. And as for getting the cane, well, that's very unlikely.'

'I wish I didn't have to go, Mum.'

'I know, love. But once you get there with all the other children, you'll be fine, I promise,' Daisy told her, swallowing a lump in her throat. 'I'll be at the school gate waiting for you when you come out and you'll be dying to tell me about all the new things you've been doing.'

A cheery rat-a-tat at the door announced the arrival of Nora, who had called in on her way to work to wish Shirley luck. 'My word, someone looks smart this morning,' she complimented, admiring Shirley's navy-blue gymslip and white blouse, both bought second-hand and made to look new by Daisy.

Shirley managed a stiff little smile but her lips were dry and her eyes like saucers in a face that was pale with nervous apprehension. 'Thank you,' she said politely.

'She's got navy-blue knickers on,' divulged Belinda, triumphant to be the bearer of such privileged information.

'She would do now that she's going to school,' was Nora's reaction. 'All schoolgirls wear those.'

'I want a pair, Mum.' Belinda didn't like to be left out.

'When you go to school you'll have them whether you like it or not,' she was told by her mother. 'This time next year you'll both be wearing navy-blue drawers.'

'A year's a long time, isn't it?' said the wistful Belinda.

'It'll come round before you know it . . . much too quickly for me,' remarked Daisy, managing to sound chirpy though there was a certain poignancy in the air, today being the end of an era as well as a new beginning. 'You're both growing up so fast I'm losing my babies.'

'Well, I'm off to work then,' announced Nora. 'See you later. Have a good day, Sherl. Ta-ta all.'

'Ta-ta,' they chorused.

Daisy and Belinda walked to the school with Shirley, who carried a navy-blue shoe bag containing a pair of plimsolls, as instructed on the school list Daisy had received in advance. It

84

was a crisp autumn morning with the promise of sunshine, though a smoky mist currently shrouded the dusty streets. There was a steady procession of children trekking towards the school, the new ones staying close to their mothers, the old hands making their own way, scuffing and pushing and showing off.

As it was Shirley's first day, Daisy was allowed inside the school to deliver her into the care of the reception teacher, a painful business for both mother and daughter. After a last brave hug, Daisy left feeling heartless. Knowing that to send a child forth was just one of life's brutal necessities didn't make her feel any the less emotional about it. Daisy hoped most fervently that the day would be kind to her first-born.

'Well, Belinda love, it's just you and me today,' she remarked, as they headed home hand in hand. When there was no reply she looked down to see that the small child was crying silently. 'Aah, what's the matter?'

'I want Shirley,' she sobbed, huge tears meandering down her cheeks.

'She's only gone to school, darling,' Daisy pointed out. 'She'll be back this afternoon.'

But the child wasn't soothed. 'I want Shirley, I want my sister,' she wailed.

The look of sheer misery on her face triggered off a memory with such painful clarity that Daisy felt winded by it. More than twenty years ago she'd said the same thing about her own sister and received a good hiding for daring to mention her. 'She'll be home before you know it,' she said kindly, wiping her daughter's eyes with a rag hanky and giving her a cuddle. 'It'll soon be time for us to come back to the school to meet her.'

Belinda seemed pacified with this and Daisy thanked God she could give her that reassurance. She herself hadn't been blessed in that way. In retrospect she could see that she'd never felt complete after losing her sister, and resolved there and then that her own daughters wouldn't be put through the misery of being parted, not while she had breath in her body. Perhaps in these enlightened times more thought was given to the agony of splitting up siblings. But no one had considered it important back in the 1930s. Feed them, keep them clean and teach them right from wrong, that had been the maxim for children in care. Their emotional wellbeing hadn't entered into the equation.

'How long till she comes home?' enquired Belinda, her voice still wobbling slightly.

'A few hours, that's all,' replied Daisy. 'She's gone to school – not emigrated.'

'Hours means ages,' she sighed.

'How about us doing something nice to make it go quicker for you?' suggested Daisy in a positive manner. 'We could go to the swings later on and have a sticky bun in a café afterwards. Would you like that?'

'Ooh, yes, please, Mum.'

The bond between siblings was a curious one, thought Daisy, because within minutes of Shirley being home from school she and Belinda would probably be scrapping like street dogs. Yet, such was the complexity of human nature, they hated to be apart. She wondered how she would have got on with her sister in adulthood had they stayed together. Would they have remained close or drifted apart? That was something she would never know.

Just when Daisy had given Nat up as a complete dead loss, he would do something to redeem himself.

This happened one evening in November. After not show-ing his face for a couple of weeks, he turned up at Daisy's place on her Saturday night off, gave her some money towards the bills, brought sweets for the girls and offered to take Daisy to the pictures. Nora was enlisted as baby-sitter, and the couple went to see *Young at Heart* with Doris Day and Frank Sinatra. All of this and chocolates too, a half-pound box no less, and he also took her for a couple of drinks at the pub afterwards.

She guessed he'd done some lucrative business deal but she knew better than to quiz him about it, and just accepted the treat graciously.

'This is lovely,' she said, sipping a gin and orange at a table in the crowded pub. 'Us having a night out together. We should do it more often.'

Reluctant as ever to commit himself to anything beyond the current moment, Nat said, 'Yeah, it would be nice but it isn't that easy, is it? Because of the girls.'

'Nora is always willing to sit with them if we want to go out on my night off,' Daisy pointed out, her joy at this rare attention from him giving her an added radiance, eyes shining, cheeks glowing prettily against her bright red coat. 'We could take the girls out sometimes too. During the day on a Saturday, for instance . . . to the park or the river.'

'Mm.'

'Don't overdo the enthusiasm.'

'You know me,' he reminded her. 'I'm not at my best with kids. I never know what to say to them.'

'These aren't just any kids, they're your daughters,' Daisy was quick to point out. 'You'd know what to say to them if you would only take the trouble to spend time with them and get to know them. They're growing faster than weeds. Surely you don't want to turn around one day to find that they're adults and you're a stranger to them.'

'Of course I don't.' He wasn't really bothered and didn't want to talk about his responsibilities when he'd gone out to enjoy himself for the evening. 'I suppose I've just never got round to spending time with them.'

'You are their father, Nat,' she said. 'You really should make the effort.'

'Yeah, yeah. Don't spoil a good night out by giving me a load of grief,' he protested. 'I'll try to be better in the future.'

'I've heard that before.'

'I mean it this time.'

'I wish I could believe that.'

He reached for her hand across the table. 'I know I'm a bit unreliable sometimes but you mean the world to me,' he said, his mood becoming tender.

'You don't love me enough to marry me, though.' She had seized the opportunity to make a point but was doing so in an affectionate manner.

'I will, one day.'

'I've waited so long, I'm beginning to lose hope.'

'It'll happen, Daisy,' he said softly, 'I promise.'

In this mood he was irresistible, and the common sense she usually had in such abundance just vanished. She could have wept with love for him. 'I believe you, thousands wouldn't,' she said lightly.

They had another drink, then walked home hand in hand. It felt utterly perfect and Daisy was content. At the bottom of the attic stairs, he commented on the fact that the whole area was in darkness as it had been the last time he was here. 'It's about time this light was fixed, isn't it?' he observed. 'Someone could fall and hurt themselves.'

'You don't have to tell me how dangerous it is,' she said. 'We have to use candles to go up and down stairs at night, and to use the sink on the landing. It's a damned nuisance, especially when one of the kids wants to go to the bathroom in the night.'

'I take it it doesn't just need a new bulb then?'

'If it was as simple as that we'd have seen to it by now,' she pointed out. 'It's a job for an electrician and the landlord's responsibility. He's supposed to be dealing with it but we're not holding our breath.'

'He can't be bothered, I suppose.'

'There's more to it than that,' she informed him. 'It's all part of his plan to get us out of here. When something needs fixing in the house, he leaves it in the hope that the inconvenience will drive us out. Some of the other long-term tenants have left. But Nora and I won't budge.'

'Wouldn't it be easier to just leave?' he suggested.

'Where would I find a place at a price I can afford?' she asked, reminded again of his lack of interest in her problems.

'It would be difficult, I suppose . . .'

'Anyway, it's downright wicked what Ellwood is doing – trying to drive decent people out of their homes,' Daisy continued. 'And you never know what stunt he's going to pull next. What with getting people to keep us awake at night with loud music and parties, employing gangster types to collect the rent in a menacing manner, and withdrawing any sort of maintenance, I don't know where it will all end.'

There was a silence, then he said worriedly, 'You know that I'm not in a position to offer you and the girls a home with me at the moment, don't you, Daisy? I would if I could but I just don't have the room.'

She was used to the fact that he shirked involvement. But for some reason it touched a raw nerve and something rose in her, something so strong it pushed aside her devotion to him so that she was able to take a clear, realistic look at the situation. Not only did he refuse to offer her and the girls a home or financial support, he didn't give them any practical help either. He never offered to speak to the landlord on her behalf, or to have a few words with the offending neighbours in the hope of making them more considerate. His children could fall down the stairs and break their necks without a light to see by and his only contribution was a feeble remark

89

about the light needing fixing. Where were his paternal instincts? Where was his sense of duty towards her? Absolutely nonexistent.

Tears swelled beneath her lids and she admonished herself for being so soft. After all, it was a long time since she'd been under any illusions about Nat. If he'd had a responsible bone in his body she'd have spotted it by now. She'd always accepted him as he was, with all his faults. But tonight, for some reason, his attitude stuck in her craw.

'I'd have to be really thick not to realise that, Nat,' she snapped. 'So you can stop panicking. The last thing I would ever do is ask you for help.'

She couldn't see his face in the dark but guessed his expression would be one of relief. He didn't even bother to make a token protest and they made their way up the darkened stairs slowly and carefully, in silence.

Because Nat had no sense of diplomacy, he made the reason for the evening's generosity glaringly obvious as soon as Nora had gone and he and Daisy were alone. He slipped his arms around her as she waited for the kettle to boil for coffee.

'Don't, Nat,' she said, pushing him away.

'Why not?'

'Because I don't want you to.'

'The girls are asleep and the bedroom door's closed,' he pointed out, insistently putting his arms around her again. 'So we've got this room to ourselves.'

'No.' Her tone was more assertive.

'Oh, I get it. It's the time of the month.'

'No, it isn't that.'

'What then?'

'I just don't want to,' she informed him briskly, pouring water on to the bottled coffee essence in the cups.

Nat wasn't easily deterred when it came to pleasures of the

90

flesh. He grabbed her by the arms roughly and pulled her round to face him. 'Come on, Daisy. Don't mess me about,' he said in a threatening manner.

She was sickened by him; even more by herself for allowing him to use her and take her for granted for so long. She'd cheapened herself because of her feelings for him and she felt dirty and stupid suddenly. 'I'm not messing you about,' she told him. 'I'm just being truthful. I don't want to do it and that's that.'

'There's a name for women who lead men on,' he declared.

'I haven't led you on.'

'Oh, not much,' he said vehemently. 'You were all over me when we were out, while I was spending money on you. Now you don't want to know.'

She was deeply hurt but her spirit remained intact. 'It was a trip to the local cinema, for heaven's sake, not a weekend at the Ritz,' she reminded him. 'And now I'm expected to show you how grateful I am.'

'There's no need to make it sound as though I'm committing some sort of a crime in expecting it,' he admonished sulkily. 'That's how these things work. I haven't noticed you putting up any objections before.'

'Maybe I'm beginning to wake up and see things in a different light,' she told him. 'After all this time I can see that the only thing that stops my relationship with you being prostitution is the fact that I do it for nothing.'

'There's no need to be vulgar, Daisy,' he rebuked primly. 'It doesn't suit you.'

'The truth can be crude.'

'Well, that's gratitude for you.' He was outraged. 'I took you out, gave you a good time, I even bought you chocolates—'

'And a couple of drinks at the pub and my cinema ticket. And you gave me money towards the bills.' She was furious now. 'As I'm not prepared to pay you in kind perhaps you'd like me to give you the money back. I'll have to repay what you've already spent on a weekly basis.' She paused for a moment, then added with emphasis, 'Unlike you, I don't have any spare cash to hand.'

'You can mock,' he chided her. 'But it all added up to quite a bit in the end.'

She marched across to the sideboard and took her purse out of her handbag. Dragging out the ten-shilling note he'd given her, she thrust it towards him. 'Here, have it back,' she demanded.

'Don't be like that.'

'You might as well take it 'cause you'll get no other form of payment from me.' She waved the note at him. 'Go on, take it. You know you want to.'

Surely even Nat wouldn't sink that low, she thought, but he said, 'All right, I will,' and snatched the money from her.

'You disgust me.' Her voice was dull with disappointment now. 'Get out.'

He walked to the door, paused for a moment, then turned and came back to her. Handing the money to her, he said in a conciliatory manner, 'Daisy, love, this is silly and beginning to get out of hand. Don't let's part on bad terms.'

'Just go.'

'You and me have been together a long time and we've always managed to patch things up before.'

'Only because I'm soft.' She didn't take the money.

'That's one of the things I love most about you,' he told her, his manner blatantly persuasive now. 'The fact that you're so warm and loving.'

'I'm also a fool,' she said coldly.

His limited patience soon ran out. 'Oh, I'm not staying here with you in this mood. I came here for pleasure not punishment,' he said irritably, walking to the door, stuffing

92

the money into his pocket. 'I'll see you around.'

The door closed behind him and Daisy heard him cursing as he fumbled his way down the stairs in the dark. She felt battered and broken inside. How can he still have such power to hurt me? she wondered, sitting in the chair with a cup of coffee. After all these years and my knowing him for what he is?

With the same certainty that she knew he would be back, she knew she would forgive him. It was no life, being in a perpetual sulk with someone you cared about. At times she wished she'd never set eyes on him but mostly she didn't regret falling in love with him. How could she when he had given her the girls who were so obviously meant to be? Anyway, it wasn't as if he was wicked. He was just extremely immature and selfish. You had to make the most of what life sent you and Nat was part of her package.

As basic and poky as it was, the 'miserable little gaff' that Alan had been so derisive about did actually begin to feel like home to June that autumn. It was a far cry from the comfortable accommodation she'd been used to, but it was surprising how quickly she adapted to it. There was a certain comfort in being one of a number in the staff quarters, all people who for one reason or another had nowhere else to live.

There were foreign waiters, and waitresses and chamber maids from all over the UK. As they shared a sitting room and kitchen, naturally camaraderie evolved. There was always company on hand if June wanted it. Obviously she couldn't stay here for ever but it suited her in the short term.

She didn't hear from Alan again, but adjusting to life without him didn't seem any easier for that. Her salvation was the job, which was far more demanding than her position at the Cliff Head had been. The atmosphere here was totally different: much busier and less personal. The well-to-do guests in this central London hotel wanted efficiency and privacy rather than personal conversation. The phone rang constantly and there were always people milling about in the foyer, many of them from abroad.

The human touch was something she missed but she enjoyed the challenge of the work, which was never less than absorbing. No matter how desperate she was feeling about the state of her personal life, while she was actually on duty, she was forced to put it to the back of her mind.

At night it tormented her, though. On her own in her lonely room she longed for Alan and wondered how he was.

Day followed day, though, and life went on. Somehow June was managing without him, albeit that she seemed merely to be skimming over the surface of everyday life.

One afternoon in early November two policemen walked into the hotel reception while she was on duty and said they were looking for Mrs June Masters.

Instantly alarmed at the thought that something must have happened to Alan, June's hand flew to her throat. 'I'm June Masters,' she said with a pounding heart. 'Has something happened to my husband?'

'Not as far as we know,' replied one of the officers, adding quickly, 'But we would like a word. Can someone take over from you here for a few minutes?'

Before June had a chance to arrange cover on the desk, the front-of-house manager bustled on to the scene and whisked her and her visitors out of sight into a small office behind reception. Policemen at the hotel were not good for business.

'So, what's all this about?' she asked through dry lips as soon as they were alone.

'You are the daughter of Margaret Grey?' The policeman needed it confirmed.

'That's right,' she said with a nod. 'Is my mother ill?'

'She's had an accident, I'm afraid,' he explained in an even

94

tone. 'She was knocked down by a car in Hounslow High Street earlier this afternoon.'

'Is she . . . is she badly hurt?'

The man hesitated, his mouth tightening slightly. 'I'm sorry to have to tell you that she died in the ambulance on the way to the hospital,' he informed her gravely.

'Oh . . .'

'The person your mother was with at the time of the accident told us she had a daughter and we tracked you down through an address book in her handbag,' he explained.

'I see.'

'I'm afraid we'll have to ask you, as her next of kin, to make a formal identification,' one of the officers told her. 'But there's no hurry. You've time for a cup of tea to steady your nerves first.'

'I'm all right,' she said, though she was breathless with shock. 'I'll just go and tell my boss what's happened, then I'll come with you.'

'If you're sure you're feeling up to it . . .?' he said kindly.

'I'm sure.'

June thought the policemen might be shocked to know that her prevailing emotion was one of relief that nothing bad had happened to Alan.

The death of her adopted mother barely touched her at the time. There had been no love lost between them anyway, but the all-consuming pain of missing Alan meant that everything else paled into insignificance. June even arranged the funeral and endured it without much emotion.

It was only when she was at the house in Hounslow where she'd grown up, sorting through her mother's things and getting the property she'd inherited, as next of kin, ready for sale that memories of the past began to flood in. Sitting at the bureau in the living room one morning, going through some family papers, she discovered a photograph of herself with her adopted parents that caused tears to flow. Not with sadness because they were both now dead but because of the agony of her life with them.

In the photograph, the three of them were in the garden of this house, standing under the lilac tree, June between the two grown-ups. Anyone else would see a picture of family contentment. But the mere sight of her father sent shivers up her spine. She still couldn't bear to look at him, and he'd been dead for four years.

Both parents had died relatively young – in their fifties – thus disproving the theory that only the good did that. It would have been hypocritical of her to pretend grief at the passing of either. It was hard to grieve for anyone you'd feared and hated. Adulthood and distance hadn't warmed her to them on her rare duty visits.

She tore the photograph up and let it flutter into the wastepaper bin. There were others that received the same treatment. She didn't want anything left to remind her of them. There were various family documents: her father's army discharge papers, her parents' marriage certificate.

Coming across a large fat brown envelope, June opened it curiously, her heart turning somersaults as she realised it was the official correspondence between her parents and the adoption authorities.

It was a weird feeling to see details of yourself in black and white; strange and rather frightening to be confronted with your background after a lifetime of ignorance. Her hand trembled as she fingered a letter, words and sentences leaping out at her.

Regarding your application to adopt legally June Rivers, currently in care at St Clare's Home for Destitute Children in Hammersmith, we feel it necessary to point out that the case of the Rivers sisters is a particularly tragic one. June may be mentally disturbed after such a sudden loss of parents and family life. It is deemed to be in the children's interest for them to remain unaware of the shocking circumstances that resulted in their being taken into the care of the authorities.

We also believe it important to June's future stability for her to be encouraged to forget her previous background, including her sister, as this may impede her progress in adapting to a new and stable family life again.

As June read other correspondence and newspaper cuttings which gave her the basic details of what the 'shocking circumstances' actually were, she shook violently from head to toe, bile rising in her throat and sending her scurrying to the bathroom. Now at last she knew why she and her sister had been abandoned, but the reason was so dreadful she wished she'd never found out. She could understand the authorities' logic in not telling two little girls about their original background. Knowing something that horrifying at such a young age could have damaged them for life.

But June did know now. And she couldn't erase the knowledge or leave it at that. She had to learn the full story. Washing her hands and face, she went back to the living room. Jotting down a few dates, she got her coat and hurried to the nearest library.

Finding 1934 in the book of old copies of a national newspaper in the reference section of the library, June began to turn the pages. The story of her early background unfolded. It was like reading cheap horror fiction but it had all actually happened. When she saw the name Morris Dodd in print, she knew with sickening certainty why she'd been haunted by the

97

memory of him for all these years. Her heart pounded at the huge significance it now had.

There was one thing she now had to do urgently. She had to find her sister, Daisy. This filled her with excitement, then despair at the impossibility of the task. Twenty years was a long time – she could be anywhere. She might not even have survived the war. St Clare's was June's only lead. It was a long shot after all these years but they just might have some idea of where she was.

'Please, God, let her still be alive,' she prayed silently as she left the library and headed for the tube station, en route for Hammersmith.

Later that same day June walked through the squalid back-streets of Notting Hill, past windows boarded up, stucco rotting on the front of terraces, fumes from the local factories mingling with the stench from wasteland used as an open rubbish dump.

It was a cold and misty November day but small children played in the street despite the weather, women stood at front doors gossiping, a crowd of young West Indian men stood on the corner engaged in conversation.

Although June's circumstances had taken a dive when she'd left Alan, the area in which she now lived was, none the less, a world apart from this, yet less than two miles away. She couldn't help but be shocked by the deprivation of the neighbourhood and was ashamed of her disgust.

She found the address in Benly Square the nuns had given her and knocked on the front door, which swung open at her touch because the lock was broken. Finding herself in a hallway that was foul with the smell of damp and stale cooking, she didn't know what to do next. The address just said number twenty Benly Square; there was nothing about a flat number.

A woman came out of one of the rooms and walked towards the front door dressed in a brown mac and carrying a shopping bag. Her eyes rose at the sight of June's smart grey suit and high-heeled court shoes.

'You looking for someone?' she asked without much interest.

June nodded. 'Daisy,' she said. 'Daisy Rivers she was. She might not be using that name now.'

'Up in the attic,' the woman informed her, and left the house.

June made her way up the creaking stairs, becoming increasingly horrified at the conditions. At the top of the attic stairs, she was greeted by a middle-aged woman with wild ginger hair and enquiring blue eyes. 'Can I help you?' she asked in a cultured voice that didn't match the ambience.

'I'm looking for Daisy,' June explained.

'She's gone to meet her little girl from school,' Nora explained pleasantly. 'She's taken her other daughter with her so there's no one in her flat at the moment.'

'Do you think she'll be long?'

'She should be back at any minute.'

'Thank you.'

'You're welcome to come and have a cup of tea in my place while you're waiting,' Nora offered, curious as to who June was but courteous enough not to enquire. 'Daisy and I are very good friends.' She gave her a wide grin. 'Well, we're more like family, really. I know she'd want me to make you welcome.'

'It's very kind of you to offer but I think I'll wait outside as she'll only be a minute,' June said, first because she was feeling emotional about the imminent reunion and needed to be on her own, and secondly because the oppressive atmosphere inside this building was making her nauseous and she was desperate for some fresh air.

'As you wish, dear,' said Nora.

'See you later then,' said June, and made her way down the broken stairs.

Relieved to be outside, despite the cold grimy atmosphere, she took a deep breath to prepare herself for the meeting. Suddenly the sound of laughter filled the air, and looking down the street she saw a small woman in a red coat – with several inches of grey skirt showing beneath it – coming towards her holding the hands of two little girls, one of them dressed in a navy-blue school raincoat. They stopped for a moment, listening to the girl in the raincoat, then there were gales of laughter.

Obviously it wasn't possible to recognise the adult from the child she remembered but she knew instinctively that the woman was Daisy, and the thing that struck June was the closeness of the trio, obviously happy to be together. On jelly legs, her heart thudding madly, June walked towards them.

Shirley was regaling her mother and sister with the story of one boy, Paul, in her class who had taken his pet mouse to school in his pocket and how it had escaped and everyone had screamed and stood on their desks, even the teacher. Daisy and Belinda had thought this hilarious.

'What happened to the mouse?'

'Paul found it and the caretaker looked after it until it was time to go home and Paul took it with him,' Shirley explained. 'Miss was very cross with him for bringing it to school and scaring everybody.'

'I expect she was,' said Daisy, imagining the teacher's embarrassment if Shirley's version of her behaviour hadn't been exaggerated.

'What's for tea, Mum?' asked Belinda.

'Fish paste sandwiches and toasted buns.'

'Toasted buns, yippee,' cried Shirley.

Immersed in her children, Daisy hadn't paid any attention to someone approaching but looked up now to see an extremely smart woman in a fitted suit and high-heeled shoes. She's out of place around here, Daisy thought, and hoped she hadn't come from the landlord with some message of doom.

'Daisy?'

'That's me,' she replied, noticing how strikingly attractive the woman was, with fine features and sleek, dark hair. 'What can I do for you?'

The woman seemed upset about something, too upset to answer; there were tears running down her cheeks.

'Shirley, love, give the lady your hanky,' said Daisy, because Shirley was the only one who had a proper handkerchief for school; the others had rag ones.

Shirley handed her the handkerchief, which seemed to make her cry even more.

'Oh, my Lord, you are in a state,' was Daisy's kind response; she was too concerned about the woman to ask how she knew her name. 'Can I help in any way?'

June stared at her.

'Whatever it is that's troubling you, you'll feel better for a cup of tea and a sit-down,' said Daisy warmly. 'You don't want to be out on the street when you're so upset, love. We only live a few doors down. So come in and have a cup of tea with us.'

'Oh, Daisy, don't you see,' said the woman, 'I'm not crying because I'm sad.'

'I dread to think what you'd be like if you were then,' quipped Daisy. 'The whole of London would be under water.'

'Daisy,' the other woman began in muffled tones, 'do you remember that you once had a sister?'

'Course I remember,' Daisy told her. 'I'm not likely to forget a thing like that.'

The woman stared at her meaningfully.

Daisy gulped, her eyes narrowing on her in a questioning manner. 'You?' she gasped.

'That's right. I'm June,' she informed her thickly. 'I'm your sister.'

'You never are,' said Daisy, staring at her in disbelief, trying to recognise something about her and remembering only that the child in her memory had had dark hair.

'I am.'

'But how—'

'I'll tell you everything all in good time,' said June. 'But for now, let me give you a hug.'

Now Daisy was weeping unashamedly. After all these years she'd come face to face with her own flesh and blood. The little girls looked on in bewilderment as the two women clutched each other, wailing loudly.

'Are we going in for tea soon?' asked Shirley at last, bringing an air of normality to the proceedings. 'It's cold out here and I'm starving.'

'Yes, love, we're going indoors for tea now.' She looked at June. 'You will join us, won't you?'

'Love to.' The terrible miasma inside the house was forgotten in the joy of the moment.

'This is your Auntie June, girls,' said Daisy, sniffing into the handkerchief.

'What, a *real* auntie?' queried Shirley. 'Not a pretend one like Nora is our pretend grannie?'

'No, this is your real auntie,' Daisy confirmed.

'Cor,' approved Shirley.

'Smashing,' added Belinda.

It was strange, thought June, an hour or so later, how the pungent hallway and landings of the dilapidated building ceased to exist once you were inside Daisy's flat, the gas fire spreading a glow over the shabby room, the curtains drawn

102

against the murky weather outside and the crumbling window sills.

Nora went to the bakers to get more buns, which were toasted with a fork on the gas fire, and they all sat around the table having tea and talking, the sweet scent of cinnamon from the buns filling the air.

Daisy had insisted that Nora stay. 'She's like a mum to me,' she'd explained to June, 'and I wouldn't want her to miss out on a special occasion like this.'

'Of course not,' June had approved.

The two sisters had exchanged basics about themselves, their jobs, their personal circumstances. June knew Daisy was an unmarried mum. June mentioned that she'd recently separated from her husband and touched on her life as a hotelier's wife but offered no details about the cause of the separation. They both agreed how fortunate it was that Daisy had kept in touch with St Clare's, who'd been able to direct June straight to her. They both had so much to say, though Daisy did mention that she had to keep her eye on the time because she was on duty this evening. June said she was having a couple of days off to sort out her late mother's affairs.

'But tell me, June,' said Daisy, when everyone had finished eating, 'why come looking for me now, after all this time?'

'I've always wanted to, of course—'

'I know that,' cut in Daisy, because they had already discussed how their upbringing had deterred them from looking for each other, 'but what actually drove you to do something about it at this particular time?'

June bit her lip, looking uncomfortable. 'It's a bit delicate, actually,' she told her.

'Come on, girls,' said Nora, taking the hint. 'Let's go and have a game of snap in my place while your mother and her sister have a chat.'

They went without argument because snap was still a big favourite with them.

'So, what is it you have to tell me that isn't suitable for little ears?' asked Daisy.

June moistened her lips. 'I've had to go through my adopted mother's papers following her death,' she explained, 'and I've found out how we came to be in St Clare's.'

'We already know,' Daisy pointed out. 'Our mother died and our father abandoned us.'

'Yes. Basically that's true,' June confirmed, 'but there was much more to it than that.'

Daisy waited for her to go on.

After taking a deep breath to try to calm herself, June asked, 'Do you remember a man called Morris Dodd?'

'Mr Dodd,' she responded, looking startled. 'Yeah, I remember him all right.'

'You remember that night he threatened us, don't you?' June guessed. 'I can tell from the look on your face.'

'It's haunted me on and off all through my life,' Daisy confided, eyes glazed as she recalled the incident. 'You and I were in bed when we heard shouting downstairs.'

'And we crept halfway down, scared to go further because we were supposed to be asleep and would have got told off if Mum had found out.'

'Mr Dodd was in the hall on his way to the front door,' Daisy continued.

'And he grabbed us and shook us and told us to go back to bed and if we ever told anyone he'd been at our house that night, he'd come after us and do something so terrible we'd wish we were dead.'

'I was so scared I nearly wet myself,' remembered Daisy. 'I still go cold when I think about it.'

'Me too,' said June. 'I can still see those eyes, glaring at us, his face close to mine. Ugh.'

'The memory of it has kept me awake many a night and I don't know what it means,' confessed Daisy.

'Neither did I until today,' June told her. 'Now I know why he was so rough with us that night.'

'And?'

She took another deep breath before uttering her next words. 'Our mother didn't die of natural causes,' she said through dry lips. 'She was murdered.'

Daisy turned pale; she was too shocked to speak.

'It gets worse,' June warned her. 'Our father was convicted of the murder. That's why we were abandoned.'

'Our father a murderer?' Daisy couldn't believe it.

'He was found guilty, yes.'

'Was he . . . was he hanged?'

'No, it wasn't considered to be premeditated so the sentence was commuted to life imprisonment,' she explained. 'You'll have to come with me to the library to read the newspaper reports of the trial to get the full story. But I don't think our father did it. Morris Dodd was our mother's lover, apparently, and I think he killed her.'

'Why do you think that?'

'Because our father claimed throughout the trial that he was innocent and Dodd killed her. Dodd denied being at our house on the night of the murder, which I reckon is the same night he scared the living daylights out of us, as we ended up in St Clare's soon after,' said June. 'That's why he was so keen to keep us quiet.'

'Ooh, June, I think you're right.'

'According to the reports, no one saw him arrive or leave the house and his wife claimed that he was with her on the night of the murder,' June went on to say. 'But we both know that he was there at the house, don't we?'

'Yeah.'

'And we are the only people alive, apart from our father

and the Dodds, who know that he was lying,' June continued. 'I don't know if our father is still alive. But I do know that you and I are the only people who can clear his name.'

'Oh, June,' gasped Daisy.

'Big responsibility, isn't it?'

'Huge,' agreed her sister.

tart or a husbandless no-hoper burdened by a couple of bastards. 'Yes, I am,' she agreed wholeheartedly, 'and every day I thank God for them. They're everything to me.'

'And you are to them,' June told her. 'It shines bright from all of you. Nora as well.'

Daisy smiled, and June couldn't remember having met anyone who exuded such warmth before. So, which of the two of them had fared better from life, she found herself wondering: a child 'favoured' by adoption, who'd grown up in a comfortable home to have good manners and refined speech, and now had a broken marriage, an inability to have children and no real friends because her childhood had robbed her of the capacity for friendship? Or Daisy, an orphanage girl struggling to raise two children on her own in poor accommodation and living from hand to mouth, but having the unqualified love of her daughters, the affection of a close woman friend and a generous heart towards everyone? The question answered itself.

'Yeah, we're a close little band, and Nora's like one of the family.' Daisy sensed a profound sadness in June that her general air of confidence couldn't hide. Presumably her broken marriage was the cause. It must be heartbreaking to have had something as precious as that and lost it, she thought, her mind drifting to her own long-standing desire for marriage to Nat, with whom she'd made her peace last week as predicted. 'She's the nearest thing I have to a mum – one that I can remember, anyway. My memories of our real mother are quite vague.'

'Mine too. Which is only natural as we lost her so young,' said June.

'And when you think about it, she must have been a bit preoccupied at the end of her life too, as she was having an affair with Morris Dodd,' Daisy pointed out, her thoughts returning to the findings in the library. 'I wonder what she did with us while she was with him.'

'Perhaps we were at school or something,' suggested June. 'It said in the paper that Morris Dodd was some sort of a sales rep. Those people can be flexible during the working day as they're out and about, so he could have seen her then, while our father was out at work.'

'The mind boggles,' said Daisy. 'An adulterous mother doesn't exactly match the cosy maternal figure I imagined her to be all these years.'

June gave an understanding nod. 'Morris Dodd was a family friend, apparently, which is how she knew him and why we remembered him being familiar to us.'

'So, let's run through it,' began Daisy, wanting to summarise the whole dreadful business. 'According to our father's evidence, Mother ended the affair but Morris Dodd is the sort of man who likes to get his own way so he went round to the house with the idea of persuading her to reconsider her decision.'

'He just burst in there apparently, and the whole thing got out of hand,' June continued. 'He confronted her in front of Dad and when she wouldn't agree to leave him, Dodd lost his temper and started knocking her about, which accounts for the shouting we heard from upstairs. Dad tried to fight him off and was knocked unconscious. When he came to, Dodd had gone and Mother was dead, strangled. Dodd must have been running from the scene of the crime when he saw us.'

'It sends shivers right through me,' said Daisy, sucking in her breath and wriggling her shoulders, 'to think what was going on downstairs while we were in bed.'

'It must have been all over by the time we crept down the stairs, though,' June speculated.

'Though Dodd tells a different story.'

June nodded. 'He denied being at the house at all that night and his alibi is watertight because his wife swore

110

under oath that he was at home with her,' she went o̶
'Because no one could prove otherwise, his version o.
events was believed and it was assumed that Dad was lying
to save his own skin.'

'Of course, we can't be absolutely certain that the night
Morris Dodd terrorised us was the night of the murder
because we were just children and it was a long time ago.'
June wanted to be realistic.

'I'm sure in my own mind, though,' Daisy responded
thoughtfully. 'I remember that nothing was ever the same
again after that.'

'No it wasn't.' June paused, sipping her coffee. 'Not that
anyone in authority will believe us. Two women suddenly
claiming to remember something they saw over twenty years
ago when they were children won't carry any weight at all.
We won't stand a chance of getting the case reopened on that
alone.'

'There is one other person besides us and our father who
knows that Dodd was lying in court.'

'His wife.'

'Exactly.'

'She's not likely to admit to perjury, though, is she?' June
pointed out.

'Not without a very strong incentive,' Daisy was forced to
agree. 'But she's the only person who can back up our story
so we have to try to find her and see if she can't somehow be
persuaded to co-operate. Don't ask me how because I haven't
a clue at this stage. But I do know we must at least try to clear
our father's name, however hopeless it seems.'

'You won't get any objections from me,' June assured her.
'But before we do anything about that side of it there's
something more important we must do.'

'Find out if our father is still alive and, if so, where he is,
then arrange to pay him a visit,' guessed Daisy.

'You've got it,' confirmed June. 'I've no idea how to set
.bout it, though. Have you?'

'Not really. But I should think the police station would be a
good starting point,' suggested Daisy. 'They'll know what the
procedure is for finding out which prison someone is in.'

Because both sisters had jobs and Daisy also had the children
to consider, they couldn't just drop everything and devote all
their time to their father's plight, as much as they both wanted
to. But they both gave the matter a great deal of thought and
did what they could within the parameters of their other
commitments.

June had access to the telephone books at work and
planned to make a list of all the Dodds in the London area. As
personal calls from work were prohibited she intended to use
a call box to contact them.

Her first task, however, was a visit to the police station
where she was informed that information about relatives in
custody could be obtained from the Home Office, who would
issue a visiting order only if the prisoner agreed to it. They
gave her the address and she got a detailed letter in the post
immediately.

Meanwhile, Daisy was keeping busy. In the hope of moving things forward with regard to finding the Dodds, she
approached the Salvation Army, having heard that they
offered a service for tracing missing people. But the job was
too big for them because she had no information beyond what
she'd read in the paper: that the Dodds had once lived in
Wembley, where the crime had taken place. The Salvation
Army officer suggested that she contact them again if she
could get more details for them to work with. It was a huge
disappointment.

The keenly awaited news from the Home Office was better.
After opening the envelope with a great deal of trepidation,

June learned that Lionel Rivers was indeed still alive and had agreed to see his daughters.

So it was that one bitterly cold afternoon in December, June and Daisy travelled together to Wormwood Scrubs.

Daisy's desire to see her father was strong, but she felt somewhat tremulous and her stomach churned horribly on the bus to the prison.

'Weird, isn't it,' she remarked to June, to take her mind off the imminent meeting which could turn out to be an ordeal, 'us being together like this? It seems unreal.'

'It is peculiar,' agreed her sister. 'The last thing I expected to be doing was going to see a father I've not seen for over twenty years – in prison.'

'I meant more in terms of us getting back together after all these years,' Daisy amended.

'Oh, I see. Yes, it does seem too good to be true.'

'You haven't said much about your childhood,' commented Daisy.

'Haven't I?' June was deliberately vague.

'I imagine from the way you've turned out, being so smart and well spoken and everything, that it was a damned sight better than mine.'

'I doubt it,' she surprised Daisy by saying.

'Oh? But you were one of the chosen few who got out of St Clare's and into a proper home,' Daisy reminded her.

'There's more to a happy life than a comfortable house, Daisy,' June pointed out.

'I realise that but—'

'Let's not talk about me,' she cut in quickly. 'Tell me about yourself.'

'There's nothing much to say really,' Daisy told her. 'I stayed at St Clare's until I was fifteen.'

'It must have been hard, having to stay there for such a

113

long time,' sympathised June. 'I remember what tartars some of the nuns were.'

'They were strict, yeah. But they had to be with all those kids to look after,' said Daisy. 'Without discipline we'd have run wild. I've a lot to thank them for. They gave me a decent upbringing and I'm grateful for that.'

'Did you stay with Catholicism after you left there?' June enquired with interest.

She nodded. 'Did you?'

'No. My adopted parents had once been practising Catholics, which was why they went to St Clare's looking for a child to adopt, but they lapsed and I didn't take it up.'

'My faith is important to me. I really need it,' Daisy went on. 'I don't know how I'd have managed without it through the bad times. When all else failed, I still had that.'

'It must be nice to have something like that to turn to.'

'It is a comfort.' Again Daisy perceived deep unhappiness in her sister but didn't pry as June had made it obvious that she'd said as much as she was going to about her past life. It was still early days in their new relationship. Daisy hoped that at some point in the future June might trust her enough to confide.

'Can you remember what our father looked like?' asked June chattily.

'I've been thinking, and all I can remember about him is that he was a big man with dark hair.'

'I remember him being big too,' said June, 'He had a loud voice and a booming laugh too.'

'Oh, yeah,' smiled Daisy. 'Now you come to mention it, I remember that too.'

Far from being large and dark, Lionel Rivers was short and stockily built, with a bald head and wispy white tufts at the side of his heavily lined countenance. He didn't have a loud voice either but was quietly spoken with sad brown eyes and a look of defeat about him. He didn't look as though he'd laughed in years, in a booming way or otherwise – which was hardly surprising considering what he'd been through, Daisy thought. He couldn't be more than about fifty but he looked like an old man.

Dressed in prison uniform of a drab grey woollen jacket and trousers with a whitish flannel shirt, he observed them with an air of bewilderment across a table in the visitors' room. 'I couldn't believe it when they told me my daughters wanted to see me,' he said, his voice shaking with emotion. 'I'm sorry to have to admit this but you're so different to how I remember you, I'm not sure which is which.'

'I'm Daisy.'

'And I'm June.'

The silence was piercing; there was so much to say but no one knew where to start. He stared from one to the other, as though searching their faces for some sign of recognition.

'It doesn't half feel queer to be looking at the two of you as women,' he said at last. 'You've always been nippers in my memory, you see.' He shook his head slowly. 'Too many years have passed since I saw you.' He sounded so sad, Daisy thought he was about to burst into tears, which made her wonder if this visit was such a good idea after all.

'I've got two little girls of my own now,' Daisy told him, struggling with her own turmoil.

'Grandchildren.' His face worked.

'That's right.'

He didn't say anything; was obviously trying to compose himself. 'That's lovely,' he uttered eventually. 'I've often thought about the two of you, wondered how you were getting on. But I never thought I'd see either of you again.'

'If we'd known what had happened, we'd have been here long before this,' Daisy was keen for him to know.

'How did you find out where I was?' he asked. 'You were supposed never to know.'

'It's a long story,' June told him. 'Too long to go into in one visiting session. The important thing is, we know why you're here and why we were taken into care.'

His eyes widened. 'Oh, I see.' He swallowed hard. 'At the time you thought I'd abandoned you, didn't you?' he muttered thickly. 'Just dumped you because I didn't want to keep you?'

They both nodded.

'It broke my heart, having you think that I would do a thing like that. But it was considered best for you to grow up believing that, rather than know the truth. There were no relatives willing to take you in, you see,' he explained. 'And I was ordered not to try and contact you or to find out where you were.' He emitted a dry, humourless laugh. 'I'd have had a job, being locked up in here.'

'We've worked all of that out for ourselves,' Daisy said gently.

'You must have been very hurt at the time, though.'

'I was,' said June.

Daisy nodded, biting back the tears. 'But that's all in the past,' she said in a positive tone. 'Now we're in the picture. We've read the reports of the murder trial in the old newspapers in the library.'

'You bothered to do that?' He sounded astonished, his face lighting up.

'It was the only way we could find out more about it,' explained June.

Lionel put his hand to his head. 'You poor things.' He looked distressed. 'It must have been a shock to read such things about your parents.'

'It was,' they confessed in unison.

'For what it's worth, I didn't kill your mother,' he said, his

116

tired brown eyes brimming with tears.

'We know that.' June was unsure how to address him. 'Lionel' didn't seem appropriate and 'Dad' was still a label she associated with a man she'd hated.

'We know it was Morris Dodd,' added Daisy.

His eyes bulged. 'How could you possibly know that?'

Between them they told him.

'Well, stone me,' was his amazed reaction.

'We want to try to clear your name and get you out of here,' Daisy informed him.

His face worked with emotion, muscles tightening, mouth twitching slightly. 'It's very kind of you to want to do that for me, but, being realistic, you'll be wasting your time after all these years.' He shook his head sagely. 'We'll never get the case reopened now. You can only get an appeal if there's new evidence. They won't consider your childhood memories to be evidence.' He cleared his throat. 'They'll say you just imagined it unless you have proof to back it up.' He rummaged in his pocket, produced a rag handkerchief and blew his nose. 'Anyway, you've got your own lives to lead. Don't waste your time on my account.'

'June and I have discussed it at length and we know they won't take our word for it,' Daisy made clear. 'We also realise that Dodd won't admit the truth. But we're thinking in terms of trying to get the truth out of his wife, somehow. We know for a fact that she lied under oath.'

'She'd never admit it,' he stated categorically.

'We think it's unlikely too, but we want to try and find the Dodds anyway,' June was firm on this point, 'see if we can't persuade her to do the right thing.'

'Look, I'm really touched that you want to do this for me but there's no need,' he tried to convince them. 'You know that I didn't murder your mother and that I didn't just abandon you because I didn't want you, and that's enough for

117

me.' He shrugged. 'I've been here so long I'm resigned to prison life. It's all I know after all this time.'

'But you're locked up for something you didn't do,' emphasised Daisy. 'Justice must be done.'

'Fine words, love, but I don't want you getting mixed up with the likes of Morris Dodd,' he told them. 'Your mother lost her life because of his vile temper so I think you should steer well clear of him. I've found you again after all these years and that's all that matters to me.'

The two women exchanged glances. This was what the justice system had done to him. It had beaten the spirit out of him and killed his appetite for normal life.

'You can't just give in,' Daisy admonished.

'It took a while but I eventually accepted my fate because I had no choice,' he explained. 'I couldn't fight back because I had no ammunition with which to do so. No one was interested in the truth. To you that might seem pathetic – to me it's plain common sense.'

'But you've got us on your side now,' Daisy encouraged.

'You can't possibly know what that means to me.' His voice was muffled by stifled tears. 'But I don't want you getting into trouble on my behalf. Come and see me every now and again when you can manage it. That'll do for me.'

'We'll be the judge of that.' Daisy fell silent, a question burning inside her. 'Do you mind if I ask you something, though it might be painful for you?'

'Fire away,' he urged her. 'I'm long past secrets.'

She chewed her bottom lip; this was a delicate matter. 'Why did our mother have an affair?' she blurted out, adding quickly, 'Sorry, I realise the subject might hurt.'

'It does, of course, though time in here has toughened me up,' he told her. 'I must stress that your mother wasn't in the habit of taking lovers. She was the last person on earth you'd expect to get involved in that sort of thing. She'd always been a good wife and mother, the homely type.'

'Having an affair with a married man isn't a very homely thing to do,' June couldn't help mentioning. 'Especially when you've a couple of young kids to look after.'

'I can't argue with you about that,' Lionel agreed dully.

'Why do you think she did it?' wondered June. 'If she cared so much about her family?'

'Morris Dodd was a charmer in those days and he turned her head,' he told them. 'I was a gardener working for the parks department of the council, always in overalls; he was a rep for a firm of stationers, earning good money; he had nice clothes and plenty of chat. He had a reputation with women – knew how to make them feel good. I got to know him in our local pub and he and his wife became family friends – well, more just acquaintances really. They weren't our usual type but he was good company in small doses. From the way he used to talk to the men in the pub I knew he didn't have much in the way of morals but that was his business. I never dreamed he would go after my wife.'

'How did you find out about the affair?' asked Daisy.

'Your mother told me,' he explained. 'Said she'd come to her senses and couldn't carry on deceiving me any longer. She said she had ended the affair with him and begged me to forgive her and give her another chance. I don't think she ever loved him. She was infatuated for a while, that's all. Anyway, I agreed to try and forgive her, for the sake of the family. And because I still loved her, despite what she'd done.' He sighed. 'What happened after that is history, as they say.'

June cleared her throat; Daisy blew her nose. They were both struggling not to break down.

Lionel stared mistily into space. 'Life was so good before she got involved with that bugger. Everything changed so suddenly I was in a state of shock for months.' He gave them a wry look. 'Now I can hardly believe I ever had any other life but this.'

'It's so sad,' murmured June almost to herself.

'Don't feel sorry for me,' he was quick to protest. 'I'm all right, honestly. I'm in good health and that's worth a lot. You mustn't worry about me.'

'Easier said than done.' Daisy paused thoughtfully. 'Do you have any idea how we might find the Dodds?'

'I've told you I don't want you getting involved with them,' he reminded her. 'He's a nasty piece of work.'

'There are two of us so we'll be quite safe,' Daisy assured him. 'If he bumped us off he'd be signing his own death warrant. He wouldn't get away with it a second time.'

'The fact of the matter is, we've decided to try to find Mr and Mrs Dodd with or without your co-operation,' June added in a tone that didn't invite argument. 'So if you've any ideas, you'll save us time by sharing them with us.'

'All right,' Lionel conceded with an eloquent sigh. 'They used to live near us in Wembley, but it's most unlikely that they'd still be there now. They wouldn't have stayed there after all the scandal, not with his affair being splashed all over the papers in connection with the murder. His wife wouldn't have stood for that.'

'No, probably not,' agreed June.

'They could be anywhere now,' he went on. 'They could have moved away from London altogether.'

'But if we had their last address it would be a start,' Daisy pointed out. 'I doubt if they'll be there now but someone in the neighbourhood might have stayed in touch with them or have some sort of a clue as to where they went. So can you remember the address?'

'That's one I'll never forget,' he told them. 'It's number three Laverstock Avenue, Wembley.'

Daisy repeated it. 'That's an easy one to remember,' she remarked.

'You be careful.'

'Don't worry,' she told him kindly. 'We won't put ourselves at risk.'

'I'll make sure of that,' June further assured him.

'I'll have to take your word on that.' He looked from one to the other. 'Anyway, that's enough about the Dodds. I want to know all about you. You've grown up into such fine women, just like your mother.'

They both shot him a look.

'She *was* basically a good woman, no matter what you may be thinking about her,' he told them. 'She was human, she made a mistake.'

Daisy couldn't help thinking about the high cost of that mistake, to them all.

'Yes, well, I think we'll have to leave the catching up until next time,' mentioned June, glancing towards the warder, who was looking at his watch. 'It's time we were going.'

'You'll be coming again then?' Lionel suggested hopefully.

'Try keeping us away,' said Daisy.

'Thank you.' His humility tore at their hearts.

As they watched him being led away, they held their tears in check. Once outside the prison, they broke down and sobbed in each other's arms.

The warders on duty near Lionel's cell heard the sound of muffled weeping despite his attempts to conceal it for fear of seeming weak. Prison life had hardened him. There had been so much pain he'd grown several skins. Over the years he'd lost all purpose in life; had just let day follow day in a state of indifference. Not feeble, just resigned. But seeing his daughters again had inspired him with new life and purpose; had given him a reason to live.

121

Naturally in the past there had been times when he'd imagined what it would be like to walk along the street again, a free man, despite the stoicism he'd needed to carry him through. He was a realist, however, and knew that freedom wasn't something he was likely to taste again, despite his daughters' best endeavours. But even if he ended his days in custody he would die a happy man having seen them again and knowing that they knew the truth about him. His tears were a glorious outpouring of joy.

'Well, I think the whole thing is downright ridiculous,' disapproved Nat one evening a week or two later. 'I don't think you should waste another minute looking for these Dodd characters. You'll never find them after all this time, not in a million years.'

It was Daisy's night off so she and June had taken the opportunity to go to Laverstock Avenue, where they had drawn a complete blank.

'Be fair, Nat,' she said in a tone of mild admonition. 'The Wembley address was just a starting point. We didn't really expect to find them there. That would have been too easy.'

'But you've just said that you knocked on every door in the streets around there and no one knew where they'd gone to. So use your loaf and give up before you waste any more time on a wild-goose chase.' Because Nat was the man in her life Daisy had confided in him about the extraordinary revelations regarding her background. 'And even if you were to find them, what good would it do? I mean, this Dodd bloke isn't likely to confess to a murder, is he?'

'We're prepared for that,' Daisy told him.

'What's the point of chasing after him then?' Nat wanted to know, his voice rising.

'Don't shout, you'll wake the children,' Daisy rebuked. 'And to answer your question, the point of chasing the Dodds

122

is because our father is in prison for something he didn't do. He's our *father, our own flesh and blood*. We can't just let him rot in prison when he's innocent without lifting a finger to help him. We have to take some sort of action.'

'I don't see why,' scoffed Nat. 'So what if he is your own flesh and blood? You haven't seen him for over twenty years. He can't possibly mean anything to you. The man's a stranger.'

'Of course he is, and he will be until we get to know him,' admitted Daisy. 'But he's been wrongfully imprisoned and we are the only people apart from him and the Dodds who know that. How can we live with ourselves if we don't do something for him? I admit it's going to be like looking for a needle in a haystack, but I'm not prepared to give up.'

'Personally,' intervened Nora, 'I think it's one of the saddest stories I've ever heard, even apart from the fact that he's the girls' father. That poor man locked up for all those years for something he didn't do – it's only natural they would want to do something to help him, even if it's only to tell that Morris Dodd that they're on to him, that he hasn't quite got away with it after all.'

Nat gave her a withering look. He thought Nora was an interfering old bag. She had far too much to say on the subject of his treatment of Daisy, and ought to learn to mind her own business. 'They were little kids when the murder happened, for God's sake,' he pointed out scathingly. 'Daisy was five years old. How can she possibly remember something that happened as far back as that?'

'I can remember my first day at school,' claimed Nora.

'Rubbish,' dismissed Nat.

'I know what I remember,' retorted Nora.

'No one can remember that far back,' argued Nat. 'Daisy probably imagined seeing the geezer at the house that night.'

'You're wrong about that,' June was quick to amend,

'because I saw him too and we can't both have imagined it. And before you say that I put ideas into her head, I didn't. She remembered it without any help from me.'

This sister of Daisy's had a bit too much to say for herself as well, Nat thought gloomily. This wasn't the first time she'd tried to put him in his place. Left alone, Daisy was as sweet as a nut. He could twist her around his little finger. But having the influence of opinionated types like Nora and June around made things more difficult for him.

'All right, so you both think you remember it, but I still think you're on a hiding to nothing in trying to clear your father's name,' he persisted.

'We know it won't be easy,' admitted Daisy. 'But we're going to give it our best shot.'

'Why are you so dead set against it anyway?' Nora wanted to know. 'It isn't as if she's asking you to help. I can't see why it matters to you one way or the other.'

'It matters to me, *my dear*,' he said with seething impatience and strong emphasis to indicate the opposite to endearment, 'because I care what happens to Daisy and I don't want her getting mixed up in something that's out of her league.'

'Cut out the squabbling, for goodness' sake,' rebuked Daisy, 'and let's see if we can't come up with something constructive between us.'

'As I've already said, I'll look in the phone book at work,' said June, 'and phone any Dodds in the London area from a call box. They have all the phone books in the library for a more thorough search, though as we haven't a clue which area they're in, that could take for ever.'

'The same thing applies to the electoral roll at the library and town hall,' Nora put in thoughtfully. 'As you don't know where they're living you'd need two lifetimes to get through the job.'

Daisy thought about this. 'I don't think they would have moved away from London, you know,' she observed. 'A different neighbourhood – yeah, definitely. But they're Londoners and the place would be in their bones, especially as they could escape from the scandal just by moving across town. A few miles up the road and you're a stranger in this city of ours. You don't need to move away from the capital to make a new start.'

'I still don't think the electoral register would be a good idea, though,' said Nora after more consideration. 'London's a densely populated place. Without knowing the actual borough, it just wouldn't be viable.'

Daisy and June nodded in agreement.

'You wouldn't believe it could be this difficult to find someone, would you?' mentioned Daisy.

'If it were easy, people wouldn't manage to stay missing and detective agencies wouldn't thrive,' Nora pointed out.

'True. Anyway, June's idea of going through the phone books is a good one,' said Daisy.

'We're frantically busy at work in the run-up to Christmas but I'm not going to let that stop me,' said June determinedly.

'I've got to work more shifts because of all the Christmas functions too,' Daisy informed them. 'I'm glad of the additional hours because of the extra dosh, but I'm going to find the time to go back to Wembley in daytime and ask around in the local shops. Someone might know something.'

'Good thinking,' approved June.

'I should forget about it altogether if I were you,' muttered Nat sulkily.

'I'm not going to do that, Nat,' asserted Daisy. 'So you may as well stop being such a doom merchant.'

'Suit yourself,' was his sharp retort. 'Frankly, I'm bored stiff with the whole flaming subject.' He threw a glare in June's direction, then looked back at Daisy. 'You've thought about nothing else but your father since your sister turned up.'

'Nat,' rebuked Daisy, flushing with embarrassment. 'Don't be so rude.'

'I'm only saying what's true,' he insisted. 'And as you obviously prefer your sister's company to mine, I might as well go down the pub.'

'Don't be like that.' Daisy looked worried now; she was only prepared to go so far in defiance of him.

'Don't leave on my account,' June told him frostily. 'It's time I was off anyway.'

'Me too,' said Nora.

And they both made hasty departures, leaving Daisy and Nat to sort out their differences in private.

'I wish you would try to be a bit nicer to my sister.' Daisy and Nat were sitting on the sofa.

'She's a stuck-up cow with her la-di-la voice and her posh clothes,' was his opinion.

'I think she speaks lovely. I could listen to her talk for hours,' Daisy said. 'Anyway, she has to be well presented in her job at a West End hotel.'

'She isn't my sort of person at all.'

'Maybe not, but she is my sister and therefore part of me,' Daisy reminded him. 'And as you're part of my life too, it would make things easier for me if you could make some sort of an effort to get along with her.'

'You haven't been the same person since she arrived on the scene,' he complained. 'You've changed.'

'Have I . . . really?'

'That's what I said.'

'It isn't intentional but I suppose June coming back into my life is bound to have an effect,' she reasoned. 'I've never had anyone of my own before.'

'You've got me.'

Even Daisy, with her huge capacity for self-delusion where Nat was concerned, could see what a gross distortion of the facts that was. She hadn't 'got him', as he put it. She never had. He appeared without prior notice at odd times and was never there when she needed him. She'd never met any of his relatives because he didn't go in for all that 'family stuff'. But there was no point in her complaining about it because he would never change. She either gave him up or accepted him as he was.

'My relationship with June is very important to me,' she said, 'but it hasn't affected my feelings for you.'

'Ooh, not much,' he disagreed. 'It's June this, June that, my father this, my father that.'

'Surely you're not jealous.'

'Do me a favour . . .'

'Be pleased for me then.'

'I am, of course,' he said rather unconvincingly. 'It's just that with your sister and Nora being around so much I never get a chance to be on my own with you.'

Privacy had never been readily available to them, given the size of the flat and the fact that the girls were always around. 'Yeah, I can see your point about that,' Daisy agreed. 'But as I never know when you're going to turn up I can't keep people away on the off chance that you'll pay me a visit, can I?'

'I suppose not.' There were no promises of reliability in the future. That wasn't his way.

'You can't complain if other people are here then, can you?' she said.

'Oh, stop yapping, woman,' he said, putting his arm around her, 'and give us a kiss.'

This wasn't a problem for her because she was still attracted to him, however deeply in the doghouse he was. But something was missing lately; she was becoming increasingly

127

conscious of a change in her attitude towards him, a need to draw back. Maybe having relatives thrust upon her suddenly had altered her. But it wasn't just that. June and her father had given Daisy's life a new meaning certainly, but subtle changes in her feelings towards Nat had begun before they'd appeared. She was irritated with him more often now, less willing to be a doormat.

But then he whispered the magic words into her ear, 'I love you, Daisy,' and she could forget all her complicated emotions and succumb to the sheer pleasure of him.

'And I love you too,' she sighed.

June sat on the tube back to Marble Arch thinking about Nat and his appalling behaviour towards Daisy, and pondering on the power of human emotions that allowed people to make such fools of themselves. An intelligent and spirited woman like Daisy would never put up with that sort of treatment were she not besotted.

Having seen the way Nat behaved towards her sister had made June reappraise Alan's virtues. He'd been no saint but he'd always treated her with respect and listened to her opinions. Whereas Nat behaved as though Daisy was some half-wit who existed purely for his convenience.

His abysmal manners obviously embarrassed her and you could tell she was hurt by his lack of interest in the girls. But still the relationship continued. Complicated things, love affairs. However crazy or unbalanced they might seem to those on the outside, only the participants knew about the indefinable ingredient that held it together.

There was one thing that June did know for sure, though. However much she might feel compelled to voice her opinion of Nat to Daisy, to do so would almost certainly damage her new adult relationship with Daisy, who would take the side of the man she loved against a sister she hardly knew. So June would hold her tongue rather than jeopardise something of such value to her, especially while it was still embryonic and delicate.

Her thoughts drifted back to Alan. She was still thinking about him as she emerged into the street, the Christmas lights shining brightly along Oxford Street, a cheering spectacle of colour and festivity which eliminated the winter gloom and made her want to cry with the pain of missing Alan. Her first Christmas without him was going to be hardly bearable, she thought, heading off down a side street to the Central Hotel in the cold December night.

Chapter Six

The next morning while June was on duty, a tall, thin man of about fifty emerged scowling from the lift, marched across to the reception desk and fixed her with a stony stare. 'I want to see the manager,' he demanded, obviously simmering with umbrage.

To save the unnecessary use of management time, receptionists here were encouraged to deal with complaints in the first instance, referring them to a higher level only if their own efforts at conciliation failed.

'Certainly, sir,' she said with immaculate manners. 'Is there a problem?'

'Ooh, not so you'd notice,' was his ironic reply.

'Perhaps you'd like to tell me about it.'

'I'm suffering from exhaustion with every possibility of pneumonia developing,' he explained through clenched teeth, pale face set in a grim expression; his short brown hair was worn in a traditional style with a side parting and greased flat to his head, making him look even sterner. 'And the appalling standards in this hotel are to blame.' His eyes rolled heavenwards in tandem with a supercilious sigh. 'Quite frankly I'd be better off sleeping in a shop doorway, and since you charge the earth for a room here, that's nothing short of a disgrace.'

'I'm so sorry to hear you're not enjoying your stay with

us,' June said in the courteous, noncommittal tone she was trained to adopt in such a situation. 'Would you like to tell me what in particular hasn't pleased you?'

'Nothing has pleased me,' he informed her brusquely. 'This place is a joke.'

Needing to get to the crux of the matter, she asked, 'Is there something wrong with your room, sir?'

'You'd be nearer the mark to ask if there's anything right with it,' he barked at her. 'I was kept awake all night by the noise. I haven't had a wink of sleep.'

'Ah, I see.' She gave a sympathetic tut. 'People come up to town for Christmas functions at this time of the year and book in here overnight. I'm afraid the festive spirit makes some of our guests a little boisterous when they come back to the hotel.'

'It wasn't the other guests who disturbed me.'

'Really?'

'No. It was the traffic.' He became incandescent with rage as he thought back on it. 'Roaring past my window all night long. I've never heard such a racket.'

'The traffic noise can be disturbing if you're not used to it,' June agreed in an understanding manner. 'Unfortunately – with the best will in the world – we can't do anything about that as the hotel is situated in London's West End. Traffic noise is par for the course around here.'

'All night?'

'It does ease off in the small hours, naturally, but it doesn't usually stop altogether.'

'Nobody told me that when I booked.'

'They must have assumed you would guess,' she suggested politely, 'this being the capital city.'

His eyes bulged at this implied criticism and June had to think fast to head off an explosion. 'What's your room number, sir?' she enquired.

'Ninety-two.'

She gave him a knowing nod. 'Now I understand. That room is on the corner of the hotel directly above the traffic lights,' she explained. 'Vehicles stop outside with their engines throbbing, then roar away when the lights change. I know what it's like because I live here at the hotel and my room is on the same corner but much higher up. The noise used to be a problem for me when I first moved in. But it doesn't bother me now that I'm used to it.'

'I'm booked in here for three more nights and I can assure you that I have no intention of getting used to it,' the man made clear with seething irritation.

'Of course not, and we wouldn't expect you to.' June was a very fair-minded woman and could usually see the customer's point of view. But she knew instinctively that this man was the type to find fault with the service at Buckingham Palace were he ever invited as a guest. She took a deep breath, keeping a grip on her professionalism. 'Would you like me to see if we have a vacant room in another part of the hotel, further away from that junction?'

'There's no point,' he snapped. 'Because the noise isn't the only thing that's wrong.'

Here comes the cause of his possible pneumonia, she thought, but said, 'Could you tell me what else is troubling you, sir, so that we can put it right? Our guests' comfort is everything to us here at the Central Hotel. If you're not happy, we're concerned.'

'My room is freezing,' he informed her. 'I've been chilled to the bone all night.'

This puzzled her because the heating in this hotel was excellent and she hadn't been notified of any problem in the boiler room. 'Oh? Is the radiator not working?'

'I wouldn't be complaining if it was, would I?' was his abrupt reply. 'It's stone-cold.'

'That's strange.' At this crucial moment in customer relations, the telephone rang. 'Please excuse me for a moment,' she said.

He frowned in reply.

'Central Hotel. Good morning,' she said in her best business voice. 'Can I help you?'

The operator's voice crackled down the line informing her of a long-distance call from Torquay. With heart pounding, June told her to put it through.

'Hello, June.'

'Alan.' She quivered from top to toe. 'How are you?'

'I'm all right. Yourself?'

'I'm fine.'

'I'll come straight to the point as I'm calling long distance,' he began.

'Look, Alan, I can't talk—'

'The fact is, June,' he went on as though her interruption hadn't registered, 'I'm calling you on impulse because I still miss you and I just can't bear the thought of Christmas without you.'

'Oh,' was the best she could manage. With the furious guest focusing her with a disapproving stare, this wasn't the time for a personal conversation.

'So, I was wondering if you might consider coming down to Torquay for the holiday,' Alan continued. 'So that we can talk things over.'

'No, Alan, that isn't a good idea.' It was a wonder to June that she didn't wither and turn to dust under the lethal glare of the disgruntled guest. It was her job to pacify him and the need to do so grew more urgent by the second. If he reported her to the management for taking a personal call when she was supposed to be giving him her undivided attention, she could lose her job, which would render her homeless as well as unemployed. 'I really can't talk now, I'm sorry,' she said *sotto voce*.

'Oh. Oh, I see.' He sounded hurt; obviously thought she was just putting him off. Although Alan was familiar with how things were on the working side of a hotel reception desk, the Cliff Head reception was a playground compared to this one, and he couldn't possibly imagine how ill-timed his call was.

'I'm on duty, Alan.' She spoke in a whisper. It wasn't possible for her to explain to him that she had every hotelier's nightmare giving her the look of death, without the man hearing her. 'It's difficult right now.'

'Oh, don't worry about me,' said the man with seething sarcasm. 'I'm only a paying guest. I should hate to interfere with your private life.'

She put her hand over the mouthpiece and looked at him anxiously. 'Sorry about this, sir. I'll be with you in a second,' she assured him.

'Don't bother to find me another room,' he roared, almost beside himself with rage now. 'I'll check out of this dump and find somewhere else to stay as the receptionist here is too busy with a personal call to attend to me. I want my money back for last night, though. I'm not paying for a room in which it's impossible to sleep.' He puffed out his lips. 'Not likely.'

A demand for a refund as well as a customer complaint about the conduct of the duty receptionist would almost certainly result in dismissal. 'I have to go now, Alan,' June said quickly, and replaced the receiver without waiting for his reaction.

She was trembling from the effect of contact with Alan as she turned her attention back to the man, though she concealed it well. 'I really am very sorry about that, sir,' she apologised again.

He gave her a curt nod.

Being accustomed to dealing with the public at large, June

135

was a consummate professional and could turn on the charm when necessary. She gave him one of her most melting smiles and behaved as though his threats to leave hadn't happened. 'Now, about the radiator in your room. It's cold, you say?'

'That's right.'

'And it's definitely turned on?'

He gave her a pitying look. 'Of course it is,' he said in a superior manner.

'That's really odd,' she said in a confiding manner, 'because the heating seems to be working well enough in the rest of the hotel.' She paused, choosing her words carefully. 'I wonder if perhaps the previous occupant of your room preferred a cool temperature and turned the radiator off.'

'How could they have done when the heating is controlled from a central point by your people?' he blasted.

'You're quite right, of course,' she conceded gracefully. 'The heating is controlled from a central point by us. But each radiator is also self-regulating and can be individually operated as long as the system is turned on, which it is in the winter.'

'Oh.'

At least he had the grace to look sheepish so she decided to help him out. 'Some of the older central heating systems don't have that individual facility,' she pointed out, 'but ours has been recently modernised.'

'I know how central heating works.' He obviously hadn't realised but would sooner die than lose face by admitting it. 'Obviously I checked to see if the radiator was turned on. And I can assure you that it was, and it was cold.'

'Yes, I understand,' she said, managing to sound convincing. 'I'll have one of our maintenance men go up to take a look.'

'Thank you.' He was noticeably more subdued.

A swift look at the hotel booking plan revealed a room

vacant in a different part of the hotel. 'As luck would have it, we've had a cancellation so I can have you moved to a quieter room if you wish, though we can't erase the noise of the traffic altogether any more than any other hotel in central London can.'

He appeared to be pondering the question.

Winning him over had become a challenge to June now. 'Or, if you'd rather, I'll ring through for the manager to come and see you if you still wish to make a formal complaint and continue with your plans to check out.' She gave him a look of concern. 'But to make sure you're not left without a bed for the night, I can ring a few hotels to find out if they have any vacancies. Most London hotels are fully booked in the run-up to Christmas with so many people coming up to town for shopping.'

The extent of her helpfulness took the sting out of his argument. Much to her relief her ploy worked. 'No, no,' he said. 'If you get me moved to a different room for tonight, I'll give it a try.' He gave her a stern look. 'But if I have so much as a hint of cause for complaint, you'll be hearing from me again.'

I bet we will, she thought, but said sweetly, 'I'll have someone move your things.'

Clearly impressed by the lengths she was prepared to go to in his interests, he became much more amenable. 'That's very nice of you,' he said. 'Thank you.'

'A pleasure,' she assured him. 'No trouble at all.' She smiled at him and decided she might as well grovel some more in the interests of customer relations. 'Might I suggest that while we're organising your move, you make yourself comfortable in the lounge and I'll have some coffee and biscuits brought to you.'

'That would be lovely.' He was smiling now and looked almost human. There was even some colour in his cheeks.

'I'll arrange everything and coffee will be along in a minute,' she said.

He nodded, then walked away towards the lounge with an air of triumph, obviously congratulating himself on winning all this attention.

But as far as June was concerned, she was the victor in this battle. Sighing with relief, she rang through to the kitchen to order his coffee.

As soon as she came off duty June went to the telephone box around the corner armed with coins, and put in a long-distance call to Torquay. Christmas with Alan was out of the question but she didn't want him to think she'd snubbed him. The mere thought of hurting him in that way upset her.

'Cliff Head Hotel, can I help you?'

Much to her annoyance June realised the voice belonged to her mother-in-law.

'Hello, Irene,' she said nervously. 'This is June.'

There was a brief silence while she digested the information. 'My God, you've got a nerve, ringing up here after what you've done to my son,' was her acerbic reaction.

'Is Alan there, please?' June wasn't prepared to waste time in conversation with Irene, since the call was costing a fortune and the money running out fast.

'No, he isn't.'

'Could you put me through to the flat then, please?'

'He isn't there either.'

'Oh. So he isn't in the hotel at all?'

'That's right. He's out on business.'

'Do you know when he'll be back?'

'No.'

'Look, I really need to speak to him urgently,' June continued, daunted but not deterred by the resistance Irene was giving her. 'He rang me earlier and I couldn't speak to him because I was on duty. It's a very busy hotel where I work and I need to explain that to him.'

'You can't if he isn't here, can you?' said the other woman unhelpfully.

'Will you tell him I called then, please?' June requested.

'Yes, I'll do that.'

'Can you explain to him why I wasn't able to speak to him?' June asked, feeling desperate now. 'I was dealing with a difficult customer when his call came through and I couldn't pay attention to him. You know how it is in a hotel reception.'

'I'll tell him.'

'Thank you . . .' The pips interrupted the conversation and the line went dead.

Her first instinct was to call again later and try to speak to Alan personally, but a call box wasn't really suitable for something of such a sensitive nature with the money running out with the speed of light. The message she'd left for him would be enough to convince him she hadn't just been putting him off.

Just as Irene was replacing the receiver after the call from June, Alan walked into reception from the restaurant where he'd been discussing something with Jack about the large private function they had booked for this evening. Despite what she'd said to June, his mother had been fully aware of his whereabouts.

Passing the desk on his way to the office, he noticed that she looked cross. 'What's up, Mother?' he asked. 'You're looking a bit rattled.'

'I'm all right,' she said innocently.

'You could turn milk sour all the way to Exeter with that face,' he teased her. 'Has someone on the phone upset you?'

'No,' she denied swiftly. 'It was someone making a

restaurant booking for next week. Just a routine call.'

He gave her a shrewd look. 'You've definitely got the look of battle about you, as though you've just been putting someone in their place.' He wasn't as cheerful as he sounded after the disappointing call he'd made to June earlier, and was just putting on a front. 'Are you sure you haven't just had a complaint?'

'What, against the Cliff Head Hotel?' She made a joke of it. 'Never let it be said.'

'Spoken like a true professional,' he approved, moving away. 'If you need me I'll be in the office.'

'All right, son.'

She had no intention of telling him about June's call. It would only unsettle him. He needed to get that dreadful woman out of his system so that he could get on with his life. And the sooner he forgot about her the better.

'I've rung all the Dodds I could find in the phone book but none of them has a Morris in the family, not even a distant relative,' June informed her sister.

'And I've had no luck in the shops around Wembley,' said Daisy, looking disappointed. 'Still, we didn't expect it to be easy, did we? We'll just have to keep trying.'

It was Sunday morning at Daisy's place. She and the girls hadn't long been back from Mass and she was peeling a pile of sprouts to go with the piece of scrag end of lamb she was cooking for lunch with roast potatoes. Shirley and Belinda were in Nora's flat, making paper chains with her.

'It's all we can do,' June agreed. 'But I thought I'd better pop over and let you know how I'd got on, even though it's a negative result.'

'I appreciate that,' Daisy said. 'It's a pity we don't have a phone we can use to save you coming over every time there's a message.'

'It's no trouble,' June assured her. 'It's only three stops on the tube.'

'Would you like to join us for lunch?' invited Daisy impulsively. 'I can easily do a few more spuds. Nora will be coming in. We always have Sunday lunch together if I'm not out working. Otherwise she gives the girls theirs.'

'I'd love to but I'm on duty at half-past twelve,' June told her.

'Another time then perhaps,' suggested Daisy.

'Thanks. I'd like that.' June paused thoughtfully. 'How come you're not working today?'

'I am. We're having a very early lunch and I'm going in to work as soon as I've eaten mine,' she explained. 'At the hotel where I work they don't start serving lunches until half-past twelve and I don't think they're likely to complain if I'm a bit late getting in today as I've agreed to stay on to serve afternoon teas and dinner tonight. As I'll be out all day until after the girls go to bed, I want to have lunch with them before I go.'

June nodded.

'I try to spend as much time as I possibly can with them, especially at this time of the year. But it's never enough.'

'Are you working over Christmas?' June enquired.

'No fear,' Daisy said. 'You?'

'No.'

'Are you doing anything exciting on Christmas Day?' Daisy asked casually.

'I've nothing planned,' June informed her gloomily. 'I suppose there might be a few of us in the staff quarters with nothing on, so maybe we'll get together for Christmas dinner. No one's said anything about it, though.'

Seeing the sadness in her sister's eyes, Daisy realised that Christmas would be difficult for her, having recently parted from her husband. She cast her eye around the room. 'This

141

isn't exactly the Ritz,' she pointed out unnecessarily, 'but we usually manage to enjoy ourselves in our own simple way at Christmas. You're very welcome to join us.'

June was more touched than Daisy could possibly know. 'I'd really love that, Daisy, but—'

'Don't feel you have to say yes,' she cut in defensively. 'I realise it isn't what you're used to.'

'I live in a basic little room in staff accommodation, for heaven's sake,' her sister reminded her, tutting to emphasise the point.

'Now you do, yes, but you have been used to better things,' Daisy went on.

'Yes, I have,' June wasn't ashamed to admit. 'But that isn't the reason I hesitated before accepting your invitation. I didn't say yes because I don't want to spoil Christmas for Nat. I'm not exactly his favourite person, am I?'

'Nat won't be here,' Daisy was quick to inform her. 'We never see him over Christmas. He goes to relatives in the East End somewhere. Some sort of a family commitment, apparently. I don't know the details.'

'And you and the girls don't go with him, not even for part of the time?' June was incredulous at this further evidence of the man's cavalier attitude.

'Nat isn't the type to take his girlfriend home to meet the family,' Daisy explained. 'That isn't his style.'

A stab of rage towards Nat whipped through June. Surely Daisy and the girls should have first call on his time at Christmas. But if her sister was upset she wasn't showing it. Probably so used to his shabby treatment as to have become immune, June guessed. 'In that case I'd love to join you,' she smiled. 'But only on the condition that I pay my share.'

'You won't get any argument from me about that,' Daisy told her with a wry grin. 'Christmas is an expensive business

142

when you've got two kids with high expectations in the Santa department.'

'That's settled then.'

'Lovely.'

Warmth towards Daisy swept over June, making her eyes feel hot and moist. 'I haven't been looking forward to Christmas one little bit this year, but you've just taken the dread out of it for me,' she said with feeling. 'And I thank you for that with all my heart.'

Daisy smiled, her cheeks flushed with pleasure. But she wasn't given to extravagant displays of sentimentality so she just said, 'We'll be delighted to have you. The more the merrier.'

Lionel Rivers lay on his bunk reading the letter for the umpteenth time, staring at the words and drinking in the joy of them. A letter in itself was a huge event for him. One like this was enough to make him shout with the pleasure of it.

It was from a friend of his daughters', someone called Nora Dove. She hoped he didn't mind her writing to him but Daisy and June had told her his story and she was so moved by it she wanted to write to offer her support and friendship. She went on to explain that she was of his generation rather than his daughters' and thought he might appreciate having someone of his own age to communicate with. She was keen to make the point that he mustn't feel under any obligation to correspond with her if he'd rather not.

She mentioned his daughters' determination to try to clear his name, adding that it might take a long time. He must take comfort in the fact that they would do everything in their power to see that justice was done. They were fine young women and he could be proud to be their father.

The letter was warm and chatty, and contained several amusing anecdotes about his granddaughters, and how they

143

and Daisy meant so much to Nora. The letter didn't spare him the grim realities of life outside altogether. She mentioned a ruthless landlord and the possibility of herself and Daisy losing their home.

'You reading that letter again?' asked Lionel's cell mate from the bunk below.'

'That's right.'

'Blimey, you must know it off by heart now,' the other man joshed. 'I haven't had a word out of you for hours and it'll be lights out soon.'

'Mm.'

'It must be from a woman to keep you that interested,' the other man went on to say.

'It's from a friend and the fact that she happens to be a woman is irrelevant,' explained Lionel. His words had a strange ring to them because it had been so long since he'd called anyone a friend. He couldn't wait to reply to her.

'There's no need to look quite so fed up, Alan,' admonished Paula Bright, a smart woman in her late twenties with short fashionably cut red hair and sparkling blue eyes. 'I realise that our parents' Christmas get-together isn't the most exciting event on your social calendar but it isn't that bad.'

'Sorry,' he apologised. 'Am I being very rude?'

'I wouldn't go so far as to say that,' she said. 'But you're not exactly lively company.'

'It's nothing personal,' he smiled, making an effort. 'I'm just not feeling very sociable this evening. But that's no excuse for bad manners.'

'Don't worry about it.' She seemed very relaxed on the subject. 'I realise that you only came to this little soirée because your parents would have given you a whole lot of grief if you hadn't.'

He gave her a knowing look. 'You too?' he said.

'Surely you don't think I enjoyed being thrown together with you at every possible opportunity when we were growing up in the hope that someday the two of us would make a go of it, do you?' she asked candidly.

'I'd never really thought about it from your point of view,' he was forced to admit.

'Too busy trying to protect yourself, I expect,' she chuckled.

'Something like that.'

'In actual fact I was about as interested in you romantically as you were in me,' she informed him. 'It was a relief to me when you got married.' She raised her eyes, tutting. 'Of course, now that you've split up with your wife, the folks will probably start to get ideas again. But you can relax in the knowledge that they're wasting their time as far as I'm concerned.'

'Oh.'

She cupped her hand behind her ear as though listening to something in the distance. 'Is that the shattering of an ego I can hear?' she chuckled.

'Just a little bruised perhaps,' he smiled, finding her candour rather entertaining.

'You men want it both ways,' she opined. 'You can't bear the idea of a woman not being interested in you even if that woman is the last person on earth you want to be with.'

'I don't think that's a gender thing,' he said. 'It's just a quirk of human nature.'

She shrugged. 'Maybe,' she conceded.

'I'm glad we've got things clear between us at last, anyway.'

'Me too.'

It was the evening of the day before Christmas Eve and he and Paula were sitting chatting at a table in the Cliff Head bar. She had come over with her parents for a seasonal drink with the Masters and other friends of her and Alan's parents.

145

The older generation were standing in a group talking nearby. Alan and Paula had drifted into conversation as a matter of course.

'I should have thought that being sociable was second nature to you, as a hotelier, whether you're in the mood or not,' she remarked, sipping her gin and tonic, blue eyes peering at him over the rim of the glass. 'It's all in a day's work to us.'

'That's true . . . up to a point.'

'But the sparkling conversation doesn't happen instinctively for a friend of the family who isn't going to pay the going rate for a room?' she suggested with a knowing twinkle in her eye. 'Am I right?'

'It isn't a conscious thing on my part but there might be something in what you say,' he returned, Paula's light-hearted manner cheering him up. 'As you say, being sociable is an automatic thing in our business.'

'Dare I ask what's made you so gloomy?' she enquired casually.

The breakdown of his marriage was the answer to that but he wasn't going to bare his soul to Paula about the fact that his wife couldn't even spare the time to talk to him on the phone or return his call. After the painful rejection she'd given him at the hotel in London, it had taken a lot of courage to call her and suggest they spend Christmas together. And she wouldn't even consider it; just put the phone down on him. Ever since then he'd been struggling to accept the truth – that it was over between them and there was no point in his trying to get her back.

He thought back to happier times. They had both been so full of hope and harmony when they'd got married. And the sad thing was he'd never noticed it slip away; still couldn't fully accept that it had. But for some reason best known to herself, June didn't want him in her life. She seemed so cold and distant now. Not the woman he had fallen in love with at all.

But now Paula was saying, 'Talk to yourself, why don't you, Paula? It seems as though that's the only way you're going to get any answers.'

'Sorry.' Alan gave her a wry grin. 'I was miles away.'

'Problems of a personal nature rather than business, I suspect,' she speculated.

He gave her his full attention. 'You're very astute.'

'Difficult guests and hotel disasters don't carry the same look of pain somehow,' she said lightly. 'I know about these things; I'm in the same line of business, remember.'

'Yes, of course.'

Her expression became more serious. 'I was sorry to hear that you and your wife had parted,' she told him. 'Even though it's probably turned our folks into dedicated matchmakers again, now that you're back in circulation. You and your wife seemed good together whenever I saw you. From what I knew of June, she seemed nice.'

'I always thought so.'

'You're speaking in the past tense, I notice,' Paula pointed out. 'And that seems a bit harsh. Just because it didn't work out for the two of you, that doesn't mean she's a lesser person than you thought she was.'

'I know that,' he corrected. 'I meant more that I feel I couldn't have ever really known her. I mean, before this happened I would have staked my life on her loyalty, on her staying with me until we were a couple of old codgers. But to just walk out like that with no warning . . .' He sighed, shaking his head. 'It still shocks me to think about it.'

'She must have had a very good reason,' was Paula's opinion. 'Or thought she had.'

Deciding he'd already said too much, he called a halt.

Despite what she'd done, it seemed disloyal to June to discuss their problems with a relative stranger.

'Yeah, I expect you're right.' He looked at her and saw shining blue eyes, a flawless skin suffused with cleverly applied make-up. A fitted black suit sat well on her trim figure. She wasn't a stunning beauty but she was attractive and sexy. 'But that's quite enough about me. Let's talk about you now. Is there anyone serious in your life?'

'I'm not about to get married, if that's what you mean,' she told him.

'I'm surprised you're not married already.'

'Most people are,' she told him. 'A man can stay single beyond the age of about twenty-five and everyone assumes he's enjoying life as a bachelor too much to want to settle down. A woman does it and they think there must be something wrong with her because she can't get a man. It never occurs to anyone that she might actually enjoy the single life.'

'I thought most women wanted to get married,' Alan said. 'Thought it was the natural thing, all part of the nesting instinct.'

'It is,' she agreed. 'Finding a husband and settling down to have babies is the life plan of the average 1950s woman. I suppose that was all I wanted too up until I was about twenty. But when it didn't happen, I got to thinking that being single wasn't so bad after all, especially as I got more involved in the management of the hotel. I'd like to meet Mr Right, of course, but if it isn't meant to be I can live with it. I realise that I'm some sort of a freak because I didn't rush up the aisle at the first opportunity.'

'I'm sure there was no lack of offers.'

'I've had a few.'

'You just didn't fancy them?'

'I've had my moments,' she said with a wicked grin. 'But

148

that doesn't mean I was ready to give up my independence and settle down just because it's the done thing. I haven't yet met anyone I'd want to give up my single status for, even if that does mean people will soon start calling me an old maid. Anyway, apart from anything else, I have to make sure it's me they want and not the hotel. Like you, Alan, I'm an only child. My parents' hotel is worth a lot of money and will be mine one day. That factor alone makes me attractive in some men's eyes.'

'You're attractive anyway,' he told her, and meant it. 'Regardless of your material assets.'

'Thank you.' She smiled, seeming pleased.

'It was never that I didn't find you attractive.' It suddenly seemed important that she knew that. 'It was just the minute I clapped eyes on June there was no one else for me.'

'Explanations aren't necessary,' Paula assured him breezily. 'As I've said, it was a mutual thing.'

'You're doing terrible things to my ego again,' he teased her.

She laughed. 'Your sense of humour didn't die altogether when June left then,' she remarked.

'Apparently not, I'm surprised to discover.'

'I suppose one of the reasons our folks were so keen for us to get together was because we each had our own assets,' she said thoughtfully. 'So they could be sure that if it did happen it wouldn't be for material gain on either side.'

'Mm.' Alan's thoughts turned to less personal matters. 'But tell me, do you still close your hotel over Christmas?'

'That's right.'

'Same here. But I'd like to throw open the doors and make a big thing of it. Do a special Christmas programme.'

'Would you get any takers, though,' she wondered, 'Christmas being a home and family time?'

'I think we might. A lot of people would probably welcome

the chance to escape from all the domestic slavery that goes on at Christmas.'

'Why don't you give it a try then?'

'Mum and Dad won't hear of it,' he explained. 'They want things to stay exactly as they have always been at the Cliff Head.' He paused, looking at her. 'I expect you have the same trouble with your folks, don't you?'

'Not at all,' she surprised him by saying. 'My parents are leaving things to me increasingly. They're content to take a back seat and let me shoulder the responsibility, glad to have some time to themselves.'

'So, you have a real say in what goes on, then?' he said thoughtfully.

'More than that, I practically run the place nowadays – with a good team of staff, of course,' she replied.

'I didn't realise your parents had retired.'

'They haven't – officially. They're still working but they've handed a lot of the responsibility over to me. They trust me to keep the place flourishing and they seem to like my new ideas. They've worked hard all their lives. Now they're only too pleased to take things a bit easier.'

'Lucky you.'

'I've no complaints.'

'I'd like to turn this place into a family hotel,' Alan said, looking around the room at the dark furnishings and décor, a few tasteful Christmas decorations dotted about, a sprig of holly here, a touch of tinsel there. 'I think we should be more child-friendly and liven the place up with entertainment and so on – something for the whole family to enjoy on holiday.'

She made a face. 'I can't see Irene and Gerald going for that one. The Cliff Head has always been a quiet, select hotel.'

'I wasn't thinking of turning it into a glorified holiday camp,' was his answer to that. 'I just want to give it some new life. It's too staid, too old-fashioned.'

'With all due respect to your parents, I agree with you. A few changes can only be a good thing,' Paula enthused. 'All of us in the hotel trade are going to have to look to our laurels over the next few years.'

'Because of the competition from holiday camps, you mean?'

'Yes, holiday camps are a worry.'

'But Butlins wouldn't appeal to the sort of people who like a hotel holiday,' Alan pointed out.

'I wouldn't bank on that,' Paula warned. 'People can easily get converted. They try a holiday camp once to see what it's like and want to go back the next year. Anyway, I think we have a much more powerful opponent looming.'

'Oh?'

'Holidays abroad.'

'Surely not.' He was sceptical. 'Only a tiny proportion of the population can afford to go abroad.'

'At the moment, yes,' she agreed. 'But foreign package holidays are getting more popular all the time. People aren't afraid of a foreign holiday if everything is organised for them and they have the security of the tour company behind them.'

'But package holidays abroad are still very much in their infancy,' he debated. 'They are only within the reach of a fraction of the market.'

'At the moment you're absolutely right,' Paula nodded. 'But they'll be a force to be reckoned with in the future if things go on as they are and the economy continues to improve. You must have read all the talk about it in the trade press.'

'I have, but I didn't think there was an immediate threat.'

'There isn't but, at the same time, we can't just sit back and expect things to stay the same for ever.' She was very confident. 'We're living in an age of prosperity and we have to bear in mind the fact that foreign holidays will get cheaper as the demand for them grows.'

'There is that.'

'Ask yourself, Alan, if you had a choice between a holiday in Spain with guaranteed sunshine, cheap drinks and entertainment laid on, or a fortnight in Torquay in a hotel with no entertainment and the possibility of tramping about the town all day in the rain, which would you choose?'

'Mm, I see your point,' he was forced to concede. 'So are you planning on doing anything about it at your place?'

'We certainly are,' she informed him brightly. 'For starters we're going to be installing an indoor swimming pool.'

'Wow!'

'That will be only our first move,' Paula explained. 'We are intending to make other improvements too, gradually. We're planning on having a games room and dancing in the dining room a couple of times a week.'

'You've really done your thinking,' he approved.

'You have to think ahead if you're to survive in business these days.' She looked at him thoughtfully. 'Is that the sort of thing you'd like to do in your dream hotel?'

'That would be a part of it,' he replied. 'And those sorts of improvements would have to be made, of course. But my dream is more to create a feeling, an atmosphere.'

'The facilities would have to come first, though.'

'Of course. But then I'd want to build something over and above that. Something that can be created only by a human touch. A welcome so warm people would want to book ahead for the following year.'

'Well, you've certainly got the enthusiasm,' she told him. 'And that's the sort of attitude that breeds success. I think you should persuade your parents to let you go ahead with it. You seem to know exactly what you want, so talk to them about it again, sell them the idea.'

How many times had June told him the same thing? How many times had he tried to get his parents to listen to his ideas? Paula was a similar age to him and she was practically running the Brights' family-owned hotel. Discontent flashed through him. It really was time he was given some credibility around here. He would talk to them, make a stand. Be determined.

'You're absolutely right,' he said, her optimism filling him with fresh hope. 'I'll raise the subject again as soon as I see the opportunity.'

'Good for you,' she said. 'I wish you luck.'

'Thanks.'

This was the first time he'd had a proper conversation with her and he was beginning to enjoy himself. At least it had taken his mind off his problems. Now that he knew her better, he liked Paula and was enjoying her company. They had plenty in common and she talked a lot of sense.

'You must let me know the outcome,' she suggested casually. 'I'd be interested to hear how you get on.'

'Yeah, I'll do that.' He gave her an uncertain smile. 'Perhaps we could meet up for a drink sometime – just for a chat.'

'I'd like that.'

'I'll give you a ring to get something arranged then, sometime in the new year,' he told her.

'I'll look forward to it.'

'In the meantime, can I get you a drink?'

'That would be lovely,' she smiled. 'I'd like a gin and tonic, please.'

'A pleasure.'

As he walked towards the bar, he was aware of approving

153

glances being cast in his direction from his parents. With June out of the way, their hopes for Paula and himself had been given a new lease of life. Fortunately, now that he and Paula understood each other, there wasn't a problem.

Chapter Seven

'It's your go, Auntie June.' Shirley passed her aunt the little plastic cup containing the dice; they were playing a game of snakes and ladders.

There were shrieks of triumphant laughter from her opponents when she landed on a snake and had to move her counter down the board. 'Oh, not again,' she wailed, entering into the spirit of rivalry with a good heart. 'I think you lot have fixed the dice to go against me.'

'Now, now,' joshed Nora. 'Don't let's have any bad sportsmanship.'

'Bad sports aren't allowed in our house, Mum says, even if they are grown-ups,' Belinda told her solemnly. 'So you'd better watch out, Auntie.'

'Ooh, hark who's talking,' retaliated June, winking at the others. 'Who was it who got a fit of the sulks when she didn't win at ludo earlier on?'

'Now then, kiddies, and that includes you, June,' began Daisy, who was so glad she'd invited her sister; she was such good fun, and wonderful with the children, 'can we have a bit less mucking about and more concentration, please? There's a serious game in progress here.'

'Yes, ma'am,' said June, making the children laugh with her mock salute.

It was the evening of Christmas Day and they'd decided on

a board game in the hope of quietening the mood before the girls' bedtime, after the excitement of the day. But June could see no sign of a slow-down; they were still as lively as a couple of puppies.

Her gaze wandered idly around the room, which was suggestive of a grotto with its dazzling festive décor. A Christmas tree glowed in the window, the ceiling was a mass of home-made paper chains and lanterns, while a plethora of cardboard Santas, snowmen and reindeers beamed from various points.

Garish and tasteless was how Alan's parents would describe it, she thought wryly. And yes, perhaps it was a bit excessive. It was also a triumph of the human spirit, in June's opinion. Scraping the money together from her meagre resources, Daisy had transformed this tatty room in a seedy tenement house into a seasonal wonder for two little girls. No child could have had a Christmas richer in goodwill. And by working all hours Daisy had ensured they didn't go short of presents either.

Never mind the fetid hallway and dangerously dark landing and stairs – inside this room the heart and spirit were so uplifted, it was all that seemed to matter.

Alan hadn't been far from June's thoughts all day and the festive season emphasised the sadness of her fractured life. But being here with this little family had eased her path through what could otherwise have been an unbearable time. In concentrating on making the occasion a happy one for the children, she'd cast out her own problems; had even managed to experience moments of genuine pleasure since she arrived last night, having come on the tube before public transport had stopped for the holiday. Nora had put her up on a camp bed in her flat as Daisy was pushed for space.

The girls had been beside themselves this morning, feverishly unwrapping parcels, then rummaging in their stockings to find an apple and orange, little packages of sweets, a comb, new hair ribbons and a few cheap sundries. The only expensive items were the roller skates that Daisy had been saving for all year. These had already made their debut on the street, the aspiring skaters clinging for dear life to walls, lamp-posts and each other. June had given them satin pyjama cases, on which their names were embroidered, complete with new pyjamas. She'd given Daisy a talcum and soap set, and a book of Betjeman poems for Nora because she knew he was a favourite of hers. She herself had received apple blossom bath cubes from Daisy and a letter-writing set from Nora.

But now the game was coming to an end and the children's reserves of energy were finally running out. Bedtime didn't bring forth its usual crop of protests tonight, though, because of the lure of the new pyjamas.

'They're absolutely whacked,' said Daisy when the three women were settled with glasses of port from the bottle June had brought with her, Daisy and Nora on the sofa, June in the armchair. 'It's been quite a day for them.'

'For me too,' added June. 'It's lovely having children around at Christmas; makes such a difference.'

Daisy gave her a questioning grin. 'You managed to survive their high spirits without losing your sanity then,' she remarked light-heartedly. 'Their boisterousness can be a bit much if you're not used to it.'

'It didn't worry me.' It was true to say that the girls' exuberance didn't bother June but she didn't feel entirely at ease with them either. Suddenly finding herself with two lively nieces was something of a challenge to someone with no experience of children, and she wasn't yet confident in her new role. Some aunts would probably consider their function to be that of an authority figure, an issuer of discipline and back-up support to the children's mother. But June, in the ardent pursuit of their love and friendship, saw herself more as a purveyor of fun and pleasure. She had to admit, though, that the playful persona she thought would appeal to their age group and win her popularity had proved difficult to sustain over a long period.

'They've worn me out today, I know that much,' Nora confessed wearily. 'I'll be asleep as soon as my head touches the pillow tonight.'

'Me too,' said Daisy, covering a yawn with her hand. 'The little perishers had us up so early this morning, it's no wonder we're exhausted.'

'Anyway.' June raised her glass. 'How about a toast? To absent friends.'

'Absent friends,' they chanted.

'Wouldn't it be great if Dad was able to spend Christmas with us next year?' said June.

'Mm,' agreed Daisy. 'I think having us visit him just before the holiday will have helped him through Christmas this year. From what he's said, visitors have been nonexistent until now, except perhaps for official prison visitors.'

'His friends have probably shunned him, thinking he was a murderer,' suggested June.

'Yeah. He's got himself a pen pal now, though, hasn't he, Nora?' smiled Daisy, turning towards her friend. 'He was tickled pink with your letter.'

'It was kind of you, Nora,' approved June.

'I probably got as much pleasure from writing it as he did receiving it.' She was quite frank about it. 'I've always enjoyed letter-writing so I was glad of an excuse to put pen to paper.'

'It was appreciated, anyway,' said June. 'And while we're on the subject of appreciation, I want to thank you both for helping me through my first Christmas without Alan. You've made me feel so welcome here, it's made all the difference.' She lifted her glass. 'To many more Christmases together.'

'I'll drink to that,' cheered Daisy, swigging her port, cheeks suffused from the alcohol and the heat from the gas fire. 'Though God knows where we'll be next year.'

Nora nodded sagely. 'Don't let's think about that, dear, not on Christmas Day,' she said.

June had gathered from what had been said that they were having trouble with their landlord but she didn't know how serious the situation actually was. 'Are things bad enough for you to move out, then?' she enquired.

Daisy sighed. 'It's getting to be that way. It depends how much more we can take of our landlord's devious tactics.'

'Didn't you say something about being determined to stand firm against him?' June queried.

'That's the plan, but we have to be realistic about it. It's all very well standing up for your rights, and we'll do that for as long as we can, but I have the kids to think of,' Daisy pointed out. 'If things get any worse we might be forced to leave here but don't ask me where we'll go because I haven't got a clue, with the housing shortage being so bad in London.'

'A hundred thousand houses were destroyed completely in London during the war, and another million were war-damaged,' Nora explained. 'That's why people like Roland Ellwood are so powerful.'

'But the war has been over for nearly ten years,' June objected. 'Surely new houses have been built.'

'Plenty of them – out in the suburbs and new towns,' Daisy told her. 'But around here the crisis is as bad as ever.'

'What about council housing?' asked June.

'Don't make me laugh,' was Daisy's quick reply. 'I've been on the waiting list for years.'

'This borough has the lowest level of council housing in London,' added the knowledgeable Nora.

'I see . . .' said June.

159

Daisy went on to tell her sister about the way some landlords were exploiting the West Indian immigrants by charging per head. 'Six to a room and sleeping in shifts. The property owners are making a fortune and the immigrants are so grateful to have a roof over their heads they pay up and think the landlords are wonderful.'

'There must be someone you can complain to about the situation,' was June's outraged reaction.

Daisy shook her head. 'There isn't, believe me. We've been down that road and it leads nowhere. The authorities have got so many homeless people to deal with, they just haven't the time to bother about the conditions people *with* homes are living under. Anyway, this place is better than some of the others. You should see the squalor some people have to live in around here – rat-infested places with no facilities and barely any sanitation.'

'Having no light on the stairs and landing is bad enough, though,' said June. 'Especially with two children needing to go up and down after dark.'

'Ellwood's probably hoping one of us will fall down the stairs and hurt ourselves; not seriously – just enough to unnerve us into moving out,' Daisy suggested. 'He's got a mind like a cash register. All he can see is the money he could make from the rooms if we weren't here.'

'I didn't realise that things were so bad,' June confessed.

'I don't suppose people outside the area do realise what it's like. Why should they?' Daisy shrugged. 'You've got to live here to know what's going on.' She gave June a shrewd look. 'And of course you were sheltered from inner city problems when you were living in Torquay.'

'You're not kidding,' she swiftly agreed. 'I'm beginning to understand just how easy I had it down in Devon.'

'If we had anywhere else to go we'd have been out of here long ago,' Daisy went on to say. 'Wouldn't we, Nora?'

160

'Not half.'

'Enough about that,' Daisy said hastily. 'It's Christmas night and not a time to be moaning and groaning. So let's talk about something else.'

But June had lapsed into thought, plans of her own coming into focus suddenly and forming an idea that would benefit them all. 'I've just realised that I can help,' she said after a while, her voice rising with excitement.

They both gave her a questioning look.

'Don't say you're thinking of trying to fix us up in the staff accommodation at the hotel where you work,' grinned Daisy, making a joke of it to lift the gloom that had crept into the atmosphere. 'Somehow I don't think the management would be too keen on that idea.'

'Don't be daft. I'm going to be moving out of staff accommodation myself soon anyway,' June explained with growing enthusiasm. 'And when I do, I can solve your problem too, make things better for us all.'

'How?' Daisy wanted to know.

'Well, my mother's little house in Hounslow came to me automatically when she died and I put it up for sale straight away because I didn't want to live in it. I've found a buyer and am just waiting for the sale to be finalised. With the money I get for it I'm going to buy somewhere else.'

'And invite us over to give us a break from this dump?' surmised Daisy.

'No. I was thinking more in terms of you all moving in with me.' Seeing the question in Nora's eyes, she added quickly, 'You too, Nora.'

'Ooh, I like the sound of that,' beamed the older woman. 'What a smashing idea.'

But Daisy reacted differently and her fierce opposition was completely unexpected to both June and Nora. Her eyes blazed, her lips tightened and an angry flush stained her

161

cheeks. 'I might not have much but I'm not a charity case yet,' she said coldly.

An abrasive silence fell over the room.

'No one is suggesting that you are,' June said at last. 'And I'm not offering charity.'

'Sounds remarkably like it to me,' snapped Daisy.

'You must have misunderstood me, then,' June was quick to point out. 'Because with the best will in the world, I'm not in a position to offer charity to anyone. I don't have any money.'

'Oh, not much,' uttered Daisy with uncharacteristic scorn. 'You've enough to buy a house and you say you've no dough. You're living in a different world.'

'Look – the only reason I can buy a house is because my adopted parents' place came to me as their next of kin,' she explained. 'I'm not saying that I'm not lucky to have it because I know that I am – *very lucky*. But it's a one-off and certainly doesn't mean I have money, as such. By the time I've paid for somewhere to live I'll be skint again, and I'll find it difficult to afford the costs of running a house on my own because I'm not on a high salary. I work in a West End hotel, yes, but I am only a receptionist. I probably don't earn much more than either of you.'

'You don't know what hardship is,' accused Daisy with unusual hostility. 'You've had it good for most of your life. Adopted by people who were well off enough to own a house, got yourself a rich husband with a part-share in some posh hotel.'

June wasn't prepared to supply her with details about her past so she just said, 'But I left all that behind me and I'm in the same boat as you are now, except that I don't have any children to support. I'm a single woman looking out for myself, just like you are. We're two of a kind.'

'Don't make me laugh,' came Daisy's cynical response.

'You'll never be the same kind as me, not with the start in life that you've had.'

'Look, Daisy, I can't help the way it worked out for us when we were children,' June reminded her. 'I didn't have any say in what happened any more than you did, and you know that in your heart.' She moved on swiftly, rather than dwell on those unhappy times. 'Anyway, when I suggested that you all move in with me, I was thinking in terms of us sharing the house, rather than my just letting you some rooms.'

'Sounds good to me,' approved Nora.

'We'd still be your lodgers.' Daisy looked extremely doubtful.

'Technically, I suppose you would be my lodgers. But what I have in mind would be more of a house-sharing arrangement, all of us on an equal footing,' June told her. 'I thought we could live like a family and split all the costs three ways: coal, gas and electric, the rates, all the running costs of the house plus any decorating and maintenance bills. It would be a joint enterprise. We'd each do our share of the chores.'

'What about rent?' asked Daisy.

'I haven't got round to thinking about that yet. But obviously if I can pay for the house outright from the sale of the other one, and you're paying your share of everything else I won't need to charge rent—' she began.

'Forget it,' cut in Daisy rudely.

'Daisy,' rebuked Nora, frowning at her.

But Daisy was at the mercy of new emotions which she could neither understand nor control, and she was deaf to Nora's protests. Her voice was shaking as she spoke. 'I'm prepared to accept any sort of a hand-out for the sake of my kids, and I'll grovel with the best of 'em for their benefit. But I won't take charity from my sister.' She shook her head in despair. 'I just can't do it.'

163

'It isn't charity, I've told you,' insisted June, distressed by this turn of events. 'You'd be the ones being charitable because you'd be doing me a favour if you move in with me. I don't want to live in a house on my own.'

'Oh, for goodness' sake,' Daisy sneered. 'Do you think I'm thick or something? You must do if you reckon I'd swallow that load of old rubbish.'

'If it would make you feel better, pay me some rent then.' June was at a loss to know what to say.

'Now you really are being patronising,' retorted Daisy through tight lips.

June was perplexed. What had seemed like a fantastic idea just a few minutes ago had turned into an explosive situation she couldn't handle. Whatever she said would be misunderstood by Daisy in this mood. 'I'm sorry you feel like that about it. I really didn't mean to upset you.'

'For heaven's sake, Daisy,' said Nora in a firm tone, 'June isn't trying to belittle you in any way. She's come up with a scheme to help us all, herself included.'

'Nora's right.' June was glad of the support. 'The idea popped into my mind just now and seemed like a practical solution for us all. You have problems with your landlord and I can't afford to rattle around in a house in my own. So the sensible thing is for us all to move in together. Even apart from the financial side, I don't fancy the idea of living by myself. It isn't as though I've got any friends in London. Sharing might be fun and it would give you and me a chance to get to know each other again after all these years.' She gave Daisy a look of defiance. 'And yes, I did think it would make things better for you. There wouldn't be any point in my asking you to move in with me otherwise, would there?'

Daisy shrugged, feigning indifference.

'You can't deny that it will be easier for you than staying on here, worried to death the whole time about what the landlord will do next,' June continued.

'Course it will be better,' confirmed Nora. 'And if you weren't so stubborn, you'd see that, Daisy.'

'I don't know yet what sort of a place I can get with the money from the sale,' June continued. 'I didn't get a fortune for my mother's house because it's out of town and anything in central London will be a lot more expensive so it won't be anything too grand. If you did decide to come in on it with me, we might have to settle for something that needs doing up to get enough room for us all at the price I can afford. But you'd certainly have more space and freedom than you have here, especially if I can get something with a little garden for the girls to play in.'

'I'm not so dim that I can't tell whether someone's being big-hearted or big-headed, you know,' expressed Daisy.

June felt as though she'd been physically slapped. 'I didn't mean to be either of those things,' she tried to make her sister understand. 'It was a spur-of-the-moment idea which would benefit me as much as you.'

Daisy pondered on this. 'Mm, maybe it would but I can't do it,' she told her.

Nora couldn't believe she was hearing this. Daisy must be having some sort of a brainstorm to behave in this way because she was usually so sensitive to other people's feelings and completely unashamed of her impecunious state. It was obvious how hurt poor June was and it was unlike Daisy to be cruel to anyone. The two of them were so different, Nora observed, Daisy so open-hearted and straightforward, June more secretive and withdrawn but equally as vulnerable, somehow. They needed each other and it tore at Nora's heart to see their new-found relationship foundering before it had got past the first post. Deciding, however, that this was a family matter and it was time she made a diplomatic exit, she said, 'Well, I'll leave you two to fight it out.'

165

'Don't go,' urged Daisy, feeling guilty for spoiling the evening for them all.

'It's time I was in bed anyway,' said Nora, affecting a yawn as she stood up. 'It's been a long day.'

'I'll come with you.' June got up and looked down at Daisy, who was sitting on the sofa looking forlorn. 'Thanks for a lovely day. It's been really great.' She paused, fiddling with her fingernails nervously. 'Look, forget the idea of us all moving in together. I should never have suggested it. The last thing I wanted to do was upset you, especially at Christmas.'

'Don't worry about it.' Daisy was very subdued.

Tension drew tight in the air. Nora could almost taste the bitterness between the sisters. Although she wanted to put her arms around them both and guide them out of this impasse, she knew she mustn't interfere. This was something they had to work out for themselves. 'G'night, love,' she said to Daisy. 'See you in the morning.'

''Night, Daisy,' added June.

''Night, both.'

As the door closed behind them, Daisy sat motionless on the sofa, feeling terrible. Looking around her, she noticed how the Christmas decorations had an irrelevant look about them now somehow. The happy day had ended on a sour note. She tried to comfort herself with the thought that it hadn't been spoiled for the children. But it didn't help.

Lying in the bed next to her sleeping daughters, listening to the now familiar sound of music and laughter from a party in the lower regions of the house, Daisy felt physically ill with remorse as she replayed the altercation in her mind and recalled how hateful she had been to June.

What made it even worse was the fact that she could see how stupid she'd been to react so negatively to the idea of them all moving in together when it was the perfect solution.

Why was it so easy for her to give yet so hard for her to take? If anyone knew about Christian charity, Daisy did, after the upbringing she'd had. She knew all about kindness and generosity, and give and take. It wasn't as though she hadn't been on the receiving end of kindness before. She'd had it in abundance from Nora. So why did it stick in her throat when it came from June?

Sibling rivalry and pride, she was ashamed to admit. But looking at the matter logically, June really did stand to gain as much as Daisy and the others from such an arrangement. It hadn't been an act of charity but an opportunity for them all. Company for June and the chance of a decent home for her and the girls and Nora. God knows, they needed it. And what had she done? Thrown it back in her sister's face, and deprived her children of a better standard of living because she was too proud to accept something in the spirit with which it was given.

She was furious with herself, and sad. Nat came into her mind for some reason and she felt a pang. Trust him not to be around when she needed him. June was right when she said they were both in the same boat. Neither had a man to love and comfort her. Nat loved her in his way – if she didn't believe that she'd have given up on him long ago – but, although it hurt to admit it, he was only a part-time lover.

But she and June did have each other. Fate had brought them together again and their relationship could become special, given time. Why throw the chance of that away just because of sisterly competition?

Weary of tossing and turning, she got up and went in the other room and curled up in the armchair with her dressing gown over her, waiting for the agonising night to end so that she could put things right.

The girls slept in the next morning after the late night. As soon as Daisy heard signs of life from across the landing, she went and tapped on Nora's door.

June opened the door in her dressing gown, looking tired and pale and extremely wary of her sister.

'You don't look as though you've had any more sleep than I have,' Daisy observed.

'I've had better nights,' was June's cool response.

Daisy bit her lip; she was full of contrition. 'Look, I'm really sorry about last night,' she said. 'I said some horrid things.'

'You're entitled to your opinion,' June told her frostily. 'I told you to forget it.'

'I know you did but I don't want to forget it.' She made a face. 'Help me out here, June. I'm trying to put things right.'

'Why the change of heart?'

'I was stupid. I don't know what got into me.' She looked at her persuasively. 'I'm sorry. And I'd really like us all to move in together. It's a brilliant idea.'

June was so thrilled she didn't bear a grudge. 'If you're sure, then that's what we'll do,' she smiled.

'As long as you let me pay my way,' Daisy made it clear in a warning tone.

'I won't have any choice about that.' June's tone was just as firm. 'As I've already said, I can't afford to keep you and the kids as well as myself. I'm only a hotel receptionist.'

'I'll have to make sure you're not out of pocket then, won't I?' said Daisy, satisfied now on this point.

'We'll work out the details when we've found somewhere. I haven't even started looking for a place yet.' She paused. 'Perhaps we could do that together, all of us.'

'That would be smashing,' enthused Daisy.

With the release of tension, they both got a fit of the giggles, hugging each other and hovering between laughter and tears.

'What's going on out here?' came Nora's throaty tones as she scuttled on to the scene in her dressing gown and slippers. 'What's all the noise about?'

Daisy grabbed hold of her and swung her round. 'We're getting out of here,' she said excitedly, linking arms with her and dancing round, lifting her knees in the air. 'We're all going to be living together . . . so what do you think of that?'

'Thank God you've come to your senses,' was Nora's enthusiastic reaction. 'It's the best bit of news I've heard in a very long time.'

In the same way as June found salvation over Christmas in Daisy and the girls and Nora, Alan found comfort in Jack Saunders' company and large quantities of alcohol drunk together in a matey fashion on Christmas Eve after work. On Christmas Day he went to his parents' house where everything was pin neat and traditional, with turkey and stuffing and perfect mince pies.

The business being a family one, shop talk was never taboo, even at Christmas. So as they lingered at the table over lunch, Alan decided to take the opportunity to raise the subject that had been on his mind ever since he'd discussed it with Paula.

'I really believe it's time for some changes at the Cliff Head,' he said in conclusion, having outlined his ideas.

'But you already know what we think about turning our hotel into a bear garden,' said Gerald.

'Bear garden, my foot. It would be a bit livelier, that's all,' corrected Alan, managing to stay calm. 'There would be no lowering of standards.'

'It's Christmas,' interrupted Irene, staidly clad in a navy-blue twinset, her hair welded into place with setting lotion. 'Not a time to talk business.'

'It's the very best time to do it,' Alan disagreed. 'We can

169

talk without being interrupted.'

'We've been through all this before, son,' pointed out his father smugly, cheeks flushed from his pre-prandial tipple. 'And your mother and I have agreed that it wouldn't be wise to introduce the changes you're proposing to the Cliff Head.'

'Why doesn't that surprise me?' Alan said cuttingly.

'Don't be facetious, dear,' requested his mother primly.

Alan looked from one to the other. 'I know you don't, personally, want to consider my ideas but give me one good solid reason why some changes wouldn't be wise from a business point of view.'

'You know why.' His father was impatient now. 'Because we are a refined hotel catering for people who want peace and quiet. We'd lose all our customers if we changed our policy.'

'We'd gain more than we'd lose.' Alan was adamant about this. 'There's a gap in the market for a family hotel. There aren't enough of them around.'

'Maybe not,' said his mother, helping herself to more Christmas pudding. 'But we are not going to add to their numbers.'

'Hear! Hear!' Gerald supported.

'So, you won't even think about it then?' said Alan, looking from one to the other.

'We already have done and the answer is no,' confirmed his father dismissively. 'So let's forget it and talk about our plans for the coming season.'

'I thought I was supposed to be a partner in the business,' Alan reminded them.

'And you are, dear,' his mother assured him. 'That isn't in question.'

'I'm questioning it.' He was really fired up now. 'I might as well be a chamber maid for all the say I get in the running of the hotel. My ideas are never even given any consideration, just dismissed out of hand.'

'That isn't fair,' his father argued. 'It's just this one thing we can't agree on.'

'No, Dad, it's everything.'

'Rubbish!'

Alan thought his father probably believed his own words so it was useless to argue the toss over that one. But he wasn't ready to give up on the main point. 'Why exactly are you so much against the ideas I've just outlined anyway?' he asked, getting heated. 'I know you're keen on all things traditional but there must be more to it than that.'

'It's Christmas, Alan,' his mother reminded him again. 'I don't want any arguments.'

'I have no intention of having an argument,' he assured her. 'I just want a straight answer to my question.'

'All right, I'll give it to you straight,' said his father, leaning back slightly in his chair and regarding his son with an air of complacency. 'Even apart from believing that a family hotel isn't right for the Cliff Head, I don't actually *want* to run the sort of place you have in mind. I would hate it.'

'Me too,' added Irene.

'But you're a sociable sort of a chap,' Alan pointed out, looking at his father. 'I should have thought you'd enjoy working in a livelier environment.'

'I might be sociable but I'm very selective about the company I keep and I'm quite happy with the way things are,' he stated. 'I don't want our refined cocktail bar to become like the public bar of some backstreet pub.'

Alan gave a dry laugh. 'You'd vet the guests before you took their booking if you could afford to turn people away, wouldn't you?' he said bitterly.

'I certainly would.' Gerald wasn't ashamed of his snobbery. 'I don't want riffraff in my hotel, neither do I want snotty-nosed kids making a racket about the place.'

'You're quite right, dear,' agreed Irene.

'It may be a very good idea in principle and right for other hoteliers, but it would never work for us,' boomed Gerald. 'So accept it once and for all, boy, and let's hear no more about it.'

In a defining moment Alan finally did exactly that: he faced up to the truth. Not only would they never agree to make the changes he wanted, it would be a disaster if they did. Anything outside of the hushed atmosphere they were used to would be anathema to them so their presence would not be conducive to the atmosphere Alan had in mind.

He'd clung to the idea because he was a man with a dream, but it was *his* dream not theirs. If he wanted a different kind of hotel he would have to do it without them. And as that was completely out of the question, he had no choice but to put it out of his mind and satisfy himself with the Cliff Head as it was, and likely to stay – in his parents' lifetime, anyway. There was certainly no point in trying to persuade them into changes that were wrong for them.

'Yes, Dad,' he said with a sigh of resignation. 'I'll do that.'

'Thank God we've got through to you at last about this,' said his father.

His mother looked relieved. 'Mince pies anyone?' she offered, smiling.

The two men answered rather absently in the affirmative and she scuttled off to the kitchen to get them. 'While we're on the subject of business,' Gerald began, 'there's a hotel and catering exhibition at Earls Court in March. I've had some literature in about it. Wondered if you fancied going.'

'I suppose it might be quite interesting.' Alan was too disappointed about the other thing to show much enthusiasm.

'It'll be worth a visit, certainly. It's always a good idea to keep up to date with what's going on in the trade.' He gave his son a wry grin. 'As long as you don't come back with more ideas for this wretched family-style hotel you're so keen on.'

Alan ignored his attempt at humour. 'Aren't you going then?' he asked.

'No. I don't fancy the London crowds,' his father explained. 'I thought you might like to go instead. Stay overnight. Give yourself a break. There won't be a problem with your getting away at that time of the year.'

'I'll think about it.'

Suddenly Alan felt about six years old. Then it had been sweets and toys, now it was a trip to London to keep his parents in his favour. Did they really not know how transparent these attempts to placate him were?

Something significant happened to him at that moment. He realised with blinding clarity what he'd known for years and not allowed himself to fully admit: he needed to find his own way, to fail or succeed for himself, away from his parents. But he was trapped. Even apart from the hideous personal complications of breaking away, he had very little in the way of material assets outside the Cliff Head.

'Here we are,' said Irene, bustling back into the room with a plate of mince pies. 'Nice and warm, straight from the oven. When we've had these we'll go in the other room and listen to the Queen's speech.'

'Lovely, dear,' enthused Gerald, helping himself to one and munching into it.

'Come on, Alan, tuck in,' urged his mother.

'I don't think I can manage one after all,' said Alan, feeling suffocated.

'Don't be silly, dear,' she admonished as though Alan was an infant. 'Of course you can manage one.'

He was so angry he wanted to slap her. 'I think I'm old enough to judge my own appetite, thank you, Mother,' he snapped.

She shot him a look. 'Don't you dare raise your voice to me,' she warned. 'A lot of hard work has gone into making

Christmas a happy time for us all.'

Her rebuke produced the desired effect and filled him with compunction. 'Sorry,' he said, taking a mince pie and forcing himself to eat it, just to keep the peace. But he longed for some breathing space from a relationship that was becoming unbearably claustrophobic.

'You're getting to be good at this, aren't you?' Jack Saunders complimented Alan when the latter beat him at a game of darts in the Gullscombe Arms on the evening of Boxing Day. 'You'd better watch yourself, mate. They'll try to rope you into the darts team if you carry on like this.'

'Fancy another game?' suggested Alan.

'You can't get enough of it now,' grinned Jack. 'But let's take a break and have another game later; leave the board free for someone else to have a go.' He paused, looking at him. 'It's my shout, as you won, so what's it to be?'

'A pint, please.'

'Coming up.'

The Gullscombe Arms was an old-world tavern in the picturesque village of Gullscombe Bay. The pub was at the centre of village life and was warm and cosy, with oak beams, fishing nets on the walls and log fires. It was Jack's local and he knew everyone by name. It wasn't too crowded tonight as some of the locals were at Boxing Day parties so the two men were able to find a table near the fire where logs were crackling.

'My folks would have a fit if they knew that I was drinking pints and getting to be red hot at the dart board,' Alan remarked, taking the top off his pint. 'Gin and tonics at the golf club are more the sort of thing they have in mind for me. And for you too, if it comes down to it, you being their restaurant manager.'

'Yeah, well, I think it's my right to do what I feel

174

comfortable with when I'm off duty, as long as it doesn't hurt anyone and is legal,' observed Jack. 'Same applies to you, in my opinion. If you enjoy a pint and a game of darts, you're perfectly entitled to have one, regardless of the social implications.'

'You're right, of course.' He made a face. 'But I must admit I find it easier not to mention these things to the folks. It causes too much trouble. They're good people and have done their best for me but our ideas and opinions don't often seem to coincide these days.'

'You'd be a bit odd if they did,' was Jack's opinion. 'Every generation has its own ideas. Anyway, we're all individuals – freethinkers, thank God.' He cast his eye around the pub. 'There's nothing nicer to me than a game of darts and a sociable pint in a pub where everyone knows my name. And if anyone objects to that, that's their problem.'

'It's different for you,' Alan pointed out. 'You're a free agent with no one to answer to.'

'So are you now that you've split up with June.'

Alan's features tightened at the mention of it but he just said, 'I do have my parents to answer to, you know.'

'Only to a certain extent,' Jack told him. 'You're a grown man, a responsible adult.'

'Because I work with them I'm still under their control,' Alan explained.

'Then you shouldn't be, not at your age,' Jack disapproved.

'It's just the way things are.'

'You can't spend your whole life doing what they want, if it isn't what you want,' Jack went on. 'I'd still be in Australia if I'd done that.'

'It took courage to come back.'

'Don't talk daft,' laughed the modest Jack. 'Where's the bottle in getting on a ship and coming home?'

'You cut your family ties and came back on your own, to

start again from scratch with no back-up,' Alan reminded him. 'That seems quite a brave thing to me.'

'My mother would probably call it selfish, going off and leaving the family like that.' He smiled with fond memories. 'Mum's a good sort, though. She wished me well and said I must do what I felt was right for me. It was traumatic for us all. I mean, Australia is the other side of the world, not near enough to go for a holiday – not unless you've got plenty of dough, anyway. But I was convinced that I had to make the move back to England while I was still young. I didn't want to go against my instincts and stay there just because it was easier, then be full of regrets on my sixty-fifth birthday because I'd been trapped by family ties.'

'I'm up to my neck in family ties at the moment.' Alan went on to tell his friend about his ideas and the frustrations he was having at the Cliff Head.

'Strike out on your own, mate,' was Jack's immediate reaction, 'if you're feeling that fed up.'

'Easier said than done,' Alan pointed out. 'Even apart from the emotional element – and make no mistake about it, my parents would be devastated if I left the partnership – what would I do if I did leave? Get a job as a hotel manager working for someone else? I don't think so.'

'You want a family hotel, so go out there and get one,' Jack suggested.

'What with? I've got a bit saved but not enough to buy a hotel, nowhere near.'

'You could raise the dough if you sold your share in the business,' advised Jack.

'If I ever were to leave, I'd give them my share, not sell it,' Alan said. 'But I couldn't walk out on them. It would break my mother's heart.'

'She's probably tougher than you think.'

'Even so . . .'

'Parents want the best for their offspring; it goes with the job, apparently, or that's how it's supposed to work. So once they got used to the idea, they'd want you to do what you know is right for you.' Knowing Alan's parents, and judging them to be extremely self-centred, Jack had grave doubts about this but kept them to himself because Alan needed encouragement to break away and live his own life. 'I'm sure they wouldn't want to hold you back once they realised how much you want to do it.'

'But how would they manage without me?'

'By employing somebody to do the job that you do, of course,' Jack replied. 'No one's indispensable.'

'I couldn't do it to them,' Alan insisted. 'They'd be absolutely devastated.'

Jack shrugged. 'So what are you going to do then? Wait until they retire or die, then do what you want with the Cliff Head? And in the meantime get increasingly frustrated and miserable? You'll grow into a crusty old sod if you don't get your life sorted out.'

'I don't have a choice.'

'You're an unattached man, Alan,' Jack reminded him firmly. 'Of course you have a choice.'

'You make it seem so simple.'

'I'm not saying it will be easy but it certainly isn't impossible, and if you stay as you are, you'll never know if you could have made it on your own. This idea of yours isn't going to go away. You're stuck with it. And taking over the Cliff Head when your folks retire won't be the same thing as making a success of something in your own right, not the same thing at all.'

'I can't just disregard obligations.'

'Look, it's natural to grow up and make your own way in the world – we all do it,' Jack reminded Alan. 'You went into the family business instead. I'm not saying there's anything wrong with that. It works very well for some people, but obviously not you, or we wouldn't be having this conversation. So, take the plunge and do something about it.'

'Everything you say is true but I couldn't desert Mum and Dad,' Alan said. 'It would be too cruel.'

Jack tutted. For years he'd watched Alan be browbeaten by the people he was so loyal to, and thought he deserved better. 'Your parents aren't disabled or even very old,' he said gently. 'They'll be fine.'

'It was different for you when you made the break,' said Alan. 'You weren't locked into a family business.'

'I was part of a family, though,' Jack was keen to point out. 'Even now, I still miss them all – Mum and Dad, my sister and brother. How do you think it feels, knowing that they're so far away and I probably won't ever see them again?'

'I didn't realise,' Alan confessed. 'You always seem so cheerful and in control.'

'That sort of thing stays inside. I made my choice and I have to get on with things. No point in going about with a long face and making other people miserable. I like my life here and you can't have everything, can you? Not many people get that.'

'Exactly,' agreed Alan. 'And I have so much more than most. A partnership in a thriving business and financial security if I stay with it.'

'None of it's worth a light if you're permanently frustrated, though, is it?'

'I'm not so sure.'

'If you don't break away and become your own man, you'll never have peace of mind,' Jack lectured.

Alan shrugged. 'Maybe not. But it's just something I'll have to live with.'

'It's your choice, but I reckon you'll live to regret it.'

'All right, Jack, you've made your point,' said Alan firmly.

'Now let's change the subject before we come to blows over it.'

'Suits me,' agreed Jack with a shrug.

'How do you fancy coming with me to London in March?' asked Alan. 'All expenses paid by the Cliff Head.'

Jack's eyes lit with interest. 'I wouldn't say no. Why, what's on?'

Alan told him about the exhibition. 'I'd be glad of the company,' he explained. 'And it'll be of interest to us both as it's our line of business. I'll arrange for you to have the time off. They can manage without you in the restaurant for a couple of days.'

'I'm game,' enthused Jack.

'Good. I'll book us some accommodation when things open up again after the holiday. In the meantime, let's have another drink. A pint for you?'

Jack nodded. 'I'll come to the bar with you,' he grinned. 'The new barmaid's quite tasty.'

Standing at the bar counter waiting to be served while Jack chatted to the barmaid, Alan reflected on the conversation they had just had. Jack talked a lot of sense and made a change of course seem so straightforward, whereas to Alan it was impossible.

June came into his mind and he knew instinctively that she would agree with Jack. He also knew that he could never make that break. The emotional ties were just too strong.

Chapter Eight

'Did you have a good Christmas, Nat?' Daisy enquired sociably.

'Yeah. It was all right,' he told her with an air of disinterest. 'How about you?'

'I had a lovely time.' Enthusiasm radiated from her. 'It was really smashing this year. One of the best Christmases I've ever had, I think.'

'Why?' His dark eyes rested on her with lurking disapproval as he took a slow, contemplative drag on his cigarette. The knowledge that Daisy was capable of having a good time without him was unsettling because it challenged his power over her. 'What did you do that made it better than usual?'

'Nothing different. Just stayed at home and did all the normal festive things with the girls and Nora,' she told him. 'But June was with us and that made it sort of special, somehow. She's ever such good company and the kids have taken to her in a big way. Having a real auntie is still a novelty to them, and she seems very fond of them.'

It was evening, a couple of days after Christmas. The girls were in bed, and Daisy and Nat were ensconced on the sofa. Daisy was enjoying the fact that she didn't have to go back to work until tomorrow night.

He laughed drily. 'Must have been a barrel-load of laughs

with that stuck-up cow under your feet all over the holiday,' he said sarcastically.

'I wish you wouldn't say such horrible things about her,' she frowned. 'You know how it upsets me. June's great. You haven't given her a chance.'

'Why should I make an effort with someone who thinks she's a cut above the rest of us?'

'She doesn't think that,' defended Daisy heatedly. 'Just because she's got a touch of class you've branded her a snob and she isn't like that at all. Far from it.'

'You're so taken with the idea of having a posh sister, you can't see what she's really like,' he said calumniously.

'That just isn't true,' she denied, her voice rising. 'You know very well that I'm the last person on earth to be impressed by someone because they're posh.' She was reminded of the altercation she'd had with June on Christmas night, which proved her point.

Even Nat could see that his accusation didn't carry any weight. 'Yeah, I s'pose so,' he muttered grudgingly.

'Anyway, I'm not going to argue with you over it.' A gleam came into her eyes and she smiled. 'Because I've got something far more exciting to tell you.'

He exhaled a cloud of smoke, looking at her thoughtfully. 'You're like a dog with two tails tonight.'

'And with very good reason.' She told him she would soon be having a change of address and gave him the details. 'Isn't it wonderful?' she enthused. 'At last I can get the girls out of this stinking hovel, get us all away from the landlord and his vile threats.'

'Where exactly will you be moving to?' Nat showed not a grain of enthusiasm.

'Not sure yet,' she told him excitedly. 'It depends where we find a house that's big enough for us all and within June's price range. We won't be moving far, though, because we all need to stay within easy reach of our jobs.'

'What's all this "we" business?' he queried disagreeably. 'It'll be your sister's house. You won't get a say in its location, or anything else for that matter.'

'We will,' she corrected. 'She wants it to be a joint venture and we're all going to have a say in everything. She's quite definite about that.'

'Use the brains you were born with, Daisy,' he warned nastily. 'You and Nora will just be lodgers.'

'No we won't.'

'Of course you will,' he insisted. 'You'll be subject to all sorts of petty rules and regulations like they are in boarding houses where the landlady lives in the house.'

'It won't be like that at all because we're going to live together as a family, on equal terms.'

'Equal terms, my arse.'

'Don't be so cynical.'

'Surely you don't really believe you're going to be equal with June?'

'Yes, I do, as it happens.'

'It'll be her house, for God's sake,' he blasted. 'Of course she's going to rule the roost.'

'The house will be hers, and she'll have the responsibility for it, obviously. But it won't be like you're suggesting.'

'Give me strength,' he sighed emphatically. 'I really don't think you should do this. It'll be a disaster.'

Naturally she was disappointed by his reaction. 'I don't know why you're getting so het up about it,' she said.

'Because you're being so blind,' he ranted on. 'Three women and two kids sharing the same house – you'll be at each other's throats in no time. And then where will you be? You'll have burned your boats with this place.'

'I certainly won't lose any sleep over that.'

'At least here you have a degree of privacy,' Nat pointed

out. 'You've got your own cooking facilities and that. All right, so the landlord is a bit of a bugger but at least he doesn't live in the house, checking up on everything you do.'

'And neither will June.' Daisy was beginning to get exasperated now. 'The three of us have discussed it thoroughly and agreed that if this thing is to work we must respect each other's privacy. The girls will probably have to share a bedroom as they do now. But we're hoping that the rest of us will have our own rooms where we can go when we want to be on our own.'

'You'll have to share the kitchen and bathroom, though . . .'

'And the living room, and sitting room if there is one,' she added with an air of defiance.

'You're asking for trouble if you go ahead with this move.' He shook his head. 'I'm telling you.'

'Why do you want to spoil it for me?' Daisy asked. 'This chance means a lot to me.'

'I'm just trying to save you from yourself,' he insisted. 'It's no good shutting your eyes to the actual reality of something like this.'

'My eyes are wide open,' she assured him. 'And I know it's going to be good.'

'Oh, well, it's your funeral,' he said in a doom-laden voice.

'Yes, it is.' She stood firm.

'Anyway, I thought you were planning to stay on here to prove that the landlord can't drive you out.'

'We're not being driven out,' she reminded him. 'We're moving out of our own accord to somewhere better, so it's not my loss.'

'Even so . . .'

'I'd be mad to turn this opportunity down,' she said with a sigh of irritation. 'It'll be so much better for the girls, especially if we can get a place with a little garden.'

'That sister of yours will have a field day, lording it over you and Nora.'

'There won't be anything like that.' Having cleared the air about this on Christmas night, she could be confident. 'I've told you, we're going to live as a family.'

'Family be buggered,' Nat scorned. 'It'll be one big battle-ground once the novelty wears off.'

She was hurt by his attitude but determined not to let him bully her into changing her mind. 'Whatever happens it's got to be better than this,' she said, waving her hand towards the room. 'And let's face it, Nat, I'm not going to get the chance of family life with the father of my children, am I? So I might as well go for the next best thing.'

'How many more times must I tell you, we'll get married eventually.' He was impatient now. 'We're all right as we are for the moment.'

'Of course we're not all right,' she disagreed. 'The situation is ridiculous.'

'Don't start—'

'I'm not starting anything; just defending myself against your unreasonable disapproval of my plans to move in with June,' she declared. 'I don't ask much from life – you know that. As long as my girls are happy, then so am I. But I'm only human and I want a decent life for them, for all of us.' She paused. 'Nothing too flash. Just somewhere reasonable to live without the constant threat of eviction.'

'I'll give you that.'

'If I wait for you to face up to your responsibilities, I'll be an old woman.'

'You're nagging again.'

'Do the right thing and I won't have to.'

'Yeah, yeah, I will.'

'And while I'm waiting for you to grow up, it's up to me to look out for myself and get the best I can for our daughters.'

'You won't find the best with your sister,' was his gruff prediction. 'I can promise you that.'

'I can't see why you're so much against it because it won't affect you, except, of course, that you'll see more of June.' She paused, her eyes narrowing in thought. 'That's it, isn't it? You'll feel uncomfortable visiting me in her house.'

'I'm not scared of her,' he objected heatedly. 'I won't like that aspect of it because I can't stand the woman, but that isn't why I think it's wrong for you. I think you're doing the wrong thing because it'll be like living in lodgings and too restricting.'

'And I'm not restricted now?'

Nat glanced around the room. 'Not as much as you will be playing happy families with your sister. Anyway, living with relatives never works out, it's a well-known fact; there are always petty squabbles.'

'Having relatives to squabble with is a first for me so I'll have to learn as I go along,' she told him. 'I'm looking forward to it, whatever you say.'

'I'm only thinking of you, Daisy.' Not true. His comments were entirely selfish. He could hardly bear to imagine what it would be like when he went to see Daisy with that high-and-mighty sister of hers hovering in the background just waiting to find fault. It was bad enough having Nora bend his ear at the slightest opportunity. With two of them on his back about the way he treated Daisy, it was going to be hellish, especially as the house would be June's. 'As I've told you before, that sister of yours has changed you. She's a bad influence, first of all filling your head with rubbish about trying to clear your ol' man's name – now this.'

'Clearing my father's name is *not* rubbish,' Daisy was quick to amend. 'We're serious about it.'

'You've got your head in the clouds if you think you can beat the system and get him out of prison.'

186

'I don't agree with you.' She wouldn't be put off. 'If we get new evidence, we can appeal and he'll be released once the truth comes out. He needs help, and June and I are all he's got. If we can find Morris Dodd and his wife we'll—'

'You're as powerless as your ol' man is, can't you see that?' he interrupted rudely. 'You don't stand a cat's chance in hell of finding them.'

Daisy couldn't deny that there was some truth in what he said. 'I know it seems hopeless but we're not going to give up,' she said. 'So you might as well face up to it and stop being such a doom merchant.'

He shrugged, stubbing out his cigarette in a saucer. 'All right, have it your own way,' he told her.

Daisy was still worried to death about her father and wouldn't rest until justice was done. But things had come to a halt for the moment. How did you find someone after more than twenty years when you had no idea where to start looking? Even a seasoned detective would be at a loss with nothing to go on at all. There was a way, she was convinced of that; something they'd yet to think of. 'I admit we're at a dead end at the moment,' she confessed. 'But we'll think of a way, given time. And it'll be easier once June and I are living in the same house because we'll have more of a chance to discuss it, to pool our ideas and work out what to do next.'

'I still say that sister of yours is bad news.' Nat just wouldn't give up. 'She unsettles you, gets you fired up about things.'

'I do have a mind of my own,' Daisy reminded him.

'I know you do. But she's the type who can manipulate anyone,' he stated categorically. 'You hardly know her, even though she's your sister.'

'That's one thing you are right about,' she conceded. 'And what better way to rectify that than to share a house with her. There'll be times when we don't see eye to eye, of course.

But I'm optimistic, and if it doesn't work out . . . well, I'll just have to cross that bridge when I come to it.' She took his arm impulsively, her mood softening as she looked into his eyes. 'Be pleased for me, eh? It would mean so much to me.'

Noticing how pretty she looked, her eyes sparkling with enthusiasm, her luxuriant hair shining in the light, his heart melted. He wasn't a romantic man and never thought in terms of 'love' as such, but he did feel something for her and still fancied her, even after all these years.

'OK, babe,' he said with a sigh of resignation. 'If it's what you really want I'll try not to spoil it for you.'

'Thanks, Nat.'

'And while we've got a bit of privacy we might as well make the most of it,' he suggested. 'There'll be precious little of it when you move house.'

'There will if I have my own bedroom,' Daisy pointed out with a giggle. 'We can shut ourselves away in there.'

'Not if the Gestapo have anything to do with it,' he said with a wry look. 'I'll be lucky if I'm allowed inside the house at all, let alone into your bedroom, with that pair of prison warders living there with you.'

'Whereas if we were to get married, we could move into a place of our own and have as much privacy as we want.' Her tone was light. She wasn't being serious; not this time.

'Yeah, yeah, I know,' he murmured into her hair. 'We're a pair, you and me. You know we'll do that, all in good time.' He paused, turning her face to his. 'Don't you?'

And because Daisy wanted to believe him she said, 'Yeah, course I do.'

The area north of Holland Park Avenue up as far as the Harrow Road – which was regarded loosely these days as Notting Hill but more usually known to its residents as North Kensington – was still riddled with building sites in the winter of 1955, as the slum clearance programme continued. Plans for major improvements and a massive road-widening scheme at Notting Hill Gate were heavily rumoured.

But at the moment, in stark contrast to its affluent neighbour Holland Park, the Notting Hill area in the majority was poor, overcrowded and grimy, with pockets of bohemia adding life and colour in some parts. Even before the Caribbeans had arrived there had been a multi-ethnic mix of Eastern European, Russian-Polish Jewish, Cypriots and so on. But the area was becoming increasingly cosmopolitan as ever larger numbers of West Indians continued to move in. Integration into the white community was still very poor.

House buying was a completely new experience for Daisy and she was surprised at the difficulty in finding somewhere suitable. There were properties for sale, of course, but many were big, brooding terraces, more suitable as letting houses than for single-family occupancy. Either that or they were in a state of neglect and needing major structural work, so couldn't be considered.

As conditions continued to deteriorate for Daisy and co. at Benly Square – a leaking sink on the landing, a faulty lavatory cistern and broken bathroom window now adding to the other miseries they had to endure – they were increasingly anxious to find a place with all possible speed.

Then one cold Sunday morning in January, with watery sunlight beaming through the clouds intermittently, they discovered number seventeen Larby Gardens, a terraced house on the hinterland of Notting Hill in the direction of Shepherd's Bush.

'So, what do you think?' asked June as they studied the house from the outside.

'Needs a lick of paint,' observed Daisy in a gross under-statement because the paint had peeled down to the bare wood in places around the windows.

'A good few gallons, I'd say,' added Nora.

'It's structurally sound, according to the agent,' June told them, 'though I'd have to get a survey done, of course.'

'Looks a bit run down,' Daisy felt obliged to point out, still rather in awe of this entire venture.

'Anything we can afford with enough bedrooms for us all isn't going to be in top-class condition,' June told them. 'We'll have to allow enough cash for furniture and decorating, remember. This is central London. It might be a run-down neighbourhood but it's still close to the West End, walking distance of Marble Arch in comfortable shoes. We can't afford to be too choosy, not unless we move further out, which none of us wants because of our work.'

'It's your money that's being spent, June,' Daisy reminded her. 'It has to be your decision.'

'Exactly,' agreed Nora.

'You know that isn't the way I want it to be.' June was adamant. 'We agreed that the choice of house would be something we were all happy with. And I really do want your honest opinion.'

Daisy looked down the street, which was a cul-de-sac full of ragged children playing and women gossiping on their doorsteps. It wasn't salubrious by any means but some of the homes showed signs of pride unknown in Benly Square. A few of the houses here even looked as though they'd been recently painted and had net curtains several shades lighter than the decaying grey lace that hung in the windows around there. Larby Gardens was only about ten minutes' walk from where they lived now, and undeniably shabby, but there was a friendly feel about it somehow, a sense of hope and possibility. 'I think it's got definite potential,' she stated.

'I like it around here,' said Shirley, looking enviously at a group of scruffy children playing marbles in the gutter nearby.

'So do I,' put in Belinda.

'We'd better go and see what it's like inside, then, hadn't we?' smiled June, the agent having given them the key as the property was empty.

Watched by a crowd of curious children who had no inhibitions about asking if Daisy's girls would be joining them as playmates, June unlocked the front door and they all trooped into a dusty hallway.

'Very promising,' was Daisy's instinctive verdict as they clattered through the empty rooms, their footsteps echoing on the bare floorboards, the air thick and musty from being closed up. 'It needs plenty of work but I think we could make this into a home. There's a nice feel about it somehow.'

'Not a bad size either,' added Nora.

As was so often the case with old terraced houses, this one was bigger than it appeared from the outside. There were four rooms upstairs and a hideous bathroom with a stained bath, and a sink that was coming away from the wall. Downstairs there were two reception rooms and an old-fashioned kitchen with a small lobby that led into the back garden. Through the window they could see that the latter was pocket-sized, and beyond the high wall at the bottom, a factory chimney towered over everything. But the house did have a garden. As tiny and overgrown as it was, it was somewhere for the children to play outside in safety.

'Cor, a garden,' shrieked Shirley in delight, as June opened the back door. 'Ooh, can we live here, please? Please, Auntie June, please say that we can.'

The three women exchanged glances.

'You two go outside and have a look while we talk about it,' she requested of them.

The little girls bounded through the door; they were well wrapped up in red coats with red and white pixie hoods that matched their gloves, and which Nora had knitted for them.

'So, what's it to be?' asked June, looking at Daisy and Nora. 'Do I go ahead and make an offer?'

Daisy cast her eye around the ancient, browning wallpaper, a flash of sunlight through the window emphasising the stains, the cracked square sink and worn-out wooden draining board. 'I feel as though I want to open all the windows and let some fresh air in,' she said excitedly. 'And tear all that awful wallpaper off and paint the walls in lovely light colours.' She paused, looking at her sister. 'But yes, I think it's right for us.'

'Hear, hear,' added Nora.

'Well, I hope you two are handy with wallpaper scrapers and paintbrushes,' grinned June, 'because you'll need to be if we take this place on. It would cost a fortune to have a professional in to do all the decorating.'

'I'm game,' smiled Daisy.

'Me too,' said Nora.

'Looks like we've found our new address then, doesn't it?' said June, looking pleased.

Daisy giggled. 'Larby Gardens, here we come,' she said, making a pattern with her finger on the dusty window.

'Cor, am I glad to take the weight off my feet,' said Jack when he and Alan finally managed to find a table to sit down to lunch on pie and chips in the cafeteria at Earls Court. 'It's a smashing exhibition but more exhausting than a week's work.'

'It's all the pushing and shoving to get through the crowds,' Alan commented, glancing around. The place was heaving; the queue at the self-service counter was snaking around the cafeteria and people were milling about with trays, trying to find somewhere to sit with their food.

'I'm enjoying it, though,' Jack remarked, shaking the ketchup bottle. 'It's really interesting.'

'It is,' nodded Alan, sprinkling salt on his chips. 'But I

think we've seen enough now, having been here all day yesterday as well as this morning.'

'Which leaves us with the rest of the afternoon free,' Jack pointed out, 'as we're not going back until tomorrow.'

'That's right.'

Pouring a dollop of ketchup on to the side of his plate, Jack said conversationally, 'I think the thing that's impressed me most here is the hotel kitchen equipment.'

'Mm.'

'Mind you, it needs to be special at the price they're asking,' he chatted on. 'The trouble with exhibitions is that they make you want everything on show.' He concentrated on his food for a few moments. 'Still, I suppose that's the whole point.'

Alan nodded but he wasn't really listening. He was tormented by the fact that he was in London and so was June. He wanted to see her *so* much. The change of address card she'd sent him recently was in his wallet and filling him with temptation. But it would be pointless to visit her. Why should he chase after a woman who didn't want him?

'What about that cocktail bar they had on display?' Jack continued to enthuse. 'Wasn't that something? Too much of a contemporary look for the Cliff Head, of course, but very smart with all that mirror glass and Formica . . . Alan, are you listening to me?'

His friend started slightly. 'No, I wasn't. Sorry.'

'At least you're honest,' was Jack's breezy reply. 'So what's making you so preoccupied?' He squinted at Alan knowingly. 'As if I didn't know.'

'It's being in the same town as her,' he admitted with a wry look. 'Naturally, she's on my mind. She is my wife, after all.'

'We're free this afternoon if you want to pay her a visit,' suggested Jack, who still thought Alan and June were made for each other.

193

'She'll probably be out at work.'

Jack shrugged. 'If she is, we'll go and see her there. You know where she works, don't you?'

'Yeah, but it might make it awkward for her,' said Alan, whose common sense was fighting with his desire to see her. 'Anyway, what would be the point? She's made it clear that it's over between us.'

'No harm in calling in for old times' sake, is there?' said Jack. 'As we're in London with time to spare, I'll go with you to make it seem more casual.'

'No. I'd better stay away.'

'It's up to you,' Jack told him with a sage look. 'But I think you'll regret it if you go back without even seeing her.'

Was it worth giving it one more try? Alan wondered. In his heart he knew he'd never forgive himself if he went back to Devon without making a final attempt. But this was her last chance. If she turned him down again this time, he would *never, ever* approach her again. And that was definite.

'You're right,' he said, his voice rising excitedly. 'I'll get a London A to Z and work out exactly where she lives when we've finished here.'

Daisy was listening to *Woman's Hour* as she worked with the scraper on the living-room walls. I'll have bigger muscles than Tarzan's by the time we've got rid of this horrible wallpaper, she thought, standing halfway up the ladder, rubbing her aching arm. But it'll be worth it in the end.

It was a March afternoon and a blustery wind whistled through the house, rattling the windows and seeming to send the dark clouds scuttling across the metal-grey skies. Daisy was alone in the house. June was out at work, Shirley was at school. It was Nora's day off and she'd taken Belinda to the park so that Daisy could get on with the decorating. Daisy had teased her; said she herself had drawn the short straw.

There had been plenty of laughter since they'd moved in here together.

Having given the walls a thorough soaking, Daisy got busy with the scraper, tearing off a sizeable strip and being rewarded with a moment of satisfaction. It was more than a month since they'd moved in and, by pulling together, had made good progress with the decorating, spurred on by a mutual desire to get the place into some sort of shape. There was still chaos on a grand scale in this room, though, with tattered curtains inherited from the previous owners, a carpet of newspaper on the bare boards, partly stripped walls and only deck chairs to sit on. When the work was finished, June was going to buy furniture and they were all very excited about that.

While she worked, Daisy listened with interest to a debate on the programme. Two women were getting quite heated about women's role in contemporary Britain. One of the debaters was a feminist whose views seemed extremely daring in that they challenged the accepted view that a woman's place was indisputably at home. The feminist speaker believed passionately that women were conditioned to enjoy a form of dedicated slavery, and that they shouldn't be made to feel guilty if they didn't enjoy being tied to the house, looking after children all day. If a woman preferred to go out to work, it didn't mean that she was flawed as a mother or loved her children less. Her opposer was rattled by this and quoted from a recent bestselling book by some doctor, who was also an expert in child care, and stated in print that the mothers of young children were not free to earn.

'Some of us don't have any choice, mate,' Daisy muttered under her breath. 'And you can't make me feel any more guilty than I already do for going out to work and leaving my girls.' As usual unmarried mothers weren't mentioned in the

195

discussion. Daisy had accepted long ago that women in her position didn't exist except to be quoted as a bad example. She was enjoying the discussion, though. It was rather refreshing to hear a different point of view.

Pushing her hair back from her brow, she looked at the clock on the mantelpiece and wondered if she could afford the time to stop for a tea break. In the end she decided to carry on working because Nora and Belinda would be back at any minute and it would soon be time to break off to collect Shirley from school anyway. Most of the local children walked to school together but Daisy wasn't ready to let her go on her own just yet.

No sooner had she denied herself a rest than there was a knock at the front door so she had to stop work anyway. Opening the door she found herself confronted by two smartly dressed men in suits and dark overcoats. Immediately her guard was up. A well-dressed man around here was either a rent man, an insurance man or a doctor; definitely officialdom of some sort.

'Yes?' she said nervously, unable to see beyond the smart clothes and their implication.

'Is June Masters in, please?' asked one of them, a young-ish, good-looking man with brown curly hair and a worried expression in his eyes.

Daisy looked at him warily and didn't reply. Good suits spelled trouble.

'Well?' he continued, looking questioningly at Daisy. 'Is she here or not?'

'Who wants to know?'

'I asked the question first.'

Years of being in thrall to rent collectors had made her ultra-sensitive about them. 'If you've come for the rent, you've come to the wrong house, mate,' she blurted out. 'We don't pay rent here. My sister owns this house.'

His face worked with astonishment and he looked very tense. 'Really?' he said.

Daisy was still afraid to admit to anything. She stared at him, pulling the door to in front of her as though to stop them entering.

'We're not gangsters about to force our way in, you know,' she was informed by the other man. 'So you're quite safe.'

'Perhaps I'd better explain,' said the first man. 'June sent me a card with her new address on it. We're in London on business and decided to call on the off chance that she might be in.'

The tone of the conversation now indicated that they weren't officials of any sort so Daisy relaxed a little. 'You know my sister well then?' she said enquiringly.

'I ought to,' he said with a half-smile. 'I'm her husband.'

'Oh, oh, I see.' He was the last person she expected it to be because he lived so far away.

He thrust his hand forward. 'Alan's the name,' he announced in a friendly manner.

'I'm Daisy,' she said, shaking his hand.

'Pleased to meet you.'

He being a relation altered things considerably. Her instinct was to invite them in and make them welcome. But would June want her estranged husband in her home? Daisy didn't know how civilised the break-up had been. If it had been a bitter parting, June wasn't going to thank Daisy for making him welcome here. 'As you've probably gathered, she's not at home at the moment,' she informed them. 'She's out at work.'

'What time are you expecting her back?'

'About five thirty.'

Alan looked at his watch. 'We'll come back later then, shall we?' he said.

'I suppose that would be best.' Daisy felt awkward. It seemed so rude not to ask them in.

'We're in London for a hotelier's exhibition,' he chose to explain. 'But we're going back to Devon first thing in the morning. It would be nice to see June before we go back, just to say hello. It didn't seem right to be so near and not call in.'

It went against the grain with Daisy to turn someone away without so much as a cup of tea on a winter's afternoon. But her name would be mud with June if she didn't want him encouraged to stay around. On the other hand, her sister had sent him her new address so she must have wanted him to know where she was, and he was going to come back later, anyway.

She was still debating the issue when Alan's companion made a timely intervention. 'We could murder a cuppa tea,' he said, winking at her. 'There's a bitter wind blowing out here and walking around the exhibition has done terrible things to our feet.'

Alan tutted and looked at him with mock disapproval, then turned back to Daisy. 'This is a friend of mine, Jack Saunders,' he informed her. 'He's a bit of a big mouth, I'm afraid.'

'So I gather.'

'We could freeze to death while you two stand there beating about the bush,' said Jack, and Daisy noticed his strong London accent. 'The two of you are sort of related and the two of us are dying for a cup of tea and a sit-down. Makes sense to put the two things together.'

Focusing her gaze on him, Daisy saw a pair of laughing blue eyes beaming at her from a fine countenance topped by short blond hair being blown flat to his head by the wind. Smiling almost despite herself, she succumbed to impulse, opened the door and invited them inside.

'Excuse the state of the place,' she said, leading them into the living room, waving her hand towards the patchy walls and indicating that they make themselves comfortable in the deck chairs that were near the fire, which she stirred into life

198

with the poker. 'As you can see, we're in the middle of doing it up.'

They nodded politely. Daisy took their coats and hung them up in the hall on the hooks that had been left by the previous occupants.

'I didn't know that June had a sister,' Alan informed her when she came back into the room.

She explained briefly about their recent reunion. 'It's a long story,' she concluded. 'I'm sure June will give you all the details.'

He nodded. 'Is it just the two of you living here?' he enquired with interest.

Daisy explained the setup.

'Cosy,' remarked Alan.

'It is, very,' said Daisy, saddened by the bitter edge to his tone; the sorrow that was very often visible in June's eyes she could now see reflected in his.

She went to the kitchen to make tea and when she came back into the room with a tray of tea and biscuits, Jack did most of the talking. Alan just added the odd polite comment. Daisy felt sorry for him. He seemed preoccupied and had a bewildered look about him; had obviously known nothing about how June had become a home owner.

'Terrible job, that, isn't it,' remarked Jack, looking at the walls, 'stripping off wallpaper?'

'Sounds as though you're speaking from experience,' Daisy replied, sitting in another deck chair with a cup of tea and a biscuit.

'From more experience than I care to think about,' he said lightly. 'I bought an old cottage and spent what seemed like the whole of the first year getting all the old wallpaper off.'

'I hope it was worth it and you've got it as you want it now,' she said chattily.

'More or less,' he replied. 'There's always something else

199

you want to do, though. By the time you get to the end of it, the beginning needs doing again.'

'Don't say that.' She made a face. 'We've only just started on this place and I feel as though I've had enough already.'

'I know the feeling.'

'We all have jobs so can only work on it at odd times,' she told him.

'I did mine that way too.'

'I shouldn't be taking this break now, to tell you the truth,' she confided. 'I wouldn't have stopped work if you hadn't arrived.'

'I bet you're glad we turned up then,' he joked.

'Ooh, yeah,' she admitted with a grin. 'Any excuse to put that damned stripper down.' She sipped her tea. 'I would have to be stopping soon anyway, though, because it's nearly time I went to collect my daughter from school.'

'You have a daughter?' he said with the note of surprise the absence of a wedding ring evoked in people.

'I have two daughters.' The sound of voices at the back door indicated the arrival of Nora and Belinda. 'One of them has just come in now.'

Belinda, a dainty, talkative child with her mother's smiling eyes, came into the room like a great bolt of energy and immediately launched into an enthusiastic account of the trip to the park and how she'd been on the swings and they'd seen some flowers which Nora had said were crocuses. Daisy gave her a hug and listened with interest, making introductions and explaining that the men were waiting for Auntie June.

They all had more tea and Daisy said she had to go and collect Shirley from school. The men talked about leaving and coming back later, whereupon Nora took it upon herself to say that they were very welcome to stay, rather than roam the streets in the cold, until June got home.

Jack astonished them all by saying, 'It's nice of you to

200

offer but if we stay we make ourselves useful, right? So have you got another one of those wallpaper strippers?'

When Daisy left, both men had their jackets off and sleeves rolled up and were working with the strippers on the walls. When she got back from school with Shirley, the wall she'd been working on was bare of wallpaper and they were making inroads into another, ably assisted by Belinda, who was collecting the strippings into a bucket and keeping up a constant flow of chatter. Daisy was infused with the warmth of the atmosphere as soon as she entered the room.

'Wow. You haven't half shifted.' She was impressed.

'We don't hang about,' grinned Jack. 'Anyway, there are two of us at it.'

'You must be supermen to have done all that in such a short time,' she teased them lightly.

'I'm the superman,' claimed Jack, making the little girls laugh by pulling a face at Alan, 'because I've had plenty of practice. Whereas my mate here doesn't have to do his own dirty work so is a bit of an amateur.'

Alan took it all in good part, even though he still seemed worried, obviously anxious about the meeting with June. 'Honestly, you'd think he had a degree in interior decorating to hear him talk,' was his jokey response. 'Just because he bought a ruin of a cottage and made it habitable.'

'What's a cottage?' Shirley wanted to know.

'A small house, love,' her mother explained.

'Like the ones in storybooks that are always in the country?' she said. 'Is yours in the country?'

'Mine's even better than that,' Jack told her. 'It's by the seaside.'

'Seaside, like Southend?' said Belinda.

'That's right,' said Jack.

'Do you make sandcastles?' she wanted to know.

'I'm a bit old to want to do that sort of thing myself,' he

told her. 'But it's a good sandy beach and children do make them there.'

'Ooh . . .' Belinda was breathless with awe.

'Sounds lovely, and I bet you've made your cottage a lot more than just habitable,' said Daisy, because Jack Saunders had the air of someone who would make a thoroughly good job of anything he took on.

'I suppose I might manage to admit to it being comfortable,' amended Alan, teasing his pal.

'You're just jealous,' joshed Jack.

'Jealous because I don't live miles from anywhere?' he returned. 'Don't kid yourself.'

'Anyway, do we have another volunteer?' asked Jack, smiling at Shirley.

'I don't mind,' said Shirley, giving him a shy look. 'But only if you'll tell us more about your cottage at the seaside.'

'It's a deal,' he agreed. 'You help your sister pick up the paper and I'll keep talking.'

'OK. I'll just go and get changed,' she said, immediately at ease with him.

'You've both done wonders in this room,' praised Nora, who had fallen under the spell of these two amiable young men.

'You certainly have,' grinned Daisy. 'You can keep it up for as long as you like.'

'Are you going to get another paint stripper and give a hand?' asked Jack.

'Afraid not,' she told him. 'I have to get ready for work in a minute.'

'Work?' he said with interest.

She told him what she did and explained that she was given a free meal at the hotel when she was on duty so wouldn't be staying for supper with the others.

'I hope you two boys will stay for a bite to eat with us,

202

though,' Nora said. 'It's nothing special but there's plenty if you'd like to join us.'

'Please stay,' chorused the little girls.

'You'll have to ask the boss about that,' Jack told her, grinning towards Alan.

'Do stay,' Shirley urged Alan, adding as an extra incentive, 'we'll show you our bedroom, if you like.'

'It's been done up and it's very pretty,' Belinda put in. 'Mummy and Auntie June and Nora painted it and put wallpaper up for us. It's got toys on it.'

'In that case, how can we say no?' said Alan.

'Hurray!' shrieked the girls, who, like their mother, were very sociable.

'You seem to have made a hit,' remarked Daisy, looking from one of the men to the other.

'If only it was that easy with bigger girls,' was Jack's light-hearted response.

'I can't believe that you'd have any trouble,' said Daisy.

'He doesn't,' Alan informed her. 'So don't listen to him. He's just trying it on.'

Daisy was amused by their banter. They were all laughing when June walked in, smiling, her face instinctively lighting up when she saw Alan, then becoming grim when the reality of the situation registered fully.

'What are you doing here?' she demanded coldly.

The laughter ended abruptly and tension crackled in the air as the couple stared at each other in stony silence.

Chapter Nine

Daisy's journey to and from work took a bit longer from Larby Gardens because she had further to walk from the station. But the extra travelling time was the last thing on her mind that night on her way home on the tube. She was lost in thought, reliving that terrible moment when June had walked in and sent the atmosphere in the house plummeting to freezing point.

Even the children had been subdued, though not for long, thanks to Jack's entertaining company. After June and Alan had made a silent departure to her room, leaving a resounding hush behind them, Jack had carried on stripping the wallpaper, chatting to the girls as though nothing untoward was happening.

Heaven knows what had happened since then. Daisy had gone to work soon after, leaving the girls in Nora's care, assisted by Jack, who was regaling them with tales of life at the seaside.

Running over June's arrival again, Daisy recalled her initial joy at seeing Alan. She'd simply lit up at the sight of him. Daisy wondered what the problem could possibly be because the couple obviously adored each other. Whatever it was it must be serious because June didn't seem like the sort of person to walk out on someone on a whim.

Her thoughts turned to Jack with whom Daisy had struck

an instant rapport. He'd made a big impression on her with his casual charm and sense of humour. His blond good looks hadn't gone unnoticed either. Oh well, they'll both be gone when I get home, she thought. June would surely have sorted things out one way or the other by now.

She was jolted out of her thoughts when someone approached her in the station foyer. 'Hello, Daisy,' he greeted her.

'Jack?' She smiled broadly, pleased but astonished to see him. 'What are you doing here?'

'That's the second time today I've heard that question,' he said with a wry grin. 'Fortunately, this time it wasn't said with quite the same venom.'

She made a face. 'Wasn't it awful?' she said, tutting. 'June was really fierce, wasn't she?'

'Enough to frighten the pants off Alan.'

'What happened after I left?' she asked, pulling her coat collar up against the strong wind as they made their way out of the station into the street.

'They stayed upstairs until supper.'

'And then . . .?'

'They came down and we all ate a meal together.'

'In agonising silence, I suppose.'

'They weren't exactly laughing and joking but they did make an effort at polite conversation so it wasn't too bad,' he told her. 'And the rest of us did enough talking to cover the tension. The kids kept things moving along. With them around there weren't any awkward silences.'

Daisy smiled affectionately at the thought of them. 'Just as well they aren't any good at keeping quiet, in this particular instance then,' she remarked.

'Absolutely.'

'So, what's happening with June and Alan?' she asked.

'They went back upstairs to June's room after the meal and

were still there when I came out,' he told her. 'I called up the stairs to them to tell them where I was going and Alan shouted down in reply. So they haven't murdered each other. That's all I know.'

'What are you doing here anyway?' she asked again. 'I thought you'd be back at your hotel by now, going to bed at a decent hour as you're going back to Devon in the morning.'

'That was the original intention. But I couldn't very well drag Alan away while he was in the middle of an emotional crisis, could I? And poor Nora looked so whacked, I told her to go to bed and not worry about staying up to entertain me,' he explained. 'I thought I might as well come and walk you home, to save sitting around at your place on my own. Nora gave me all the gen so that I knew where to meet you.'

'It's very kind of you,' Daisy said as they left the station lights behind and began to stride out against the wind, passing a staggering drunk, a tramp in a shop doorway and a crowd of Teddy boys hanging around on a street corner.

'It wasn't kindness that inspired me to come,' he confessed.

'No? What then?'

'I enjoyed your company so much earlier, I wanted some more of it.'

'At least you're honest,' she approved. 'And I'm flattered.'

They walked on in comfortable silence for a while, then: 'I shouldn't really say this but I'm going to stick my neck out and say it anyway,' he began hesitantly. 'Is it a good idea for you to be out on the streets on your own at this time of night with so many dodgy characters about?'

'No choice, I'm afraid,' she informed him chirpily. 'Anyway, I'm used to it so it doesn't worry me.'

'Wouldn't a daytime job be better for you?'

Daisy explained her situation and her reasons for working unsociable hours.

'Where's the kids' father?' Jack asked.

'He's around and we're still together,' she said, adding in the defensive way that had become almost second nature to her, 'We'll be getting married, eventually.'

'Doesn't he worry about you being out on your own at night in such a dangerous part of London?' he queried. 'I know I would if you were my girlfriend.'

'I don't think Nat ever gives it a thought, to be perfectly honest,' she replied. 'We're Londoners; urban life is what we know. Anyway, it isn't as dangerous as it might seem to an outsider. It can't be because I always get home safe and sound.'

'I'm not a complete outsider, you know,' he pointed out. 'I haven't always lived out in the sticks in deepest Devon. I'm originally from Hackney.'

Which explained the accent, she noted, but said, 'You've lived away for quite a while, though, haven't you? So you've probably got a bit out of touch with the way things are here.'

'Are you suggesting that I've become a bit of a yokel?' he grinned, teasing her.

'I wasn't, actually.' She paused, giggling. 'But I think you might look rather fetching in a smock.'

'Cheeky,' he admonished good-humouredly. 'We don't all have straw in our hair down there, you know.'

'And it isn't all pimps and prostitutes up here,' she countered quickly.

'I suppose I asked for that,' he laughed. 'But seriously, though, you must admit that this part of London does have a reputation for being a bit rough.'

'Things go on around here, so I've heard. But they don't affect me or my children,' Daisy said. 'I just get on with my life and let other people get on with theirs. Being out on my own at night isn't a problem.'

'As you say, I'm probably out of touch with how things are here now that I'm a country boy,' he conceded.

She nodded. 'You really like it down there then?'

'Love it.'

'Is it living by the sea that appeals to you in particular?'

'I enjoy having the ocean on my doorstep, yeah, sure. But I like the general feeling of space I get from living on the seashore,' Jack explained. 'I spent some time in Australia. I think that gave me a taste for the outdoors.'

'You wouldn't come back to London to live then?'

'It would have to be something really special to make me do that,' he told her. 'My folks are all settled in Australia so I don't have any family ties here now. I'm still a London boy at heart and I don't suppose I'll ever lose that. But I've got used to the slower pace of life down there. Clean air, not so much traffic. And the countryside is beautiful.'

'It sounds wonderful.'

'It is,' he confirmed. 'And my cottage is in a fantastic location.' He paused, turning to her with a wry look. 'Sorry, I'm probably being boring. I'm afraid I get a bit carried away with enthusiasm for the place.'

'You're not being at all boring.' She couldn't believe he would ever be that. 'But I must admit, I can't imagine you living miles from anywhere. You're far too sociable.'

'I'm no hermit, believe me,' he quickly put her right. 'I'm out at work a lot of the time and it's only ten minutes into town on my motorbike.'

'A motorbike eh?'

'My pride and joy.'

'What is it with men and motorbikes?'

'The speed, the freedom . . .'

'The wind in your hair?'

'Yeah, that too,' he laughed.

'You're building up a picture of a fabulous way of life.'

'It'll do for me.'

They moved on to other things. She told him about her job

and asked about his. He told her a bit about the Cliff Head and his position there.

'And you are best mates with Alan, despite the fact that his parents own the hotel?' she remarked. 'Some people might be put off by that.'

'The fact that he's the boss doesn't interfere with our friendship at all,' Jack told her. 'He doesn't pull rank on me when we're off duty or ram his position down my throat, that's why. We wouldn't be mates at all if he did and he knows it. We hit it off from the start. We're the same age and have similar views about things. It was only natural we should get pally.'

'You seem to know June quite well too.'

'Not as well as I know him but I was friendly with them as a couple before she did her disappearing act,' he explained. 'He turned to me then. The poor bloke was beside himself.'

'What happened to split them up?'

'No idea. And from what he's said, I don't think Alan knows either. She just went, out of the blue, leaving him completely shattered.' He paused thoughtfully. 'But you're her sister – hasn't she talked to you about it?'

'Hardly at all. She said that her husband was the son of a hotelier in Torquay and she left him but she's never said why, and she makes it clear she doesn't want to talk about it.'

'It's all very odd.'

'Mm.'

'Naturally there's been gossip,' he mentioned. 'Some people think his parents drove her out. But I think there's more to it than that. She's too strong-minded to be driven out of anywhere, and she's certainly a match for them.'

'She didn't get on with them, then?'

'They didn't get on with her, to be more precise, especially his mother. She gave June a really hard time. I've watched her in action. I've seen her put June through it over the years.'

210

'Didn't Alan stick up for her?'

'He did if he caught his mother at it,' he told her. 'But she was as nice as pie to June when he was around. Far too clever to let him get wind of what was really happening. June must have told him about it, I suppose, but maybe she didn't tell him just how bad it was. June's always struck me as a caring sort of a woman, despite what she's done to Alan. Maybe she didn't want to come between mother and son.'

'You could be right.'

'Anyway, I still don't think that was why she left,' Jack went on to say. 'But I'm convinced she must have had a very good reason to walk out like that. I worked with them for a long time. I've seen how they were together. She always seemed loyal and absolutely devoted to him. But you're her sister, you know what she's like.'

'I don't actually.' Daisy briefly explained the unusual situation with June and herself. 'I'm still getting to know her. She seems very deep; keeps things close to her chest.'

'Mm, you're probably right. Anyway, I hope they can patch their marriage up,' he said. 'They were a great team and Alan hasn't been the same man since she went.'

'Perhaps they're getting back together as we speak,' she suggested.

'If talking has anything to do with it, they will be,' he grinned. 'They've been at it long enough. He'll have to call it a day soon so that we can go back to the hotel to bed.'

'You're not staying at the hotel where June works, I take it, or she wouldn't have been so surprised to see you.'

'Alan didn't want to crowd her,' explained Jack. 'We only came to the house on the spur of the moment.'

'He seems very genuine to me.'

'He is.'

They'd reached the house and he stopped outside and turned to her, the wind blowing his hair about. 'In case Alan's

211

ready to leave and drags me off in a hurry and I don't get a chance to mention it,' he began, smiling uncertainly, 'I just want to say how much I've enjoyed meeting you.'

'The same goes for me too.' She shivered against the wind that was whipping around the buildings and sweeping litter along the pavement. 'It's been lovely.'

'And those daughters of yours are a couple of smashers,' he continued.

'Thank you.' She smiled broadly. Compliments about her children always pleased her.

'I wish you all the best for the future.'

'The same to you,' Daisy responded, noticing that his mood had become formal but oddly intimate somehow. 'When London seems especially hectic and the tube impossibly crowded, I'll think of you with envy in your cottage by the sea.'

'Anyway,' he said with a note of finality, thrusting his hand towards her. 'It's been a pleasure.'

'Likewise,' she said, shaking a hand that felt firm and strong.

'Come on then, let's go and see if those two have made any progress towards a reunion,' he said, and they walked up to the front door together.

'If you didn't want me to find you, why send me your change of address?' Alan wanted to know.

'How many more times must I tell you,' replied June impatiently. 'It was in case of an emergency. I just didn't feel able to move house without letting you know my address.'

'If you really wanted it to be over between us, you would have moved without giving me a second thought.'

'I was just being responsible. You could have had an accident or been seriously ill and needed to contact me,' she went on to explain. 'Or you could have wanted to file for divorce. There are any number of reasons why you needed to know where I was. It just didn't seem right not to tell you.'

'You didn't find it necessary when you left,' he reminded her. 'I had to use my own methods to track you down and only did so then because of luck.'

She lowered her eyes in shame. 'I know. That was really bad of me,' she admitted. 'I would have let you know eventually. You beat me to it, that's all.'

'Let's put all that behind us and you come home, June,' he begged for the umpteenth time.

'Alan, we've been going over this for hours and I've told you I'm not coming back,' she insisted. 'I can't. My life is here in London now.'

'The reason we've been going over it for hours is because we both want the same thing – to be back together. But you won't admit it for some reason best known to yourself.'

They were in her bedroom, not yet refurbished, the walls suffused with wallpaper darkened with age, the floorboards bare. He was sitting in a wicker chair near the sash window. They'd been talking for a long time but not only about their marriage. There had been a mutual exchange of news. She'd told him about the bizarre circumstances that had led to the reunion with Daisy, and their hopes to clear their father's name. She'd explained how she came to buy this house. He'd given her an update about things at the Cliff Head.

'Apart from anything else,' she said now, 'I need to be in London with Daisy to do what we can for our father.'

'So stay here for a while longer, and then come back,' Alan suggested. 'If I knew you were coming back eventually, I could live with that.'

'I'm not coming back, Alan,' she repeated. 'Not ever. So you must try to accept it.' She had to force the words out. 'When I made the decision to leave you, it was for good.'

His expression was grim. He stared at her, then looked

213

down at his hands as though pondering. When he spoke again, his tone was sad but positive. 'OK, I'll do what you want and go away and get on with my life without you. I won't come after you again. But don't expect me to believe that it's what you really want because I know that it isn't.' He raised his eyes to meet hers and added vehemently, 'I'll never believe that. Not ever.'

'That's up to you.'

The silence was painfully tense until Alan changed the subject completely. 'About this business of your father – I admire you for being willing to have a go and I don't want to put you off, but I think you should prepare yourself for disappointment. It all seems a bit pie-in-the-sky to me.'

'It is, extremely,' June agreed. 'We've got nothing to go on at all. But because Daisy and I know that he's innocent we have the motivation to keep trying. It could take years to find these people, and we might never do it but we can't give up. Can you understand that?'

'Yes, I think so. Just be careful.'

She nodded. His mood was now one of dull resignation and she guessed that he had, at last, accepted their separation as permanent. He was finished with shouting and pleading. He was going to make the best of his life without her. It broke her heart.

Noises from downstairs drifted up.

'Sounds as though the others are back,' Alan said, standing up with a purposeful air and a heartbreaking show of dignity. 'So I'd better be on my way.'

'Yes.'

'It isn't fair to keep Jack hanging about any longer,' he said lamely, in an effort to delay the inevitable.

'No it isn't.' She swallowed hard. 'Could you make my apologies to him for me, please?' Dangerously close to tears, she could barely trust herself to speak. 'I'd rather not go down and see him off. I'm sure he won't mind.'

'Of course he won't,' he said coolly, and left the room quietly while June remained where she was, sitting stiffly on the edge of the bed.

'No luck with June then?' observed Jack as he and Alan headed for the station.

'Does it look like it?'

'All right, no need to bite my head off, mate,' Jack retaliated. 'Just making conversation.'

'Save your breath,' was Alan's sharp response. 'I'm not in the mood for a chat.'

'Suits me fine,' said Jack, who knew Alan far too well to be offended.

'Good.'

Jack was concerned about his friend, of course, and hated to see him miserable. But thoughts of someone else were filling his mind as they walked through the dingy streets of Notting Hill, occasionally splashed with neon and the sound of jazz music drifting from some basement.

Daisy had made a huge impression on him and his heart lifted at the memory of her: her beaming smile, the things she'd said, the way she was with her children. She wasn't smart or glamorous but she was so richly endowed with warmth and vitality, a natural beauty radiated from her. Her sex appeal was magnetic, all the more so because it was completely uncontrived.

He longed to see her again but knew such feelings were pointless. Apart from the obvious geographical problem, she was still involved with the children's father, and therefore not available. She was as good as married, and married women were off limits as far as he was concerned. It was a pity, though, because he'd really taken a shine to her.

He was recalled to the present by Alan. 'Sorry I've been

such a pain, snapping your head off and keeping you waiting all that time at June's place.'

'No problem,' Jack was able to assure him honestly. If Alan hadn't decided to call on June, Jack would never have met Daisy. He'd probably never see her again but he felt richer for having briefly made her acquaintance.

Daisy was having much the same thoughts about him as she heated milk for cocoa in the kitchen. Meeting Jack had been a real tonic. He'd made her feel light-hearted and vibrant, somehow. It was a pity she wouldn't be seeing him again because he was such a smashing bloke. Ah well, ships that pass in the night, she thought wistfully. She'd not thought it possible to be so profoundly affected by a complete stranger. She barely knew him but he'd felt special to her. Her feelings for him weren't entirely platonic either, she admitted, grinning to herself. She'd been involved with Nat for so long she'd forgotten how exhilarating it was to fancy someone new.

Her mind drifted on to the other events of the evening and she was sad as she remembered Alan coming downstairs looking gloomy but proud, and leaving the house with Jack so quietly. He and June had obviously not managed to work things out.

The house felt achingly silent now. Usually at this time when she got back from work, she, June and Nora would have a cup of cocoa together and a chat before they went to bed. Nora had obviously been exhausted by the tension of it all but was probably lying awake worrying about it. June definitely wouldn't be asleep after such a trauma.

Suddenly decisive, Daisy heated more milk and made three mugs of cocoa, put them on a tray and carried it upstairs. Pausing outside June's room, she could just hear the low sound of stifled sobbing. June was obviously struggling very

216

hard not to be heard. They had a strict house rule here: the privacy of someone's bedroom was sacrosanct. This was where you went when you wanted to be left alone and everyone respected that. If Daisy went in, she would be intruding. But her heart ached for her sister and she wanted to help. Surely it was permissible to bend the rules under the circumstances.

Holding the tray with one hand with her arm supporting it, she tapped tentatively on the door.

No reply.

She knocked again. 'I've brought you some cocoa, June,' she called.

All was silent.

'Can I come in?'

As the request was ignored and the crying continued, Daisy dispensed with house rules altogether and followed her instincts, turning the door handle and looking cautiously into the room. Her sister was lying face down on the bed, her body heaving.

'Oh, June, love.' Putting the tray on the dressing table, Daisy went over to the bed and sat down, putting a comforting arm around her sister's shoulders. 'You and Alan weren't able to sort things out then?'

'No, and we never will. We can't ever get back together, and I've told him that,' she spluttered. 'He shouldn't have come here. All he's done is upset us both.'

'Perhaps you shouldn't have let him know where you are if you feel that strongly about it,' was Daisy's cautious suggestion.

June turned over and sat up, mopping her face with a handkerchief. 'I couldn't just cut myself off from him altogether. It wouldn't have been fair,' she said, her voice muffled with tears. 'He needed to know my address, even if only because he wants to start divorce proceedings.'

'There is that, I suppose,' Daisy agreed.

'Sorry you've all been made to feel awkward in the house,' she apologised, sniffing into her hanky. 'And about my imitation of Niagara Falls.'

'Don't be silly,' Daisy assured her. 'I was out at work so I wasn't affected. And everyone's entitled to a good old weep now and again. I'm your sister. I want to be here for you.'

'And I'm your friend and the same goes for me,' added Nora, entering the room. 'The last thing I want to do is intrude but I heard you crying and I heard Daisy come in.' She paused, looking at June. 'I want to help, June.' She picked up the tray and offered the cocoa mugs to them.

June seemed to recover and managed a watery smile after moistening her mouth with the hot, sweet liquid. 'That means a lot to me,' she told them, her eyes glistening with fresh tears. 'I've never had any real friends before.'

'I am surprised,' expressed Daisy. 'You being so confident and everything.'

'That doesn't necessarily bring friends.' She didn't enlighten them as to the reason for her friendless state. She hated to talk about it, and, besides, she didn't want to burden them with her past. 'None that I was close to, anyway. I suppose Alan was the best friend I ever had. And even then there was always . . .' her voice tailed off.

'Always what?' urged Daisy.

'Nothing.'

'As Alan obviously means so much to you, and vice versa, is there no chance of your getting back together?' asked Daisy with feeling. 'It seems such a terrible waste. Anyone can see the two of you still love each other.'

'Love isn't always enough,' said June thickly.

'Surely it's the main ingredient, though,' suggested Daisy hopefully. 'If you've got that, the rest can be sorted out. Or am I just being naïve?'

'You are rather,' muttered June.

'You might feel better if you talk about it, dear,' suggested Nora kindly. 'A trouble shared and all that. It goes without saying that nothing you say will go any further.'

'There's nothing to say, honestly,' she insisted, composing herself suddenly, as though fearing they might persuade her to say something she would later regret. 'It's over between Alan and me, and that's that.'

Daisy knew that June's demons, whatever they were, had not been exorcised by her leaving Alan. She was still a very tormented woman. 'Well, you obviously know your own mind. And being completely selfish, we'd have missed you like mad if you'd gone back to Devon,' she said in an effort to lift the atmosphere as June obviously didn't want to confide.

'By the way,' began June, taking this opportunity to make something clear, 'if anything ever happened and I did have to sell up and go away for any reason at all, I would make sure you weren't left without a home.' She paused and added most emphatically, 'You have my word on that.'

'That's nice of you,' said Daisy.

'Yes,' added Nora.

'So, having cleared that up, let's talk about something more cheerful,' June suggested, trying without success to convince them that she was feeling better.

'One good thing has come out of today,' Daisy grinned, determined to cheer them all up.

They both looked at her enquiringly.

'All the old wallpaper has been stripped off in the living room, thanks to our visitors.'

'It is true what they say about an ill wind then,' said Nora with a chuckle.

Even June attempted a smile at Daisy's down-to-earth way of getting things back to normal.

As the air warmed and softened to spring and then summer, the occupants of number seventeen Larby Gardens lived in harmony together. Rooms turned from dingy and old-fashioned to fresh and contemporary as the decorating progressed. Furniture was bought, carpets laid and home-liness added with pictures, ornaments and lamps.

June paid for all of this from the money she'd put by from the sale of her mother's house, but everything else was shared: the chores, the bills, the decisions. Meals were eaten together whenever possible against a clamour of conversa-tion, with the children making their contributions. Late-night cocoa continued to be a regular habit. Naturally there were differences of opinion but generally speaking they got on well.

But the long-term co-existence of human beings was rarely that simple, and Daisy's first falling-out with her sister was over Nat, and was very painful for them both.

'I don't know why you put up with it,' June blurted out one night when he'd not been near for a fortnight, then turned up just before bedtime, expecting Daisy to make supper for him, and had gone off in a huff when she'd refused. 'It's disgusting the way he treats you. Ignoring your existence for weeks on end, then turning up just when he feels like it. He's got a flaming cheek.'

Daisy wasn't easily offended and could take any amount of criticism about herself, but when it came to Nat, her defence mechanism went into top gear. 'My relationship with Nat is my business,' she told June sharply.

Having managed to restrain herself from saying too much about Nat's offhand behaviour towards her sister for all these months, now that she had spoken out, June couldn't stop.

'I'm only thinking of you,' she went on. 'That man has no right to treat you the way he does. You shouldn't stand for it.'

'It's got nothing to do with you.'

'It's pathetic, the way you let him get away with it,' June ranted on with her sister's interests at heart. 'You're not soft or stupid, so why keep him in your life when he obviously doesn't have a serious thought in his head as regards his intentions towards you? Why don't you just tell him to get lost?'

Daisy was furious. 'I don't have to explain myself to you,' she retaliated, her cheeks almost matching her red dressing gown. 'I don't tell you how to run your life so don't try and tell me how to run mine.'

'Girls, girls,' intervened Nora worriedly. They were in the living room, ready to go to bed, and until a few moments ago the atmosphere between them had been as jovial as ever. 'Calm down, both of you, before you say something you'll really regret.'

'You agree with me, surely?' said June, turning to Nora for support. 'You must be able to see how that dreadful man is using her.'

Indeed she could and had said so many times. But now wasn't the time to take sides. 'My opinion doesn't come into it.' She was treading warily. 'As Daisy says, it's her business. Only she knows how she feels about Nat. I think the two of you should agree to differ on this one.'

But June was too fired up in her sister's defence to stop now. 'You're an attractive and intelligent woman, Daisy. You can do a lot better than Nat Barker,' she went on. 'You're much too good for him.'

'Like you're too good for Alan. Is that what you do, June – judge people; give them points out of ten for good behaviour and character?' retorted Daisy, who wasn't normally sarcastic or cynical; this issue was beyond the intellect and was rooted entirely in the emotions. Words were flowing out of her mouth, almost as though someone else was saying them. 'Is

221

that why you left him, because he didn't measure up to your high standards?'

'My marriage to Alan has nothing to do with this,' she declared hotly.

'Oh, no, when it comes to your private life, you don't want it mentioned, do you? You clam up completely and no one's allowed to say a word. Yet you think you have the right to lecture me.' Daisy glared at her across the hearth. 'You are in no position to comment on my relationship with Nat since you couldn't even keep your own marriage together.'

'That has nothing to do with this issue,' June insisted. 'I can't stand by and see Nat treat you so badly.'

'How dare you preach to me?' said Daisy through clenched teeth. 'Nat is the man I chose, the man I fell in love with. Whether I stay with him or not is my decision, *not yours*. It's nothing to do with you so keep your big nose out of my business.'

'You must be able to see—'

'I do have eyes in my head and a brain,' Daisy roared. 'Of course I can see that he isn't perfect, and that he pushes his luck with me something rotten. What do you think I am? Some sort of halfwit?'

'Haven't I just said the opposite to that?' June replied angrily. 'It's because I know that you're an intelligent woman and worth better, I think you should get rid of him.'

'And as I've just said, what I choose to do about Nat is my business and nobody else's, certainly not yours,' Daisy told her. 'People are people, a mixture of everything, and we all have some good and bad in us. Not only the decent, well-behaved ones are lovable, you know.'

'Now you're suggesting that *I'm* a halfwit.'

'If the cap fits . . .'

June didn't reply to this, just looked at Daisy in outrage, cheeks scarlet in her otherwise pale countenance.

'To hear you talk anyone would think you were an expert on men,' Daisy ranted.

'I've never claimed that.'

'You couldn't very well, could you? Because you wouldn't have a leg to stand on.' Daisy was out of control, driven on by her protective instincts towards Nat and her right to live her life in the way she chose. 'And even if you did have a more impressive track record in that direction, you'd still have no right to tell me what to do. I know you own this house and I'm just a lodger but that doesn't mean you can interfere in my life.'

June was further enraged by this suggestion. 'This has nothing to do with the house,' she denied hotly. 'I've told you that I never think of you and Nora as lodgers. This is a personal thing.'

Daisy stood up, her voice shaking with emotion. 'Be that as it may, Nat is the man I love and the father of my children, so I would thank you to respect that fact in future. Whatever he does, however badly he behaves, it has *nothing whatsoever* to do with you. Is that clear? It's my life, so just leave me alone to get on with it in the way that I choose.'

And with that she rushed from the room.

Ashen-faced and shaky, June looked at Nora contritely. 'I don't know what came over me,' she said, biting her lip. 'It all just came pouring out.'

'Nat has the same effect on me and I've had plenty of words with Daisy about him in the past,' Nora told her. 'But I try to keep shtoom now because she's very sensitive about it and won't hear a word against him.' She sighed. 'And what she says is quite true, of course. It isn't any of our business. Daisy's no fool. She knows in her heart that Nat is no good for her but she loves him. And us being critical doesn't help because she knows she can never give him up. He can twist her around his little finger.'

'It makes me so mad.'

'Me too, but it'll never change. It's been going on too long. So we might as well accept it and keep our opinions to ourselves.'

June looked worried. 'I don't know what to do, Nora,' she confessed, raking her hair with her fingers anxiously and biting her lip. 'The last thing I want is to be at war with Daisy.'

'Give her a few minutes to calm down, then go up and see her,' suggested Nora.

'Yes, I think I shall have to,' agreed June. 'Because I can't leave it like this.'

Daisy was sitting up in bed looking at a magazine when June made a cautious entry, having tapped on the door first.

'If you've come to say more horrible things about Nat, then you're wasting your time because I don't want to hear them so I won't listen,' she said, holding the magazine open and keeping her eyes fixed on it.

'I've come to apologise actually,' June said sheepishly.

'Oh.' Now Daisy put the magazine down and looked at her sister, waiting for her to go on.

'I shouldn't have said those things,' June admitted ruefully. 'I really am very sorry.'

'You're right, you shouldn't have said all that stuff,' Daisy responded coolly.

'You said some pretty rotten things to me too, you know,' June pointed out.

'Only after serious provocation.'

'I suppose you're right.'

'You shouldn't have got me fired up like that,' Daisy told her, her tone becoming warmer. 'You can't expect to say things like that to someone about their man and not expect them to retaliate.'

'In future then the least said the soonest mended when it comes to Nat,' suggested June.

'I think we need more than just that to keep the peace between us on the subject,' Daisy informed her.

'Meaning . . .?'

'Whether you like it or not, Nat is the man in my life,' she began, 'and he comes to this house as a guest of mine.'

June waited.

'So I'd appreciate it if you could treat him with courtesy, in the same way as I do when your friends come to the house,' Daisy requested.

'I'm always polite to him.'

Daisy gave a dry laugh. 'In an arctic sort of way,' she pointed out. 'You could make him feel welcome when he's here, rather than painfully uncomfortable.'

'Point taken.'

'Good.'

'I'm sorry about just now, Daisy, I really am,' said June, keen to make amends. 'I went too far.'

'Yes, you did, and I hope you truly realise that.'

'I do.' June paused. 'And I really don't think of you and Nora as lodgers. I think of us all as friends sharing a house.'

Daisy was ashamed now. 'Yeah, I know you do,' she sighed. 'I was angry . . . I said things I didn't mean.'

'We both did.'

'Except for the things you said about Nat.' Daisy gave her sister a questioning look. 'You did mean those, didn't you?'

'I'm sorry, Daisy.' June made a face. 'There's no point in my lying about it. But I will make an effort to make him feel more welcome here.'

'Thanks. Live and let live, eh?'

June nodded. 'Friends again?' she asked hopefully.

'Yeah, course we are,' said Daisy, sitting up and giving her sister a hug. 'It'll take more than a man to split us up.'

But June sensed that this was a fragile peace that needed looking after. She knew she must tread carefully on the subject of Nat or risk losing Daisy.

And Daisy knew that Nat would remain a sore point between them even if he wasn't mentioned. The fact that June was absolutely right in everything she said about him didn't make any difference. He was Daisy's man and she would defend him against anyone.

Chapter Ten

On duty one evening in late July, Daisy served roast beef to the wrong table, knocked a jug of water over on another and got more coffee in the saucers than the cups when pouring. When she compounded the whole shoddy performance by dropping a pile of dirty plates on to the hotel kitchen floor, sending broken china and food leftovers flying everywhere, the head waiter suggested, quite forcibly, that she go home as she obviously wasn't fit for work.

'Anyone can see that you're ill.' He was a small immaculate man of Italian extraction, with dark hair greased close to his head and a neat moustache. He'd lived in London for most of his life and spoke perfect English.

'I'm all right, honestly, and I'm sorry I've been so careless.' She was afraid for her job. 'I'll be more careful from now on so it won't happen again.'

'It certainly won't happen again tonight because you're going off duty right now,' he announced, far more concerned about the smooth running of the hotel restaurant than a sick member of staff. A complaint about the service would mean a reprimand for him from the manager. 'You shouldn't have come in to work if you weren't feeling well.'

'I didn't want to let you down,' she said weakly. 'Anyway, I need the money.'

'You're not doing yourself or us any favours by being

here,' he insisted in a firm but not wholly unkind manner. 'It's no wonder you dropped the plates – you're shivering too much to hang on to anything.'

'I can't afford to take time off work. You know I have two kids to feed,' she reminded him.

'You'll just have to manage with sick pay from the State because you're certainly no good to us around here,' he insisted. 'You should be at home in bed.'

'I'll be all right, really—'

'Go home before you pass out, girl.' He was ordering her to go now.

Although she protested some more, Daisy knew he was right because she did feel terrible. In the staff room, changing out of her black and white uniform, her teeth were chattering and she was covered in goose pimples but her skin was hot and painful. Every bit of her hurt, and when she took off her black cap, with its starched white trim, it felt as though she was making a flesh wound on her scalp. She hadn't felt well for the last couple of days, ever since she'd got drenched in a heavy summer shower while out shopping at Portobello market and her clothes had dried on her. She seemed to be more susceptible to chills than most people; she always had been and put it down to her weak chest.

But now she headed for the tube and home, feeling worse by the second.

'Into bed with you,' Nora said when Daisy stumbled into the house, feeling faint.

'We'll bring you up a hot drink and some aspirin in a minute,' said June.

'The girls—' Daisy began.

'The girls are fast asleep,' Nora assured her. 'So go to bed before we have to pick you up off the floor.'

'Come on,' urged June, taking her sister's arm gently. 'Let me help you into bed.'

228

'There's no need for all this fuss,' she insisted. 'I'll be fine after a good night's sleep.'

But sleep wasn't for Daisy that night. As her condition worsened, she thrashed about in the sheets, shivering but soaked in sweat, her chest hurting, head aching, breathing painful. Nora and June were so alarmed the next morning, neither of them went to work. June rushed out to the phone box and called the doctor, who diagnosed pneumonia.

At the sight of an ambulance, a crowd gathered to watch the barely conscious Daisy being carried out of the house on a stretcher. June went with her in the ambulance and Nora stayed with the girls, who were pale with fright and staying very close to her. She put a comforting arm firmly round each one.

'I don't want Mummy to go away,' said Shirley tearfully, as the ambulance doors were closed.

'Nor do I,' added Belinda shakily, huge tears rolling down her cheeks.

'You want her to get better, though, don't you?'

They nodded.

'That's why she has to go to the hospital for a little while,' Nora explained. 'So that the doctors can make her better. I know that you two are going to be very brave.'

'I don't like it when Mummy's ill,' said Shirley. 'It makes me feel funny inside.'

'It makes me scared,' Belinda whispered.

'There, there, you two. She'll be back home before you know it,' said Nora, saying a silent prayer and trying not to show the little girls how worried she was.

Over the next day or so, Daisy wasn't aware of very much at all. Drifting in and out of consciousness, she realised in a vague sort of way that she was in hospital but was too ill to take notice or ask questions. But when the drugs started to work and her confusion began to clear a little, the first thing

229

she said was, 'My children – where are they?'

'Your daughters are at home with your sister,' the nurse assured her calmly.

'But she has to go to work.'

'She's taken compassionate leave to look after them, apparently,' explained the nurse, a middle-aged woman of large proportions, with a nice smile and a kindly manner.

'My eldest is on school holidays,' muttered Daisy worriedly. 'The two of them together are quite a handful. My sister isn't used to coping with them on her own.'

'I'm sure she'll manage.' The nurse was very soothing. 'They're only children, not wild animals. And your friend helps out when she gets home from work, I believe.' At Daisy's querying look, she went on, 'We had a chat when they came to see you and they told me all about it. You were asleep. They asked me to give you their love when you were awake and taking notice.'

Daisy tried to sit up but fell back weakly against the pillows. 'I'm needed at home,' she said anxiously. 'I've got to get out of here.'

'You'll go when the doctor says you're ready.' The nurse was kind but firm. 'And that won't be for a while yet. You'll soon know how weak you are if you try to get out of that bed, my dear. So stop fretting.'

And Daisy felt too frail to argue.

'Will you eat your lunch, please, girls?' requested June of her nieces as they all sat at the kitchen table.

'No.' The gleam of rebellion was strong in Shirley's eyes.

'We don't like sausages,' added Belinda.

'Yes, you do,' June disagreed patiently. 'They're one of your favourites.'

'We only like them when Mummy's here,' said Shirley in truculent mood.

230

'We don't like *your* sausages,' added Belinda, fixing June with a hostile stare. 'We only like Mummy's; we're not eating your mouldy old sausages.'

'We want our mum,' announced Shirley, her little mouth set determinedly. 'We don't like you.'

'We hate you,' supported Belinda.

'You're horrible,' Shirley declared.

'Yeah,' was Belinda's contribution.

June guessed that part of the reason for their appalling behaviour was that they were missing their mother and taking it out on her. But she sensed also that they were testing her – and winning hands down at the moment, she was forced to admit. They were at an age of physical perfection, smooth-skinned and unblemished. She ached with love for them. They were so alike to look at, with the same shiny brown hair and their mother's beautiful tawny eyes, though theirs were currently simmering with resentment.

Although she was ostensibly calm, June was actually in despair, her nerves shattered by the monsters her nieces had become since she'd been in charge. It seemed feeble for a grown woman to have to admit but, without actual maternal experience, she felt vulnerable to the point of being almost afraid of these small children. Ridiculous, she knew, but she just didn't have Daisy's natural armoury which would enable her to be in a position of control with the girls. This whole miserable experience was particularly upsetting because until June had become a temporary substitute for Daisy, she'd prided herself on the rapport she was beginning to have with them. Maybe she'd never felt completely at ease but after her initial confusion as to her function, she'd settled into the role of indulgent aunt, giving them presents, attention and fun, and it had seemed to work very well.

Until these past few days, when they'd given her hell, arguing the toss about every single thing, from the food she

231

gave them to having a bath and what clothes they would wear. At first she'd treated them with the gentle touch, sensitive to the fact that they were missing their mother. When they'd responded to this with mutiny, she'd tried being firm, but their enmity had continued. Yet Nora had no trouble with them at all. June couldn't bear to imagine what a battle there would be at bedtime if Nora wasn't at home then to give her some support.

She and Nora had agreed that June should be the one to take time off work to look after them as she was allowed some compassionate leave with pay – only for a limited period but long enough for Daisy to get back on her feet, she hoped. The important thing was that Daisy was over the worst and expecting to be discharged from hospital in a few days.

June was disappointed in herself for failing so miserably as Daisy's stand-in. She wanted so much to make the children feel secure and loved in her care. Not having any children of her own, from the minute she'd first set eyes on them she'd wanted to play a special part in their lives. It was Daisy's job to administer discipline, her own to supply pleasure. And what was her peculiar reward? Anarchy.

Working at the hotel was a holiday compared to looking after two stroppy kids. She'd sooner be dealing with tedious, unreasonable hotel guests than these two little horrors. They knew they had the upper hand and she didn't seem able to turn things around.

'OK, so you don't like me,' she said now in response to their hurtful utterings. 'Well, I don't like you very much at the moment either. But we're stuck with each other until your mother is better so let's try and get along, shall we?'

They stared at her in stony silence.

'All right, I'll do a deal with you.' Daisy would be appalled at such blatant bribery but she wasn't here, and June was desperate. 'You eat your lunch and I'll buy you some sweets when we go out to the shops. How about that?' She gave them a smile, forcing her tone to be softly persuasive, despite her sorely tried patience. 'And we could take a picnic to the park later on too, if you're good girls and eat your lunch. Would you like that?'

Shirley gave June a defiant look and pushed her plate away so violently it shot across the table. She then got up and ran towards the kitchen door. Belinda followed.

At that moment something snapped inside June. After days of torture from these horrors, she had finally had enough. Acting on instinct, she fled to the door and stood in front of it facing them, barring their way. 'Oh, no,' she told them with an air of grim command. 'You're not going anywhere. You're going to sit back at the table.' She paused, staring at them. *'Now.'*

Pale with shock at the dramatic change in their pushover aunt's manner, they did as she said without a word of argument, their sullenness now tinged with awe.

'Right,' June began, looking down at them from a standing position with her arms folded. She wasn't shouting; her manner of quiet assertiveness was far more effective. 'I've had it up to here with you two these past few days. You've been rude, disobedient and downright horrid and I'm not going to put up with any more of it, do you understand?'

Four tawny eyes rested on her; two little pink mouths began to tremble.

'I've taken the trouble to cook sausages and beans for your lunch because I know that you like them,' she went on. 'I could have given you something you don't like, like mince or liver. But, fool that I am, I made your favourite, which you now choose to say you don't like. All right, if you don't want what I've given you, don't eat it but you'll get nothing else. When you're hungry enough you'll eat what I put in front of you even if it's just a bit of dry bread; that's how nature

233

works, you see. Meanwhile, there'll be no sweets, no park, no treats at all until you have both said sorry to me for your disgusting behaviour and promised to stop all this silly nonsense.'

They said nothing. Just sat close together, holding hands, staring at her, their eyes like great brown saucers against their sudden pallor.

'You might as well do as I ask because I'm going to make you sit there until you're ready to apologise to me for being nasty little brats your mother would be ashamed of,' she told them. 'I know that you're upset because your mum isn't around and you want to make me suffer for it.' She drew in her breath and turned up the volume. 'I've made allowances for all of that but now I have had enough.'

They sat there without moving. Neither said a word. The appearance of tears in their eyes twisted June's heart and she wanted to hug them better. But that must wait until later. All would be lost if she showed signs of weakening now. She could see that she'd been wrong to think she could be just their pal, someone who could be relied on for fun and pleasure. They were small children who looked to adults for authority. She could be their friend, yes, but they needed to know who was boss. Discipline gave them guidelines and made them feel secure, however bitter the pill was to swallow. Better she destroy any bond she might have with them and start again from scratch by taking a hard line than let them run rings around her. If she gave in now, they would lose all respect for her.

'So, what's it to be?'

Silence.

'I've got all the time in the world,' she told them, looking at her watch. 'I've taken days off work to look after you so I can wait here all afternoon if necessary.'

She wasn't as confident as she sounded. She was a novice

when it came to child psychology. Heaven only knew what her next move would be if this didn't work. With her heart in her mouth, she sat down at the table and waited.

Shirley was the first to crumble. The trembling lip began to wobble and she bowed her head and wept silently, followed soon after by her sister, who wailed loudly.

'You won't get round me that way,' said June, suspecting that they would because her heart was breaking for them. 'You can cry all you like but you're not leaving here until I've heard you both say sorry.'

She was surprised to observe that even at this tender age, pride was a problem. 'Sorry,' mumbled Shirley at last, head down, words barely audible.

'What was that, Shirley?' asked June. 'I didn't hear what you said.'

'Sorry.' Slowly she looked up at June, who watched all the defiance slip away, leaving the child looking forlorn but relieved. June had to bite back her own tears. 'I'm sorry I've been naughty, Auntie June. I'll be good now, I promise.'

'I'm sorry too, Auntie June,' echoed Belinda.

'That's better.' Swallowing hard, June opened her arms to them. 'Come here, come on, both of you,' she said thickly.

They both climbed on to her lap and cuddled into her, their lithe little bodies trembling. She held them close for a long time, knowing instinctively that the three of them had passed some sort of a watershed.

'Can we have our sausages and beans now please, Auntie June?' requested Shirley.

'Course you can, darling,' she said to them. 'But they'll be cold by now. I'll warm them up for you.'

'Thank you, Auntie June,' said Belinda.

'It's a pleasure.' Such was the strength of her love for her nieces at that particular moment, she knew she would brave fire and flood for them if ever it was necessary. These past few days had taught her that motherhood was not always a picnic but it had not lessened her longing for children of her own.

That evening they all went to the hospital to see Daisy. A maximum of two visitors at the bedside was the usual rule but the understanding sister turned a blind eye so that they could have a few minutes all together.

'How are you feeling, dear?' asked Nora.

'Fine,' said Daisy, who still looked ghastly. She was paper-white and skinny, with dark circles under her eyes and a general look of frailty about her.

'When are you coming home, Mum?' Belinda was eager to know.

'Very soon, I hope,' sighed Daisy wistfully. 'I miss you all so much. They're ever so good to me in here and everything, but I'm fed up with being stuck in hospital. I'll recover quicker at home.'

'It isn't wise to rush things, though,' warned Nora. 'You'll end up back in here if you do that.'

'We have to be realistic, Nora,' was Daisy's answer to that. 'I've got the girls to think about. June can't have time off work to look after them for too long.'

'But I can do it for a bit longer,' June assured her.

'And if she can't, I will,' Nora offered. 'We'll manage between us somehow. The important thing is for you to get well.'

'Even when you do come home, you'll have to take it easy for a while, I should think,' suggested June. 'You're not going to be able to get back to normal right away.'

'Don't you start,' Daisy responded in jovial admonition. 'I've had enough of that from the doctors. They've really been giving me earache about how I mustn't overdo things when they discharge me from here. I know they mean well

236

but they don't have a clue about what life is like for someone like me – well, they wouldn't, would they, being professionals with healthy salaries and sick pay when they're ill?' She paused and brushed a tired hand across her brow. 'All I hear from them is, "You need to go away on holiday and get some sea air and plenty of rest and good food to build yourself up." I mean, I ask you. How can I do any of those things? I need to get back to work as soon as possible and start earning again.'

'You won't be able to go back to work for a while, surely?' June was worried by her attitude.

'Let's just say that I won't be sitting about the house for any longer than I absolutely have to. But let's wait and see how I feel.' Daisy smiled at them all. 'That's quite enough about me. How are you all getting on?'

'We're missing you like mad, of course, and we can't wait for you to come home,' Nora told her. 'But everything's under control at the house and running smoothly.'

Daisy looked at her daughters, who were sitting either side of the bed, each holding one of her hands. She then fixed her gaze on June. 'How have they been behaving?' she asked lightly. 'Not giving you any trouble, I hope?'

A look passed between June and the children. She perceived a moment of apprehension as they wondered if she was going to spill the beans.

'No trouble at all,' she said to Daisy, then looked towards the children. 'We're getting along just fine, aren't we, girls?'

'Yes, Auntie June,' they chorused, looking relieved and beaming broadly at June and then their mother.

June smiled too. She wasn't naïve enough to expect it to be all plain sailing between herself and her nieces because human relations were never that easy, but she did feel a definite bond with them now. Something had happened this afternoon that would live on into the future; she could sense it and it warmed her heart.

But now another visitor arrived for Daisy and her face lit up with joy.

'Nat,' she said, beaming at him. 'How lovely to see you. It's good of you to come.'

Seeing this as their cue to make a diplomatic exit, June and Nora said their goodbyes and left with the children.

Daisy was shocked at the extent of her weakness when she got home from the hospital. Being in such a feeble state made her angry with herself. She'd expected to be back at work in a few days but she hardly had the strength to get out of bed, let alone go to work. It was as much as she could do to look after the girls and she didn't feel as though she was doing that properly.

Feeling this fragile wasn't like Daisy at all. She was a fighter; she had inner strengths and, no stranger to bad health, she usually managed to carry on however ill she felt. If she did have to take to her bed, it was never for long.

But this was different. It wasn't the illness itself but the aftermath, and she didn't seem to get any stronger despite all the beef tea and egg custards she was consuming to build herself up. Being at the mercy of extreme physical limitations made her low in spirits too. She just didn't seem able to cope with anything. Everything was too much effort; even taking care of her beloved daughters seemed beyond her. She was literally dragging herself around, even though she insisted that June go back to work.

'I don't think I'd better leave you. You're in no fit state to cope on your own just yet,' was June's reaction to that.

'For goodness' sake, June,' Daisy responded sharply, 'you've been absolutely brilliant and I'm really grateful to you for looking after the girls for me, but I'm back home now and I'm not an invalid.'

'But—'

'Look, June, the best thing for me is to get back into the swing of things.' She was trying to convince herself as much as June. 'I'll never get my strength back by taking it easy. The sooner we return to normal around here the better for us all. I want to go to work again in a day or two.'

But after almost passing out on Saturday when they were all out shopping in Portobello market, Daisy knew she must accept that recovery was going to take longer than she'd expected, and be patient.

'I know you like to be some sort of a superwoman but even you can't beat nature, Daisy,' said Nora that night after the girls had gone to bed. 'You simply have to let it take its course.'

'I know. But it's dragging on and I feel such a burden to the rest of you,' confided Daisy, tears running down her cheeks and making her feel worse because crying seemed like weakness.

'You're not being, so you can put that out of your mind,' June assured her.

'You've both been wonderful,' Daisy told them. 'But I'm not pulling my weight around here.'

'You've not heard us complaining, have you?' June was keen to point out. 'You've been ill and you need time to recover. So stop being so impatient.'

However, Daisy wouldn't be fully assured. 'I appreciate your support. But not only do I need to get back to work of an evening, I need to be more energetic during the day too. It's the school holidays. Belinda starts school in September and I want to take the girls out and about a bit before then.' She looked at Nora. 'We always go to Southend for the day around this time.'

'And we will do when you're feeling up to it.'

'It's no fun for them having me sitting about with hardly the strength to tie their hair ribbons for them, is it?' Daisy

239

went on. 'I feel like a complete dead loss.'

'Oh, for goodness' sake,' rebuked Nora, 'you've only been home from hospital a few days. Nature will take longer to heal you if you fight it and go against how you feel.' She sighed, giving a worried tut. 'I know it isn't possible to have one, but the doctors were right when they said you need a holiday. It wouldn't do the girls any harm either, after all the disruption they've had. You and the girls need to get right away from here for a couple of weeks.'

'There are lots of things the girls and I need, Nora,' Daisy told her. 'But we're not going to get them so there's no point in thinking about them, is there?'

'I suppose not,' agreed Nora.

June had gone quiet, mulling something over. The next morning when she went out to get a Sunday paper, she then went to a telephone box and made a long-distance call.

Alan and Jack were having a drink together at the Cliff Head bar that Sunday night after work. The bar was closed and they had the place to themselves. They chatted about business for a while, moving on to some basic male observations about Marilyn Monroe, whose new film, *The Seven Year Itch*, had just come out. They enjoyed a spot of light-hearted crudity on the subject of sex, like most men when they were in all-male company.

'Talking of women,' said Alan, becoming more serious, 'I had a phone call from June this morning.'

'That sounds promising,' responded Jack.

'No. My relationship with her is well and truly over,' Alan said with a wry look. 'Her call had nothing to do with her and me.'

'What did she want then?'

'A favour,' he explained. 'She wants me to try and find some holiday accommodation for her sister, Daisy, and the

240

little girls, for a couple of weeks.'

'Really?'

'Mm. Daisy's been ill, apparently.'

'Oh dear.' Jack was immediately concerned. 'Nothing serious, I hope.'

'Serious enough to put her in hospital. She's had pneumonia.'

Jack frowned. 'God, poor Daisy. How is she now?'

'She's at home, but very weak and run-down, apparently,' Alan informed him. 'So June's trying to arrange a holiday for her and the girls, to try to get her back on her feet.'

'We're fully booked here at this time of the year, I suppose,' Jack surmised.

Alan nodded. 'June said the Cliff Head wouldn't be suitable for them anyway,' he said. 'It's too quiet, too expensive and too restricting for the children. I agree with her about that. I mean, we don't actually ban children but we don't make them particularly welcome either.'

'What sort of place is Daisy looking for?' Jack enquired, his interest growing.

'Daisy isn't looking for anything,' Alan explained. 'In fact, she knows nothing about it yet. June wants to get everything arranged before she tells her so that she'll feel she can't refuse, if it's all booked up. Daisy can't afford a holiday so June is footing the bill. But Daisy is funny about that sort of thing, apparently. She's very proud and won't accept charity.'

'What a kind thing for June to do,' commented Jack.

'I thought so too.'

'Any luck with the accommodation?'

'None at all, so far. I've been on the phone to quite a few places, but it being the height of the season, all the hotels are booked up, which is why June's turned to me. She wants to get something organised double sharp because she and Nora are afraid that Daisy will go back to work before she's properly recovered and suffer a relapse. I've still got a few

241

more places I can try. June's going to ring me tomorrow to find out if I've had any luck.'

'You need look no further,' announced Jack with a broad smile. 'Daisy and the girls can stay at my cottage.'

Alan gave him a questioning look.

'They'll all have to share my spare room and I'll have to get a couple of camp beds for the girls,' Jack went on enthusiastically, 'but I'd love to have them.'

Stroking his chin thoughtfully, Alan said, 'It's very good of you to offer, mate, but I'm not sure if that's the sort of thing June has in mind. I think she was thinking more in terms of a B. and B. on the seafront.'

'My place is on the seafront.'

'Here in Torquay, close to all the amenities, I mean,' Alan clarified. 'June wants me to keep an eye on them and make sure they're all right while they're here, with Daisy having been so ill. June can't go away with them because she can't get the time off work.'

'I'll look after them if they stay with me,' offered Jack. 'And you won't get a healthier place than Gullscombe Bay.'

'You seem very keen,' was Alan's shrewd observation.

Actually Jack couldn't believe his luck in being given a chance to see Daisy again, and he wasn't going to let the opportunity pass him by. 'Just trying to help, mate.'

'That's why you look as though you've just come into money, is it?' his friend joshed.

'All right, I admit it. I did take a fancy to Daisy when we were in London,' Jack confessed. 'But there would be no funny business if she stayed with me, I can promise you that. I genuinely want to help and I can't think of a better place to convalesce than Gullscombe Bay. Ideal for the kids too, with the safe beach being so close to the cottage.'

'But you'd be at work a lot of the time and they'd be stuck out there on their own, miles from everything,' Alan objected.

'Daisy is a town girl; she might feel too isolated.'

'Obviously I'd have to have some time off to look after them and entertain them,' Jack pointed out with a grin. 'But I've got some holidays owing to me.'

'At the height of our busy season, you must be joking.' Alan didn't look pleased.

'I've got a good deputy,' Jack reminded him. 'And I wouldn't take all that much time off – just a few evenings, and the odd day or two. I'm at home for part of the day anyway so they wouldn't be too lonely.'

'I'm relieved to hear you're not planning on deserting us for the whole two weeks,' said Alan ruefully. 'But I'm beginning to wish I'd never mentioned it.'

'I don't believe that,' challenged Jack. 'You'd do anything to please June.'

'Once that might have been true, but not now,' Alan said. 'But I'll pass on your invitation to her when she rings me tomorrow, see what she thinks about it.'

'I'll look forward to hearing her reaction,' beamed Jack.

A few days later, over breakfast, Daisy read a letter that had come for her in the post. She smiled, then frowned, then glared at her sister and said, 'You've been meddling, haven't you?'

'Meddling?'

'Don't try and tell me that this letter from Jack Saunders, inviting me and the kids for a holiday at his cottage, isn't your doing because I won't believe you.'

'I had nothing to do with that,' June denied truthfully.

'How did Jack know that I'd been ill then, if you didn't tell him?' Daisy wanted to know.

June bit her lip and held up her hands in a gesture of surrender. 'All right, I admit it. I got on the phone to Alan and asked him to find some accommodation for you. And before

243

you go up in the air about it, I didn't tell you because I knew you would squash the whole idea even though it will be so good for you,' she explained. 'Anyway, Jack got to hear about it and offered for you to stay at his cottage. I really didn't have anything to do with that part of it. But knowing what your reaction would be to anyone doing anything for you at all, I asked Alan to ask Jack to write to you and invite you properly. Apparently he's dead keen for you and the girls to go. He's crazy about where he lives and wants to show it off.'

'You had no right to do this, June,' rebuked Daisy.

'She was only thinking of you, love,' intervened Nora, while the two little girls ate their cornflakes, listening.

'What am I, some hard-up half-wit who isn't capable of organising her own life, or something?' erupted Daisy, tears swelling beneath her lids. She was touched by June's attempts to help and that made her feel worse because she didn't have the means to accept and she felt so damned helpless. This weakness was making her spiteful to people who didn't deserve it and she hated herself but couldn't stop. 'I've had pneumonia, I haven't lost the use of my brain.'

'Look, I think you need a holiday, so I tried to organise one for you and I can pay the costs out of the money I had left over between selling my mother's house and buying this one,' June spelled out for her. 'I acted on impulse and Alan seemed the obvious person to approach as he's in a position to find out about seaside accommodation. Is that such a crime?'

At the word 'seaside' the children's interest was aroused.

'The seaside,' said Shirley excitedly. 'Are we going to Southend for the day?'

'The seaside, goodee,' enthused Belinda. 'Can we have a bucket and spade?'

Seeing those young eyes shining with hope, Daisy was filled with shame. She was spoiling everything for them as well as June because of her stupid pride. What right did she

244

have to deprive them of a holiday, and June the pleasure of giving? June wanted to help her because she was her sister. If the situation was reversed she would want to do the same thing for her.

She remembered how upset she'd been initially when June had offered them a home. She'd grown closer to her since then; knew her well enough to recognise this for what it was – a kind gesture with no ulterior motive.

'Better than a day at Southend,' Daisy informed them with a tearful smile. 'Much, much better. Two whole weeks at the seaside in Devon thanks to your lovely Auntie June.'

Forgetting the table manners Daisy had been at pains to teach them since they were old enough to understand such things, they slipped off their chairs and tore around the kitchen, then up and down the hall, shrieking with delight. 'We're going to the seaside, the seaside, the seaside!'

'Sorry about just now, June,' said Daisy. 'I was an idiot. I think I must be touchy because I'm feeling so low physically. I didn't mean to be horrible.' She put her hand on her sister's arm. 'It's ever so good of you to do this for us and I really do appreciate it.'

'It's a pleasure,' beamed June, getting up and hugging her.

'Why are Mummy and Auntie June crying, Nora?' asked Shirley, looking worried.

'Because they're happy,' Nora explained.

'That's all right then,' said Shirley, looking happy too.

Predictably, the one person who wasn't happy about the forthcoming holiday was Nat.

'You're going to Devon to stay with some bloke,' he disapproved sternly, that same evening. 'Daisy, how could you?'

They were on the sofa in the living room; smart and comfy

now, it had been refurbished with bright contemporary wall-paper and a red carpet. The girls were in bed. June was washing her hair and Nora was in her room writing a letter.

'It isn't how you're making it sound,' she told him, having already given him full details of the holiday and how it had come about. 'Jack's offered to put the girls and me up, that's all. It's perfectly innocent.'

'You might be gullible enough to believe that, but I'm certainly not,' he barked.

'So, without knowing anything about him, you've got him down as a rapist, have you?'

'I didn't say that.'

'You're questioning my morals then?'

'No. I'm just saying that he's a man and he'll make the most of having you in the house.'

'And you think I'm daft enough to fall into his arms?'

'No. I'm just pointing out what could happen.'

'That is sick,' objected Daisy. 'You shouldn't judge other people by your own standards.'

'You're trying to tell me that you're going to be sharing a house with an unattached man for two weeks and nothing like that will happen?' he said cynically.

'Yes, I am telling you exactly that,' she said with emphasis. 'What do you take me for? A tramp? Such a thing hadn't even occurred to me.'

'Then it should have,' he warned her. 'You know nothing about the man. You don't know what he's capable of.'

'He seemed thoroughly decent to me on the one occasion that I met him.' She didn't add that she'd liked Jack a lot and knew somehow that he was to be trusted, because Nat would deliberately misunderstand her feelings. 'Anyway, June knows him quite well and she wouldn't have me stay with someone who isn't trustworthy. He'll be out at work a lot of the time anyway, apparently, and he's giving us the complete run of his house while he's out. Frankly, I think it's very kind of him.'

'Huh.'

'You're jealous, aren't you?' Daisy accused. 'That's what this is all about.'

'Well, how would you feel if I told you I was going away for a fortnight with a woman?' Nat challenged her.

'I wouldn't like it at all,' she admitted. 'But I'm not going away with a man. I'm simply using his house.' She sighed. 'Look, I've been ill and I've been advised to take a holiday by the doctors. Thanks to my sister's generosity and the kindness of one of her husband's friends, the girls and I can have one.'

'I don't think you should go.'

'Don't you want me to get better?'

'You'll get better if you stay here, eventually,' he said. 'Nature will take its course wherever you are.'

Daisy was very tired suddenly. 'You're probably right and the last thing I want to do is upset you, Nat,' she told him wearily. 'But I've been given this opportunity and I feel I must take it.'

'Even though I don't want you to.'

'If you won't change your mind, yes. I'm feeling so rotten I have to do something about it. Let's face it, I'm not much use to anyone as I am now, especially our little girls, the poor lambs. First I give them a scare when I'm carted off to hospital, then I'm like a wet weekend when I come home. I owe it to them to try and speed up my recovery. I've been so bad-tempered with them lately. Anyway, even apart from all of that, a holiday at the seaside will be really smashing for them. Surely you want something nice for your daughters.'

As mean and self-centred as Nat was, he wasn't entirely without feelings, and the sight of Daisy looking so pale and pinched touched something inside him. 'Yeah, course I do,' he said with a change of attitude.

247

'Really?'

'Yeah. You go and enjoy yourself.'

'Thanks, Nat,' she beamed.

He reached into his pocket and took out some notes. 'Here's some spending money for you, an' all,' he said, handing her a few pound notes. 'And I want you to come back with some colour in your cheeks, do you understand?'

'Oh, Nat, are you sure about this?' she queried, looking at the money.

Giving her one of his most dazzling smiles, he said, 'Go on. Take it before I change my mind.'

'You're all right, Nat Barker, do you know that?' she told him, slipping her arms around him.

'Glad you think so,' he muttered, looking bewildered. He was astonished by his own impulsive generosity, and was wondering what had come over him.

'You never cease to surprise me,' she told him. 'It's no wonder I still love you, even after all these years.'

'I make it my policy not to be too predictable,' he said, back on form with the chat. 'You might start to take me for granted if I did that.'

'Never.'

'And I intend to make sure it stays that way.'

'If this is how you're going to do it, you won't hear me complaining.'

Daisy had decided to go to Devon whatever Nat thought about it because she knew it was the right thing for everyone at the house. But having his blessing meant that she could go away with an easy mind and enter into the spirit of the holiday with the same enthusiasm as her excited daughters.

Chapter Eleven

The road from Torquay to Gullscombe Bay wound through lush green countryside, the soft undulating hills a patchwork of thickly wooded slopes and rich expanses of grassland. There were picturesque villages with cob-walled, thatched cottages, and stone-built bridges over clear streams. When the road became coastal – high above sea level – tantalising glimpses of the sea could be caught through the trees. Daisy had never seen anything like it before, and the girls were breathless with awe, shrieking with delight at every new view of the ocean.

'I thought they couldn't get any more excited than they were when June and Nora saw us off on the train,' Daisy confided to Jack, who had met them at Torquay station and was driving them to his cottage in a black Ford Anglia, she in the front with him, the girls in the back, 'but I was wrong because they've reached such a pitch now, I think they might explode.'

'There's nothing quite like the enthusiasm of childhood, is there?' he smiled.

'I'm not so sure about that because I'm nearly as bad as they are,' she admitted. 'None of us has been further than Southend until now, so this is all quite stunning for us.'

'You wait till you see Gullscombe Bay,' he said, sounding as thrilled to be showing them the area as they were to see it.

'We'll be there in a minute. It seems to be taking for ever because I'm used to whizzing to and fro on my motorbike.'

Daisy turned to observe his clean-cut profile, a summer tan making him look even more wholesome than she remembered, especially with the white sports shirt he was wearing with lightweight fawn slacks. 'You have a car as well as a motorbike then?'

'No. This little motor belongs to a pal of mine. He's given me the use of it while you're here,' Jack explained, deeming it wise to alter the facts slightly so as not to mention that he had actually hired the car from a friend who had a car-hire firm, and paid the going rate for it because he wanted Daisy and the girls to travel in comfort while they were on holiday. He'd been warned by Alan, who'd been briefed by June, to be extremely cautious about anything with so much as a hint of charity.

'That's very nice of him but won't he be needing it himself?' she enquired.

'No. He has another vehicle he can use.' At least that was no lie.

'Two cars. Wow.' She was impressed. 'I can see that the scenery around here isn't the only thing that's different from what I'm used to. I don't know anyone with one car, let alone two.'

Jack didn't reply to that; just concentrated on the road. 'We're about to turn into Gullscombe Bay now.' His voice rose with enthusiasm. 'It's just round the bend.'

They turned a corner and began to descend a steep hill. Daisy gasped at the sight ahead of them. Golden sands fringed the sea round a bay flanked by red cliffs, the turquoise ocean shimmering in the afternoon sun and dotted with little white sailing boats. At the foot of the hill there were huge expanses of meadow edged with sand dunes leading to the beach. A little further on they came to Gullscombe Bay village, a pretty gathering of whitewashed thatched houses with a pub, a general store with a Post Office sign, and a church, all set around a village green.

Driving down a narrow track towards the seashore, Jack turned off the road and pulled up outside a cottage, the like of which Daisy had seen before only in picture books.

'Well, what do you think?' asked Jack proudly as she and the girls got out of the car and stared at the little whitewashed house with a blue door, a thatched roof and 'Seagull Cottage' written in bold letters on a sign on the front wall above a dazzling abundance of hollyhocks and wallflowers.

'It's beautiful, *really beautiful*,' breathed Daisy, turning to her wide-eyed daughters. 'Isn't it, girls?'

They nodded vigorously.

'Before we go inside, I want to show you what it's like out the back.' He looked at Daisy excitedly and grinned at the girls. 'Come on, follow your Uncle Jack.'

He led them through a blue wooded door at the side of the property into a garden with rolling lawns, bordered by trees and shrubs between which the sea could be seen. Going out of a gate at the bottom, they came to wide steps sloping down gently to a sandy beach, the cries of the gulls rising above the whisper of the sea at low tide.

'Cor,' gasped Shirley.

'The sea is in the back garden,' said Belinda in wonder.

'Not quite,' said Jack proudly. 'But almost.'

'So what do you think of that, eh, girls?' asked Daisy. 'Are we lucky to be here, or what?'

'Ooh, yeah,' enthused Shirley.

'Very lucky,' added her sister.

'It's safe for bathing,' Jack told Daisy. 'There aren't any strong currents in the shallow waters so you can let them paddle without any worries.'

Belinda was jumping up and down now with excitement.

251

'Can we go in the water? Can we, please, Mum? Can we?'

'When we've got our stuff out of the car and got changed, we'll go and dip our toes in,' promised Daisy.

'I expect you'd like something to eat too,' suggested Jack. 'I don't suppose you've had any lunch.'

'We haven't but I'm not expecting you to feed us,' Daisy was quick to point out. She thought he was doing quite enough by letting them stay and she wasn't prepared to impose further on his good nature. 'I saw a shop in the village. I can pop over there and get us something.'

'Don't be so silly.' He was outraged at the suggestion. 'I've got plenty of food in.'

Realising that to insist would be bad manners, she said graciously, 'Thank you. You're very kind.'

Inside the cottage there were wooden beams against buttercup-yellow walls in a living room with soft squashy sofas and French doors leading to the garden. Up a rickety wooden staircase, Jack showed them into a pretty room with low ceilings, a sea view and three beds, two of which were camp beds.

'I'm sorry you have to share,' he apologised, guessing it would embarrass Daisy if he were to give her his room and sleep on the sofa himself, as willing as he was to do this. 'I only have the one spare bedroom.'

'Don't apologise, for goodness' sake,' Daisy urged him. 'We're very grateful to be able to stay here. You've done us proud and I really do appreciate it.'

'It gives me a chance to show off my cottage,' he said lightly, and stepped towards the door. 'I'll leave you to sort yourselves out then. The bathroom is just along the landing and when you come downstairs I'll show you where everything else is.'

She smiled in thanks and told him they'd join him down there in a few minutes.

There were only two room downstairs – the kitchen and the living room – but both were of a reasonable size. The kitchen was quarry-tiled and oak-beamed, with a long farmhouse-style table. Jack made a pot of tea for Daisy and gave the girls a real treat: chilled lemonade with ice cubes from his fridge.

'I have to go to work now,' he explained to Daisy, 'but there's plenty of food so help yourselves to anything you fancy. There's fresh bread in the bread bin – and stuff to go with it in the fridge – ham, cheese, corned beef pie and so on. The larder's quite well stocked as well.'

'Sounds as though you've been having a busy time at the shops,' she said.

'Well, you do when you've got guests coming to stay, don't you?'

Having guests to stay didn't feature in Daisy's life but she just said, 'Yeah, I suppose so.' She hadn't expected this sort of hospitality and found herself in an awkward position. She didn't want to offend Jack but neither did she want to sponge on him. 'Look, Jack. It's very kind of you to put us up, but as I said just now, I don't expect you to feed us as well. So, let me give you some money.'

'Right. Since you've brought the subject up, we might as well get it sorted out here and now so that we both know where we are,' he said, his expression becoming grave. 'And this is how it will work. I want you to treat this place as your home for the next two weeks. That means having anything you want to eat and drink. But you are my guests so I want no talk of money.'

She bit her lip. 'Well, if you're sure . . .'

'I am, so let's hear no more about it,' he told her firmly. 'I won't be here all of the time because of work commitments but I've arranged to take some time off later on, to show you around the area.' He paused, spreading his hands, his blue eyes resting on Daisy. 'Please, please, make yourselves at home.' He winked at her. 'If you look in the ice-making compartment of the fridge you'll find something the kids might enjoy later on. I've arranged to get off early tonight so I'll be back about eight and I'll bring something from the hotel kitchen for our evening meal. OK?'

Without causing offence there wasn't much else Daisy could say except, 'Thank you so much.'

'Thanks aren't necessary because it's my pleasure.' He paused thoughtfully. 'My work number is on the pad by the telephone on the living-room windowsill. Any problem, or anything you want to know, give me a call.'

'Will do,' she said, and he left by the kitchen door.

Pressured by the girls for an immediate investigation of the ice box, they found a block of strawberry and vanilla ice cream which Shirley and Belinda were told they couldn't have until after they'd eaten some lunch. Daisy was just setting out some crusty bread and butter with fresh cheese and thick slices of ham and luscious tomatoes when Jack came back and popped his head around the door. 'I forgot to tell you that there are some deck chairs in the shed.' He grinned at the girls. 'There's a couple of buckets and spades in there too.'

The girls beamed. 'Bucket and spades ... for us?' said Shirley. One treat after another – she could hardly believe it.

'Well, I didn't buy them for your mother,' he grinned. 'I think the deck chair is more up her alley.'

Daisy laughed, realising it was the first time she'd done so properly since her illness. 'Oh, Jack, this is so kind of you.' She turned to the girls. 'What do you say to Uncle Jack?'

'Thank you very much, Uncle Jack,' they chorused with delight.

'You're welcome,' he said, and left.

A few minutes later they heard his motorbike roar away. Daisy had to admit to being glad of this time to themselves to get used to the place. Although she felt very much at ease with Jack, he was little more than a stranger and she might have felt a bit awkward with him hovering over them so soon after their arrival.

What a kind and generous man he was. And with such a lovely home. His standard of living and the fact that he had modern refinements only dreamed of by Daisy – such as a fridge, a telephone, and a small television set in the corner of the living room – reminded her that he was in a management position and was therefore in a different league to her as a waitress. He was a smashing bloke, though, with no airs and graces.

Roaring through the lanes on his Harley-Davidson, the high speed causing an invigorating rush of cold air on his face around his goggles, Jack was thinking of Daisy and hoping he'd done the right thing in leaving her and the girls on their own so soon after they'd arrived.

Some people might think it was rather a rude thing to do but he'd given the matter some thought and decided to make himself scarce with the idea that she might feel more relaxed with the run of the place to herself, initially. He'd thought it best not to take the whole night off work too, to give them a chance to get settled in. Daisy needed to rest and enjoy the sea air for a few days, with just her children as much as possible. He smiled fondly, thinking of her tinkly laugh and the way she moved, quickly but with grace. Completely without the trappings of glamour that made most women look attractive, she had her own brand of natural beauty with her pert little face and slender body.

He smiled at the thought of the girls. Buying the buckets and spades had probably given him more pleasure than they'd had from receiving them. It was really important to him that they all had a good holiday. The weather had given them a warm welcome anyway, and he just couldn't wait to get back from work tonight to see them all again.

'I need more water for the moat,' announced Shirley, about to trail down to the sea with her bucket for the umpteenth time.

'Don't go out too far,' warned Daisy. 'You can't swim, remember. So stay at the edge.'

'Can me and Sherl learn to swim in the sea, Mum?' Belinda requested.

Her mother pondered the question. 'It might not be a bad idea to give it a try while we're here,' she said, settled in a deck chair on the sand, watching her daughters play. Both girls were proudly sporting bright yellow swimsuits that Nora had bought them as holiday treats. Daisy was less daring in a rather shapeless cotton dress she'd bought years ago in Portobello market. 'The school will be taking you to the swimming baths for lessons when you're a bit older but the sooner you can swim the better so I'll give it some thought.'

'I love it here, Mum,' enthused Belinda, looking around at the golden sand that was only lightly sprinkled with people, the bay being uncommercialised and off the beaten track.

'So do I,' added Shirley. 'I want to stay here for ever.'

Those were Daisy's sentiments exactly. She'd felt she belonged here from the minute they'd arrived. Realistically, it was too soon to feel any significant change in her health but she fancied that the air agreed with her. Being in such a weak state, she had been exhausted by the journey but after just one afternoon in the fresh air she felt stronger and more energetic. The girls' pasty London complexions were already beginning to glow with colour too.

'It's certainly a lovely place,' she agreed with her daughters.

Thank you so much, June and Jack, for giving us all this, she said silently, raising her face to the sun, its warmth softened by a light summer breeze. She couldn't remember feeling this relaxed in a very long time.

Observing his visitor across the table, Lionel Rivers thought she had one of the friendliest faces he'd ever seen, with her sparkling blue eyes and warm, engaging smile. Initially she'd seemed rather odd to look at: bright, disorderly hair, tall gangling frame and freckled face that was so much smaller than the rest of her. But the instant she smiled, he stopped noticing anything else.

'I'm glad you agreed to let them issue me with a visiting order,' Nora explained in her deep husky voice. 'I didn't want you to be without visitors as the girls couldn't make it this time.'

'I've been looking forward to meeting you at last,' he said, and she saw genuine pleasure in his warm brown eyes. 'Though I feel as if I know you already because of your letters.'

'I feel like that about you too.'

He frowned. 'I hope there's nothing wrong with the girls to keep them away.'

'Quite the reverse,' she was pleased to be able to assure him. 'Daisy's away on holiday in Devon and June's tied up at work so we decided between us that it would be a good idea for me to meet my pen pal on my day off.'

'I really am very grateful to you for coming.' He cast a disapproving eye around the room. 'But I don't like the idea of you, or the girls, having to come to such an awful place.'

'It doesn't worry me, dear,' Nora said, dismissing the subject by moving on, bringing him up to date with news of his daughters and telling him how Daisy's holiday had come about.

'I didn't even know she'd been ill,' Lionel said with concern.

'It happened only recently, and they'd have mentioned it next time they came to visit you, I expect,' she told him. 'Don't worry about Daisy. She'll be all right. She's tough. She's had to be, the amount of illness she's had in her life.'

'Really?'

She told him about Daisy's poor health. 'She's got stamina, though, that one. Never gives in. I've known her go to work when she's been half dead with bronchitis before now. She struggled on at work this time until they sent her home. She takes her responsibilities towards the girls very seriously.'

'Doesn't their father help her at all with their upkeep?' he wondered.

'No. Not on a regular basis,' Nora explained. 'He slips her a few bob now and again but that's about all.'

'Sounds as though you don't like him.'

'I don't. Because of the way he treats Daisy,' she admitted. 'The man's a complete dead loss. She knows he is too, in her heart, though she'd never admit it or give him up.' She shrugged, sighing. 'That's love for you.'

'It's weird to find out all these things about your own daughter at such a late stage,' Lionel told her.

'I'm sure it must be.'

'Finding them again is a dream come true, though.' He knew that Nora was fully in the picture about his family history. 'I thought I'd lost them for ever all those years ago. It was the worst moment of my life when I was told they were being taken into care. It was all so sudden. One minute I had a wife and family, the next I had no one. The girls were whisked out of the house sharpish, as soon as the police came. I wasn't even allowed to say goodbye to them before they carted me off to the nick.'

'It seems cruel but I suppose the authorities were acting in the children's best interests,' she said, her eyes moist with tears as she stared at this sad-eyed man whose face was lined beyond his years and who had a gentleness about him despite his tough appearance. The Rivers' story was one of the most poignant she'd ever heard. 'They would have needed to get the children away from the murder scene, and putting them into care was the only option they had with your wife dead, you in prison and no relatives willing to take them on.'

'They had no choice, I know that.' His eyes became glazed as he looked back. 'Losing my wife and being banged up for a murder I didn't do was bad enough, but losing my girls was the hardest blow of all. I thought they would think I'd abandoned them, which they did, of course.'

'It's all clear now as far as that's concerned, though,' Nora pointed out cheerfully.

'Yeah, thank God. Knowing that they don't think I stopped loving them has made me a happy man, and I'm so lucky to have them back in my life, even if that means only a brief visit now and then.'

'They're pleased to have found you too, and each other.' They'd been speaking in low voices but Nora lowered hers even more now against the prying ears of the warders. 'And although there's no movement at the moment, they are both still determined to clear your name and get you out of here.'

'It's good of them to want to do all that for me, but I'm not holding my breath.'

'That's very wise,' she said, nodding sagely. 'It was a long time ago and the people concerned could be anywhere by now. They might even be dead.'

'Which is what I told them,' he made clear. 'Anyway, I'm so used to prison life I'd probably be like a fish out of water if I ever did get out of here.'

'You'd be bound to feel strange at first, of course,' she told him. 'But now that you've got some family to help you, you'd soon adjust. You've got your daughters and granddaughters out there to welcome you.' She paused and gave him a shy

259

grin. 'And me, of course. I'm part of the furniture.'

He smiled at her. 'Your letters mean a lot to me,' he said. 'They keep me going.'

'Good'. Nora paused thoughtfully, leaning towards him in a confidential manner. 'Look, even though it wouldn't be wise to bank on anything, you mustn't stop hoping. Just because nothing's happening at the moment, that doesn't mean it's been forgotten. The girls won't rest until they've found the Dodds. Daisy reckons they need just one break that'll set the whole thing in motion, and she's convinced that they'll get it sooner or later. That's Daisy for you – she always looks on the bright side and that's what you must do.'

Lionel nodded. 'You're sort of a mum to my daughters, then?' he assumed.

'Not to both of them. June and I are just friends because I haven't know her for so long. But I am like a mum to Daisy. She seems to want that. Daisy's strong but June has a tougher edge somehow. She isn't as open as Daisy so you can't get close to her.'

They were interrupted by the warder telling them that time was up.

'Thanks ever so much for coming,' Lionel said.

'It was a pleasure,' Nora smiled. 'I'll come again sometime if you'd like me to.'

'Yes, please.'

'I'll sort something out with the girls then, as you're only allowed a certain number of visits,' she told him.

He nodded in approval.

It was heartbreaking to see him being taken away, battered by the way life had treated him but retaining a proud stance, shoulders squared, chin up. She could see a lot of his younger daughter in him.

Nora's empathy for Lionel was strong because she'd had her share of loneliness; she knew what it was like to feel like an outsider. Until Daisy had come into her life she'd felt isolated from people because she was a spinster. It was the recognition of how true friendship had changed her life for the better that had inspired her to write to Lionel. She hoped she could give to him some of what his daughter had given her.

'Morning, madear,' the proprietor of the Gullscombe Bay village shop greeted Daisy in her rich Devonian accent. 'Another lovely day. You've certainly brought some good weather with you.'

'We seem to have – so far, anyway, Mrs Graham,' agreed Daisy. 'Let's hope it lasts.'

A plump-faced woman of middle years, with rosy cheeks and a fresh complexion, the shopkeeper turned her attention to Shirley and Belinda, to whom she'd taken a liking this past week. 'And how are my little maids today?' she asked.

'Very well, thank you, Mrs Graham,' they chanted politely, making their mother swell with pride at their lovely manners.

'That's good.' She turned to Daisy. 'Your usual this morning, madear?'

'Please.'

The other woman took a cottage loaf out of a basket, wrapped it in tissue paper and put it on the counter with a pint of milk. 'Anything else?'

'I think I'll take some apples and bananas too, please,' Daisy requested.

'Pick out what you want then, madear,' Mrs Graham instructed, 'and I'll weigh them up.'

While Daisy helped herself from the wooden trays and handed the fruit to the shopkeeper, Belinda asked in a proud tone, 'Do you know what I can do, Mrs Graham?'

'No, what's that, pet?' the woman smiled.

'I can swim.'

261

'Can you really?' Mrs Graham was most impressed. 'That's very good indeed.'

'She can't do it on her own yet.' Her sister's competitive streak went into top gear. 'She can only do it with the water wings on, same as me.'

'It's still swimming,' insisted Belinda.

'Not proper swimming until we can do it on our own,' argued Shirley. 'Uncle Jack says.'

Daisy gave Mrs Graham a wry grin. 'There's no shortage of sibling rivalry between these two.'

'No harm in a spot of healthy competition,' the shopkeeper pointed out.

'Jack's been helping me to teach them to swim,' Daisy told her. 'It would be good if they could do it before we go back. Once they've learned they've got it for ever.'

'If anyone can teach them, Jack will. He's got the patience of a saint, that man,' enthused Mrs Graham. 'You won't hear a bad word about him in this village.'

'Everyone seems to like him.'

'That's because he does so much for the people around here,' she confided. 'In the winter he clears the snow for the old folk; he even gets the coal in for them. And that's just two examples of the sort of man he is. Nothing's too much trouble.'

Jack was a local hero in these parts, Daisy had already gathered that. Gullscombe Bay was a small community, barely touched by tourism. There were no hotels or boarding houses. A few of the residents offered bed and breakfast in the summer but that was about it. Because Daisy and the girls were guests of the village hero, who had made it generally known that she was here to convalesce, they were being given the red-carpet treatment by the locals, many of whom had stories of courage and kindness to tell about Jack. Everything from rescuing a drowning man to lobbying the council to get

262

more streetlights put up in the village.

'I've noticed that,' she agreed. 'It's very good of him to let us stay with him.'

'You're enjoying your holiday then.' It was a statement rather than a question since it would never occur to this local woman that any visitor to the area could do anything but enjoy themselves.

'I'll say we are,' enthused Daisy. 'We love it here. We won't want to go back when the time comes. Still, I won't think about that yet, as we've still got a week left.'

'Let's hope the weather stays fine.'

Daisy nodded, handing the woman some money. Daisy hadn't the means of knowing for sure but she believed that rain, shine, hail or storm, she would enjoy being in Gullscombe Bay.

'You're certainly looking a lot better than when you arrived,' observed the shopkeeper, handing Daisy her change. 'You looked quite poorly then.'

'I'm feeling heaps better now,' Daisy was pleased to be able to report.

After some more idle chat, she and the girls left the shop and walked across the village green and down the lane to the cottage. One of the highlights of the day for Daisy was walking to the shop every morning with the girls to get fresh bread and milk. She loved the smell of the sea in the morning air, the friendliness of the people she met and the fresh taste of the food when they got back to the cottage. The walk before breakfast gave them an appetite and they'd got into the habit of having just-baked bread and butter with fresh fruit or jam instead of the porridge and cornflakes they had in the mornings at home.

At the beginning Jack had offered quite insistently to do the morning trip to the shop but when Daisy explained how much she enjoyed it, he let her carry on while he had an extra half-hour in bed. There was a very relaxed atmosphere between them. Not once had he made her feel like a lodger in his house. Quite the opposite; he made her feel as though he was honoured to have her and the girls in the house.

So far, with such good weather, they'd been able to have breakfast in the garden looking out over the sea. It was the most wonderful start to the day. She could understand why Jack had settled here. It was the sort of place you never wanted to leave.

It was mid-afternoon and the residents of Seagull Cottage were all in the shallow waters of the sea. Even Daisy was wearing a swimsuit now, a flowery little one-piece she'd bought in Torquay when Jack had taken them in the car the other day for a look round. Because holidays away had been unknown to her until now, she hadn't owned such a thing before.

'Come on then, Shirley,' Jack instructed. 'Let's have some action here. Swim from your mum to me.'

The little girl looked doubtful. 'Not without the water wings,' she told him.

'You can do it on your own, I promise you,' he encouraged. 'That's why we took them off, so that you can try.'

'I'm scared to do it without them.'

'You've nothing to be scared of because you're ready to do it on your own now,' he promised her. 'Honestly, I wouldn't suggest you do it if I wasn't sure that you can. But I'm here to catch you if you can't manage.'

'Go on, love,' urged Daisy. 'Give it a try.'

Shirley tried and floundered, waving her arms in a panic.

'It's all right, I've got you,' said Jack, holding her firm until she was steady on her feet. Keen for her not to be put off by the failure, he suggested she should try again right away.

264

'Push yourself off from the bottom, come on, swim from Mummy to me.'

It worked. It was only a matter of a few yards but she did actually move through the water without artificial aid. By the end of the session she was swimming on her own and loving it, her sister almost ready to dispense with the water wings too.

Afterwards they got dried and had tea and scones in the garden. When they'd finished eating, the children went off to play on the sand where the adults could keep an eye on them.

'They can never have enough of the beach,' observed Daisy. 'Whenever it's time to go, it's too soon for them. I'm sure if we stayed till midnight I'd still have a battle to get them to come home.'

'That's all most kids want on holiday,' Jack remarked, 'sea, sand and sunshine.'

'They've never had it before,' she said. 'They are two happy little girls, thanks to you.'

'I do have an ulterior motive.'

She squinted at him, shielding her eyes from the sun with her hand. 'Yeah? What's that then?'

'I get to show off my little corner of the world,' he laughed.

'And understandably so,' she smiled. 'Gullscombe Bay has three more devoted fans now.'

'Good. Oh, and by the way,' he said, and Daisy sensed a sudden uneasiness in his manner, 'I'm not working tonight. I've got a night off.'

'Lovely,' she beamed. 'I'll cook for us.' She felt awkward suddenly and bit her lip. 'Sorry, I'm being presumptuous. You're probably going out – on a hot date or something.'

He looked at her, his heart melting at her smile and her shining eyes, her skin now suffused with a light tan, her brown hair bleached by the sun and blowing off her face in the light warm breeze. She'd even lost that raw skinniness she'd had when she first arrived. He'd made a point of studying her reaction to the news that he was going to be at home this evening, ever careful not to encroach upon her privacy. All week he'd given her the run of the cottage so she would feel completely at home without him around.

Now, halfway through the holiday, the time was right for him to get to know her better; before it was too late. He had nothing specific in mind for Daisy. He wasn't planning on making a move on her or anything because he knew she was involved with someone else. He just wanted to be with her because he was so smitten. There was no future in it but he couldn't help the way he felt.

'No hot date,' he informed her. 'Just a quiet night in . . . something good to eat and a bottle of wine, perhaps.'

'Wine, at home?' She looked surprised. 'I thought people only had wine at wedding receptions, or when they're staying at a posh hotel like the one where I work.' She gave him one of her delicious grins. 'But I'm forgetting, you being a restaurant manager you'd have more sophisticated tastes than me.'

'Don't be daft,' he said in a tone of light admonition. 'I just thought it would be a nice idea to make the meal a bit special, you being on holiday.'

'It's a lovely idea.'

'So if you tell me what you fancy to eat I'll pop into town on the bike and do some shopping.'

'You choose the food and I'll cook it,' she said, smiling into his eyes. 'Deal?'

'Deal,' he replied with a tender look.

That same evening June answered a knock at the door to find Nat Barker standing on the step. Naturally she was puzzled.

'Daisy's still away on holiday,' she reminded him.

'I know that,' he told her. 'I was just wondering if you'd heard from her.'

'No, not yet,' she replied. 'I expect we'll get a postcard in due course. I take it you haven't heard either.'

He shook his head, then enquired, 'Well, aren't you going to ask me in?'

She spread her hands, looking at him. 'Daisy isn't here so what would be the point?'

'So that we don't have to talk in full view of the neighbours is as good a reason as any,' he suggested. 'And also because I'm as good as your brother-in-law. I think that in itself warrants a cup of tea, don't you?'

'No,' was her frank reply. 'And you're about as likely to be my brother-in-law as the Duke of Edinburgh is.'

'Ooh,' he said, shaking his head disapprovingly and sucking in his breath, 'Daisy won't be pleased to hear that you kept me waiting on the doorstep, not pleased at all.'

He was right about that. June had promised Daisy that she'd be more sociable to Nat and she must keep that promise even though Daisy wasn't here. 'Come on in then,' she said with reluctance, ushering him into the living room.

'The sergeant major not about tonight then?' he said when she brought him a cup of tea a few minutes later.

'If you mean Nora, she's gone to her poetry group,' June informed him coolly. 'And I'd rather you didn't call her names, if you don't mind. The least she deserves is respect from you, considering she's been helping Daisy to raise your daughters for years with no assistance from you whatever.'

Nat shrugged indifferently. 'Poetry group, eh?' he said with a mocking grin.

'That's right,' she confirmed briskly. 'Nora likes that sort of thing. She's a very erudite woman.'

'That sounds like some sort of glue.'

'It means knowledgeable.'

'Yeah, well, books and stuff suit her,' he commented cynically. 'Both are as boring as hell.'

June didn't reply. She perched on the edge of an armchair opposite him, feeling intensely irritated and wondering again what Daisy saw in him. She supposed he was good-looking in a greasy sort of way but he had no dress sense whatever and, to her eyes, looked ridiculous with his quiffed hair, gaudy tie and royal-blue suit with a long jacket. It would be rude of her to leave him here on his own and she didn't want to give him any opportunity to make trouble between her and Daisy. But she didn't feel comfortable in the same room with him.

'Each to their own,' she said, keeping her temper, 'and Nora is very clever and well read.'

'She's a sad old bag.'

'Right, that's it.' This was justifiable grounds for eviction. 'I won't have my friends insulted in my own house. So get out. Go on, push off.'

'I haven't finished my tea yet.'

'Too bad. I want you out of here right now.'

'Look, I'm sorry,' he apologised, sounding unexpectedly contrite. 'I overstepped the mark.'

'It's no more than I've come to expect from you,' June said, 'as normal decent behaviour seems to be beyond you.'

'That's a bit strong,' he objected. 'Anyone would think I was some sort of ruffian to hear you talk.'

'I wonder why that is,' was her ironic retort.

Nat looked at her with a gleam in his eye. He hated the sight of the snooty cow and the way she looked down on him. He'd come here on impulse, as he'd been passing the end of the street, with no ulterior motive other than idling away a few minutes on his way to the pub. But with Daisy out of the way, he could see the perfect opportunity to bring her superior sister down a peg or two.

'Look, I know there's no love lost between us,' he said in a tone of fake conciliation, 'but can't we bury the hatchet for Daisy's sake? I know she would like us to get on better.'

June gave him a shrewd look. She didn't trust him an inch but if they could come to some understanding whereby they got along better, even if only in front of Daisy, it would make life easier for them all. If he was prepared to make an effort then so was she. 'OK. If you really mean it, I'm prepared to give it a try,' she told him.

'Good, I'm glad that's settled.' He looked at her innocently but was actually planning his next move. 'It's next Saturday Daisy gets back, isn't it?'

'That's right,' she confirmed. 'She's halfway through the holiday now. I hope she's enjoying herself. She's had a rough time and deserves a break.'

'Yeah, I hope she has a good time, an' all.' He fixed her with his dark, somnolent eyes. 'I know you don't think much of me but I do care about her, you know.'

'Don't make me laugh,' she said. 'You don't give a toss about her. There's only one person you care about and that's yourself.'

'Here, that's not very nice.' He looked peeved. 'I thought we'd agreed to call a truce.'

'Yes, we did,' she admitted, 'but if we're going to stay at peace we'd better steer clear of the subject of your feelings for Daisy.' She stood up. 'Anyway, I don't want to seem rude but I do have things to do.'

He drained his teacup and stood up.

She turned to lead him to the front door when she felt his arms slip around her from behind.

'What the hell do you think you're doing?' she gasped, turning to him and wrenching away.

'Come on, June, you know you want to,' he taunted.

'You must be off your head—'

'You don't like me but you do fancy me,' he interrupted. 'And don't deny it because I won't believe you.'

'You must be joking.'

'You women are all the same,' he persisted. 'You can't resist a bad boy.'

'Ugh!' She stared at him in disgust. 'I'd sooner be savaged by a mad Alsatian.'

'Don't give me that,' he persisted suggestively, coming towards her again. 'Why fight it when you know you won't win? What harm is there, eh? Daisy will never know.'

June whacked her hand across his face so hard it stung her. Caught unawares, he reeled back. 'You spiteful cow,' he muttered.

'Now get out,' she said, marching towards the door and opening it. 'Go on, get out – *now*.'

His eyes were simmering with rage. Such was his vanity, he'd planned only to get her interested, then make a fool of her by turning her down. The way she'd turned the tables on him was the ultimate humiliation. 'I'll get you for this,' he threatened. 'I can promise you that.'

'Just go,' she said, putting her hands on his chest and pushing him through the doorway.

'You'll pay for this, you bitch,' was his parting shot, and the haunting image she saw as she shut the door on him was his venomous eyes glaring at her.

Behind the closed door June was trembling, his threats making her shiver. How could someone as genuinely good-hearted as Daisy have got mixed up with such a brute? she wondered. Daisy really ought to have her eyes opened about the sort of man he was. But June knew that she could never hurt her sister by telling her what her beloved Nat had just done.

Chapter Twelve

'Thanks for helping us out with the wine, Paula. You're a pal.'
Alan was talking to his friend in the Cliff Head reception,
having just removed a dozen bottles of white wine from the
boot of her car. 'We've usually got plenty in stock but our
suppliers let us down at the last minute.' He tutted, giving her
a wry grin. 'And, of course, Sod's law being as it is, everyone
wants white wine tonight.'

'Isn't it always the way?'

'Yeah. Still, thanks to you we can stay in favour with the
customers.' He put the cardboard box containing the wine
down on the counter and looked at her, raising his eyes in a
gesture of self-deprecation. 'A decent-class hotel without any
white wine, I ask you.'

'These things happen in the most well-run establishments,'
she reminded him. 'And I'm sure you'd help us out in similar
circumstances.'

'Course we would.' He paused, looking at her. 'You should
have let me come to get it, though, to save you driving over.'

'I was glad of the break,' she admitted. 'It's always so
hectic on a Saturday night at our place.'

'Same here.' He glanced towards the wine. 'So, how much
do we owe you?'

'I don't know off the top of my head,' she said casually.
'I'll find out the trade price and let you know.'

'OK.' Saturday night was in full swing at the Cliff Head and Alan needed to get back to work but he didn't want to be rude. 'Can I get you a drink?' he offered. 'It's the least I can do after you've gone to such trouble on our behalf.'

'Thanks, Alan, but no. I've had a breather but I mustn't stop to socialise.' She threw him a knowing look. 'And neither, I suspect, must you.'

'I am a bit pushed,' he was forced to admit. 'Jack's got the night off.'

Her brows rose. 'The restaurant manager off duty on a Saturday night at the height of the season?'

Alan made a face. 'I'm a soft touch to have agreed to it, I know, but he's got people staying with him,' he explained. 'My wife's sister and her two children, as a matter of fact.' He leaned towards her, becoming confidential. 'I think he's fallen for my sister-in-law, actually. I haven't been able to get a sensible word out of him since she's been here. It's Daisy this, Daisy that . . .'

'He must be smitten to ask for a Saturday night off at this time of the year.'

Alan nodded. 'I didn't make an issue of it, though, because he's such an asset to this place and he never pushes his luck about time off as a rule.'

Unexpectedly, he found himself noticing how attractive Paula looked in a pale blue summer suit with a pencil skirt and high-heeled court shoes. Since they'd cleared the air last Christmas, their friendship had blossomed and they met up for a meal or a drink on a regular basis. They had all the right ingredients for a friendship, being in the same line of business, having parents who were friends, and sharing a similar sense of humour.

But meeting her clear blue eyes now and feeling the stirrings of a physical response, he wondered if, perhaps, there could be something more for them. He and June were

272

no longer at daggers drawn but she'd made it clear there was no future for them together. So maybe there could be one for him with Paula. Unlike Jack, Alan didn't enjoy the single life.

'How about dinner one evening soon?' he suggested. 'Once Jack's visitors have gone back to London and his mind is on the job again, I'll be able to get away, especially on a weekday evening.'

'That would be lovely, Alan,' she accepted graciously. 'I'd really like that.'

'I'll give you a ring soon to get something arranged then.'

'Sure.'

At that moment his mother sailed on to the scene from the direction of the restaurant. 'Alan, I've had to send— Oh, hello, Paula.' She looked from one to the other, beaming as she misread the situation. 'How nice to see you, dear. I didn't realise you were here.'

'I'm just on my way out,' Paula told her, making as though to leave. 'Nice to see you again, Mrs Masters. You're looking well. See you soon, Alan.'

'I'll ring you,' he said, smiling after her as she swung across the foyer in her high-heeled shoes.

His mother was looking very pleased with herself. 'You two seem to be getting along very well lately,' she observed.

'She came with the wine we needed, that's all,' Alan explained. 'It wasn't a social visit.'

'That doesn't alter the fact that the two of you seem to get on well now,' she persisted.

He shrugged and changed the subject. 'You wanted me for something?'

'Yes, so I did. I came to tell you that Chef isn't feeling well so I've sent him home. The sous-chef will have to take over.'

'Wonderful,' Alan said with irony. 'That's all we need.' He sighed. 'Oh, well, it's all in a night's work, I suppose.'

273

Daisy was feeling extremely happy and relaxed. The children were asleep in bed and she and Jack were having coffee in the living room at the cottage after dining on steak and salad, followed by chocolate eclairs, and all washed down with a bottle of wine.

Daisy had never talked to a man so much in her life – certainly not to Nat. There was something about Jack that made her want to confide. She was so much at ease she even told him about her background and her plans to get her father's name cleared. She told him everything.

Unlike Nat, Jack didn't react by immediately pouring scorn on the idea. But he was a little circumspect. 'Whilst I can understand your wanting to find this Morris Dodd and his wife, I think you should treat the whole thing with caution,' he told her. 'I mean, even if you do find him, he isn't going to put his hands up to the murder, is he? And he'll see you and your sister as a threat, turning up out of the blue after all these years. He could get nasty.'

'We've already thought of that and we'll be careful, of course,' she assured him. 'But it's his wife we're planning on dealing with, rather than him.'

'She isn't likely to admit to anything either.'

'Maybe not, but she holds the key to our father's freedom and the restoration of his good name,' Daisy pointed out. 'So I believe there must be some way to get her to admit that she lied under oath, and give us the evidence we need to get Dad's case reopened.'

Jack leaned back with his arms folded, considering the matter. 'The last thing I want to do is put you off because I can tell how much this means to you,' he began, 'but facts have to be faced. She's already committed perjury; she isn't going to change her story after all this time, is she? She'll be too scared of the consequences.'

'I know all that, Jack. But I'm still convinced that if we can only find the Dodds, we'll somehow be able to see that justice is done.' She shrugged, making a face. 'I admit we've come to a dead end at the moment but we're not going to give up because we *know* that the pair of them lied in court. That's got to give us a strong case for an appeal.'

'If you can get them to admit it, yes it will,' he said. 'And I agree with you that she's more likely to be persuaded to open up than he is. He was unfaithful to her, after all.'

'Exactly,' agreed Daisy. 'Look at this whole thing from Mrs Dodd's point of view: because of the murder the world knew that her husband had been cheating on her. That must have been extremely humiliating. Being betrayed by your husband is painful enough, I should imagine. Having everyone know about it must have been excruciating.'

'No doubt about that.'

'Even though she lied for him, she must have felt resentful towards him. Any woman would,' Daisy went on. 'And the fact that she knew he wasn't at home with her at the time of the murder, as they both claimed, must have made her wonder if he did actually do it, whatever lies he told her about that. Over the years she might have become bitter about it and be ready to shop him – with a little encouragement.'

'Not at the expense of her own liberty.' Jack didn't want Daisy to fool herself about this.

'I know it's a long shot.'

'They might not even still be together,' he pointed out.

'We've thought of that too, and I know that when you consider all the drawbacks, our chances of success don't look good.' She pondered for a moment. 'But all I can say is, I've got a feeling about this whole thing.' Her voice rose with ardour. 'If it takes the rest of my life I'll see my father's name cleared.' She paused, guessing his thoughts. 'Even if it is posthumously.'

There was obviously no point in trying to talk her out of it so he wanted to be helpful. 'You say you've come to a dead end in your search for them?'

'Yeah,' she sighed. 'If we had any idea of the area to look it would help, but we haven't a flaming clue.' She told him what they'd done so far.

'Quite a task.'

'You can say that again. The trouble is, neither June nor I have much spare time. We both have demanding jobs and I've got the girls to consider. But, as I said, we'll get it sorted out. I don't know when but we'll do it.'

Infected by her optimism, Jack believed her suddenly. She was the sort of person who would do anything she set her mind to. 'Yes, I think you will too,' he said.

'Oh.' She sounded surprised because of the odds stacked against a successful outcome. 'It's encouraging to know that someone's got faith in me.'

She was wearing a white sleeveless top with a round neck and a full floral skirt, her hair shining in the light. She looked so pretty, he couldn't help telling her so.

'Thank you.' She smiled, blushing. 'Flattery will get you everywhere.' The way he looked at her made her feel different – sort of beautiful and special. Warmth flowed between them like a living thing. She couldn't remember feeling this good in a very long time, if ever. But compunction hovered, nudging her into making sure that Nat didn't get forgotten. 'I'm not used to it because Nat isn't the complimentary type.'

'And talking of Nat,' he said, as though acknowledging the other man's place in her life, 'what does he think about these plans you have to help your father?'

'He doesn't approve.'

'Worried it might be risky for you, I suppose.'

'No, it isn't that,' she corrected with characteristic honesty. 'He just thinks it's a stupid idea that won't get a result.'

'You won't get any help from him then?'

Daisy puffed out her lips, shaking her head. 'Opposition is all I'll get from him,' she said with emphasis. 'Apart from anything else, he can't stand the sight of my sister so is against anything I do with her.'

'Tell me . . . are you actually engaged to him?' came Jack's tentative enquiry.

'Yeah, I suppose you could say that's what we are. I always think of us in that way.'

'You don't wear a ring, though.'

In the early days a ring had been promised but never materialised. But she just said, 'No. But we are seriously committed to each other.'

Jack nodded without comment.

'Poor old Nat is always in the doghouse with June and Nora over something or other,' she found herself saying without any prior intention. 'Neither of them likes him. They don't think he treats me right.'

'Really?' Jack said in a querying tone. 'And do they have a fair point?'

'He's not perfect, I'm the first to admit that,' she told him. 'He tends to be a bit too casual about things. But that's just his way. We can't all be steady and reliable, can we? It'd be a boring old world if we were.'

This Nat character sounded like a right cretin and obviously didn't value the prize he had in Daisy, thought Jack, finding himself angry about it. If the man had any sense or serious intentions he'd have married her years ago. But he spared her feelings and said, 'It certainly would.'

'Have you ever been married?' she asked conversationally.

'No.'

'Would you like to be?'

'Not especially, no. I'm quite happy as I am,' he informed her. 'I suppose I've got a bit selfish and set in my ways. You get used to pleasing yourself when you're on your own.'

'Yeah, I suppose you would.'

'Anyway,' he began, changing the subject, 'you're enjoying your stay in Gullscombe Bay?'

'I'll say. It's beautiful here. No wonder you made it your home. It's enough to tempt anyone. The idea of going back to Notting Hill isn't in the least appealing, I can tell you. The way I feel at the moment, I could happily stay away indefinitely.'

'Really?' He couldn't hide his enthusiasm.

'Yeah, really,' she confirmed with a wistful look. 'But I have to go back, of course.'

'Why?'

She threw him a puzzled look. 'I should have thought that was obvious,' she told him. 'My life is in London.'

'It doesn't have to be.'

'No, it doesn't have to be. But it is. I'm a Londoner, Jack.'

'So am I.'

'But it's where I belong. Everything I know is there,' she pointed out. 'Being here has made me understand why people move away from the city to places like this and I feel I'd like to do the same. But that's just the holiday atmosphere getting to me. Being realistic, it's just a holiday place, somewhere I'd love to come again for a visit. But not a place I could live in.'

'I've made it my home,' he reminded her.

'It's different for you,' she objected. 'You're a single man with only yourself to consider. Even apart from the fact that I couldn't leave Nat, I have the girls to support so I have to have steady work. And London is where the work is.'

He could hardly bear the thought of her leaving and wanted to beg her to stay. But he had no right. Her life was in London and she obviously thought the world of this Nat person. 'Yeah, of course it is,' he said in an understanding manner. 'It's just that . . . well, you seem to have taken the place so much to your heart and it obviously agrees with you. I suppose my enthusiasm for the area got a bit out of hand.'

'That's understandable.'

'It's true about the place being good for you, though,' he added. 'You're hardly recognisable from the pale, sickly woman I met off the train a week ago.'

'I feel different too.'

'You're very beautiful, Daisy,' he blurted out.

'Here, leave off,' she said, embarrassed to find herself on the receiving end of his admiration for the second time. 'I think you've had one too many to drink.'

'I haven't—'

'Well, I think I have,' she cut in quickly because she was enjoying the attention rather too much and needed to come down to earth. 'I think it's time I went to bed.' She gave him a wry grin. 'After we've done the dishes, naturally.'

'I'll see to that,' he offered. 'You cooked the meal so it's only fair that I do the washing up.'

'Are you sure?'

'Quite sure,' he confirmed. 'You go to bed.'

She stood up. 'I'll have to take you up on that,' she said, stifling a yawn, 'before I get too sleepy to get up the stairs. All this fresh air knocks me out. I'll see you in the morning.'

'Yeah.'

'Thanks for a lovely evening.'

'Thank *you*, Daisy.'

''Night, Jack.'

''Night, Daisy.'

Daisy slipped into bed, her head swimming with happy memories of today and excited thoughts of tomorrow. That was how it was since she'd been in Gullscombe Bay. Each new day was a fresh treat to be anticipated with pleasure. This must be why people are so keen to go away on holiday, she thought, because it's just one long round of fun and recreation. How could you not be happy in surroundings like these, going to sleep every night to the soothing sound of the sea and waking up to it every morning?

Who was she kidding? It wasn't just the environment that was making her feel so happy and alive. It was going to sleep at night knowing that she would see *him* the next morning. She wanted to go on doing it, to go on being with him and feeling like this. Refusing to spoil the moment by dwelling on the sobering thought that it would end all too soon, she lay back on the pillow and drifted into a peaceful sleep.

Downstairs Jack was humming softly to himself as he washed the dishes and put them to drain on the draining board. It was so good having Daisy here, he was literally dreading her departure. As he'd said to her, living alone had made him selfish and set in his ways. But he didn't feel selfish when he was with her. He wanted to put himself out for her benefit; enjoyed her appreciation of every little thing. Having the kids around was great fun too, their youthful exuberance filling the house with noise and laughter. Their energy and nonstop chatter was positively uplifting to him. Selfish he might be but he couldn't do enough for this little family. The trouble was, he wanted to go on doing it, and this time next week they'd be back in London.

The trio had breathed new life into him, and the cottage was never going to be the same after they'd gone. The thought of their departure was so depressing he blotted it out of his mind and looked forward to tomorrow and waking up knowing that Daisy and the girls were in the house.

The next morning the unthinkable happened. They awoke to find rain trickling down the windows and forming puddles in the garden. Jack insisted on going to the shop, which opened for a few hours on a Sunday morning, to get the milk and bread to save Daisy a drenching as she had recently been ill.

Breakfast was eaten indoors, but by the time they'd finished and done the dishes, the rain had stopped. It was still overcast, though, so Jack suggested a walk along the beach. He had to go to work a bit later on but had time to spare for a stroll.

So, with sweaters over their summer clothes, they set off around the bay, the girls stopping every so often to collect shells in their buckets, Daisy observing the patches of woodland that fringed the shore. Having spent most of the time on the beach up until now, they hadn't walked as far as this before so this bit of the landscape was new to her.

'Well, has the place lost some of its magic now that you've seen it in the rain?' asked Jack.

'Not on your life,' she assured him. 'The rain has freshened everything up and made it even better.'

'You won't say that if it rains every day for the rest of your holiday,' he grinned.

'You can bet I won't,' she admitted with a smile. 'But I'm sure I'll still love the place whatever the weather.'

'Let's hope the sun comes out so you're not put to the test,' he remarked casually.

They ambled on in comfortable silence. The girls were dragging behind, poking about in the rock pools.

'Wow! What a lovely house,' enthused Daisy as a large stone-faced property came into view through the trees. 'It's huge. Is it a private house or some sort of an institution?'

'It's a private house,' Jack informed her. 'I believe they call it a gentleman's residence. It's known as Gullscombe Manor.'

'It's beautiful,' she breathed, noticing a turreted roof and a veranda facing the sea.

'It used to be,' he corrected as they stared at the property, the rear of which was facing them. 'But it's been empty for ages and just left to rot.'

'Who owns it?'

'A wealthy businessman; retired now, though, and getting on a bit in years,' he told her. 'He's got pots of money.'

'You'd need it to maintain a place like that,' was Daisy's opinion.

'You're right there.'

'So what happened to the owner?'

'No one knows for sure. Rumour has it that he's gone to live with his married daughter in Exeter.'

'What, just moved out and left the place?'

Jack nodded. 'They say he went a bit soft in the head after his wife died,' he explained. 'They'd lived there all their married life and he just couldn't cope with being there after she'd gone. It's all a bit sad really.'

'Mm. But surely one of his family could make sure the place was looked after,' Daisy suggested. 'Either that or sell it rather than leave it to deteriorate.'

'You'd think so, wouldn't you?' he agreed. 'Maybe he can't bring himself to take the final step of selling it. And perhaps his daughter doesn't fancy living in such a remote spot.'

'It's probably something like that,' remarked Daisy. 'But it's a terrible shame for it to be so neglected.' She paused, squinting at the house. 'What's it like at the front?'

'We'll go and have a look if you like,' he said. 'There's no one around to object.'

Having called to the girls, and helped them on with their shoes, they climbed up a sloping path through the trees into the gardens, which were extensive and very overgrown. Making their way through the long wet grass to the front, they came to a gravel forecourt at the end of a driveway leading to the road.

The house entrance was imposing, with wide stone steps leading up to double doors on which the varnish was dull and faded. Daisy peered through one of the dirty windows to see a large room with dust sheets covering the furniture.

'I bet the spiders are having a whale of a time in there with all those cobwebs,' she said, shivering at the thought. 'It's creepy, as though it's got caught in a time warp, as though life suddenly stopped in there.'

'That is what happened when his wife died,' Jack told her. 'He just upped and left.'

'What will happen to it ultimately, I wonder?'

'I suppose eventually it'll be sold,' he suggested. 'Or the owner's daughter and her husband will take it over.'

'It certainly needs urgent attention, so let's hope something happens sooner rather than later,' she commented. 'Before it gets any worse.'

'Mm.' Noticing that the skies were darkening, Jack said, 'Anyway, I think it's about to chuck it down with rain so we'd better find some shelter.'

He was right. The heavens opened and they made a dash for the only protection they could find, the veranda at the back of the house. It was an attractive structure with mosaic tiles underfoot and intricate laced metalwork arched between the supporting pillars. There were glass doors leading into the house through which they could see a spacious room in which dust covers were a dominant presence.

'This is handy for us, and very pretty too,' observed Daisy as the downpour drenched the gardens and bounced on to some decrepit wooden garden furniture. She turned and peered through the glass doors. 'They must have really lived in style. The rooms are enormous.'

'You wouldn't buy a place like this unless you could afford to live in style, would you?' he mentioned.

'No, not unless you bought it for commercial use,' she remarked casually, 'to change into a nursing home or something.'

Jack nodded, looking at his watch.

'Oh dear. Are you going to be late for work?' Daisy looked worried.

'Not yet. But I do need to keep an eye on the time,' he told her. 'Alan's being very good about my having time off, but I don't want to upset him, especially as I want some time off next week.'

'Don't get into trouble at work on our account,' she advised him. 'You don't have to stay home from work because of us. The girls and I will be fine on our own.'

'I know that but I want to spend time with you,' he said, taking her hand and squeezing it in a sudden impulse. 'I enjoy your company.'

'The feeling's mutual,' she blurted out, instinctively moving closer to him. 'I just don't want you to put yourself out any more than you already have.'

The atmosphere changed from warm and friendly to vibrantly intimate but was shattered almost instantly by the two girls running out into the rain in sheer devilment.

'Come back in here, you two,' called Daisy. 'Your clothes will get soaked.'

Shirley raised her face to the rain. 'It feels lovely, Mum,' she called, lifting her arms. 'It's washing my face and making the garden smell nice.'

Belinda copied her sister, tilting her head back to let the rain soak her face and hair. 'It doesn't feel cold, does it, Sherl?'

'No. It feels smashing.'

Daisy could understand them being inspired to do this because she too was tempted to run out into the rain. She felt so alive she wanted to touch the elements. But the sensible, maternal side of her nature prevailed. 'I'm sure it's really good fun but come into the shelter just the same,' she said with as much authority as she could muster in her carefree mood. 'We're going in a minute, as soon as the rain eases off a bit.'

They did as she said, and stood dripping on the veranda, giggling at the sheer boldness of getting soaked through with their clothes on.

Jack smiled. 'What it's like to be a kid, eh?' he said. 'They make you remember, bring it all back.'

'Those two aren't concerned with practicalities like drying wet clothes or catching cold,' Daisy said. 'Kids just follow their instincts. And boring old Mum had to go and spoil it all by being sensible.' She sighed. 'Still, childhood is short enough. I want them to enjoy it to the full.'

The rain stopped quite suddenly and they headed back towards the cottage, the girls running on ahead, eager now to get changed into dry clothes.

'Oh, by the way,' Jack said as they walked along the beach and the cottage came into view, 'I've been thinking about your search for the Dodds and I've got a suggestion.'

'Oh, yeah?'

'You've been thinking in terms of finding a way of finding them, which, as you've indicated, is an impossible task when you've no idea at all where they might be, and both you and June have other commitments. Right?'

'Yes, that's right,' she confirmed. 'We can't afford a private detective.'

'Maybe you should change your strategy altogether and have them come to you,' he told her intriguingly.

'How on earth would we do that?'

'This is how . . .' he began.

The following week passed all too quickly. After the rain on Sunday, the sun reappeared on Monday, and Daisy and the girls returned to their glorious outdoor routine. They were joined by Jack whenever he could get away from the hotel and Daisy was aware of a tacit closeness growing between them.

He arranged to have the whole day off on Friday as it was their last day. In the morning he drove Daisy and the girls into Torquay to buy gifts to take home. They didn't have much money but, because Jack had refused to take anything for their food, they were able to afford a few modest presents.

The many gift shops were filled with novelty items and they had fun choosing what to buy. Daisy bought a jewellery box made of seashells for June to put on her dressing table, and a china cat with ginger fur and luminous green eyes for Nora because she was very fond of cats. For Nat she purchased a cigarette case.

Shirley bought her aunt and surrogate grannie each a comb in a leather case with 'Torquay' boldly displayed in gold letters. Belinda treated them each to a large, Cellophane-wrapped pink seashell filled with sweets that looked like pebbles.

They all had a good laugh in one of the shops at a hideous duck ornament that looked as though it had been thrown together. It had a bright yellow beak that was crooked and shaped in such a way as to give the impression that the bird was laughing.

'Honestly, some of the stuff they expect you to part with your money for,' disapproved Daisy, but she couldn't help but smile at the grinning artefact.

'You don't like it then?' said Jack.

'Of course I don't. How could anyone like such a shoddy piece of workmanship? Whoever made it must have been drunk when they put it together. The whole thing's lopsided.'

'This probably makes me the king of bad taste but it actually appeals to me,' he confessed, picking it up and examining it more closely. 'I like it.'

286

'You can't possibly like it,' said Daisy in disbelief. 'You're teasing us.'

'No. I'm not, honest. I really think he's great,' he told the amazed Daisy with a devilish grin. 'And at least you wouldn't be miserable with it in the house because it makes you laugh just to look at it.'

'You laugh with the sheer awfulness of it,' was Daisy's opinion.

'I gather you're not going to take it back to London as a souvenir of Torquay then?'

'Not on your life,' she replied without hesitation.

Because they were catching an early train back to London the next morning, Daisy needed to have all but the last-minute packing done before they went to bed that night. This created an air of gloom because it reminded them that their departure was imminent and meant they had to come off the beach earlier than usual.

Still at least Jack wasn't working, and as it was their last night he and Daisy agreed that the girls could stay up to eat with them. So while Daisy bathed the girls and did the bulk of the packing, Jack went to get fish and chips for them all from a shopping parade further up the coast that was just a few minutes away on his motorbike.

When he got back Daisy had laid the table and the girls were in a silly mood, giggling and spluttering behind their hands.

'Have you two got ants in your pants again?' he asked, making them laugh all the more.

When they all sat down at the table and he saw a package wrapped in fancy paper by the side of his plate, he began to understand.

'I've had the devil's own job keeping them quiet about it all afternoon,' Daisy explained.

'What's this?'

'Just a little something to say thank you for giving us such a wonderful holiday,' she told him.

He looked at her sternly and then the girls. 'You shouldn't have,' he said, looking delighted despite his protests. 'There's really no need. I've loved having you.'

'Open it then,' urged Shirley.

'Go on,' added Belinda, jumping up and down in her seat.

The removal of the wrapping revealed a book on the history of motorcycles. Jack was so touched by their thoughtfulness, he couldn't speak for a moment.

'Don't you like it?' Shirley looked anxious.

'I love it.' He got up and gave them each a hug. 'I really love it. It's so kind of you.'

'We think you deserve it for putting up with us for two weeks, don't we, girls?' said Daisy.

The girls nodded, still seeming a bit odd, he thought. There was still plenty of giggling going on.

'We did our secret shopping when you'd had enough of trailing around the shops and went for coffee and left us to it,' Daisy explained.

'I knew I shouldn't have let you loose on Torquay town on your own,' he joshed. 'But thank you all very much for the book. I shall treasure it, always.'

'Um, that isn't quite all,' said Daisy, looking at Shirley, who left the room and returned with another package.

'This is an extra thing that Mum thought you might like,' she said, handing it to him.

Curiously he tore off the wrapping paper. A roar of laughter went up as he held up the laughing duck ornament.

'Something to remember us by,' Daisy grinned. 'You might have awful taste in ornaments but you're a wonderful host.'

Now there were tears clearly visible in his eyes and they were not entirely from laughing.

'Thank you.' His gaze focused on Daisy and they both knew that this was her gift to him and it was an adult thing. Then he looked at the children and added, 'I shall put him on the kitchen windowsill to cheer me up when I'm washing the dishes. I shall think of you all every time I look at him.'

Even the girls picked up on the emotion in the air and were subdued.

'Come on then, everyone,' urged Daisy in a rousing tone to get things back to normal. 'Eat your fish and chips before they get cold.'

'The holiday's gone so quick, I can hardly believe it's over,' said Daisy to Jack later that evening after the children had gone to bed. 'This time tomorrow the girls will be in their own beds at home.'

He nodded gloomily. 'And you?' he said in a querying tone. 'Will you be seeing Nat?'

'Depends if he remembers we're coming home and comes round,' she told him.

'Will you go to his place if he doesn't turn up?'

'No.' She wasn't in the mood to go into much detail about the peculiar nature of her relationship with Nat, especially as she knew Jack would disapprove. 'I'm tied because of the girls so he always comes to me. It's a habit we've slipped into over the years.'

'I see.'

They were in the living room, having a last cup of coffee together, she on the sofa, he in an armchair. They'd been sitting here talking since the girls went to bed, the tension becoming unbearable for Daisy as the evening drew to a close.

'Well, I suppose I'd better be making my way towards bed as we've got to be up early in the morning,' she said, finishing her coffee and standing up.

He got up too, his blue eyes fiercely bright. 'I don't want you to go, Daisy,' he said quickly.

'I can't stay up all night,' she said.

'That isn't what I mean . . .'

She met his eyes. 'I know,' she said softly, 'and I don't want to leave tomorrow either.'

'Marry me, Daisy,' he blurted out.

'What!'

'I love you and I want to marry you.'

She stared at him, his words echoing in the silence. He was as shocked as she was by his proposal.

'Don't be daft, Jack,' she said at last. She was thrilled by what he'd said but it was too sudden, too impossible to be taken seriously. 'Don't mess about.'

He shook his head, as though in disbelief at this unexpected turn of events. 'I had no intention of proposing to you. It just sort of came out. But I'm serious,' he said, his eyes never leaving her face. 'I've fallen in love with you. And I think . . . well, I hope that you feel the same about me.'

She bit her lip, absently combing her hair back from her brow with her fingers. 'Maybe I do feel something but it'll be just a holiday thing.' She was afraid of the strength of her feelings. Here with Jack everything seemed possible but, as the mother of two children, she had to keep her feet planted firmly on the ground. 'All this sunshine and fresh air has gone to my head.'

'It's more than that and we both know it,' he contradicted ardently. 'Don't go back to London. Stay here with me.'

Overwhelmed, she tried to keep things light to hide how deeply she felt for him. 'If I were to stay here, the novelty would soon wear off for you, believe me, under the strain of everyday life and having two noisy kids under your feet.'

'Why not stay and give me the chance to prove you wrong?' he suggested.

She shook her head. 'I can't, Jack. It's all happened too fast. I can't be irresponsible, not with two kids relying on me.'

'Look, this might sound a bit sloppy but I felt something special for you when we first met back in the spring,' he confessed. 'I know we haven't known each other long but these past two weeks have been the most wonderful time of my life. And I know you well enough to know that I love you and I want to be with you . . . and the girls – for the rest of my life.'

Suddenly Daisy didn't want to protest. She didn't want to be sensible and think about the impossibility of a future for her and Jack. She didn't want to consider tomorrow and the parting she knew must come. No one had ever looked at her in the way Jack was looking at her now, as though she was the most important person on earth. All she could think of was what she could see in Jack's eyes, and knew she would never see again after tonight. The only thing that seemed to matter was her feelings for him at this moment.

'Come here,' she said, reaching out for him.

'No, Jack, no,' Daisy said, pulling away from him and dragging her blouse into place. 'I can't do this.'

'All right, don't panic,' he told her, drawing back quickly, his voice quivering slightly. 'I'm not going to force you into anything.'

'I shouldn't have led you on. I'm sorry,' she said, her hands trembling as she sat at the far end of the sofa, doing up her blouse. 'I got carried away.'

'Things got a bit out of hand, that's all,' he assured her. 'It wasn't your fault.'

'I hope you don't think I make a habit of leading men on.'

'Of course not. Why would I think that?'

'It's all right, it's just me being ultra-sensitive,' she told him with a wry look. 'Being an unmarried mum brands you in the eyes of most people.'

'Not in mine,' he said. 'Things moved faster than we intended but it was only natural. We're a pair, you and me. We have a wonderful future ahead of us, you, me and the girls.'

Reality hit home like a physical blow. What was she doing allowing things to go this far? Had she lost her mind? 'No, Jack. Now is all there is,' she stated solemnly. 'I have to go home tomorrow.'

'Surely you're not going back to London as though nothing's changed.' He was distraught.

'Nothing's changed as far as my life there is concerned.' She was ignoring her heart and speaking from her mind because she knew she must be sensible. 'This . . . us, is lovely but it isn't the stuff of real life.'

'What we have is about as real as it gets,' he argued.

'I know it feels like that now but . . .' The sound of a child's voice calling to her from upstairs brought her even more firmly down to earth. When she came back downstairs, having given Shirley a drink of water, settled her and been reminded of her serious responsibilities, she was even more convinced that she must control these bewildering new feelings. 'There can't be a future for us and I shouldn't have let you think otherwise.'

Jack got up and paced around the room. 'You and I are right together,' he declared, standing still and looking down at her sitting stiffly on the sofa. 'Surely that's the most important thing.'

'In a sentimental love story it would be, but this isn't fiction and I'm not some teenager with no responsibilities. I have to go home tomorrow and get on with my life.'

'So, I mean nothing to you?'

'You know that isn't true. You mean the world to me,' she was quick to assure him. 'But nothing can come of it.'

292

'You're saying it's over between us then?'

'Oh, Jack, what is there to be over?' she said, spreading her hands in a gesture of helplessness. 'We've had two weeks together, that's all.'

'Don't trivialise something that means a lot to me,' he admonished sharply.

'It means a lot to me too,' Daisy made clear, 'but I'm a realist and I know that holiday romances rarely last.'

'This isn't just a holiday romance,' he insisted. 'We were drawn to each other when we met last spring. Now that we know each other better it's developed into something special. You must admit that's true.'

'I don't deny feeling something special for you, but I have commitments.'

'Nat, I suppose.'

'That's right,' she said, but there were many more confusing elements to it than that.

'You're not married to him,' he reminded her. 'You're not even officially engaged.'

'No, but he is the father of my children.'

'Are you in love with him?' he blurted out.

Once she would have said yes without hesitation. But she'd been disillusioned with Nat and much less besotted even before she'd met Jack, who was a better man than Nat would ever be. She still cared for Nat, despite all his faults, but she wasn't in love with him. Not now. But to marry her daughters' father was her long-held dream. There was a completeness in it somehow and she didn't feel able to let it go.

'I still feel something for him, yes.'

'That doesn't sound like a proclamation of love to me,' Jack said, his anger rising. 'It sounds more as though he's a habit you're afraid to break.'

'Don't get cross, please, Jack.' Daisy's eyes were full of regret. 'What you and I have shared this past two weeks has

293

been wonderful, like nothing I have experienced before. And I'll never forget it. But that doesn't mean it will last.'

'I don't agree.' He was adamant. 'We have all the right ingredients to make it work.'

'There are too many complications . . .'

'Nothing that can't be resolved,' he told her. 'You'd be happy living here. I know it's right for you. The girls would love it and there's a school the other side of the village. It's a good place to bring children up. And think how healthy you've felt since you've been here. The air agrees with you. You've said so yourself.'

Daisy knew he was right and she wanted to stay more than anything. But her down-to-earth nature just wouldn't allow her to cut the ties with her other life. She'd never had any real stability and was afraid to leave her home and her job for a man she hardly knew and a relationship that could fizzle out under the strain of everyday life. Thinking she was in love with Jack wasn't enough to build a whole new life. She was a realist, used to hardship and disappointment. She couldn't believe that her life would change.

'And what would I do for money?' She was so accustomed to supporting herself and the girls, she couldn't imagine anything else. 'Move in here and sponge off you?'

'How can you sponge off me if you're my wife?' he wanted to know. 'I want to marry you, to look after you and support you . . . and the girls. So you wouldn't have to go out to work.'

'Oh . . .' She'd never imagined a man would ever be this caring to her. 'You're such a good man, Jack.'

'Of course, if you wanted to go out to work, I wouldn't try and stop you,' he added quickly. 'An experienced waitress is always in demand in Torquay. But you wouldn't have to work. The choice would be yours.'

'It's mostly seasonal work around here, I should imagine,'

she commented. 'Anyway, as I'm not staying, that's neither here nor there.'

'Why do you have to go back to Nat?' He was fighting for her now so the truth must be told. 'If he was going to marry you he'd have done it years ago.'

'That is one way of looking at it.'

'Why keep fooling yourself then?'

She sighed. 'I suppose it's because Nat and I go back a long way and he's the girls' father,' she tried to explain, thinking it through as she spoke because she was still very confused.

'I can see that his being the girls' dad would create a bond between you and I would never want to come between a man and his children. But if he made you happy, this thing that's grown between us this past fortnight wouldn't be there, and we wouldn't be having this conversation.'

In a moment of clarity, she realised that happiness wasn't something she'd ever expected to have with Nat. It was the familiar pattern of her life that was drawing her back – a case of the devil she knew, perhaps. 'You can't just snatch what seems good in the moment and hope for the best for the future, not when you've got two kids.'

'You're entitled to grab the chance of happiness, though.'

'That isn't my way, Jack.'

He wasn't ready to give up. 'Would it make any difference if I was prepared to move to London to be with you?'

'No. London isn't the issue,' she told him. 'Anyway, you'd hate living there.'

'Yes, but I'd do it if it meant having you,' he stated gravely. 'That's how much you mean to me.'

Daisy was shocked by the depth of his feelings for her. No one had ever felt that much for her before and it was a huge responsibility. Marriage and a proper family life was all she'd ever wanted. Now she was being offered it and she wasn't in a position to take it. She wanted to seize the moment and accept Jack's proposal. He'd shown her what it felt like to be truly loved by a man. But she still felt bound to the father of her children.

'Jack, you're a great bloke and you'll always be very special to me but I'm going to stay with my old life,' she said. 'It's what I know; what I'm used to.'

Something about her tone must have finally convinced him that she wasn't going to change her mind because his manner became one of cool resignation. 'It's your decision, of course. But I think it's the wrong one.'

'I'm sorry.'

'Don't be,' he said coldly. 'I don't have the right to make you do anything you don't want to do.'

'Jack—'

'I have no claim on you.'

'No, but—'

'It's a simple misunderstanding.' His manner was piercingly abrupt and she knew how much she had hurt him. 'I really believed that you and I had something.'

'And we do,' she told him with emphasis. 'But it can't be permanent.'

'It could be if you wanted it,' he declared briskly. 'But you don't, so let's forget it.'

'Don't be like that, Jack, please.' She felt awful.

'Would you like a drink of something before you go to bed?' he offered, ever the gentleman.

'No, thanks,' Daisy said. 'But I would like you to stop behaving like the perfect host.'

It was as though he'd shut himself off from her. 'I'll go on up to bed if you don't want anything,' he said in a formal tone. 'See you in the morning.'

'Yeah,' she said dismally to his retreating back.

She stayed where she was for a while, too distressed to

move. Eventually she made her way slowly up the stairs. Pausing outside his room, she reached for the door handle and almost touched it. But common sense finally prevailed and she moved on to the room she shared with her daughters and closed the door quietly behind her. She suspected that she'd just made the biggest mistake of her life but felt forced by circumstances to stand by her decision.

Chapter Thirteen

Daisy and the girls were out shopping with June and Nora in Portobello market. Weaving their way through the Saturday morning crowds, they purchased the weekend supply of fruit and vegetables, fresh flowers to brighten up the house, some fish and eggs, a joint of meat for Sunday dinner and a variety of other eatables.

They lingered at an antique stall where an oddly dressed man in a jauntily angled straw hat and a long black tailcoat was in the middle of an entertaining spiel on a rare item, a fine china cricket cage, which he claimed had been especially made for a rich oriental gentleman over two hundred years ago. According to the flamboyant trader's story, the man's servants would have collected the insects and put them into the cage where they would chirrup musically for the entertainment of their owner.

The crowd were taking a lively interest in what he was saying until the price of the unusual artefact was mentioned.

'Five quid for that piece o' junk? Don't make me laugh,' said someone.

'You'd have to pay me to take that lump o' rubbish off your hands,' added another.

'You want your head tested, mate, if you think anyone'll pay two bob for that, let alone five nicker,' came another disparaging utterance.

'Not very nice for the poor little crickets, being caged in,' was a typically soft-hearted reaction from Nora as the crowd began to disperse. 'Downright cruel, I reckon.'

'Have we finished then?' asked Daisy, as they were all weighed down with shopping bags.

Nora examined the list. 'Yes, that's about it for today,' she confirmed.

'I must just pop down to Notting Hill Gate to get my skirt from the dry-cleaner's,' June told them. 'I need it for work on Monday. You can start walking home if you like. I'll catch you up.'

'No. Let's all take a wander down there and have a cuppa coffee and a bun in the ABC,' suggested Daisy.

As the idea was greeted with approval, they left the market crowds behind and walked to the bustling shopping parade at Notting Hill Gate. While June went to Sketchleys, the others had a look round Woolworth's. Moving on past the Gaumont Cinema on their way to the teashop, Daisy noticed a sign in the window of an antique dealer's which read, 'STREET WIDENING MEANS WE MUST MOVE – STOCK CLEARANCE SALE.'

There were similar announcements in several of the shops around here.

'We won't recognise the old place when they've finished knocking it about, will we?' remarked Daisy.

'I hope we still can.' Nora looked concerned. 'It could do with smartening up but I hope they don't change it beyond recognition when they do finally do it.'

' "When" being the operative word,' expressed Daisy, because the Notting Hill Gate road widening and redevelopment scheme had been on the cards for years. 'The council have been talking about it for long enough.'

'Have they really?' enquired June, who had met them outside Woolworth's.

'The idea goes back to the last century,' informed the knowledgeable Nora, who was a member of a local history society and took a keen interest in local affairs. 'But it wasn't finally approved until the nineteen thirties, then it had to be postponed because of the outbreak of war. The latest news I've heard is that it's definitely scheduled to go ahead in the next year or two.'

'I'll believe that when I see it,' was Daisy's opinion.

'I think most people feel like that about it,' said Nora.

They reached the ABC – proudly declaring itself to be 'London's Popular Caterers' on the awning outside – and settled down at a table in the cafeteria with their elevenses.

'Just think, Daisy, a little over a week ago you were living it up by the seaside,' mentioned June conversationally, spreading a small pat of butter on her currant bun and trying, unsuccessfully, to make it reach the edges.

'I wouldn't call what we did "living it up" exactly,' said Daisy, sipping her coffee. 'It was all simple pleasure. But, yes, we were enjoying ourselves, weren't we, girls?'

'Cor, yeah,' enthused Shirley.

'I wish we were still there,' sighed Belinda.

'Are you telling us that you'd rather be at the seaside with Mummy than here at home with your Auntie June and me?' teased Nora.

'I'd rather we were all at Gullscombe Bay seaside than here,' the child clarified. 'You and Auntie June too.'

'So would I,' said her sister.

'Maybe the three of you can go again next year as you liked it so much,' suggested June, winking at the girls, then looking meaningfully at Daisy.

'We'll see.' Daisy was noncommittal but she knew she wouldn't go again. It would be far too complicated.

June gave her a close look. 'You did enjoy yourself, didn't you, Daisy?'

'Yeah, of course I did. Why?'

'Because the girls haven't stopped talking about it since they got back,' June pointed out. 'But you've been noticeably quiet.'

'I've told you, I had a wonderful time.'

'You certainly look better for it, anyway,' approved Nora.

'Positively blooming,' agreed June. 'Back at work and ready to take the world on.'

'That's right,' confirmed Daisy.

'Why so quiet then?' persisted June.

'Probably an anticlimax,' suggested Nora.

'You got on all right with Jack, didn't you?' June was being persistent because she wanted to make sure there had been no problems with the holiday she'd arranged for her sister. 'And everything was all right with the accommodation?'

'Everything was perfect at the cottage, and Jack and I got on like a house on fire.' Daisy hadn't been able to stop thinking about him all week, his wide smile, his warm eyes. Anticlimax wasn't the word for how she'd felt this past week. Hell would be nearer to it, without Jack around. Knowing she'd made the right decision – or rather the only possible decision – didn't help much either.

Nat had picked up on her mood this past week. He'd accused her of being preoccupied and not paying enough attention to him, which he thought was a bit much as he'd agreed to her going away and had even shelled out some spending money. He hadn't seemed particularly pleased with the cigarette case she'd brought back for him either; he preferred to use fags straight from the packet, apparently. She'd been irritated by his ingratitude; had found herself comparing him to Jack. That was unfair and pointless, and would have to stop.

But now she found herself wondering what Jack would be doing at this moment. She looked at the big clock on the wall.

It was eleven o'clock. He wouldn't have gone to work yet so he might have gone for a swim or be tinkering with that motorbike of his. Whatever he was doing, she wished she was still there with him.

June recalled her to the present, waving her hand in front of Daisy's eyes. 'Penny for them,' she said.

'I was just wondering,' she fibbed – because what had happened between her and Jack was too precious and delicate to talk about at the moment, and the subject she was about to raise needed discussion anyway – 'if you've thought any more about that idea I mentioned to you about finding the Dodds? The one that Jack came up with?'

'Yes, I've thought about it.' June pondered for a moment. 'And although it's a bit of a long shot, I think we should do it. I don't know why we didn't think of it before.'

'Me neither.' Daisy turned to Nora. 'What do you think?'

'It's worth a try.'

'Good,' said Daisy. 'Let's have a proper discussion about it tonight when I get back from work.'

The two other women nodded in agreement.

'In the meantime, let's finish here and get the shopping home,' Daisy suggested. 'I'm on duty at four o'clock this afternoon to serve the teas so it would be useful to me if we could have our lunch a bit early, if that's all right with you.'

'Sure,' agreed June.

'Suits me,' added Nora.

They left the café soon after, chatting in a friendly manner. But Daisy wasn't paying attention to what was being said; her thoughts were lingering on a certain cottage by the sea.

Jack was thinking about Daisy at that time too. He was washing his hands at the kitchen sink after messing about with his motorbike when he noticed the laughing duck grinning at him from the windowsill.

303

He dried his hands and picked it up, remembering the moment he'd received it and feeling again the joy that had filled the house at that time. It brought Daisy so close to him he could hear her laugh, smell her hair, feel her skin. He put the ornament back on the windowsill, smiling despite the mood of melancholy that had settled over him since Daisy and the girls had left. He couldn't have Daisy and that broke his heart. But they'd had two wonderful weeks together and if that was all there was, it was better than nothing.

Grinning to himself as he recalled Daisy's disgust at his taste in ornaments, he made a cup of coffee and took it into the garden to read the newspaper in the sunshine until it was time to get ready for work.

One autumn morning in the back garden of a small house in a quiet Ruislip street, a thin, grey-haired woman wearing a floral apron over a dowdy grey jumper and skirt, was pegging the last of her washing on the line. She was hoping that her next-door neighbour – who was also in her garden doing the same thing – wouldn't try to engage her in conversation over the fence. It was a Monday morning so washing was flapping in the wind in rear gardens the length of the street.

Her hopes were dashed when the neighbour said, 'Good morning.'

'G'morning,' responded Eileen Dodd coolly.

'Looks like it's gonna be a good drying day,' commented the neighbour in a friendly manner.

'Mm.'

'And thank God for that too,' the woman went on. 'Nothing worse than a wet Monday, is there? Wet washing all over the place, making everything steamy and damp. It always gives me the right hump.'

'Yeah.' Eileen kept her eyes down; she never looked at anyone when she spoke to them.

'There won't be many more nice days now that the summer is over,' the neighbour went on.

'I suppose not.' Eileen was moving towards the kitchen door as she spoke, in her eagerness to avoid any further dialogue. 'Ta-ta for now.'

'Ta-ta dear,' said the neighbour. 'See you again.'

Indoors Eileen made a sandwich with cold meat from yesterday's joint for her lunch, poured herself a cup of tea and went into the living room to eat it, her hand trembling slightly from the fright she had just had at being forced into conversation. That was what she had come down to: she was so introverted that just a few words with a next-door neighbour left her nerves in tatters. Any sort of social intercourse was difficult for Eileen, who was in her fifties and hadn't a friend in the world. It was just her and her husband, Morris, against the rest of the world.

Though that wasn't strictly true, she thought, slowly eating her sandwich. Morris wasn't with her against the world. He had a life of his own outside the house. As a representative for a fancy goods company, he met lots of people in the course of his work; he enjoyed a drink and a chat at the local, too. A gregarious man like Morris was never short of company.

Eileen hadn't always been a recluse. Years ago she'd had a normal life in Wembley with a happy marriage – or so she'd thought – and a social life.

Her life had changed so suddenly it was hardly believable in retrospect. One minute they'd been living an ordinary life in a quiet suburban street, the next they were the talk of the neighbourhood, her husband implicated in a murder case and his betrayal of his wife made public property by the newspapers. Immediately after the trial, they'd fled to an area where they weren't known. Morris would have been quite happy to stay put but she hadn't been able to cope with the shame, the gossip, the humiliation.

She'd known nothing of her husband's adultery with Rose Rivers until after the murder. The devastation she'd felt then still sent shock waves through her whenever it came into her mind. Rose had been a neighbour and friend. Suddenly she was Morris's dead lover. The whole terrible business had torn the heart out of Eileen; she'd never got over it.

The scandal of being associated with a murder investigation had never appeared to worry Morris. He'd even seemed to enjoy the notoriety. 'I've done nothing to be ashamed of, Eileen, except for being unfaithful to you, and that's nothing to do with anyone else,' he would say to her as she became increasingly reclusive. 'Lionel Rivers killed his wife, not me, and he's doing time for it. So there's no need for either of us to hide away. Nobody around here knows about our past, anyway.'

It was as though he actually believed that neither of them had done anything wrong in lying under oath. He'd made a great performance of regret over the death of his lover and remorse at his adultery when giving evidence at Lionel Rivers' trial. After that he just carried on with his life as though nothing much had happened, as though having his wife commit perjury for him was no more than her duty.

At the time, he'd told her it would make things easier if she said he was at home with her when the murder had taken place. She was to tell the court that he'd come home early from the pub because he'd not been feeling well and had got home just after nine, having left the pub just before nine, as verified by the barman. He'd told her that he'd walked the streets for hours, after leaving the pub, working out how he was going to end his affair with Rose Rivers. But he couldn't prove where he'd been at that time and people might get the wrong idea. He was at pains to convince her that the only reason he'd asked her to say he'd been home at the earlier time instead of much later on, after she'd gone to bed, was not because he'd done the murder. Oh, no. It was just to prevent the police putting two and two together and making five.

In retrospect, she could see that she'd been extremely gullible to have believed him, and she didn't think she ever had, not in her heart. But telling herself what he said was true had been more acceptable than the alternative. It was hardly bearable for a woman to suspect that she was married to a murderer. As well as the horror, fear and revulsion, there were practical considerations. She was reliant on him to provide for her. If he'd gone to prison, her life would have been ruined as well as his because she would have had no means of support. Only the poorest or most exceptional married women had gone out to work back in those days before the war.

So she'd complied with his wishes, telling herself she was merely preventing complications and not protecting a murderer. Once the lies had been uttered in court, there had been no going back. She'd never forget the sheer terror of knowing that she had committed a criminal offence. She'd tried to blot out her crime and get on with life in an area where no one knew them. But compunction and fear had plagued her constantly, making her bitter and depressed. The Dodds' home had become a battleground for its occupants.

Then one night during an argument, Morris had confessed to the murder in a fit of temper. He'd even boasted about it. Even though he'd let it slip in a moment of reckless rage, he'd not been too concerned because he'd known his secret was safe with her. As he'd taken great pains to point out, she had too much to lose to open her mouth. If she went to the police she'd go down with a prison sentence for perjury.

So she'd remained silent, the past standing between them, a chilling and tangible presence. They coexisted with cold indifference and occasional violent arguments. She'd grown to hate him more with every passing day, loathing him for his arrogance, his unfaithfulness, his cruelty and cowardice in letting someone else pay the price for his crime. They slept in separate bedrooms and any sort of physical contact between them was carefully avoided apart from when he lost his temper and knocked her about. She guessed he made other arrangements in the sexual department. That didn't bother her. After the terrible things he'd done, continued adultery was nothing.

The only thing that kept them together was mutual fear. She was afraid of life without him as breadwinner; he feared she might put them both in jail if he wasn't on hand to remind her of the serious consequences for herself should she get tempted to unburden her guilty conscience.

Self-loathing for her weakness had made her withdraw into herself. Even when she was forced to work during the war, she'd not mixed with her workmates at the factory. The people around here knew nothing of her past but she still felt set apart from them, whilst at the same time longing for friendship. Her only outings were to the local shops, an occasional visit to the doctor and dentist and a rare trip to a hairdresser's for a perm. If she happened to meet a neighbour she couldn't avoid while she was out, she greeted them briefly then escaped into the security of her home. Fortunately, in this quiet suburban neighbourhood, people tended to keep to themselves anyway. The loneliness was terrible, though. It nagged away at her like a physical pain day after day.

But now she finished her lunch and picked up the newspaper, which they had delivered every day because Morris liked to read it in the evening. She always looked through it; it helped pass the time in her isolation.

Some film star called James Dean had been killed in a car crash at the age of just twenty-four, she noted. She'd read about him in the paper but not seen any of his films because she never went to the cinema. There was also an article about the new television programme called *Double Your Money* with Hughie Green. That was something she did have experience of, because Morris had done so well with sales recently, he'd bought a television set for the opening of commercial television, a week or so ago.

She flicked through the rest of the paper absently, thinking she must get on and wash the dishes, then give the kitchen a thoroughly good clean prior to the washing being dry enough to iron. Very much a slave to routine, she hated to deviate from her daily pattern. She was about to put the paper down on the coffee table ready for Morris to look at tonight, when something towards the back, in the personal column, leaped out at her. She blinked, thinking she must have imagined it. She stared hard at the print again, finding it difficult to focus because her hands were shaking so much.

'Would Eileen Dodd, last heard of at number three Laverstock Avenue, Wembley, in the 1930s please get in touch with Box No. 3350.'

Her initial reaction was a feeling of hope for escape from the prison she was in. One of her old friends from Wembley must want to get in touch with her for a reunion. It must be that. Who else would be trying to contact her? Warmth spread through her. How good it felt to have someone seeking her company, someone she'd have something in common with because she'd known them when her life had been normal. She'd had some good friends in Wembley at one time. But she hadn't been able to face them after what had happened so had cut herself off from them. When she and Morris had left the area they hadn't said goodbye to anyone or left a forwarding address.

But now someone was looking for her. On the heels of joy came disappointment. She couldn't respond to this. Anyone she knew from Wembley would know about her past. They didn't know the whole truth, of course, but they knew about Morris's public betrayal of her. She would be a laughing stock all over again and she simply couldn't face it.

But she looked longingly at the advertisement. Here was a chance to have company after all these years in the wilderness. To visit friends for tea, to go shopping with someone, all the ordinary everyday things other women took for granted. She stared at the words through a blur of tears as she accepted that she couldn't reply to it.

As a precaution, she carefully tore the advertisement out of the paper. If Morris spotted it he would force her to reply to it to see if there was anything of a financial nature in it for them, as was often the case when someone was being traced in this way. He would humiliate her all over again. She then screwed the piece of paper up and stuffed it in her apron pocket, collected her cup and plate and went to the kitchen to wash them.

'It doesn't look as though our plan is going to bear fruit, does it?' said Daisy gloomily, over a cup of bedtime cocoa one night in mid-October.

'It doesn't seem too hopeful,' agreed her sister, who was sitting on the sofa in her dressing gown with her legs curled under her. 'It's been two weeks since the advertisement went into the paper. If she was going to take the bait she'd have done so by now.'

'Not necessarily,' disagreed Nora. 'She could be busy and still trying to find the time to get down to writing a letter. For all we know she might be out at work all day.'

'That's true,' said Daisy. 'We have no idea what her circumstances are. Or even if she's alive.'

'Maybe she smelled a rat,' suggested June. 'Or her husband saw the advertisement and he did. It could be that they're staying well clear, to be on the safe side.'

'I honestly don't think it's that,' was Daisy's opinion. 'As we agreed when we decided to give this a try, they wouldn't connect a notice in the personal column of a national newspaper with the murder. They'd think in terms of the police if anything had arisen about that. Anyway, it's such a long while ago she wouldn't expect anything to happen about it after all this time.'

'She'll think it's a friend or relative she's lost touch with, as we planned,' said Nora. 'That's the sort of thing personal columns are made up of. Unless, of course, they think someone's left them some money.'

'In which case they definitely would have got in touch,' reasoned Daisy.

'Maybe she just didn't see it,' was another idea of Nora's. 'It could be that she doesn't read that particular paper. I think if she did see it, she couldn't help but be intrigued. I mean, you would be, wouldn't you? That's just natural human curiosity.'

'Perhaps the second entry will bring us a result,' suggested Daisy hopefully. 'We got cheap rates for having it in twice so it isn't as if it cost us all that much more.'

'If it doesn't work we could think in terms of trying another one of the nationals,' said June.

There was a murmur of agreement from the others.

'It's going in on Friday this time instead of Monday,' mused Nora. 'Being a different day of the week might help. Some people have days when they don't have time to look at the paper and other days when they do.'

'Fingers crossed for Friday then,' said June.

'And in the meantime,' yawned Daisy, finishing her cocoa and standing up, 'my bed is calling.'

The others were of similar opinions so they took their cups into the kitchen, turned off the lights and went upstairs to bed.

★ ★ ★

June couldn't sleep but it wasn't thoughts of finding the Dodds that were keeping her awake. It was Alan. Every time she closed her eyes she could see his face, his warm eyes, his tender smile. The images just wouldn't go away. She wondered if she would ever stop missing him. Even now, more than a year since she'd left, she still wasn't over him.

Inevitably he would find someone else. Indeed, that was why she'd left, so that he could have a chance of a normal family life with a 'proper' woman. Maybe he was already seeing someone. She wouldn't blame him. The thought hurt even though she knew she was being unreasonable. Weary of tossing and turning, she got out of bed and made her way quietly downstairs, careful not to disturb anyone. She was in the kitchen waiting for the kettle to boil when her sister appeared.

'Another one who's tired of counting sheep, eh?' June surmised.

'That's right.'

'What's keeping you from your beauty sleep then?'

'Nothing in particular,' fibbed Daisy, because if she were to tell June the truth – that she'd been kept awake tonight and many other nights since her holiday by thoughts of Jack, whose marriage proposal she had turned down because she'd been afraid to let go of the past and move into a new, unfamiliar world – June would erupt into a fury of disapproval. Daisy had enough trouble coping with the decision herself; the last thing she needed was an argument about it. 'How about you?'

'I don't know what it is,' lied June, because she was dangerously close to confiding in her sister about the series of events that had led to her decision to leave Alan. She wanted to tell her everything she'd kept locked inside her for so many years. But to share the hideous secrets of her past in a weak moment would make her feel vulnerable and she knew she would regret it.

'Tea is supposed to keep you awake,' mentioned Daisy. 'But I'm going to have one anyway.'

'I'll risk it too,' said June.

They drank their tea at the kitchen table in a comfortable silence, each lost on her own thoughts. Then they made their way back upstairs to bed.

Alan was awake too that night, thinking first about June, then wondering what to do about Paula, whom he'd been seeing with increasing regularity since the late summer.

He cast his mind back to the previous evening. He and Paula had been out to a restaurant and he'd driven her home afterwards to the smart block of flats overlooking the sea where she lived. They'd sat in his car talking about business, as they so often did, and discussing the pros and cons of living on the job, which she preferred not to do. Although the conversation hadn't been of an intimate nature, he'd felt a change in the air and sensed that they'd been just a hair's breadth away from becoming lovers.

She'd invited him in for coffee. He'd wanted to accept but had politely declined because he'd known what would happen if he had, and wasn't sure if he wanted all the emotional upheaval that a change from friends to lovers would entail. He wasn't in love with Paula but he liked and respected her far too much to have an affair with her without commitment.

They were both on their own. He was lonely and so, he suspected, was she. His wife didn't want him. From the signals Paula was giving out lately she obviously wouldn't be adverse to a change in their relationship. So why not?

Looking at the question logically, he could see that Paula was the way forward for him. They would be good for each other. June wasn't going to change her mind, and he couldn't avoid a serious attachment for the rest of his life just because his marriage had failed.

One thing he did know for sure: he and Paula could no longer be just friends. It wouldn't work that way now that another element had made itself known. He sighed, sensing a certain inevitability about the situation.

'Oh no, not again,' complained Morris Dodd, staring through a large hole in the newspaper he was reading. 'I wish you wouldn't keep tearing great lumps out of the paper before I've had a chance to look at it, Eileen.'

'I didn't think it would matter as there was nothing of interest on the other side,' she told him. 'It was only an advert for cough mixture. I did check.'

'That isn't the point,' he grumbled. 'It makes the paper in such a mess and you know how I hate that.'

'Sorry.'

'It isn't as if it's the first time you've done it lately,' he went on irritably.

'I've said I'm sorry.'

'What was so important you had to tear it out, anyway?' he demanded.

'A recipe,' she lied.

'Oh really. Surely you could have left the paper intact until after I'd read it,' he admonished sternly. 'You could have torn your bloody stupid recipe out any time.'

'I can't see that it matters as there was nothing you'd want to see on the other side.'

'Well, it does matter to me,' he growled. 'You can do what you like with the bloody paper when I've looked at it but until then show a bit of respect, will you? As I pay the newsagent's bill I think I'm entitled to that much.'

'All right, there's no need to go on about it.'

He scowled at her, grunted and went back to the paper

314

while Eileen stared absently at the wooden box in the corner. There was a serious play on the television and Morris didn't enjoy drama, apart from *Dixon of Dock Green*. Although the television set was still something of a novelty, Morris was selective in his viewing. He didn't like anything more demanding than sport, light comedy and variety shows.

Something seemed to have attracted his attention now, though, and he put the paper on his lap and stared at the screen. Eileen found herself observing him and thinking that he could still be considered an attractive man even though he was now in his fifties, and despite the fact that his dark hair was thinning and his figure gargantuan from his greedy appetite for food. He'd never been good-looking in the traditional sense – his dark eyes were too small, his nose too long. It was his personality that attracted women. He had a magnetism about him that was still very much in evidence, she guessed, even though it did nothing for her.

Eileen was having trouble concentrating on the television screen tonight, on account of what had really been on the bit she'd torn out of Morris's newspaper. Whoever it was who was looking for her must be serious about finding her to have put the notice in the paper again. Advertising in a national newspaper wasn't cheap. As well as being intriguing it was also rather worrying because if they put it in again and she missed it for some reason, Morris would spot it and take the matter out of her hands. The thought made her stomach churn.

But now he was bored with both the paper and the television apparently. 'I'm going out, down the pub,' he announced, getting up purposefully.

There was nothing new in that. It was Friday night and he always went out on Fridays. Whether he really went to the pub or had something of a more intimate nature lined up, she neither knew nor cared.

'All right,' she said indifferently.

'Don't wait up.'

'I won't.'

After the front door had closed behind him, she stayed where she was for a while, lost in thought. Eventually, she got up, went over to the sideboard and picked up her handbag. Hesitating for only a moment, she opened it and took out the crumpled piece of newspaper she'd removed earlier today and looked at it for a long time. Then, with her heart palpitating fit to burst, she took a writing pad out of the drawer, sat down at the table and began to write a letter, her hand trembling with a mixture of nervous apprehension and excitement.

Chapter Fourteen

Answering a knock at the front door one morning a week or so later, Eileen was confronted by two young women smiling at her on the doorstep.

'Yes?' she greeted in a cool, questioning manner.

'Good morning,' smiled the smarter of the two, who was tall, dark and slim, and carrying a small, brown attaché case.

'What do you want?' tutted Eileen, who wasn't about to indulge in doorstep small talk.

'We represent the Smithsons Vacuum Cleaner Company and we're in this area to tell people about the launch of our revolutionary new machine—'

'No thank you,' Eileen interrupted sharply. 'I already have a very good vacuum cleaner and I don't want another one.'

'But ours is no ordinary cleaner—'

'I never buy anything at the door.'

'And we don't sell at the door,' said the other woman, who was a tiny little thing, a bit on the shabby side, with big eyes and a shock of brown wind-blown hair.

'Why are you here then?'

The little woman moved closer to the door, which Eileen was about to close. 'Just for an informal chat.' She spread her hands. 'As you can see we have no cleaner with us to sell to you.'

'I don't care what sales pitch you're using,' the astute

Eileen made clear. 'I said no and I mean it.'

'Would we be right in thinking that the man of the house isn't home at this time of the day?' the dark woman enquired.

'Of course he isn't at home,' was Eileen's sharp retort. 'He's out earning his living, like any other responsible man.'

'That's why we call on people during the day, initially. We like to speak to the lady of the house about our product,' said the little woman, her manner becoming chummy. 'As women, we all know that men haven't a clue about how housework is done so we prefer to speak to the people who actually do the job. A sensible idea, don't you think, Mrs, er . . .'

'Dodd,' she said without thinking. 'And yes, it is a good idea but I'm still not going to buy a cleaner.'

'Look, I'll be straight with you.' The small woman moved her head forward and spoke to Eileen in a confiding manner. 'My colleague and I have to do a certain amount of preliminary presentations in the course of a working day, or we're in deep trouble back at the office. So . . .' she paused, smiling persuasively, 'I wonder if you could do us a favour and give us a few minutes of your time just so that we can put you down on our list of definite visits and stay sweet with the management.'

Eileen gave them full marks for persistence. She'd been married to a salesman for long enough to know that without tenacity you got nowhere in the job. Morris didn't sell door to door but the same principle applied to any form of selling. 'I'm too busy,' she said firmly. 'I'm sorry.'

'Ten minutes maximum,' the dark-haired woman requested insistently. 'Just let us come in to show you a few brochures, tell you how this new concept in cleaners works. Just so that we can put you down on our activity report for today.'

'And talk me into buying one of your cleaners at the same time,' was Eileen's cynical response.

'No, not at all,' denied the little one, who had a very pretty

318

smile Eileen couldn't help noticing. 'Honestly, that isn't what we have in mind.'

'My husband has all the spending power in this house anyway, so you'd be on to a loser.'

'The men usually do,' the small woman agreed in an understanding manner. 'They earn the money so they say how it's going to be spent – that's the way it seems to work in most of the homes that we visit, anyway. So our policy is to tell the lady of the house about the cleaner and if they like what we have to say and are interested in seeing the cleaner, we come back in the evening when the husband is at home to do a demonstration for them both. In your case, of course, that won't happen because you've told us that you definitely don't want to buy one, and we respect that. So we'll just run through some brochures with you, fill in our time sheet and be on our way.'

'There wouldn't be any point in your coming back at another time with the cleaner because my husband won't buy from anyone selling door to door, anyway,' Eileen stated.

'That's perfectly understandable,' said the dark woman in a matey tone. 'Some of the door-to-door salespeople around give the rest of us a bad name by talking people into buying all sorts of rubbish. But we're not like that. Oh no. And in your case, all we want is your co-operation in keeping the boss off our backs. Just the chance to go through our brochures with you. You've nothing to lose except ten minutes of your time.'

Eileen looked from one to the other; she was beginning to weaken under the influence of their friendly enthusiasm. It was a refreshing change to have females selling at the door. Most of those working on the knocker were men who wouldn't take no for an answer until she slammed the door in their faces.

These two were persistent but nice with it, somehow. She

thought of the lonely day ahead of her with not a soul to talk to. What harm could there be in letting them in for a few minutes to show her some brochures and tell her about their product? At least it would be human contact, and she'd made it clear that she wasn't going to buy from them.

'Ten minutes then,' she said, opening the door wider to let them in. 'When your time's up, you're out. Understand?'

'We understand,' said the small woman.

'Come on then, let's have a look at your brochures,' requested Eileen when she'd shown the two sales reps into the living room and offered them a seat.

The dark women opened her attaché case to reveal that it was empty. 'We don't have any brochures,' she said, turning the case upside down and shaking it to illustrate her point, her attitude now deadly serious.

'No brochures?' Eileen looked puzzled and somewhat annoyed. 'Why bother to talk me into letting you in then? How can you sell your cleaner without the product itself, or any sales literature?'

'We're not here to sell you a vacuum cleaner, Mrs Dodd,' said the little one.

'No?' Eileen was baffled. 'Then why—'

'We're here about this,' the dark woman told her, handing Eileen a newspaper cutting.

Eileen stared at it for a moment. 'You?' she said, looking from one to the other. 'You put that in the paper?'

'That's right,' the little one confirmed.

She gave them both a studious look, searching for some sort of recognition. 'I don't know you, so what was the advertisement all about?'

'We needed to find you urgently,' explained the dark-haired one. 'And now we have, thanks to your putting your address on your letter.'

'So it was all a trick to get into my house.' Eileen looked frightened now.

'Afraid so,' confirmed Daisy. Had they just knocked at her door and told her who they were, it would have been immediately slammed in their faces, which was why the rather elaborate subterfuge had been necessary.

'Who are you?' she demanded, her grey eyes darting from one to the other. 'What do you want with me?'

'I'm Daisy Rivers and this is my sister, June.'

Eileen's eyes popped. Her face flushed momentarily, then became bloodless. She sat down heavily on the sofa as though her legs had buckled beneath her. 'Rose Rivers's daughters,' she gasped, her hand flying to her head. 'I would never have known you.'

'Well, you wouldn't do, would you?' June pointed out. 'Being that we were just little kids when you last saw us.'

'What,' Eileen began in a dry anxious voice, 'do you want with me after all this time?'

'Justice,' announced Daisy.

'Justice?' Eileen echoed fearfully, her eyes clouded with worry.

'That's right,' confirmed June. 'Our father has been in prison for over twenty years for the murder of our mother because you lied under oath to give your husband an alibi. And we intend to see to it that you put things right.'

The older woman sprang to her feet. She was visibly trembling. 'Get out,' she ordered in a quivering voice. 'Get out of my house this minute, before I call the police.'

Daisy gave her a hard look. 'We're not going anywhere until you've heard what we have to say,' she told her in a commanding tone. 'So sit down.'

'How dare you tell me what to do in my own house?'

'Sit down,' repeated Daisy.

'I could have you done for slander, saying I lied under

321

oath,' protested Eileen weakly.

'You won't, though, will you? Because you know what we're saying is true.'

'I didn't do it,' Eileen insisted, sinking down on the sofa. 'I don't know what's made you think I did.'

'We don't just *think* you lied,' June amended evenly, 'we *know* you did.'

'Don't be ridiculous, you can't do.'

'We know that you were lying about your husband being at home with you at the time of our mother's murder because he was at the house where we lived,' Daisy informed her. 'And we know that because we saw him there.'

'Rubbish.'

'He saw us too,' June enlightened her. 'He threatened us with terrible things if we told anyone we'd seen him.'

From the look of sheer horror on Eileen's face it was obvious that Morris had told her nothing of his encounter with them that terrible night.

'He didn't tell you anything about that, did he?' surmised June.

'There was nothing to tell me,' she bluffed. 'Because he wasn't at that house that night. As I told the court at the trial, he was at home with me.'

'Look,' began Daisy, stepping forward and looking down at her, 'all three of us know that isn't true so let's stop messing about.'

'Get out,' ordered Eileen again.

'It was your husband who murdered our mother and you damned well know it,' persisted Daisy. 'And it's time that terrible wrong was put right.'

'You've been imagining things,' claimed Eileen. 'You were just children back then. You couldn't possibly remember something that happened then, not after all this time.'

'We couldn't forget a thing like that,' June told her. 'Your husband put the fear of God into us in his anxiety to make sure we didn't spill the beans about his being there. We were too young to be questioned anyway so he was safe. As children we were powerless and no threat to him even though he was worried enough to terrorise us into keeping quiet. He made one fatal mistake, though. He didn't take into account the fact that one day we would grow up to be adults, and we would remember, and understand.'

'Childhood fantasies, nothing more,' Eileen taunted, becoming braver as she considered the flimsiness of their evidence. 'No one would believe a story like that.'

'Why did you commit perjury for such a man?' Daisy wanted to know. 'A man who had been unfaithful to you and humiliated you publicly, a man who killed his lover in a fit of rage. Was it because you were afraid of what he'd do to you if they didn't send him down for murder, was that it?'

'Or were you afraid of losing your breadwinner and your comfortable life?' added June.

The older woman didn't reply; she just sat there staring at her hands.

'If you were to make a confession to the police about what you've done and make it clear that your husband put pressure on you to lie for him, the courts might be lenient with you,' suggested Daisy hopefully.

Eileen clasped her head as though in pain. 'Stop it, stop saying these terrible things,' came her anguished cry. 'You tricked your way into my home and now you're behaving in a threatening manner. I could have the law on you.'

'You won't, though.' Daisy was confident about that. 'Because you wouldn't want to draw attention to yourself. You had enough of that in the past, when you lived in Wembley.'

'You've got nothing on me and my husband,' Eileen insisted, composing herself, 'so get out of my house.'

'We'll go,' complied Daisy. 'But just one thought before we leave, Mrs Dodd. For all these years you've thought you'd got away with what you've done, believing it was just a matter between you and your conscience, that no one else knew. But you won't be able to rest easy any longer because you know that we know the truth, and one way or another we'll see that justice is done. You could make things easier for yourself by telling the police the truth because it's going to come out anyway, I promise you.'

'You're talking rubbish,' Eileen blustered. 'No one would take you seriously if you were to come out with your outlandish story.' She narrowed her eyes on Daisy. 'And you know that. Otherwise you'd have gone to the police already.'

She was right, of course, but Daisy wasn't going to admit it. 'What does it feel like to live with a murderer, knowing that you helped to put an innocent man behind bars, and robbed two little girls of their father?' she asked.

'I don't know what that feels like because I haven't experienced it.' Eileen was adamant. 'And if you stay here all day you won't get me to say different, so you might as well sling your hook.'

'We're going,' Daisy told her, moving towards the living-room door. 'But you haven't seen the last of us or heard the last of this matter, believe me.'

'We'll be back,' added June.

And they walked to the front door and let themselves out, leaving Eileen sitting on the sofa.

'You're bound to be disappointed that nothing more constructive came out of it,' said Nora that evening when, over cocoa, the three of them were doing a post-mortem on the incident. 'But we all knew she wouldn't admit to anything right away, didn't we? It was unrealistic to think that she would. It'll take time.'

'I suppose so, but it's such an anticlimax,' complained Daisy. 'I thought we were home and dry when we found out where the Dodds lived. But we're no further forward. Unless she admits she was lying we don't have a case. We got her rattled and we can do so again and again, but we can't make her confess.'

'What should our next move be, do you think?' wondered June.

'I honestly don't know,' confessed Daisy. 'It needs more thought. The one thing we mustn't do is give up now we've come this far.' She looked at June. 'Do you agree?'

'Absolutely.'

Daisy burst out laughing as she remembered something. 'I wonder what our chances are as vacuum cleaner sales reps,' she giggled.

'As you managed to get through the door without so much as a brochure between you, or a cleaner to demonstrate, you must have had some sort of a flair,' smiled Nora.

'We were pretty convincing,' boasted Daisy.

'All that stuff you gave her about us being in trouble at the office if she didn't let us in to do a presentation was nothing short of genius,' grinned June. 'I almost believed it myself.'

'I had to think on my feet when she seemed determined not to let us in.'

'It was brilliant,' complimented June.

Daisy's mood became grim again. 'Seriously, though, we have to think of a way to finish the job we've started. Now that we've come this close and found Eileen Dodd, there must be a way to get her to admit the truth.'

The other two women nodded in agreement but none of them knew the answer.

Nat came to the house late one night a few days later. He said he just happened to be passing and had called in to see Daisy.

'She isn't home from work yet,' June told him at the door.

'I'll come in and wait then,' he took it on himself to announce. 'She shouldn't be long.'

'Why don't you go and meet her?' suggested June, who didn't feel comfortable with him in the house after that disgusting incident in the summer when Daisy had been away on holiday. It hadn't been mentioned but she could tell by the way he looked at her sometimes that he hadn't forgiven her for rejecting him. 'She can't be further than the end of the street and she'll be thrilled to have you walk the rest of the way home with her.'

'Nah. It isn't worth it,' he said. 'She'll be here in a minute.'

Not wishing to be found quarrelling with him by her sister, June invited him in with reluctance, offered him a seat in the living room, and made herself scarce in the kitchen so that she didn't have to be alone with him. Nora was upstairs getting ready for bed and would probably come down in her dressing gown for a cup of cocoa later when Daisy got in.

June used the time to wash some cups from earlier and tidy the kitchen. She was drying her hands at the sink when the door opened and Nat swaggered in with a purposeful air.

'You after a cup of tea?' she asked. 'I thought you'd wait and have one with Daisy.'

'I don't want a cuppa tea.'

As his manner suggested that he'd come into the kitchen for some definite purpose, she said, 'What do you want then?'

'Isn't it obvious?'

'Not to me, no.'

'Surely you didn't think I'd forgotten what happened between us in the summer.'

'Nothing happened.'

'Exactly,' he said, coming towards her with a horrible smile on his face. 'And I aim to change that.'

326

'Daisy will be in any minute, so don't try anything.' She tried to sound firm but her voice was shaking.

'I'm not worried about Daisy.'

There was something very stage-managed about the way he was behaving that June found disconcerting.

'You touch me and I'll scream for Nora,' she warned. 'I mean it, so don't come any closer.'

But he moved so swiftly she didn't have a chance to do anything as he pushed her backwards against the sink, pressing his body against hers and clamping his hand over her mouth. Her heart sank as she distantly heard the sound of the front door opening and closing and Daisy's cheerful voice calling out, 'Hello, you lot, I'm home.'

June struggled but the element of surprise and his physical strength meant she didn't stand a chance. He dragged her arms around his neck and put his face to hers for a few horrible seconds, the smell of his sweat and stale cigarette smoke making her nauseous. She heard the kitchen door open and almost immediately he sprang away from her.

'Daisy,' he said, as though shocked to see her. 'Thank God you're back. She's been coming on to me for months . . . just wouldn't take no for an answer. Perhaps she'll stop now you've caught her at it.'

'Don't listen to him,' said June, observing with dismay the horror in her sister's eyes. 'He's lying because he wants to come between you and me. He knew you'd be home from work at any minute and he set this whole thing up.'

June reeled at the disgust exuding from Daisy as she looked from one to the other, then back at June, her eyes narrowed. 'Don't try and make any more of a fool of me than you already have,' she said to her sister icily.

'Daisy, no, it isn't what you think.'

'You're nothing but a tart, a filthy, rotten tart. I don't know why I ever trusted you.'

'It was him, please believe me . . .' June could feel her truthful words distorted to sound like lies by the damning appearance of the situation. 'He tried it on with me while you were away in Devon and he's done this to get back at me for turning him down then. He isn't interested in me. He just wants to hurt me by turning you against me.'

'I know now why you've never had a good word to say for him,' Daisy went on through gritted teeth. 'You wanted him for yourself so you tried to turn me against him and break us up, you scheming cow.'

'That just isn't true.' June's voice was ragged with emotion. 'Can't you see what he's up to?'

'I can see what's been going on under my nose. That was made very clear to me as soon as I opened this door.' She turned to Nat, who was looking triumphant. 'And as for you, I don't suppose you put up much of a fight against her. So get out of my sight. I never want to see you again.'

'What on earth's going on here?' asked Nora, appearing in her red dressing gown. 'You'll wake the children up in a minute with all this shouting.'

'Did you know about it?' asked Daisy.

'Know about what?'

'That these two have been at it like rabbits every time my back is turned,' she explained.

'Daisy, what are you saying?' was Nora's shocked response.

'You obviously didn't know. Well, they've been having an affair behind my back.'

'No!' gasped Nora.

'Yes. It's true, and I've just caught them at it.' She looked from Nat to June, her eyes full of hurt. 'You're welcome to each other and I want nothing more to do with either of you,' she said, and fled from the room.

Daisy sat on the edge of her bed, staring dismally at the floor. A grinding pain in the pit of her stomach was dragging her down, and she wasn't sure which hurt the most, Nat's betrayal or June's. She decided it was definitely the latter. She remembered that she herself has almost succumbed to temptation with Jack in the summer and knew how easily these things could happen. Nat had been unable to resist June's advances in the same way as Daisy had almost yielded to her passion for Jack.

Nobody was immune to this sort of thing. What cut so deep with Daisy was June's deceit in pretending to disapprove of Nat and trying to turn Daisy against him when all the time she fancied the pants off him herself.

There was a tap on the bedroom door.

'Go away.'

June came in anyway and stood tentatively just beside the closed door. 'I swear to God, Daisy, that it wasn't the way it seemed down there tonight,' she told her.

Her sister shrugged.

'Nat doesn't want me any more than I want him,' June went on to say, keeping her voice low because the girls were asleep in the next room. 'He hates the sight of me and I wouldn't have him if he came with the crown jewels as part of the package.'

'That's why you had your arms wrapped around him, is it?' said Daisy, looking up. 'God knows what I'd have seen if I'd been a few minutes later.'

'It was all a put-up job, can't you see that?' June tried to convince her. 'This is his revenge on me for turning him down in the summer, and he only came on to me then to try and make a fool of me.'

'Don't make things worse by telling me a pack of lies.'

'I am not lying,' June told her. 'He knew exactly what time you'd be in from work tonight, and that you'd go straight to the kitchen if there was no one in the living room. You can't deny that's true. He came in and grabbed hold of me just seconds before you walked in so that you would see what he wanted you to see. He's trying to break us up, Daisy.'

'I know he isn't perfect but he isn't devious enough to come up with such a plan.'

'He is, Daisy, believe me.'

Daisy didn't respond; she sat staring at her feet, leaning forward slightly, her hands resting on her knees. 'I was so happy when you came back into my life, June,' she said sadly. 'After all those years, it was a dream come true for us to be together. The only thing that spoiled it was your disapproval of Nat, and you and I agreed to differ about that.' She looked up, her huge eyes heavy with disappointment. 'I'm not glamorous or sophisticated like you. There's only ever been one man in my life.' She paused, forced by her honest nature to correct this. 'Well, two actually. I got pretty close to Jack Saunders back in the summer.'

'Oh, really?' gasped June.

'You might find this hard to believe, but Jack asked me to marry him,' Daisy continued.

'Why on earth would I find that hard to believe?' June asked in astonishment.

'Because I'm not beautiful or refined.'

'Don't put yourself down,' admonished June angrily. 'You're very beautiful in a way that doesn't need make-up or smart clothes, as I do, and your manners are fine. This is what Nat's done to you. He's destroyed your sense of self-worth.'

'Maybe he has, I don't know. Anyway, that isn't the issue,' she went on. 'I was very tempted by Jack's offer, I admit. He's a really gorgeous bloke and I think the world of him. But in the end I chose the father of my children, the man I've been with for so long and who I believe does actually love me, despite what you think of him. And you have to wreck that for me.'

'Daisy, about tonight—'

'I feel sick to my stomach,' Daisy went on as though June hadn't spoken. 'To think that my sister, my own flesh and blood, could try to steal him from me.'

'I didn't—'

'Just leave it, will you?' Daisy cut in, putting her hands to her head wearily. 'I don't want to talk about it any more except to say that me and the girls will be moving out of here as soon as I can find somewhere else.'

'Oh, Daisy, no, you can't . . .'

'Surely you can see that I can't stay here now,' Daisy told her. 'I don't want to share a roof with someone I can't trust.'

'You've got it all wrong.'

'Can you go now, please?' Daisy requested. 'Tell Nora I won't be down for cocoa tonight.'

Knowing it was useless to argue, a very dejected June left the room.

'You can cut the atmosphere in our place with a knife, the way those daughters of yours are carrying on, and I'm stuck in the middle of it,' Nora told Lionel, a week or so later. 'I think I'd be more comfortable sharing a cell with you than I am at home at the moment.'

He grinned. He enjoyed Nora's company and had grown to look forward to her visits. 'I very much doubt that. But what's the trouble at your place, then?'

She gave him a brief outline of what had happened. 'They're only speaking to each other when it can't be avoided and being polite in front of the children. It's breaking my heart to see them destroying something that means so much to them both. Finding each other after all those years apart was a gift. And now they're like two cats, wanting to scratch

331

each other's eyes out the whole time.' She shook her head worriedly. 'Daisy's even looking for somewhere else to live.'

'Oh dear.' Lionel could see how concerned she was. 'Which one of them do you think is to blame?'

'Certainly not June. Daisy's being stubborn but it isn't really her fault either. Nat's the culprit here,' she had no hesitation in telling him. 'He obviously set the whole thing up, as June said, to break the sisters up. He's jealous of Daisy's relationship with June. June wouldn't be interested in him if he was the last man on earth. Neither she nor I can stand the sight of him. But Daisy can't see that. She's got a blind spot where he's concerned.'

'Have you tried talking to her?'

'I certainly have,' she told him. 'And she just accuses me of taking June's side because she knows I don't like Nat either. He's just using her and she can't see it – doesn't want to see it. I tell you, Lionel, it's given me no end of grief over the years, watching the way that man treats your daughter.'

'Daisy always strikes me as such a sensible sort of a girl too, not the type to be easily taken in,' he mentioned.

'Her feelings for Nat cut across her intellect, I think,' Nora explained. 'In every other area of her life she's full of common sense and she certainly doesn't let people trample on her. She's tough and independent, and has her eyes wide open about everything except this awful man she's got herself involved with.'

'I only wish I was in a position to do something to help.' He stroked his chin, looking worried. 'But I'm helpless being stuck in here . . .'

'You wouldn't be able to help even if you weren't stuck in here,' she pointed out. 'No one can help them on this one. The girls have to sort it out for themselves. And unless Daisy faces up to what Nat is really like, I can't see it having a happy conclusion. And as she hasn't been able to see the truth about him after all these years, it isn't very likely to happen now.'

'What a shame.'

'It's an absolute tragedy.' Seeing how concerned he was she wondered if she'd done the right thing in telling him. 'Maybe I shouldn't have burdened you with it.'

'Don't be daft. I want news of my family, the bad as well as the good,' he assured her. 'I want to feel involved, even though I can't actually be there to help.'

Nora looked at him and saw hardship written all over that lined and craggy countenance. She so much wanted him to enjoy the pleasures of freedom again, to go out for a walk and feel the sun on his face. How good it would be if the girls were able to make this possible for him. They'd asked Nora not to tell him that they'd located the Dodds, partly because they didn't want to raise his hopes too high at this stage and also because he'd been so wary of them getting involved with Morris Dodd, it might worry him.

Anyway, with the girls being at loggerheads, Nora didn't know what would happen about their plans to help their father, except that they would continue, somehow, bad friends or not.

'You want to know about your family – I'll tell you what your granddaughters have been up to, then, shall I?' she suggested to cheer him up.

'Yes, please,' he said eagerly.

Ever since her falling out with June, Daisy had been studiously polite to her and very careful not to be rude to her in front of the children. So she was shocked to hear what Shirley had to say one morning at breakfast.

'Why are you and Auntie June always cross with each other now, Mummy?' she asked.

'What makes you think we're cross with each other?'

333

'You look cross and you don't seem to like each other much now,' she replied.

'We like each other,' said Daisy, exchanging a glance with her sister. 'Don't we, June?'

'Yes. Course we do.'

'Why are you being so horrid to one another then?' the child wanted to know.

'None of your business,' Daisy told her quickly. 'Now finish your breakfast, both of you. It's nearly time to go to school.'

'You're not supposed to be mean to people.' Shirley was determined to have her say. 'That's what you always tell me and Belinda when we have an argument. And that's what the nuns tell us at Sunday school.'

'Yeah, they do,' was Belinda's predictable contribution.

'Stop yapping, for goodness' sake, and finish your toast,' said Daisy, because she didn't want to have a lengthy discourse with a couple of children about something they weren't old enough to understand.

Daisy hated what was happening between her and June. It was tearing her apart. The barrier between them was more unbearable with every passing day. She wasn't an unforgiving woman; she wanted to put the whole thing behind them and carry on as before. But every time she thought of June and Nat together, anger flared towards June for destroying her trust. This battle was about Daisy and June rather than Daisy and Nat.

She'd valued the warmth of the burgeoning friendship with her sister and had looked forward to becoming closer in the future. All that had been swept away by June's betrayal. The last thing Daisy wanted was to move out of here, to drag the girls away from a home where they were happy to some awful little bedsit somewhere. But after what had happened, and the bitter resentment it had caused, she didn't think it would be fair to any of them to stay on. Every time she looked at June, she became angry and spiteful, and she didn't want to be like that.

Things had been going so well, too. Why had June had to destroy what they had? Was June to blame, though? she found herself wondering. Was it possible she could be telling the truth, after all? No, it couldn't be. Daisy had seen her and Nat together. You didn't have your arms wrapped around a man's neck if you were trying to fight him off. Anyway, Nat might be a bit of a bugger – and Daisy wasn't naïve enough to believe that he never flirted with other women – but he wasn't so lacking in principles that he'd go after her sister.

What about that story June had come out with about him setting the whole thing up with the deliberate intention of coming between the sisters to get back at June? No. It was too far-fetched to be true. Only a fool would believe such a story. Her racing thoughts stilled for a moment. Maybe that could work both ways; only a fool would make up such a story. And June certainly wasn't one of those.

Nat hadn't been near since the incident two weeks ago. Daisy knew him too well to think that he'd taken her literally when she'd told him she never wanted to see him again. He'd turn up eventually, like the proverbial bad penny. He'd be waiting for her to cool down before he dared to show his face.

She decided suddenly that she wasn't prepared to wait for him, with resentment and suspicion eating away at her day after day. If he wouldn't come to her, she'd go to him and have this thing out once and for all. And the sooner the better.

Turning her mind to more immediate matters, she checked that the children had had enough to eat and got them ready for school, feeling slightly better for having made the decision to take some positive action.

Chapter Fifteen

Eileen was stirring gravy in a saucepan on the stove for the evening meal when there was a knock at the front door. She muttered a mild expletive because the liquid was at the crucial thickening stage and would go lumpy if left unstirred. Hearing Morris answer the door, however, she relaxed.

'The window cleaner wants paying,' he informed her, coming into the kitchen.

'Oh,' she said in surprise, continuing to stir. 'I didn't even realise he'd been.'

'He did the windows this morning, apparently,' he said, sounding bored. 'You must have been out shopping or something.'

She tutted. 'If I leave this now, to come to see to him, it'll be ruined.'

In a tone of mild irritation, Morris said, 'All right, tell me where the money is and I'll deal with it.' Domestic expenses such as window cleaning came out of Eileen's housekeeping money.

'You'll have to get it out of my purse,' she told him absently, her concentration focused on the contents of the saucepan. 'It's in my handbag on the sideboard, I think.'

'Right.' He headed off in search of the handbag.

She heard him talking to the window cleaner briefly before he shut the front door. A few minutes later, he marched into the kitchen seething with aggression, and waved a screwed-up scrap of newspaper under her nose.

'Perhaps you'd like to explain this,' he demanded, scowling at her. 'It fell out of your bag when I got your purse out.'

She was so startled, she dropped the wooden spoon on the floor and splashed gravy all over the cooker top, splattering her hand and staining the front of her apron. 'Junk has a habit of building up in my bag,' she said, blowing on her scalded hand and managing to recover sufficiently to look unconcerned about his discovery. 'Stick it in the bin for me, would you?'

'This isn't just a bit of handbag junk,' he stated, his eyes narrowed on her accusingly. 'It's a newspaper cutting with your name on it.'

'Is it?' She turned the gas off under the saucepan and bent down to pick the spoon up off the floor, trying to gather her wits and find a way out of this.

'You know perfectly well it is,' he snapped.

Morris was no fool and she'd been stupid to deny it. But she'd been caught unawares and panicked because she was terrified he would find out that the Rivers sisters had tracked them down because she'd responded to their advert and put her address on the letter. 'All right, so I know what it is,' she confessed. 'That isn't a crime, is it?'

'Who's looking for you?' He gave her a hard look. 'Have you been left some money or something?'

'Don't be ridiculous,' she protested. 'Who do I know with anything to leave?'

It was such a valid point he couldn't argue with it. 'What is it all about then and why did you say nothing to me about it?' he wanted to know.

'I don't know what it's all about because I didn't reply to it,' she continued to lie. 'And I didn't tell you because it didn't seem worth mentioning.'

He narrowed his eyes on her suspiciously. 'Your name in the paper, not worth mentioning? Don't take me for a mug, Eileen. You know damned well who's looking for you.'

'Why would I lie about it?'

'I don't know, but I intend to find out.'

'There's nothing to find out.'

'You're up to something, and I'll find out what it is one way or another,' he warned her. 'So you might as well make things easy for yourself and tell me.'

'I don't know who put that advertisement in the paper but it's obviously someone from the old days, wanting a get-together or something,' she tried to fob him off, a strong sense of self-preservation forcing the lies out of her. 'And because I don't want to see anyone from the past, I didn't bother to follow it up.'

'Why keep the advert hidden in your handbag, then?' Morris demanded.

'It wasn't hidden. It just happened to be in there.' She cursed herself for forgetting the advertisement was in her bag and telling Morris to look in there. If he discovered the truth he'd lose his temper and that meant bruises aplenty for her. 'I wouldn't have told you to go to my bag if I was hiding anything in there, would I?'

There was a brief hiatus while he pondered on this. 'I suppose not.' He was still doubtful, though. 'But you bothered to tear it out of the paper so you must have considered it important.'

'I was curious, naturally. Anyone would be, seeing their name in the newspaper.'

She didn't manage to convince him. 'You're keeping something from me,' he growled, gripping her arms so hard she cried out in pain. 'And I won't give up until you tell me what it is.'

'Morris, please . . . you're hurting me.'

'I think you did answer that advert.' He put his face close to hers. 'So tell me who's looking for you. Tell me, woman, before I break both your arms.'

'I don't know.'

Stars exploded in her head as he punched her face; she cowered back from him.

'There's plenty more where that came from if you don't tell me the truth,' he warned her.

'Don't hit me any more, please,' she begged.

'I'll stop when you tell me the truth.'

He hit her again, then took hold of her arms and held them so tight she could feel them bruising. 'There's nothing to tell.' Her voice was little more than a gasp.

'Do yourself a favour and tell me what's been going on,' he demanded, 'or I'll beat it out of you.'

Despite her dread of the brutality she knew from past experience he was capable of, she had a sudden unexpected surge of spirit, the misery of more than twenty years culminating in a blaze of fury. She knew she had no choice but to tell him the truth but she decided not to do so meekly, since he would punish her anyway. 'All right, I'll tell you,' she said, her voice rising with new courage. 'But you'll wish I hadn't.'

'Get on with it.'

'It was June and Daisy Rivers – the daughters of your dead lover,' she announced, her tone heavy with malice now. He'd been smug for too long. She wanted to see him suffer, and enjoyed seeing him struck with horror, eyes wide, mouth dropping open.

'Those little brats,' he gasped at last, letting go of Eileen in the shock of the moment. 'How did they find us?'

She told him. 'And they're not little brats now, Morris. Far from it,' she informed him with relish. 'They're women now. Intelligent women too.'

'What did they want with you?'

'Justice for their father.'

'What!'

'They know you killed their mother,' she told him with a note of triumph in her voice, the danger this posed to herself cast to one side in the pleasure of seeing the arrogant swine knocked off his perch. 'They saw you at the Rivers's house on the night of the murder so they know that we both lied under oath. They know, Morris.' Her voice rose, becoming shrill and hysterical as she recognised the gravity of the situation for them both. 'They know the truth.'

He couldn't hide his fear. 'They're bluffing,' he said. 'They must be.'

'You didn't tell me that someone besides Rose and Lionel Rivers knew you were at the house that night, did you?' she blurted out. 'You said no one could ever find out.'

'I didn't count a couple of little kids,' he was quick to point out. 'And I still don't. They can't possibly remember seeing me there after all this time.'

'They do.'

'Even if they do, who would believe them?' he scorned. 'Not a bloody soul, that's who. So I hope you haven't been opening your big mouth and admitting anything.'

'I'm not a complete idiot.'

'You were fool enough to put our address on your letter, though, weren't you?' he taunted.

'How was I to know they were behind the advert?'

'You should have been more careful.'

'I realise that now.'

'You've got as much to lose as I have in all this, remember,' he reminded her. 'If I go down, so do you.'

'As if I could ever forget.'

'And if it does happen it'll be because of your stupidity.'

Stress always inflamed Morris's temper. Rose Rivers had lost her life because of it and Eileen had sustained her share

341

of injuries over the years. Now she took the full brunt as he looked at her with contempt, then pushed her hard against the wall and aimed one punishing blow after another at her face, her chest, her stomach.

'How dare you keep secrets from me?' he said, hitting her again and again. 'If those two come here again, I want to know about it. Understand? They can't prove anything so don't give them what they need by opening your mouth.'

She tried to get away but he dragged her back and hit her again in the stomach. 'I won't say anything, I promise,' she gasped at last, her hands raised to protect her head. 'But please stop hitting me . . . please.'

'You lied to your husband and that's wrong,' Another blow to the face.

'I'm sorry, I'm sorry . . .'

'You will be when I've finished with you.'

The violence continued until his anger finally abated and she was slumped on the floor, leaning against the wall, head down and sobbing quietly.

'You can stop snivelling and get my dinner,' he told her, walking to the door and turning, showing not a hint of remorse. 'I've been out working all day and I need a good meal when I get home. I don't expect to be kept waiting, either.'

The door closed after him. Slowly Eileen got up, her body racked with pain. She rinsed her face under the tap, wincing with the pain of a swollen eye and lip. The ruined gravy was poured down the sink and she got out the Bisto to make some more. She found herself with the chilling thought that one of these days her husband was going to go too far and she'd end up like Rose Rivers. In her dejected state, she didn't really care.

That same evening Daisy got the tube to Paddington and

walked briskly along the main road towards Nat's place. It was typical November weather, bitterly cold, with a greyish mist shrouding everything. She was shivering despite the thick sweater she was wearing under her coat.

She couldn't afford to take the night off work but had decided that this was important enough to lose money for. Having made the decision to take action this morning, she wanted to get on with it, and there was no point in trying to find Nat at home during the day. Nora minded the children in the evenings anyway so that wasn't a problem.

The streets seemed even scruffier and more sinister around here than the ones Daisy was used to. Marauding yobs were out in force, looking for trouble, drunks staggered out of pubs, young couples were locked in clinches in shop doorways, and there were overflowing rubbish bins everywhere. Daisy had only ever been to Nat's place once or twice and that was years ago, but she was able to find the dilapidated flatlet house.

The front door wasn't locked so she went in and knocked on the door of the ground-floor flat where he lived. A blonde of about thirty opened the door with a small child clutching at her skirt.

'Yeah?' she said.

Daisy frowned, wondering who the woman was. 'Is Nat in, please?' she asked.

'Nat?'

'That's right. Is he at home at the moment?'

'Never 'eard of anyone called Nat.'

Wondering if she'd come to the wrong house, Daisy looked around her and was sure she hadn't. She looked back at the woman whose dark roots matched her black sweater and tight skirt. 'Nat Barker,' she said hopefully.

'Oh, Mr Barker, I know 'im,' the woman told her. 'He lived here before we moved in six months ago.'

'He's moved out?' Daisy couldn't believe he would change his address without telling her.

'Well, he certainly ain't dossing down here with us, dear,' the blonde said. 'We've hardly got enough room for ourselves, let alone having a lodger about the place.'

Daisy's throat was so constricted she could hardly swallow. 'Do you happen to know where he moved to?' she managed to utter at last.

'Over Queens Park way somewhere, as far as I remember. Dunno exactly where, though.'

'He didn't leave a forwarding address then?' muttered the shocked Daisy.

'No, nothing like that.' The woman thought for a moment. 'You could ask him in there,' she suggested, pointing at the door of the flat opposite. 'I think they were quite matey so he might have an address.'

Numb with shock, Daisy walked to the other flat and knocked on the door.

Afterwards Daisy couldn't remember getting to Queens Park that night. She was weak from the shock, and bitterly hurt to think that Nat would have done something as major as moving house without telling her, the woman in his life for more than seven years.

Admittedly she wasn't in the habit of visiting him, but she needed to know where he was in case of an emergency. He was the father of her children, for goodness' sake.

She'd forgiven him most things over the years but he'd have to have a damned good explanation for this, she thought, as she came out of the station and walked down a street of towering Victorian terraced houses converted into flats. The house she was looking for was smarter than Nat's previous address, she noticed with surprise. She pushed the front door open and knocked on the first door she came to because the

344

neighbour from Nat's old address had only given her the house number.

A heavily pregnant young woman wearing a red maternity smock answered the door.

'Sorry to bother you but can you tell me which flat Nat Barker lives in, please?' enquired Daisy politely. 'I've been given this address but not the actual flat number.'

The woman, who had long black hair and dark eyes, fixed her with a steady gaze. 'What do you want him for?' she asked in a chilly manner.

Daisy bristled. She was having a terrible night. She'd just discovered that her long-standing boyfriend had moved house without telling her and now some stranger had the cheek to pry into her personal affairs. 'I think that's my business, don't you?' was her brisk reply. 'So can you please tell me where I can find him?'

There was silence for a moment as the woman considered the matter. 'Nat,' she shouted into the flat, 'come here. There's someone to see you.'

To Daisy's utter astonishment he appeared.

'Daisy . . .' He was clearly as shocked to see her as she was to see him. 'What are you doing here?'

'I might ask you the same thing,' came her sharp reply. 'How could you do such a thing – change your address without telling me?'

'I can explain—'

'Why should he tell you where he lives?' demanded the other woman, throwing Daisy a glare.

'You'd better ask him that,' she suggested.

'Who is she, Nat?' asked the woman, turning to him. 'And why should you explain anything to her?'

'Never mind who I am,' snapped Daisy, resenting the stranger's proprietary attitude towards Nat. 'Who are you? That's what I'd like to know.'

'That's easily sorted,' she replied, exuding confidence and pausing briefly before continuing as though to create the maximum effect. 'I'm Nat's wife.'

The hallway spun around her. Daisy gripped the stair banisters to steady herself, cold sweat suffusing her skin, her legs buckling.

'You can't be,' she muttered.

'I can and I am.'

'You're lying.'

'With him standing next to me?' she said in a mocking tone. 'Don't be such a silly cow.'

Daisy stared at her, still unable to take it in but knowing with sickening certainty that it was true.

'I don't understand,' she said numbly.

'Nothing complicated about it,' the woman went on breezily. 'He's my husband. We've been married for six months and have a baby due in a few weeks' time.'

'A baby.'

The woman patted her bump with both hands, looking at Daisy with a half-smile. 'Well, this ain't the result of too many doughnuts, mate,' she said.

'Oh, Nat,' gasped Daisy, looking at him with disbelief. 'How could you?'

And she turned and rushed out of the house.

'I couldn't just let you go like that, not after all the years we've been together,' said Nat, having chased after Daisy and persuaded her to go into the nearest pub with him so that he could explain.

'Won't you be in trouble with your . . . with your . . .' she could hardly bear to utter the title she had believed would belong to her one day, 'with your wife for chasing after me? You'll certainly have some explaining to do.'

'I can handle Marge, don't worry.'

Daisy emitted a humourless laugh. Her pain and humiliation went too deep for tears. 'All these years I thought that the only reason you wouldn't marry me was because you didn't want to marry anyone,' she said bitterly. 'And then you go and marry someone else. How's that for a punch in the throat?'

'I didn't want to get married and I didn't intend to marry Marge,' he informed her.

'But you went ahead and did it, just the same.'

'When she got pregnant I didn't have any choice in the matter,' he told her.

'I got pregnant, twice,' she reminded him. 'But you didn't feel obliged to do the decent thing by me, did you? And that hurts, Nat, that really hurts.'

'Marge has a very persistent father,' he explained.

'So if I'd had a dad to twist your arm, you'd have married me then, is that what you're saying?' she suggested.

'Not exactly, no.'

'Why did it work for her then?'

'Marge's dad is a powerful man around here,' he said. 'He owns several other houses besides the one we live in.'

'Ah, so that's it.' She gave him a knowing look. 'She has something I could never give you – money.'

'It isn't like that,' he denied somewhat unconvincingly.

'What then?'

'Her ol' man put on the pressure for me to marry her and he's the sort of bloke you don't defy if you value your health. He employs morons to deal with people who don't do what he wants. And they don't go in for small injuries, I can tell you.'

Daisy didn't believe a word of it. He'd married Marge because he saw something in it for himself. He was just using her as he'd used Daisy for so long. But at least Marge got to raise her child within the security of marriage. 'How blind can you get?' she said dully. 'All these years I thought I was

347

the woman in your life when I was actually just your bit on the side.'

'No, Daisy, you were never that.' He looked suitably outraged at the suggestion.

'You must have been deceiving me for months,' she went on, her eyes narrowing in thought. 'No wonder you stayed away for weeks at a time. You had other fish to fry. God knows how many women there have been over the years, and I was too dim to suspect anything.' She paused, pondering, then added almost to herself, 'I suppose I knew in my heart there must be others but I didn't want to believe it so I deceived myself into thinking that I was the only one.'

He looked sheepish and didn't deny it.

'I don't suppose you ever loved me,' she went on. 'I was a fool to think you did.'

'I did love you, Daisy,' he claimed. 'I still do.'

'Don't make things worse by piling on the lies.' Her voice was hard. 'You've been found out so there's no point.'

He shrugged. 'I'm a bloke and we ... well, these things just sort of happen,' he said lamely. 'It's different for men than it is for women. It's the way we're made.'

'Don't tar the whole of your gender with the same brush as yourself,' she admonished.

'You and me go back a long way, Daisy, and you are the only woman I've ever really loved.'

'How come you're married to Marge then?'

'I made a mistake and the choice was taken out of my hands, I told you.'

She took a large swallow of her gin and orange, looking at him. 'I don't think you're capable of loving anyone but yourself,' she told him. 'I don't suppose you even love your wife, the poor cow.'

He didn't say anything, just swigged his beer. 'You've every right to be upset,' he said after a while.

'You're not kidding.' She gave him a questioning look. 'One thing that does puzzle me: why bother to go on seeing me when you didn't want me?'

'I did want you.'

'But you had a wife, and a child on the way, a nice home and a rich father-in-law,' she pointed out. 'Why not be straight with me and tell me it was over?'

'I couldn't bring myself to end it, I suppose,' he told her. 'So I carried on seeing you.'

'In other words, you wanted to have your cake and eat it.'

'A woman would see it that way, I suppose.'

'Anyone with a scrap of decency in them would see it that way,' she amended.

With her perception altered by events, she saw him with a new and truthful eye. He was a flashily dressed man with greasy sideburns and a paunch around his middle, a chancer who cared for no one but himself. He wasn't even much to look at, if the truth be told. 'The reason I came looking for you tonight was because I was going to ask you to be honest with me about what happened between you and June,' she explained. 'Now that I know the sort of deception you are capable of, I don't suppose I need to.'

'I wanted to bring her down off her high horse,' he blurted out in a rare burst of honesty. 'I don't like her attitude. She thinks she's God's gift.'

'She's been telling the truth all along, hasn't she?'

He hesitated for only a second before nodding his head. Lying was like breathing to Nat, but even he could see that there was no point in continuing with the pretence now. 'I didn't fancy her,' he was keen to assure Daisy. 'The idea was to get her interested and then laugh in her face. I wanted to make her feel put down in the same way she always makes me feel, turning her nose up, the superior bitch. But she didn't want to know, turned me down flat. So I decided to get

349

even with her by making trouble for her with you. That's why I set that scam up the other night.'

'Surely you've got better things to do with your time, now that you're a married man,' Daisy disapproved.

'My life and my feelings for you haven't ended just because I've married Marge, you know,' he informed her. 'I still have a life outside the home.'

'I bet you do,' she said harshly. 'If you hadn't been rumbled you'd have carried on seeing me, wouldn't you?'

He met her eyes. 'If I could have got away with it, yeah, I expect I would,' he admitted without shame.

'It's about time you grew up, Nat Barker,' she told him. 'My daughters have got more sense than you.'

'Our daughters,' he corrected.

'*My* daughters,' she countered, her voice rising. 'You've never wanted to be bothered with them, never been anything of a father to them.'

'Only because I'm no good with kids, you know that's the reason,' he defended.

'I know that you've never made any effort with them,' she said.

'Don't go on about it.'

'I'm not going to go on at you about anything ever again,' she made clear. 'I just hope you make a better job of fatherhood with your new baby than you ever did with Shirley and Belinda. Your poor wife doesn't know what she's letting herself in for with you. I wish her the best of luck.'

'Daisy, please, don't be so hard,' he urged her. 'It just isn't like you to be so nasty.'

'No, it isn't. And I should have been harder and nastier a long time ago as far as you were concerned. My biggest regret is that I didn't allow myself to see through you before,' she said, finishing her drink and standing up to go. 'You're a cheat and a liar and I never want to see you again.'

She left the pub with him in hot pursuit.

'Daisy, we can't part bad friends like this,' he said, taking her arm.

She pulled away from him and stared into his face. 'Don't you ever touch me again,' she ordered, her voice distorted with rage. 'Not ever!'

'But—'

'If you ever come near me or my girls again,' she said through gritted teeth, 'I'll go to the law and have a court order taken out against you.'

'Now you're just being bloody ridiculous,' he objected, moving back.

'You've got a wife at home waiting for you,' she reminded him tartly. 'So go to her and leave us alone. You're not fit to breathe the same air as my daughters or my sister or my dear friend Nora. So go away, you pathetic little man.'

'Don't worry,' he countered. 'I wouldn't want to come near you or your bastard brats again anyway.'

That was too much for even Daisy's patience. She clenched her fist and drove it hard into his face. 'That's for calling my daughters names,' she informed him, and walked away, leaving him looking after her with his handkerchief held to his bleeding nose.

When the parish priest went into the church to lock up he saw a woman sitting in the pew with her head bowed. He caught her eye and gave her a tentative smile.

'Are you waiting to lock up, Father?' she asked. It wasn't her local church so this priest was a stranger.

'When you're ready,' he said. 'No hurry.'

'I'll just be a few more minutes.'

'Take as long as you like.' He looked at her kindly. 'Is there anything I can do to help? I'm a good listener.'

'Thanks, Father. But not this time.'

He nodded and walked away, disappearing through the door to the vestry.

Daisy had never been able to define what the inside of a church meant to her. But she did know that part of it was a sense of belonging that dated back to the orphanage chapel. It was something familiar, something she'd grown up with. The atmosphere had comforted her as a child and still did today. She breathed in the lingering smell of incense and candlewax around her, finding it soothing.

She'd come in here on impulse tonight, passing the church on her way to the station after leaving Nat. Every nerve in her body had been stretched to the limit; she'd been full of disgust for him and humiliation for the years of self-delusion, believing that she and Nat had a future together.

But now, sitting here in tune with her spiritual self, she felt calmer and more able to clarify her thoughts. She'd been young and hungry for love when she'd fallen for Nat, dazzled by his confidence and colourful looks. She could see now that she'd clung on to what she'd thought they had, blinding herself to the truth even though the magic of that young love had gone long ago. She'd not allowed herself to move on from those immature feelings.

Looking back over the peculiar nature of their relationship and the fact that she had been excluded from so much of his life, it should have been obvious to her that there was more to him than she knew about. She could only assume that she hadn't wanted to face up to that so had told herself that it wasn't Nat's way to be bound by the normal rules of court-ship because he was unconventional, a free spirit. He'd let her down so many times, she should have been tough in the face of this ultimate humiliation. But she wasn't and the pain was profound.

Somewhere at the back of her mind, though, she recognised something else which she couldn't quite identify but could feel growing. It was a lightness of heart that felt remarkably like relief and something beyond that too – a kind of strength. Only now could she fully accept that loving Nat, or thinking she loved him, had been a burden; it had held her back, stunted her emotional growth. It had made her lose a good man she could have had a future with, and caused a serious rift between herself and her sister.

She would never deny that there had been good times with Nat, and he had given her her greatest gift: her lovely daughters. But he had been a negative influence in her life for a long time. Now it was over. It was the end of an era. She had to get on with her life without him. And there was one thing she must do before anything else. Maybe it was too late to put things right with Jack. But not with June.

As she got up to leave, the priest appeared and came over to her.

'Feeling better?' he asked.

'Much better, thank you,' she was able to say truthfully. 'Good night, Father.'

'Good night.'

Facing the altar, she genuflected, then turned and walked to the back of the church, her footsteps echoing on the stone floor in the silent building. She pushed open the heavy door and walked out into the cold night air.

June and Nora were in the living room having their cocoa when Daisy finally got home. She came straight to the point.

'I've been a complete idiot,' she told them, sitting down and looking from one to the other. 'Can you ever forgive me?'

'I'll go and get you some cocoa,' offered Nora, with the idea of making a diplomatic exit.

'No, don't go, Nora,' Daisy requested. 'I want you to stay and hear what I have to say.'

Nora sat back down and listened while Daisy told them

353

about the events of the evening.

'Daisy, love, I'm so sorry,' said Nora, removing her spectacles and rubbing the lens with the corner of her cardigan. 'I know I've sometimes upset you by speaking my mind about Nat but I wouldn't have had this happen to you for the world.'

'Nor me,' added June.

'I know you wouldn't and it's all right,' Daisy assured them. 'I feel OK about it now.'

'Are you sure?' asked Nora.

'Yeah. I'm very hurt, of course. It was one hell of a shock and I was shattered. But I think I needed something like this to make me face up to what I've known deep down all along and what the two of you have tried to make me see: that Nat doesn't live by the same rules as the rest of us.' Even now she couldn't bring herself to be unnecessarily hateful about him. 'I feel better now that it's finally over. It was never a proper relationship, even though I tried to tell myself it was.'

The two women looked at her in silence, a palpable sense of relief settling over the room.

'I'll go and get you that cup of cocoa now,' said Nora.

'Thanks, Nora.' Daisy managed a smile. 'And thanks, both of you, for not saying I told you so.'

Nora chortled. 'It's more than we dare do,' she told her. 'We're used to keeping quiet when it comes to Nat.'

'Not any more,' Daisy told them. 'That's all over and done with. From now on the shortcomings of Nat Barker are not unmentionable in this house.'

'Thank God for that,' said Nora, and disappeared into the kitchen to make Daisy some cocoa.

Hyped up by what had happened, Daisy didn't feel ready to go to bed when she'd finished her cocoa. June was upset on Daisy's behalf and feeling wakeful also, so they stayed up talking after Nora had gone to bed. Sitting either side of the dying embers of the fire, Daisy talked about Nat.

'I was young when I met him,' she said, in a reminiscent mood. 'Young and lonely and desperate for love, I suppose. I was very well looked after at St Clare's but there wasn't much love about.' She paused. 'So I fell for Nat in a big way.'

June gave her an understanding nod.

'Leaving the orphanage was worse than being there. Much worse. OK, so there are no home comforts in an institution but there was security and constant companionship. Coming into the outside world after all those years was a real shock to the system, I can tell you. I've never felt so alone as I did then.' Her eyes were glazed as she thought back on it. 'I had absolutely no one.'

'Didn't they do any sort of follow-up, to make sure you were all right?' enquired June.

'Oh, yeah, they did that. An aftercare officer used to visit me now and again to make sure I was surviving,' she explained. 'But they couldn't cure the grinding loneliness. Although I never felt loved at St Clare's, I never felt lonely either. But when I left there I felt as though I'd lost everything because my security had gone. I was fifteen and on my own in the world, or that's what it felt like. I missed St Clare's dreadfully.' She looked at her sister. 'You weren't there for long enough to remember much about it, I suppose.'

'No. But I know all about feeling alone and unloved.'

June had indicated before that her childhood had somehow been lacking. But as she'd made it obvious that she didn't want to talk about it, Daisy didn't like to press her. 'Really?' she said.

Meeting her sister's sympathetic eyes, June felt comforted. She'd never told anyone the truth about her childhood, not even Alan. She couldn't bear to talk about it because to do so evoked the painful memories she'd spent the whole of her adult life trying to blot out. But now she sensed that the time had come to bring it all out into the open. Suddenly she knew that she needed to face the memories if she was ever to erase her fear of them. 'Contrary to what you might expect, my life was hell after I left St Clare's.'

'Why?'

'Downright wicked are the only words I can think of to describe the people who adopted me.'

'No!' Daisy was shocked. 'How can that be? I mean, surely if they wanted a child desperately enough to adopt one, they would love and cherish it.'

'Oh, they claimed to love me,' June said, bitterness creeping into her tone. 'When they were beating me, they told me it was for my own good, that it would make me into a better person, and I would thank them for it one day.'

'They beat you?'

'On a regular basis.' She looked grim. 'But the beatings I could take.'

'There were worse things?'

June cleared her throat, finding it difficult to say the words after keeping it all locked away for so long. 'Mental torture, and lots of it, though I didn't know that was what it was called at the time, of course,' she explained. 'They constantly told me that I was a useless human being and they wished they'd never taken me on. They used to lock me in my bedroom for hours on end, whole weekends sometimes, as a punishment for something as small as being a few minutes late back from school because I'd been chatting to the other kids on the way home. They got even stricter about that as I grew older.'

'That's terrible.'

'It was, I can tell you. I wasn't allowed to have any friends at all outside of school hours.' June gave Daisy a wry look. 'I don't suppose they'd have allowed me to go to school if it

356

hadn't been against the law to keep me home.'

'Why didn't they want you to mix?'

'They didn't want me corrupted by the other kids, was what they said. I believed them; kids believe anything adults tell them, don't they? Later I realised it was because they saw outside influences as a threat to their control over me.'

'I can't understand why they went to the trouble of adopting a child, as they obviously weren't suited to parenthood.'

'That's often puzzled me too,' said June thoughtfully. 'I can only think it must have been because they wanted someone to control, to manipulate. They probably even convinced themselves they were doing the best thing for me. They must have convinced the authorities that they were good people. I imagine that couples wanting to adopt were vetted, even in those days when there were so many children in care.'

'You must have been relieved when you were old enough to leave home.'

'Phew, I'll say I was. I left when I was fifteen,' she explained. 'Like you I was alone and in lodgings at that tender age.'

'What happened? Did you reach a point at home when you'd had enough so you just walked out?' Daisy enquired.

'No.' June turned very pale and Daisy could see that she was trembling. 'No, it wasn't like that. Something happened that made it impossible for me to stay there.'

'Oh . . .' Daisy didn't want to pry but she sensed that June needed to talk about whatever it was that still troubled her so deeply. She waited, hoping her sister would feel able to confide.

June stared at her shaking hands. 'I've never told a soul. I don't know if I can,' she began, looking up and biting her lip. 'It's just too awful to put into words. You'll be very shocked, Daisy.'

'Don't tell me if you'd rather not,' said her sister kindly.

357

'But it might help. And don't worry about shocking me. After tonight, I can face anything.'

There was a silence. June pushed her fingers distractedly through her hair. 'My adoptive father used to . . . to get fresh with me.' She paused, unable to continue. 'And then one time he raped me,' she finally managed to get out in a rush. 'And I got pregnant as a result.'

Daisy couldn't pretend not to be appalled. 'Oh, June, that's awful!' she gasped.

'That isn't all,' she went on, her skin paper-white but suffused with red blotches on her cheeks and neck. 'They made me have an abortion.'

The gasp emitted by Daisy filled the silent room.

'That's the bit I knew would upset you, you being a Catholic.' June was very distressed.

'I can't help it.'

'I had no choice in the matter,' June went on. 'I didn't know what was going to happen when they took me to this woman's house. Not until she took me into a room and locked the door. By that time it was too late. I struggled but there were three strong adults against a fifteen-year-old girl. My parents held me down. Even though I didn't want to carry a baby of that monster's, I didn't want to do that, believe me.'

'You don't have to justify yourself to me,' Daisy assured her. 'I'm not going to judge you.'

'I had a miscarriage that night but I was very ill for days afterwards, terrible pains, floodings, a fever,' she continued. 'I thought I was going to die. I think they did too but they daren't call a doctor because questions would have been asked.'

'They ought to have been reported for breaking the law,' said the outraged Daisy. 'Was there nobody you could turn to?'

'Nobody at all because they'd never allowed me to have

friends,' she explained. 'I wouldn't have said anything anyway because the shame was too great.'

'I can imagine.'

'Anyway, as soon as I was well enough after the abortion, I left,' she went on. 'I wasn't safe at home with him around. My mother wanted me out of the way by that time, too. She couldn't face up to what he was like and blamed me for the whole thing; she said I'd encouraged him. It was probably the only way she could bring herself to stay with him.'

'That's quite a story,' said Daisy.

'It's the reason why I left Alan,' June told her.

'Really?' Daisy was puzzled. 'Was it still haunting you and coming between you then?'

'It has always haunted me and always will do. But I was able to cope with it until Alan and I started to try for a baby and I couldn't get pregnant,' she explained. 'Obviously because of the damage caused by the abortion.'

'You don't know that for sure.'

'I can be pretty certain, though. I mean, what else could be stopping me from conceiving?'

'Any number of things.'

'With the abortion damage being the most likely.' June was in little doubt. 'Anyway, when Alan started talking about seeking medical advice, I knew it was time for me to leave. I couldn't risk having my past come out.'

'Surely, whatever the doctors discovered would have been confidential between you and them, wouldn't it?' suggested Daisy. 'I don't think it would be ethical for a doctor to discuss a patient's details with anyone else, even a husband.'

'But I would have had to lie to Alan about it,' she pointed out. 'And I didn't want to do that. I lied to him about my reasons for leaving him but I had to do that so that he would get on with his life without me.'

'So he still doesn't know why you left?'

'Of course not. I could hardly tell him a thing like that, could I? It's better this way. With me out of the picture he can find a woman who can give him the child he wants. He deserves that. He's a really decent bloke. What right do I have to stop him having kids?'

'Sounds as though you still love him.'

'Desperately,' June admitted. 'I walked out on him because I love him and want the best for him.'

'Sounds like cock-eyed logic to me,' Daisy disapproved. 'You could at least have given him the chance of an opinion on the matter.'

'I know what I did was right for him.'

'I suppose that's the important thing,' sighed Daisy. 'When it comes down to it, you have to trust your own judgement about something as personal as that.'

'Mm.' June threw her a look. 'So what do you think of your smart sophisticated sister now you know the truth about her?'

'I think it's sad,' was Daisy's honest reply. 'Sad that you've had such a rotten life. And kids growing up in an orphanage are always thought of as the hard-done-by ones.'

'I'm glad I've told you.'

'I'm glad it's helped.'

Something happened to June at that moment, and she broke down, the stifled pain of the past finally culminating in a great outpouring of grief.

Daisy went over to her and held her while she sobbed. 'You're not on your own any more,' she said, stroking her hair. 'And neither am I. We've got each other now. We were given a gift when fate brought us together again. We nearly lost that when we fell out over Nat. We mustn't let anything come between us ever again.'

'Definitely not,' agreed June, in a muffled tone, but feeling better for having let go. 'Nothing will part us now.'

'And now that we're friends again, we have a job to finish,' Daisy reminded her.

June nodded, blowing her nose and composing herself. 'We need to work out our next move,' she said shakily. 'Not that we have many options.'

'I was wondering,' began Daisy, 'if perhaps we should give some more thought to the one lead we do have.'

'Go straight to the organ grinder, you mean?' suggested June, catching on.

'Exactly,' Daisy confirmed. 'It might be a bit risky but there will be two of us. And I really do think it's our only hope.'

'What exactly do you have in mind?'

'This is my plan . . .' began Daisy.

'Good evening, Mrs Dodd,' said Daisy, when Eileen answered the door.

She gasped and shrank back. 'Oh, no. Not you two again,' she complained. 'I thought I'd made it clear that I don't want to see you around here again.'

'You made it very clear,' confirmed June.

'Why are you here then?'

'We've come to see your husband,' explained Daisy. 'Is he at home this evening?'

Eileen looked guarded and very frightened. 'No, he isn't,' she said, and went to close the door.

'I don't believe you,' said Daisy, stepping forward and pushing her foot against it.

'Clear off.'

'We're going to pester the life out of you until we do see him, so you might as well get it over with,' Daisy told her.

'What do you want with him?' Eileen's wary eyes rested on them suspiciously. 'I made our position very clear the last time you were here.'

'Let us in and you can listen to what we have to say,' Daisy said in reply.

A booming voice came from inside the house: 'Who is it, Eileen?'

'Just a couple of Jehovah's Witnesses,' she lied.

'Tell them to bugger off,' Morris bellowed back at her. 'I'm waiting for my pudding.'

Daisy moved forward and shouted into the house, 'It isn't Jehovah's Witnesses, Mr Dodd. It's Daisy and June Rivers and we're not going to go away until we've seen you so you might as well let us in.'

In an instant he was at the door, his beady little eyes darting from one to the other in search of recognition, not quite able to hide his fear. 'My wife's already told you that you're not welcome here, so clear off.'

Daisy found it an eerie experience to see him again after all these years. He'd been a shadowy image in her mind, except for those evil eyes, which had remained vivid. She couldn't stop imagining what his plump, stubby hands had done to their mother. Anger imbued her, which she knew she must control or ruin their plan. 'You'll regret it if you don't listen to what we have to say,' she told him.

'You've got nothing on me,' he responded with an air of indifference that didn't quite come off.

'We wouldn't be here if we hadn't,' Daisy pointed out.

'Shush, all of you,' Eileen urged them, looking into the street and peering both ways. 'There's no need to let the whole neighbourhood know our business.'

'The whole world will know your business if you don't let us in,' said June.

'You'd better do what they say, Morris,' Eileen advised him nervously.

'Oh, all right,' he tutted, moving aside to let them in and leading them into the living room where he stood with his back to the fire. 'I won't offer you a seat because you won't be stopping. Just say what you have to say and get out.'

The sisters stood just inside the door 'How does it feel to see us again after all these years, Mr Dodd?' Daisy asked.

'It doesn't feel like anything in particular,' he replied with nonchalance that didn't ring true. 'You were nothing to me then and you're nothing now. Just the kids of a neighbour where we once lived, that's all.'

'Looking at you is like looking at the devil himself,' Daisy told him.

'For me too,' added June.

'My sister and I are the only people living who saw you at the house that night,' Daisy reminded him. 'Apart from our father, of course. And he's out of the picture for the moment.'

'Just temporarily,' June put in.

'I dunno what you're going on about,' Morris blustered. 'As I said just now, you've got nothing on me.'

'That's where you're wrong,' said Daisy, hoping to goad him into losing his temper which, from what they'd heard, shouldn't be too difficult.

'Very wrong,' June backed her up.

'We have something very incriminating,' Daisy went on. 'We have our own personal experience and the police will be interested to hear what we have to say about having seen you at our house on the night of our mother's murder.'

'You didn't see me there,' he denied. 'And if you think you did you're barmy.'

'We intend to leave no stone unturned to clear our father's name,' threatened Daisy. 'So be warned.'

'I knew there would be trouble.' Eileen was deathly white, her voice shaking. 'You shouldn't have done it, Morris.'

'Shut up, you stupid cow,' he bellowed at her. 'Keep your big mouth shut.'

'That's what you said to us that night,' Daisy reminded him.

'Rubbish!' he exclaimed. 'You were just a couple of snotty-nosed kids. You couldn't possibly remember anything as far back as that. This is just something you've dreamed up.'

'We wouldn't make a thing like that up.'

'There was only us and you in that hallway that night,' June reminded him. 'How could we know about it if we weren't actually there – that's the line the police will take.'

Daisy pointed to her head. 'It's all up here,' she informed him. 'And we intend to use it.'

'You know as well as I do that no one will believe such a story,' he challenged.

They did know that, which was why they needed Eileen to back them up and that was what they hoped to achieve with this visit. 'They'll have to look into what we have to say, whether they believe us or not,' Daisy bluffed. 'Especially as there are two of us.'

He narrowed his eyes on her. 'If you're so sure, why are you here bothering us?' he enquired. 'Why don't you just have done with it and go to the police?'

'It's only recently been possible but that's another story,' said June. 'We're here now because we wanted to see you, to see if you can look us in the eye after what you've done.'

'I've done nothing to be ashamed of.'

'I can believe that too, because you're the sort of man who wouldn't be ashamed of committing murder and letting someone else take the blame.' Daisy's tone was hard. 'We'll see you punished for it. No matter how long it takes, you'll pay for what you've done.'

'Do something, Morris,' cried Eileen in a panic. 'Do something or we'll both go down.'

His wife's fear seemed to enrage him and he replied with

his fist, hard across her mouth, which immediately spurted with blood. 'I've told you to shut your big gob. Now perhaps you'll do what you're told,' he roared.

'Are you going to let him get away with that, Eileen?' challenged Daisy.

'He's murdered one woman,' put in June. 'You might be the next. He's certainly capable of it.'

'Stop them, Morris,' wailed Eileen, holding a handkerchief to her bleeding lip.

In reply he struck her across the face so hard she fell to the floor. He then lunged towards her with the idea of aiming more blows. But Daisy intervened.

'That's enough of that,' she said, dragging him away with June's help.

He swung round, his fists flying. 'Get out of my house, the pair of you,' he ordered, his voice shaking with rage. 'Your mother was scum anyway, leading me on, then turning cold. She deserved everything she got.'

'You admit you killed her then?' said Daisy.

'Yeah, I admit it.' He was shouting now, his face red with fury and his eyes wild; he'd obviously lost control as the sisters had hoped he would. 'And bloody good riddance to her too. She should never have played us off one against the other.'

Daisy was about to strike him but was pre-empted by him aiming a blow to her face that made her see stars.

'You animal.' She tried to push him away but he was too strong for her, especially as she was still dazed from the blow. 'Get off of me.'

'Leave her alone,' shouted June, trying to drag him off her sister and failing against his strength.

Suddenly help came from an unexpected source.

'Haven't you done enough damage to these women, you evil bugger?' said Eileen, struggling up from the floor and grabbing him by his other arm so that, between them, she and

365

June were able to hold him back from Daisy. 'You robbed them of their parents when they were just little kids, and now you're trying to beat them up.'

'Shut up, Eileen.'

'No, I won't shut up,' she said, her voice distorted as she started to sob.

'You bloody well will.'

'You've ruined the childhood of these two women, and you've wrecked my life too,' she told him. 'But you've made my life a misery for long enough, I tell you. I'd sooner be in a prison cell than have to live another day with you.'

'Eileen,' he said in a warning tone, struggling to get free but failing because there were three women holding him now. 'What are you talking about?'

'I'm going to tell the police what you made me do, and get the case reopened so you will have to pay for your crime,' she said, her voice strong suddenly, despite the fact that she was crying.

'Don't make me laugh,' he scorned 'You won't have the bottle.'

'I will, you know. I'm going to tell the truth – that I lied under oath because you told me you hadn't done the murder,' she went on as though he hadn't spoken. 'I would never have lied if I'd known the truth. By the time I found out what you'd done I was caught in a trap that you'd put me in. Well, no more. Enough's enough.'

'You wouldn't dare.'

'Watch me.'

'You'll go down with me,' he warned.

'So what? I'm living in a prison now,' she told him. 'A real one can't be worse than the hell of a life I live with you.'

He made one last bid to get away and broke free, but Eileen landed him a blow to the face so hard he was stunned into immobility.

'Come on, girls,' she said to the astonished sisters. 'Let's go to the police station.'

While Morris was still gathering his wits from the shock of his wife's unprecedented violence, the three women fled from the house into the bitter night. They stopped only long enough for Daisy to grab a coat from the hallstand for Eileen.

Chapter Sixteen

Jack strode out along the beach, the cold January wind stinging his face, the tangy salt air filling his lungs and clearing his head. It was late Sunday morning and he didn't have to go on duty until this evening as they didn't open the restaurant for lunches in the winter. After a good hard walk, he'd have a sociable hour in the Gullscombe Arms, then go back to the cottage for a bite to eat followed by a leisurely browse through the Sunday papers by the fire until it was time to go to work. Smashing!

The sea breeze felt more like a gale this morning, the sky a great rolling dome of grey, the ocean rough and dark. The surf was so thunderous, each breaking wave seemed to shake the ground beneath his feet. Definitely not the sort of weather to attract the average person to the beach, but Jack had a curious fondness for it on wild winter days when the life force was so breathtakingly tangible. He found it invigorating and uplifting, especially as he was dressed for the elements, the hood of his duffel coat pulled right up over his ears.

There was hardly anyone about – just a man throwing sticks for a dog in the curve of the bay and a group of youngsters exploring the rock pools around the bottom of the cliffs, their high, youthful voices carried on the wind. Rock pools were like a magnet to kids, he thought, reminded of last summer and how Shirley and Belinda had loved poking about in them, looking for shells.

Of course, everything had been drenched in sunshine then: his life as well as the landscape, for that brief interlude when Daisy and her daughters had been a part of it. That was almost half a year ago, and nothing had been the same for him since. He didn't sit about feeling sorry for himself; that wasn't his way. He worked hard, went for long walks, tinkered with his motorbike and was his usual sociable self to anyone he encountered. He even dated women occasionally. But the dull ache of missing Daisy didn't go away.

He walked on with his head bent against the wind, passing Gullscombe Manor, more visible now than in summer because the trees were bare. Every time he passed this spot he thought of Daisy and how they'd sheltered from the rain on the veranda. He'd felt so close to her then; had really believed they had something worth nurturing.

But now, something attached to a post outside the house caught his eye and he halted in his step, peering at it. It looked like an estate agent's FOR SALE board but he couldn't see the details from this distance. Inspired by mild curiosity to take a closer look, he made his way up the sloping path through the trees.

It was an estate agent's board but with an auction notice pasted across it. He'd heard through the village grapevine that the owner had recently died. His descendants obviously wanted to dispose of the place as quickly as possible and it would go for a song at auction. There couldn't be much demand for a ruin like that, no matter how beautiful it had once been, because it would need such a huge injection of cash to return it to its former glory. So somebody would get a bargain.

A memory popped into his mind of a casual comment Daisy had made when they'd been here together, about the potential of the place for use as something other than a private house. He stood still, mulling a sudden idea over, then walked purposefully across the garden and down the slope to the beach. His step gathered momentum to such an extent that he was practically running back to the cottage in a fever of rising excitement. Stopping for only long enough to collect his crash helmet and goggles, he jumped on his motorbike and roared away towards town.

Alan and Jack were having a drink in a Torquay pub an hour or so later, Jack having turned up at Alan's flat in ebullient mood, saying he needed to speak to him urgently and in private away from the Cliff Head. When Alan heard what he had to say, his reaction was one of astonishment.

'You're saying that you want the two of us to go into partnership to buy Gullscombe Manor and turn it into a hotel that we will run together?' He was excited by the prospect, even though he wasn't in a position to consider such a proposition.

'That's exactly what I'm saying.' Jack was full of it. 'A great idea, isn't it?'

'But it's a wreck of a place,' Alan pointed out.

'Which is why it will go dirt cheap at auction.'

'It would need to go for practically nothing since it'll cost a fortune to restore,' was Alan's shrewd response. 'Even more to convert into a hotel.'

'If we got it at a low enough price, we should be able to manage it.' Jack's fervour was intense. 'Surely you can see how perfect the place would be as a hotel. The building and grounds, the location, everything.'

'Yeah, I can see the potential.' Alan would be a fool to deny it. 'I can also visualise the terrific amount of work it would take to renovate it and turn it into a hotel. And building work costs money, lots of it.'

'Just think, though, Alan, we could make it into a family hotel, the sort of place you've always dreamed of having,' Jack effused, his faith in the project causing him to ignore the obstacles Alan was putting in the way. 'It's the perfect setting, in extensive grounds with direct access to a safe beach. What could be better?'

'It's a good position but—'

'I know we could make a success of this,' Jack cut in excitedly. 'We could put in a swimming pool and a games room, all that sort of thing.'

'Just one minor point,' said Alan with irony. 'How are we supposed to fund this project?'

'By my selling my cottage and you could either raise money on your share in the Cliff Head or use your savings and get a bank loan if that isn't enough, based on the reputation you will have built up from running the Cliff Head.' He'd worked it all out on the way into town. 'I know when we were talking once you said that your savings wouldn't be anywhere near enough to get your own hotel, but as there would be the two of us sharing the cost, and we'd be starting something from scratch with no goodwill to pay for, you wouldn't need so much.'

'I can't believe you'd sell your cottage.' Alan shook his head slowly. 'You love that place.'

'I do. Very much. But it is only bricks and mortar when it comes down to it.'

'That isn't what you said when you were doing it up,' Alan reminded him.

'I know what I said, but when an opportunity like this comes up, you have to adapt, don't you?' Jack told him. 'Anyway, the thing I love most about the cottage is that it's on the seashore at Gullscombe Bay. If I moved to the manor I'd still be on the bay and in an even better position.'

Alan couldn't help but be infected by his friend's enthusiasm but he had to be realistic. 'It's a nice dream, mate,' he sighed wistfully.

'It's more than just a dream.' Jack was deadly serious. 'This is a sound business idea.'

'It is, I agree. But it will have to stay just a dream for me,' he said. 'I can't come in with you on it, Jack. I couldn't do that to my folks. As I told you before, if I ever left the Cliff Head I would give them my share. But I still wouldn't do it because I know they'd be devastated.'

'I thought that might be your reaction.' Jack couldn't hide his disappointment. 'And the last thing I want to do is interfere in a family matter.' He paused, sipping his beer. 'But I will say this. You were my first choice as a business partner for two reasons. Partly because I believe we'd make a great team. And also because I know you're fed up and frustrated at the Cliff Head and need to do something in your own right, away from your parents. Well, mate, you'll never get a better chance than this.'

Because Alan wanted to seize this opportunity with both hands, he was beginning to delude himself into thinking it might be possible. 'Would it really be a viable proposition, do you think?' he asked.

'I'm as certain as I can be at such an early stage,' said Jack without hesitation. 'Obviously we'd have to find out what the reserve price is and work out some figures. But if we can get the finance side of things sorted, I don't see how the actual project can fail, not with us two at the helm, being both experienced in the hotel trade and having the same ideas for what we want in a hotel. Gullscombe Bay is a natural beauty spot badly in need of a hotel. Taking over the manor house would mean we could open one without spoiling the landscape. We'd keep everything as it is now as far as possible, with necessary changes inside done tastefully.' His enthusiasm was growing with every word. 'I could raise more money by selling my motorbike too, if necessary.'

'But that's your hobby – the love of your life,' said his amazed companion.

'It is, but I'd sell it to get this project off the ground,' Jack told him gravely. 'Harley-Davidsons fetch a good price, even old ones like mine.'

'I can't believe you'd be willing to sell your cottage *and* your bike.'

'That's how much I want to do this.'

'But you've never shown any interest in having your own hotel before,' mentioned Alan.

'I haven't thought about it until now, and I'm not interested in owning just any hotel,' he explained. 'But now that I've thought of this Gullscombe Manor thing, I can't let it go. The idea's too good.' He drank his beer, looking thoughtful. 'Anyway, I've been drifting for too long – going to work and coming home, messing about with the bike. I need a challenge in my life and I can't see a better one than this coming along – *ever*.'

'It's certainly got the makings.'

Jack put his pint glass down, looking at his friend closely. 'I want you to come in with me on this, Alan. But if you really don't feel able to, I'm still going to go ahead and bid for it at auction.'

'If things were different I'd jump at the chance of coming in with you on it.'

'I know you would, mate. But I'll have to find someone else as a partner.' Jack's thoughts were racing ahead. 'I won't be able to raise enough cash on my own. It's too big a project.'

Alan nodded.

'Still, I've got plenty of contacts in the hotel trade,' Jack continued. 'I should be able to arouse some interest.'

'I really wish it could be me.' Alan couldn't bring himself to

374

let go of the idea completely. 'I'm long overdue a challenge.'

Jack looked at him. 'You wouldn't be going to the outback of Australia, you know,' he pointed out. 'You'd only be a few miles up the coast. You'd still be able to see your folks on a regular basis.'

'They wouldn't want to see me if I left their business,' Alan told him rucfully.

'*Their* being the operative word.' Jack didn't want to give up on Alan either. 'It's their business and not yours.'

'When they retire, things will be different. I'll be able to put my own stamp on the place then.'

'It'll still be a business they've built up,' persisted Jack.

'I'll just have to live with that.' Alan was resigned now. 'Because I just couldn't hurt them in that way.'

'We've been over this before and you know my feelings on the subject,' said Jack.

Alan sighed. 'It's easy for you to say but things aren't that simple when relatives are involved.'

'After leaving my family at the other side of the world, I think I know how difficult it is,' Jack reminded him. 'It's your decision, of course, but I wouldn't be a true mate if I didn't say that I think you're missing out on the chance of a lifetime. Not just because I'm certain that the two of us could make a go of it but also because I really do believe you need to break away from your parents' apron strings.'

'You're probably right,' agreed Alan. 'But it's actually doing it that's the problem.'

'I think you might be underestimating them, you know,' Jack went on sagely. 'They'll be upset at first, naturally, but they'd get used to it eventually. They might even be proud of you for having a go.'

'Sorry, mate, the answer still has to be no.'

Jack shrugged. 'OK. I've said my piece, I'll shut up about it now.'

'I hope it works out for you.'

'Me too.' His enthusiasm rose again. 'If it doesn't, it certainly won't be for the lack of trying. I've got a real good feeling about this one.'

'Keep me posted,' said Alan enviously.

'I'll do that,' said Jack.

During the winter months there was usually maintenance work of some sort in progress at the Cliff Head. General repairs, painting and decorating – bits of building work that couldn't be done when guests were around. It was Alan's sole responsibility to organise all of this. He decided what needed doing and when; he did the costings, found the tradesmen, did the hiring.

Or that was how it was supposed to work. But one morning a few days after Jack's proposition, Alan was given cause seriously to question his authority when he arrived in reception to find an argument in progress. The altercation was between his parents and the proprietor of the small building firm Alan had hired to do various jobs around the hotel.

'You were supposed to be here by nine o'clock this morning and you roll in now at turned ten o'clock,' Alan's mother was admonishing the man. 'It really isn't good enough.'

'Sorry we were a bit late, missus.' He was a stockily built, square-jawed man who spoke with a rich Devon brogue. 'But I had a bit o' trouble with the van this morning. I just couldn't get her going – had to get a mechanic out to her in the end.'

'Excuses, excuses,' she said.

'It in't just an excuse,' he protested, looking miffed but staying patient. 'It's the God's honest truth.'

'You builders are all the same,' Irene went on rudely. 'Unreliable, the lot of you.'

'Look, I've said I'm sorry,' he said, less patiently. 'I can't do more. So if you'll excuse us, me and the lads have to get on with our work.'

'My wife's right.' Gerald wasn't going to be left out. 'We want this job finished before this summer season, not next. The way you're carrying on, it still won't be done this time next year.'

'We'll be finished by the completion date we gave you,' the man assured him. 'We'll be out of your way well before you open for Easter.'

'I should damned well think so too, the price you're charging us.' Alan's mother was in her element. There was nothing she enjoyed more than flaunting her power.

And to hell with the consequences, thought Alan, observing the builder's annoyance which was increasing, understandably. Good jobbing builders were hard to find. They could pick and choose the work they took on in this age of prosperity, with so many people having property renovated and extended. If Alan's mother's vicious tongue lost them this one they wouldn't get anyone to finish the work before the start of the season because all the reputable builders were booked up for months ahead.

'It's all right, Mother,' Alan said, winking surreptitiously at the builder, whose name was Bill. 'I'll take over now.'

But she was in the mood for a battle and there was no stopping her now she'd got the taste. 'You're nothing but a bunch of layabouts, the lot of you,' she accused the man, whose two employees were standing quietly beside him.

'Here, you wanna watch what you're saying,' Bill objected, his brown eyes hardening as his anger grew. 'That in't fair.'

'As I'm paying your wages, I'll decide what's fair,' she argued. 'You come and go when you please with no consideration for us at all. You can't deny that.'

'I certainly do deny it.'

'Do you think we're blind or something?' Gerald put in.

'Do you think we don't notice what time you turn up for work in the mornings?'

'You obviously don't pay attention to what time we finish at night or we wouldn't be having this conversation,' Bill pointed out. 'Anyway, I'm self-employed. I don't have to account to you about time-keeping. As long as the job is finished by the specified date, I'm within my rights.'

'As we're paying you, we have a right to some kind of reliability,' Irene argued.

Now she'd pushed the man too far. 'Right, that's it,' he retaliated. 'As you're obviously not happy with our way of working, we'll get out of your way. We've enough work to last us for a year ahead. We're not staying here to be insulted by the likes of you.'

'Now you're being ridiculous,' said Irene.

'You listen to me, missus,' said Bill, observing her coldly. 'We've plenty of customers waiting to have work done, people who appreciate us and treat us with respect. So you can pay us for what we've done so far and get some other mug to finish the job for you because we in't doing it.' He paused. 'If you can find anyone who'll put up with your attitude.'

'Don't be hasty, Bill,' intervened Alan worriedly. 'My mother doesn't mean what she says.'

'Oh yes I do,' she made plain, undermining her son's authority completely. 'Never mind you walking out on us, you're sacked, the lot of you.'

Alan was so angry he couldn't speak. Hiring and firing building staff was his job and she'd ignored him altogether; behaved as though he wasn't even there. This sort of thing wasn't unusual and he normally accepted it as an occupational hazard. But in a sudden moment of clarity he saw it with a fresh eye.

He could now see with absolute certainty how right Jack

378

was when he said that Alan needed to break away from the family business. While he worked with his parents he would never amount to anything. He would always be twelve years old in their eyes, and he had had enough.

'Ignore my mother,' he said to Bill at last. 'I'm the one you deal with around here.'

'Really, Alan—' began Irene.

'Shut up, Mother,' he blasted.

'How dare you—' she began.

'Don't you dare speak to your mother like that,' added his father.

Had Alan not been so furious, he might have felt embarrassed at having to endure this public humiliation. But he was beyond that sort of sensitivity. He looked from one parent to the other. 'Fine, you deal with it then. I'll keep out of it altogether.' He turned to Bill. 'Sorry about this, mate,' he said.

Bill gave him a nod to let him know that he had no quarrel with him personally. He'd seen Alan humiliated by his parents too many times to bear a grudge.

'I'll leave you to it, then,' Alan announced to his parents, turning to go.

'There's no need for that,' said Irene, looking worried now. 'You can't just go off.'

'Watch me.' He paused, looking at them. 'And when you've finished with Bill, can you come up to my flat, please? I have something to say to you.'

And with that he headed for the lift.

'Your behaviour was utterly disgraceful, Alan,' reproached Irene, perched stiffly on the edge of an armchair in her son's flat a few minutes later. 'I was thoroughly ashamed.'

'I wasn't proud of your appalling behaviour, either,' was her son's unexpected response.

'What!' She wasn't used to having him answer her back

and it shocked her. 'In what way did I behave badly?'

'Apart from being unnecessarily rude to the builders, you went over my head completely with them,' he told her. 'And it just isn't on.'

'I had to step in and deal with the situation because you're too damned soft with people who do work for us,' she said. 'You let them do exactly what they like.'

'You have to let them know who's boss,' added his father, standing with his back to the window, dominating the room. 'You can't let them make the rules. You can't allow them to win.'

'But they have won, haven't they?' Alan pointed out heatedly. 'You've sacked them and now there's no one to do the work we urgently need doing. So we're the losers, no doubt about that. They're not bothered because they've got plenty of jobs lined up, like all decent builders these days. About the only people who aren't booked up are cowboys, and there are plenty of those about.'

'You'll soon find someone reputable to finish the job,' was his mother's confident answer.

'Oh, no. Not me,' Alan put her straight. 'You took over from me, remember.'

'Only temporarily,' she told him.

'It's a permanent arrangement as far as I'm concerned,' he informed her. 'The job's all yours from now on. You've humiliated me once too often.' He shook his head. 'But never again.'

'Don't be ridiculous,' rebuked his father. 'It's your job to sort this out.'

'Not any more,' he said. 'I quit.'

They stared at him in bewilderment.

'You mean you're going to leave the job of finding another builder to us?' suggested Irene nervously, at last.

'I'm leaving everything to you from now on.' He forced

himself to stay calm. 'I'm leaving the Cliff Head.'

Two pairs of eyes widened in horror.

'Now you really are being silly,' said his mother as though Alan was a recalcitrant child. 'Resigning just because you're in a temper because I paid the builder off.'

Alan looked from one to the other and when he spoke it was in a quiet, reasonable tone. 'That isn't the reason I'm leaving. That just forced me to take a close look at myself and my place in this business as well as my position as an adult human being. I'm not leaving the business in a fit of pique. I'm leaving because I need to do something on my own without the two of you looking over my shoulder the whole time.'

'We don't do that—' began his mother.

'With respect, you do, all the time,' Alan corrected firmly. 'Anyway, an interesting opportunity has come up for me and I've decided to take it.'

'You can't leave,' ordered Irene.

'I can and I will,' Alan told his parents in a definite tone. 'It's something I have to do. I need to prove myself.'

'And what are we supposed to do without you?' asked his mother aggressively.

'You won't have any trouble managing without me. You can run this place standing on your heads, as you've told me so often,' he reminded them. 'I wouldn't go if I wasn't absolutely certain of that.'

'You always have been selfish,' accused his father, hitting out unreasonably.

'I'm what you made me, which is one of the reasons why I have to get away,' Alan tried to explain. 'I'll never know what I'm really capable of if I stay here.'

'Rubbish,' said his mother.

'Absolutely,' supported his father.

'You'll be better off financially without me because I'm

giving you my share of the business,' Alan went on to say. 'You can take on a manager to replace me and you won't have to pay him a share of the profits as you do me. I'll be moving out of the flat so you can offer the manager accommodation, too. It'll be an attractive opportunity and you shouldn't have any trouble finding someone suitable.'

'Moving out of your flat,' gasped Irene, realising at last that he was serious.

'I won't be far away, though,' he assured her. 'Just a few miles down the coast.'

'Where, exactly?'

He outlined his plans.

'I see.' Her eyes were as cold and hard as stones.

'What will you use for money?' his father enquired coolly.

'I'll use my savings and get a loan for the rest,' he explained. 'It's such a good proposition, I should be able to persuade the bank to lend me what I need.'

'And get yourself into debt with huge interest charges,' warned his father.

'If I have to, yes,' Alan confirmed.

'And if you don't get Gullscombe Manor at the auction, you'll want to stay on here, I suppose?' his mother mocked.

'Oh no. Whatever happens, I'm leaving the Cliff Head,' he made clear. 'It's something I now know I must do. If the Gullscombe Manor thing falls through I shall find something else. I'll find a way to use my experience.'

His mother burst into tears. 'I never thought my own son would be so uncaring of his parents,' she said through dramatic sobs. 'I thought we'd brought you up to respect family values.'

'You have,' he said in a softer tone, because he wasn't an unkind man and he did love his parents. 'My striking out on my own doesn't mean I don't still respect family values. I'll still be a good son to you, if you'll let me. The only thing that will change is that we won't be working together.'

'We gave you everything a child could possibly want . . .' she went on woefully.

'Yes, you did,' he agreed. 'But as an adult I need something else – independence.'

'I've always prided myself on being a good mother.' She just wouldn't let go.

'And you have been,' he assured her. 'I wouldn't dream of saying otherwise.'

'The Cliff Head has always been a family firm,' she rambled on tearfully. 'We've worked hard to make it into a good business for you to eventually inherit. As soon as you were old enough we made you a partner.'

'I know all that and I appreciate everything you've done for me. But I've worked hard too, and I think I've made a valuable contribution to the business,' he asserted. 'But I've gone as far as I can here now. I need a new challenge, my own space, and the chance to see if I can succeed or fail in my own right.'

'You can do that here,' came his mother's muffled suggestion. 'We won't stand in your way.'

He chewed his lip, looking at them. 'You will, without even realising it,' he said. 'The original idea was for you to gradually stand back and leave more of the responsibility to me. But it hasn't happened. This place is in your blood. You just can't let go and leave things to me, which is why we had that scene downstairs just now and why you won't consider any of my ideas for the place. This is *your* hotel with your plans and opinions. You're a part of the place and it's part of you because you built it and made it what it is. I want to do the same thing with a very different kind of hotel from this. So why not let me go with your blessing so that we can stay friends? Wish me well and take an interest. I'd really like that. I'm sure any advice you have to offer will be useful.'

But Irene's tone hardened even more and her tears stopped as suddenly as they'd started. 'We'll have the accountant work out a reasonable price for your share of the business and you'll be paid what you're owed,' she announced through tight lips.

'There's no need for that,' protested Alan. 'I've told you, I don't want any money from you. You can have my share of the Cliff Head and welcome.'

'You'll get what you're entitled to,' she said in an acerbic manner.

'I don't want it.'

'As you were so keen to point out,' she went on coldly, 'you've worked hard and made a contribution. I'm not having you say that we've done you out of anything – that we haven't been fair.'

'Surely you know me better than that.' He was very hurt. 'I would never say any such thing.'

'To eliminate any possibility of that, we will pay you for your share of the business,' she insisted. 'But there'll be no question of us staying friends. You want to leave, so go ahead. But you'll be paid off and all ties between us cut.'

'Mother!' He was shocked. He'd known they wouldn't be pleased but hadn't expected to be banished from their lives altogether. 'Now you're just being vindictive.'

'Steady on, Irene,' warned Gerald.

But she was far too engrossed in her own self-pity to take any notice of him. 'As you've just said, Alan, your father and I can run this place standing on our heads so there's no need for you to stay around for a minute longer,' she blasted at him, her tone increasing in speed with the swell of her temper. 'You can get out of here right away, and any contact we have in the future will be through a solicitor. If you let us have a forwarding address, the money you are owed for your share in the business will be sent to you when the amount has been decided. It will *not* be negotiable.'

Alan felt as though he'd been physically beaten. He looked at his father. 'Does that go for you too? Or are you going to stand up to her for once?'

Gerald looked at his wife. 'Don't you think you're being a bit harsh, dear?' he said in cautious admonition. 'They boy's entitled to a change.'

'You do what you like, Gerald,' she told him with a look that forbade disagreement. 'I've said my piece and I won't change my mind.'

'But, dear—'

'I've told you where I stand on this one, Gerald,' she confirmed. 'He's letting us down and I want no more to do with him. If you feel differently, that's up to you.'

Gerald studied his son's face, unable to hide a fleeting look of regret before saying, 'You heard what your mother said. We want you out of here right away.' His voice quivered slightly with emotion. 'So get yourself and your stuff out.'

Upset but not defeated, Alan said, 'OK. I'll go. I'm sure Jack will put me up at his cottage until something permanent can be sorted out.' He paused, looking at them. 'But aren't you just the tiniest bit proud of your son for finally having the courage to do something for himself?'

'You're no son of mine,' was his mother's parting shot before marching from the room, followed by his father.

For a long time Alan couldn't move; he just stood frozen in the centre of the room, so tense his limbs ached. He felt as though the heart had been ripped out of him; it was a terrible thing to happen between a man and his parents. But there was a new strength there too, a sense that he'd finally grown up. As much as he wanted to go after them, he knew he couldn't go back on what he'd said. To reverse his decision now would be the act of a coward.

Walking over to the window, he stared idly across the bay,

385

the sea black and choppy on this winter's day, banks of low cloud obliterating the horizon altogether. But this view always soothed him, however bad the weather. Thinking back on what had been said, he decided not to refuse the money his mother insisted on paying him. It would make them feel better about cutting him out of their lives, he thought miserably, because they could fuel their grudge by telling themselves that they'd given him something to which he wasn't entitled. Anyway, if he was honest, he reckoned he'd earned it for all the hard work he'd put in over the years, as well as the humiliation they'd made him suffer.

June came into his mind as she often did at odd moments because she was never far from his thoughts. He knew instinctively that she would support him in his current plans and wished more strongly than ever that she was here to go forward with him.

He turned back into the room, sad at the thought of leaving here but strong in the belief that he'd done the right thing. A fresh start was long overdue. The excitement of the new project was clouded by the rift with his parents, though. The last thing he wanted was them out of his life.

Maybe they'd have a change of heart when they'd calmed down and thought the whole thing through, he found himself hoping. But being realistic, he doubted it. His mother could be very stubborn when she wanted her own way about something, and he couldn't give in to her over this, as tempting as that was. He emitted a long sigh, sadly accepting the fact that this really was a parting of the ways.

Chapter Seventeen

Things moved fast in the Lionel Rivers case after Eileen Dodd's confession. Morris's arrogance earned him an early arrest. He was far too conceited to believe that his wife would actually go through with her threat to shop him so made no attempt to escape and was arrested at home later that night.

The fact that Eileen had obviously punished herself over the years and had finally come forward and confessed went in her favour and she received only a suspended sentence for perjury and conspiring to pervert the course of justice.

As for Lionel – his release wasn't immediate because the formalities had to be adhered to and his appeal had to go through the normal channels. Despite his daughters constantly badgering the authorities to hurry things along, it was February before everything was finalised.

On a bitterly cold morning with heatless sun glinting on the frosty rooftops of West London, Daisy and June stood at the prison gates, both dressed in warm coats and fur-lined boots.

'We've waited a long time for this,' said June, her breath turning to steam as she spoke.

'Not nearly as long as Dad has,' her sister pointed out, stamping her feet because her toes were turning numb.

'That's true enough,' agreed June, hugging herself against the cold.

'I feel nervous,' Daisy confessed. 'Excited and happy but a bit scared too. It's such a traumatic thing for anyone to deal with. It'll take time for Dad to adjust to life on the outside.'

'I feel churned up too,' admitted June. 'I hope we don't have to wait much longer because the butterflies in my stomach are multiplying by the moment.'

Just then the small door in the heavy prison gates opened and Lionel Rivers stepped out into freedom. Wearing the smart suit and overcoat his daughters had brought him for this occasion, he stood looking around him with a bewildered expression as the door slammed shut behind him.

Both feeling oddly shy, his daughters walked slowly towards him.

Daisy was too choked up to say anything coherent and only managed a tearful, 'Hello, Dad.'

'Hi, Dad,' said June.

He didn't speak; just looked at them, his eyes brimming with tears. 'Thank you, girls,' he muttered thickly at last. 'Thank you for making this happen.'

That did it; the barriers were down and with one accord they threw their arms around him, all three of them weeping with joy and relief.

'Today is your day, Dad,' Daisy said when she'd recovered sufficiently to speak. 'You can do whatever you like. Get drunk, paint the town red, anything. You deserve it.'

'The only thing I want to do is go home to your place for a cup of tea and the chance to get to know you better,' he told them.

Moist-eyed but smiling, they walked away from the prison in the winter sunlight, a proud father and his two beloved daughters.

One Sunday lunchtime several months later, Daisy said, 'More apple pie, Dad? There's plenty.'

'Thank you, dear, but I couldn't manage another morsel,' he said, patting his stomach. 'It was lovely, though.'

'Nora made the pudding today,' Daisy informed him. 'June and I were in charge of the dinner.'

'You all did very well,' he complimented in his gracious way. 'The whole meal was delicious.'

'It's all down to teamwork,' she grinned. 'I enjoy making Sunday dinner into a family occasion now that we're all together again. I hate to miss it when I'm working Sunday lunchtime.'

'It's good of you to put up with me every Sunday,' said her father.

He was far too self-effacing, in Daisy's opinion, and it upset her. Prison seemed to have robbed him of all his self-esteem. 'We don't "put up" with you, Dad,' she corrected. 'We enjoy having you.'

'We do,' confirmed June.

'Very much so,' added Nora.

'The whole idea of your getting a place just around the corner from us was so that we could see plenty of you,' Daisy reminded him. 'And if you get lonely living on your own, you're welcome to come back here.'

'It's kind of you to offer but you don't have room.' His soft brown eyes had had a worried look about them since he'd been out of prison.

'I suppose not,' agreed June, because she didn't want to patronise him by denying the facts. 'But we managed when you first came out of prison.'

'I wouldn't have imposed on you then if I'd had anywhere else to go.'

'You weren't imposing,' Daisy was keen to make clear.

'Perhaps not. But you and June had to share a bedroom because you gave yours up for me,' he reminded her. 'That's all right in the short term but not as a permanent arrangement.

389

Anyway, there's no need for it, thanks to my compensation money.'

'Just as long as you know that we always like to see you,' Daisy told him.

It was late summer and Morris Dodd was now serving a life sentence for the murder of Rose Rivers. Some people thought he'd got off too lightly, and should have been hanged as Ruth Ellis was last year for killing her lover. Daisy wasn't vindictive enough to wish that on him, or anyone. He was being punished and that was good enough for her.

As there had been no question about her father's wrongful imprisonment, his claim for compensation had been dealt with swiftly. He hadn't received a fortune, but enough to buy a small house in the next street. No amount of money could give him back what prison had taken from him, though: his confidence. He'd been shaky for ages after his release and was still finding it difficult to settle, though he didn't say much about it. Daisy thought it might help if he had a job more suited to him rather than the one in a factory he insisted on doing because there was nothing available in his own field.

Daisy, June and the girls made sure he never lacked for company, but it was Nora to whom he turned for friendship. Being such different types, Daisy didn't think they had much in common besides their age but they got on surprisingly well. Eager for him to be integrated back into the community, Nora had dragged Lionel off to various local associations, none of which he'd continued with except the gardening club, which he enjoyed, already having an interest because of the nature of his work before prison. Nora hadn't been a gardening enthusiast before but she went with him to keep him company and, typical of her, became keen. Between the two of them they kept his tiny garden and theirs a picture.

But now Daisy was recalled to the present by Nora, who was nudging her and saying, 'So what do you think, Daisy?'

'About what?' she asked, startled slightly.

'Cor, dear, oh dear, you're a dreamer today,' she said. 'I was just suggesting that we all go over to the park after dinner as it's such a lovely afternoon.'

'Can we, Mum?' urged Shirley.

'Go on, Mum, say yes,' coaxed Belinda.

'OK,' agreed Daisy absently. 'I'm on duty later on, though, so I won't be able to stay for very long.'

June gave her a studious look. 'Are you all right?' she asked. 'You seem very distant.'

'I'm fine,' she nodded, but there was something on her mind apart from her father, and she just couldn't let it go.

However, the subject of the job Lionel had taken in a factory because there were no vacancies in the council's parks department came up, and a discussion ensued on which she tried hard to concentrate. June pointed out that he didn't have to do that job. He could manage for a while on his compensation.

'I'm only fifty-two,' he reminded her. 'I'm not ready to be put out to grass yet. I need something definite to do, a proper purpose to the day.'

'But you hate it at the factory.'

'Yeah, but I'd sooner do that than be sitting on my arse at home all day.'

'You could afford to take some time to look for something more suitable,' June persisted. 'Isn't that right, Daisy? Daisy . . .?'

'What?'

'What *is* the matter with you?'

'Nothing, sorry. I'm listening now, honest.'

June repeated what she'd said and Daisy agreed. But she wasn't paying proper attention. Something about the shaft of sunlight pouring into the room through the window had set off a chain of memories about last summer and who had made that time, a year ago, so very special for her. Here the sun shining through the net curtains made dappled patterns on the wall. She recalled the effect of the same thing in Jack's cottage where there had been no need for net curtains. She remembered the feeling of fresh air and light and space, the prettiness of Gullscombe Bay. So vivid were her recollections, she could almost smell the air and taste the salt on her lips.

How ironic it had all turned out to be. She'd rejected Jack, only to have Nat betray her in the cruellest possible way. Dear Jack, just the thought of him made her feel warm inside. She must have been mad to turn him down.

She looked around the table at this cluster of loved ones, everyone interrupting each other in the way people do when they're close. It still gave her pleasure to see her father in their midst, her daughters sitting either side of the grandfather they'd taken to their hearts so readily. They all meant so much to her.

But there was something missing in her life, and it was that which dominated her thoughts all afternoon and right through her waitressing shift. By the time she got home from work that night, she had come to a decision. She asked June and Nora if they could do her rather a big favour this coming weekend . . .

The following Saturday her stomach churned throughout the train journey and she was visibly trembling in the taxi from Torquay station to Gullscombe Bay. What she was about to do was crazy; just to turn up at Jack's door without warning. It was a huge gamble but something she felt compelled to do. By arriving unannounced, she believed she would get a genuine reaction and know if he still wanted her.

It was mid-afternoon. Sunshine bathed the landscape and gave her a feeling of *déjà vu* because it had been like this when Jack had driven her to Gullscombe Bay that first time with the girls. Now, seeing the bay through the trees at the top of the hill brought tears to her eyes. It was so good to be back.

Her heart was pounding, partly with excitement, partly with nerves when she paid the taxi driver and walked up the path to the cottage, carrying a small overnight bag. With a shaky hand, she lifted the heavy metal knocker and let it fall with a resounding thud on the front door.

In all her agonising about whether or not he would still want her, she had never imagined the possibility of being greeted at the door by anyone but him. So her spirits plummeted when she found herself staring into the sparkling brown eyes of a youngish woman with honey-blonde hair and smoothly tanned shoulders gleaming beneath a yellow sundress.

'Yes?' said the woman, smiling enquiringly at the little woman with the big worried eyes. 'Can I help you?'

Daisy cursed her impulsive behaviour. Not only had she off-loaded her responsibilities for the weekend, she was now about to cause trouble for Jack by turning up on his doorstep. Having an ex of her husband's on the doorstep with an overnight bag would be about as welcome to this woman as a smack in the mouth.

'I was looking for Jack, actually, Jack Saunders.' She wasn't about to get into deeper waters by lying about it but she felt extremely awkward.

Just then two small children appeared, a boy and a girl. 'How long till we can go down on the beach, Mummy?' asked the little boy. 'I'm dying to go in the sea.'

Mummy – Daisy's thoughts went into top gear. These children were about the same age as her own daughters, and it was only a year since she'd last seen Jack. Surely he wouldn't have . . .? No, she couldn't believe that he'd had a wife and kids he hadn't told her about. Not Jack.

'I'll only be a few minutes,' the woman told the children. 'Go and wait for me in the back garden. Don't get impatient and go without me down to the beach.'

The children hurried away and their mother gave Daisy a conspiratorial look. 'The beach here is very safe but I won't let them go down there by themselves. They're not quite big enough yet. They might wander into the sea and go too far out.'

Daisy nodded in an understanding manner which, knowing the beach so well, she could do truthfully.

'So you want to see Jack,' the woman went on, seeming unconcerned.

'If he's around . . .' Daisy felt terrible.

'He isn't, I'm afraid.'

'Oh well, it doesn't matter,' she told her, anxious to get away under the circumstances. 'I just thought I'd call on the off chance that he might be in.'

The woman looked at the overnight bag and gave Daisy a querying look.

'I thought I'd look him up but as he isn't in, it doesn't matter.' She felt really embarrassed now, as well as having a horrible ache in her heart.

'It isn't that he isn't in,' explained the woman. 'It's just that he doesn't live here any more.'

'What!' Daisy couldn't believe it.

'My husband and I bought the place from him earlier this year,' she said. 'We live in London. This is our holiday cottage, our little bolt hole. The children and I have been down here for most of the school summer holidays. My husband just comes down at the weekends.'

'Oh.' Daisy felt weak with relief. On the heels of this glorious feeling came concern for Jack. Something very dramatic must have happened for him to sell the cottage he loved so much.

'You seem surprised.'

'I'm absolutely shocked,' she confirmed. 'This place was his pride and joy. I can't imagine there could be anything bad enough to make him sell up and leave here.'

'It wasn't anything bad – quite the opposite, as far as I know.' She gave Daisy a close look. 'But you've obviously been travelling and must be feeling a bit weary. So why not come inside and I'll tell you exactly where you can find him over a cup of tea.'

'But your children are waiting to go to the beach.'

'It won't hurt them to wait a little longer,' she said, ushering Daisy into the cottage. 'They're not exactly deprived.'

'In that case, thank you very much indeed,' said Daisy politely, and followed the woman inside, eager to hear what she had to say.

'It doesn't look much like the beginnings of a swimming pool to me, mate,' said Jack, grinning at the leader of the team who were installing a swimming pool in the grounds of Gullscombe Manor. 'It looks more like something from the Battle of the Somme, as though you're digging in for trench warfare.'

'Give us a chance,' defended the man, who was bare-chested and wearing shorts. 'We've only just started the job. It'll be lovely when it's finished. Just like the pictures in the brochure.'

'Yeah, I know,' sighed Jack. 'I suppose I'm getting impatient for things to be finished.'

'I told you at the start the pool wouldn't be ready for this season,' the man reminded him.

'You did. I'm just over-anxious to have everything in place so that when we start promoting the hotel we can truthfully offer a full range of facilities,' said Jack. 'My partner and I have put all our money into this project and we have to make it work as a commercial proposition.'

'Just as well to get the pool done now,' the man chatted on with a strong Devon accent. 'While you're in a state of chaos, having a few more workmen around and a lump of the garden dug up won't make much difference.'

'You're right there.' Dressed in shorts and a T-shirt, his skin deeply tanned, Jack looked towards the house. It had scaffolding all around it. The whole place was crawling with workmen and had been for the past few months. Builders were repairing outside walls, knocking down internal ones, fitting en suite bathrooms, making one of the downstairs rooms into a bar and another into a restaurant. And to add to all that, work on the swimming pool had just begun.

'Sometimes when I look at it I feel as though it'll never be finished. The renovations seem to have been going on for ever.'

'You're bound to feel like that,' sympathised the man, speaking with a cigarette in the corner of his mouth. 'You're having a lot of work done all at the same time. You can't do that without inconvenience.'

'My partner and I won't know ourselves when we're not tripping over builders' rubble every time we move about inside.'

'Living in the middle of it doesn't help,' he commiserated.

'We've no choice,' Jack confided. 'As we're paying the mortgage on this place it would be financial suicide to pay out for other accommodation as well.'

'There are worse places to live than this, chaos or no chaos,' the man commented. 'It's a lovely spot you've got here.' He looked out across the bay, the sea shining in the sun.

'It is.'

'If I didn't live around here I'd come here for my holidays myself,' the man chortled.

396

'Let's hope lots of people from the towns and cities feel the same way as you and me,' agreed Jack, following the other man's gaze and looking out to sea, shading his eyes against the sun.

A movement on the edge of the wooded area caught his attention. Someone emerged from the trees and was heading for the gardens. A woman carrying a holdall. That was odd because this was private property. This time next year hotel guests would be trailing up and down the beach path all day but whoever that person was, she was trespassing.

He stared, squinting at the slight figure struggling up the slope. Even at this distance there was something achingly familiar about the way she moved. Now he really was getting delusions, he told himself, imagining every woman he saw to be Daisy. But it really did look like her. She lifted her hand and waved and he knew that it was her. He didn't know how or why. *But it was her*. She'd come back. She really had come back to him.

Leaving the man staring after him, he tore across the garden to meet her, smiling fit to bust.

When Daisy saw him coming she dropped her bag on to the ground and ran to meet him, her laughter ringing out across the gardens. Everything she needed to know was there in his eyes. Words weren't necessary for either of them.

The swimming pool installer watched with interest as the couple clung to each other, making a romantic picture with the sea behind them. 'It's like something out of a bloomin' film,' he muttered to himself. 'Canoodling is all very well in its place but some of us have work to do.'

And he jumped down into the trench to talk to the men who were digging down there.

Alan was full of Jack's reunion with Daisy when he and Paula were dining in a Torquay restaurant that evening. 'Apparently she just turned up out of the blue, appeared on the beach path like a dream come true,' he told her excitedly. 'He thought he was seeing things at first. But no, it really was her. You should see him, Paula, he's like a ruddy teenager.'

She smiled. 'I can imagine. So what happens next?' she enquired conversationally. 'Will she leave London and come to live at Gullscombe Bay?'

'I don't know what their long-term plans are,' he told her. 'But he certainly can't up sticks and go to live in London now that we've taken on the manor, can he?'

'Not really, no.'

'So I suppose she will move to Devon,' he surmised. 'She's got to go back to London tomorrow, apparently, because of her two little girls. She's left them with her sister and her friend for the weekend, with her father helping out.'

'Her sister being your wife, of course?'

'Well, yes,' he confirmed, and went on to repeat what Daisy had told him about how they'd cleared their father's name.

'Quite a story.'

'Phew, I'll say. That's typical of June, though, to take on something like that,' he said in a tone of admiration. 'She's a very determined woman when she decides to do something.'

'Like when she decided to leave you,' Paula pointed out.

'Ouch, that's a bit harsh.'

'Yes, it was a bit bitchy,' she admitted, making a face. 'I'm sorry, Alan.'

He shrugged. 'That's all right,' he assured her. 'I'm the one who should apologise. I was going on about her, which is rude of me when I'm out with you for the evening, especially after what she did to me. I just didn't realise I was doing it.' He gave her a persuasive smile. 'Am I forgiven?'

'Sure.'

'Good.'

Breaking some bread to eat with her soup, she asked, 'Why are you so thrilled about Jack and Daisy getting back together?'

'Because he's crazy about her,' he explained. 'He's a good friend and I care about him.'

She gave him a shrewd look. 'It isn't because Daisy is your sister-in-law and her being together with Jack will give you contact with your wife, then?'

'Of course not,' he was rather too quick to deny.

Paula chewed her bread in thoughtful silence, then made an observation that took him aback. 'It isn't working out for us, is it, Alan?'

His soup spoon was poised in mid-air. 'Why . . . what makes you say that?'

'There's nothing there,' was her frank reply.

'I wouldn't say that.'

'As much as we both want it and as hard as we try, we just can't produce that magic ingredient.'

'That's just because we don't see enough of each other.' He was fighting against rejection even though he knew what she was saying was true. 'What with all the organisation for the manor and doing a job as well, I just never get any time as I only have the one night off a week.'

Both he and Jack still had jobs because they needed incomes until they opened the hotel for business next spring and got money that way. Jack had stayed on as restaurant manager at the Cliff Head since Alan's parents had no quarrel with him. Alan worked as a barman in a Torquay pub. It was quite a comedown after his previous position but it brought in enough cash for him to pay his way, and he actually rather enjoyed the job.

'It isn't just that, Alan, and we both know it,' came her candid opinion. 'I think if we'd been able to see more of each other we'd probably have ended our affair long before this.'

'Is that what you're leading up to, Paula?' he asked. 'You want to end it?'

She reached across the table and took his hand. 'I'm only doing what we both know is inevitable,' she told him in a tone of sad resignation. 'Let's finish it while we're still friends, which is what we should have stayed. Things were fine between us then.'

'And they still are.' He was reluctant to face facts because it would mean the awful loneliness of not having a female in his life again.

'No, they're not, Alan,' she disagreed, removing her hand and sipping a glass of wine.

'Is there someone else?' he enquired. 'Is that it?'

'Not for me,' was her cryptic reply.

'What's that supposed to mean?'

'You're the one with someone else.'

'I've not been seeing anyone else,' he denied hotly. 'I wouldn't do that to you.'

'I know. But you're still in love with your wife, Alan.' It was a categorical statement. 'That was what I meant.'

'June and I are finished, you know that.'

'You're still in love with her, though.'

'What makes you say that with such certainty?'

She gave a dry laugh. 'You should see yourself,' she told him. 'You light up when you mention her name.'

'Do I, really?' He hadn't realised his feelings were so obvious.

'Absolutely,' she confirmed. 'This probably isn't a conscious thing but I believe the reason you're so delighted about Jack's reconciliation with Daisy is because it brings June closer to you. Even if you don't see her, having Daisy around means you'll get news of her. It will give you contact with her again.'

'That isn't fair,' he protested. 'I am genuinely pleased for Jack's sake. You're making me sound selfish.'

'I don't mean to. And I'm not saying that your having a personal interest is intentional,' she explained. 'I know that you're pleased for Jack's sake. But I think that some of the pleasure comes from the reason I've mentioned, even if only subconsciously.'

He lowered his eyes for a moment because he couldn't honestly deny it. 'Even if it were true, it's only thoughts,' he pointed out. 'I'm not going to try and get her back or anything. June and I are history. I accepted that long ago.'

'You're not over her, though.'

'It isn't easy when you've been married to someone.'

'I accept that.' She looked at him over the small floral centrepiece of roses and sweet peas. 'Maybe there's a woman out there somewhere who can make you light up in the same way as June does. But that woman isn't me.'

Alan wasn't going to insult her intelligence by denying it. 'I'm so sorry, Paula,' he said, looking sheepish. 'You're a lovely person and I'm very fond of you . . .' His voice tailed off.

'The feeling's mutual so let's part while we can still do it in a civilised manner,' she said, to avoid any further embarrassment. 'We'll see each other around, as we always have, and I'll follow the progress of Gullscombe Manor Hotel with interest. But let's not try to force something that's never going to happen.'

He sighed. 'What can I say?'

'Nothing,' she said. 'Just finish your soup before it gets cold. Then you can tell me how the renovations are coming along at the manor.'

They chatted amiably over the rest of the meal but the atmosphere wasn't relaxed. They were both deeply disappointed. Disappointed because they had failed to find

401

something they both needed and had hoped for in each other.

Daisy was extremely impressed with Jack's plans for Gullscombe Manor. 'I think it's a wonderful idea. It'll be fabulous when it's finished,' she enthused.

'It had better be after all the chaos and expense,' he told her. 'Though it is sometimes hard to imagine the finished product with all this mess everywhere.'

They were sitting on the veranda, surrounded by scaffolding and builders' materials, including a cement mixer and a mechanical digger. Looking beyond the incipient swimming pool, they could see the lights coming on all around the bay, a necklace glowing in the dusk. 'I can visualise it already,' she said. 'It's in such a wonderful position.'

'I hope you realise that you're to blame for all of this,' he teased her.

'Why?'

'When I saw that the place was up for auction I remembered you saying something about the possibility of someone buying it for commercial reasons,' he explained. 'That was my inspiration.'

'Let's hope it'll be a success, then,' she said, 'or I'll be in dead trouble.'

'I'm that pleased to see you I can't imagine ever being angry with you about anything.'

'I feel the same.' She paused. 'But I nearly died when I found out you'd moved from the cottage.'

'You couldn't have been more amazed than I was when I saw you coming up the path,' Jack said. 'You still haven't told me what actually made you do it.'

'Well, we were all sitting around the table last Sunday dinner time and I suddenly wondered what I was doing there when I could be here with you,' she admitted. 'I couldn't get it off my mind all day so decided to make the necessary arrangements to turn up on your doorstep. That way, if you'd found someone else at least I'd have known.'

'No chance of that,' he assured her. 'I still want to marry you.'

'I'd have been very disappointed if you'd changed your mind,' she said softly.

'On a practical note, though,' he began, 'one of us is going to have to move.'

'I'll come here.' Her smile darkened into a frown. 'It'll be hard leaving the others and I'll miss them like mad but you can't have everything you want in life, and the girls and I belong with you.' She shrugged. 'You're obviously not in a position to move to London now, are you?'

'Well, no.' He waved his hand towards the house. 'Anyway, I want you to be a part of all this, to work in the new business with me. If you'd like that, of course,' he added, because Jack wasn't the type to take anything for granted.

'I'd love it,' she was quick to assure him. 'But how will Alan feel about it?'

'He'll be all for it, I should think. We're going to need plenty of willing hands, and who better to fill the breach than a member of the family with a special interest in the place.'

'Family,' she echoed. 'It sounds lovely.'

'Husband and wife working together. I hope you won't find that too much.'

'I could never have too much of you.'

'Time will tell.'

'If I say it myself, I'm a good waitress,' she mentioned, her thoughts moving on. 'Or wouldn't that be a fitting job for the wife of one of the proprietors?'

'Daisy,' he said, leaning forward and holding her hands, 'we are all going to have to muck in to make this place a success. We will be taking on staff but there'll be times when

403

they're not around and we'll have to get on and do their work. I'll scrub the floors if I haven't got someone to do it. There'll be no standing on ceremony. We'll be part of a team.'

'Sounds great.' There was so much to think about and she did have to consider the girls' needs. 'Where will we live now that you've sold the cottage?'

'It'll have to be here at the manor somewhere. Even apart from the fact that I'll need to be on hand, I put all my money into this place so I can't afford to take on anything else.' He pondered for a moment. 'We're having the outhouses made into staff accommodation and making the attics into flats for management. Alan and I were going to have one of those each but that won't be suitable for us because of the girls.' He paused again, remembering something. 'There's an old gardener's cottage in the grounds that could be done up.'

'Sounds promising.'

'Leave it to me,' he assured her. 'I'll sort something nice out for us. The main thing is for us to set the date.'

'I can't wait.' She hesitated, looking worried suddenly. 'But I want to tell the others about it before I actually set the date, if you don't mind. I want to talk it over with them, you know. Obviously they'll be upset at the idea of me and the girls being so far away. I'm not happy about that aspect of it either. But I won't keep you waiting long because the sooner the better as far as I'm concerned.'

'Me too,' he enthused. 'I won't want you to go back to London tomorrow.'

'It won't be like when I left before, though, will it?' she pointed out tenderly. 'Because this time we both know that I'll be coming back.'

'So, what do you think of Daisy's news, then, Lionel?' asked Nora, a week or so later when they called in for a drink at the local pub after their weekly visit to the gardening club.

404

'I'm dead chuffed for her,' he enthused. 'This Jack sounds like a genuine sort of a bloke. I can't wait to meet him.'

'I'm looking forward to meeting him again too. I've only ever seen him once but he seemed like an absolute sweetheart when he came to the house before,' Nora told him, sipping a glass of stout. 'From what's been said, I get the idea that he's devoted to Daisy and the girls. You could tell they liked each other when he came to the house that time.'

'Sounds to me as though he's genuinely fond of her,' he said.

'I'm so pleased she's found someone decent at last,' Nora went on. 'She needs a bit of cherishing after the way that Nat fella treated her. As well as all the abuse she's had to endure as an unmarried mother.'

'Bad, was it?'

'Awful. It's disgusting the way people behave towards women in Daisy's position,' Nora declared. 'Even the midwife treated her like dirt when she had the girls. Wouldn't let her have anything to help with the pain because she wasn't married. I really gave her a mouthful over that.'

'I wish I'd been around at that time,' he said. 'I'd have given her what for.'

'Nat could have saved her from such a lot of pain by marrying her but he wouldn't do it.' She made a face. 'Still, it's just as well. He'd probably have been a lousy husband, anyway.'

'At least she's found someone nice now.'

'Mm. Although I'm pleased for her I'm devastated for myself,' Nora admitted, swallowing hard on a lump in her throat. 'She and the girls have been a part of my life for so long, their going away is bound to leave an awful gap. I've got so used to them being there, it never occurred to me that one day they wouldn't be.'

'We're all going to miss them and that's a fact,' Lionel

agreed in a sympathetic manner. 'I feel as though I'm just getting to know Daisy and she's going away.' He paused. 'It's a weird feeling having to get to know your daughters from scratch when they're grown women. I haven't always known how to handle it, you know . . . being a bloke.'

'You're doing fine.'

'I feel as though I'm beginning to get there.' He shrugged. 'And now Daisy's off.'

'It's a shame,' Nora commiserated. 'I wouldn't dream of spoiling it for her by telling her but I'm absolutely dreading her going.'

'Still, we'll keep each other company,' he encouraged, patting her hand in a friendly manner.

'I know,' she said, rummaging in her pocket for her handkerchief and sniffing into it.

'And we'll have June.'

'Yes, of course we will. I've grown fond of June,' Nora told him. 'But we're not as close as Daisy and I are. Me and Daisy have been together a long time, since before she had the kids, even.' She raised her eyes in self-derision. 'But what must you think of me, worrying about myself when Daisy's got the chance of a better life? She deserves a break and I couldn't be more pleased for her. I just wish she wasn't going to be so far away.'

'You wouldn't be human if you didn't feel as you do. And I certainly don't think bad of you for being sad about it. I'm grateful to you for being so good to her over the years. I was certainly no help.'

'Don't start beating yourself up about something that wasn't your fault,' she admonished kindly.

He gave her a lopsided grin. 'You're a good friend, Nora,' he told her in a warm tone. 'As much as I love my daughters, I need someone of my own age to talk to.'

'Same here,' she enthused. 'I didn't realise just how much

406

until you joined the family. However much we love the others, we are of a different generation and, as such, our ideas are different.' She paused thoughtfully. 'Of course, it doesn't always follow that you'll get on with someone just because you're in the same age group, but I felt comfortable with you right away, when I came to see you in prison that first time. Yet we're very different.'

'You're a lot brainier than I am, for a start.'

'Don't be daft,' she laughed. 'I'm curious about things so I take the trouble to find out more about them, that's all.'

'It isn't all down to that. You're an intelligent woman,' he insisted. 'But you don't shove it down my throat.'

'You'd soon tell me if I did.'

'Not half.'

A sudden commotion at the bar halted the conversation as a crowd of Teds came in and an argument erupted because the management were refusing to serve them with alcohol on the grounds that they were under age. The Teds denied it rowdily, even though the landlord was pointing out the undeniable fact that if they were eighteen they wouldn't have greased quiffs, long sideburns and a DA haircut but an army short back and sides.

'There's one good thing about Daisy going away,' Nora confided to Lionel as the Teds made a noisy exit. 'With all the trouble around here between the Teds and the immigrant community, with fights on the streets almost every night of the week, Daisy and the girls are better off out of it. At least she won't have to be out on her own late at night any more, travelling back from work.'

He nodded in agreement. 'You can feel the hostility simmering in the air, can't you?' he observed. 'As though violence is about to erupt at any minute.'

'I know what you mean.'

'Black and white don't mix around here, and from what

407

I've heard, all the trouble isn't only down to the Teds,' he confided. 'The older generation aren't blameless. There are plenty of fascists stirring things up.'

'And the Teds jump at the chance of an excuse for a fight,' agreed Nora.

'Exactly. After doing a long stretch in the nick, I reckon I'm pretty tough, but even I don't like being out on the streets on my own of a night in this area,' he confessed. 'And I hate to think of Daisy doing that journey.'

'I've worried about it for years,' said Nora. 'Even before we had a racial problem around here, the streets were full of dodgy characters after dark.'

'Thank God that's coming to an end for Daisy. She'll have someone to look out for her from now on.'

'Daisy will do her whack in that hotel business, though. She's been independent for too long to sit back and let a man keep her.'

'It'll be a better life for her, though.'

'Definitely.' Nora finished her drink, looking at him. 'You must have found London a very different place after all those years locked away,' she remarked chattily.

'I still do,' Lionel told her. 'Especially as I wasn't from around here, and Wembley was a whole lot quieter.'

'You wouldn't want to go back to Wembley?'

He shook his head vigorously. 'No fear. Even apart from the bad memories, there's nothing for me there now,' he said. 'Whereas here, I do have people. I know Daisy's going away but there's still June . . .' He paused. 'And you.'

'We all need people nearby who care about us,' she said. 'I think one of the reasons Daisy and I got friendly so quickly was because neither of us had anyone else, unless you count that waste of space, Nat.'

He nodded.

'Sometimes it used to seem as though it was just Daisy and

me against the rest of the world,' she went on. 'A spinster and an unmarried mum. Both outsiders.'

'And now you've got an ex-con in the gang as well,' he said with a grin.

She threw back her head and laughed. 'At least you can joke about it,' she chuckled.

'Just about.'

'Do you feel properly settled now?'

'No,' he replied without hesitation. 'I'm glad to be out of the nick, of course, and I value my freedom, naturally. But I still feel restless. I don't feel as though I belong.'

'Is that because you hate the job in the factory?'

'That doesn't help.'

'Can't you find something else?'

'No.'

'I thought there was supposed to be loads of jobs about.' She was puzzled. 'That's the impression I get from reading the paper, anyway.'

'There is plenty of work about but not in the parks department,' he informed her. 'There's nothing at all in that line at the moment. Still, beggars can't be choosers. So the factory will do me for the moment.'

'Hardly a beggar, Lionel, as you got your compensation,' she pointed out. 'Surely you've enough to live on until more suitable work comes up.'

'That money will soon fritter away if I sit on my backside all day doing nothing,' he said. 'I want to keep it in case of an emergency. One of the girls might suddenly need help, and if that happens, I want to be able to step in. Anyway, I want to give Daisy the best wedding ever. It's traditional for the bride's parents to shoulder most of the expense. Walking my daughter down the aisle is something I never thought I'd do. It'll be my proudest moment.'

'I can understand how you feel,' she remarked. 'But after

all you've been through, you're entitled not to have to do work you loathe.'

'I'll be all right,' Lionel assured her perkily. 'Don't you worry about me. The important thing is being free, and all thanks to my lovely daughters.' He smiled at her. 'With backup support from you, as well.'

'I was just baby-sitter and general dogsbody,' she explained. 'They did it all. You can be very proud of those girls of yours. They're fighters, both of them.'

'You don't have to tell me,' he said, his eyes soft with affection for them.

'I wonder who they get it from?' she grinned knowingly.

'God knows,' he said in his usual modest way.

Attracted by a sudden clatter, she looked towards the door as a couple of the Teds burst back in and swaggered over to the bar, insisting to the landlord that they were over eighteen and deferred from army service.

'Drink up, Lionel. I think we'd better get out of here, sharpish,' Nora suggested. 'It looks as though there's going to be trouble.'

'It does, an' all,' he agreed, draining his glass and standing up to go.

They hurried to the door and went out on to the streets that had such a dangerous feel to them lately.

Chapter Eighteen

Daisy's wedding was everything she'd always dreamed of and thought she'd never have: a long dress, bridesmaids, church bells, a reception with a four-piece band – the works. Even the weather smiled on her. Being early December it was cold, but one of those glorious winter days with a dry crisp feel to it and sunshine glinting on everything.

'Happy?' asked Jack as they smooched around the dance floor at the wedding reception in the functions room of the Gullscombe Arms.

'Need you ask?' She was radiant in an ivory satin dress of a simple design with a fitted bodice, long sleeves and a high neckline suitable for a winter wedding. Her hair was taken back into a chignon and adorned with cream satin flowers attached to a billowing veil. 'Are you?'

'Are you a Catholic?' was his answer to that.

She laughed. 'It's been a great day, hasn't it?' she said. 'Thank you.'

'You're thanking *me*?'

'I certainly am. Not only for marrying me but also for doing it the way I wanted it, in a Catholic church, and all that that entails.' As a non-Catholic, it had been necessary for Jack to take some instruction from the priest beforehand, during which he had agreed to allow any children of the marriage to be raised in the faith; standard procedure in a mixed marriage.

'I'd have married you in a phone box if it was what you wanted, and could be arranged,' he smiled. 'And the other stuff wasn't a problem.'

They'd chosen to marry in Devon rather than the church in London where Daisy and the girls attended Mass because they had both wanted the reception to be in Gullscombe Bay, where they had fallen in love, and would be living. Fortunately the parish priest here hadn't had a problem with Daisy having two children out of wedlock, and had been happy to marry them. She wasn't divorced – that was the important thing as far as the Catholic Church was concerned. The Manor wasn't quite ready to host a wedding reception so they'd decided on the village pub instead.

Shirley and Belinda had been bridesmaids, June a matron of honour and Alan the best man. Because Jack was so popular in the village, the wedding had turned into something of a community event and many of Gullscombe Bay's residents were here this evening. It was surprising the amount of people you could get into a village pub.

'It's been such a smashing day, I don't want it to end,' she sighed.

'There'll be plenty more good days for us,' he told her. 'This is just the beginning.'

'I know it is and I'm really looking forward to our life together,' she assured him. 'But today is so special I feel as though I want to hang on to it.'

'That's understandable and I hate to bring you down to earth but it'll be time to get changed out of your wedding finery soon,' he reminded her. 'We don't want to be too late getting away.'

'I'll go and get changed after this dance.' They were staying overnight in a Torquay hotel before travelling to the Lake District tomorrow for a week. June, Nora and Lionel were all taking time off work and staying on here to look after the girls while they were away. They were staying at Gullscombe Manor and making a sort of holiday of it. 'I'm still a bit worried about going away and leaving the girls, you know,' she confessed.

'They'll have a whale of a time with June and Nora and your dad,' Jack said to reassure her. 'They're so used to them they won't even notice that we're not around. Especially as they'll get spoiled rotten.'

'I know I'm being soft,' she went on. 'But I've never left them for as long as that before.'

'It's only a week, and we'll make it up to them when we get back,' he promised her.

'You're so sweet to them.'

'It's no effort, I can assure you, because I think the world of them. You and I need a honeymoon, a little time away on our own. But after that, whenever we go away it'll be all of us together as a family.'

'I love you, Mr Saunders,' she chuckled.

'The feeling is mutual, Mrs Saunders,' he said, holding her very close.

One thing that was casting a dark shadow over Daisy's perfect day was the thought of living so far away from Nora and June and her father. She knew she couldn't have everything and that Jack and the girls must be her priority now, but the thought of them not being close by gave her a tight ache inside.

'Brings tears to your eyes to watch them, doesn't it?' June remarked to Alan as they sat together watching the newly-weds dancing. June and Alan were alone at the table; everyone else in their party had gone off – some to dance, others to mingle. Shirley and Belinda – resplendent in red velvet bridesmaids' dresses – were bopping with Nora and their grandfather close to the band; they'd been at it for ages and

413

showed no sign of flagging. 'I've never seen a couple more right for each other than Daisy and Jack.'

'Just like us,' he said.

She forced a dry laugh to keep the tone light and hide the depth of her feelings for Alan, which were frightening in their intensity since seeing him again. Having been among the main participants in today's proceedings, they had been in each other's company for most of the time, albeit not on their own until now. 'Let's hope they don't end up the same way,' she said.

'It doesn't have to be like this, you know, June.'

'Alan, don't . . .'

'I still love you,' he burst out, unable to hold his feelings back.

She started visibly from the profound effect his sudden declaration had on her. But she daren't let a few sweet words allow her to lose track of the facts. 'Weddings have a romantic effect on people,' she said lightly, cheeks suffused with pink, folds of pale lemon satin so perfect with her dark colouring. 'They're known for it. It's got something to do with all the emotion floating about in the atmosphere.'

'I'd rather you didn't trivialise something that's so important to me,' he admonished.

'I didn't mean to trivialise it,' she explained. 'But this isn't the time to bring up our feelings for each other; not in a room full of people.'

'As far as I know, there is no special time to tell someone you love them,' was his simple answer to that.

It was what she wanted to hear so much, her good intentions weakened. 'Are you saying that even after the terrible thing I did to you, you'd still be willing to take me back?'

He met her eyes. 'Yes, that's exactly what I'm saying,' he affirmed. He had planned never to ask her back again but seeing her today, that resolution had disappeared.

414

'Alan, you don't understand—'

'Things are different now that I've made the break from the Cliff Head. I'm a different person, much more able to stand on my own two feet,' he cut in, having always suspected that his parents had been a contributing factor in June's decision to leave him, even though she'd denied it. 'It couldn't have been easy for you, working so close with my folks. I know my mother could be difficult at times.'

June felt like a different person too, since unburdening herself to Daisy about her past. The scars were still there but, bringing it out into the open had lessened the feeling of isolation and made her braver about her thoughts and memories. Being with Alan again was like being held in two loving arms and she wanted more of it, much more. That was all very well, she reminded herself, but nothing had changed as far as her reasons for leaving him were concerned.

Seeing the genuine warmth in his eyes, however, she felt a surge of hope and experienced a defining moment. There was only one way she and Alan stood a chance of happiness together and that entailed doing something that carried a huge risk. She decided to take that risk.

'Alan, we need to talk . . .'

'I'm all for that and the sooner the better—'

But at that crucial moment there was a noisy interruption.

'This is the best day ever, Auntie June,' announced Shirley, breathless from dancing, cheeks flushed with excitement. 'It's better than Christmas.'

'Mummy looks ever so pretty, doesn't she?' added Belinda. 'She looks like a film star.'

'I think so too,' agreed June.

'And you two look like little princesses,' said Alan, smiling at their shining faces, red velvet hair bands decorated with small white satin flowers adorning their heads. 'You're the prettiest bridesmaids I've ever seen.'

415

They beamed. This was their first taste of glamour.

'Come and dance,' urged Shirley, tugging at June's hand. 'And you, Uncle Alan.'

Nora and Lionel arrived back at the table just as the band struck up with 'Rock Around the Clock'.

'Phew, thank God for a sit-down,' said Nora, grinning at June and Alan. 'It's your turn now. Those kids will keep you at it until you're on your knees.'

June smiled at Alan and they allowed themselves to be led on to the floor to dance rock 'n' roll style. When they returned to the table the others were there so a private conversation wasn't possible. Anyway, Alan had to attend to his duties as best man, organising a send-off for the departing bride and groom.

Clouds of confetti showering the happy couple, they departed to cheers from the crowd gathered outside the pub. June stood beside Alan as they watched Jack's black Ford Anglia, with a 'Just Married' sign on the back, disappear out of sight. June was imbued with a mixture of emotions. She was happy for Daisy but sad that she was going to be living so far away. They would still see each other occasionally but it wouldn't be the same.

A hand holding hers recalled her to the present and she glanced down to see Shirley looking somewhat forlorn.

'What's the matter, poppet?' she asked.

'Nothing.' But she was brushing tears from her eyes with the back of her hand.

'They'll be back before you know it,' June comforted her, guessing what the problem was. 'And in the meantime, you and me and Nora and Granddad are all going to have such fun together.'

'Just because it's wintertime doesn't mean we can't go out and about,' Alan added. 'I'll take you all out in my car and you can help me show Nora and your granddad the area.'

'We have to go to school,' Belinda reminded him. Daisy had moved to Devon a couple of weeks ago so that she could be on hand for the wedding preparations. The girls had started at the village school right away. Daisy had wanted them to be settled in their new school before she went away on honeymoon.

'Yes, but we'll still have the rest of the weekend and the evenings,' June pointed out.

'Will you meet us from school?' enquired Shirley.

'Every day,' promised June, 'and I'll have Nora and Granddad with me.'

'And Uncle Alan?' asked Belinda hopefully.

'You'd better ask him,' suggested June, turning to him. 'But he does have to go to work.'

'I'm sure I can arrange things so that I can be at the school gate when you come out,' he told her.

This cheered both the children.

'Let's go and do some more dancing!' cried Shirley.

'Yeah!' added her echo.

And they all trooped back inside the hall.

'About that talk you were suggesting,' began Alan.

'That'll have to wait until they've all gone to bed tonight,' June whispered.

All the major structural work at Gullscombe Manor was done. Just the finishing touches were left to do before they opened for business at Easter: some of the decorating and the furnishings and fittings. June and her father and Nora were being accommodated in the rooms that were ready, albeit that the furnishings weren't complete.

What was to be the main visitors' lounge was more or less complete. It was a large, elegant room with huge bay windows, velvet curtains in a soft orange shade, wood-panelled walls, russet-patterned carpet and plenty of soft seating and subdued lighting. They'd had central heating installed throughout the building but had also had the original iron-work fireplace restored in the main lounge.

It was in this room, around midnight that same night, sitting either side of the dying embers of a log fire, that June told Alan everything.

'That was why I left,' she said in conclusion. 'Not because I didn't love you but because I didn't want to deprive you of the chance to have children. I just couldn't bring myself to tell you the truth. When you followed me to London, I had to pretend I didn't love you because I wanted you to give up all hope of my coming back so that you could get on with your life with someone else.'

He sat very still, his expression inscrutable. She felt physically ill with fear – sick and giddy – because she wanted him back so much, but only if he still wanted her, knowing the truth. It was expecting a lot of any man and she wouldn't blame him for not having her back after what she'd done. But it was the only way they could go forward together.

'I feel so hurt, June,' he said at last, looking at her with a grim expression.

'I'm sure you must do,' she said. 'I'm not proud of what happened. But I was just a young girl and I didn't have any power over the situation.'

'I'm not talking about that,' he was quick to amend with emphasis. 'I'm referring to the fact that you didn't trust me enough to confide in me about all the terrible things that had happened to you.' He looked at her sadly, shaking his head. 'To keep it all to yourself and then just go off like that, leaving me worried and wondering what I'd done wrong . . .'

'It was unforgivable, I know.' She bit her lip so hard it hurt. 'But I just couldn't tell you the truth, Alan, I was too ashamed to tell anyone. I kept it all locked up inside until it all came pouring out to Daisy one night.'

418

'You couldn't possibly know how I felt after you left.'

'I think I can because I was equally as devastated,' she told him. 'Looking back on it, it was crazy. But leaving seemed like the only decent thing to do at that time. You were pushing for us to take medical advice when I already knew the reason we couldn't have a child. Had I known before we got married that I wasn't going to be able to get pregnant I would never have married you. I didn't want to stop you having kids.'

'And it never occurred to you, I suppose, that I married you because you were the woman I loved, not because I wanted a baby-making machine.'

'Come on, Alan, you were dead keen for us to have a baby when we'd been married for a while,' she reminded him. 'You must admit that.'

'Yes, I did want us to have a family, I admit it. It's a natural thing and I'm not going to deny it,' was his candid reply. 'But I didn't want children more than I wanted you as my wife.'

'Are you speaking in the past tense?'

'No,' he said. 'The same thing still applies. If it isn't possible for us to have kids, I can accept that.'

She couldn't believe how lucky she was. 'Oh, Alan,' she said, smiling.

He gave her a sharp look. 'There is a condition, though,' he began sternly.

'Oh, dear,' she uttered nervously, waiting for him to go on.

'There are to be no more secrets between us.' He looked very grave.

'There won't be—'

'I'm serious about this, June,' he cut in grimly. 'I need to know that you'll tell me in future when there's a problem. I can't cope unless I can have your word on this.'

'I promise.'

'Good. Now that that's settled, can we be a couple again?' he asked with a hesitant smile. 'Will you move into

Gullscombe Manor on a permanent basis, not just as a temporary guest?'

'Try stopping me,' she beamed.

'And as we're already married you can move in right away,' he suggested.

'I'll have to go back to London to clear up a few things, give my notice in at work and so on,' she said. 'But, yes, I can move in tonight, if you like.'

'Oh, yes,' he grinned, and as though of one mind they rose and moved towards each other.

'When you said you wanted me to tell you anything at all that's worrying me, did you mean everything?' she asked him later.

'Absolutely everything,' Alan confirmed.

'In that case, I have to tell you that there's one aspect of moving back to Devon that I'm not happy about.'

'What's that?'

'Being so far away from my father and Nora,' June explained. 'I don't want to leave Dad because I've only just found him and was enjoying getting to know him properly, and Nora because she's a true friend. She's already lost Daisy and the girls; with me gone as well she's going to be so lonely. I promised both her and Daisy that I would never leave them without a home so I'll have to work something out so that Nora's got somewhere to live.' She thought about this. 'I'll sell the house and get a flat or something for her because I won't leave her homeless.'

'And the fact that you're going to do the right thing by her doesn't make you feel any better?' he guessed.

'No, not really. The thought of leaving her and Dad makes me want to weep. We've all become so close, you see,' she told him. 'It's spoiling things for me a bit.'

He pondered the question for a while. 'Well, we can't have

our reunion spoiled, can we? Not when the problem can be easily solved,' he said mysteriously.

Gullscombe Manor Hotel was ready to open in March. The rooms were all furnished, the cocktail bar fitted, an alcohol licence obtained and they were fully booked for Easter, following an extensive national advertising campaign.

Both Nora and Lionel had jumped at the chance of moving to Devon and joining the team at the hotel. Lionel was in his element looking after the grounds and doing any small maintenance jobs that didn't need an expert from outside. Nora's sharp brain made her a natural for the office, June was in reception and Daisy was in charge of the waiting staff. Jack and Alan were at the helm as joint managing directors. Versatility was of the essence here. They all worked as a team and helped out wherever they were needed in the hotel, regardless of job titles.

Daisy and Jack and the girls lived in the renovated gardener's cottage in the grounds, June and Alan were in an attic flat while Nora and Lionel both had rooms at the back of the house. The family atmosphere was strong among this group.

The children thrived in the healthy environment with so much space to run and play, and a more personal atmosphere at the village school than they'd been used to in London. Daisy was able to work flexible hours that fitted in with their routine and they always knew where to find her if she was on duty after school hours.

All ideas were discussed and suggestions welcomed. Daisy's brain wave of having a reception in the new bar of the hotel just prior to its opening, for local businessmen and other hoteliers in the area and the local press, was greeted with approval by them all. So the invitations went out and the acceptances came pouring in. They were planning a prestigious event and were all very excited.

When there was no response at all to one particular invitation, however, June decided to take action . . .

'You,' gasped Irene Masters one afternoon when she answered a knock at the door to find June standing on the step. Being out of season she'd guessed she'd find her mother-in-law at home. 'I didn't think you'd ever have the nerve to show your face here again. I suppose Alan sent you.'

'Not at all. He doesn't even know I'm here,' she informed her in an even tone.

'Why have you come then?' she demanded, looking at June with hostility.

'I need to talk to you and Gerald.'

'Well, we don't want to speak to you.'

'Look, it really is important or I wouldn't have come, so may I come in, please? It won't take long.' This was a much more confident June than the one who used to inwardly quiver in Irene's formidable presence. 'Just ten minutes or so . . .'

Irene tutted and sighed, then with seething irritation she ushered June into the living room, a lavishly appointed chamber with deep-pile carpet and lace-curtained bay windows overlooking the sea. Gerald was sitting in an armchair reading the newspaper.

'Well, well, you're quite a stranger,' he said, looking up in surprise as June entered the room; he was noticeably less hostile towards her than his wife.

She nodded. 'How have you been, Gerald?' she asked politely.

'Not so bad, thanks.' He squinted at her over the top of his spectacles. 'We heard that you and Alan were back together.'

'The local grapevine is still in good working order then.'

'That's enough chatter,' intervened Irene, throwing June an

422

icy stare. 'Just say what you have to say and leave us in peace.'

June fixed her with a steady gaze. It felt so good not to be afraid of her. 'We have a mutual dislike of each other, and that's one thing we do agree on. Right?'

Irene nodded. Gerald made no comment.

'But we all care about Alan,' continued June. 'Well, I assume, as his parents, you must feel something for him even if you do have a funny way of showing it.'

This enraged Irene. 'How dare you?' she exploded. 'I won't be insulted in my own house.'

'I've come here to ask you to come to the reception we're having at Gullscombe Manor on Friday night,' she went on as though Irene hadn't spoken. 'You haven't replied to our invitation which probably means that you intend to hurt Alan by staying away.'

'Whether we go or not is our business,' snapped Irene. 'It has nothing to do with you.'

'I'm Alan's wife, which means it's everything to do with me,' June asserted. 'I'm not prepared to stand by and see him get hurt. Don't you think you've done enough of that already?'

'I think you'll find the boot's on the other foot there,' objected Irene. 'How do you think we felt when he told us he wanted to leave the family business?'

'Alan didn't do that to hurt you. He just needed to do something for himself and I admire him for it,' June replied.

'Yes, well, you're not a parent, are you? So you can't possibly know what it feels like to have your only son turn his back on you,' Irene went on.

'From what I've heard it was you who turned your back on him,' June corrected. 'You wanted to keep him at your beck and call indefinitely, and when he acted like a grown-up and showed some initiative, you were mean-spirited enough to cut

423

him out of your life altogether.'

'We gave him what he was owed.'

'This isn't about money.' June was becoming heated. 'This is about Alan's right to make something of himself as a person as well as someone's son. It's a normal human desire. Anyway, you left him with no choice. You wouldn't give him the respect he needed here so he had to break away.'

'I want you to leave—' Irene began.

'Not until you've heard me out.' June was adamant. 'Alan hasn't said as much to me but I know that your approval of our new venture would mean a lot to him and I suspect that you're going to deprive him of that. That's why we haven't had a reply. You didn't even have the decency to decline the invitation. You're just going to let him keep on hoping that you'll be there and spoil it for him by not turning up on the night.'

'You don't know that,' was Irene's sharp response.

'I'm willing to bet on it.'

'He does actually want us to be there, then?' Gerald seemed pleased at the idea.

'Of course he wants you to be there. You're his parents, for goodness' sake, and you're important to him.' June paused, looking from one to the other, then continuing in a more conciliatory manner, 'Look . . . his leaving the Cliff Head had nothing at all to do with his feelings for you.'

'You don't betray people you care about,' announced Irene.

'He didn't betray you.' Her voice rose with exasperation. 'I wasn't around at the time but I know Alan and I know that that would be the last thing he intended. From what I can gather he was really upset about the rift between you. He didn't want it and still doesn't. He'd give a lot to be on good terms with you again.'

'Do you think we're enjoying it?' demanded Irene cuttingly. 'He's our only son, for heaven's sake.'

'And a son to be proud of, too. He's worked so hard to make a success of Gullscombe Manor,' June went on, 'serving in a pub to bring in money and organising all the renovations for the hotel at the same time. Both he and Jack have worked their socks off this past year or so. Between the lot of us we are going to make a success of it.'

'You don't need us then, do you?' said Irene miserably.

'No, we don't need you,' was June's frank response. 'And your being at the reception on Friday night will make no difference to the success of the hotel because that's going to happen anyway. But it would make Alan so happy if you were there.' She paused, feeling an unexpected surge of pity for them. 'Look, you've made your own success with the Cliff Head, now it's Alan's turn to shine. So why not come along to the party and give him your support? It will mean so much to him, even if you just stay for an hour.' Another pause and she heard herself say, 'I'd like you to be there too.'

Gerald looked at Irene. 'What do you think?' he asked.

'I'll give it some thought,' she said, looking at June. 'That's all I'm prepared to say.'

'Fair enough,' agreed June, and allowed Gerald to show her to the door without further comment. She'd done what she could. It was up to them now. But she hoped they would find it in their hearts to be there because Alan's happiness was the most important thing in her life.

Daisy had never been to anything as posh as the reception before, and she was enjoying every moment. Having always, until recently, had clothes that were years old and from a market stall, it was fun being able to have nice things and she felt good in a turquoise figure-hugging cocktail dress with a boat-shaped neck, which she was wearing with high-heeled shoes. With the hotel still being in its infancy, they couldn't afford to be reckless with money but, as Jack's wife, the standard of living for her and her daughters had risen dramatically. And as she worked hard alongside him, she wasn't troubled by the independent spirit she'd developed after so many years on her own.

'If my waitress friends at the hotel where I used to work could see me now,' she said to June as they sipped champagne together in between mingling with the guests, 'they'd be green with envy.'

'Full of admiration, more like,' corrected June, who was much more used to this sort of thing than her sister. She thought Daisy had coped brilliantly with the new etiquette required of her in her position as the wife of one of the principles. Making the transition from waitress to management couldn't have been easy but she'd slipped into it as though born to it.

This evening they had brought in their newly appointed staff to look after the guests so that they were free to socialise.

'I could get used to this sort of thing,' Daisy told her sister.

'That's just as well because there'll be more of it in the future,' said June.

'We've all been working so hard to get the place ready, we haven't had the chance to be glamorous.'

'You've made up for that tonight, though,' complimented June, looking approvingly at her sister's radiant face glowing with a dusting of make-up, her hair worn loose and casual.

'You look nice too.'

June was wearing a red satin dress with a low neck and short sleeves and a gently flared skirt, her hair taken back into a pleat.

'Thanks, kid.' She looked around to see Nora and Lionel engaged in conversation with the landlord of the Gullscombe Arms and his wife. Nora had splashed out on a green dress and jacket, her hair cut shorter now and properly styled for

426

the occasion while Lionel looked spruce in a suit. 'It all seems to be going very well. Everyone seems to be enjoying themselves.'

Daisy nodded. 'I still have to pinch myself to make sure that this is all really happening to me,' she said. 'It's such a different life from before. And the best part is that we're all here together. The thought of living so far away from you all was spoiling it for me when I got married.'

'I think we're all relieved about that.'

'You and Alan seem to be getting on well,' Daisy remarked casually.

'Better than ever now that everything's out in the open,' June told her. 'Alan's changed too, now that his parents aren't pulling his strings.'

Daisy sighed. 'Everything's so perfect, I keep thinking that it's too good to last.'

'That's what years of trouble and hardship have done to you. Fearing the worst becomes a habit, I suppose. But you'll get more confident in time. Nothing's going to go wrong, Daisy. This is your life now, yours and the girls', here in Gullscombe Bay with Jack and the rest of us.'

'Yeah, I know.'

Jack appeared at Daisy's side, looking dashing in a dark suit and crisp white shirt. 'Come on, you two, get mingling. That's enough of all this sisterly nattering,' he joshed. 'This might seem like a night off but you are actually working. Socialising with all the local business people. Putting Gullscombe Manor Hotel on the map so that if they ever need a function or a conference, they'll immediately think of us.'

'All right, slave driver,' smiled Daisy. 'We were just taking a little break.'

'Just kidding,' he grinned. 'You carry on chatting if it makes you happy.'

Noticing that June was looking around anxiously, Daisy

asked her if anything was wrong.

'Some people I was hoping would turn up haven't done so, that's all,' she explained.

'There's bound to be a few who can't make it.'

June nodded.

'Anyway, enough of all this family rabbiting,' said Jack with a hearty grin. 'I must go and fly the flag for our hotel.'

Daisy watched him go, smiling affectionately after him. Nora and Lionel drifted over and the four of them talked about how well everything was going.

Jack appeared at June's side a little while later. 'Your missing guests have just turned up,' he informed her with a knowing look.

'Irene and Gerald?'

'The very ones,' he confirmed. 'Alan's talking to them in reception.'

'Thank goodness for that.' She shot him a look because she hadn't told anyone about her visit to Irene and Gerald. 'But how did you know it was them I was talking about? Have you added mind-reading to all your other talents?'

'Just a lucky guess. You and I have been friends a long time, remember,' he said, cocking his head and winking at her. 'I was hoping they'd turn up too, for Alan's sake. So now that they have, we can relax and enjoy ourselves.'

She nodded cheerfully.

'There's a couple of people over there looking a bit lost,' said Daisy, glancing across the room. 'I'll go over and make them feel welcome.'

'You're a natural for this sort of thing, a real asset,' was Jack's tender reply

Chapter Nineteen

Their first season surpassed all expectations and the hotel was fully booked right through until September. It was hectic, fulfilling and, at times, fraught with problems. Apart from the minor mishaps that arise in any business, a summer flu bug gave them a major staff shortage in the middle of high season, and a storm left them without electricity thus threatening to leave the guests without their evening meal. Fortunately, the power was restored at the eleventh hour and dinner was delayed rather than non-existent. But the experience was a salutary lesson and they had their own generator installed to avoid similar inconvenience in the future.

With a great deal of hard work, flexibility and an unflagging sense of humour on the part of the management team, they overcame these and other crises without the guests perceiving so much as a hint of the chaos that reigned behind the scenes.

Although they weren't planning to close for the winter, there were mixed opinions about Alan's idea of putting on a special Christmas programme. Mainly because they weren't sure if there would be sufficient bookings to make a party of it, Christmas being traditionally a time for hearth and home. In the end they decided to test the market by advertising, with the idea of not taking any bookings at all if there wasn't enough interest to make it financially viable and to create a festive atmosphere.

But the idea of a work-free Christmas with log fires, lashings of festive food, Santa Claus, a Boxing Day treasure hunt and various other social events appealed to a lot of people and the hotel was fully booked for Christmas and the New Year. Hosting the event was exhausting but enjoyable too, and a friendly atmosphere prevailed throughout the hotel.

In the quiet times during the winter they kept business ticking over by hosting conferences and seminars as well as keeping the restaurant open to non-residents all year. They also hosted special weekends for hobby societies and specialist groups. They had such enthusiasts as ballroom dancers, keep fitters, aspiring artists and writers, all of whom provided their own programme of events so only required food and accommodation. The introduction of the Gullscombe Manor Special Cabaret Weekends with dinner dances and first-class entertainment proved to be enormously popular too.

The following year, as their second frantic summer season advanced towards its end, they were quietly confident that their hotel was becoming established.

'I reckon we'll all be ready for the pace to slow down a bit when the busy season finally ends,' Daisy said to Jack one morning in September.

'You're not kidding,' he agreed. 'We're all shattered.'

They were finishing breakfast in the kitchen of their cottage, a warm and cosy, oak-beamed room where the four of them ate their meals, talked things over and generally congregated. A shaft of autumn sunlight was shining through the window and lying cheerily across the corner of the solid wooden table that used to adorn the kitchen at Seagull Cottage. This house wasn't yet such a triumph to DIY as the other one because Jack hadn't had time to get busy on it. But it had had a certain amount of refurbishment and was comfortable enough and very pretty with stone-faced walls and leaded-light windows. At the moment Daisy and Jack were enjoying a quiet few minutes alone together because the girls had finished their breakfast and were upstairs getting ready for school.

'We won't have time to take it easy for long, though, will we? Because no sooner will things have slowed down after the summer season than it'll be time to organise the Christmas programme,' she pointed out.

He nodded. 'The hotel certainly doesn't give us time to get fat and lazy,' he observed.

'I don't mind, though,' she told him. 'I enjoy being busy.'

'No regrets then?'

'You're joking.' She was emphatic. 'This is the best thing that's ever happened to me. Even apart from loving every minute of being married to you, I enjoy being part of a business. After all those years slogging away as a waitress, actually helping to run a hotel is really exciting.'

'Hard work, though.'

'Not half,' she agreed. 'It's certainly destroyed all my illusions about management having it easy.'

As they were finishing their coffee they heard the clunk of the letter box as the morning paper came through the door and dropped on to the mat.

'I'll get it, love,' offered Daisy. 'I've finished my coffee anyway.'

When she came back into the room, she was looking somewhat distracted.

'Something the matter?' he asked.

She handed him the newspaper.

'Blimey,' was his shocked response as he took in the violent scenes on the front page of race riots in the Notting Hill Gate region of London. 'Thank God you're out of that area.'

'I never thought things would get so bad,' she told him.

431

'I've noticed a few reports in the paper of racial attacks around there this past couple of weeks, but it seems to have escalated into a full-scale battle now.'

'This is shocking!' he exclaimed, reading on. 'They're fighting with anything they can lay their hands on. Cars have been torched, people knifed.'

'Let's have another look at the paper, please, Jack?' she asked with growing anxiety.

He handed it back to her and she read of a place she didn't recognise as the one she'd lived in for most of her adult life. This was a war zone, a place of petrol bombs, stabbings and fights with broken bottles, knives, sticks, iron bars and bicycle chains. Ordinary, decent people were confined to home because they were too afraid to leave their houses. In Paddington a house had been set on fire by a petrol bomb. 'It makes me want to weep,' Daisy said, her eyes fixed on the newsprint and pictures of policemen struggling with rioters. 'Who would have thought it would come to this, eh? I mean, trouble had been brewing for ages before I left there. Street fights between the Teds and the West Indians were par for the course around there. You couldn't not be aware of the racial tension if you lived there, even if you weren't involved, because it was all around you. But I didn't realise that feelings were running that high, probably because it was outside of my circle. Live and let live has always been my motto. And you only get to the heart of the culture of an area in so far as it affects yourself, don't you?'

'In a big crowded place like London that's probably true,' Jack agreed. 'Around here you only have to have a cross word with someone and the whole village knows about it.'

'Thinking about it, though,' she went on thoughtfully, 'the bad atmosphere was getting worse towards the end of my time there.'

'You must be glad you're away from it all.'

'I wouldn't want to still be living there, but I'll always be a Londoner at heart, wherever I live,' she told him. 'I have a special feeling for the place no matter how rough things get there. It has nothing to do with buildings or living conditions. It's an emotional thing. There's something about the place I can't shake off.'

'Oh.' He looked disappointed.

'Don't get all upset,' she said affectionately. 'Here is where I want to be. My home now is wherever you are.'

'That's all right then.' He seemed reassured.

'But I still miss London from time to time,' she continued. 'Don't you?'

'Yeah, course I do, sometimes. But not as much as you do, I suspect.' He gave a casual shrug. 'You know how attached I am to this part of the world.'

She raised her eyes, grinning. 'I couldn't fail to know that, and I'm very fond of it too,' she told him. 'But I think I'll always need to go back to London every so often to keep in touch with my roots, such as they are.'

'I can understand that.'

'And while we're on the subject of London,' she went on to say, remembering something, 'I've been meaning to tell you that June has asked me if I'll go with her when she goes to see the gynaecologist in Harley Street in a couple of months' time.'

'Has she got to go again?' He seemed surprised. 'Nothing wrong, is there?'

'Nothing new,' she told him. 'Still the same problem, the lack of a pregnancy.'

'I thought that was all in the lap of the gods now that she and Alan have both had tests and know that there's nothing wrong with either of them.'

'It is. There's no medical reason why June can't get pregnant. She's been given all sorts of advice about the right sort of diet, and told the most fertile times during her menstrual cycle and so on to increase her chances,' she informed him. 'This next appointment is just a follow-up.'

'I see.'

'I don't know if there's anything else they can do but if there is, June will jump at it. She'll do anything to have a baby, though she does try to accept that it might never happen.'

'Is Alan not going with her to the specialist this time?' queried Jack.

'He will if she wants him to,' Daisy replied. 'But she seems to want me to go with her instead. It's a woman thing, I think. She wants to make a shopping trip of it as it will be so near to Christmas.'

'She's still desperate to have a baby then?'

'God, yes. Everything's perfect except for that one thing. She and Alan are happy, the hotel's doing well and we're all here together. It's just that one thing that's spoiling it for her. And she knows that Alan would love a child, even though he keeps telling her not to worry about it.'

'Still, she's getting medical advice from someone who really knows their stuff.'

'Exactly. When she finally plucked up the courage to see a doctor, Alan insisted on the best, and this one is a specialist in fertility problems.' Daisy paused, looking at Jack. 'Anyway, love, do you mind if I go with her? You'll have to look after the girls but I'll only be away for a couple of days. And Nora will give you a hand.'

'Of course I don't mind,' he was quick to assure her. 'It'll be a nice break for you.' He paused, glancing towards the paper. 'As long as you keep away from Notting Hill Gate. It's too dangerous there at the moment.'

'We're not going until early December,' she told him. 'The trouble will be over long before then. The police have got it under control now, according to the paper.'

'Yeah, I expect you're right.'

'June suggested that we stay in the hotel where she used to work,' she went on. 'It's very central.'

'Good idea,' he approved. 'You go with my blessing and I hope you have a lovely time.'

'And in the meantime, I must take the girls to school.'

'I'd offer to take them for you but I know you enjoy going yourself.'

'You bet. One of the highlights of my day is that walk to the village school, especially on a glorious morning like this,' she said, glancing towards the window through which the sea could be seen beyond the hotel gardens. The cottage was tucked away at the far side of the tennis courts with just enough distance for its inhabitants to enjoy their privacy.

'On your way then, woman,' he joshed in the easy way they had with each other. 'Take your daughters to school and leave the old man to read the paper in peace.'

'You're gorgeous, do you know that?'

'You're only saying that because it's true,' he joked.

She brushed her lips against his hair then headed for the stairs. 'Time for school, you two,' she called up to the girls. 'So get yourselves down here sharpish.'

The West End of London was a seething mass of people when the Rivers sisters joined the crowds in Oxford Street one Friday afternoon in December. They'd got an early train from Devon and, as June's appointment wasn't until the next morning, they had the rest of today free for shopping, which they entered into with gusto.

'I don't know how we're going to get all this stuff back to Devon,' said June as they took a break for tea in Selfridges, piling their store bags on the floor beside them.

'We'll manage,' said Daisy, sinking her teeth into a buttered toasted teacake. 'Being in London at this time of the year is too good an opportunity to miss. I've certainly made inroads into my Christmas shopping list. I got some lovely things for the girls.'

'I've done well too,' said June, sipping her tea.

'That's a smashing wristwatch you got for Alan.'

'I think he'll be pleased.'

They fell into a comfortable silence. 'Aren't you going to eat your teacake?' Daisy enquired eventually as she made short work of hers.

'No, I'm not all that hungry,' June told her. 'I shouldn't have bought it.'

'It won't go to waste with me around,' grinned Daisy. 'But you ought to have something to keep your strength up if we're going to do some more shopping.'

June made a face. 'I hate to be a wet blanket but would you mind if I call it a day now?' she asked.

'Oh?' Daisy was surprised because they'd both been looking forward to doing their Christmas shopping. She squinted at her sister, noticing that she was looking rather pale. 'Are you OK?'

'I'm fine but I'm feeling a bit shattered after the early start this morning,' she explained. 'I'd like to go back to the hotel when I've finished my tea, if you don't mind. But you stay and do some more shopping if you like and I'll see you back at the hotel later.'

June hadn't been her usual self since they'd left home; she'd been quiet and preoccupied, Daisy thought. Probably had the doctor's appointment on her mind. 'I think I will wander around the shops for a little while longer,' she said. 'Though I won't be able to carry much more.'

'I'm sure you'll be able to manage a few more packages for those daughters of yours,' grinned June.

'Hello, Jack, it's Daisy.'

'Hello, love.' His voice was warm with pleasure and surprise to hear from her. 'Are you enjoying yourself?'

'I'm have a smashing time,' she told him. 'I'm just calling to find out if everything's OK.'

'Everything's fine.'

'The girls all right?'

'Good as gold,' he said. 'But you should be concentrating on enjoying yourself, not worrying about us.'

'I've got a few minutes to spare while June's in with the doctor so I thought I'd give you a call,' she explained. 'Just wanted to hear your voice.'

'It's lovely to hear yours. I've missed you.'

'I've missed you too,' she confessed. 'But I can't stay long because I'm in a phone box and the money I put in won't last long and I've no more change. I'll see you tonight.'

'I'll be at the station to meet you.'

'Can't wait.'

'Me neither.'

'Bye, then,' she said quickly as the coins were used and the line went dead.

She realised that she was smiling as she replaced the receiver. Just a few words with Jack was all it took to lift her spirits, she thought, as she crossed the road to the consultant's rooms. She'd been feeling a bit tense before the call. She hadn't wanted to worry Jack with it, but the trip had been rather a strain because June had been in such a strange mood. Her longing for a baby was really beginning to drag her down and Daisy was worried about her.

The waiting room was a far cry from the sort of doctor's waiting room Daisy was used to, she thought, as she went in and sat down on a sofa. Instead of hard chairs and well-thumbed, out-of-date magazines, here the seats were soft and the reading material new and of the thick glossy variety with photographs of beautiful homes and gardens.

She was immersed in a picture of a luxurious bedroom when the consultant's door opened and June came out. Oh Lord, she thought when she saw that her sister's face was wet with tears. She must have had bad news.

'June, love,' she said in concern, going towards her.

'Daisy, I've got the most amazing news,' she said shakily.

'Oh?' Daisy was wary.

'I'm pregnant.'

'What!'

'Isn't it wonderful?' She was smiling now and Daisy realised that the tears she'd seen were those of joy.

'But I thought . . .' The details could wait until later, she decided, hugging her sister, tears springing to her own eyes. 'That's the best news ever. Congratulations.'

Because their train didn't leave until late that afternoon, they had time to spare after lunch so decided on a nostalgia trip to Notting Hill Gate. Leaving their luggage at the hotel, they headed for Marble Arch tube station.

'I thought you'd seemed quiet ever since we left home,' remarked Daisy on the train, returning to the subject that was filling both their minds. 'I assumed you were fretting because you couldn't get pregnant when in actual fact you were preoccupied because you thought you might be. You're a dark horse.'

'I was dying to tell you but afraid that if I actually said the words out loud I would somehow be tempting providence. I know it's silly but I was scared to hope after waiting so long,' she explained. 'My periods have never been regular so being late is nothing new for me. I've been feeling a bit sick but that could have been anything.'

'I thought you were nervous about the doctor's appointment and that's why you didn't want much to eat.'

'That was part of it but I was feeling queasy too,' she said. 'Anyway, I told the consultant all this and he examined me and gave me the good news.' She shook her head, smiling. 'I still can't believe it.'

'You will do once you start expanding,' laughed Daisy, getting up as the train rumbled into Notting Hill Gate station.

It was a typical December afternoon: cold and still, a smoky haze hanging over everything. In contrast to the brightly lit West End shops and all the colourful Christmas decorations, the streets looked grey and dismal as they walked from the station to Larby Gardens, through run-down areas juxtaposed with pockets of affluence so characteristic of London. Passing through a shabby neighbourhood with the smell of poverty about it, it seemed to Daisy, who could now view the area from a broader perspective, having been away, that this bit of London had been forgotten by the affluent era.

In Larby Gardens, they stood outside their old house, staring at it like sightseers on their first trip to the capital. To Daisy's surprise she found the experience curiously unemotional, though they had had some good times there. Portobello market was as vibrantly vulgar as ever and evoked happy memories for them both. It also reminded Daisy of Nat, but she felt nothing more than a moment of sadness as she remembered the humiliating ending of a relationship that had once meant so much to her. He was her past, the same as this city. She would always want to come here to visit but she belonged in Devon now with Jack, and felt able to draw a line under her life here.

Thinking of her life in Gullscombe, a warm glow spread through her. As well as having her beloved Jack with her, she had all the other people who mattered most to her. The girls were thriving and her dad was happy and settled. She smiled, thinking of him and Nora, who were great pals and spent most of their spare time together. They sometimes reminded

Daisy of an old married couple, the way they teased each other and joked around, but there had been no talk of anything other than friendship. It might change at some time in the future – who could say? And if it didn't they still had something really special.

On the way back to the station, snatches of jazz and calypso music drifted out of the drinking clubs. The pubs were closing after the lunchtime session and people were straggling out and talking in groups in the street. A gang of Teds were congregated outside a seedy-looking café with filthy net curtains at the windows.

'I wonder if they're plotting another riot,' said June.

'Now, June, we don't know for sure that the Teds started the riots,' Daisy pointed out in a tone of gentle admonition.

'I didn't think there was any doubt about it,' was June's answer. 'That's what we've been led to believe.'

'According to the papers they were to blame but Dad reckons the Teds were just convenient scapegoats,' Daisy told her. 'He used to listen to what was being said in the pubs when we lived there. They were at the centre of the riots, no one can deny that, but it might not have been all their fault. Dad said they were used by the fascists to stir up racial trouble. The Teds jumped at the chance of a fight and got all the blame – that's Dad's theory, anyway.'

While they'd been talking some black youths had come out of a West Indian café and the atmosphere became threatening as the two gangs walked towards each other.

'Whatever the truth of it, the trouble obviously isn't over,' observed June. 'The riots have finished but the fighting hasn't.'

'You're right,' said Daisy, and they hurried away from a brawl in the making.

'It's quite frightening,' commented June. 'A relief to be away from there.'

'I'll say,' agreed Daisy. 'I'm glad to have got the girls out of that area before all the big trouble started. They love it in Gullscombe with Jack and me and the rest of the gang.'

'You only have to look at them to see that,' June remarked.

'Of course, your baby will know nothing of living in a place like this, will it?'

'Neither will it have to suffer any of the problems we had, Daisy.'

'No. Thank goodness.'

'Still, it turned out all right for us in the end, didn't it?' June reminded her cheerfully, linking arms with her sister. 'And the future is bright for us all.'

'Especially now that you've had such good news,' said Daisy.

'Yes,' June smiled, and they walked to the tube station, arm in arm, glad to be together and going home.

THE SOVIET CRUCIBLE

VAN NOSTRAND POLITICAL SCIENCE SERIES

Editor

FRANKLIN L. BURDETTE
University of Maryland

LONDON, K.—*How Foreign Policy Is Made*

PLISCHKE, E.—*Conduct of American Diplomacy*

DIXON, R. G., JR., and PLISCHKE, ELMER—*American Government: Basic Documents and Materials*

SPROUT, HAROLD and MARGARET—*Foundations of National Power*, 2nd Ed.

LANCASTER, LANE W.—*Government in Rural America*, 2nd Ed.

JORRIN, M.—*Governments of Latin America*

TORPEY, WILLIAM G.—*Public Personnel Management*

PLISCHKE, ELMER—*International Relations: Basic Documents*

LINEBARGER, P. M. A., DJANG, C., and BURKS, A. W.—*Far Eastern Governments and Politics—China and Japan*, 2nd Ed.

GOODMAN, WILLIAM—*The Two-Party System in the United States*

WATKINS, J. T., IV, and ROBINSON, J. W.—*General International Organization: A Source Book*

SWARTZ, WILLIS G.—*American Governmental Problems*

BAKER, BENJAMIN—*Urban Government*

DILLON, CONLEY H., LEIDEN, CARL, and STEWART, PAUL D.—*Introduction to Political Science*

ZINK, HAROLD, PENNIMAN, HOWARD R., and HATHORN, GUY B.—*American Government and Politics: National, State, and Local*

ZINK, HAROLD—*Modern Governments*

HENDEL, SAMUEL—*The Soviet Crucible: Soviet Government in Theory and Practice*

THE SOVIET CRUCIBLE

Soviet Government in Theory and Practice

Edited with Introductory Notes by

SAMUEL HENDEL

*Professor of Government,
The City College of New York*

D. VAN NOSTRAND COMPANY, INC.

PRINCETON, NEW JERSEY

TORONTO   LONDON

NEW YORK

D. VAN NOSTRAND COMPANY, INC.
120 Alexander St., Princeton, New Jersey (*Principal office*)
257 Fourth Avenue, New York 10, New York

D. VAN NOSTRAND COMPANY, LTD.
358, Kensington High Street, London, W.14, England

D. VAN NOSTRAND COMPANY (Canada), LTD.
25 Hollinger Road, Toronto 16, Canada

Published simultaneously in Canada by
D. VAN NOSTRAND COMPANY (Canada), LTD.

Library of Congress Catalogue Card No. 59-8657

PRINTED IN THE UNITED STATES OF AMERICA

1066815

TO
STEVEN AND LINDA
WITH LOVE

"Revolutions," wrote Leon Trotsky—who made no small contribution to the art and to the commentary—"are always verbose." And what is true of revolutions generally is even truer of the Bolshevik revolution. Probably more has been written about the "October" revolution, and its philosophic and historical background and aftermath, than about any other revolution in the history of man.

This, obviously, poses some difficulties for an editor of a Book of Readings. Clearly, anything resembling consensus on what ought to be included is precluded. At the same time, it becomes all the more necessary for the editor to state the presuppositions and premises that guided his selections.

No serious and conscientious student of Soviet affairs would deny that wide differences of opinion—often tenably supported—exist among scholars and writers regarding the development, nature, and prospects of the Soviet system. A basic premise on which this book proceeds, accordingly, is that understanding is likely to be enhanced by recognizing and giving consideration to variant positions on complex and controversial issues affecting the U.S.S.R.

It is another premise that both the form and substance of Soviet rule in the U.S.S.R. were considerably affected and influenced by *peculiarly Russian* history and circumstances. Selections deal, therefore, with the Tsarist heritage generally and, in greater depth, with the history of Russia from about the end of serfdom to the Bolshevik revolution.

A fundamental assumption, reflected in the plan of this book, is that a knowledge of Marxist and Leninist theory is of great importance for a true understanding of the Soviet order; for, while Leninist theory, in vital respects, departed from Marxist theory—and Marxist-Leninist theory has, in some fundamentals, been attenuated or discarded in Soviet practice— theory not only played an important role in organizing the Bolshevik revolution and state but is part of the ethos of Soviet society. It has, as Edward Hallett Carr has written, "the status of a creed which purports to inspire every act of state power"; so that even the process of emasculation requires appropriate genuflection. Certainly, Marxist-leninist theory—however distorted—continues to inspire Communist-led revolutionary movements. As Lenin wrote: "Without a revolutionary theory, there can be no revolutionary movement." Moreover, Marxist-Leninist theory merits evaluation as a body of doctrine claiming scientific validity and universal applicability. (There is an important school of thought which denies that theory has much, if any, relevance to Soviet practice. This position is represented.)

Selection of readings was further guided by the conviction that the basis for the non-democratic and totalitarian character of Soviet institutions was largely laid—however unwittingly on the part of some who participated in the process—by the end of 1921 with the failure of the World Revolution, the loss by the Bolsheviks of even militant working class support, the destruction of all opposition parties, and the outlawry of factions within the Communist Party. Certainly, this dictatorial basis was fairly definitively established by the end of 1928 when Stalin, after a series of internecine Party struggles, had obtained a position of almost unchallengeable power (although its apogee was probably not reached until some years thereafter). Accordingly, the process by which the Bolshevik Revolution "went wrong," abandoned so-called proletarian democracy, and then intra-Party democracy, is closely examined.

Totalitarianism having taken root with the triumph of Stalin, the book shifts to analyses and appraisals, largely contemporary, of the Soviet political, economic and, to a lesser extent, social systems. Apart from limitations of space which precluded detailed chronological treatment, this is in accord with the intended emphasis on the fundamental character and spirit of Soviet institutions. Similarly, little or no attention is devoted to details of organization and structure of Soviet institutions. These details are of real importance to the specialist but are not likely to be long remembered by the non-specialist.

On the political side, the Soviet System is examined from five focal points of interest: The provisions of the Constitution; The extent to which these represent reality and myth in Soviet practice; The role of terror as a system of power (including Khrushchev's own analysis of the part it played in the Stalin era); Who rules in Russia?; The problem of non-violent and orderly succession.

In a thoroughly planned economy there is a close interrelationship and interdependence between politics and economics beyond anything known under capitalism. The fact is, too, that the belief of Soviet leaders in the ultimate triumph of socialism throughout the world is based, in major part, upon its alleged superiority as an economic system over capitalism. The Soviet economic system—its successes, failures and prospects—is fully and rigorously considered, analyzed and evaluated.

The final section has a twofold concern: with the impact of Soviet totalitarianism on the beliefs, loyalties, habits and social behavior of the Soviet people; and, additionally, with the durability of Soviet totalitarianism—a subject which has aroused considerable speculation since the death of Stalin and has obvious external as well as internal importance.

It will be observed that the book contains no detailed and systematic discussion of Soviet policies affecting some particular groups and social areas. In light of the need to make choices, this proved unavoidable. Similarly, there is no treatment of Soviet foreign policy or of American foreign policy concerned with the U.S.S.R. Here, too, exclusion was unfortunately necessary. Although internal policy was unquestionably affected by Soviet external policy in a process of interaction, to do justice to foreign policy—its history, motivations, and limitations—requires another volume.

It is not pretended that the use of diverse sources on many aspects of Soviet theory and practice suggests neutrality. The book reflects a strong bias in favor of democracy and against dictatorship. Nevertheless, the attempt has been made to set forth—so far as practical—significant and divergent opinions, including the official Soviet view, on *many* of the great issues discussed. Inevitably, this has meant the inclusion of some of the most distinguished, as well as authoritative, writers in the Soviet field. It is hoped that the varied and conflicting opinions—sometimes among seminal scholars—will make clear the complexities of the subject matter, encourage wider reading, and tend to raise the level of discourse about the U.S.S.R. to a more informed and sophisticated plane.

I am, of course, tremendously indebted to the authors and publishers whose materials are reprinted in this volume. Acknowledgment of permission is specifically made at appropriate points in this book. Separate mention must be made, however, of permission to quote the following: Ivan Turgenev's "The Threshold," from *A Treasury of Russian Life and Humor,* edited by John Cournos, published by Coward-McCann, Inc., 1943; Alexander Pushkin's "To Chaadayev," from *The Poems, Plays and Prose of Pushkin,* edited by Avrahm Yarmolinsky, published by Random House, Inc., 1936; and Vladimir Kirillov's "We," from *Russian Literature Since the War,* edited by Joshua Kunitz, and published by Boni & Gaer, Inc., 1948.

I am grateful to many of my students who, over a period of fifteen years in my classes on Government and Politics in the U.S.S.R., subjected my ideas to critical examination and raised challenging questions. In particular, I am indebted to two such students, Robert Scheer, who worked closely with and assisted me in the difficult late stages of assembling the material for the manuscript, and Morton Schwartz, who made some useful suggestions.

I am also grateful to many scholars in the Soviet field who gave me the benefit of their criticism and advice; but especially to R. N. Carew Hunt, Charles B. McLane, and John G. Stoessinger who made detailed suggestions. I am appreciative of the counsel of my colleagues at The City

College, Hillman M. Bishop, Ivo Ducachek, and John Herz. My thanks go to Theodore Shabad, who assisted me in tracking down recent amendments to the Soviet constitution; to Dr. Bernard L. Koten, of the Library for Intercultural Studies, for his helpfulness; and to my secretary, Mrs. Mathilda Lerner, who was burdened with typing chores.

The aid of my wife, Clara, with the many tasks in preparing the manuscript was considerable. Even more valuable were her help in the search for suitable materials, her unfailing encouragement and patience, and her practical and sage advice which often resolved what for a time appeared to be insuperable difficulties.

SAMUEL HENDEL

Contents

xi

LIST OF ILLUSTRATIONS

I

TOWARD AN UNDERSTANDING OF THE U.S.S.R.

1. A Plea for Objectivity

"Impartiality is a dream; honesty is a duty."

GAETANO SALVEMINI

"Seek simplicity, and distrust it."

A. N. WHITEHEAD

"There is no ill which may not be dissipated, like the dark, if you let in a stronger light upon it. . . . If the light we use is but a paltry and narrow taper, most objects will cast a shadow wider than themselves."

HENRY DAVID THOREAU

"If we begin with certainties, we shall end in doubts; but if we begin with doubts, and are patient in them, we shall end in certainties."

FRANCIS BACON

Chapter 1

A PLEA FOR OBJECTIVITY

Books on Soviet theory and practice are "as the sands of the seashore." Those conforming to official Soviet explanations and rationalizations are uncritically laudatory and often involve distortions of historical fact. At the other extreme are the reports of critics of the U.S.S.R. who picture communism as "a gigantic chamber of intellectual and moral horrors." To be sure, the story abounds in horror. "But this," as Isaac Deutscher writes, "is only one of its elements; and even this, the demonic, has to be translated into terms of human motives and interests." Moreover, consideration should proceed with some understanding and appreciation of the special history, geography, and circumstances which—to an important degree—shaped Soviet policies and institutions. Desirable, too, is avoidance of the oversimplifications often characteristic of extreme cold-war partisanship and pressures.

It must be recognized, however, that even the serious and fair-minded student of Russian affairs confronts many difficulties. For one, pre-revolutionary Russian history is little known in the West except in superficial and imaginative fashion. For another, Marxist-Leninist theory, which purports to be the basis of Soviet practice, is ambiguous and inconsistent in significant segments, and is seldom read except in crudely excerpted form; and the extent of its real influence on Soviet practice is seriously controverted.

Other difficulties derive from the complexity and dynamism of the Soviet system which extends over a vast land mass of more than 8 million square miles and a great variety of peoples who number over 210 millions. In little more than forty years of history the Soviet Union has passed through several more or less clearly differentiated phases of development in its economic, military, religious, minority, educational policies and programs—to name but a few. Then, too, close and detailed knowledge of the background, experience, thinking, and motivations of Soviet leaders is not generally available as it is in respect to their Western counterparts.

Secrecy and censorship (as well as expunging and distortion)—continue to impede the process of gathering reliable information and data about the Soviet system. On the other hand, there has been some noteworthy relaxation and improvement in these areas in recent years. In general, in fields

3

having little or no military significance, there is little doubt that much official Soviet information is substantially complete and accurate. (A discussion specifically "On the Reliability of Soviet Statistics"—particularly economic statistics—appears in Chapter 15.)

Notwithstanding formidable difficulties it is, I believe, fair to say that the extent to which Russian policy, and hence Russia itself, is "a riddle wrapped in a mystery inside an enigma," is greatly exaggerated. Even Churchill, who used the phrase with respect to Soviet foreign policy, added "but perhaps there is a key. That key is Russian national interest." Apart from the proceedings at high levels, which are shrouded in great secrecy, there is a considerable body of dependable knowledge and information about many aspects of Soviet life. This is, in no small part, due to the work of devoted scholars, journalists, diplomats, and many others who brought to their writing and comments about the U.S.S.R. a high degree of intellectual integrity and objectivity.

The Berman article is reprinted here as one provocative analysis of the sources and dangers of American misconceptions about the U.S.S.R. It should be added that some Western scholars would take issue with some of his comments—on the viability and durability of the Soviet system, for example. Some of these differences are reflected in various sections of this book.

THE DEVIL AND SOVIET RUSSIA

Harold J. Berman [*]

An old lady who could never bring herself to speak ill of anyone was asked what she thought of the Devil. "Well," she replied after a pause, "he is very hard-working!"

The old lady understated the Devil's virtues. He is also very intelligent. He knows how to win friends and influence people. In the words of Bishop Emrich of Michigan, writing on *Some Neglected Aspects of Communism,* "the Devil is not a derelict on 'skid row.' He is not a 'bum'; for this type of person is weak, pathetic, disorganized, lacking in will, sick, and not strong enough to stand against a single policeman. . . . The Devil is quite different. . . . He is patient . . . well organized, disciplined, persuasive, and attractive."

[*] Professor of Law at Harvard Law School; research associate and member of the executive committee of the Russian Research Center of Harvard University. He is the author of several books on Soviet law, as well as a book of essays entitled *The Russians in Focus.* The selection originally appeared in *The American Scholar,* Vol. 27 (Spring, 1958), pp. 147-152. By permission.

What makes him the Devil, says Bishop Emrich, is that "with all his virtues he is going in the wrong direction; and since he possesses virtues, he goes in the wrong direction effectively. The Devil, says traditional Christian thought with profound insight, is a fallen angel."

In both Soviet and American thinking there is a strong strain of puritanism which tends to turn opponents into enemies, enemies into devils, and devils into ugly monsters. An American reading what is printed in Soviet literature about life in the United States can only laugh at the fantastic caricatures that are presented to the Russian people as sober realities. It is a bitter truth that Russians who get a chance to read what is written about life in the Soviet Union in American newpapers, magazines and books—and today more and more Russians get that chance—also find, often, not reality but a ridiculous distortion of reality.

In August and September of 1955, I met in Moscow about ten United States senators and representatives who were taking advantage of the new "Geneva spirit" to get a firsthand glimpse of what they previously had known mainly from newspaper accounts and committee reports. Without exception they manifested great surprise, often amounting to amazement, at what they saw. In particular they said they had expected to find the morale of the people and the standard of living much lower than they appeared to be.

In May of 1957 in Moscow, I told this to the head of one of the largest American communications networks, and I added that I thought the American congressmen had expected to find barbed wire in the streets and people walking around with their heads hanging and their bodies bent. He replied, "Well, that's what I had expected to find."

Of the dozens of American tourists whom I met during two visits to Russia, the overwhelming majority said they found conditions of life in Russia much better than they had anticipated. The list includes newspaper editors, businessmen, college professors, college students, agricultural experts, women television broadcasters—and American specialists on Soviet affairs! Many of them said, half in despair and half in jest, "What am I going to say when I get back to the United States?"

It is not for the Russians to complain, of course, if Americans have too black a picture of their country; the Soviet policy of secrecy has been one of the important contributing causes of our misconceptions. But our own press and radio, our own political propaganda and our own scholarship also bear an important share of the responsibility.

Yet the real reason is deeper—deeper than Soviet secrecy, deeper than American one-sidedness in reporting. The fact is that together with a great deal of rubbish there are also excellent accounts of daily life in the Soviet Union by American correspondents in Russia, and there are many American books which analyze Soviet institutions in an objective and scholarly manner. But American readers of these reports and books all too often simply reject, subconsciously, those images which conflict with their pre-conceptions.

Two years ago an American newspaper correspondent in Moscow wrote an account of the May Day parade in which he described people singing and dancing in the streets and enjoying themselves thoroughly. His newspaper published the account, but at the same time it ran an editorial in which it portrayed an embittered Russian people forced by their hated government to demonstrate in favor of a revolution which they did not want.

The correspondent, in recounting this to me, said that he thereupon wrote a letter to his editor in which he said, "I was there—I saw it—they were not bitter, they were happy, they were having a good time." The editorial writer wrote back, in effect, that they may have appeared happy, but that actually they could not have been happy, in view of the evils of the system under which they live.

It is probably fruitless to argue about whether or not Russians are happy. It is of critical importance, however, to recognize that *the notion that because communism is evil the people who live under it must be wretched is based on a false conception of evil.*

It is a false conception of evil which assumes that men who believe in evil doctrines—such as the doctrine of world revolution or the doctrine of the dictatorship of the proletariat—cannot at the same time work to accomplish great humanitarian benefits. It is an elementary fact, for example, that under the leadership of the Communist party of the Soviet Union the number of doctors in Russia increased from about 20,000 in 1917 to about 300,000 in 1957, and that in the same period and under the same leadership illiteracy declined from over 50 per cent to less than 5 per cent.

It is a false conception of evil which assumes that men who ordered the shooting of Hungarian women and children attempting to flee from terror could not at the same time sponsor a series of reforms designed to humanize conditions of detention in Soviet labor camps and to improve the system of criminal trials in the interest of the accused. The assumption sounds so plausible—yet it is contradicted not only in the particular case of the Soviet leadership in 1956 but also countless times in history. Did not Cromwell, the great restorer of English liberties, treat the Irish with barbaric cruelty? Did not Americans who fought for the inalienable rights of "all men" at the same time buy and sell slaves?

A group of prominent American lawyers visited Russia in 1956 in order to observe the Soviet legal system in operation. One of them later published an account of his impressions, the gist of which was that the Soviet legal system, despite some superficial resemblances to the legal systems of civilized countries, is *necessarily* a sham and a farce since the political leaders can and do rely heavily on force and secrecy as instruments of policy, and have absolute power to change the law as they will. Further, he argued, where there is no belief in God there can be no just system for the adjudication of disputes. In view of the satisfaction which all righteous people can derive from this reasoning, it is disconcerting to note that the great system of Roman law was developed under tyrants who employed terror against their enemies, who had absolute power, and who did not believe in God.

Is it really possible that Joseph Stalin, a cruel despot who ordered hundreds of thousands of people suspected of political opposition sent to labor camps in remote regions of Siberia without even the pretense of a fair trial, at the same time established a system of law and justice designed to operate fairly and objectively in nonpolitical cases? It is not only possible: it is a fact. But why should it appear strange?

Our notion that the tyrant can only do wrong is linked, as I have suggested, to our puritan tradition, with its fire-and-brimstone concept of hell. It is linked also to our national immaturity which leads us to see moral issues in terms of black and white, "good guys" versus "bad guys." It is linked, in addition, to an unconscious desire to cover up our own lack of high common purpose by creating an external symbol of evil, a Moby Dick, through which we find a release from our frustrations.

The fire-and-brimstone theory of totalitarianism, popularized in Orwell's *1984* and expounded in learned terms by many of our leading scholars, is comforting to us. Like the Pharisee we can say, "God, I thank thee, that I am not as other men are, extortioners, unjust, adulterers, or even as this publican."

Such self-righteousness blinds us to the true nature of evil. In the Bible the Devil tempts Christ with bread, with power over all the kingdoms of the world, and with miracles. So the totalitarian state offers its followers economic security, political power and sensational technological progress —all in return for one thing: absolute subservience to the high priest of these gods, the party.

But why speak of the positive achievements of the Soviet system, people often ask, when the most important feature of that system is the lack of freedom to defy the party line? And even granting that American writers have exaggerated the violence, injustice, bureaucracy and poverty of life under the Soviet regime, why should we advertise that fact? Don't we thereby weaken ourselves in our fight against communism?

The first answer is that if we have begun to test truth in terms of how useful it is politically, we have already lost the most important battle in the fight against communism. The second answer is that it is only by giving full credit to the positive achievements of the Soviet system that we can prepare ourselves to meet its challenge.

The Soviet system as it exists in popular imagination—with 20 million prisoners in Siberian labor camps, workers ground down by management, every tenth person an informer, people afraid to talk about anything—is no challenge to us at all. Such a system could not survive a single major crisis.

The Soviet system which actually has been created is quite different. It is a working totalitarianism, a viable totalitarian order, capable of surviving the death of its leading personalities, capable, very likely, of surviving even a defeat in war. It is a system which gives promise of achieving the very goals it has set for itself: economic security, political power and technological progress—by the very means it proclaims: absolute subservience to party discipline and the party line.

The challenge of this system is that it meets certain real needs of twentieth-century man—the need for unity and the need for a common social purpose.

It is of no use to fight communism by showing that the materialist aims which it proclaims can be achieved better by democratic means, since the underlying appeal of communism is not only in its aims but also—and primarily—in the process of mobilizing people to achieve those aims. By creating a mobilized social order, the Communist party provides peaceful outlets for service, self-sacrifice, discipline and other virtues usually associated with military life.

If we really want to defeat communism, there is only one way to do it. That way is so obvious one would be embarrassed to speak of it if it were not for the fact that it is the one thing that people who talk about fighting communism generally fail to mention. We must construct a social order in which the goals of justice, mercy and morality take precedence over economic security, political power and technological progress, and we must freely, through voluntary associations, pour into that social order the same spirit of service, self-sacrifice and common purpose that under the Soviet system is induced by party discipline.

Otherwise, Khrushchev's prediction that our grandchildren will be Communists may well come true (though of course they would not call themselves Communists but true democrats), and one of the most cherished American illusions may finally be disproved—that good always triumphs over evil in the end.

II

THE HERITAGE

2. The Tsarist Heritage

TO CHAADAYEV

Not long we basked in the illusion
Of love, of hope, of quiet fame;
Like morning mists, a dream's delusion,
Youth's pastimes vanished as they came.
But still, with strong desires burning,
Beneath oppression's fateful hand,
The summons of the fatherland
We are impatiently discerning;
In hope, in torment, we are turning
Toward freedom, waiting her command. . . .
Thus anguished do young lovers stand
Who wait the promised tryst with yearning.
While freedom kindles us, my friend,
While honor calls us and we hear it,
Come: to our country let us tend
The noble promptings of the spirit. . . .
Comrade, believe: joy's star will leap
Upon our sight, a radiant token;
Russia will rouse from her long sleep;
And where autocracy lies, broken,
Our names shall yet be graven deep.

ALEXANDER PUSHKIN

Chapter 2

THE TSARIST HERITAGE

The form and content of Soviet rule in the U.S.S.R. were considerably affected and influenced by peculiarly Russian history and circumstances —this is undeniable. Can it be doubted, for example, that had a proletarian revolution come to England it would have established institutions and pursued internal policies different in fundamental respects from those which were, in fact, established and pursued in Russia? Early in the twentieth century, England was a country with a powerful industrial base, a large middle class, a mature proletariat, a high degree of literacy, and a developed tradition of democracy. Russia, on the other hand, was then a relatively backward, predominantly agricultural, and largely illiterate country with a long history of despotism and fanaticism—whose Fundamental Laws proclaimed the monarch an "unlimited autocrat" to whom obedience was "ordained by God himself."

This history gave substance to Alexander Herzen's prophetic comment in 1851 that "communism is the Russian autocracy turned upside down," and to the statement of William Henry Chamberlin that "the monarchical absolutism of Nicholas I was the natural parent of the revolutionary absolutism of Lenin." That is not to say that choices made and fortuitous circumstances could not and did not alter the course of Soviet history. It is only to suggest that events must be appraised in the context of the historic background in which they occurred. Some light is shed on that historic background in the broad canvas spread by William Henry Chamberlin and in the detailed story, beginning in 1857, told by George Vernadsky. Historians differ, of course, in their interpretations of Tsarist history but few challenge Mr. Chamberlin's basic thesis. Some of Professor Vernadsky's characterizations of leading figures and policies meet with greater dissent.

11

THE SOVIET UNION CANNOT ESCAPE
RUSSIAN HISTORY

William Henry Chamberlin*

The Soviet Union cannot escape Russian history. . . . From the moment when the Russians emerge on the historical stage one finds them engaged in grim struggles, first for existence, then for the realization of certain goals of expansion.

Geographically Russia was a bulwark of Europe against Asia and it bore some of the hardest blows inflicted by nomadic invaders from the East. In the early Kiev period of Russian history, in the tenth, eleventh and twelfth centuries, there are records in the old chronicles of constant fighting with the wandering peoples of the steppe, the Polovtsi and Pechenegi.

Russia was submerged in the flood of Tartar conquest in the thirteenth century. The Tartar rule was gradually shaken off during the fourteenth and fifteenth centuries. But Russian history for centuries was an almost continuous series of wars, regular and irregular, declared and undeclared, now with Oriental peoples like the Turks and the Tartars, now with the Western neighbors, Swedes, Poles, Lithuanians, who barred the Russian thrust towards the Baltic Sea.

These wars were an important cause of the wretched poverty of the Russian people. They strained to the limit the human and material resources of the medieval Muscovite state. "The state swelled and the people grew thin." In this brilliant phrase Klyuchevsky summarizes the results of Russia's slow and painful expansion of its frontiers during the seventeenth century. This expansion, like so many episodes in Russian history, was accompanied by a vast sacrifice of human lives. The last available penny was screwed out of the people in taxes, often with the aid of the knout, a peculiarly brutal Russian form of whip. A grotesque situation arose when people voluntarily wished to become serfs, in order to escape tax obligations. This method of tax-evasion became so prevalent that it was made punishable by whipping with the formidable knout. To be compelled to remain free by the threat of being beaten within an inch of your life if you preferred to become a serf: here was a characteristic grim Russian paradox.

With most of its territory a vast plain, Russia lacked natural frontiers.

* Former foreign correspondent in the U.S.S.R., author of many books on the Soviet Union including *Russia's Iron Age* and *The Russian Revolution*. This selection is reprinted from chapters 1 and 2 of *The Russian Enigma* by William Henry Chamberlin, Copyright, 1943, by Charles Scribner's Sons, with permission of the publisher.

It was always vulnerable to land invasion. On four critical occasions its national independent existence hung in the balance as a result of foreign war, sometimes complicated by domestic turmoil. . . . From 1240, when the wild Tartar horsemen of Baty slaughtered the people of Kiev, until 1941 and 1942, when the Germans wrought the same scenes of carnage and destruction with modern weapons, Russia has always lived under the overhanging threat of war.

There were some periods of fairly prolonged external peace, especially in the nineteenth century. But foreign war, actual or threatened, has always been a major force in Russian national development. This constant military pressure was not the only cause that made the Russian Tsar the most complete autocrat in Europe. But it was an important cause. And the organization of the country almost on the basis of an armed camp helped to clamp down the institution of serfdom in Russia. During the early Middle Ages the Russian peasants could move freely, at stated times, from one landlord's estate to another. But during the sixteenth and seventeenth centuries there was increasing pressure to attach the peasant to the service of a single master.

This was the result not only of the greed of the landlord class, but of the military exigencies of the time. The theory was put forward that, as the gentry had to fight in the Tsar's army, the peasants were under an obligation to support, or, in the old Russian phrase, to "feed" the gentry. Peter the Great lent a certain validity to this crude Russian conception of the "social contract" by issuing a series of regulations that added up to a national labor service act. This Tsar of unbounded energy demanded that every young noble should serve the state, either in the armed forces or in the civil administration. . . .

Of course freedom from the threat of foreign invasion was not the only factor that made for the strengthening of American democracy and individualism. The inherited British tradition of political self-government and the sovereignty of law, the absence of any large unassimilable indigenous population, the high standard of literacy, all played their part. But the almost universal American assumption of political democracy and of respect for the constitutional rights of the individual would have been subjected to a much graver strain if our history had been heavily checkered with major wars. . . .

It is difficult for the American, accustomed to the ideas of separation of church and state, of freedom of opinion on religious questions, to understand either the curious mixture of state control and other-wordly mysticism in the Russian Orthodox Church or the doctrinaire atheism of the Communists. There is no parallel in American history for the passionate fanaticism that impelled tens of thousands of dissident Russian Old Believers, in the seventeenth century, to burn themselves alive as a protest against the wickedness of the world, and as a means of escaping from this wickedness and from the persecution of their belief. Both the absolutism of the autocracy and the absolutism of the revolutionary regime are alien to the Western mind, with its traditions of tolerance.

Russia, on its side, scarcely experienced the effect of three great movements which became part of the common heritage of Western Europe and America: the Renaissance, the Reformation and the French Revolution. Each of these movements, in its own way, contributed to the liberation of the human personality, to the strengthening of individualism. . . .

The roots of many Soviet actions and institutions may be sought and found in events and developments that occurred as far back as the days of Ivan the Terrible (1547-1584) and Peter the Great (1689-1725). There is historic justice and appropriateness in the fact that these two strongest figures in the long line of Tsars have been restored to official favor in the Soviet Union and commended to the admiration of the Russian people. Stalin is indebted to both these rulers for many models of policy, especially in such matters as carrying out a thorough liquidation of undesired or suspected individuals and classes.

If one were called on to name a single dominant element in Russian history from the Middle Ages to the present time it would be the unlimited power of the ruler. The Russian Tsar was an autocrat in a measure unparalleled in European countries. He was absolute master of the lives and property of his subjects, like a Turkish Sultan or a Tartar Khan.

Of course democracy, in the modern sense of the term, did not exist in medieval Europe. A network of privileges and distinctions separated the noble from the serf, the knight from the commoner, the wealthy merchant or master craftsman from the poorer classes in the cities. But in this European society there was a system of checks and balances, at least among the higher classes. The Church possessed independent authority and could sometimes bring the haughtiest monarch to his knees in repentance. The nobility often acted as a check on the Crown, the free cities on the nobility. The privileged orders were a counterpoise to each other and to the king. In the absence of any single all-controlling absolutism was the germ of future representative government.

Very different was the situation in Russia. No Tsar went to Canossa to perform public penance. No medieval Russian sovereign found himself obliged to limit his own authority by signing a charter at the demand of rebellious barons. No court would have protected a subject who refused to pay an exorbitant tax or to surrender a piece of property which the Tsar desired. Many Tsars were assassinated in palace conspiracies. But no Russian ruler was judged and sentenced to death by a revolutionary court of his subjects, like Charles I in England and Louis XVI in France.[1]

---

[1] There might have been such a scene in Russian history after the Bolshevik Revolution if it had not been for the exigencies of the Civil War. Nicholas II, his wife, son

The last *zemsky sobor,* the Russian equivalent for a parliament, met in 1649. After that time no national representative assembly was held in Russia until 1906. The upsurge of the revolutionary movement in 1905 induced Nicholas II to promulgate a Constitution, which provided for a Duma, or elected parliament. But this body was quickly reduced to a pale and unrepresentative shadow by arbitrary changes in the election law as soon as the revolutionary tide subsided and the autocracy again felt itself securely in the saddle.

It is not only in the retrospect of modern times that the Russian autocracy seems un-European in its unlimited power. A number of foreigners who visited Russia in the sixteenth and seventeenth centuries reported their impressions of a despotism that went far beyond anything with which they were familiar in their own countries. Ivan the Terrible made a show of his power to a visiting English merchant by ordering one of his courtiers to leap to certain death. When the Tsar asked whether the British sovereign (Queen Elizabeth) possessed similar power the British visitor drily replied that Her Majesty had better use for the necks of her subjects.

There is little trace in Russian thinking of any idea that subjects possessed any rights against the Tsar until the great intellectual awakening and flowering of Russian culture in the nineteenth century.[2] And even then it was deeply significant for the future course of events that the majority of Russian revolutionary theorists were not so much interested in protecting the individual against the state as in using the power of the state to transform society along collectivist lines. Many of these theorists preached what Lenin practised: the remaking of the social order through the dictatorship of a picked revolutionary minority. Had it not been for the autocracy of the Tsars, with its blighting effect on the conception of individual rights and liberties, the dictatorship of the Communist Party might never have come into operation. The one was a natural sequel to the other.

What were the roots of this despotism, unlimited in theory until the Constitution of 1905, although it was moderated in practice by the emergence of a gradually enlarging intelligent public opinion in the latter part of the nineteenth century? At the time when Kiev, the old city on the Dnieper, was the centre of Russian political life, in the tenth and eleventh centuries, Constantinople was the metropolis which the Russians knew best, through trade, through war and through religion. It was through the Greek Orthodox Church that the Russians were converted to Christianity. The

---

and four daughters were simply butchered in the cellar of their place of confinement in Ekaterinburg (now Sverdlovsk) without any formalities of indictment and trial because it was feared that they might be rescued by the advancing anti-Bolshevik forces.

[2] Peter the Great defined his own power in the following expansive terms: "His Majesty is an autocratic monarch, responsible to no one for his policies. He has power and authority to govern his state and lands as a Christian ruler according to his will and understanding."

Byzantine Empire was the state to which they naturally looked as a model.

And this Byzantine influence was entirely in favor of autocracy. The Byzantine Emperor was an absolute ruler, who was sometimes assassinated, but was never subjected to regular control by nobles, parliament or church. The Patriarch of Constantinople never assumed the independence of the Pope of Rome. This spiritual association with Constantinople was emphasized again at a later period. A Russian monk sent a message of greeting to Ivan III, who married a Byzantine Princess, and hailed him as sovereign of "the third Rome" that would never perish. Constantinople, the "second Rome," had just fallen to the Turks.

The Tartar conquest of the thirteenth century also worked in favor of the autocratic principle. Contrary to a general impression abroad, there was not much racial intermingling between Tartars and Russians. After the first orgy of killing and pillaging was over, the Tartar khans were satisfied if the Russian princes rendered tribute and paid occasional visits to the Tartar Court to render homage and seek confirmation of their titles. But the Asiatic despotism of the Tartar conquerors naturally had its effect upon the Russians. Moreover, the Tartar rule isolated Russia from the West and deepened the chasm between Russian and European civilization.

And in the further course of Russian history the forces that made for diversity of political life in Europe were blotted out. Russia became a primitive totalitarian state before the word was used in political terminology.

At one time there was a good deal of lusty, turbulent freedom in the two large trading towns of northwestern Russia, Novgorod and Pskov, which had belonged to the Hanseatic League. But eventually both sank to the level of ordinary provincial towns under the levelling despotism of the Muscovite Tsars. Ivan III took away the great bell that had once called the people of Pskov together for meeting, as a sign that such dangerous liberty was no longer to be permitted. Employing a method that has frequently been applied to undesired classes and groups in the Soviet Union, Ivan deported a considerable number of the Pskov citizens and replaced them with new settlers from Moscow. Ivan the Terrible mercilessly decimated the population of the two cities in reprisal for disloyalty, actual or suspected.

The boyars, as the older Russian nobles were called, also suffered at the hands of this stern Tsar. Ivan, who had been slighted by the boyars as a boy and nourished an implacable hatred for the whole order, built up a terrorist political police devoted to his service. Its members, the *oprichniki*, ranged over the country, clothed in black and displaying their formidable emblem, a dog's head and a broom. This symbolized their mission: to sniff out disloyalty and purge the land of treason.

There was no legal restraint on what the *oprichniki* could do. They were empowered to kill boyars, suspected of treason (the word sabotage was not known in Ivan's day), to violate their wives and seize their estates. The result of this policy was to break the inherited power and prestige of the old nobility and to transfer much of the land, then the principal source of wealth, to a new class, selected by the Tsar for his personal terrorist service and completely dependent on him for favor and advancement. Stalin followed a similar policy, against a different political and social background, when he exterminated many of the surviving Old Bolsheviks and replaced them with henchmen of his own. . . .

Twenty years after Ivan's death Russia was plunged into the crisis of the Troubled Times (1603-1613). The ruthless Ivan, as lustful as he was cruel, had married six times, in defiance of the canons of the Orthodox Church. He was succeeded by his son Fyodor, a weakling in body and mind. When Fyodor died childless, a cunning and ambitious boyar, Boris Godunov, had gained enough influence to insure his election as Tsar by a national assembly. A younger half-brother of the late Tsar Fyodor named Dmitry had died some years earlier. There was a strong suspicion that he had been murdered by order of Boris, in order to pave the way for the latter's accession to the throne.

But the ghost of Dmitry proved fatal to the ambition of Boris to found a dynasty of his own. A young adventurer who gave himself out as the escaped Dmitry found a hospitable reception and political support in Poland. He invaded Russia with a band of followers, accompanied by some Polish troops. This episode touched off the stormy decade of the Troubled Times (1603-1613). This is one of the most obscure and chaotic periods in Russian history. Every disintegrating force in the country was let loose. Cossacks swept up from the South to take part in pillage and devastation. Serfs rebelled and killed their masters. Swedes and Poles intervened. Rival Tsars were chosen and assassinated.

The existence of the Muscovite state seemed to be at stake. But the Russian people displayed their qualities of toughness, resilience, determination not to be ruled by foreigners. Bit by bit order emerged from chaos. A movement to clear the country of the foreigners and restore a strong central government found leaders in Prince Pozharsky, an aristocrat and Kuzma Minin, a man of the common people.

A national assembly, held in 1613, elected a new Tsar, Michael Romanov, first of a dynasty that endured for three centuries. Peace and the opportunity to recover from the ravages of the Troubled Times were purchased by the cession to Poland of some Russian territory in the neighborhood of Smolensk. But from that time on the balance of power, as between Russia and Poland, steadily inclined towards the former. The unlimited despotism of the Tsars was a blighting influence on many aspects of Russian life. But it was more conducive to military success and territorial expansion than the aristocratic anarchy of Poland, where the king was almost powerless and the peasants were held in serfdom. The Polish ruling class, the country gentry, developed a disastrous habit of engaging in factional quarrels which laid the country open to foreign intrigue and intervention, weakened its power of resistance, and was an important cause of the final tragedy, the partition of Poland between Russia, Austria and Prussia towards the end of the eighteenth century.

The Muscovite state gained a valuable ally against Poland in the Cossacks, who had established a wild, free, military republic in the valley of the Dnieper. These Cossacks were in many cases runaway serfs, peasants of the bolder type who preferred frontier fighting to the bondage which prevailed in the settled interior of Russia. They settled along the ill-defined southern fringe of the growing Russian Empire and served both as a spearhead for attack and a screen for defense against Turks and Tartars. The spirit and appearance of these Russian frontiersmen are admirably preserved in a painting by the great artist, Repin, which shows the Cossacks in their camp preparing a defiant reply to the Turkish Sultan.

The Cossacks of the Dnieper had been under Polish rule. But contempt for constituted authority was second nature to the Cossack. The arrogance of the Polish nobility, the uncertain delimitation of Cossack rights and privileges, the difference of religious faith (the Cossacks were Orthodox, the Poles were Roman Catholics) were among the causes of a big Cossack uprising, led by Bogdan Khmelnitsky, in 1648. An extraordinarily spirited equestrian statue of Khmelnitsky in a central square of Kiev still commemorates the anarchical liberty of this medieval Cossack community.

This uprising finally led to the detachment from the Polish state of all land east of the Dnieper and of the city of Kiev, on the western bank. After wavering between Russia, Poland and Turkey, the Cossacks, although with some misgivings and backslidings, accepted Russian rule as the least of the three evils. For some time the Cossacks represented the sole element of turbulent freedom in the despotic Russian state. Stenka Razin and Emilian Pugachev, leaders of the two greatest serf rebellions, were both Cossacks from the Don.

It is worth noting that periods of internal calm in Russian history are broken by terrific explosions of mass revolt. One such explosion began in 1669 under the leadership of Razin, a picturesque Robin Hood type of bandit whose memory is preserved in one of the most haunting of Russian folksongs. His forces rolled up the valley of the Volga, getting reinforcements of fugitive serfs. But he was defeated near Simbirsk, in the Middle Volga region. His motley hordes, with their ill-assorted arms, could not cope with the Government troops, which had received some training from European instructors. His final downfall was hastened by division among the Don Cossacks themselves. The wealthier disliked his primitive levelling tendencies. He was captured and executed in 1671.

Pugachev's revolt ran much the same course as Razin's, although it covered a wider area, including the valley of the Kama, the main tributary of the Volga. His rebellion foreshadowed the Bolshevik Revolution that was to occur a century and a half later inasmuch as it rallied the same forces of discontent that Lenin would mobilize in 1917. Along with discontented serf peasants Pugachev found supporters among the early Russian "proletarians," the laborers in the ironworks of the Urals, and among the Bashkirs, Chuvashes and other non-Russian peoples who live in the valley of the Volga and in the land between the Volga and the Urals. But Pugachev was crushed by the trained soldiers of Catherine II. And after his defeat and execution there were no more big serf revolts. The country was more efficiently policed, communications improved, and the old Cossack *volnost* (an almost untranslatable Russian word meaning uncontrolled liberty) was tamed. As the majority of the Cossacks became well-to-do farmers they lost their rebel spirit and became faithful soldiers of the Tsar, dashing horsemen in war, auxiliary police against strikers and peasant rioters in peace.

When serfdom was abolished, in 1861, it was not under the pressure of a peasant insurrection. It was better, as Tsar Alexander II told a gathering of reluctant landowners, that serfdom should be abolished from above than from below. Perhaps it was because serfdom was abolished in this way, and with a good deal of consideration for the interests of the landowners, that many peasant grievances remained unredressed. Russia, as the experiences of 1905 and 1917 proved, remained ripe for agrarian rebellion.

One very important element in Russia's past heritage is the marked time-lag in the cultural development of the nation. No European country of corresponding population and political importance was so barren in free and questioning minds. During the centuries when religion was the first concern of men's minds in Europe, there was no Russian Thomas Aquinas, Loyola, Pascal, Luther, Calvin or Huss. The most serious schism in the Russian Church took place in the seventeenth century, when the Patriarch Nikon introduced changes in the prayer books and ritual to bring Russian practice into line with that of other churches of the Orthodox rite. These changes were stubbornly and suspiciously resisted by some of the clergy and parishioners, who were known as Old Believers. It is significant of the intellectual sterility of the time in Russia that no important question of theological belief or church organization was involved in this schism, although each side maintained its viewpoint with uncompromising determination and was prepared to give or receive the crown of martyrdom.

There was, to be sure, a certain psychological background for the schism. The Old Believers were averse to all the foreign innovations and administrative changes that took place in the latter part of the seventeenth century and reached their culmination in the reign of Peter the Great. Moussorgsky's magnificent opera, *Khovanstchina,* far too little known outside of Russia, gives an unforgettable imaginative picture of the clash between old and new in Russia on the eve of Peter's reforms and finds its climax in a scene of self-immolation on the part of the Old Believers.

The Russian Church was weakened by the schism. And it lost its last chance to function as even a modest counterpoise to the absolutism of the state when Peter the Great abolished the Patriarchate and placed the Church under the administrative authority of a layman, the Procuror of the Holy Synod.

So Russia did not share the mighty ferment of ideas that coincided in Europe with the struggle between Roman Catholicism and Protestantism. It also missed the humanistic culture of the Renaissance. Until the nineteenth century Russia conveys the impression of a nation asleep, so far as cultural life is concerned. There is no fourteenth-century Russian Dante, no sixteenth-century Russian Shakespeare, no seventeenth-century Russian Newton, no eighteenth-century Russian Voltaire.

Now and then a European would bring into semi-Asiatic Russia some western influence. Scotch and German soldiers of fortune helped to impart the elements of drill and discipline to the raw Russian levies. Italian architects, of whom Rastrelli was the most famous, designed churches and palaces. Skilled artisans were induced to come to Russia, especially in the time of Peter the Great, to teach industrial arts and crafts to the Russians. But there was only a very dim and pale Russian reflection of the humanist movement of the West, of the rediscovery of the Greek and Latin classics, because there were so few Russian scholars. Russia was a force to be reckoned with politically and militarily long before it was able to make a notable contribution to European cuture.

A similar unevenness of development is visible in the Soviet Union in the third decade of its existence. The Soviet accomplishment in building up industrial and military power is out of all proportion to the manifestations of original creative thought under the Communist dictatorship.

Russia was sufficiently part of Europe to be drawn into the wars of the French Revolution and of the Napoleonic period. But the French Revolution aroused no such response in Russia as in the countries of Western and Central Europe. The autocracy, the noble-serf social relation, remained unchanged. The most visible reflection of the influence of the French Revolution in Russia was the unsuccessful revolt of the Decabristi in 1825. They were a group of officers who had imbibed progressive ideas from service abroad in countries which had felt the impact of the French revolutionary changes.

The reign of Peter the Great (1689-1725) marked the transition from the Moscow to the St. Petersburg period in Russian history. That revolutionary autocrat shifted the capital from old, semi-Oriental Moscow to the new capital which he built on the shore of the Gulf of Finland in the style of a European city and gave his own name. A giant of a man, gifted with enormous mental and physical energy, Peter strove mightily to de-barbarize Russia, to bring it up to the level of the European civilization of the time. It was both a personal and perhaps a characteristic national tragedy that the means which he used to promote this debarbarization were often extremely cruel and oppressive and won him, in the eyes of some of his more conservative and superstitious subjects, the reputation of being the anti-Christ forecast in the Book of Revelations.

From early boyhood Peter broke away from the conventional life of a Muscovite Tsar, secluded in a palace and surrounded with Oriental ceremony. He loved to talk and carouse with the adventurous riffraff of foreigners who lived in the "German Village," a settlement where foreigners were segregated by order of the Government so that they would not con-taminate Orthodox Russians with their strange ways and ideas. He learned to smoke, a heathenish sin in the eyes of the bearded boyars who practised almost all the other vices. He conceived a very unroyal fondness for work-ing with his hands. Ships, guns, machines, all the material things in which the West excelled Russia, fascinated the young ruler.

He was the first Tsar who left his own country to travel in Europe. The story of how he worked incognito in a Dutch shipyard and got into a fistfight with a fellow-worker is one of the few internationally well-known anecdotes of Russian history. Peter was far from housebroken and, with his boon companions, he left behind him a trail of rowdy devastation in the house which was assigned for his residence in England. The sequel was a bill for damages and some shocked and disapproving comment.

Peter returned to Russia brimming over with plans for the modern-ization of the country. He encountered a mutiny of the *streltsi*, which he promptly quelled, cutting off the heads of the ringleaders with his own hand. There was nothing gentle about Peter. His son Aleksei, who did not sympathize with his innovating plans, died as a result of torture which was inflicted in order to make him disclose the accomplices in a suspected plot. V. O. Klyuchevsky, most eloquent and philosophical of Russian historians, sums up the paradox of Peter as reformer in the following sentences:

His beneficent actions were accomplished with repelling violence. Peter's reform was a struggle of despotism with the people, with its sluggishness. He hoped through the threat of his authority to evoke initiative in an enslaved society, and through a slave-owning nobility to introduce into Russia European science, popular education, as the neccessary condition of social initiative. He desired that the slave, remaining a slave, should act consciously and freely. The inter-action of despotism and freedom, of education and slavery—this is the political squaring of the circle, the riddle which we have been solving for two centuries from the time of Peter, and which is still unsolved. . . .

Although Peter's quick and lively mind seized on many Western dis-coveries and methods of administration and adapted them for use in Russia, he made no attempt to introduce into Russia the element of individual

freedom and initiative which contributed much to the scientific and technical progress of the West. The autocracy became stronger than ever. There
was no loosening of the chains of serfdom. There was no experimenting
with elected representative bodies. The Church was reduced almost to
the status of a department of the state.

Throughout the eighteenth century the extension of Russia's frontiers
proceeded with the inexorable finality of an expanding glacial ice-cap.
The growing weakness of Russia's neighbors, the Poles in the West, the
Tartars and Turks in the South and Southwest, favored this extension.
Under the reign of Peter's most distinguished successor, Catherine II, Russia
reached its natural southern frontier, the Black Sea, and swallowed up the
greater part of Poland. It maintained and somewhat improved its western
boundary under the shock of the Napoleonic War. During the nineteenth
century Russia made no very considerable territorial gain in Europe, but
the Empire was rounded out with new conquests in the Caucasus and
Central Asia.

More important than any political and military developments was
the amazing cultural awakening of Russia in the nineteenth century. There
was a flowering of imagination and of creative thought that is all the more
impressive because of the previous sterile nature of the Russian intellectual
soil. There were a few pioneers of the future Russian culture, like the
poet-scientist, M. V. Lomonosov, who helped to establish the Russian
literary language in the eighteenth century. But if everything written in
Russian before 1800 (old sagas and folksongs excepted) were destroyed by
some natural catastrophe, the loss would scarcely be perceptible, except to
specialized students. Russia entered the nineteenth century with an intellectual past remarkably blank for a people so numerous and, as the future
would show, so gifted artistically. There had been no achievements up to
this time in literature or art (the inherited Byzantine ikon-painting excepted), in science and philosophy that could challenge comparison with
those of England and France, Germany and Italy. Several causes account
for this retarded cultural growth.

There was the long sleep enforced by the Tartar Conquest. There
was the chronic exhaustion of national strength and wealth by a long series
of wars. The unlimited autocracy was itself no encouragement to free
speculation. This might also be said of a state religion that was at once
dogmatic and conservative. Cities are the centres of intellectual life, and
Russia up to very modern times possessed very few genuine cities, only
garrison towns and large trading villages.

The nineteenth century was an era of noteworthy cultural and material
progress for all Europe. And Russia was caught up in the wave of this
progress. Its two glowing lyric poets, Pushkin and Lermontov, rank with
Byron and Shelley among the leading figures in the romantic movement.
Both Russian poets found much of their inspiration in the life and legends

of the Caucasus, with its magnificent mountain scenery and its medley of picturesque tribes.

In the field of the novel Russia, with its four masters, Tolstoy, Dostoevsky, Turgenev, and Gogol, and its many lesser writers, such as Goncharov, Saltikov-Shchedrin, Chekhov, Gorky, Andreev, easily surpassed the contemporary achievement of any European country, with the possible exception of France. In music it achieved a position second only to Germany, with such composers as Tschaikovsky, Moussorgsky, Rimsky-Korsakov, Rubinstein, Borodin, Glinka and many others. Scientists, such as Metchnikov, Mendeleev and Pavlov, artists like Repin, historians ranging from the old-fashioned courtly Karamzin at the beginning of the century to the brilliant and profoundly thoughtful Klyuchevsky at the end, all made their contribution to this great century of Russian cultural achievement.

This was no mere emergence of individual men of genius and talent. The Russian educated class steadily increased in numbers, although it remained relatively small because of the great masses of illiterate and semiliterate peasants and the still more backward non-Russian Oriental peoples of the Empire. But the quality of this young Russian intelligentsia was out of all proportion to its numbers. In breadth of intellectual interest, in spontaneity and keenness of literary and artistic appreciation, in receptivity to new ideas, the Russian intellectual, the writer, teacher, physician, scientist, artist or student often compared very favorably with men and women of similar educational background in other countries.

To what was, for Russia, a discovery of European art, literature, philosophy, science, social and economic theories the Russian intelligentsia brought an exhilarating sense of new learning, a generous enthusiasm, such as Europe's own humanists felt when they began to decipher the masterpieces of Greece and Rome. Ivan Karamazov, the intellectual among the three brothers of Dostoevsky's mighty novel, apostrophizes Europe in these glowing words:

Precious are the dead that lie there. Every stone over them speaks of such burning life in the past, of such passionate faith in their work, their truth, their struggle and their science that I know I shall fall on the ground and kiss those stones and weep over them.

It is scarcely an exaggeration to say that only in the nineteenth century did Russians begin to come alive as human beings. The personalities of Tsars and Tsarinas, positive or negative, had always been important because of the absolutist character of the government. A few progressive-minded nobles and distinctive generals convey a sense of definite character. But until the nineteenth century the poverty of individual personality in Russia matched the poverty in cultural achievement. Then the ice that seemed to freeze the Russians of earlier generations commenced to crack. Figures of world significance began to emerge.

Perhaps the best known Russian of the last century was Count Leo

Tolstoy. Descendant of an old aristocratic family, author of the two great novels, *War and Peace* and *Anna Karenina,* he attracted international attention by the philosophy of nonviolence, renunciation of wealth, abstinence and simple living which he preached and practised during the later period of his life. He was a successor of Rousseau and a precursor of Gandhi, with whom he had much in common spiritually and intellectually. In his attitude, bordering on anarchism, of rejecting the power of the state, in his repudiation of violence between man and man, Tolstoy expressed the unconscious aspirations of the peasants whom he knew on his estate, and who regarded taxes and military conscription as two of the principal curses of their lives.

Tolstoy escaped exile or imprisonment because of his aristocratic antecedents and because of his international prestige. But he was excommunicated by an officially controlled Church, although he might reasonably have been regarded as a most sincere Christian. Other independent minds were not so fortunate. Alexander Herzen, perhaps the most eloquent Russian publicist of his time, found that he could write freely only in London. N. G. Chernishevsky, a man who might have ranked with Mill and Spencer because of his encyclopedic learning and his fondness for social theory, was broken by a period of long exile in Siberia.

One of the most lovable figures in the revolutionary movement was Prince Peter Kropotkin. He gave up a promising scientific career to take up the hunted, persecuted life of the revolutionary. For a time he was imprisoned in the grim fortress of Peter and Paul, in St. Petersburg. His escape, after he had been transferred to a hospital, was one of the spectacular episodes of the struggle between the revolutionaries and the police. To Darwin's hard law of the survival of the fittest in a world of struggle, Kropotkin opposed a theory of mutual aid, for which he tried to find support in science and in history. Forced to live in exile for many years Kropotkin returned to Russia, an old man, after the Revolution. He found a new form of dictatorial state instead of the voluntary association of free communes of which he had dreamed, and died, sad and disappointed, in 1921.

Another striking figure was Michael Bakunin. Like Kropotkin, he was an Anarchist by conviction. But, unlike the humane and scholarly Prince, he reveled in violent action and was willing to resort to any kind of force and intrigue in order to gain his objective: the total overthrow of existing society and the substitution of anarchist communism. It is psychologically significant that this great Russian Anarchist, who yearned for the destruction of the state, as the source of all evil, who fought on more than one barricade in European insurrections, tried to create secret revolutionary organizations, based on the principle of absolute authority of the leaders. It was this very principle, successfully carried into practice by Lenin, that laid the foundation for the Communist dictatorship.

It was not only dangerous political thinkers like Herzen, Bakunin and Kropotkin who felt the stern hand of the Tsar's police. Authors like Dostoevsky and Turgenev also found themselves in difficulties. Because he had joined a discussion club which was suspected of seditious tendencies, Dostoevsky, under the reactionary rule of Nicholas I, was condemned to death. At the last moment the sentence was commuted to four years of penal servitude in Siberia. Curiously enough, Dostoevsky emerged from this experience not an embittered rebel, but a mystical Christian. His views became more conservative and nationalist in his later years and he satirized the revolutionaries savagely in his novel, *The Possessed*. The Westernized liberal Turgenev was so much harassed by police surveillance that he preferred to spend much of his life abroad.

Yet, although the autocratic system pressed heavily on the individual, especially upon the individual of liberal or radical views, the nineteenth century was still the freest and most progressive period in Russian history. No European country grew so visibly in mental stature between 1800 and 1900. No European land owes so large a part of its heritage of civilization to the effort of a single century. One recalls the enthusiastic words of Gogol, who likened Russia's forward movement to the galloping of a troika, a Russian carriage or sleigh, drawn by three horses:

And, Russia, art thou not also flying onward like a spirited troika that nothing can overtake? The road is smoking beneath thee, the bridges rumble, everything falls back and is left behind. Russia, whither fliest thou? Answer! She gives no answer. The ringing of the bells melts into music. The air, torn to shreds, whirs and rushes like the wind. Everything on earth is flying by. The other states and nations, looking askance, make way for her and stand aside.

The absence of an old cultural tradition lent a quality of reckless boldness to Russia's newly emancipated thinkers. Herzen, the coiner of expressive phrases, described Russia as "the land of outward slavery and inward freedom." Severely curbed by police and censors, the Russian intellectual was free from the invisible West European restraints of custom and convention. From the extremism of autocracy it was an easy step to the opposite pole of extremism: revolutionary dictatorship.

In the heritage of the Russian past one can find many seeds of the great revolution that was to shatter the political and social order, and many foreshadowings of the regime that was to emerge from that revolution. The traditional unlimited power of the government was an excellent preparation for the Communist dictatorship. The Russian folk pattern of bearing great poverty and hardship stoically over long periods of time and then flaring up in an outburst of wild revolt was favorable to the success of a group of determined revolutionaries who would take advantage of one of these moods of all-out rebellion and then lay a heavy yoke of their own on the masses of the people.

The essential newness of Russian conscious thinking on social and economic problems, the exclusion of most educated Russians from positions of practical responsibility, worked in favor of doctrinaire extremism. Russia had missed the individualist aspects of such movements as the Reformation, the Renaissance and the French Revolution. It was less touched than any large European power by the general trend towards parliamentarism and liberalism. Among the obvious causes of the Revolution were the intolerable strain and dislocation imposed by the First World War, the contrasts of wealth and poverty in the country, the hard living conditions of most of the industrial workers and peasants, the discontent of the non-Russian nationalities.

Less obvious, but no less important as a cause was the comparative absence, in Russian historical experience, of anything that would cultivate a strong sense of an individual's right to personal liberty and private property. No Russian was safe against arrest for political reasons. Only a minority of the peasants owned their land on an individual property basis. The number of persons with a conscious personal stake in the avoidance of violent change was smaller than in any other European country. On the very eve of its fall the Tsarist system impressed most observers as a bulwark of conservatism and reaction. But it was also a powder-magazine of violent revolution. . . .

The Bolshevik Revolution made Russia more enigmatical than ever, in the eyes of the outside world. The downfall of Tsarism was generally welcomed in democratic countries. But many of the theories and acts of the victorious revolutionaries seemed harsh and repelling. The denial of political and civil liberties, the "liquidation" of whole classes of the population, the attempt to realize professedly humane ultimate ends by immediate means that were often ruthless and brutal, inspired doubts and questionings, even in the minds of many who were originally sympathetic with the Revolution. . . .

FROM 1857 TO 1914

GEORGE VERNADSKY *

ALEXANDER II

Public opinion had already made itself felt during the life of Emperor Nicholas I, despite all the efforts of censorship and police. Following his death, it could no longer be restrained, the more so because the new emperor, Alexander II, was by nature different from his father. It cannot be

* At Yale University. Author of *The Expansion of Russia; Lenin, Red Dictator,* and *Political and Diplomatic History of Russia.* The selection is from chapters 10, 11, and 12 of *A History of Russia,* Copyright 1929, 1930, and 1944, by Yale University Press. By permission.

said that his political views differed greatly from those of his father. He had, in fact, the same ideals of enlightened absolutism; but he was of a much gentler and more tolerant disposition. Alexander had been educated in much more humane spirit. His preceptor was the poet Zhukovsky, one of the most noble characters of the first half of the nineteenth century.

The patriotic feelings of Alexander, as of many of his contemporaries, were deeply hurt by the outcome of the Crimean War. Reforms in Russia seemed inevitable, as the old *régime* had proved itself incapable of organizing the defense of Russia. This was admitted prior to his death by Nicholas I, who told Alexander: "I am handing you command of the country in a poor state." The basic defect of the old *régime* was the institution of serfdom. It was consequently natural that the reforms of Alexander II should start with this matter, the more so because the solution of the question had been prepared during the reign of Nicholas I.

In January, 1857, a secret Committee on Peasant Reform was organized. It was composed of several of the highest officials of the Government, but the fear of taking decisive action retarded its work. A decisive step was taken at the initiative of Alexander in the late autumn of 1857, when the emperor authorized the governor-general of Vilna to organize "Provincial Committees" of the nobility in the Lithuanian provinces for the discussion of the terms of the proposed peasant reforms on December 2, 1857. Following this move there was no possibility of retreat; the reforms became inevitable. The nobles of other provinces were forced to request the Government's authorization to form similar committees. Their motives were clearly expressed in the famous speech of Alexander II to the nobility of Moscow: "Better that the reform should come from above than wait until serfdom is abolished from below." . . .

The basic principles of the reform were as follows: Household serfs were to be freed within a period of two years without redemption, but were to receive nothing on gaining their freedom. Peasant serfs were to receive not only their personal freedom, but also certain allotments of land. In determining the dimensions of each peasant's share, the amount of land worked by peasants for their own use under conditions of serfdom was taken into consideration. The serfs had worked both their own lands and the lands of their owner. The area of the allotments granted to the peasants following the reform was equal approximately to the area retained by the landowner. Thus, under the terms of the reform of 1861, the peasants received grants of land which, prior to the reform, had absorbed only half of their labor.

By the terms of the emancipation, the land which the peasants received did not become their private property. It continued to be regarded as the property of the landowner, but was held for the benefit of the peasant. The peasants, though now freedmen, were called upon to pay for the use of this land or to perform certain services for the landowner. The Government, however, was willing to help, if both the landowners and the peasants desired to terminate this relationship. Help was provided in the form of a long-term credit to purchase the land. In those cases where estate-owners agreed to sell the land to their former serfs, the Government paid the landowners the cost of the land with an interest-bearing bond, and this sum was imposed upon the peasant in the form of deferred payments over a period of years. The cost was computed on the basis of the annual payment of the peasant, being worth 6 per cent of the cost of the land. The deferred payments were added to the head tax of the peasant.

The appointed period was forty-nine years. Within twenty years following 1861 about 85 per cent of landowners actually sold to the peasants their part of land in each estate with the above-mentioned assistance of the Government. Even in this case the peasant did not receive the land in complete personal ownership, but each peasant commune or village received the whole area of land in communal ownership under collective responsibility for the redemption payments of all the members of the commune. Special government agents named for the purpose of putting the reform into operation, called mediators, drew up charter deeds for the land in the name of a whole commune. The commune itself divided the land among its members according to the size of families. These subdivisions took place periodically every few years.

Thus, even following the reforms, the peasant did not become an individual property owner or an individual possessing full civil rights, but remained subject to the authority of the commune. Actually the peasants became dependent upon those government bureaucratic agencies which concerned themselves with peasant affairs. It is necessary to add that outside of the commune each peasant could purchase land on the basis of full ownership. This situation is important for the understanding of future events. It explains the continued juridical isolation of the peasants even following the reform. It also preserved in their consciousness the memory of serfdom. The firm bonds of the commune did not permit changes in the manner of owning land. The peasants never forgot that the commune had only half of the former estate. The reform of 1861 seemed incomplete and they dreamed of completing it. Another idea connected with the land commune was that the land was not the property of individuals but was granted in the form of an allotment to serve the uses of the individual. Thus, land within the whole state was regarded by the peasant as a fund which could be drawn upon for further allotments until it was used up. These were the embryonic ideas of the subsequent revolution.

The reform of 1861 was tragically inadequate. There were two ways of really solving the question finally. The first was to leave the possession as well as the ownership of the land with the land-owner. The peasant in this case would have received merely his personal freedom. In the majority of cases, however, under the pressure of necessity, the landowner would have been forced to sell part of his land to his former serfs. The Government could have assisted in this transaction, in the favor of the individual peasants, and not of the communes. The actual result would have been almost the same as it was by the reform of 1861, but the psychological results would have been quite different. Instead of thousands of peasant communes there would have been created millions of peasant landowners. The ideas of a "general fund" and of "allotments" would have been avoided. It was toward this result that the later reforms of Stolypin were directed, but the reforms of Stolypin came forty-five years too late (1906).

The other possibility, in introducing the reform of 1861, was to take all the land away from the estate-owners and to divide it among the peasants. This would have been the simplest solution, which would have prevented all the later upheavals in Russia. If the partition of land had been completed in 1861, there would have been no need for it in 1918 and in that case the Russian revolution would never have been accompanied by such riots as it actually was.

However, in spite of its incompleteness, the reform of 1861 was an ambitious effort which changed the whole old order. After the peasant reform, it seemed easier to start with other reforms which, taken together, completely changed the nature of the Russian state. The other leading "great reforms" of Alexander II were the reforms of the Zemstvo, the towns, the courts, and the military service.

The reform of the Zemstvo in 1864 created for the first time since that of the early Moscow state, real local self-government without regard to class. The basis of the reform consisted in granting to elected representatives of each county (Uyezd) control over the schools, medical affairs, and roads. The elective law provided for the division of electors into three *curias:* the private landowners (nobles and merchants); peasant communes; and townspeople. The representatives elected an "Executive Committee" known as the *Uprava* for a term of three years. The representatives of the Uyezd formed a provincial assembly which elected a provincial Zemstvo Committee (*Uprava*). Following the general spirit of the Zemstvo reforms, similar measures were introduced for town government in 1870. The electors were likewise divided into three *curias,* according to a property census; the amount of taxes paid was totaled and divided into three equal parts, each having an equal number of representatives. Both the Zemstvo and the town authorities succeeded in carrying out work of great cultural importance in Russia prior to the Revolution of 1917.

Of no less significance was the new judicial reform of 1864, of which S. I. Zarudny was the chief promoter. Its basic principles were: the improvement of court procedure; the introduction of the jury and the organization of lawyers into a formal bar. Despite some drawbacks of the Russian courts following 1864, they undoubtedly reached considerable efficiency, and in this respect Russia could be favorably compared with the most progressive European countries. It is necessary, however, to note here the difference between the façade and the foundation of the new Russian state. The peasants in the vast majority of small civil litigations did not use the new courts and had to be content with the "volost" courts, especially organized for them, and from the reign of Alexander III until 1912, they also had to accept the jurisdiction of the "Land Captains."

The last of the major reforms was the introduction of universal military service in 1874. The law of military service was practically the only one of the laws of this time which affected equally all the classes of the Russian people. Here there was no difference between the façade and the structure; it was profoundly democratic in spirit. The recruits were granted privileges only according to their family position. The only son, the only grandson, or only supporter of a family, received full privileges and were registered in the reserve of the second category, that is, in practice, prior to the World War, they were never called into service. With respect to the term of service and promotion, special privileges were recognized in favor of individuals having secondary education. Class differences were not in any way reflected in privileges of military service, with the exception of the selection of the Guards officers from the aristocratic circles of society. The society created by the reforms of Alexander II lasted in its general character until 1905, and in part until 1917. . . .

The internal policy of Alexander II did not bring about political peace in Russia. In spite of his far-reaching social and administrative reforms, he had to face bitter political opposition and direct revolutionary movements. The political opposition to the Government came primarily from the nobility. The idea was current that the nobility, having been deprived of its social and economic privileges, should receive in exchange political privileges, that is, a part of the governing power. This idea appeared during the preparation of the peasant reforms among members of the Provincial Committees who were discontented with the radicalism of the Revising Commission. In addition to the political programs of the nobles, other plans, looking to the reorganization of Russia along constitutional and democratic lines, were advanced, as a continuation of "Decembrist" tradition.

The revolutionary idea was chiefly current among the "Raznochintsi" —that is, individuals of no definite class: the children of peasants and merchants having received secondary or higher education; the children of the clergy who did not desire to enter the church; the children of small civil servants who did not desire to continue the vocation of their fathers; and the children of impoverished nobles. These Raznochintsi rapidly formed a new social class, the so-called "intelligentsia," which included many members of the nobility. The intellectuals grew rapidly with the reforms of Alexander II. The institution of the legal bar, the growth of newspapers and magazines, the increased number of teachers, etc., contributed to the growth. The intelligentsia consisted of intellectual people in general, but at first it consisted primarily of people connected with the publication of papers and magazines or connected with universities. The university students contributed the greatest number of radical and revolutionary leaders. The majority of the students consisted of men who had no means whatsoever. The average student lived in a state of semi-starvation, earning his way through the university by giving lessons or by copying. The majority of the students had no notion of sport and no taste for it. Lack of physical exercise and consequent ill-health had a crushing effect upon the psychology of the students.

The leaders of the intelligentsia desired not only radical political changes but also a social revolution, in spite of the fact that Russian industry was too undeveloped to supply a firm basis for socialism. The Government was criticized for not being radical enough. The more moderate criticism was expressed in the legalized press, while the more bitter criticism appeared in revolutionary organs published abroad, the best known of which was *Kolokol* (The Bell), published by Herzen in London. Revolutionary propaganda against the Government immediately took a harsh tone. In 1862 there appeared a proclamation to the youth of Russia calling for terrorism and the murder of members of the Government and supporters of its policy. The appearance of this proclamation was contemporaneous with a number of cases of incendiarism in St. Petersburg. The Government took decisive steps; several individuals were arrested and exiled. At the same time the Polish revolutionary leaders were preparing an uprising in Poland. The activity of the Russian revolutionary leaders was connected with the Polish movement. The Polish revolution broke out in 1863. Just prior to this uprising the Russian Government had started a more liberal policy in Poland. The introduction of the reform had been put in the hands of a prominent Polish statesman, Marquis Wielopolski. The radical elements in Poland decided to *sabotage* the policy of moderate reform. The uprising was suppressed by military force, after which the last remnants of Polish independence were abrogated. . . .

A new wave of antigovernment activity arose in the 1870's. Among the liberal circles of society, the desire grew for elective representation not only in local self-government (Zemstvos and towns) but also in the central agencies of government. The institution of a parliament was to complete the unfinished reforms. This movement became particularly strong following the Turkish War of 1877-78, when the liberated Bulgaria received a constitution. The desire for a constitution in Russia became clearly expressed. The activity of the revolutionary organizations in Russia during this period likewise increased. Their activity may be divided into two periods. From 1870 to 1875 the radical intellectuals abstained from direct struggle against the Government, but undertook preparatory propaganda among the masses of the people. Many members of the intellectuals of that time went "to the people," living among the peasants and workmen, teaching schools or becoming agricultural or industrial laborers.

The Government, fearing the results of the propaganda, oppressed the movement by arresting participants in it. At times the peaceful members of the movement suffered arrest together with the real propagandists. In many cases persons were tried and imprisoned or exiled on the mere suspicion and action by the police. The Government's measures aroused the bitterest feeling among the radical intellectuals. In the middle of the 1870's, the revolutionaries began to use terrorism and to make attempts against members of the Government. In 1879, in Lipetsk in central Russia, the leaders of the revolutionary movement met in secret conference. An Executive Committee was elected at this meeting for the purpose of opposing the Government. This Executive Committee decided to abandon all attempts against individual members of the Government and to bend every effort upon assassinating the head of the Government, Emperor Alexander II. From that time on, Alexander II was the object of a manhunt by revolutionaries. Attempts were made in rapid succession, one after the other, but were without success until the attempt made in St. Petersburg in the spring of 1881, which resulted in the death of Alexander II on March 13, 1881.

The assassination of Alexander II occurred on the very day when the emperor signed a *ukaz* calling for Representative Committees to advise the State Council. This was the "constitution" drawn up by Loris Melikov, the Minister of the Interior. Melikov's idea was that the revolutionary activity of the intellectuals could not be stopped by police measures alone. In his opinion the revolutionaries had the moral support of the moderate classes of society who were discontented with the autocratic policy of the Government. Melikov believed that the Government should placate the moderate elements of the opposition by means of granting a moderate constitution. This measure, he believed, would deprive the revolutionaries of the moral support of these classes. The assassination of Alexander II prevented the execution of this plan. His son and successor, Alexander III, withdrew the constitution of Melikov, and the *ukaz* signed by Alexander II was never published.

ALEXANDER III AND NICHOLAS II

The impression made upon Alexander III by the assassination of his father lasted during his life. He retained a distrust for all popular movements and influenced by Constantine Pobiedonostsev, expressed a firm belief in the infallibility of the principle of autocracy. The political program of Alexander III was extremely simple. It consisted in opposing all liberal and revolutionary movements in Russia and in satisfying, to a certain degree, the urgent economic demands of the Russian people. These principles of policy were handed down by Alexander to his son Nicholas, who ascended the throne on the death of his father in 1894. It was only under the pressure of the revolution of 1904-5 that Nicholas agreed to grant a constitution; but up to the second revolution of 1917, and probably to his very death in 1918, Nicholas retained a belief in the principles of policy laid down by his father. . . .

Soon after Nicholas' coronation, intrigues sprang up among his ministers and the grand dukes, whom Nicholas never succeeded in mastering and putting in their proper place. Nicholas did not like to admit that anyone exercised any influence upon him. In fact, however, he was constantly under someone's influence, until he became completely dominated by his wife, Alexandra Feodorovna. An episode illustrating Nicholas' character took place in Moscow during his coronation. Because of the incompetence of the police, a panic occurred at the distribution of gifts in honor of the occasion, in which over one thousand people were crushed to death. This accident took place at the very height of the coronation festivities. There is no doubt that if it had occurred at the coronation of Alexander III, he would have immediately canceled all further celebration. Nicholas, however, had the idea of showing his firmness and made no change of plans. Even the ball at the French Ambassador's the same evening was not canceled. As a matter of fact this was not firmness but tactlessness.

While it is possible to define the internal policy pursued by Alexander III, the same cannot be done for the reign of Nicholas II. His policy consisted simply in continuing by inertia the policy of his father. The internal policy of Alexander III consisted first of all in strengthening governmental control in all directions where free public opinion could be expected to manifest itself. Pursuant to this policy, the laws regarding local self-government were revised. The power of the Government, in the person of the provincial governors, was strengthened as against the power of the Zemstvos. According to the new laws of 1890, the peasants elected only candidates for the Zemstvo, while the governor chose representatives from among these candidates. This law was repealed in 1906. In order to extend governmental supervision over the peasants, the office of "Zemsky Nachalnik" or Land Captain, appointed by the Government from the nobility, was created in 1889. The Zemsky Nachalniks had administrative power in local affairs as well as the function of judge over the peasantry.

Many measures were also taken to repress the intellectuals. The universities were reorganized in 1884. Education became subject to government control. Censorship of the press was strengthened and the majority of newspapers and magazines became subject to the "preliminary censorship" of government agents. The political tendencies of the intellectuals became subject to redoubled watchfulness by the police. Persons who were suspected were subject to police supervision. Attempts at political conspiracies were mercilessly crushed. In 1887 the police discovered a plot to assassinate Alexander III. The guilty parties were executed, among them Alexander

Ulianov, Lenin's eldest brother. In order to grant the police greater freedom, many provinces of Russia were declared in a state of "special protection." This enabled the administration to suspend the normal laws of procedure with respect to political prisoners. Several of the territories of Russia, inhabited by non-Russian peoples, also fell under suspicion. The Government began a policy of forcible "Russianization." This policy was applied particularly to Poland. Measures were also taken against the cultural dominance of the Germans in the Baltic provinces where they formed a minority of the population. Only the landowning class, the Barons, were Germans. The religious life was also subject to restrictions. The Christian dissenters, the evangelical sects, Stundo-Baptists, and Catholics were equally affected. Particular suspicion was leveled against the Jews.

The Jewish question had arisen in Russia in the eighteenth century. A great many Jews had become subjects of the Russian state, following the division of Poland and the annexation of the southwestern Russian territories, which had a large Jewish population. According to the laws of 1804, the Jews were forbidden to settle in the central Russian provinces. The statutes fixed a "pale of settlement" where alone Jews could live. This included the western and southern provinces. Under Alexander III the conditions under which the Jews lived were subjected to further restriction. They were forbidden to settle outside the towns and villages, even within the territories which they might inhabit. The line of demarcation was further restricted in 1887 when the city of Rostov-on-Don was excluded from the pale. In 1891 seventeen thousands Jews were deported from Moscow. Furthermore, a quota of Jews, limited to their proportion of the population, was introduced in government educational institutions. With few exceptions the Jews were not admitted to governmental service.

Seeking to hold the various classes under close observation, the Government searched for a group in society upon which it could itself depend. This group was the Russian nobility. During the reigns of Alexander III and Nicholas II, the Government attempted to secure the support of the nobility by granting it special privileges in respect to local self-government and local justice. In addition a number of financial privileges were granted to the nobility. The dependence of the internal policy upon the nobility was a fatal political error. The Russian nobility was politically dead after the reforms of Alexander II and the beginning of the democratization of Russian life. The attempt to bring it back into political life was an attempt to revive a corpse. Even when the nobility had been a powerful force in Russia, in the eighteenth and the first half of the nineteenth century, the interests of the imperial power seldom agreed with those of the nobility. It was an act of political shortsightedness to seek to establish a close union between the Government and the nobility at a time when the nobility no longer possessed any vitality. This mistaken policy only brought about further discontent with the Government on the part of other classes.

However, it would be unjust to point only to the negative aspects of Russian policy in the last quarter of the nineteenth century for it must be admitted that the Government also carried out reforms improving the social and economic conditions of the majority of the people. Many measures were directed toward the improvement of the condition of the peasantry. First, in the beginning of 1882, a decree was issued ordering compulsory sale to peasants of land on those estates where the sale had not been completed following the emancipation. Furthermore, the instalments to be paid by the peasants for the land were lowered and the head tax was abolished (1886). New regulations were issued making it easy for peasants to rent government lands and aiding them to migrate to the free lands in the eastern part of the Empire. It was partly to further migration that the Siberian railroad was begun in 1892. The reign of Alexander III also marked the beginning of labor legislation in Russia. In 1882 government inspection of factories was instituted and the Government undertook to regulate the conditions of the workers. At the same time the working day of minors and women was limited by law. Labor legislation was continued during the reign of Nicholas II.

The Government also undertook reforms of the finances. The finances of Russia were greatly improved under Nicholas I, but since that time two wars and expensive internal reforms had succeeded in shaking them and the currency had already depreciated. The Government was fortunate in having such a brilliant statesman as Witte. He succeeded in reorganizing Russian finances and in reintroducing gold into circulation in 1897.

All these government measures directed toward improving the economic condition of the country could not, however, outweigh the irritation caused by the police supervision instituted by the Government. The internal policy of Alexander III succeeded in suppressing social discontent and political opposition only for a short time. Actually, in the course of the reign of Alexander III and the first half of the reign of Nicholas II, everything was quiet; but during the second half of the reign of Nicholas II, the accumulated social discontent expressed itself in a violent explosion. . . .

The war with Japan in 1904-1905 resulted in a series of defeats for Russia. The Japanese fleet showed itself to be considerably stronger than the Russian, whose vessels were less well constructed and had weaker armaments. The Japanese fleet soon succeeded in blockading Port Arthur. Soon after the Japanese troops were landed on the mainland.

The Russian army was considerably stronger than the Japanese in numbers. As regards quality, the Russian troops were not inferior to the Japanese. Nevertheless, the war on land was as unfortunate for Russia as the war on the sea. The first failures might be explained by the difficulty of rapidly concentrating Russian troops at the distant battlefield. The whole army depended upon the Siberian railway, which was not even completed. There was no line around Lake Baikal. But the subsequent defeats must be explained on psychological grounds. The Russian army went into battle without enthusiasm. The deep dissatisfaction of the Russian people with the Government could not fail to be reflected in the army. The war was unpopular in Russia from the very beginning. Its objects were not understood by the Russian people. It did not seem to them to affect the vital interests of the country, while every Japanese soldier understood that the war concerned the vital interests of Japan. . . .

The revolutionary sentiments of the Russian people in 1904-1905 expressed themselves in the most diverse forms. The political activity of the intellectuals took the form of lectures on politics, the organization of societies of a semipolitical nature, and, in some cases, of riots on the part of students. The liberal landowners, members of the local (Zemstvo) administration, organized conferences to discuss reforms and a deputation from one of these congresses was sent to the emperor on June 19, 1905. The workers took recourse to strikes, the chief aims of which were political, rather than economic, reforms. The discontent of the peasantry found expression in agrarian riots, which resulted frequently in the destruction of landowners' houses or even in the murder of the landowners. Finally, following the termination of the Japanese war, disorder spread to the army. The soldiers were affected by socialist propaganda and in many cases revolted against their officers. Socialist agitators urged the formation of councils composed of soldiers, an idea which in 1917 proved fatal to the Russian army. Riots spread from the army to the navy, and on the battleship *Potemkin* the sailors succeeded in temporarily seizing control in June, 1905.

The whole period was characterized by a series of assassinations of governmental officials by terrorists. The Government first attempted to deal with the revolutionary sentiments of the people by suppressing disorders with armed force and by disrupting the revolutionary organizations. The Department of Police introduced secret agents in revolutionary organizations for the purpose of securing evidence against their leaders. The government agents sometimes became leaders of the revolutionary parties and took so active a part in the movement that it became impossible for the Government to determine where revolution began and where provocation ended. It was under circumstances of this kind that the Minister of the Interior, Plehve, was assassinated. The Department of Police also attempted to get control over the workers' movement by satisfying their economic demands and thus drawing them away from political activity. Zubatov, an agent of the secret police, succeeded in the spring of 1902 in organizing the workers along purely economic lines in Moscow and was ordered by Plehve to introduce his system all over Russia.

Following the death of Plehve and the dismissal of Zubatov, the workers' organization continued to develop of its own momentum. Its new leader, the priest Gapon, thought of petitioning the Tsar in person to effect the reforms demanded by the workers. On January 22, 1905, a huge crowd of workmen made their way to the Winter Palace in St. Petersburg to appeal to Nicholas II. The day had a tragic end, for, notwithstanding the fact that the workmen were peacefully inclined and unarmed, the crowd was dispersed by gunfire, as a result of which several hundred people were killed or wounded. "Bloody Sunday," as this day came to be called, became a decisive turning point in the history of the opposition of the working classes. It had as its immediate result their alliance with the socialist working class parties. The Government by this time realized that it had no plan to alleviate the situation and no firm support among the people. It consequently decided upon concessions in the matter of political reform. But even in this it moved unwillingly. On August 19, 1905, the order was given to call a national congress, the imperial Duma, which was to have deliberative, but not legislative, functions. This was, however, a half-measure which satisfied no one.

In the autumn of 1905, the situation became critical. A general strike was called throughout Russia. In the cities even the electricity and water supply were cut off; all railroads came to a standstill, with the exception of the Finland Railway. The leadership of the revolutionary group in St. Petersburg was taken by a special council composed of the leaders of the Socialist parties and representatives of the workers. This was the so-called Soviet of Workers' Deputies which was to take a prominent part in the events of 1917. At the first session of the Soviet the number of workers' representatives was only forty. It was increased later to five hundred. The chairman of the Soviet was a lawyer, Khrustalev-Nosar, but the actual leader was the vice-president Bronstein, subsequently known as Trotsky. It should be noted that the pseudonyms employed by many revolutionary leaders were assumed for self-protection against the espionage of the government police. All revolutionary instructions were signed by fictitious names.

The majority of the Soviet was in the hands of the Mensheviks, of whom Trotsky was a prominent member. The Bolsheviks failed to capture control of the first Soviet and regarded it with suspicion. Soviets were formed in some other cities, Moscow, Odessa, and elsewhere; but before they achieved any important results, the Government decided to make far-reaching political concessions. At the initiative of Count Witte, a manifesto, which amounted practically to capitulation by the Government, was issued October 30, 1905.

By this manifesto the imperial Government promised that it would grant to the Russian nation: (1) the fundamental principles of civil liberty —inviolability of person, and liberty of thought, speech, assembly, and organization; (2) democratic franchise; (3) the principle that no law could henceforth be made without the consent of the Duma. A new Prime

Minister, Count Witte, with power to appoint assistants from opposition circles, was named to carry the manifesto into effect. This was the first time in Russia that a united cabinet was formed.

The manifesto was an embodiment of the principal demands of the liberal opposition. The hope was that it would stop the revolutionary activity of this opposition. In this regard the manifesto was an attempt to unite the Government and the Liberal parties against the imminent social revolution. For this reason leaders of the social movement who desired revolution at all costs were opposed to the manifesto. Their arguments were that the Government was not sincere in its promises, that it desired only to stop the revolutionary movement, and that as soon as conditions permitted, it would rescind the manifesto. The Government indeed did hope that the manifesto would stop the revolution; but it was not true that it wished to withdraw the concessions. In fact, it did not do so after its real victory over the revolutionaries. Count Witte, the head of the Government and the author of the manifesto, personally believed in the necessity for reform and had naturally no intentions of retraction. Only the inexperience of the leaders of the Russian liberal movement can explain the decision of the liberal groups to decline all the invitations of Count Witte to enter his ministry. The result was that the manifesto of October 30 did not stop the revolutionary movement at once.

The Socialist parties desired only the triumph of their revolutionary doctrines. The leader of the Bolsheviks, Lenin, who came to Russia following the manifesto of October 30, became the staunchest opponent of the Government's policy. The strikes went on; a second railroad strike lasted from the end of November to the middle of December, and an armed insurrection occurred in Moscow at the end of December, 1905. The irreconcilable policy of the revolutionaries was not supported, however, by the majority of the people, who were fairly well satisfied with the program set forth in the manifesto. The Government was enabled to retake control of the situation. The Soviets were disbanded and the riots were suppressed by force. In several cities *pogroms* against Jews took place, organized by the so-called "Union of the Russian People," a reactionary group whose ideology was of the same pattern as that of German Nazism.

The insurrection at Moscow was not fully suppressed when the Government published a decree on December 24 on the procedure for elections. At the beginning of March, there appeared a manifesto concerning the organization of the new Parliament, which was to be formed of two Houses: the state Duma and the state Council, the first consisting of members elected by the nation, and the second of members half of whom were appointed by the emperor and half elected by the nobility, Zemstvos, and university faculties. The electoral law gave the right of suffrage to the majority of the people, but it was neither equal nor direct. The voters were divided into groups: The workers in several large cities chose their electors to the

Duma separately; the peasants chose electors who formed electoral colleges together with the electors chosen by the large landowners. These councils selected the deputies to the Duma. The electoral law artificially isolated the peasants and the workers and gave them a considerable rôle in the elections. This policy was prompted by the desire on the part of the Government to draw the peasants and the workers away from the opposition parties.

As a further means of appeasing the peasantry, Count Witte had the idea of expropriating the large estates and handing over the lands to the peasants. This project was developed by one of Witte's ministers, Kutler, who subsequently took a prominent part in the financial reorganization of the Soviet Government. The expropriation of large land holdings, however, was bitterly opposed by the estate-owners. Witte did not have enough power to insist upon the measures he proposed, and was forced to cancel his project. This failure reacted upon the operation of the electoral law which was primarily a bid to the peasantry. Just as in the case of the earlier attempts to organize the workers in a manner favorable to the Government, it merely succeeded in stirring up social movements without either satisfying or being able to control them.

The elections to the first Duma took place in March, 1906. On May 10 the state Council and Duma were opened by Nicholas II. The majority of the Duma consisted of opposition deputies; of 490 members, 187 belonged to the Liberal party and 85 to the moderate labor group. The Constitutional Democrats, led by I. Petrunkevich (the other leader, P. Miliukov, being removed under a specious pretext from the list of voters), was the strongest party represented. The Socialist parties boycotted the elections, while the Nationalist and Conservative parties were defeated at the polls and secured only a small number of seats. The results of the elections were disappointing to the Government.

Finding a hostile group in control of the state Duma, Nicholas II immediately dismissed Count Witte and appointed Goremykin in his place. The new Prime Minister was a typical civil servant of the old *régime*. He was chosen, not because he had initiative and political convictions, but, on the contrary, because he lacked these qualities and was ready to execute the orders of the emperor. The appointment of Goremykin was a great political error. The relations between the Government and the Duma rapidly took on an unfriendly character.

The principal point of dispute between the Government and the Duma was the agrarian problem. Its discussion in the Duma aroused the passions of all groups. An agrarian bill, sponsored by the Constitutional Democrats, proposed the expropriation of the large estates and the transfer of land to the ownership of the peasants, granting compensation to the owners. This led to increased agitation against the Duma by the reactionaries. Nicholas II faced the problem of either submitting to the Duma and displeasing the nobility, or of dismissing it and provoking the hostility of the Liberals. On July 21 the Duma was dissolved. As a concession to the Liberals, Goremykin was dismissed and a new man, Stolypin, was appointed Prime Minister.

Stolypin had been Minister of the Interior in the Cabinet of his predecessor in office. He began his service to the Crown as a governor of one of the southern provinces. Before that he had managed his own estates. He had a profound comprehension of the agrarian problem in Russia and possessed the qualities of an outstanding statesman. He was firm, patriotic, and a man of ideas. The opposition parties did not support Stolypin and his program, but they were obliged to reckon with him. Following the dissolution of the Duma, the opposition groups were undecided as to their course. Their psychology was not that of peaceful parliamentary opposition, but that of revolution. They dreaded the possibility of the Government's canceling the whole program of reform and plainly distrusted the emperor. After the dissolution, members of the Duma issued an appeal to the Russian nation to resist the Government by refusing to pay taxes and to refuse conscription into the army. The appeal had no effect upon the people. Its only result was that its authors lost the right of voting in the subsequent elections.

Stolypin first tried to attract some of the leading members of the moderate liberal groups into his Cabinet. They refused to cooperate with him, and he was obliged to draw upon professional bureaucrats. His agrarian policy consisted primarily in destroying the communal ownership of land instituted by the reforms of 1861, and in encouraging peasant ownership of individual farms.

On November 22 the decree abrogating the peasant commune was published. Each peasant was given the right to receive his share of the common land in full ownership. Simultaneously, measures were taken to finance the purchase by the peasantry of Crown lands. Stolypin's measures were an attempt to repair the defects in the reform of 1861 and to create in Russia a new class of small landowners to form the basis for the new state. This program was deemed incompatible with the agrarian bill introduced by the first Duma. The expropriation of nearly all land, the basis of that proposal, was calculated to solve the whole agrarian problem at one stroke. Stolypin's reform required a score of years to produce lasting results.

When the second Duma gathered on March 5, 1907, it proved to be even more hostile to the Government than was the first. The second Duma had a stronger left wing than the first one (180 Socialists); Lenin had abruptly changed his tactics, and the Socialists did not boycott the Duma. The conflict between the Government and the Duma in 1907 was more acute than in 1906. The Government now had a practical program of reform which the Duma did not possess. Fifty-five socialist deputies were charged with organizing a plot against the emperor and the second Duma was dissolved in June, 1907. In order to suppress similar expressions of opposition, the electoral law was changed. The large landowners were given preference over the peasants in selecting representatives to the electoral colleges. The third Duma, elected in November, 1907, had a membership different from that of its predecessors. The majority of deputies now belonged to parties of the right, and the liberal and socialist deputies were in the minority. The result of the two years of political conflict was the victory of Stolypin and the Moderate parties. The new *régime,* it seemed, had succeeded in entrenching itself firmly. However, it was not a true parliamentary government that emerged from the revolutionary period of 1905-1906. . . .

Following the revolutionary period, characterized by the bitter struggle between the Government and the Duma, there began a period of relative quiet. The third Duma sat without interruption through the whole period of its legal existence, from 1907 to 1912, and the elections of 1912 resulted in a triumph of the conservative nationalist groups.

While the political conflict between the Government and the Duma was temporarily solved by the reformed electoral law of 1907, there remained the more troublesome question of dealing with the aftermath of the revolutionary spirit of 1905. The dissatisfaction of that period found continued expression in a number of assassinations of prominent government officials. Premier Stolypin adopted a course of merciless suppression of revolutionary terrorism. Those accused of political crimes were subject to trial by a court-martial, and when found guilty were punished by death. Stolypin's policy in this regard met with severe criticism from the opposition, but was supported by the majority of the conservative members of the Duma. The greatest number of executions during this period occurred in 1908, when the total number reached 782. After this year the number steadily decreased, and in 1911 seventy-three sentences were passed.

Just as political equilibrium seemed to have been reached, Stolypin was assassinated in September, 1911. His place was taken by the Minister of Finance, Kokovtsev. Like his predecessor, he was a Moderate Constitutionalist. He was faced with the constitutional problem of overriding the power of veto vested in the state Council organized at the same time as the Duma, and consisting only partially of elected members. One-half of the members of the Council were appointed by the emperor, and the Prime Minister had little influence in their selection. The Court circles of reactionary aristocrats were irreconcilably opposed to the Duma and succeeded in carrying out their policies without consulting the Prime Minister by direct influence upon the emperor. But notwithstanding irritating incidents of this kind, the Duma proved itself capable of bringing about many favorable changes in the country. Of great importance was the legislation concerning the peasantry, by which the precarious legal status of the peasants was done away with and their civil rights were equalized with those of other citizens.

The reform of local justice was an important measure in this connection. By virtue of the law of June 28, 1912, the general judicial system was to be gradually extended over the peasant population. The Land Captain was displaced in judicial matters by a justice of the peace. The Duma also undertook to organize the educational system and provided for an annual increase of 20,000,000 rubles in the educational budget, which grew steadily from 44,000,000 in 1906 to 214,000,000 in 1917. The number of pupils in the primary schools rose from 3,275,362 in 1894 to 8,000,000 in 1914. Thus on the eve of the war over half of all children of school age in Russia were receiving instruction. It was estimated by the educational committee of the Duma that universal education in Russia would be reached in 1922. The war and the revolution, however, prevented realization of this program. . . .

The creation of the new capitalist structure was accompanied by a rapid economic development of the country. The basic factor of economic development, as in the preceding period, was the rapid growth of population. From the middle of the nineteenth century to the beginning of the twentieth century, the population of Russia doubled. During the first fifteen years of the twentieth century, the population increased 30 per cent. In 1914 it totaled 175,000,000.

Particularly significant was the growth of city population. In 1851 there were less than three and a half million people in the towns or less than 6 per cent of the total population. In 1897 the town population had risen to sixteen and one-third millions or 13 per cent of the whole population, and in 1914 to 17.5 per cent. These figures indicate the growth of the industrial population as compared with the agricultural. According to the census of 1897, 74.2 per cent of the population was agricultural, and 13.3 per cent industrial. Thus, in spite of the growth of the cities and of industry, about three-quarters of Russia's population before the First World War was occupied in agriculture. . . .

The ownership of land in Russia, following the peasant reforms of 1861, underwent great changes. Land rapidly passed into the ownership of the peasants. The peasantry not only retained the lands distributed in 1861, but also acquired new lands by purchase. Thus, simultaneous with the growth of area under cultivation in Russia during the fifty years preceding the First World War, a radical change in the social structure of the agricultural population took place. As a result of the Stolypin reforms of 1906, the peasant communes began to disintegrate, and in 1911 six million households had acquired personal possession of the land. Russia was moving with great strides toward small landownership by citizens possessing equal rights with the rest of the population.

The industrialization of Russia which began in the second half of the nineteenth century increased rapidly until 1914, and in some branches of industry until 1917. We will trace this process briefly. . . .

The Russian cotton industry, prior to the First World War, occupied fourth place in world production. It was exceeded only by Great Britain, the United States, and Germany. In 1905 the Russian cotton industry employed 7,350,683 spindles and 178,506 looms. By 1911 the productive forces of the industry had grown to 8,448,818 spindles and 220,000 looms. The increased production of Russian cotton factories was absorbed partly by the home market and partly by foreign trade. The increase of internal consumption may be illustrated by the fact that in 1890 the per capita consumption of cotton cloth in Russia was 2.31 pounds and in 1910, 4.56 pounds. . . . The metallurgical industries showed a similar development. In 1900, around 1,500,000 tons of pig iron were produced in Russia. By 1914 production had grown to over 3,500,000 tons. . . .

The growth of industrial production was reflected also in mining. Eighty-five per cent of the coal used in Russia was of domestic extraction. The chief center of coal mining was the Donets basin which supplied 55 per cent of Russia's needs for coal. In 1900, 11,000,000 tons were mined in the Donets basin and in 1913 the production rose to 25,000,000 tons.

The exploitation of forests served both domestic needs and foreign trade. In 1904, 13,200,000 rubles worth of lumber was exported. By 1913 exports reached 164,900,000 rubles. Of great importance also was the production of oil, chiefly in the neighborhood of Baku. In 1860 oil production in the Baku area hardly exceeded 160,000 tons. In 1905 production rose to over 7,000,000 tons and in 1913 to around 9,000,000 tons. . . .

Even more rapid than the expansion of industry was the development of railroads in Russia. In the middle of the nineteenth century, the total length of railroads in operation in Russia did not exceed 660 miles. In 1912 the Russian railroad system comprised 40,194 miles and was second only to that of the United States. The greatest achievement was the completion of the great Trans-Siberian Railroad, from 1892 to 1905. Its construction was one of the most daring railroad projects of our time. The length of the line from Moscow to Vladivostok is 5,542 miles. In the construction of this line it was necessary to overcome the greatest natural and technical difficulties—the frozen subsoil and the wildness of the territories penetrated. The cost of the Trans-Siberian Railroad exceeded $200,000,000. It was originally a single-track line, but during the First World War a second line was laid down.

The rapid expansion of Russian industry was accompanied by the creation of a working class on a scale previously unknown in Russia. . . . It was only in 1902 that the Government assented to the legalization of some unions and it was only after the Revolution of 1905 that labor unions were permitted on a large scale by the Law of March 4, 1906.

The Government artificially retarded the development of labor unions and thereby unwittingly fostered the formation of illegal revolutionary organizations. But while restricting the development of labor unions, the Government made efforts to satisfy the principal needs of the workers by means of legislation. Labor legislation in Russia goes back to the 1880's in the reign of Alexander III. In 1897 day work was limited to eleven and a half hours and night work to ten hours. Night work was forbidden for children under seventeen, and children under twelve were not allowed to engage in industrial work of any kind. The legislation of the twentieth century introduced workers' accident compensation in 1903, health insurance in 1912, and accident insurance in 1912. The condition of the working class gradually improved, thanks to increasing wages, particularly in Petrograd and Moscow. At the end of the nineteenth century, the average wage of the Russian worker was only 187 rubles a year. By 1913 it had risen to 300 rubles and in some branches of industry in Petrograd and Moscow to five times this sum. In many factories the low money wages were augmented by free lodgings, hospital services, and factory schools. . . .

In the eighteenth and the first half of the nineteenth century, Russian culture centered chiefly around the large cities and the nobles' estates. From the middle of the nineteenth century, the basic elements of modern civilization, as, for example, education and medical care, spread far and wide, reaching the lowest levels of the city population and the peasant huts. A prominent part in this movement was played by the Zemstvos and city organizations introduced by the reforms of Alexander II. . . .

Over two-thirds of the expenditures of the Zemstvos were for public health and education. The Zemstvo department of Public Health in 1914 expended 82,000,000 rubles. The rural population, prior to 1864 when the Zemstvos were introduced, was almost wholly lacking in medical care. Fifty years later, at the eve of the First World War, the Zemstvos had covered the rural territories with hospitals and dispensaries. The average radius of the medical districts was ten miles. . . .

The expenditure of the Zemstvos on public education in 1914 was 106,000,000 rubles. Most of these sums were expended upon primary schools. In 1914 there were fifty thousand Zemstvo schools with eighty thousand teachers and three million school children. The Zemstvos paid particular attention to the construction of new schools corresponding to modern pedagogical ideas and hygienic requirements. Besides primary education, the Zemstvos also organized their own system of secondary education for the training of teachers and organized courses for the improvement of teaching methods. The Zemstvos likewise organized extension courses and built libraries. In 1914 there were 12,627 rural public libraries in thirty-five of the forty-three Zemstvo governments.

III

THE THEORY

THE THRESHOLD

"To you who desire to cross this threshold, do you know what awaits you here?"

"I know," replied the girl.

"Cold, hunger, abhorrence, derision, contempt, abuse, prison, disease, and death!"

"I know, I am ready. I shall endure all suffering, all blows."

"Not from enemies alone, but also from relatives, from friends."

"Yes, even from them."

"Very well. You are ready for the sacrifice. You shall perish, and nobody will ever know whose memory to honor."

"I need neither gratitude nor compassion. I need no home."

"Are you ready even to commit a crime?"

The girl lowered her head.

"I am ready for crime, too—"

The voice lingered for some time before resuming its questions.

"Do you know," it said at length, "that you may be disillusioned in that which you believe at present, that you may discover that you were mistaken, and that you ruined your young life in vain?"

"I know this, too."

"Enter!"

The girl crossed the threshold, and the heavy curtain fell behind her.

"Fool!" said someone, gnashing his teeth.

"Saint!" someone uttered in reply.

IVAN TURGENEV

Chapter 3

THE ROLE OF THEORY

What is the relation of Marxist theory to Soviet practice? Historic connection apart, has Marxist theory profoundly influenced the policies of the Soviet leaders? There is a school of thought, typified by W. W. Rostow's position in The Dynamics of Soviet Society, which maintains that Soviet policies and practices have been primarily and essentially a consequence of a singleminded effort by Soviet leaders to maintain their own absolute internal power over Russian society and extend their power vis-à-vis the external world. In this view, "what is left of Marxism is what has been found useful . . . to support the maintenance and enlargement of power by the regime at home and abroad."

Other Western scholars, while recognizing that Marxist theory, in vital respects, has been subordinated, attenuated, or abandoned in the crucible of Soviet practice, have attributed significant influence to the continuity of theory and its impact on policy. Isaac Deutscher, for example, in his Russia After Stalin, defines the content of the Stalin era as a "mutual interpenetration of modern technology and Marxist socialism with Russian barbarism." (Editor's emphasis.) He argues that before the Soviet regime could embrace certain policies, it "would first have to ban the works of Marx, Engels, and Lenin, that is to say to destroy its own birth certificate and ideological title deeds." And, as R. N. Carew Hunt tells us, the Soviet leaders "have been nurtured" in the Marxist creed since birth, "and it would be strange indeed if they have remained unaffected." It is of some significance, too, that Julian Towster, in the opening words of his Political Power in the U.S.S.R., finds it possible to assert: "So great is the stress placed upon the interrelation of theory and practice in the Soviet state that an understanding of its operative constitutional order would lack coherence without due attention to avowed theory."

But, whatever the merit of either position, Marxist theory is so deeply embedded in the ethos of Soviet society that even attenuation requires obeisance. It has, as Edward Hallett Carr in his Soviet Impact on the West makes clear, "the status of a creed which purports to inspire every act of

47

state power and by which every such act can be tested and judged." More-
over, it has had "a remarkable capacity to inspire loyalty and self-sacrifice
in its adherents; and this success is beyond doubt due in part to its bold
claim . . . to be the source of principles binding for every form of human
activity including the activity of the state." (On the role of ideology in
Soviet society today, see the Bauer, Inkeles, and Kluckhohn Reading, in
chapter 19.) Certainly, theory played a vital role in the making of the
Bolshevik and other Communist revolutions and continues to play a part in
Communist-led revolutionary movements throughout the world.

In the circumstances, a pertinent and continuing inquiry with which
the reader should be concerned throughout is: "What is the relation of
Marxist theory to Soviet practice?"

THE PRIORITY OF POWER

W. W. Rostow*

A converging series of influences made Lenin and the hard core of
the Bolshevik Party he dominated choose that course which would increase
their own direct short-run power, as opposed to any other possible goal
open to them, at moments of decision. The means to power early became,
in fact, an end in themselves—a result implicit in Lenin's conception and
organization of the Bolshevik Party and fully evident in the policy of the
Soviet regime by 1921. This fundamental transition appears to have substantial roots in the philosophic bases of Marxism, in Russian history, and
in the personalities of the men who dominated the Bolshevik group initially
and who subsequently proved best capable of surviving in power.

The concept of the priority of power, which is used throughout the
following essay, is a shorthand phrase for a complex phenomenon. It appears important that this conception be distinguished from the notion that,
psychologically, the rulers of the Soviet state are motivated, in a personal
sense, simply by the desire for power. Indeed, there is an evident enjoyment of power present in the lives of Lenin, Stalin, and the others who
made the Russian Revolution of November 1917; and they certainly belong
with those many figures of history who found it easy to believe that, if
power remained concentrated in their hands, larger beneficent purposes
would be served. More than that, one of the dynamic, self-reinforcing
processes to be discerned in this story is the progressive selection of men

* Author of *The Prospects for Communist China* and *An American Policy in Asia.*
This selection is reprinted from pp. 7-11 of *The Dynamics of Soviet Society* by W. W.
Rostow. By permission of W. W. Norton & Company, Inc., Copyright 1952, 1953, by
Massachusetts Institute of Technology.

who had a respect for power, knew how to use it, and were prepared to take risks in order to achieve it. And there is an equally consistent process of elimination of those unwilling to resolve their conflicts between idealism and their own power position, or less able in the pursuit of the latter. The love of personal power is a legitimate element in the analysis; but we do not attempt to pierce behind it to the deeper psychological roots of the behavior of the chief Bolsheviks; and, more important, this element in the analysis is not taken to be the sole root for the priority of power that has consistently dominated the behavior of the Russian Communists. This essay is not simply a Newtonian elaboration on the theme of personal power maximization.

The priority of power is based, in the first instance, on a combination of Marx's view that there was a determinable form which future history would take and Lenin's conception of the Communist Party as a chosen instrument for the achievement of Marx's prognosis. The Party thus acquired in its own eyes both legitimacy of status and the moral right to force the "correct" historical path—against the will of the majority and against the will, even, of the industrial working men who were designed to be the primary beneficiaries of the whole revolutionary development. In prerevolutionary Russia this essentially conspiratorial conception attracted emotional support due to the frustration of economic, social, and political reform by the tsarist state which led many reformers to concentrate their energy on the task of overthrowing by violence that autocratic regime. The overthrow of a regime by force is, essentially, a problem in the strategy and tactics of power. Further, since the "correct" line is always arguable, in its Russian context this conception had the consequence of moving the Communist Party itself toward a dictatorial form of rule, in which, in the end, one man's judgment would determine the line; and, in the anarchic state of revolutionary and postrevolutionary Russia, the right to lay down the "correct" line was likely to rest with him who knew best how to conduct a struggle for power. The bases for the priority of power lie, then, in converging aspects of the history of Russia and Communism, as well as in the personal characteristics of Soviet leaders. It is inseparably bound up with one aspect of Communist ideology, and gathered its initial emotional force from that fact. The reader should constantly bear in mind that this essay is not based on a simple opposition of ideology and a lust for power. Both conceptions are much more complex than common usage would credit; and, in the Soviet case, they partially converged.

Communist ideology also included, however, a fairly explicit set of economic, social, and political goals, incorporated in the aspirations and programs of various revolutionary groups. Some of these specific goals converged with the effective pursuit of power—for example, the nationalization of industry. Some of them conflicted—for example, the placing of political authority directly in the hands of trade unions and the Soviets, those

Bolshevik-dominated organizations of workers and soldiers on whom the November Revolution was built. The inner core of consistency in the story of the Russian Communists is the priority they were prepared to give to the maintenance and expansion of their own power over other lines of policy, including their willingness to go to any lengths judged to be required to organize and control the Russian peoples in an effort to secure their own continued ascendancy as a regime. In the end, the society they have organized represents a projection out onto an entire state and its peoples of the form and concepts of organization created largely by Lenin for the operation of the Communist Party itself.

Despite the impressive continuity of the priority of power the manner in which it has been exercised has, of course, changed. Lenin, in the immediate postrevolutionary days, may be seen groping among the conflicting leads offered to him by the complex and contradictory heritage of Russian Marxism. There are, in his performance as a political leader, certain unresolved contradictions which, for some historians, justify for Lenin a higher moral status than for Stalin; for example, the relative freedom in which he left Soviet intellectual and cultural life, his unwillingness to use the death penalty against fellow Communists, the bonhomie with which he led the Communist Party (except when seriously challenged), and the relative freedom within the Communist Party for open controversy in his day. There are some real differences between the rule of Lenin and that of Stalin which are of historical interest. On balance, however, in the key decisions he made, the priority of power over other goals, including goals professed by Russian Communists, is evident in Lenin.

Stalin, in this context, appears less hampered than Lenin by the problem of overriding those elements in the Communist heritage which conflicted with the priority of power. His performance has a massive consistency, both in the extensive changes he brought about in the decade after 1928 and in the subsequent stability of the policies and institutions he elaborated. Increasingly, in the years before Stalin's death, one sensed that the Soviet regime was operating less from a conscious and fresh set of decisions, in which alternative possibilities were examined in the light of relatively fixed principles (including the priority of power among them), than from habits and procedures built into heavy inflexible bureaucratic structures. The historical roots of the priority of power and the living experiences which brought it to life seemed far distant from the Soviet Union, enshrined, at best, in such ritualistic documents as the *Short History of the Communist Party of the Soviet Union* and in the youthful memories of the middle-aged and elderly men who now rule Russia. Like almost all else in the Soviet Union, the priority of power as the dominant test for policy appears to have been bureaucratized.

The interaction of the pursuit of power, thus defined, with the problems and resistances it met resulted in decisions which had, in turn, their consequences; and these consequences created new situations (often in the form of increased resistance) which required further decision. It is essential to this argument that the secondary consequences of given decisions did not lie fully within the control of the Soviet regime and were not, in all cases, either fully predictable or compatible with its primary purposes. The successive application of the priority of power thus yielded an unfolding sequence of decisions which shaped modern Soviet society and, in particular, shaped the institutional form it has assumed since the late 1930's. To understand the present position of that society and the alternatives for it which the future may hold, it is, therefore, necessary to look back to the process by which it has arrived at its present position.

One might have expected that the study of the first professedly Marxist regime in history would constitute an exercise in the analysis of the relations between the economy on the one hand and the social, political, and cultural superstructure on the other. On the contrary, the philosophical implication of the priority of power has been that Hegel, having been allegedly turned on his head by Marx, is set right side up again by Lenin and Stalin. We are examining a peculiarly persistent and single-minded effort to use the maximum powers of a modern state to produce throughout the society it controls the economic, social, political, and cultural changes believed desirable for the maintenance and expansion of power by a small co-optive group. The *de facto* ideology of the Soviet Union would now more nearly identify the Great Leader and the State as the prime movers of history than the play of economic forces or even the interplay of economic, social, political, and cultural forces. The dilution of executive authority since Stalin's death is unlikely to alter this conception, unless much more drastic changes occur within the Soviet Union. But if our view of the history of society as a fully interacting process is correct, the actual course of the society is not to be determined or understood solely in terms of its political process, even when power is wielded absolutely with the full mechanisms available to a modern state. And, in fact, the evolution of Soviet society consists in large part of a sequence of interactions between the aims of Soviet rulers and the limitations imposed on them not only by Russia's geographical position and natural resources, but also by the stage of Russian history and economic development at which they came to power and by profound cultural forces in Russian society which are capable of only slow change.

Put more precisely, the forms which the efficient pursuit of power has taken have been more heavily determined by certain abiding or slow-changing aspects of the Russian scene than by the ideological or other presuppositions which the Soviet rulers brought to their self-designated mission. Those who seek to consolidate and enlarge their power wish their people to work hard and efficiently on the tasks they set. If men are to execute assigned tasks, their motivating interests must be taken into account, as well as the accretion within them of a long cultural heritage. In fact, men appear to be governed less in their actions by a conscious, rational calculus among alternatives than by habits, customs, and attitudes deeply ingrained in their heritage and personal experience, and tenaciously held. The existence of these forces embedded in cultures does not eliminate the need for men to exercise choice among alternatives; but it limits the range over which those choices are likely to be found acceptable. Lenin said of the Russian peasant: ". . . he is as he is, and will not become different in the near future . . . the transformation of the peasant's psychology and habits is something that requires generations." Although the motivations and cultural outlook of men are certainly subject to change over time, the ruler who wishes prompt as well as efficient performance must take men as he finds them. This, essentially, the Soviet regime has done. Despite varying efforts to shape more profoundly the human beings within Soviet society to its purposes, the regime has generally sought efficiency and conformity from the Russian peoples as it found them and as they have evolved in the past thirty-five years under influences longer lived and more complex than the policy of the Soviet state alone. The consequence of the regime's pragmatic decision, over the years, has helped give a distinct and persistent Russian character to the forms of Communist dictatorship; but it is an important conclusion of this analysis . . . that the Russian mannerisms of the Soviet regime do not imply an identification of the regime's interests with those of the Russian peoples or the Russian nation.

We are thus convinced that the story of Soviet Russia is not only a lesson in the awful potential of totalitarian rule in the context of modern societies; it is also a lesson in the limitations of even the maximum exercise of political power in the face of the nature of cultures and ultimately the resistance, often passive, of men.

THE IMPORTANCE OF DOCTRINE

R. N. CAREW HUNT*

MYTHS AND THE MASSES

Virtually all analysts would agree that in the years of struggle before the October Revolution the Bolsheviks took the theory which lay behind their movement in deadly earnest; there is also general agreement that in the 1920's the doctrine acted as a stimulus to the workers, who took pride

* At St. Antony's College, Oxford University. Author of *The Theory and Practice of Communism; Marxism Past and Present;* and *A Guide to Communist Jargon.* The selection is from *Problems of Communism,* Vol. 7 (March-April 1958), pp. 11-15. By permission.

in building up their country. In the 1930's, however, the situation changed. Stalin assumed absolute power. The machinery of the state and of the secret police was greatly strengthened, and all prospect of establishing a genuine classless society disappeared. With the Stalin-Hitler Pact, if not before, the Soviet Union entered an era which can plausibly be represented as one of naked power politics, perpetuated after World War II in the aggressive and obstructive policies pursued by the regime. Hence it is sometimes argued that Communist ideology has now ceased to possess any importance; that it is simply a top-dressing of sophistries designed to rationalize measures inspired solely by Soviet interests; and that apart from a few fanatics, such as may be found in any society, no one believes in the doctrine any longer, least of all the leaders themselves.

Yet such unqualified assertions are erroneous. Consider, first, the outlook of the ordinary Soviet citizen *vis-à-vis* the ideology. Day in, day out, he is subjected to intensive and skillfully devised propaganda through every known medium, designed to demonstrate that the ideology on which the Soviet Union is based makes it the best of all possible worlds, and that on this account it is encircled with jealous enemies bent on its destruction. The Soviet leadership has always considered it essential that every citizen possess as deep an understanding of Communist principles as his mind is capable of assimilating, and those holding positions of consequence are obliged recurrently to pass through carefully graded schools of political instruction.

It is significant that whenever the leaders feel themselves in a tight corner—as in the recent aftermath of destalinization and the intervention in Hungary—their invariable reaction is to intensify indoctrination in an attempt to refocus public attention on "first principles." As hard-headed men they would certainly not attach such importance to indoctrination if they did not know that it paid dividends—and experience has proved that the persistent repetition of a body of ideas which are never challenged is bound to influence the minds of their recipients. Of course, the present generation does not react to the formal ideology with the same fervor as did its forebears who made the revolution, and there are doubtless those who view official apologetics with a large degree of cynicism. But between total commitment and total disillusionment there are many intermediate positions; it is quite possible for a man to regard much of what he is told as nonsense while still believing that there is something of value behind it, especially if he identifies that "something" with the greatness of his country as "the first socialist state" and believes in its historic mission.

LEADERSHIP CREDENCE—A HOPE OR A HABIT?

More significant, in the present context, than the attitude of the ordinary citizen is that of the ruling elite which is responsible for policy.

What its top-ranking members believe is a question which no one, of course, can answer positively. But before surmising, as do some analysts, that the Soviet leadership cannot possibly believe in the myths it propounds, we should remind ourselves that no class or party ever finds it difficult to persuade itself of the soundness of the principles on which it bases its claim to rule.

The Soviet leaders are fortified in this conviction by the very nature of their creed. They have been nurtured in it from birth, and it would be strange indeed if they had remained unaffected. It has become second nature to these men to regard history as a dialectical process—one of incessant conflict between progressive and reactionary forces which can only be resolved by the victory of the former. The division of the world into antagonistic camps, which is an article of faith, is simply the projection onto the international stage of the struggle within capitalistic society between the bourgeoisie, which history has condemned, and the proletariat, whose ultimate triumph it has decreed. The leaders seem to be confident that history is on their side, that all roads lead to communism, and that the contradictions of capitalism must create the type of situation which they can turn to their advantage.

Democratic governments desirous of recommending a certain policy normally dwell upon its practical advantages. But in the Soviet Union this is not so. Any important change of line will be heralded by an article in *Pravda,* often of many columns, purporting to show that the new policy is ideologically correct because it accords with some recent decision of a party congress, or with Lenin's teaching, or with whatever other criterion may be adopted. How far the policy in question will have been inspired by considerations of ideology as opposed to others of a more mundane nature can never be precisely determined. This, however, is not an exclusive feature of the Communist system; in politics, as for that matter in personal relations, it is seldom possible to disentangle all the motives which determine conduct. The policies of any party or government are likely to reflect its political principles even if they are so framed as to strengthen its position, and there is no reason why the policies adopted by the Soviet leaders should constitute an exception.

Analysts of the "power politics" school of thought hold that the Kremlin leaders are concerned solely with Soviet national interest, and merely use the Communist movement to promote it. Yet here again the difficulty is to disengage factors which are closely associated. The future of the Communist movement cannot be disassociated from the fortunes of the Soviet Union. If the Soviet regime were to collapse, that movement would count for little, and whether it would long survive even in China is doubtful. Recognizing this, non-Russian Communist parties generally have remained subservient to Moscow even when threatened with large-scale defections of rank-and-file members in the face of particularly odious shifts in the Moscow line. . . .

INEFFICIENCY—AN INDEX OF IDEOLOGY

Indeed, . . . the attitude of the Soviet leaders *must* be attributed, at least in part, to the theoretical principles which distinguish Communist regimes from other forms of dictatorship. Certainly the leaders shape and phrase their domestic and foreign policies to fit the general framework established by these principles, and the latter often do not allow much room for maneuver. In fact, their application may sometimes weaken rather than strengthen the country.

To take a simple example, much waste would be avoided if small traders were permitted to operate on a profit basis; the fishmonger, for instance, would have an incentive to put his fish on ice, which he frequently fails to do to the discomfort of the public. Allowance of profits, however, would constitute a return to private enterprise, which cannot be tolerated.

Similarly, in the Communist view it has long been regarded as indefensible to subordinate a higher to a lower form of socialized enterprise. Thus, while it has been apparent for years that Soviet agriculture would be more efficient if the Machine Tractor Stations were handed over to the collective farms, the issue has been consistently dodged, because the MTS are fully state-owned organs and therefore "higher" than the farms, which still belong in part to the peasants. When the economist Venzher advocated this measure some years ago, he was slapped down at once by Stalin, the fact that it had already been adopted in Yugoslavia only making his suggestion the more objectionable. Just two years ago Khrushchev launched an extensive program to strengthen the organization and power of the MTS. Very recently, however, he indicated that the regime was—at long last—prepared to yield to practical necessity on this point; in a speech on farm policy, he advocated the transfer of farm machinery to the collectives, and although his proposals are not yet legalized, it would appear that a number of MTS have already been dissolved.*

The principle of hierarchy has not been repudiated, however, and still governs other aspects of agricultural organization—for example, the relative status of the two forms of agricultural enterprise. From the standpoint of productive efficiency the collective farms are bad, but the state farms are worse. Nonetheless, the latter represent a "higher type" of organization, and thus the present virgin lands campaign has been based upon them.

* Editor's note: The plan was legalized and put into operation in April 1958.

DOGMATISM IN FOREIGN POLICY

. . . The argument can be carried further. By its behavior throughout
its history, the Soviet Union has incurred the hostility, or at least the
suspicion, of the entire free world. Yet there was no practical reason why
it should have done so. After the October Revolution the Bolshevik regime
was faced with appalling domestic problems, and it had nothing to gain
by courting the animosity of the West. The Soviet leaders might well have
built up their country in accordance with the principles to which they were
committed without exciting such widespread hostility. What governments
do at home is commonly regarded as their own affair. Fundamentally,
the regime in Yugoslavia is as Communist as that of the Soviet Union,
and was established with an equal ruthlessness. But Tito, having asserted
his independence from Moscow, has muffled his attacks on the West, and
in turn the Western governments have demonstrated their desire—albeit
tempered with caution—to believe in his good faith.

What no country will tolerate is the attempt, deliberately engineered
by a foreign power, to overthrow its form of government; this has been the
persistent aim and effort of the Soviet regime in defiance of its express
diplomatic guarantees of non-interference. It is hard to see how this
strategy has assisted the development of Soviet Russia, and that it has never
been abandoned cannot be dissociated from those messianic and catastro-
phic elements in the Communistic creed which influence, perhaps impel, the
Soviet drive for world power.

In conclusion, it is frequently stated that communism has created an
ideological cleavage between the West and the Soviet bloc. Yet this statement would be meaningless if the issue today were, as some believe, simply
one of power politics. An ideology is significant only if it makes those who
profess it act in a way they would not otherwise do. The fact that large
numbers of persons accept communism would not constitute a danger if
it did not lead them to support policies which threaten the existence of
those who do not accept it. It is true that many people, especially in
backward countries, call themselves Communists without having any clear
idea of what it means. Yet the movement would not be the force it has
become were there not in every country men and women who sincerely
believe in the ideas behind it, which form collectively what we call its
ideology.

To represent this ideology as a species of opium with which the Soviet
leaders contrive to lull the people while taking care never to indulge in it
themselves is to attribute to them an ability to dissociate themselves from
the logic of their system—an ability which it is unlikely they possess. For
the concepts which make up that system, fantastic as many of them appear

to be, will be found on examination to be interrelated, and to be logical extensions of the basic principles to which all Communists subscribe.

To turn it the other way around, Communists claim a theoretical justification for the basic principles in which they believe. But these principles must be translated into appropriate action; and action, if directed by the rulers of a powerful country like the Soviet Union, will take the form of *Realpolitik*. There is no yardstick which permits a measure of the exact relationship between power politics and ideology in the policies which result; but surely neither factor can be ignored.

Chapter 4

MARXISM

Apart from the relevance of Marxist theory to Soviet practice there is, of course, the question of the soundness and acuteness of its analyses and prophecies.

Extreme claims have been made for the validity of Marx's theories. Marx himself stated in 1852:

I cannot claim to have discovered the existence of classes in modern society or their strife against one another. Petty bourgeois historians long ago described the evolution of class struggles, and political economists showed the economic physiology of the classes. I have added as a new contribution the following propositions: 1. That the existence of classes is bound up with certain phases of material production; 2. That the class struggle leads necessarily to the dictatorship of the proletariat; 3. That this dictatorship is but the transition to the abolition of all classes and to the creation of a society of the free and equal.

Marx's co-worker, Engels, insisted that "With the same certainty with which from a given mathematical proposition a new one is deduced, with that same certainty can we deduce the social revolution from the existing social conditions and the principles of political economy."

These broad claims and prophecies are carried to absurd (and probably un-Marxist) lengths in the official (Short) History of the Communist Party of the Soviet Union, *edited by a commission of its Central Committee, in which it is affirmed that mastery of Marxist theory "enables the Party to find the right orientation to any situation" and "to understand the inner connection of current events." Equally fatuous is* Pravda's *assertion that "The Party's decisions, like its entire policy, have always been based upon knowledge of the objective laws of social development, with sober account of all forces, both international and domestic."*

Many modern scholars, although rejecting much of Marx's theory, have nevertheless recognized him as one of the great seminal thinkers in the history of man who greatly enriched our understanding of society and improved our research methodology. Serious students of philosophy, history, economics, and politics, therefore, will examine Marxist theory with a view to its insights and contributions as well as its defects.

MANIFESTO OF THE COMMUNIST PARTY [1]

KARL MARX AND FRIEDRICH ENGELS

In 1847, Marx and Engels were requested to prepare a theoretical and practical party program for the Communist League, a workingmen's association. The Manifesto *was completed in 1848 on the eve of the French Revolution of that year. Written when Marx was 30 and Engels only 28 years of age, the* Manifesto *contains in developed or undeveloped form the fundamentals of Marxist theory. Professor Sidney Hook has called it "undoubtedly the most influential political pamphlet of all time." "What is truly astonishing," he added, "is the extent to which the* Manifesto, *after a century, reads like a contemporary document."*

From the PREFACE by Friedrich Engels (1888):

The Manifesto being our joint production, I consider myself bound to state that the fundamental proposition, which forms its nucleus, belongs to Marx. That proposition is: That in every historical epoch, the prevailing mode of economic production and exchange, and the social organisation necessarily following from it, form the basis upon which is built up, and from which alone can be explained, the political and intellectual history of that epoch; that consequently the whole history of mankind (since the dissolution of primitive tribal society, holding land in common ownership) has been a history of class struggles, contests between exploiting and exploited, ruling and oppressed classes; that the history of these class struggles forms a series of evolutions in which, nowadays, a stage has been reached where the exploited and oppressed class—the proletariat—cannot attain its emancipation from the sway of the exploiting and ruling class—the bourgeoisie —without, at the same time, and once and for all, emancipating society at large from all exploitation, oppression, class distinctions and class struggles. . . .

A spectre is haunting Europe—the spectre of Communism. All the powers of old Europe have entered into a holy alliance to exorcise this spectre: Pope and Czar, Metternich and Guizot, French Radicals and German police-spies.

Where is the party in opposition that has not been decried as communistic by its opponents in power? Where the Opposition that has not hurled back the branding reproach of Communism, against the more advanced opposition parties, as well as against its reactionary adversaries?

Two things result from this fact:

[1] The included footnotes were added by Engels in 1888.

I. Communism is already acknowledged by all European powers to be itself a power.

II. It is high time that Communists should openly, in the face of the whole world, publish their views, their aims, their tendencies, and meet this nursery tale of the spectre of Communism with a manifesto of the party itself. . . .

I. BOURGEOIS AND PROLETARIANS [2]

The history of all hitherto existing society[3] is the history of class struggles.

Freeman and slave, patrician and plebeian, lord and serf, guildmaster and journeyman, in a word, oppressor and oppressed, stood in constant opposition to one another, carried on an uninterrupted, now hidden, now open fight, a fight that each time ended, either in a revolutionary reconstitution of society at large, or in the common ruin of the contending classes.

In the earlier epochs of history, we find almost everywhere a complicated arrangement of society into various orders, a manifold gradation of social rank. In ancient Rome we have patricians, knights, plebeians, slaves; in the Middle Ages, feudal lords, vassals, guild-masters, journeymen, apprentices, serfs; in almost all of these classes, again, subordinate gradations.

The modern bourgeois society that has sprouted from the ruins of feudal society, has not done away with class antagonisms. It has but established new classes, new conditions of oppression, new forms of struggle in place of the old ones.

Our epoch, the epoch of the bourgeoisie, possesses, however, this distinctive feature: It has simplified the class antagonisms. Society as a whole is more and more splitting up into two great hostile camps, into two great classes directly facing each other—bourgeoisie and proletariat.

From the serfs of the Middle Ages sprang the chartered burghers of the earliest towns. From these burgesses the first elements of the bourgeoisie were developed.

---

[2] By bourgeoisie is meant the class of modern capitalists, owners of the means of social production and employers of wage-labour; by proletariat, the class of modern wage-labourers who, having no means of production of their own, are reduced to selling their labour power in order to live.

[3] That is, all *written* history. In 1847, the pre-history of society, the social organisation existing previous to recorded history, was all but unknown. Since then Haxthausen discovered common ownership of land in Russia, Maurer proved it to be the social foundation from which all Teutonic races started in history, and, by and by, village communities were found to be, or to have been, the primitive form of society everywhere from India to Ireland. The inner organisation of this primitive communistic society was laid bare, in its typical form, by Morgan's crowning discovery of the true nature of the *gens* and its relation to the *tribe*. With the dissolution of these primæval communities, society begins to be differentiated into separate and finally antagonistic classes. I have attempted to retrace this process of dissolution in *The Origin of the Family, Private Property and the State.*

The discovery of America, the rounding of the Cape, opened up fresh ground for the rising bourgeoisie. The East-Indian and Chinese markets, the colonisation of America, trade with the colonies, the increase in the means of exchange and in commodities generally, gave to commerce, to navigation, to industry, an impulse never before known, and thereby, to the revolutionary element in the tottering feudal society, a rapid development.

The feudal system of industry, in which industrial production was monopolised by closed guilds, now no longer sufficed for the growing wants of the new markets. The manufacturing system took its place. The guild-masters were pushed aside by the manufacturing middle class; division of labour between the different corporate guilds vanished in the face of division of labour in each single workshop.

Meantime the markets kept ever growing, the demand ever rising. Even manufacture no longer sufficed. Thereupon, steam and machinery revolutionised industrial production. The place of manufacture was taken by the giant, modern industry, the place of the industrial middle class, by industrial millionaires—the leaders of whole industrial armies, the modern bourgeois.

Modern industry has established the world market, for which the discovery of America paved the way. This market has given an immense development to commerce, to navigation, to communication by land. This development has, in its turn, reacted on the extension of industry; and in proportion as industry, commerce, navigation, railways extended, in the same proportion the bourgeoisie developed, increased its capital, and pushed into the background every class handed down from the Middle Ages.

We see, therefore, how the modern bourgeoisie is itself the product of a long course of development, of a series of revolutions in the modes of production and of exchange.

Each step in the development of the bourgeoisie was accompanied by a corresponding political advance of that class. An oppressed class under the sway of the feudal nobility, it became an armed and self-governing association in the mediæval commune; here independent urban republic (as in Italy and Germany), there taxable "third estate" of the monarchy (as in France); afterwards, in the period of manufacture proper, serving either the semi-feudal or the absolute monarchy as a counterpoise against the nobility, and, in fact, corner-stone of the great monarchies in general—the bourgeoisie has at last, since the establishment of modern industry and of the world market, conquered for itself, in the modern representative state, exclusive political sway. The executive of the modern state is but a committee for managing the common affairs of the whole bourgeoisie.

The bourgeoisie has played a most revolutionary rôle in history.

The bourgeoisie, wherever it has got the upper hand, has put an end to all feudal, patriarchal, idyllic relations. It has pitilessly torn asunder the motley feudal ties that bound man to his "natural superiors," and has left no other bond between man and man than naked self-interest, than callous "cash payment." It has drowned the most heavenly ecstasies of religious fervour, of chivalrous enthusiasm, of philistine sentimentalism, in the icy water of egotistical calculation. It has resolved personal worth into exchange value, and in place of the numberless indefeasible chartered freedoms, has set up that single, unconscionable freedom—Free Trade. In one word, for exploitation, veiled by religious and political illusions, it has substituted naked, shameless, direct, brutal exploitation.

The bourgeoisie has stripped of its halo every occupation hitherto honoured and looked up to with reverent awe. It has converted the physician, the lawyer, the priest, the poet, the man of science, into its paid wage-labourers.

The bourgeoisie has torn away from the family its sentimental veil, and has reduced the family relation to a mere money relation.

The bourgeoisie has disclosed how it came to pass that the brutal display of vigour in the Middle Ages, which reactionaries so much admire, found its fitting complement in the most slothful indolence. It has been the first to show what man's activity can bring about. It has accomplished wonders far surpassing Egyptian pyramids, Roman aqueducts, and Gothic cathedrals; it has conducted expeditions that put in the shade all former migrations of nations and crusades.

The bourgeoisie cannot exist without constantly revolutionising the instruments of production, and thereby the relations of production, and with them the whole relations of society. Conservation of the old modes of production in unaltered form, was, on the contrary, the first condition of existence for all earlier industrial classes. Constant revolutionising of production, uninterrupted disturbance of all social conditions, everlasting uncertainty and agitation distinguish the bourgeois epoch from all earlier ones. All fixed, fast-frozen relations, with their train of ancient and venerable prejudices and opinions, are swept away, all new-formed ones become antiquated before they can ossify. All that is solid melts into air, all that is holy is profaned, and man is at last compelled to face with sober senses his real conditions of life and his relations with his kind.

The need of a constantly expanding market for its products chases the bourgeoisie over the whole surface of the globe. It must nestle everywhere, settle everywhere, establish connections everywhere.

The bourgeoisie has through its exploitation of the world market given a cosmopolitan character to production and consumption in every country. To the great chagrin of reactionaries, it has drawn from under the feet of industry the national ground on which it stood. All old-established national industries have been destroyed or are daily being destroyed. They are dislodged by new industries, whose introduction becomes a life and death question for all civilised nations, by industries that no longer work up indigenous raw material, but raw material drawn from the remotest zones; industries whose products are consumed, not only at home, but in every quarter of the globe. In place of the old wants, satisfied by the production of the country, we find new wants, requiring for their satisfaction the products of distant lands and climes. In place of the old local and national seclusion and self-sufficiency, we have intercourse in every direction, universal interdependence of nations. And as in material, so also in intellectual production. The intellectual creations of individual nations become common property. National one-sidedness and narrow-mindedness become more and more impossible, and from the numerous national and local literatures there arises a world literature.

The bourgeoisie, by the rapid improvement of all instruments of production, by the immensely facilitated means of communication, draws all nations, even the most barbarian, into civilisation. The cheap prices of its commodities are the heavy artillery with which it batters down all Chinese walls, with which it forces the barbarians' intensely obstinate hatred of foreigners to capitulate. It compels all nations, on pain of extinction, to adopt the bourgeois mode of production; it compels them to introduce what it calls civilisation into their midst, *i.e.,* to become bourgeois themselves. In a word, it creates a world after its own image.

The bourgeoisie has subjected the country to the rule of the towns. It has created enormous cities, has greatly increased the urban population as compared with the rural, and has thus rescued a considerable part of the population from the idiocy of rural life. Just as it has made the country dependent on the towns, so it has made barbarian and semi-barbarian countries dependent on the civilised ones, nations of peasants on nations of bourgeois, the East on the West.

More and more the bourgeoisie keeps doing away with the scattered state of the population, of the means of production, and of property. It has agglomerated population, centralised means of production, and has concentrated property in a few hands. The necessary consequence of this was political centralisation. Independent, or but loosely connected provinces, with separate interests, laws, governments and systems of taxation, became lumped together into one nation, with one government, one code of laws, one national class interest, one frontier and one customs tariff.

The bourgeoisie, during its rule of scarce one hundred years, has created more massive and more colossal productive forces than have all preceding generations together. Subjection of nature's forces to man, machinery, application of chemistry to industry and agriculture, steam-navigation, railways, electric telegraphs, clearing of whole continents for cultivation, canalisation of rivers, whole populations conjured out of the ground —what earlier century had even a presentiment that such productive forces slumbered in the lap of social labour?

We see then that the means of production and of exchange, which served as the foundation for the growth of the bourgeoisie, were generated in feudal society. At a certain stage in the development of these means of production and of exchange, the conditions under which feudal society produced and exchanged, the feudal organisation of agriculture and manufacturing industry, in a word, the feudal relations of property became no longer compatible with the already developed productive forces; they became so many fetters. They had to be burst asunder; they were burst asunder.

Into their place stepped free competition, accompanied by a social and political constitution adapted to it, and by the economic and political sway of the bourgeois class.

A similar movement is going on before our own eyes. Modern bourgeois society with its relations of production, of exchange and of property, a society that has conjured up such gigantic means of production and of exchange, is like the sorcerer who is no longer able to control the powers of the nether world whom he has called up by his spells. For many a decade past the history of industry and commerce is but the history of the revolt of modern productive forces against modern conditions of production, against the property relations that are the conditions for the existence of the bourgeoisie and of its rule. It is enough to mention the commercial crises that by their periodical return put the existence of the entire bourgeois society on trial, each time more threateningly. In these crises a great part not only of the existing products, but also of the previously created productive forces, are periodically destroyed. In these crises there breaks out an epidemic that, in all earlier epochs, would have seemed an absurdity —the epidemic of over-production. Society suddenly finds itself put back into a state of momentary barbarism; it appears as if a famine, a universal war of devastation had cut off the supply of every means of subsistence; industry and commerce seem to be destroyed. And why? Because there is too much civilisation, too much means of subsistence, too much industry, too much commerce. The productive forces at the disposal of society no longer tend to further the development of the conditions of bourgeois property; on the contrary, they have become too powerful for these conditions, by which they are fettered, and no sooner do they overcome these fetters than they bring disorder into the whole of bourgeois society, endanger the existence of bourgeois property. The conditions of bourgeois society are too narrow to comprise the wealth created by them. And how does the bourgeoisie get over these crises? On the one hand by enforced destruction of a mass of productive forces; on the other, by the conquest of new markets, and by the more thorough exploitation of the old ones. That is to say, by paving the way for more extensive and more destructive crises, and by diminishing the means whereby crises are prevented.

The weapons with which the bourgeoisie felled feudalism to the ground are now turned against the bourgeoisie itself.

But not only has the bourgeoisie forged the weapons that bring death to itself; it has also called into existence the men who are to wield those weapons—the modern working class—the proletarians.

In proportion as the bourgeoisie, *i.e.*, capital, is developed, in the same proportion is the proletariat, the modern working class, developed—a class of labourers, who live only so long as they find work, and who find work only so long as their labour increases capital. These labourers, who must sell themselves piecemeal, are a commodity, like every other article of commerce, and are consequently exposed to all the vicissitudes of competition, to all the fluctuations of the market.

Owing to the extensive use of machinery and to division of labour, the work of the proletarians has lost all individual character, and, consequently, all charm for the workman. He becomes an appendage of the machine, and it is only the most simple, most monotonous, and most easily acquired knack, that is required of him. Hence, the cost of production of a workman is restricted, almost entirely, to the means of subsistence that he requires for his maintenance, and for the propagation of his race. But the price of a commodity, and therefore also of labour, is equal to its cost of production. In proportion, therefore, as the repulsiveness of the work increases, the wage decreases. Nay more, in proportion as the use of machinery and division of labour increases, in the same proportion the burden of toil also increases, whether by prolongation of the working hours, by increase of the work exacted in a given time, or by increased speed of the machinery, etc.

Modern industry has converted the little workshop of the patriarchal master into the great factory of the industrial capitalist. Masses of labourers, crowded into the factory, are organised like soldiers. As privates of the industrial army they are placed under the command of a perfect hierarchy of officers and sergeants. Not only are they slaves of the bourgeois class, and of the bourgeois state; they are daily and hourly enslaved by the machine, by the over-looker, and, above all, by the individual bourgeois manufacturer himself. The more openly this despotism proclaims gain to be its end and aim, the more petty, the more hateful and the more embittering it is.

The less the skill and exertion of strength implied in manual labour, in other words, the more modern industry develops, the more is the labour of men superseded by that of women. Differences of age and sex have no longer any distinctive social validity for the working class. All are instruments of labour, more or less expensive to use, according to their age and sex.

No sooner has the labourer received his wages in cash, for the moment escaping exploitation by the manufacturer, than he is set upon by the other portions of the bourgeoisie, the landlord, the shopkeeper, the pawnbroker, etc.

The lower strata of the middle class—the small tradespeople, shopkeepers, and retired tradesmen generally, the handicraftsmen and peasants

—all these sink gradually into the proletariat, partly because their diminutive capital does not suffice for the scale on which modern industry is carried on, and is swamped in the competition with the large capitalists, partly because their specialised skill is rendered worthless by new methods of production. Thus the proletariat is recruited from all classes of the population.

The proletariat goes through various stages of development. With its birth begins its struggle with the bourgeoisie. At first the contest is carried on by individual labourers, then by the work people of a factory, then by the operatives of one trade, in one locality, against the individual bourgeois who directly exploits them. They direct their attacks not against the bourgeois conditions of production, but against the instruments of production themselves; they destroy imported wares that compete with their labour, they smash machinery to pieces, they set factories ablaze, they seek to restore by force the vanished status of the workman of the Middle Ages.

At this stage the labourers still form an incoherent mass scattered over the whole country, and broken up by their mutual competition. If anywhere they unite to form more compact bodies, this is not yet the consequence of their own active union, but of the union of the bourgeoisie, which class, in order to attain its own political ends, is compelled to set the whole proletariat in motion, and is moreover still able to do so for a time. At this stage, therefore, the proletarians do not fight their enemies, but the enemies of their enemies, the remnants of absolute monarchy, the landowners, the non-industrial bourgeois, the petty bourgeoisie. Thus the whole historical movement is concentrated in the hands of the bourgeoisie; every victory so obtained is a victory for the bourgeoisie.

But with the development of industry the proletariat not only increases in number; it becomes concentrated in greater masses, its strength grows, and it feels that strength more. The various interests and conditions of life within the ranks of the proletariat are more and more equalised, in proportion as machinery obliterates all distinctions of labour and nearly everywhere reduces wages to the same low level. The growing competition among the bourgeois, and the resulting commercial crises, make the wages of the workers ever more fluctuating. The unceasing improvement of machinery, ever more rapidly developing, makes their livelihood more and more precarious; the collisions between individual workmen and individual bourgeois take more and more the character of collisions between two classes. Thereupon the workers begin to form combinations (trade unions) against the bourgeoisie; they club together in order to keep up the rate of wages; they found permanent associations in order to make provision beforehand for these occasional revolts. Here and there the contest breaks out into riots.

Now and then the workers are victorious, but only for a time. The real fruit of their battles lies, not in the immediate result, but in the ever expanding union of the workers. This union is furthered by the improved means of communication which are created by modern industry, and which place the workers of different localities in contact with one another. It was just this contact that was needed to centralise the numerous local struggles, all of the same character, into one national struggle between classes. But every class struggle is a political struggle. And that union, to attain which the burghers of the Middle Ages, with their miserable highways, required centuries, the modern proletarians, thanks to railways, achieve in a few years.

This organisation of the proletarians into a class, and consequently into a political party, is continually being upset again by the competition between the workers themselves. But it ever rises up again, stronger, firmer, mightier. It compels legislative recognition of particular interests of the workers, by taking advantage of the divisions among the bourgeoisie itself. Thus the ten-hour bill in England was carried.

Altogether, collisions between the classes of the old society further the course of development of the proletariat in many ways. The bourgeoisie finds itself involved in a constant battle. At first with the aristocracy; later on, with those portions of the bourgeoisie itself whose interests have become antagonistic to the progress of industry; at all times with the bourgeoisie of foreign countries. In all these battles it sees itself compelled to appeal to the proletariat, to ask for its help, and thus, to drag it into the political arena. The bourgeoisie itself, therefore, supplies the proletariat with its own elements of political and general education, in other words, it furnishes the proletariat with weapons for fighting the bourgeoisie.

Further, as we have already seen, entire sections of the ruling classes are, by the advance of industry, precipitated into the proletariat, or are at least threatened in their conditions of existence. These also supply the proletariat with fresh elements of enlightenment and progress.

Finally, in times when the class struggle nears the decisive hour, the process of dissolution going on within the ruling class, in fact within the whole range of old society, assumes such a violent, glaring character, that a small section of the ruling class cuts itself adrift, and joins the revolutionary class, the class that holds the future in its hands. Just as, therefore, at an earlier period, a section of the nobility went over to the bourgeoisie, so now a portion of the bourgeoisie goes over to the proletariat, and in particular, a portion of the bourgeois ideologists, who have raised themselves to the level of comprehending theoretically the historical movement as a whole.

Of all the classes that stand face to face with the bourgeoisie today, the proletariat alone is a really revolutionary class. The other classes decay and finally disappear in the face of modern industry; the proletariat is its special and essential product.

The lower middle class, the small manufacturer, the shopkeeper, the artisan, the peasant, all these fight against the bourgeoisie, to save from extinction their existence as fractions of the middle class. They are therefore not revolutionary, but conservative. Nay more, they are reactionary, for they try to roll back the wheel of history. If by chance they are revolutionary, they are so only in view of their impending transfer into the proletariat; they thus defend not their present, but their future interests; they desert their own standpoint to adopt that of the proletariat.

The "dangerous class," the social scum (*Lumpenproletariat*), that passively rotting mass thrown off by the lowest layers of old society, may, here and there, be swept into the movement by a proletarian revolution; its conditions of life, however, prepare it far more for the part of a bribed tool of reactionary intrigue.

The social conditions of the old society no longer exist for the proletariat. The proletarian is without property; his relation to his wife and children has no longer anything in common with bourgeois family relations; modern industrial labour, modern subjection to capital, the same in England as in France, in America as in Germany, has stripped him of every trace of national character. Law, morality, religion, are to him so many bourgeois prejudices, behind which lurk in ambush just as many bourgeois interests.

All the preceding classes that got the upper hand, sought to fortify their already acquired status by subjecting society at large to their conditions of appropriation. The proletarians cannot become masters of the productive forces of society, except by abolishing their own previous mode of appropriation, and thereby also every other previous mode of appropriation. They have nothing of their own to secure and to fortify; their mission is to destroy all previous securities for, and insurances of, individual property.

All previous historical movements were movements of minorities, or in the interest of minorities. The proletarian movement is the self-conscious, independent movement of the immense majority, in the interest of the immense majority. The proletariat, the lowest stratum of our present society, cannot stir, cannot raise itself up, without the whole superincumbent strata of official society being sprung into the air.

Though not in substance, yet in form, the struggle of the proletariat with the bourgeoisie is at first a national struggle. The proletariat of each country must, of course, first of all settle matters with its own bourgeoisie.

In depicting the most general phases of the development of the proletariat, we traced the more or less veiled civil war, raging within existing society, up to the point where that war breaks out into open revolution, and where the violent overthrow of the bourgeoisie lays the foundation for the sway of the proletariat.

Hitherto, every form of society has been based, as we have already seen, on the antagonism of oppressing and oppressed classes. But in order to oppress a class, certain conditions must be assured to it under which it can, at least, continue its slavish existence. The serf, in the period of serfdom, raised himself to membership in the commune, just as the petty bourgeois, under the yoke of feudal absolutism, managed to develop into a bourgeois. The modern labourer, on the contrary, instead of rising with the progress of industry, sinks deeper and deeper below the conditions of existence of his own class. He becomes a pauper, and pauperism develops more rapidly than population and wealth. And here it becomes evident, that the bourgeoisie is unfit any longer to be the ruling class in society, and to impose its conditions of existence upon society as an over-riding law. It is unfit to rule because it is incompetent to assure an existence to its slave within his slavery, because it cannot help letting him sink into such a state, that it has to feed him, instead of being fed by him. Society can no longer live under this bourgeoisie, in other words, its existence is no longer compatible with society.

The essential condition for the existence and sway of the bourgeois class, is the formation and augmentation of capital; the condition for capital is wage-labour. Wage-labour rests exclusively on competition between the labourers. The advance of industry, whose involuntary promoter is the bourgeoisie, replaces the isolation of the labourers, due to competition, by their revolutionary combination, due to association. The development of modern industry, therefore, cuts from under its feet the very foundation on which the bourgeoisie produces and appropriates products. What the bourgeoisie therefore produces, above all, are its own grave-diggers. Its fall and the victory of the proletariat are equally inevitable.

II. PROLETARIANS AND COMMUNISTS

In what relation do the Communists stand to the proletarians as a whole?

The Communists do not form a separate party opposed to other working class parties.

They have no interests separate and apart from those of the proletariat as a whole.

They do not set up any sectarian principles of their own, by which to shape and mould the proletarian movement.

The Communists are distinguished from the other working class parties by this only: 1. In the national struggles of the proletarians of the different countries, they point out and bring to the front the common interests of the entire proletariat, independently of all nationality. 2. In the various stages of development which the struggle of the working class against the bourgeoisie has to pass through, they always and everywhere represent the interests of the movement as a whole.

The Communists, therefore, are on the one hand, practically, the most advanced and resolute section of the working class parties of every country, that section which pushes forward all others; on the other hand, theoretically, they have over the great mass of the proletariat the advantage of clearly understanding the line of march, the conditions, and the ultimate general results of the proletarian movement.

The immediate aim of the Communists is the same as that of all the other proletarian parties: Formation of the proletariat into a class, overthrow of bourgeois supremacy, conquest of political power by the proletariat.

The theoretical conclusions of the Communists are in no way based on ideas or principles that have been invented, or discovered, by this or that would-be universal reformer.

They merely express, in general terms, actual relations springing from an existing class struggle, from a historical movement going on under our very eyes. . . .

You are horrified at our intending to do away with private property. But in your existing society, private property is already done away with for nine-tenths of the population; its existence for the few is solely due to its non-existence in the hands of those nine-tenths. You reproach us, therefore, with intending to do away with a form of property, the necessary condition for whose existence is the nonexistence of any property for the immense majority of society. . . .

Just as, to the bourgeois, the disappearance of class property is the disappearance of production itself, so the disappearance of class culture is to him identical with the disappearance of all culture.

That culture, the loss of which he laments, is, for the enormous majority, a mere training to act as a machine.

But don't wrangle with us so long as you apply, to our intended abolition of bourgeois property, the standard of your bourgeois notions of freedom, culture, law, etc. Your very ideas are but the outgrowth of the conditions of your bourgeois production and bourgeois property, just as your jurisprudence is but the will of your class made into a law for all, a will whose essential character and direction are determined by the economic conditions of existence of your class. . . .

Abolition of the family! Even the most radical flare up at this infamous proposal of the Communists.

On what foundation is the present family, the bourgeois family, based? On capital, on private gain. In its completely developed form this family exists only among the bourgeoisie. But this state of things finds its complement in the practical absence of the family among the proletarians, and in public prostitution.

The bourgeois family will vanish as a matter of course when its complement vanishes, and both will vanish with the vanishing of capital.

Do you charge us with wanting to stop the exploitation of children by their parents? To this crime we plead guilty.

But, you will say, we destroy the most hallowed of relations, when we replace home education by social.

And your education! Is not that also social, and determined by the social conditions under which you educate, by the intervention of society, direct or indirect, by means of schools, etc.? The Communists have not invented the intervention of society in education; they do but seek to alter the character of that intervention, and to rescue education from the influence of the ruling class.

The bourgeois claptrap about the family and education, about the hallowed co-relation of parent and child, becomes all the more disgusting, the more, by the action of modern industry, all family ties among the proletarians are torn asunder, and their children transformed into simple articles of commerce and instruments of labour.

But you Communists would introduce community of women, screams the whole bourgeoisie in chorus.

The bourgeois sees in his wife a mere instrument of production. He hears that the instruments of production are to be exploited in common, and, naturally, can come to no other conclusion than that the lot of being common to all will likewise fall to the women.

He has not even a suspicion that the real point aimed at is to do away with the status of women as mere instruments of production.

For the rest, nothing is more ridiculous than the virtuous indignation of our bourgeois at the community of women which, they pretend, is to be openly and officially established by the Communists. The Communists have no need to introduce community of women; it has existed almost from time immemorial.

Our bourgeois, not content with having the wives and daughters of their proletarians at their disposal, not to speak of common prostitutes, take the greatest pleasure in seducing each other's wives.

Bourgeois marriage is in reality a system of wives in common and thus, at the most, what the Communists might possibly be reproached with is that they desire to introduce, in substitution for a hypocritically concealed, an openly legalised community of women. For the rest, it is self-evident, that the abolition of the present system of production must bring with it the abolition of the community of women springing from that system, *i.e.,* of prostitution both public and private.

The Communists are further reproached with desiring to abolish countries and nationality.

The working men have no country. We cannot take from them what they have not got. Since the proletariat must first of all acquire political supremacy, must rise to be the leading class of the nation, must constitute itself *the* nation, it is, so far, itself national, though not in the bourgeois sense of the word.

National differences and antagonisms between peoples are vanishing gradually from day to day, owing to the development of the bourgeoisie, to freedom of commerce, to the world market, to uniformity in the mode of production and in the conditions of life corresponding thereto.

The supremacy of the proletariat will cause them to vanish still faster. United action, of the leading civilised countries at least, is one of the first conditions for the emancipation of the proletariat.

In proportion as the exploitation of one individual by another is put an end to, the exploitation of one nation by another will also be put an end to. In proportion as the antagonism between classes within the nation vanishes, the hostility of one nation to another will come to an end.

The charges against Communism made from a religious, a philosophical, and, generally, from an ideological standpoint, are not deserving of serious examination.

Does it require deep intuition to comprehend that man's ideas, views, and conceptions, in one word, man's consciousness, changes with every change in the conditions of his material existence, in his social relations and in his social life?

What else does the history of ideas prove than that intellectual production changes its character in proportion as material production is changed? The ruling ideas of each age have ever been the ideas of its ruling class.

When people speak of ideas that revolutionise society, they do but express the fact that within the old society the elements of a new one have been created, and that the dissolution of the old ideas keeps even pace with the dissolution of the old conditions of existence.

When the ancient world was in its last throes, the ancient religions were overcome by Christianity. When Christian ideas succumbed in the 18th century to rationalist ideas, feudal society fought its death-battle with the then revolutionary bourgeoisie. The ideas of religious liberty and freedom of conscience merely gave expression to the sway of free competition within the domain of knowledge.

"Undoubtedly," it will be said, "religion, moral, philosophical and juridical ideas have been modified in the course of historical development. But religion, morality, philosophy, political science, and law, constantly survived this change."

"There are, besides, eternal truths, such as Freedom, Justice, etc., that are common to all states of society. But Communism abolishes eternal truths, it abolishes all religion, and all morality, instead of constituting them on a new basis; it therefore acts in contradiction to all past historical experience."

What does this accusation reduce itself to? The history of all past society has consisted in the development of class antagonisms, antagonisms that assumed different forms at different epochs.

But whatever form they may have taken, one fact is common to all past ages, *viz.,* the exploitation of one part of society by the other. No wonder, then, that the social consciousness of past ages, despite all the multiplicity and variety it displays, moves within certain common forms, or general ideas, which cannot completely vanish except with the total disappearance of class antagonisms.

The Communist revolution is the most radical rupture with traditional property relations; no wonder that its development involves the most radical rupture with traditional ideas.

But let us have done with the bourgeois objections to Communism.

We have seen above, that the first step in the revolution by the working class is to raise the proletariat to the position of ruling class, to establish democracy.

The proletariat will use its political supremacy to wrest, by degrees, all capital from the bourgeoisie, to centralise all instruments of production in the hands of the state, *i.e.,* of the proletariat organised as the ruling class; and to increase the total of productive forces as rapidly as possible. . . .

When, in the course of development, class distinctions have disappeared, and all production has been concentrated in the hands of a vast association of the whole nation, the public power will lose its political character. Political power, properly so called, is merely the organised power of one class for oppressing another. If the proletariat during its contest with the bourgeoisie is compelled, by the force of circumstances, to organise itself as a class; if, by means of a revolution, it makes itself the ruling class, and, as such sweeps away by force the old conditions of production, then it will, along with these conditions, have swept away the conditions for the existence of class antagonisms, and of classes generally, and will thereby have abolished its own supremacy as a class.

In place of the old bourgeois society, with its classes and class antagonisms, we shall have an association, in which the free development of each is the condition for the free development of all.

[Section III, "Socialist and Communist Literature," is omitted.]

A CONTRIBUTION TO THE CRITIQUE
OF POLITICAL ECONOMY

KARL MARX*

My investigations led to the conclusion that legal relations as well as forms of State could not be understood from themselves, nor from the

---

* The excerpt is from the Preface of the work, first published in 1859. In it, according to Lenin, "Marx gives an integral formulation of the fundamental principles of materialism as applied to human society and its history."

so-called general development of the human mind, but, on the contrary, are rooted in the material conditions of life, the aggregate of which Hegel, following the precedent of the English and French of the eighteenth century, grouped under the name of "civil society"; but that the anatomy of civil society is to be found in political economy. . . . The general conclusion I arrived at—and once reached, it served as the guiding thread in my studies —can be briefly formulated as follows: In the social production of their means of existence men enter into definite, necessary relations which are independent of their will, productive relationships which correspond to a definite stage of development of their material productive forces. The aggregate of these productive relationships constitutes the economic structure of society, the real basis on which a juridical and political superstructure arises, and to which definite forms of social consciousness correspond. The mode of production of the material means of existence conditions the whole process of social, political and intellectual life. It is not the consciousness of men that determines their existence, but, on the contrary, it is their social existence that determines their consciousness.

At a certain stage of their development the material productive forces of society come into contradiction with the existing productive relationships, or, what is but a legal expression for these, with the property relationships within which they had moved before. From forms of development of the productive forces these relationships are transformed into their fetters. Then an epoch of social revolution opens. With the change in the economic foundation the whole vast superstructure is more or less rapidly transformed. In considering such revolutions it is necessary always to distinguish between the material revolution in the economic conditions of production, which can be determined with scientific accuracy, and the juridical, political, religious, aesthetic or philosophic—in a word, ideological forms wherein men become conscious of this conflict and fight it out.

Just as we cannot judge an individual on the basis of his own opinion of himself, so such a revolutionary epoch cannot be judged from its own consciousness; but on the contrary this consciousness must be explained from the contradictions of material life, from the existing conflict between social productive forces and productive relationships. A social system never perishes before all the productive forces have developed for which it is wide enough; and new, higher productive relationships never come into being before the material conditions for their existence have been brought to maturity within the womb of the old society itself. Therefore, mankind always sets itself only such problems as it can solve; for when we look closer we will always find that the problem itself only arises when the material conditions for its solution are already present or at least in process of coming into being.

In broad outline, the Asiatic, the ancient, the feudal and the modern bourgeois modes of production can be indicated as progressive epochs in the economic system of society. Bourgeois productive relationships are the last antagonistic form of the social process of production—antagonistic in the sense not of individual antagonism, but of an antagonism arising out of the conditions of the social life of individuals; but the productive forces developing within the womb of bourgeois society at the same time create the material conditions for the solution of this antagonism. With this social system, therefore, the pre-history of human society comes to a close.

THE MATERIALIST CONCEPTION OF HISTORY

George Plekhanov*

Plekhanov, a brilliant polemicist, known as the "father of Russian Marxism," was one of the founders (in 1883) and the intellectual leader of the "Emancipation of Labor," the first Russian Marxist organization. He collaborated closely with Lenin in establishing (in 1900) and in editing "Iskra" (The Spark) but soon broke sharply with him and later denounced the Bolshevik seizure of power. Notwithstanding, Lenin in 1921, said: "It seems to me fitting to remark, for the benefit of the young members of the Party, that one cannot become an intelligent and genuine Communist without having studied—I say advisedly studied—all that Plekhanov has written on philosophy, for it is the best of its kind in international Marxist literature."

The methods by which social man satisfies his needs, and to a large extent these needs themselves, are determined by the nature of the implements with which he subjugates nature in one degree or another; in other words, they are determined by the state of his productive forces. Every considerable change in the state of these forces is reflected in man's social relations, and, therefore, in his economic relations, as part of these social relations. The idealists of all species and varieties held that economic relations were functions of *human nature*; the dialectical materialists hold that these relations are functions of the *social productive forces*. . . .

Man makes history in striving to satisfy his needs. These needs, of course, are originally imposed by nature; but they are later considerably modified quantitatively and qualitatively by the character of the artificial environment. The productive forces at man's disposal determine all his social relations. First of all, the state of the productive forces determines the relations in which men stand towards each other in the social process

* The selection is from George Plekhanov, *The Materialist Conception of History*, International Publishers Co., Inc., 1940, *passim*. By permission. This essay was first published in 1897.

of production, that is, their *economic relations*. These relations naturally
give rise to definite interests, which are expressed in *law*. "Every system of
law protects a definite interest," Labriola says. The development of productive forces divides society into classes, whose interests are not only different,
but in many—and, moreover, essential—aspects are diametrically antagonistic. This antagonism of interests gives rise to conflicts, to a struggle
among the social classes. The struggle results in the replacement of the
tribal organization by the *state* organization, the purpose of which is to protect the dominant interests. Lastly, social relations, determined by the
given state of productive forces, give rise to common *morality*, the morality,
that is, that guides people in their common, everyday life.

Thus the law, the state system and the morality of any given people
are determined *directly* and *immediately* by its characteristic economic relations. These economic relations also determine—but *indirectly* and *medi-
ately*—all the creations of the mind and imagination: art, science, etc.

To understand the history of scientific thought or the history of art in
any particular country, it is not enough to be acquainted with its economics.
One must know how to proceed from economics to *social psychology*, without a careful study and grasp of which a materialist explanation of the history of ideologies is impossible.

That does not mean, of course, that there is a social soul or a collective
national "spirit," developing in accordance with its own special laws and
manifesting itself in social life. "That is pure mysticism," Labriola says. All
that the materialist can speak of in this case is the prevailing state of sentiment and thought in the particular social class of the particular country at
the particular time. This state of sentiment and thought is the result of
social relations. Labriola is firmly persuaded that it is not the forms of
man's consciousness that determine the forms of his social being, but, on
the contrary, the forms of his social being that determine the forms of his
consciousness. But once the forms of his consciousness have sprung from the
soil of social being, they become a part of history. Historical science cannot
limit itself to the mere anatomy of society; it embraces the *totality of phenomena* that are *directly* or *indirectly* determined by social economics, including the work of the imagination. There is no historical fact that did
not owe its origin to social economics; but it is no less true to say that there
is no historical fact that was not preceded, not accompanied, and not succeeded by a definite state of consciousness. Hence the tremendous importance of social psychology. For if it has to be reckoned with even in the
history of law and of political institutions, in the history of literature, art,
philosophy, and so forth, not a single step can be taken without it.

When we say that a given work is fully in the spirit of, let us say, the
Renaissance, it means that it completely corresponds with the then prevailing sentiments of the classes which set the tone in social life. So long as the
social relations do not change, the psychology of society does not change

either. People get accustomed to the prevailing beliefs, concepts, modes of thought and means of satisfying given esthetic requirements. But should the development of productive forces lead to any substantial change in the economic structure of society, and, as a consequence, in the reciprocal relations of the social classes, the psychology of these classes will also change, and with it the "spirit of the times" and the "national character." This change is manifested in the appearance of new religious beliefs or new philosophical concepts, of new trends in art or new esthetic requirements. . . .

How does law arise? It may be said that all law represents the supersession or modification of an older law or custom. Why are old customs superseded? Because they cease to conform to the new "conditions," that is, to the new actual relations in which men stand towards each other in the social process of production. Primitive communism disappeared owing to the development of productive forces. However, productive forces develop but gradually. Hence the new actual relations of man to man in the social process of production also develop but gradually. And hence, too, the restrictiveness of the old laws or customs, and, consequently, the need to provide a corresponding *legal* expression for the new *actual* (economic) relations of men also develop but gradually. The instinctive wisdom of the reasoning animal usually follows in the wake of these actual changes. If old laws hamper a section of society in attaining its material aims, in satisfying its urgent wants, it will infallibly, and with the greatest ease, become conscious of their restrictiveness: this requires very little more intelligence than is necessary for the consciousness that tight shoes or heavy weapons are uncomfortable. But, of course, from being conscious of the restrictiveness of an existing law to *consciously striving to abolish it* is a very far cry.

At first, men simply try to get round it in each particular case. Let us recall what used to happen in our country in large peasant families, when, under the influence of nascent capitalism, new sources of earnings arose which were not equal for all members of the family. The customary family code thereupon became restrictive for the lucky ones who earned more than the others. But it was not so easy for these lucky ones to make up their minds to revolt against the old custom, and they did not do so all at once. For a long time they simply resorted to subterfuge, concealing part of their earnings from the elders. But the new economic system grew gradually stronger, and the old family life more and more shaken: those members of the family who were interested in its abolition grew bolder and bolder; sons more and more frequently separated off from the common household, and in the end the old custom disappeared and was replaced by a new custom, arising out of the new conditions, the new *actual* relations, the new *economics* of society.

Man's cognition of his situation more or less lags, as a rule, behind the development of the new actual relations which cause that situation to change. But it does keep in the wake of the actual relations. Where man's conscious striving for the abolition of old institutions and the establishment of a new legal system is weak, there the way for the new system has not yet been properly *paved by the economics of the society*. . . .

All positive law is a defense of some definite interest. How do these interests arise? Are they a product of human will and human consciousness? No, they are created by man's economic relations. Once they have arisen, interests are reflected in one way or another in man's *consciousness*. In order to defend an interest, there must be consciousness of it. Hence every system of positive law may and should be regarded as a product of consciousness. It is not man's consciousness that calls into being the interests that the law protects, and, consequently, it is not man's consciousness that determines the content of law; but the state of social consciousness (social psychology) in the given era does determine *the form which the reflection of the given interest takes in the mind of man*. Unless we take the state of the social consciousness into account we shall be absolutely unable to explain the history of law.

In this history, it is always essential to draw a careful distinction between *form* and *content*. In its *formal* aspect, law, like every ideology, is subject to the influence of all, or, at least of some of, the other ideologies: religious beliefs, philosophical concepts, and so on. This in itself hinders to some extent—and sometimes to a very large extent—the disclosure of the dependence between men's legal concepts and their mutual relations in the social process of production. But that is only half the trouble. The real trouble is that *at different stages of social development a given ideology is subject to the influence of other ideologies in very unequal degrees*. For example, ancient Egyptian, and partly Roman, law was under the sway of religion; in more recent history law has developed (we repeat, and request it to be noted, that we are here speaking of the *formal* aspect) under the strong influence of philosophy. Philosophy had to put up a big fight before it succeeded in eliminating the influence of religion on law and substituting its own influence. This fight was nothing but a reflection in the realm of ideas of the social struggle between the third estate and the clergy, but, nevertheless, it greatly hampered the formation of a correct view of the origin of legal institutions, for, thanks to it, these institutions seemed to be the obvious and indubitable product of a struggle between abstract ideas. . . .

The origin of the symbolical custom by which a woman cuts off her braid on the grave of a brother is to be explained by the history of the family; and the explanation of the history of the family is to be sought in the history of economic development. . . . If the conservatives passionately uphold the old customs, it is because in their minds the idea of an advantageous, precious and customary social system is firmly associated with the idea of these customs. If the innovators detest and scoff at these customs, it is because in their minds the idea of these customs is associated with the idea of restrictive, disadvantageous and objectionable social relations. Consequently, *the whole point lies in an association of ideas.* When we find that a particular tie has survived not only the relations which gave rise to it, but also cognate rites that arose from these same relations, we have to conclude that in the minds of the innovators it was not so strongly associated with the idea of the old, detested order as other customs were. Why so? To answer this question is sometimes easy, but at others it is quite impossible for lack of the necessary psychological data. But even when we are constrained to admit that the question is unanswerable—at least, in the existing state of our knowledge—we must nevertheless remember that the point does not lie in the *force of tradition,* but in definite associations of ideas produced by definite actual relations of men in society.

The history of ideologies is to a large extent to be explained by the rise, modification and breakdown of associations of ideas under the influence of the rise, modification and breakdown of definite combinations of social forces. . . .

From the standpoint of the theory of factors, human society is a heavy load which various "forces"—morality, law, economics, etc., etc.—drag each in its own way along the path of history. From the standpoint of the modern materialist conception of history, the whole thing assumes a different aspect. It turns out that the historical "factors" are mere abstractions, and when the mist surrounding them is dispelled, it becomes clear that men do not make several distinct histories—the history of law, the history of morals, the history of philosophy, etc.—but only one history, the history of their own social relations, which are determined by the state of the productive forces in each particular period. *What is known as ideologies is nothing but a multiform reflection in the minds of men of this single and indivisible history.*

THE ROLE OF THE INDIVIDUAL IN HISTORY

GEORGE PLEKHANOV*

There cannot be the slightest doubt that the materialist conception of the human will is quite compatible with the most vigorous practical activity. . . . *The "disciple" serves as an instrument of this necessity and cannot help doing so,* owing to his social status and to his mentality and temperament, which were created by his status. This, too, is an *aspect of necessity.* Since his social status has imbued him with this character and no other, he

* The selection is from George Plekhanov, *The Role of the Individual in History* (International Publishers Co., Inc., 1940), *passim.* By permission. This essay was first published in 1898.

not only serves as an instrument of necessity and cannot help doing so, but he *passionately desires, and cannot help desiring,* to do so. . . .

While some subjectivists, striving to ascribe the widest possible role to the "individual" in history, refused to recognize the historical progress of mankind as a process expressing laws, some of their later opponents, striving to bring out more sharply the coherent character of this progress, were evidently prepared to forget that *men make history, and, therefore, the activities of individuals cannot help being important in history.* . . .

By virtue of particular traits of their character, individuals can influence the fate of society. Sometimes this influence is very considerable; but the possibility of exercising this influence, and its extent, are determined by the form of organization of society, by the relation of forces within it. The character of an individual is a "factor" in social development only where, when, and to the extent that social relations permit it to be such.

We may be told that the extent of personal influence may also be determined by the talents of the individual. We agree. But the individual can display his talents only when he occupies the position in society necessary for this. Why was the fate of France in the hands of a man who totally lacked the ability and desire to serve society? Because such was the form of organization of that society. It is the form of organization that in any given period determines the role and, consequently, the social significance that may fall to the lot of talented or incompetent individuals.

But if the role of individuals is determined by the form of organization of society, how can their social influence, which is determined by the role they play, contradict the conception of social development as a process expressing laws? It does not contradict it; on the contrary, it serves as one of its most vivid illustrations. . . .

No matter what the qualities of the given individual may be, they cannot eliminate the given economic relations if the latter conform to the given state of productive forces. But the personal qualities of individuals make them more or less fit to satisfy those social needs which arise out of the given economic relations, or to counteract such satisfaction. The urgent social need of France at the end of the eighteenth century was the substitution for the obsolete political institutions of new institutions that would conform more to her economic system. The most prominent and useful public men of that time were those who were more capable than others of helping to satisfy this most urgent need. . . .

Let us assume that Robespierre was an absolutely indispensable force in his party; but even so, he was not the only force. If the accidental fall of a brick had killed him, say, in January, 1793, his place would, of course, have been taken by somebody else, and although this person might have been inferior to him in every respect, nevertheless, events would have taken *the same course* as they did when Robespierre was alive. For example, even under these circumstances the Gironde would probably not have escaped defeat; but it is possible that Robespierre's party would have lost power somewhat earlier. . . . In short, it may have fallen sooner or perhaps later, but it certainly would have fallen, because the section of the people which supported Robespierre's party was totally unprepared to hold power for a prolonged period. At all events, results "opposite" to those which arose from Robespierre's energetic action are out of the question. . . .

Owing to the specific qualities of their minds and characters, influential individuals can change the *individual features of events and some of their particular consequences,* but they cannot change their general *trend,* which is determined by other forces. . . .

In order that a man who possesses a particular kind of talent may, by means of it, greatly influence the course of events, two conditions are needed: First, this talent must make him more conformable to the social needs of the given epoch than anyone else. If Napoleon had possessed the musical gifts of Beethoven instead of his own military genius he would not, of course, have become an emperor. Second, the existing social order must not bar the road to the person possessing the talent which is needed and useful precisely at the given time. This very *Napoleon* would have died as the barely known General, or Colonel, *Bonaparte* had the older order in France existed another seventy-five years.[1] . . .

It has long been observed that great talents appear everywhere, whenever the social conditions favorable to their development exist. This means that every man of talent who *actually appears,* every man of talent who becomes a *social force,* is the product of *social relations.* Since this is the case, it is clear why talented people can, as we have said, change only individual features of events, but not their general trend; *they are themselves the product of this trend; were it not for that trend they would never have crossed the threshold that divides the potential from the real.* . . .

Thus, the personal qualities of leading people determine the individual features of historical events; and the accidental element, in the sense that we have indicated, always plays some role in the course of these events, the trend of which is determined, in the last analysis, by so-called general causes, *i.e.,* actually by the development of productive forces and the mutual relations between men in the social-economic process of production. Casual phenomena and the personal qualities of celebrated people are ever so much more noticeable than deep-lying general causes. The eighteenth century pondered but little over these general causes, and claimed that history was explained by the conscious actions and "passions" of historical personages. . . .

At the present time we must regard the development of productive forces as the final and most general cause of the historical progress of man-

[1] Probably Napoleon would have gone to Russia, *where he had intended to go just a few years before the Revolution.* Here, no doubt, he would have distinguished himself in action against the Turks or the Caucasian highlanders, but nobody here would have though that this poor, but capable, officer could, under favorable circumstances, have become the ruler of the world.

kind, and it is these productive forces that determine the consecutive changes in the social relations of men. Parallel with this *general* cause there are *particular* causes, *i.e., the historical situation* in which the development of the productive forces of a given nation proceeds and which, in the last analysis, is itself created by the development of these forces among other nations, *i.e.,* the same general cause.

Finally, the influence of the *particular* causes is supplemented by the operation of *individual* causes, *i.e.,* the personal qualities of public men and other "accidents," thanks to which events finally assume their *individual features.* Individual causes cannot bring about fundamental changes in the operation of *general and particular* causes which, moreover, determine the trend and limits of the influence of individual causes. Nevertheless, there is no doubt that history would have had different features had the individual causes which had influenced it been replaced by other causes of the same order. . . .

A great man is great not because his personal qualities give individual features to great historical events, but because he possesses qualities which make him most capable of serving the great social needs of his time, needs which arose as a result of general and particular causes. Carlyle, in his well-known book on heroes and hero-worship, calls great men *beginners.* This is a very apt description, A great man is precisely a beginner because he sees *further* than others, and desires things *more strongly* than others. . . .

Bismarck said that we cannot make history and must wait while it is being made. But who makes history? It is made by the *social man,* who is its *sole "factor."* The social man creates his own, social, relationships. But if in a given period he creates given relationships and not others, there must be some cause for it, of course; it is determined by the state of his productive forces. No great man can foist on society relations which *no longer* conform to the state of these forces, or which *do not yet* conform to them.

MARX'S ECONOMIC DOCTRINE

V. I. LENIN*

MARX'S ECONOMIC DOCTRINE

"It is the ultimate aim of this work to reveal the economic law of motion of modern society" (that is to say, capitalist, bourgeois society), writes Marx in the preface to the first volume of *Capital*. The study of the production relationships in a given, historically determinate society, in their genesis, their development, and their decay—such is the content of Marx's economic teaching. In capitalist society the dominant feature is the production of *commodities,* and Marx's analysis therefore begins with an analysis of a commodity.

Value

A commodity is, firstly, something that satisfies a human need; and, secondly, it is something that is exchanged for something else. The utility of a thing gives it *use-value.* Exchange-value (or simply, value) presents itself first of all as the proportion, the ratio, in which a certain number of use-values of one kind are exchanged for a certain number of use-values of another kind. Daily experience shows us that by millions upon millions of such exchanges, all and sundry use-values, in themselves very different and not comparable one with another, are equated to one another. Now, what is common in these various things which are constantly weighed one against another in a definite system of social relationships? That which is common to them is that they are *products of labour.* In exchanging products, people equate to one another most diverse kinds of labour. The production of commodities is a system of social relationships in which different producers produce various products (the social division of labour), and in which all these products are equated to one another in exchange.

Consequently, the element common to all commodities is not concrete labour in a definite branch of production, not labour of one particular kind, but *abstract* human labour—human labour in general. All the labour power of a given society, represented in the sum total of values of all commodities, is one and the same human labour power. Millions upon millions

---

* The selection is from V. I. Lenin, *The Teachings of Karl Marx,* International Publishers Co., Inc., 1930, pp. 18-30. By permission of the publisher. This essay, written by Lenin for a Russian encyclopedia, was completed in November 1914. It presents in summary Marx's doctrines in their most revolutionary—and, from the Bolshevik point of view, most acceptable—form.

of acts of exchange prove this. Consequently, each particular commodity represents only a certain part of *socially necessary* labour time.

The magnitude of the value is determined by the amount of socially necessary labour, or by the labour time that is socially requisite for the production of the given commodity, of the given use-value. ". . . Exchanging labour products of different kinds one for another, they equate the values of the exchanged products; and in doing so they equate the different kinds of labour expended in production, treating them as homogeneous human labour. They do not know that they are doing this, but they do it." As one of the earlier economists said, value is a relationship between two persons, only he should have added that it is a relationship hidden beneath a material wrapping. We can only understand what value is when we consider it from the point of view of a system of social production relationships in one particular historical type of society; and, moreover, of relationships which present themselves in a mass form, the phenomenon of exchange repeating itself millions upon millions of times. "As values, all commodities are only definite quantities of congealed labour time."

Having made a detailed analysis of the twofold character of the labour incorporated in commodities, Marx goes on to analyse the *form of value and of money*. His main task, then, is to study the *origin* of the money form of value, to study the *historical process* of the development of exchange, beginning with isolated and casual acts of exchange ("simple, isolated, or casual value form," in which a given quantity of one commodity is exchanged for a given quantity of another), passing on to the universal form of value, in which a number of different commodities are exchanged for one and the same particular commodity, and ending with the money form of value, when gold becomes this particular commodity, the universal equivalent. Being the highest product of the development of exchange and of commodity production, money masks the social character of individual labour, and hides the social tie between the various producers who come together in the market. Marx analyses in great detail the various functions of money; and it is essential to note that here (as generally in the opening chapters of *Capital*) what appears to be an abstract and at times purely deductive mode of exposition in reality reproduces a gigantic collection of facts concerning the history of the development of exchange and commodity production.

Money . . . presupposes a definite level of commodity exchange. The various forms of money (simple commodity equivalent or means of circulation, or means of payment, treasure, or international money) indicate, according to the different extent to which this or that function is put into application, and according to the comparative predominance of one or other of them, very different grades of the social process of production. [*Capital,* Vol. I.]

Surplus Value

At a particular stage in the development of commodity production, money becomes transformed into capital. The formula of commodity circulation was C-M-C (commodity—money—commodity); the sale of one commodity for the purpose of buying another. But the general formula of capital, on the contrary, is M-C-M (money—commodity—money); purchase for the purpose of selling—at a profit. The designation "surplus value" is given by Marx to the increase over the original value of money that is put into circulation. The fact of this "growth" of money in capitalist society is well known. Indeed, it is this "growth" which transforms money into *capital*, as a special, historically defined, social relationship of production. Surplus value cannot arise out of the circulation of commodities, for this represents nothing more than the exchange of equivalents; it cannot arise out of an advance in prices, for the mutual losses and gains of buyers and sellers would equalise one another; and we are concerned here, not with what happens to individuals, but with a mass or average or social phenomenon.

In order that he may be able to receive surplus value, "Moneybags must . . . find in the market a commodity whose use-value has the peculiar quality of being a source of value"—a commodity, the actual process of whose use is at the same time the process of the creation of value. Such a commodity exists. It is human labour power. Its use is labour, and labour creates value. The owner of money buys labour power at its value, which is determined, like the value of every other commodity, by the socially necessary labour time requisite for its production (that is to say, the cost of maintaining the worker and his family). Having bought labour power, the owner of money is entitled to use it, that is to set it to work for the whole day—twelve hours, let us suppose. Meanwhile, in the course of six hours ("necessary" labour time) the labourer produces sufficient to pay back the cost of his own maintenance; and in the course of the next six hours ("surplus" labour time), he produces a "surplus" product for which the capitalist does not pay him—surplus product or surplus value.

In capital, therefore, from the viewpoint of the process of production, we have to distinguish between two parts: first, constant capital, expended for the means of production (machinery, tools, raw materials, etc.), the value of this being (all at once or part by part) transferred, unchanged, to the finished product; and, secondly, variable capital, expended for labour power. The value of this latter capital is not constant, but grows in the labour process, creating surplus value. To express the degree of exploitation of labour power by capital, we must therefore compare the surplus value, not with the whole capital, but only with the variable capital. Thus, in the example just given, the rate of surplus value, as Marx calls this relationship, will be 6:6, *i.e.,* 100%.

There are two historical prerequisites to the genesis of capital: first, accumulation of a considerable sum of money in the hands of individuals living under conditions in which there is a comparatively high development of commodity production. Second, the existence of workers who are "free" in a double sense of the term: free from any constraint or restriction as regards the sale of their labour power; free from any bondage to the soil or to the means of production in general—*i.e.,* of propertyless workers, of "proletarians" who cannot maintain their existence except by the sale of their labour power.

There are two fundamental ways in which surplus value can be increased: by an increase in the working day ("absolute surplus value"); and by a reduction in the necessary working day ("relative surplus value"). Analysing the former method, Marx gives an impressive picture of the struggle of the working class for shorter hours and of government interference, first (from the fourteenth century to the seventeenth) in order to lengthen the working day, and subsequently (factory legislation of the nineteenth century) to shorten it. Since the appearance of *Capital,* the history of the working-class movement in all lands provides a wealth of new facts to amplify this picture.

Analysing the production of relative surplus value, Marx investigates the three fundamental historical stages of the process whereby capitalism has increased the productivity of labour; (1) simple cooperation; (2) division of labour, and manufacture; (3) machinery and large-scale industry. How profoundly Marx has here revealed the basic and typical features of capitalist development is shown by the fact that investigations of the so-called "kustar" industry* of Russia furnish abundant material for the illustration of the first two of these stages. The revolutionising effect of large-scale machine industry, described by Marx in 1867, has become evident in a number of "new" countries, such as Russia, Japan, etc., in the course of the last fifty years.

But to continue. Of extreme importance and originality is Marx's analysis of the *accumulation of capital,* that is to say, the transformation of a portion of surplus value into capital and the applying of this portion to additional production, instead of using it to supply the personal needs or to gratify the whims of the capitalist. Marx pointed out the mistake made by earlier classical political economy (from Adam Smith on), which assumed that all the surplus value which was transformed into capital became variable capital. In actual fact, it is divided into *means of production* plus variable capital. The more rapid growth of constant capital as compared with variable capital in the sum total of capital is of immense importance in the process of development of capitalism and in that of the transformation of capitalism into Socialism.

The accumulation of capital, accelerating the replacement of workers

* Small-scale home industry of a predominantly handicraft nature.

by machinery, creating wealth at the one pole and poverty at the other, gives birth to the so-called "reserve army of labour," to a "relative over-abundance" of workers or to "capitalist overpopulation." This assumes the most diversified forms, and gives capital the possibility of expanding production at an exceptionally rapid rate. This possibility, in conjunction with enhanced facilities for credit and with the accumulation of capital in the means of production, furnishes, among other things, the key to the understanding of the *crises* of overproduction that occur periodically in capitalist countries—first about every ten years, on an average, but subsequently in a more continuous form and with a less definite periodicity. From accumulation of capital upon a capitalist foundation we must distinguish the so-called "primitive accumulation": the forcible severance of the worker from the means of production, the driving of the peasants off the land, the stealing of the communal lands, the system of colonies and national debts, of protective tariffs, and the like. "Primitive accumulation" creates, at one pole, the "free" proletarian: at the other, the owner of money, the capitalist.

The *"historical tendency of capitalist accumulation"* is described by Marx in the following well-known terms:

The expropriation of the immediate producers is effected with ruthless vandalism, and under the stimulus of the most infamous, the baset, the meanest, and the most odious of passions. Self-earned private property [of the peasant and the handicraftsman], the private property that may be looked upon as grounded on a coalescence of the isolated, individual, and independent worker with his working conditions, is supplemented by capitalist private property, which is maintained by the exploitation of others' labour, but of labour which in a formal sense is free. . . . What has now to be expropriated is no longer the labourer working on his own account, but the capitalist who exploits many labourers. This expropriation is brought about by the operation of the immanent laws of capitalist production, by the centralisation of capital. One capitalist lays a number of his fellow capitalists low.

Hand in hand with this centralisation, concomitantly with the expropriation of many capitalists by a few, the co-operative form of the labour process develops to an ever-increasing degree; therewith we find a growing tendency towards the purposive application of science to the improvement of technique; the land is more methodically cultivated; the instruments of labour tend to assume forms which are only utilisable by combined effort; the means of production are economised through being turned to account only by joint, by social labour; all the peoples of the world are enmeshed in the net of the world market, and therefore the capitalist régime tends more and more to assume an international character. While there is thus a progressive diminution in the number of the capitalist magnates (who usurp and monopolise all the advantages of this transformative process), there occurs a corresponding increase in the mass of poverty, oppression, enslavement, degeneration, and exploitation; but at the same time there is a steady intensification of the wrath of the working class—a class which grows ever more numerous, and is disciplined, unified, and organised by the very mechanism of the capitalist method of production. Capitalist monopoly becomes a fetter upon the method of production which has flourished with it and under it. The centralisation of the means of production and the socialisation of labour reach a point where they prove incompatible with their capitalist husk. This bursts asunder. The knell of capitalist private property sounds. The expropriators are expropriated. [*Capital,* Vol. I.]

. . . The impoverishment and the ruin of the agricultural population lead, in their turn, to the formation of a reserve army of labour for capital. In every capitalist country, "part of the rural population is continually on the move, in course of transference to join the urban proletariat, the manufacturing proletariat. . . . (In this connection, the term "manufacture" is used to include all non-agricultural industry.) This source of a relative surplus population is, therefore, continually flowing. . . . The agricultural labourer, therefore, has his wages kept down to the minimum, and always has one foot in the swamp of pauperism" (*Capital,* Vol. I). The peasant's private ownership of the land he tills constitutes the basis of small-scale production and causes the latter to flourish and attain its classical form. But such petty production is only compatible with a narrow and primitive type of production, with a narrow and primitive framework of society. Under capitalism, the exploitation of the peasant "differs from the exploitation of the industrial proletariat only in point of form. The exploiter is the same: capital. The individual capitalists exploit the individual peasants through mortgages and usury, and the capitalist class exploits the peasant class through state taxation" (*Class Struggles in France*). "Peasant agriculture, the smallholding system, is merely an expedient whereby the capitalist is enabled to extract profit, interest, and rent from the land, while leaving the peasant proprietor to pay himself his own wages as best he may. . . ."

In agriculture as in industry, capitalism improves the production process only at the price of the "martyrdom of the producers."

The dispersion of the rural workers over large areas breaks down their powers of resistance at the very time when concentration is increasing the powers of the urban operatives in this respect. In modern agriculture, as in urban industry, the increased productivity and the greater mobility of labour are purchased at the cost of devastating labour power and making it a prey to disease. Moreover, every advance in capitalist agriculture is an advance in the art, not only of robbing the worker, but also of robbing the soil. . . . Capitalist production, therefore, is only able to develop the technique and the combination of the social process of production by simultaneously undermining the foundations of all wealth—the land and the workers. [*Capital,* Vol. I.]

SOCIALISM

From the foregoing it is manifest that Marx deduces the inevitability of the transformation of capitalist society into Socialist society wholly and exclusively from the economic law of the movement of contemporary society. The chief material foundation of the inevitability of the coming of Socialism is the socialisation of labour in its myriad forms, advancing ever more rapidly, and conspicuously so, throughout the half century that has elapsed since the death of Marx—being especially plain in the growth of large-scale production, of capitalist cartels, syndicates, and trusts; but also in the gigantic increase in the dimensions and the power of finance capital. The intellectual and moral driving force of this transformation is the proletariat, the physical carrier trained by capitalism itself. The contest of the proletariat with the bourgeoisie, assuming various forms which grow continually richer in content, inevitably becomes a political struggle aiming at the conquest of political power by the proletariat ("the dictatorship of the proletariat"). The socialisation of production cannot fail to lead to the transfer of the means of production into the possession of society, to the "expropriation of the expropriators." An immense increase in the productivity of labour; a reduction in working hours; replacement of the remnants, the ruins of petty, primitive, individual production by collective and perfected labour—such will be the direct consequences of this transformation.

THE PHILOSOPHIC AND ECONOMIC THEORIES OF MARXISM

R. N. CAREW HUNT*

I. THE PHILOSOPHIC THEORY OF MARXISM

Marxism consists of three elements:

1. A dialectical philosophy borrowed from Hegel but transformed into dialectical materialism, from which in turn historical materialism derives.

2. A system of political economy, of which the dynamic part is the labour theory of value, the theory of surplus value and the conclusions drawn from them.

3. A theory of the State and of revolution. . . .

Dialectic and Formal Logic

. . . As a revolutionary, Marx was naturally attracted to the dialectic because it represented everything as being in the state of becoming something else, and to this day Communists are taught that it constitutes a mode of reasoning which is somehow superior to that of formal logic, which is represented as conceiving of everything in fixed and unchangeable terms

* At St. Antony's College, Oxford University. The selection is from chapters IV and V of R. N. Carew Hunt, *The Theory and Practice of Communism* (New York: The Macmillan Company, fifth revised edition, 1957), copyright by the author, and used with the permission of the publisher.

and as thus providing a convenient intellectual instrument for reactionaries. Thus, Engels says that the dialectic transcends the narrow horizon of formal logic and contains the germ of a more comprehensive view of the world: and that while the latter is all very well "for every-day purposes," it is inadequate to give "an exact representation of the universe"; though the claim of the dialectic to perform this rests on no more secure foundation than that in Marxist hands it can be twisted to explain anything. . . .

Hegel's belief that change is always effected by the fruitful conflict of what he called, indifferently, contradictions or oppositions led him to challenge what he regarded as the barren conflict of affirmation and denial made by formal logic.[1] Unfortunately, he did not at all clearly define what he meant by contradictions, and those to which he refers are of many different kinds. In a given situation, there may be forces that make for peace and others that make for war, and it is doubtless permissible to represent these as contradictions which "exist in unity."[2] But there are other types of contradiction which are by their very nature irreconcilable. If, for example, the statement that "All men are mortal" does not exclude the contrary statement that "Some men are immortal," it is meaningless. But few writers on dialectical materialism distinguish between the various types of contradiction—between what Jules Monnerot, in his able treatment of this problem, calls *contradictions motrices* and *contradictions paralysantes*.[3]

Marxists habitually describe as contradictory any sequences of events that are in some vague sense contrary to one another; and at the same time imply that the contradictions between them are reconcilable, and that it is only outmoded formal logic which asserts the contrary. Yet while it is legimate to regard dialectical logic as a development of formal logic, it contains no new function, and the opposition which Marxists set up between it and formal logic is quite unjustifiable. We may accept it if we like; but its rejection in no way commits us, as Marxists would have it, to regarding everything as fixed and static, and of thus being forever incapable of taking into account the fluidity of the subject matter of thought and of making new judgments as changes in it require them. In fact, Marxists do not hesitate to use such expressions as "Feudalism" and "Capitalism" as fixed terms, as indeed they have to do. They talk continually of the "logic of contradiction," but none of their writings from Marx to Stalin contains any example of reasoning which does not assume that given one thing, another follows from it, which is how we all normally argue.[4] . . .

[1] On Hegel's treatment of the Law of Contradiction see Hans Kelsen, *The Political Theory of Bolshevism* (California University Press, 1949), pp. 14-17.

[2] George H. Sabine, *History of Political Theory* (ed. 1948), pp. 532-535.

[3] Jules Monnerot, *Sociologie du Communisme* (Paris, 1949), pp. 214 f.; see also the German Social Democrat, Edouard Conze, *An Introduction to Dialectical Materialism* (n.d.), p. 57, and for a criticism of Conze, David Guest's *A Textbook of Dialectical Materialism* (1939), pp. 78 f.

[4] Julien Benda, *Trois Idoles Romantiques* (Paris, 1948), p. 162.

All Marxist theoreticians are committed to applying the dialectic to any problem with which they may be dealing, though the result is often totally to obscure it; and the commonest criticism of any scheme that has miscarried is that its authors failed to carry out beforehand a correct dialectical analysis of the situation. For it is on the dialectic that the *Conclusion* of the official *Short History of the Communist Party of the Soviet Union* bases the claim which it makes for the Marxist doctrine, "the power of which," as it declares, lies in the fact that "it enables the Party to find the right orientation to any situation, to understand the inner connection of current events, to foresee their course, and perceive not only how and in what direction they are developing in the present, but how and in what direction they are bound to develop in the future." Without some knowledge of this mode of reasoning it is thus scarcely possible to understand Marxist literature at all. But by reason of its official adoption, it has degenerated into a barren scholasticism such as is taught in all communist centres of learning under the guise of instruction in the art of thinking, of which the best that can be said is that it may perhaps encourage beginners to think historically. Yet we may accept the dialectic as a description of the part played in human affairs by conflicting tendencies and purposes, without necessarily accepting it as a universal law. In the first sense it can be applied with genuine force to the analysis of society, as no one who has read Marx will dispute, and critics like Max Eastman go too far when they condemn it as completely valueless and as a redundant element of Marxist theory.[1]

But although the dialectic may give us valuable insights into the history of human development, the Marxist claim that it constitutes the only scientific approach to reality cannot be allowed. It is not, in fact, scientific at all, and it is only in Russia that scientists are required to set out their ideas in pseudo-dialectical jargon, for which Engel's *Anti-Dühring* provides the model.[2] Marxists argue, indeed, that the processes of nature are governed by the dialectic, though if this be so, it is strange that all the great scientific discoveries should have been made without apparent reference to it. Thus, to take the illustration borrowed from Hegel and used by Engels in Ch. xiii of his *Anti-Dühring,* a grain of barley germinates and dies, and from it there arises a plant which is "the negation of the grain." This plant grows, and finally produces a stalk at the end of which are further grains of barley. "As soon as these are ripened the stalk dies and is in turn negated"; and as a result of this "negation of the negation," the original grain of barley is multiplied tenfold. But such changes cannot justly be represented as contradictions, nor does the emergence of ten grains of barley from a single grain constitute a "qualitative" change (since the

[1] Cp. Karl Mannheim, *Ideology and Utopia* (1936), pp. 115-116.
[2] See Monnerot, p. 215: but cp. J. B. S. Haldane, *Dialectical Materialism and Modern Science* (n.d.), and J. D. Bernal, *The Foundations of Necessity* (1949), pp. 370 f., 410 f., 423 f.

grains remain barley), or issue in a "higher reformulation," such as the dialectic is understood to effect. In fact, the seed-flower-fruit cycle simply brings us back to where we started.[1]

Again, the world of the scientist is not one in which everything is in a state of becoming, for if it were, most scientific investigation would have to be abandoned. As it is, the scientist is aware that the phenomena with which he is dealing change so imperceptibly as to justify him in regarding them as static, and his work becomes possible only because he can, for all practical purposes, isolate them into closed systems. He will, of course, consider his particular group of phenomena in their relation to others; but the idea that they can be comprehended only as a part of the Whole is one which belongs to metaphysics rather than to science. And, finally, there is, as Röpke points out, a profound gulf between the attempt to comprehend the world through the critical intelligence, as the scientist seeks to do within his own field, and the attempt to identify that intelligence with the world. For the process of becoming and our idea of that process are different things, and science lends no warrant to the notion that it is possible to establish a mystical union between the two.[2]

Marx's Materialism and His Theory of Knowledge

Marx rejected, or at least believed he had rejected, the whole of Hegel's idealist philosophy while retaining his dialectic method. He had many faults to find with Hegel's system, but his fundamental criticism of it is contained in a famous passage in the Introduction to the first volume of *Capital:*

> My own dialectic method is not only different from the Hegelian, but is its direct opposite. For Hegel . . . the thinking process is the demiurge (creator) of the real world, and the real world is only the outward manifestation of "the Idea." With me, on the other hand, the ideal is nothing else than the material world reflected by the human mind and translated into terms of thought.

. . . But what Marx does is to take over the essential property of that Absolute upon which, in Hegel's system, both mind and nature depend, and apply it to a material world of which he had declared mind to be simply a by-product. The Marxist version of the dialectic is indeed open to serious objection. The dialectic can properly be applied to the development of ideas through the conflict of contradictions, and Hegel provides a rational explanation of that development. Yet, although dialectical materialism can point to something analogous to contradictions in the material world, not only are these analogies altogether arbitrary, but even if they were not, it would still remain a complete mystery why the material world should exhibit them. Dialectical materialism in fact asserts that matter is

---

[1] Sidney Hook, *The "Laws" of the Dialectic* (*Polemic*, November-December, 1946), pp. 9 f.

[2] Wilhelm Röpke, *Le Crise de Nôtre Temps* (Neuchâtel, 1947), p. 68; Benda, pp. 166 f.

matter, but that it develops as ideas do. Only while we can see why ideas develop as they do, as for example in discussion, there is no conceivable reason why material things should develop in the same way. Eastman maintains, however, that Marx was by no means as successful in getting rid of Hegel as he had supposed, and that having declared the world to be made up of unconscious matter, he then found himself obliged to read into matter the very essence of Hegel's Absolute, so that his system is in fact a return to the animism of primitive man which attributes human values to trees and other material objects.[1]

This criticism is perhaps less applicable to Marx than it is to Engels, who both in his *Anti-Dühring* and in his *Dialectics of Nature* maintained that natural processes are dialectical, as modern dialectical materialists continue to do. There are indeed passages in *Capital* which suggest that Marx held the same view, and indeed if the dialectic is a universal principle, it is hard to see upon what grounds the order of nature is to be excluded from its operation. Marx's real interest, however, was in the process of social development, and this he certainly believed to be dialectical. Unfortunately, for a writer who claimed that his work was scientific, he took altogether insufficient pains to make himself understood, and was often obscure and careless in expression. Thus it is not always clear whether his dialectic is one of material economic forces or of the class struggle to which their development gives rise; and his anxiety to stress the importance of the former led him frequently to use language which suggests that they somehow possess the property of developing dialectically, so that by throwing the emphasis upon them rather than upon the human framework within which they can alone operate, he exposed himself to the charge of endowing his material universe with qualities which transcend its physical nature and belong to the order of metaphysics. . . .

Historical Materialism

Historical materialism, or the materialist interpretation of history, is simply dialectical materialism applied to the particular field of human relations within society. The dialectic supplies the clue to the whole process. In the preface to his *Critique of Political Economy* Marx starts by asking what is the principle that governs all human relations, and his answer is that it is the common end which all men pursue, that is, the production of the means to support life, and next to production, the exchange of things produced. Man has to live before he can start to think. Hence the ultimate determinant of social change is not to be found in his ideas of eternal truth and social justice, but in changes in the mode of production and exchange. . . .

Marx distinguishes five economic forms, or modes, of production—primitive communal, slave, feudal, capitalist and socialist. Under the first,

---

[1] Max Eastman, *Marxism. Is it a Science?*, p. 23.

the means of production are socially owned. Under the second, the slave-owner owns them. Under the third, the feudal lord partially owns them, as his men have some property. Under the fourth, the capitalist owns the means of production, but not his men, whom he can no longer dispose of as he pleases, though they are compelled to work for him. Under the fifth, which has not yet come into existence, the workers themselves will own the means of production and, with the abolition of the contradictions inherent in Capitalism, production will reach its fullest development. Both from the point of view of production and of freedom, each of these stages represents an advance upon its predecessor, this being in accordance with the dialectic principle that every new stage takes up whatever was of value in that which it has "negated"—the principle that had led Hegel to declare in the Introduction to his *Philosophy of History* that, "The Oriental World knows only *one* that is free, the Greeks and Romans recognize that *some* are free, the German nations have attained to the knowledge that *all* are free." Thus, Marx commends the early capitalists because they had broken down the barriers imposed by Feudalism, but argues that the system has outlived its usefulness and has become an obstacle to the further development of the productive forces.

To understand social revolutions we have therefore to distinguish between changes in the productive forces and the various ideological forms in which men become conscious of the conflict and fight it out. The real cause is always the former; but men are seldom aware of this, and will believe that they are fighting for religion, political liberty or any other ideological motive. Marxists contend that it is, indeed, on the basis of this illusion that most history has been written, the true cause of revolutions having been thus concealed until Marx revealed it. They have to adopt this position because it is an article of their faith that every great movement in history—the rise of Islam, the Renaissance or any other—was ultimately due to an economic cause.

This, then, was the theory which Engels claimed, at Marx's graveside, to have made as great a contribution to the science of social relations as had Darwin's theory to natural science.

Just as Darwin discovered the law of evolution in organic nature, so Marx discovered the law of evolution in human history; he discovered the simple fact, hitherto concealed by an overgrowth of ideology, that mankind must first of all eat and drink, have shelter and clothing, before it can pursue politics, religion, science, art, etc.; and that therefore the production of the immediate material means of subsistence, and consequently the degree of economic development attained by a given people or during a given epoch, form the foundation upon which State institutions, the legal conceptions, the art and even the religious ideas of the people concerned have been evolved, and in the light of which these things must be explained, instead of vice versa as had hitherto been the case.[1]

[1] *Selected Works*, II, p. 153; see also Engels' preface to the 1885 German edition of Marx's *Eighteenth Brumaire*, in which he makes a somewhat similar claim, *ibid.*, pp. 223-224.

The Class Struggle

We have seen that the productive forces at any given period always develop appropriate forms of productive relations, and that, except among the most primitive communities, these are always relations of exploitation which divide society into classes. It is, however, characteristic of Marx that having devoted the greater part of his life to writing about the class struggle he should never have defined what he meant by a class, a question that he raised in the last chapter of the third volume of *Capital*, but without answering it. He recognizes, however, that classes are not homogeneous, and that there will be as many of them as there are well-marked degrees of social status. But he is not much concerned with their functional differences, because, for the purpose of the class struggle, he holds that all classes are ultimately divisible into two, one of which controls the means of production, while the other does not, and that the antagonism to which this gives rise creates a profound contradiction. Yet it is through this very contradiction that progress is effected, since, as we have seen, it is through the conflict of thesis and antithesis that we reach the synthesis which brings us one step nearer to our goal.[1]

The force which lies behind the dialectic of history and moves the world is not therefore the clash of nations, as Hegel and the majority of historians had supposed, but the clash of classes or the class struggle. Class interest thus takes the place of national interest, which is always found upon examination to be no more than the interest of the ruling class. Marx did not pretend to have discovered the class struggle; but he claimed to have proved that the existence of classes is bound up with a "particular historic phase in the history of production," that it must inevitably lead to the dictatorship of the proletariat, and that the dictatorship will be a transitional stage which will end with the abolition of all classes and the establishment of a classless society.[2]

The class struggle is thus held to offer an explanation of phenomena for which traditional history cannot account, and in particular of the trend towards increasing productivity. Men work blindly within a social system which forces them to act in accordance with what they believe to be their class interest, and it is vain to blame them for so doing. As all are caught in the network, they can do nothing to change its nature. This is one of the reasons why Marx does not believe in social technology, and incidentally why Marxism is no guide to the practice of government, as Lenin was later to discover. Yet all the time the class struggle is inevitably leading to the transformation of society. As the productive forces change, the class which

---

[1] On the class struggle see K. R. Popper, *The Open Society and its Enemies* (1945), II, pp. 103 f.; Venable, *Human Nature*, pp. 98 f.; J. L. Gray, *Karl Marx and Social Philosophy in Social and Political Ideas of the Victorian Age* (ed. F. J. C. Hearnshaw, 1933), pp. 141 f.

[2] Letter to Weydemeyer of March 5th, 1852, *Correspondence*, p. 57.

has hitherto controlled them is confronted by a new class, which claims to be able to administer them more efficiently; and just as the merchants and craftsmen were able to challenge the feudal lord of the later Middle Ages, so will the wage-earner challenge the capitalist and wrest economic power from him. Thus there will be brought about the final emancipation of mankind, seeing that there is no class below the proletariat, which is at the bottom of the social scale. But to accelerate this process, the class-consciousness of the worker must first be developed, that is, he must be made to realize his class interest and become conscious of that same power with which Hegel had endowed the nation. The class-conscious proletarian is thus the worker who is not only aware of his class situation, but is also proud of his class and assured of its historic mission.

Yet Marx nowhere seeks to prove that the worker *is*, in fact, fitted for the role assigned to him; nor does it occur to him that the negation of Capitalism may lead to the emergence of a wholly new class which is strictly speaking neither capitalist nor proletarian. The belief in human perfectibility that he had inherited from the eighteenth century led him to believe that a classless society, inherently desirable on ethical grounds, must be the next stage in social evolution; while as a revolutionary and agitator he saw in the working-class movement the only available instrument for the achievement of this aim in the immediate future, and was thus induced to regard it as the final "negation of the negation."

The belief in the class struggle as the "inner essence" of history vitiates the thinking of Marxists by leading them to attribute to the proletariat attitudes and judgments which are, in fact, confined to little groups of revolutionaries.[1] The classical economists were in the habit of generalizing widely about a class of factors of production which they called "labour," and to which they opposed an equally chimerical general monopoly of employers. But this classification breaks down upon analysis. So also does the Marxist version of the class struggle. It is, in fact, a myth, and the very exhortation of the workers to unite is an admission that there is no natural proletarian solidarity, as is attested by the relations in any particular country between male and female labour, skilled and unskilled, white and coloured. Still less is there an identity of interests between workers in different countries. Measures which perpetuate the poverty of the workers in one country are beneficial to those in another; while in no advanced country will the workers accept cheap foreign labour. And, again, all experience has hitherto proved that whenever the existence of any country appears to be threatened from without, its preservation is regarded as the dominant interest by all classes.[2]

---

[1] Max Eastman, *Stalin's Russia and the Crisis of Socialism* (1940), p. 217.

[2] L. H. Robbins, *The Economic Basis of the Class Struggle* (1939), pp. 17 f.; Franz Borkenau, *Socialism, National or International* (1942), pp. 14 f.

Finally, Marx's thesis that all conflict among men arises from the class struggle, albeit of undoubted tactical value as calculated to convince the masses that their misfortunes are attributable to the capitalist system and will disappear with the victory of the proletariat, is none the less fallacious. For the supreme source of conflict in life is the inevitable opposition between the claims of the individual and those of society—a conflict which is not reducible to the class struggle and cannot be dialectically resolved (even were it desirable that it should be) because it is a part of the unchanging human situation.

Criticism of Historical Materialism

Marx's philosophy of history is regarded, even by his critics, with a greater respect than any other part of his doctrine, though it did not exert much influence until after his death. It rests on two theses. The first is that economic causes are fundamental, and the second that they operate in accordance with the dialectic principle. The latter is nowadays accepted only by Marxists, but the former commands a much wider allegiance.

The claim that the dialectic furnishes the clue to history cannot, indeed, be seriously defended, even if we are prepared to accept it as an explanation of the processes of thought. Any proposition, such as that "All property is theft," can be developed dialectically because it supplies a starting point. But as Karl Federn points out in his most valuable study, history proceeds as an unending stream of which no one knows the beginning or the end. It provides no *terminus a quo,* and thus makes it impossible to determine which of its stages are thesis, antithesis or synthesis.[1] Any historical event can be shown with equal plausibility to be a synthesis of two contradictory elements in the past, or as a thesis for which some other event will then be chosen to provide the antithesis. Thus, the Norman Conquest can be represented as a synthesis of Roman and Anglo-Saxon cultures, or as a thesis of which the age of the Plantagenets and that of the Tudors are respectively the antithesis and the synthesis. Such irresponsible treatment simply reduces history to a game for which the only qualifications are a lively imagination and much ignorance.

Further, we have seen that the dialectic, as used by Hegel, is essentially an optimistic doctrine, since every synthesis is an advance towards the Absolute; while Marx similarly contends that every successive stage of society which arises on account of the internal contradictions of the preceding stage constitutes a "higher" form. If history were a continuous record

---

[1] Karl Federn, *The Materialistic Conception of History* (1939), pp. 209 f.; for a recent statement of the Marxist thesis see Jean Bruhat, *Destin de l'Histoire* (Paris, 1948); see also M. M. Bober, *Karl Marx's Interpretation of History* (Harvard University Press, 1927), pp. 297-315; for a well-reasoned statement of the Marxist case see R. Mondolfo, *Il materialismo storico in Federico Engels* (1912, ed. Florence, 1952); H. B. Acton, *The Illusion of the Epoch* (1955), pp. 107 f.

of progress, this would be well enough. But it is as much a tale of dissolution and decay; and to this part of it the dialectic cannot be applied.[1]

Again, the dialectical approach to history becomes extremely dangerous when it is accepted *de fide,* as it offers no objective standard as to the sense and rationality of action; and the fanatical devotion to it of the Russian leaders is certainly a hindrance to them rather than a help. The inter-war years abound in examples of policies, allegedly based on dialectical analyses, which served neither Russian nor communist interests. A notable instance was the discovery that the pre-condition of a communist victory in Germany was that Hitler should enjoy what it was assumed would be only a brief spell of authority. The Communists were therefore instructed to attack the Social Democrats instead of combining with them against the common enemy, with the result that he came into power and crushed them both.[2] Similarly, the line which Stalin imposed upon the Chinese Communists, in support of which a whole literature of theoretical justification was forthcoming, proved singularly unfortunate. They were ordered to adopt a policy which lay beyond their power to carry out, or at least to do so as Stalin desired, and thus played into the hands of the Kuomintang which wellnigh exterminated them. The party was driven into the remoter districts, to emerge many years later under conditions which had never been foreseen, and are unlikely to have been viewed by Moscow with entire satisfaction.[3]

But Marx's first thesis, that the economic factor is fundamental for all social institutions and particularly for their historical development, is of much greater importance. It has exercised a profound influence, and all modern writers are indebted to him even if they do not know it. Any return to pre-Marxist social theory is inconceivable. Indeed, as K. R. Popper points out, his thesis is sound enough so long as we use the term "fundamental" loosely and do not lay too much stress upon it; and practically all social studies will profit if they are conducted against the background of the "economic conditions" of society. In this qualified sense his "economism" represents a valuable advance in the methods of social science, and has suggested many lines of enquiry that have greatly extended our knowledge.[4]

None the less, it is open to serious criticism in the extreme form in which Marx presented it. He asserts in the *Critique of Political Economy* that there are two factors in production, the productive forces and the pro-

---

[1] John Plamenatz, *What is Communism?* (1946), pp. 39-40.
[2] A. L. Rowse, *The Use of History* (1946), pp. 136-137.
[3] Stalin defended his policy in his speech to the Central Committee of August 1st, 1927, printed in *Marxism and the National and Colonial Question,* pp. 232 f. For a criticism of it see Harold R. Isaacs, *The Tragedy of the Chinese Revolution* (1938, revised edition, Stanford, 1951) and Robert C. North, *Moscow and the Chinese Communists* (Stanford, 1953), pp. 66-121.
[4] Popper, II, p. 99.

ductive relations which derive from them. Conceived in purely economic terms, they constitute the substructure, which is primary; while all the manifestations of the mind of Man as reflected in his religion, laws, institutions and the like, constitute the superstructure, which is secondary. In other words, the mind and all that it creates is a part of the superstructure which is determined by the economic substructure. We are therefore left to suppose, as was pointed out above, that the productive forces somehow develop automatically, though in fact they *are developed, e.g.,* by new discoveries, the responsible agency being the intelligence of Man and the use which he makes of it.[1] As Koestler put it, "Marxist society has a basement-production and an attic-intellectual-production; only the stairs and lifts are missing." [2]

That Marx was aware of this difficulty is shown by the many passages in which he treats the political and social institutions of the superstructure as a part of the substructure, as indeed he is obliged to do if he is to make sense of his theory, since it is obvious that it is only in proportion as men reach a certain level of political and social development that they are likely to make discoveries or possess the resources to exploit them. His disciples do likewise, and, as John Plamenatz says, no good Marxist will ever hesitate to include elements of the superstructure in the substructure whenever he finds it convenient to do so.[3] The truth is that while Marx was ultimately led to admit an interconnection between the two, he never clearly worked out what it was, and that if he had attempted to do so he would have had to abandon his theory.

Now it is quite certain that the forms of production have far-reaching consequences and are of the greatest importance in history. But, as Federn observes, the question is whether it is true that the intellectual, cultural and political forms of any community not only depend for their existence upon economic production, but are in all their modifications also determined by it. When Marx said that "men must be able to live in order to be able to make history," he did not simply mean that society depends on production for its existence, as this would have been a view that no one would have contested. Air is an essential condition of life. But if a scientist should succeed in proving that institutions and opinions depend upon the particular composition of the atmosphere, he would have made a very important discovery indeed. What Marx meant was that the way in which men produce determines the entire complex of ideas and institutions which make up the social order.[4]

The proofs which Marxists adduce to substantiate this are taken either from pre-history or from history; the method is to show that an economic

[1] Federn, pp. 15 f.; but cp. Bober, pp. 11-27.
[2] *The Yogi and the Commissar* (1945), p. 70.
[3] Plamenatz, p. 35.
[4] Federn, pp. 30 f.

change occurred at a certain time, that some decades or centuries later a change took place in the ideas or institutions of the same people, and then to attribute the second change to the first. Thus, Karl Kautsky accounts for Puritanism in England by saying that "the transition from a natural to a monetary system of economy caused the lower classes to fall a prey to a sombre Puritanism." Why this should be so is not explained; in fact, the transition to a monetary economy had been completed by the fourteenth century, whereas Puritanism did not appear until towards the end of the sixteenth century. Again, Antonio Labriola explains why the aborigines of North America did not attain a high degree of civilization on the ground that it was the Europeans who introduced wheat and domestic animals which had previously been lacking. But not only were there other forms of food, but vast herds of bison roamed the North American plains which the Red Indians might have tamed, just as did the Negroes the buffalo and the Mongols the yak. That they did not do so was simply because it was not among their gifts.[1]

Marxist writers thus forever repeat the truism that men must eat and clothe themselves before they can undertake political activity and the like. But this is to confuse the condition of such activity with its cause. It is significant that it is to primitive society that they turn whenever possible for their illustrations, since the more primitive a community, the greater will be the part which physical necessity plays in its life—as is equally true of the individual. As civilization advances, men become possessed of more complex desires which cannot be so easily related to elemental needs, such as the love of power which has led to so many conflicts. But having decided that every movement must have an economic cause, Marxists do not study the movement in order to find out what really lies behind it, but look round for any economic cause that may possibly explain it.[2]

In finding such a cause they are assisted by the equivocal use that they make of the concept of "historical necessity" which Marx and Engels borrowed from Hegel. "Necessity" means something—whether good or bad is immaterial—which is bound to occur because it is the inevitable result of a cause. Yet Marxists commonly apply it in the quite different sense of "desirable." Thus, we are told that England had a liberal constitution because she needed strong personalities to develop her commercial empire; whereas it would be far nearer the truth to say that because she had a free constitution, and other countries had not, the strong personalities had full scope and were in a position to found it. Again, the emergence of a great man at a critical period in a nation's history is attributed to "necessity," so that Engels points out that Napoleon "did not come by chance, and that if he had not come another man would have taken his place." Yet

[1] *Ibid.*, pp. 36-38, 40-41.
[2] Federn, p. 73.

no great man emerged to save the civilization of Greece and Rome.[1] But then Marxists invariably belittle the role of "so-called great men," arguing that they do no more than identify themselves with conditions which are independent of them. As Croce puts it, "Homer had sung, Plato had philosophized, Jesus and Paul had transformed moral consciousness quite unaware that they were simply the instruments of an economic process to which all their work was ultimately reducible."[2] For to concede that such men shape history would be inconsistent with the principle that it is determined by economic forces, and these last have, therefore, to be made responsible for their emergence. Thus, Hessen maintains that Newton was not inspired to discover the law of gravitation by being hit on the head by an apple as the discovery was demanded by the economic needs of his time.[3]

Nor do Marxists make any allowance for the contingent element that enters into history. Bertrand Russell gives some brilliant examples of seemingly fortuitous events which have had a decisive influence. It was, as he points out, touch and go whether the German Government would allow Lenin to return to Russia in 1917, and if the particular minister had said "No" when in fact he said "Yes," it is difficult to believe that the Russian revolution would have taken the course it did. Again, if Genoa had not ceded Corsica to France in 1768, Napoleon, born there in the year following, would have been an Italian and would have had no career in France. Yet it can scarcely be seriously maintained that without him the history of France would have been the same.[4]

The social relations which form the subject-matter of history are, in fact, far too complex to be determined by any single cause. Historical materialism does not explain why peoples living under similar conditions of production have developed widely divergent civilizations.[5] It does not explain why the Christian religion was independently accepted by races as different as the civilized Romans and the semi-barbarous Slavs and Irish. Nor, incidentally, does it explain why totally different ideologies should be held by men who share the same cultural background, so that the founders of Socialism, including Marx and Engels themselves and most of the leaders of the nineteenth-century labour movement, should have belonged to the bourgeoisie. As Federn puts it, the relation between the economic substructure and the superstructure resembles that between the soil of a field

[1] *Op. cit.*, pp. 220-222.

[2] *Sul Problema Morale dei nostri Tempi* in *Pensiero Politico e Politica Attuale* (Bari, 1946, pp. 7-8).

[3] B. Hessen, *The Economic Roots of Newton's Principia* (1931). On the general Marxist thesis all manifestations of intellectual and artistic activity are determined by the state of the productive forces in any given age; see Plekhanov, *In Defence of Materialism* (ed. 1947), pp. 200 f.

[4] *Freedom and Organization* (1935), pp. 228-229.

[5] Bober, pp. 278 f.

and the plants growing in it. We know that the plants sprang from the soil, and that if there were no soil there would be no plants; but we do not know who sowed the seeds, or where they come from, or why those plants grow there and not others.[1]

Finally, Marx had no right to appeal to economics in support of his theory. As L. H. Robbins points out, economics is not, as was once held, the study of the causes of material welfare, but of those aspects of behaviour which arise from the scarcity of means to achieve given ends. As to whether the ends in themselves are good or bad, it is strictly neutral; but if the attainment of one set of ends involves the sacrifice of others, it has an economic aspect.[2] The notion, entertained by men like Carlyle and Ruskin, that economics is concerned with purely material ends is false, though they may perhaps be excused for having held it, as it was generally accepted by the economists of their day. Nor can it be argued, save on the basis of the crudest Benthamite psychology, that the economic motive always prevails.

Again, economics is not to be confused with technology. It is not interested in technique as such, but only in so far as it is one of the influences that determine scarcity. The manner in which men will apply the various skills of which they become masters will largely depend upon considerations which are psychological and have nothing to do with economics. But Marx's economic interpretation of history explains all major events by changes in the *technique of production,* thus implying that ultimate valuations are merely its by-products, and without taking into account the very different ways in which men may use it. His doctrine, as Robbins puts it, "is a general statement about the causation of human motive which, from the point of view of economic science, is sheer metaphysics. The label 'materialist' fits the doctrine. The label 'economic' is misplaced. Economics may well provide an important instrument for the elucidation of history. But there is nothing in economic analysis which entitles us to assert that all history is to be explained in 'economic' terms, if 'economic' is to be used as equivalent to the technically material. The materialist interpretation of history came to be called the economic interpretation of history, because it was thought that the subject-matter of economics was the cause of material welfare. Once it is realized that this is not the case, the materialist conception must stand or fall on its own merits. Economic science lends no support to its doctrines." [3]

·   ·   ·   ·   ·

The claim that historical materialism rests upon scientific laws contained the implication that history was an exact science, and that it was thus possible to foretell its future development. Yet neither Marx nor

[1] Federn, p. 100.
[2] *The Nature and Significance of Economic Science* (1932), pp. 7 f., 24-25.
[3] *Ibid.,* pp. 43-44.

Engels was a historian, and the value of their work lies solely in their penetrating observation of a certain number of contemporary facts. In his
Capital Marx does indeed make considerable use of history to support conclusions at which he had arrived independently, but the book in no way
proves historical materialism to be true, and in fact, assumes that as it is
self-evident no proof is required. His anxiety to represent history as an
exact science, and his "historicism" which made him believe that the main
function of science was to predict the future, led him, however, constantly
to maintain that society was governed by "inexorable laws" operating independently of the will of man, and thus beyond his power to change. "When
a society," he says in the Introduction to *Capital*, "has discovered the natural law that determines its own movement . . . it can neither overleap the
natural phases of its evolution nor shuffle out of them by a stroke of the
pen." All it can do "is to shorten and lessen the birth pangs." But this committed him to a view of history not altogether consistent with that implied
by his theory of knowledge as *Praxis,* of which the function is to "change
the world," so that, as he and Engels both declare, "History does nothing"
seeing that "man makes his own history, even though he does not do so on
conditions chosen by himself." [1] Doubtless what they both wished to convey
was that man was able to become the master of his destiny; but in their
desire to stress the scientific character of their doctrine they succeeded in
making a great many people think that they meant the exact opposite, and
that the course of history was wholly predetermined.[2]

By the nineties Engels had become aware of this, and in a letter to
Joseph Bloch he admits that many contemporary Marxists were turning out
"a rare kind of balderdash":

> According to the materialist conception of history, [he says], the determining
> element . . . is *ultimately* the production and reproduction in real life. More than
> this neither Marx nor I have ever asserted. If, therefore, somebody twists this into
> the statement that the economic element is the *only* determining one, he transforms
> it into a meaningless, abstract and absurd phrase. The economic situation is the
> basis, but the various elements of the superstructure . . . also exercise their in-
> fluence upon the historical struggle, and in many cases preponderate in determin-
> ing their form. There is an interaction of all those elements in which, amid all the
> endless *hosts* of accidents . . . the economic movement finally asserts itself as
> necessary . . . Marx and I are ourselves partly to blame for the fact that younger
> writers sometimes lay more stress on the economic factor than is due to it. We had
> to emphasize this main principle in opposition to our adversaries, who denied it,
> and we had not always the time, the place or the opportunity to allow the other
> elements involved in the interaction to come into their rights.[3]

Marxist writers hold that the above puts the whole matter in a just
perspective. Yet, in fact, Engels has to admit an interaction between the
superstructure and the substructure, which is, indeed, assumed by the ap-

[1] Hook, *From Hegel to Marx*, pp. 38 f.
[2] Edmund Wilson, *To the Finland Nation* (1940), pp. 180 f.
[3] September 21st, 1890, *Correspondence*, pp. 475-476.

peal, "Workers of the World Unite!"; for if there were none, it was useless
to preach revolution, and there would be nothing for the proletariat to do
save passively to await the working out of the dialectical process, of which
it was the ultimate beneficiary. But he does not seek to explain its nature,
and repeats that the "economic situation" is the basis which always "ultimately" asserts itself. His concession, as T. D. Weldon puts it, is "an elaborate attempt to have it both ways, to accept the incompleteness of the Marxist hypothesis and to pass this off as a matter of no great moment." [1] In
practice, Marxists habitually write as if economic factors were the sole determinants, and rarely if ever make allowances for any others.

As, however, Marx and Engels are concerned with the origin of the
superstructure rather than with its influence upon the development of
society, they tend to assign to it a purely passive role. In his *Dialectical and
Historical Materialism* (1938) Stalin goes further, and insists that once a
superstructure has arisen, it becomes "a most potent force which facilitates
. . . the progress of society." Indeed "new social ideas and theories arise
precisely because they are necessary to society, because it is impossible to
carry out the urgent tasks of the development of the material life of society
without their organizing, mobilizing and transforming action." [2] He returned to this theme in his *Concerning Marxism in Linguistics* (1950):
"The superstructure is a product of the basis, but this does not mean that
it merely reflects it, that it is passive, neutral, indifferent to the fate of its
basis, to the fate of classes, to the character of the system. On the contrary,
having come into being, it becomes an exceedingly active force, actively
assisting its basis to take shape and consolidate itself, and doing everything
it can to help the new system finish off and eliminate the old basis and the
old classes." [3]

This would seem to be a more positive view than that of Marx and
Engels. Yet two points should be noted. First, Stalin is only able to represent the superstructure as a "potent force" because, as all Marxists do, he
attributes to the substructure or base the property of being able to produce
"new ideas and theories" whenever the material needs of society require
them, though no explanation is given as to why this should be so. Secondly,
as he was himself largely responsible for the form the superstructure had
assumed in Russia, he could very well represent it as playing an "active"
role, and indeed could scarcely do otherwise. [4]

While therefore Marx and Engels have much to say about the power
of men to transform nature and, in so doing, to transform themselves and
the society in which they live, and while both maintain that it is in the
knowledge of external reality and the power to use that knowledge for

[1] *States and Morals* (1946), p. 158.
[2] *History of the Communist Party of the Soviet Union* (Moscow, 1943), pp. 116-117.
[3] P. 4.
[4] For a full discussion of Stalin's views see Henri Chambre, *Marxism en Union
Soviétique* (Paris, 1955), pp. 457-483.

definite ends that human freedom consists, they never resolve the central problem. If man is to be in any real sense the master of his destiny, it can be only through his ideas and opinions. But these belong to the super-structure, and the form they take is determined by the substructure. All they will admit is that an interaction takes place between the two, though upon what principle they do not tell us. But once an interaction has been conceded, the whole thesis is undermined, since we are no longer dealing with a purely economic factor, but with one which has been itself in part determined by non-economic factors. To say after this that the economic factor must always be decisive is meaningless.

The common-sense view is surely this. Man is a being endowed with intelligence, and this develops as he rises in the scale of civilization. Through it he provides himself with the means of subsistence, and at the same time with the laws, art forms and the like that he regards as necessary for his security and well-being. The two are part of the same process, and there is no occasion to bring them into opposition and to make the one dependent upon the other. If it be true that the way in which men think and the various institutional and other forms to which their ideas give rise are influenced by the manner in which they make their living, the converse is equally true. Marx is a good servant but a bad master. He was quite right in drawing attention to the importance of the economic factor, which had been seriously neglected, but he gave it an undue prominence and thus over-simplified the complexity of the social situation, as his followers have continued to do to this day. . . .

II. MARXIST ECONOMICS

. . . We have already seen that it is the Marxist contention that at some remote and unspecified period of history society became divided into two classes, one of which obtained control over the means of production, while the other possessed nothing but its labour power. This labour power, which Marx calls "variable capital," the capitalist (the contemporary rep-resentative of the possessing class) buys and sets to work on the various means of production—raw materials, machinery and the like—that consti-tute what he calls "constant capital." Now, labour possesses the unique property of being able to produce more than is required for its subsistence and replacement. The worker receives as wages only what is sufficient to maintain him; and if it took a whole day's work to produce this, the ques-tion of surplus value would not arise, nor incidentally would it be to any-one's advantage to employ him. What, in fact, happens is that a man works for ten hours, and in the first, say, five of these (which constitute what Marx calls "socially necessary labour") he produces all the value he is to receive as wages. Of the value produced during the second five hours he gets nothing, and it is stolen from him by his employer. The difference between the value created during the period of socially necessary labour and that created during the period in excess of it is what Marx calls "surplus value," and is the measure of the worker's "exploitation." Thus the value produced by the worker far exceeds the value of his means of subsistence, that is, the value of his labour power which he receives from the capitalist as wages. But by remunerating labour in the form of wages, the division between paid and unpaid labour time is concealed.

Variable capital, *i.e.*, labour, alone produces value, and constant capital produces none. Machinery is simply "stored up labour," that is, something upon which labour has already been expended. Sources of wealth, such as unworked mineral deposits, have, indeed, an exchange value, because people are prepared to give money for them, but this is only on account of their potential value, that is, the value they will have when labour is applied to them. Orthodox economic theory teaches that the production of anything that has value calls for the cooperation of four agents—land (raw materials), labour, capital and organization (management)—and that each agent receives its share of the product: land as rent, labour as wages, capital as interest and management (or more strictly the element of uncertainty which enters into production) as profits. Marx rejects this view and isolates labour from the other agents of production. It alone is the source of value, and is alone entitled to the value it is alleged to create.

In the first volume of *Capital* Marx argues that as profit is created solely by surplus value, and as labour is the sole value-producing agency, the rate of profit will depend upon what he calls the "organic composition of capitals," that is, the proportion of labour (variable capital) to machinery (constant capital) employed in a given undertaking; and that it will thus tend to fall in proportion as technological improvements lead to the employment of less labour. Yet although this conclusion logically followed from his premises, it was demonstrably false in practice. Marx was aware of the difficulty, to which he refers in a letter to Engels of August 1862.[1] But he did not face it at the time, and set it aside for further treatment. There the matter rested until 1883, when he died.

Engels had seriously miscalculated the time that would be needed to put in order the unpublished portion of *Capital,* and the second and third volumes did not appear until 1885 and 1894 respectively. Meanwhile, as E. H. Carr has pointed out, certain followers of the German economist Rodbertus had accused Marx of plagiarizing from the works of their master, and Engels had retorted by challenging them to produce the solution to the above problem, thus drawing increased attention to it.[2] It was, indeed, eagerly awaited, but when it appeared in the third volume it caused widespread disillusionment. For it was now contended that although the rate of profit did depend on the relation of variable to constant capital if the

[1] *Briefwechsel,* III, p. 77.
[2] Carr, *Karl Marx,* pp. 270-271.

whole capital of the world was taken into account (and of this no proof was given), this did not apply to the profits of particular businesses, which tended to equalize themselves according to the state of trade. As Joan Robinson points out, Marx's demonstration simply amounts to the tautology that if wages are constant (and elsewhere he denies that they are) the rate of profit will fall as capital per man increases.[1]

What, after all this, is left of the labour theory of value? We are asked to believe that there is an abstract property called "value" which belongs to any labour-produced commodity, and which, while purporting to be its exchange value, does not, in fact, correspond to its price or even to its average price. And we are further asked to believe that there is a second abstraction, called "surplus value," which determines profits in general but not profits in particular, and bears no relation to the standard of wages of the workers whose exploitation it is supposed to measure. Marx first says that the value of a commodity corresponds to the amount of labour put into it, and if he had stuck to this, he would, as Plamenatz points out, at least have made clear in what sense he was using the term. But he then goes on to call this value "exchange value," and to spend many pages describing just how the value of one commodity is expressed in terms of another, thus inevitably suggesting that they do actually tend to exchange in accordance with the relative amounts of labour required to produce them. He then has to confess that they do not, in fact, exchange in this manner, and would only do so if the same proportions of capital and labour were employed in their production; and thus, he ends by confusing both himself and his readers.[2] Actually, he is ultimately driven to admit that exchange value is governed by the market, that is, by the law of supply and demand, which makes nonsense of his theory that it is derived from labour only. . . .

Marx's economic doctrine may be summarized as follows. Labour alone creates value. All profits are derived from unpaid labour time. Capitalists are driven by competition to accumulate capital, which becomes concentrated in fewer and fewer hands, with the result that the smaller businesses disappear and their owners are driven back into the working-class. The accumulation of capital in the form of labour-saving devices reduces the use of human labour and at the same time the profits of the capitalists, who are therefore compelled to offset their losses by intensifying the exploitation of their workers, over whom the increase of unemployment has given them an even stronger hold and who are now prepared to work on any terms. Hence the misery of the workers, eventually almost the entire population, will progressively become more and more unendurable. This will lead them to combine for their own protection, and so create a force which will eventually destroy the whole system.

It has been necessary to dwell upon Marx's theory of value at some

---

[1] *An Essay on Marxian Economics* (1949), p. 36.
[2] Plamenatz, pp. 33-34.

length because he regarded it, as do all Marxists, as the cornerstone of his system, though it only introduces an element of confusion, and he has nothing of importance to say which could not have been expressed equally well without it. We have seen that it is not a theory of value at all, and that his value and surplus value are pure abstractions. It is in fact a theory of exploitation, designed to show that the propertied class has always lived on the labour of the non-propertied class. It is therefore on the assumption that labour—by which is meant wage-labour—is the only value-producing agency, that the theory stands or falls. But it is a false assumption because, as is characteristic of Marxist dogmas, it concentrates upon one single factor in a highly complex situation to the exclusion of all others. Thus capital is itself a product of labour. Someone has laboured to produce it, and has then decided to forego the immediate consumption of the value created in order to create further value, as it is clearly in the interests of society that he should do. As, however, not everyone is willing to do this, the owner of capital finds himself in possession of something that has a scarcity value and thus commands its market price. The Marxist argument that capital produces value only when labour is applied to it is simply that of the medieval Schoolmen. Labour without capital is equally unproductive. The capitalist system is open to abuses like any other. Yet those who desire to abolish it would do well to reflect that the only alternative to the profit-and-loss motive that has so far shown any indication of being equally effective is the fear of punishment imposed by a totalitarian State.

Moreover, as Popper points out, the whole of Marx's theory of value is redundant. For if we assume, as is fundamental to his case, a free market in which there is always a greater supply of labour than there is a demand for it, the law of supply and demand becomes sufficient to explain all the phenomena of "increasing misery" without bringing value into it.[1] Marx was on strong grounds so long as he restricted himself to the conditions prevailing under *laissez-faire* Capitalism at the time when he was writing, and his analysis of these conditions was an important contribution to the study of social relations. He was quite right in pointing out that labour was not receiving its fair share; but he failed to see that there might be other ways of dealing with the problem than by revolution, and that he himself had provided one of the most effective of these by calling upon the workers to unite. The organization of labour, collective bargaining and State intervention in its various forms were to revolutionize the situation and to make nonsense of the law of increasing misery, save in so far as it applies to Russia, where the promise of the millennium remains unfulfilled and all verbs, it has been said, are conjugated in the future tense.

Nor did Marx discern that the middle-class, so far from being crushed out of existence, would greatly increase in strength. The capitalist to whom

[1] *Op. cit.*, II, pp. 165.

Engels had first called his attention was commonly the owner of his business. But the great extension of jointstock companies in the second half of the century—following in this country upon the Companies Act of 1862, which extended the principle of limited liability—had the effect of creating a new type of capitalist in the person of the shareholder, who had no part in the management of the concern, which he delegated to paid officials. The result was at least temporarily to broaden the basis of the capitalist system by creating a new middle-class which had an interest in retaining it either as investors concerned with their dividends, or as members of the managerial salariat, whose lower ranks felt themselves superior to the proletariat from which they had been largely recruited.

Keynes has described *Capital* as "an obsolete economic text book . . . not only scientifically erroneous, but without interest or application for the modern world." [1] Yet the modern world continues to take an interest in it, for, like every great revolutionary treatise, its power lies rather in its central idea than in the arguments used to support it, which may often enough be found untenable. To the Victorians the capitalist system appeared the embodiment of permanence and stability, and, in general, this belief persisted up to 1914. From that conflict many held that it had emerged even stronger than ever. Yet, as Carr has shown, its character had changed. The old-fashioned Capitalism—what Marx called "bourgeois Capitalism"—had broken down, partly because it had evolved away from a free competitive system of individuals and small units into a highly organized system of large-scale enterprises; and partly because of the increasing strength and organization of the workers, who were bound to resent the old privileged order, and to insist that the new order should contain increasing elements of Socialist-planned economy which made for a more equal distribution of goods. This transformation had taken place over most of Western Europe by the First World War; after that war Capitalism in the older sense never came back, and there was an uneasy interregnum during which the two rival systems jostled one another without finding any working compromise.[2] These years were marked by violent economic crises, accompanied by greater mass unemployment than had been known since the Industrial Revolution started. The concentration of capital proceeded; while labour continued to organize itself, though it is claimed that the workers did not thereby become revolutionary-minded. Then came the Second World War, and few will contend that the capitalist system is the stronger for it. Many of Marx's prophecies have, indeed, been falsified. Yet, looked at objectively, it is too early to say that his central thesis has been disproved; and we should do well to recall Jung's observation upon Columbus, who "by using

---

[1] *Essays in Persuasion* (New York, 1932), p. 300.
[2] *Problems of Writing Modern Russian History* (*The Listener,* October 7th, 1948, pp. 548 f.).

subjective assumptions, a false hypothesis, and a route abandoned by modern navigation, nevertheless discovered America."

For, when every criticism has been made, *Capital* remains a very great book, and if the greatness of a book is to be measured by its influence, one of the most important ever written. Marx presents a view of the world which cannot be disregarded—a world in which, as Edmund Wilson puts it, "commodities bear rule and make men their playthings." His highly abstract reasoning provides the clue to this economic labyrinth. "It is," Wilson says, "his great trick to hypnotize us by the shuttling of the syllogisms which he produces with so scientific an air, and then suddenly to remind us that these principles derive solely from the laws of human selfishness which are as unfailing as the force of gravitation." The exposition of his theory is always followed by a documented picture of the capitalist laws at work, until "we feel that we have been taken for the first time through the real structure of our civilization, and that it is the ugliest that ever existed—a state of things where there is very little to choose between the physical degradation of the workers and the moral degradation of the masters." [1]

But this account of the matter is not altogether satisfactory. Marx does indeed hold that the capitalist system is morally objectionable, though he fails to show how its evils will be removed by getting rid of the capitalists, as they certainly have not been in the Soviet Union. Yet he is careful not to ascribe these evils to the capitalists themselves, nor to impute to such persons a larger share of original sin than other members of the community possess. For they are, like the workers they exploit, the prisoners of a system. They have to operate in accordance with its laws, and these are not "laws of human selfishness," but the laws which govern the development of the productive forces, and which demand that it must inevitably take the particular historical form it has done, though they will equally inevitably end by destroying it. It is true that Communist propaganda is designed to convince the workers that capitalism is simply the expression of the selfish interests of a minority which deliberately exploits the majority for its own advantage. But this was not Marx's teaching—at least when he was writing seriously.

[1] *Op. cit.,* pp. 271-272.

A BRIEF PSYCHOLOGICAL CRITIQUE

SIGMUND FREUD*

The strength of Marxism obviously does not lie in its view of history or in the prophecies about the future which it bases upon that view, but in its clear insight into the determining influence which is exerted by the economic conditions of man upon his intellectual, ethical and artistic reactions. A whole collection of correlations and causal sequences were thus discovered, which had hitherto been almost completely disregarded. But it cannot be assumed that economic motives are the only ones which determine the behaviour of men in society. The unquestionable fact that different individuals, races and nations behave differently under the same economic conditions, in itself proves that the economic factor cannot be the sole determinant. It is quite impossible to understand how psychological factors can be overlooked where the reactions of living human beings are involved; for not only were such factors already concerned in the establishment of these economic conditions, but, even in obeying these conditions, men can do no more than set their original instinctual impulses in motion —their self-preservative instinct, their love of aggression, their need for love, and their impulse to attain pleasure and avoid pain. In an earlier lecture we have emphasised the importance of the part played by the super-ego, which represents tradition and ideals of the past, and which will resist for some time the pressure exerted by new economic situations. . . .

It is probable that the so-called materialistic conceptions of history err in that they underestimate this factor. They brush it aside with the remark that the "ideologies" of mankind are nothing more than resultants of their economic situation at any given moment or superstructures built upon it. That is the truth, but very probably it is not the whole truth. Mankind never lives completely in the present; the ideologies of the super-ego perpetuate the past, the traditions of the race and the people, which yield but slowly to the influence of the present and to new developments, and, so long as they work through the super-ego, play an important part in man's life, quite independently of economic conditions. . . .

And, finally, we must not forget that the mass of mankind, subjected

* Reprinted from pp. 243-244, 95-96, 244-245 of *New Introductory Lectures on Psychoanalysis* by Sigmund Freud, Copyright, 1933, by Sigmund Freud. By permission of W. W. Norton & Company, Inc.

though they are to economic necessities, are borne on by a process of cultural development—some call it civilisation—which is no doubt influenced by all the other factors, but is equally certainly independent of them in its origin; it is comparable to an organic process, and is quite capable of itself having an effect upon the other factors.

Chapter 5

Marxism into Leninism

Although Lenin did assert that "in no sense do we regard the Marxist theory as something complete and unassailable," he generally severely castigated socialists who, in his view, departed from Marx, once writing: "You cannot eliminate even one basic assumption, one substantial part of this philosophy of Marxism (it is as if it were a solid block of steel) without abandoning objective truth, without falling into the arms of the bourgeois-reactionary falsehood."

Lenin's insistence upon his own rigid orthodoxy did not, in the judgment of Professor Sabine, prevent him from being "responsible for the most considerable changes that any follower of Marx ever made in the master's teaching."

Bolshevism before 1917, and the nature and significance of Lenin's contributions to theory and to preparation for revolution—as well as his divergencies from Marx—are examined in the pages that follow.

This material has more than just an historic importance. It was Lenin, above any other single individual, whose conceptions shaped the Bolshevik Party, who "made" the Bolshevik revolution and supplied its theoretical justification; and it was his ideas and policies which often decisively shaped the Soviet system in a formative period with consequences that persist to this day. Soviet Russia is more in the image of Lenin than of Marx. The "downgrading" of Stalin has served only to enhance Lenin's importance within the U.S.S.R. and to Communist movements throughout the world. Lenin's ideas and practices merit, therefore, the most careful study.

BOLSHEVISM BEFORE 1917

MERLE FAINSOD*

An acute observer of Russian society in the late nineteenth and early twentieth centuries might have found the potential of revolution in every corner of the realm. Had he predicted that it would be the Bolsheviks who would ultimately inherit the Tsar's diadem, most of his contemporaries would probably have dismissed him as mad. Until 1917, the tiny handful of revolutionaries who followed the Bolshevik banner appeared to be swallowed in the vastness of Russia. Lenin, in a speech before a socialist youth meeting in Zurich on January 22, 1917, expressed strong doubts that he would "live to see the decisive battles of this coming revolution." The sudden rise of Bolshevism from insignificance to total power was as great a shock to the Bolshevik leaders as it was to those whom Bolshevism displaced.

Yet it would be the height of superficiality to treat the triumph of Bolshevism as a mere accident. The great crises of history are rarely accidents. They have their points of origin as well as their points of no return. The doctrine, the organizational practices, and the tactics which Bolshevism developed in its period of incubation enabled it to harness the surge of revolutionary energy released by deeper forces of social unrest and war. If in the process Bolshevism also succeeded in replacing the lumbering, inefficient police absolutism of Tsardom and the short-lived democratic experiment of the Provisional Government by the first full-scale venture in modern totalitarianism, that result too was implicit in the doctrinal, organizational, and tactical premises on which the structure of Bolshevism was built.

THE DEVELOPMENT OF DOCTRINE

Until the 1880's the Russian revolutionary movement, as was natural in a country so predominantly agricultural, revolved around the peasant and his fate. Whatever may have been the tactical divergences among Narodnik intellectuals—whether they dedicated themselves to agitation or terror—their whole orientation was toward Ilya of Murom, the peasant hero of the folk poems (byliny), who, as Masaryk puts it, "when the country is in straits

* Professor of Government at Harvard University. Author of *Smolensk Under Soviet Rule; International Socialism and the World War;* and of many articles on the U.S.S.R. Reprinted by permission of the publishers from chapter 2 of Merle Fainsod's *How Russia Is Ruled* (Cambridge, Mass.: Harvard University Press, Copyright, 1953, by The President and Fellows of Harvard College). For footnote references, see original source.

. . . awakens from his apathy, displays his super-human energy, and saves the situation." Even the industrial awakening of the seventies did little to disturb this fundamental preoccupation with the peasant and his destiny.

Narodnik philosophers from Herzen to Lavrov and Mikhailovsky were not unaware of Marx and Engels; indeed, the Narodniks were largely responsible for translating Marx and Engels into Russian and introducing them to a wide audience of the intelligentsia. For the Narodniks, however, the stages of industrialization and proletarianization which Marx and Engels described were dangers to be avoided rather than paths to be traversed. Nor were Marx and Engels themselves at first certain that the course of economic development in Russia would have to recapitulate that of the West. In a letter which Marx wrote in 1877 to a Russian publication, *Notes on the Fatherland,* he referred to his theory of capitalist development as not necessarily everywhere applicable and spoke of Russia as having "the best opportunity that history has ever offered to a people to escape all the catastrophes of capitalism." By 1882 Marx and Engels began to qualify their views on the possibility of Russian exceptionalism. In an introduction to a new Russian translation of the *Communist Manifesto,* they saw the capitalist system in Russia "growing up with feverish speed." They still thought, however, that the mir might "serve as a starting-point for a communist course of development" but only "if the Russian revolution sounds the signal for a workers' revolution in the West, so that each becomes the complement of the other."

By 1892 Engels had in effect written off the mir as a Narodnik illusion. In a letter to Danielson, the Narodnik translator of *Capital,* Engels commented, "I am afraid that we shall soon have to look upon your mir as no more than a memory of the irrecoverable past, and that in the future we shall have to do with a capitalistic Russia." In a brief reference to earlier hopes, he continued, "If this be so, a splendid chance will unquestionably have been lost." To the end of their lives, Marx and Engels remained warm admirers of the Narodnaya Volya and its courageous revolutionary Narodnik successors. Terror, for Marx and Engels, had a special justification in the struggle against Russian absolutism, and they deplored the efforts of their own Russian Marxist followers to discredit the Narodnik revolutionaries. Indeed, one of the last interventions of Engels in Russian affairs was his attempt in 1892 to arrange a merger of Narodniks and Marxists into a single party. The effort, needless to say, failed.

THE BEGINNINGS OF RUSSIAN MARXISM

Russian Marxism as an independent political movement originated in the split in 1879 of the Narodnik organization *Zemlya i Volya* (Land and Freedom). The seceders, who stood for propaganda and agitation as opposed to terrorism, established a rival organization, the *Chërnyi Peredel*

(Black Repartition), to propagate their doctrines. One of their leaders was Plekhanov, soon to be known as the father of Russian Marxism, but then still clinging to the Narodnik belief in the peasant as the driving force of revolution. The roundup of revolutionaries which followed the assassination of Alexander II in 1881 caused Plekhanov to flee abroad. His break with Zemlya i Volya on the issue of terror, the apparent bankruptcy of Narodnik policies in the reaction which followed 1881, and the manifest failure of the peasantry to respond either to agitation or terror impelled Plekhanov to reëxamine his views. The search for a new faith led him to Marxism. In 1883 Plekhanov, Paul Axelrod, Leo Deutsch, and Vera Zasulich, all of whom had been members of the Chërnyi Peredel, joined in establishing the first Russian Marxist organization, the group known as *Osvobozhdenie Truda* (Emancipation of Labor). Plekhanov from the beginning was the intellectual leader of the group. In a series of brilliantly written polemical works, he laid the doctrinal foundations for Russian Marxism.

Russian Marxism thus emerged out of disillusionment with the Narodnik infatuation with the peasantry. As a result, it quickly took on a strong anti-peasant orientation. "The main bulwark of absolutism," argued the 1887 program of the Emancipation of Labor group, "lies in the political indifference and the intellectual backwardness of the peasantry." In a later pamphlet by Plekhanov, *The Duty of the Socialists in the Famine,* the point was put even more strongly:

> The proletarian and the muzhik are political antipodes. The historic role of the proletariat is as revolutionary as the historic role of the muzhik is conservative. The muzhiks have been the support of oriental despotism for thousands of years. The proletariat in a comparatively short space of time has shaken the "foundations" of West European society.

Since peasant worship still exercised a powerful hold on the minds of the Russian revolutionary intelligentsia, the task of Plekhanov, and later of Lenin, was to undermine this faith and to turn the attention of the intellectuals from the village to the city, where capitalism was taking root and a new industrial proletariat was in process of creation. There, argued Plekhanov, was the coming revolutionary force. The challenge to the Narodniks was summed up in his famous dictum: "The revolutionary movement in Russia can triumph only as a revolutionary movement of the working class. There is not, nor can there be, any other way!"

The sharp antithesis which Plekhanov made between revolutionary worker and backward peasant had great polemical value in combating the influence of Narodnik ideology. But it also meant that the Social-Democratic movement turned its back on the countryside. Its long-term legacy was an attitude of suspicious distrust toward the peasantry which affected both the Bolshevik and Menshevik wings of Russian Social-Democracy and was never altogether extirpated. Even so perceptive and skillful a revolutionary engineer as Lenin did not really sense the revolutionary potential of the peasantry until the peasant risings of the 1905 revolution forced him to reëxamine the tenets of his faith.

The first problem of the early Russian Marxists was to win acceptance for their proposition that Russia was launched on an irreversible course of capitalist development and that the Narodnik dream of skipping the stage of capitalism and leaping directly from the mir to socialism was nothing but a mirage. The struggle in its inception was a battle of books and pamphlets. The polemic of the Marxists against the Narodniks was even welcomed by the government, since in its eyes the Narodniks were still dangerous revolutionaries and the Marxists were viewed as essentially a rather harmless literary group.

The diffusion of Marxism among the intellectuals of the nineties was also attended by confusion about its content and significance. For many of the "fellow-travelers" of the Legal Marxist period, "Marxist" was hardly more than a generic name for the protagonists of the industrial development which appeared to be in full triumph in the early nineties. Even Peter Struve, who counted himself a Marxist in that period and drafted the manifesto of the First Congress of the Russian Social-Democratic Labor Party, held in Minsk in 1898, could end his "Critical Remarks on the Problem of the Economic Development of Russia" (1894) with the appeal: "Let us recognize our backwardness in culture and let us take our lessons from capitalism." For still others, the so-called Economists of the late nineties, Marxism meant little more than "bread and butter" trade unionism, bargaining with employers for that extra kopeck on the ruble for which Lenin had such fierce contempt. Other professed Marxists—and by 1899 Struve had become one of them—responded to Bernstein's challenge to orthodox Marxism by establishing a Russian branch of Critical Revisionism, a movement which was to lead them from Marxism to idealism and to an eventual break with the Social-Democratic Party.

In the face of these divergent trends (later to be described as deviations), the doctrinal problem which Plekhanov and Lenin faced in the nineties was to buttress the orthodox Marxian analysis and to reassert its revolutionary content. In the international socialist controversies of the period, Plekhanov and Lenin took their stand with Kautsky, the guardian of the true faith, against the heterodoxies of Bernstein. In Russia they denounced the objectivism of the Legal Marxists and the reformist tendencies of Economism and Critical Revisionism. For both Plekhanov and Lenin, Marxism was a revolutionary creed not to be diluted by opportunistic waverings.

During this period, Plekhanov was still the master and Lenin the pupil. Both considered themselves orthodox Marxists. Marx's panorama of capitalist development seemed to imply that the socialist revolution stood its greatest chance of success in those countries in which the processes of industrialization were most highly advanced and in which the working class formed a substantial part of the population. How apply such a recipe for a successful socialist revolution to Russia with its nascent industrialism, its weakly developed proletariat, and its overwhelmingly peasant population? Confronted with Russia's industrial backwardness, both Plekhanov and Lenin agreed that the first order of business was to achieve a bourgeois-democratic revolution in Russia. With the further development of Russian capitalism, Russia would become ripe for a successful proletarian revolt. In this analysis they merely followed the familiar two-stage sequence laid down in the *Communist Manifesto*. Plekhanov, the theorist, was to remain loyal to this formulation for the rest of his life. Lenin, the activist, was to find it increasingly uncongenial, and though he continued for many years to pay it verbal tribute, his whole revolutionary career was essentially an escape from its confines.

THE PROBLEM OF INDUSTRIAL BACKWARDNESS

The question of the shape and pace of the Russian revolution was to produce furious controversies among Social-Democrats of all shades. The heart of the problem was Russia's industrial backwardness and the political consequences to be drawn from it. The Social-Democratic Labor Party based itself on a weak and still-undeveloped industrial proletariat. What was the role of the party to be? Should it attempt to seize power at the first promising opportunity or would it have to wait patiently until Russia's industrialization matched that of the most advanced Western nations? If it limited its immediate activities to organizing the proletariat and helping the bourgeoisie to overthrow the autocracy, would the party not be strengthening its most dangerous enemy by surrendering to it the power of the state? If, on the other hand, the party emphasized its hostility to the bourgeoisie and its role as capitalism's gravedigger, would the bourgeoisie not be driven to unite its fortunes with those of the autocracy? Questions such as these might be argued in terms of Marxian exegesis, but the answers that were evolved depended more on temperament than on theory.

The Menshevik wing of Russian Social-Democracy, with which Plekhanov was finally to ally himself, saw the arrival of socialism in Russia as the climax of a long process of development. The Menshevik response to the challenge of industrial backwardness was to preach the postponement of the socialist revolution until industrial backwardness had been overcome. Strongly influenced by orthodox Western Marxism and impressed by the weakness of the Russian industrial proletariat, the Mensheviks concluded that a socialist Russia was a matter of the distant future and that the immediate task was to clear the way for a bourgeois, middleclass revolution. Their first charge as good Marxists was to help the bourgeoisie to carry out its own historical responsibilities. They were therefore prepared to conclude alliances with liberal bourgeois forces who opposed the autocracy and to join them in fighting for such limited objectives as universal suffrage, constitutional liberties, and enlightened social legislation. Meanwhile, they awaited the further growth of capitalism in Russia to establish the conditions for a successful socialist revolution. Essentially, the Mensheviks had their eye on Western European models; they expected to march to power through legality and to be the beneficiaries of the spontaneous mass energy which the creation of a large industrial proletariat would release.

At the opposite extreme from the Menshevik conception was the theory of "permanent revolution" developed by Parvus and adopted by Trotsky during and after the 1905 revolution. For Parvus and Trotsky, the industrial backwardness of Russia was a political asset rather than a liability. As a result of backwardness and the large role played by state capitalism, the Russian middle class was weak and incapable of doing the job of its analogues in Western Europe. Thus, according to Parvus' and Trotsky's dialectic of backwardness, the bourgeois revolution in Russia could be made only by the proletariat. Once the proletariat was in power, its responsibility was to hold on to power and keep the revolution going "in permanence" until socialism was established both at home and abroad. The Russian revolution, Trotsky thought, would ignite a series of socialist revolutions in the West. This "permanent revolution" would offset the resistance which developed. Thus Trotsky's prescription for Russia's retarded economy was a new law of combined development. The two revolutions bourgeois-democratic and proletarian-socialist—would be combined, or telescoped, into one. The working class would assert its hegemony from the outset and leap directly from industrial backwardness into socialism. Implicit in the Trotsky-Parvus formula was a clear commitment to the theory of minority dictatorship for Russia. An industrial proletariat which was still relatively infinitesimal in numbers was called upon to impose its will and direction on the vast majority of the population. Out of such theoretical brick and straw, the edifice of Soviet totalitarianism was to be constructed.

The position of Lenin and the Bolshevik wing of the Russian Social-Democratic Party was much closer in spirit to Trotsky than to the Mensheviks, though the verbal premises from which Lenin started seemed indistinguishable from the Menshevik tenets. Like the Mensheviks, Lenin proclaimed that Russia was ripe for only a bourgeois-democratic revolution. His *Two Tactics of Social-Democracy in the Democratic Revolution* (1905) contained at least one formulation which Mensheviks would wholeheartedly have endorsed:

> The degree of economic development of Russia (an objective condition) and the degree of class consciousness and organization of the broad masses of the proletariat

(a subjective condition inseparably connected with the objective condition) make the immediate complete emancipation of the working class impossible. Only the most ignorant people can ignore the bourgeois nature of the democratic revolution which is now taking place. . . . Whoever wants to arrive at socialism by a different road, other than that of political democracy, will inevitably arrive at absurd and reactionary conclusions, both in the economic and the political sense. If any workers ask us at the given moment why not go ahead and carry out our maximum program we shall answer by pointing out how far the masses of the democratically disposed people still are from socialism, how undeveloped class antagonisms still are, how unorganized the proletarians still are.

Again, in the same pamphlet, Lenin reiterated: "We Marxists should know that there is not, nor can there be, any other path to real freedom for the proletariat and the peasantry, than the path of bourgeois freedom and bourgeois progress."

While dicta such as these can be and have been cited to establish a basic area of agreement between Mensheviks and Bolsheviks on the two-stage perspective of the Russian revolution, the kinship was more illusory than real. Plekhanov summed up one of the important differences when he observed to Lenin, "You turn your behind to the liberals, but we our face." For Lenin, as for Trotsky, the bourgeois liberals were a weak and unreliable reed. Like Trotsky, Lenin came to believe that the proletariat would have to take leadership in completing the bourgeois revolution; but unlike both Trotsky and the Mensheviks, Lenin looked to an alliance with the peasantry to provide the proletariat with a mass base.

In this rediscovery of the strategic significance of the peasantry, Lenin reclaimed the Narodnik heritage which both he and Plekhanov had done so much to repudiate in the nineties. In the essay on *Two Tactics,* Lenin declared:

Those who really understand the role of the peasantry in a victorious Russian revolution would not dream of saying that the sweep of the revolution would be diminished if the bourgeoisie recoiled from it. For, as a matter of fact, the Russian revolution will begin to assume its real sweep . . . only when the bourgeoisie recoils from it and when the masses of the peasantry come out as active revolutionaries side-by-side with the proletariat.

The first task was to consolidate "the revolutionary-democratic dictatorship of the proletariat and the peasantry." After this was achieved, the socialist revolution would become the order of the day. Lenin's formula thus envisaged two tactical stages: first, the alliance of proletariat and peasantry to complete the democratic revolution, and second, an alliance of the proletariat and village poor to initiate the socialist revolution.

Given Lenin's activist temperament, it was inevitable that he should feel greater affinity for Trotsky's revolutionary dynamism than for the Mensheviks' passive fatalism. As the excitement of the 1905 revolution mounted, we find him speaking the language of Trotsky: "From the democratic revolution we shall at once, and just in accordance with the measure of our strength, the strength of the class-conscious and organized proletariat, begin to pass to the socialist revolution. We stand for uninterrupted revolution. We shall not stop half way." Despite many intervening conflicts, the bond with Trotsky was to be sealed by the experiences of 1917. The dialectic of backwardness was "resolved" by the Bolshevik seizure of power.

Out of that adventure a new theory of revolution was to be developed with world-wide applications. Stalin has given it authoritative exposition:

Where will the revolution begin? . . .

Where industry is more developed, where the proletariat constitutes the majority, where there is more culture, where there is more democracy—that was the reply usually given formerly.

No, objects the Leninist theory of revolution; *not necessarily where industry is more developed,* and so forth. The front of capitalism will be pierced where the chain of imperialism is weakest, for the proletarian revolution is the result of the breaking of the chain of the world imperialist front at its weakest link; and it may turn out that the country which has started the revolution, which has made a breach in the front of capital, is less developed in a capitalist sense than other, more developed, countries, which have, however, remained within the framework of capitalism.

Thus Marx, who turned Hegel on his head, was himself turned on his head. Industrial backwardness was transformed from obstacle to opportunity. The concept of the dictatorship of the proletariat shifted from a weapon of the majority into a tool of minorities. Consciousness triumphed over spontaneity, and the way was cleared for the organized and disciplined revolutionary elite capable of transmuting the grievances of a nation into a new formula of absolute power.

ORGANIZATION: THE ELITE PARTY

The organizational conception embodied in Bolshevism was essentially an incarnation of this elitist ideal. "Give us an organization of revolutionaries," said Lenin, "and we shall overturn the whole of Russia!" It was Lenin who forged the instrument, but the seeds of his conspiratorial conceptions were planted deep in Russian history and were nurtured by the conditions of the revolutionary struggle against the autocracy. Pestel among the Decembrists, Bakunin, Nechayev, Tkachev, and the Narodnik conspirators of the seventies and early eighties, all provided organizational prototypes of the professional revolutionary as the strategic lever of political upheaval. It was a tradition from which Lenin drew deep inspiration even when he found himself in profound disagreement with the particular programs which earlier professional revolutionaries espoused. His works are filled with tributes to the famous revolutionaries of the seventies (figures like Alekseyev, Myshkin, Khalturin, and Zhelyabov). In developing his own conceptions of party organization in *What Is to Be Done?* he refers to "the magnificent organization" of the revolutionaries of the seventies as one "which should serve us all as a model." Lenin's conviction that Russian Marxism could triumph only if led by a disciplined elite of professional revolutionaries was reënforced by his own early amateur experiences as a member of the Petersburg League of Struggle for the Emancipation of the Working Class. This organization was easily penetrated by the police, and the first effort of Lenin and his collaborators in 1895 to publish an underground paper—"The Workers' Cause"—resulted in the arrest of Lenin and his chief associates and a quick transfer of domicile to Siberia.

It is against this background that the organizational conceptions of Lenin took shape. By 1902, with the publication of *What Is to Be Done?* they were fully developed. In this essay, the seminal source of the organizational philosophy of Bolshevism, Lenin set himself two main tasks: (1) to destroy the influence of Economism with its repudiation of revolutionary political organization and its insistence on trade unionism as the basic method of improving the welfare of the working class, and (2) to build an organized and disciplined revolutionary Marxist party which would insure the triumph of socialism in Russia.

The polemic against the Economists clearly revealed Lenin's elitist preconceptions. More than a quarter of a century earlier Tkachev had written: "Neither in the present nor in the future can the people, left to their own resources, bring into existence the social revolution. Only we revolutionists can accomplish this . . . Social ideals are alien to the people; they belong to the social philosophy of the revolutionary minority." Now Lenin was to repeat:

> The history of all countries shows that the working class, exclusively by its own effort, is able to develop only trade union consciousness. . . . This [Social-Democratic] consciousness could only be brought to them from without. . . . The theory of socialism . . . grew out of the philosophic, historical, and economic theories that were elaborated by the educated representatives of the propertied classes, the intellectuals . . . quite independently of the spontaneous-growth of the labor movement. . . .
> Our task, the task of Social-Democracy, is to *combat spontaneity,* to *divert* the labor movement from its spontaneous, trade unionist striving to go under the wing of the bourgeoisie, and to bring it under the wing of revolutionary Social-Democracy.

To accomplish this objective, Lenin sought to weld together a disciplined party of devoted adherents, "a small, compact core, consisting of the most reliable, experienced and hardened workers, with responsible agents in the principal districts and connected by all the rules of strict secrecy with the organization of revolutionaries." . . . [Editor's note: The article next ensuing is a substantial excerpt from Lenin's *What Is to Be Done?*]

Democratic management, Lenin held, was simply inapplicable to a revolutionary organization. *What Is to Be Done?* disclosed the profoundly elitist and anti-democratic strain in Lenin's approach to problems of organization. It also made clear that in Lenin's new model party, leadership would be highly centralized, the central committee would appoint local committees, and every committee would have the right to coöpt new members. But it still left a precise blueprint to be worked out. This was the task which Lenin undertook to perform at the Second Party Congress of the Russian Social-Democratic Labor Party, which met in Brussels and then in London in the summer of 1903. Lenin prepared for this Congress with a meticulous attention to detail of which he alone among his revolutionary contemporaries was capable. His one desire was to construct a compact majority which would dominate the Congress and build a party willing "to devote to the revolution not only their spare evenings, but the whole of their lives."

The foundations seemed to be well laid. The rallying point of the "compact majority" was *Iskra* (The Spark), a journal which had been established abroad in 1900 largely on Lenin's initiative. Wisely, Lenin and his young associates, Martov and Potresov, enlisted the coöperation of Plekhanov and other members of the Emancipation of Labor group as co-editors. The association generated its own sparks; Lenin has provided a vivid record of the conflict in his "How the Spark Was Nearly Extinguished." But the quarrels for supremacy were composed; Lenin still needed the prestige of the older generation of revolutionaries in mobilizing adherents to the *Iskra* platform. Meanwhile, Lenin retained control of the secret agents who smuggled *Iskra* into Russia and maintained the closest connections with the underground organizations which distributed the journal. This organization of *Iskra* men was to provide the core of Lenin's majority at the Second Congress.

When the Second Congress assembled in Brussels in 1903, thirty-three votes, a clear majority of the fifty-one official votes, belonged to the *Iskra* faction. The remaining eighteen delegates represented a collection of Bundists (members of the All-Jewish Workers' Union of Russia and Poland), Economists, and miscellaneous uncommitted representatives, whom the Iskraites described contemptuously as "the Marsh" because they wallowed in a quagmire of uncertainty. The Iskraites appeared to be in full control. They named the presidium and easily pushed through their draft program and various resolutions on tactics.

The next order of business was the adoption of the party rules, and here trouble developed. The Iskraites were no longer united; Lenin and Martov offered rival drafts. The initial issue was posed by the definition of party membership. Lenin's draft of Paragraph One read: "A Party member is one who accepts its program and who supports the Party both financially and *by personal participation in one of the Party organizations.*" Martov's formulation defined a party member as "one who accepts its program, supports the Party financially and renders it regular personal assistance under the direction of one of its organizations." To many of the delegates, the difference in shading between the two drafts appeared slight, but as the discussion gathered momentum, the differences were magnified until a basic, and ultimately irreconcilable, question of principle emerged.

The issue was the nature of the party. Lenin wanted a narrow, closed party of dedicated revolutionaries operating in strict subordination to the center and serving as a vanguard of leadership for the masses of workers who would surround the party without belonging to it. Martov desired a broad party open to anyone who believed in its program and was willing to work under its direction. Martov conceded the necessity of central leadership, but he also insisted that party members were entitled to have a voice in its affairs and could not abdicate their right to think and influence party policy.

As the debate raged, the *Iskra* group fell apart. Plekhanov rallied to Lenin's defense; the Leninist formula seemed to him admirably adapted to protect the party against the infiltration of bourgeois individualists. Axelrod and Trotsky supported Martov. To Axelrod it seemed that Lenin was dreaming "of the administrative subordination of an entire party to a few guardians of doctrine." And after the Congress had adjourned, Trotsky, in a sharp attack on Lenin, provided the classic formulation of the opposition. In Lenin's view, he pointed out, "the organization of the Party takes the place of the Party itself; the Central Committee takes the place of the organization; and finally the dictator takes the place of the Central Committee." It was to turn out a more somber and tragic vision of things to come than Trotsky realized at the time.

At the Congress, Martov's draft triumphed by a vote of twenty-eight to twenty-two. But Lenin had not yet shot his last bolt. He still retained the leadership of a majority of the Iskraites, though his group was now a minority in the Congress. This minority was soon transformed into a majority by a series of "accidents" to which Lenin's parliamentary maneuvering and planning contributed. When the Congress rejected the Bundist claim to be the sole representative of the Jewish proletariat, the five delegates of the Bund withdrew from the Congress. Their departure was followed by the withdrawal of the delegates from the League of Russian Social-Democrats, an Economist-dominated organization, which the Congress voted to dissolve on Lenin's motion. With the exit of these two groups, the *Iskra* majority became the Congress majority and proceeded to elect its representatives to the central party organs. It was this triumph which gave Lenin's caucus the title of Bolsheviks (the majority men), while his defeated opponents became known as Mensheviks (the minority men).

But the triumph was short-lived. The central party institutions elected by the Second Congress consisted of the editors of *Iskra*, the Central Committee in Russia, and a Party Council of five members (two representing *Iskra*, two the Central Committee, and a fifth elected by the Congress). The Board of Editors of *Iskra* was given power equal to and indeed above that of the Central Committee. Disputes between *Iskra* and the Central

Committee were to be settled by the Party Council. Lenin, Plekhanov, and Martov were elected as editors of *Iskra*. Martov refused to serve unless the original editorial board, which included Axelrod, Zasulich, and Potresov, was restored. Lenin and Plekhanov were thus left in exclusive control. The Central Committee in Russia was composed entirely of Bolsheviks, and they were given power to coöpt other members. The party apparatus appeared to be safely in Bolshevik hands when Plekhanov, out of a desire to heal the breach with his old associates, acceded to Martov's conditions and insisted on the restoration of the original *Iskra* board. Lenin promptly withdrew, and at one stroke *Iskra* was transformed into an organ of Menshevism.

Differences now began to develop in the Bolshevik Central Committee in Russia; a majority group emerged which advocated a policy of conciliation toward the Mensheviks. Three Mensheviks were coöpted into the Central Committee, and in the summer of 1904 this strategic power position, which Lenin had regarded as impregnable, passed over to the opposition. After all his careful planning and apparent triumph, Lenin was left isolated and alone, betrayed by his own nominees in Russia, alienated from the leading figures of the emigration, and the chief target of abuse in the party organ which he had been primarily instrumental in establishing.

After a temporary fit of utter discouragement, Lenin rallied and began once more to gather his forces. The remnants of the faithful in the emigration were welded into a fighting organization. Connections were reestablished with the lower party committees in Russia, and a new body, the Bureau of the Committee of the Majority, was established to coordinate the work of Lenin's supporters. Toward the end of 1904 a new paper, *Vperëd* (Forward), was founded as the organ of the bureau. A second effort to capture control of the party organization was now in the full tide of preparation. But this time the Mensheviks were wary and refused to attend the so-called Third Congress of the Social-Democratic Labor Party, which assembled on Lenin's initiative in London in May 1905. The Mensheviks met separately in Geneva.

The 1905 revolution brought Bolsheviks and Mensheviks closer together. Responding to the *élan* of the uprising, Mensheviks became more militant and Bolsheviks seemed to abandon their distrust of uncontrolled mass organization. As Lenin put it, "The rising tide of revolution drove . . . differences into the background. . . . In place of the old differences there arose unity of views." Joint committees were formed in many cities, and finally a Joint Central Committee was created on a basis of equal representation to summon a "Unity" Congress. Both parties were flooded with new members for whom the old quarrels were ancient history and the practical tasks of the moment were paramount. The misgivings of the leaders were swept aside in a widespread yearning for unity.

The Fourth so-called "Unity" Congress, which took place at Stockholm in 1906, reflected this surge from below. Thirty-six thousand workers took part in the election of delegates. Menshevism flourished on legality, and of the one hundred eleven voting delegates selected, sixty-two were Mensheviks and forty-nine Bolsheviks. As a result, the Mensheviks dominated the proceedings. They wrote the program and resolutions and controlled the leading party organs. The Central Committee elected by the Congress was composed of seven Mensheviks and three Bolsheviks; the editorial board for the central party newspaper (which never appeared) was composed exclusively of Mensheviks. Perhaps the most important organizational action taken at the Congress was the admission of the Bund and the Polish and Latvian Social-Democratic parties as constituent units in the united party. The Polish and Latvian parties joined as autonomous organizations operating in their respective territorial areas; the Bund renounced its claim to be the sole representative of the Jewish proletariat on the understanding that it would be permitted to retain its program of national cultural autonomy and to organize Jewish workers without respect to territorial boundaries. The admission of these groups introduced an additional complication into the power structure of the party. Given the relatively even distribution of strength between Mensheviks and Bolsheviks in this period, the balance of power now shifted to the Bund and the Polish and Latvian Social-Democrats, and their votes became of crucial significance in shaping the party's future course.

Although Lenin suffered defeat at the Stockholm Congress, he continued to maneuver for ascendancy. The Bolshevik factional apparatus was maintained, and funds to finance the apparatus were partly obtained through "expropriations" (robberies and holdups). The effort to capture local organizations was continued, and Menshevik policies were attacked with relentless ferocity. As a result of this activity, the Bolsheviks registered marked gains at the Fifth Congress, held in London in 1907. While the precise strength of the Bolshevik and Menshevik blocs is still in dispute, all accounts agree that the Bolsheviks achieved a slight preponderance over the Mensheviks at the Congress.

This did not mean, however, that the Bolsheviks controlled the Congress. The real power of decision rested with the Bund and the Polish and Latvian Social-Democrats, who exercised a role of balance between the conflicting Russian factions. On the whole, the Mensheviks attracted Bundist support, while the Bolsheviks were dependent on the Poles and Latvians for such majorities as they obtained. While the Bolsheviks failed to secure the support of the national delegates in their efforts to condemn the work of the Menshevik Central Committee and of the Duma fraction of the party and were themselves condemned for their sponsorship of "expropriations," they were able to defeat the Mensheviks on a number of important resolutions. The Menshevik policy of cooperating with the Kadets was repudiated. The proposal of Axelrod and other leading Mensheviks to call a non-party labor congress and to transform the Social-Democratic Party into a broad, open labor party was denounced by Lenin as "Liquidationism" and decisively rejected by the Congress. But the Bolsheviks were unable to achieve a dependable, monolithic majority, and the elections to the Central Committee yielded five Bolsheviks, four Mensheviks, two Bundists, two Polish Social-Democrats, and one Latvian Social-Democrat.

During the period of reaction and repression which accumulated momentum after the London Congress, both Menshevik and Bolshevik segments of the party underwent a serious crisis. Party membership crumbled away, and police spies penetrated such remnants of the organizational apparatus as remained. The crisis was particularly acute for the Mensheviks. Potresov, in a letter to Axelrod toward the end of 1907, reflected an almost hopeless despondency:

> Complete disintegration and demoralisation prevail in our ranks. Probably this is a phenomenon common to all parties and fractions and reflects the spirit of the times; but I do not think that this disintegration, this demoralisation have anywhere manifested themselves so vividly as with us Mensheviks. Not only is there no organisation, there are not even the elements of one.

The situation within Bolshevik ranks was not much better. "In 1908," notes the Bolshevik historian Popov, "the Party membership numbered not tens and hundreds of thousands, as formerly, but a few hundreds, or, at best, thousands." The plight of the Moscow organization was not atypical. From the end of 1908 to the end of 1909, membership declined from five hundred to one hundred fifty; in the next year the organization was completely destroyed when it fell under the control of a police spy. The Bolsheviks, by virtue of their conspiratorial traditions and tight discipline, made a better adjustment than the Mensheviks to the rigors of illegal existence, but even Bolshevik vigilance could not prevent the secret agents of the police from penetrating the underground hierarchy and rising to high places in the party apparatus. Meanwhile, the leaders of both the Bolshevik and Menshevik factions fled abroad once more where they were soon engaged in resurrecting old quarrels and giving birth to new differences.

Both factions fell victim to internal dissension. The Mensheviks divided between the "Liquidators" (as Lenin dubbed them), who counseled the abandonment of the underground party and concentration on legal work in the trade unions and the Duma, and the "Party" Mensheviks, who continued to insist on the necessity of an illegal organization. Bolshevism spawned in rapid succession a bewildering series of controversies. First, there were the "Duma Boycotters," led by Bogdanov, at that time one of Lenin's closest associates. On this issue Lenin joined with the Mensheviks and supported party participation in the election of the Third Duma. Then there were the "Otzovists" and "Ultimatumists," the former demanding the immediate recall or withdrawal of the Duma party delegation and the latter insisting that an ultimatum be dispatched to the delegation with the proviso that its members should immediately be recalled if the instructions contained in the ultimatum were rejected. Lenin again opposed both tendencies. Next came the philosophical heresies, the Neo-Kantian "Machism" of Bogdanov and the "God-Creator" religionism of Lunacharsky and Gorky. These were heresies that Lenin endured as long as the heretics were enrolled in his political camp; they became intolerable only when Bogdanov and the rest challenged his control of the party faction. Finally, there were the Bolshevik "Conciliators" who insisted that peace be made with the Mensheviks after Lenin had determined that a final split was essential.

In the parlance of latter-day Bolshevism, each of these "deviations" had to be "liquidated" if Lenin was to build the party in his own image. He was determined to accomplish precisely that task. The first act took place in the summer of 1909 at an enlarged editorial conference of *Proletarii,* the organ of the Bolshevik caucus. Again Lenin made careful advance preparations, and equipped with the necessary votes, he carried a resolution declaring that Boycottism, Otzovism, Ultimatumism, God-Construction, and Machism were all incompatible with membership in the Bolshevik faction. Over bitter protest, Bogdanov was ousted from the Bolshevik central leadership where he had been second only to Lenin, and he and his associates were declared "to have placed themselves outside the faction." Expelled from the fold, the dissidents proceeded to declare themselves "true Bolsheviks," established a new journal utilizing an old name, *Vperëd,* and became known during the next years as Vperëdist Bolsheviks.

Having disposed of the Vperëdists, Lenin confronted the new opposition of the so-called Conciliators, or Party Bolsheviks, who called for reconciliation with the expelled faction and unity with the Mensheviks. At a plenary session, held in January 1910, of the Central Committee elected by the London Congress, Lenin received a sharp rebuff when the Conciliators turned against him. The conference voted to discontinue the Bolshevik paper *Proletarii* as well as the Menshevik *Golos Sotsial-Demokrata* (Voice of the Social-Democrat) and to replace both with a general party organ, *Sotsial-Demokrat,* which would have two Menshevik editors, Martov and Dan, two Bolshevik editors, Lenin and Zinoviev, and one representative of the Polish Social-Democrats, Warski, to break any deadlocks that might develop.

Again the attempt at "unity" miscarried. With the support of Warski, Lenin won control of the new party journal and denied the Menshevik editors the right to publish signed articles in what was supposed to be the organ of the united party. Martov replied by attempting to discredit Lenin through an exposure of the seamy side of Bolshevism—the holdups, the counterfeiting, and "expropriations" which Lenin had allegedly sanctioned and defended.

Lenin now moved toward an open and irrevocable break. Despite the protest of the Bolshevik Conciliators, he summoned an All-Russian Party

Conference which met in Prague in January 1912 to ratify the split. Although the conference was dominated by a carefully selected group of Lenin's most reliable supporters, the uneasiness of the delegates in the face of Lenin's ruthless determination to move toward schism manifested itself in a belated decision to invite Plekhanov, Trotsky, and others to attend. To Lenin's great relief, both Plekhanov and Trotsky refused on the ground that the conference was too one-sided and imperiled party unity. Martov and the Menshevik Liquidators were not invited. The Bund and the Polish and Latvian Social-Democrats also stayed away.

The "Rump Parliament" proceeded to assume all the rights and functions of a party congress (indeed, Lenin called it The Sixth Congress of the Russian Social-Democratic Labor Party). The old Central Committee created by the London Congress was declared dissolved, and a new "pure" Bolshevik Central Committee was elected from which all Bolshevik Conciliators were excluded. The Prague Conference marked the decisive break with Menshevism and the turning point in the history of Bolshevism as an independent movement. There were to be many subsequent attempts to bring the Bolsheviks back into the fold of a united party, but all were doomed to failure. The last effort, sponsored by the International Socialist Bureau of the Second International, was slated to take place at the Vienna Congress of the Second International in August 1914. War intervened, and the congress was never held. By an ironical turn of events, the International which attempted to close the breach in the Russian party was itself split by the Bolsheviks whom it tried to bring to heel.

The early organizational history of Bolshevism, which has been briefly summarized here, holds more than historical interest. The experience of the formative years left an ineradicable stamp on the character and future development of the party. It implanted the germinating conception of the monolithic and totalitarian party. The elitism which was so deeply ingrained in Lenin, the theory of the party as a dedicated revolutionary order, the tradition of highly centralized leadership, the tightening regimen of party discipline, the absolutism of the party line, the intolerance of disagreement and compromise, the manipulatory attitude toward mass organization, the subordination of means to ends, and the drive for total power —all these patterns of behavior which crystallized in the early years were destined to exercise a continuing influence on the code by which the party lived and the course of action which it pursued.

WHAT IS TO BE DONE?
BURNING QUESTIONS OF OUR MOVEMENT

V. I. Lenin*

This document, completed and published in 1902, is one of the most important in all Marxist-Leninist literature. Lenin's theoretical and practical conceptions of the nature, structure, and role of the Party had a most profound influence in shaping the Bolshevik movement. Although Lenin's elitist conception of the Party was then intended to apply only to the period before the seizure of power and only in the conditions of Russian autocracy, it remains an attribute of the Party organization to this day.

Without a revolutionary theory there can be no revolutionary movement. This cannot be insisted upon too strongly at a time when the fashionable preaching of opportunism is combined with absorption in the narrowest forms of practical activity. . . .

The Russian workers will have to undergo trials immeasurably severe; they will have to take up the fight against a monster, compared with which anti-Socialist laws in a constitutional country are but pigmies. History has now confronted us with an immediate task which is *more revolutionary than all the immediate tasks* that confront the proletariat of any other country. The fulfilment of this task, the destruction of the most powerful bulwark, not only of European, but also (it may now be said) of Asiatic reaction, places the Russian proletariat in the vanguard of the international revolutionary proletariat. We shall have the right to count upon acquiring the honourable title already earned by our predecessors, the revolutionaries of the seventies, if we succeed in inspiring our movement—which is a thousand times wider and deeper—with the same devoted determination and vigour.

I. THE SPONTANEITY OF THE MASSES AND THE CLASS-CONSCIOUSNESS OF SOCIAL-DEMOCRACY

The Beginning of the Spontaneous Movement

. . . Strikes occurred in Russia in the seventies, and in the sixties (and also in the first half of the nineteenth century), and these strikes were ac-

---

* The selection is from the pamphlet by the same title (International Publishers Co., Inc., 1929), *passim*. By permission of the publisher.

companied by the "spontaneous" destruction of machinery, etc. Compared with these "revolts" the strikes of the nineties might even be described as "conscious," to such an extent do they mark the progress which the labour movement had made since that period. This shows that the "spontaneous element," in essence, represents nothing more nor less than consciousness in an *embryonic form*. Even the primitive rebellions expressed the awakening of consciousness to a certain extent: The workers abandoned their age-long faith in the permanence of the system which oppressed them. They began . . . I shall not say to understand, but to sense the necessity for collective resistance, and emphatically abandoned their slavish submission to their superiors. But all this was more in the nature of outbursts of desperation and vengeance than *struggle*. The strikes of the nineties revealed far greater flashes of consciousness: Definite demands were put forward, the time to strike was carefully chosen, known cases and examples in other places were discussed, etc. While the revolts were simply uprisings of the oppressed, the systematic strikes represented the class struggle in embryo, but only in embryo. Taken by themselves, these strikes were simple trade union struggles, but not yet Social-Democratic struggles. They testified to the awakening antagonisms between workers and employers, but the workers were not and could not be conscious of the irreconcilable antagonism of their interests to the whole of the modern political and social system, *i.e.*, it was not yet Social-Democratic consciousness. In this sense, the strikes of the nineties, in spite of the enormous progress they represented as compared with the "revolts," represented a purely spontaneous movement.

We said that *there could not yet be* Social-Democratic consciousness among the workers. This consciousness could only be brought to them from without. The history of all countries shows that the working class, exclusively by its own effort, is able to develop only trade-union consciousness, *i.e.*, it may itself realise the necessity for combining in unions, to fight against the employers and to strive to compel the government to pass necessary labour legislation, etc.

The theory of Socialism, however, grew out of the philosophic, historical and economic theories that were elaborated by the educated representatives of the propertied classes, the intellectuals. The founders of modern scientific Socialism, Marx and Engels, themselves belonged to the bourgeois intelligentsia. Similarly, in Russia, the theoretical doctrine of Social-Democracy arose quite independently of the spontaneous growth of the labour movement; it arose as a natural and inevitable outcome of the development of ideas among the revolutionary Socialist intelligentsia. At the time of which we are speaking, *i.e.*, the middle of the nineties, this doctrine not only represented the completely formulated programme of the Emancipation of Labour group but had already won the adhesion of the majority of the revolutionary youth in Russia.

Hence, simultaneously we had both the spontaneous awakening of the masses of the workers—the awakening to conscious life and struggle, and the striving of the revolutionary youth, armed with the Social-Democratic theories, to reach the workers. In this connection it is particularly important to state the oft-forgotten (and comparatively little-known) fact that the early Social-Democrats of that period, *zealously carried on economic agitation* (being guided in this by the really useful instructions contained in the pamphlet *Agitation* that was still in manuscript) but they did not regard this as their sole task. On the contrary, *right from the very beginning* they brought up the general historical tasks of Russian Social-Democracy, and particularly the task of overthrowing the autocracy. . . .

Bowing to Spontaneity

. . . Since there can be no talk of an independent ideology being developed by the masses of the workers in the process of their movement* then *the only choice is:* Either bourgeois, or Socialist ideology. There is no middle course (for humanity has not created a "third" ideology, and, moreover, in a society torn by class antagonisms there can never be a non-class or above-class ideology). Hence, to belittle Socialist ideology *in any way,* to *deviate from it in the slightest degree* means strengthening bourgeois ideology. There is a lot of talk about spontaneity, but the *spontaneous* development of the labour movement leads to its becoming subordinated to bourgeois ideology, it means developing *according to the programme* of the *Credo,* for the spontaneous labour movement is pure and simple trade unionism, is *Nur-Gewerkschaftlerei,* and trade unionism means the ideological subordination of the workers to the bourgeoisie. Hence, our task, the task of Social-Democracy, is to *combat spontaneity,* to *divert* the labour movement, with its spontaneous trade-unionist striving, from under the wing of the bourgeoisie, and to bring it under the wing of revolutionary Social-Democracy. . . .

But why, the reader will ask, does the spontaneous movement, the movement along the line of least resistance, lead to the domination of bourgeois ideology? For the simple reason that bourgeois ideology is far older in origin than Social-Democratic ideology; because it is more fully developed and because it possesses *immeasurably* more opportunities for becoming widespread. And the younger the Socialist movement is in any given country, the more vigorously must it fight against all attempts to entrench non-Socialist ideology, and the more strongly must it warn the workers against those bad counsellors who shout against "exaggerating the conscious elements," etc. . . .

* This does not mean, of course, that the workers have no part in creating such an ideology. But they take part not as workers, but as Socialist theoreticians, like Proudhon and Weitling; in other words, they take part only to the extent that they are able, more or less, to acquire the knowledge of their age and advance that knowledge. . . .

II. TRADE-UNION POLITICS AND SOCIAL-DEMOCRATIC POLITICS

Political Agitation and Its Restriction by the Economists

. . . Social-Democrats lead the struggle of the working class not only for better terms for the sale of labour power, but also for the abolition of the social system which compels the propertyless class to sell itself to the rich. Social-Democracy represents the working class, not in its relation to a given group of employers, but in its relation to all classes in modern society, to the state as an organised political force. Hence, it not only follows that Social-Democrats must not confine themselves entirely to the economic struggle; they must not even allow the organisation of economic exposures to become the predominant part of their activities. We must actively take up the political education of the working class, and the development of its political consciousness. . . .

All and sundry manifestations of police tyranny and autocratic outrage, in addition to the evils connected with the economic struggle, are equally "widely applicable" as a means of "drawing in" the masses. The tyranny of the Zemstvo chiefs, the flogging of the peasantry, the corruption of the officials, the conduct of the police towards the "common people" in the cities, the fight against the famine-stricken and the suppression of the popular striving towards enlightenment and knowledge, the extortion of taxes, the persecution of the religious sects, the severe discipline in the army, the militarist conduct towards the students and the liberal intelligentsia—all these and a thousand other similar manifestations of tyranny, though not directly connected with the "economic" struggle, do they, in general, represent a *less* "widely applicable" method and subject for political agitation and for drawing the masses into the political struggle? The very opposite is the case. Of all the innumerable cases in which the workers suffer (either personally or those closely associated with them) from tyranny, violence, and lack of rights, undoubtedly only a relatively few represent cases of police tyranny in the economic struggle as such. Why then should we beforehand *restrict* the scope of political agitation by declaring *only one* of the methods to be "the most widely applicable," when Social-Democrats have other, generally speaking, not less "widely applicable" means? . . .

Revolutionary Social-Democracy always included, and now includes, the fight for reforms in its activities. But it utilises "economic" agitation for the purpose of presenting to the government, not only demands for all sorts of measures, but also (and primarily) the demand that it cease to be an autocratic government. Moreover, it considers it to be its duty to present this demand to the government, not on the basis of the economic struggle *alone,* but on the basis of all manifestations of public and political life. In a word, it subordinates the struggle for reforms to the revolutionary struggle for liberty and for Socialism, in the same way as the part is subordinate to the whole. . . .

III. THE PRIMITIVENESS OF THE ECONOMISTS
AND THE ORGANISATION OF REVOLUTIONISTS

Primitive Methods and Economism

. . . These people, who cannot pronounce the word "theoretician" without a contemptuous grimace, who describe their genuflections to common lack of training and ignorance as "sensitiveness to life," reveal in practice a failure to understand our most imperative *practical* task. To laggards they shout: Keep in step! don't run ahead! To people suffering from a lack of energy and initiative in organisational work, from lack of "plans" for wide and bold organisational work, they shout about the "tactics-process"! The most serious sin we commit is that we *degrade* our political and *our organisational* tasks to the level of immediate, "palpable," "concrete" interests of the every-day economic struggle; and yet they keep singing to us the old song: Give the economic struggle itself a political character. We say again: This kind of thing displays as much "sensitiveness to life" as was displayed by the hero in the popular fable who shouted to a passing funeral procession: May you never get to your destination. . . .

Workers, average people of the masses, are capable of displaying enormous energy and self-sacrifice in strikes and in street battles, with the police and troops, and are capable (in fact, are alone capable) of *determining* the whole outcome of our movement—but the struggle against the *political* police requires special qualities; it can be conducted only by *professional* revolutionists. And we must not only see to it that the masses "advance" concrete demands, but also that the masses of the workers "advance" an increasing number of such professional revolutionists from their own ranks. Thus we have reached the question of the relation between an organisation of professional revolutionists and the pure and simple labour movement. . . .

Organisation of Workers, and Organisation of Revolutionists

It is only natural that a Social-Democrat who conceives the political struggle as being identical with the "economic struggle against the employers and the government," should conceive "organisation of revolutionists" as being more or less identical with "organisation of workers." . . .

It is the fact that on questions of organisation and politics the Economists are forever lapsing from Social-Democracy into trade unionism. The political struggle carried on by the Social-Democrats is far more extensive and complex than the economic struggle the workers carry on against the employers and the government. Similarly (and indeed for that reason), the organisation of revolutionary Social-Democrats must inevitably *differ* from the organisations of the workers designed for the latter struggle. The workers' organisations must in the first place be trade organisations; secondly, they must be as wide as possible; and thirdly, they must be as public as conditions will allow (here, of course, I have only autocratic Russia in mind). On the other hand, the organisations of revolutionists must be comprised first and foremost of people whose profession is that of revolutionists (that is why I speak of organisations of *revolutionists,* meaning revolutionary Social-Democrats). . . .

In countries where political liberty exists the distinction between a labour union and a political organisation is clear, as is the distinction between trade unions and Social-Democracy. The relation of the latter to the former will naturally vary in each country according to historical, legal and other conditions—it may be more or less close or more or less complex (in our opinion it should be as close and simple as possible); but trade-union organisations are certainly not in the least identical with the Social-Democratic party organisations in those countries. In Russia, however, the yoke of autocracy appears at first glance to obliterate all distinctions between a Social-Democratic organisation and trade unions, because *all* trade unions and *all* circles are prohibited, and because the principal manifestation and weapon of the workers' economic struggle—the strike—is regarded as a crime (and sometimes even as a political crime!). Conditions in our country, therefore, strongly "impel" the workers who are conducting the economic struggle to concern themselves with political questions. They also "impel" the Social-Democrats to confuse trade unionism with Social-Democracy. . . .

The workers' organisations for carrying on the economic struggle should be trade-union organisations; every Social-Democratic worker should, as far as possible, support and actively work inside these organisations. That is true. But it would be far from being to our interest to demand that only Social-Democrats be eligible for membership in the trade unions. The only effect of this, if it were attempted, would be to restrict our influence over the masses. Let every worker who understands the necessity for organisation, in order to carry on the struggle against the employers and the government, join the trade unions. The very objects of the trade unions would be unattainable unless they united all who have attained at least this elementary level of understanding, and unless they were extremely wide organisations. The wider these organisations are, the wider our influence over them will be. They will then be influenced not only by the "spontaneous" development of the economic struggle, but also by the direct and conscious action of the Socialists on their comrades in the unions. But a wide organisation cannot be a strictly secret organisation (since the latter demands far greater training than is required for the economic struggle). How is the contradiction between the necessity for a large membership and the necessity for strictly secret methods to be reconciled? . . .

In order to achieve this purpose, and in order to guide the nascent trade-union movement in the direction the Social-Democrats desire, we must first fully understand the foolishness of the plan of organisation with which the St. Petersburg Economists have been occupying themselves for nearly five years. That plan is described in the Rules of a Workers' Fund, of July, 1897 and also in the Rules for a Trade Union Workers' Organisation, of October, 1900. The fundamental error contained in both these sets of rules is that they give a detailed formulation of a wide workers' organisation and confuse the latter with the organisation of revolutionists. . . .

A small, compact core, consisting of reliable, experienced and hardened workers, with responsible agents in the principal districts and connected by all the rules of strict secrecy with the organisations of revolutionists, can, with the wide support of the masses and without an elaborate set of rules, perform *all* the functions of a trade-union organisation, and perform them, moreover, in the manner Social-Democrats desire. Only in this way can we secure the *consolidation* and development of a *Social-Democratic* trade-union movement, in spite of the gendarmes.

It may be objected that an organisation which is so loose that it is not even formulated, and which even has no enrolled and registered members, cannot be called an organisation at all. That may very well be. I am not out for names. But this "organisation without members" can do everything that is required, and will, from the very outset, guarantee the closest contact between our future trade unionists and Socialism. Only an incorrigible utopian would want a *wide* organisation of workers, with elections, reports, universal suffrage, etc., under autocracy.

The moral to be drawn from this is a simple one. If we begin with the solid foundation of a strong organisation of revolutionists, we can guarantee the stability of the movement as a whole, and carry out the aims of both Social-Democracy and of trade unionism. If, however, we begin with a wide workers' organisation, supposed to be most "accessible" to the masses, when as a matter of fact it will be most accessible to the gendarmes, and will make the revolutionists most accessible to the police, we shall neither achieve the aims of Social-Democracy nor of trade unionism; . . .

It is far more difficult to catch ten wise men than it is to catch a hundred fools. And this premise I shall defend no matter how much you instigate the crowd against me for my "anti-democratic" views, etc. As I have already said, by "wise men," in connection with organisation, I mean *professional revolutionists,* irrespective of whether they are students or workingmen. I assert: 1. That no movement can be durable without a stable organisation of leaders to maintain continuity; 2. that the more widely the masses are drawn into the struggle and form the basis of the movement, the more necessary is it to have such an organisation and the more stable must it be (for it is much easier then for demagogues to side-track the more backward sections of the masses); 3. that the organisation must consist chiefly of persons engaged in revolution as a profession; 4. that in a country with a despotic government, the more we *restrict* the membership of this organisation to persons who are engaged in revolution as a profession and who have been professionally trained in the art of combating the political police, the more difficult will it be to catch the organisation; and 5. the *wider* will be the circle of men and women of the working class or of other classes of society able to join the movement and perform active work in it. . . .

We can never give a mass organisation that degree of secrecy which is essential for the persistent and continuous struggle against the government. But to concentrate all secret functions in the hands of as small a number of professional revolutionists as possible, does not mean that the latter will "do the thinking for all" and that the crowd will not take an active part in the movement. On the contrary, the crowd will advance from its ranks increasing numbers of professional revolutionists, for it will know that it is not enough for a few students and workingmen waging economic war to gather together and form a "committee," but that professional revolutionists must be trained for years; the crowd will "think" not of primitive ways but of training professional revolutionists. The centralisation of the secret functions of the *organisation* does not mean the concentration of all the functions of the *movement*. The active participation of the greatest masses in the dissemination of illegal literature will not diminish because a dozen professional revolutionists concentrate in their hands the secret part of the work; on the contrary, it will *increase tenfold.*

Only in this way will the reading of illegal literature, the contribution to illegal literature, and to some extent even the distribution of illegal literature *almost cease to be secret work,* for the police will soon come to realise the folly and futility of setting the whole judicial and administrative machine into motion to intercept every copy of a publication that is being broadcast in thousands. This applies not only to the press, but to every function of the movement, even to demonstrations. The active and widespread participation of the masses will not suffer; on the contrary, it will benefit by the fact that a "dozen" experienced revolutionists, no less professionally trained than the police, will concentrate all the secret side of the work in their hands—prepare leaflets, work out approximate plans and appoint bodies of leaders for each town district, for each factory district, and for each educational institution (I know that exception will be taken to my "undemocratic" views, but I shall reply to this altogether unintelligent objection later on).

The centralisation of the more secret functions in an organisation of revolutionists will not diminish, but rather increase the extent and the quality of the activity of a large number of other organisations intended for wide membership and which, therefore, can be as loose and as public as possible, for example, trade unions, workers' circles for self-education, and the reading of illegal literature, and Socialist, and also democratic, circles for *all other sections of the population,* etc., etc. We must have *as large a number as possible* of such organisations having the widest possible variety of functions, but it is absurd and dangerous to *confuse these with organisations of revolutionists,* to erase the line of demarcation between them, to dim still more the already incredibly hazy appreciation by the masses that to "serve" the mass movement we must have people who will devote themselves exclusively to Social-Democratic activities, and that such people must *train* themselves patiently and steadfastly to be professional revolutionists.

Aye, this consciousness has become incredibly dim. The most grievous sin we have committed in regard to organisation is that *by our primitiveness we have lowered the prestige of revolutionists in Russia.* A man who is weak and vacillating on theoretical questions, who has a narrow outlook, who makes excuses for his own slackness on the ground that the masses are awakening spontaneously, who resembles a trade-union secretary more than a people's tribune, who is unable to conceive a broad and bold plan, who is incapable of inspiring even his enemies with respect for himself, and who is inexperienced and clumsy in his own professional art—the art of combating the political police—such a man is not a revolutionist but a hopeless amateur!

Let no active worker take offence at these frank remarks, for as far as insufficient training is concerned, I apply them first and foremost to myself. I used to work in a circle that set itself a great and all-embracing task: and every member of that circle suffered to the point of torture from the realisation that we were proving ourselves to be amateurs at a moment in history when we might have been able to say—paraphrasing a well-known epigram: "Give us an organisation of revolutionists, and we shall overturn the whole of Russia!" And the more I recall the burning sense of shame I then experienced, the more bitter are my feelings towards those pseudo-Social-Democrats whose teachings bring disgrace on the calling of a revolutionist, who fail to understand that our task is not to degrade the revolutionist to the level of an amateur, but to *exalt* the amateur to the level of a revolutionist.

The Scope of Organisational Work

. . . If we had such an organisation, the more secret it would be, the stronger and more widespread would be the confidence of the masses in the party, and, as we know, in time of war, it is not only of great importance to imbue one's own adherents with confidence in the strength of one's army, but also the enemy and all *neutral* elements; friendly neutrality may sometimes decide the outcome of the battle. If such an organisation existed on a firm theoretical basis, and possessed a Social-Democratic journal, we would have no reason to fear that the movement will be diverted from its path by the numerous "outside" elements that will be attracted to it. . . .

Our very first and most imperative duty is to help to train working-class revolutionists who will be on the same level *in regard to party activity* as intellectual revolutionists (we emphasise the words "in regard to party activity," because although it is necessary, it is not so easy and not so imperative to bring the workers up to the level of intellectuals in other respects). Therefore, attention must be devoted *principally* to the task of *raising* the workers to the level of revolutionists, but without, in doing so, necessarily *degrading* ourselves to the level of the "labour masses." . . .

A workingman who is at all talented and "promising," *must not be left* to work eleven hours a day in a factory. We must arrange that he be maintained by the party, that he may in due time go underground, that he change the place of his activity, otherwise he will not enlarge his experience, he will not widen his outlook, and will not be able to stay in the fight against the gendarmes for several years. As the spontaneous rise of the labouring masses becomes wider and deeper, it not only promotes from its ranks an increasing number of talented agitators, but also of talented organisers, propagandists, and "practical workers" in the best sense of the term (of whom there are so few among our intelligentsia). In the majority of cases, the latter are somewhat careless and sluggish in their habits (so characteristic of Russians).

When we shall have detachments of specially trained working-class revolutionists who have gone through long years of preparation (and, of course, revolutionists "of all arms") no political police in the world will be able to contend against them, for these detachments will consist of men absolutely devoted and loyal to the revolution, and will themselves enjoy the absolute confidence and devotion of the broad masses of the workers. The *sin* we commit is that we do not sufficiently "stimulate" the workers to take this path, "common" to them and to the "intellectuals," of professional revolutionary training, and that we too frequently drag them back by our silly speeches about what "can be understood" by the masses of the workers, by the "average workers," etc. . . .

"Conspirative" Organisation and "Democracy"

. . . Against us it is argued: Such a powerful and strictly secret organisation, which concentrates in its hands all the threads of secret activities, an organisation which of necessity must be a centralised organisation, may too easily throw itself into a premature attack, may thoughtlessly intensify the movement before political discontent, the ferment and anger of the working class, etc., are sufficiently ripe for it. . . .

It is precisely at the present time, when no such organisation exists yet, and when the revolutionary movement is rapidly and spontaneously growing, that we *already observe* two opposite extremes (which, as is to be expected, "meet") *i.e.,* absolutely unsound Economism and the preaching of moderation, and equally unsound "excitative terror," which strives artificially to "call forth symptoms of its end in a movement that is developing and becoming strong, but which is as yet nearer to its beginning than to its end" [V. Zasulich, in *Zarya*, Nos. 2-3, p. 353]. And the example of *Rabocheye Dyelo* shows that *there are already* Social-Democrats who give way to both these extremes. This is not surprising because, apart from other reasons, the "economic struggle against the employers and the government" *can never* satisfy revolutionists, and because opposite extremes will always arise here and there. Only a centralised, militant organisation, that consistently carries out a Social-Democratic policy, that satisfies, so to speak, all revolutionary instincts and strivings, can safeguard the movement against making thoughtless attacks and prepare it for attacks that hold out the promise of success.

It is further argued against us that the views on organisation here expounded contradict the "principles of democracy." Now while the first mentioned accusation was of purely Russian origin, this one is of *purely foreign* origin. And only an organisation abroad (the League of Russian Social-Democrats) would be capable of giving its editorial board instructions like the following:

> *Principles of Organisation.* In order to secure the successful development and unification of Social-Democracy, broad democratic principles of party organisation must be emphasised, developed and fought for; and this is particularly necessary in view of the anti-democratic tendencies that have become revealed in the ranks of our party. [*Two Congresses,* p. 18.]

. . . Every one will probably agree that "broad principles of democracy" presupposes the two following conditions: first, full publicity and second, election to all functions. It would be absurd to speak about democracy without publicity, that is a publicity that extends beyond the circle of the membership of the organisation. We call the German Socialist Party a democratic organisation because all it does is done publicly; even its party congresses are held in public. But no one would call an organisation that is hidden from every one but its members by a veil of secrecy, a democratic organisation. What is the use of advancing *"broad* principles of democracy" when the fundamental condition for this principle *cannot be fulfilled* by a secret organisation. "Broad principles" turns out to be a resonant, but hollow phrase. . . .

Nor is the situation with regard to the second attribute of democracy, namely, the principle of election, any better. In politically free countries, this condition is taken for granted. "Membership of the party is open to those who accept the principles of the party programme, and render all the support they can to the party"—says paragraph 1 of the rules of the German Social-Democratic Party. And as the political arena is as open to the public view as is the stage in a theatre, this acceptance or non-acceptance, support or opposition, is announced to all in the press and at public meetings. Every one knows that a certain political worker commenced in a certain way, passed through a certain evolution, behaved in difficult periods in a certain way; every one knows all his qualities, and consequently, knowing all the facts of the case, *every party member can decide for himself whether or not to elect this person for a certain party office.* The general control (in the literal sense of the term) that the party exercises over every act this person commits on the political field brings into being an automatically operating mechanism which brings about what in biology is called "survival of the fittest." "Natural selection," full publicity, the principle of election and general control provide the guarantee that, in the last analysis, every political worker will be "in his proper place," will do the work for which he is best fitted, will feel the effects of his mistakes on himself, and prove before all the world his ability to recognise mistakes and to avoid them.

Try to put this picture in the frame of our autocracy! Is it possible in Russia for all those "who accept the principles of the party programme and render it all the support they can," to control every action of the revolutionist working in secret? Is it possible for all the revolutionists to elect one of their number to any particular office when, in the very interests of the work, he *must conceal his identity* from nine out of ten of these "all"? Ponder a little over the real meaning of the high-sounding phrases that *Rabocheye Dyelo* gives utterance to, and you will realise that "broad democracy" in party organisation, amidst the gloom of autocracy and the domination of the gendarmes, is nothing more than a *useless and harmful toy*. It is a useless toy, because as a matter of fact, no revolutionary organisation has ever practiced *broad* democracy, nor could it, however much it desired to do so. It is a harmful toy, because any attempt to practice the "broad principles of democracy" will simply facilitate the work of the police in making big raids, it will perpetuate the prevailing primitiveness, divert the thoughts of the practical workers from the serious and imperative task of training themselves to become professional revolutionists to that of drawing up detailed "paper" rules for election systems. . . .

The only serious organisational principle the active workers of our movement can accept is: Strict secrecy, strict selection of members, and the training of professional revolutionists. If we possessed these qualities, "democracy" and something even more would be guaranteed to us, namely: Complete, comradely, mutual confidence among revolutionists. And this something more is absolutely essential for us because, in Russia, it is useless to think that democratic control can serve as a substitute for it. It would be a great mistake to believe that because it is impossible to establish real "democratic" control, the members of the revolutionary organisation will remain altogether uncontrolled. They have not the time to think about the toy forms of democracy (democracy within a close and compact body enjoying the complete mutual confidence of the comrades), but they have a lively sense of their *responsibility,* because they know from experience that an organisation of real revolutionists will stop at nothing to rid itself of an undesirable member. Moreover, there is a very well-developed public opinion in Russian (and international) revolutionary circles which has a long history behind it, and which sternly and ruthlessly punishes every departure from the duties of comradeship (and does not "democracy," real and not toy democracy, represent a part of the conception of comradeship?). Take all this into consideration and you will realise that all the talk and resolutions that come from abroad about "anti-democratic tendencies" has a nasty odour of the playing at generals that goes on there.

STATE AND REVOLUTION

V. I. LENIN

This pamphlet, written during World War I and completed while Lenin was in exile following the March revolution, is presented here in abridged and rearranged form.

In his Preface, dated August 1917, Lenin wrote: "The unheard-of horrors and miseries of the protracted war are making the position of the masses unbearable and increasing their indignation. An international proletarian revolution is clearly rising. The question of its relation to the state is acquiring a practical importance."

So far as the impact on the Russian revolution was concerned, with some ambiguity, he commented that "The Revolution is evidently completing the first stage of its development" and added, "but, generally speaking, this revolution can be understood in its totality only as a link in the chain of Socialist proletarian revolutions called forth by the imperialist war."

Marx's doctrines are now undergoing the same fate which, more than once in the course of history, has befallen the doctrines of other revolutionary thinkers and leaders of oppressed classes struggling for emancipation. During the lifetime of great revolutionaries, the oppressing classes have invariably meted out to them relentless persecution, and received their teaching with the most savage hostility, most furious hatred, and a ruthless campaign of lies and slanders. After their death, however, attempts are usually made to turn them into harmless saints, canonizing them, as it were, and investing their name with a certain halo by way of "consolation" to the oppressed classes, and with the object of duping them; while at the same time emasculating and vulgarizing the real essence of their revolutionary theories and blunting their revolutionary edge. At the present time the bourgeoisie and the opportunists within the Labor Movement are co-operating in this work of adulterating Marxism. They omit, obliterate, and distort the revolutionary side of its teaching, its revolutionary soul, and push to the foreground and extol what is, or seems, acceptable to the bourgeoisie. . . .

THE STATE AS THE PRODUCT OF THE IRRECONCILABILITY OF CLASS ANTAGONISMS

Let us begin with the most popular of Engels' works, *The Origin of the Family, Private Property, and the State*. Summarizing his historical analysis Engels says:

The State in no way constitutes a force imposed on Society from outside. Nor is the State "the reality of the Moral Idea," "the image and reality of Reason," as Hegel asserted. The State is the product of Society at a certain stage of its development. The State is tantamount to an acknowledgment that the given society has become entangled in an insoluble contradiction with itself, that it has broken up into irreconcilable antagonisms, of which it is powerless to rid itself. And in order that these antagonisms, these classes with their opposing economic interests, may not devour one another and Society itself in their sterile struggle, some force standing, seemingly, above Society, becomes necessary so as to moderate the force of their collisions and to keep them within the bounds of "order." And this force arising from Society, but placing itself above it, which gradually separates itself from it—this force is the State.

Here, we have, expressed in all its clearness, the basic idea of Marxism on the question of the historical role and meaning of the State. The State is the product and the manifestation of the irreconcilability of class antagonisms. When, where and to what extent the State arises, depends directly on when, where and to what extent the class antagonisms of a given society cannot be objectively reconciled. And, conversely, the existence of the State proves that the class antagonisms *are* irreconcilable. . . .

According to Marx, the State is the organ of class *domination,* the organ of oppression of one class by another. Its aim is the creation of order which legalizes and perpetuates this oppression by moderating the collisions between the classes. But in the opinion of the petty-bourgeois politicians, the establishment of order is equivalent to the reconciliation of classes, and not to the oppression of one class by another. To moderate their collisions does not mean, according to them, to deprive the oppressed class of certain definite means and methods in its struggle for throwing off the yoke of the oppressors, but to conciliate it. . . .

But what is forgotten or overlooked is this:—If the State is the product of the irreconcilable character of class antagonisms, if it is a force standing above society and "separating itself gradually from it," then it is clear that the liberation of the oppressed class is impossible without a violent revolution, and without the destruction of the machinery of State power, which has been created by the governing class and in which this "separation" is embodied. . . .

BOURGEOIS DEMOCRACY

In capitalist society, under the conditions most favorable to its development, we have a more or less complete democracy in the form of a democratic republic. But this democracy is always bound by the narrow framework of capitalist exploitation, and consequently always remains, in reality, a democracy only for the minority, only for the possessing classes, only for the rich. Freedom in capitalist society always remains more or less the same as it was in the ancient Greek republics, that is, freedom for the slave owners. The modern wage-slaves, in virtue of the conditions of capitalist exploitation, remain to such an extent crushed by want and poverty that they "cannot be bothered with democracy," have "no time for politics"; so that, in the ordinary peaceful course of events, the majority of the population is debarred from participating in public political life. . . .

Democracy for an insignificant minority, democracy for the rich—that is the democracy of capitalist society. If we look more closely into the mechanism of capitalist democracy, everywhere—in the so-called "petty" details of the suffrage (the residential qualification, the exclusion of women, etc.), in the technique of the representative institutions, in the actual obstacles to the right of meeting (public buildings are not for the "poor"), in the purely capitalist organization of the daily press, etc., etc.—on all sides we shall see restrictions upon restrictions of democracy. These restrictions, exceptions, exclusions, obstacles for the poor, seem slight—especially in the eyes of one who has himself never known want, and has never lived in close contact with the oppressed classes in their hard life, and nine-tenths, if not ninety-nine hundredths, of the bourgeois publicists and politicians are of this class! But in their sum these restrictions exclude and thrust out the poor from politics and from an active share in democracy. Marx splendidly grasped the *essence* of capitalist democracy, when, in his analysis of the experience of the Commune, he said that the oppressed are allowed, once every few years to decide which particular representatives of the oppressing class are to represent and repress them in Parliament! . . .

In a democratic Republic, Engels wrote, "wealth wields its power indirectly, but all the more effectively," first, by means of "direct corruption of the officials" (America); second, by means of "the alliance of the government with the stock exchange" (France and America). At the present time, imperialism and the domination of the banks have reduced to a fine art both these methods of defending and practically asserting the omnipotence of wealth in democratic Republics of all descriptions. . . .

We must also note that Engels quite definitely regards universal suffrage as a means of capitalist domination. Universal suffrage, he says (summing up obviously the long experience of German Social-Democracy), is "an index of the maturity of the working class; it cannot, and never will, give anything more in the present state." The petty-bourgeois democrats such as our Socialist-Revolutionaries and Mensheviks and also their twin brothers, the Social-Chauvinists and opportunists of Western Europe, all expect a "great deal" from this universal suffrage. They themselves think and instil into the minds of the people the wrong idea that universal suffrage in the "present state" is really capable of expressing the will of the majority of the laboring masses and of securing its realization. . . .

Take any parliamentary country, from America to Switzerland, from France to England, Norway and so forth; the actual work of the State is done behind the scenes and is carried out by the departments, the chancelleries and the staffs. Parliament itself is given up to talk for the special purpose of fooling the "common people." . . .

Two more points. First: when Engels says that in a democratic republic, "not a whit less" than in a monarchy, the State remains an "apparatus for the oppression of one class by another," this by no means signifies that the *form* of oppression is a matter of indifference to the proletariat, as some anarchists "teach." A wider, more free and open form of the class struggle and class oppression enormously assists the proletariat in its struggle for the annihilation of all classes.

Second: only a new generation will be able completely to scrap the ancient lumber of the State—this question is bound up with the question of overcoming democracy, to which we now turn.

DICTATORSHIP OF THE PROLETARIAT

The forms of bourgeois States are exceedingly various, but their substance is the same and in the last analysis inevitably the *Dictatorship of the Bourgeoisie.* The transition from capitalism to Communism will certainly bring a great variety and abundance of political forms, but the substance will inevitably be: the *Dictatorship of the Proletariat.* . . .

The State is a particular form of organization of force; it is the organization of violence for the purpose of holding down some class. What is the class which the proletariat must hold down? It can only be, naturally, the exploiting class, i.e., the bourgeoisie. The toilers need the State only to overcome the resistance of the exploiters, and only the proletariat can guide this suppression and bring it to fulfillment, for the proletariat is the only class that is thoroughly revolutionary, the only class that can unite all the toilers and the exploited in the struggle against the bourgeoisie, for its complete displacement from power. . . .

But the dictatorship of the proletariat—that is, the organization of the advance-guard of the oppressed as the ruling class, for the purpose of crushing the oppressors—cannot produce merely an expansion of democracy. *Together* with an immense expansion of democracy—for the first time becoming democracy for the poor, democracy for the people, and not democracy for the rich—the dictatorship of the proletariat will produce a series of restrictions of liberty in the case of the oppressors, exploiters and capitalists. We must crush them in order to free humanity from wage-slavery; their resistance must be broken by force. It is clear that where there is suppression there must also be violence, and there cannot be liberty or democracy. . . .

The replacement of the bourgeois by the proletarian State is impossible without a violent revolution. . . . There is [in *Anti-Dühring*] a disquisition on the nature of a violent revolution; and the historical appreciation of its role becomes, with Engels, a veritable panegyric on violent revolution. . . . Here is Engels' argument:

> That force also plays another part in history (other than that of a perpetuation of evil), namely a *revolutionary* part; that, as Marx says, it is the midwife of every old society when it is pregnant with a new one; that force is the instrument and the means by which social movements hack their way through and break up the dead and fossilized political forms—of all this not a word by Herr Dühring. Duly, with sighs and groans, does he admit the possibility that for the overthrow of the system of exploitation force may, perhaps, be necessary, but most unfortunate if you please, because all use of force, forsooth, demoralizes its user! And this is said in face of the great moral and intellectual advance which has been the result of every victorious revolution! . . . And this turbid, flabby, impotent, parson's mode of thinking dares offer itself for acceptance to the most revolutionary party which history has known!

In the *Communist Manifesto* are summed up the general lessons of history, which force us to see in the State the organ of class domination, and lead us to the inevitable conclusion that the proletariat cannot overthrow the bourgeoisie without first conquering political power, without obtaining political rule, without transforming the State into the "proletariat organized as the ruling class"; and that this proletarian State must begin to wither away immediately after its victory because in a community without class antagonisms, the State is unnecessary and impossible.

WHAT IS TO REPLACE THE SHATTERED STATE MACHINERY?

In 1847, in the *Communist Manifesto*, Marx was as yet only able to answer this question entirely in an abstract manner, stating the problem rather than its solution. To replace this machinery by "the proletariat organized as the ruling class," "by the conquest of democracy"—such was the answer of the *Communist Manifesto*. . . .

Refusing to plunge into Utopia, Marx waited for the experience of a mass movement to produce the answer to the problem as to the exact forms which this organization of the proletariat as the dominant class will assume and exactly in what manner this organization will embody the most complete, most consistent "conquest of democracy." Marx subjected the experiment of the [Paris] Commune, although it was so meagre, to a most minute analysis in his *Civil War in France*. . . .

The Commune was the direct antithesis of the Empire. It was a definite form . . . of a Republic which was to abolish, not only the monarchical form of class rule, but also class rule itself.

What was this "definite" form of the proletarian Socialist Republic? What was the State it was beginning to create? "The first decree of the [Paris] Commune was the suppression of the standing army, and the substitution for it of the armed people," says Marx. . . . But let us see how, twenty years after the Commune, Engels summed up its lessons for the fighting proletariat. . . .

Against this inevitable feature of all systems of government that have existed hitherto, viz., the transformation of the State and its organs from servants into the lords of society, the Commune used two unfailing remedies. First, it appointed to all posts, administrative, legal, educational, persons elected by universal suffrage; introducing at the same time the right of recalling those elected at any time by the decision of their electors. Secondly, it paid all officials, both high and low, only such pay as was received by any other worker. The highest salary paid by the Commune was 6,000 francs (about £240).

Thus was created an effective barrier to place-hunting and career-making, even apart from the imperative mandates of the deputies in representative institutions introduced by the Commune over and above this. . . .

The lowering of the pay of the highest State officials seems simply a naive, primitive demand of democracy. One of the "founders" of the newest opportunism, the former Social-Democrat, E. Bernstein, has more than once exercised his talents in the repetition of the vulgar capitalist jeers at "primitive" democracy. Like all opportunists, like the present followers of Kautsky, he quite failed to understand that, first of all, the transition from capitalism to Socialism is impossible without "return," in a measure, to "primitive" democracy. How can we otherwise pass on to the discharge of all the functions of government by the majority of the population and by every individual of the population. And, secondly, he forgot that "primitive democracy" on the basis of capitalism and capitalist culture is not the same primitive democracy as in pre-historic or pre-capitalist times. Capitalist culture has created industry on a large scale in the shape of factories, railways, posts, telephones, and so forth: and *on this basis* the great majority of functions of "the old State" have become enormously simplified and reduced, in practice, to very simple operations such as registration, filing and checking. Hence they will be quite within the reach of every literate person, and it will be possible to perform them for the usual "working man's wage." This circumstance ought to and will strip them of all their former glamour as "government," and, therefore, privileged service.

The control of all officials, without exception, by the unreserved application of the principle of election and, *at any time,* re-call; and the approximation of their salaries to the "ordinary pay of the workers"—these are simple and "self-evident" democratic measures, which harmonize completely the interests of the workers and the majority of peasants; and, at the same time, serve as a bridge leading from capitalism to Socialism. . . .

To organize our whole national economy like the postal system, but in such a way that the technical experts, inspectors, clerks and, indeed, all persons employed, should receive no higher wage than the working man, and the whole under the management of the armed proletariat—this is our immediate aim. This is the kind of State and the economic basis we need. This is what will produce the destruction of parliamentarism, while retaining representative institutions. This is what will free the laboring classes from the prostitution of these institutions by the capitalist class. . . .

For the mercenary and corrupt parliamentarism of capitalist society, the Commune substitutes institutions in which freedom of opinion and discussion does not become a mere delusion, for the representatives must themselves work, must themselves execute their own laws, must themselves verify their results in actual practice, must themselves be directly responsible to their electorate. Representative institutions remain, but parliamentarism as a special system, as a division of labor between the legislative and the executive functions, as creating a privileged position for its deputies, *no longer exists.* Without representative institutions we cannot imagine a democracy, even a proletarian democracy; but we can and *must* think of democracy without parliamentarism, if our criticism of capitalist society is not mere empty words, if to overthrow the supremacy of the capitalists is for us a serious and sincere aim, and not a mere "election cry" for catching working men's votes. . . .

The dictatorship of the proletariat, the period of transition to Communism, will, for the first time, produce a democracy for the people, for the majority, side by side with the necessary suppression of the minority constituted by the exploiters. Communism alone is capable of giving a really complete democracy, and the fuller it is the more quickly will it become unnecessary and wither away of itself. In other words, under capitalism we have a State in the proper sense of the word: that is, a special instrument for the suppression of one class by another, and of the majority by the minority at that. Naturally, for the successful discharge of such a task as the systematic suppression by the minority of exploiters of the majority of exploited, the greatest ferocity and savagery of suppression is required, and seas of blood are needed, through which humanity has to direct its path, in a condition of slavery, serfdom and wage labor.

Again, during the *transition* from capitalism to Communism, suppression is *still* necessary; but in this case it is suppression of the minority of exploiters by the majority of exploited. A special instrument, a special machine for suppression—that is, the "State"—is necessary, but this is now a transitional State, no longer a State in the ordinary sense of the term. For the suppression of the minority of exploiters, by the majority of those who were *but yesterday* wage slaves, is a matter comparatively so easy, simple and natural that it will cost far less bloodshed than the suppression of the risings of the slaves, serfs or wage laborers, and will cost the human race far less. And it is compatible with the diffusion of democracy over such an overwhelming majority of the nation that the need for any *special machinery* for *suppression* will gradually cease to exist. The exploiters are unable, of course, to suppress the people without a most complex machine for performing this duty; but *the people* can suppress the exploiters even with a very simple "machine"—almost without any "machine" at all, without any special apparatus—by the simple *organization of the armed masses* (such as the Councils of Workers' and Soldiers' Deputies, we may remark, anticipating a little).

Finally, only under Communism will the State become quite unnecessary, for there will be *no one* to suppress—"no one" in the sense of a *class*, in the sense of a systematic struggle with a definite section of the population. We are not utopians, and we do not in the least deny the possibility and inevitability of excesses by *individual persons,* and equally the need to suppress such excesses. But, in the first place, for this no special machine, no special instrument of repression is needed. This will be done by the armed nation itself, as simply and as readily as any crowd of civilized people, even in modern society, parts a pair of combatants or does not allow a woman to be outraged. And, secondly, we know that the fundamental social cause of excesses which violate the rules of social life is the exploitation of the masses, their want and their poverty. With the removal of this chief cause, excesses will inevitably begin to "wither away." We do not know how quickly and in what stages, but we know that they will be withering away. With their withering away, the State will also wither away.

THE "WITHERING AWAY" OF THE STATE

Engels' words regarding the "withering away" of the State enjoy such a popularity, are so often quoted, and reveal so clearly the essence of the common adulteration of Marxism in an opportunist sense that we must examine them in detail. Let us give the passage from which they are taken.

The proletariat takes control of the State authority and, first of all, converts the means of production into State property. But by this very act it destroys itself, as a proletariat, destroying at the same time all class differences and class antagonisms, and with this, also, the State.

Engels speaks here of the *destruction* of the capitalist State by the proletarian revolution, while the words about its withering away refer to the remains of a *proletarian* State *after* the Socialist revolution. The capitalist State does not wither away, according to Engels, but is *destroyed* by the proletariat in the course of the revolution. Only the proletarian State or semi-State withers away after the revolution. . . .

A general summary of his views is given by Engels in the following words:—

Thus, the State has not always existed. There were societies which did without it, which had no idea of the State or of State power. At a given stage of economic development which was necessarily bound up with the break up of society into classes, the State became a necessity, as a result of this division. We are now rapidly approaching a stage in the development of production, in which the existence of these classes is not only no longer necessary, but is becoming a direct impediment to production. Classes will vanish as inevitably as they inevitably arose in the past. With the disappearance of classes the State, too, will inevitably disappear. When organizing production anew on the basis of a free and equal association of the producers, Society will banish the whole State machine to a place which will then be the most proper one for it—to the museum of antiquities side by side with the spinning-wheel and the bronze axe.

FIRST PHASE OF COMMUNIST SOCIETY: SOCIALISM

It is this Communist society—a society which has just come into the world out of the womb of capitalism, and which, in all respects, bears the stamp of the old society—that Marx terms the first, or lower, phase of Communist society.

The means of production are now no longer the private property of individuals. The means of production belong to the whole of society. Every member of society, performing a certain part of socially-necessary labor, receives a certificate from society that he has done such and such a quantity of work. According to this certificate, he receives from the public stores of articles of consumption, a corresponding quantity of products. After the deduction of that proportion of labor which goes to the public fund, every worker, therefore, receives from society as much as he has given it.

"Equality" seems to reign supreme. . . . But different people are not equal to one another. One is strong, another is weak; one is married, the other is not. One has more children, another has less, and so on.

With equal labor [Marx concludes] and, therefore, with an equal share in the public stock of articles of consumption, one will, in reality, receive more than another, will find himself richer, and so on. To avoid all this, "rights," instead of being equal, should be unequal.

The first phase of Communism, therefore, still cannot produce justice and equality; differences and unjust differences in wealth will still exist, but the *exploitation* of one man by many, will have become impossible, because it will be impossible to seize as private property the *means of production,* the factories, machines, land, and so on. . . .

"He who does not work neither shall he eat"—this Socialist principle is *already* realized. "For an equal quantity of labor an equal quantity of products"—this Socialist principle is also already realized. Nevertheless, this is not yet Communism, and this does not abolish "bourgeois law," which gives to unequal individuals, in return for an unequal (in reality) amount of work, an equal quantity of products.

This is a "defect," says Marx, but it is unavoidable during the first phase of Communism; for, if we are not to land in Utopia, we cannot imagine that, having overthrown capitalism, people will at once learn to work for society *without any regulations by law;* indeed, the abolition of capitalism does not *immediately* lay the economic foundations for such a change. . . .

The State is withering away in so far as there are no longer any capitalists, any classes, and, consequently, any *class* whatever to suppress. But the State is not yet dead altogether, since there still remains the protection of "bourgeois law," which sanctifies actual inequality. For the complete extinction of the State complete Communism is necessary.

THE HIGHER PHASE OF COMMUNIST SOCIETY: COMMUNISM

Marx continues:

In the higher phase of Communist society, after the disappearance of the enslavement of man caused by his subjection to the principle of division of labor; when, together with this, the opposition between brain and manual work will have disappeared; when labor will have ceased to be a mere means of supporting life and will itself have become one of the first necessities of life; when with the all-round development of the individual, the productive forces, too, will have grown to maturity, and all the forces of social wealth will be pouring an uninterrupted torrent—only then will it be possible wholly to pass beyond the narrow horizon of bourgeois laws, and only then will society be able to inscribe on its banner: "From each according to his ability; to each according to his needs."

Only now can we appreciate the full justice of Engels' observations when he mercilessly ridiculed all the absurdity of combining the words "freedom" and "State." While the State exists there can be no freedom. When there is freedom there will be no State.

The economic basis for the complete withering away of the State is that high stage of development of Communism when the distinction between brain and manual work disappears; consequently, when one of the principal sources of modern *social* inequalities will have vanished—a source, moreover, which it is impossible to remove immediately by the mere conversion of the means of production into public property, by the mere expropriation of the capitalists.

This expropriation will make it possible gigantically to develop the forces of production. And seeing how incredibly, even now, capitalism *retards* this development, how much progress could be made even on the basis of modern technique at the level it has reached, we have a right to say, with the fullest confidence, that the expropriation of the capitalists will result inevitably in a gigantic development of the productice forces of human society. But how rapidly this development will go forward, how soon it will reach the point of breaking away from the division of labor, of the destruction of the antagonism between brain and manual work, of the transformation of work into a "first necessity of life"—this we do not and *cannot* know.

Consequently, we are right in speaking solely of the inevitable withering away of the State, emphasizing the protracted nature of this process, and its dependence upon the rapidity of development of the *higher phase* of Communism; leaving quite open the question of lengths of time, or the concrete forms of this withering away, since material for the solution of such questions is not available.

The State will be able to wither away completely when society has realized the formula: "From each according to his ability; to each according to his needs"; that is when people have become accustomed to observe the fundamental principles of social life, and their labor is so productive, that they will voluntarily work *according to their abilities*. "The narrow horizon of bourgeois law," which compels one to calculate, with the pitilessness of a Shylock, whether one has not worked half-an-hour more than another, whether one is not getting less pay than another—this narrow horizon will then be left behind. There will then be no need for any exact calculation by society of the quantity of products to be distributed to each of its members; each will take freely "according to his needs." . . .

The scientific difference between Socialism and Communism is clear. That which is generally called Socialism is termed by Marx the first or lower phase of Communist society. In so far as the means of production become public property, the word Communism is also applicable here, providing that we do not forget that it is not full Communism. . . .

By what stages, by means of what practical measures humanity will proceed to this higher aim—this we do not and cannot know. But it is important that one should realize how infinitely mendacious is the usual capitalist representation of Socialism as something lifeless, petrified, fixed once for all. In reality, it is only with Socialism that there will commence a rapid, genuine, real mass advance, in which first the majority and then the *whole* of the population will take part—an advance in all domains of social and individual life.

LENIN AND COMMUNISM

GEORGE H. SABINE*

LENIN'S RELATION TO MARXISM

Lenin's Marxism was in the last degree dogmatic and orthodox, supported by the *ipsissima verba* of the master and designed in large part to provide a creed for a fighting organization of professional revolutionists. Yet it was responsible for the most considerable changes that any follower of Marx ever made in the master's teaching. Lenin professed a regard, almost a reverence, for theory as an indispensable part of the equipment of a revolutionary movement. He conceived of theory as a guide to action, not as a body of statically true doctrine, but as a mass of suggestive ideas, to be recognized and picked out in a concrete situation, to be used in assessing its possibilities, and to be modified in the application. There is no doubt that Lenin was a genius in adapting both his thought and his action to circumstances, while at the same time he continued to pursue what he believed to be the essentials of his program.

It was this remarkable combination of suppleness and rigidity that made him an incomparable leader. He could follow a policy almost to the breaking-point but not quite; he could change before either his followers or his opponents knew that a crisis had occurred; he could give way when he must and come back when he could; and always he could make a change of front appear as the logical next step in a prearranged program of advance. Often it is difficult to tell what was a valid application of principles, what was legitimate recognition of new facts, and what was sheer opportunism. Opportunism in respect to the philosophy of Marx was the theme of Lenin's bitterest and most constant condemnation. Yet the changes that he made even in Marxian theory were certainly very considerable, and it is doubtful whether Lenin himself always appreciated their extent.

Stalin[1] has said that there are three interpretations of Lenin's relation to Marx, all at least partially correct. The first is that he reverted from the final form of Marx's philosophy, stated mainly in *Capital*, to its more revolutionary form contained in the early pamphlets. It is true that one of Lenin's chief purposes was to save Marxism from the opportunists and

---

* Professor Emeritus of Philosophy at Cornell University. The selection is from pp. 719-738, 741-742 of *A History of Political Theory*, First Edition, by George H. Sabine. By permission of Henry Holt & Co., Inc., Copyright 1937.

[1] *Leninism*, Eng. trans. by E. and C. Paul (London, 1928), p. 13,

make it again a revolutionary creed, and references to *Capital* were comparatively few in his works. But in itself this says nothing about Lenin; he was certainly not interested in substituting one literary tradition for another. The second interpretation is that he adapted Marxism to the state of affairs in Russia, and this also is true, since his life was spent as a leader of one branch of the Russian socialist party and most of what he wrote had to do with that party or with the Russian Revolution. But this interpretation, if taken as a sufficient account of his work, is equivalent to saying that, from his own point of view, Lenin's work was a failure. For he certainly believed that Marxism was a general social philosophy having more than merely a national application. The third interpretation of Lenin's work is that it brought Marx down to date, taking account of the further evolution of capitalist society and reformulating the theory and the tactics of Marxism in the light of developments of which Marx saw only the beginning. From this point of view Lenin's philosophy is regarded as Marxism in the latest or imperialist stage of the capitalist system, and the modifications which he made are merely the perfecting of the system. This is certainly the light in which Lenin himself would wish his ideas to be viewed.

It is true that some of Lenin's most important and characteristic doctrines had to do with the organization and tactics proper to the Russian socialist party and that the part which he was finally able to play in Russia in 1917 depended upon his leadership, during the preceding fifteen years, of one wing of that party. Organized in 1898 as the organ of the urban proletariat and largely with the purpose of substituting revolutionary mass-tactics for sporadic acts of violence, the party at once divided into two factions which, by the accident of their relative strength in the party convention of 1903, came to be known as Bolshevik and Menshevik (majority and minority, respectively). The differences between the two factions turned upon the nature of the organization most suitable to the new party, and Lenin led the group that stood for a tight organization under rigid discipline, not too large for secrecy, and providing leadership for the less class-conscious but potentially revolutionary masses in the trade-unions and among the workers. This question of party organization formed the subject of Lenin's first important work, the pamphlet entitled *What Is To Be Done?* The conclusion reached is suggested in the following passage:

A small, compact core, consisting of reliable, experienced and hardened workers, with responsible agents in the principal districts and connected by all the rules of strict secrecy with the organizations of revolutionists, can, with the wide support of the masses and without an elaborate set of rules, perform all the functions of a trade-union organization, and perform them, moreover, in the manner Social Democrats desire.

TRADE-UNIONIST AND SOCIALIST IDEOLOGY

Though *What Is To Be Done?* has to do chiefly with the question of organization, it touches, and very characteristically, upon important points of Marxian theory. Lenin's opponents objected that his limited, rigidly disciplined party was a virtual denial of the Marxian principle that the relations of production in capitalism form the proletarian class and its characteristic revolutionary ideology. Hence, they argued, a revolutionary movement must arise spontaneously; it cannot be "made," since neither force nor exhortation can run ahead of the underlying industrial conditions upon which the proletarian state of mind depends. Lenin met this argument, which had certainly the color of sound Marxism, with a flat denial. The argument, he asserted, confuses the mentality of trade-unionism with that of socialism. Spontaneously the workers do not become socialists but trade-unionists; socialism has to be brought to them from the outside by middle-class intellectuals.

We said that *there could not yet be* Social-Democratic consciousness among the workers [in the Russian strikes in the 1890's]. This consciousness could only be brought to them from without. The history of all countries shows that the working class, exclusively by its own effort, is able to develop only trade-union consciousness, *i.e.,* it may itself realize the necessity for combining in unions, to fight against the employers and to strive to compel the government to pass necessary labor legislation, etc.

The socialist theory of Marx and Engels, he continued, was created by educated representatives of the bourgeois intelligentsia and it was introduced into Russia by the same group. A trade-union movement is incapable of developing an ideology for itself and in consequence the choice must lie between allowing it to fall a prey to the ideology of the middle class or indoctrinating it with the ideology of socialist intellectuals.

It is true that this contrast between socialism and the spontaneously developed mentality of the working class was not altogether of Lenin's making and that he was able to quote a passage from Kautsky to support it. It referred to a deep-seated uncertainty in Marx's philosophy: the relation between the nonvoluntary effects of economic conditions in producing a mentality characteristic of social classes and the voluntary efforts of individuals to modify or direct the ideological results of those conditions. Many critics had asked, If socialism is inevitable, why work for it? The vigor of socialist parties had sometimes been sapped by too much dependence on natural growth. Though Lenin was touching an old question, he was raising it in a peculiarly provocative form. For if the growth of capitalist production creates in the proletariat only the mentality that makes trade-union tactics possible, the Marxian principle that all ideology is a superstructure built upon the foundation of production-relations apparently ought to imply that trade-unionism is the final answer of the proletariat to capitalism.

Nothing could be farther from Marx's meaning. On the other hand, if socialism and a socialist ideology must be produced by a bourgeois intelligentsia and introduced into the proletariat "from the outside," what can it mean to say that material conditions of production and not "ideas" are the effective causes of social revolution? And still more difficult to understand, why should capitalist production, which creates the opposed bourgeois and proletarian classes and their ideologies, bring into existence a middle-class intelligentsia devoted to the task of making an ideology for the proletariat? Either the class-struggle does not wholly determine the mentality of the class or else it produces in the middle class a perverted form of class-consciousness that devotes itself to the destruction of the class.

Lenin's conception of the party and its relation to a proletarian movement was intelligible in the light of the situation in Russia, but it was doubtfully Marxian. Marx's emphasis had always been upon the evolution of class-consciousness under the influence of the relations of production, and apparently he always assumed that his own philosophy represented the ideology that capitalist production tended to create in the working-class. This philosophy can only "shorten and lessen the birth-pangs"; it cannot help a society to "overleap the natural phases of evolution." Lenin's conception was in principle quite different. Not only in Russia—a country in which, as he repeatedly said, Marxism is peculiarly in danger of being perverted by the ideas of the petty bourgeoisie—but everywhere the working class is unable to work out an ideology of its own. It is hung between two ideologies, that of the bourgeoisie and that of the middle-class socialist intelligentsia. Its fate is to be captured by one or the other and the essential tactical problem of the party is to capture it.

The argument ran parallel to one that Marx had used in another connection, that the peasantry and petty bourgeoisie, having no future in a developing capitalist society, must fall under the control either of capitalists or proletarians and ultimately of the latter. Lenin used this argument of the proletariat itself. The result is that for him the rôle of the party became enormously more important, since it became responsible for a spread of socialist ideology that Marx regarded as largely a normal result of the class-struggle itself, and that the rôle of intellectuals in the party was correspondingly magnified, since they had to bring this ideology to the working class "from the outside." This explains the great importance that Lenin always attached to theory as the guide of tactics. The party became a picked body of the intellectual and moral élite, in the midst of all working-class movements, to be sure, and providing leadership, but always distinguishable from the body of workers. It seems clear that, even as early as 1902, and quite without reference to imperialist capitalism, Lenin had evolved a theory of the party which does not follow from anything in Marx and is even incompatible with what most socialists thought that Marx meant.

THE SOLIDARITY OF THE PARTY

The communist party thus becomes a staff-organization in the struggle of the proletarian class for power, and Marxism is the creed that holds it together, the guide of its action, and the subject-matter by which it extends the circle of class-consciousness. Ideal union through the principles of Marxism and material union through rigid organization and discipline were the two foundationstones upon which, from the beginning of his career, Lenin proposed to build a revolutionary movement. Two passages may be placed side by side to show how constantly this purpose was maintained. The first is from his pamphlet, *One Step Forward, Two Steps Backward,* published in 1904:

> The proletariat has no weapon in the struggle for power except organization. . . . Constantly pushed down to the depths of complete poverty the proletariat can and will inevitably become an unconquerable force only as a result of this: that its ideological union by means of the principles of Marxism is strengthened by the material union of an organization, holding together millions of toilers in the army of the working class.

The second is from a resolution adopted at a congress of the Communist International in 1920:

> The Communist Party is part of the working class: its most progressive, most class-conscious and therefore most revolutionary part. The Communist Party is created by means of selection of the best, most class-conscious, most self-sacrificing, and far-sighted workers. . . . The Communist Party is the lever of political organization, with the help of which the more progressive part of the working class directs on the right path the whole mass of the proletariat and the semi-proletariat.[2]

Obviously within the party individual freedom, not only of action but of opinion, must be strictly subordinated to discipline and unity of command. For ideology is itself part of the class-struggle, an ideal agency of discipline and organization. Nothing can surpass the dogmatism with which at all times, from 1902 on, Lenin asserted the integrity of the Marxian philosophy and its revolutionary value.

> To belittle socialist ideology *in any way,* to *deviate from it in the slightest degree,* means strengthening bourgeois ideology.[3]

Freedom of criticism is opportunism, eclecticism, and absence of principle, a kind of "Bernstein revisionism."

[2] These two passages are quoted by W. H. Chamberlin, *The Russian Revolution, 1917-1921,* Vol. II (New York, 1935), p. 361.
[3] *What Is To Be Done?* The italics are Lenin's.

We are marching in a compact group along a precipitious and difficult path, firmly holding each other by the hand. We are surrounded on all sides by enemies, and are under their almost constant fire. We have combined voluntarily; especially for the purpose of fighting the enemy and not to retreat into the adjacent marsh. . . . And now several in our crowd begin to cry out—let us go into this marsh! [4]

In part, then, "theory" meant for Lenin a creed, a dogma to be held integrally and unswervingly as part of the tactics of battle. Yet it would be easy to quote an equal number of passages in which he asserted that theory is the guide of action, subject to the vicissitudes of life and circumstance and to be changed remorselessly as occasion demands. In the pamphlet *One Step Forward, Two Steps Backward,* he tells of his delight in the seemingly discouraging wrangling of party-conferences:

Opportunity for open fighting. Opinions expressed. Tendencies revealed. Groups defined. Hands raised. A decision taken. A stage passed through. Forward! That's what I like! That's life! It is something different from the endless, wearying intellectual discussions, which finish, not because people have solved the problem, but simply because they have got tired of talking.[5]

This fixed faith in the constancy of principles, coupled with freedom of controversy within the bounds fixed, is almost like scholasticism. . . .

IMPERIALIST CAPITALISM

The outbreak of the World War turned Lenin's attention more definitely toward international affairs and led to the formulation of his theory of the imperialist war and of communism in the imperialist stage of capitalism, which must be regarded as his chief contribution to Marxist theory.[6] The war brought to a head all the smoldering differences that had divided socialists for years, such as the support of national interests, the voting of war-credits, and participation in bourgeois governments. After a little hesitation nearly all socialists fell in behind their national governments. Lenin, an exile in Switzerland, stood out and belabored the opportunism and chauvinism of the Second International for its betrayal of socialism. In this he continued the attacks which he had been making for years upon every form of revisionism, only now he included in his condemnation nearly all socialists everywhere, except his own wing of the Russian party and a few other dissenters like Karl Liebknecht and Rosa Luxemburg in Germany. From the beginning Lenin argued that the attempt to apportion guilt among the belligerent nations was nonsense, that all were dominated

---

[4] *Ibid.*

[5] Quoted by Lenin's wife, N. K. Krupskaya, *Memories of Lenin,* Eng. trans. by E. Verney (New York, 1930), pp. 102 f.

[6] See the *Collected Works,* Vols. XVIII and XIX, especially *Under a Stolen Flag, Socialism and War* (with G. Zinoviev), *Imperialism: The Highest Stage of Capitalism;* also Bukharin's *Imperialism and World Economy* (New York, 1929). These were written in 1915 and first published after the March Revolution in 1917.

by the same kind of economic motives, and that the war was essentially a capitalist quarrel about the division of booty. In this quarrel the working class of no nation has any vital concern; certainly, he said, the Russian workers have no interest in taking away the spoils of one young robber (Germany) in order to give it to two old ones (England and France). But Lenin was at no time a pacifist. His object from the first was to "turn the imperialist war into a civil war."

The "betrayal of socialism" by the socialists was obviously an anomaly from the point of view of Marx's philosophy as it was commonly understood. For the class-struggle ought to have been growing sharper and society more clearly divided into bourgeoisie and proletariat as capitalism developed. Hence Lenin, as the most rigid of Marxians and the enemy of all revisionism, must supplement the theory to account for what appeared like a gross exception. He began with an unquestionable historical fact: the period after 1871 was mainly one in which socialist parties had grown by peaceful means to a size where they could hope to succeed by parliamentary tactics. Inevitably there was an infiltration of petty bourgeois membership and ideology, and the substitution of trade-union for revolutionary tactics. But since ideology must follow the relations of production, this fact itself needs to be traced back to the inherent development of the capitalist system. This Lenin accomplished by supposing that in the successful imperialist countries the expansion of markets and the increase of production had enabled a small part of the workers, especially in the skilled trades, to profit. This produced between 1871 and 1914 a kind of backwash in the class-struggle. A small but influential part of the workers joined with the capitalists to exploit the great mass of unskilled workers, especially workers in backward countries and colonies. The ideology of this movement was petty bourgeois. It fell a victim to the illusion of peaceful evolution and the harmony of class-interests. This theory may well have been suggested to Lenin by Engels' observations on the British labor-movement and the effect of foreign trade upon it.

This secondary movement in the class-struggle was thus due to the peculiar qualities of capitalism in the period, and these in turn corresponded definitely to a certain stage in the development of the capitalist system as a whole. In his description of this imperialist stage of capitalism Lenin assembled a number of characteristics that had been described by many authors before him, both socialist and non-socialist, expanding Marx's account of capitalist accumulation. The units in which industry is organized steadily tend to grow larger until they become monopolies, either of a whole industry or of a vertical string of related industries. The market becomes world-wide and prices both of commodities and of labor tend to be fixed in the world-market. Competition practically ceases within the nation and so loses the power to keep down prices, while more and more it assumes the form of rivalry between national monopolies. At the same time tariffs cease to nourish infant industries and become weapons in national trade-wars. With the formation of industrial combinations banking capital is fused with industrial capital, and industry comes more and more under bankers' control. Capital itself becomes a significant item of export. The steady pressure for larger markets and the demand for raw materials, both inherent in the expansion of capitalist production, result in an international scramble for undeveloped territory and the control of backward peoples. In international politics the vital question becomes the partition of exploitable territory and population; in internal politics capitalist control becomes more direct, with the result that parliamentary institutions become more and more a sham. Reduced to its essentials an imperialist war, such as that begun in 1914, is a struggle between syndicates of German capitalists with their subsidiaries and syndicates of allied French and English capitalists with their subsidiaries for the control of Africa. To be sure, eddies and backwashes occur, as in the hope of Russian capitalists to get Constantinople or of the Japanese to exploit China; in the backward nations there are even *bona fide* nationalist movements, as in Serbia or India.

THE IMPERIALIST WAR

Now the purpose of Marxian theory is to provide a guide to proletarian tactics, and tactics must be fitted to the nature of the epoch in which they are used. The theory of imperialist capitalism enabled Lenin to advance a new theory of the significant periods in the evolution of European society. The turning-points he took to be 1871—fixed apparently by the Paris Commune, the last important revolutionary outbreak—and 1914, the beginning of the first imperialist war. Between the French Revolution and 1871 capitalism was on an ascending curve and the bourgeoisie was a progressive class, compared with the remnants of feudalism which it displaced. In this period it produced its characteristic—and, in their time and place, its valuable—social and political consequences, notably the democratization of government and the liberation of nationalities. The proletariat was in a process of formation and was therefore obliged to adjust itself to the expanding power of the bourgeoisie. Consequently it was sound socialist tactics to inquire, as Marx did in 1859, whether the international interests of the proletariat would be best served by the success of Austria or France. War in this period was, by and large, an agency in the forming and freeing of nationalities, and socialists could logically cooperate with this process. The period from 1871 to 1914 was, so to speak, the flat top of the curve, the age of capitalist domination and incipient decay, in which the class-struggle was confused by a false appearance of conciliation and the capitalist organization of society took on the monopolist and imperialist characteristics just described.

In 1914 the World War signalized the end of this period, the beginning of the precipitate fall of the curve of capitalism. The bourgeoisie has now become a decaying and reactionary class, interested not in production but in consumption, with the typical psychology of the *rentier*,[7] and following a policy imposed on it by finance-capitalism. In this period there must occur a series of imperialist convulsions, of which the war is the first but not necessarily the last, and in it the situation has again become definitely revolutionary from the point of view of a proletarian party. In 1914 a progressive bourgeoisie is ridiculous; there can be no question of an alliance between the proletariat and any group of national imperialist capitalists; the purpose of the working class must be the overthrow—almost certainly by violence[8]—of international finance capitalism.

By this very able supplementation and extension of Marx's analysis of capitalism, Lenin could interpret the existing national and international situation by means of the categories provided in the Marxian system. The opposing interests of imperialist national groupings could be presented as the outgrowth of "contradictions" between the productive forces of industry and the restraints imposed on it by an outworn ideology, and the imminence of a proletarian revolution could be deduced as Marx had already deduced it in the 1840's. According to Lenin, the contradiction in 1914 lies substantially between the international nature of industry and the restraints imposed by national political divisions. The ruling class which controls production, and labor as well, is divided into national groups with competing interests that have no counterpart in the system of production itself. National states, under the control of these artifical groupings, have become a clog upon the normal development of production. The new ideology of national solidarity and self-sufficiency, with the corresponding policies of tariff-exclusion and national monopoly, stands square across the path of expansion appropriate to the economic system, and this expansion appears in the perverted form of imperialist annexation. Inevitably, according to the theory, the underlying forces of production must assert their mastery. The war will centralize political power, destroy small states, and expand monopoly. But it will also bring the class-struggle, as one of the permanent forces of capitalist society, back to its normal proportions, temporarily distorted by imperialism.

The war severs the last chain that binds the workers to the masters, their slavish submission to the imperialist state. The last limitation of the proletariat's philosophy is being overcome: its clinging to the narrowness of the national state, its patriotism. The interests of the moment, the temporary advantage accruing to it from the imperialist robberies and from its connections with the imperialist state,

---

[7] Cf. Bukharin's analysis of Böhm-Bawerk's theory of value as representing the ideology of a consuming class; *The Economic Theory of the Leisure Class*, New York, 1927. The book was written in 1914 before the War and first published in 1919.

[8] Kautsky was arguing that the peaceful development of a world-economy within the capitalist system was possible.

become of secondary importance compared with the lasting and general interests of the class as a whole, with the idea of a social revolution of the international proletariat which overthrows the dictatorship of finance capital with an armed hand, destroys its state apparatus and builds up a new power, a power of the workers against the bourgeoisie.[9]

The plan of Lenin's revision, it should be noted, was that already followed by Engels in 1895 when he acknowledged, in editing Marx's pamphlet on the French Revolution of 1848, that capitalism "still had great capacity for expansion" beyond what he and Marx supposed at the earlier date. But the theory also has a remarkable capacity for expansion. What is foretold by means of it is always the end, and the revision consists in putting in new intermediate stages between the present and the end. This is hardly scientific prediction, as dialectical materialists like to believe. A predetermined end that arrives by an unknown path and after an interval of time that cannot be specified belongs rather to the realm of vitalist evolution than to that of scientific prediction. There are, of course, probabilities that make a proletarian revolution more or less likely and that give it more or less chance of success if it occurs. Such probabilities depend in no way upon dialectic, and conversely the supposed necessity of the proletarian revolution seems to have nothing to do with probability. It is envisaged as a tendency, or drive, or force directed toward a result, and capable of persisting against setbacks and counter currents. This is the sort of quality that vitalists have always attributed to the vital force and that Hegel attributed to the Idea, but there is little about it that is empirical or scientific.

BOURGEOIS AND PROLETARIAN REVOLUTION

Lenin's theory of capitalist imperialism supplied additional justification for the revolutionary tactics which he had always advocated. In 1917 the March Revolution, and his return to Russia in April, turned his attention toward the question of revolution in Russia. It led at once to an even more daring departure from what had been thought to be the implications of Marxism. The revolution which had created the Kerensky government was, by Marxian standards, a bourgeois revolution; it took power from the old nobility and gave it to the middle class. It was a settled principle of Marxism that any revolution, bourgeois or proletarian, occurs not through a sporadic application of force but must be prepared by the proper political and economic development. It followed that the bourgeois revolution must be "completed" before the proletarian revolution could properly be begun. It was this settled interpretation of Marxism that, to the astonishment of his followers and finally of Marxists everywhere, Lenin proceded to set aside as antiquated. He at once perceived that

[9] Bukharin, *Imperialism and World Economy,* Eng. trans., p. 167.

the essence of the situation in Russia was what he called "dual power," the existence side by side of the bourgeois Provisional Government and the soviets.[10] With the insight of a tactical genius he saw in this situation the possibility of an immediate revolution by the combined workers and peasants, if only these two forces could be held together. The soviets he chose to interpret as the embryo of a revolutionary dictatorship following a type set by the Paris Commune of 1871, thus spreading over them the aegis of Marxian theory, though Marxists had been, and still were, a small minority among their members.

The conception that a time of preparation must elapse between the bourgeois and the proletarian revolutions Lenin boldly relegated to "the archive of 'Bolshevik' pre-revolutionary antiques," and in the name of "living Marxism."

It is necessary to acquire that incontestable truth that a Marxist must take cognizance of living life, of the true facts of reality, that he must not continue clinging to the theory of yesterday, which, like every theory, at best only outlines the main and the general, only approximately embracing the complexity of life. . . . Whoever questions the "completeness" of the bourgeois revolution from the old viewpoint, sacrifices living Marxism to a dead letter. According to the old conception, the rule of the proletariat and peasantry, their dictatorship, can and must follow the rule of the bourgeoisie. In real life, however, things have already turned out otherwise; an extremely original, new, unprecedented interlocking of one and the other has taken place.[11]

That Lenin grasped "living life" was perhaps proved by the success of the new revolution a few months later, but it was also true that he had made a great departure from what Marx's philosophy had always been thought to mean. Nothing in the whole system was better settled than the proposition that a revolutionary ideology can be created only by the training of the proletariat in capitalist industry. The theory that politics depends upon the relations of production implies this. Marx had said that the final purpose of *Capital* was to show that no nation could "overleap the natural phases of evolution." Engels in the *Anti-Dühring* had used three chapters to show that force can do no more than supplement a revolutionary situation prepared by economic development. In 1915 Lenin had believed that a socialist revolution in Russia was impossible, though he hoped for a democratic republic there and for socialist revolutions in more advanced countries.[12] Even in 1917, before coming to Russia, he thought of a Russian revolution as a temporary expedient which might indeed fail, but which might succeed until the situation could be saved by its becoming "a prologue to the world socialist revolution." [13] His change of position, as he frankly

---

[10] *On Dual Power* and *Letters on Tactics, Collected Works,* Vol. XX, Bk. I, pp. 115 ff. Lenin had been in Petrograd less than a week.

[11] *Ibid.,* p. 121.

[12] *Collected Works,* Vol. XVIII, pp. 81 f.; 198.

[13] *Ibid.,* Vol. XX, Book I, pp. 85 f.

admitted, was an inspiration of the moment. On the other hand, it was merely an extension of the changes in Marxian theory that he had made years before. He had always considered socialist ideology as the creation of the intelligentsia rather than as a spontaneous product of industrial relations, and he had always contemplated a situation in which this ideology was actually possessed by a very small proportion of workers.

Lenin's rather abrupt reversal of an important part of traditional Marxism was helped also by his theory of capitalist imperialism. For from this point of view it was possible to argue that the chances of a revolution in any single country depended upon the international situation as well as upon its internal condition. The strain of war might well break capitalism "at its weakest point," and this need not be in those countries where capitalism itself is most highly developed. Probably, however, what carried conviction among Lenin's Russian followers in 1917 was their belief that proletarian revolution was imminent throughout Europe and that the revolution in Russia was merely a "prologue." In 1924 Trotsky and his followers still held that a proletarian revolution could not permanently succeed or be carried through completely in a single country, though by that time the continued existence of the revolutionary government had made this view a "deviation." In 1925 Stalin argued that the limitation on communism in one country was merely the risk of interference from the outside. In effect this leaves little or nothing of the older idea that societies pass through a normal series of industrial stages and that their political history and ideology follow their economic development. Thus Stalin has argued that a proletarian revolution differs from a bourgeois revolution partly by the fact that the former brings a socialist economy into existence, while a capitalist economy precedes the latter, and Bukharin has argued that in periods of revolution the course of development goes from ideology to technology, thus reversing the normal order.[14] The older theory remains, if at all, only as applied to the whole international development of capitalism and the revolutionary ideology.

The relation of socialism to political democracy forms a special phase of this general question about the preparation of the proletarian revolution, and here, too, there was a substantial difference between Lenin and Marx, or at least what other Marxists supposed that Marx meant. When Lenin returned to Russia he was the leader of a minority even among the socialists, who were themselves a minority in the bourgeois government. In Russia at large the industrial proletariat was of course a tiny minority in the whole population, and Lenin never doubted that success would fall to the party that could gain the support, or at least the acquiescence, of the peasants. He made no secret of his opposition to the Provisional Government, but until July he did not favor armed resistance to it. He repeatedly

---

[14] Stalin, *Leninism*, Eng. trans. by E. and C. Paul (London, 1928), p. 20; Bukharin, *Historical Materialism* (New York, 1925), p. 262.

denied that his group was for seizure of power by a minority or for economic reforms not ripe "in the consciousness of an overwhelming majority." But such phrases have to be taken in the light of his theory of the party, held since 1903, which contained no implication of majority-rule as a political institution. In August he came out flatly with the assertion that in politics majority-rule is a "constitutional illusion." The permanent force is the domination of a class; majority-rule is impossible unless the interests of the ruling class happen to coincide with the interests of the majority, and history is full of cases where the more organized, more class-conscious, better armed minority has forced its will upon a majority.

At the decisive moment and in the decisive place you *must prove the stronger one*, you must *be victorious.*[15]

Even in the evolution that leads up to decisive moments, majority-rule had for Lenin no virtue as a political right. It was rather a scheme of skillful compromise by which the leading minority keeps in touch with its followers.

The task of a truly revolutionary party is not to declare the impossible renunciation of all compromises, but to be able *through all compromises,* as far as they are unavoidable, to remain true to its principles, to its class, to its revolutionary task.[16]

This was in fact Lenin's most astonishing and most valuable quality as a leader, and he referred to his compromises on occasion as "democracy," but obviously they had no relation to democracy as an institution.[17] The truth is that democracy had no significant place in Lenin's conception of political evolution. On the other hand, most Marxists would have agreed that Kautsky accurately represented Marx's opinion when he said, in criticism of the Russian Revolution, that "the education of the masses, as well as of their leaders, in democracy is a necessary condition of socialism. . . ."

Lenin's Marxism presents the anomaly of being at once the most dogmatic assertion of orthodox adherence to the principles of the master and at the same time the freest rendering of it on points where circumstances required its modification. For him Marxism was at once the creed of a party, having the function of all creeds that give unity to a militant organization, and also a guide to action, to be shaped at need to new occasions. Yet the creed itself stood in the way of frankly empirical revision or the abandonment of parts in the light of new facts; if it were revised it

---

[15] *Collected Works,* Vol. XXI, Bk. I, p. 68. Lenin's italics.

[16] *Collected Works, ibid.,* p. 152.

[17] A striking example was Lenin's adoption in November, 1917, of a land-policy which he took whole from his opponents and which he fully expected to fail. For the time being he was powerless to do anything else so he made a virtue of "democracy." The later coercion of the peasants was perfectly logical from his point of view. See W. H. Chamberlin, *The Russian Revolution,* Vol. 1, p. 326.

must develop its own changes dialectically. The revisions which Lenin made were sometimes perilously close to abandonment. Retaining the strictest letter of economic determinism, according to which politics and every form of ideology must be explained ultimately by the economic system, he magnified both the rôle of the party and of the middle-class intellectual in the party, while he minimized the spontaneous creation of a socialist ideology in the proletariat by the relations of production. He abandoned the belief that capitalist development in any single country, with its attendant political manifestations, runs through a normal or standard series of stages, so that, as Marx had said, "A country in which industrial development is more advanced than in others, simply presents those others with a picture of their own future." Much of the plausibility of the contention that this was merely an extension of Marxism depended on the expectation that the proletarian revolution was about to become general, and this proved to be a mistake. In the future the theory can again be made to square with any state of the facts by adding more stages to the development of capitalism. What Lenin's career illustrated most obviously was not precision of theory but the enormous power in a crisis of a leader with character and insight, aided by even a small group of self-confident and disciplined men who are willing relentlessly to follow their convictions. This surely is a result which no logic can deduce from dialectical materialism, unless indeed it be the logic of faith.

GERMAN MARXISM AND RUSSIAN COMMUNISM

JOHN PLAMENATZ*

There is a side of Lenin's teaching which, though it adds nothing important to Marxism and no longer inspires the behavior of the Communist Party, is yet well worth studying for the insight it gives us into the character of the greatest revolutionary of our age. Lenin has been called a realist, and indeed was one, and yet was also a Utopian simpler and more credulous than most. If we look at *The State and the Revolution,* perhaps the most often read of all his pamphlets, we can see how narrow the understanding and how little the foresight of the man who, more than any other, has changed our modern world.

The State and the Revolution consists of quotations from Marx and Engels so put together and explained as to justify the revolutionary Marx-

* Fellow of Nuffield College, Oxford. Author of *The Revolutionary Movement in France, 1815-71.* The selection is from pp. 240-247 of the book by the same title, published by Longmans, Green & Co., Inc., 1954. By permission of the publisher.

ism of the Bolsheviks and confound all their critics. The too ample commentary on the quotations is a rude[1] defence of the "pure doctrine" against the Majority socialists in Germany and the Mensheviks in Russia. Lenin's pamphlet seeks to prove, against the German Social-Democrats, that Marx and Engels never ceased to be revolutionary socialists, but does not offer us a coherent theory of the state. On the contrary, it draws attention to what might otherwise have escaped notice—to the absence of any such theory in the writings of Marx and Engels; it also draws attention to other faults invisible to Lenin, to the reckless assertions and bad logic of the two men who seemed to him the most profound of thinkers.

We can find in Lenin's pamphlet arguments—as if by anticipation—against much that happened in Russia after 1920 and that Trotsky later condemned. The pamphlet is, of course, still printed in Russia and approved by the authorities, who do not think it dangerous to themselves. It is an authorized text subject to official interpretation, and therefore not to be taken literally. It has proved easy enough to teach the youth of Russia to admire it without drawing from it any inconvenient practical consequences. They are made familiar with it, and the familiarity breeds a kind of careless reverence not far removed from contempt.[2] But the fact remains that the pamphlet can be taken literally, and that those who so take it, if they happen to be Marxists, will soon find themselves looking at the Russia of Stalin through the eyes of Trotsky.

Marx produced two doctrines of the state, and would neither explain how they are connected nor abandon one of them. He said that the state is an instrument of class oppression, and also that it is often a parasitic growth on society, making class oppression possible even when the government is not the agent of any class. Lenin accepted both these doctrines without noticing that they are incompatible or attempting to adjust them to one another. He also accepted the theory of Engels that the state emerges as soon as there arise in society classes with irreconcilable interests, its function being to keep the peace between them. Lenin, like Engels, never thought it necessary to explain how it is that the peace cannot be kept except by sacrificing the interests of all classes but one to that one class. Nor did he explain how the keeping of peace within society differs from

[1] Marx was a most rude and scornful controversialist, and his disciples have mostly imitated his manners, whose freedom from "bourgeois hypocrisy" they have greatly admired. It seems not to have occurred to them that discourtesy, by causing men from motives of vanity to defend the indefensible and to waste time on irrelevancies, is a serious obstacle in the search for truth. Or if it has occurred to them, they have disregarded it in practice.

[2] We, too, are brought up in the same way. When we are young we are taught to admire the saying: "Sell all that thou hast and give to the poor." When we first hear it, it can do us no harm, for we are children with nothing to sell and nothing to give. And when we grow up, we quickly discover that the advice is impracticable. This process of inoculation against the impossible virtues, which we ought to admire but not to practise, is a usual part of nearly all education. Whether it is necessary, the psychologist must decide.

the conciliation of interests; he merely said, repeating Engels, that the function of the state is to keep the peace between "irreconcilable" classes, and to keep it in the interest of only one class among them. Lenin had fewer doubts than either of his masters and was never tempted to question their assumptions; he therefore never pondered their curious doctrine that, though the social classes have *irreconcilable* (and not merely different) interests, it is somehow possible to keep the peace between them. He quietly accepted in the way of doctrine whatever they offered him, including this far from self-evident assumption that to maintain social peace and order is not to conciliate interests. For the difference between these two functions he had never a thought to spare.[3]

In *The State and the Revolution,* Lenin repeats, again following Engels, that the existence of armies and police forces is proof enough that class interests cannot be reconciled. Special instruments must, he thinks, be created to maintain the supremacy of the ruling class. The alternative hypothesis, which is perhaps more plausible, that these instruments were first created in the common interest and then enabled those who controlled them to become a ruling class, never occurs to him, though he also repeats the argument of Engels that the state arises out of the need to hold class antagonisms in check, a need presumably felt by all the classes and whose satisfaction is therefore a common interest.

On the basis of this theory of the state—or, rather, of this collection of

---

[3] Interests are not solid things of determinate shapes, which, like the parts of a jig-saw puzzle, either can or cannot be fitted into each other. How is one man's interest reconciled with another's? There are two words of uncertain meaning in this question—"interest" and reconciled." A man's interests can surely be no more than the objects of his more persistent desires, the things for whose sake he works and makes sacrifices; and the interests of a class merely the objects of the most persistent desires common to persons having more or less the same status in society. The interests, whether of individuals or classes, very frequently conflict; if one man gets all he wants another must often get less, and so it must also be with classes. How are interests "reconciled"? They are "reconciled," presumably, whenever the men or classes that pursue them observe the rules whose general observance is social peace. How then, if the rules are observed, can interests be irreconcilable? We can perhaps say, as many philosophers have done, that the more rules are observed because they are felt to be just, the greater the harmony between men's interests; and that, conversely, the more they are observed from fear of punishment, the less that harmony. This, at least, is a distinction which makes sense; but, in that case, what becomes of the "irreconcilable" interests of different classes in a society where, say, bourgeois morality prevails? Let us suppose for a moment that some travellers' tales are true, and that American workers really do not mind their employers being ten or a hundred or even a thousand times richer than themselves, that they would rather keep their one chance in ten thousand of becoming rich than have governments, however democratically elected, take over the factories they work in; let us also suppose that they require no more of governments than that they should tax the rich to give everyone modest provision against ill-health, unemployment, and old age. Are their interests and those of their employers "irreconcilable" still? What could be meant by calling them so? When classes are at peace and little force is required to keep that peace, surely the man who calls their interests "irreconcilable" merely betrays his desire that there should be disputes where there are none, or that what disputes there are should be more bitter.

ideas about the state—Lenin seeks to establish as orthodox Marxism two propositions neglected or denied by the German Majority Socialists: 1. that the bourgeois state and all its instruments must be destroyed by the proletariat, and 2. that it is the "dictatorship of the proletariat" (that is, the proletarian and not the bourgeois state) which is destined to "wither away." There are interesting corollaries of these propositions, but they are the two major theses of the pamphlet. . . .

The bourgeois state must be destroyed because it cannot be used for proletarian purposes. Lenin's assumption is that every ruling class dominates society in its own peculiar way, and therefore requires its own political institutions, its peculiar instruments of government. The bourgeois state has a natural tendency to grow stronger and more elaborate, to become an always fatter parasite feeding on the body of society. It maintains an army, a police force and a bureaucratic machine, whose interests cannot be those of society as a whole. The bourgeois find it easy to tolerate this parasite, because, while it exists, it maintains the conditions of their economic and social supremacy.

The dictatorship of the proletariat, the workers' state or "half-state" (as Lenin sometimes called it), is not a growing parasite whose function is to maintain the social conditions of class exploitation; it is the instrument of the workers and peasants, of the great majority, who use it to destroy the last traces of class exploitation.

It is therefore the dictatorship of the proletariat and not the bourgeois state that will wither away. The workers' state is strongest at the moment of its birth, and must from that moment weaken until it dies. Lenin called it a "half-state" because its function is not to perpetuate the conditions of its own life but to destroy them. It is repressive and therefore a state; but it is also the instrument of the great majority. In the words of Lenin: "Since the majority of the people themselves suppress their oppressors, a 'special force' for suppression is no longer necessary! In this sense the state begins to wither away." In the bourgeois state, the minority exploit the majority, and the condition of this exploitation is the growing strength of certain instruments of government, of organizations that perpetuate themselves because their members have corporate interests of their own. In the proletarian state the majority suppress the minority, and, being the majority, have no need to use for instruments organizations that are self-perpetuating and parasitic. On the contrary, the organizations they use are democratically controlled, and they gradually disappear as the work of suppression is completed.

Lenin, when he wrote *The State and the Revolution,* had never had even a day's administrative experience. He had been for years a member of the Russian Social-Democratic Party, an undisciplined and quarrelsome body, and had later created his own Bolshevik organization; but he had never taken even a subordinate part in government. That is why he could write,[4] only a few months before the Bolshevik revolution, that "the great majority of the functions of the old state power have been so simplified and can be reduced to such simple operations of registration, filing and checking, that they can be easily performed by every literate person." Lenin believed that capitalism makes the tasks of government easier. Why, then, has the bourgeois state become so massive? Lenin's answer is that successive revolutions have made it so; that the parasite has fed on its host and is swollen with its blood. This was the simple answer that satisfied Lenin in 1917, when he still refused to believe that the spread of industry makes society so complex that only a large, varied and highly trained administration can control it. "We ourselves," he said, "the workers, shall organize large-scale production on the basis of what capitalism has already created . . . we shall reduce the role of state officials to a simple carrying out of our instructions as responsible, revocable, and modestly paid 'managers.' . . . Overthrow the capitalists . . . smash the bureaucratic machine of the modern state—and you will have a mechanism of the highest technical equipment, free from the parasite, capable of being operated by the workers themselves, who will hire their own technicians, managers and bookkeepers, and pay them all—as, indeed, all state officials in general— ordinary workmen's wages." Only a Bolshevik could have been so innocent in the summer of 1917.

The German Social-Democrats, of course, knew better. They had outgrown Marxism, though not the vanity that made them cling to their reputations as leading Marxists. They had hitherto not needed to reject the more irresponsible utterances of Marx and Engels; it had been enough to take little notice of them. But with the Bolsheviks in the ascendant, and their own extremists restive, they had learnt to dislike what they had previously ignored. Above all, they had come to dislike the phrase "the dictatorship of the proletariat," and now wanted to minimize its importance. Experience had taught them that the bourgeois state is not merely an instrument of class oppression, that it is not a mere parasite feeding on the social body, that the departments of the state established by the old society would be necessary to the new one; they knew, in short, what we all know when we have no special motive for refusing to admit the obvious; they knew that the government of modern industrial society is altogether too difficult to be entrusted to persons not specially trained for it. They knew that direct rule by the workers is impossible, and that the most to be hoped for is as much responsibility to them as the devices of democracy will allow. The administrative machine must not be smashed; it must be preserved and adapted to new uses. For without it socialism is impossible—socialism

---

[4] The explanation falls short of the truth. In matters so simple common sense can enlighten us even when we have no experience. Such blindness as Lenin's is the effect not of inexperience but of devotion to false doctrines.

which requires so great an intervention of public authority in the daily business of our lives. . . .

It is odd that Marx's description of the Commune, his disingenuous account of a government inspired by the doctrines of his great rival Proudhon, should have been the stone that broke in two the great international socialist movement most of whose leaders called themselves Marxists. What is less odd—for nothing is more usual than that men's actions should give the lie to their doctrines—is that, within a year or two of writing *The State and the Revolution,* Lenin should have proved that Kautsky was right after all. Lenin soon found himself obliged to establish a highly centralized administrative machine in Russia, finding that he could not govern without it. The constitution of the new Bolshevik state was federal, but that federalism was a mere pretence; all real power belonged to the closely disciplined Communist Party. Most of the old departments of state were brought to life again, albeit under new names; and the political police were soon more active than they had been under the Tsars.

Chapter 6

ENDS AND MEANS

The ultimate end envisaged by Marx of a stateless, classless society, "when, along with the all-round development of individuals, the productive forces too have grown, and all the springs of social wealth are flowing more freely," from which there will have vanished all need for organized force, and in which men will be content to contribute to society in accordance with their abilities and be rewarded according to need—however Utopian and visionary, and, in the minds of some, undesirable—is of undoubted nobility. It is an end which revolutionary anarchists and evolutionary socialists, as well as Communists, accept.

Even the more immediate theoretical end of the Communist philosophy, that is, socialism—ownership in common of the basic means of production and distribution and a planned economy—finds support among many reformists, Christian socialists, and others.

A major distinguishing characteristic of the Communist Party lies in the means it was prepared to and did in fact use and justify to seize and hold power. In State and Revolution, *Lenin, it will be recalled, insisted upon "the necessity of fostering among the masses" the belief that "the replacement of the bourgeois by the proletarian state is impossible without a violent revolution." (In this, he explicitly rejected Marx's "exceptionalism." Marx had said in 1872—a position later echoed by Engels—that "we do not deny that there are certain countries, such as the United States and England . . . in which the workers may hope to secure their ends by peaceful means.")*

Apart from Lenin's belief that capitalist power made violent proletarian revolution necessary, he insisted, in general, "that morality is wholly subordinated to the interests of the class struggle of the proletariat"—a position that was more fully developed and theoretically justified by Trotsky in Their Morals and Ours. *The far-reaching implications and consequences of the Leninist view of the relation of ends and means are discussed by Morris Raphael Cohen and Harold J. Laski.*

172

Parenthetically, reference must be made to the contemporary views of the Soviet leadership on the necessity for violent revolution to overturn capitalism and achieve socialism—although obviously these had no bearing on the tactics pursued in the Bolshevik revolution or on the theoretical position for years thereafter. In his Report for the Central Committee of the Communist Party to the 20th Congress, in February, 1956, Khrushchev stated, in pertinent part, as follows:

In connection with the radical changes in the world arena new prospects are also opening up in respect to the transition of countries and nations to socialism. . . . It is probable that more forms of transition to socialism will appear. Moreover, the implementation of these forms need not be associated with civil war under all circumstances. . . .

There is no doubt that in a number of capitalist countries the violent overthrow of the dictatorship of the bourgeoisie and the sharp aggravation of class struggle connected with this are inevitable. But the forms of social revolution vary. It is not true that we regard violence and civil war as the only way to remake society. . . . Leninism teaches us that the ruling class will not surrender its power voluntarily. And the greater or lesser degree of intensity which the struggle may assume, the use or the non-use of violence in the transition to socialism depends on the resistance of the exploiters, on whether the exploiting class itself resorts to violence, rather than on the proletariat.

In this connection the question arises of whether it is possible to go over to socialism by using parliamentary means. No such course was open to the Russian Bolsheviks, who were the first to effect this transition. . . . Since then, however, the historical situation has undergone radical changes which make possible a new approach to the question. The forces of socialism and democracy have grown immeasurably throughout the world, and capitalism has become much weaker. The mighty camp of socialism with its population of over 900 million is growing and gaining in strength. Its gigantic internal forces, its decisive advantages over capitalism, are being increasingly revealed from day to day. Socialism has a great power of attraction for the workers, peasants, and intellectuals of all countries. The ideas of socialism are indeed coming to dominate the minds of all toiling humanity. . . .

In these circumstances the working class, by rallying around itself the toiling peasantry, the intelligentsia, all patriotic forces, and resolutely repulsing the opportunist elements who are incapable of giving up the policy of compromise with the capitalists and landlords, is in a position to defeat the reactionary forces opposed to the popular interest, to capture a stable majority in parliament, and transform the latter from an organ of bourgeois democracy into a genuine instrument of the people's will. . . . In the countries where capitalism is still strong and has a huge military and police apparatus at its disposal, the reactionary forces will of course inevitably offer serious resistance. There the transition to socialism will be attended by a sharp class, revolutionary struggle.

Whether the present position of the Central Committee of the Communist Party of the Soviet Union represents a decisive break with Lenin on the necessity for violent overthrow of capitalism has been controverted. There are those who believe that the Communists are convinced of the superiority of socialism and of its ultimate appeal, that they appreciate the dangers of war, and therefore are prepared to eschew revolutionary methods.

On the other hand, typical of an opposing view is that of Stefan T. Possony who wrote:

The Communists did not forswear violence at all, provided you go to the trouble of reading the fine print. . . . The need for the application of violence against bourgeois nations with strong military and police force was reaffirmed. On the assumption that the Communists will not succeed in talking the United States into dismantling its security forces, this country will remain a strong power. Hence it will have to be subjected to violence—or else the world revolution will have to be called off. The Communists continue to proclaim that the revolution will occur. Hence if logic means anything, nonviolent methods of revolution, while perhaps feasible in some countries without military and police forces, are not applicable to the United States.

COMMUNIST ETHICS

V. I. LENIN*

First of all, I shall deal here with the question of Communist ethics.

You must train yourselves to be Communists. The task of the Young Communist League is to organise its practical activity in such a manner that in studying, in organising and consolidating itself, and in fighting on, it will be training itself and all those who regard it as their leader. It will thus be training Communists. The whole work of training, educating, and instructing the present-day youth must be directed towards imbuing them with Communist ethics.

But is there such a thing as Communist ethics? Is there such a thing as Communist morality? Of course there is. It is frequently asserted that we have no ethics, and very frequently the bourgeoisie makes the charge that we Communists deny all morality. That is one of their methods of confusing the issue, of throwing dust into the eyes of the workers and peasants.

In what sense do we deny ethics, morals?

In the sense in which they are preached by the bourgeoisie, which deduces these morals from god's commandments. Of course, we say that we do not believe in god. We know perfectly well that the clergy, the landlords, and the bourgeoisie all claimed to speak in the name of god, in order to protect their own interests as exploiters. Or, instead of deducing their ethics from the commandments of morality, from the commandments of god, they deduced them from idealistic or semi-idealistic phrases which in substance were always very similar to divine commandments.

We deny all morality taken from superhuman or non-class conceptions.

* From a speech delivered at the Third All-Russian Congress of the Young Communist League of the Soviet Union on October 2, 1920.

We say that this is a deception, a swindle, a befogging of the minds of the workers and peasants in the interests of the landlords and capitalists.

We say that our morality is wholly subordinated to the interests of the class-struggle of the proletariat. We deduce our morality from the facts and needs of the class-struggle of the proletariat.

The old society was based on the oppression of all the workers and peasants by the landlords and capitalists. We had to destroy this society. We had to overthrow these landowners and capitalists. But to do this, organisation was necessary. God could not create such organisation.

Such organisation could only be created by the factories and workshops, only by the trained proletariat, awakened from its former slumber. Only when this class had come into existence did the mass movement commence which led to what we have to-day—to the victory of the proletarian revolution in one of the weakest countries in the world—a country which for three years has resisted the attacks of the bourgeoisie of the whole world. We see how the proletarian revolution is growing all over the whole world. And we can say now, on the basis of experience, that only the proletariat could have created that compact force which is carrying along with it the once disunited and disorganised peasantry—a force which has withstood all the attacks of all the exploiters. Only this class can help the toiling masses to unite their forces, to close their ranks, to establish and build up a definitely Communist society and finally to complete it.

That is why we say that a morality taken from outside of human society does not exist for us; it is a fraud. For us morality is subordinated to the interests of the proletarian class-struggle.

THEIR MORALS AND OURS

LEON TROTSKY*

This essay was Trotsky's reply to the charge that Stalin, Lenin, and Trotsky were equally amoral. It was published in 1938 in America. "Written as a polemic at a particular time," according to its editor, "Trotsky's pamphlet is unquestionably one of his enduring contributions to Marxism. It is the first systematic exposition of the Marxist conception of the relation between means and ends as a dialectical interrelation." It is probably true that although Trotsky was then in exile from the U.S.S.R.—his attack on Stalin and Stalinism apart—his justification of Bolshevik "amorality" would be found unexceptional by the Communist leaders.

* The selection is from *Their Morals and Ours* (Mexico: Pioneer Publishers Co.), *passim*. By permission of the publisher.

This pamphlet was written many years after the Revolution. But during the civil and international war that followed, Trotsky wrote The Defence of Terrorism *(completed May, 1920). There he gave expression to some of the ideas he was later to develop more fully and systematically, inter alia, "The revolution does require of the revolutionary class that it should attain its end by all methods at its disposal—if necessary, by an armed rising: if required, by terrorism," and "Terror can be very efficient against a reactionary class which does not want to leave the scene of operations."*

Bourgeois evolutionism halts impotently at the threshold of historical society because it does not wish to acknowledge the driving force in the evolution of social forms: *the class struggle.* Morality is one of the ideological functions in this struggle. The ruling class forces *its* ends upon society and habituates it into considering all those means which contradict its ends as immoral. That is the chief function of official morality. It pursues the idea of the "greatest possible happiness" not for the majority but for a small and ever diminishing minority. Such a regime could not have endured for even a week through force alone. It needs the cement of morality. The production of this cement constitutes the profession of the petty-bourgeois theoreticians and moralists. They radiate all the colors of the rainbow but in the final analysis remain apostles of slavery and submission.

"MORAL PRECEPTS OBLIGATORY UPON ALL"

Whoever does not care to return to Moses, Christ or Mohammed; whoever is not satisfied with eclectic *hodge-podges* must acknowledge that morality is a product of social development; that there is nothing immutable about it; that it serves social interests; that these interests are contradictory; that morality more than any other form of ideology has a class character.

But do not elementary moral precepts exist, worked out in the development of mankind as a whole and indispensable for the existence of every collective body? Undoubtedly such precepts exist but the extent of their action is extremely limited and unstable. Norms "obligatory upon all" become the less forceful the sharper the character assumed by the class struggle. The highest form of the class struggle is civil war which explodes into mid-air all moral ties between the hostile classes.

Under "normal" conditions a "normal" man observes the commandment: "Thou shalt not kill!" But if he kills under exceptional conditions for self-defense, the jury acquits him. If he falls victim to a murderer, the court will kill the murderer. The necessity of courts as well as that of self-defense, flows from antagonistic interests. In so far as the state is concerned, in peaceful times it limits itself to legalized killings of individuals so that in time of war it may transform the "obligatory" commandment, "Thou shalt not kill!" into its opposite. The most "humane" governments, which in peaceful times "detest" war, proclaim during war that the highest duty of their armies is the extermination of the greatest possible number of people. . . .

This vacuity in the norms obligatory upon all arises from the fact that in all decisive questions people feel their class membership considerably more profoundly and more directly than their membership in "society." The norms of "obligatory" morality are in reality filled with class, that is, antagonistic content. The moral norm becomes the more categoric the less it is "obligatory upon all." The solidarity of workers, especially of strikers or barricade fighters, is incomparably more "categoric" than human solidarity in general.

The bourgeoisie, which far surpasses the proletariat in the completeness and irreconcilability of its class consciousness, is vitally interested in imposing *its* moral philosophy upon the exploited masses. It is exactly for this purpose that the concrete norms of the bourgeois catechism are concealed under moral abstractions patronized by religion, philosophy, or that hybrid which is called "common sense." The appeal to abstract norms is not a disinterested philosophic mistake but a necessary element in the mechanics of class deception. The exposure of this deceit which retains the tradition of thousands of years is the first duty of a proletarian revolutionist. . . .

THE CRISIS IN DEMOCRATIC MORALITY

. . . At the extreme left wing of the "left" fraternity stands a small and politically completely insignificant grouping of German émigrés who publish the paper *Neuer Weg* (The New Road). Let us bend down lower and listen to these "revolutionary" indicters of Bolshevik amoralism. In a tone of ambiguous pseudo praise the *Neuer Weg* proclaims that the Bolsheviks are distinguished advantageously from other parties by their absence of hypocrisy—they openly declare what others quietly apply in fact, that is, the principle: "the end justifies the means." But according to the convictions of *Neuer Weg* such a "bourgeois" precept is incompatible with a "healthy socialist movement." "Lying and worse are not permissible means of struggle, as Lenin still considered." The word "still" evidently signifies that Lenin did not succeed in overcoming his delusions only because he failed to live until the discovery of *The New Road*.

In the formula, "lying and worse," "worse" evidently signifies—violence, murder, and so on, since under equal conditions violence is worse than lying; and murder—the most extreme form of violence. We thus come to the conclusion that lying, violence, murder are incompatible with a "healthy socialist movement." What, however, is our relation to revolution? Civil war is the most severe of all forms of war. It is unthinkable not only without violence against tertiary figures but, under contemporary technique, without killing old men, old women and children. Must one be reminded of Spain? The only possible answer of the "friends" of republican Spain sounds like this: Civil war is better than fascist slavery. But this completely correct answer merely signifies that the *end* (democracy or socialism) justifies, under certain conditions, such *means* as violence and murder. Not to speak about lies! Without lies war would be as unimaginable as a machine without oil. In order to safeguard even the session of the Cortes (February 1, 1938) from fascist bombs the Barcelona government several times deliberately deceived journalists and their own population. Could it have acted in any other way? Whoever accepts the end: victory over Franco, must accept the means: civil war with its wake of horrors and crimes.

But, after all, do not lying and violence "in themselves" warrant condemnation? Of course, even as does the class society which generates them. A society without social contradictions will naturally be a society without lies and violence. However there is no way of building a bridge to that society save by revolutionary, that is, violent means. The revolution itself is a product of class society and of necessity bears its traits. From the point of view of "eternal truths" revolution is of course "anti-moral." But this merely means that idealist morality is counter-revolutionary, that is, in the service of the exploiters.

"Civil war," will perhaps respond the philosopher caught unawares, "is however a sad exception. But in peaceful times a healthy socialist movement should manage without violence and lying." Such an answer however represents nothing less than a pathetic evasion. There is no impervious demarcation between "peaceful" class struggle and revolution. Every strike embodies in an unexpanded form all the elements of civil war. Each side strives to impress the opponent with an exaggerated picture of its resoluteness to struggle and its material resources. Through their press, agents, and spies the capitalists labor to frighten and demoralize the strikers. From their side, the workers' pickets, where persuasion does not avail, are compelled to resort to force. Thus "lying and worse" are an inseparable part of the class struggle even in its most elementary form. It remains to be added that the very conception of *truth* and *lie* was born of social contradictions. . . .

THE "AMORALISM" OF LENIN

The Russian "Social Revolutionaries" were always the most moral individuals: essentially they were composed of ethics alone. This did not prevent them, however, at the time of revolution from deceiving the Russian peasants. In the Parisian organ of Kerensky, that very ethical socialist who was the forerunner of Stalin in manufacturing spurious accusations against the Bolsheviks, another old "Social Revolutionary" Zenzinov writes: "Lenin, as is known, taught that for the sake of gaining the desired ends communists can, and sometimes must 'resort to all sorts of devices, manœuvres and subterfuge' . . ." (*New Russia*, February 17, 1938, p. 3). From this they draw the ritualistic conclusion: Stalinism is the natural offspring of Leninism.

Unfortunately, the ethical indicter is not even capable of quoting honestly. Lenin said: "It is necessary to be able . . . to resort to all sorts of devices, manœuvres, and illegal methods, to evasion and subterfuge, *in order to penetrate into the trade unions, to remain in them, and to carry on communist work in them at all costs.*" The necessity for evasion and manœuvres, according to Lenin's explanation, is called forth by the fact that the reformist bureaucracy, betraying the workers to capital, baits revolutionists, persecutes them, and even resorts to turning the bourgeois police upon them. "Manœuvres" and "subterfuge" are in this case only methods of valid self-defense against the perfidious reformist bureaucracy. . . .

Norman Thomas speaks about "that strange communist amorality in which nothing matters but the party and its power" (*Socialist Call*, March 12, 1938, p. 5). . . . In the eyes of Thomas and his kind the party is only a secondary instrument for electoral combinations and other similar uses, not more. His personal life, interests, ties, moral criteria exist outside the party. With hostile astonishment he looks down upon the Bolshevik to whom the party is a weapon for the revolutionary reconstruction of society, including also its morality. To a revolutionary Marxist there can be no contradiction between personal morality and the interests of the party, since the party embodies in his consciousness the very highest tasks and aims of mankind. It is naive to imagine that Thomas has a higher understanding of morality than the Marxists. He merely has a base conception of the party. . . .

The clerks of the ruling classes call the organizers of this party "amoralists." In the eyes of conscious workers this accusation carries a complimentary character. It signifies: Lenin refused to recognize moral norms established by slave-owners for their slaves and never observed by the slave-owners themselves; he called upon the proletariat to extend the class struggle into the moral sphere too. Whoever fawns before precepts established by the enemy will never vanquish that enemy!

The "amoralism" of Lenin, that is, his rejection of supra-class morals, did not hinder him from remaining faithful to one and the same ideal throughout his whole life; from devoting his whole being to the cause of the oppressed; from displaying the highest conscientiousness in the sphere of ideas and the highest fearlessness in the sphere of action; from maintaining an attitude untainted by the least superiority to an "ordinary" worker, to a defenseless woman, to a child. Does it not seem that "amoralism" in the given case is only a pseudonym for higher human morality? . . .

DIALECTICAL INTERDEPENDENCE OF END AND MEANS

A means can be justified only by its end. But the end in its turn needs to be justified. From the Marxist point of view, which expresses the historical interests of the proletariat, the end is justified if it leads to increasing the power of man over nature and to the abolition of the power of man over man.

"We are to understand then that in achieving this end anything is permissible?" sarcastically demands the Philistine, demonstrating that he understood nothing. That is permissible, we answer, which *really* leads to the liberation of mankind. Since this end can be achieved only through revolution, the liberating morality of the proletariat of necessity is endowed with a revolutionary character. It irreconcilably counteracts not only religious dogma but all kinds of idealistic fetishes, these philosophic gendarmes of the ruling class. It deduces a rule for conduct from the laws of the development of society, thus primarily from the class struggle, this law of all laws.

"Just the same," the moralist continues to insist, "does it mean that in the class struggle against capitalists all means are permissible: lying, frame-up, betrayal, murder, and so on?" Permissible and obligatory are those and only those means, we answer, which unite the revolutionary proletariat, fill their hearts with irreconcilable hostility to oppression, teach them contempt for official morality and its democratic echoers, imbue them with consciousness of their own historic mission, raise their courage and spirit of self-sacrifice in the struggle. Precisely from this it flows that *not* all means are permissible. When we say that the end justifies the means, then for us the conclusion follows that the great revolutionary end spurns those base means and ways which set one part of the working class against other parts, or attempt to make the masses happy without their participation; or lower the faith of the masses in themselves and their organization, replacing it by worship for the "leaders." Primarily and irreconcilably, revolutionary morality rejects servility in relation to the bourgeoisie and haughtiness in relation to the toilers, that is, those characteristics in which petty-bourgeois pedants and moralists are thoroughly steeped.

These criteria do not, of course, give a ready answer to the question as to what is permissible and what is not permissible in each separate case. There can be no such automatic answers. Problems of revolutionary morality are fused with the problems of revolutionary strategy and tactics. The living experience of the movement under the clarification of theory provides the correct answer to these problems. . . .

Two classes decide the fate of modern society: the imperialist bourgeoisie and the proletariat. The last resource of the bourgeoisie is fascism, which replaces social and historical criteria with biological and zoological standards so as thus to free itself from any and all restrictions in the struggle for capitalist property. Civilization can be saved only by the socialist revolution. To accomplish the overturn, the proletariat needs all its strength, all its resolution, all its audacity, passion and ruthlessness. Above all it must be completely free from the fictions of religion, "democracy" and transcendental morality—the spiritual chains forged by the enemy to tame and enslave it. Only that which prepares the complete and final overthrow of imperialist bestiality is moral, and nothing else. The welfare of the revolution—that is the supreme law! . . .

WHY I AM NOT A COMMUNIST

Morris Raphael Cohen*

What distinguishes present-day Communists is not . . . their professed ultimate goal or their analysis of our economic ills, but their political remedy or program—to wit, the seizure of power by armed rebellion and the setting up of a dictatorship by the leaders of the Communist Party. To be sure, this dictatorship is to be in the name of the *proletariat,* just as the fascist dictatorship is in the name of *the whole nation.* But such verbal tricks cannot hide the brute facts of tyrannical suppression necessarily involved in all dictatorship. For the wielders of dictatorial power are few, they are seldom if ever themselves toilers, and they can maintain their power only by ruthlessly suppressing all expression of popular dissatisfaction with their rule. And where there is no freedom of discussion, there is no freedom of thought.

This program of civil war, dictatorship, and the illiberal or fanatically intolerant spirit which war psychology always engenders may bring more miseries than those that the Communists seek to remove; and the arguments to prove that such war is desirable or inevitable seem to me patently inadequate.

Communists ignore the historic truth that civil wars are much more destructive of all that men hold dearest than are wars between nations; and all the arguments that they use against the latter, including the "war to end war," are much more cogent against civil wars. Wars between nations are

* Late Professor of Philosophy, The City College of New York. President of the American Philosophical Association, 1929. Author of *Reason and Nature; Law and the Social Order; Faith of a Liberal;* and other works. The selection is from Morris Raphael Cohen, "Why I Am Not a Communist," *Modern Monthly* (April, 1934), Vol. 8, No. 3. Reprinted with permission of the administrators of the estate of Morris Raphael Cohen.

necessarily restricted in scope and do not prevent—to a limited extent they even stimulate—co-operation within a community. But civil wars necessarily dislocate all existing social organs and leave us with little social capital or machinery to rebuild a better society. The hatreds which fratricidal wars develop are more persistent and destructive than those developed by wars that terminate in treaties or agreements.

Having lived under the tyranny of the Czar, I cannot and do not condemn all revolutions. But the success and benefits of any revolution depend on the extent to which—like the American Revolution of 1776, the French Revolution of 1789, and the anti-Czarist Revolution of March 1917—it approximates national unanimity in the co-operation of diverse classes. When armed uprisings have been undertaken by single oppressed classes, as in the revolt of the gladiators in Rome, the various peasant revolts in England, Germany, and Russia, the French Commune of 1871, or the Moscow uprising of 1905, they have left a deplorably monotonous record of bloody massacres and oppressive reaction. The idea that armed rebellion is the only or the always effective cure for social ills seems to me no better than the old superstition of medieval medicine that blood-letting is the only and the sovereign remedy for all bodily ills.

Communists may feel that the benefits of the Revolution of 1917 outweigh all the terrific hardships which the Russian people have suffered since then. But reasonable people in America will do well to demand better evidence than has yet been offered that they can improve their lot by blindly imitating Russia. Russian breadlines, and famine without breadlines, are certainly not *prima facie* improvements over American conditions. [Editor's note: The article was written in 1934.] At best a revolution is a regrettable means to bring about greater human welfare. It always unleashes the forces that thrive in disorder, the brutal executions, imprisonments, and, what is even worse, the sordid spying that undermines all feeling of personal security. These forces, once let loose, are difficult to control and they tend to perpetuate themselves. If, therefore, human well-being, rather than mere destruction, is our aim, we must be as critically-minded in considering the consequences of armed revolution as in considering the evils of the existing regime.

One of the reasons that lead Communists to ignore the terrific destruction which armed rebellion must bring about is the conviction that "the revolution" is inevitable. In this they follow Marx, who, dominated by the Hegelian dialectic, regarded the victory of the proletariat over the bourgeoisie as inevitable, so that all that human effort can hope to achieve is "to shorten and lessen the birth pangs" of the new order. There is, however, very little scientific value in this dialectic argument, and many Communists are quite ready to soft-pedal it and admit that some human mistake or misstep might lead to the triumph of fascism. The truth is that the dialectic method which Marx inherited from Hegel and Schelling is an outgrowth of speculations carried on in theologic seminaries. The "system" of production takes the place of the councils or the mills of the gods. Such Oriental fatalism has little support in the spirit and method of modern science. Let us therefore leave the pretended dialectic proof and examine the contention on an historical basis.

Historically, the argument is put thus: When did any class give up its power without a bloody struggle? As in most rhetorical questions, the questioner does not stop for an answer, assuming that his ignorance is conclusive as to the facts. Now, it is not difficult to give instances of ruling classes giving up their sovereignty without armed resistance. The English landed aristocracy did it in the Reform Bill of 1832; and the Russian nobility did it in 1863 when they freed their serfs, though history showed clearly that in this way not only their political power but their very existence was doomed (for money income has never been so secure as direct revenue from the land, and life in cities reduced the absolute number of noble families). In our own country, the old seaboard aristocracy, which put over the United States Constitution and controlled the government up to the Jacksonian era, offered no armed resistance when the backwoods farmers outvoted them and removed church and property qualifications for office and for the franchise.

But it is not necessary to multiply such instances. It is more important to observe that history does not show that any *class* ever gained its enfranchisement through a bloody rebellion carried out by its own unaided efforts. When ruling classes are overthrown it is generally by a combination of groups that have risen to power only after a long process. For the parties to a rebellion cannot succeed unless they have more resources than the established regime. Thus the ascendancy of the French bourgeoisie was aided by the royal power which Richelieu and Colbert used in the seventeenth century to transform the landed barons into dependent courtiers. Even so, the French Revolution of 1789 would have been impossible without the co-operation of the peasantry, whose opposition to their ancient seigneurs was strengthened as the latter ceased to be independent rulers of the land. This is in a measure also true of the supposedly purely Communist Revolution in Russia. For in that revolution, too, the peasantry had a much greater share than is ordinarily assumed. After all, the amount of landed communal property (that of the crown, the church, etc.) which was changed by the peasants into individual ownership may have been greater than the amount of private property made communal by the Soviet regime. Even the system of collective farms is, after all, a return to the old *mir* system, using modern machinery. The success of the Russian Revolution was largely due to the landlords' agents who, in their endeavor to restore the rule of the landlords threw the peasantry into the arms of the Bolshevists.

Indeed, the strictly Marxian economics, with its ideology of surplus-value due to the ownership of the means of production, is inherently inapplicable to the case of the peasant who cultivates his own piece of ground.

Even more important, however, is it to note that no amount of repetition can make a truth of the dogma that the capitalist class alone rules this country and like the Almighty can do what it pleases. It would be folly to deny that, as individuals or as a class, capitalists have more than their proportionate share of influence in the government, and that they have exercised it unintelligently and with dire results. But it is equally absurd to maintain that they have governed or can govern without the co-operation of the farmers and the influential middle classes. None of our recent constitutional amendments—not the income-tax amendment, not the popular election of the United States Senators, not woman suffrage, neither prohibition nor its repeal—nor any other major bit of legislation can be said to have been imposed on our country in the interests of the capitalist class. The farmers, who despite mortgages still cling to the private ownership of their land, are actually the dominant political group even in industrial states like New York, Pennsylvania, and Illinois.

The Communist division of mankind into workingmen and capitalists suffers from the fallacy of simplism. Our social structure and effective class divisions are much more complicated. As the productivity of machinery increases, the middle classes increase rather than decrease. Hence a program based entirely on the supposed exclusive interests of the proletariat has no reasonable prospect. Any real threat of an armed uprising will only strengthen the reactionaries, who are not less intelligent than the Communist leaders, understand just as well how to reach and influence our people, and have more ample means for organization. If our working classes find it difficult to learn what their true interests are and do not know how to control their representatives in the government and in the trade unions, there is little prospect that they will be able to control things better during a rebellion or during the ensuing dictatorship.

If the history of the past is any guide at all, it indicates that real improvements in the future will come like the improvements of the past—namely, through co-operation among different groups, each of which is wise enough to see the necessity of compromising with those with whom we have to live together and whom we cannot or do not wish to exterminate.

I know that this notion of compromise or of taking counsel as the least wasteful way of adjusting differences is regarded as hopelessly antiquated and bourgeois, but I do not believe that the ideas of so-called Utopian socialists have really been refuted by those who arrogate the epithet "scientific" to themselves. The Communists seem to me to be much more Utopian and quite unscientific in their claims that the working class alone can by its own efforts completely transform our social order.

I do not have very high expectations from the efforts of sentimental benevolence. Yet I cannot help noticing that the leaders of the Communists and of other revolutionary labor movements—Engels, Marx, Lassalle, Luxemburg, Liebknecht, Lenin, and Trotsky—have not been drawn to it by economic solidarity. They were not workingmen nor even all of workingmen's families. They were driven to their role by human sympathy. Sympathy with the sufferings of our fellow men is a human motive that cannot be read out of history. It has exerted tremendous social pressure. Without it you cannot explain the course of nineteenth-century factory legislation, the freeing of serfs and slaves, or the elimination of the grosser forms of human exploitation. Though some who regard themselves as followers of Karl Marx are constantly denouncing reformers who believe in piecemeal improvement and hope rather that things will get worse so as to drive people into a revolution, Marx himself did not always take that view. Very wisely he attached great importance to English factory legislation which restricted the number of hours per working day, for he realized that every little bit that strengthens the workers strengthens their resistance to exploitation. Those who are most oppressed and depressed, the inhabitants of the slums, do not revolt—they have not energy enough to think of it. When, therefore, Mr. Strachey and others criticize the socialists for not bringing about the millennium when they get into power, I am not at all impressed. I do not believe that the socialists or the Labor Party in England have been free from shameful error. But neither have the Communists, nor any other human group, been free from it. Trite though it sounds, it is nevertheless true that no human arrangement can bring about perfection on earth. And while the illusion of omniscience may offer great consolation, it brings endless inhumanity when it leads us to shut the gates of mercy. Real as are our human conflicts, our fundamental identity of interest in the face of hostile nature seems to me worthy of more serious attention than the Communists have been willing to accord it.

If liberalism were dead, I should still maintain that it deserved to live, that it had not been condemned in the court of human reason, but lynched outside of it by the passionate and uncompromisingly ruthless war spirit, common to Communists and Fascists. But I do not believe that liberalism is dead, even though it is under eclipse. There still seems to me enough reason left to which to appeal against reckless fanaticism.

It is pure fanaticism to belittle the gains that have come to mankind from the spirit of free inquiry, free discussion, and accommodation. No human individual or group of individuals can claim omniscience. Hence society can only suffer serious loss when one group suppresses the opinions and criticisms of all others. In purely abstract questions compromise may often be a sign of confusion. One cannot really believe inconsistent principles at the same time. But in the absence of perfect or even adequate knowledge in regard to human affairs and their future, we must adopt an experimental attitude and treat principles not as eternal dogmas, but as hypotheses, to be tried to the extent that they indicate the general direction of solution to specific issues. But as the scientist must be ever ready to modify his own hypothesis or to recognize wherein a contrary hypothesis has merits or deserves preference, so in practical affairs we must be prepared to learn from those who differ with us, and to recognize that however contradictory diverse views may appear in discourse they may not be so in their practical applications.

Thus, the principles of Communism and individualism may be held like theologic dogmas, eternally true and on no occasion ever to be contaminated one by the other. But in fact, when Communists get into power they do not differ so much from others. No one ever wished to make everything communal property. Nor does anyone in his senses believe that any individual will ever with impunity be permitted to use his "property" in an antisocial way when the rest of the community is aroused thereby. In actual life, the question how far Communism shall be pushed depends more upon specific analyses of actual situations—that is, upon factual knowledge. There can be no doubt that individualism à la Herbert Hoover has led millions to destruction. Nevertheless, we must not forget that a Communist regime will, after all, be run by individuals who will exercise a tremendous amount of power, no less than do our captains of industry or finance today. There is no real advantage in assuming that under Communism the laboring classes will be omniscient. We know perfectly well how labor leaders like John Lewis keep their power by bureaucratic rather than democratic methods. May it not be that the Stalins also keep their power by bureaucratic rather than democratic methods?

Indeed the ruthless suppression of dissent within the Communist Party in Russia and the systematic glorification of the national heroes and military objectives of Czarist days suggest that the Bolshevik Revolution was not so complete a break with the Russian past as most of its friends and enemies assumed in earlier days. In any event we have witnessed in the history of the Communist movement since 1917 a dramatic demonstration of the way in which the glorification of power—first as a means of destroying a ruling class, then as a means of defending a beleaguered state from surrounding enemies, and finally as a means of extending Communism to neighboring lands—comes imperceptibly to displace the ends or objectives which once formed the core of Communist thought. Thus, one by one, the worst features of capitalist society and imperialism, against which Communism cut its eye teeth in protest—extreme inequality in wages, speed-up of workers, secret diplomacy, and armed intervention as a technique of international intercourse—have been taken over by the Soviet Union, with only a set of thin verbal distinctions to distinguish the "good" techniques of Communism from the corresponding "bad" techniques used by capitalism. As is always the case, the glorification of power dulls the sense of righteousness to which any movement for bettering the basic conditions of human living must appeal.

The Communist criticism of liberalism seems to me altogether baseless and worthless. One would suppose from it that liberalism is a peculiar excrescence of capitalism. This is, however, not true. The essence of liberalism—freedom of thought and inquiry, freedom of discussion and criticism—is not the invention of the capitalist system. It is rather the mother of Greek and modern science, without which our present industrial order and the labor movement would be impossible. The plea that the denial of freedom is a temporary necessity is advanced by all militarists. It ignores the fact that, when suppression becomes a habit, it is not readily abandoned. Thus, when the Christian Church after its alliance with the Roman Empire began the policy of "compelling them to enter," it kept up the habit of intolerant persecution for many centuries. Those who believe that many of the finer fruits of civilization were thereby choked should be careful about strengthening the forces of intolerance.

When the Communists tell me that I must choose between their dictatorship and Fascism, I feel that I am offered the choice between being shot and being hanged. It would be suicide for liberal civilization to accept this as exhausting the field of human possibility. I prefer to hope that the present wave of irrationalism and of fanatical intolerance will recede and that the great human energy which manifests itself in free thought will not perish. Often before, it has emerged after being swamped by passionate superstitions. There is no reason to feel that it may not do so again.

"POWER TENDS TO CORRUPT. . . ."

Harold J. Laski*

The Marxian view of a secretly armed minority assuming power at a single stroke is unthinkable in the modern state. It would have to imply either the existence of a government so weak that it had practically ceased to be a government at all, or, what is perhaps an equivalent, a population actively sympathetic to the revolutionary minority. The resources of publicity in modern civilization make impossible the private preparation of the gigantic effort assumed by the Marxian hypothesis.

* Late Professor of Political Science at the London School of Economics. Author of *Communism; Reflections on the Revolution of Our Time; Faith, Reason and Civilization;* and many other books. The selection is from pp. 42-45 of *Karl Marx: An Essay,* first published in America by the League for Industrial Democracy in 1933. By permission of the publisher.

But this is only the beginning of the difficulty. Marx assumed throughout his analysis a system of compact states the life of which was mainly determined by economic considerations, and each relatively independent of its neighbors. Each of these assumptions is only partially true of the modern world. A State like England, which is wholly dependent on foreign trade, could not undergo a successful revolution except upon the assumption that her neighbors viewed its results with benevolence. Such an attitude on the part, for instance, of America is very unlikely, and the rupture of Anglo-American trade would be fatal to any revolution in this country. Nor is that all. It is quite clear that the division a revolution would imply must, in its workings, be very partially determined by economic considerations.

In a country like America, for example, there would be at least three other factors of vital importance. An American communist revolution would have to cope with problems of distance which would probably render it abortive at a very early stage. It would not, as in France, be a matter of the immense impact of the capital on the life of the nation; Washington is relatively insignificant in the perspective of America. To control the whole continent would involve controlling the most complicated railway system in the world. And even if that difficulty could be surmounted, a complex of nationalist differences would have to be assuaged. German, French, English, Irish, Polish, these have their special characteristics which the American capitalist has been able to exploit to their common disadvantage; it is difficult to see how an appeal to a communist minority of each would result in the transcendence of these differences. Even then, the religious problem remains; and the hold of the churches upon the mind, particularly, of the Latin peoples would not be easy to loosen. For Marx, insisting only upon the economic motive, it is easy to ignore these difficulties, but it is far too narrow an outlook not to realize at the outset that appeal can be made to other incentives every whit as strong. And even if it were argued that Marx could in our own time assume that the day of such prejudice as nationality and religion engender is passing (which is doubtful), and that the barriers built by economic difference are now alone important, his conclusions would not follow. For in a period of universal suffrage, it ought then to be possible to capture the seat of power at the polls, and throw upon the capitalist the onus of revolting against a socialist democracy.

There are, however, other approaches to the problem which Marx did not adequately consider. There is, in the first place, the general result upon society of the practice of violence, particularly when the destructive nature of modern warfare is borne in mind; and, in the second, there is the special psychological result upon the agents of the opposing forces in such a regime. Marx did not consider these possibilities, in part because he judged that, in any case, the conflict was inevitable, and also because he was convinced that whatever sacrifices had to be made would be ultimately justified by the

result. Such an attitude is, of course, simply an instance of his general failure to weigh sufficiently the substance of a political psychology. In part,
also, it is the corollary of a determinism which the facts in issue at no point
justify. For it is obvious that if revolution, with its attendant violence, is
justified for any cause in which you happen to believe profoundly, no modern state can hope for either security or order.

The war has shown clearly that the impulses of savagery which are
checked by peace are, when loosed, utterly destructive of the foundations of
a decent existence. If life became an organized and continuous jacquerie,
civilization could quite easily be reduced to the state where, as in Mr. Wells's
imaginary but far from impossible picture, some aged survivor may tell of
an organized Europe as a legend which his grandchildren cannot hope to
understand. Violence, on the grand scale, in fact, so far from proving an
avenue to communism, would be the one kind of existence in which the
impulses demanded by a communist state had no hope of emergence. For
the condition of communism is the restraint of exactly those appetites which
violence releases; and Marx has nowhere indicated how this difficulty could
be met.

Even beyond this issue, a further point must be raised. Marx has assumed the seizure of power, and a period of rigorous control until the
people are prepared for communism. But he has not shown what approximate length that period is to be, nor what certainty we have that those who
act as controllers of the dictatorship will be willing to surrender their power
at the proper time. It is a commonplace of history that power is poisonous
to those who exercise it; there is no reason to assume that the Marxian dictator will in this respect be different from other men. And, *ex hypothesi,* it
will be more difficult to defeat his malevolence since his regime will have
excluded the possibility of opposition. No group of men who exercise the
powers of a despot can ever retain the habit of democratic responsibility.
That is obvious, for instance, in the case of men like Sir Henry Maine and
Fitzjames Stephen, who, having learned in India the habit of autocratic
government, become impatient on their return to England of the slow
process of persuasion which democracy implies.

To sit continuously in the seat of office is inevitably to become separated from the mind and wants of those over whom you govern. For the
governing class acquires an interest of its own, a desire for permanence, a
wish, perhaps, to retain the dignity and importance which belong to their
function; and they will make an effort to secure them. That, after all, is
only to insist that every system of government breeds a system of habits;
and to argue as a corollary therefrom that the Marxian dictatorship would
breed habits fatal to the emergence of the regime Marx had ultimately in
view. The special vice of every historic system of government has been its
inevitable tendency to identify its own private good with the public welfare.

To suggest that communists might do the same is no more than to postulate their humanity. And it may be added that if they surrender power at a reasonable time, the grounds for so doing, being obviously in their nature noneconomic, would thereby vitiate the truth of the materialistic interpretation of history.

IV

TOWARD THE BOLSHEVIK TRIUMPH

We, the countless, redoubtable legions of Toil,
We've conquered vast spaces of oceans and lands,
Illumined great cities with suns of our making,
Fired our souls with proud flames of revolt.
Gone are our tears, our softness forgotten,
We banished the perfume of lilac and grass,
We exalt electricity, steam and explosives,
Motors and sirens and iron and brass. . . .
Our arms, our muscles cry out for vast labors,
The pain of creation glows hot in our breast
United, we sweeten all life with our honey,
Earth takes a new course at our mighty behest.
We love life, and the turbulent joys that intoxicate,
We are hard, and no anguish our spirit can thaw.
We—all, We—in all, We—hot flames that regenerate,
We ourselves, to ourselves, are God, Judge, and Law.

VLADIMIR KIRILLOV

"I am compelled to reject Bolshevism for two reasons: First, because the price mankind must pay to achieve Communism by Bolshevik methods is too terrible; and secondly because, even after paying the price, I do not believe the result would be what the Bolsheviks profess to desire."

BERTRAND RUSSELL

"Instead of being a destructive force, it seems to me that the Bolsheviki were the only party in Russia with a constructive program and the power to impose it on the country."

JOHN REED in *Ten Days That Shook the World*

Chapter 7

WAR AND REVOLUTIONS

The First World War which linked Russia with the French and British democracies against imperial Germany at the outset aroused considerable support among the Russian people for their government in its war effort. The detailed process by which enthusiasm turned to bitter discontent and then disaffection is traced by John S. Curtiss in the pages that follow.

The fundamental and historic backwardness and inequities of Russia's political, economic, and social structures and, more immediately, the privations of war, the inequalities of burdens, the incompetency and corruption of the imperial court, military inefficiency, and widespread agitation, culminated in March 1917 in the collapse of Tsardom in what has been called "one of the most leaderless, spontaneous, anonymous revolutions of all time"; "elemental, and for that reason all the more conclusive."

The Bolshevik revolution, on the other hand, was carefully premeditated and planned. It is interesting to speculate on which of the decisions made during the War, and particularly after the March revolution, strengthened the Bolshevik position. (It is probably true that while the Bolsheviks never commanded majority support, at the time of the November revolution, "the active masses of workers and soldiers were, in the main, on the side of the coup, or at least regarded it with friendly neutrality"—as William Henry Chamberlin wrote.) Such speculation may provide some insight on Bolshevik success in Russia and have importance in relation to revolutionary movements and ferment elsewhere in the world.

The "indifference" with which the arbitrary dissolution of the Constituent Assembly was received by the nation after the freest and most equal election in all its history was further evidence of the people's lack of deep understanding of or commitment to democracy. The critical decision on land having apparently already been made, the majority of peasants were not prepared to fight to preserve democracy, for, to them, as Michael T. Florinsky wrote, "freedom did not mean the introduction of parliamentary institutions about which they knew nothing, but the immediate division

. . . of the landed estates in which they saw the real reason for their poverty and misery." That this "indifference" was to turn into "sullen discontent" with the program of collectivization did not alter the immediate situation.

THE RUSSIAN REVOLUTIONS OF 1917

JOHN S. CURTISS*

THE RUSSIAN EMPIRE IN THE FIRST WORLD WAR

Background of the War. . . . In June, 1914, when the Austrian Archduke Francis Ferdinand was assassinated with the complicity of Serbian terrorists, the Russian government at first warned the Serbs to make amends. But when Austria-Hungary presented an ultimatum apparently designed to lead to war against Serbia, and when Vienna quickly declared war, Russia sought to protect her small ally against the Austrians. The Russians began partial mobilization against Austria, but then, under pressure from his generals, the Tsar reluctantly agreed to full mobilization, knowing that this might well lead Germany to declare war. Germany did so on July 19/ August 1, 1914.[1] From a Balkan quarrel the war had become a general one.

The First Months of the War. When war came, Russia was stronger than ever before. There was considerable popular support for the government, and political conflict almost vanished. The Duma, in an outburst of patriotism, voted full support and gave the government a free hand. The people responded well to the call for mobilization. Even most of the socialists gave their support. As for the Bolshevik group in the Duma, who sharply opposed the war, it was quickly arrested and exiled to Siberia.

The Russian army, thoroughly reorganized after the Japanese war, had more artillery and machine guns than before, and an excellent spirit. But, in spite of belief in victory in a few months, the army was poorly prepared to fight the best military power in the world. The Russians had far fewer guns per division than the Germans, and no heavy field guns. Even worse, the Russians, with feeble facilities for making ammunition, had only 1,000 shells per gun, while the Germans had 3,000 per gun and ample capacity to make more. The Russians were also woefully lacking in machine guns, with only 4,100 in the whole army. Their supply and medical system were primitive, their communications weak, and their aviation was far inferior to the

* Professor of History, Duke University. The selection is from pp. 21-87 of *The Russian Revolutions of 1917* (Princeton, N. J.: D. Van Nostrand Co., Inc., 1957). By permission of the publisher.
[1] The first date is that of the old Russian calendar, the other is the same date corresponding to the new Soviet calendar (identical with that of the West).

Germans. Against the Austrians the Russians could more than hold their own, but from the beginning the Germans far outclassed them.

Even more disastrous, the Russian high command was poorly organized. It was only on the second day that the Grand Duke Nicholas, uncle of the Tsar, was named commander-in-chief, much to his surprise. He himself stated that at first he wept copiously because he did not know how to perform his new duties. Although he had some success, his appointment was unfortunate. His chief-of-staff, General Ianushkevich, had had no field experience, and other high commanders were also poorly trained. V. A. Sukhomlinov, the Minister of War, was either extremely incompetent or a traitor. . . .

The Russian Disasters of 1915. By the spring of 1915 the Russians, in spite of heavy losses, had pushed to the crest of the Carpathians and even through some of the passes to the Hungarian plain. The Russians depended chiefly upon the bayonet, as their ammunition was almost gone. With their extended lines and almost silent cannon the Russians invited a German counter-stroke, which came suddenly in April, 1915. With massed guns and heavy air attacks the Teutons cut the Russian army to pieces, whole units surrendering in confusion. The Germans pursued relentlessly, striking along the whole front, and threatened to entrap the Russians in Poland. The Russian cannon were limited at best to one shell per gun per day. Even the infantry lacked rifle ammunition, and reserve troops often had no rifles, but were forced to lie unarmed under fire until the rifles of the killed and wounded could be made available. Yet the Russian army held together under these demoralizing conditions, and late in the fall the Germans halted their offensive on a line running from just west of Riga to the corner of Galicia.

Naturally, the Russian losses during this period were immense. At the height of the German drive, the killed and wounded numbered 235,000 per month, and 200,000 prisoners were lost each month. During 1915 alone, the Russians lost some 2,000,000 men killed and wounded, and 1,300,000 prisoners, bringing the total losses since the outbreak of the war to 4,360,000. It is no wonder that the British General Knox, who was with the Russian forces, stated that the army had come through a trial that "would have been fatal to most armies." The remnants of the army, although replenished in numbers, were inferior in quality, as the great quantities of regular officers and noncoms put out of action could never be replaced. Moreover, the morale of the Russians never could be restored.

Political Results of the Defeats. Inevitably, news of the difficulties of the army filtered back to the Duma as early as January, 1915. At that time the members sharply questioned Sukhomlinov, the Minister of War, only to be told that the supply situation was satisfactory. The Duma could do nothing, even though it was sure that this answer was untrue. The leading political figures of the country met and repeatedly urged basic reforms in the government, only to be snubbed by the Tsar. The movement for reform grew, however, and early in the summer of 1915 two-thirds of the Duma organized the Progressive Bloc, headed by P. N. Miliukov, to ask necessary reforms and the "Ministry of Confidence" that was so widely demanded. When the Duma reconvened on June 19, 1915, there was a fierce attack upon the reactionary and incompetent ministers, who had opposed the mobilization of the public forces to support the war. As a result, the Tsar replaced three of the worst with able and respected conservatives. . . . The hopes of the Progressive Bloc were high.

The Sway of Rasputin. The Empress Alexandra, a fanatical believer in the autocratic power of the Emperor, had long been under the influence of Rasputin, who urged her to combat the progressive tendencies. She had already expressed her hatred of Guchkov. In August, she and Rasputin persuaded the Tsar to dismiss the Grand Duke Nicholas, the commander-in-chief, and go to the front and take command himself. When the news leaked out, there was general consternation in the Duma, as the Tsar had no military training. Moreover, his absence from Petrograd would leave the government without a head. The feeling grew so strong that the ministers, under strong pressure from the Duma and the general public, on August 21 sent the Tsar a joint letter urging him to reconsider his decision. Only the aged Goremykin, the submissive Premier, opposed the protest. The letter, however, failed to deter the Tsar, who left for Headquarters on August 23. The ministers did not learn of his departure until two days later. By this act Nicholas cut himself off from the ministers. In reality, he turned over his political powers to the Empress, whom he encouraged to dabble in matters of state. The Empress, in turn, was firmly under the influence of Rasputin. And, thus, the great empire was dominated by a debauched and ignorant peasant, with whom no decent man could cooperate. The Empress, trusting firmly in him, threw herself into the work of running the state with dire results. The doom of the Empire was sealed.

The Brusilov Offensive in 1916. In spite of the fatal turn in political life, the Russian army made a remarkable recovery over the winter of 1915-1916. The troops were rested and re-equipped, and heavy contingents of new men were added to the ranks. . . . In fact, as the German army also had improved greatly since 1914, the improved Russian army was even more inferior to the Germans than before. None the less, it was decided to take the offensive in 1916, to relieve the Allies, hard pressed in France, and especially to succor the Italians after the rout at Caporetto.

The Russian commanders facing the Germans had little hope of success, but Brusilov, commander in Galicia, was sure of success against the Austrians and was given command of the offensive. Thanks to effective artillery fire and numerical superiority, the Russians quickly overwhelmed the Austrians on a wide front and captured 400,000 prisoners. But with German aid the Austrians again halted the Russians with heavy losses. The **Rus-**

sians had diverted large German forces from France and had saved Italy. Moreover, Brusilov's success had finally lured Rumania into the war on the allied side—although Rumania soon experienced disaster. But in spite of these successes, the offensive was unwise. In 1916 the Russians lost more than 2,000,000 men killed and wounded, and 350,000 prisoners. Even more important, the morale of the Russian army was ruined beyond repair, and its collapse seemed certain. The army was ripe for revolution.

Ministerial Leapfrog. After the Tsar had gone to the front, the internal situation worsened rapidly. The country's economy began to display alarming signs of weakness. Inflation, slow at first, soon gained momentum, and prices soared. For the swollen populations of the cities this brought great hardship, as wages, pitifully low at best, lost their purchasing power. The misery of the working people was intensified by a growing shortage of food. The peasants found it unprofitable to sell their grain for inflated money, especially as there were few manufactured goods to buy with it. In addition, the railroads proved unable to cope with the enormous problem of supplying the huge army as well as the civilian population, and often available food supplies could not be transported. Food riots and strikes became more frequent, although the government dealt severely with the participants. A fuel shortage added to the woes of the urban inhabitants. As for the peasants, they were fairly docile, but they were more and more disgusted with the war, which had taken so many of their men and was constantly taking more.

Under these circumstances, able administration was imperative. It was not, however, supplied. Instead, the Empress, egged on by Rasputin, campaigned for the removal of the able men appointed by the Tsar in the summer of 1915. Two of them were dismissed in September, and a few months later two others went. Polivanov, the capable Minister of War, was especially hated by the Empress, who wrote to her husband: "A greater traitor than Sukhomlinov." When Nicholas finally gave in and removed him, she wrote: "Oh, the relief! Now I can sleep well." More and more the reputable men of Russia found it impossible to work under the influence of Rasputin, who, steeped in debauchery, was surrounded by a crowd of unprincipled adventurers. During the last eighteen months of the empire, the public was regaled with the spectacle of the "ministerial leap-frog," as one corrupt politician succeeded another in the positions of power, while Rasputin pulled the strings. In December, 1915, Nicholas removed old Goremykin because of his inability to cope with the strong opposition to him. His successor, however, was Stürmer, a shady and disreputable politician for whom nobody had a good word. This appointment caused consternation at home and abroad, as he was incorrectly believed to be pro-German. He kept his post for almost a year. At first he posed as a friend of the Duma, to the great delight of the public.

But as the governmental scandals grew ever more noisome, and as the inability of the administration to deal with the food situation became more obvious, public opinion grew more and more vehement against Stürmer's government. Finally, the naming of A. D. Protopopov as Minister of Interior outraged Duma and public alike. Even the Tsar protested against him, but the urging of the Empress and Rasputin won out. It was not long before Protopopov's proven connections with Rasputin infuriated the citizenry, while his unbalanced mental state made him obviously unfit for the key post of Minister of Interior. Feeling ran so high that he did not dare appear before the Duma, over which he had once presided. In November, 1916, the Tsar decided to dismiss him, but the Empress in despair fought for him, and Protopopov remained in power until the end.

The Rising Tide of Unrest. Protopopov failed signally in his efforts to control the situation. In October, 1916, he sought to smash a city-wide strike in Petrograd by using two regiments of the garrison to reinforce the police. The troops, however, fired, not on the strikers, but on the police—an ominous note. Reports from the front frequently stressed that the soldiers wanted only peace and bread. Opposition to the war was so great that some officers feared to lead their troops in action lest they be shot by their own men. Protests demanding basic reforms were adopted by the *zemstvos* and the town governments, by the financial interests, by the nobility, and countless other organized groups. The situation grew so menacing that members of the Tsar's family met in secret to consider deposing the Tsar and the Empress as a means of avoiding the coming revolution. Generals and members of the Duma conferred concerning similar action, but nobody dared to take the lead.

On November 1, 1916, the Duma met for the first time in five months. Miliukov, leader of the Progressive Bloc, delivered a scathing attack on "the dark forces" around the throne, ending each part of his indictment with the question: "Is this stupidity or is it treason?" He was followed by several of the conservatives, who furiously denounced Rasputin and Stürmer. The latter, terrified, dared not challenge the Duma, in spite of the great wrath of the Empress. For once the Tsar acted independently by dismissing Stürmer and replacing him with a decent man, who insisted on removing Protopopov. The frantic Empress went to Headquarters, however, and secured the Tsar's promise to keep him, so that the dismissal of Stürmer brought little improvement. Fresh speeches in the Duma condemning Rasputin and his henchmen showed the enormous dissatisfaction of the Russian educated public, but produced no change in the government. The only result was further to infuriate the Empress, who demanded that the Tsar dismiss the Duma. "Russia loves to feel the whip."

One consequence of the speeches in the Duma was that several of the highest nobility of Russia decided to assassinate Rasputin in order to save the regime. Prince Yusupov, related to the Tsar by marriage, and the Grand Duke Dimitry, nephew of the Tsar, plied Rasputin with poisoned wine, and when that failed to take effect, he was shot and his body dumped into the river. When the corpse was recovered, the Tsar and the Empress attended his funeral upon the palace grounds. Rasputin's removal had no effect upon the political life of the land, which continued to drift toward revolution.

THE FIRST REVOLUTIONARY MONTHS

The Mounting Crisis. In the first two months of 1917, dissatisfaction in Russia grew rapidly. The inflation advanced at a fast pace, with severe effects upon the working population, which showed its exasperation by an increasing number of strikes. The food shortages angered all, especially the women who had to wait in line for hours in the bitter cold, sometimes to find that there was no food to be had. In the rising popular fury the radical parties played little part, as the Mensheviks were still supporting the war and the Bolsheviks, with their chief figures in exile abroad or in Siberia, could accomplish little. The revolutionary movement was thus largely spontaneous and unexpected, even though it had long been foreseen. . . .

The Uprising. The insurrection began almost unnoticed. Early in March, 1917, a strike of workers of Petrograd's great Putilov Works turned thousands of men onto the streets, to demonstrate against the government and to appeal to the workers of other plants. March 8, International Woman's Day, regularly celebrated by the workers, brought thousands of women from the breadlines to swell the crowds. Red flags and banners with the slogan "Down with the Autocracy!" made their appearance. The police, however, had no great trouble in dispersing the crowds, and the unrest seemed no greater than on previous occasions. By the 9th there were nearly 200,000 strikers in the streets, demonstrating in the center of the city. Cossacks called out to disperse the crowds refused to charge them, and on one occasion they bowed to the crowd which applauded their inactivity. But the unrest apparently still was not threatening: the British ambassador cabled London: "Some disorders occurred today, but nothing serious."

On March 10 the movement grew in intensity, and the Tsar wired General Khabalov, commander of the garrison, to disperse the crowds with rifle fire. The next day preparations were made to subdue the demonstrations. Police with machine guns were placed in the upper stories of buildings overlooking main thoroughfares, and regiments of the garrison fired with considerable effect on crowds in several parts of the city. The government seemed to have won. But that night the troops in their barracks decided not to shoot down the crowds in the future. When ordered to march on the morning of the 12th, one of the regiments refused, shot the commander, and poured into the streets to join the crowds. Other regiments were quickly won over to the revolution. Together with the workers they hunted down the police and broke into the arsenals, where 40,000 rifles were captured and distributed to the workers. While these events were occurring, M. V.

Rodzianko, President of the Duma, wired the Tsar, warning him of the seriousness of the situation and urging immediate reforms to avert a catastrophe. Nicholas said impatiently to his Court Chamberlain: "That fat Rodzianko has written me some nonsense, to which I shall not even reply."

Victory of the Revolution. By nightfall of March 12 it was all over. As the revolution surged ahead, General Khabalov sought to bring into play his special reserve of troops, but found himself able to collect no more than six companies. This force was sent to drive back the victorious crowds, but on contact with the insurrectionists they melted away, the men going over to the crowds, and the officers into hiding. Finally, late in the day, Khabalov, with less than two thousand men, took refuge in the Winter Palace, only to be asked to leave by the Grand Duke Michael. They went to the nearby Admiralty building, to disperse completely on the following day. The revolution was in full control of Petrograd. The overturn was marked by few excesses and by light casualties. Aside from burning the police stations and hunting down the police, the crowds shed little blood. In all, 1,315 persons, chiefly soldiers and citizens, were killed or wounded. In the rest of the vast Russian Empire, the revolution spread rapidly, with little fighting. . . .

The Revolutionary Government. The Duma was in session when the disorders began, but on March 12 they were prorogued by order of the Tsar, prepared well in advance. The deputies hesitated whether to obey the order of dismissal, but after some thought they accepted it, lest they give aid and comfort to the revolutionaries. They moved from their official meeting place to a room across the hall, where they organized as an unofficial committee with the purpose "of restoring order and to deal with institutions and individuals." In the meantime, as early as March 9, some of the revolutionary leaders, with memories of 1905, suggested the election of a Soviet of Workers' Deputies, and several factories did hold elections. It was only on March 12, however, that the Soviet assembled in the Tavrida Palace, across the hall from the meeting of the Duma committee. After it had been joined by delegates from the garrison regiments, it changed its name to Soviet of Workers' and Soldiers' Deputies. Both the Soviet and the Duma were visited by hordes of workers and soldiers, who looked to them for leadership. The Soviet busied itself with the practical matters of the moment —patrolling the streets, feeding the soldiers who had joined the revolution, and similar matters, while the Duma leaders sought to preserve an effective government for the country.

Most of the Duma leaders were convinced monarchists, who felt that a Tsar was essential, even though the abdication of Nicholas II could not be avoided. So it was decided to send a delegation to the Tsar to ask him to abdicate, naming his brother Michael as regent. With some difficulty two of them made their way to the Tsar, who had come part way back to the capital. Before they arrived, Nicholas had heard from all the leading generals that his abdication was essential, so when the delegates appeared he surprised them by readily abdicating in favor of Michael. Back in Petrograd, however, the Duma leaders found it impossible to persuade the masses to accept *any* Tsar and barely escaped violence when they came out for Michael. Nevertheless, on March 16 a group of the Duma leaders, headed by Miliukov, visited Michael to urge him to take the throne. The Grand Duke, however, realizing the public hostility to a monarchy, refused to take the crown except from a Constituent Assembly. Hence, Russia became a republic *de facto,* although the formal declaration of the republic came much later.

Formation of the Provisional Government. The members of the Duma committee felt that they had no right to form a government, but as they realized that if they did not, the leaders of the Soviet, more radical in their outlook, would do so, they decided to take power, "otherwise others will take it, those who have already elected some scoundrels in the factories." Miliukov, especially, sought to establish the authority of the new government by negotiating with the leaders of the Soviet. The latter, however, did not desire to rule, as they were men inexperienced in governmental affairs. Moreover, they were moderate socialists, who believed that at this moment the revolution was bourgeois in character, as the workers were too weak to set up the dictatorship of the proletariat. Hence, the Soviet chiefs felt that power should be entrusted to the leaders of the bourgeoisie, drawn from the ranks of the Duma.

Consequently, on March 14, the leaders of the Duma and the Soviet conferred about the powers and program of the new government, which took office on March 16. The Premier of the Provisional Government was Prince G. E. Lvov, a noted liberal; Guchkov was Minister of War, and Miliukov was Foreign Minister. Alexander Kerensky took the post of Minister of Justice. He was nominally a right-wing Socialist Revolutionary, although he was basically conservative. But his enthusiasm for the revolutionary overturn and his inspiring speeches had made him a popular hero and had won him election to the Soviet. He joined the Provisional Government while retaining his membership in the Soviet for the purpose of serving as a link between the two bodies.

The program of the new regime, approved by the Soviet, provided for a full amnesty, broad civil liberties, and complete legal equality of all. Trade unions and strikes were declared legal. The manifesto promised immediate preparation for a constituent assembly, to be elected by universal, direct, equal, and secret voting. Local government was also to be elected. Finally, the soldiers were promised full civil rights, upon condition that firm discipline was observed. This program, which was necessarily a compromise between the Duma and the Soviet, said nothing about the vital issues: the war, and the distribution of land to the peasants. On these points no agreement was possible.

Like its program, the government itself was an uneasy compromise between the Soviet and the leaders of the former Duma. The latter, drawn from the middle-class parties, were quite conservative and instinctively distrusted the masses and the Soviet which represented them. For its part, the Soviet had no great confidence in the Provisional Government. Backed as it was by the vast majority of the workers and the soldiers of the Petrograd garrison, the Soviet undertook to support the Provisional Government only as long as the latter remained true to the cause of the revolution. It compelled the government to arrest the Tsar.

Order No. 1. One of the first acts of the Soviet was to issue its famous Order No. 1 to the troops, to ensure that they would not be used for counter-revolutionary purposes. It was drawn up on March 14 at the suggestion of some of the soldiers. It provided for the election of committees of soldiers in all army units, which were to obey the Soviet and were to keep control of the arms, which were not to be turned over to the officers. The troops were to obey their officers and the Provisional Government, but only insofar as their orders were not in conflict with those of the Soviet. Saluting off duty and elaborate honors to officers were abolished, and the officers were forbidden to be harsh toward their men. These instructions were in part a symptom of the distrust of the officers felt by the rank and file, who had seen that their officers had given no support to the revolution. Discipline in the army had begun to crumble well before the fall of the Tsar. Nevertheless, Order No. 1 doubtless contributed much to the further collapse of the authority of the commanders and of the discipline essential to any effective body of troops. Thus, the Provisional Government lacked effective military support and was dependent for its authority upon the backing of the Soviet.

An Era of Good Feeling. Although in the first weeks after the fall of the monarchy the dualism or divided control of the state held latent the seeds of conflict, matters for a time went fairly smoothly. The Soviet, which grew to over three thousand members, was dominated largely by the soldier delegates, who were usually noncommissioned officers, company clerks, or other partly educated persons, who were not especially radical in their views. Most of them were under the influence of the Socialist Revolutionaries, who supported the war and were not eager for further radicalism. For the most part the workers were led by the Mensheviks, who also supported the war. The latter were convinced that Russia was by no means ready for a proletarian dictatorship, so they were quite ready to let the upper classes represented by the Provisional Government run the country. Even the Bolsheviks did not take an extreme stand at this time.

Kamenev and Stalin, who returned from Siberia during these early days, in their *Pravda* editorials held that, while the war was imperialist in nature, until a general peace became possible there should be no attempt to make a separate peace, and the Russian army should continue to defend the country. And, indeed, even if the Bolsheviks *had* been inspired by the radical views of Lenin, who was fretting in exile in Switzerland, they were too few in numbers and too weak in influence to disturb the relative calm. . . .

The Moderate Attitude of the Masses. In general, the army, although it had long since lost any enthusiasm for the war, still thought along traditional lines of its duty to defend the country. . . .

As early as March, 1917, the peasants began to call for peasant Soviets to consider the land question. Nevertheless, they still remembered their punishment in 1906 and 1907 too well to act rashly, and for a time they were willing to wait. The workers, who had immediately gained the eight hour day as a result of the revolution, also were not yet ready for further insurrection. In March, 1917, factory committees, elected by the workers, were set up, to represent the workers in negotiating with the employers. Although there was much friction between committees and employers, in the early spring the committees were seeking higher wages for the employees rather than confiscation of the factories. As yet the moderate socialists had not been replaced by the militant Bolsheviks who later dominated the committees, and the workers were not in a revolutionary frame of mind.

The Rising Conflict Over Foreign Policy. At first the Provisional Government took the position that the revolution had changed nothing in Russia's foreign policy. Miliukov, the Foreign Minister, hastened to assure the Allies that Russia stood by her treaty obligations and warmed their hearts by stating that the Tsar had been overthrown because his government had not been able to wage war with sufficient energy—a far from correct statement. Miliukov was especially interested in obtaining Constantinople and the Dardanelles for Russia, which had been promised by the secret treaties of 1915. The moderate socialists who dominated the Soviet, however, felt that the war was essentially imperialistic in character and hoped that the peoples of the other warring states would also overturn their governments and demand peace.

With this end in view, on March 27 the Soviet issued a "Manifesto to the Peoples of the World," calling on them to oppose actively the annexationist policies of their governments. The Russian democracy, the manifesto promised, would resist to the death all efforts of its ruling classes to pursue such a policy. The peoples of the West, especially in Germany, should rise in revolution against kings, landowners, and bankers, and thus bring about a revolutionary peace. But until this should happen, the Soviet declared, the Russian revolution would not retreat before conquering bayonets nor allow itself to be crushed by outside force. This manifesto was widely hailed by the socialist press, which strongly demanded a peace "without annexations and indemnities."

Miliukov, however, did not share this attitude. Early in April he issued a press interview stating that Russia was fighting to unite the Ukrainian

parts of the Austro-Hungarian Empire with Russia and to gain Constantinople and the Straits. These objectives, he declared, could not be regarded
as annexation. This utterance aroused a storm of protest. Conflict was
averted, however, when the Provisional Government published a "Declaration on War Aims" renouncing annexations and upholding self-determination. It added, however, that Russia should not "emerge from the great
struggle humiliated, undermined in her vital strength." The Provisional
Government stated its determination "to protect national rights while
strictly fulfilling the obligations assumed toward the Allies." In these vague
phrases Miliukov saw support for his design to win Constantinople.

Lenin's Return. The news of the fall of the monarchy and the forming
of the Provisional Government found Lenin in Switzerland, where he had
spent much of the war years. During this period he had formulated his attitude toward the war. Capitalism, he held, must inevitably lead to imperialism, and imperialism is bound to produce war for the interests of the capitalists. In such a conflict the working class had no interest, but should
strive to transform the war into a civil war. The socialists of Europe who
had supported their nation's cause after Serajevo were thus traitors to the
proletariat. Only a true Marxist party could be trusted to end the war in
the interests of the working class. . . .

Swiss socialist leaders arranged with the German government to let
him and a number of other Russian exiles travel across Germany in a sealed
car to Denmark; from there he made his way to Sweden and Finland, and
on April 16 he reached Petrograd. Although he had expected to be arrested by the Provisional Government, to his surprise he was met by a
deputation from the Soviet and a guard of honor at the Finland Station.
He impatiently turned from his official welcome to address the throngs of
people in a fiery speech ending with the words: "Long live the socialist
revolution!"

The April Theses. On April 17, the day after his arrival, Lenin presented his revolutionary program to two gatherings: one of Bolsheviks, and
the second of Bolsheviks and Mensheviks together. The program, known
as the April Theses, contained ten points. It declared that the war was still
an imperialistic one, to be ended by the overthrow of capitalism and fraternization of the soldiers with the enemy. The revolution, he held, should
immediately take the power from the hands of the bourgeoisie and give it
to the proletariat and poorer peasants. No support should be given to the
Provisional Government, which should be replaced by the Soviet of Workers' Deputies. All large estates were to be nationalized and turned over to
the Soviets of Farmhands' Deputies.

This program, in particular as it concerned the war, horrified even the
Bolshevik leaders, who felt that it was utterly unrealistic. The Mensheviks
regarded Lenin as so visionary as to be ludicrous and felt joy at his imprac-
ticability. His program was promptly rejected by the Bolsheviks, 12 to 2,

and *Pravda* wrote that his proposals were based upon an incorrect analysis of the revolution. But Lenin was not dismayed by this reception. He pushed his program in incessant speeches to streams of men and women who came to hear him, and so simple and so logical did his points of "End the war" and "All land to the peasants" seem that he won their complete support. His propaganda enjoyed such success among the masses that his party swung over to his side, and at an All-Russian Conference of Bolsheviks in May it strongly approved the program that it had rejected three weeks before. Thus, the lines began to form for a struggle between the Provisional Government and the masses, urged on by Lenin.

THE MOUNTING CRISIS

The Fall of Miliukov. Miliukov's trickery in attempting to cover his annexationist aims with vague words soon came out into the open. When it was discovered that the Allies had not heard of the "Declaration of War Aims," there was a strong demand that he communicate it officially to them. He did so on May 1, but accompanied the Declaration with a covering note, in which he affirmed that Russia was determined to carry the war "to a decisive conclusion," in order to obtain "sanctions and guarantees" which would make new wars impossible. ("Sanctions and guarantees" sounded ominously like annexations.) Finally, he again promised to "fulfill Russia's obligations to her Allies." When, on May 3, this note became public, it was taken as a deliberate challenge to the wishes of the public. The people felt that their strivings for peace had been nullified by the obstinate Foreign Minister.

A crisis of extreme seriousness resulted, with mass demonstrations in front of the seat of the Provisional Government. Although some of the demonstrators supported Miliukov, most of them, including fully armed regiments, carried banners demanding peace without annexations and indemnities, the end of the war, and the dismissal of Miliukov. On the next day, there were even stronger demonstrations, in which there were demands for the end of the Provisional Government. General L. G. Kornilov, commander of the Petrograd garrison, wanted to use his troops to smash the demonstration, but severe bloodshed was averted by the Petrograd Soviet, which ordered that no regiment should come out into the streets without an order signed by the Soviet. Kornilov, angered by this check upon his authority, resigned his command and went to the front.

The demonstration was quickly checked by the orders of the Soviet. The Provisional Government hastened to calm the public by issuing its explanation of Miliukov's note, which it sent to the Allied ambassadors. It practically disavowed Miliukov's interpretation and repeated the pacifist phrases of the earlier declarations. As Miliukov held to his views, he now had to give up the Foreign Ministry, and he refused a lesser post. Likewise Guchkov, Minister of War, also resigned, in part because of poor health, and partly from despair with the trend of events. These resignations led to a reorganization of the Provisional Government, which reformed with nine ministers from the former Duma (chiefly Cadets), and six moderate socialists from the Soviet. It was hoped that this coalition would end the friction between the Soviet and the Provisional Government. The result, however, was to transfer the disharmony into the midst of the government itself. Probably the chief figure in the new regime was Kerensky, the Minister of War. . . .

The Lull Before the Storm. The Provisional Government, and especially the Cadet party, which was rapidly absorbing the other conservative parties, seemed little concerned over the rise of the Bolsheviks. . . . The Bolsheviks, while growing, remained a considerable minority, while the moderate socialists remained in control of the Soviet. But here, too, the reality was not reassuring to the moderates. While the masses out of habit voted for socialists, at the same time they often would vote for Bolshevik resolutions. Nevertheless, when the First Congress of Soviets met on June 16, 1917, the Bolsheviks and allied groups had only 137 out of the 1,090 members. Tseretelli, a moderate leader of the Petrograd Soviet, was sufficiently encouraged by the lack of Bolshevik strength to declare in his speech that the government was secure, "as there is no political party in Russia which at the present time would say: 'Give us power.'" But at this point Lenin spoke from his seat: "Yes, there is!" . . .

The Military Debacle. On July 1, 1917, the Russian offensive began in Galicia. The Russians, with great superiority in numbers and thanks to an unprecedented artillery preparation, penetrated the Austrian lines at several points near Lvov and took several thousand prisoners. Soon, however, they encountered unexpected resistance. The attack, which on other fronts had had no success, bogged down after twelve days. On July 19, the Germans and Austrians began a counter-drive which met almost no opposition as the Russians fled headlong. All discipline vanished and the rout intensified, accompanied by terrible outrages inflicted on the civilians as the troops fled. Finally the line stabilized after all Galicia had been given up; but it was the decision of the enemy rather than Russian resistance that ended the retreat. General Kornilov, who was appointed to command the Southwest Front on July 20, demanded the death penalty in the front areas, and immediately used machine guns and artillery on masses of deserters and mutineers. On July 25, the Provisional Government restored the death penalty and set up special military tribunals to deal with major offenses. But not even these measures accomplished much, for the morale of the army was ruined beyond repair.

The July Insurrection. While the Russian offensive was continuing, violence erupted in Petrograd. The masses of workers, already very hostile toward the Provisional Government, and the soldiers of the garrison, fearful that they might be sent to the front, grew impatient with the apparent timidity of the Bolshevik leadership. On July 16 the First Machine Gun Regiment, an especially radical unit, marched forth, although both the Soviets and the Bolsheviks sought to restrain them. The revolutionary call of the soldiers was eagerly obeyed by other troop units and by hundreds of thousands of workers, whom the Bolsheviks reluctantly led, in order to keep them from getting completely out of hand. On July 17, perhaps 500,000 in huge columns poured through the streets with banners demanding "All Power to the Soviets!" and "Down with the Provisional Government!" They converged on the Tavrida Palace, seat of the Central Executive Committee of the Soviets, to demand that this body assume power in place of the Provisional Government. Feelings ran extremely high, as the demonstrators, augmented by a large force of fierce sailors from Kronstadt, armed to the teeth, streamed through the streets. Occasional shots were fired, at which the demonstrators, believing themselves under attack from neighboring buildings, broke into the houses to hunt for snipers. Several score of persons were killed, and over one hundred wounded. Some of the ministers had narrow escapes. Kerensky was almost captured on the first day, and Victor Chernov, the socialist Minister of Agriculture, escaped death at the hands of sailors only through the intervention of Trotsky.

In the meantime, in the palace, the Central Executive Committee, composed chiefly of Mensheviks and Socialist Revolutionaries, was beset by masses of furious armed men who demanded that they take power—something they refused to do. A stalemate developed as frustrated soldiers and workers threatened the frightened but stubborn leaders of the Soviet to induce them to take power. But the long discussions proved fruitless, and the Bolsheviks, who could easily have seized all Petrograd by giving the order, failed to do so, so that eventually the demonstrators grew weary and went home. The sailors boarded their ships and went back to Kronstadt, and the Central Executive Committee could breathe more freely.

Reaction Against Lenin and the Bolsheviks. The tide of revolt receded as quickly as it had risen. Several of the Guards regiments, which had not taken part in the demonstration, were informed on July 17 that the Minister of Justice had documentary proof that Lenin was a German agent. The Guards, convinced by this, at once put themselves at the orders of the government and the Central Executive Committee. The danger was now over, and on the following day government forces raided and wrecked the offices and plant of *Pravda* and occupied without a struggle the Fortress of Peter and Paul and the Bolshevik headquarters. On July 19 a Bolshevik leaflet announced that the demonstration was at an end.

The documents charging Lenin and other Bolshevik leaders with treason were published in the newspapers, much to the annoyance of Kerensky, who claimed that this had prevented Lenin's capture and punishment.

Other ministers were very dubious about the documents and their source. The middle classes, however, were easily convinced of the correctness of the charges, as they remembered that Lenin had left Switzerland in a German train. Warrants were issued for his arrest, and also for Zinoviev and Kamenev. But Lenin and Zinoviev hid, although they protested their innocence. Lenin at first wanted to stand trial, but as he was persuaded by his associates that he might be murdered in prison, he escaped to Finland, where the Russian police could not follow. He stayed in Helsingfors until autumn. Trotsky and several other Bolsheviks were arrested, but were soon released.

It is perhaps worth stating that most historians of repute do not believe that Lenin was a German agent, even though the Germans had enabled him to return to Russia. . . .

Government Policy After the July Days. The Provisional Government took advantage of its improved position to take further action. Legislation was adopted against incitement to mutiny. Regiments that had taken the lead in the uprising were disbanded and the men sent to the front, in some cases with the use of force. Several of the Bolshevik newspapers were closed and circulation of such publications among the troops was forbidden. . . .

The moderate and the conservative elements of Russia had been granted a new lease of life by the unexpected outcome of the July Days. Neither group, however, took advantage of the opportunity to satisfy the enormous popular demand for peace and land, which was the basis of the strength of the Bolsheviks. The moderate Left continued to advocate prosecution of the war to victory and urged that the land and other problems be deferred until the Constituent Assembly, which, it must be said, they did little to hasten. Thus, they did nothing of significance to win the masses from the Bolsheviks and, hence, remained without any real popular following. As for the Right—landowners, capitalists, army officers, and other upper-class elements—they had never accepted the revolutionary regime in their hearts, and now that the rabble had been subdued, they felt that they discerned the delightful possibility of a strong man—a military dictatorship—to sweep aside all this rubbish of socialists and soviets and to establish sound law and order again, as before the revolution.

THE KORNILOV MOVEMENT

The Illusion of Calm. Although the collapse of the July demonstration had apparently ended all danger from the Bolsheviks, the improvement in the government's position was largely on the surface, while underneath the situation grew worse. On instructions from Lenin, the Bolsheviks concentrated their efforts on the factory committees, which were becoming more and more aggressive. The factory workers found that the rapid inflation raised prices far more than they could raise their wages, and the poorer paid were especially hard hit. The declaration of the textile workers that their children were dying like flies as a result of hunger was not entirely rhetoric. Hence, the lot of the workers became unbearable and they turned to the factory committees for redress and to the Bolsheviks for leadership. . . .

To add to the woes of the government, the national minorities became increasingly self-assertive. As Poland and most of the Baltic states were held by the Germans, they were not an active problem; but both Finland and the Ukraine were becoming restless. . . .

The Kerensky Government. The coalition formed after the July Days failed to endure, for on July 21 Prince Lvov resigned his post as Premier in disapproval of the socialist policy of Chernov, Minister of Agriculture, and others. Kerensky thereupon took office as Premier. After much negotiating and scheming a new government was installed in early August, with eleven socialists and seven nonsocialists. In spite of the preponderance of socialists, however, the new government was more conservative than its predecessor, as the socialists, frightened by the events of July, had lost all trace of revolutionary zeal. More and more, Kerensky dominated the scene. . . .

The Rise of General Kornilov. . . . General L. G. Kornilov, the new commander-in-chief, was a dashing soldier who had won great fame by his exploits in the war as well as by his spectacular personality. A Siberian, with somewhat Mongolian features, he was followed with devotion by a bodyguard of wild Caucasian cavalrymen, whose language he knew. In May, as commander of the Petrograd garrison, he had wished to smash the demonstration against Miliukov, and when the Soviet had prevented this he had resigned to go to the front. Kornilov's reputation as a Napoleonic figure had been further enhanced by his ruthless measures in dealing with the routed troops after the disastrous July offensive. He was greatly admired by Boris Savinkov, the former Socialist Revolutionary who had become head of the Ministry of War under Kerensky, and as Kerensky felt that Kornilov would be successful in reviving the fighting spirit of the army, the general had been named commander-in-chief on July 31. Kornilov's conditions for taking over this post, amounting to a virtual free hand with the army, as well as the extension of full military control to the rear military areas, indicated that he would be a difficult person to handle. The friction caused by this stand was soon eliminated when Kornilov agreed to a compromise, but the incident gave a hint of trouble to come.

Kornilov's Dictatorial Tendencies. Kornilov, who had little knowledge of politics, soon became a storm center. He was instinctively hostile to all socialists, whether extreme or mild, and he disliked Kerensky, although he promised to work with him. The Leftist press, which saw in him a danger to the revolution, attacked him strongly, asking that he be replaced by a general more in sympathy with the revolutionary cause. Conservatives and reactionaries became his enthusiastic allies. The Union of Cossack Troops warned that the consequences for the army would be disastrous if he were removed—an opinion voiced by other military organizations. . . .

The Moscow State Conference. Kornilov's *coup d'état* was already taking shape by August 25. It gained even greater momentum as a result of the Moscow State Conference, which took place on August 25-28. Ironically enough, this meeting, whose purpose was to demonstrate the unity of all behind the government, met in a Moscow without streetcars and without lights; even the restaurants were not functioning, thanks to a one-day general strike called by the Bolsheviks. The Conference, far from supporting Kerensky's government, turned into an overt demonstration of the Right, whose hostility toward Kerensky was plain to see. . . .

The Preliminaries to the Uprising. The outcome of the Moscow State Conference was to confirm Kornilov and his supporters in the belief that Kerensky could never restore order in Russia, for which Kornilov was the essential man. Rodzianko, Miliukov, and other leaders of the Duma period, energetically enrolled landowners and financial magnates in well financed organizations to further the cause, while generals and officers built up organizations of officers and military cadets to support the march on Petrograd by uprisings at the right moment. Kornilov's chief-of-staff later claimed that there were thousands in Petrograd waiting to strike in support of the movement. On September 6, Savinkov, head of the War Ministry under Kerensky, with the latter's approval, visited Kornilov at Headquarters and approved the commander's demands for introducing the death penalty in the rear, Savinkov also told him that as a Bolshevik uprising was expected within a few days, he should send a cavalry corps to the capital to protect the Provisional Government.

This request, which Kornilov had already anticipated by sending troops, was part of the political scheme to which Savinkov was a party. Kerensky was to be invited to dismiss the government and form a new one in which he, Kornilov, and Savinkov would be the dominant figures. If Kerensky refused, the troops were to be brought into play. Unfortunately for the success of the scheme, V. N. Lvov, a lesser political figure, undertook to persuade Kerensky to cooperate, and thereby gave the Premier warning. Kerensky, realizing that if the scheme went through his freedom, if not his life, would be in danger, at once took steps against the conspiracy. After arresting Lvov, on September 9 he ordered Kornilov to resign and asked for support from the Soviet and from the ministers. The Soviet at once gave him full support, but the Cadet ministers resigned from the government, apparently hoping to cause its collapse. . . .

The Collapse of the Movement. Undismayed by Kerensky's opposition, Kornilov persisted in his undertaking, issuing a blast against the Provisional Government, charging it with collaborating with the Germans and ruin-

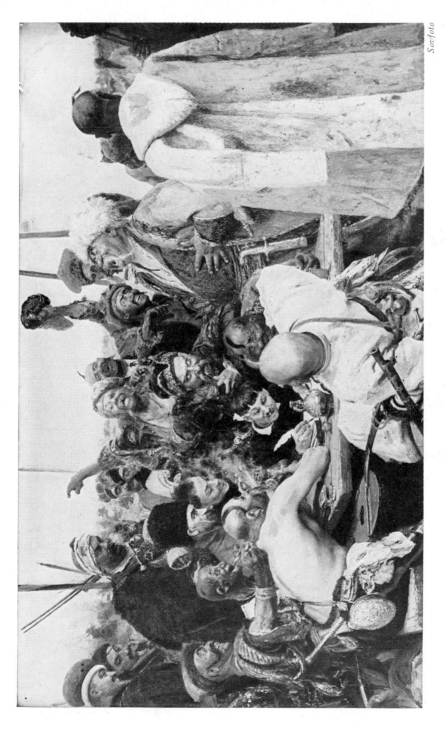

The Zaporozhye Cossacks. The Cossacks are composing a provocative letter to Sultan Mahomet IV of Turkey. The painting is by the Russian artist Ilya Repin.

Peter the Great.

Tsar Nicholas II and his family.

The Bolshevik attack on the Winter Palace. The artist V. Kuznetsov shows the Bolsheviks storming the headquarters of the Provisional Government in November 1917.

The first Russian Revolution of 1905, "Barricades in Moscow," from a painting by I. Vladimirov.

Lenin addressing armed workers and peasants in 1919.

ing the army and the country. He appealed to the populace in a manifesto full of nationalist and religious phrases, which, however, had already lost their potency. With almost complete support from the Allies, and even aided by a British unit of armored cars, whose men had donned Russian uniforms, he was certain of success. Most of the army leaders were with him, he was sure of the Wild Division and the Cossacks, and he counted on the aid of other disciplined troops. The garrison of Petrograd seemed to have no great enthusiasm for fighting for Kerensky. As for the Petrograd populace, he felt that they, unorganized and leaderless, would remain in sullen apathy, "an indifference that submits to the whip." General Krymov and the other field commanders were ordered to advance on Petrograd.

As soon as the Soviet in Petrograd realized the approaching danger, it hastened to act. Despairing of Kerensky's leadership, the Soviet leaders threw themselves into the work of defending the capital. On September 9, moderate socialists and Bolsheviks combined in a "Committee for Struggle against Counter-Revolution" to defeat Kornilov. The garrison was put in a state of readiness, neighboring troops were called to their aid, and large numbers of eager sailors from Kronstadt arrived, with more coming from other parts of the fleet. Under Bolshevik leadership the Petrograd workers were mobilized. Trenches were dug, barbed wire was strung, barricades were built in the city streets. The Red Guards from the factories, who had been disarmed after the July Days, were again given weapons, and turned out, full of fight. Strong detachments were sent to break up the officers' organizations that had planned to rise as Krymov's forces approached. The conspiratorial center in the Hotel Astoria was taken without difficulty, and a sweeping series of arrests and searches eliminated other groups of plotters. A colonel sent by Kornilov to direct the movement fled to Finland. In all, some 7,000 arrests were made by the Soviet, thus ending all danger of an officers' uprising in Petrograd.

The Failure of the Troop Movements. Not content to await the arrival of the attacking forces, the Soviet had sent word to the railway workers to impede the movement of the hostile troops. At the orders of their union the men cut telegraph wires, put locomotives out of commission, blocked tracks by tipping over freight cars, tore up rails. As the troop trains progressed, they were switched off in the wrong direction and finally halted, isolated and helpless. . . .

The Aftermath of the Kornilov Coup. Kerensky, who had been saved by the spontaneous action of the Soviet and the Bolsheviks, was far from happy about his position after the episode. He now realized that, with the power of the Right destroyed, the Left had gained greatly in strength. Hence, he sought to use the remaining conservatives as a counterweight to the now rising popular forces. To replace Kornilov as commander-in-chief Kerensky named, not one of the generals in sympathy with the revolution, but General Alexeev, who had been hand-in-glove with Kornilov. Moreover, Kerensky ordered that, until Alexeev arrived at Headquarters, the army should continue to obey Kornilov's orders. Alexeev promptly cancelled the movement of strong revolutionary forces to subdue Kornilov's Headquarters garrison. It was only with the greatest reluctance that he had the insurgent general arrested on September 14, along with his most obvious supporters. The arrested men were transferred to a town in the Ukraine, where they were nominally imprisoned. The jailers were none other than Kornilov's devoted Caucasian bodyguard.

An extraordinary investigating committee was sent out to gather evidence against the conspirators, but they showed no willingness to take action and soon released all but the five chief participants. It was obvious that Kerensky's government was not willing to deal harshly with the insurgents. To the masses of soldiers and workers, who had been willing to risk their lives to suppress the Kornilov insurrection, this tenderness toward the defeated generals seemed as treasonable as the uprising itself.

THE AFTERMATH OF THE KORNILOV AFFAIR

Another Chance for Kerensky. After the threat from Kornilov had been removed, Kerensky, although his prestige was badly shaken by his unwillingness to punish the rebels, still had an opportunity to bring the government into line with the aspirations of the people. It is conceivable that if he had accepted reality and had decided to support the demand for peace and had approved a land program satisfactory to the peasants, a more violent revolutionary outbreak could still have been avoided. A moderate democratic regime was perhaps still possible. Instead of making a sharp change in direction, however, the government remained much as before. It still depended on the old Central Executive Committee of the Soviet which had been elected in the earlier, conservative period and which did not represent the feelings of the masses. The Socialist Revolutionaries and the Mensheviks who composed it had been left behind by the rapid march of events. Beneath the surface the Soviets were beginning to swing to the Bolsheviks, while peasants and soldiers were no longer willing to support the war and to wait for a much-postponed Constituent Assembly to deal with the land problem. The appeal of the Right to counter-revolutionary force had made the masses far more impatient with the inaction of the government and more ready to decide the issue by a new resort to the enormous revolutionary force that still remained.

More than ever the government of Russia centered in Kerensky. After the crisis was over, the ministers, who had tendered their resignations, remained in office for a time on a day-to-day basis. In September 14, a Directory or inner cabinet of five men, headed by Kerensky, was set up to determine policy. On the same day, Russia was proclaimed a republic. This step, which merely recognized what had long been obvious, met with strong opposition on the part of the conservatives, who asserted that it exceeded the powers of the Provisional Government. Many felt that beneath the legalistic basis for the protest there lingered a strong hope on the part of the conservatives that somehow the monarchy could be restored. . . .

The Failure of the Socialist Revolutionaries. Kerensky's failure to take advantage of the collapse of the Right was paralleled by the failure of his party—the Socialist Revolutionaries. This party, the largest political organization in Russia before the revolution, expanded enormously after the fall of the Tsar. It had long enjoyed the support of the teeming peasant millions, and now that many of these millions were in uniform and had rifles in their hands their political activity had greatly increased. They joined the Socialist Revolutionary party in such numbers that the party was not able to digest the huge mass. Several of its most effective leaders had died shortly before the revolution, leaving Victor Chernov, a theorist and writer rather than a practical politician, to deal with the vital problems of the times. Other Socialist Revolutionary leaders, especially those like Kerensky, who had represented the party in the Duma, became more and more conservative and lost touch with the masses. . . .

The Split in the Ranks of the SR's. While the Socialist Revolutionary leaders for the most part were becoming more conservative, the rank and file were becoming more and more radical. In May, 1917, the SR's held their Third All-Russian Congress, at which, in spite of a strong tendency of the Right faction to secede, Chernov's program was adopted, calling for a just and speedy peace and for a positive socialist policy of labor and agrarian legislation. This evidence that the bulk of the party wanted to follow a progressive policy was lost on the leaders, except Chernov, who before long was forced from power. . . .

The Breakdown of the Army and Navy. To the millions of Russian soldiers, suffering from hunger and cold in the trenches, the Kornilov insurrection added a new and more infuriating grievance. The soldiers had been distrustful of their officers, most of whom had taken no part in the struggle for the overthrow of the Tsar. The men were convinced that the war was an imperialistic struggle for Constantinople and Galicia, and when the July offensive was attempted, it confirmed these beliefs. Now they had seen their highest commanders, who had insistently demanded the death penalty as punishment for desertion and mutiny, rise in rebellion against the revolution. Many of the other officers had sought to aid the Kornilov mutiny and few had taken a stand against it. Moreover, after the rank and file of the army, together with the populace of Petrograd, had suppressed this revolt, it became clear that none of the guilty leaders—to say nothing of the lesser culprits—would pay with his life. . . .

Fraternization with the enemy became common—in part induced by Bolshevik or German propaganda, but often a spontaneous expression of distaste for the business of killing. Any active measures against the enemy were bitterly opposed: when artillerymen, less infected with the mutinous spirit, opened fire on the enemy lines, thus inviting retaliation against the Russian trenches, the Russian infantry cut the telephone wires to the batteries and even beat the gunners if they persisted in firing. Violence against officers increased after the Kornilov affair. Numerous officers were arrested by their men or were forced to resign. In some cases, privates or corporals were elected to replace them. Riots occasionally occurred, in which officers were beaten or killed. Sometimes enlisted men fired into the quarters of their officers at night or threw hand-grenades into the officers' mess. Even the soldiers' committees and the commissars with the troops were not immune from attack if they tried to uphold the authority of the officers.

The Russian navy was an especially radical part of the armed forces. Kronstadt had become a hotbed of revolt early in the revolution and remained so, in spite of all that Kerensky could do. The naval bases at Helsingfors and Sveaborg were also radical. The crews of all the ships of the Baltic fleet were strongly behind the Bolsheviks and would have played a big role in the Kornilov affair if stubborn fighting had developed. The Black Sea fleet, on the other hand, for some time maintained its discipline under Admiral Kolchak, and in the spring of 1917 it even supported the war. But eventually it, too, succumbed to the revolutionary virus. By the middle of June the sailors began disarming their officers. Kolchak threw his sword into the sea rather than give it up and resigned his command in disgust. By October, 1917, the Black Sea fleet was as radical as the Baltic fleet.

The Rising Peasant Movement. In the early days of the revolution the peasants had not taken the law into their own hands, but had apparently decided to wait for the Constituent Assembly to deal with the land problem. In the meantime, Chernov, Minister of Agriculture, took steps to prepare the basis for a future transfer of the land of the landowners to the peasants. But Chernov was forced from office with little to show for his efforts, and the Constituent Assembly was repeatedly postponed. The peasants, whose conviction remained firm that the land should go to him who tilled it, grew weary of waiting. . . .

In the autumn months of 1917 the climax was reached. More and more frequently the peasants marched in a body to the estates of the landowners, broke into the manor houses, and pillaged without mercy. If the gentry submitted without resistance, they were usually permitted to go in peace. The livestock, implements, furniture, and other useful articles, as well as the land, were divided up by the peasants, who then usually burned the manors and other buildings, to make sure that the owners would not return. Often much wanton damage was done: the leaves of fine library books were torn out for cigarette paper, and paintings by famous artists were cut from their frames to make canvas trousers. . . .

The Upsurge of the Workers. The factory workers had been, from the beginning of the revolution, the most radical element in Russia. Repeatedly, in Petrograd, the proletarians had given proof of their readiness to seek an extreme solution of their difficulties. After the frustration of the masses in the July Days, the workers had been somewhat subdued, and their units of Red Guards had been largely disarmed by the government. But their grievances had not been remedied, but rather had become more burdensome as the galloping inflation cut sharply into the buying power of their wages. Food riots grew increasingly frequent.

To make matters worse, after midsummer there were increasingly frequent closings of factories, which threw harassed men out of work. Probably, in most cases, these shutdowns were caused by such unavoidable factors as shortages of fuel or raw materials like steel, rubber, and cotton. But the desperate workers were always prone to think that the closings were lockouts intended to compel the workers to reduce their wage demands, especially as the employers were known to have expressed wrath on this score. The remark allegedly made by Riabushinsky, a great industrialist, rang from one end of Russia to the other: "Perhaps . . . we need the bony hand of hunger, the poverty of the people, which would seize by the throat all these false friends of the people, all those democratic Soviets and committees." Whether it was said or not, it was widely believed, and it infuriated the workers, who needed little to anger them. . . .

The Rising Power of the Bolsheviks. With soldiers, peasants, and workers in a militant frame of mind, the Bolsheviks found themselves in a steadily improving position. They could gain little support among the peasants, but the soldiers, both at the front and in the garrisons in the rear, were turning to them and rejecting less radical advisers. Likewise the workers, who had never believed the charges against Lenin, in the fall of 1917 almost completely gave their allegiance to the Bolsheviks. . . .

Control of the workers and the garrison troops led inevitably to control of the Soviets through their frequent elections. On September 12 the Bolsheviks obtained a majority in the Petrograd Soviet, and on October 8 it elected Trotsky as its president. The Moscow Soviet was won by the Bolsheviks on September 18, and many of the provincial Soviets were coming under their control.

The party of Lenin was strong not only in the two capitals, but also in the Volga towns, the industrial centers of the Urals, the Donets Basin, and in other industrial towns of the Ukraine. Moreover, the Bolsheviks had as allies the Left Socialist Revolutionaries, who had a considerable following in the army and among the peasants. Thus, the Bolsheviks had effective support in many important areas of Russia and need no longer fear that a Red Petrograd would be opposed by the rest of the country.

Lenin's Insistence on an Uprising. Lenin, still in Finland, was immensely cheered by the results of the Kornilov insurrection. In the latter part of September, he wrote a letter to the Central Committee of the Bolshevik party demanding the seizure of power and reviving the slogan "All Power to the Soviets." This letter, however, was promptly rejected by the Central Committee as unrealistic. He followed this with two secret letters to the Central Committee saying that the time was ripe for seizure. His arguments, however, failed to sway the committee. . . .

Another letter, "The Crisis Is Ripe," repeated his earlier arguments that the Bolsheviks now had strong support from the masses and added a new argument: the revolution in Germany, he declared, was fast approaching and would back up the revolt in Russia. To show his sincerity and determination, Lenin offered his resignation to the Central Committee in order that he might have freedom of action. The offer was refused, but Lenin continued to oppose the decision of his party by writing to various local organizations of the Bolsheviks and to the populace to urge support for his program.

One of Lenin's most effective strokes was a pamphlet, *Can the Bolsheviks Hold State Power?* In it he strove to refute the arguments of some of the more moderate Bolsheviks, who held that, even if an insurrection should prove successful, it would not be supported by the rest of the country and in the end would be drowned in a sea of blood. Lenin, however, argued that if a few hundred thousand landowners and Tsarist officials could rule Russia for centuries, the Bolsheviks, who already enjoyed the support of great masses of the people, could hold power. Especially, he stated, when the lowly and the poor began to see that the new Soviet government would suppress the rich and strip them of their wealth, which would be given to the needy poor, then "no power of the capitalists and kulaks . . . can conquer the people's revolution."

Gradually, Lenin's persistent urging won out over the doubts of his fellow Bolsheviks. On October 22, he returned to Petrograd in disguise and on the following day he spoke at a crucial meeting of the Central Committee. His passionate emphasis on the need for an uprising and his reproaches of "indifference" to this question turned the tide in his favor, albeit with difficulty. The vote was ten to two in favor of an insurrection, with Zinoviev and Kamenev opposed. The Central Committee also named a Political Bureau to carry out the preparations for the revolt. . . .

On October 29, Lenin again presented his arguments to an enlarged meeting of the Central Committee. He told the Bolsheviks that there would be either a dictatorship of the Right or the Left, and that the party should not be guided solely by the feelings of the masses, who were inclined to waver from one side to the other. He also expressed faith in the coming German revolution. Once more he won, but again Zinoviev and Kamenev voiced their doubts, which may have been shared by others present. Kamenev then resigned from the Central Committee. Two days later a letter from Zinoviev and Kamenev appeared in Maxim Gorky's *Novaia Zhizn,* announcing that the Bolsheviks were preparing an armed uprising, which the signers felt was a dangerous mistake. Lenin, infuriated, condemned their action as "strike-breaking" and "a crime." He followed this up with a letter to the Central Committee, which met without him on November 2, asking that the two be expelled from the party.

Nevertheless, an effort was made to patch the matter up. Kamenev resigned from the Central Committee, which enjoined the two members to refrain from further public opposition to the policy of the party. Lenin's demand for their expulsion from the party was not dealt with. Lenin seems to have been satisfied with the action taken, for on November 6, when the Central Committee met to prepare for the revolutionary action on the morrow, Kamenev resumed his seat as though he had never resigned. Lenin's policy was about to be applied.

THE OVERTHROW OF THE PROVISIONAL GOVERNMENT

Bolshevik Preparations. The Bolshevik leaders, who, on October 23, had decided to undertake an armed insurrection, at first did little to prepare for it. On October 22, a proposal of the Mensheviks for the formation of a Military Revolutionary Committee to coordinate the defense of Petrograd, chiefly against the advancing Germans, offered a convenient way to organize the uprising. The Military Revolutionary Committee, as it was finally set up by the Petrograd Soviet, became a sort of general staff for the insurrection. Thanks to a boycott of the committee by the moderate socialists, the Bolsheviks completely controlled it. The Left Socialist Revolutionaries and Anarchists in the committee deferred to the Bolsheviks. Thus, the latter, headed by Trotsky, were able freely to prepare the troops of the garrison of Petrograd and of the surrounding towns, to expand and equip the Red Guards, and in other ways to get ready. . . .

The Fortress of Peter and Paul, which sprawled on the river bank across from the Winter Palace, appeared to be an obstacle to Bolshevik success. After many discussions as to how to win control of its neutral garrison, Trotsky, on November 5, casually went to the fortress and, finding a soldiers' meeting in progress, promptly addressed it. The soldiers, who were probably wavering already, needed little urging to join the insurrectionary forces. Thus, one of the government's main strongholds fell without a shot being fired. Moreover, the arsenal of Peter and Paul contained large stocks of rifles, which were promptly turned over to the Red Guards, who were among the most active forces at the disposal of the Military Revolutionary Committee. . . .

The Government Acts. Finally, in a meeting on November 5, the government decided to strike against the Bolshevik menace. The forces of junkers (military cadets) in Petrograd were to be called out to close the Bolshevik newspapers, to arrest the leading Bolsheviks, and to subdue the Military Revolutionary Committee. Reliable troops were to be brought to the capital, including junkers from the school at Oranienbaum, shock troops, and artillery. On November 6, the government forces moved. The junkers seized the printing shop where *Pravda* was published, scattered the type, and confiscated some 8,000 copies. The cruiser *Aurora,* anchored in the Neva near the Winter Palace, was ordered to put to sea for a training cruise. A Woman's Battalion of Death moved into the Winter Palace, the seat of the government, along with some junkers and a few Cossacks. Junkers seized and raised several of the main bridges and occupied important government buildings, including the main telephone and postal building. This show of force, like many of the actions of the Provisional Government, was both ineffectual and late. The reaction was immediate and strong.

The Attack on the Provisional Government. The Military Revolutionary Committee at once counter-attacked. Troops were ordered to retake and guard the printing establishments, which by 11 o'clock were again in Red hands. The orders to the *Aurora* were countermanded, and it again dropped anchor. Sailors from its crew landed and helped the Red Guards seize and lower the bridges. . . .

At night the Red forces moved to attack, quickly overrunning the main railway stations and the remaining bridges. Torpedo boats from the Baltic fleet moved into the Neva to aid in the assault. On the morning of November 7, the State Bank and the main telephone station were taken, with very little bloodshed. The government now held little of the city but the Winter Palace. The vastly superior forces of the attackers and their high discipline had overwhelmed the weak and dispirited defenders. It must be said, however, that the Red forces were poorly led, as for hours they failed to make use of their opportunity to crush the defenders at once. But not even the gift of much precious time could save the government.

Kerensky's Flight. In the interim Kerensky was in the Winter Palace trying to obtain reinforcements. Several regiments of Don Cossacks promised their support, but failed to appear. When Kerensky telephoned them over a secret wire that was still functioning, they repeatedly assured him that they "were getting ready to saddle the horses." But the horses were never saddled. Likewise, Kerensky's own party, the Socialist Revolutionaries, could provide him with no armed forces.

Eventually, therefore, the Premier realized that the government's position was hopeless and decided to flee Petrograd, hoping to bring back troops to retake the capital. One of his aides requisitioned a car belonging to a Secretary of the American Embassy, and thus, flying the American flag, Kerensky escaped through the Bolshevik patrols to go for help.

The Fall of the Winter Palace. . . . The insurgents moved slowly toward the Winter Palace and, early in the evening, summoned it to surrender. Most of the military men there, realizing the hopelessness of the situation, urged acceptance, but the ministers refused to submit. They shut themselves up in the palace, defended by a small force of junkers and the Woman's Battalion of Death. Barricades of firewood were thrown up in the palace square, and the tiny force settled down for a siege. Part of the garrison had already slipped away, and the morale of those that remained was not high. . . .

For the most part the fighting consisted of rather aimless firing, while groups of men filtered in through the innumerable entrances to the palace. At first, the defenders were able to disarm the attackers, but as the latter increased in numbers they succeeded in disarming the garrison.

Finally, the last remnants of junkers sought to stand outside the inner room where the ministers were sitting, but they were quickly ordered to surrender. Antonov, the Red leader, promptly arrested the ministers and sent them off under guard to the Fortress of Peter and Paul. Passing through the infuriated crowd, they were almost lynched, but their guards succeeded in delivering them unharmed. A few days later they were put under house arrest in their homes, and before long they were given their freedom. The revolution was still relatively humane.

There was still opposition to the Bolshevik revolution in Petrograd. The moderate socialists—Mensheviks and Socialist Revolutionaries—resigned from the Congress of Soviets in protest against the overthrow of the government. After vainly trying a protest march, they withdrew to the city Duma, where, with delegates from the Council of the Republic and the old Central Executive Committee, they formed a Committee for the Salvation of the Fatherland and the Revolution. But it could do little but issue angry protests and appeal for support against the lawless action of the Bolsheviks. The new revolutionary regime held Petrograd. . . .

The Revolution in the Rest of Russia. In Moscow, in contrast to Petrograd, there was long and stubborn fighting. . . . In the rest of the country, especially in the main Russian areas, the change in power occurred more easily. Although in some places it took weeks, it was almost bloodless, as there were few to fight for the fallen government. In some of the minority areas, however, more enduring opposition regimes were set up. . . .

The attempt to use the army as a center of opposition failed. The Soviet government proceeded to establish complete control over all the command posts, so that a threat from that direction was no longer possible. Indeed, the army as an organized force was rapidly going out of existence, as a vast flood of deserters moved homeward. Only the Cossacks, the Georgians, and the [Ukrainian] *Rada* remained in defiance of the Soviet authorities. They, indeed, were too weak to be a threat, as they were menaced by attack from the sketchy Soviet military forces. The Soviet government was accepted throughout the rest of the vast territory of Russia, and no effective challenge to its power was visible anywhere in this expanse.

THE FIRST MEASURES OF THE SOVIET GOVERNMENT

First Steps of the New Regime. On November 7, while the fighting for Petrograd was still going on, Lenin made his first public appearance before the Petrograd Soviet. To it he proclaimed in triumph the coming of "the workers' and peasants' revolution" which he had long predicted. He then sketched the immediate program of the victors: the destruction of the old governing machine and the creation of a new one, the immediate ending of the war, and the satisfying of the peasants by a decree wiping out the property rights of the nobility. Then, turning to the international scene, he hailed the movement of the workers "which is already beginning to develop in Italy, England, and Germany," and closed with the cry: "Long live the world socialist revolution!"

Secession of the Moderates. Lenin did not appear before the Second Congress of Soviets when it met that evening. As had been expected, it was predominantly Bolshevik: some 390 out of the total membership of 850 were followers of Lenin, with more than 100 of the Left Socialist Revolutionaries, who were allied with the Bolsheviks. There were not more than 80 Mensheviks, including members of the Jewish *Bund,* while the pro-Kerensky Socialist Revolutionaries had a mere 60 delegates. From the beginning, the moderates refused to accept the revolutionary overturn and bitterly denounced the insurrection as treason to the revolution. Representatives of the army joined the attack by terming the uprising a betrayal of the army and a crime against the people. The Mensheviks, the Socialist Revolutionaries, and the Bund followed these utterances by walking out of the Congress in protest against the revolt, whose cannon could be heard in the distance. . . .

Lenin's Proposals. Lenin, who had spent the night resting beside Trotsky, appeared before the Congress of Soviets on November 8. After several preliminary speeches, Lenin rose, to receive a loud ovation. He then read a "proclamation to the peoples and the governments of all the fighting nations." It contained a pledge to abolish secret diplomacy and to publish immediately the secret treaties with the Allies, as well as a renunciation of the special privileges granted to Russia. The proclamation went on to propose an armistice lasting three months, and appealed to the working people of England, France, and Germany to take "decisive, energetic, and persistent action" to bring about a successful peace and at the same time to achieve the liberation of the masses of exploited working people "from all slavery and exploitation." After a brief discussion the proposal was adopted with vast enthusiasm: one delegate who ventured to vote against it felt it safer to drop his opposition. The Congress then sang the *"Internationale,"* the anthem of international revolutionary socialism.

The next point on the agenda was land for the peasants. A short decree proposed by Lenin abolished private landholding at once and without compensation. Private, state, crown, and church lands were to be turned over to land committees and Soviets of Peasants' Deputies for distribution to the peasants. The rules for the distribution of the land were set forth in an Instruction appended to the decree. The Instruction, which Lenin had obtained from a compilation of peasant resolutions prepared by the Soviet of Peasants' Deputies, provided for a complete ban on private ownership of land, prohibition of the buying and selling of land, and for the use of the land solely by persons who would work it with their own and their families' labor. This measure, which would promote a mass of small peasant farms, was contrary to accepted Marxist views. Hence, there was some objection to it from Bolshevik members of the Congress. Lenin, however, frankly stated that this was a Socialist Revolutionary proposal which he felt it necessary to adopt in order to win the support of the peasant masses. On this basis, the Congress approved it.

The Formation of the Soviet Government. While the above measures were readily approved, it proved more difficult to form the revolutionary government. In spite of the secession of the moderate socialists and their opposition to the revolutionary overturn, the Left Socialist Revolutionaries and the Menshevik Internationalists were extremely eager to have a coalition of all socialist parties instead of a purely Leftist government. Likewise *Vikzhel,* the railway workers' union, insisted on a coalition, threatening to stop all rail traffic unless agreement were reached. The demand for an all-socialist government was also warmly endorsed by many of the Bolsheviks. Consequently, in spite of the scorn of Lenin and Trotsky for the moderates, it was necessary to try to form a coalition. But while this was being attempted a government was needed, and so an all-Bolshevik cabinet was set up. Several posts were offered to the Left Socialist Revolutionaries, but they refused to enter the government. So the Council of People's Commissars was approved, with Lenin as President, Trotsky as Commissar for Foreign Affairs, and Rykov as Commissar for Internal Affairs. Most of the other appointees were men who were not well known; among them was Joseph Stalin, Commissar for Nationalities.

A Coalition Government? The possibilities of a coalition regime were explored at length at a conference that met on November 11, 1917. The negotiations lasted for some time, but because of the stiff demands of the moderate socialists they produced no result. At first the socialists insisted that the Military Revolutionary Committee be dissolved and that Lenin and Trotsky be excluded from the government. Later, after the Bolsheviks had consolidated their power in both Moscow and Petrograd, there was less pressure for a coalition and Lenin was able to overcome the moderate Bolsheviks. Nevertheless, on November 17, five of the Bolsheviks of the Central Committee—among them Zinoviev, Kamenev, and Rykov—resigned in protest against the rejection of a coalition. There were also resignations from the cabinet over the same issue.

Lenin was not dismayed by this revolt within his party. He answered it with a furious manifesto from the Central Committee upholding his course and terming the dissenters "waverers and doubters." Such men counted for little, he said, when the Soviet government was supported by "millions of workers in the towns, soldiers in the trenches, peasants in the villages, ready to achieve at any cost the victory of peace and the victory of socialism." This ended the revolt.

None the less, in November the Bolsheviks reached an understanding with the Left Socialist Revolutionaries, and 108 delegates from the Peasant Congress were added to the Soviet Executive Committee. On December 22, the Left Socialist Revolutionaries accepted three posts in the Council of People's Commissars. Thus, a coalition of a sort was finally established, although not so broad in its makeup as the one that had been demanded.

Miscellaneous Actions of the Soviet Government. From the first days of its existence, the new government wrestled with a whole series of problems and wrote a remarkable record of achievements—many of which, it must be said, existed only on paper. Almost immediately there was a sweeping strike of government workers, who refused to recognize the new order. For a regime without a shred of experience in governing this proved most difficult, especially as the State Bank was among the striking institutions. For days the government could obtain no funds, and only the use of force and the opening of the vaults made money available to the Bolshevik rulers of Russia. On December 27, all banks were nationalized and occupied by forces of troops, while the vaults and safe deposit boxes were opened by a commissar. Eventually, the funds of the striking civil servants ran out and they returned to duty in January, 1918.

Economic Measures. During the first few months, decrees flowed forth in a rapid stream. One of the first was a decree directed to the working people, informing them that economic power had been transferred to them. The nationalization of banks was next, followed by a ban on dividends and securities. On February 10, 1918, a decree annulled all debts of the Russian government, including foreign debts. Contrary to Bolshevik doctrine, Lenin was in no hurry to nationalize industry and even wanted the managerial personnel to continue to work on fairly generous terms. Nevertheless, "workers' control" meant supervision and much outright interference by the workers, so that the conditions in the factories became chaotic. When this led to the shutting down of enterprises, the Supreme Economic Council, created on December 15, had the power to nationalize them.

There was a general levelling down of the standard of living—in part by the ever rising inflation, and in part by decree: members of the Council of Commissars were restricted to 500 rubles per month, with allowances for dependents, and to one room for each member of the family. The ending of private ownership of multiple dwellings was another levelling measure: the city Soviets took them over and sought to equalize the housing facilities, often moving families from the slums into the half-empty apartments of wealthy citizens. The food situation proved to be the most insoluble problem. Try as they would, the Soviet authorities could not obtain more bread for the cities, and the amounts issued on rations fell drastically. To the hungry workers there was left only the consolation that the hated "bourgeois" were faring even worse than they.

Political and Social Legislation. Important political and social decrees were also issued during the first months. To cope with secret enemies of the regime, drunken mobs that invaded mansions in search of liquor, and food speculators, on December 20 Felix Dzerzhinsky, a fanatical Polish Communist, became head of the All-Russian Extraordinary Commission, whose name, abbreviated to *Cheka,* became dreaded throughout Russia. A system of revolutionary tribunals was set up to deal with political cases, while new, informal "people's courts" dispensed ordinary justice by common sense rather than law books. The Soviet legislators also found time to reform the Russian alphabet and the calendar. Sweeping new laws made marriage and divorce equally easy to obtain and legalized all children, whether born of registered or informal unions. The full legal equality of men and women was also proclaimed.

The Church and the Revolution. . . . Many of the measures of the new regime angered the churchmen, who hoped ardently for its overthrow, and on February 1, 1918, the Patriarch issued a pastoral letter to the people. It strongly indicted the Soviet leaders for having caused violence and outrages. "Your acts are not merely cruel, they are the works of Satan, for which you will burn in hell fire in the life hereafter. . . ." To this he added his anathema. To the believers, he issued a call to organize in defense of the church, for "the gates of Hell shall not prevail against it."

This, however, did not deter the Soviet authorities, who on February 5, 1918, published a law by which "the church was separated from the state, and the school from the church." Religion was made a private matter for the citizens, and no religious functions or ceremonies were permitted in any institution of government, whether national or local. Religious teaching was barred from all schools, public and private alike. Even the theological schools were ordered closed. The property of churches and religious societies was nationalized, although church buildings might be turned over to congregations of believers for free use for public worship.

This measure was strongly opposed by the leaders of the Orthodox church, but, in spite of their angry protests, the government put it into effect. There were some demonstrations in opposition to it, and occasional riots, at times accompanied by bloodshed. But the government persisted in its purpose. Perhaps the fact that the churches remained open and no attempt was made to prevent divine worship explains why this legislation, which was unfavorable to the Russian church, did not produce any effective explosions of popular wrath.

The Problem of the Constituent Assembly. One of the worst dilemmas for the Bolsheviks was caused by the Constituent Assembly. The Provisional Government had promised to convene this body speedily, but nothing was done about it for months. Finally, the government set November 25 as the date for the elections. Thus, when the Bolsheviks took power they were in a quandary. Before they had seized power, one of their effective slogans had been for "Speedy Convocation of the Constituent Assembly!" But, while they were on record as wanting it to meet soon, Lenin and the other Bolsheviks had reason to believe that vast numbers of peasants as usual would vote for the Socialist Revolutionaries. It seemed likely that the new Soviet government would be challenged by a body in which the Bolsheviks would be only a minority. Lenin firmly held that the Soviets, which excluded the propertied classes, were a higher form of democracy than a body elected by universal suffrage. His solution was to postpone the elections, but it was decided to hold them and to convene the Assembly, which should, however, be dissolved if it proved troublesome.

The Result of the Elections. Although the Bolsheviks made no effort to dominate the elections, which began on November 25, the Cadet party was especially handicapped by the fact that many of their leaders were in hiding or in prison, and their newspapers were largely suppressed. The voting gave the Bolsheviks only 175 of the 707 elected members of the Constituent Assembly. The SR's (Socialist Revolutionaries) had 410—a substantial majority—and most of the other delegates were anti-Bolshevik. Yet the figures do not tell the whole story. The Bolsheviks were now in alliance with the Left SR's, who had had a majority of the Peasant Congress. Although the Left SR's had only 40 out of the 410 SR delegates, it seems probable that their following in the country was far stronger than their representation in the Constituent Assembly.

Above all, the realities of power favored the Bolsheviks. They had full majorities in Petrograd and Moscow and their strength was great in other industrial centers. Their government had the positions of power in the cities and in the army, while the opposition's strength lay chiefly in the unorganized millions of peasants. Moreover, the Bolsheviks were united and determined, with a clearcut program which seemed to meet the needs of the people. The opposition was unorganized and lacked driving force. Also, it was unable to offer an alternative to the program that the Bolsheviks were already carrying out.

The Attitude of the Bolsheviks. The Bolsheviks, realizing that the Constituent Assembly would become the focal center for all anti-Bolshevik elements, whether socialist or upper class, were determined not to permit it to play the counter-revolutionary role that the French National Assembly had played in 1848. On December 11, 1917, the Soviet government forcibly prevented an attempt of former ministers of the Provisional Government to convene the Assembly ahead of time. Shortly thereafter, Lenin wrote his "Theses on the Constituent Assembly," published in *Pravda* on December 26, 1917. Here he stated that a Constituent Assembly had been highly desirable after the fall of the Tsar, when the revolution was still in its moderate or "bourgeois" stage. Now, however, the revolution was in its socialist stage, with the Bolsheviks establishing the dictatorship of the proletariat and its allies, the poorer peasantry. As for the bourgeoisie, they were in open counter-revolution. Hence, any attempt to treat the Constituent Assembly from a purely theoretical, legalistic point of view was treason to the proletariat. Either the Assembly would declare its acceptance of the Soviet government and its program, or else the crisis that would result "can be solved only by revolutionary means."

In order to cut the ground from beneath the feet of the Constituent Assembly, it was decided to have the Third Congress of Soviets meet three days after the opening of the Assembly, and the Congress of Peasant Deputies a few days later. On January 16, the Central Executive Committee drafted a Declaration of Rights of the Toiling and Exploited People, for adoption by the Assembly. It opened with a declaration that Russia was a republic of Soviets, to which all power belonged, and a statement that it was a "free union of free nations, as a federation of national Soviet republics." There followed a long pronouncement for the Constituent Assembly to make, upholding Soviet policy and legislation. Finally, two paragraphs stated that, as the Constituent Assembly had been elected on the basis of party lists compiled before the changed situation after the fall of the Provisional Government, "it would be basically incorrect to set itself up against the Soviet power. . . ." Furthermore, the Assembly, supporting the Soviet regime, would recognize that its role was merely to be "the general working out of the fundamental principles of the socialist reconstruction of society."

The Dissolution of the Constituent Assembly. Lenin and his followers, then, had already made up their minds to deal rigorously with the Constituent Assembly unless it proved to be tame and toothless. Nevertheless, realizing that this body, advocated for decades by Russian liberals and revolutionaries, might enjoy immense prestige in the eyes of the populace, they did not want to shock public opinion by unnecessarily brutal treatment of it. It was permitted to meet, but the vicinity of the Tavrida Palace was surrounded by heavily armed troops, and the galleries were crowded with soldiers and sailors with rifles, pistols, and cartridge belts. For their part, the SR's had sought the support of some regiments, but as they refused to let them come out under arms, even those soldiers who sympathized with the moderates refused their appeal. A demonstration of civilian sympathizers with the Assembly—largely intellectuals and other white-collar workers—occurred, but it met the well-armed troops and was dispersed by gunfire, with some loss of life.

When the meeting opened, Sverdlov, a veteran Bolshevik, seized temporary control in order to read the Declaration of the Rights of the Toiling and Exploited People. After briefly urging the Assembly to adopt it, he withdrew to his seat. The big bloc of SR's now took over, electing Chernov as permanent chairman, in spite of Bolshevik warnings that they should support the program of active socialism. The session dragged on for almost twelve hours. At midnight the crucial vote was taken on the Bolshevik declaration, which lost, 237 to 138. Later, the Bolsheviks withdrew from the meeting, because of its "counter-revolutionary majority." The Left SR's withdrew an hour later. Not long before daybreak the sailor in command of the guard, apparently under orders from Lenin, asked that the meeting adjourn "because the guard is tired." There was a brief flurry of activity, during which a resolution on land and an appeal to the Allies for peace were read and declared approved. Neither of these differed greatly from the measures taken by the Second Congress of Soviets after the fall of the Kerensky government. Then, a little before five in the morning, the meeting adjourned until late afternoon.

The Constituent Assembly never met again. The Central Executive Committee, after a strong speech by Lenin, declared that it was dissolved, and an armed guard at the doors prevented it from reconvening. There was scarcely any protest against the dissolution: The Constituent Assembly had given no heroic leadership to the people and had failed to gain effective support. Probably if it had been convened six months before, the result would have been far different.

Chapter 8

THE CRUSHING OF OPPOSITION

In the months following the Bolshevik revolution, its leaders antici-pated that the revolt in Russia would unleash a socialist revolution in the West. Pending this anticipated revolution, Lenin insisted that the govern-ment come to terms with the Germans. After some serious indecision and wrangling in the Party—which touched off a German military attack—Lenin finally won out and the Treaty of Brest-Litovsk was signed on March 3, 1918. Under this treaty, Russia lost more than 1¼ million square miles of territory containing a population of 62 millions, half of her industrial plants, and a third of her best farm area. Three days later, Lenin stated:

The revolution will not come as quickly as we expected. History has proved this, and we must be able to take this as a fact, we must be able to reckon with the fact that the world Socialist revolution cannot begin so easily in the advanced countries as the revolution began in Russia—the land of Nicholas and Rasputin, the land in which the overwhelming majority of the population was quite in-different to the conditions of life of the people in the outlying regions. In such a country it was quite easy to start a revolution, as easy as lifting a feather.

Thereafter, however, Lenin alternated between optimism and pessimism on the prospects of revolution in the West.

The "peace" of Brest-Litovsk set off a chain of developments that al-most encompassed the destruction of Bolshevik power. During the next few years the Soviets were engaged in civil war with forces ranging from the monarchist-restorationists at the extreme right to the left Social Revo-lutionaries. Many of these forces had the support—financial and otherwise —of Allied powers. And some of these powers, including Japan, Great Britain, France, and the United States sent military forces into Russia. The justification was the necessity of re-establishing an Eastern front in the desperate war against Germany, but the record is clear that other consid-erations—territorial spoils, fear of revolution, or detestation of the Bol-sheviks—also played a part.

Of course, the effort to destroy the Bolshevik régime was never massive and coordinated, and the Americans, particularly, did much to balk annex-

227

ationist ambitions. The consequences, however, were to leave a residue of great bitterness in the U.S.S.R. against the interventionist powers and create an encirclement psychosis which, whatever its uses for propaganda purposes, also was grounded in history.

During the period of civil war and intervention—which endured into 1922—the Bolsheviks outlawed all opposition parties (socialist as well as nonsocialist) and imposed a ban on factions within the Communist Party itself. Why? Marxian theory had not suggested that the dictatorship of the proletariat might be equated with the rule of one *socialist party. And, according to Lenin, the dictatorship of the proletariat was to bring with it "a widening of the practical utilization of democracy by those oppressed by capitalism, by the laboring classes, as has never yet been seen in the whole world."*

Many explanations have been offered for the failure of proletarian "democracy." One explanation placed responsibility on the internal and external foes of Bolshevism: ". . . Soviet 'totalitarianism' was not inevitable nor necessarily implicit in the Bolshevism of 1917-18 but was forced upon it, with death as the alternative, by the decisions of Russian democrats and the Western Democracies." Another, proffered by W. W. Rostow, suggested that "the maintenance of the internal power machine has had a clear priority over any other goal of Soviet policy." Another may be inferred from Merle Fainsod's Bolshevism Before 1917, *in which he holds that "the early organizational history of Bolshevism . . . implanted the germinating conception of the monolithic and totalitarian party."*

The democratic failure has been explained, additionally, for example, by the weakness and backwardness of the Russian economy and proletariat, and the basic incompatibility between large-scale economic planning and any form of democracy. Recently, in this latter vein, R. N. Carew Hunt wrote: "What Lenin early came to see was that a nation-wide planned economy was incompatible with the parliamentary democracy of the West. If production is to be planned, some body of persons must do the planning, and this becomes impossible if the plan is liable to be reversed at any moment by a vote in a popular assembly." And, finally, there are the distinctive contributions made to this discussion in the excerpts from the writings of Isaac Deutscher and Leonard Schapiro in these pages.

Varied explanations of the disparity between Marxist theory and Soviet practice have been alluded to in the hope that they will induce an appreciation of the complexities of judgment involved and encourage the reader to explore the problem further. It may be suggested, too, that important implications extending beyond the U.S.S.R. may ensue from the acceptance of one or another explanation.

DEFEAT IN VICTORY

Isaac Deutscher*

The years of world war, revolution, civil war, and intervention had resulted in the utter ruin of Russia's economy and the disintegration of her social fabric. From a ruined economy the Bolsheviks had had to wrest the means of civil war. In 1919, the Red Army had already used up all stocks of munitions and other supplies. The industries under Soviet control could not replace them by more than a fraction. Normally southern Russia supplied fuel, iron, steel, and raw materials to the industries of central and northern Russia. But southern Russia, occupied first by the Germans and then by Denikin, was only intermittently and during brief spells under Soviet control. When at last, at the end of 1919, the Bolsheviks returned there for good, they found that the coal-mines of the Donets valley were flooded and the other industries destroyed. Deprived of fuel and raw materials, the industrial centres of the rest of the country were paralysed. Even towards the end of 1920, the coal-mines produced less than one-tenth and the iron- and steel-works less than one-twentieth of their pre-war output. The production of consumer goods was about one-quarter of normal. The disaster was made even worse by the destruction of transport. All over the country railway tracks and bridges had been blown up. Rolling stock had not been renewed, and it had only rarely been kept in proper repair, since 1914. Inexorably transport was coming to a standstill. (This, incidentally, was one of the contributory causes of the Red Army's defeat in Poland. The Soviets had enlisted five million men, but of these less than 300,000 were actually engaged in the last stages of the Polish campaign. As the armies rolled onward, the railways were less and less capable of carrying reinforcements and supplies over the lengthening distances.) Farming, too, was ruined. For six years the peasants had not been able to renew their equipment. Retreating and advancing armies trampled their fields and requisitioned their horses. However, because of its technically primitive character, farming was more resilient than industry. The muzhik worked with the wooden *sokha,* which he was able to make or repair by himself.

The Bolsheviks strove to exercise the strictest control over scarce resources; and out of this striving grew their War Communism. They nationalized all industry. They prohibited private trade. They dispatched

* Author of *Stalin: A Political Biography; Soviet Trade Unions;* and *Russia in Transition.* This selection is from chapter XIV of *The Prophet Armed* (New York: Oxford University Press, Inc., 1954). Reprinted by permission of the publisher.

workers' detachments to the countryside to requisition food for the army and the town-dwellers. The government was incapable of collecting normal taxes; it possessed no machinery for doing so. To cover government expenses, the printing-presses produced banknotes day and night. Money became so worthless that wages and salaries had to be paid in kind. The meagre food ration formed the basic wage. The worker was also paid with part of his own produce, a pair of shoes or a few pieces of clothing, which he usually bartered away for food.

This set of desperate shifts and expedients looked to the party like an unexpectedly rapid realization of its own programme. Socialization of industry would have been carried out more slowly and cautiously if there had been no civil war; but it was, in any case, one of the major purposes of the revolution. The requisitioning of food, the prohibition of private trade, the payment of wages in kind, the insignificance of money, the government's aspiration to control the economic resources of the nation, all this looked, superficially, like the abolition of that market economy which was the breeding-ground of capitalism. The fully grown Communist economy about which Marxist text-books had speculated, was to have been a natural economy, in which socially planned production and distribution should take the place of production for the market and of distribution through the medium of money. The Bolshevik was therefore inclined to see the essential features of fully fledged communism embodied in the war economy of 1919-20. He was confirmed in this inclination by the stern egalitarianism which his party preached and practised and which gave to war communism a romantic and heroic aspect.

In truth, war communism was a tragic travesty of the Marxist vision of the society of the future. That society was to have as its background highly developed and organized productive resources and a superabundance of goods and services. It was to organize and develop the social wealth which capitalism at its best produced only fitfully and could not rationally control, distribute, and promote. Communism was to abolish economic inequality once for all by levelling up the standards of living. War communism had, on the contrary, resulted from social disintegration, from the destruction and disorganization of productive resources, from an unparalleled scarcity of goods and services. It did indeed try to abolish inequality; but of necessity it did so by levelling down the standards of living and making poverty universal.[1]

The system could not work for long. The requisitioning of food and the prohibition of private trade for the time being helped the government to tide over the direst emergencies. But in the longer run these policies aggravated and accelerated the shrinkage and disintegration of the economy. The peasant began to till only as much of his land as was necessary to keep

[1] The reader will find a detailed and instructive account of war communism in E. H. Carr, *The Bolshevik Revolution,* vol. ii.

his family alive. He refused to produce the surplus for which the requisitioning squads were on the look-out. When the countryside refuses to produce food for the town, even the rudiments of urban civilization go to pieces. The cities of Russia became depopulated. Workers went to the countryside to escape famine. Those who stayed behind fainted at the factory benches, produced very little, and often stole what they produced to barter it for food. The old, normal market had indeed been abolished. But its bastard, the black market, despoiled the country, revengefully perverting and degrading human relations. This could go on for another year or so; but, inevitably the end would be the breakdown of all government and the dissolution of society. . . .

Matters came to a head on 12 January 1920, when Lenin and Trotsky appeared before the Bolshevik leaders of the trade unions and urged them to accept militarization. Trotsky defended his own record. If his Commissariat, he said, had "pillaged" the country and exacted severe discipline. it had done so to win the war. It was a disgrace and a "sin against the spirit of the revolution" that this should now be held against him, and that the working class should be incited against the army. His opponents were complacent about the country's economic condition. The newspapers concealed the real state of affairs. "It is necessary to state openly and frankly in the hearing of the whole country, that our economic condition is a hundred times worse than our military situation ever was. . . . Just as we once issued the order 'Proletarians, to horse!', so now we must raise the cry 'Proletarians, back to the factory bench! Proletarians, back to production!' " [2] The nation's labour force continued to shrink and degenerate. It could not be saved, reconstituted, and rehabilitated without the application of coercive measures. Lenin spoke in the same vein. Yet the conference almost unanimously rejected the resolution which he and Trotsky jointly submitted. Of more than three score Bolshevik leaders only two men voted for it. Never before had Trotsky or Lenin met with so striking a rebuff.

Trotsky's strictures on the complacency of his critics were not unjustified. The critics did not and could not propose any practical alternative. They, too, clung to war communism and disavowed only the conclusion Trotsky had drawn from it. He had little difficulty therefore in exposing their inconsistency. Yet there was a certain realism and valuable scruple in their very lack of consistency. Trotsky's opponents refused to believe that the wheels of the economy could be set in motion by word of military command, and they were convinced that it was wrong for a workers' state to act as a press gang towards its own working class.[3] . . . They argued that compulsory labour was inefficient. "You cannot build a planned economy,"

[2] Trotsky, *Sochinenya*, vol. XV, pp. 27-52.
[3] This controversy filled the pages of *Ekonomicheskaya Zhizn* and *Pravda* throughout January 1920.

exclaimed Abramovich, the Menshevik, "in the way the Pharaohs built their pyramids." [4] Abramovich thus coined the phrase, which years later Trotsky was to repeat against Stalin. . . .

For a time the Polish war blunted the edge of this controversy. Peril from without once again induced people to accept without murmur policies which, before, had aroused their intense resentment. At the height of the war, Trotsky, surrounded by a team of technicians, made a determined effort to set the railways in motion. By this time the stock of locomotives had been almost entirely wasted. Engineers forecast the exact date—only a few months ahead—when not a single railway in Russia would be working. Trotsky placed the railway men and the personnel of the repair workshops under martial law; and he organized systematic and rapid rehabilitation of the rolling stock. He went into the repair workshops to tell the workers that the country was paying for their slackness in blood: the paralysis of transport had encouraged the Poles to attack. "The situation of the worker," he declared, "is grievous in every respect . . . it is worse than ever. I would deceive you if I were to say that it will be better to-morrow. No, ahead of us are months of heavy struggle until we can lift our country out of this terrible misery and utter exhaustion, until we can stop weighing our bread ration on the chemist's scales." [5] When the railwaymen's trade union raised objections to his action, he dismissed its leaders and appointed others who were willing to do his bidding. He repeated this procedure in unions of other transport workers. Early in September he formed the *Tsektran*, the Central Transport Commission, through which he brought the whole field of transport under his control. The Politbureau backed him to the hilt as it had promised. To observe electoral rights and voting procedures in the unions seemed at that moment as irrelevant as it might seem in a city stricken with pestilence. He produced results and surpassed expectations: the railways were rehabilitated well ahead of schedule—"the blood circulation of the economic organism was revived"—and he was acclaimed for the feat.[6]

But no sooner had the Polish war been concluded than the grievances and dissensions exploded anew and with greater force than before. He himself provoked the explosion. Flushed with success, he threatened to "shake up" various trade unions as he had "shaken up" those of the transport workers. He threatened, that is, to dismiss the elected leaders of the unions and to replace them by nominees who would place the nation's economic interest above the sectional interests of the workers. He grossly overstepped the mark. Lenin now bluntly dissociated himself from Trotsky and per-

---

[4] *Tretii Vserossiskii Syezd Profsoyuzov*, p. 97.

[5] See his speech at the Muromsk workshops of 21 June 1920 in *Sochinenya*, vol. xv, p. 368.

[6] For the famous Order no. 1042 concerning the railways see op. cit., pp. 345-7. Later in the year Trotsky was placed at the head of special commissions which took emergency action to rehabilitate the industries of the Donets valley and of the Urals.

suaded the Central Committee to do likewise. The Committee openly called
the party to resist energetically "militarized and bureaucratic forms of work":
and it castigated that "degenerated centralism" which rode roughshod over
the workers' elected representatives. It called on the party to re-establish
proletarian democracy in the trade unions and to subordinate all other
considerations to this task.[7] A special commission was formed to watch that
these decisions were carried out. Zinoviev presided over it, and, although
Trotsky sat on it, nearly all its members were his opponents.[7] . . .

The deeper ill which afflicted the whole system of government, and of
which this tug-of-war was merely a symptom, lay in the frustration of the
popular hopes aroused by the revolution. For the first time since 1917 the
bulk of the working class, not to speak of the peasantry, unmistakably
turned against the Bolsheviks. A sense of isolation began to haunt the ruling group. To be sure, the working class had not come to regret the revolution. It went on to identify itself with it; and it received with intense
hostility any openly counter-revolutionary agitation. "October" had so
deeply sunk into the popular mind that Mensheviks and Social Revolutionaries now had to preface their criticisms of the government with an
explicit acceptance of the "achievements of October." Yet the opposition to
current Bolshevik policies was just as intense and widespread. The Mensheviks and Social Revolutionaries, who in the course of three years had
been completely eclipsed and had hardly dared to raise their heads, were
now regaining some popular favour. People listened even more sympa-
thetically to anarchist agitators violently denouncing the Bolshevik régime.
If the Bolsheviks had now permitted free elections to the Soviets, they would
almost certainly have been swept from power.[8]

The Bolsheviks were firmly resolved not to let things come to that pass.
It would be wrong to maintain that they clung to power for its own sake.
The party as a whole was still animated by that revolutionary idealism of
which it had given such abundant proof in its underground struggle and in
the civil war. It clung to power because it identified the fate of the republic
with its own fate and saw in itself the only force capable of safeguarding
the revolution. It was lucky for the revolution—and it was also its mis-
fortune—that in this belief the Bolsheviks were profoundly justified. The
revolution would hardly have survived without a party as fanatically devoted to it as the Bolsheviks were. But had there existed another party
equally devoted and equally vigorous in action, that party might, in con-

[7] See the report of the Central Committee in *Izvestya Tsentralnovo Komiteta RKP*,
no. 26, 1920, and G. Zinoviev, *Sochinenya*, vol. vi, pp. 600 ff.

[8] Many Bolshevik leaders explicitly or implicitly admitted this. See Lenin, *Sochinenya*,
vol. xxxii, pp. 160, 176, 230 and *passim;* Zinoviev in *Desyatyi Syezd RKP*, p. 190. In a
private letter to Lunacharsky (of 14 April 1926) Trotsky describes the "menacing discontent" of the working class as the background to the controversy of 1920-1. *The Trotsky
Archives.*

sequence of an election, have displaced Lenin's government without convulsing the young state. No such party existed. The return of Mensheviks and Social Revolutionaries would have entailed the undoing of the October Revolution. At the very least it would have encouraged the White Guards to try their luck once again and rise in arms. From sheer self-preservation as well as from broader motives the Bolsheviks could not even contemplate such a prospect. They could not accept it as a requirement of democracy that they should, by retreating, plunge the country into a new series of civil wars just after one series had been concluded.

Nor was it by any means likely that a free election to the Soviets would return any clear-cut majority. Those who had supported Kerensky in 1917 had not really recovered from their eclipse. Anarchists and anarcho-syndicalists, preaching a "Third Revolution," seemed far more popular among the working class. But they gave no effective focus to the opposition; and they were in no sense pretenders to office. Strong in criticism, they possessed no positive political programme, no serious organization, national or even local, no real desire to rule a vast country. In their ranks honest revolutionaries, cranks, and plain bandits rubbed shoulders. The Bolshevik régime could be succeeded only by utter confusion followed by open counter-revolution. Lenin's party refused to allow the famished and emotionally unhinged country to vote their party out of power and itself into a bloody chaos.

For this strange sequel to their victory the Bolsheviks were mentally quite unprepared. They had always tacitly assumed that the majority of the working class, having backed them in the revolution, would go on to support them unswervingly until they had carried out the full programme of socialism. Naïve as the assumption was, it sprang from the notion that socialism was the proletarian idea *par excellence* and that the proletariat, having once adhered to it, would not abandon it. That notion had underlain the reasoning of all European schools of Socialist thought. In the vast political literature produced by those schools the question of what Socialists in office should do if they lost the confidence of the workers had hardly ever been pondered. It had never occurred to Marxists to reflect whether it was possible or admissible to try to establish socialism regardless of the will of the working class. They simply took that will for granted. For the same reason it had seemed to the Bolsheviks as clear as daylight that the proletarian dictatorship and proletarian (or Soviet) democracy were only two complementary and inseparable aspects of the same thing: the dictatorship was there to suppress the resistance of the propertied classes; and it derived its strength and historic legitimacy from the freely and democratically expressed opinion of the working classes. Now a conflict arose between the two aspects of the Soviet system. If the working classes were to be allowed to speak and vote freely they would destroy the dictatorship. If the dictatorship, on the other hand, frankly abolished proletarian democracy it would deprive itself of historic legitimacy, even in its own eyes. It would cease to be a proletarian dictatorship in the strict sense. Its use of that title would henceforth be based on the claim that it pursued a policy with which the working class, in its own interest, ought and eventually must identify itself, but with which it did not as yet identify itself. The dictatorship would then at best represent the idea of the class, not the class itself.

The revolution had now reached that cross-roads, well known to Machiavelli, at which it found it difficult or impossible to fix the people in their revolutionary persuasion and was driven "to take such measures that, when they believed no longer, it might be possible to make them believe by force." For the Bolshevik party this involved a conflict of loyalties, which was in some respects deeper than any it had known so far, a conflict bearing the seeds of all the turbulent controversies and sombre purges of the next decades.

At this cross-roads Bolshevism suffered a moral agony the like of which is hardly to be found in the history of less intense and impassioned movements. Later Lenin recalled the "fever" and "mortal illness" which consumed the party in the winter of 1920-1, during the tumultuous debate over the place of the trade unions in the state. This was an important yet only a secondary matter. It could not be settled before an answer had been given to the fundamental question concerning the very nature of the state. The party was wholly absorbed in the controversy over the secondary issue, because it was not altogether clearly aware of the primary question and was afraid to formulate it frankly in its own mind. But as the protagonists went on arguing they struck the great underlying issue again and again and were compelled to define their attitudes.

It is not necessary here to go into the involved and somewhat technical differences over the trade unions, although the fact that the drama of the revolution revealed itself in a seemingly dry economic argument significantly corresponded to the spirit of the age.[9] Suffice it to say that, broadly speaking, three attitudes crystallized. The faction led by Trotsky (and later by Trotsky and Bukharin) wanted the trade unions to be deprived of their autonomy and absorbed into the machinery of government. This was the final conclusion which Trotsky drew from his conflicts with the trade unions. Under the new dispensation, the leaders of the unions would, as servants of the state, speak for the state to the workers rather than for the workers to the state. They would raise the productivity and maintain the discipline of labour; they would train workers for industrial management; and they would participate in the direction of the country's economy.

At the other extreme the Workers' Opposition, led by Shlyapnikov and Kollontai, protested against the government's and the party's tutelage over the unions. They denounced Trotsky and Lenin as militarizers of

[9] A detailed account of the debate can be found in Deutscher, *Soviet Trade Unions (Their place in Soviet labour policy)*, pp. 42-59.

labour and promoters of inequality. In quasi-syndicalist fashion they demanded that trade unions, factory committees, and a National Producers' Congress should assume control over the entire economy. While Trotsky argued that the trade unions could not in logic defend the workers against the workers' state, Shlyapnikov and Kollontai already branded the Soviet state as the rampart of a new privileged bureaucracy.

Between these two extremes, Lenin, Zinoviev, and Kamenev spoke for the main body of Bolshevik opinion and tried to strike a balance. They, too, insisted that it was the duty of the trade unions to restrain the workers and to cultivate in them a sense of responsibility for the state and the nationalized economy. They emphasized the party's right to control the unions. But they also wished to preserve them as autonomous mass organizations, capable of exerting pressure on government and industrial management.

Implied in these attitudes were different conceptions of state and society. The Workers' Opposition and the so-called *Decemists* (the Group of Democratic Centralism) were the stalwart defenders of "proletarian democracy" *vis-à-vis* the dictatorship. They were the first Bolshevik dissenters to protest against the method of government designed "to make the people believe by force." They implored the party to "trust its fate" to the working class which had raised it to power. They spoke the language which the whole party had spoken in 1917. They were the real Levellers of this revolution, its high-minded, Utopian dreamers. The party could not listen to them if it was not prepared to commit noble yet unpardonable suicide. It could not trust its own and the republic's fate to a working class whittled down, exhausted, and demoralized by civil war, famine, and the black market. The quixotic spirit of the Workers' Opposition was apparent in its economic demands. The Opposition clamoured for the immediate satisfaction of the workers' needs, for equal wages and rewards for all, for the supply, without payment, of food, clothing, and lodging to workers, for free medical attention, free travelling facilities, and free education.[10] They wanted to see fulfilled nothing less than the programme of full communism, which was theoretically designed for an economy of great plenty. They did not even try to say how the government of the day could meet their demands. They urged the party to place industry, or what was left of it, once again under the control of those factory committees which had shown soon after the October Revolution that they could merely dissipate and squander the nation's wealth. It was a sad omen that the people enveloped in such fumes of fancy were almost the only ones to advocate a full revival of proletarian democracy.

Against them, Trotsky prompted the party to cease for the time being the advocacy and practice of proletarian democracy and instead to con-

---

[10] *Desyatyi Syezd RKP*, p. 363; A. M. Kollontai, *The Workers' Opposition in Russia*.

centrate on building up a Producers' Democracy. The party, to put it more plainly, was to deny the workers their political rights and compensate them by giving them scope and managerial responsibility in economic reconstruction. At the tenth congress (March 1921), when this controversy reached its culmination, Trotsky argued:

> The Workers' Opposition has come out with dangerous slogans. They have made a fetish of democratic principles. They have placed the workers' right to elect representatives above the party, as it were, as if the party were not entitled to assert its dictatorship even if that dictatorship temporarily clashed with the passing moods of the workers' democracy. . . . It is necessary to create among us the awareness of the revolutionary historical birthright of the party. The party is obliged to maintain its dictatorship, regardless of temporary wavering in the spontaneous moods of the masses, regardless of the temporary vacillations even in the working class. This awareness is for us the indispensable unifying element. The dictatorship does not base itself at every given moment on the formal principle of a workers' democracy, although the workers' democracy is, of course, the only method by which the masses can be drawn more and more into political life.[11]

The days had long passed when Trotsky argued that the Soviet system of government was superior to bourgeois parliamentarianism because under it the electors enjoyed, among other things, the right to re-elect their representatives at any time and not merely at regular intervals; and that this enabled the Soviets to reflect any change in the popular mood closely and instantaneously, as no parliament was able to do. His general professions of faith in proletarian democracy now sounded like mere saving clauses. What was essential was "the historical birthright of the party" and the party's awareness of it as the "indispensable unifying element." Euphemistically yet eloquently enough he now extolled the collective solidarity of the ruling group in the face of a hostile or apathetic nation.

Lenin refused to proclaim the divorce between the dictatorship and proletarian democracy. He, too, was aware that government and party were in conflict with the people; but he was afraid that Trotsky's policy would perpetuate the conflict. The party had had to override trade unions, to dismiss their recalcitrant leaders, to break or obviate popular resistance, and to prevent the free formation of opinion inside the Soviets. Only thus, Lenin held, could the revolution be saved. But he hoped that these practices would give his government a breathing space—his whole policy had become a single struggle for breathing spaces—during which it might modify its policies, make headway with the rehabilitation of the country, ease the plight of the working people, and win them back for Bolshevism. The dictatorship could then gradually revert to proletarian democracy. If this was the aim, as Trotsky agreed, then the party must reassert the idea of that democracy at once and initiate no sweeping measures suggesting its abandonment. Even though the régime had so often had recourse to co-

[11] *Desyatyi Syezd RKP,* p. 192. See also p. 215.

ercion, Lenin pleaded, coercion must be its last and persuasion its first resort.[12] The trade unions ought therefore not to be turned into appendages of the state. They must retain a measure of autonomy; they must speak for the workers, if need be against the government; and they ought to become the schools, not the drill-halls, of communism. The administrator —and it was from his angle that Trotsky viewed the problem—might be annoyed and inconvenienced by the demands of the unions; he might be right against them in specific instances; but on balance it was sound that he should be so inconvenienced and exposed to genuine social pressures and influences. It was no use telling the workers that they must not oppose the workers' state. That state was an abstraction. In reality, Lenin pointed out, his own administration had to consider the interests of the peasants as well as of the workers; and its work was marred by muddle, by grave "bureaucratic distortions," and by arbitrary exercise of power. The working class ought therefore to defend itself, albeit with self-restraint, and to press its claims on the administration. The state, as Lenin saw it, had to give scope to a plurality of interests and influences. Trotsky's state was implicitly monolithic.

The tenth congress voted by an overwhelming majority for Lenin's resolutions. Bolshevism had already departed from proletarian democracy; but it was not yet prepared to embrace its alternative, the monolithic state.

．　　　．　　　．　　　．　　　．

While the congress was in session the strangest of all Russian insurrections flared up at the naval fortress of Kronstadt, an insurrection which, in Lenin's words, like a lightning flash illumined reality.

The insurgents, sailors of the Red Navy, were led by anarchists. Since the end of February they had been extremely restless. There had been strikes in nearby Petrograd; a general strike was expected; and Kronstadt was astir with rumours of alleged clashes between Petrograd workers and troops. The crews of the warships were seized by a political fever reminiscent of the excitement of 1917. At meetings they passed resolutions demanding freedom for the workers, a new deal for the peasants, and free elections to the Soviets. The call for the Third Revolution began to dominate the meetings, the revolution which was to overthrow the Bolsheviks and establish Soviet democracy. Kalinin, President of the Soviet Republic, made a flat-footed appearance at the naval base; he denounced the sailors as "disloyal and irresponsible" and demanded obedience. A delegation of the sailors sent to Petrograd was arrested there.

Soon the cry "Down with Bolshevik tyranny!" resounded throughout Kronstadt. The Bolshevik commissars on the spot were demoted and imprisoned. An anarchist committee assumed command; and amid the sailors' enthusiasm the flag of revolt was hoisted. "The heroic and generous Kron-

---

[12] *Desyatyi Syezd RKP.*, pp. 208 ff.

stadt," writes the anarchist historian of the insurrection, "dreamt of the liberation of Russia. . . . No clear-cut programme was formulated. Freedom and the brotherhood of the peoples of the world were the watchwords. The Third Revolution was seen as a gradual transition towards final emancipation; and free elections to independent Soviets as the first step in this direction. The Soviets were, of course, to be independent of any political party—a free expression of the will and the interests of the people." [13]

The Bolsheviks denounced the men of Kronstadt as counterrevolutionary mutineers led by a White general. The denunciation appears to have been groundless. Having for so long fought against mutiny after mutiny, each sponsored or encouraged by the White Guards, the Bolsheviks could not bring themselves to believe that the White Guards had no hand in this revolt. Some time before the event, the White émigré press had indeed darkly hinted at trouble brewing in Kronstadt; and this lent colour to the suspicion. The Politbureau, at first inclined to open negotiations, finally resolved to quell the revolt. It could not tolerate the challenge from the Navy; and it was afraid that the revolt, although it had no chance of growing into a revolution, would aggravate the prevailing chaos. Even after the defeat of the White Guards, numerous bands of rebels and marauders roamed the land from the northern coasts down to the Caspian Sea, raiding and pillaging towns and slaughtering the agents of the government. With the call for a new revolution bands of famished Volga peasants had overrun the *gubernia* of Saratov, and later in the year Tukhachevsky had to employ twenty-seven rifle divisions to subdue them.[14] Such was the turmoil that leniency towards the insurgents of Kronstadt was certain to be taken as a sign of weakness and to make matters worse.

On 5 March Trotsky arrived in Petrograd and ordered the rebels to surrender unconditionally. "Only those who do so," he stated, "can count on the mercy of the Soviet Republic. Simultaneously with this warning I am issuing instructions that everything be prepared for the suppression of the mutiny by armed force. . . . This is the last warning." [15] That it should have fallen to Trotsky to address such words to the sailors was another of history's ironies. This had been his Kronstadt, the Kronstadt he had called "the pride and the glory of the revolution." How many times had he not stumped the naval base during the hot days of 1917! How many times had not the sailors lifted him on their shoulders and wildly acclaimed

[13] Alexander Berkman, *Der Aufstand von Kronstadt*, pp. 10-11.

[14] See the correspondence between S. Kamenev, Shaposhnikov, and Smidovich with the commander of the Saratov area, and Tukhachevsky's report to Lenin of 16 July 1921. *The Trotsky Archives*. And here is a characteristic message sent to Lenin from Communists in the sub-Polar region on 25 March 1921: "The Communists of the Tobolsk region in the North are bleeding white and sending their fiery farewell greetings to the invincible Russian Communist Party, to our dear comrades and our leader Lenin. Perishing here, we carry out our duty towards the party and the Republic in the firm belief in our eventual triumph." Ibid.

[15] Trotsky, *Sochinenya*, vol. xvii, book 2, p. 518.

him as their friend and leader! How devotedly they had followed him to the Tauride Palace, to his prison cell at Kresty, to the walls of Kazan on the Volga, always taking his advice, always almost blindly following his orders! How many anxieties they had shared, how many dangers they had braved together! True, of the veterans few had survived; and even fewer were still at Kronstadt. The crews of the *Aurora,* the *Petropavlovsk,* and other famous warships now consisted of fresh recruits drafted from Ukrainian peasants. They lacked—so Trotsky told himself—the selfless revolutionary spirit of the older classes. Yet even this was in a way symbolic of the situation in which the revolution found itself. The ordinary men and women who had made it were no longer what they had been or where they had been. The best of them had perished; others had become absorbed in the administration; still others had dispersed and become disheartened and embittered. And what the rebels of Kronstadt demanded was only what Trotsky had promised their elder brothers and what he and the party had been unable to give. Once again, as after Brest, a bitter and hostile echo of his own voice came back to him from the lips of other people; and once again he had to suppress it.

The rebels ignored his warning and hoped to gain time. This was the middle of March. The Bay of Finland was still icebound. In a few days, however, a thaw might set in; and then the fortress, bristling with guns, defended by the whole Red Navy of the Baltic, assured of supplies from Finland or other Baltic countries, would become inaccessible, almost invincible. In the meantime even Communists joined in the revolt, announcing that they had left "the party of the hangman Trotsky." The fortress, so Trotsky (or was it Tukhachevsky?) resolved, must be seized before ice floes barred the approach. In feverish haste picked regiments and shock troops were dispatched to reinforce the garrison of Petrograd. When the news of the mutiny reached the tenth congress, it aroused so much alarm and anger that most of the able-bodied delegates rushed straight from the conference hall in the Kremlin to place themselves at the head of the shock troops which were to storm the fortress across the Bay of Finland. Even leaders of the Workers' Opposition and *Decemists* who, at the congress, had just raised demands not very different from those the rebels voiced, went into battle. They, too, held that the sailors had no right to dictate, hands on triggers, even the justest of demands.

White sheets over their uniforms, the Bolshevik troops, under Tukhachevsky's command, advanced across the Bay. They were met by hurricane fire from Kronstadt's bastions. The ice broke under their feet; and wave after wave of white-shrouded attackers collapsed into the glacial Valhalla. The death march went on. From three directions fresh columns stumped and fumbled and slipped and crawled over the glassy surface until they too vanished in fire, ice, and water. As the successive swarms and lines of attackers drowned, it seemed to the men of Kronstadt that the perverted Bolshevik revolution drowned with them and that the triumph of their own pure, unadulterated revolution was approaching. Such was the lot of these rebels, who had denounced the Bolsheviks for their harshness and whose only aim it was to allow the revolution to imbibe the milk of human kindness, that for their survival they fought a battle which in cruelty was unequalled throughout the civil war. The bitterness and the rage of the attackers mounted accordingly. On 17 March, after a night-long advance in a snowstorm, the Bolsheviks at last succeeded in climbing the walls. When they broke into the fortress, they fell upon its defenders like revengeful furies.

On 3 April Trotsky took a parade of the victors. "We waited as long as possible," he said, "for our blinded sailor-comrades to see with their own eyes where the mutiny led. But we were confronted by the danger that the ice would melt away and we were compelled to carry out . . . the attack." [16] Describing the crushed rebels as "comrades," he unwittingly intimated that what he celebrated was morally a Pyrrhic victory. Foreign Communists who visited Moscow some months later and believed that Kronstadt had been one of the ordinary incidents of the civil war, were "astonished and troubled" to find that the leading Bolsheviks spoke of the rebels without any of the anger and hatred which they felt for the White Guards and interventionists. Their talk was full of "sympathetic reticences" and sad, enigmatic allusions, which to the outsider betrayed the party's troubled conscience.[17]

.   .   .   .   .

The rising had not yet been defeated when, on 15 March, Lenin introduced the New Economic Policy to the tenth congress. Almost without debate the congress accepted it. Silently, with a heavy heart, Bolshevism parted with its dream of war communism. It retreated, as Lenin said, in order to be in a better position to advance. The controversy over the trade unions and the underlying issue at once died down. The cannonade in the Bay of Finland and the strikes in Petrograd and elsewhere had demonstrated beyond doubt the unreality of Trotsky's ideas: and in the milder policies based on the mixed economy of subsequent years there was, anyhow, no room for the militarization of labour.

The controversy had not been mere sound and fury, however. Its significance for the future was greater than the protagonists themselves could suppose. A decade later Stalin, who in 1920-1 had supported Lenin's

[16] Trotsky, *Sochinenya*, vol. xvii, book 2, p. 523.

[17] André Morizet, *Chez Lénine et Trotski*, pp. 78-84 and V. Serge, *Mémoires d'un Révolutionnaire*, chapter iv, describe the Kronstadt period from the standpoint of foreign Communists in Russia. Both writers accepted the party's case, although both sympathized with the rebels.

"liberal" policy, was to adopt Trotsky's ideas in all but name. Neither Stalin nor Trotsky, nor the adherents of either, then admitted the fact: Stalin—because he could not acknowledge that he was abandoning Lenin's attitude for Trotsky's; Trotsky—because he shrank in horror from his own ideas when he saw them remorselessly carried into execution by his enemy. There was hardly a single plank in Trotsky's programme of 1920-1 which Stalin did not use during the industrial revolution of the thirties. He introduced conscription and direction of labour; he insisted that the trade unions should adopt a "productionist" policy instead of defending the consumer interests of the workers; he deprived the trade unions of the last vestige of autonomy and transformed them into tools of the state. He set himself up as the protector of the managerial groups, on whom he bestowed privileges of which Trotsky had not even dreamt. He ordered "Socialist emulation" in the factories and mines; and he did so in words unceremoniously and literally taken from Trotsky.[18] He put into effect his own ruthless version of that "Soviet Taylorism" which Trotsky had advocated. And, finally, he passed from Trotsky's intellectual and historical arguments ambiguously justifying forced labour to its mass application. . . .

The Bolshevik party still defended the principle of proletarian democracy against Trotsky; but it continued to depart from it in practice.

It was only in 1921 that Lenin's government proceeded to ban all organized opposition within the Soviets. Throughout the civil war the Bolsheviks had harassed the Mensheviks and Social Revolutionaries, now outlawing them, now allowing them to come into the open, and then again suppressing them. The harsher and the milder courses were dictated by circumstances and by the vacillations of those parties in which some groups leaned towards the Bolsheviks and others towards the White Guards. The idea, however, that those parties should be suppressed on principle had not taken root before the end of the civil war. Even during the spells of repression, those opposition groups which did not plainly call for armed resistance to the Bolsheviks still carried on all sorts of activities, open and clandestine. The Bolsheviks often eliminated them from the Soviets or reduced their representation by force or guile. It was through the machinery of the Soviets that Lenin's government organized the civil war; and in that machinery it was not prepared to countenance hostile or neutral elements. But the government still looked forward to the end of hostilities when it would be able to respect the rules of Soviet constitutionalism and to readmit regular opposition. This the Bolsheviks now thought themselves unable to do. All opposition parties had hailed the Kronstadt rising; and so the Bolshe-

---

[18] At the beginning of 1929, a few weeks after Trotsky's expulsion from Russia, the sixteenth party conference proclaimed "Socialist emulation," quoting *in extenso* the resolution written by Trotsky and adopted by the party in 1920. The author's name was not mentioned, of course.

viks knew what they could expect from them. The more isolated they themselves were in the nation the more terrified were they of their opponents. They had half-suppressed them in order to win the civil war; having won the civil war they went on to suppress them for good.

Paradoxically, the Bolsheviks were driven to establish their own political monopoly by the very fact that they had liberalized their economic policy. The New Economic Policy gave free scope to the interests of the individualistic peasantry and of the urban bourgeoisie. It was to be expected that as those interests came into play they would seek to create their own means of political expression or try to use such anti-Bolshevik organizations as existed. The Bolsheviks were determined that none should exist. "We might have a two-party system, but one of the two parties would be in office and the other in prison"—this dictum, attributed to Bukharin, expressed a view widespread in the party. Some Bolsheviks felt uneasy about their own political monopoly; but they were even more afraid of the alternative. Trotsky later wrote that he and Lenin had intended to lift the ban on the opposition parties as soon as the economic and social condition of the country had become more stable. This may have been so. In the meantime, however, the Bolsheviks hardened in the conviction, which was to play so important a part in the struggles of the Stalinist era, that any opposition must inevitably become the vehicle of counter-revolution. They were haunted by the fear that the new urban bourgeoise (which soon flourished under the N.E.P.), the intelligentsia, and the peasantry might join hands against them in a coalition of overwhelming strength; and they shrank from no measure that could prevent such a coalition. Thus, after its victory in the civil war, the revolution was beginning to escape from its weakness into totalitarianism.

Almost at once it became necessary to suppress opposition in Bolshevik ranks as well. The Workers' Opposition (and up to a point the *Decemists* too) expressed much of the frustration and discontent which had led to the Kronstadt rising. The cleavages tended to become fixed; and the contending groups were inclined to behave like so many parties within the party. It would have been preposterous to establish the rule of a single party and then to allow that party to split into fragments. If Bolshevism were to break up into two or more hostile movements, as the old Social Democratic party had done, would not one of them—it was asked—become the vehicle of counter-revolution?

In the temper of the party congress of 1921 there was indeed something of that seemingly irrational tension which had characterized the congress of 1903. A split similarly cast its shadow ahead—only the real divisions were even more inchoate and confused than in 1903. Now as then Trotsky was not on the side of the controversy to which he would eventually belong. And now as then he was anxious to prevent the split. He therefore raised no objection when Lenin proposed that the congress should prohibit organized groups or factions within the party; and he himself disbanded the faction he had formed during the recent controversy.[19] This was not yet strictly a ban on inner party opposition. Lenin encouraged dissenters to express dissent. He liberally invited them to state their views in the Bolshevik newspapers, in special discussion pages and discussion sheets. He asked the congress to elect the leaders of all shades of opposition to the new Central Committee. But he insisted that opposition should remain diffuse and that the dissenters should not form themselves into solid leagues. He submitted a resolution, one clause of which (kept secret) empowered the Central Committee to expel offenders, no matter how high their standing in the party. Trotsky supported the clause, or, at any rate, raised no objection to it; and the congress passed it. It was against Shlyapnikov, Trotsky's most immitigable opponent, that the punitive clause was immediately directed; and against him it was presently invoked. It did not occur to Trotsky that one day it would be invoked against himself.

The arrangement under which opposition was permitted provided it remained dispersed could work as long as members of the party disagreed over secondary or transient issues. But when the differences were serious and prolonged it was inevitable that members of the same mind should band together. Those who, like the Workers' Opposition, charged the ruling group with being animated by "bureaucratic and bourgeois hostility towards the masses" could hardly refrain from concerting their efforts against what they considered to be a sinister and formidably organized influence within the party. The ban on factions could thus at first delay a split only to accelerate it later. . . .

When he was still at the threshold of his career, Trotsky wrote: "A working class capable of exercising its dictatorship over society will tolerate no dictator over itself." By 1921 the Russian working class had proved itself incapable of exercising its own dictatorship. It could not even exercise control over those who ruled in its name. Having exhausted itself in the revolution and the civil war, it had almost ceased to exist as a political factor. Trotsky then proclaimed the party's "historical birthright," its right to establish a stern trusteeship over the proletariat as well as the rest of society. This was the old "Jacobin" idea that a small, virtuous and enlightened minority was justified in "substituting" itself for an immature people and bringing reason and happiness to it, the idea which Trotsky had abjured as the hereditary obsession of the *Decembrists,* the *Narodniks,* and the Bolsheviks. This "obsession," he himself had argued, had reflected the atrophy or the apathy of all social classes in Russia. He had been convinced that with the appearance of a modern, Socialist working class that atrophy had been overcome. The revolution proved him right. Yet after their paroxysms of energy and their titanic struggles of 1917-21 all classes

---

[19] Among the leaders of the faction were, apart from Trotsky and Bukharin, Dzerzhinsky, Andreev, Krestinsky, Preobrazhensky, Rakovsky, Serebriakov, Pyatakov and Sokolnikov.

of Russian society seemed to relapse into a deep coma. The political stage, so crowded in recent years, became deserted and only a single group was left on it to speak boisterously on behalf of the people. And even its circle was to grow more and more narrow.

When Trotsky now urged the Bolshevik party to "substitute" itself for the working classes, he did not, in the rush of work and controversy, think of the next phases of the process, although he himself had long since predicted them with uncanny clear-sightedness. "The party organization would then substitute itself for the party as a whole; then the Central Committee would substitute itself for the organization; and finally a single dictator would substitute himself for the Central Committee."

The dictator was already waiting in the wings.

THE ORIGIN OF THE COMMUNIST AUTOCRACY

LEONARD SCHAPIRO*

LENINISM TRIUMPHANT

Lenin had first formulated his doctrine on the organization of the social democratic party in 1902. This is what he wrote in September of that year to a party worker in a letter which was reproduced and widely circulated:

While in the matter of ideology and of practical *control* of the movement and of the revolutionary struggle we need the *maximum possible centralization* for the proletariat, so far as concerns *information* on the movement the centre needs the *maximum possible decentralization*. . . . We must centralize control over the movement. We must likewise . . . *decentralize* as much as possible the *responsibility before the party* of each individual member. . . . We must particularly bear in mind . . . the *centre will be powerless* if we do not at the same time put into effect the *maximum decentralization* both as regards responsibility to the centre, and as regards information at the centre on all the wheels and little cogs of the party machine. . . . In order that the centre should be able not only to advise, to persuade, and to argue (as we have been doing up till now) but really to direct the orchestra, it is essential for it to know in detail who plays what fiddle and where, what instrument he has studied and is studying, and where, who is playing out of tune, and where, and why (when the music begins to grate on the ear), and who should be transferred, and how and whither he should be transferred in order to get rid of the discord, and so forth.[1]

* Reprinted by permission of the publishers from chapter XVIII of Leonard Schapiro's *The Origin of the Communist Autocracy* (Cambridge, Mass.: Harvard University Press, 1955); and also by permission of the London School of Economics and Political Science.
[1] *Lenin*, Vol. V, pp. 179-92. Cf. his "Chto delat?," *Lenin*, Vol. IV, pp. 359-508. The first edition of this work carried as its epigraph a quotation from Lassalle: "The party strengthens itself by purging itself."

This plan, though designed for the purposes of revolution, was not substantially altered after the revolution had been accomplished. It was not, however, until 1921, with the development of the party Secretariat and Orgbureau, that it began to be put into practice. Nor was it until 1921 that Lenin was able to achieve the other fundamental principle of his scheme of party organization, the monopoly of control over proletariat and peasantry. The latter was only accomplished with the elimination from the political scene of socialist opponents, and especially of the Mensheviks, whose influence in the trade unions presented the most serious competition to the Communists.

Before the revolution the conflict between the two wings of Russian social democracy had centred much more on questions of organization and method than on questions of theory. With the coming of the February Revolution, Bolsheviks and Mensheviks alike did not scruple to jettison theoretical principles to which each had previously adhered. The same process can be observed after the October Revolution, during the years of the civil war. Once again, it was much less dispute over the theory of marxism which divided Bolsheviks and Mensheviks than questions of organization and method. The Mensheviks, in particular, had in practice abandoned, within a year of the revolution, the most cherished tenet of orthodox Russian marxists, that a socialist revolution should only take place after a long period of "bourgeois" democracy, by conceding the "historical necessity" of the October Revolution. In introducing his New Economic Policy Lenin did little more than take over and put into practice a doctrine evolved by the Mensheviks—after first removing the Mensheviks from the political scene.

Even in the case of relations between the Bolsheviks and the Socialist Revolutionaries, it was to some extent true that what divided the two parties was more often disagreement over methods of government than widely divergent theoretical beliefs. The left wing of the Socialist Revolutionaries immediately accepted the Bolshevik revolution, and only broke with the Bolsheviks on the question of the tactics to be adopted in preserving the revolutionary government in power. But even the rest of the party, who at first repudiated the Bolshevik revolution, accepted it in the end when they found that their struggle against the revolutionary government was helping a counter-revolutionary government to power. The capitulation of many of their number to the Communists, and the hesitations of those who did not capitulate, proved this beyond doubt. Lenin had in turn accepted, at any rate temporarily, the socialist revolutionary theory of land distribution to the peasantry, and had abandoned the bolshevik programme of immediate nationalization. Once again, as before the revolution, the main source of conflict between Lenin and Russian socialism proved to be questions of organization and method—such as the *Vecheka,* the uncontrolled bureaucracy, or the subordination of the trade unions to centralized party control. Above all, the great majority of socialists were not prepared to tolerate the suppression of democratic liberties. The victory of the Bolsheviks over the socialists can of course in large measure be explained by the constant use of force. But there were other causes at work which were also of importance in helping to assure this victory.

The first reason was the war with Germany. The efforts of the Second International had not yet by the summer of 1914 produced unity in the ranks of the great majority of Russian social democrats who rejected Lenin's authoritarian tactics. But on the eve of the war it seemed as if Lenin's tactics were at last going to bring about in Russian social democracy the cohesion which it had hitherto lacked. The war put an end to this movement, which, had it succeeded, might well have left Lenin and his followers by the wayside as an offshoot of the main trend of Russian politics, of little more historical importance than Tkachev before him. For the division caused by the war brought the internationalist wings of both Mensheviks and Socialist Revolutionaries much nearer to Lenin's group of extremists in the Second International than to their own "defensist" colleagues, who appeared to them to be betrayers of socialist principles. In Russia, during the critical and chaotic months between March and November 1917, large sections of both the Socialist Revolutionaries and of the Mensheviks, namely, the Left Socialist Revolutionaries and Martov's Internationalists, occupied positions much closer to the Bolsheviks than to the "defensists" in their respective parties. When they realized that Lenin's policy had led not to the promised revolutionary war, but to Brest-Litovsk, they broke with the Bolsheviks, but it was by then too late. Moreover, even among the "defensist" socialists, if one excepts a few realists like Plekhanov, or romantic patriots like Savinkov, there were many whose outward support of national defence was nevertheless qualified by demands for such action as made effective defence impossible. Their attitude only served to strengthen the hands of the Bolsheviks.

Equally important for the victory of bolshevism was the advantage which the Bolsheviks derived from the moral scruples of their socialist opponents. It is now a commonplace to argue that the Provisional Government, headed by the socialist Kerensky, could easily have prevented the bolshevik revolution by taking effective and timely action against a mere handful of men and their skeleton organization. But, to argue thus is to look at the Bolsheviks through the eyes of 1921, or 1951, and not of 1917. In August or September 1917 the Provisional Government, largely composed of socialists and headed by a socialist prime minister, was understandably reluctant to use the methods of the overthrown autocracy against ostensibly socialist opponents, however extremist their views or actions. When it was goaded into taking some steps against the Bolsheviks after the abortive rising of July 1917, its measures were half-hearted and quite ineffective. It was not for nothing that the bolshevik leaders subsequently maintained that their coup d'état in November 1917 had proved easy beyond expectation.

The hesitation of their political opponents to take up arms against the Bolsheviks played as great a part in their retention of power after 1917. The Mensheviks rejected armed opposition from the first, though a minority of the party was for a short time in favour of it, and a few individuals broke with their party and joined one or other of the anti-bolshevik forces or conspiracies. As regards the party as a whole, such a course was foreign to their tradition, their temperament, and be it said their capabilities. The case of the Socialist Revolutionaries was different. They were neither a marxist nor a proletarian party and the peasants whom they represented had given them an ostensible mandate in the elections to the Constituent Assembly against the bolshevik usurpation of power. Unlike the Mensheviks, many of their number were in November 1917 anxious to fight to victory against Germany and the Central Powers, and the bolshevik surrender outraged their patriotic sentiments. Even the internationalist Left Socialist Revolutionaries were not devoid of such sentiment. Their indignation at the treaty of Brest-Litovsk, though primarily due to what they regarded as the betrayal of the cause of world revolution, was not untinged with the romantic notions harboured by their intelligentsia of the enraged Slav masses rising against the invading West. Moreover, violence had always been an influential factor in socialist revolutionary tradition. Yet, the story of the Socialist Revolutionaries' struggle against the Bolsheviks is one of indecision, hesitation, disunity, and divided loyalty. The refusal of the Central Committee of the main party to take up arms in defence of the Constituent Assembly, at a time when there were still armed forces available to support the attempt, lost them an opportunity which never recurred, and dealt a great blow to their prestige.

The treaty of Brest-Litovsk goaded them at last into co-operation with the forces of the Western Allies and into an armed struggle against the Bolsheviks. But the weak governments which the Socialist Revolutionaries set up fell, and were replaced by military dictatorships. By November 1918 the ill-assorted partnership of inexperienced and doctrinaire socialists on the one hand, and politically illiterate and reactionary army officers on the other, had come to an end. The Socialist Revolutionaries' insistence on the adoption of a full socialist policy in the midst of a civil war had contributed not a little to the debâcle. Moreover, in November 1918 the defeat of Germany removed the circumstance which in the eyes of many Socialist Revolutionaries had alone justified armed struggle against the Bolsheviks. The fight against Lenin's government could now no longer be viewed as a means of restoring the Eastern front against Germany, but became open civil war. A number of the party capitulated to the Bolsheviks, preferring political extinction to a struggle which, though it might defeat the Bolsheviks, would do so at the cost of putting reactionary monarchists into power.

Within Russia the remnants of the party organization renounced re-course to arms for the duration of the civil war. From the end of 1918 onwards the armed activity against the Communists by Socialist Revo-lutionaries inside Russia was limited to the participation of individuals in the fighting in the civil war and in a few conspiratorial organizations, while abroad groups of émigrés endeavoured to enlist the support of the Western Allies for more effective intervention. The party organization waited to lead a popular rising on a national scale, which never came. Thus, of the opponents of the Bolsheviks during the years of the civil war, those who had moral authority to justify their resistance, the socialists, hesitated to use the method of the coup d'état. The reactionary White Armies, which remained in the field against the Bolsheviks, had no such scruples. But they, in turn, lacked the moral authority which could have won them popular support, and might have ensured their success.

These were the negative reasons for the Bolsheviks' success. There were positive reasons as well. In contrast to their socialist opponents, the Bolsheviks were resolute, and bold in decision. Under Lenin's leadership, and because of it, they were not afraid to jettison their doctrine where the all-important question of power was involved—not afraid, in fact, of that "opportunism" for which Lenin so frequently reviled his socialist op-ponents. Besides this, the personality of Lenin, his political skill as well as his clarity of thought and incisiveness in the analysis of a situation, were without rival anywhere on the Russian political scene. Among social demo-crats, certainly Plekhanov, perhaps Martov, were his equals as theorists. Neither of them even approximated to Lenin as a political leader. Among the Socialist Revolutionaries there is no single name that even invites comparison with Lenin, whether as a theorist or as a political leader. But perhaps Lenin's greatest achievement for bolshevism was his success in harnessing to marxism the smouldering passions of the Russian people, which centuries of autocracy had engendered. It is true that in the last few years before the war it was marxism in its moderate, Western form of trade unionism and parliamentary democracy that seemed at long last to be tak-ing some root in Russia. But this was only the beginning of a new process in a country in which habits of constitutionalism and legality still remained to be formed. The more traditional instinctive form of Russian socialism was not menshevik marxism, but the *Narodnik* mystique of the Socialist Revolutionaries, with its belief that it was Russia's destiny to follow a path quite distinct from that of capitalist Europe, and its faith in the natural socialism of the Russian peasant; and with its sense of the dark forces of anarchy which could so easily be conjured up.

In Russia [wrote Bakunin] the robber is the only true revolutionary. . . . The robbers in the woods, in the cities and in the villages, robbers all over Russia, and robbers imprisoned in the innumerable jails throughout the country make up one, indivisible, closely linked world,—the world of the Russian revolution. . . . He who wishes to plot revolution in earnest in Russia, he who desires a popular revolution, must enter this world.

There was not a Russian socialist, Bolshevik, Menshevik, or *Narodnik,* who did not know the significance of this world. But whereas all Mensheviks and the majority of Socialist Revolutionaries recoiled from it in horror, hoping to exorcise it in the end from Russian society, Lenin was not afraid of alliance with it.

The victory of the Bolsheviks in November 1917 did not, however, mean the victory of a united party. The struggles which reached their culmination at the Tenth Party Congress in March 1921 need have caused no surprise. Lenin's rapid and sudden switches of doctrine in response to the exigencies of policy placed considerable strain on the loyalty of his bewildered followers. One need only recall as instances the sudden abandonment and discard of the two orthodox phases of revolution: the repeated promise of revolutionary war jettisoned in favour of an immediate peace on any terms in March 1918; the rapid ending of workers' control, and the sudden and unheralded switch from war communism to the New Economic Policy. To anyone who based his conduct on a political theory it was no easy matter to follow Lenin through the many mutations of his policy. Yet for all this, it was not solely or primarily from the failure of Lenin's followers to realize as rapidly as Lenin the practical reasons for his switches of theory, that the most serious opposition arose inside the Russian communist party.

There was nothing peculiar to Russia in the fact that a revolutionary theory should have undergone a change when once the attempt had been made to put it into practice. Nor is the difference between political programmes before and after the coming into office of the party which sponsors them confined to revolutionary parties. Lenin's departures from his promises, or from marxist doctrine, could not by themselves have engendered the feverish excitement which characterized the Russian communist party during 1921. Indeed, some of the most fundamental departures both from orthodox theory and from party promises took place without arousing any serious opposition within the communist party at all. Perhaps this ready acceptance by the Russian Communists of the need to subordinate theory to keeping in power is best illustrated by their attitude to that all important question, the state in a socialist society.

It will be recalled that the Russian social democrats, alone of all European marxists, had accepted as an item of their programme the "dictatorship of the proletariat." Marx had used this phrase almost casually, on isolated occasions, to designate the temporary form which the struggle of the proletariat with its opponents would take immediately after its seizure of power. He had never defined or elaborated the shape which he thought a revolutionary government would assume in practice. But, since in Marx's conception the proletarian revolution was to take place at a moment when the vast exploited majority finally rose against a small minority of exploiters, it was plain that this dictatorship would be temporary and short-lived. Moreover, since the seizure of power by the proletariat would inaugurate the advent of the classless society, and since the state existed only as a device for preventing class conflict from erupting into violence, it followed, in marxist analysis, that the state must begin to wither away progressively from the moment that the proletariat had seized and consolidated its power.

On the very eve of the bolshevik revolution Lenin still fully accepted this analysis. In his *State and Revolution*, written in August and September 1917 while he was in hiding—a work written with care and much thought, and a statement of principles to which he attached the utmost importance —Lenin fully accepted the classical marxist analysis. "The proletarian state," he wrote, "will begin to wither away immediately after its victory, since in a society without class contradictions, the state is unnecessary and impossible." True, it would not, as the anarchists demanded, simply be abolished overnight. But neither, according to Lenin, would it resemble, while it lasted, the state which it had overthrown, with its police and other machinery of repression. Supported as it would be by the overwhelming mass of the population, it would enforce its will "almost without any special machinery." [2]

These words, it should be emphasized, were not part of the demagogy with which the Bolsheviks captured the support of the masses between March and November 1917, since *State and Revolution* was not published until the spring of 1918. By the time Lenin's words were published, the *Vecheka* had been active for several months, and not even the most sanguine marxist could have discerned any signs of the state beginning to wither away. When the question of "withering away" came up in March 1918, at the Seventh Party Congress, Lenin now impatiently brushed it aside. "One may well wonder when the state will begin to wither away. . . . To proclaim this withering away in advance is to violate historical perspective." It was Bukharin, the Left Communist, who had raised the question. Many years passed before the question was raised again. The Left Communists, the Democratic Centralists, the Workers' Opposition,—all accepted the need for the terror, the *Vecheka,* the unbridled powers of the executive. The reason was not, perhaps, far to seek. The Bolsheviks, so far from winning over the great majority of the country after they had seized power, as doctrine demanded, remained a small, unpopular minority, ruling by force. Their survival in sole power depended upon the state and the apparatus which they had created, and few Communists were prepared to question the necessity for this survival.

Thus, so far as one of the most fundamental departures from marxist theory was concerned, the realities of power operated to dictate its ac-

[2] *Lenin,* Vol. XXI, pp. 388, 431-2.

ceptance, and without much discussion at that. The same proved to be the case with some other crucial questions of marxist theory which did cause some division within the communist party during the civil war. The Left Communists were opposed to Lenin not only on the question of peace, but also on fundamental questions of economics and politics. But, when once Lenin's peace policy appeared to be justified in practice, their opposition on questions of theory faded away. The Democratic Centralists, who opposed a fairly reasoned alternative to Lenin's doctrine of party organization, capitulated at the Tenth Party Congress in March 1921 without firing a shot. Yet both these groups included some of the best intellectuals in the party. The main struggles on questions of theory—on the New Economic Policy, on socialism in one country, on the nature and meaning of the October Revolution, on the withering away of the state, on dialectical materialism—all lay ahead. But by the time these debates began to develop, in 1923 and in the succeeding years, questions of theory had largely become a screen or an instrument for a struggle to capture, or resist, the party apparatus among the men who had in 1921 helped to create it.

Indeed, so little did questions of doctrine animate the Russian Communists for some time after the October Revolution, that the biggest departure from marxism of all passed unnoticed. The main opposition within the communist party, the Workers' Opposition and the general discontent loosely linked with it, only came to a head at the end of 1920, with the virtual end of the civil war. This was not surprising. Until then the Soviet régime had been engaged in a life and death struggle for survival, of which the issue was at no time certain. The common danger created unity, and discontent with such matters as over-centralization, or interference in trade union affairs was assuaged by the faith that these were temporary, if necessary evils, which would be put right when the danger had been averted. The failure to analyse the theoretical implications of policy was understandable during the civil war, while the existence of the new state was in danger. But the blindness to questions of theory continued after the civil war, when the Soviet state was no longer in peril from outside attack, but the communist monopoly of power was threatened from the inside. When in March 1921 the foundation of the future state structure was laid, it became apparent that no one within the communist party had grasped the theoretical issues which were at stake, perhaps not even Lenin. For what now took place was no less than a reversal in practice of the very basis of marxist teaching, that the political machine is the mere reflection or superstructure of the economic structure. Henceforward, political power was to control the economic form of society.

The coup d'état of November 1917 had been accepted as a proletarian revolution, cutting short the democratic phase—that is, accepted as such by the Communists; the Mensheviks, who continued to believe that the October

Revolution, in spite of appearances, remained in essence a bourgeois, democratic revolution, nonetheless accepted its "historical necessity." The first impact of Lenin's unorthodox decision to seize power had thrown his followers into confusion. But the confusion did not last long. The unexpected failure of their opponents to rally and overthrow the new communist government was probably as powerful an advocate for the correctness of Lenin's decision as any theoretical doctrine. So long as war communism remained the official policy, the virtual one party state which existed in the country after the peace of Brest-Litovsk might have appeared to many to be justified as the correct political superstructure for the putting into effect of extreme socialist policies.

But by the spring of 1921 war communism had failed. It was now to be replaced by an economic system in which there would be room for private capitalist enterprise and interests. Marxist logic therefore demanded that the political machine corresponding to such an economic system should be composed of parties representing the interests of the various classes which were now to be tolerated, in a state which was no longer regarded even in theory as a one class state. Lenin himself had conceded this theoretical necessity in 1905, when he had argued that so long as the revolution had not emerged from the democratic, and therefore multi-class stage, government should take the form of a coalition dictatorship of the peasantry and the proletariat. Yet, in 1921 no serious opinion within the communist party was prepared to challenge the monopoly of all political power by their own proletarian party, though many Communists were ready to criticize the abuses which proceeded from the monopoly. In this respect the simple mutineers at Kronstadt, who at all events demanded political freedom for all workers' and peasants' parties, may be said to have proved themselves better marxists than the Communists.

The question can be looked at from another aspect in which marxist theory plays no part. The Bolsheviks had never proclaimed the one party state as their avowed policy before the revolution. The seizure of power had been ostensibly accomplished in the name of the soviets in which several parties were represented. When Lenin's decision to govern alone became apparent immediately after the October Revolution it even provoked a short-lived crisis inside the bolshevik ranks. For some years to come the fiction that the Communists were but one party among many was maintained. The suppression of the socialists was, with the exception of the short period between June and November 1918, invariably bolstered by charges such as "counter-revolution," or speculation: it was not action openly taken against political opponents. The communist policy of defaming the political integrity of all socialists dates from this time. Up to 1921 it was not difficult for the Communists to justify to themselves their decision to take, and keep, power alone. The socialists had after all failed to achieve between March and November 1917 a solid and efficient government, and had then repudiated the Bolsheviks, who were at any rate prepared to take the responsibility for decisive action. The peace with Germany had been bitterly opposed by Mensheviks and Socialist Revolutionaries alike. Was it not logical that the Communists should take upon themselves the burden of government alone? The Socialist Revolutionaries had for a time even sided with the anti-bolshevik forces in the civil war.

But all these factors had ceased to exist in 1921. The socialist parties inside Russia, or those of them who still had an opportunity of voicing their views, were vying with one another in their loyalty to the ideals of the revolution as such, while condemning the excess of the Communists. There was not the remotest threat of any right wing or counter-revolutionary restoration. Long after 1921, though deprived of all political power and though many of their number were in prison or exiled, the intelligentsia and the middle-class continued to serve the Soviet state. The emigré socialists and *Kadety* even developed a whole philosophy of collaboration with the Communists in order to build up Russia, and many of them returned to implement what they considered to be their duty. There was opposition inside Russia, to be sure. But as the programme of the Kronstadt insurgents, which was typical of this opposition, shows, it was opposition not to Soviet government but to the Communists' monopoly of power, and to their party's illegal methods of preserving it.

Those, and there are many,[3] who justify the Communists' elimination of their socialist opponents in 1921 by the necessity of safeguarding the "revolution" from its enemies ignore two essential facts: first, that enmity against the Communists was not enmity against the revolution, i.e., the Soviet form of government, but against the methods of communist rule in the name of that revolution. It was therefore not only an enmity of the Communists' own creation, but one which it was in their power to remove without danger to the revolution, though with undoubted risk to their own monopoly of power. To be sure, Lenin and the Communists identified "the revolution" with themselves. But it was an identification made by them alone, which did not correspond to facts. Secondly, that a large number,

---

[3] See e.g. *Deutscher*, [Stalin], p. 226, "It was true enough that concern for the revolution compelled Bolshevism to take the road chosen by the tenth congress . . ."; *Carr*, [The Bolshevik Revolution], *I*, p. 183. The latter concludes that the demise of the legal opposition "cannot fairly be laid at the door of one party. If it was true that the Bolshevik régime was not prepared after the first few months to tolerate an organized opposition, it was equally true that no opposition party was prepared to remain within legal limits. The premise of dictatorship was common to both sides of the argument." This judgment ignores not only the Mensheviks, but most of the Socialist Revolutionaries as well. The premise of dictatorship was certainly common to both sides in Lenin's "argument" with Denikin. But what relation to fact does such an assertion bear in the case of Martov and the Mensheviks, whose policy was founded upon the need to "remain within legal limits"? Or in the case of the Samara Socialist Revolutionaries, who gave up the fight for fear it might assist the victory of a right wing dictatorship? The charge that the Mensheviks were not prepared to remain within legal limits is part of the Bolsheviks' case; it does not survive an examination of the facts.

perhaps even the majority, of the conscious proletariat, were in early 1921 menshevik or menshevik sympathizers. The revolutionary nature of this party's policy, which accorded political freedom to workers and peasants alone, and advocated large scale nationalization of industry and state control of foreign trade, cannot be conjured away, as is normally done by apologists of Lenin's policy, by describing it as "bourgeois." The socialists were not eliminated in 1921 because they were counter-revolutionary. They were described as counter-revolutionary in order to justify their elimination.

The fate of the socialists was sealed when it became apparent that in their criticism of communist methods they were speaking much the same language as the many malcontents inside the communist party. The realization of the extent of the support which the Kronstadt mutineers could muster, even inside the communist party within the naval garrison, had come as a grave shock. But different considerations applied to the Workers' Opposition. There was no vestige in their programme of any quarrel with the communist leaders for their treatment of socialist opponents, or of the peasantry. It was a mixture of the early syndicalism which the Communists had abandoned, utopianism, and nostalgia for the lost enthusiasm of the first months. They combined with it some well-founded criticism of the abuses of bureaucracy and of excessive party discipline and control. The communist leaders may have been right in seeing in the existence of this critical group a potential party split. The moral case for the Workers' Opposition was perhaps not very strong. They demanded freedom for themselves, but had no thought of conceding it to others. When they complained of control by the centre over the communist committees in the trade-unions, they did not pause to think that those same communist committees for which they demanded more freedom of action did not hesitate to impose their will on a trade union membership, some fourteen times their number, which was bitterly opposed to them. They accepted the state of affairs in which a party of a few hundred thousand could impose its will by force on millions of workers who did not support them. But they did not realize that if a minority party is to survive in sole power against the will of the great majority, it can only do so if it maintains the strictest discipline and control by its leaders over its own members. Once again the Kronstadt mutineers proved themselves more mature politicians than the Workers' Opposition.

But if the communist leaders were right in sensing in the Workers' Opposition a danger of a party split, they were wrong in attempting to identify the views of this opposition with menshevism. It is true that one of the fundamental differences between bolshevism and menshevism, which had even preceded the formal split in 1903, had been disagreement on the value of the spontaneous effort of the masses. The Mensheviks, following Plekhanov, and Lavrov before him, believed that the revolution must be the work of the masses themselves. Lenin had replaced this view by the doctrine that, left to themselves, the masses will be content with palliative reforms, and must therefore be led on to revolution by a party of professional revolutionaries. This difference of view was reflected in the rival formulas put forward for incorporation in the party statute by Lenin and Martov at the Second Congress in 1903—Lenin's, confining membership to those who "personally participate in one of the party organizations," i.e. put themselves under party discipline; and Martov's, extending it much more widely to all who "co-operate" with the party "under the direction of one of its organizations." The Mensheviks were concerned with the relations between the social democratic party and the proletariat as a whole, or, in other words, with the nature of and, more important, the degree of leadership which the party of the proletariat should exercise over that proletariat. It was in this context that, in opposition to Lenin, they claimed that a greater degree of initiative should be left to the workers themselves as distinct from the party which claimed to speak in their name.

But the Workers' Opposition were concerned with an entirely different question, the relation of the party at a low level to the party at a higher level. They were not concerned with the workers outside that party, who formed the majority. It is true that in their demands for less restriction on the freedom of local party and trade union committees, for example, the Workers' Opposition may have appeared at times to be speaking the same language as the Mensheviks. But the Mensheviks wanted free elections in the trade unions, which would have put socialist, but not communist majorities into power. The Workers' Opposition did not seek to alter the rigged elections which ensured communist majorities, but merely sought to safeguard the local trade union committee or cell from being replaced by central nominees. It was also true that Mensheviks and Workers' Opposition shared in common a somewhat romantic faith in the superiority of the proletariat actually engaged in manual labour over the professional party bureaucrat, or the intellectual. But in basic political aims the two were poles apart.

The balance sheet of political support was not an encouraging one for the communist party in March 1921. Among the peasantry it had lost most, if not all, the support or at least neutrality which had once played an important part in achieving victory both in November 1917 and in the civil war. Even among the proletariat dislike of the Communists had grown. With it grew the popularity of the socialist parties, notably of the Mensheviks. No communist leader could have had any doubt, and some, such as Zinoviev, openly admitted, that in any free election to any soviet, or trade union committee, in March 1921 the number of communist candidates elected would have been small. It was true that much of this unpopularity was due to privations brought about by the civil war. But it was also true that much of it was due to the revolt of the Russian people against the unfairness, the violence, and the illegality with which the Communists suppressed all who did not accept their rule without question. The Kronstadt revolt proved this beyond any doubt.

In these circumstances there were only two policies open to Lenin. Either to resign himself to his failure to win over the majority, to moderate the policy by which his monopoly of power had been secured and to accept the consequent loss of that monopoly. Or, to preserve his monopoly of political power at all costs, and at the same time make the task of preserving it easier by removing, at the price of sacrificing communist doctrine, some of the economic causes of discontent. He chose the second course. But it was plain that this policy could only be successfully achieved by a disciplined party, united, if necessary by force, for the difficult task which now confronted it. There could be no room for party democracy. The trade union discussion, which had revealed the personal rivalries dividing the party as well as the wide divergence of view on fundamental questions of policy, had proved that. The views of the Democratic Centralists, of Preobrazhensky or Krestinsky, of Shlyapnikov or Kollontai, suffered from the contradiction that they stood for two incompatible aims: *both* a democratic communist party, *and* the exclusion of all other parties from power. It was this circumstance more than any other which determined their quick collapse at the Tenth Party Congress.

Lenin easily steered his policy to victory at this congress. He was still the outstanding figure in the party, much as he had been in 1917. There was no rival leader within sight who could have succeeded in rallying the discontented inside the party around himself and in raising a revolt against Lenin; even if there had been anyone, which there was not, who had the courage to assume such a rôle. The only possible candidate would have been Trotsky. But Trotsky was much too close in outlook to Lenin on the vital question of communist monopoly of power to have thought of such a course. Moreover, his personal popularity was already seriously impaired in 1921 by policies associated with his name. Nor is there the slightest reason to suppose that he ever contemplated such a move for a moment. The Workers' Opposition lacked any leaders of note, the intellectual Democratic Centralists had no thought of struggle, and certainly no stomach for it. It was therefore easy for Lenin to carry the leaders of his party with him, in spite of the misgivings which some of them uttered, and perhaps many more felt.

It is plain that in 1921, as in 1917, many followed Lenin without completely realizing where he was leading them. The full significance of his policy then may have been no more apparent than had been the full significance of the seizure of power. In November 1917 a number of bolshevik leaders cavilled when they discovered that what they had believed to be seizure of power by the soviets was in reality seizure of power by the bolshevik party. In 1921 those who followed Lenin believed that what was being achieved was the consolidation of the power of the communist party.

Many of them were to rebel once again, in 1923, when they discovered that what had really taken place was the consolidation in power of the central party apparatus. But it was then too late.

Thus once again, in 1921 as in 1917, the personal qualities and influence of Lenin proved the decisive factor. In 1917 the political immaturity and inexperience of the Russian parties had played into the hands of anyone both resolute enough to seize power, and untroubled by the doubts and hesitancies which beset the more scrupulous. After 1918 Lenin's democratic opponents had no armed forces at their disposal. Their sole hope of overthrowing the Communists might have been in alliance with the White Armies. The overwhelming majority of them had not been prepared to accept such an alliance for fear that the only outcome would be the downfall of the revolution, and the restoration of the monarchy. The population, distracted by hardships of every kind, was able to achieve no more than a peasant guerrilla war and the Kronstadt revolt.

In 1921 the fate of the country lay in the hands of Lenin. He had a chance of burying past enmities and of carrying the vast majority of the country with him in an attempt to build up ruined Russia on the basis of co-operation and legal order, and not of the dictatorship of an unpopular minority. It is difficult to escape the conclusion that a greater man than Lenin would have seized this chance. But Lenin's genius lay in the technique of grasping and holding power. He was a great revolutionary, but not a statesman. His conviction that he and his followers alone held the secret of successful rule in their hands was, to a large extent, the product of the struggle by which he had achieved his position. But from his fateful decision in the spring of 1921 flowed all the consequences of the one party dictatorship which became apparent in the subsequent years of Soviet history.

Two main consequences derived from Lenin's political policy of 1921, both of enormous importance for the future history of Soviet Russia. The first was the emergence of what Engels has so well described as the "conventional hypocrisy." During the civil war there was at any rate some justification for the view that "he who is not with us is against us." In the heat of battle it was possible for the Communists to see in those socialists who were fighting against them enemies of the revolution, without seeming to do undue violence to truth. After 1921, the lumping together of Mensheviks, Workers' Opposition, serious theoretical critics, and malcontents inside the communist party as counter-revolutionaries was a falsification, and everyone knew it.

The acceptance of this official lie by almost the entire leadership of the communist party inevitably led to the result that whoever among them was strong enough to exploit it in his own interest had the rest of them at his mercy. What is the difference between the attempt by Lenin to expel Shlyapnikov, in 1921, and the expulsion of Trotsky six years later, if both

can be justified by the same argument—that the stability of the dictatorship is the supreme law? But this, in turn, leads to the second main consequence of Lenin's policy. For, who has the power to decide by what faction
the stability of the régime is to be best served? Clearly, he who manipulates
the apparatus of the party, and can thereby ensure both the necessary majorities at the centre and implicit obedience to central orders throughout
the country. The malignant figure of the General Secretary, Stalin, has become only too familiar in its portrayal by disappointed oppositionists,
defeated by the apparatus which he controlled. But it was Lenin, with
their support, who equipped him with the weapons, and started him upon
his path.

V

TOWARD THE DICTATORSHIP OF STALIN

9. The Triumph of Stalin

O great Stalin, O leader of the peoples,
Thou who broughtest man to birth,
Thou who fructifiest the earth,
Thou who restorest the centuries,
Thou who makest bloom the spring,
Thou who makest vibrate the musical chords.
Thou, splendor of my spring, O thou,
Sun reflected by millions of hearts. . . .
Translation of Uzbek poem in Pravda, August 28, 1936

"Comrades! The cult of the individual acquired such monstrous size chiefly because Stalin himself, using all conceivable methods, supported the glorification of his own person. This is supported by numerous facts. One of the most characteristic examples of Stalin's self-glorification and of his lack of even elementary modesty is the edition of his *Short Biography,* which was published in 1948.

"This book is an expression of the most dissolute flattery, an example of making a man into a godhead, of transforming him into an infallible sage, 'the greatest leader,' 'sublime strategist of all times and nations.' Finally no other words could be found with which to lift Stalin up to the heavens.

"We need not give here examples of the loathsome adulation filling this book. All we need to add is that they all were approved and edited by Stalin personally and some of them were added in his own handwriting to the draft text of the book."

NIKITA S. KHRUSHCHEV, February 25, 1956

Chapter 9

THE TRIUMPH OF STALIN

One of the more interesting and important questions is why and how Stalin was able to emerge from a position of relative obscurity to one of unexcelled power in the history of the modern world. (While it is probably true that Stalin was far abler than some critics have suggested, he was, when compared with certain other of the Bolshevik leaders, a gray mediocrity, hardworking, pedestrian, and uninspired.) A more serious, and related, question is how did it happen that, under the aegis of a theory which was designed to liberate man from exploitation, so crass and pervasive a dictatorship could arise and develop.

Relevant, of course, to these questions are the explanations considered or suggested in the previous section. But there are additional and variant explanations offered by Isaac Deutscher, Leon Trotsky, John Plamenatz, and Sidney Hook which merit consideration.

A few words should be added in regard to the historic circumstances under which Stalin consolidated his power—apart from those dealt with in the pages that follow. By 1928, under the New Economic Policy (NEP) —which had abolished requisitioning from the peasantry, encouraged private trade and small-scale enterprise while the "commanding heights" of industry remained under state administration—productivity had been restored to prewar levels. However, the grain surplus available for urban consumption or export was only at one-third prewar level. In the minds of Stalin and other Soviet leaders, NEP did not provide an adequate basis for large-scale investment in, and subsidization of, a massive industrialization. Moreover, a large class of peasant proprietors and business entrepreneurs presented at least a potential threat to the regime. Stalin decided to embark, therefore, upon wholesale collectivization of agriculture to support industrialization.

The first five-year plan, which went into effect on October 1, 1928, engendered tremendous enthusiasm and a spirit of sacrifice, particularly among the youth. On the other hand, it resulted in massive and sullen

263

attended private departmental conferences and even the meetings of the Council of Commissars. This system was devised as a method of training an *élite* for the civil service; but as a result of it the Rabkrin was able to keep its eye on every wheel of the governmental machine.[1]

The whole bizarre scheme of inspection was one of Lenin's pet ideas. Exasperated by the inefficiency and dishonesty of the civil service, he sought to remedy them by extreme and ruthless "control from below," and the Commissariat was to be the means. The choice of Stalin for the job gives a measure of Lenin's high confidence in him, for the Inspectorate was to be a sort of a super-government, itself free from every taint and blemish of officialdom.

Lenin's cure proved as bad as the disease. The faults of the civil service, as Lenin himself frequently pointed out, reflected the country's appalling lack of education, its material and spiritual misery, which could be cured only gradually, over the lifetime of at least a generation. The Rabkrin would have had to be a commissariat of angels in order to rise, let alone raise others, above the dark valley of Russian bureaucracy. With his characteristic belief in the inherent virtues of the working classes, Lenin appealed to the workers against his own bureaucracy. The mill of officialdom, however, turned the workers themselves into bureaucrats. The Commissariat of the Inspectorate, as Lenin was to discover later on, became an additional source of muddle, corruption, and bureaucratic intrigue. In the end it became an unofficial but meddlesome police in charge of the civil service. But let us not run ahead of our story. Suffice it to say here that, as the head of the Inspectorate, Stalin came to control the whole machinery of government, its working and personnel, more closely than any other commissar.

His next position of vantage was in the Politbureau. Throughout the civil war, the Politbureau consisted of five men only: Lenin, Trotsky, Stalin, Kamenev, and Bukharin. Ever since the break between Bolsheviks and Social Revolutionaries, this had been the real government of the country. Lenin was the recognized leader of both government and party. Trotsky was responsible for the conduct of the civil war. Kamenev acted as Lenin's deputy in various capacities. Bukharin was in charge of press and propaganda. The day-to-day management of the party belonged to Stalin. The Politbureau discussed high policy. Another body, which was, like the Politbureau, elected by the Central Committee, the Organization Bureau (Orgbureau), was in charge of the party's personnel, which it was free to call up, direct to work, and distribute throughout the army and the civil service according to the demands of the civil war. From the beginning of 1919 Stalin was the only permanent liaison officer between the Politbureau and

---

[1] See Lenin, *Sochinenya*, vol. xxvii, pp. 14-20; *Letters of Lenin*, pp. 455-6, 474-5. Zinoviev's speeches in *8 Syezd RKP* (*b*), pp. 162-3, 501, 225-6, and 290-1; and *Kratkii Otchet Narkom. R.K.I.*

the Orgbureau. He ensured the unity of policy and organization; that is, he marshalled the forces of the party according to the Politbureau's directives. Like none of his colleagues, he was immersed in the party's daily drudgery and in all its kitchen cabals.

At this stage his power was already formidable. Still more was to accrue to him from his appointment, on 3 April 1922, to the post of General Secretary of the Central Committee. The eleventh congress of the party had just elected a new and enlarged Central Committe and again modified the statutes. The leading bodies of the party were now top-heavy; and a new office, that of the General Secretary, was created, which was to coordinate the work of their many growing and overlapping branches. It was on that occasion, Trotsky alleges, that Lenin aired, in the inner circle of his associates, his misgivings about Stalin's candidature: "This cook can only serve peppery dishes." [1] But his doubts were, at any rate, not grave; and he himself in the end sponsored the candidature of the "cook." Molotov and Kuibyshev were appointed Stalin's assistants, the former having already been one of the secretaries of the party. The appointment was reported in the Russian press without any ado, as a minor event in the inner life of the party.

Soon afterwards a latent dualism of authority began to develop at the very top of the party. The seven men who now formed the Politbureau (in addition to the previous five, Zinoviev and Tomsky had recently been elected) represented, as it were, the brain and the spirit of Bolshevism. In the offices of the General Secretariat resided the more material power of management and direction. In name the General Secretariat was subordinate to the illustrious and exalted Politbureau. But the dependence of the Politbureau on the Secretariat became so great that without that prop the Politbureau looked more and more like a body awkwardly suspended in a void. The Secretariat prepared the agenda for each session of the Politbureau. It supplied the documentation on every point under debate. It transmitted the Politbureau's decisions to the lower grades. It was in daily contact with the many thousands of party functionaries in the capital and the provinces. It was responsible for their appointments, promotions, and demotions. It could, up to a point, prejudice the views of the Politbureau on any issue before it came up for debate. It could twist the practical execution of the Politbureau's decisions, according to the tastes of the General Secretary. Similar bodies exist in any governmental machinery but rarely acquire independent authority. What usually prevents them from transgressing their terms of reference is some diffusion of power through the whole system of government, effective control over them, and, sometimes, the integrity of officials. The over-centralization of power in the Bolshevik leadership, the lack of effective control, and, last but not least, the personal

[1] L. Trotsky, *Mein Leben,* p. 450.

ambitions of the General Secretary, all made for the extraordinary weight that the General Secretariat began to carry barely a few months after it had been set up.

The picture would be incomplete without mention of another institution, the Central Control Commission, that came to loom large in Bolshevik affairs. Its role *vis-à-vis* the party was analogous to that of the Commissariat of the Inspectorate *vis-à-vis* the governmental machine: it audited party morals. It was formed at the tenth congress, in 1921, on the demand of the Workers' Opposition, with which the congress had otherwise dealt so harshly. It was in charge of the so-called purges. These, too, were initiated by the tenth congress, on the demand of the Opposition. They were intended to cleanse the party periodically of careerists, who had climbed the band-wagon in great numbers, of Communists who had acquired a taste for bourgeois life, and commissars whose heads had been turned by power. Lenin adopted the idea and intended to use it in order to stop his followers departing from the party's puritanic standards. But he also turned one edge of the purges against "anarcho-syndicalists," waverers, doubters, and dissidents, against the real initiators of the new practice.

The procedure of the purges was at first very different from what it became in later years. The purges were no concern of the judiciary. They were conducted by the party's local control commissions before an open citizens' forum, to which Bolsheviks and non-Bolsheviks had free access. The conduct of every member of the party, from the most influential to the humblest, was submitted to stern public scrutiny. Any man or woman from the audience could come forward as a witness. The Bolshevik whose record was found to be unsatisfactory was rebuked or, in extreme cases, expelled from the party. The Control Commission could impose no other penalties than these.

The original motive behind the purges was almost quixotic. It was to enable the people to crack periodically a whip over their rulers. But, since the ruling party was convinced that in all essentials of policy it could not really submit to popular control, these new devices for reviving popular control were *a priori* irrelevant and could not but prove ineffective. They illustrated the party's already familiar dilemma: its growing divorce from the people and its anxiety to preserve its popular character; the dilemma that underlay Lenin's pathetic experiments with his party in the last two years of his political activity. The purges were to serve as a substitute for real elections; they were to remove corrupted members, without removing the party, from power.[1]

---

[1] The purges provided a good cover for all sorts of private vendettas. In May 1922, Lenin wrote in a letter to Stalin: ". . . the purging of the party revealed the prevalence, in the majority of local investigation committees, of personal spite and malice. . . . This fact is incontrovertible and rather significant." In the same letter Lenin complained about the lack of partymen with "an adequate legal education . . . capable of resisting all purely local influences." See *The Essentials of Lenin*, vol. ii, p. 809.

The Central Control Commission in Moscow soon became the supreme court of appeal for the victims of the purges all over the country. Originally, it was to be independent from the Central Committee and the Politbureau. Later it was put on an almost equal footing with the Central Committee; and the two bodies regularly held joint sessions. The General Secretariat was the co-ordinating link between them. Thus, unofficially, Stalin became the chief conductor of the purges.

Lenin, Kamenev, Zinoviev, and, to a lesser extent, Trotsky, were Stalin's sponsors to all the offices he held. His jobs were of the kind which could scarcely attract the bright intellectuals of the Politbureau. All their brilliance in matters of doctrine, all their powers of political analysis would have found little application either at the Workers' and Peasants' Inspectorate or at the General Secretariat. What was needed there was an enormous capacity for hard and uninspiring toil and a patient and sustained interest in every detail of organization. None of his colleagues grudged Stalin his assignments. As long as Lenin kept the reins of government they looked upon him merely as Lenin's assistant; and all of them readily accepted Lenin's leadership. Neither they nor Lenin noticed in time the subtle change by which Stalin was gradually passing from the role of assistant to that of coadjutor.

.   .   .   .   .

Less than two months after Stalin's appointment to the post of General Secretary, the reins of government slipped from Lenin's hands. By the end of May 1922, he suffered his first stroke of arteriosclerotic paralysis. Almost speechless, he was taken out of the Kremlin to the country-side, near Moscow. Not until the middle of the autumn did he recover sufficiently to return to office; and then his activity was very short. At the end of the autumn a second stroke put him out of action; and at the end of the winter, in March 1923, a third stroke removed him finally from the political scene, though his body still wrestled with death until 21 January 1924.

The impact of Lenin's illness on the Bolshevik leadership can hardly be exaggerated. The whole constellation ceased, almost at once, to shine with the reflected light of its master mind or to move in the familiar orbits. Lenin's disciples and satellites (only Trotsky belonged to neither of these categories) began to feel for their own, independent ways. Gradually they were shedding those characteristics of theirs that were merely imitative, their second, and better, nature. The negative side of Lenin's overwhelming and constant influence on his followers now became strikingly apparent. Just how overwhelming it had been can be seen from the circumstance, attested by Trotsky, that during the years of their apprenticeship with their leader, Zinoviev and Kamenev had acquired even Lenin's handwriting. They were now to go on using his handwriting without the inspiration of his ideas.

Stalin was in a sense less dependent on Lenin than were his colleagues;

his intellectual needs were more limited than theirs. He was interested in
the practical use of the Leninist gadgets, not in the Leninist laboratory of
thought. His own behaviour was now dictated by the moods, needs, and
pressures of the vast political machine that he had come to control. His political philosophy boiled down to securing the dominance of that machine
by the handiest and most convenient means. In an avowedly dictatorial
régime, repression often is the handiest and most convenient method of
action. The Politbureau may have been thrown into disarray by Lenin's
disappearance; the General Secretariat was not. On the contrary, since it
had no longer to account for what it did to the vigilant and astute super-
visor, it acted with greater firmness and self-confidence. The same was
true of the Workers' and Peasants' Inspectorate. . . .

.   .   .   .   .

It was about this time that a triumvirate, composed of Stalin, Zinoviev,
and Kamenev, formed itself within the Politbureau. What made for the
solidarity of the three men was their determination to prevent Trotsky
from succeeding to the leadership of the party. Separately, neither could
measure up to Trotsky. Jointly, they represented a powerful combination
of talent and influence. Zinoviev was the politician, the orator, the dema-
gogue with popular appeal. Kamenev was the strategist of the group, its
solid brain, trained in matters of doctrine, which were to play a paramount
part in the contest for power. Stalin was the tactician of the triumvirate and
its organizing force. Between them, the three men virtually controlled the
whole party and, through it, the Government. Kamenev had acted as
Lenin's deputy and presided over the Moscow Soviet. Zinoviev was the
chairman of the Soviet of Petersburg, soon to be renamed Leningrad. Stalin
controlled most of the provinces. Zinoviev was, in addition, the President
of the Communist International, whose moral authority in Russia was then
great enough to make any pretender strive for its support.

Finally, the three men represented, as it were, the party's tradition.
Their uninterrupted association with Bolshevism dated back to the split of
1903; and they held seniority in leadership. Of the other members of the
Politbureau, apart from Trotsky, Bukharin was considerably younger, and
Tomsky, the leader of the trade unions, had only recently become a member
of it. Seniority carried with it the halo of a heroic past, distinguished by
unflagging devotion to Bolshevism. The three men refused now to follow
that "ex-Menshevik," Trotsky, who, after an association with the party
which had lasted only five years, had come to be commonly regarded as
Lenin's successor. This motive, the only one that made for their solidarity,
impelled them to act in concert. As the other members of the Politbureau
walked each his own way, the triumvirs automatically commanded a majority. Their motions and proposals, on which they usually agreed before

every session of the Politbureau, were invariably carried. The other members were bound hand and foot by the discipline of the Politbureau—any attempt by one of them to discuss their inner controversies in public would have appeared as an act of disloyalty. . . .

·   ·   ·   ·   ·

Since the promulgation of the N.E.P. in 1921, Russia's economy was beginning to recover. But the process was slow and painful. Industry was still unable to meet the country's most essential needs. It failed to supply the countryside with the goods that would induce peasants to sell food. Low wages, unemployment, and starvation were driving the working class to despair. Since trade unions refused to take up the workers' demands, discontent exploded in "unofficial" strikes. The restive mood penetrated into the ruling party. Clandestine opposition groups were discovered within its ranks. Some of these groups were half Menshevik; others were wholly Bolshevik and consisted of remnants of the oppositions that had been banned in 1921 as well as of new elements. Their main plank was the demand for freedom of criticism inside the party. Some of the dissenters were expelled, others imprisoned. These were the first instances of clandestine opposition among Communists. So far, the secret groups had acted without concert and lacked leadership. The triumvirs feared a link-up between their rivals and the discontented rank and file.[1]

They reacted to the crisis in a self-contradictory manner. They put before the Central Committee a motion about the need to restore democracy and freedom of discussion for the members of the party. On the other hand, they mobilized the political police against the secret oppositions. The police found that ordinary Bolsheviks often refused to co-operate in tracing the opposition groups. Dzerzhinsky asked the Politbureau to authorize the police to take action against uncooperative Bolsheviks, too. At this point the fight between Trotsky and the triumvirs entered a new phase. Without making it quite clear whether he thought that Dzerzhinsky's demand should be granted, Trotsky attacked the triumvirate. What had happened, he stated, was symptomatic of the party's state of mind, its sense of frustration, and its distrust of the leaders. Even during the civil war "the system of appointment [from above] did not have one-tenth of the extent that it has now. Appointment of the secretaries of provincial committees is now the rule." He granted that there was a grain of demagogy in the demands for a workers' democracy, "in view of the incompatibility of a fully developed workers' democracy with the régime of the dictatorship." But the discipline of the civil war ought to have given place to "a more lively and broader party responsibility." Instead, "the bureaucratization of the party machine had developed to unheard of proportions; and criticism and dis-

[1] J. Stalin, *Sochinenya*, pp. 354-61; N. Popov, *Outline History*, vol. ii, pp. 194-204.

content, the open expression of which was stifled, were driven underground, assuming uncontrollable and dangerous forms." [1]

The triumvirs evaded the issues raised by Trotsky and charged him with malevolence, personal ambition, neglect of his duties in the Government, and so on. They accused him of trying to establish himself as Lenin's successor.[2] This last charge was, in a sense, true, for the fight over the succession was inherent in the situation. Yet this as well as the other charges were beside the point, for the crisis in the party, as Trotsky diagnosed it, was a fact.

In the middle of this exchange forty-six prominent Communists issued a declaration the gist of which was identical with Trotsky's criticisms.[3] . . . It is not certain whether Trotsky directly instigated their demonstration. So far he conducted his dispute with the triumvirs behind the closed doors of the Politbureau. The party at large was under the impression that he had all the time been whole-heartedly behind the official policy. He thus had the worst of both worlds: he had been burdened with responsibility for a policy to which he had been opposed; and he had done nothing to rally in time those who might have supported him.

In November the alarm caused by the crisis led the triumvirs to table a motion in favour of democratic reform in the party. As in the Georgian affair, so now Stalin agreed to make any verbal concession to Trotsky. The motion was carried by the Politbureau unanimously. Trotsky had no choice but to vote for it. On 7 November, the sixth anniversary of the revolution, Zinoviev officially announced the opening of a public discussion on all issues that troubled the Bolshevik mind. The state of siege in the party, so it might have seemed, was at last being lifted.

This was not the case. The state of affairs against which the opposition rose was not merely the result of Stalin's or the other triumvirs' ambition and ill will. It had deeper roots. The revolution had saved itself by building up a massive political machine. The apathy, if not the hostility, of the masses drove it to rely increasingly on rule by coercion rather than by persuasion. Who could say with any certainty that the time had now come to reverse all this, to scrap or even curb the political machine, and to rely on the soundness of popular opinion? Who could be sure that this would not have impaired the safety of the revolution? If a workers' democracy was needed, did that mean that the Mensheviks and the Social Revolutionaries were to be allowed to come back? Most of Stalin's critics, including Trotsky, agreed that the Mensheviks should remain outlawed. In their view, the time had not yet come to lift the state of siege in the republic—they wanted it to be lifted in the party only. But was it at all possible that the party should be an island of freedom in a society doomed, for good or evil, to

[1] M. Eastman, *Since Lenin Died*, Appendix IV, pp. 142-3.
[2] N. Popov, *Outline History*, vol. ii, pp. 144-96.
[3] N. Popov, *Outline History*, vol. ii, pp. 144-96.

dictatorial rule? Apart from all this, the massive dictatorial machine had now a vested interest in self-perpetuation, which it was able to identify with the broader interest of the revolution. Both sides in the dispute were aware of the dilemma; but while to one of them, the opposition, that awareness was a source of weakness, to the other it was a source of strength.

Trotsky consequently demanded not more than a limited reform, to be promulgated from above, a degree of administrative liberalism. He had been careful so far to refrain from any appeal to public opinion, even Communist opinion, against the rulers. Yet he felt the need for bringing the dispute into the open. The official inauguration of a public discussion gave him the opportunity to do so, the opportunity, that is, to appeal to public opinion against the rulers and to do so with the rulers' own formal permission. His inconsistency, real or apparent, was dictated by deeper considerations. He believed that it should be possible to strike a balance between dictatorship and freedom, that it should be possible to restrict or broaden the one or the other, according to circumstances. He hoped that with Russia's economic recovery and the progress of socialism, the régime would be able to rely less and less upon coercion and more and more upon willing support. The revolution should be able to recapture its own youth. The divorce between the revolution and the people, he thought, was of a temporary character. The triumvirs, and especially Stalin, were far less hopeful.

Here we touch the root of most of the differences between Trotskyism and Stalinism. Both insisted on their basic loyalty to the Marxist outlook; and there is no reason to doubt the sincerity of their professions. For both factions to claim allegiance to Marxism and Leninism was as natural as it is for Protestants and Catholics to swear by Christianity. In the one case as in the other the professions of faith, common to both sides, offer almost no clue to their antagonism. What underlay Trotsky's attitude was a cautious and yet very real revolutionary optimism, a belief that, if only the rulers pursued the right Socialist policy, the working classes would support them. This belief had indeed been implicit in the Marxist philosophy; and Stalin never openly contradicted it. But between the lines of his policies there is always present a deep disbelief in the popularity of socialism, and even more than that: an essentially pessimistic approach to man and society. . . .

Meanwhile the one text of Lenin that might have removed the earth from under Stalin's feet, his will, was still unknown to the party and to himself. Only in May, four months after Lenin's death, was it read out at a plenary session of the Central Committee, which was to decide whether the document should be made public at the forthcoming congress of the party. "Terrible embarrassment paralysed all those present," so an eyewitness describes the scene.[1] "Stalin sitting on the steps of the rostrum looked small and miserable. I studied him closely; in spite of his self-control

[1] B. Bazhanov, *Stalin, der Rote Diktator*, pp. 32-4.

and show of calm, it was clearly evident that his fate was at stake." In the atmosphere of the Leninist cult, it seemed almost sacrilegious to disregard Lenin's will. At this, for him, fateful moment he was saved by Zinoviev. "Comrades," so Zinoviev addressed the meeting, "every word of Ilyich [Lenin] is law to us. . . . We have sworn to fulfil anything the dying Ilyich ordered us to do. You know perfectly well that we shall keep that vow." (Many among the audience drop their eyes—they cannot look the old actor in the face.) "But we are happy to say that in one point Lenin's fears have proved baseless. I have in mind the point about our General Secretary. You have all witnessed our harmonious co-operation in the last few months; and, like myself, you will be happy to say that Lenin's fears have proved baseless." Kamenev followed with an appeal to the Central Committee that Stalin be left in office. But if this was to happen it was not advisable to publish Lenin's will at the congress. Krupskaya protested against the suppression of her husband's testament, but in vain. Trotsky, present at the meeting, was too proud to intervene in a situation which affected his own standing too. He kept silent, expressing only through his mien and grimaces his disgust at the scene. Zinoviev's motion that the testament should not be published, but only confidentially communicated to picked delegates, was then passed by forty votes against ten. Stalin could now wipe the cold sweat from his brow. He was back in the saddle, firmly and for good.

The solidarity of the triumvirs stood this extraordinary test because both Zinoviev and Kamenev were as convinced that they had nothing to fear from Stalin as they were afraid of Trotsky. Zinoviev, the President of the Communist International, was still the senior and the most popular triumvir. Kamenev was conscious of his intellectual superiority over his partners. Both looked upon Stalin as upon their auxiliary; and, though they were sometimes uneasy about a streak of perversity in him, neither suspected him of the ambition to become Lenin's sole successor. Nor, for that matter, did any such suspicion enter the mind of the party as a whole. It was not, on the other hand, very difficult to arouse in the party distrust of Trotsky. The agents of the triumvirate whispered that Trotsky was the potential Danton or, alternatively, the Bonaparte of the Russian revolution. The whispering campaign was effective, because the party had, from its beginnings, been accustomed to consult the great French precedent. It had always been admitted that history might repeat itself; and that a Directory or a single usurper might once again climb to power on the back of the revolution. It was taken for granted that the Russian usurper would, like his French prototype, be a personality possessed of brilliance and legendary fame won in battles. The mask of Bonaparte seemed to fit Trotsky only too well. Indeed, it might have fitted any personality with the exception of Stalin. In this lay part of his strength.

The very thing which under different circumstances would have been a liability in a man aspiring to power, his obscurity, was his important asset.

The party had been brought up to distrust "bourgeois individualism" and to strive for collectivism. None of its leaders looked as immune from the former and as expressive of the latter as Stalin. What was striking in the General Secretary was that there was nothing striking about him. His almost impersonal personality seemed to be the ideal vehicle for the anonymous forces of class and party. His bearing seemed of the utmost modesty. He was more accessible to the average official or party man than the other leaders. He studiously cultivated his contacts with the people who in one way or another made and unmade reputations, provincial secretaries, popular satirical writers, and foreign visitors. Himself taciturn, he was unsurpassed at the art of patiently listening to others. . . .

Nor did Stalin at that time impress people as being more intolerant than befitted a Bolshevik leader. He was, as we have seen, less vicious in his attacks on the opposition than the other triumvirs. In his speeches there was usually the tone of a good-natured and soothing, if facile, optimism, which harmonized well with the party's growing complacency. In the Politbureau, when matters of high policy were under debate, he never seemed to impose his views on his colleagues. He carefully followed the course of the debate to see which way the wind was blowing and invariably voted with the majority, unless he had assured his majority beforehand. He was therefore always agreeable to the majority. To party audiences he appeared as a man without personal grudge and rancour, as a detached Leninist, a guardian of the doctrine who criticized others only for the sake of the cause. He gave this impression even when he spoke behind the closed doors of the Politbureau. In the middle of the struggle Trotsky still described Stalin to a trusted foreign visitor as "a brave and sincere revolutionary."[1] A few descriptions of scenes in the Politbureau give a vivid glimpse of Stalin, the good soul:

> When I attended a session of the Politbureau for the first time [writes Bazhanov] the struggle between the triumvirs and Trotsky was in full swing. Trotsky was the first to arrive for the session. The others were late, they were still plotting. . . . Next entered Zinoviev. He passed by Trotsky; and both behaved as if they had not noticed one another. When Kamenev entered, he greeted Trotsky with a slight nod. At last Stalin came in. He approached the table at which Trotsky was seated, greeted him in a most friendly manner and vigorously shook hands with him across the table.[2]

During another session, in the autumn of 1923, one of the triumvirs proposed that Stalin be brought in as a controller into the Commissariat of War, of which Trotsky was still the head. Trotsky, irritated by the proposal, declared that he was resigning from office and asked to be relieved from all posts and honours in Russia and allowed to go to Germany, which then seemed to be on the brink of a Communist upheaval, to take part in

[1] M. Eastman, *Since Lenin Died*, p. 55.
[2] B. Bazhanov, *Stalin, der Rote Diktator*, p. 21.

the revolution there. Zinoviev countered the move by asking the same for himself. Stalin put an end to the scene, declaring that "the party could not possibly dispense with the services of two such important and beloved leaders."[1]

He was slowly stacking his cards and waiting. The opposition, though again condemned by the thirteenth congress in May 1924, was still a factor to be reckoned with. The attitude of the Communist International had also to be considered. The leaders of European communism, Germans, Poles, and Frenchmen, had either protested against the discrediting of Trotsky or attempted to persuade the antagonists to make peace. It took Zinoviev a lot of wire-pulling to silence those "noises off." He had behind him the prestige of the only victorious Communist party, the international myth, so to say, of the October revolution, from which only very few Communists dared to break away. He also had at his disposal the treasure of the International, to which the Russian party was the greatest single contributor and on which some European parties were, up to a point, dependent. Enough that by using all means of pressure, after the expulsion or demotion of many Communist leaders, the triumvirate succeeded in extracting a pronouncement against the Russian opposition from the fifth congress of the International, which sat in Moscow in June and July 1924. Stalin, who had so far kept aloof from the Comintern, addressed in private its Polish commission and castigated the Poles for their bias in favour of Trotsky.[2]

Dissension among the triumvirs was yet another reason for Stalin's caution. Not until a year later, in 1925, did they fall out; but even now personal jealousies troubled their relations. Zinoviev and Kamenev began to feel that Stalin was tightening his grip on the party machine and excluding them from control. Stalin was envious of their authority in matters of doctrine. Shortly after the condemnation of Trotsky, he made his first public attack, irrelevant in content, on Kamenev's doctrinal unreliability.[3] Each of the triumvirs had enough ground to think that a split between them might drive one of them to join hands with Trotsky against the others. This motive did not impel Zinoviev and Kamenev, who eventually were to coalesce with Trotsky, to soften their attacks on him; but it did enter into Stalin's tactical calculations. As a tactician he proved himself superior to his partners.

Finally, he was still waiting for the adversary to make the blunders that were inherent in his attitude. Trotsky had accepted the Leninist cult, even though his rational mind and European tastes were outraged by it. The uniform of Lenin's disciple was, anyhow, too tight for him. The Leninist *mystique,* however, had already grown too powerful for anybody who wanted to get the hearing of a Communist audience to ignore it, let

[1] *Ibid.,* p. 52.
[2] J. Stalin, *Sochinenya,* vol. vi, pp. 264-72.
[3] *Ibid.,* p. 257.

alone challenge it. Trotsky thus involved himself in fighting on ground where he was weak. The triumvirs hurled at him old anti-Trotskyist quotations from Lenin and, what was even more embarrassing to him, his own strictures on Lenin which he had uttered twelve or fifteen years ago. In the mind of the young Communist, the selection of such quotations added up to a picture of Trotsky malevolently opposing Lenin at every turn of events, from the split in 1903 to the debates over Brest Litovsk and the trade unions. In the light of the Leninist dogma, Trotsky stood condemned.

For Trotsky to reject the dogma would have meant to appeal against the party to non-communist opinion. This was the one thing that Stalin could be quite sure Trotsky would not do. Outside the party, formless revolutionary frustration mingled with distinctly counter-revolutionary trends. Since the ruling group had singled out Trotsky as a target for attack, he automatically attracted the spurious sympathy of many who had hitherto hated him. As he made his appearance in the streets of Moscow, he was spontaneously applauded by crowds in which idealistic Communists rubbed shoulders with Mensheviks, Social Revolutionaries, and the new *bourgeoisie* of the N.E.P., by all those indeed who, for diverse reasons, hoped for a change.[1] Precisely because he refused to rally in his support such mixed elements, he showed timidity and hesitancy in almost every move he made. He could not stop opposing the triumvirs who had identified themselves with the party; and yet even in his rebellion he still remained on his knees before the party. Every move he made was thus a demonstration of weakness. Stalin could afford to wait until his rival defeated himself through a series of such demonstrations.

It is here that the knot was tied which was to be cut only in the tragic purge trials twelve and thirteen years later. It is here, too, that the most important clue to the understanding of those trials is to be found. At the congress in May 1924, Trotsky, facing the implacably hostile phalanx of party secretaries, was on the point of surrendering to his critics and abjuring the opposition. Krupskaya, Radek, and others exhorted the antagonists to make peace. Zinoviev, however, was not to be persuaded. He demanded that Trotsky should surrender in his thoughts as well as in his deeds, that he should admit that he had been wrong in his criticisms. In the history of Bolshevism this was the first instance where a member of the party was vaguely charged with a "crime of conscience," a purely theological accusation. Its motive was tactical, not theological: Trotsky, submitting to party discipline but not recanting, still seemed to the triumvirs a formidable foe. Zinoviev therefore added to the terms of his submission an obviously unacceptable point, which would compel Trotsky to go on waging the unequal struggle. Thus, the first suggestion of a "crime of conscience" against the party was made by the man who, twelve years later, was to go to his death with appalling recantations of his own "crimes of conscience." Stalin, at

[1] M. Eastman, *Since Lenin Died*, p. 128, and B. Bazhanov, *Stalin, der Rote Diktator.*

least in appearance, had nothing to do with that. He repeatedly stated that
the only condition for peace was that Trotsky should stop his attacks. He
repeatedly made the gesture that looked like the stretching out of his hand
to his opponent.

Trotsky's reply to Zinoviev was pregnant with the tragedy that was to
overwhelm Zinoviev and Kamenev even more cruelly than himself:

> The party [Trotsky said] in the last analysis is always right, because the party
> is the single historic instrument given to the proletariat for the solution of its
> fundamental problems. I have already said that in front of one's own party nothing
> could be easier than to acknowledge a mistake, nothing easier than to say: all my
> criticisms, my statements, my warnings, my protests—the whole thing was a mere
> mistake. I, however, comrades, cannot say that, because I do not think it. I know
> that one must not be right *against* the party. One can be right only with the party,
> and through the party, for history has created no other road for the realization of
> what is right. The English have a saying: "Right or wrong—my country." With
> far greater historic justification we may say: right or wrong, on separate particular
> issues, it is my party. . . .[1]

These words of the leader of the opposition resembled less the words
a patriotic Englishman might use than those of a medieval heretic, con-
fessing his heresy, rueful and yet stubborn in his conviction, able to see no
salvation beyond the Church and yet none in the Church either. Stalin
sarcastically dismissed Trotsky's statement, saying that the party made no
claim to infallibility. . . .

∙   ∙   ∙   ∙   ∙

Stalin first formulated his ideas on socialism in one country in the autumn of 1924. Belief in socialism in one country was soon to become the
supreme test of loyalty to party and state. In the next ten or fifteen years
nobody who failed that test was to escape condemnation and punishment.
Yet, if one studies the "prolegomena" to this article of Stalinist faith, one
is struck by the fact that it was first put forward by Stalin almost casually,
like a mere debating point, in the "literary discussion." For many months,
until the summer of the next year, none of Stalin's rivals, neither the other
triumvirs nor Trotsky, thought the point worth arguing. Nor was Stalin's
own mind fixed. In his pamphlet *The Foundations of Leninism*, published
early in 1924, he stated with great emphasis that, though the proletariat of
one country could seize power, it could not establish a Socialist economy in
one country. . . .

He now stated [later in 1924] that the efforts of Russia alone would
suffice for the *complete* organization of a Socialist economy. A Socialist
economy—this had so far been taken for granted—was conceivable only
as an economy of plenty. This presupposed a highly developed industry

---

[1] *13 Syezd Vsesoyuznoi Komunisticheskoi Partii,* pp. 166 and 245. See also M. Eastman, *Since Lenin Died,* pp. 88-9.

capable of ensuring a high standard of living for the whole people. How then, the question arose, could a country like Russia, whose meagre industry had been reduced to rack and ruin, achieve socialism? Stalin pointed to Russia's great assets: her vast spaces and enormous riches in raw materials. A proletarian government could, in his view, through its control of industry and credit, develop those resources and carry the building of socialism to a successful conclusion, because in this endeavour it would be supported by a vast majority of the people, including the peasants.

This, the most essential, part of Stalin's formula was very simple. It proclaimed in terms clear to everybody the self-sufficiency of the Russian revolution. It was true that Stalin begged many a question. He did not even try to meet the objections to his thesis that were raised later by his critics. One objection that most peasants, attached as they were to private property, were certain to put up the strongest resistance to collectivism, he simply dismissed as a heretical slander on the peasantry. Nor did he seriously consider the other argument that socialism was possible only on the basis of the intensive industrialization already achieved by the most advanced western countries; and that Russia by herself would not be able to catch up with those countries. According to his critics, socialism could beat capitalism only if it represented a higher productivity of labour and higher standards of living than had been attained under capitalism. The critics deduced that if productivity of labour and standards of living were to remain lower in Russia than in the capitalist countries then socialism would, in the long run, fail even in Russia. Nor did Stalin ever try to refute their forecast that in an economy of scarcity, such as an isolated Russian economy would be, a new and glaring material inequality between various social groups was certain to arise.

But, whatever the flaws in Stalin's reasoning, flaws that were obvious only to the most educated men in the party, his formula was politically very effective. It contained, at any rate, one clear and positive proposition: we are able to stand on our own feet, to build and to complete the building of socialism. This was what made the formula useful for polemical and practical purposes. It offered a plain alternative to Trotsky's conception. For a variety of reasons, however, Stalin did not present his thesis in that plain and clear-cut form. He hedged it round with all sorts of reservations and qualifications. One reservation was that the victory of socialism in Russia could not be considered secure so long as her capitalist environment threatened Russia with armed intervention. Socialism in a single state could not be beaten by the "cheap goods" produced in capitalist countries of which his critics spoke; but it might be defeated by force of arms. In the next few years Stalin himself constantly held that danger before Russia's eyes and thereby seemed to weaken his own case. Moreover, he went on to express, though with ever decreasing confidence, a belief in the proximity of international revolution. He proclaimed the absolute self-sufficiency of

Russian socialism in one half of his thesis and disclaimed it in the other.

The strangeness of that passionate ideological dispute does not end here. As the controversy developed, Stalin ascribed to his critics the view that it was not possible to build socialism in Russia. He then presented the issue as one between those who believed in the "creative force" of the revolution and the "panic mongers" and "pessimists." Now the issue was not as simple as that. His critics were beyond question not guilty of the things imputed to them. They, too, asserted that it was possible and necessary to organize the country's economy on Socialist lines. Trotsky in particular had, since the end of the civil war, urged the Politbureau to begin gearing up the administration for planned economy; and in those early days he first sketched most of the ideas that were later to be embodied in the five-year plans.[1]

The student of the controversy may thus often have the uncanny feeling that its very object is indefinable; that, having aroused unbounded passion and bitterness, it simply vanishes into thin air. Stripped of polemical distortions and insinuations, the debate seems in the end, to the student's astonishment, to centre on a bizarre irrelevancy. The point was not whether socialism could or should be built but whether the building could be *completed* in a single isolated state.

"TESTAMENT"

V. I. LENIN

In mid-December 1922, Lenin suffered a stroke and felt the nearness of death. On December 25, he dictated a memorandum to his secretary to be made known to the Party in the event of his death. On December 30, he turned his attention to a conflict in Georgia (U.S.S.R.) and in his notes spoke of "the hastiness and administrative impulsiveness" of Stalin and added that "it behooves us to hold Stalin . . . politically responsible for this genuine Great Russian nationalistic campaign." On January 4, 1923, he dictated a postscript to his "Testament."

Subsequently, in the early months of 1923, when Lenin had recovered

---

[1] N. Bukharin in his *Kritika Ekonomicheskoi Platformy Oppozitsii*, entirely devoted to a criticism of Trotsky's, Piatakov's, and Preobrazhensky's economic ideas, quotes Trotsky's letter to the Central Committee (8 October 1923), in which Trotsky summed up his policy as follows: "Planned economy; severe concentration of industry; severe reduction of costs" (p. 54). In his *Novyi Kurs*, published later in the year, Trotsky urged the subordination of financial and monetary policy to the needs of industrialization (ibid., pp. 71-2). This brought upon him the charge that he advocated the "dictatorship of industry" and "super-industrialization." See N. Bukharin, op. cit., pp. 3, 53-4.

somewhat from his illness, he launched a devastating attack on Stalin. His March 4 article in Pravda, *without direct mention of Stalin, bitterly assailed the Workers' and Peasants' Inspectorate, which Stalin headed. The next day, Lenin "broke off" all personal relations with Stalin and prepared for his denunciation. But soon, thereafter, Lenin became incapacitated again. He died on January 21, 1924.*

The "Testament," although known to the Soviet leaders, was not published in the Soviet press until May 18, 1956, when a part of it first appeared in Komsomolskaya Pravda, *the Young Communist newspaper, to explain what was behind the attack on the "cult of the individual."*

By the stability of the Central Committee, of which I spoke before, I mean measures to prevent a split, so far as such measures can be taken. For, of course, the White Guard in *Russkaya Mysl* (I think it was S. E. Oldenburg) was right when, in the first place, in his play against Soviet Russia he banked on the hope of a split in our party, and when, in the second place, he banked for that split on serious disagreements in our party.

Our party rests upon two classes, and for that reason its instability is possible, and if there cannot exist an agreement between those classes its fall is inevitable. In such an event it would be useless to take any measures or in general to discuss the stability of our Central Committee. In such an event no measures would prove capable of preventing a split. But I trust that is too remote a future, and too improbable an event, to talk about.

I have in mind stability as a guarantee against a split in the near future, and I intended to examine here a series of considerations of a purely personal character.

I think that the fundamental factor in the matter of stability—from this point of view—is such members of the Central Committee as Stalin and Trotsky. The relation between them constitutes, in my opinion, a big half of the danger of that split, which might be avoided, and the avoidance of which might be promoted, in my opinion, by raising the number of members of the Central Committee to fifty or one hundred.

Comrade Stalin, having become General Secretary, has concentrated an enormous power in his hands; and I am not sure that he always knows how to use that power with sufficient caution. On the other hand, Comrade Trotsky, as was proved by his struggle against the Central Committee in connection with the question of the People's Commissariat of Ways and Communications, is distinguished not only by his exceptional abilities—personally he is, to be sure, the most able man in the present Central Committee—but also by his too far-reaching self-confidence and a disposition to be too much attracted by the purely administrative side of affairs.

These two qualities of the two most able leaders of the present Central Committee might, quite innocently, lead to a split; if our party does not take measures to prevent it, a split might arise unexpectedly.

I will not further characterize the other members of the Central Committee as to their personal qualities. I will only remind you that the October episode of Zinoviev and Kamenev was not, of course, accidental, but that it ought as little to be used against them personally as the non-Bolshevism of Trotsky.

Of the younger members of the Central Committee, I want to say a few words about Bukharin and Pyatakov. They are in my opinion, the most able forces (among the youngest) and in regard to them it is necessary to bear in mind the following: Bukharin is not only the most valuable and biggest theoretician of the party, but also may legitimately be considered the favorite of the whole party; but his theoretical views can only with the very greatest doubt be regarded as fully Marxist, for there is something scholastic in him (he never has learned, and I think never has fully understood, the dialectic).

And then Pyatakov—a man undoubtedly distinguished in will and ability, but too much given over to administration and the administrative side of things to be relied on in a serious political question.

Of course, both these remarks are made by me merely with a view to the present time, or supposing that these two able and loyal workers may not find an occasion to supplement their knowledge and correct their onesidedness.
December 25, 1922

Postscript: Stalin is too rude, and this fault, entirely supportable in relations among us Communists, becomes insupportable in the office of General Secretary. Therefore, I propose to the comrades to find a way to remove Stalin from that position and appoint to it another man who in all respects differs from Stalin only in superiority—namely, more patient, more loyal, more polite and more attentive to comrades, less capricious, etc. This circumstance may seem an insignificant trifle, but I think that from the point of view of preventing a split and from the point of view of the relation between Stalin and Trotsky which I discussed above, it is not a trifle, or it is such a trifle as may acquire a decisive significance.
January 4, 1923

THE REVOLUTION BETRAYED

LEON TROTSKY*

THE SOVIET THERMIDOR

1. **Why Stalin Triumphed** . . . A political struggle is in its essence a struggle of interests and forces, not of arguments. The quality of the leadership is, of course, far from a matter of indifference for the outcome of the conflict, but it is not the only factor, and in the last analysis is not decisive. Each of the struggling camps moreover demands leaders in its own image.

The February revolution raised Kerensky and Tseretelli to power, not because they were "cleverer" or "more astute" than the ruling tsarist clique, but because they represented, at least temporarily, the revolutionary masses of the people in their revolt against the old regime. Kerensky was able to drive Lenin underground and imprison other Bolshevik leaders, not because he excelled them in personal qualifications, but because the majority of the workers and soldiers in those days were still following the patriotic petty bourgeoisie. The personal "superiority" of Kerensky, if it is suitable to employ such a word in this connection, consisted in the fact that he did not see farther than the overwhelming majority. The Bolsheviks in their turn conquered the petty bourgeois democrats, not through the personal superiority of their leaders, but through a new correlation of social forces. The proletariat had succeeded at last in leading the discontented peasantry against the bourgeoisie.

The consecutive stages of the great French Revolution, during its rise and fall alike, demonstrate no less convincingly that the strength of the "leaders" and "heroes" that replaced each other consisted primarily in their correspondence to the character of those classes and strata which supported them. Only this correspondence, and not any irrelevant superiorities whatever, permitted each of them to place the impress of his personality upon a certain historic period. . . .

It is sufficiently well known that every revolution up to this time has been followed by a reaction, or even a counter-revolution. This, to be sure, has never thrown the nation all the way back to its starting point, but it has always taken from the people the lion's share of their conquests. The victims of the first reactionary wave have been, as a general rule, those pioneers, initiators, and instigators who stood at the head of the masses in

* The selection is from Chapter 5 and the Appendix of the book by the same title, written by Trotsky in 1936 (New York: Pioneer Publishers, 1945). By permission of the publisher.

the period of the revolutionary offensive. In their stead people of the second line, in league with the former enemies of the revolution, have been advanced to the front. Beneath this dramatic duel of "coryphées" on the open political scene, shifts have taken place in the relations between classes, and, no less important, profound changes in the psychology of the recently revolutionary masses. . . .

A revolution is a mighty devourer of human energy, both individual and collective. The nerves give way. Consciousness is shaken and characters are worn out. Events unfold too swiftly for the flow of fresh forces to replace the loss. Hunger, unemployment, the death of the revolutionary cadres, the removal of the masses from administration, all this led to such a physical and moral impoverishment of the Parisian suburbs that they required three decades before they were ready for a new insurrection.

The axiomlike assertions of the Soviet literature, to the effect that the laws of bourgeois revolutions are "inapplicable" to a proletarian revolution, have no scientific content whatever. The proletarian character of the October revolution was determined by the world situation and by a special correlation of internal forces. But the classes themselves were formed in the barbarous circumstances of tsarism and backward capitalism, and were anything but made to order for the demands of a socialist revolution. The exact opposite is true. It is for the very reason that a proletariat still backward in many respects achieved in the space of a few months the unprecedented leap from a semifeudal monarchy to a socialist dictatorship, that the reaction in its ranks was inevitable. This reaction has developed in a series of consecutive waves. External conditions and events have vied with each other in nourishing it. Intervention followed intervention. The revolution got no direct help from the west. Instead of the expected prosperity of the country an ominous destitution reigned for long. Moreover, the outstanding representatives of the working class either died in the civil war, or rose a few steps higher and broke away from the masses. And thus after an unexampled tension of forces, hopes and illusions, there came a long period of weariness, decline and sheer disappointment in the results of the revolution. The ebb of the "plebeian pride" made room for a flood of pusillanimity and careerism. The new commanding caste rose to its place upon this wave.

The demobilization of the Red Army of five million played no small role in the formation of the bureaucracy. The victorious commanders assumed leading posts in the local Soviets, in economy, in education, and they persistently introduced everywhere that regime which had ensured success in the civil war. Thus on all sides the masses were pushed away gradually from actual participation in the leadership of the country.

The reaction within the proletariat caused an extraordinary flush of hope and confidence in the petty bourgeois strata of town and country, aroused as they were to new life by the NEP, and growing bolder and bolder.

The young bureaucracy, which had arisen at first as an agent of the proletariat, began now to feel itself a court of arbitration between the classes.
Its independence increased from month to month.

The international situation was pushing with mighty forces in the
same direction. The Soviet bureaucracy became more self-confident, the
heavier the blows dealt to the world working class. Between these two facts
there was not only a chronological, but a causal connection, and one which
worked in two directions. The leaders of the bureaucracy promoted the
proletarian defeats; the defeats promoted the rise of the bureaucracy. The
crushing of the Bulgarian insurrection and the inglorious retreat of the
German workers' party in 1923, the collapse of the Esthonian attempt at
insurrection in 1924, the treacherous liquidation of the General Strike in
England and the unworthy conduct of the Polish workers' party at the installation of Pilsudski in 1926, the terrible massacre of the Chinese revolution in 1927, and, finally, the still more ominous recent defeats in Germany and Austria—these are the historic catastrophes which killed the faith
of the Soviet masses in world revolution, and permitted the bureaucracy to
rise higher and higher as the sole light of salvation. . . .

Two dates are especially significant in this historic series. In the second
half of 1923, the attention of the Soviet workers was passionately fixed upon
Germany, where the proletariat, it seemed, had stretched out its hand to
power. The panicky retreat of the German Communist Party was the
heaviest possible disappointment to the working masses of the Soviet Union.
The Soviet bureaucracy straightway opened a campaign against the theory
of "permanent revolution," and dealt the Left Opposition its first cruel
blow. During the years 1926 and 1927 the population of the Soviet Union
experienced a new tide of hope. All eyes were now directed to the East
where the drama of the Chinese revolution was unfolding. The Left Opposition had recovered from the previous blows and was recruiting a phalanx of new adherents. At the end of 1927 the Chinese revolution was
massacred by the hangman, Chiang-kai-shek, into whose hands the Communist International had literally betrayed the Chinese workers and peasants. A cold wave of disappointment swept over the masses of the Soviet
Union. After an unbridled baiting in the press and at meetings, the
bureaucracy finally, in 1928, ventured upon mass arrests among the Left
Opposition.

To be sure, tens of thousands of revolutionary fighters gathered around
the banner of the Bolshevik-Leninists. The advanced workers were indubitably sympathetic to the Opposition, but that sympathy remained passive. The masses lacked faith that the situation could be seriously changed
by a new struggle. Meantime the bureaucracy asserted: "For the sake of an
international revolution, the Opposition proposes to drag us into a revolutionary war. Enough of shake-ups! We have earned the right to rest.
We will build the socialist society at home. Rely upon us, your leaders!"

This gospel of repose firmly consolidated the *apparatchiki* and the military and state officials and indubitably found an echo among the weary workers, and still more the peasant masses. Can it be, they asked themselves, that the Opposition is actually ready to sacrifice the interests of the Soviet Union for the idea of "permanent revolution?" In reality, the struggle had been about the life interests of the Soviet state. The false policy of the International in Germany resulted ten years later in the victory of Hitler —that is, in a threatening war danger from the West. And the no less false policy in China reinforced Japanese imperialism and brought very much nearer the danger in the East. But periods of reaction are characterized above all by a lack of courageous thinking.

The Opposition was isolated. The bureaucracy struck while the iron was hot, exploiting the bewilderment and passivity of the workers, setting their more backward strata against the advanced, and relying more and more boldly upon the kulak and the petty bourgeois ally in general. In the course of a few years, the bureaucracy thus shattered the revolutionary vanguard of the proletariat.

It would be naïve to imagine that Stalin, previously unknown to the masses, suddenly issued from the wings fully armed with a complete strategical plan. No indeed. Before he felt out his own course, the bureaucracy felt out Stalin himself. He brought it all the necessary guarantees: the prestige of an old Bolshevik, a strong character, narrow vision, and close bonds with the political machine as the sole source of his influence. The success which fell upon him was a surprise at first to Stalin himself. It was the friendly welcome of the new ruling group, trying to free itself from the old principles and from the control of the masses, and having need of a reliable arbiter in its inner affairs. A secondary figure before the masses and in the events of the revolution, Stalin revealed himself as the indubitable leader of the Thermidorian bureaucracy, as first in its midst. . . .

Personal incidents in the interval between these two historic chapters were not, of course, without influence. Thus the sickness and death of Lenin undoubtedly hastened the denouement. Had Lenin lived longer, the pressure of the bureaucratic power would have developed, at least during the first years, more slowly. But as early as 1926 Krupskaya said, in a circle of Left Oppositionists: "If Ilych were alive, he would probably already be in prison." The fears and alarming prophecies of Lenin himself were then still fresh in her memory, and she cherished no illusions as to his personal omnipotence against opposing historic winds and currents.

The bureaucracy conquered something more than the Left Opposition. It conquered the Bolshevik party. It defeated the program of Lenin, who had seen the chief danger in the conversion of the organs of the state "from servants of society to lords over society." It defeated all these enemies, the Opposition, the party and Lenin, not with ideas and arguments, but with its own social weight. The leaden rump of the bureaucracy outweighed the head of the revolution. That is the secret of the Soviet's Thermidor.

2. The Degeneration of the Bolshevik Party. The Bolshevik party prepared and insured the October victory. It also created the Soviet state, supplying it with a sturdy skeleton. The degeneration of the party became both cause and consequence of the bureaucratization of the state. It is necessary to show at least briefly how this happened.

The inner regime of the Bolshevik party was characterized by the method of *democratic centralism*. The combination of these two concepts, democracy and centralism, is not in the least contradictory. The party took watchful care not only that its boundaries should always be strictly defined, but also that all those who entered these boundaries should enjoy the actual right to define the direction of the party policy. Freedom of criticism and intellectual struggle was an irrevocable content of the party democracy. The present doctrine that Bolshevism does not tolerate factions is a myth of the epoch of decline. In reality the history of Bolshevism is a history of the struggle of factions. And, indeed, how could a genuinely revolutionary organization, setting itself the task of overthrowing the world and uniting under its banner the most audacious iconoclasts, fighters and insurgents, live and develop without intellectual conflicts, without groupings and temporary factional formations? The farsightedness of the Bolshevik leadership often made it possible to soften conflicts and shorten the duration of factional struggle, but no more than that. The Central Committee relied upon this seething democratic support. From this it derived the audacity to make decisions and give orders. The obvious correctness of the leadership at all critical stages gave it that high authority which is the priceless moral capital of centralism.

The regime of the Bolshevik party, especially before it came to power, stood thus in complete contradiction to the regime of the present sections of the Communist International, with their "leaders" appointed from above, making complete changes of policy at a word of command, with their uncontrolled apparatus, haughty in its attitude to the rank and file, servile in its attitude to the Kremlin. But in the first years after the conquest of power also, even when the administrative rust was already visible on the party, every Bolshevik, not excluding Stalin, would have denounced as a malicious slanderer anyone who should have shown him on a screen the image of the party ten or fifteen years later.

The very center of Lenin's attention and that of his colleagues was occupied by a continual concern to protect the Bolshevik ranks from the vices of those in power. However, the extraordinary closeness and at times actual merging of the party with the state apparatus had already in those first years done indubitable harm to the freedom and elasticity of the party regime. Democracy had been narrowed in proportion as difficulties increased. In the beginning, the party had wished and hoped to preserve freedom of political struggle within the framework of the Soviets. The civil war introduced stern amendments into this calculation. The opposition parties were forbidden one after the other. This measure, obviously in conflict with the spirit of Soviet democracy, the leaders of Bolshevism regarded not as a principle, but as an episodic act of self-defense.

The swift growth of the ruling party, with the novelty and immensity of its tasks, inevitably gave rise to inner disagreements. The underground oppositional currents in the country exerted a pressure through various channels upon the sole legal political organization, increasing the acuteness of the factional struggle. At the moment of completion of the civil war, this struggle took such sharp forms as to threaten to unsettle the state power. In March 1921, in the days of the Kronstadt revolt, which attracted into its ranks no small number of Bolsheviks, the tenth congress of the party thought it necessary to resort to a prohibition of factions—that is, to transfer the political regime prevailing in the state to the inner life of the ruling party. This forbidding of factions was again regarded as an exceptional measure to be abandoned at the first serious improvement in the situation. At the same time, the Central Committee was extremely cautious in applying the new law, concerning itself most of all lest it lead to a strangling of the inner life of the party.

However, what was in its original design merely a necessary concession to a difficult situation, proved perfectly suited to the taste of the bureaucracy, which had then begun to approach the inner life of the party exclusively from the viewpoint of convenience in administration. Already in 1922, during a brief improvement in his health, Lenin, horrified at the threatening growth of bureaucratism, was preparing a struggle against the faction of Stalin, which had made itself the axis of the party machine as a first step toward capturing the machinery of state. A second stroke and then death prevented him from measuring forces with this internal reaction.

The entire effort of Stalin, with whom at that time Zinoviev and Kamenev were working hand in hand, was thenceforth directed to freeing the party machine from the control of the rank-and-file members of the party. In this struggle for "stability" of the Central Committee, Stalin proved the most consistent and reliable among his colleagues. He had no need to tear himself away from international problems; he had never been concerned with them. The petty bourgeois outlook of the new ruling stratum was his own outlook. He profoundly believed that the task of creating socialism was national and administrative in its nature. He looked upon the Communist International as a necessary evil which should be used so far as possible for the purposes of foreign policy. His own party kept a value in his eyes merely as a submissive support for the machine

Together with the theory of socialism in one country, there was put into circulation by the bureaucracy a theory that in Bolshevism the Central

Committee is everything and the party nothing. This second theory was in any case realized with more success than the first. Availing itself of the death of Lenin, the ruling group announced a "Leninist levy." The gates of the party, always carefully guarded, were now thrown wide open. Workers, clerks, petty officials, flocked through in crowds. The political aim of this maneuver was to dissolve the revolutionary vanguard in raw human material, without experience, without independence, and yet with the old habit of submitting to the authorities. The scheme was successful. By freeing the bureaucracy from the control of the proletarian vanguard, the "Leninist levy" dealt a death blow to the party of Lenin. The machine had won the necessary independence. Democratic centralism gave place to bureaucratic centralism. In the party apparatus itself there now took place a radical reshuffling of personnel from top to bottom. The chief merit of a Bolshevik was declared to be obedience. Under the guise of a struggle with the Opposition, there occurred a sweeping replacement of revolutionists with *chinovniks*.[1] The history of the Bolshevik party became a history of its rapid degeneration. . . .

Of the Politburo of Lenin's epoch there now remains only Stalin. Two of its members, Zinoviev and Kamenev, collaborators of Lenin throughout many years as émigrés, are enduring ten-year prison terms for a crime which they did not commit. Three other members, Rykov, Bukharin and Tomsky, are completely removed from the leadership, but as a reward for submission occupy secondary posts. And, finally, the author of these lines is in exile. The widow of Lenin, Krupskaya, is also under the ban, having proved unable with all her efforts to adjust herself completely to the Thermidor.

[Editor's note: Zinoviev and Kamenev were executed in August 1936. Tomsky committed suicide on August 23, 1936, when "implicated" in the same case, and Rykov and Bukharin were executed in March 1938. Trotsky died on August 21, 1940, in Mexico City, from wounds inflicted by an assassin.]

The members of the present Politburo occupied secondary posts throughout the history of the Bolshevik party. If anybody in the first years of the revolution had predicted their future elevation, they would have been the first in surprise, and there would have been no false modesty in their surprise. For this very reason, the rule is more stern at present that the Politburo is always right, and in any case that no man can be right against the Politburo. But, moreover, the Politburo cannot be right against Stalin, who is unable to make mistakes and consequently cannot be right against himself.

Demands for party democracy were through all this time the slogans of all the oppositional groups, as insistent as they were hopeless. The above-

[1] Professional governmental functionaries.

mentioned platform of the Left Opposition demanded in 1927 that a special law be written into the Criminal Code "punishing as a serious state crime every direct or indirect persecution of a worker for criticism." Instead of this, there was introduced into the Criminal Code an article against the Left Opposition itself.

Of party democracy there remained only recollections in the memory of the older generation. And together with it had disappeared the democracy of the soviets, the trade unions, the co-operatives, the cultural and athletic organizations. Above each and every one of them there reigns an unlimited hierarchy of party secretaries. The regime had become "totalitarian" in character several years before this word arrived from Germany. "By means of demoralizing methods, which convert thinking communists into machines, destroying will, character and human dignity," wrote Rakovsky in 1928, "the ruling circles have succeeded in converting themselves into an unremovable and inviolate oligarchy, which replaces the class and the party." Since those indignant lines were written, the degeneration of the regime has gone immeasurably farther. The G.P.U. has become the decisive factor in the inner life of the party. If Molotov in March 1936 was able to boast to a French journalist that the ruling party no longer contains any factional struggle, it is only because disagreements are now settled by the automatic intervention of the political police. The old Bolshevik party is dead, and no force will resurrect it. . . .

In spite of the October revolution, the nationalization of the means of production, collectivization, and "the liquidation of the kulaks as a class," the relations among men, and that at the very heights of the Soviet pyramid, have not only not yet risen to socialism, but in many respects are still lagging behind a cultured capitalism. In recent years enormous backward steps have been taken in this very important sphere. And the source of this revival of genuine Russian barbarism is indubitably the Soviet Thermidor, which has given complete independence and freedom from control to a bureaucracy possessing little culture, and has given to the masses the well-known gospel of obedience and silence.

We are far from intending to contrast the abstraction of dictatorship with the abstraction of democracy, and weigh their merits on the scales of pure reason. Everything is relative in this world, where change alone endures. The dictatorship of the Bolshevik party proved one of the most powerful instruments of progress in history. But here too, in the words of the poet, "Reason becomes unreason, kindness a pest." The prohibition of oppositional parties brought after it the prohibition of factions. The prohibition of factions ended in a prohibition to think otherwise than the infallible leaders. The police-manufactured monolithism of the party resulted in a bureaucratic impunity which has become the source of all kinds of wantonness and corruption.

3. The Social Roots of Thermidor. We have defined the Soviet Thermidor as a triumph of the bureaucracy over the masses. We have tried to disclose the historic conditions of this triumph. The revolutionary vanguard of the proletariat was in part devoured by the administrative apparatus and gradually demoralized, in part annihilated in the civil war, and in part thrown out and crushed. The tired and disappointed masses were indifferent to what was happening on the summits. These conditions, however, important as they may have been in themselves, are inadequate to explain why the bureaucracy succeeded in raising itself above society and getting its fate firmly into its own hands. Its own will to this would in any case be inadequate; the arising of a new ruling stratum must have deep social causes. . . .

We must now prolong our analysis of the conditions of the transition from capitalism to socialism, and the role of the state in this process. Let us again compare theoretic prophecy with reality. "It is still necessary to suppress the bourgeoisie and its resistance," wrote Lenin in 1917, speaking of the period which should begin immediately after the conquest of power, "but the organ of suppression here is now the majority of the population, and not the minority as has heretofore always been the case. . . . In that sense the state *is beginning to die away*." In what does this dying away express itself? Primarily in the fact that "in place of special institutions of a privileged minority (privileged officials, commanders of a standing army), the majority itself can directly carry out" the functions of suppression. Lenin follows this with a statement axiomatic and unanswerable: "The more universal becomes the very fulfillment of the functions of the state power, the less need is there of this power." The annulment of private property in the means of production removes the principal task of the historic state—defense of the proprietary privileges of the minority against the overwhelming majority.

The dying away of the state begins, then, according to Lenin, on the very day after the expropriation of the expropriators—that is, before the new regime has had time to take up its economic and cultural problems. Every success in the solution of these problems means a further step in the liquidation of the state, its dissolution in the socialist society. The degree of this dissolution is the best index of the depth and efficacy of the socialist structure. We may lay down approximately this sociological theorem: The strength of the compulsion exercised by the masses in a worker's state is directly proportional to the strength of the exploitive tendencies, or the danger of a restoration of capitalism, and inversely proportional to the strength of the social solidarity and the general loyalty of the new regime. Thus the bureaucracy—that is, the "privileged officials and commanders of a standing army"—represents a special kind of compulsion which the masses cannot or do not wish to exercise, and which, one way or another, is directed against the masses themselves.

the Constituent Assembly during its brief hours of life—the "fundamental task" of the new regime was thus defined: "The establishment of a socialist organization of society and the victory of socialism in all countries." The international character of the revolution was thus written into the basic document of the new regime. No one at that time would have dared present the problem otherwise! In April 1924, three months after the death of Lenin, Stalin wrote, in his brochure of compilations called *The Foundations of Leninism:* "For the overthrow of the bourgeoisie, the efforts of one country are enough—to this the history of our own revolution testifies. For the final victory of socialism, for the organization of socialist production, the efforts of one country, especially a peasant country like ours, are not enough—for this we must have the efforts of the proletarians of several advanced countries." These lines need no comment. The edition in which they were printed, however, has been withdrawn from circulation.

The large-scale defeats of the European proletariat, and the first very modest economic successes of the Soviet Union, suggested to Stalin, in the autumn of 1924, the idea that the historic mission of the Soviet bureaucracy was to build socialism in a single country. . . .

The "theory" of socialism in one country—a "theory" never expounded, by the way, or given any foundation, by Stalin himself—comes down to the sufficiently sterile and unhistoric notion that, thanks to the natural riches of the country, a socialist society can be built within the geographic confines of the Soviet Union. With the same success you might affirm that socialism could triumph if the population of the earth were a twelfth of what it is. In reality, however, the purpose of this new theory was to introduce into the social consciousness a far more concrete system of ideas, namely: the revolution is wholly completed; social contradictions will steadily soften; the kulak will gradually grow into socialism; the development as a whole, regardless of events in the external world, will preserve a peaceful and planned character. Bukharin, in attempting to give some foundation to the theory, declared it unshakably proven that "we shall not perish owing to class differences within our country and our technical backwardness, that we can build socialism even on this pauper technical basis, that this growth of socialism will be many times slower, that we will crawl with a tortoise tempo, and that nevertheless we are building this socialism, and we will build it." We remark the formula: "Build socialism even on a pauper technical basis," and we recall once more the genial intuition of the young Marx: with a low technical basis "only want will be generalized, and with want the struggle for necessities begins again, and all the old crap must revive. . . ."

Socialism must inevitably "surpass" capitalism in all spheres—wrote the Left Opposition in a document illegally distributed in March 1927— "but at present the question is not of the relation of socialism to capitalism in general, but of the economic development of the Soviet Union in relation to Germany, England and the United States. What is to be understood by the phrase 'minimal historic period'? A whole series of future five-year plans will leave us far from the level of the advanced countries of the West. What will be happening in the capitalist world during this time? . . . If you admit the possibility of its flourishing anew for a period of decades, then the talk of socialism in our backward country is pitiable tripe. Then it will be necessary to say that we were mistaken in our appraisal of the whole epoch as an epoch of capitalist decay. Then the Soviet Republic will prove to have been the second experiment in proletarian dictatorship since the Paris Commune, broader and more fruitful, but only an experiment. . . . Is there, however, any serious ground for such a decisive reconsideration of our whole epoch, and of the meaning of the October revolution as a link in an international revolution? No! . . . In finishing to a more or less complete extent their period of reconstruction [after the war] . . . the capitalist countries are reviving, and reviving in an incomparably sharper form, all the old pre-war contradictions, domestic and international. This is the basis of the proletarian revolution. It is a fact that we are building socialism. A greater fact, however, and not a less—since the whole in general is greater than the part—is the preparation of a European and world revolution. The part can conquer only together with the whole. . . . The European proletariat needs a far shorter period for its take-off to the seizure of power than we need to catch up technically with Europe and America. . . . We must, meanwhile, systematically narrow the distance separating our productivity of labor from that of the rest of the world. The more we advance, the less danger there is of possible intervention by low prices, and consequently by armies. . . . The higher we raise the standard of living of the workers and peasants, the more truly shall we hasten the proletarian revolution in Europe, the sooner will that revolution enrich us with world technique, and the more truly and genuinely will our socialist construction advance as a part of European and world construction." This document, like the others, remained without answer—unless you consider expulsions from the party and arrests an answer to it. . . .

To be sure, the isolation of the Soviet Union did not have those immediate dangerous consequences which might have been feared. The capitalist world was too disorganized and paralyzed to unfold to the full extent its potential power. The "breathing spell" proved longer than a critical optimism had dared to hope. However, isolation and the impossibility of using the resources of world economy even upon capitalistic bases (the amount of foreign trade has decreased from 1913 four to five times) entailed, along with enormous expenditures upon military defense, an extremely disadvantageous allocation of productive forces, and a slow raising of the standard of living of the masses. But a more malign product of isolation and backwardness has been the octopus of bureaucratism.

The juridical and political standards set up by the revolution exercised a progressive action upon the backward economy, but upon the other hand they themselves felt the lowering influence of that backwardness. The longer the Soviet Union remains in a capitalist environment, the deeper runs the degeneration of the social fabric. A prolonged isolation would inevitably end not in national communism, but in a restoration of capitalism.

If a bourgeoisie cannot peacefully grow into a socialist democracy, it is likewise true that a socialist state cannot peacefully merge with a world capitalist system. On the historic order of the day stands not the peaceful socialist development of "one country," but a long series of world disturbances: wars and revolutions. Disturbances are inevitable also in the domestic life of the Soviet Union. If the bureaucracy was compelled in its struggle for a planned economy to dekulakize the kulak, the working class will be compelled in its struggle for socialism to debureaucratize the bureaucracy. On the tomb of the latter will be inscribed the epitaph: "Here lies the theory of socialism in one country."

TROTSKYISM

John Plamenatz[*]

As an indictment of Stalinism, Trotsky's account of Soviet Russia is formidable. So much so, indeed, that some version or other of it has been adopted by nearly all Stalin's more plausible critics. But the account is not only an attack on Stalinism; it is also an apology for Trotsky and Lenin. For it was their revolution that Stalin betrayed, misunderstood and corrupted.

As an apology for the Bolshevik revolution, Trotsky's account is not impressive. It makes the assumptions that Lenin made about the condition of western capitalism and the prospect of immediate world revolution. Trotsky, no more than Lenin, understood how it was that the German Social-Democrats, nourished on Marxism and enjoying in their own country incomparably greater working-class support than the Bolsheviks had ever done in Russia, could not make a proletarian revolution. He, too, spoke of treachery and corruption in a bourgeois environment. It never occurred to him that the German workers, knowing the 'sham democracy' of the bourgeois better than he did, might have learnt to like it and to prize the benefits it brought them. Every sign of disorder in Germany seemed to him

* Fellow of Nuffield College, Oxford. The selection is from pp. 303-305 of *German Marxism and Russian Communism*, Longmans, Green & Co., Inc., 1954. By permission of the publisher.

to announce the coming proletarian revolution in the West—the revolution so much needed by the Bolsheviks to justify their desperate hazard of 1917 but which the German workers felt they could do without. Blinded by Marxism, Trotsky even mistook the great and rapid increase in the number of civil servants in western countries for evidence that bourgeois repression was increasing as bourgeois predominance grew less secure. Though he survived Lenin by many years, he would not—perhaps because he dared not—recognize the emergence of the democratic welfare state. That state has, no doubt, inefficiencies and injustices peculiar to itself, but they are not faults that lead to proletarian revolution. The welfare state is no more bourgeois than the Communist state is proletarian. These old-fashioned categories no longer apply, but the Communist still believes that they do, and therefore systematically misdescribes the world he lives in.[1]

The Bolshevik revolution was never betrayed, for both Lenin and Trotsky miscalculated when they made it. They quite misread the situation in the West; for there never was reasonable hope of proletarian revolution in Germany, or in any other major industrial country during or after the First World War. The Bolshevik revolution was premature and the coming of Stalinism, whose causes Trotsky described so well, was therefore (on Marxian premises) inevitable. If Marxism is true, not all the valiant efforts of Lenin and Trotsky could have prevented the emergence of some such system as Stalin later stood for. The 'objective conditions' of his success were created by the Bolshevik revolution—which was itself a betrayal of Marxism but which no Marxist could betray.

Nor were these efforts as valiant as Trotsky, after his quarrel with Stalin, tried to make them out. In *Two Tactics*, the long and elaborate pamphlet in which Lenin first put forward the doctrine of 'uninterrupted revolution,' there is nothing said about the Russian workers and Social-Democrats slightly anticipating in their country a movement soon to sweep the whole capitalist world. That argument was lightly touched upon in 1905, but was not made much of until many years later, when it seemed to Lenin that war was exhausting all the Great Powers and that Tsardom had not long to live. The doctrine of 'uninterrupted revolution' was revived, and this argument used to defend it against the Mensheviks. Trotsky himself, who was a more lucid and consistent advocate of 'uninterrupted revolution' than Lenin, long thought it inevitable in Russia whatever happened elsewhere.

Moreover, most of the evil consequences of premature revolution were

---

[1] Not only the Communist but the westerner also. We still commonly speak of England and France as capitalist countries, though they are no longer capitalist in the sense understood by Marx and his contemporaries. The political and social theorist cannot avoid using words with several or changing meanings, but he can take care not to treat an argument which is valid when a word is used in one sense as if it were valid when it is used in another. Communists, whether followers of Trotsky or Stalin, usually neglect this simple precaution.

already apparent before Lenin died. They were, indeed, consequences of courses that the Bolsheviks had felt themselves driven to in their 'valiant efforts' to retain power. They had had to fight hard to defeat numerous enemies, and most of the institutions that Trotsky afterwards considered preclusive of socialism had been created to give victory to the Bolsheviks. After the civil war they had somewhat relaxed their hold on an almost stifled economy but had kept all their instruments of coercion; and Trotsky for one had never suggested that they could do without them. His strong dislike for these instruments was not evident until there was no longer a hope of his using them.

There can be no doubt that Stalin was right and Trotsky wrong in the dispute between them about the imminence of proletarian revolution outside Russia. There was not, after 1920, even the glimmer of a hope of it in any great industrial country. Had the Bolsheviks exerted themselves to stimulate it, they would have failed miserably and have united all the Powers against them. Western governments were willing enough to let the Bolsheviks play the masters in exhausted Russia, provided they kept their hands off the rest of Europe. It did not greatly concern them who killed whom, or how many millions starved, in so remote, impoverished and barbarous a country. They were too much occupied with their own quarrels and too little recovered from the effects of war to embark on new adventures in Russia. They had, for a time, while they thought the Whites might beat the Reds, thrust their little fingers just a short way into the Russian mess, but had got nothing for themselves or their friends by doing so. Russia, they now thought, was best left alone. She was the victim of a dreadful and catching disease, and should be kept away from other nations and allowed to cure herself as best she might. The western governments wanted to have as little to do with her as possible, and she was therefore safe from them. Only the reckless policy advocated by Trotsky could have caused them to change their minds, and drive the Bolsheviks out of Russia before they had time to make her and themselves formidable.

REFLECTIONS ON THE RUSSIAN REVOLUTION

Sidney Hook*

DEMOCRACY AND THE DICTATORSHIP OF THE PARTY

The key to the Russian economy, to the evolution of Russian culture since the early years of the revolution, to its ghastly purges and juridical

* Professor of Philosophy, New York University. Author of *From Hegel to Marx* and *Marx and the Marxists.* The selection is from pp. 165-168 of *Reason, Social Myths and Democracy* (New York: The Humanities Press). By permission of the publisher.

frame-ups, is to be found in the character of the Russian state power. The Russian state is marked by the concentration of all political and economic power in the hands of the Communist Party. Other political parties of the working class are forbidden, even in the "democratic" Stalin Constitution. The organization of factions within the Communist Party is punishable by exile to concentration camps or by death. The Soviets and Parliament have the same function in Russia as the Reichstag [under Hitler] in Germany —emphatic rubber stamps for policies decided by the Political Committee of the Party. Begun as a dictatorship of a class, the Russian Revolution developed through the dictatorship of the Communist Party into the dictatorship of the Secretariat. Questions of causation are always tangled knots, but I think it can be established that, given the conditions in which the Russian Revolution was begun, the only *controllable* factor that led to the degeneration of the Russian Revolution and its Thermidorian regime was the abrogation of working-class and peasant democracy, signalized by the suppression of all other political parties and the concentration of all power in the hands of the Communist Party.

Let us cast a glance in this light at the various reasons given by Trotsky for the Soviet Thermidor. The immaturity of the productive forces, the belatedness of the world revolution, the decimation of the best fighters and the idealists, the weakening of morale, the death of Lenin—none of them was in the control of the Bolshevik party. And if together they constitute a sufficient explanation of the Thermidor, then degeneration and betrayal were unavoidable no matter who was at the helm or what political forms prevailed. Trotsky, however, is far from establishing a direct and relevant connection between any or all of these factors and the corruption of socialist program and ideals in the Soviet Union. But there is one factor which he does mention as having a direct bearing upon the emergence of Stalinism from Bolshevism, whose importance, however, he immediately proceeds to deny by subordinating it to those mentioned above. "It is absolutely indisputable that the domination of a single party served as the juridical point of departure for the Stalinist totalitarian system. But the reason for this development lies neither in Bolshevism nor in the prohibition of other parties as a temporary war measure, but the number of defeats of the proletariat in Europe and Asia" (*Stalinism and Bolshevism*, 1938).

Domination here is a weak word. A political party can *dominate* even in a democracy which offers it a mandate after the give and take of free discussion. What Trotsky means is the exclusive *dictatorship* of the party, and on other occasions he has not hesitated to say so. The more forcibly the Communist Party exercised its dictatorship over other working-class parties, the more pervasive became the dictatorship of the Secretariat within the Communist Party itself. Times without number Trotsky has maintained that had genuine democratic processes prevailed in the Soviet and in the Party, Stalin's policies would not have prevailed. That is to say, were there Soviet, or even Party, democracy, Stalin's policies would not have prevailed *even though* the revolution was delayed, Lenin dead, and the productive forces undeveloped. Trotsky's policies were quite different from those of Stalin's and they were based every whit as much upon recognition of the objective situation in Russia and in the world generally. But on Trotsky's own analysis, the failure to adopt them was due *not* to the common objective situation but to the absence of workers' and party democracy. Were Trotsky to deny this, he would be admitting that the defeat of his policies was necessary, inevitable, and justifiable, and the denial would make nonsense of his eloquent criticisms of the strangulation of the Soviets and Party under Stalin.

Despite his cosmic optimism, even Trotsky acknowledges that there will always be some periods in which the objective situation is unfavorable, as was true in 1924. Where contrary policies are advocated to meet the situation, absence of workers' and party democracy means that the policy of those who have the dictatorial power in their hands will be adopted, irrespective of whether it is an intelligent one or whether it leads to a *cul de sac*. Even if we assume identity of interests between the dictators and the rank and file, we cannot assume infallibility on the part of the dictating bureaucracy in adopting appropriate measures to realize the common interests.

On every concrete question on which Trotsky has been defeated in Russia, the proximate cause has been, not the level of the productive forces at home or the political situation abroad, but the denial of equal rights of assembly, agitation, and publication to him and to his followers, and the persecution, imprisonment, and often the execution of those of his followers who have tried to exercise these rights. Had Trotsky's policies been turned down in a genuinely functioning workers' and party democracy, the factors he mentions might be relevant in explaining why the electorate refused to give him its confidence. But as it was, Stalin's policies, which led directly to the Thermidor, prevailed because the dictatorship *of* the party was transformed into a dictatorship *over* the party.

It does not require much perspicacity to realize that the dictatorship of a political party cannot for long be effective without its own internal organization becoming dictatorial. The necessity of *controlling* the mass of the population over whom the party wields a dictatorship, of effectively combating enemies, real and alleged, of imposing a uniform ideology, compels the party to assume a military, sometimes called monolithic, structure. The interests of the non-party masses which cannot be openly expressed because of the absence of free political institutions, naturally tend to express themselves in differences within the party itself, in factional groupings of various sorts.

But the dictatorship of the party cannot be effectively wielded unless the facts and appearance of division in its own ranks are concealed from the non-party masses. To conceal this division and to parade the maximum amount of unity, the ruling group in the party must regulate and control the expression of opinion among the rank and file. It must exercise an even stricter supervision of the party press than it does of the non-party press. Now in order to exercise the proper supervision the leading group must itself be unified. Dissidents are isolated, gagged into silence, exiled, deported, and shot. The rule of the leading group must be fortified by a mythology which glorifies "the leader," "the beloved disciple," "the man of iron" who tops the pyramidal structure and whose word on any subject is law. Opposition of any kind is equated with treason. Decisions are "unanimously" approved; failure, no matter for what reason, becomes sabotage; silence today, a sign of betrayal tomorrow; the instruments of one purge become the victims of another. Historical variations may appear at some points in this evolution from the dictatorship *of* a political party to the dictatorship *over* the party. The general pattern of Russian development, however, fits the facts: from the outlawing of other working-class political parties, to the prohibition of factions in the Communist Party . . . to ruthless police terror against *all* dissidents under Stalin.

VI

THE SOVIET POLITICAL SYSTEM

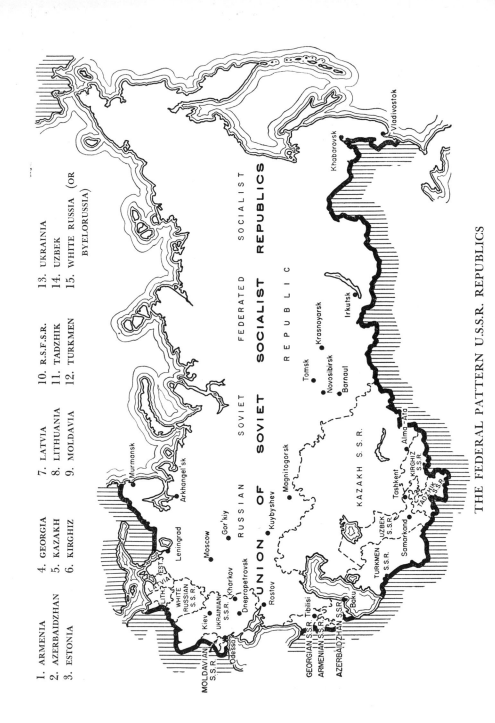

THE FEDERAL PATTERN U.S.S.R. REPUBLICS

1. ARMENIA
2. AZERBAIDZHAN
3. ESTONIA

4. GEORGIA
5. KAZAKH
6. KIRGHIZ

7. LATVIA
8. LITHUANIA
9. MOLDAVIA

10. R.S.F.S.R.
11. TADZHIK
12. TURKMEN

13. UKRAINIA
14. UZBEK
15. WHITE RUSSIA (OR
    BYELORUSSIA)

Chapter 10

THE SOVIET CONSTITUTION

The first Soviet Constitution, which went into effect on July 19, 1918, on the eve of civil war and intervention, was limited in its application to the Russian Socialist Federated Soviet Republic. By its terms,

The principal object of the Constitution of the RSFSR . . . consists in the establishment of the dictatorship of the urban and rural proletariat and the poorest peasantry, in the form of the strong All-Russian Soviet power, with the aim of securing the complete suppression of the bourgeoisie, the abolition of the exploitation of man by man, and the establishment of socialism, under which there shall be neither class divisions nor State authority.

Although it provided disproportionate representation for the proletariat, it made no mention of the Communist Party, which did not then enjoy a legal monopoly of power.

The first All-Union Constitution, which was approved by the Second Congress of Soviets on January 31, 1924, was closely patterned after the 1918 Constitution. The U.S.S.R. was declared "a trustworthy bulwark against world capitalism, and a new decisive step along the path of the union of the workers of all countries in a World Socialist Soviet Republic." The Constitution stated that each Republic "retains the right of free withdrawal from the Union."

The 1924 Constitution was replaced by the "Stalin" Constitution, in effect December 5, 1936, which eliminated all disproportionate representation (see Articles 134, 135, and 136) and, on the other hand, accorded to the Communist Party a special position (see Article 126). Speaking generally, the Soviet Constitution—which is set forth in the pages immediately following and which merits careful reading—in form, structure, and definition of fundamental rights and duties of citizens—would appear to be one of the most advanced and forward-looking in the world. To what extent this is reality and to what extent myth are the subjects of the discussion next ensuing.

305

CONSTITUTION

(FUNDAMENTAL LAW)

OF THE UNION OF SOVIET SOCIALIST REPUBLICS

*As Amended and Added to
at the Ninth Session
of the Supreme Soviet of the U.S.S.R.,
Fourth Convocation*
(December 1957)

CHAPTER I. THE SOCIAL STRUCTURE

Article 1.—The Union of Soviet Socialist Republics is a socialist state of workers and peasants.

Article 2.—The political foundation of the U.S.S.R. is the Soviets of Working People's Deputies, which grew and became strong as a result of the overthrow of the power of the landlords and capitalists and the conquest of the dictatorship of the proletariat.

Article 3.—All power in the U.S.S.R. belongs to the working people of town and country as represented by the Soviets of Working People's Deputies.

Article 4.—The economic foundation of the U.S.S.R. is the socialist system of economy and the socialist ownership of the instruments and means of production, firmly established as a result of the liquidation of the capitalist system of economy, the abolition of private ownership of the instruments and means of production, and the elimination of the exploitation of man by man.

Article 5.—Socialist property in the U.S.S.R. exists either in the form of state property (belonging to the whole people) or in the form of co-operative and collective-farm property (property of collective farms, property of co-operative societies).

Article 6.—The land, its mineral wealth, waters, forests, mills, factories, mines, rail, water and air transport, banks, communications, large state-organized agricultural enterprises (state farms, machine and tractor stations and the like), as well as municipal enterprises and the bulk of the dwelling-houses in the cities and industrial localities, are state property, that is, belong to the whole people.

Article 7.—The common enterprises of collective farms and co-operative organizations, with their live-stock and implements, the products of the collective farms and co-operative organizations, as well as their common buildings, constitute the common, socialist property of the collective farms and co-operative organizations.

Every household in a collective farm, in addition to its basic income from the common collective-farm enterprise, has for its personal use a small plot of household land and, as its personal property, a subsidiary husbandry on the plot, a dwelling-house, live-stock, poultry and minor agricultural implements—in accordance with the rules of the agricultural artel.

Article 8.—The land occupied by collective farms is secured to them for their use free of charge and for an unlimited time, that is, in perpetuity.

Article 9.—Alongside the socialist system of economy, which is the predominant form of economy in the U.S.S.R., the law permits the small private economy of individual peasants and handicraftsmen based on their own labour and precluding the exploitation of the labour of others.

Article 10.—The personal property right of citizens in their incomes and savings from work, in their dwelling-houses and subsidiary husbandries, in articles of domestic economy and use and articles of personal use and convenience, as well as the right of citizens to inherit personal property, is protected by law.

Article 11.—The economic life of the U.S.S.R. is determined and directed by the state national-economic plan, with the aim of increasing the public wealth, of steadily raising the material and cultural standards of the working people, of consolidating the independence of the U.S.S.R. and strengthening its defensive capacity.

Article 12.—Work in the U.S.S.R. is a duty and a matter of honour for every able-bodied citizen, in accordance with the principle: "He who does not work, neither shall he eat."

The principle applied in the U.S.S.R. is that of socialism: "From each according to his ability, to each according to his work."

CHAPTER II. THE STATE STRUCTURE

Article 13.—The Union of Soviet Socialist Republics is a federal state, formed on the basis of a voluntary union of equal Soviet Socialist Republics, namely:

The Russian Soviet Federative Socialist Republic
The Ukrainian Soviet Socialist Republic
The Byelorussian Soviet Socialist Republic
The Uzbek Soviet Socialist Republic
The Kazakh Soviet Socialist Republic

The Georgian Soviet Socialist Republic
The Azerbaijan Soviet Socialist Republic
The Lithuanian Soviet Socialist Republic
The Moldavian Soviet Socialist Republic
The Latvian Soviet Socialist Republic
The Kirghiz Soviet Socialist Republic
The Tajik Soviet Socialist Republic
The Armenian Soviet Socialist Republic
The Turkmen Soviet Socialist Republic
The Estonian Soviet Socialist Republic

Article 14.—The jurisdiction of the Union of Soviet Socialist Republics, as represented by its higher organs of state power and organs of state administration, embraces:

a) Representation of the U.S.S.R. in international relations, conclusion, ratification and denunciation of treaties of the U.S.S.R. with other states, establishment of general procedure governing the relations of Union Republics with foreign states;

b) Questions of war and peace;

c) Admission of new republics into the U.S.S.R.;

d) Control over the observance of the Constitution of the U.S.S.R., and ensuring conformity of the Constitutions of the Union Republics with the Constitution of the U.S.S.R.;

e) Confirmation of alterations of boundaries between Union Republics;

f) Confirmation of the formation of new Autonomous Republics and Autonomous Regions within Union Republics;

g) Organization of the defence of the U.S.S.R., direction of all the Armed Forces of the U.S.S.R., determination of directing principles governing the organization of the military formations of the Union Republics;

h) Foreign trade on the basis of state monopoly;

i) Safeguarding the security of the state;

j) Determination of the national-economic plans of the U.S.S.R.;

k) Approval of the consolidated state budget of the U.S.S.R. and of the report on its fulfilment; determination of the taxes and revenues which go to the Union, the Republican and the local budgets;

l) Administration of the banks, industrial and agricultural institutions and enterprises and trading enterprises of all-Union importance; over-all direction of industry and construction under Union Republic jurisdiction.

m) Administration of transport and communications of all-Union importance;

n) Direction of the monetary and credit system;

o) Organization of state insurance;

p) Contracting and granting of loans;

q) Determination of the basic principles of land tenure and of the use of mineral wealth, forests and waters;

r) Determination of the basic principles in the spheres of education and public health;

s) Organization of a uniform system of national-economic statistics;

t) Determination of the principles of labour legislation;

u) Establishment of the principles of legislation concerning the judicial system and judicial procedure, and of the principles of the criminal and civil codes.

v) Legislation concerning Union citizenship; legislation concerning rights of foreigners;

w) Determination of the principles of legislation concerning marriage and the family;

x) Issuing of all-Union acts of amnesty.

Article 15.—The sovereignty of the Union Republics is limited only in the spheres defined in article 14 of the Constitution of the U.S.S.R. Outside of these spheres each Union Republic exercises state authority independently. The U.S.S.R. protects the sovereign rights of the Union Republics.

Article 16.—Each Union Republic has its own Constitution, which takes account of the specific feature of the Republic and is drawn up in full conformity with the Constitution of the U.S.S.R.

Article 17.—The right freely to secede from the U.S.S.R. is reserved to every Union Republic.

Article 18.—The territory of a Union Republic may not be altered without its consent.

Article 18-a.—Each Union Republic has the right to enter into direct relations with foreign states and to conclude agreements and exchange diplomatic and consular representatives with them.

Article 18-b.—Each Union Republic has its own Republican military formations.

Article 19.—The laws of the U.S.S.R. have the same force within the territory of every Union Republic.

Article 20.—In the event of divergence between a law of a Union Republic and a law of the Union, the Union law prevails.

Article 21.—Uniform Union citizenship is established for citizens of the U.S.S.R.

Every citizen of a Union Republic is a citizen of the U.S.S.R.

Article 22.—The Russian Soviet Federative Socialist Republic includes the Autonomous Soviet Socialist Republics: Bashkirian, Buryat-Mongolian*,

---

* Decree of Presidium of Supreme Soviet, dated July 7, 1958, renamed as Buryat—subject to ratification by the Supreme Soviet.

Daghestan, Kabardino-Balkarian, Karelian, Komi, Mari, Mordovian, North Ossetian, Tartar, Udmart, Chechen-Ingush, Chuvash, Yakut; Autonomous Regions: Adygei, Gorny Altai, Jewish, Kalmyk*, Karachai-Cherkess, Tuva and Khakass.

Article 24.—The Azerbaiijan Soviet Socialist Republic includes the Nakhichevan Autonomous Soviet Socialist Republic and the Nagorny Karabakh Autonomous Region.

Article 25.—The Georgian Soviet Socialist Republic includes the Abkhazian Autonomous Soviet Socialist Republic, the Ajarian Autonomous Soviet Socialist Republic and the South Ossetian Autonomous Region.

Article 26.—The Uzbek Soviet Socialist Republic includes the Kara-Kalpak Autonomous Soviet Socialist Republic.

Article 27.—The Tajik Soviet Socialist Republic includes the Gorny Badakhshan Autonomous Region.

Article 28.—The decision of questions relating to the Regional and Territorial Administrative Structure of Union Republics is left to the jurisdiction of Union Republics.†

CHAPTER III. THE HIGHER ORGANS OF STATE POWER IN THE UNION OF SOVIET SOCIALIST REPUBLICS

Article 30.—The highest organ of state power in the U.S.S.R. is the Supreme Soviet of the U.S.S.R.

Article 31.—The Supreme Soviet of the U.S.S.R. exercises all rights vested in the Union of Soviet Socialist Republics in accordance with Article 14 of the Constitution, in so far as they do not, by virtue of the Constitution, come within the jurisdiction of organs of the U.S.S.R. that are accountable to the Supreme Soviet of the U.S.S.R., that is, the Presidium of the Supreme Soviet of the U.S.S.R., the Council of Ministers of the U.S.S.R., and the Ministries of the U.S.S.R.

Article 32.—The legislative power of the U.S.S.R. is exercised exclusively by the Supreme Soviet of the U.S.S.R.

Article 33.—The Supreme Soviet of the U.S.S.R. consists of two Chambers: the Soviet of the Union and the Soviet of Nationalities.

Article 34.—The Soviet of the Union is elected by the citizens of the U.S.S.R. voting by election districts on the basis of one deputy for every 300,000 of the population.

* Decree of Presidium of Supreme Soviet, dated July 29, 1958, reorganized as Kalmyk Autonomous Soviet Socialist *Republic*—subject to ratification by the Supreme Soviet.
† This 1957 amendment accounts for the hiatus in Article numbers.

Article 35.—The Soviet of Nationalities is elected by the citizens of the U.S.S.R. voting by Union Republics, Autonomous Republics, Autonomous Regions, and National Areas on the basis of 25 deputies from each Union Republic, 11 deputies from each Autonomous Republic, 5 deputies from each Autonomous Region and one deputy from each National Area.

Article 36.—The Supreme Soviet of the U.S.S.R. is elected for a term of four years.

Article 37.—The two Chambers of the Supreme Soviet of the U.S.S.R., the Soviet of the Union and the Soviet of Nationalities, have equal rights.

Article 38.—The Soviet of the Union and the Soviet of Nationalities have equal powers to initiate legislation.

Article 39.—A law is considered adopted if passed by both Chambers of the Supreme Soviet of the U.S.S.R. by a simple majority vote in each.

Article 40.—Laws passed by the Supreme Soviet of the U.S.S.R. are published in the languages of the Union Republics over the signatures of the President and Secretary of the Presidium of the Supreme Soviet of the U.S.S.R.

Article 41.—Sessions of the Soviet of the Union and of the Soviet of Nationalities begin and terminate simultaneously.

Article 42.—The Soviet of the Union elects a Chairman of the Soviet of the Union and four Vice-Chairmen.

Article 43.—The Soviet of Nationalities elects a Chairman of the Soviet of Nationalities and four Vice-Chairmen.

Article 44.—The Chairmen of the Soviet of the Union and the Soviet of Nationalities preside at the sittings of the respective Chambers and have charge of the conduct of their business and proceedings.

Article 45.—Joint sittings of the two Chambers of the Supreme Soviet of the U.S.S.R. are presided over alternately by the Chairman of the Soviet of the Union and the Chairman of the Soviet of Nationalities.

Article 46.—Sessions of the Supreme Soviet of the U.S.S.R. are convened by the Presidium of the Supreme Soviet of the U.S.S.R. twice a year.

Extraordinary sessions are convened by the Presidium of the Supreme Soviet of the U.S.S.R. at its discretion or on the demand of one of the Union Republics.

Article 47.—In the event of disagreement between the Soviet of the Union and the Soviet of Nationalities, the question is referred for settlement to a conciliation commission formed by the Chambers on a parity basis. If the conciliation commission fails to arrive at an agreement or if its decision fails to satisfy one of the Chambers, the question is considered for a second time by the Chambers. Failing agreement between the two Chambers, the Presidium of the Supreme Soviet of the U.S.S.R. dissolves the Supreme Soviet of the U.S.S.R. and orders new elections.

Article 48.—The Supreme Soviet of the U.S.S.R. at a joint sitting of the two Chambers elects the Presidium of the Supreme Soviet of the U.S.S.R., consisting of a President of the Presidium of the Supreme Soviet of the U.S.S.R., sixteen Vice-Presidents, a Secretary of the Presidium and fifteen members of the Presidium of the Supreme Soviet of the U.S.S.R.

The Presidium of the Supreme Soviet of the U.S.S.R. is accountable to the Supreme Soviet of the U.S.S.R. for all its activities.

Article 49.—The Presidium of the Supreme Soviet of the U.S.S.R.:
a) Convenes the sessions of the Supreme Soviet of the U.S.S.R.;
b) Issues decrees;
c) Gives interpretations of the laws of the U.S.S.R. in operation;
d) Dissolves the Supreme Soviet of the U.S.S.R. in conformity with

Article 47 of the Constitution of the U.S.S.R. and orders new elections;
e) Conducts nation-wide polls (referendums) on its own initiative or on the demand of one of the Union Republics;
f) Annuls decisions and orders of the Council of Ministers of the U.S.S.R. and of the Councils of Ministers of the Union Republics if they do not conform to law;
g) In the intervals between sessions of the Supreme Soviet of the U.S.S.R., releases and appoints Ministers of the U.S.S.R. on the recommendation of the Chairman of the Council of Ministers of the U.S.S.R., subject to subsequent confirmation by the Supreme Soviet of the U.S.S.R.;
h) Institutes decorations (Orders and Medals) and titles of honour of the U.S.S.R.;
i) Awards Orders and Medals and confers titles of honour of the U.S.S.R.;
j) Exercises the right of pardon;
k) Institutes military titles, diplomatic ranks and other special titles;
l) Appoints and removes the high command of the Armed Forces of the U.S.S.R.;
m) In the intervals between sessions of the Supreme Soviet of the U.S.S.R., proclaims a state of war in the event of military attack on the U.S.S.R., or when necessary to fulfil international treaty obligations concerning mutual defence against aggression;
n) Orders general or partial mobilization;
o) Ratifies and denounces international treaties of the U.S.S.R.;
p) Appoints and recalls plenipotentiary representatives of the U.S.S.R. to foreign states;

q) Receives the letters of credence and recall of diplomatic representatives accredited to it by foreign states;

r) Proclaims martial law in separate localities or throughout the U.S.S.R. in the interests of the defence of the U.S.S.R. or of the maintenance of public order and the security of the state.

Article 50.—The Soviet of the Union and the Soviet of Nationalities elect Credentials Committees to verify the credentials of the members of the respective Chambers.

On the report of the Credentials Committees, the Chambers decide whether to recognize the credentials of deputies or to annul their election.

Article 51.—The Supreme Soviet of the U.S.S.R., when it deems necessary, appoints commissions of investigation and audit on any matter.

It is the duty of all institutions and officials to comply with the demands of such commissions and to submit to them all necessary materials and documents.

Article 52.—A member of the Supreme Soviet of the U.S.S.R. may not be prosecuted or arrested without the consent of the Supreme Soviet of the U.S.S.R., or, when the Supreme Soviet of the U.S.S.R. is not in session, without the consent of the Presidium of the Supreme Soviet of the U.S.S.R.

Article 53.—On the expiration of the term of office of the Supreme Soviet of the U.S.S.R., or on its dissolution prior to the expiration of its term of office, the Presidium of the Supreme Soviet of the U.S.S.R. retains its powers until the newly-elected Supreme Soviet of the U.S.S.R. shall have formed a new Presidium of the Supreme Soviet of the U.S.S.R.

Article 54.—On the expiration of the term of office of the Supreme Soviet of the U.S.S.R., or in the event of its dissolution prior to the expiration of its term of office, the Presidium of the Supreme Soviet of the U.S.S.R. orders new elections to be held within a period not exceeding two months from the date of expiration of the term of office or dissolution of the Supreme Soviet of the U.S.S.R.

Article 55.—The newly-elected Supreme Soviet of the U.S.S.R. is convened by the outgoing Presidium of the Supreme Soviet of the U.S.S.R. not later than three months after the elections.

Article 56.—The Supreme Soviet of the U.S.S.R., at a joint sitting of the two Chambers, appoints the Government of the U.S.S.R., namely, the Council of Ministers of the U.S.S.R.

CHAPTER IV. THE HIGHER ORGANS OF STATE POWER IN THE UNION REPUBLICS

Article 57.—The highest organ of state power in a Union Republic is the Supreme Soviet of the Union Republic.

Article 58.—The Supreme Soviet of a Union Republic is elected by the citizens of the Republic for a term of four years.

The basis of representation is established by the Constitution of the Union Republic.

Article 59.—The Supreme Soviet of a Union Republic is the sole legislative organ of the Republic.

Article 60.—The Supreme Soviet of a Union Republic:

a) Adopts the Constitution of the Republic and amends it in conformity with Article 16 of the Constitution of the U.S.S.R.;

b) Confirms the Constitutions of the Autonomous Republics forming part of it and defines the boundaries of their territories;

c) Approves the national-economic plan and the budget of the Republic and forms the economic administrative Regions.

d) Exercises the right of amnesty and pardon of citizens sentenced by the judicial organs of the Union Republic;

e) Decides questions of representation of the Union Republic in its international relation;

f) Determines the manner of organizing the Republic's military formations.

Article 61.—The Supreme Soviet of a Union Republic elects the Presidium of the Supreme Soviet of the Union Republic, consisting of a President of the Presidium of the Supreme Soviet of the Union Republic, Vice-Presidents, a Secretary of the Presidium and members of the Presidium of the Supreme Soviet of the Union Republic.

The powers of the Presidium of the Supreme Soviet of a Union Republic are defined by the Constitution of the Union Republic.

Article 62.—The Supreme Soviet of a Union Republic elects a Chairman and Vice-Chairmen to conduct its sittings.

Article 63.—The Supreme Soviet of a Union Republic appoints the Government of the Union Republic, namely, the Council of Ministers of the Union Republic.

CHAPTER V. THE ORGANS OF STATE ADMINISTRATION OF THE UNION OF SOVIET SOCIALIST REPUBLICS

Article 64.—The highest executive and administrative organ of the state power of the Union of Soviet Socialist Republics is the Council of Ministers of the U.S.S.R.

Article 65.—The Council of Ministers of the U.S.S.R. is responsible and accountable to the Supreme Soviet of the U.S.S.R., or, in the intervals between sessions of the Supreme Soviet, to the Presidium of the Supreme Soviet of the U.S.S.R.

Article 66.—The Council of Ministers of the U.S.S.R. issues decisions and orders on the basis and in pursuance of the laws in operation, and verifies their execution.

Article 67.—Decisions and orders of the Council of Ministers of the U.S.S.R. are binding throughout the territory of the U.S.S.R.

Article 68.—The Council of Ministers of the U.S.S.R.:

a) Co-ordinates and directs the work of the all-Union and Union-Republican Ministries of the U.S.S.R. and of other institutions under its jurisdiction and exercises direction over the Economic Councils of the economic administrative Regions through the Union Republic Councils of Ministers.

b) Adopts measures to carry out the national-economic plan and the state budget, and to strengthen the credit and monetary system;

c) Adopts measures for the maintenance of public order, for the protection of the interests of the state, and for the safeguarding of the rights of citizens;

d) Exercises general guidance in the sphere of relations with foreign states;

e) Fixes the annual contingent of citizens to be called up for military service and directs the general organization of the Armed Forces of the country;

f) Sets up, whenever necessary, special Committees and Central Administrations under the Council of Ministers of the U.S.S.R. for economic and cultural affairs and defence.

Article 69.—The Council of Ministers of the U.S.S.R. has the right, in respect of those branches of administration and economy which come within the jurisdiction of the U.S.S.R., to suspend decisions and orders of the Councils of Ministers of the Union Republics and the Economic Councils of the economic administrative Regions and to annul orders and instructions of Ministers of the U.S.S.R.

Article 70.—The Council of Ministers of the U.S.S.R. is appointed by the Supreme Soviet of the U.S.S.R. and consists of: the chairman of the U.S.S.R. Council of Ministers; the first vice-chairmen of the U.S.S.R. Council of Ministers; the vice-chairmen of the U.S.S.R. Council of Ministers; Ministers of the U.S.S.R.; the chairman of the U.S.S.R. Council of Ministers' State Planning Committee; the chairman of the U.S.S.R. Council of Ministers' Soviet Control Commission; the chairman of the U.S.S.R. Council of Ministers' State Committee on Labor and Wages; the chairman of the U.S.S.R. Council of Ministers' State Scientific and Technical Committee; the chairman of the U.S.S.R. Council of Ministers' State Committee on Aviation Technology; the chairman of the U.S.S.R. Council of Ministers' State Committee on Defense Technology; the chairman of the U.S.S.R. Council of

Ministers' State Committee on Radio Electronics; the chairman of the U.S.S.R. Council of Ministers' State Committee on Shipbuilding; the chairman of the U.S.S.R. Council of Ministers' State Committee on Construction; the chairman of the U.S.S.R. Council of Ministers' State Committee on Foreign Economic Relations; the chairman of the U.S.S.R. Council of Ministers' State Committee on State Security; the chairman of the Board of the U.S.S.R. State Bank; the director of the U.S.S.R. Council of Ministers' Central Statistical Administration.

The U.S.S.R. Council of Ministers includes the chairmen of the Union Republic Councils of Ministers ex officio.

Article 71.—The Government of the U.S.S.R. or a Minister of the U.S.S.R. to whom a question of a member of the Supreme Soviet of the U.S.S.R. is addressed must give a verbal or written reply in the respective Chamber within a period not exceeding three days.

Article 72.—The Ministers of the U.S.S.R. direct the branches of state administration which come within the jurisdiction of the U.S.S.R.

Article 73.—The Ministers of the U.S.S.R., within the limits of the jurisdiction of their respective Ministries, issue orders and instructions on the basis and in pursuance of the laws in operation, and also of decisions and orders of the Council of Ministers of the U.S.S.R., and verify their execution.

Article 74.—The Ministries of the U.S.S.R. are either all-Union or Union-Republican Ministries.

Article 75.—Each all-Union Ministry directs the branch of state administration entrusted to it throughout the territory of the U.S.S.R. either directly or through bodies appointed by it.

Article 76.—The Union-Republican Ministries, as a rule, direct the branches of state administration entrusted to them through corresponding Ministries of the Union Republics; they administer directly only a definite and limited number of enterprises according to a list confirmed by the Presidium of the Supreme Soviet of the U.S.S.R.

Article 77.—The following Ministries are all-Union Ministries: Foreign Trade; Merchant Marine; Transportation; Medium Machine Building; Transport Construction; Chemical Industry; Power Plants.

Article 78.—The following Ministries are Union Republic Ministries: Internal Affairs; Higher Education; Geology and Conservation of Mineral Resources; Public Health; Foreign Affairs; Culture; Defense; Communications; Agriculture; Trade; Finance; Grain Products.

CHAPTER VI. THE ORGANS OF STATE ADMINISTRATION OF THE UNION REPUBLICS

Article 79.—The highest executive and administrative organ of the state power of a Union Republic is the Council of Ministers of the Union Republic.

Article 80.—The Council of Ministers of a Union Republic is responsible and accountable to the Supreme Soviet of the Union Republic, or, in the intervals between sessions of the Supreme Soviet of the Union Republic, to the Presidium of the Supreme Soviet of the Union Republic.

Article 81.—The Council of Ministers of a Union Republic issues decisions and orders on the basis and in pursuance of the laws in operation of the U.S.S.R. and of the Union Republic, and of the decisions and orders of the Council of Ministers of the U.S.S.R., and verifies their execution.

Article 82.—The Council of Ministers of a Union Republic has the right to suspend decisions and orders of the Councils of Ministers of its Autonomous Republics and to annual decisions and orders of the Executive Committees of the Soviets of Working People's Deputies of its Territories, Regions and Autonomous Regions and of the Economic Councils of the economic administrative Regions.

Article 83.—The Council of Ministers of a Union Republic is appointed by the Supreme Soviet of the Union Republic and consists of:
The Chairman of the Council of Ministers of the Union Republic;
The First Vice-Chairmen of the Council of Ministers;
The Vice-Chairmen of the Council of Ministers;
The Ministers;
The Chairman of the State Planning Commission;
The Chairman of the State Committee of the Council of Ministers of the Union Republic on Construction and Architecture;
The Chairman of the State Security Committee under the Council of Ministers of the Union Republic.

Article 84.—The Ministers of a Union Republic direct the branches of state administration which come within the jurisdiction of the Union Republic.

Article 85.—The Ministers of a Union Republic, within the limits of the jurisdiction of their respective Ministries, issue orders and instructions on the basis and in pursuance of the laws of the U.S.S.R. and of the Union Republic, of the decisions and orders of the Council of Ministers of the U.S.S.R. and the Council of Ministers of the Union Republic, and of the orders and instructions of the Union-Republican Ministries of the U.S.S.R.

Article 86.—The Ministries of a Union Republic are either Union-Republican or Republican Ministries.

Article 87.—Each Union-Republican Ministry directs the branch of state administration entrusted to it, and is subordinate both to the Council of Ministers of the Union Republic and to the corresponding Union-Republican Ministry of the U.S.S.R.

Article 88.—Each Republican Ministry directs the branch of state administration entrusted to it and is directly subordinate to the Council of Ministers of the Union Republic.

Article 88-a.—The Economic Councils of the economic administrative Regions direct the branches of economic activity entrusted to them and are directly subordinate to the Union Republic Council of Ministers.

The Economic Councils of the economic administrative Regions, within the bounds of their competence, make decisions and issue directives on the basis and in execution of the laws of the U.S.S.R. and the Union Republic and of the decrees and directives of the U.S.S.R. Council of Ministers and the Union Republic Council of Ministers.

CHAPTER VII. THE HIGHER ORGANS OF STATE POWER IN THE AUTONOMOUS SOVIET SOCIALIST REPUBLICS

Article 89.—The highest organ of state power in an Autonomous Republic is the Supreme Soviet of the Autonomous Republic.

Article 90.—The Supreme Soviet of an Autonomous Republic is elected by the citizens of the Republic for a term of four years on a basis of representation established by the Constitution of the Autonomous Republic.

Article 91.—The Supreme Soviet of an Autonomous Republic is the sole legislative organ of the Autonomous Republic.

Article 92.—Each Autonomous Republic has its own Constitution, which takes account of the specific features of the Autonomous Republic and is drawn up in full conformity with the Constitution of the Union Republic.

Article 93.—The Supreme Soviet of an Autonomous Republic elects the Presidium of the Supreme Soviet of the Autonomous Republic and appoints the Council of Ministers of the Autonomous Republic, in accordance with its Constitution.

CHAPTER VIII. THE LOCAL ORGANS OF STATE POWER

Article 94.—The organs of state power in Territories, Regions, Autonomous Regions, Areas, Districts, cities and rural localities (stanitsas, villages, hamlets, kishlaks, auls) are the Soviets of Working People's Deputies.

Article 95.—The Soviets of Working People's Deputies of Territories, Regions, Autonomous Regions, Areas, Districts, cities and rural localities (stanitsas, villages, hamlets, kishlaks, auls) are elected by the working people of the respective Territories, Regions, Autonomous Regions, Areas, Districts, cities or rural localities for a term of two years.

Article 96.—The basis of representation for Soviets of Working People's Deputies is determined by the Constitutions of the Union Republics.

Article 97.—The Soviets of Working People's Deputies direct the work of the organs of administration subordinate to them, ensure the maintenance of public order, the observance of the laws and the protection of the rights of citizens, direct local economic and cultural affairs and draw up the local budgets.

Article 98.—The Soviets of Working People's Deputies adopt decisions and issue orders within the limits of the powers vested in them by the laws of the U.S.S.R. and of the Union Republic.

Article 99.—The executive and administrative organ of the Soviet of Working People's Deputies of a Territory, Region, Autonomous Region, Area, District, city or rural locality is the Executive Committee elected by it, consisting of a Chairman, Vice-Chairmen, a Secretary and members.

Article 100.—The executive and administrative organ of the Soviet of Working People's Deputies in a small locality, in accordance with the Constitution of the Union Republic, is the Chairman, the Vice-Chairman and the Secretary elected by the Soviet of Working People's Deputies.

Article 101.—The executive organs of the Soviets of Working People's Deputies are directly accountable both to the Soviets of Working People's Deputies which elected them and to the executive organ of the superior Soviet of Working People's Deputies.

CHAPTER IX. THE COURTS AND THE PROCURATOR'S OFFICE

Article 102.—In the U.S.S.R. justice is administered by the Supreme Court of the U.S.S.R., the Supreme Courts of the Union Republics, the Courts of the Territories, Regions, Autonomous Republics, Autonomous Regions and Areas, the Special Courts of the U.S.S.R. established by decision of the Supreme Soviet of the U.S.S.R., and the People's Courts.

Article 103.—In all Courts cases are tried with the participation of people's assessors except in cases specially provided for by law.

Article 104.—The Supreme Court of the U.S.S.R. is the highest judicial organ. The Supreme Court of the U.S.S.R. is charged with the supervision of the judicial activities of all the judicial organs of the U.S.S.R. and of the Union Republics within the limits established by law.

Article 105.—The Supreme Court of the U.S.S.R. is elected by the Supreme Soviet of the U.S.S.R. for a term of five years. The Supreme Court of the U.S.S.R. includes the Chief Justices of the Supreme Courts of the Union Republics, ex officio.

Article 106.—The Supreme Courts of the Union Republics are elected by the Supreme Soviets of the Union Republics for a term of five years.

Article 107.—The Supreme Courts of the Autonomous Republics are elected by the Supreme Soviets of the Autonomous Republics for a term of five years.

Article 108.—The Courts of Territories, Regions, Autonomous Regions and Areas are elected by the Soviets of Working People's Deputies of the respective Territories, Regions, Autonomous Regions or Areas for a term of five years.

Article 109.—People's Courts are elected by the citizens of the districts on the basis of universal, direct and equal suffrage by secret ballot for a term of three years.

Article 110.—Judicial proceedings are conducted in the language of the Union Republic, Autonomous Republic or Autonomous Region, persons not knowing this language being guaranteed the opportunity of fully acquainting themselves with the material of the case through an interpreter and likewise the right to use their own language in court.

Article 111.—In all Courts of the U.S.S.R. cases are heard in public, unless otherwise provided for by law, and the accused is guaranteed the right to defence.

Article 112.—Judges are independent and subject only to the law.

Article 113.—Supreme supervisory power to ensure the strict observance of the law by all Ministries and institutions subordinated to them, as well as by officials and citizens of the U.S.S.R. generally, is vested in the Procurator-General of the U.S.S.R.

Article 114.—The Procurator-General of the U.S.S.R. is appointed by the Supreme Soviet of the U.S.S.R. for a term of seven years.

Article 115.—Procurators of Republics, Territories, Regions, Autonomous Republics and Autonomous Regions are appointed by the Procurator-General of the U.S.S.R. for a term of five years.

Article 116.—Area, district and city procurators are appointed by the Procurators of the Union Republics, subject to the approval of the Procurator-General of the U.S.S.R., for a term of five years.

Article 117.—The organs of the Procurator's Office perform their functions independently of any local organs whatsoever, being subordinate solely to the Procurator-General of the U.S.S.R.

CHAPTER X. FUNDAMENTAL RIGHTS AND DUTIES OF CITIZENS

Article 118.—Citizens of the U.S.S.R. have the right to work, that is, the right to guaranteed employment and payment for their work in accordance with its quantity and quality.

The right to work is ensured by the socialist organization of the national economy, the steady growth of the productive forces of Soviet society, the elimination of the possibility of economic crises, and the abolition of unemployment.

Article 119.—Citizens of the U.S.S.R. have the right to rest and leisure.

The right to rest and leisure is ensured by the establishment of an eight-hour day for industrial, office, and professional workers, the reduction of the working day to seven or six hours for arduous trades and to four hours in shops where conditions of work are particularly arduous; by the institution of annual vacations with full pay for industrial, office, and professional workers, and by the provision of a wide network of sanatoria, holiday homes and clubs for the accommodation of the working people.

Article 120.—Citizens of the U.S.S.R. have the right to maintenance in old age and also in case of sickness or disability.

This right is ensured by the extensive development of social insurance of industrial, office, and professional workers at state expense, free medical service for the working people, and the provision of a wide network of health resorts for the use of the working people.

Article 121.—Citizens of the U.S.S.R. have the right to education.

This right is ensured by universal compulsory seven-year education; by extensive development of ten-year education, by free education in all schools, higher as well as secondary, by a system of state grants for students of higher schools who excel in their studies; by instruction in schools being conducted in the native language, and by the organization in the factories, state farms, machine and tractor stations, and collective farms of free vocational, technical and agronomic training for the working people.

Article 122.—Women in the U.S.S.R. are accorded equal rights with men in all spheres of economic, government, cultural, political and other public activity.

The possibility of exercising these rights is ensured by women being accorded an equal right with men to work, payment for work, rest and leisure, social insurance and education, and by state protection of the interest of mother and child, state aid to mothers of large families and unmarried mothers, maternity leave with full pay, and the provision of a wide network of maternity homes, nurseries and kindergartens.

Article 123.—Equality of rights of citizens of the U.S.S.R., irrespective of their nationality or race, in all spheres of economic, government, cultural, political and other public activity, is an indefeasible law.

Any direct or indirect restriction of the rights of, or conversely, the establishment of any direct or indirect privileges for, citizens on account of their race or nationality, as well as any advocacy of racial or national exclusiveness or hatred and contempt, are punishable by law.

Article 124.—In order to ensure to citizens freedom of conscience, the church in the U.S.S.R. is separated from the state, and the school from the church. Freedom of religious worship and freedom of anti-religious propaganda is recognized for all citizens.

Article 125.—In conformity with the interests of the working people, and in order to strengthen the socialist system, the citizens of the U.S.S.R. are guaranteed by law:
  a) freedom of speech;
  b) freedom of the press;
  c) freedom of assembly, including the holding of mass meetings;
  d) freedom of street processions and demonstrations.
These civil rights are ensured by placing at the disposal of the working people and their organizations printing presses, stocks of paper, public buildings, the streets, communications facilities, and other material requisites for the exercise of these rights.

Article 126.—In conformity with the interests of the working people, and in order to develop the organizational initiative and political activity of the masses of the people, citizens of the U.S.S.R. are guaranteed the right to unite in public organizations: trade unions, co-operative societies, youth organizations, sport and defence organizations, cultural, technical and scientific societies; and the most active and politically-conscious citizens in the ranks of the working class, working peasants and working intelligentsia voluntarily unite in the Communist Party of the Soviet Union, which is the vanguard of the working people in their struggle to build communist society and is the leading core of all organizations of the working people, both public and state.

Article 127.—Citizens of the U.S.S.R. are guaranteed inviolability of the person. No person may be placed under arrest except by decision of a court or with the sanction of a procurator.

Article 128.—The inviolability of the homes of citizens and privacy of correspondence are protected by law.

Article 129.—The U.S.S.R. affords the right of asylum to foreign citizens persecuted for defending the interests of the working people, or for scientific activities, or for struggling for national liberation.

Article 130.—It is the duty of every citizen of the U.S.S.R. to abide by the Constitution of the Union of Soviet Socialist Republics, to observe the laws, to maintain labour discipline, honestly to perform public duties, and to respect the rules of socialist intercourse.

Article 131.—It is the duty of every citizen of the U.S.S.R. to safeguard and fortify public, socialist property as the sacred and inviolable foundation of the Soviet system, as the source of the wealth and might of the country, as the source of the prosperity and culture of all the working people.

Persons committing offences against public, socialist property are enemies of the people.

Article 132.—Universal military service is law.

Military service in the Armed Forces of the U.S.S.R. is an honourable duty of the citizens of the U.S.S.R.

Article 133.—To defend the country is the sacred duty of every citizen of the U.S.S.R. Treason to the Motherland—violation of the oath of allegiance, desertion to the enemy, impairing the military power of the state, espionage—is punishable with all the severity of the law as the most heinous of crimes.

CHAPTER XI. THE ELECTORAL SYSTEM

Article 134.—Members of all Soviets of Working People's Deputies— of the Supreme Soviet of the U.S.S.R., the Supreme Soviets of the Union Republics, the Soviets of Working People's Deputies of the Territories and Regions, the Supreme Soviets of the Autonomous Republics, the Soviets of Working People's Deputies of the Autonomous Regions, and the Area, District, City and rural (stanitsa, village, hamlet, kishlak, aul) Soviets of Working People's Deputies—are chosen by the electors on the basis of universal, equal and direct suffrage by secret ballot.

Article 135.—Elections of deputies are universal: all citizens of the U.S.S.R. who have reached the age of eighteen, irrespective of race or nationality, sex, religion, education, domicile, social origin, property status or past activities, have the right to vote in the election of deputies, with the exception of insane persons and persons who have been convicted by a court of law and whose sentences include deprivation of electoral rights.

Every citizen of the U.S.S.R. who has reached the age of twenty-three is eligible for election to the Supreme Soviet of the U.S.S.R., irrespective of race or nationality, sex, religion, education, domicile, social origin, property status or past activities.

Article 136.—Elections of deputies are equal: each citizen has one vote; all citizens participate in elections on an equal footing.

Article 137.—Women have the right to elect and be elected on equal terms with men.

Article 138.—Citizens serving in the Armed Forces of the U.S.S.R. have the right to elect and be elected on equal terms with all other citizens.

Article 139.—Elections of deputies are direct: all Soviets of Working People's Deputies, from rural and city Soviets of Working People's Deputies to the Supreme Soviet of the U.S.S.R., are elected by the citizens by direct vote.

Article 140.—Voting at elections of deputies is secret.

Article 141.—Candidates are nominated by election districts.

The right to nominate candidates is secured to public organizations and societies of the working people: Communist Party organizations, trade unions, co-operatives, youth organizations and cultural societies.

Article 142.—It is the duty of every deputy to report to his electors on his work and on the work of his Soviet of Working People's Deputies, and he may be recalled at any time upon decision of a majority of the electors in the manner established by law.

CHAPTER XII. ARMS, FLAG, CAPITAL

Article 143.—The arms of the Union of Soviet Socialist Republics are a sickle and hammer against a globe depicted in the rays of the sun and surrounded by ears of grain, with the inscription "Workers of All Countries, Unite!" in the languages of the Union Republics. At the top of the arms is a five-pointed star.

Article 144.—The state flag of the Union of Soviet Socialist Republics is of red cloth with the sickle and hammer depicted in gold in the upper corner near the staff and above them a five-pointed red star bordered in gold. The ratio of the width to the length is 1:2.

Article 145.—The Capital of the Union of Soviet Socialist Republics is the City of Moscow.

CHAPTER XIII. PROCEDURE FOR AMENDING THE CONSTITUTION

Article 146.—The Constitution of the U.S.S.R. may be amended only by decision of the Supreme Soviet of the U.S.S.R. adopted by a majority of not less than two-thirds of the votes in each of its Chambers.

Chapter 11

MYTH AND REALITY

In an extraordinary speech that Stalin delivered on November 25, 1936 —set forth herein—after extolling the virtues of the Soviet economic and social systems, he declared that "the Constitution of the U.S.S.R. is the only thoroughly democratic constitution in the world"—a viewpoint echoed by Andrei Vyshinsky, who affirmed that "Soviet democracy and the Soviet state are a million times more democratic than the most democratic bourgeois republic."

The whole question could perhaps be dismissed with the statement that these affirmations must rest on a particular definition of democracy and that the Russians are free to define democracy any way they please. But, in light of the great attraction and appeal of the democratic concept throughout the world—attested to by the use of the term "People's Democracy"—it may be well to consider whether the Russian claim can be supported by any meaningful, rational, and consistent definition of democracy.

To begin with, no honest observer could seriously claim that Soviet practice conforms to the criteria suggested, for example, by Robert M. MacIver:

It was a necessary condition of democracy everywhere that opposing doctrines remained free to express themselves, to seek converts, to form organizations, and so compete for success before the tribunal of public opinion. Any major trend of opinion could thus register itself in the character and in the policies of government.

The "ritualistic exercises in unanimity" of the kind described by Frederick L. Schuman, and reflected in the statistics of the March 16, 1958, elections to the Supreme Soviet (in the pages hereafter), cannot be said to meet these tests. And, it must be noted, in this connection, that Stalin did concede that the 1936 Constitution "leaves unchanged the present leading position of the Communist Party of the U.S.S.R.,"—that is to say, its monopoly of power concentrated in few hands.

What then are the bases upon which the claim of the Soviet regime to democracy may be urged? It is believed that a careful reading of the Stalin

326

and Aleksandrov speeches will indicate that the claim rests upon two propositions.

The first of these is that the Communist Party (through its leadership) has served the interests of the Soviet people by strengthening the power of the nation and bringing to the people great economic and social benefits.

It must be conceded that under the domination of the Communist Party, the U.S.S.R. has realized great advances in industrialization and education, in some cultural areas, and in the eradication of many forms of discrimination and inequality characteristic of the Tsarist period. But, the price paid in suffering and hardship has also been of tremendous magnitude.

Whether the benefits conferred *outweighed the suffering* imposed *is a matter of some importance—which is discussed at various points in this volume—but surely has no relevance to the existence or nonexistence of political democracy in the Soviet Union. The essence of political democracy, in* any *meaningful sense, must certainly lie in* self-government *rather than in service to the interests of the people (although it is of course probably true that in the long run self-government alone will provide good government). If democracy does not involve self-government, but only good government, then the term not only loses all connection with its historic connotations but may be reduced to a manifest absurdity to describe the most thorough-going dictatorship provided only that it is benevolent or enlightened (or, perhaps, only claims to be so).*

The second proposition upon which the Communist claim to democracy may be said to rest is that, because of the "great concord" of the Soviet peoples and in the absence of hostile or antagonistic classes, "there are no grounds for the existence of several parties, and therefore for the existence of freedom of such parties in the U.S.S.R." As recently as April 26, 1958, Nikita Khrushchev, speaking in Kiev, reaffirmed this position of Stalin: "The Party and the people in our country are as one. So why do the Soviet people need other parties? Or are they to be created especially for the people in capitalist countries who are not satisfied with the socialist system?"

Whether it is true in fact that Russia has a classless society in any sense is certainly questionable. (See section in Chapter 13 entitled Who Rules in Russia?*) But, conceding the absence of antagonistic classes in the U.S.S.R. and a "great concord" of the Soviet people on the* ends *defined by Marxism—a large concession for the sake of argument—can it serve to equate the power of a small group of leaders within one Party with "democracy"? Is it really possible to argue in light of the known facts of Soviet history that at all times during the Party's (or Stalin's) monopoly of power, all of the Soviet people were agreed on the* means *to be used to achieve the agreed ends? Were all "as one" on the tempo of industrialization, or on "socialism in one country"; or on aid to World Revolution; or on the dissolution of*

*the Comintern; or on the official attitude toward religion, art, and litera-
ture? Did (and do) good socialists disagree among themselves about these
and myriad other questions—especially in light of occasional drastic shifts
in policy—without finding any legal means to express dissent from official
policy? The answer to these questions is in part given by Khrushchev's
own denunciation of the wanton purges of the 30's based, concededly, on
nothing more than honest disagreement with Stalin.*

*In expressing the viewpoint that in no meaningful sense is it possible
to speak of political democracy in the U.S.S.R., it is not suggested that the
Soviet Constitution as a whole is devoid of significance beyond clothing
"the realities of arbitrary power in the protective garb of tradition and
legitimacy." It does establish the economic basis of the Soviet state and
mark the aspiration for a free and equal society. Whether this will remain
no more than aspiration depends upon many complex factors with which,
in one way or another, various sections of this book are concerned.*

ON THE NEW SOVIET CONSTITUTION

JOSEPH V. STALIN*

THE NEW SOCIETY

The complete victory of the socialist system in all spheres of the national economy is now a fact. This means that exploitation of man by
man is abolished—liquidated—while the socialist ownership of the implements and means of production is established as the unshakable basis of
our Soviet society. (*Loud applause.*)

As a result of all these changes in the national economy of the U.S.S.R.,
we have now a new socialist economy, knowing neither crises nor unemployment, neither poverty nor ruin, and giving to the citizens every possibility to live prosperous and cultured lives.

Such, in the main, are the changes which took place in our economy
during the period from 1924 to 1936. Corresponding to these changes in
the sphere of the economy of the U.S.S.R., the class structure of our society
has also changed. As is known, the landlord class had already been liquidated as a result of the victorious conclusion of the Civil War.

As for the other exploiting classes, they shared the fate of the landlord
class. The capitalist class has ceased to exist in the sphere of industry. The
kulak class has ceased to exist in the sphere of agriculture. The merchants

* From a speech delivered to the Extraordinary Eighth Congress of Soviets on November 25, 1936.

and speculators have ceased to exist in the sphere of distribution. In this way, all exploiting classes are proved to have been liquidated. . . .

What do these changes signify? They signify, first, that the dividing line between the working class and the peasantry, as well as that between these classes and the intelligentsia, is becoming obliterated and that the old class exclusiveness is disappearing. This means that the distance between these social groups is more and more diminishing. They signify, secondly, that the economic contradictions between these social groups is subsiding, is becoming obliterated. They signify, finally, that the political contradictions between them are also subsiding, becoming obliterated. Such is the position concerning the changes in the sphere of class structure in the U.S.S.R.

The picture of the changes in social life in the U.S.S.R. would be incomplete without a few words regarding the changes in another sphere. I have in mind the sphere of national interrelations within the U.S.S.R. As is well known, the Soviet Union comprises about sixty nations, national groups and nationalities. The Soviet state is a multi-national state. . . .

The very absence of the exploiting classes which are the principal organizers of strife among the nationalities, the absence of exploitation, breeding mutual distrust and fanning nationalist passions, the fact that the power is held by the working class, which is the enemy of all enslavement and the faithful bearer of ideas of internationalism, the materialization in reality of mutual aid of the peoples in all fields of economic and social life, and finally the high development of the national culture of the peoples of the U.S.S.R., culture that is national in form and socialist in content—as a result of all these and similar factors, the peoples of the U.S.S.R. have radically changed their characteristics. Their feeling of mutual distrust has disappeared. The feeling of mutual friendship has developed, and thus fraternal cooperation of the peoples has been established in the system of a single union state. As a result, we now have a fully formed multi-national socialist state, which has passed all tests and which has a stability which any national state in any part of the world may well envy. (*Loud applause.*) . . .

THE NEW CONSTITUTION

How are these changes in the life of the U.S.S.R. reflected in the draft of the new Constitution? In other words, what are the main specific features of the draft Constitution submitted for consideration at the present congress? . . .

The draft of the new Constitution of the U.S.S.R. proceeds from the fact of the abolition of the capitalist system, from the fact of the victory of the socialist system in the U.S.S.R.

The main foundation of the draft of the new Constitution of the

U.S.S.R. is formed of the principles of socialism and its chief mainstays, already won and put into practice, namely, the socialist ownership of land, forests, factories, shops and other implements and means of production; abolition of exploitation and exploiting classes; abolition of poverty for the majority and luxury for the minority; abolition of unemployment; work as an obligation and duty and the honor of every able-bodied citizen according to the formula: "He who does not work, neither shall he eat," *i.e.*, the right of every citizen to receive guaranteed work; the right to rest and leisure; the right to education, etc. The draft of the new Constitution rests on these. . . .

The draft of the new Constitution of the U.S.S.R. proceeds from the fact that antagonistic classes no longer exist in our society, that our society consists of two friendly classes: the workers and peasants, that precisely these toiling classes are in power, that the state guidance of society (dictatorship) belongs to the working class as the advanced class of society, that the Constitution is needed to consolidate the social order desired by and of advantage to the toilers. Such is the third specific feature of the draft of the new Constitution. . . .

The draft of the new Constitution of the U.S.S.R. is profoundly international. It proceeds from the premise that all nations and races have equal rights. It proceeds from the premise that color or language differences, differences in cultural level or the level of state development as well as any other difference among nations and races, cannot serve as grounds for justifying national inequality of rights.

It proceeds from the premise that all nations and races irrespective of their past or present position, irrespective of their strength or weakness, must enjoy equal rights in all spheres, economic, social, state and the cultural life of society. Such is the fourth feature of the draft of the new Constitution. The fifth specific feature of the draft of the new Constitution is its consistent and fully sustained democracy. From the viewpoint of democracy, the bourgeois constitutions may be divided into two groups. One group of constitutions openly denies or virtually negates equality of the rights of citizens and democratic liberties. The other group of constitutions willingly accepts and even advertises democratic principles, but in doing so makes such reservations and restrictions that democratic rights and liberties prove to be utterly mutilated.

They talk about equal suffrage for all citizens but immediately limit it by residential, educational and even by property qualifications. They talk about equal rights of citizens, but immediately make the reservation that this does not apply to women, or only partly applies to them, etc. A specific feature of the draft of the new Constitution of the U.S.S.R. is that it is free from such reservations and restrictions.

Active and passive citizens do not exist for it; for it all citizens are active. It recognizes no difference in the rights of men and women, "of fixed abode" and "without fixed abode," with property or without property, educated or uneducated. For it all citizens are equal in their rights. Neither property status nor national origin, nor sex, nor official standing, but only the personal capabilities and personal labor of every citizen determine his position in society.

Finally, there is one other specific feature in the draft of the new Constitution. Bourgeois constitutions usually limit themselves to recording the formal rights of citizens without concerning themselves about the conditions for exercising these rights, about the possibility of exercising them, the means of exercising them. They speak about equality of citizens but forget that real equality between master and workman, between landlord and peasants, is impossible if the former enjoy wealth and political weight in society, while the latter are deprived of both; if the former are exploiters and the latter are exploited.

Or again: they speak of free speech, freedom of assemblage and of the press, but forget that all these liberties may become empty sound for the working class if the latter is deprived of the possibility of having at its command suitable premises for meetings, good printshops, sufficient quantity of paper, etc.

A specific feature of the draft of the new Constitution is that it does not limit itself to recording formal rights of citizens, but transfers the center of gravity to questions of the guarantee of these rights, to the question of the means of exercising them. It does not merely proclaim the equality of the rights of citizens but ensures them by legislative enactment of the fact of liquidation of the regime of exploitation, by the fact of liberation of citizens from any exploitation.

It not only proclaims the right to work, but ensures it by legislative enactment of the fact of non-existence of crises in Soviet society, and the fact of abolition of unemployment. It not merely proclaims democratic liberties but guarantees them in legislative enactments by providing definite material facilities. It is clear, therefore, that the democracy of the new Constitution is not the "usual" and "generally recognized" democracy in general, but socialist democracy. . . .

BOURGEOIS CRITICS OF THE CONSTITUTION

A few words about bourgeois criticism of the draft Constitution. . . . As for the allegation that the Constitution of the U.S.S.R. is an empty promise, a Potemkin village, I would like to refer to a number of established facts which speak for themselves. . . .

After organizing industry and agriculture on new, socialist lines, with a new technical basis, Soviet power brought about such a state of affairs that now agriculture in the U.S.S.R. produces one and a half times more than in pre-war times, industry produces seven times more than pre-war, and the national income has increased fourfold compared to pre-war. All of these are facts and not promises. (*Prolonged applause.*)

The Soviet power abolished unemployment, carried into life the right to work, the right to rest and leisure, and the right to education, ensured better material and cultural conditions for workers, peasants and intellectuals, ensured the introduction of universal, direct and equal suffrage with secret ballot for citizens. All of these are facts and not promises. (*Prolonged applause.*)

Finally, the U.S.S.R. produced a draft of the new Constitution which is not a promise but is a record and legislative enactment of these universally known facts, a record and legislative enactment of what has already been achieved and won. . . .

There is [another] group of critics. . . . This group charges that the draft makes no change in the existing position of the U.S.S.R.; that it leaves the dictatorship of the working class intact, does not provide for freedom of political parties, and preserves the present leading position of the Communist Party of the U.S.S.R. And, at the same time, this group of critics believes that the absence of freedom for parties in the U.S.S.R. is an indication of the violation of the fundamental principles of democracy.

I must admit the draft of the new Constitution really does leave in force the regime of the dictatorship of the working class, and also leaves unchanged the present leading position of the Communist Party of the U.S.S.R. (*Loud applause.*)

If our venerable critics regard this as a shortcoming of the draft Constitution, this can only be regretted. We Bolsheviks, however, consider this as a merit of the draft Constitution. (*Loud applause.*) As for freedom for various political parties, we here adhere to somewhat different views.

The party is part of the class, its vanguard section. Several parties and consequently freedom of parties can only exist in a society where antagonistic classes exist whose interests are hostile and irreconcilable, where there are capitalists and workers, landlords and peasants, kulaks and poor peasants.

But in the U.S.S.R. there are no longer such classes as capitalists, landlords, kulaks, etc. In the U.S.S.R. there are only two classes, workers and peasants, whose interests not only are not antagonistic but, on the contrary, amicable. Consequently there are no grounds for the existence of several parties, and therefore for the existence of freedom of such parties in the U.S.S.R. There are grounds for only one party, the Communist Party, in the U.S.S.R. Only one party can exist, the Communist Party, which boldly defends the interests of the workers and peasants to the very end. And there can hardly be any doubt about the fact that it defends the interests of these classes. (*Loud applause.*)

They talk about democracy. But what is democracy? Democracy in capitalist countries where there are antagonistic classes is in the last analysis democracy for the strong, democracy for the propertied minority. Democracy in the U.S.S.R., on the contrary, is democracy for all. But from this it follows that the principles of democracy are violated not by the draft of the new Constitution of the U.S.S.R. but by the bourgeois constitutions.

That is why I think that the Constitution of the U.S.S.R. is the only thoroughly democratic constitution in the world.

THE PATTERN OF SOVIET DEMOCRACY

G. F. ALEKSANDROV*

All the critics of Soviet democracy are united in one requirement that these people wish to set for so-called "pure," "genuine" democracy. The foreign press—not only newspapers and magazines, but a large number of the books issued in recent years—tiresomely poses one and the same question: if the Bolsheviks are right and they are indeed carrying out democratic principles, why is there only one political party in the Soviet Union? Is not the constant struggle of several parties the sign of "true" democracy? Is not freedom of speech, of assembly, of thought concerning the social system and government policy, not better assured if several political parties compete; if the government policy is carefully considered from the point of view of the interests of various social groups, various political principles and various parties?

This question, as is self-evident, presents several aspects: does the presence of two or more parties bespeak the democratic structure of society? Is the view, widely held today among bourgeois politicians, true that the more parties there are fighting for power, the more perfect and broader the democracy? And finally, do the arrows of the modern critics of Soviet democracy hit the mark when they consider it undemocratic for the people to have a single party?

As is known, the very concept of "democracy" means popular sovereignty in general. The majority of those discussing the question of democracy agree that by democracy is meant a system of political relations within society which assures the development of society and its institutions in the interests of the people and with the participation of the people itself. Glimmers of this thought shine through even the haziest reasoning of the most mystically inclined modern bourgeois philosophers. Consequently,

* Member of the Academy of Sciences of the U.S.S.R. Author of *The History of Western Philosophy*. The selection is from pp. 21-26 of the translation by Leo Gruilow of a speech delivered at a session of the Academy of Sciences on December 4, 1946, and widely distributed in the U.S.S.R. Reprinted with the permission of the publisher, Public Affairs Press, Washington, D. C.

from the historical and social points of view, the character of democracy is revealed not by whether the form of government and the state system are connected with the existence of one, two, or more parties, but by the content of political institutions, the nature of the state and the nature of the internal and foreign policies followed by the state and its governments. For example, who does not know of the abundance of political organizations and the existence of a sharp struggle among social classes and groups in Athens of the fifth and fourth centuries, B.C.? Or of the struggle of various social classes and cliques in ancient Rome? Yet who dares term those cities and the countries they represented, with their slaveholding system of life, examples of democratic organization of society, on the basis of the abundance of competing political groupings?

But is it worth while turning to such ancient examples to prove the falsity, the contrived nature and the artificiality of this "argument" of critics of Soviet democracy? To expose this "argument," constantly cited, lo, these more than twenty years, by all sorts of political sharpers, one can turn to modern history and even to the present situation in those very United States of America or in Great Britain, where in recent years one could gather a whole harvest of all sorts of newly-come "critics," "investigators" and just plain political rowdies—specialists in "democracy."

English and American politicians and social scientists often cite their countries as examples for others, as countries of basically two parties and thereby presumably completely democratic. But in politics one cannot take reasoning of this sort on faith. Why, many labor members of Parliament themselves consider that the Labor and Conservative parties of England *do not differ in principle* on many quite important contemporary questions. Some call themselves Conservative and carry out a frankly imperialistic, expansionist policy; others call themselves Labor, socialists, the workers' party, but often, particularly in the field of foreign relations, carry out the very same policy.

The same can be said concerning the U.S.A. More than thirty years ago Lenin pointed out that the two bourgeois parties in America were distinguished by particular stability and vigor after the civil war over slavery in 1860-65. The party of former slaveholders is the so-called "Democratic Party." The party of the capitalists, standing for emancipation of the Negroes, developed into the "Republican Party."

After the emancipation of the Negroes, the difference between the two parties grew less and less. The struggle of these parties was conducted primarily over the question of higher or lower tariffs. This struggle did *not possess serious* significance for the masses of the people. The people were deceived and deflected from their vital interests by means of the effective and empty *duels* of the two bourgeois parties. This so-called 'two-party system' prevailing in America and England, was one of the most powerful means of hindering the rise of an independent workers', i.e., a truly socialistic, party.[1]

[1] Lenin, *Collected Works* (Russian Edition), Vol. XVI, p. 190.

However, if the modern supporters of "two-party democracy" do not hesitate to put to us any—in their opinion—"tricky" questions, then, on the basis of mutual politeness and those same democratic principles, we Soviet people, in turn, would like to put a few questions to the variegated "specialists" in democracy, to those who love to pose questions: if the existence of two, three or more parties corresponds to a truly democratic way of life, then why, for instance, do the Laborites fight the Conservatives on questions, yet fly into a fury at the mere mention of the English Communists? If the existence of several parties is the real sign of genuine democracy, it would seem sensible and logical to encourage and support any opposition movement in England, and to afford an opportunity for free expression of the views of parties which have not obtained a majority in Parliament. Yet everybody knows that as a matter of fact the Laborites are not guided by this principle; as a matter of fact they strive to dislodge the Conservative Party and, if they could, apparently they would be happy to obtain all the seats in Parliament now held by Conservatives, without particular concern that the existence of one party in Parliament would be a "violation" of democratic principles. No, apparently when the democratic or undemocratic character of the state is discussed, the question is not whether there is one or several parties. Who will believe that certain Laski-type theoreticians of the Labor Party and the other various lovers of "defending" democracy are interested in the existence of their political foes and extension of their foes activity? Yet only thus must one interpret the passionate argument for the necessity of preserving a system of two or more parties in order to preserve democracy! No, the point is merely that today the Laborites still lack the strength to finish off their political foes in the electoral struggle and to win over the whole of society to their side.

That is why it seems entirely probable that the thesis of identity between democracy and the struggle of two or more parties within society is the thesis of those who today are in no position to win over to their side the majority of society; the thesis of those who know that in the conditions of bourgeois society, that is, in the conditions in which society lives and develops on the basis of a struggle of diverse social classes, there can be no place for a single party which would express with equal success the interests of opposed social classes. As long as antagonistic class society exists, the struggle among various political parties, expressing the struggle of classes, is inevitable. In this and only in this lies the essence of the question so often asked in foreign literature: is democracy compatible with a one-party system? Is not the existence of several parties in society the sign of true, genuine democracy?

We Soviet people give a clear and unequivocal answer: no, it is not. The democratic or anti-democratic nature of public life, of a state, of a government's policy, is determined not by the number of parties but by the substance of the policy of this state, of these parties—by whether this or that policy is carried out in the interests of the people, in the interests of its overwhelming majority, or in the interests of its minority. That is how matters stand with regard to the first question—whether democracy coincides with the existence of one or several parties in society.

It is natural that all the arguments of the foreign "specialists" in democracy revolve around the question of one party in the Soviet Union. For what relationship does the realization of the truly democratic principles of socialist society bear to the position of leadership held in this society by the one and only party, namely, the Communist Party? . . .

Soviet democracy expresses the principles of a socialist society. As is known, socialist society begins where and when the exploiting classes—landowners, manufacturers, financial magnates, bankers, kulaks, speculators and other social groups living on unearned income—cease to exist, and society begins to develop on the basis of a friendly alliance of the workers, peasants and intelligentsia. As long as exploiting classes exist, they strive to protect their political interests in society, to create their political organizations and to have their own parties for the protection of their private interests and the subordination of the interests of society to the interests of the given clique or social group. But after the new social order, namely, the socialist order, triumphs in all fields, no place remains in society for the classes oppressing other classes: the time comes of a great concord of the people and the creation of the deepest unity of all society. In this period the former need and the former necessity for the existence of divergent political parties disappears.

That party which is best able to express the deepest fundamental interests of the whole of society and can point the way to the quickest practical plan for establishing the foundations of a new life—a life without exploiters and parasites; that party which, by its organizational work, is able to rally around it all of society, and lead it along the new paths of building communism; that party, finally, which by its devoted, self-sacrificing service to the people has won unquestionable and undisputed authority throughout the whole of society—that particular party can express historically the deepest desires, life aims and ideals of the tremendous majority of the population of the country. It is precisely in this historical situation that the necessity and any possibility for the existence of divergent parties in society disappears completely. In the Soviet Union such a single party really exists and works for the welfare of the people—the party of the Communists, the Leninist party, guided by its leader, Comrade Stalin. The Soviet people have linked themselves with the party of the Bolsheviks and have adopted its program and ideas for their own.

Any other party that might arise in Soviet society could have only one program: a program of return to the past, to the old, to the life liquidated by our people: a program of struggle against socialism.

THE POLITY OF OLIGARCHY

FREDERICK L. SCHUMAN*

1. UNION OF SOVIETS

. . . In the Soviet system of power, elected law-makers have long been dominated by executive policy-makers named by the Party, with the shadow of terror never remote. In turn, the Party—and State and nation as well— have been dominated during most of four decades by the Leader, even though the great and good Lenin and the great and bad Stalin are now both dead and the "cult of the individual" has given way to *Kollectivnost:* collective or collegial leadership. Here, as elsewhere among men, the naked and ugly realities of power have been suitably garbed in seemly raiment to persuade those from whom obedience is expected that the regime is not a mere aggregation of arbitrary and self-chosen despots but is a dedicated group of guardians of a Supreme Law, devoted to Political Truth, Civic Virtue, and the Common Good. The devices of bourgeois "constitution-alism" have often fulfilled this function in the West. They were borrowed early by the Marxist rulers of Muscovy to serve this need and were elaborated into "the most democratic constitution in the world" precisely during the bloodiest years of the terror. . . .

Between 1929 and 1935 the economic and social order of the U.S.S.R. underwent the most drastic transformation that has ever occurred in a similar period in any major community. In the Soviet Union, as elsewhere, political practices deeply imbedded in the habits of rulers and ruled change less rapidly than the texture of social living and the activities by which men and women earn their daily bread. Political vocabularies, with their sacred stereotypes and highly emotionalized symbols and slogans, are modified even more slowly. Political man, even when a citizen of a revolutionary State, is a conservative animal. Communists, however, pride themselves on their energy as innovators and swear by the Marxist dictum that political institutions are but the superstructure of class relations flowing out of prevailing modes of production. The collectivization of agriculture and the tremendous upsurge of industrialization, accompanied by crises and convulsions, transformed Soviet society and economy almost beyond

* Woodrow Wilson Professor of Government, Williams College. Author of *The Commonwealth of Man; Night Over Europe;* and *Europe on the Eve.* The selection is reprinted from chapter 7 of *Russia Since 1917* by Frederick L. Schuman, by permission of Alfred A. Knopf, Inc. Copyright 1957 by the author.

recognition. The Party leadership therefore concluded in the course of the Second Five Year Plan that the constitutional structure dating from the early period of the NEP was no longer appropriate to the needs of a new epoch.

The Seventh All-Union Congress of Soviets voted on February 6, 1935, to appoint a Constitution Commission to draw up an amended text embodying equal suffrage, direct election, secret ballot, and recognition of "the present relation of class forces" in the light of the growth of socialist industry, the end of the kulaks, and the triumph of collectivization. On the next day the CEC named a Commission of 31 to draft a new document. Stalin became its president. In June 1936 the completed draft was published in hundreds of thousands of copies and in all languages of the U.S.S.R. General discussion was encouraged and almost demanded by the Party leaders. Over half a million meetings were held, attended by no less than 36,000,000 people. After many thousands of proposed changes were sifted out, 150 were given serious consideration and 43 were adopted.

At the Extraordinary Eighth Congress of Soviets on November 25, 1936, Stalin delivered a lengthy address on the revised draft. He dwelt first on the changes of recent years which had "eliminated all the exploiting classes"; "transformed the proletariat into the working class of the U.S.S.R., which has abolished the capitalist economic system, has established the socialist ownership of the instruments and means of production, and is directing Soviet society along the road to communism"; converted the peasants into collective farmers, "emancipated from exploitation"; and established a new Soviet Intelligentsia, serving the masses. The new Constitution, continued Stalin, must not be a program of the future—e.g., the achievement of communism—but a "summary of the gains already achieved"—e.g., socialism. . . .

On December 1, 1936, the deputies unanimously adopted a Resolution (*Izvestia,* December 2, 1936) approving the draft and appointing an Editorial Commission of 220 members to put it in final form. . . .

For these gains, declared Y. A. Yakovlev, "we are obliged to the best Leninist, the creator of the new Constitution, the great son of the Soviet people of whom our nation is proud, who in the family of every worker and peasant is called the father of toilers—our leader, Comrade Stalin!" (Ovation.)

In addressing the Congress on the same day, Nikita S. Khrushchev, a member of the Politburo, declared (*Izvestia,* December 2, 1936):

> The Fascists, especially the German, are now shouting about their triumph over Marxism, but this "triumph" is one of jesters and clowns of the Middle Ages. And here we are accepting our Constitution and celebrating the victory of Marxism-Leninism-Stalinism, a victory which is not only ours but is also that of toilers the world over. . . . The German Fascists have illusions about the breakdown of our Socialist State and they rave about seizing lands to the East. . . . If the Fascists

Lenin and Stalin in 1922.

Premier G. M. Malenkov and N. S. Khrushchev at a collective farm in 1954.

Rules on elections to the Supreme Soviet are being read to collective farmers **in** Kirghiz.

A meeting of workers in Moscow in 1950 as Stalin consents to stand for election to the Supreme Soviet.

The Twentieth Congress of the Communist Party in 1956.

A meeting of the Supreme Soviet of the Russian Socialist Federated Soviet Republic in the Kremlin.

and 1 for each National Region. Its membership was 574 at the outset and 713 by 1941. [Its membership was 640 in 1958.] All federal legislation requires a majority vote in each house. The two chambers, meeting jointly, choose a Presidium of 42 members, headed by a President (Kalinin). The Presidium has 15 (originally 11) Vice-Presidents, one for each Union Republic. The Supreme Soviet is normally convened by its Presidium twice a year, with special sessions meeting on the call of the Presidium or of any one of the Republics. The Supreme Soviet appoints the Union Sovnarkom, consisting at the outset of 25 Union Commissariats and 15 Union-Republican Commissariats.

The Soviet Constitution, unlike that of the United States, does not purport to establish what is generally termed a "presidential" system of government. Its scheme (on paper) comes closer to a "parliamentary" system, comparable to that of the United Kingdom, the French Republic, the Weimar Republic, and other Continental democracies. . . .

On paper this design for power establishes a completely democratic system of government by all modern definitions of democracy. It was currently hailed in the U.S.S.R. as "the most democratic constitution in the world." To what extent and in what sense, if any, it has been a vehicle of democracy in its actual operation will be considered below. . . .

2. THE SOCIALIST STATE

. . . Here the fiction of the "dictatorship of the proletariat" confronted the fact of rulership by a managerial elite. Here the juridical theory of a government by Soviets, local, regional, and national, faced the practice of the monolithic and monopolistic oligarchy of the Party. Within the Party, Lenin's concept of "democratic centralism," postulating the responsibility of the leaders to the led, gave way to Stalin's totalitarian machine, ruthlessly exacting obedience from the led to the leaders. Within the leadership, collective deliberations and decisions often gave way, prior to Stalin's demise, to a species of Cæsarism.

Any account of government in the U.S.S.R. must, if it is to do justice to reality, simultaneously take account of the paradoxes and avoid their exaggeration into the totality of Soviet political experience. Whether the comments to follow will achieve this goal is doubtful, but they will at least be directed toward its attainment.

As regards the "federal" character of the Soviet Union and of its largest unit, the Russian Socialist Federated Soviet Republics, Communist publicists claimed from the outset that Soviet federalism represented the final resolution of the "nationality problem" of the Tsarist Empire, with its scores of ethnic groups and its pogroms, oppressions, and efforts at "Russification." A new day allegedly dawned, suffused with the light of tolerance, equality, and brotherhood among equals—reflected, as of 1941, in the formal existence within the RSFSR of 15 "Autonomous Soviet Socialist Republics (ASSR), of 6 "autonomous regions" (AR), and 9 "National Districts," plus 2 ASSR's (Adzhar and Abkhazian) and 1 AR (South Ossetian) in Georgia, 1 ASSR (Nakhichevan) and 1 AR (Nagorno-Karabakh) in Azerbaijan, 1 ASSR (Kara-Kalpak) in Uzbekistan, and 1 AR (Gorno-Badakhan) in Tadjikistan.

Within these far-flung Eurasian areas of mixed populations and many national minorities, peace and harmony were officially declared to be assured by autonomy and "self-determination" for all, each enjoying its own language and culture "national in form, but proletarian in content," and all united in a federation of "Union Republics"—ultimately 16 in number, including Estonia, Latvia, Lithuania, and Moldavia, annexed in 1940, and reduced to 15 in July 1956 with the absorption of the Karelo-Finnish SSR, the smallest in population, into the RSFSR. . . .

To what degree has "Soviet federalism" been a reality and to what degree a fiction among the national groups of the U.S.S.R.? The letter of the law is clear. Art. 123 of the Constitution of 1936 asserts:

> Equality of rights of citizens of the U.S.S.R., irrespective of their nationality or race, in all spheres of economic, State, cultural, social, and political life, is an indefeasible law. Any direct or indirect restriction of the rights of, or, conversely, any establishment of direct or indirect privileges for, citizens on account of their race or nationality, as well as any advocacy of racial or national exclusiveness or hatred and contempt, is punishable by law.

In pursuit of this aspiration, Soviet policy-makers brought literacy to the "backward peoples" of the Caucasus and Central Asia, often in Latin alphabets to begin with and later in Cyrillic alphabets. The forgotten men of Transcaucasia, Turkestan, and remote Siberia not only learned how to read and write their own tongues but came into possession of schools, libraries, hospitals, and factories, with resulting living standards far above those of other Asian peoples beyond the Soviet frontier. In all the ordinary social and civic relationships among human beings, Soviet society—in this respect, at least, conforming to the highest ideals of Christianity and liberalism—achieved at times an approximation to complete freedom from racial and national prejudice and discrimination.

But if the question be posed as to whether "federalism" in the Western sense—i.e., a formula for uniting separate sovereignties into a union in which each yields certain powers to a common authority and retains all others in local autonomy—is a reality of political life in the U.S.S.R., the only possible verdict must be a negative one. . . .

The Soviet scheme of government embodies on paper many of the attributes of federalism. The 1936 Constitution describes the U.S.S.R. as "a federal State formed on the basis of the voluntary association of Soviet Socialist Republics, having equal rights" (§13). Twenty-three federal powers are enumerated, with all others left to the Republics (§§14-15). The

Soviet equivalent of Article VI of the American Constitution is found (cf. Appendix) in §§19, 20, 105, and 130, by which the primacy of federal law is assured. Amendments to the Union Constitution (§146) require a two-thirds vote of each chamber of the Supreme Soviet but do not, as in the United States, require ratification by state legislatures—i.e., the Supreme Soviets of the Union Republics. These, however, are equally represented in the Soviet of Nationalities and in theory (§17) could secede if dissatisfied with a constitutional amendment. In a semantic *tour de force,* Stalin and his collaborators, in framing the Union Constitution of 1936, provided for an unqualified right of secession. "Of course," commented Stalin (November 25, 1936) in a masterpiece of understatement, "none of our Republics would actually raise the question of seceding from the U.S.S.R."

In practice Soviet "federalism" has been, from beginning to end, a pretense. Repeatedly over the years boundaries have been changed (e.g., the transfer of the Crimea from the RSFSR to the Ukraine in February 1954, and the absorption of the Karelo-Finnish SSR into the RSFSR in July 1956), the division of powers has been altered, and whole populations have been uprooted not through any "federal" procedure of decision-making but by joint decrees of the Union Sovnarkom or Council of Ministers and the Central Committee of the Party. In his indictment of Stalin (February 24-5, 1956), Khrushchev noted indignantly that in 1943-4, on the order of the *Vozhd,* all the people of the Karachai AR, and of the Kalmyk, Chechen-Ingush, and Kabardino-Balkar ASSR's were deported to Asia, along with the inhabitants of the Crimean Tartar and Volga German ASSR's, both unmentioned by Khrushchev.

The Ukrainians avoided meeting this fate only because there were too many of them and there was no place to which to deport them. . . . Not only a Marxist-Leninist but also no man of common sense can grasp how it is possible to make whole nations responsible for inimical activity, including women, children, old people, Communists, and Komsomols, to use mass repression against them, and to expose them to misery and suffering for the hostile acts of individual persons or groups of persons.

In Stalin's last years, moreover, anti-Semitism and other forms of discrimination against minority peoples became a marked feature, despite semantic disguises, of the official conduct of Soviet policy-makers. In happier days to come, federalism may be given practical meaning in the public law and political life of the U.S.S.R. During most of the unhappy past it has been a fiction or a fraud.*

* Joshua Kunitz, in his otherwise perceptive and illuminating essay "The Jewish Problem in the USSR" (*Monthly Review,* March and April 1953), argues that *popular* anti-Semitism was widespread after 1945 but that no *official* anti-Semitism existed. It is doubtless true that no individuals were persecuted or discriminated against because of Jewish origin *per se,* provided that they were willing to renounce their Jewish religious and cultural heritage. But Party and Government alike, prior to Stalin's demise, savagely attacked not only political Zionism, or even the slightest supicion thereof, but suppressed

A like judgment is warranted by the record on many other aspects of the theory of Soviet governance in contrast to the practice of the arts of power by the oligarchs. On paper the Soviet Constitution establishes a "parliamentary" system on the British and Continental model. Cabinets in both the U.S.S.R. and the Union Republics are chosen by, and from, the freely elected members of legislative bodies and may, in principle, be altered or displaced by the deputies who appoint them. In fact any such relationship is wholly contrary to reality. The persisting pattern of Soviet public life, still unaltered in 1957 despite hopes and prospects of change, was formerly established by the oligarchs in 1937. Its genesis therefore merits review.

The first election held under the 1936 Constitution took place on December 12, 1937, for the new Supreme Soviet. In preparation for the event the old federal CEC appointed a Central Electoral Commission, which directed a hierarchy of local commissions in registering voters and candidates, conducting propaganda, supervising the preparation of ballots, envelopes, and ballot boxes, counting the ballots, and announcing the results. Electoral districts, established at least 45 days before the election, were to be fixed by the CEC and subsequently by the Supreme Soviet itself. For purposes of registering voters and casting and counting ballots (but not for purposes of representation) the RSFSR was divided into 93,927 precincts, of which 2,047 were on boats. The population of some of the urban precincts was as large as 150,000, while districts in the lesser Republics varied between 5,000 and 20,000 inhabitants.

Candidates were proposed in the constituencies by trade unions, cooperatives, Komsomol units, cultural societies, army regiments, collective farms, and the primary organizations of the Party, with the latter in most instances advising other groups in areas where it was decided not to nominate a Party member. No candidate could be nominated by an individual, but all voters were entitled to attend meetings where nominees were proposed. Efforts of church congregations to propose candidates were disallowed by the Electoral Commission. Procedure conformed closely to the Election Regulations later issued by the Supreme Soviet. Voting lists were compiled by agents of city and rural Soviets on the basis of house rolls, membership lists of collective farms, and personal canvassing. In the absence of any residence requirement, all temporary and permanent inhabitants were listed alphabetically in each precinct. Those moving before election day or engaged in travel were granted certificates by local Soviets, entitling them to vote wherever they might be. The lists thus compiled were posted in local Soviet HQ 30 days before the election. All citizens were entitled to complain of omissions or errors, with each complaint to be

all manifestations of Hebrew or Yiddish culture, even to the extent of executing, on trumped-up charges, numerous Yiddish writers and artists. Amends have since been made. The realities of 1948-53, however, suggest that Kunitz's dichotomy is a distinction without a difference. Cf. Solomon M. Schwarz: *The Jews in the Soviet Union* (Syracuse University Press, 1953).

dealt with inside of 3 days by the Soviet Executive Committee, with appeal to the People's Courts, which were required to reach a decision in open hearings within 3 days in the presence of the complainant and a representative of the Soviet.

Qualifications for candidates were the same as those for voters, except that no candidate could be a member of an Electoral Commission and each was required to consent in writing to be a nominee. The names of proposed candidates were to be published in the local press 25 days before the election. Ballots were to be printed 15 days before the election. In most districts several candidates were proposed, usually by acclamation in the various nominating groups. But in all districts only one candidate for each seat in the Soviet of the Union and the Soviet of Nationalities (1,143 in all) appeared on the ballot. Of the total thus nominated, 37 were dropped and replaced by others, on the order of the Central Electoral Commission. This elimination of all but one candidate normally took place within the 10 days between the publishing of names and the printing of ballots. The procedure was nowhere set forth by law or decree. It amounted to a highly informal "primary," inevitably guided by the local Party members. The choice of deputies was thus made not at the election but during the campaign in the name of a "bloc of Party and non-Party people." Of the 569 candidates for the Soviet of the Union, 81% (and of the 574 candidates for the Soviet of Nationalities, 71%) were members or candidates of the Party. Others were designated as "non-Party Bolshevists."

Soviet theory continued to anticipate multiple nominations for membership in the Supreme Soviet. The statutes provided for "run-off" elections two weeks after the original polling if less than half of the registered voters cast ballots or if no candidate received an absolute majority. While it does not appear that this familiar democratic device, or the constitutional right of popular recall, has ever been applied to federal offices, the possibility of at least 3 candidates for a single seat was clearly contemplated. Mayors of cities were at this period elected by popular choice through secret ballot from among four or five candidates. The same was true for members of village and urban Soviets, in which non-Party members usually constitute two-thirds or three-quarters of the deputies.

If the first federal election day was a gala occasion, the preceding nation-wide campaign to get out the vote had all the earmarks of an educational crusade. . . . The goals were unanimity now and solidarity forever. Polls were open from 6 A.M. until midnight. Moscow and other cities were aglow with bunting, garlands, and flags. Stalin, Molotov, and Voroshilov voted in precinct 58 of the Lenin election district of the capital. Others voted by millions in town and countryside, in lonely villages and remote valleys, in Arctic outposts and desert oases, on ships at sea, and even at railway stations, where booths were set up for passengers in transit.

Of the 93,639,458 enfranchised Soviet citizens, 90,319,436, or 96%, cast ballots. Of the ballots for deputies to the Soviet of the Union, 636,808 were invalid and 632,074 had names crossed out. In electing the members of the Soviet of Nationalities, the voters cast 1,487,582 invalid ballots and crossed out names in 562,402 instances. . . .

The pattern thus established was followed undeviatingly up to the 40th anniversary of the October Revolution. To Western liberals, it is a travesty of representative democracy, since there can plainly be no effective freedom or representation or democracy in ritualistic exercises in unanimity. To many Russians, unfamiliar with Western ways or disposed to regard them as "bourgeois frauds," the ceremonials perhaps recall with nostalgia and gratitude the age-long search of the Slavs for unity in the face of schisms within and hostility from without—reflected paradoxically in the *liberum veto* in the Diet of the old Kingdom of Poland and in the requirement of unanimity for major decisions in the ancient Russian *Veche* or Assembly. As recently as 1956, when portents of a new dispensation were numerous, only one name for each office appeared on Soviet ballots, even in neighborhood "elections" of judges of the local People's Courts and of their two lay assistants, all chosen for two-year terms and most of them, incidentally, women.

On March 14, 1954, the ritual was repeated, with 120,727,826 voters (out of 120,750,816) choosing 708 and 639 deputies, respectively, for the two chambers of the Supreme Soviet, of whom 1,050 were Party members, 297 were non-Party, and 348 were women, with the proportions of non-Party deputies and women deputies almost identical in the two houses. [Editor's note: For the results of the March 1958 election see the following article.]

Soviet legislative procedure has, thus far, followed a comparable pattern. Soviet "law-makers" are not salaried officials but part-time deputies with other jobs, paid travel expenses and *per-diem* allowances out of public revenue. On the federal, Republican, and local levels, they hear and consider legislative proposals presented by the Ministers, listen to reports and speeches, rarely advance proposals of their own, discuss bills in committees, but in their final "decisions" always vote unanimously in favor of whatever projects the Party leadership has resolved to adopt as public policy. Their function, not unlike that of Western parliamentarians in this respect, is to reflect local expectations, demands, grievances, and hopes, and to act as *liaison* agents between the Party leadership and administrative bureaucracy, on the one hand, and their constituents on the other. But they have possessed, thus far, no powers of decision, save insofar as their advice may influence the judgment of the top-level oligarchs whose ultimate conclusions have long been sacrosanct on the premise (long unquestioned but vaguely acknowledged to be dubious and dangerous since Stalin's demise) that the Party is infallible and therefore above criticism or challenge. . . .

3. THE RIGHTS OF MAN

Within the limits of oligarchy, what are the realities and what are the fictions of the "constitutional rights" of Soviet citizens as elaborately set forth in Chapters X and XI of the Charter of 1936? The answer is less simple than many Western commentators have assumed. "Real liberty," declared Stalin to Roy Howard (cf. *Izvestia*, December 8, 1936), "can be had only where exploitation is destroyed, where there is no oppression of one people by another, where there is no unemployment and pauperism, where a person does not shiver in fear of losing tomorrow his job, home, bread. Only in such a society is it possible to have real, and not paper, liberty, personal and otherwise."

This "reality" proved meaningless over many years to the millions of Soviet citizens arrested by agents of the OGPU, NKVD, or MVD and consigned to forced-labor camps in Siberia and the Far North, where only the hardiest survived the rigors of arduous work, meager diet, miserable living conditions, and systematic terrorization and exploitation—pending the amnesties, relaxations, and "mellowing" of the police-state regime since Stalin's death.

Many other rights solemnly guaranteed by the Supreme Law of Soviet-land remained "dead letters" during most of the two decades after 1936. Freedom of speech, press, assembly, and association (§§125, 126) and inviolability of persons, homes, and correspondence (§§127, 128) were often honored more in the breach than in the observance, as was acknowledged at Party Congress XX and thereafter. The same was true of intellectual, scientific, and academic freedom, particularly in the black years of Stalin's posturing as the infallible source of all truth and taste—when the *Vozhd* and his agents felt in duty bound to impose "Socialist Realism" on writers, artists, and musicians, Lysenko's fantasies on biologists, "Marxist physics" on other scientists, etc. Political privileges (§§134-42) have been less rights than duties, and have, in any case, only a tangential relationship to public policy-making and the selection of representatives. The independence of the courts (§112) and the protection of the individual against arbitrary arrest, imprisonment, or execution (§§111, 127, 128) remained fictitious so long as the MVD possessed the right to punish alleged political offenders without public trial, so long as the criminal code permitted penalization "by analogy" of acts not defined as crimes but held dangerous to the State, so long as the death penalty was prescribed (as in the act of August 7, 1932) for theft of public property, and so long as the full rigors of the criminal code were made applicable (as in the act of April 7, 1935) to juvenile delinquents.

Freedom of conscience and worship (§124), or the lack thereof, have undergone many vicissitudes during the four decades of Soviet power. The sequence began with open persecution by a regime of atheists of many churchmen and believers during the years when the established Orthodox Church, smarting from Soviet disestablishment and dispossession of most of its wealth, championed Autocracy and the cause of the White Armies. The charter of 1936 re-enfranchised the clergy. The "League of the Militant Godless," founded in 1925 and directed by Emilian Yaroslavsky, claimed 10,000,000 members by 1932 but had declined to 3,000,000 by 1940. When Communist efforts to extirpate religion had clearly failed and the new Church patriotically rallied to the defense of the State against the Nazi invaders, the League was dissolved and its publishing facilities were transferred to the Orthodox priesthood. On September 12, 1943, an officially sponsored *Sobor* elected Metropolitan Sergei of Moscow Patriarch of all Russia. Upon his death a new *Sobor* in January 1945 elected Metropolitan Alexei as Patriarch. Meanwhile, in October of 1943 a State Council on Church Affairs, headed by Georgi Karpov, was set up to promote "genuine religious freedom."

Any congregation willing to pay the salary of a cleric and the costs of building maintenance may conduct services in church, mosque, or synagogue. But religious instruction of the young outside of home is still (1957) forbidden. No church receives any financial aid from the State save for the restoration and upkeep of ecclesiastical structures of historic or artistic importance—most of which, however, are without congregations and have been converted into museums. Under these circumstances religious life languishes despite formal freedom of worship.

Soviet citizens enjoy certain other "constitutional rights" that are more substance than shadow. Individual and collective property rights, along with rights of ownership and inheritance of income, personal property, savings, and private houses (§§7-10), appear to be well respected within the limits already indicated. The major social gains of the Revolution are embodied (§§118-20) in the rights to work, to paid vacations, to insurance against illness and old age, and to free dental and medical service, including access to hospitals and sanatoria. The social-insurance system, administered by the trade unions, and socialized medicine, directed by the Ministry of Health, are among the significant contributions of the Soviet State to the welfare of the people. The number of physicians increased from 20,000 in 1913 to 63,000 in 1928, 141,000 in 1941 (January 1), and 299,000 in 1955 (July 1), with lesser health workers, including *feldshers* (medical aides) and nurses, increasing from 393,200 in 1941 to 731,100 in 1955. Death rates declined from 18.3 per thousand population in 1940 to 9.6 in 1950, 9.0 in 1953, and 8.4 in 1955, while birth rates for the corresponding years were reported as 31.7, 26.5, 24.9, and 25.6.

Equality of rights for women, including equal access to all vocations and identical status with men as to salaries, vacations, social insurance, and education, plus "pre-maternity and maternity leave with full pay" (§122), is also a fact and not a fiction. Early Soviet legislation made marriage and

apartments for all of the faculty and much of the student body of 22,000. The Stalinist State, having in some measure expiated the crimes committed in its name by educating Russia, was in process, four decades after 1917, of ceasing to be a Stalinist State.

OFFICIAL RETURNS ON 1958 ELECTION TO SUPREME SOVIET

CENTRAL ELECTION COMMISSION*

Throughout March 17-18 the Central Election Commission received from all the constituency election commissions for the elections to the Soviet of the Union and the Soviet of Nationalities the complete figures on the returns of the elections to the fifth U.S.S.R. Supreme Soviet.

The total electorate for the U.S.S.R. has been established at 133,836,-325, of which 133,796,091, or 99.97 per cent of the total, took part in the elections of the U.S.S.R. Supreme Soviet deputies.

In all the constituencies for elections to the Soviet of the Union the candidates of the people's Communist and non-Party bloc polled 133,214,-652, or 99.57 per cent of the total number of ballots cast, while 580,641 ballots were cast against the candidates for deputy to the Soviet of the Union. Under Article 88 of the Regulations Governing the Elections to the U.S.S.R. Supreme Soviet, 798 ballots were declared invalid.

In all the constituencies for elections to the Soviet of Nationalities the candidates of the people's Communist and non-Party bloc polled 133,431,-524, or 99.73 per cent of the total number of votes cast, while 363,736 ballots were cast against them. Under Article 88 of the Regulations Governing the Elections to the U.S.S.R. Supreme Soviet 831 ballots were declared invalid.

For the Union Republics the returns of the elections to the U.S.S.R. Supreme Soviet are as follows:

* This is from an official translation of an announcement that appeared in *Pravda* on March 19, 1958.

| Union Republic | Number of voters | Went to the Polls | |
		In figures	In percentage of voters
Russian Federation.....	76,271,336	76,243,637	99.96
Ukraine..............	27,989,652	27,984,894	99.98
Byelorussia...........	5,277,630	5,276,902	99.99
Uzbekistan...........	4,409,068	4,408,655	99.99
Kazakhstan...........	5,282,391	5,282,055	99.99
Georgia..............	2,547,637	2,547,588	99.99
Azerbaijan...........	2,111,707	2,111,243	99.98
Lithuania............	1,736,751	1,735,999	99.96
Moldavia............	1,697,111	1,696,659	99.97
Latvia...............	1,528,864	1,527,687	99.92
Kirghizia............	1,162,353	1,162,180	99.99
Tajikistan...........	1,070,965	1,070,945	99.99
Armenia.............	1,009,013	1,008,853	99.98
Turkmenia...........	856,251	856,174	99.99
Estonia..............	885,596	882,620	99.66
Total for U.S.S.R.:	133,836,325	133,796,091	99.97

| Union Republic | Voted for Candidates of Communist and Non-Party Bloc | | | |
| | Soviet of the Union | | Soviet of Nationalities | |
	In figures	In percentage of ballots cast	In figures	In percentage of ballots cast
Russian Federation.....	75,785,506	99.40	75,988,512	99.67
Ukraine.............	27,936,040	99.83	27,946,035	99.86
Byelorussia..........	5,268,396	99.84	5,267,110	99.81
Uzbekistan..........	4,399,674	99.80	4,400,279	99.81
Kazakhstan..........	5,261,950	99.62	5,256,038	99.51
Georgia.............	2,546,296	99.95	2,545,960	99.94
Azerbaijan...........	2,105,964	99.75	2,107,898	99.84
Lithuania............	1,734,404	99.91	1,734,133	99.89
Moldavia............	1,685,349	99.33	1,694,271	99.86
Latvia...............	1,526,275	99.91	1,526,183	99.90
Kirghizia............	1,158,144	99.65	1,157,300	99.58
Tajikistan...........	1,068,926	99.81	1,067,900	99.72
Armenia.............	1,006,625	99.78	1,007,300	99.85
Turkmenia...........	852,428	99.56	853,632	99.70
Estonia.............	878,675	99.55	878,973	99.59
Total for U.S.S.R.:	133,214,652	99.57	133,431,524	99.73

In all the constituencies for elections to the Soviet of Nationalities from the autonomous republics, autonomous regions and national areas, of the total electorate of 11,618,853 people 11,616,306, or 99.98 per cent of the total, went to the polls. The candidates of the people's Communist and non-Party bloc running in these constituencies polled 11,500,546, or 99.43 per cent of the total number of ballots cast, while 65,704 ballots

were cast against the candidates running for deputy to the Soviet of Nationalities from the autonomous republics, autonomous regions and national areas. Under Article 88 of the Regulations Governing the Elections
to the U.S.S.R. Supreme Soviet 56 ballots were declared invalid.

The Central Election Commission has examined the materials for each
constituency individually and under Article 38 of the Regulations Governing the Elections to the U.S.S.R. Supreme Soviet has registered the election
of deputies to the U.S.S.R. Supreme Soviet in all 1,378 constituencies. This
includes 738 deputies elected to the Soviet of the Union and 640 deputies
elected to the Soviet of Nationalities.

Chapter 12

The Role of Terror

In Chapter 6, entitled "Ends and Means," the discussion was concerned primarily with the theoretical position of Lenin and Trotsky on the interrelation of Marxist ends and revolutionary and terrorist means in the seizure and holding of power. In this section, we are principally concerned with the institutionalization of terror as a system of power in the U.S.S.R.

One of the most provocative explanations of the role of terror in a modern state appears in Barrington Moore, Jr., Terror and Progress, U.S.S.R. *He suggests that organized terror*

. . . does not stem from any particular type of economic structure, but from the attempt to alter the structure of society at a rapid rate and from above through forceful administrative devices. The essence of the situation appears to lie in the crusading spirit, the fanatical conviction in the justice and universal applicability of some ideal about the way life should be organized, along with a lack of serious concern about the consequences of the methods used to pursue this ideal. . . . The attempt to change institutions rapidly nearly always results in opposition by established interests. The more rapid and more thorough the change, the more extensive and bitter is the opposition likely to be. Hence organized terror becomes necessary. . . .

Whether spontaneous or forced, a rapid pace of change is likely to produce wide-spread human suffering. Hence the situation in which a socialist regime comes to power is crucial in determining the probabilities of terror, as is widely recognized in socialist writings. If the socialists are content to take over the situation left by their predecessors without making fundamental changes, relatively little terror may be needed. This was the situation originally anticipated in Marxist theory, where terror would merely brush away the remnants of the old order. If, on the other hand, socialism is to be dynamic after it has come to power, it is likely to require the constant application of terror, both against the population at large and dissidents within its own ranks. Its commitment to terror is as great as its commitment to change that goes against the habits and desires of various sectors of the population.

TERROR AS A SYSTEM OF POWER

MERLE FAINSOD*

Terror is the linchpin of modern totalitarianism. What distinguishes twentieth-century totalitarianism from earlier patterns of more primitive dictatorship is not the use of terror and a secret police as instruments of control but rather their high development as an organized system of power. With the emergence of totalitarianism, terror has become elaborately institutionalized, has developed its own bureaucratic apparatus and specialized professionalisms, and has spread its net over the whole range of society. The large-scale organizational rationalization of the totalitarian terror machine introduces a new dimension of cold-blooded efficiency and calculated violence in comparison with which even the Jacobin terror takes on the character of a spontaneous and chaotic *Jacquerie.*

This does not mean that terror is the only method by which a totalitarian regime maintains itself in power. Loyalty and devotion must also be elicited. The skillful totalitarian dictator weaves a complex web of controls in which indoctrination and incentives have their appointed places. Agitation and propaganda may rally fanatic support, and appeals to self-interest may enlist the energies of the ambitious and bind their fortunes to the regime. When discontent accumulates, "loyalty" to the regime may be consolidated by providing scapegoats on whom frustrated aggression may exhaust itself. The shrewd totalitarian dictatorship may go further and permit ventilation of grievances of a nonpolitical and nonorganized character. It may even institutionalize such expression as the Soviet dictatorship does when it sanctions criticism of bureaucratic malpractice or inefficiency. Such criticism may play a constructive role in strengthening the regime since it accomplishes the triple function of draining off aggression on the part of its subjects, prodding the bureaucracy to improve its performance, and sustaining the illusion that the supreme leadership is genuinely concerned about popular annoyances and vexations.

Yet ultimately the totalitarian dictator must depend on terror to safeguard his monopoly of power. Behind the totalitarian façade, the instrument of terror can always be found, ready for use when needed, operative, above all, even when not visible by the mere fact that it is known to exist.

* Professor of Government at Harvard University. Reprinted by permission of the publishers from chapter 13 of Merle Fainsod's *How Russia is Ruled* (Cambridge, Mass.: Harvard University Press, Copyright, 1953, by the President and Fellows of Harvard College). For footnote references, see original source.

Because the totalitarian regime provides no legitimate channel for the expression of political dissent, its constant concern is to prevent or eliminate its illegal existence. To accomplish this purpose, it recruits its specialists in espionage and terror and uses fear as a political weapon. The secret police becomes the core of totalitarian power, an omnipresent and pervasive force which envelops every sector of society in an ominous cloud of suspicion and insecurity. The task of the secret police is to serve as the eyes and ears of the dictatorship, as well as its sword. It must not only hear what people say; it must also be prepared to diagnose their souls and plumb their innermost thoughts. It must transform every citizen into a potential watchdog and informer to check and report on his friends and neighbors. It must sow distrust, for distrust will discourage organization and revolt.

THE DEFENSE OF TERROR

The practice of totalitarian terror generates its own underlying theoretical justifications. The role of terror in Communist ideology furnishes a prime example. Violence is accepted as implicit in the class struggle. As Lenin said in defending the dissolution of the Constituent Assembly, "Violence when it is committed by the toiling and exploited masses is the kind of violence of which we approve." This instrumental attitude toward violence prepares the way for its sanctification when employed by the Party in the name of the working class and by the Party leadership in the name of the Party.

The rationalization of terror embraces two central propositions. The first emphasizes the safety of the Revolution as the supreme law. In the words of Lenin, "The Soviet Republic is a fortress besieged by world capital . . . From this follows our right and our duty to mobilize the whole population to a man for the war." The second emphasizes the intransigence of the enemies of the Revolution, the necessity of crushing them completely if the Revolution itself is not to be destroyed. "What is the 'nutritive medium,'" asks Lenin,

which engenders counterrevolutionary enterprises, outbreaks, conspiracies, and so forth? . . . It is the medium of the bourgeoisie, of the bourgeois intelligentsia, of the kulaks in the countryside, and, everywhere, of the "non-Party" public, as well as of the Socialist-Revolutionaries and the Mensheviks. We must treble our watch over this medium, we must multiply it tenfold. We must multiply our vigilance, because counterrevolutionary attempts from this quarter are absolutely inevitable, precisely at the present moment and in the near future.

In essence, Stalin's defense of terror, delivered in an interview with a visiting Foreign Workers' Delegation on November 5, 1927, covers much the same ground, though with notably less frankness.

The GPU or Cheka is a punitive organ of the Soviet government. It is more or less analogous to the Committee of Public Safety which was formed during the Great French Revolution . . . It is something in the nature of a military-political tribunal set up for the purpose of protecting the interests of the revolution from attacks on the part of the counterrevolutionary bourgeoisie and their agents . . .

People advocate a maximum of leniency; they advise the dissolution of the GPU . . . But can anyone guarantee that the capitalists of all countries will abandon the idea of organizing and financing counterrevolutionary groups of plotters, terrorists, incendiaries, and bomb-throwers after the liquidation of the GPU . . . ?

. . . We are a country surrounded by capitalist states. The internal enemies of our revolution are the agents of the capitalists of all countries . . . In fighting against the enemies at home, we fight the counterrevolutionary elements of all countries . . .

No, comrades, we do not wish to repeat the mistakes of the Parisian Communards. The GPU is necessary for the Revolution and will continue to exist to the terror of the enemies of the proletariat.

The real significance of Stalin's theory of Soviet terror did not become fully manifest until the period of the Great Purge in the thirties. The liquidation of the Old Bolsheviks made it altogether clear that the salient role of terror in Stalinist ideology was to serve as a bulwark of defense for his own monopoly of Party leadership. Since this involved establishing a regime of terror within the Party, Stalin was faced with the problem of reconciling his innovation with the traditional notion that terror was reserved for the class enemy. The problem was neatly and ruthlessly solved by identifying any form of opposition to Stalin with counterrevolution and foreign espionage. The formula of capitalist encirclement proved elastic enough to embrace the enemy inside the Party as well as the enemy outside. Stalin put it as follows:

It should be remembered and never forgotten that as long as capitalist encirclement exists there will be wreckers, diversionists, spies, terrorists, sent behind the frontiers of the Soviet Union by the intelligence services of foreign states . . .

It should be explained to our Party Comrades that the Trotskyites, who represent the active elements in the diversionist, wrecking and espionage work of the foreign intelligence services . . . have already long ceased to serve any idea compatible with the interests of the working class, that they have turned into a gang of wreckers, diversionists, spies, assassins, without principles and ideas, working for the foreign intelligence services.

It should be explained that in the struggle against contemporary Trotskyism, not the old methods, the methods of discussion, must be used, but new methods, methods for smashing and uprooting it.

After the Great Purge, Stalin again faced the problem of reconciling the retention of these strong-arm methods with the claim that antagonistic classes had ceased to exist in the Soviet Union. In his report to the Eighteenth Party Congress in 1939, Stalin addressed himself to the issue, "It is sometimes asked: 'We have abolished the exploiting classes; there are no longer any hostile classes in the country; there is nobody to suppress; hence

there is no more need for the state; it must die away— Why then do we
not help our socialist state to die away? . . . Is it not time we relegated
the state to the museum of antiquities?" Again Stalin rested his case for
the retention of the terror apparatus on the allegation of capitalist encirclement:

> These questions not only betray an underestimation of the capitalist encircle-
> ment, but also an underestimation of the role and significance of the bourgeois states
> and their organs, which send spies, assassins and wreckers into our country and
> are waiting for a favourable opportunity to attack it by armed force. They like-
> wise betray an underestimation of the role and significance of our socialist state
> and of its military, punitive and intelligence organs, which are essential for the
> defense of the socialist land from foreign attack.

Writing in 1950, after a considerable expansion of Soviet power as a result
of World War II, Stalin remained committed to "the conclusion that in
the face of capitalist encirclement, when the victory of the socialist revolution has taken place in one country alone while capitalism continues to
dominate in all other countries, the country where the revolution has
triumphed must not weaken but must strengthen in every way its state,
state organs, intelligence agencies, and army if it does not want to be destroyed by capitalist encirclement." Behind these rationalizations was the
crystallization of a system of government in which terror had become the
essential ingredient. Defended originally as an expression of the class interests of the proletariat, its edge was first turned against all opponents of
Communist ascendancy and finally against any appearance of challenge to
the domination of the ruling clique.

THE CREATION OF THE CHEKA

The genealogy of the Bolshevik apparatus of terror reaches back to
the first weeks after the seizure of power. In pre-Revolutionary days, the
Bolsheviks had occasion to acquire an intimate familiarity with the operations of the Tsarist *Okhrana* or secret police; the lessons they learned then
were later to be applied and amplified. Lenin quickly decided that the
Bolsheviks would have to develop their own Okhrana. In a memorandum
dated December 19-20, 1917, he called on Dzerzhinsky, the commandant
of Smolny, to organize the struggle against counterrevolution and sabotage.
On December 20, the Council of People's Commissars approved a decree
establishing the Cheka or All-Russian Extraordinary Commission. Dzerzhinsky was made the first chairman of the eight-member commission.
One of its early acts was an appeal "to all local soviets to proceed immediately to the organization of similar commissions." Workers, soldiers, and
peasants were instructed to inform the Cheka "about organizations and
individual persons whose activity is harmful to the Revolution." At the
same time, a system of revolutionary tribunals was established to investi-

gate and try offenses which bore the character of sabotage and counter-revolution. The judges of the revolutionary tribunals were to fix penalties in accordance with "the circumstances of the case and the dictates of the revolutionary conscience."

In the confusion of the first months of the Bolshevik Revolution, terror was far from being a monopoly of the specialists in terror. The Cheka was still in its organizational phase, and its regime was singularly mild compared with what was to come. Acts of violence against the bourgeoisie were common, but they were usually committed by revolutionary mobs and undisciplined sailors and soldiers and were not ordinarily officially authorized and inspired. The early death sentences of the Cheka were imposed on bandits and criminals. As the White forces began to rally their strength, the Cheka spread its net more widely and turned to sterner measures. On February 22, 1918, the Cheka ordered all local soviets "to seek out, arrest, and shoot immediately all members . . . connected in one form or another with counterrevolutionary organizations . . . (1) enemy agents and spies, (2) counterrevolutionary agitators, (3) speculators, (4) organizers of revolt . . . against the Soviet government, (5) those going to the Don to join the . . . Kaledin-Kornilov band and the Polish counterrevolutionary legions, (6) buyers and sellers of arms to equip the counterrevolutionary bourgeoisie . . . all these are to be shot on the spot . . . when caught red-handed in the act."

The terror began to gather momentum. Gorky's newspaper *Novaya Zhizn'* (New Life) reported, "Executions continue. Not a day, not a night passes without several persons being executed." On the night of April 11, 1918, the Cheka staged a mass raid on anarchist centers in Moscow; several hundred were arrested and approximately thirty were killed while resisting arrest. Though the curve of Cheka activity was rising, its operations still remained on a limited scale.

The terror was given a sharp impetus by the effort of the Left SR's to seize power in Moscow soon after the assassination of the German Ambassador Mirbach on July 6, 1918. Large-scale arrests of Left SR's followed, and at least thirteen were shot. As the punitive actions of the Cheka increased, the SR's replied in kind. On August 30, 1918, Uritsky, the head of the Petrograd Cheka, was assassinated, and Lenin was seriously wounded. The attack on Uritsky and Lenin unleashed mass reprisals. In Petrograd alone, more than five hundred "counterrevolutionaries and White Guards" were immediately shot. The slaughter in Moscow included "many Tsarist ministers and a whole list of high personages." The President of the Provincial Soviet of Penza reported, "For the murder from ambush of one comrade, Egorov, a Petrograd worker, the Whites paid with 152 lives. In the future firmer measures will be taken against the Whites." The prominent Chekist Latsis declared,

We are no longer waging war against separate individuals, we are exterminating the bourgeoisie as a class. Do not seek in the dossier of the accused for proofs as to whether or not he opposed the soviet government by word or deed. The first question that should be put is to what class he belongs, of what extraction, what education and profession. These questions should decide the fate of the accused. Herein lie the meaning and the essence of the Red Terror.

The demonstrative massacres which followed the attack on Lenin were designed to strike fear into the hearts of all opponents of the Bolsheviks. The terror was mainly directed against the former nobility, the bourgeoisie, the landowners, the White Guards, and the clergy. But it was by no means confined to these groups. The SR's and Mensheviks, too, felt its sharp edge, and peasants who resisted the requisitioning of grain or who deserted from the Red Army were also among its victims. The Red Terror had its counterpart on the White side; the victims in this grim competition were numbered in the tens of thousands and perhaps hundreds of thousands.

As the Cheka broadened the scope of its activities, it also jealously resisted any interference with its claimed authority. Its tendency to set itself above and beyond the law aroused concern even in Bolshevik circles. At the Second All-Russian Conference of Commissars of Justice held in Moscow July 2-6, 1918,

> Comrade Lebedev . . . pointed out that granting the necessity for the existence of the Extraordinary Commissions, it was nevertheless important to delimit their sphere of activity . . . Otherwise we shall have a state within a state, with the former tending to widen its jurisdiction more and more. . .
>
> Comrade Terastvatsaturov said that . . . in the provinces the question of the activities of the Extraordinary Commissions is a very acute one. The Commissions do everything they please . . . The president of our Cheka in Orel said: "I am responsible to no one; my powers are such that I can shoot anybody."

The reply of Krestinsky, the Commissar of Justice, emphasized the difficulty of imposing restraints on the Cheka. "So long as the Cheka functions," concluded Krestinsky, "the work of justice must take a secondary place, and its sphere of activity must be considerably curtailed." The Cheka was vigorous and effective in asserting its prerogatives both against local soviet authorities and the Commissariat of Justice. The Chekist Peters put it bluntly, "In its activity the Cheka is completely independent, carrying out searches, arrests, shootings, afterwards making a report to the Council of People's Commissars and the Soviet Central Executive Committee."

After the end of the Civil War and the inauguration of the NEP, an effort was made to impose legal limits and restraints on Cheka operations. On the initiative of V. M. Smirnov, an Old Bolshevik of the Left Opposition, the Ninth Congress of Soviets, meeting in December 1921, adopted a resolution, which, after expressing gratitude for the "heroic work" of the Cheka "at the most acute moments of the Civil War," recommended that curbs be imposed on its powers.

THE GPU

On February 8, 1922, VTsIK (the All-Russian Central Executive Committee) issued a decree abolishing the Cheka and its local organs and transferring its functions to a newly created State Political Administration (GPU), which was to operate "under the personal chairmanship of the People's Commissar for Interior, or his deputy." . . .

The mass incidence of OGPU arrests during the period of the First Five Year Plan was most widely felt in the countryside. The commitment to collectivize and mechanize agriculture involved a decision to liquidate the kulaks as a class, on the ground that they were inveterate enemies of Soviet power and could be counted on to sabotage collectivization. Stalin estimated in November 1928 that the kulaks constituted about 5 per cent of the rural population, or more than one million of the twenty-five million peasant families. The OGPU was assigned the task of ejecting them from their land, confiscating their property, and deporting them to the North and Siberia. Some of the more recalcitrant were shot when they resisted arrest or responded with violence to efforts to dispossess them. The great majority became wards of the OGPU and were sentenced to forced labor in lumber camps or coal mines, or on canals, railroads, and other public works which the OGPU directed. At one stroke, the OGPU became the master of the largest pool of labor in the Soviet Union. Its own enterprises expanded rapidly to absorb them; those for whom no work could be found in the OGPU industrial empire were hired out on contract to other Soviet enterprises encountering difficulty in mobilizing supplies of free labor.

The mass deportation of the kulaks meant a tremendous growth in the network of OGPU forced labor camps. At the same time, the jurisdiction of the OGPU over ordinary criminals was enlarged. All prisoners serving sentences of more than three years were transferred to OGPU care, even if the crimes were not of a political character. No official statistics were made available on the population of the camps in the early thirties, but some indication of the magnitudes involved is provided by the fact that Belomor, the canal project connecting Leningrad and the White Sea, alone utilized more than two hundred thousand prisoners. By the end of the First Five Year Plan, forced labor had become a significant factor in manning the construction projects of the Soviet economy.

THE NKVD AND THE GREAT PURGE

The powers of the OGPU were concurrently enhanced. It was given authority to enforce the obligatory passport system introduced in large areas of the Soviet Union at the end of 1932. In July 1934 the OGPU was transformed into the People's Commissariat of Internal Affairs, or NKVD.

The enlarged activities of the NKVD included responsibility for state security, all penal institutions, fire departments, police (militia), convoy troops, frontier guards, troops of internal security, highway administration, and civil registry offices (vital statistics). The reorganization of 1934-35 involved a consolidation of the repressive machinery of the Soviet state. For the first time, all institutions of detention were placed under one jurisdiction. The secret police and their supporting military formations were united with the ordinary police. A formidable structure of power was cemented.

Some contemporary commentators tended to view the reorganization as an effort to impose limits on the arbitrary authority of the secret police. The bases for these hopes were twofold. In July 1933 a new office, the Procuratorship of the U.S.S.R., was established, and among its duties was "the supervision . . . of the legality and regularity of the actions of the OGPU." The statute creating the NKVD appeared to restrict its judicial powers. A special council attached to the NKVD was vested with authority "to issue orders regarding administrative deportation, exile, imprisonment in corrective labor camps for a term not exceeding five years." No mention was made of any NKVD authorization to inflict the death penalty. The statute seemed clearly to imply that criminal cases not disposed of administratively by the NKVD were to be transferred to the courts for trail and that crimes such as treason and espionage, which involved the possibility of the death penalty, were to be triable by the Military Collegium of the Supreme Court or other military tribunals. Whatever may have been the intent behind these measures to restrict the NKVD, subsequent events testified to their futility. In the Great Purge touched off by the assassination of Kirov, legal forms lost all significance. The arbitrary power of the NKVD reached previously unattained heights; the "Yezhovshchina" (as the worst phase of the purge became known after its sponsor, the NKVD head Yezhov) entered the language as a symbol of lawlessness run riot.

Before 1934 the victims of the OGPU-NKVD were largely former White Guards, the bourgeoisie, political opponents of the Bolsheviks, Nepmen, members of the old intelligentsia, and kulaks. During the late twenties and early thirties, some members of the Trotsky-Zinoviev and Right oppositions were also arrested by the OGPU and condemned to administrative exile or confinement in political *isolators;* but as Anton Ciliga, who was sentenced to one of the latter, records, the political prisoners received "special treatment," had books at their disposal, held meetings and debates, published prison news sheets, and lived a relatively privileged existence compared with the wretched inhabitants of the forced labor camps. Until 1934, the Party was largely exempt from the full impact of the OGPU-NKVD terror; the relatively few oppositionists who were confined in OGPU prisons were still treated with comparative humanity.

In December 1934, when Kirov was assassinated by Nikolayev, allegedly a former member of the Zinoviev opposition, a new era in NKVD history opened. The "liberal" regime which the imprisoned "oppositionists" enjoyed came to an abrupt end. The concentrated power of the NKVD was now directed toward uprooting all actual or potential opposition in the Party. For the first time, the Party felt the full brunt of the terror.

The murder of Kirov was followed by drastic reprisals. Nikolayev and a group of his alleged confederates were charged with having formed a so-called Leningrad Center to organize the assassination and were condemned to death. More than a hundred persons who had been arrested prior to Kirov's death as "counterrevolutionaries" were promptly handed over to military commissions of the Supreme Court of the U.S.S.R. for trial, were found guilty of preparing and carrying out terrorist acts, and were instantly shot. This demonstrative massacre was accompanied by the arrest and imprisonment, on charges of negligence, of twelve high NKVD officials in Leningrad. In the spring of 1935, thousands and perhaps tens of thousands of Leningrad inhabitants who were suspected of harboring opposition sentiments were arrested and deported to Siberia. In the sardonic nomenclature of exile and concentration camp, they came to be referred to collectively as "Kirov's assassins."

Zinoviev, Kamenev, and all the principal leaders of the Zinoviev group were also arrested and transferred to the political *isolator* at Verkhne-Uralsk. During the summer of 1935, Zinoviev, Kamenev, and an assortment of lesser figures were secretly tried for plotting against the life of Stalin. According to Ciliga, "Two of the prisoners were shot: one collaborator of the G.P.U. and one officer of the Kremlin Guard. The others escaped with sentences ranging between five and ten years." Stalin, in addressing the graduates of the Red Army Academies at the Kremlin on May 4, 1935, observed,

> These comrades did not always confine themselves to criticism and passive resistance. They threatened to raise a revolt in the Party against the Central Committee. More, they threatened some of us with bullets. Evidently, they reckoned on frightening us and compelling us to turn from the Leninist road . . . We were obliged to handle some of these comrades roughly. But that cannot be helped. I must confess that I too had a hand in this.

During 1935 the purge gathered momentum, but its proportions were still relatively restricted. The dissolution of the Society of Old Bolsheviks on May 25, 1935, was an ominous portent of things to come. On May 13, some two weeks earlier, the Party Central Committee had ordered a screening of all Party documents in order to "cleanse" the Party of all opposition elements. As Zhdanov stated in a report at the plenum of the Saratov *kraikom*, "Recent events, particularly the treacherous murder of Comrade Kirov, show clearly how dangerous it is for the Party to lose its vigilance . . . I have to remind you that the murderer of Comrade Kirov, Nikolayev, committed his crime by using his Party card." By December 1, 1935, 81.1

per cent of all Party members had been subjected to screening, and 9.1 per cent of these were reported as expelled. On December 25 the Central Committee of the Party, dissatisfied with the modest results of the verification of Party documents, ordered a new purge. Beginning February 1, 1936, all old Party cards were to be exchanged for new cards; the issuance of new Party documents was to serve as the occasion for a rigorous unmasking of enemies who had survived the earlier screening. The bite of the first phase of the purge is indicated by the striking decline of Party membership from 2,807,786 in January 1934 to 2,044,412 in April 1936. In a little over two years, more than one out of every four members and candidates disappeared from the Party rolls. Their fate can be inferred from the diatribes which the Soviet press of the period directed against "wreckers, spies, diversionists and murderers sheltering behind the Party card and disguised as Bolsheviks."

The Great Purge reached its climax in the period 1936-1938. Its most dramatic external manifestation was the series of show trials in the course of which every trace of Old Bolshevik opposition leadership was officially discredited and exterminated. The first of the great public trials took place in August, 1936. Zinoviev, Kamenev, Ivan Smirnov, and thirteen associates were charged with organizing a clandestine terrorist center under instructions from Trotsky, with accomplishing the murder of Kirov, and with preparing similar attempts against the lives of other Party leaders. All sixteen were executed. In the course of the trial, the testimony of the accused compromised many other members of the Bolshevik Old Guard. A wave of new arrests followed. On August 23, 1936, Tomsky, hounded by a sense of impending doom, committed suicide.

In January 1937 came the Trial of the Seventeen, the so-called Anti-Soviet Trotskyite Center, which included such prominent figures as Pyatakov, Radek, Sokolnikov, Serebryakov, and Muralov. This time the accused were charged with plotting the forcible overthrow of the Soviet government with the aid of Germany and Japan, with planning the restoration of capitalism in the U.S.S.R., and with carrying on espionage, wrecking diversive, and terrorist activities on behalf of foreign states. Again, the trial was arranged to demonstrate that Trotsky was the *éminence grise* who inspired, organized, and directed all these activities. The prisoners in the dock fought for their lives by playing their assigned role in a drama designed to destroy Trotsky's reputation. Radek and Sokolnikov were rewarded with ten-year prison sentences. Two minor figures were also sentenced to long prison terms. The remaining thirteen were shot.

On June 12, 1937, *Pravda* carried the announcement of the execution of Marshal Tukhachevsky and seven other prominent generals of the Red Army "for espionage and treason to the Fatherland." This time no public trial was held. The Party press merely declared that the executed generals had conspired to overthrow the Soviet government and to reëstablish "the yoke of the landowners and industrialists." The conspirators were alleged to be in the service of the military intelligence of "a foreign government," to which they were supposed to have indicated their readiness to surrender the Soviet Ukraine in exchange for assistance in bringing about the downfall of the Soviet government. Besides Tukhachevsky, the Deputy People's Commissar of Defense, the list of the executed included General Yakir, Commander of the Leningrad Military District; General Uborevich, Commander of the Western Military District; General Kork, Commander of the War College in Moscow; General Primakov, Budënny's Deputy Commander of Cavalry; Feldman, head of the Administration of Commanding Personnel in the Defense Commissariat; Putna, the former Soviet military attaché in Great Britain; and Eideman, President of the Central Council of *Osoaviakhim,* the civilian defense agency. Gamarnik, who served as the Party's watchdog over the army in his capacity as head of the Political Administration of the Red Army (PUR), committed suicide to avoid arrest. The execution of Tukhachevsky and his associates was the prelude to a mass purge of the Soviet armed forces in the course of which the top commanding personnel was particularly hard hit.

The slaughter of the Old Guard continued with the Trial of the Twenty-one, the so-called Anti-Soviet Bloc of Rights and Trotskyites, in March 1938. Among the prisoners in the dock were Bukharin, Rykov, and Krestinsky, all former members of the Politburo; Yagoda, the former head of the NKVD; Rakovsky, the former chairman of the Council of People's Commissars in the Ukraine and Soviet ambassador to England and France; Rosengoltz, the former People's Commissar of Foreign Trade; Grinko, the former People's Commissar of Finance; and Khodjayev, the former chairman of the Council of People's Commissars of Uzbekistan. The indictment against them embraced the usual combination of treason, espionage, diversion, terrorism, and wrecking. The bloc headed by Bukharin and Rykov was alleged to have spied for foreign powers from the earliest days of the Revolution, to have entered into secret agreements with the Nazis and the Japanese to dismember the Soviet Union, to have planned the assassination of Stalin and the rest of the Politburo, and to have organized innumerable acts of sabotage and diversion in order to wreck the economic and political power of the Soviet Union. If the testimony of Yagoda is to be believed, he not only murdered his predecessor in office, Menzhinsky, but also tried to murder his successor, Yezhov; he facilitated the assassination of Kirov, was responsible for the murder of Gorky, Gorky's son, and Kuibyshev; he admitted foreign spies into his organization and protected their operations; he planned a palace coup in the Kremlin and the assassination of the Politburo.

If these lurid tales strain the credulity of the reader, they nevertheless represent the version of oppositionist activity which Stalin and his faithful lieutenants found it expedient to propagate. Without access to the archives of the Kremlin and the NKVD, it is doubtful whether the web of fact and fancy behind the show trials will ever be authoritatively disentangled. The hatred of the former leaders of the opposition for Stalin can be taken for granted. That their hatred carried them to the point of conspiring together to overthrow him is not unlikely, though the evidence adduced at the trails to support the charge is lame and unconvincing. What appears singularly implausible are the allegations that Old Bolsheviks who had given their lives to the Communist cause would plot with the Nazis to restore capitalism in the Soviet Union, would function as their puppets and espionage agents, and arrange to hand over large portions of the Soviet Union to them as compensation for dethroning Stalin. . . .

The crescendo of the Great Purge was reached in the second period, which extended from late September 1937, when Yezhov was appointed head of the NKVD, until the end of July 1938, when Lavrenti Beria was designated as Yezhov's deputy and eventual successor. The announcement of Yezhov's removal did not come until December, but meanwhile Beria assumed *de facto* command of the NKVD organization, and early in 1939 Yezhov disappeared and was probably liquidated.

The period of the Yezhovshchina involved a reign of terror without parallel in Soviet history. Among those arrested, imprisoned, and executed were a substantial proportion of the leading figures in the Party and governmental hierarchy. The Bolshevik Old Guard was destroyed. The roll of Yezhov's victims included not only former oppositionists but many of the most stalwart supporters of Stalin in his protracted struggle with the opposition. No sphere of Soviet life, however lofty, was left untouched. Among the purged Stalinists were three former members of the Politburo, Rudzutak, Chubar, and S. V. Kossior, and three candidate members, Petrovsky, Postyshev, and Eikhe. An overwhelming majority of the members and candidates of the Party Central Committee disappeared. The senior officer corps of the armed forces suffered severely. According to one sober account, "two of five marshals of the Soviet Union escaped arrest, two of fifteen army commanders, twenty-eight of fifty-eight corps commanders, eighty-five of a hundred and ninety-five divisional commanders, and a hundred and ninety-five of four hundred and six regimental commanders." The havoc wrought by the purge among naval commanding personnel was equally great. The removal of Yagoda from the NKVD was accompanied by the arrest of his leading collaborators, Agranov, Prokofiev, Balitsky, Messing, Pauker, Trilisser, and others. The Commissariat of Foreign Affairs and the diplomatic service were hard hit. Among the Old Guard, only Litvinov, Maisky, Troyanovsky, and a few lesser lights survived. Almost every commissariat was deeply affected.

The purge swept out in ever-widening circles and resulted in wholesale removals and arrests of leading officials in the union republics, secretaries of the Party, Komsomol, and trade-union apparatus, heads of industrial trusts and enterprises, Comintern functionaries and foreign Communists, and leading writers, scholars, engineers, and scientists. The arrest of an important figure was followed by the seizure of the entourage which surrounded him. The apprehension of members of the entourage led to the imprisonment of their friends and acquaintances. The endless chain of involvements and associations threatened to encompass entire strata of Soviet society. Fear of arrest, exhortations to vigilance, and perverted ambition unleashed new floods of denunciations, which generated their own avalanche of cumulative interrogations and detentions. Whole categories of Soviet citizens found themselves singled out for arrest because of their "objective characteristics." Old Bolsheviks, Red Partisans, foreign Communists of German, Austrian, and Polish extraction, Soviet citizens who had been abroad or had relations with foreign countries or foreigners, and "repressed elements" were automatically caught up in the NKVD web of wholesale imprisonment. The arrests mounted into the millions; the testimony of the survivors is unanimous regarding crowded prison cells and teeming forced labor camps. Most of the prisoners were utterly bewildered by the fate which had befallen them. The vast resources of the NKVD were concentrated on one objective—to document the existence of a huge conspiracy to undermine Soviet power. The extraction of real confessions to imaginary crimes became a major industry. Under the zealous and ruthless ministrations of NKVD examiners, millions of innocents were transformed into traitors, terrorists, and enemies of the people.

How explain the Yezhovshchina? What motives impelled Stalin to organize a blood bath of such frightening proportions? In the absence of revealing testimony from the source, one can only venture hypotheses. Stalin's desire to consolidate his own personal power appears to have been a driving force. The slaughter of the Bolshevik Old Guard may be viewed partly as a drastic reprisal for past insubordination; it was more probably intended as a preventive measure to end once and for all any possibility of resistance or challenge from this direction. The extension of the purge to the Stalinist stalwarts in the Party and governmental apparatus is much more difficult to fathom. It is possible that many fell victim to the system of denunciations in the course of which their loyalty to Stalin was put in question, that a number were still involved in official or personal relationships with former oppositionists, that some were liquidated because they displayed traces of independence in their dealings with the Supreme Leader, that others were merely suspected of harboring aspirations toward personal power, and that still others simply furnished convenient scapegoats to demonstrate the existence of a conspiracy that reached into the highest circles.

Implicit in any understanding of the Yezhovshchina is a theory of the role of terror in Stalin's formula of government. The consolidation of personal rule in a totalitarian system depends on the constant elimination of all actual or potential competitors for supreme power. The insecurity of the masses must be supplemented by the insecurity of the governing elite who surround the Supreme Dictator. The too strongly entrenched official with an independent base of power is by definition a threat to the dictator's total sway. The individuals or groups who go uncontrolled and undirected are regarded as fertile soil for the growth of conspiratorial intrigue. The function of terror thus assumes a two-fold aspect. As prophylactic and preventive, it is designed to nip any possible resistance or opposition in the bud. As an instrument for the reinforcement of the personal power of the dictator, it is directed toward ensuring perpetual circulation in the ranks of officeholders in order to forestall the crystallization of autonomous islands of countervailing force.

The manipulation of terror as a system of power is a delicate art. A dictator in command of modern armaments and a secret police can transform his subjects into robots and automatons, but if he succeeds too well, he runs the risk of destroying the sources of creative initiative on which the survival of his own regime depends. When terror runs rampant, as it did at the height of the Yezhovshchina, unintended consequences follow. Fear becomes contagious and paralyzing. Officials at all levels seek to shirk responsibility. The endless belt of irresponsible denunciations begins to destroy the nation's treasury of needed skills. The terror apparatus grows on the stuff on which it feeds and magnifies in importance until it overshadows and depresses all the constructive enterprises of the state. The dictator finds himself caught up in a whirlwind of his own making which threatens to break completely out of control.

As the fury of the Yezhovshchina mounted, Stalin and his intimates finally became alarmed. Evidence accumulated that the purge was overreaching itself and that much talent sorely needed by the regime was being irretrievably lost. The first signal of a change of policy was given in a resolution of the January 1938 plenum of the Party Central Committee entitled "Concerning the Mistakes of Party Organizations in Excluding Communists from the Party, Concerning Formal-Bureaucratic Attitudes toward the Appeals of Excluding Members of the VKP(b), and Concerning Measures to Eliminate these Deficiencies." The resolution identified a new culprit, the Communist-careerists, who sought to make capital out of the purge by securing promotions through provocatory denunciations of their superiors. It was these careerists, the resolution charged, who were primarily responsible for sowing suspicion and insecurity within Party ranks and for decimating the Party cadres. The resolution concluded with a ten-point program designed to put an end to mass expulsions and to secure the rehabilitation of former members who had been expelled as the result of slanders. The immediate effect of this resolution was to produce a new purge of so-called Communist-careerists. At the same time, the

Party press began to carry stories of the reinstatements of honest Communists who had been the unfortunate victims of unjustified denunciations.

The third and final phase of the Great Purge involved the purging of the purgers. In late July 1938 Yezhov's sun began to set when Beria took over as his deputy. In December, Yezhov was ousted as head of the NKVD and appointed Commissar for Inland Water Transport, from which post he soon disappeared unmourned but not forgotten. During the same month came the sensational announcement of the arrest, trial, and shooting of the head of the NKVD of Moldavia and a group of his examiners for extracting false confessions from innocent prisoners. The enemies of the people, it now appeared, had wormed their way into the NKVD apparatus itself and had sought to stir up mass unrest and disaffection by their brutal persecution of the guiltless.

It was now the turn of Yezhov and his collaborators to play the role of scapegoat for the excesses of the purge. A wave of arrests spread through the NKVD organization. The prisons began to fill with former NKVD examiners; many prisoners who had been tortured by these same examiners had the welcome experience of greeting their former tormentors as cellmates in prisons and forced labor camps. The "Great Change," as it was soon to become known, was marked by a substantial amelioration in prison conditions and examining methods. According to Beck and Godin, "Prisoners were released by the thousands, and many were restored to their old positions or even promoted." A new era appeared to have dawned.

Stalin now presented himself in the guise of the dispenser of mercy and justice. Excesses of the purge were blamed on subordinate officials who had exceeded their authority, saboteurs who had tried to break the indissoluble link which bound Leader and people, and careerists and counterrevolutionaries who had insinuated themselves into the Party and NKVD organizations in order to subvert and undermine the Soviet regime. At the Eighteenth Congress in 1939, Zhdanov reeled off case after case of so-called slanderers and calumniators who had tried to advance themselves in the Party by wholesale expulsions of honest Party members. Quoting from Stalin, he repeated, "Some of our Party leaders suffer from a lack of concern for people, for members of the Party, for workers . . . As a result of this heartless attitude towards people . . . discontent and bitterness are artificially created among a section of the Party, and the Trotskyite double-dealers artfully hook on to such embittered comrades and skillfully drag them into the bog of Trotskyite wrecking." Zhdanov called for a change in Party Rules to ensure "an attentive approach and careful investigation of accusations brought against Party members," which would "protect the rights of Party members from all arbitrary procedure," and "abolish the resort to expulsion from the Party . . . for trifling misdemeanours."

Thus, the pressure of the purge was temporarily relaxed as Stalin sought to enlist the energies and loyalties of the new governing elite whom he had promoted to positions of responsibility over the graves of their predecessors. Again, as in the collectivization crisis earlier, Stalin demonstrated his remarkable instinct for stopping short and reversing course at the brink of catastrophe.

The full circle of the Great Purge offers a remarkable case study in the use of terror. Arrests ran into the millions. The gruesome and harrowing experiences of the victims blackened the face of Stalinist Russia. The havoc wrought in leading circles appeared irreparable. Yet despite the damage and the hatred engendered, the dynamic momentum of the industrialization program was maintained. The arrests of responsible technicians and officials frequently produced serious setbacks in production, but as their replacements acquired experience, order was restored, and production began to climb again. While many functionaries reacted to the purge by shunning all responsibility, others responded to the fear of arrest by working as they had never worked before. Terror functioned as prod as well as brake. The acceleration in the circulation of the elite brought a new generation of Soviet-trained intelligentsia into positions of responsibility, and Stalin anchored his power on their support. Meanwhile, Stalin emerged from the purge with his own position consolidated. The major purpose of decapitating the Bolshevik Old Guard had been accomplished. Every rival for supreme power who was visible on the horizon had been eliminated. The Party and the nation were thoroughly intimidated. The purgers had been purged and the scapegoats identified. The ancient formula of protecting the infallibility of the Leader by punishing subordinates for their excessive ardor was impressively resurrected.

The moving equilibrium on which Stalin balanced his power structure entered a new phase. The temporary lifting of the blanket of fear was designed to restore morale, to revive hope and initiative, and to reforge the bonds between regime and people which the purge had dangerously strained. But the mitigation of the terror involved no abandonment of the system. For the totalitarian dictator, terror is an indispensable necessity, and its invocation is a guarantee that no organized force will rise to challenge his undisputed rule. The Stalinist refinement on the use of terror as a system of power involved oscillating phases of pressure and relaxation which varied with the dictator's conception of the dangers which he confronted. The essence of control was never abandoned. At the same time, when the pressure became too great, a mirage of security and stability was held out in order to enlist the energy and devotion of the oncoming generations. It is a system which devours many of its servants, but as in games of chance, since the winners and survivors are highly rewarded and cannot be identified in advance, the ambitions of the players are periodically renewed, and the regime bases its strength on their sacrifices.

As the Great Purge drew to a close, the major efforts of the NKVD were concentrated against elements which might prove unreliable in the event that the Soviet Union became involved in war. After the Soviet-Nazi pact and the partition of Poland, the NKVD undertook wholesale arrests in the newly occupied areas. The victims ran into the hundreds of thousands and included whole categories of people whose "objective characteristics" could be broadly construed as inclining them to anti-Soviet behavior. The great majority were deported to forced labor camps in the Soviet North, from which the survivors were amnestied by the terms of the Polish-Soviet pact concluded after the Nazi attack on the Soviet Union. The Soviet occupation of the Baltic States in June 1940 was also followed by large-scale NKVD arrests and deportations of so-called anti-Soviet elements.

After the Nazi invasion, the NKVD engaged in widespread roundups of former "repressed" people and others whose records aroused suspicion of disloyalty to the Soviet regime. The Volga-German Autonomous Republic was dissolved, and its inhabitants were dispatched to forced labor camps or exile in the far reaches of Siberia. With the turning of the tide at Stalingrad and the advance of the Soviet armies westward, the NKVD found new victims among the population of the reoccupied areas. Many were arrested on the ground of actual or alleged collaboration with the Germans, and the forced labor camps reaped a new harvest. A number of the national minorities served as a special target of NKVD retribution because of their alleged disloyalty. The Kalmyk and Chechen-Ingush Republics were dissolved. The Crimean Tatars were penalized for their "traitorous" conduct by the abolition of the Crimean Autonomous Republic. The Autonomous Republic of the Kabards and Bolkars was dismembered, leaving only the Kabardinian ASSR. Meanwhile, German war prisoners accumulated, and the NKVD took over the responsibility of running the camps in which they were confined.

After the capitulation of the Nazis, the NKVD confronted the vast new assignment of sifting the millions of Soviet citizens who found themselves in Germany and Austria at the end of the war. Most of them were war prisoners and *Ostarbeiter* who had been shipped west by the Germans as forced labor. Some, however, had retreated with the German armies in order to escape Soviet rule. Others had fought in Nazi military uniform or in separate anti-Soviet military formations such as the Vlasov Army. The latter when caught received short shrift; the great majority were executed. All of these elements on whom the NKVD could lay its hands were rounded up at assembly points and subjected to intensive interrogations by the NKVD before being shipped back to the Soviet Union. The NKVD followed a calculated policy of treating the "returners" as contaminated by their contact with the West. In order to isolate them from the Soviet populace, large numbers were dispatched to forced labor camps on suspicion of disloyalty or traitorous conduct.

Much less is known about police activities inside the Soviet Union since the end of the war. Large-scale deportations have been reported from the border areas of Esthonia, Latvia, Lithuania, Karelia, and the Western Ukraine; the native population has been shifted to remote areas in Siberia and replaced by Russians, frequently war veterans, brought in from other regions. From reports in the Soviet press of campaigns against collective farm abuses, of cases of venality and corruption among bureaucrats and industrial administrators, of purges of the Party apparatus and among intellectuals, it can be inferred that the secret police continues to claim its victims in widely diversified strata of Soviet society. While the available information is too sparse to justify any sweeping conclusions, there have been no indications thus far of any repetition of the mass retributions of the 1936-1938 period, except for the large-scale campaigns against so-called "untrustworthy" elements in the border regions. Elsewhere, if the testimony of escaped Soviet citizens is to be given credence, the secret police makes its presence felt by individual rather than group arrests. Its arbitrary power and pervasive organization help to sustain its reputation as the most feared weapon in the Soviet arsenal of power. . . .

FORCED LABOR

. . . Estimates of the number of people confined in forced labor camps in the Soviet Union run a wide gamut, even within the same period. The Soviet government has not seen fit to release any official statistics. Most estimates represent the guesses of former prisoners who escaped from the Soviet Union and whose personal experience was ordinarily confined to one or a few camps or even sections of camps. Beck and Godin, in an account of the Great Purge which is distinguished by its sobriety and restraint, estimated the total number of prisoners "living in detention under the NKVD" during the Yezhovshchina as between seven and fourteen million. Alexander Weissberg, a distinguished scientist who was imprisoned in Kharkov during the Yezhovshchina, hazarded the guess that between 5 and 6 per cent of the local population was arrested in the 1937-1939 period. By projecting this percentage to the country at large, Weissberg arrived at a total of nine million arrests, of which two million represented criminal charges and seven million were attributable to the purge. After reviewing a wide variety of estimates by former inmates of forced labor camps, Dallin and Nicolaevsky, in a work devoted exclusively to forced labor, concluded that the totals ranged in different periods from seven to twelve million. In the nature of things, these estimates are not susceptible to precise corroboration.

Perhaps the most revealing collection of unquestionably authentic data on the role of forced labor in the Soviet economy is contained in an official Soviet document entitled "State Plan of Development of the National Economy of the U.S.S.R. for 1941." This classified Soviet document, which was captured by the Nazis in the rapid advance of the first months of the war, contains a detailed statement of economic targets for 1941; it also includes a rich assortment of material on the economic activities of the NKVD. The 1941 plan lists a projected capital investment of 37,650,-000,000 rubles, exclusive of capital investments of the Commissariats for Transportation, Defense, and Navy. Out of this sum, the NKVD accounted for 6,810,000,000 rubles, or about 18 per cent. In presenting the 1941 economic plan, Voznesensky, the chairman of Gosplan, reported the total capital investment planned for 1941 as 57,000,000,000 rubles. The NKVD share of this total was approximately 12 per cent. On the basis of the 1941 capital investment data, Naum Jasny reached the conclusion that the NKVD was expected to account for 17 per cent of the total 1941 construction and that the number of concentration camp inmates engaged in NKVD construction projects alone would approximate 1,172,000. The 1941 plan indicated that lumbering was the second most important industrial activity of the NKVD. The total share of the NKVD in this industry was about 12 per cent, but this percentage was substantially exceeded in the northern areas of the U.S.S.R. In Archangelsk *oblast,* it was 26 per cent; in the Khabarovsk *krai* and the Karelo-Finnish Republic, more than 33 per cent; in Murmansk *oblast,* more than 40 per cent; and in the Komi Autonomous Republic, more than 50 per cent. Other NKVD industrial targets mentioned in the plan included 5,300,000 tons of coal out of a total 191,000,000 tons; 250,000 tons of oil out of a total 35,000,000 tons; 150,000 tons of chrome ore out of a total of 370,000; and 82,000,000 bricks to be produced in the Khabarovsk and Maritime *krais.*

It should be noted that the captured version of the 1941 plan is incomplete. Data on gold production and armaments were not included and were apparently reserved for separate supplements which circulated among a very restricted group. Information from other sources indicates that gold mining was virtually an NKVD monopoly; the vast development in the Kolyma region was administered by the NKVD through its subsidiary *Dalstroi* and was largely manned by forced labor. On the basis of sober reading of the reports of former inmates of the concentration camps in the Kolyma area, it would appear that Dalstroi utilized from two hundred thousand to four hundred thousand forced laborers in the 1941 period. This, it should be stressed, is a conservative figure. The estimate of Dallin and Nicolaevsky runs from one and a half to two million prisoners.

The 1941 plan does not list the number of camp inmates. The data on the economic activities of the NKVD, however, make it possible to arrive at a fairly reliable estimate of aproximately three and a half million. This total applies only to forced labor confined in prison camps under direct NKVD jurisdiction. It does not include persons hired out to other enterprises. It does not include persons sentenced to exile in remote areas who remained under NKVD supervision even though they lived and worked under the same conditions as the rest of the population. Nor does it include the arrested who were being held for investigation and sentence in remand prisons or those serving terms of confinement in ordinary prisons. It does not include workers penalized for tardiness or absenteeism by being compelled to work at their jobs at substantially reduced pay. And it takes no account of the degree of compulsion which is ordinarily attached to job assignments and transfers of so-called "free" labor in the Soviet system. It is obvious that estimates of "forced labor" will vary widely, depending on the categories which are included.

Since 1941, no authoritative internal source comparable to the State Plan has become available. The accounts of released prisoners for subsequent years indicate that large contingents of new forced laborers have been steadily flowing into the camps, but estimates must be speculative to a high degree, and no attempt will be made here to undertake even a crude estimate of the present population of the forced labor camps. Reports that the MVD has been charged with the sole responsibility for the building and operation of all atomic developments and the large-scale construction projects launched under the postwar Five Year Plans point toward a continuing reliance on forced labor as an essential aspect of the Soviet system.

The role of forced labor in the Soviet economy has given rise to sharp controversy. Those who view the concentration camps as an asset to the Soviet economy argue that the MVD derives a substantial profit from the exploitation of slave labor, that the productivity of the concentration camp inmates is considerably in excess of the cost of their upkeep, and that the profits realized from the use of slave labor are "an important element of the government's industrialization fund." The accelerated development of the Soviet North and other remote areas, it is contended, would have been impossible had the government been forced to rely on free labor.

Those who regard the concentration camps as a liability to the Soviet economy are usually ready to concede that the existence of large pools of forced labor has facilitated the exploitation of resources in regions where primitive conditions and hardships are barriers to the recruitment of free labor. But they also point out that the productivity of slave labor is considerably less than that of free workers and that the alleged profits involved disappear when full account is taken of the expense of maintaining the MVD apparatus, both outside and inside the camps. They also stress the high mortality rates in the camps and the great losses involved for the Soviet economy when scarce skilled workers, highly qualified engineers and other professionally trained experts, whose education has involved high costs for the state, are utilized as unskilled laborers.

The initial impetus for the establishment of concentration camps was provided by political rather than economic considerations. The arrests of hundreds of thousands or millions of Soviet citizens were not originally planned as a method of obtaining slave labor power. The large-scale economic enterprises of the NKVD-MVD were developed in order to exploit the prisoners whom the secret police had accumulated. As these enterprises were established, they acquired a momentum of their own. The manpower that they consumed had to be replaced by new contingents, and the NKVD-MVD encountered no great difficulty in finding pretexts for replenishments. A system of power in which the security of the leadership is founded on the insecurity of its subjects demands a continuous crop of fresh victims. The regime of forced labor serves to ensure that the leadership will at least derive some advantage from this process.*

THE HAZARDS OF TERROR

The reliance on terror as an instrument of dominion has its elements of danger. It is not easy to control. A secret police develops its own laws of growth. The more discord it discovers or develops, the more indispensable it becomes. Its tendency is always to extend its own sovereignty, to seek to emancipate itself from all external controls, to become a state within a state, and to preserve the conditions of emergency and siege on which an expansion of its own power depends. Once terror becomes an end in itself, there is no easy and natural stopping place. From the viewpoint of the leadership, there is an even greater worry, the fear that as the secret police apparatus emancipates itself from external controls, it becomes a menace to the security of the highest Party leaders themselves. It is a risk of which the Party leadership has been aware and against which it has taken precautions. Every effort is apparently made to ensure the subordination of the MVD to the central Party organization. Employees are required to be Party members. The secretaries of the Party organizations in the MVD are used as the eyes and ears of the Party Central Committee to ensure loyalty to the Party. The Special Section in the secretariat of the Central Committee is presumed to have a particularly close supervisory relationship to the secret police. Special groups of the Party Control Committee are assigned to watch over the MVD. In these and perhaps other ways, the Party leadership seeks to safeguard itself against the possibility that "the avenging sword of the Revolution" may turn against the revolutionary leadership itself.

Thus far, no head of the Soviet secret police has succeeded in using his position as a platform from which to strike out for supreme power. The first director of the Cheka and OGPU was Felix Dzerzhinsky, an Old Bolshevik of unimpeachable idealism whose whole career documented the

* Editor's footnote: Available evidence suggests that forced labor camps have been largely liquidated since the death of Stalin. But Professor Fainsod's account remains a vivid part of the historic tragedy.

proposition that there is no fanaticism so terrible as that of the pure idealist. Dzerzhinsky gave no evidence of Napoleonic ambitions and died in 1926 without attaining Politburo status. His successor, Menzhinsky, was a much lesser figure, and though he continued as head of the OGPU until 1934, he never moved beyond the second rank of Party leaders. Yagoda, who came next, was removed from office in 1936 and executed in 1938. His successor, Yezhov, was relieved of his duties in 1938 and disappeared in 1939, presumably a scapegoat for the excesses of the Great Purge. Neither Yagoda nor Yezhov could be counted in the front ranks of Party leaders. Beria, who succeeded Yezhov, was the first head of the NKVD to enter the Politburo, where he became an outstanding figure. His rise to power, however, gave every evidence of reflecting Stalin's tutelage rather than any independent leverage which his position as head of the NKVD afforded. Thus far, the vigilance of the ruling group has been proof against all dreams of utilizing the terror apparatus as the road to supremacy. The proposition that Beria may carve a new path has still to be tested.

Even if the Party leadership is successful in imposing its mastery on the secret police, there are other disadvantages in a regime of terror which are not so amenable to skillful manipulation. A system which relies on a large secret police as a basic core of its power is highly wasteful of manpower. The main occupation of the secret police is that of spying, investigating, examining, guarding, and controlling others. Large numbers of talented people are removed from productive work. There is always the hazard that the secret police will run amok and do serious and perhaps unintended harm to the productive and administrative machinery of the state. The atmosphere of universal suspicion which terror breeds is not ordinarily conducive to creative thinking and displays of individual initiative. If the weight of terror becomes too great and the penalty of any administrative failure or mistake is MVD detention, it becomes difficult to persuade people to take responsibility. Even those driven by fear of the secret police to work as they have never worked before begin to crack under the strain. It is no easy task to apply terror and at the same time to hold it in leash.

Perhaps the most subtle danger in a police regime of the Soviet type is its impact on the quality of political decisions at the very highest level. The MVD is one of the main pillars that sustains the regime. It is also a primary source of intelligence regarding both domestic and international developments. Since the MVD apparatus lives and grows on emergency and danger, its justification hinges upon the maintenance of a state of siege. Consequently, the intelligence that filters through the MVD to the top political leadership is apt almost unconsciously to emphasize the storms that are brewing, the plots against the regime, and sinister threats at home and abroad. The risk which the Party leadership faces is that it too will become the unconscious victim of the Frankenstein's monster which it has created. The ultimate hazard of terror as a system of power is that it ends by terrorizing the master as well as the slave.

[EDITOR'S NOTE: *On July 10, 1953, some few months after the death of Stalin on March 5, 1953, it was officially announced that Beria had been dismissed as head of the MVD and was being held for trial. On December 16, the Soviet State Prosecutor issued a statement that Beria (and accomplices) had confessed during the course of investigation to "having committed a number of State crimes." Among the crimes charged were that Beria had been "an agent of foreign capital, directed toward the subversion of the Soviet state" with links to foreign Intelligence services "as far back as the civil war"; had striven "to place the Ministry of Internal Affairs above the party and Government, to seize power and to liquidate the Soviet worker-peasant regime with a view to restoring capitalism and securing the revival of the bourgeoisie." It was also charged that Beria had attempted "to subvert the collective-farm system and to create food difficulties in our country" and "to sow hatred and discord between the peoples of the U.S.S.R."*

On December 23, it was briefly announced that the accused had been tried (behind closed doors) before a tribunal headed by Marshal Ivan S. Konev, that all had been found guilty, and shot.]

STALIN AND THE CULT OF THE INDIVIDUAL

NIKITA S. KHRUSHCHEV*

This denunciation of Stalin and of "the cult of the individual" was delivered on February 24-25, 1956, before a closed session of the XXth Congress of the Communist Party of the Soviet Union and first published in the United States, after release by the United States Department of State on June 4, 1956. Its authenticity has never been officially acknowledged. However, it has been widely credited in the Communist press of the world. Eugene Dennis, General Secretary of the National Committee of the Communist Party of the United States, for instance, wrote in the Daily Worker *on June 18, 1956, "The Khrushchev report on Stalin tells a tragic story."*

In Russia itself, a long "Resolution of the Central Committee of the Communist Party of the Soviet Union," published in Pravda *on July 2, 1956, read in part: "For more than three years now our Party has been*

* First Secretary of the Communist Party of the Soviet Union and Chairman of the Council of Ministers of the U.S.S.R. The text of this speech is reprinted with permission in abridged form from the version published in *The New Leader* on July 16, 1956, and in its pamphlet titled "The Crimes of the Stalin Era," with the footnote annotations by Boris I. Nicolaevsky, author of *Letter of an Old Bolshevik* and co-author of *Forced Labor in Soviet Russia*.

waging a consistent struggle against the cult of the person of J. V. Stalin, persistently overcoming its harmful consequences. Naturally this question occupied an important place in the work of the XXth Congress of the CPSU and in its decisions." The next day, Pravda commented editorially, "As is well known, at the XXth Congress of the Communist Party of the Soviet Union the question of the cult of the individual and its consequences was examined in detail."

It may be said, finally, that during a visit made to the U.S.S.R. by this editor in June 1957, every one with whom he raised the question seemed aware of the document and its general contents.

Comrades! In the report of the Central Committee of the party at the 20th Congress, in a number of speeches by delegates to the Congress, as also formerly during the plenary CC/CPSU [Central Committee of the Communist Party of the Soviet Union] sessions, quite a lot has been said about the cult of the individual and about its harmful consequences.

After Stalin's death the Central Committee of the party began to implement a policy of explaining concisely and consistently that it is impermissible and foreign to the spirit of Marxism-Leninism to elevate one person, to transform him into a superman possessing supernatural characteristics, akin to those of a god. Such a man supposedly knows everything, sees everything, thinks for everyone, can do anything, is infallible in his behavior. Such a belief about a man, and specifically about Stalin, was cultivated among us for many years.

The objective of the present report is not a thorough evaluation of Stalin's life and activity. Concerning Stalin's merits, an entirely sufficient number of books, pamphlets and studies had already been written in his lifetime. The role of Stalin in the preparation and execution of the Socialist Revolution, in the Civil War, and in the fight for the construction of socialism in our country, is universally known. Everyone knows this well.

At present, we are concerned with a question which has immense importance for the party now and for the future—with how the cult of the person of Stalin has been gradually growing, the cult which became at a certain specific stage the source of a whole series of exceedingly serious and grave perversions of party principles, of party democracy, of revolutionary legality.

Because of the fact that not all as yet realize fully the practical consequences resulting from the cult of the individual, the great harm caused by the violation of the principle of collective direction of the party and because of the accumulation of immense and limitless power in the hands of one person, the Central Committee of the party considers it absolutely necessary to make the material pertaining to this matter available to the 20th Congress of the Communist Party of the Soviet Union.

Allow me first of all to remind you how severely the classics of

Marxism-Leninism denounced every manifestation of the cult of the individual. In a letter to the German political worker, Wilhelm Bloss, Marx stated: "From my antipathy to any cult of the individual, I never made public during the existence of the International the numerous addresses from various countries which recognized my merits and which annoyed me. I did not even reply to them, except sometimes to rebuke their authors. Engels and I first joined the secret society of Communists on the condition that everything making for superstitious worship of authority would be deleted from its statute. . . ."

The great modesty of the genius of the Revolution, Vladimir Ilyich Lenin, is known. Lenin had always stressed the role of the people as the creator of history, the directing and organizational role of the party as a living and creative organism, and also the role of the Central Committee.

Marxism does not negate the role of the leaders of the working class in directing the revolutionary liberation movement. While ascribing great importance to the role of the leaders and organizers of the masses, Lenin at the same time mercilessly stigmatized every manifestation of the cult of the individual, inexorably combated the foreign-to-Marxism views about a "hero" and a "crowd," and countered all efforts to oppose a "hero" to the masses and to the people. . . .

During Lenin's life the Central Committee of the party was a real expression of collective leadership of the party and of the nation. Being a militant Marxist-revolutionist, always unyielding in matters of principle, Lenin never imposed by force his views upon his co-workers. He tried to convince; he patiently explained his opinions to others. Lenin always diligently observed that the norms of party life were realized, that the party statute was enforced, that the party congresses and the plenary sessions of the Central Committee took place at the proper intervals.

In addition to the great accomplishments of V. I. Lenin for the victory of the working class and of the working peasants, for the victory of our party and for the application of the ideas of scientific Communism to life, his acute mind expressed itself also in this—that he detected in Stalin in time those negative characteristics which resulted later in grave consequences. Fearing the future fate of the party and of the Soviet nation, V. I. Lenin made a completely correct characterization of Stalin, pointing out that it was necessary to consider the question of transferring Stalin from the position of the Secretary General because of the fact that Stalin is excessively rude, that he does not have a proper attitude toward his comrades, that he is capricious and abuses his power.

In December 1922, in a letter to the Party Congress,[1] Vladimir Ilyich wrote: "After taking over the position of Secretary General, Comrade Stalin accumulated in his hands immeasurable power and I am not certain

_____

[1] The full text of this document is commonly known as "Lenin's Testament," although Lenin himself did not use that term. [It appears in Chapter 9 of this book.] [All footnotes are by Boris I. Nicolaevsky.]

whether he will be always able to use this power with the required care."

This letter—a political document of tremendous importance, known in the party history as Lenin's "testament"—was distributed among the delegates to the 20th Party Congress. You have read it and will undoubtedly read it again more than once. You might reflect on Lenin's plain words, in which expression is given to Vladimir Ilyich's anxiety concerning the party, the people, the state, and the future direction of party policy. . . .

This document of Lenin's was made known to the delegates at the 13th Party Congress, who discussed the question of transferring Stalin from the position of Secretary General. The delegates declared themselves in favor of retaining Stalin in this post, hoping that he would heed the critical remarks of Vladimir Ilyich and would be able to overcome the defects which caused Lenin serious anxiety.

Comrades! The Party Congress should become acquainted with two new documents, which confirm Stalin's character as already outlined by Vladimir Ilyich Lenin in his "testament." These documents are a letter from Nadezhda Konstantinovna Krupskaya to [Leo B.] Kamenev, who was at that time head of the Political Bureau, and a personal letter from Vladimir Ilyich Lenin to Stalin.

I will now read these documents:

LEV BORISOVICH! [2]
Because of a short letter which I had written in words dictated to me by Vladimir Ilyich by permission of the doctors, Stalin allowed himself yesterday an unusually rude outburst directed at me. This is not my first day in the party. During all these 30 years I have never heard from any comrade one word of rudeness. The business of the party and of Ilyich are not less dear to me than to Stalin. I need at present the maximum of self-control. What one can and what one cannot discuss with Ilyich I know better than any doctor, because I know what makes him nervous and what does not, in any case I know better than Stalin. I am turning to you and to Grigory [E. Zinoviev] as much closer comrades of V. I. and I beg you to protect me from rude interference with my private life and from vile invectives and threats. I have no doubt as to what will be the unanimous decision of the Control Commission, with which Stalin sees fit to threaten me; however, I have neither the strength nor the time to waste on this foolish quarrel. And I am a living person and my nerves are strained to the utmost.

N. KRUPSKAYA

Nadezhda Konstantinovna wrote this letter on December 23, 1922. After two and a half months, in March 1923, Vladimir Ilyich Lenin sent Stalin the following letter:[3]

[2] This letter has first come to light now. It has never before been mentioned in the literature of this field. It sheds considerable light on Stalin's real relations with Lenin in the last months of the latter's life. It shows that Stalin started baiting Krupskaya, Lenin's wife, immediately after Lenin suffered his second stroke (December 16, 1922) and systematically continued doing so right up to Lenin's death. . . .

[3] The existence of this letter was known from Trotsky's memoirs, but the full text has never previously been available. . . .

To Comrade Stalin:

Copies for: Kamenev and Zinoviev.

Dear Comrade Stalin!

You permitted yourself a rude summons of my wife to the telephone and a rude reprimand of her. Despite the fact that she told you that she agreed to forget what was said, nevertheless Zinoviev and Kamenev heard about it from her. I have no intention to forget so easily that which is being done against me, and I need not stress here that I consider as directed against me that which is being done against my wife. I ask you, therefore, that you weigh carefully whether you are agreeable to retracting your words and apologizing or whether you prefer the severance of relations between us.

SINCERELY: LENIN

MARCH 5, 1923

(Commotion in the hall.)

Comrades! I will not comment on these documents. They speak eloquently for themselves. Since Stalin could behave in this manner during Lenin's life, could thus behave toward Nadezhda Konstantinovna Krupskaya —whom the party knows well and values highly as a loyal friend of Lenin and as an active fighter for the cause of the party since its creation—we can easily imagine how Stalin treated other people. These negative characteristics of his developed steadily and during the last years acquired an absolutely insufferable character.

As later events have proven, Lenin's anxiety was justified: In the first period after Lenin's death, Stalin still paid attention to his advice, but later he began to disregard the serious admonitions of Vladimir Ilyich.

When we analyze the practice of Stalin in regard to the direction of the party and of the country, when we pause to consider everything which Stalin perpetrated, we must be convinced that Lenin's fears were justified. The negative characteristics of Stalin, which, in Lenin's time, were only incipient, transformed themselves during the last years into a grave abuse of power by Stalin, which caused untold harm to our party.

We have to consider seriously and analyze correctly this matter in order that we may preclude any possibility of a repetition in any form whatever of what took place during the life of Stalin, who absolutely did not tolerate collegiality in leadership and in work, and who practiced brutal violence, not only toward everything which opposed him, but also toward that which seemed, to his capricious and despotic character, contrary to his concepts.

Stalin acted not through persuasion, explanation and patient cooperation with people, but by imposing his concepts and demanding absolute submission to his opinion. Whoever opposed this concept or tried to prove his viewpoint and the correctness of his position was doomed to removal from the leading collective and to subsequent moral and physical annihilation. This was especially true during the period following the 17th Party Congress, when many prominent party leaders and rank-and-file party workers, honest and dedicated to the cause of Communism, fell victim to Stalin's despotism.

We must affirm that the party had fought a serious fight against the Trotskyites, rightists and bourgeois nationalists, and that it disarmed ideologically all the enemies of Leninism. This ideological fight was carried on successfully, as a result of which the party became strengthened and tempered. Here Stalin played a positive role.

The party led a great political-ideological struggle against those in its own ranks who proposed anti-Leninist theses, who represented a political line hostile to the party and to the cause of socialism. This was a stubborn and a difficult fight but a necessary one, because the political line of both the Trotskyite-Zinovievite bloc and of the Bukharinites led actually toward the restoration of capitalism and capitulation to the world bourgeoisie. Let us consider for a moment what would have happened if in 1928-1929 the political line of right deviation had prevailed among us, or orientation toward "cotton-dress industrialization," or toward the kulak, etc. We would not now have a powerful heavy industry, we would not have the *kolkhozes,* we would find ourselves disarmed and weak in a capitalist encirclement.

It was for this reason that the party led an inexorable ideological fight and explained to all party members and to the non-party masses the harm and the danger of the anti-Leninist proposals of the Trotskyite opposition and the rightist opportunists. And this great work of explaining the party line bore fruit; both the Trotskyites and the rightist opportunists were politically isolated; the overwhelming party majority supported the Leninist line and the party was able to awaken and organize the working masses to apply the Leninist party line and to build socialism.

Worth noting is the fact that, even during the progress of the furious ideological fight against the Trotskyites, the Zinovievites, the Bukharinites and others, extreme repressive measures were not used against them. The fight was on ideological grounds. But some years later, when socialism in our country was fundamentally constructed, when the exploiting classes were generally liquidated, when the Soviet social structure had radically changed, when the social basis for political movements and groups hostile to the party had violently contracted, when the ideological opponents of the party were long since defeated politically—then the repression directed against them began.

It was precisely during this period (1935-1937-1938) that the practice of mass repression through the Government apparatus was born, first against the enemies of Leninism—Trotskyites, Zinovievites, Bukharinites, long since politically defeated by the party—and subsequently also against many honest Communists, against those party cadres who had borne the heavy load of the Civil War and the first and most difficult years of industrialization and collectivization, who actively fought against the Trotskyites and the rightists for the Leninist party line.

Stalin originated the concept "enemy of the people." This term automatically rendered it unnecessary that the ideological errors of a man or men engaged in a controversy be proven; this term made possible the usage of the most cruel repression, violating all norms of revolutionary legality, against anyone who in any way disagreed with Stalin, against those who were only suspected of hostile intent, against those who had bad reputations. This concept "enemy of the people" actually eliminated the possibility of any kind of ideological fight or the making of one's views known on this or that issue, even those of a practical character. In the main, and in actuality, the only proof of guilt used, against all norms of current legal science, was the "confession" of the accused himself; and, as subsequent probing proved, "confessions" were acquired through physical pressures against the accused. This led to glaring violations of revolutionary legality and to the fact that many entirely innocent persons, who in the past had defended the party line, became victims.

We must assert that, in regard to those persons who in their time had opposed the party line, there were often no sufficiently serious reasons for their physical annihilation. The formula "enemy of the people" was specifically introduced for the purpose of physically annihilating such individuals.

It is a fact that many persons who were later annihilated as enemies of the party and people had worked with Lenin during his life. Some of these persons had made errors during Lenin's life, but, despite this, Lenin benefited by their work; he corrected them and he did everything possible to retain them in the ranks of the party; he induced them to follow him.

In this connection the delegates to the Party Congress should familiarize themselves with an unpublished note by V. I. Lenin directed to the Central Committee's Political Bureau in October 1920. Outlining the duties of the Control Commission, Lenin wrote that the commission should be transformed into a real "organ of party and proletarian conscience."

As a special duty of the Control Commission there is recommended a deep, individualized relationship with, and sometimes even a type of therapy for, the representatives of the so-called opposition—those who have experienced a psychological crisis because of failure in their Soviet or party career. An effort should be made to quiet them, to explain the matter to them in a way used among comrades, to find for them (avoiding the method of issuing orders) a task for which they are psychologically fitted. Advice and rules relating to this matter are to be formulated by the Central Committee's Organizational Bureau, etc. . . .

An entirely different relationship with people characterized Stalin. Lenin's traits—patient work with people, stubborn and painstaking education of them, the ability to induce people to follow him without using compulsion, but rather through the ideological influence on them of the whole collective—were entirely foreign to Stalin. He discarded the Leninist method of convincing and educating, he abandoned the method of ideological struggle for that of administrative violence, mass repressions and terror. He acted on an increasingly larger scale and more stubbornly through punitive organs, at the same time often violating all existing norms of morality and of Soviet laws.

Arbitrary behavior by one person encouraged and permitted arbitrariness in others. Mass arrests and deportations of many thousands of people, execution without trial and without normal investigation created conditions of insecurity, fear and even desperation.

This, of course, did not contribute toward unity of the party ranks and of all strata of working people, but, on the contrary, brought about annihilation and the expulsion from the party of workers who were loyal but inconvenient to Stalin.

Our party fought for the implementation of Lenin's plans for the construction of socialism. This was an ideological fight. Had Leninist principles been observed during the course of this fight, had the party's devotion to principles been skillfully combined with a keen and solicitous concern for people, had they not been repelled and wasted but rather drawn to our side, we certainly would not have had such a brutal violation of revolutionary legality and many thousands of people would not have fallen victim to the method of terror. Extraordinary methods would then have been resorted to only against those people who had in fact committed criminal acts against the Soviet system.

Let us recall some historical facts.

In the days before the October Revolution, two members of the Central Committee of the Bolshevik party—Kamenev and Zinoviev— declared themselves against Lenin's plan for an armed uprising.[4] In addition, on October 18 they published in the Menshevik newspaper, *Novaya Zhizn,* a statement declaring that the Bolsheviks were making preparations for an uprising and that they considered it adventuristic. Kamenev and Zinoviev thus disclosed to the enemy the decision of the Central Committee to stage the uprising, and that the uprising had been organized to take place within the very near future.

This was treason against the party and against the Revolution. In this connection, V. I. Lenin wrote: "Kamenev and Zinoviev revealed the decision of the Central Committee of their party on the armed uprising to Rodzyanko[5] and Kerensky[6] . . ." He put before the Central Committee the question of Zinoviev's and Kamenev's expulsion from the party.

However, after the Great Socialist October Revolution, as is known,

[4] Gregory E. Zinoviev (1883-1936) and Leo B. Kamenev (1883-1936), who in 1917 were members of the Party Central Committee, voted at this October 10, 1917 meeting against Lenin's proposal to organize an insurrection. . . .

[5] Mikhail V. Rodzyanko (1859-1924), President of the Third and Fourth Dumas, and a leader in the democratic February Revolution. He played a prominent role in its first days, but later vanished completely from the political scene. Lenin and other Bolsheviks concocted a completely false story that he had inspired behind-the-scenes reactionary forces which influenced the policies of the Provisional Government in 1917.

[6] Alexander F. Kerensky (born 1881) was President of the Provisional Government from July to October 1917.

Zinoviev and Kamenev were given leading positions. Lenin put them in positions in which they carried out most responsible party tasks and participated actively in the work of the leading party and Soviet organs. It is known that Zinoviev and Kamenev committed a number of other serious errors during Lenin's life. In his "testament" Lenin warned that "Zinoviev's and Kamenev's October episode was of course not an accident." But Lenin did not pose the question of their arrest and certainly not their shooting.

Or, let us take the example of the Trotskyites. At present, after a sufficiently long historical period, we can speak about the fight with the Trotskyites with complete calm and can analyze this matter with sufficient objectivity. After all, around Trotsky were people whose origin cannot by any means be traced to bourgeois society. Part of them belonged to the party intelligentsia and a certain part were recruited from among the workers. We can name many individuals who, in their time, joined the Trotskyites; however, these same individuals took an active part in the workers' movement before the Revolution, during the Socialist October Revolution itself, and also in the consolidation of the victory of this greatest of revolutions. Many of them broke with Trotskyism and returned to Leninist positions. Was it necessary to annihilate such people? We are deeply convinced that, had Lenin lived, such an extreme method would not have been used against any of them.

Such are only a few historical facts. But can it be said that Lenin did not decide to use even the most severe means against enemies of the Revolution when this was actually necessary? No; no one can say this. Vladimir Ilyich demanded uncompromising dealings with the enemies of the Revolution and of the working class and when necessary resorted ruthlessly to such methods. You will recall only V. I. Lenin's fight with the Socialist Revolutionary organizers of the anti-Soviet uprising, with the counterrevolutionary kulaks in 1918 and with others, when Lenin without hesitation used the most extreme methods against the enemies. Lenin used such methods, however, only against actual class enemies and not against those who blunder, who err, and whom it was possible to lead through ideological influence and even retain in the leadership. Lenin used severe methods only in the most necessary cases, when the exploiting classes were still in existence and were vigorously opposing the Revolution, when the struggle for survival was decidedly assuming the sharpest forms, even including a civil war.

Stalin, on the other hand, used extreme methods and mass repressions at a time when the Revolution was already victorious, when the Soviet state was strengthened, when the exploiting classes were already liquidated and socialist relations were rooted solidly in all phases of national economy, when our party was politically consolidated and had strengthened itself both numerically and ideologically.

It is clear that here Stalin showed in a whole series of cases his intolerance, his brutality and his abuse of power. Instead of proving his political correctness and mobilizing the masses, he often chose the path of repression and physical annihilation, not only against actual enemies, but also against individuals who had not committed any crimes against the party and the Soviet Government. Here we see no wisdom but only a demonstration of the brutal force which had once so alarmed V. I. Lenin.

Lately, especially after the unmasking of the Beria gang, the Central Committee looked into a series of matters fabricated by this gang.[7] This revealed a very ugly picture of brutal willfulness connected with the incorrect behavior of Stalin. As facts prove, Stalin, using his unlimited power, allowed himself many abuses, acting in the name of the Central Committee, not asking for the opinion of the Committee members nor even of the members of the Central Committee's Political Bureau; often he did not inform them about his personal decisions concerning very important party and government matters.

Considering the question of the cult of an individual, we must first of all show everyone what harm this caused to the interests of our party. Vladimir Ilyich Lenin had always stressed the party's role and significance in the direction of the socialist government of workers and peasants; he saw in this the chief precondition for a successful building of socialism in our country. Pointing to the great responsibility of the Bolshevik party, as ruling party of the Soviet state, Lenin called for the most meticulous observance of all norms of party life; he called for the realization of the principles of collegiality in the direction of the party and the state.

Collegiality of leadership flows from the very nature of our party, a party built on the principles of democratic centralism. "This means," said Lenin, "that all party matters are accomplished by all party members—directly or through representatives—who, without any exceptions, are subject to the same rules; in addition, all administrative members, all directing collegia, all holders of party positions are elective, they must account for their activities and are recallable."

It is known that Lenin himself offered an example of the most careful observance of these principles. There was no matter so important that Lenin himself decided it without asking for advice and approval of the majority of the Central Committee members or of the members of the Central Committee's Political Bureau. In the most difficult period for our

---

[7] This statement by Khrushchev is not quite true: Investigation of Stalin's terrorist acts in the last period of his life was initiated by Beria. On April 4, 1953, Beria announced the release of all those arrested in the so-called "doctors' plot" and the commitment for trial of those who fabricated it, led by Deputy Minister of State Security Ryumin, who was accused of torturing the prisoners (the first time such an accusation had been made openly against functionaries of the MGB). Khrushchev, who now depicts himself as having well-nigh initiated the probe of Stalin's torture chambers, actually tried to block it in the first months after Stalin's death.

party and our country, Lenin considered it necessary regularly to convoke congresses, party conferences and plenary sessions of the Central Committee at which all the most important questions were discussed and where resolutions, carefully worked out by the collective of leaders, were approved.

We can recall, for an example, the year 1918 when the country was threatened by the attack of the imperialistic interventionists. In this situation the 7th Party Congress was convened in order to discuss a vitally important matter which could not be postponed—the matter of peace. In 1919, while the civil war was raging, the 8th Party Congress convened which adopted a new party program, decided such important matters as the relationship with the peasant masses, the organization of the Red Army, the leading role of the party in the work of the soviets, the correction of the social composition of the party, and other matters. In 1920 the 9th Party Congress was convened which laid down guiding principles pertaining to the party's work in the sphere of economic construction. In 1921 the 10th Party Congress accepted Lenin's New Economic Policy and the historical resolution called "About Party Unity."

During Lenin's life, party congresses were convened regularly; always, when a radical turn in the development of the party and the country took place, Lenin considered it absolutely necessary that the party discuss at length all the basic matters pertaining to internal and foreign policy and to questions bearing on the development of party and government.

It is very characteristic that Lenin addressed to the Party Congress as the highest party organ his last articles, letters and remarks.[8] During the period between congresses, the Central Committee of the party, acting as the most authoritative leading collective, meticulously observed the principles of the party and carried out its policy. So it was during Lenin's life. Were our party's holy Leninist principles observed after the death of Vladimir Ilyich?

Whereas, during the first few years after Lenin's death, party congresses and Central Committee plenums took place more or less regularly, later, when Stalin began increasingly to abuse his power, these principles were brutally violated. This was especially evident during the last 15 years of his life. Was it a normal situation when over 13 years elapsed between the 18th and 19th Party Congresses, years during which our party and our country had experienced so many important events? These events demanded categorically that the party should have passed resolutions pertaining to the country's defense during the Patriotic War [World War II] and to peacetime construction after the war. Even after the end of the war a Congress was not convened for over seven years. Central Committee

---

[8] It was, of course, very characteristic of Lenin that he addressed his last articles, letters and notes to the Congress; but it is even more characteristic of the methods employed by the Communist dictatorship that these documents are still unpublished today under Khrushchev.

plenums were hardly ever called. It should be sufficient to mention that during all the years of the Patriotic War not a single Central Committee plenum took place. It is true that there was an attempt to call a Central Committee plenum in October 1941, when Central Committee members from the whole country were called to Moscow. They waited two days for the opening of the plenum, but in vain. Stalin did not even want to meet and talk to the Central Committee members. This fact shows how demoralized Stalin was in the first months of the war and how haughtily and disdainfully he treated the Central Committee members.

In practice, Stalin ignored the norms of party life and trampled on the Leninist principle of collective party leadership. Stalin's willfulness *vis-à-vis* the party and its Central Committee became fully evident after the 17th Party Congress which took place in 1934.

Having at its disposal numerous data showing brutal willfulness toward party cadres, the Central Committee has created a party commission under the control of the Central Committee Presidium; it was charged with investigating what made possible the mass repressions against the majority of the Central Committee members and candidates elected at the 17th Congress of the All-Union Communist Party (Bolsheviks).

The commission has become acquainted with a large quantity of materials in the NKVD archives and with other documents and has established many facts pertaining to the fabrication of cases against Communists, to false accusations, to glaring abuses of socialist legality, which resulted in the death of innocent people. It became apparent that many party, Soviet and economic activists, who were branded in 1937-1938 as "enemies," were actually never enemies, spies, wreckers, etc., but were always honest Communists; they were only so stigmatized and, often, no longer able to bear barbaric tortures, they charged themselves (at the order of the investigative judges—falsifiers) with all kinds of grave and unlikely crimes.

The commission has presented to the Central Committee Presidium lengthy and documented materials pertaining to mass repressions against the delegates to the 17th Party Congress and against members of the Central Committee elected at that Congress. These materials have been studied by the Presidium of the Central Committee.

It was determined that of the 139 members and candidates of the party's Central Committee who were elected at the 17th Congress, 98 persons, *i.e.,* 70 per cent, were arrested and shot (mostly in 1937-1938). (Indignation in the hall.) What was the composition of the delegates to the 17th Congress? It is known that 80 per cent of the voting participants of the 17th Congress joined the party during the years of conspiracy before the Revolution and during the civil war; this means before 1921. By social origin the basic mass of the delegates to the Congress were workers (60 per cent of the voting members).

For this reason, it was inconceivable that a congress so composed would have elected a Central Committee a majority of whom would prove to be enemies of the party. The only reason why 70 per cent of Central Committee members and candidates elected at the 17th Congress were branded as enemies of the party and of the people was because honest Communists were slandered, accusations against them were fabricated, and revolutionary legality was gravely undermined.

The same fate met not only the Central Committee members but also the majority of the delegates to the 17th Party Congress. Of 1,966 delegates with either voting or advisory rights, 1,108 persons were arrested on charges of anti-revolutionary crimes, *i.e.,* decidedly more than a majority. This very fact shows how absurd, wild and contrary to common sense were the charges of counterrevolutionary crimes made out, as we now see, against a majority of participants at the 17th Party Congress. (Indignation in the hall.)

We should recall that the 17th Party Congress is historically known as the Congress of Victors. Delegates to the Congress were active participants in the building of our socialist state; many of them suffered and fought for party interests during the pre-Revolutionary years in the conspiracy and at the civil-war fronts; they fought their enemies valiantly and often nervelessly looked into the face of death.

How, then, can we believe that such people could prove to be "two-faced" and had joined the camps of the enemies of socialism during the era after the political liquidation of Zinovievites, Trotskyites and rightists and after the great accomplishments of socialist construction? This was the result of the abuse of power by Stalin, who began to use mass terror against the party cadres.

What is the reason that mass repressions against activists increased more and more after the 17th Party Congress? It was because at that time Stalin had so elevated himself above the party and above the nation that he ceased to consider either the Central Committee or the party.

While he still reckoned with the opinion of the collective before the 17th Congress, after the complete political liquidation of the Trotskyites, Zinovievites and Bukharinites, when as a result of that fight and socialist victories the party achieved unity, Stalin ceased to an ever greater degree to consider the members of the party's Central Committee and even the members of the Political Bureau. Stalin thought that now he could decide all things alone and all he needed were statisticians; he treated all others in such a way that they could only listen to and praise him.

After the criminal murder of Sergei M. Kirov, mass repressions and brutal acts of violation of socialist legality began. On the evening of December 1, 1934 on Stalin's initiative (without the approval of the Political Bureau—which was passed two days later, casually), the Secretary of the Presidium of the Central Executive Committee, Yenukidze, signed the following directive:

1. Investigative agencies are directed to speed up the cases of those accused of the preparation or execution of acts of terror.

2. Judicial organs are directed not to hold up the execution of death sentences pertaining to crimes of this category in order to consider the possibility of pardon, because the Presidium of the Central Executive Committee of the U.S.S.R. does not consider as possible the receiving of petitions of this sort.

3. The organs of the Commissariat of Internal Affairs are directed to execute the death sentences against criminals of the above-mentioned category immediately after the passage of sentences.

This directive became the basis for mass acts of abuse against socialist legality. During many of the fabricated court cases, the accused were charged with "the preparation" of terroristic acts; this deprived them of any possibility that their cases might be re-examined, even when they stated before the court that their "confessions" were secured by force, and when, in a convincing manner, they disproved the accusations against them.

It must be asserted that to this day the circumstances surrounding Kirov's murder hide many things which are inexplicable and mysterious and demand a most careful examination. There are reasons for the suspicion that the killer of Kirov, Nikolayev, was assisted by someone from among the people whose duty it was to protect the person of Kirov.

A month and a half before the killing, Nikolayev was arrested on the grounds of suspicious behavior but he was released and not even searched. It is an unusually suspicious circumstance that when the Chekist assigned to protect Kirov was being brought for an interrogation, on December 2, 1934, he was killed in a car "accident" in which no other occupants of the car were harmed.[9] After the murder of Kirov, top functionaries of the Leningrad NKVD were given very light sentences, but in 1937 they were shot. We can assume that they were shot in order to cover the traces of the organizers of Kirov's killing. (Movement in the hall.)

Mass repressions grew tremendously from the end of 1936 after a telegram from Stalin and [Andrei] Zhdanov, dated from Sochi on September 25, 1936, was addressed to Kaganovich, Molotov and other members of the Political Bureau. The content of the telegram was as follows:

We deem it absolutely necessary and urgent that Comrade Yezhov be nominated to the post of People's Commissar for Internal Affairs. Yagoda has definitely proved himself to be incapable of unmasking the Trotskyite-Zinovievite bloc. The OGPU is four years behind in this matter. This is noted by all party workers and by the majority of the representatives of the NKVD.[10]

---

[9] Kirov did not permit a secret-police guard to be maintained around him, but he had in his office in Leningrad's Smolny Institute an elderly man named Borisov who acted more or less as his orderly. This Borisov would have been a most inconvenient eye-witness for the organizers of the murder. On December 2, he was called to the Leningrad NKVD to receive orders; on the way, he was killed in an auto crash in which no one else was injured. This mysterious episode was noted in a number of accounts of the Kirov murder; Khrushchev's report provides further confirmation.

[10] This telegram is an exceptionally important document, showing that Stalin felt that mass repressions within the Communist party were four years overdue—that is, they

Strictly speaking, we should stress that Stalin did not meet with and, therefore, could not know the opinion of party workers.

This Stalinist formulation that the "NKVD is four years behind" in applying mass repression and that there is a necessity for "catching up" with the neglected work directly pushed the NKVD workers on the path of mass arrests and executions.

We should state that this formulation was also forced on the February-March plenary session of the Central Committee of the All-Union Communist Party (Bolsheviks) in 1937. The plenary resolution approved it on the basis of Yezhov's report, "Lessons flowing from the harmful activity, diversion and espionage of the Japanese-German-Trotskyite agents," stating:

> The plenum of the Central Committee of the All-Union Communist Party (Bolsheviks) considers that all facts revealed during the investigation into the matter of an anti-Soviet Trotskyite center and of its followers in the provinces show that the People's Commissariat of Internal Affairs has fallen behind at least four years in the attempt to unmask these most inexorable enemies of the people.

The mass repressions at this time were made under the slogan of a fight against the Trotskyites. Did the Trotskyites at this time actually constitute such a danger to our party and to the Soviet state? We should recall that in 1927, on the eve of the 15th Party Congress, only some 4,000 votes were cast for the Trotskyite-Zinovievite opposition while there were 724,000 for the party line. During the 10 years which passed between the 15th Party Congress and the February-March Central Committee plenum, Trotskyism was completely disarmed; many former Trotskyites had changed their former views and worked in the various sectors building socialism. It is clear that in the situation of socialist victory there was no basis for mass terror in the country.

Stalin's report at the February-March Central Committee plenum in 1937, "Deficiencies of party work and methods for the liquidation of the Trotskyites and of other two-facers," contained an attempt at theoretical justification of the mass terror policy under the pretext that as we march forward toward socialism class war must allegedly sharpen. Stalin asserted that both history and Lenin taught him this.

Actually Lenin taught that the application of revolutionary violence is necessitated by the resistance of the exploiting classes, and this referred to the era when the exploiting classes existed and were powerful. . . .

Stalin deviated from these clear and plain precepts of Lenin. Stalin put the party and the NKVD up to the use of mass terror when the exploiting classes had been liquidated in our country and when there were no serious reasons for the use of extraordinary mass terror.

---

should have begun in 1932, when Stalin first demanded execution of members of the opposition group headed by Ryutin, Gorelov and others but was defeated both in the Politburo and at the Central Committee plenum which met from September 28 to October 2, 1932. On Stalin's demand, Henry Yagoda was removed from the post of People's Commissar for Internal Affairs and, on September 26, 1936, replaced by Nikolai I. Yezhov.

This terror was actually directed not at the remnants of the defeated exploiting classes but against the honest workers of the party and of the Soviet state; against them were made lying, slanderous and absurd accusations concerning "two-facedness," "espionage," "sabotage," preparation of fictitious "plots," etc.

At the February-March Central Committee plenum in 1937 many members actually questioned the rightness of the established course regarding mass repression under the pretext of combating "two-facedness." . . .

Using Stalin's formulation, namely, that the closer we are to socalism the more enemies we will have, and using the resolution of the February-March Central Committee plenum passed on the basis of Yezhov's report, the *provocateurs* who had infiltrated the state-security organs together with conscienceless careerists began to protect with the party name the mass terror against party cadres, cadres of the Soviet state and the ordinary Soviet citizens. It should suffice to say that the number of arrests based on charges of counterrevolutionary crimes had grown ten times between 1936 and 1937.

It is known that brutal willfulness was practiced against leading party workers. The party statute, approved at the 17th Party Congress, was based on Leninist principles expressed at the 10th Party Congress. It stated that, in order to apply an extreme method such as exclusion from the party against a Central Committee member, against a Central Committee candidate and against a member of the Party Control Commission, "it is necessary to call a Central Committee plenum and to invite to the plenum all Central Committee candidate members and all members of the Party Control Commission"; only if two-thirds of the members of such a general assembly of responsible party leaders find it necessary, only then can a Central Committee member or candidate be expelled.

The majority of the Central Committee members and candidates elected at the 17th Congress and arrested in 1937-1938 were expelled from the party illegally through the brutal abuse of the party statute, because the question of their expulsion was never studied at the Central Committee plenum.

Now, when the cases of some of these so-called "spies" and "saboteurs" were examined, it was found that all their cases were fabricated. Confessions of guilt of many arrested and charged with enemy activity were gained with the help of cruel and inhuman tortures.

At the same time, Stalin, as we have been informed by members of the Political Bureau of that time, did not show them the statements of many accused political activists when they retracted their confessions before the military tribunal and asked for an objective examination of their cases. There were many such declarations, and Stalin doubtless knew of them.

The Central Committee considers it absolutely necessary to inform the Congress of many such fabricated "cases" against the members of the party's Central Committee elected at the 17th Party Congress.

An example of vile provocation, of odious falsification and of criminal violation of revolutionary legality is the case of the former candidate for the Central Committee Political Bureau, one of the most eminent workers of the party and of the Soviet Government, Comrade Eikhe who was a party member since 1905. (Commotion in the hall.)

Comrade Eikhe was arrested on April 29, 1938 on the basis of slanderous materials, without the sanction of the Prosecutor of the U.S.S.R., which was finally received 15 months after the arrest.

Investigation of Eikhe's case was made in a manner which most brutally violated Soviet legality and was accompanied by willfulness and falsification.

Eikhe was forced under torture to sign ahead of time a protocol of his confession prepared by the investigative judges, in which he and several other eminent party workers were accused of anti-Soviet activity.

On October 1, 1939 Eikhe sent his declaration to Stalin in which he categorically denied his guilt and asked for an examination of his case. In the declaration he wrote: "There is no more bitter misery than to sit in the jail of a government for which I have always fought."

A second declaration of Eikhe has been preserved which he sent to Stalin on October 27, 1939; in it he cited facts very convincingly and countered the slanderous accusations made against him, arguing that this provocatory accusation was on the one hand the work of real Trotskyites whose arrests he had sanctioned as First Secretary of the West Siberian Krai [Territory] Party Committee and who conspired in order to take revenge on him, and, on the other hand, the result of the base falsification of materials by the investigative judges.

Eikhe wrote in his declaration:

. . . I am now alluding to the most disgraceful part of my life and to my really grave guilt against the party and against you. This is my confession of counter-revolutionary activity. . . . The case is as follows: Not being able to suffer the tortures to which I was submitted by Ushakov and Nikolayev—and especially by the first one—who utilized the knowledge that my broken ribs have not properly mended and have caused me great pain, I have been forced to accuse myself and others.

The majority of my confession has been suggested or dictated by Ushakov, and the remainder is my reconstruction of NKVD materials from Western Siberia for which I assumed all responsibility. If some part of the story which Ushakov fabricated and which I signed did not properly hang together, I was forced to sign another variation. . . .

It would appear that such an important declaration was worth an examination by the Central Committee. This, however, was not done, and the declaration was transmitted to Beria while the terrible maltreatment of the Political Bureau candidate, Comrade Eikhe, continued.

On February 2, 1940 Eikhe was brought before the court. Here he did not confess any guilt and said as follows:

In all the so-called confessions of mine there is not one letter written by me with the exception of my signatures under the protocols, which were forced from me. I have made my confession under pressure from the investigative judge, who from the time of my arrest tormented me. After that I began to write all this nonsense. . . . The most important thing for me is to tell the court, the party and Stalin that I am not guilty. I have never been guilty of any conspiracy. I will die believing in the truth of party policy as I have believed in it during my whole life.

On February 4 Eikhe was shot. (Indignation in the hall.)

It has been definitely established now that Eikhe's case was fabricated; he has been posthumously rehabilitated.

Comrade Rudzutak, candidate-member of the Political Bureau, member of the party since 1905, who spent 10 years in a Tsarist hard-labor camp, completely retracted in court the confession which was forced from him. The protocol of the session of the Collegium of the Supreme Military Court contains the following statement by Rudzutak:

. . . The only plea which he places before the court is that the Central Committee of the All-Union Communist Party (Bolsheviks) be informed that there is in the NKVD an as yet not liquidated center which is craftily manufacturing cases, which forces innocent persons to confess; there is no opportunity to prove one's non-participation in crimes to which the confessions of various persons testify. . . .

He was not even called before the Central Committee's Political Bureau because Stalin did not want to talk to him. Sentence was pronounced on him in 20 minutes and he was shot. (Indignation in the hall.)

After careful examination of the case in 1955, it was established that the accusation against Rudzutak was false and that it was based on slanderous materials. Rudzutak has been rehabilitated posthumously.

The way in which the former NKVD workers manufactured various fictitious "anti-Soviet centers" and "blocs" with the help of provocatory methods is seen from the confession of Comrade Rozenblum, party member since 1906, who was arrested in 1937 by the Leningrad NKVD.

During the examination in 1955 of the Komarov case Rozenblum revealed the following fact: When Rozenblum was arrested in 1937, he was subjected to terrible torture during which he was ordered to confess false information concerning himself and other persons. He was then brought to the office of Zakovsky,[11] who offered him freedom on condition that he make before the court a false confession fabricated in 1937 by the NKVD concerning "sabotage, espionage and diversion in a terroristic center in Leningrad." (Movement in the hall.) With unbelievable cynicism, Zakovsky told about the vile "mechanism" for the crafty creation of fabricated "anti-Soviet plots."

[11] Leonid Zakovsky, one of the most prominent figures in the *Yezhovshchina*, was chief first of the Leningrad section (1934-38) and then of the Moscow section of the NKVD. He was notorious for his merciless employment of torture followed by execution. After Yezhov's removal and Beria's rise to power, Zakovsky was arrested and disappeared.

"In order to illustrate it to me," stated Rozenblum, "Zakovsky gave me several possible variants of the organization of this center and of its branches." . . . Said Zakovsky:

You, yourself, will not need to invent anything. The NKVD will prepare for you a ready outline for every branch of the center; you will have to study it carefully and to remember well all questions and answers which the Court might ask. This case will be ready in four-five months, or perhaps a half year. During all this time you will be preparing yourself so that you will not compromise the investigation and yourself. Your future will depend on how the trial goes and on its results. If you begin to lie and to testify falsely, blame yourself. If you manage to endure it, you will save your head and we will feed and clothe you at the Government's cost until your death.

This is the kind of vile things which were then practiced. (Movement in the hall.) . . .

Many thousands of honest and innocent Communists have died as a result of this monstrous falsification of such "cases," as a result of the fact that all kinds of slanderous "confessions" were accepted, and as a result of the practice of forcing accusations against oneself and others. . . . In those years repressions on a mass scale were applied which were based on nothing tangible and which resulted in heavy cadre losses to the party.

The vicious practice was condoned of having the NKVD prepare lists of persons whose cases were under the jurisdiction of the Military Collegium and whose sentences were prepared in advance. Yezhov would send these lists to Stalin personally for his approval of the proposed punishment. In 1937-1938, 383 such lists containing the names of many thousands of party, Soviet, Komsomol, Army and economic workers were sent to Stalin. He approved these lists.

A large part of these cases are being reviewed now and a great part of them are being voided because they were baseless and falsified. Suffice it to say that from 1954 to the present time the Military Collegium of the Supreme Court has rehabilitated 7,679 persons, many of whom were rehabilitated posthumously.

Mass arrests of party, Soviet, economic and military workers caused tremendous harm to our country and to the cause of socialist advancement. Mass repressions had a negative influence on the moral-political condition of the party, created a situation of uncertainty, contributed to the spreading of unhealthy suspicion, and sowed distrust among Communists. All sorts of slanderers and careerists were active.

Resolutions of the January plenum of the Central Committee, All-Union Communist Party (Bolsheviks), in 1938 had brought some measure of improvement to the party organizations. However, widespread repression also existed in 1938.[12] . . .

[12] Khrushchev gives a completely incorrect appraisal of the decisions adopted by the January 1938 Central Committee plenum. The published version of one resolution did contain criticism of several incorrect expulsions from the Party, but the criticism was

Facts prove that many abuses were made on Stalin's orders without reckoning with any norms of party and Soviet legality. Stalin was a very distrustful man, sickly suspicious; we know this from our work with him. He could look at a man and say: "Why are your eyes so shifty today?" or "Why are you turning so much today and avoiding to look me directly in the eyes?" The sickly suspicion created in him a general distrust even toward eminent party workers whom he had known for years. Everywhere and in everything he saw "enemies," "two-facers" and "spies." Possessing unlimited power, he indulged in great willfulness and choked a person morally and physically. A situation was created where one could not express one's own will.

When Stalin said that one or another should be arrested, it was necessary to accept on faith that he was an "enemy of the people." Meanwhile, Beria's gang, which ran the organs of state security, outdid itself in proving the guilt of the arrested and the truth of materials which it falsified. And what proofs were offered? The confessions of the arrested, and the investigative judges accepted these "confessions." And how is it possible that a person confesses to crimes which he has not committed? Only in one way —because of application of physical methods of pressuring him, tortures, bringing him to a state of unconsciousness, deprivation of his judgment, taking away of his human dignity. In this manner were "confessions" acquired.

When the wave of mass arrests began to recede in 1939, and the leaders of territorial party organizations began to accuse the NKVD workers of using methods of physical pressure on the arrested, Stalin dispatched a coded telegram on January 20, 1939 to the committee secretaries of *oblasts* and *krais,* to the central committees of republic Communist parties, to the People's Commissars of Internal Affairs and to the heads of NKVD organizations. This telegram stated:

The Central Committee of the All-Union Communist Party (Bolsheviks) explains that the application of methods of physical pressure in NKVD practice is permissible from 1937 on in accordance with permission of the Central Committee of the All-Union Communist Party (Bolsheviks) . . . It is known that all bourgeois intelligence services use methods of physical influence against the representatives of the socialist proletariat and that they use them in their most scandalous forms.

The question arises as to why the socialist intelligence service should be more humanitarian against the mad agents of the bourgeoisie, against the deadly enemies of the working class and of the *kolkhoz* workers. The Central Committee of the All-Union Communist Party (Bolsheviks) considers that physical pressure should still be used obligatorily, as an exception applicable to known and obstinate enemies of the people, as a method both justifiable and appropriate.

---

curious: The plenum found that Party organizations had been guilty of expelling people on false denunciations "by masked two-facers," but that the NKVD organs led by Yezhov had exposed these criminal attempts and, after rehabilitating the innocent victims, punished the culprits. In other words, this was a resolution which praised the Yezhov purge. Khrushchev had to falsify his account because it was at this plenum that he himself was first elected a candidate member of the Politburo.

Thus, Stalin had sanctioned in the name of the Central Committee of the All-Union Communist Party (Bolsheviks) the most brutal violation of socialist legality, torture and oppression, which led as we have seen to the slandering and self-accusation of innocent people. . . .

The power accumulated in the hands of one person, Stalin, led to serious consequences during the Great Patriotic War.

When we look at many of our novels, films and historical "scientific studies," the role of Stalin in the Patriotic War appears to be entirely improbable. Stalin had foreseen everything. The Soviet Army, on the basis of a strategic plan prepared by Stalin long before, used the tactics of so-called "active defense," i.e., tactics which, as we know, allowed the Germans to come up to Moscow and Stalingrad. Using such tactics, the Soviet Army, supposedly thanks only to Stalin's genius, turned to the offensive and subdued the enemy. The epic victory gained through the armed might of the land of the Soviets, through our heroic people, is ascribed in this type of novel, film and "scientific study" as being completely due to the strategic genius of Stalin. . . . What are the facts of this matter?

[Editor's note: Khrushchev proceeds to show that Stalin ignored repeated warnings of impending German attack and adds that "despite these particularly grave warnings, the necessary steps were not taken to prepare the country properly for defense and to prevent it from being caught unawares."]

The result was that already in the first hours and days the enemy had destroyed in our border regions a large part of our Air Force, artillery and other military equipment; he annihilated large numbers of our military cadres and disorganized our military leadership; consequently we could not prevent the enemy from marching deep into the country.

Very grievous consequences, especially in reference to the beginning of the war, followed Stalin's annihilation of many military commanders and political workers during 1937-1941 because of his suspiciousness and through slanderous accusations.[13] During these years repressions were instituted against certain parts of military cadres beginning literally at the company and battalion commander level and extending to the higher military centers; during this time the cadre of leaders who had gained military experience in Spain and in the Far East was almost completely liquidated.

The policy of large-scale repression against the military cadres led also to undermined military discipline, because for several years officers of all

---

[13] We now know from revelations by former members of the German secret police that Stalin wiped out a vast part of the command personnel of the Red Army on the basis of false documents which Stalin's personal secretariat had received from Nazi agents. The false documents on the basis of which Marshal Tukhachevsky and his closest colleagues were executed were turned over by Nazi agents to L. Z. Mekhlis, a trusted member of Stalin's personnel secretariat, who flew to Berlin for that purpose in May 1937.

ranks and even soldiers in the party and Komsomol cells were taught to "unmask" their superiors as hidden enemies. (Movement in the hall.) It is natural that this caused a negative influence on the state of military discipline in the first war period.

And, as you know, we had before the war excellent military cadres which were unquestionably loyal to the party and to the Fatherland. Suffice it to say that those of them who managed to survive, despite severe tortures to which they were subjected in the prisons, have from the first war days shown themselves real patriots and heroically fought for the glory of the Fatherland; I have here in mind such comrades as Rokossovsky (who, as you know, had been jailed), Gorbatov, Maretskov (who is a delegate at the present Congress),[14] Podlas (he was an excellent commander who perished at the front), and many, many others. However, many such commanders perished in camps and jails and the Army saw them no more.

All this brought about the situation which existed at the beginning of the war and which was the great threat to our Fatherland. It would be incorrect to forget that, after the first severe disaster and defeat at the front, Stalin thought that this was the end. In one of his speeches in those days he said: "All that which Lenin created we have lost forever."

After this Stalin for a long time actually did not direct the military operations and ceased to do anything whatever. He returned to active leadership only when some members of the Political Bureau visited him and told him that it was necessary to take certain steps immediately in order to improve the situation at the front.

Therefore, the threatening danger which hung over our Fatherland in the first period of the war was largely due to the faulty methods of directing the nation and the party by Stalin himself.

However, we speak not only about the moment when the war began, which led to serious disorganization of our Army and brought us severe losses. Even after the war began, the nervousness and hysteria which Stalin demonstrated, interfering with actual military operation, caused our Army serious damage.

Stalin was very far from an understanding of the real situation which was developing at the front. This was natural because, during the whole Patriotic War, he never visited any section of the front or any liberated city except for one short ride on the Mozhaisk highway during a stabilized situation at the front. To this incident were dedicated many literary works full of fantasies of all sorts and so many paintings. . . .

[14] Marshal Konstantin K. Rokossovsky, [formerly] Poland's Defense Minister, was arrested in 1937 in Leningrad, where he was a corps commander. He was repeatedly subjected to brutal beatings in the course of interrogation and then sent to a concentration camp, from which he was released shortly before the outbreak of war in 1941. The same fate overtook the other military commanders mentioned by Khrushchev: Colonel-General Alexander V. Gorbatov, now commander of the Baltic Military District; Marshal Kirill A. Meretskov, now commander of the Northern Military District, and many others.

The tactics on which Stalin insisted without knowing the essence of the conduct of battle operations cost us much blood until we succeeded in stopping the opponent and going over to the offensive.

The military know that already by the end of 1941, instead of great operational maneuvers flanking the opponent and penetrating behind his back, Stalin demanded incessant frontal attacks and the capture of one village after another.

Because of this, we paid with great losses—until our generals, on whose shoulders rested the whole weight of conducting the war, succeeded in changing the situation and shifting to flexible-maneuver operations, which immediately brought serious changes at the front favorable to us.

All the more shameful was the fact that, after our great victory over the enemy which cost us so much, Stalin began to downgrade many of the commanders who contributed so much to the victory over the enemy, because Stalin excluded every possibility that services rendered at the front should be credited to anyone but himself.

Stalin was very much interested in the assessment of Comrade Zhukov as a military leader. He asked me often for my opinion of Zhukov. I told him then, "I have known Zhukov for a long time; he is a good general and a good military leader."

After the war Stalin began to tell all kinds of nonsense about Zhukov, among others the following, "You praised Zhukov, but he does not deserve it. It is said that before each operation at the front Zhukov used to behave as follows: He used to take a handful of earth, smell it and say, 'We can begin the attack,' or the opposite, 'The planned operation cannot be carried out.'" I stated at that time, "Comrade Stalin, I do not know who invented this, but it is not true." It is possible that Stalin himself invented these things for the purpose of minimizing the role and military talents of Marshal Zhukov.

In this connection, Stalin very energetically popularized himself as a great leader; in various ways he tried to inculcate in the people the version that all victories gained by the Soviet nation during the Great Patriotic War were due to the courage, daring and genius of Stalin and of no one else. . . .

Not Stalin, but the party as a whole, the Soviet Government, our heroic Army, its talented leaders and brave soldiers, the whole Soviet nation—these are the ones who assured the victory in the Great Patriotic War. (Tempestuous and prolonged applause.) . . .

Comrades, let us reach for some other facts. The Soviet Union is justly considered as a model of a multinational state because we have in practice assured the equality and friendship of all nations which live in our great Fatherland.

All the more monstrous are the acts whose initiator was Stalin and which are rude violations of the basic Leninist principles of the nationality policy of the Soviet state. We refer to the mass deportations from their native places of whole nations, together with all Communists and Komsomols without any exception; this deportation action was not dictated by any military considerations.

Thus, already at the end of 1943, when there occurred a permanent break-through at the fronts of the Great Patriotic War benefiting the Soviet Union, a decision was taken and executed concerning the deportation of all the Karachai from the lands on which they lived.

In the same period, at the end of December 1943, the same lot befell the whole population of the Autonomous Kalmyk Republic. In March 1944, all the Chechen and Ingush peoples were deported and the Chechen-Ingush Autonomous Republic was liquidated. In April 1944, all Balkars were deported to faraway places from the territory of the Kabardino-Balkar Autonomous Republic and the Republic itself was renamed the Autonomous Kabardian Republic.[15]

The Ukrainians avoided meeting this fate only because there were too many of them and there was no place to which to deport them. Otherwise, he would have deported them also. (Laughter and animation in the hall.)

Not only a Marxist-Leninist but also no man of common sense can grasp how it is possible to make whole nations responsible for inimical activity, including women, children, old people, Communists and Komsomols, to use mass repression against them, and to expose them to misery and suffering for the hostile acts of individual persons or groups of persons.

After the conclusion of the Patriotic War, the Soviet nation stressed with pride the magnificent victories gained through great sacrifices and tremendous efforts. The country experienced a period of political enthusiasm. The party came out of the war even more united; in the fire of the war, party cadres were tempered and hardened. Under such conditions nobody could have even thought of the possibility of some plot in the party.

And it was precisely at this time that the so-called "Leningrad affair" was born. As we have now proven, this case was fabricated. Those who innocently lost their lives included Comrades Voznesensky, Kuznetsov, Rodionov, Popkov, and others.

As is known, Voznesensky and Kuznetsov were talented and eminent leaders. Once they stood very close to Stalin. It is sufficient to mention that Stalin made Voznesensky first deputy to the chairman of the Council of Ministers and Kuznetsov was elected Secretary of the Central Committee. The very fact that Stalin entrusted Kuznetsov with the supervision of the state-security organs shows the trust which he enjoyed.

How did it happen that these persons were branded as enemies of the people and liquidated?

[15] Khrushchev does not mention two Soviet republics liquidated during the war on Stalin's orders whose populations were deported to Siberia and Kazakhstan, *i.e.,* the autonomous Volga German and Crimean Republics.

Facts prove that the "Leningrad affair" is also the result of willfulness which Stalin exercised against party cadres. Had a normal situation existed in the party's Central Committee and in the Central Committee Political Bureau, affairs of this nature would have been examined there in accordance with party practice, and all pertinent facts assessed; as a result, such an affair as well as others would not have happened.

We must state that, after the war, the situation became even more complicated. Stalin became even more capricious, irritable and brutal; in particular his suspicion grew. His persecution mania reached unbelievable dimensions. Many workers were becoming enemies before his very eyes. After the war, Stalin separated himself from the collective even more. Everything was decided by him alone without any consideration for anyone or anything. . . .

The question arises: Why is it that we see the truth of this affair only now, and why did we not do something earlier, during Stalin's life, in order to prevent the loss of innocent lives? It was because Stalin personally supervised the "Leningrad affair," and the majority of the Political Bureau members did not, at that time, know all of the circumstances in these matters and could not therefore intervene. . . .

The willfulness of Stalin showed itself not only in decisions concerning the internal life of the country but also in the international relations of the Soviet Union.

The July plenum of the Central Committee studied in detail the reasons for the development of conflict with Yugoslavia. It was a shameful role which Stalin played here. The "Yugoslav affair" contained no problems which could not have been solved through party discussions among comrades. There was no significant basis for the development of this "affair"; it was completely possible to have prevented the rupture of relations with that country. This does not mean, however, that the Yugoslav leaders did not make mistakes or did not have shortcomings. But these mistakes and shortcomings were magnified in a monstrous manner by Stalin, which resulted in a break of relations with a friendly country.

I recall the first days when the conflict between the Soviet Union and Yugoslavia began artificially to be blown up. Once, when I came from Kiev to Moscow, I was invited to visit Stalin, who, pointing to the copy of a letter lately sent to Tito, asked me, "Have you read this?"

Not waiting for my reply, he answered, "I will shake my little finger—and there will be no more Tito. He will fall. . . ."

Let us also recall the "affair of the doctor-plotters." (Animation in the hall.) Actually there was no "affair" outside of the declaration of the woman doctor Timashuk, who was probably influenced or ordered by someone (after all, she was an unofficial collaborator of the organs of state security) to write Stalin a letter in which she declared that doctors were applying supposedly improper methods of medical treatment.

Such a letter was sufficient for Stalin to reach an immediate conclusion that there are doctor-plotters in the Soviet Union.[16] He issued orders to arrest a group of eminent Soviet medical specialists. He personally issued advice on the conduct of the investigation and the method of interrogation of the arrested persons. He said that the academician Vinogradov should be put in chains, another one should be beaten. Present at this Congress as a delegate is the former Minister of State Security, Comrade Ignatiev. Stalin told him curtly, "If you do not obtain confessions from the doctors we will shorten you by a head." (Tumult in the hall.)

Stalin personally called the investigative judge, gave him instructions, advised him on which investigative methods should be used; these methods were simple—beat, beat and, once again, beat.

Shortly after the doctors were arrested, we members of the Political Bureau received protocols with the doctors' confessions of guilt. After distributing these protocols, Stalin told us, "You are blind like young kittens; what will happen without me? The country will perish because you do not know how to recognize enemies."

The case was so presented that no one could verify the facts on which the investigation was based. There was no possibility of trying to verify facts by contacting those who had made the confessions of guilt. We felt, however, that the case of the arrested doctors was questionable. We knew some of these people personally because they had once treated us. When we examined this "case" after Stalin's death, we found it to be fabricated from beginning to end. . . .

In organizing the various dirty and shameful cases, a very base role was played by the rabid enemy of our party, an agent of a foreign intelligence service—Beria, who had stolen into Stalin's confidence. In what way could this *provocateur* gain such a position in the party and in the state, so as to become the First Deputy Chairman of the Council of Ministers of the Soviet Union and a member of the Central Committee Political Bureau? It has now been established that this villain had climbed up the Government ladder over an untold number of corpses. . . .

The indictment in the Beria case contains a discussion of his crimes. Some things should, however, be recalled, especially since it is possible that not all delegates to the Congress have read this document. I wish to recall Beria's bestial disposition of the cases of Kedrov,[17] Golubev, and Golubev's

---

[16] The case of the "doctors' plot" was concocted on Stalin's orders in the winter of 1952-53 by the then Minister of State Security, S. D. Ignatiev, and his deputy, Ryumin. Several dozen of the leading doctors in Moscow were arrested, headed by the top specialists of the Kremlin hospital who treated Stalin and all the Soviet chieftains. They were officially charged with using improper medical techniques in order to murder their patients. Specifically, they were accused of having poisoned Andrei A. Zhdanov and Alexander S. Shcherbakov and of attempting to poison Marshals Konev, Vasilevsky, Govorov and others. . . .

[17] Mikhail S. Kedrov (1878-1940), a Bolshevik since the early 1900s, was in 1907-08 director of the legal Bolshevik publishing house in St. Petersburg, which published among other works the first collection of Lenin's political articles, *During Twelve Years*. . . .

adopted mother, Baturina—persons who wished to inform the Central Committee concerning Beria's treacherous activity. They were shot without any trial and the sentence was passed *ex post facto,* after the execution.

Here is what the old Communist, Comrade Kedrov, wrote to the Central Committee through Comrade Andreyev (Comrade Andreyev was then a Central Committee secretary):

> . . . My torture has reached the extreme. My health is broken, my strength and my energy are waning, the end is drawing near. To die in a Soviet prison, branded as a vile traitor to the Fatherland—what can be more monstrous for an honest man? And how monstrous all this is! Unsurpassed bitterness and pain grips my heart. No! No! This will not happen; this cannot be, I cry. Neither the party, nor the Soviet Government, nor the People's Commissar, L. P. Beria, will permit this cruel, irreparable injustice. I am firmly certain that, given a quiet, objective examination, without any foul rantings, without any anger and without the fearful tortures, it would be easy to prove the baselessness of the charges. I believe deeply that truth and justice will triumph. I believe. I believe.

The old Bolshevik, Comrade Kedrov, was found innocent by the Military Collegium. But, despite this, he was shot at Beria's order. (Indignation in the hall.)

Beria also handled cruelly the family of Comrade Ordzhonikidze. Why? Because Ordzhonikidze had tried to prevent Beria from realizing his shameful plans. Beria had cleared from his way all persons who could possibly interfere with him. Ordzhonikidze was always an opponent of Beria, which he told to Stalin. Instead of examining this affair and taking appropriate steps, Stalin allowed the liquidation of Ordzhonikidze's brother and brought Ordzhonikidze himself to such a state that he was forced to shoot himself.[18] (Indignation in the hall.)

Beria was unmasked by the party's Central Committee shortly after Stalin's death. As a result of the particularly detailed legal proceedings, it was established that Beria had committed monstrous crimes and Beria was shot.

The question arises why Beria, who had liquidated tens of thousands of the party and Soviet workers, was not unmasked during Stalin's life. He was not unmasked earlier because he had utilized very skillfully Stalin's weaknesses; feeding him with suspicions, he assisted Stalin in everything and acted with his support.

Comrades: The cult of the individual acquired such monstrous size chiefly because Stalin himself, using all conceivable methods, supported the glorification of his own person. This is supported by numerous facts. One of the most characteristic examples of Stalin's self-glorification and of

[18] Official Soviet statements during the past three years have gradually lifted the veil of secrecy from the death of Grigory K. (Sergo) Ordzhonikidze (1886-1937). The original version published in the Soviet press attributed his death on February 18, 1937 to heart disease. This can now be finally discarded—as can any confidence in the official bulletins of Soviet doctors. Nor can one trust the latest statement, that he shot himself. . . .

his lack of even elementary modesty is the edition of his *Short Biography,* which was published in 1948.

This book is an expression of the most dissolute flattery, an example of making a man into a godhead, of transforming him into an infallible sage, "the greatest leader, sublime strategist of all times and nations." Finally, no other words could be found with which to lift Stalin up to the heavens.

We need not give here examples of the loathesome adulation filling this book. All we need to add is that they all were approved and edited by Stalin personally and some of them were added in his own handwriting to the draft text of the book.

What did Stalin consider essential to write into this book? Did he want to cool the ardor of his flatterers who were composing his *Short Biography?* No! He marked the very places where he thought that the praise of his services was insufficient. . . . Thus writes Stalin himself:

> Although he performed his task as leader of the party and the people with consummate skill and enjoyed the unreserved support of the entire Soviet people, Stalin never allowed his work to be marred by the slightest hint of vanity, conceit or self-adulation. . . .
>
> Stalin's military mastership was displayed both in defense and offense. Comrade Stalin's genius enabled him to divine the enemy's plans and defeat them. The battles in which Comrade Stalin directed the Soviet armies are brilliant examples of operational military skill. . . .

And when Stalin himself asserts that he himself wrote the *Short Course of the History of the All-Union Communist Party (Bolsheviks),* this calls at least for amazement. Can a Marxist-Leninist thus write about himself, praising his own person to the heavens?

Or let us take the matter of the Stalin Prizes. (Movement in the hall.) Not even the Tsars created prizes which they named after themselves. . . .

And was it without Stalin's knowledge that many of the largest enterprises and towns were named after him? Was it without his knowledge that Stalin monuments were erected in the whole country—these "memorials to the living"? . . . Consider, yourself, was Stalin right when he wrote in his biography that ". . . he did not allow in himself . . . even a shadow of conceit, pride, or self-adoration"? . . .

In speaking about the events of the October Revolution and about the Civil War, the impression was created that Stalin always played the main role, as if everywhere and always Stalin had suggested to Lenin what to do and how to do it. However, this is slander of Lenin. (Prolonged applause.)

I will probably not sin against the truth when I say that 99 per cent of the persons present here heard and knew very little about Stalin before the year 1924, while Lenin was known to all; he was known to the whole party, to the whole nation, from the children up to the graybeards. (Tumultuous, prolonged applause.)

All this has to be thoroughly revised so that history, literature and the fine arts property reflect V. I. Lenin's role and the great deeds of our Communist party and of the Soviet people—the creative people. (Applause.)

Comrades! The cult of the individual has caused the employment of faulty principles in party work and in economic activity; it brought about rude violation of internal party and Soviet democracy, sterile administration, deviations of all sorts, covering up the shortcomings and varnishing of reality. Our nation gave birth to many flatterers and specialists in false optimism and deceit.

We should also not forget that, due to the numerous arrests of party, Soviet and economic leaders, many workers began to work uncertainly, showed over-cautiousness, feared all which was new, feared their own shadows and began to show less initiative in their work.

Take, for instance, party and Soviet resolutions. They were prepared in a routine manner, often without considering the concrete situation. This went so far that party workers, even during the smallest sessions, read their speeches. All this produced the danger of formalizing the party and Soviet work and of bureaucratizing the whole apparatus.

Stalin's reluctance to consider life's realities and the fact that he was not aware of the real state of affairs in the provinces can be illustrated by his direction of agriculture. All those who interested themselves even a little in the national situation saw the difficult situation in agriculture, but Stalin never even noted it. Did we tell Stalin about this? Yes, we told him, but he did not support us. Why? Because Stalin never traveled anywhere, did not meet city and *kolkhoz* workers; he did not know the actual situation in the provinces. . . .

And when he was once told during a discussion that our situation on the land was a difficult one and that the situation of cattle breeding and meat production was especially bad, a commission was formed which was charged with the preparation of a resolution called "Means toward further development of animal breeding in *kolkhozes* and *sovkhozes*." We worked out this project.

Of course, our proposals of that time did not contain all possibilities, but we did chart ways in which animal breeding on *kolkhozes* and *sovkhozes* would be raised. We had proposed then to raise the prices of such products in order to create material incentives for the *kolkhoz*, MTS [machine-tractor station] and *sovkhoz* workers in the development of cattle breeding. But our project was not accepted and in February 1953 was laid aside entirely.

What is more, while reviewing this project Stalin proposed that the taxes paid by the *kolkhozes* and by the *kolkhoz* workers should be raised by 40 billion rubles; according to him the peasants are well off and the *kolkhoz* worker would need to sell only one more chicken to pay his tax in full.

Imagine what this meant. Certainly, 40 billion rubles is a sum which the *kolkhoz* workers did not realize for all the products which they sold to the Government. In 1952, for instance, the *kolkhozes* and the *kolkhoz* workers received 26,280 million rubles for all their products delivered and sold to the Government.

Did Stalin's position, then, rest on data of any sort whatever? Of course not. In such cases facts and figures did not interest him. If Stalin said anything, it meant it was so—after all, he was a "genius," and a genius does not need to count, he only needs to look and can immediately tell how it should be. When he expresses his opinion, everyone has to repeat it and to admire his wisdom.

But how much wisdom was contained in the proposal to raise the agricultural tax by 40 billion rubles? None, absolutely none, because the proposal was not based on an actual assessment of the situation but on the fantastic ideas of a person divorced from reality. . . .

If we are to consider this matter as Marxists and as Leninists, then we have to state unequivocally that the leadership practice which came into being during the last years of Stalin's life became a serious obstacle in the path of Soviet social development. Stalin often failed for months to take up some unusually important problems, concerning the life of the party and of the state, whose solution could not be postponed. During Stalin's leadership our peaceful relations with other nations were often threatened, because one-man decisions could cause, and often did cause, great complications.

In the last years, when we managed to free ourselves of the harmful practice of the cult of the individual and took several proper steps in the sphere of internal and external policies, everyone saw how activity grew before their very eyes, how the creative activity of the broad working masses developed, how favorably all this acted upon the development of economy and of culture. (Applause.)

Some comrades may ask us: Where were the members of the Political Bureau of the Central Committee? Why did they not assert themselves against the cult of the individual in time? And why is this being done only now?

First of all, we have to consider the fact that the members of the Political Bureau viewed these matters in a different way at different times. Initially, many of them backed Stalin actively because Stalin was one of the strongest Marxists and his logic, his strength and his will greatly influenced the cadres and party work.

It is known that Stalin, after Lenin's death, especially during the first years, actively fought for Leninism against the enemies of Leninist theory and against those who deviated. Beginning with Leninist theory, the party, with its Central Committee at the head, started on a great scale the work of socialist industrialization of the country, agricultural collectivization and the cultural revolution.

At that time Stalin gained great popularity, sympathy and support.

The party had to fight those who attempted to lead the country away from the correct Leninist path; it had to fight Trotskyites, Zinovievites and rightists, and the bourgeois nationalists. This fight was indispensable. Later, however, Stalin, abusing his power more and more, began to fight eminent party and Government leaders and to use terroristic methods against honest Soviet people. . . .

In the situation which then prevailed I have talked often with Nikolai Alexandrovich Bulganin; once when we two were traveling in a car, he said, "It has happened sometimes that a man goes to Stalin on his invitation as a friend. And, when he sits with Stalin, he does not know where he will be sent next—home or to jail."

It is clear that such conditions put every member of the Political Bureau in a very difficult situation. And, when we also consider the fact that in the last years the Central Committee plenary sessions were not convened and that the sessions of the Political Bureau occurred only occasionally, from time to time, then we will understand how difficult it was for any member of the Political Bureau to take a stand against one or another unjust or improper procedure, against serious errors and shortcomings in the practices of leadership. As we have already shown, many decisions were taken either by one person or in a roundabout way, without collective discussion. . . .

One of the oldest members of our party, Klimenti Yefremovich Voroshilov, found himself in an almost impossible situation. For several years he was actually deprived of the right of participation in Political Bureau sessions. Stalin forbade him to attend the Political Bureau sessions and to receive documents. When the Political Bureau was in session and Comrade Voroshilov heard about it, he telephoned each time and asked whether he would be allowed to attend. Sometimes Stalin permitted it, but always showed his dissatisfaction.

Because of his extreme suspicion, Stalin toyed also with the absurd and ridiculous suspicion that Voroshilov was an English agent. (Laughter in the hall.) It's true—an English agent. A special tapping device was installed in his home to listen to what was said there. (Indignation in the hall.) By unilateral decision, Stalin had also separated one other man from the work of the Political Bureau—Andrei Andreyevich Andreyev. This was one of the most unbridled acts of willfulness.

Let us consider the first Central Committee plenum after the 19th Party Congress when Stalin, in his talk at the plenum, characterized Vyacheslav Mikhailovich Molotov and Anastas Ivanovich Mikoyan and suggested that these old workers of our party were guilty of some baseless charges. It is not excluded that had Stalin remained at the helm for another several months, Comrades Molotov and Mikoyan would probably have not delivered any speeches at this Congress.

Stalin evidently had plans to finish off the old members of the Political

Bureau. He often stated that Political Bureau members should be replaced by new ones.

His proposal, after the 19th Congress, concerning the election of 25 persons to the Central Committee Presidium, was aimed at the removal of the old Political Bureau members and the bringing in of less experienced persons so that these would extol him in all sorts of ways. We can assume that this was also a design for the future annihilation of the old Political Bureau members and, in this way, a cover for all shameful acts of Stalin, acts which we are now considering.

Comrades! In order not to repeat errors of the past, the Central Committee has declared itself resolutely against the cult of the individual. We consider that Stalin was excessively extolled. However, in the past Stalin doubtless performed great services to the party, to the working class and to the international workers' movement.

This question is complicated by the fact that all this which we have just discussed was done during Stalin's life under his leadership and with his concurrence; here Stalin was convinced that this was necessary for the defense of the interests of the working classes against the plotting of enemies and against the attack of the imperialist camp.

He saw this from the position of the interest of the working class, of the interest of the laboring people, of the interest of the victory of socialism and communism. We cannot say that these were the deeds of a giddy despot. He considered that this should be done in the interest of the party, of the working masses, in the name of the defense of the revolution's gains. In this lies the whole tragedy! . . .

We should, in all seriousness, consider the question of the cult of the individual. We cannot let this matter get out of the party, especially not to the press. It is for this reason that we are considering it here at a closed Congress session. We should know the limits; we should not give ammunition to the enemy; we should not wash our dirty linen before their eyes. I think that the delegates to the Congress will understand and assess properly all these proposals. (Tumultuous applause.)

Comrades! We must abolish the cult of the individual decisively, once and for all; we must draw the proper conclusions concerning both ideological-theoretical and practical work. It is necessary for this purpose:

First, in a Bolshevik manner to condemn and to eradicate the cult of the individual as alien to Marxism-Leninism and not consonant with the principles of party leadership and the norms of party life, and to fight inexorably all attempts at bringing back this practice in one form or another.

To return to and actually practice in all our ideological work the most important theses of Marxist-Leninist science about the people as the creator of history and as the creator of all material and spiritual good of humanity, about the decisive role of the Marxist party in the revolutionary fight for the transformation of society, about the victory of communism.

In this connection we will be forced to do much work in order to examine critically from the Marxist-Leninist viewpoint and to correct the widely spread erroneous views connected with the cult of the individual in the sphere of history, philosophy, economy and of other sciences, as well as in literature and the fine arts. It is especially necessary that in the immediate future we compile a serious textbook of the history of our party which will be edited in accordance with scientific Marxist objectivism, a textbook of the history of Soviet society, a book pertaining to the events of the Civil War and the Great Patriotic War.

Secondly, to continue systematically and consistently the work done by the party's Central Committee during the last years, a work characterized by minute observation in all party organizations, from the bottom to the top, of the Leninist principles of party leadership, characterized, above all, by the main principle of collective leadership, characterized by the observance of the norms of party life described in the statutes of our party, and, finally, characterized by the wide practice of criticism and self-criticism.

Thirdly, to restore completely the Leninist principles of Soviet socialist democracy, expressed in the Constitution of the Soviet Union, to fight willfulness of individuals abusing their power. The evil caused by acts violating revolutionary socialist legality which have accumulated during a long time as a result of the negative influence of the cult of the individual has to be completely corrected.

Comrades! The 20th Congress of the Communist Party of the Soviet Union has manifested with a new strength the unshakable unity of our party, its cohesiveness around the Central Committee, its resolute will to accomplish the great task of building communism. (Tumultuous applause.)

And the fact that we present in all their ramifications the basic problems of overcoming the cult of the individual which is alien to Marxism-Leninism, as well as the problem of liquidating its burdensome consequences, is an evidence of the great moral and political strength of our party. (Prolonged applause.)

We are absolutely certain that our party, armed with the historical resolutions of the 20th Congress, will lead the Soviet people along the Leninist path to new successes, to new victories. (Tumultuous, prolonged applause.)

Long live the victorious banner of our party—Leninism! (Tumultuous, prolonged applause ending in ovation. All rise.)

Chapter 13

WHO RULES IN RUSSIA?

Few serious students of Soviet affairs would maintain that significant political power resides in the mass of the Russian people—except in an inchoate sense—or even in the millions of Communist Party members as a whole. While E. H. Carr and Milovan Djilas, in the excerpts that follow, both see power concentrated in a ruling group which, in Carr's phrase "finds its institutional embodiment in the Party," they disagree on whether there may be said to be a ruling class *in Russia and on the extent to which there is fluidity in Soviet society and the ruling group.*

Merle Fainsod concerns himself principally with the position of the Communist Party in the post-Stalin era. As Fainsod explains, "the major thrust of the Khrushchev reforms has been to reinforce the authority of the party apparatus in every direction." Typical of the Communist need to relate practice to theory is Khrushchev's justification of the primacy of the Party. In an interview with Iverach McDonald, foreign editor of The Times *of London, on January 31, 1958, Khrushchev linked decentralization of industry with the transition to a communist society under which "many organs of state administration will gradually wither away. Thus the army, the court, the Prosecutor's office and other organs will wither away." He further maintained that "Already now social life is developing exactly along lines following from the theoretical principles of Marxism-Leninism," and added:*

So, in these conditions, in order to utilize most rationally the available material and other resources, the Party's role is increasing. The Party has a stronger foundation than the government organs. It has arisen and exists not as a result of some obligations of a legislative kind. Its development is conditioned by circumstances following from political views of people, that is, from propositions of a moral factor. And humanity will always need moral factors.

WHO RULES IN SOVIET SOCIETY?

E. H. CARR*

The victors of 1917 thought they were establishing a dictatorship of the proletariat, or, a shade more realistically, a dictatorship of the proletariat and the peasantry. Just as the peasants were encouraged to seize the land, so the workers were encouraged to take over the factories. "Workers' control" was the slogan of the hour. Workers' control did not work, and without it the dictatorship of the proletariat ceased to be a reality and became a symbol. It was replaced by what? The answer is clear. By the dictatorship of the party (a phrase used at the time by Lenin and others, though afterwards rejected as heretical) and later by the dictatorship of the party machine. In other words, if we want to identify the ruling group in Soviet society, we have to look not for a class but for a party.

The Marxist class analysis of society was a product of the nineteenth century. Few people are convinced by the famous generalization with which the Communist Manifesto opens, that all history has been the history of class struggles. Marx took what he correctly diagnosed as the most significant feature of contemporary society in Western Europe and sweepingly extended it to other periods, where its application was by no means so clear. Marx never explained what he meant by a class: it probably seemed so obvious a phenomenon of the world in which he lived as not to require definition. But I will take Lenin's definition: "Classes are groups of people of such a kind that one group can appropriate the labor of another, thanks to the difference of their position in the specific structure of the social economy."

This takes account of the two cardinal factors in class. Class is primarily based on common economic interest, but it also acquires a quasi-permanent character conferred on it by social tradition or convention. I have never been altogether happy about the application of the class analysis to countries like the United States where, for historical reasons, this quasi-permanent character is weak or non-existent, or to countries like Czarist Russia where the major divisions of society were not economic, but legal and constitutional; and I feel sure that it is altogether misleading as an explanation of the structure of Soviet society. There is no ruling class in Soviet Russia.

* Fellow, Trinity College, Cambridge. Author of the monumental *A History of Soviet Russia; Studies in Revolution; The Soviet Impact on the Western World,* and many scholarly articles on Soviet affairs. The selection is from *The Nation,* Vol. 181 (October 1, 1955), pp. 278-280. By permission.

There is a ruling group which finds its institutional embodiment in the party.

This is, I think, significant. A class is an economic formation, a party a political formation. I shall not argue that economic factors play a smaller role in the life of society than in the nineteenth century. But what I would maintain is that the clear-cut line of demarcation between economics and politics which dominated all economic thinking in the nineteenth century, including that of Marx, is out of date. In Soviet Russia, at any rate, economics means politics, and the structure of Soviet society must be analyzed in terms not of economic class but of political party.

As I have said, the dictatorship of the proletariat was replaced by the dictatorship of the party when workers' control collapsed in the factories. And workers' control collapsed because the workers lacked the necessary technical engineering and managerial skills. One of the first tasks of the party, of the ruling group, was to find the technicians and white-collar workers of all grades to put industry back into production; and the attitude to be adopted to these "specialists," as they were called, was a constant pre-occupation of party literature. And when, a few years later, the even more desperate problem was tackled of mechanizing agriculture and introducing modern methods of cultivation, the difficulty once more was to provide not only machinery but skilled personnel to use it and organize its use. It was precisely those specialists who, being indispensable to the regime, came to occupy a leading—and sometimes equivocal—position in the ruling group of what was still called a workers' state; and to study the party's attitude toward them is an important part of the analysis of Soviet society.

From the outset the attitude of the party toward specialists was utterly different from its position on the nepmen. The nepmen, and *a fortiori* the *kulak*, was *ex hypothesi* an enemy of the regime, pursuing aims incompatible with it, tolerated only so long as he had to be. A loyal nepman or a loyal *kulak* was an impossibility; no nepman or *kulak* could conceivably be admitted to the party. The specialist, on the other hand, though by his origins he might be a class enemy like the nepman, was pursuing the aims of the regime whose servant he was. His origins might make him suspect. But he could be, and often was, loyal; and as time went on more and more specialists became party members. Thus, for the specialist, origin was not the determining factor. He might be bourgeois by origin but he was not bourgeois in function. He did not enjoy the economic independence of the *entrepreneur*. On the contrary, he was politically dependent on the government and on the party. If he was successful, success was rewarded not by increased profits but by promotion to a bigger and better job. The soft-pedalling of world revolution, the proclamation of "socialism in one country," and the policy of industrialization eased the process of the assimilation for the specialist. By the end of the nineteen-twenties he had become, by and large, a loyal servant of the regime; the avenues of promotion and of party membership were wide open to him.

I do not think that up to this time the specialist had any important influence on decisions of policy. These were still taken by the old party leadership, by the survivors of the pre-revolutionary party intelligentsia. But in the nineteen-thirties, when a new generation grew up which had never known pre-revolutionary Russia, and when sons of workers had clambered up the educational ladder to the top, the distinctions began to fade. The taint of bourgeois origin was no longer acutely felt; and the whole group of white-collar workers—party officials, government officials, managers, technicians, teachers, doctors, lawyers, and intellectuals of all kinds—began gradually to coalesce. Official pronouncements began to extol the member of this new intelligentsia; the Stalin constitution enfranchised him irrespective of his origin; the party statute of 1939 gave him a status in the party side by side with the worker and the peasant.

It is in this new intelligentsia, recruited from different class origins, and not constituting a class in the Marxist or Leninist sense of the term, that we must look for the ruling group in Soviet society. This is the group which has substituted itself for the dictatorship of the proletariat; the only theoretical justification for the substitution is that its *raison d'etre* and its purpose—the cementing force which holds it together—is the industrialization of the country. In this respect, it still carries the dynamic of the proletarian revolution; and to this long-term purpose the immediate welfare of the worker, to say nothing of the peasant, will be ruthlessly sacrificed. The ruling group remains pledged to the eradication of everything bourgeois from Soviet society. It if still tolerates a handful of nepmen, it tolerates them because it must. It is engaged in a desperate uphill struggle to turn the *kolkhoz* worker into a good Socialist—a struggle only halted by the still more desperate need to induce him to feed the towns for a meager return in the form of consumer goods. This is the core of the problem which any ruling group that stands for industrialization has to face.

One more question: How far does this ruling group constitute a closed and privileged social order? . . . Every ruling group looks after its own, including its own children; and, when good educational facilities are scarce, it will see to it that its children get the best. But the essential facts about Soviet society is that it is the society of an expanding economy; and educational facilities, too, are expanding rapidly. In an expanding society policies of exclusion do not work and do not last. The child of the worker does not, it is true, start level with the child of the party official or of the industrial manager. But the gulf is not unbridgeable, and it seems likely to narrow if the Soviet economy continues to expand at anything like its present rate. So long as this goes on, Soviet society and the ruling group will remain fluid and we shall see further changes. Meanwhile, we only confuse ourselves by attempting to equate the present regime in Russia with anything we have seen in the past—whether with a Czarist autocracy or with a Victorian bourgeoisie. It is a new phenomenon in history, with new merits and new vices, and we had better try to see it for what it is.

THE NEW CLASS

Milovan Djilas*

Everything happened differently in the U.S.S.R. and other Communist countries from what the leaders—even such prominent ones as Lenin, Stalin, Trotsky, and Bukharin—anticipated. They expected that the state would rapidly wither away, that democracy would be strengthened. The reverse happened. They expected a rapid improvement in the standard of living—there has been scarcely any change in this respect and, in the subjugated East European countries, the standard has even declined. In every instance, the standard of living has failed to rise in proportion to the rate of industrialization, which was much more rapid. It was believed that the differences between cities and villages, between intellectual and physical labor, would slowly disappear; instead these differences have increased. Communist anticipations in other areas—including their expectations for developments in the non-Communist world—have also failed to materialize.

The greatest illusion was that industrialization and collectivization in the U.S.S.R., and destruction of capitalist ownership, would result in a classless society. In 1936, when the new Constitution was promulgated, Stalin announced that the "exploiting class" had ceased to exist. The capitalist and other classes of ancient origin had in fact been destroyed, but a new class, previously unknown to history, had been formed. . . .

The roots of the new class were implanted in a special party, of the Bolshevik type. Lenin was right in his view that his party was an exception in the history of human society, although he did not suspect that it would be the beginning of a new class.

To be more precise, the initiators of the new class are not found in the party of the Bolshevik type as a whole but in that stratum of professional revolutionaries who made up its core even before it attained power. . . .

The once live, compact party, full of initiative, is disappearing to

* Partisan leader during the war and former Vice-President of Yugoslavia under Tito, he broke with Yugoslav Communism and was expelled from the Party in 1954. He is presently in prison as a result of attacks on the Yugoslav regime. The selection is from the book and chapter titled *The New Class* (New York: Frederick A. Praeger, Inc., 1957). By permission of the publisher.

become transformed into the traditional oligarchy of the new class, ir-
resistibly drawing into its ranks those who aspire to join the new class and
repressing those who have any ideals.

The party makes the class, but the class grows as a result and uses the
party as a basis. The class grows stronger, while the party grows weaker;
this is the inescapable fate of every Communist party in power. . . .

The movement of the new class toward power comes as a result of the
efforts of the proletariat and the poor. These are the masses upon which
the party or the new class must lean and with which its interests are most
closely allied. This is true until the new class finally establishes its power
and authority. Over and above this, the new class is interested in the
proletariat and the poor only to the extent necessary for developing production and for maintaining in subjugation the most aggressive and rebellious
social forces. The monopoly which the new class establishes in the name
of the working class over the whole of society is, primarily, a monopoly
over the working class itself. . . .

As defined by Roman law, property constitutes the use, enjoyment,
and disposition of material goods. The Communist political bureaucracy
uses, enjoys, and disposes of nationalized property.

If we assume that membership in this bureaucracy or new owning
class is predicated on the use of privileges inherent in ownership—in this
instance nationalized material goods—then membership in the new party
class, or political bureaucracy, is reflected in a larger income in material
goods and privileges than society should normally grant for such functions.
In practice, the ownership privilege of the new class manifests itself as an
exclusive right, as a party monopoly, for the political bureaucracy to
distribute the national income, to set wages, direct economic development,
and dispose of nationalized and other property. This is the way it appears
to the ordinary man who considers the Communist functionary as being
very rich and as a man who does not have to work. . . .

Membership in the Communist Party before the Revolution meant
sacrifice. Being a professional revolutionary was one of the highest honors.
Now that the party has consolidated its power, party membership means that
one belongs to a privileged class. And at the core of the party are the all-
powerful exploiters and masters. . . .

In Stalin's victory Trotsky saw the Thermidoric reaction against the
revolution, actually the bureaucratic corruption of the Soviet government
and the revolutionary cause. Consequently, he understood and was deeply
hurt by the amorality of Stalin's methods. Trotsky was the first, although he
was not aware of it, who in the attempt to save the Communist movement
discovered the essence of contemporary Communism. But he was not
capable of seeing it through to the end. He supposed that this was only a
momentary cropping up of bureaucracy, corrupting the party and the revolution, and concluded that the solution was in a change at the top, in a

"palace revolution." When a palace revolution actually took place after Stalin's death, it could be seen that the essence had not changed; something deeper and more lasting was involved. The Soviet Thermidor of Stalin had not only led to the installation of a government more despotic than the previous one, but also to the installation of a class. . . .

Without relinquishing anything it created under Stalin's leadership, the new class appears to be renouncing his authority for the past few years. But it is not really renouncing that authority—only Stalin's methods which, according to Khrushchev, hurt "good Communists." . . .

In view of the significance of ownership for its power—and also of the fruits of ownership—the party bureaucracy cannot renounce the extension of its ownership even over small-scale production facilities. Because of its totalitarianism and monopolism, the new class finds itself unavoidably at war with everything which it does not administer or handle, and must deliberately aspire to destroy or conquer it. . . .

The fact that the seizure of property from other classes, especially from small owners, led to decreases in production and to chaos in the economy was of no consequence to the new class. Most important for the new class, as for every owner in history, was the attainment and consolidation of ownership. The class profited from the new property it had acquired even though the nation lost thereby. The collectivization of peasant holdings, which was economically unjustified, was unavoidable if the new class was to be securely installed in its power and its ownership. . . .

The establishment of the ownership of the new class was evidenced in the changes in the psychology, the way of life, and the material position of its members, depending on the position they held on the hierarchical ladder. Country homes, the best housing, furniture, and similar things were acquired; special quarters and exclusive rest homes were established for the highest bureaucracy, for the elite of the new class. The party secretary and the chief of the secret police in some places not only became the highest authorities but obtained the best housing, automobiles, and similar evidence of privilege. Those beneath them were eligible for comparable privileges, depending upon their position in the hierarchy. The state budgets, "gifts," and the construction and reconstruction executed for the needs of the state and its representatives became the everlasting and inexhaustible sources of benefits to the political bureaucracy. . . .

Open at the bottom, the new class becomes increasingly and relentlessly narrower at the top. Not only is the desire necessary for the climb; also necessary is the ability to understand and develop doctrines, firmness in struggles against antagonists, exceptional dexterity and cleverness in intra-party struggles, and talent in strengthening the class. . . .

Just as under Stalin, the new regime, in excuting its so-called liberalization policy, is extending the "socialist" ownership of the new class. Decentralization in the economy does not mean a change in ownership, but only gives greater rights to the lower strata of the bureaucracy or of the new class. If the so-called liberalization and decentralization meant anything else, that would be manifest in the political right of at least part of the people to exercise some influence in the management of material goods. At least, the people would have the right to criticize the arbitrariness of the oligarchy. This would lead to the creation of a new political movement, even though it were only a loyal opposition. However, this is not even mentioned, just as democracy in the party is not mentioned. Liberalization and decentralization are in force only for Communists; first for the oligarchy, the leaders of the new class; and second, for those in the lower echelons. This is the new method, inevitable under changing conditions, for the further strengthening and consolidation of monopolistic ownership and totalitarian authority of the new class. . . .

The new class instinctively feels that national goods are, in fact, its property, and that even the terms "socialist," "social," and "state" property denote a general legal fiction. The new class also thinks that any breach of its totalitarian authority might imperil its ownership. Consequently, the new class opposes *any* type of freedom, ostensibly for the purpose of preserving "socialist" ownership. Criticism of the new class's monopolistic administration of property generates the fear of a possible loss of power. . . .

In defending its authority, the ruling class must execute reforms every time it becomes obvious to the people that the class is treating national property as its own. Such reforms are not proclaimed as being what they really are, but rather as part of the "further development of socialism" and "socialist democracy." . . .

This is a class whose power over men is the most complete known to history. For this reason it is a class with very limited views, views which are false and unsafe. Closely ingrown, and in complete authority, the new class must unrealistically evaluate its own role and that of the people around it.

Having achieved industrialization, the new class can now do nothing more than strengthen its brute force and pillage the people. It ceases to create. Its spiritual heritage is overtaken by darkness.

While the new class accomplished one of its greatest successes in the revolution, its method of control is one of the most shameful pages in human history. Men will marvel at the grandiose ventures it accomplished, and will be ashamed of the means it used to accomplish them.

When the new class leaves the historical scene—and this must happen—there will be less sorrow over its passing than there was for any other class before it. Smothering everything except what suited its ego, it has condemned itself to failure and shameful ruin.

THE PARTY IN THE POST-STALIN ERA

Merle Fainsod*

In the period since Stalin's death, pressures for the loosening of party controls have again become visible on the Soviet scene. This restiveness has been many-sided. In the intellectual realm it has expressed itself in a demand for "creative freedom" and liberation from bureaucratic party direction.[1] In the military sphere—if the charges against Marshal Zhukov are true—resistance to party controls has taken the form of "curtailing the work of party organizations, political organs and military councils" and "of abolishing the leadership and control of the party, its Central Committee and Government over the Army and the Navy."[2] In the economic sector, as the recent public discussion of industrial reorganization made clear, there is widespread insistence by factory directors and enterprise managers on the need for greater autonomy in conducting their operations.[3]

These symptoms of dissatisfaction over restrictive party controls may be viewed as part of a larger pattern of pluralistic forces which are seeking expression in Soviet society. Rapid industrialization, educational advances, and the growth of professionalism in different walks of Soviet life have operated in varying degrees to create points of resistance to monolithic party control. Indeed, these developments have led some to contend that there is an inevitable conflict between the imperatives of an industrial society and the functions traditionally assigned to the party in Soviet society, and that the party is destined to become obsolete as the pressures for democratization and freedom spawned by education and industrialization come into ascendancy. Arguing the conflict thesis more cautiously, Barrington Moore Jr. concluded in 1954 that the forces which have been set in motion by industrialization will compel the party men to give ground to the engineer-administrator and that "if peace should continue for a decade or more, the rationalist or the traditionalist forces in Soviet society, or some unstable combination of the two, may do their work of erosion upon the Soviet totalitarian edifice."[4]

* The selection is from *Problems of Communism*, Vol. 7 (January-February 1958), pp. 7-13. By permission.
[1] See, *e.g.*, Khrushchev's speech in *Pravda*, August 28, 1957.
[2] *Pravda*, November 2, 1957.
[3] See "The Soviet Industrial Reorganization," by Alec Nove, in *Problems of Communism*, No. 6, November-December 1957.
[4] Barrington Moore, Jr., *Terror and Progress U.S.S.R.*, Harvard University Press, Cambridge, Mass., 1954, pp. 31, 231.

Meanwhile, a half decade of history has unfolded since Stalin's death. How has the party apparatus responded to challenges to its authority? Is there any evidence that its power has been undermined? Have there been any perceptible changes in the role of the party, and if so, how can those changes be defined?

THE PARTY MACHINE

One lesson of the last five years would appear by now to be undeniable. Control of the party apparatus remains the key to supreme power in the Soviet system. The step-by-step ascent of Khrushchev to a position of undisputed leadership represents a striking recapitulation of the Stalinist experience. Starting, like Stalin before him, from a position of relative weakness in the Presidium, Khrushchev has used the powers of the secretarial office to install his friends in key posts in the party and governmental apparatus, to pack the Central Committee with his supporters, and to transform his preponderance in the Central Committee into domination of the Presidium.

The present composition of the Presidium dramatizes the ascendancy of the party Secretariat. Of the fifteen full members, no less than ten— Khrushchev, Aristov, Beliaev, Brezhnev, Kuusinen, Furtseva, Suslov, Mukhitdinov, N. G. Ignatov, and Kirichenko—also serve as secretaries of the Central Committee. One other, F. R. Kozlov, occupies the important post of First Secretary of the Leningrad organization. The four remaining members of the Presidium—Bulganin, Mikoyan, Voroshilov, and Shvernik— represent holders from the old Stalinist Politburo whose power has been effectively neutralized by the new arrivals. Of the eight alternate members of the Presidium, one, Pospelov, is a secretary of the Central Committee and four others serve as first secretaries in the republic and regional party apparatus—Kalnberzin in Latvia, Mazurov in Belorussia, Mzhavanadze in Georgia, and Kirilenko in Sverdlovsk. Of the three remaining alternates, Korotchenko, a former party **apparatchik,** occupies the post of Chairman of the Ukrainian Supreme Soviet, while only two, Pervukhin and Kosygin, hold ministerial positions and can be classified as managerial or technical in their primary orientation.*

When the composition of the present-day Presidium is compared with the Politburo under Stalin, or even with the enlarged Presidium which came into being after the Nineteenth Party Congress in October 1952, some interesting contrasts are evident. Stalin's high command contained representatives of the police in the persons of Beria and later S. D. Ignatiev; at

* Editor's footnote: In November 1958, Beliaev was relieved of his secretarial post, while retaining membership in the Presidium, to enable him to devote more time to Party leadership in Kazakhstan. In March 1958, Koslov was made a First Deputy Premier; and, in September, Bulganin was ousted from the Presidium. At present (November 1958), Pervuhkin is the U.S.S.R.'s Ambassador to East Germany.

present there are no representatives of the police ministries in the top structure of party authority. While Stalin's inner circle included no professional army officers (unless Voroshilov is so regarded), Khrushchev for a brief period enlisted the services of Marshal Zhukov, only to cast him aside when he loomed as a potential competitor for supreme power. Stalin's Presidium included some of the Soviet Union's outstanding economic administrators; Khrushchev has demoted them to a lower order of influence and status in the party hierarchy. Under Khrushchev, more than ever before, the Presidium has become the inner sanctum of the party functionaries. For those who looked to the "managerial revolution" to make its influence felt in the highest reaches of the Soviet power structure, there can be little comfort in these developments.

An analysis of the composition of the Central Committee elected at the Twentieth Party Congress reveals a similar pattern of domination by the party secretariat. While the Central Committee includes a substantial group of ministers and a sprinkling of army officers, diplomats, and party ideologists, the party functionaries are clearly the most numerous group. Well over half of the membership consists of Central Committee secretaries and members of the Central Committee apparatus, secretaries of the republic party organizations, and first secretaries of the regional party committees. To the extent that this apparatus operates as a disciplined phalanx responsive to Khrushchev's leadership, it enables him to impose his will on all the leading party organs.

THE SPREADING TENTACLES

Khrushchev's authority is not confined to party circles alone. As part of his drive for power, a well-planned campaign was successfully executed to place his supporters in strategic posts in the governmental apparatus. While many examples could be cited, a few must suffice. The head of the political police (KGB), General I. A. Serov, was an associate of Khrushchev's in the Ukraine and his rise to prominence has paralleled Khrushchev's. The Procurator-General since June 1953 has been R. A. Rudenko, a former subordinate of Khrushchev's in the Ukraine. On February 1, 1956, S. N. Kruglov was replaced as Minister of Internal Affairs by N. P. Dudorov, who was also a Khrushchev subordinate in the Ukraine and was later brought to Moscow as chief of the construction section of the Central Committee Secretariat. The head of Gosplan and first deputy chairman of the U.S.S.R. Council of Ministers, I. I. Kuzmin, headed the machine-building section of the Central Committee apparatus until he was lifted by Khrushchev to his new pinnacle. While the projection of party functionaries into key administrative posts was primarily designed to consolidate Khrushchev's grip on the governing machinery, its effect was also to underline the central importance of the party apparatus in Khrushchev's formula of governance.

The rise of Khrushchev has been accompanied by a renewed emphasis on the leading role of the party in Soviet society. On July 6, 1956, Pravda proclaimed: "As for our country, the Communist Party was, is, and will be the only ruler of thought, the inspirer of ideas and aspirations, the leader and organizer of the people in the entire course of their struggle for communism . . ." This militant reiteration of the vanguard role of the party has been accompanied by an effort to pour new vitality into party life. On the ideological front, it has expressed itself in a drive to recapture revolutionary momentum and élan by stressing the triumphs of the regime at home and abroad. But it has proved no easy matter to recreate the evangelical fervor and messianic dedication of the early revolutionary years, and the shrill demands of the party press for ideological commitment reveal undertones of concern at the lack of ardor and militancy in party ranks.[5]

With a view to securing greater mass support, the party has altered its recruitment policy to attract more collective farmers and production workers into its ranks. Under the recruitment directives now in force, the party seeks to enlist "the best people" in every occupational group.[6] While the party remains basically an association of the directing cadres of the Soviet Union, its stress on the recruitment of "outstanding" kolkhozniks and factory workers is designed to sink firmer roots into the lower reaches of Soviet society and to prevent the estrangement of the masses from the top party stratum.

REFORMS FROM ABOVE

The campaign to breathe new life into the party has also been attended by a so-called "democratization" drive. The professed objectives have included wider participation of party members in party activities and discussions, secret elections of party bureaus and secretaries, punctilious observance of party rules in calling meetings and conferences, and broader scope for initiative at the grass roots. While scattered reports of local party meetings make clear that some highly embarrassing and challenging questions were put in the wake of Khrushchev's "secret" attack on Stalin at the Twentieth CPSU Congress, nothing that has happened thus far indicates any real impairment of central control over the party rank and file. With a few minor exceptions, "elections" below continue to ratify the nominations

[5] Thus *Pravda* noted on February 22, 1957, ". . . we cannot shut our eyes to the fact that in Soviet society, too, there are still people poisoned by petty-bourgeois survivals, who take at face value the profusion of bourgeois propaganda about the 'delights' of bourgeois democracy and the bourgeois way of life."

[6] For an excellent treatment of recent changes in recruitment policy, see T. H. Rigby, "Social Orientation of Recruitment and Distribution of Membership in the Communist Party of the Soviet Union." *The American Slavic and East European Review,* New York. October 1957, pp. 275-90.

of higher party organs, and discussions have followed the traditional course of "unanimously" approving central resolutions. Power has remained safely in the hands of the central party functionaries.

Under pressure from the center, the number of paid functionaries has been reduced, and the party apparatus itself has been reorganized to secure greater efficiency and more adequate control. As an accompaniment to the agricultural reforms initiated in the fall of 1953, the party embarked on a drastic reorganization of its rural organization with the objective of bringing the leadership closer to the grass roots.[7] The fulcrum of intensive control was shifted from the raion, or district center, to the MTS (machine-tractor stations). Each raion was divided into zones—one for each MTS station—and a district party secretary was assigned to each zone with headquarters at the MTS. Party instructors were transferred from the raion centers to the MTS, with each instructor responsible for one or at most two collective farms.

Since then a number of other steps have been taken to simplify the party structure. The political departments (politotdels) at Machine-Tractor Stations have been abolished, and the system of special Central Committee organizers in important industrial enterprises has also been liquidated. There has been a contraction in the number of paid secretaries in primary (i.e., the lowest-level) party organizations. At the republic and oblast level, sections of the party apparatus have been combined, and at the raion, or district, level there has been some tendency to replace sectional organization of the secretariat by a pool of party instructors, each of whom is assigned to one or more primary organizations with responsibility for all aspects of their work.[8]

The major thrust of the Khrushchev reforms has been to reinforce the authority of the party apparatus in every direction. Beginning with the reassertion of party controls in the MVD after the arrest of Beria, all efforts to weaken party controls in any sector of Soviet life have been sternly rebuffed. The rebuke administered early in 1954 to party officials in the Ministry of Construction who violated the party decree prohibiting the acceptance of payments or bonuses from economic organizations furnished a striking example.[9] **Pravda** seized the occasion to re-emphasize the independence of the party hierarchy and to indicate that party officials who allowed themselves to become "tools in the hands of administrative organizations" would be severely punished. The tendency under Khrushchev has been to stress the party's economic responsibilities and to gear agitational and propaganda activities much more directly to production objectives. As Khrushchev put it at the Twentieth Congress:

[7] *Pravda*, September 13 and 15, 1953; March 6 and 21, 1954.

[8] See T. Uldzhabaev. "Soversherstvuem rabotu partiinovo apparata" (We Improve the work of the party apparatus), *Partiinaia Zhizn*, No. 14 (July 1957), pp. 20-27.

[9] See *Partiinais Zhizn*, No. 3 (May 1954), pp. 47-50.

Economic development is one of the most important facets of our party work. The work of a party official should be judged primarily by those results attained in development of the economy for which he is responsible . . . Unfortunately, many party organizations draw an absurd distinction between party political work and economic activity. One still meets so-called party "officials" who consider party work one thing and economic work and state administration another. One can even hear complaints from such functionaries that they are being diverted from so-called "pure party work" and compelled to study economics, technology, farming and production. Such a conception of the tasks of party work is fundamentally wrong and harmful. The Communist Party of the Soviet Union is the ruling party and everything that happens on our Soviet soil is of vital interest to the party as a whole and to each Communist. A Communist has no right to be a detached bystander. This is why the party demands that party cadres not separate party work from economic work and that they supervise the economy in a concrete and competent manner . . .[10]

THE POLITICS OF ECONOMICS

The curious history of Khrushchev's role in the recent struggle over industrial reorganizations may serve to illustrate his determination to centralize control of the economy in the hands of the party apparatus. At the Central Committee plenum in December, 1956, a decision was approved to broaden the powers of the Economic Commission and to install Pervukhin and other leading economic administrators in controlling posts within it. The effect of this move was to strengthen the authority of elements in the Presidium identified with the state rather than the party machine. Against the background of later developments, it now appears clear that the scheme was not palatable to Khrushchev. Departing from his usual custom, he delivered no report to the Plenum nor did he associate himself with the plan. Perhaps reluctant to do battle so soon after the Hungarian and Polish debacles, he apparently acceded to the demands of his rivals in the Presidium to fortify the power of the Economic Commission and even allowed the Supreme Soviet to ratify the reorganization scheme on February 12, 1957.

Yet the very next day a specially summoned session of the Central Committee convened to hear a report by Khrushchev, which proposed a radically different approach to the managerial problem. Apparently now assured of overwhelming support in the Central Committee, Khrushchev counterattacked with a plan designed to emasculate the Economic Commission and to place control of the economy securely in the hands of the party apparatus.

The resolution approved by the Central Committee was cautiously worded. It spoke merely of "reorganizing the work of the State Economic Commission" and "of the need to increase the role of the State Planning Commission (Gosplan) in planning and managing the country's national economy." [11] It called for a reduction of the central apparatus of the

[10] *Pravda.* February, 15, 1956.
[11] *Pravda,* February 16, 1957.

ministries and for a transfer of personnel and functions to new regional organs of administration which would be closer to production and provide for integrated development of economic areas. But its political thrust lay elsewhere. By weakening the power of the central governmental bureaucracy and initiating a major rorganization of the central planning organs, it cleared the way for a purge of Khrushchev's opponents in the ministries and the installation of his friends in key posts. By pitting local and regional managerial personnel against the central ministries, it permitted Khrushchev to enlist new support on a country-wide scale. Above all, by dispersing ministerial authority in the localities, it left the field free for the party apparatus as the primary integrating and centralizing force.

The subsequent unfolding of the plans for industrial reorganization made all this unmistakably clear. The law approved by the Supreme Soviet on May 10, 1957, abolished the Economic Commission and established Gosplan as the dominant economic planning agency.[12] By a decree of the Presidium of the Supreme Soviet a week earlier, I. I. Kuzmin, one of Khrushchev's subordinates in the Central Committee apparatus, had already been installed as chairman of Gosplan and first vice-chairman of the U.S.S.R. Council of Ministers.[13] The process of tightening Khrushchev's grip on the central government machinery was completed when, as a follow-up on the purge of the "anti-party group" in the last week of June 1957, Kakanovich, Molotov, Pervukhin, and Saburov were removed as first vice-chairmen of the U.S.S.R. Council of Ministers and Malenkov was dismissed as a deputy chairman.

With the emphasis on administrative decentralization in the economic sphere, the integrating role of the party apparatus bulked larger than ever before. Of this Khrushchev showed himself fully aware. Noting in his speech to the Supreme Soviet on May 7, 1957 that "under the new structure of management, where local agencies are granted extensive rights, there may arise tendencies toward autarchy . . ." and temptations to satisfy "local needs" at the expense of the interests of the state as a whole, he made clear that the party, as well as other agencies subordinate to it, would have as one of its main missions the "struggle against such harmful . . . tendencies." [14] In the words of the Central Committee resolution, one of the effects of the reorganization would be "to enhance the role of local party and Soviet organizations . . . in economic development." [15] The party hierarchy was counted on to remain a binding force.

The most recent vindication of the doctrine of party supremacy is to be found in the Zhukov affair. While the purge of the popular World War II hero may be interpreted as primarily an assertion of Khrushchev's undisputed ascendancy, Soviet press commentary makes clear that the issue was

[12] *Pravda,* May 11, 1957.
[13] *Ibid.*
[14] *Pravda,* May 8, 1957.
[15] *Pravda,* February 18, 1957.

precipitated by friction between the party's political apparatus in the armed forces and the more professionally-oriented officers who followed Marshal Zhukov in subordinating political indoctrination to combat-training and military control. The Central Committee resolution on the improvement of party and political work in the Soviet Army and Navy charged that Marshal Zhukov had "pursued a policy" of underestimating and curtailing party leadership of the Army and Navy. Noting "serious shortcomings in practical party and political work" in the armed forces, the resolution reminded the military command:

The chief well-spring of the might of our Army and Navy lies in the fact that the Communist Party—the guiding and directing force of Soviet society—is their organizer, leader and instructor. We must always remember V. I. Lenin's directive that the "policy of the military establishment, as of all other establishments and institutions, is pursued in strict accordance with the general directives given to the party through its Central Committee and under its direct control." [16]

This reaffirmation of party hegemony epitomizes the road which Khrushchev has traveled during the last five years. Embodying himself in the party and proclaiming its right to unchallenged leadership, he has raised his entourage of party functionaries to heights of power which they could hardly have dreamed of a half-decade ago. The victory of Khrushchev represents the triumph of the **apparatchiki** in its purest and most unadulterated form.[17]

A PYRRHIC VICTORY?

How secure is the victory and what role can we envisage for the party in the years ahead? Stalin became General Secretary of the party at the age of 43. Khrushchev begins his reign at 63. In the eyes of the more ambitious members of the younger generation of **apparatchiki,** his must appear a transitional regime, destined before not very long to give way to a different set of governing arrangements, and replete with all the temptations to maneuver and intrigue which any short-term **modus vivendi** accentuates. Moreover, the very terms of settlement by which the succession struggle has been resolved, the reinforcement of the prerogatives and status of the party apparatus, has undoubtedly left a legacy of bruised feelings and unfulfilled aspirations in other quarters. To intellectuals who welcomed the destalinization campaign as promising a new charter of liberties, the tightening of party bonds has come as a rude awakening. To officers in the armed

---

[16] *Pravda,* November 2, 1957.

[17] Khrushchev's determination to increase the authority of the party apparatus has also been manifested in a new policy on the arts, marked by a tightening of party controls, a reaffirmation of the principle of partiinost ("party-mindedness"), purges of the editorial boards of literary and scholarly journals which allowed themselves to become mouthpieces for "unhealthy sentiments and tendencies," *etc.*

forces who saw the rise of Marshal Zhukov as a symbol of military independence, his demotion signalizes a renewed effort to subordinate the military forces to party control. To factory managers throughout the Union the autonomy promised by regionalization was no doubt more than welcome, but the injunction to reinvigorate party controls at the enterprise level may well be interpreted as withdrawing with one hand what had been granted by the other. To magnify the powers of the party apparatus is to run the risk of estrangement from other groups who see their interests threatened by excessive party tutelage.

It may turn out that the consolidation of the **apparatchiki** under Khrushchev has only served to arrest long-term trends which will eventually operate to undermine party controls. But there is danger in being excessively sanguine on this score, at least over the short-run. The imperatives of industrialization impose their own patterns of rationalized management in any society which sets maximum productivity as a primary goal, but they do not abolish the distinction between technical men and political men. Those who run the factories do not necessarily aspire to run the state, and their interests may be accommodated within a framework of totalitarian party control without yielding them political power. There is no iron law which dictates incompatibility between one-party rule and a highly-developed industrial society.

Nor is the domination of the party apparatus inevitably destined to give way to military rule. Bonapartism will always remain a threat as long as the armed forces bulk so important on the Soviet scene, but a military **coup d'etat** requires a degree of conspirational secrecy and an **esprit de corps** in officer ranks which the whole pattern of party controls in the armed forces is calculated to discourage and prevent. Soviet educational progress has produced striking technological and scientific achievements, but we must not forget that it is associated with a system of political indoctrination which instills subservience to party commands. Heartening as it has been to note signs of ferment and criticism among Soviet students and intellectuals in recent years, these remain somewhat marginal phenomena, and it may be a long time before they build up into the insistent and organized demand for political liberty which would represent a real danger to the regime.

Yet change there is, and change there will continue to be. The party apparatus under Khrushchev is not what it was when Stalin seized power, and it may well be different tomorrow from what it is today. Better-educated than their Stalinist predecessors, more technically-oriented in their training and experience, the present-day party functionaries have had to learn to balance zealotry with the pragmatic skills required to manage a complex industrial society. They confront a nation which has been to school, which has mastered the technical arts of an industrial civilization, which is dissatisfied with its living standard, and which faces the future with sharpened expectations, the more urgent because they have been so long postponed. How the party apparatus responds to these aspirations may well determine its ability to survive.

The brute weapons of Stalinist mass terror are no longer readily at hand, and, even if available, are unlikely to be mobilized, except as an act of desperation. The problems which today's party leadership must resolve call for a subtler policy of accommodation, in which social forces already set in motion are manipulated by incentives and persuasion, rather than the cruder forms of repression. But however skillfully the present apparatus channels the social currents which are flowing, it must live with the knowledge that its authority rests on a precarious equilibrium created by a dictator who is no longer young. Even if Khrushchev's apparatus copes successfully with the difficult domestic and international problems which loom before it, it cannot for long postpone its own appointment with destiny. The test of its power will come with the next succession crisis— that periodic **malaise** of the totalitarian party state for which no therapy of legitimacy has yet been devised.

Chapter 14

THE PROBLEM OF SUCCESSION

Harrison E. Salisbury explains what he regards as a "fatal flaw in the Soviet system," namely, that Russia has developed no constitutional means resting on popular participation and consent for transmitting governmental power. He queries whether "a modern technological state" can afford "the fantastic price of a murderous struggle for power each time a transition in leadership is required."

FATAL FLAW IN THE SOVIET SYSTEM

HARRISON E. SALISBURY*

Today, the whole world once ruled by Stalin with an iron hand is in a state of profound transition. Within the Soviet Union itself there has been a continuous process of change since Stalin's death. In the hinterland even more powerful forces for change are at work. Two events have directed attention with special force toward a re-examination of the factors which underlie what is gradually revealing itself as a general crisis of communism.

The first of these events was the latest leadership crisis in Moscow. This struggle for power, from which Nikita S. Khrushchev, with the aid of Marshal Georgi K. Zhukov, emerged victorious, again emphasized that communism as it developed under Stalin in Russia is not a genuine system of government but merely a mechanism of rule. It has no formal structure for transferring power peacefully and smoothly from one leader or group of leaders to another. The only way a new ruler can arise is by a test of force. Whether, in a nuclear age, Russia or any nation can afford to be governed

* Formerly the *New York Times* correspondent in Moscow. The selection is from *New York Times Magazine,* August 25, 1957, pp. 13 ff. By permission of *The New York Times* and Harrison E. Salisbury.

427

by so primitive a method is one of the questions which thoughtful Europeans are studying with especial care.

The second event which has placed communism as a means of government under new scrutiny is the publication of the fascinating analysis by the eccentric former Yugoslav Communist leader, Milovan Djilas, which he calls "The New Class." It is Mr. Djilas' conclusion that communism has given birth to a new class of Communist bureaucrats whom he regards as the worst class of all time, worse than the bourgeoisie whom they replaced or the feudal lords who preceded the bourgeoisie.

The Djilas critique appears at a special moment in history—a moment when the educated, knowledgeable peoples of many countries in Eastern Europe are themselves asking how much longer they must suffer a kind of government which falls vastly short of their expectations and needs. There are young people in many East European countries, including some within the Soviet Union, who have been challenging the basic postulates of Communist rule as it has long been practiced.

There are writers and poets who are writing novels and sonnets whose themes come closer and closer to being: "How long, O Lord, how long?" One does not need to agree with Djilas to understand readily that he has given voice and form to the bitter antagonism which communism has aroused against itself among many peoples.

The reason for this general crisis of communism lies in a basic flaw in the Soviet scheme: It constitutes a rule without a system, a meting out of justice without laws, a land where, in the end, only the man with the loaded revolver says who is the boss.

The transfer of power from one ruler to another has always been a risky thing in Russia. There was no well-established tradition under the Czars. Violence, more often than not, attended the accession of a new ruler to the throne. Indeed, an acid-penned English observer once noted that in England the throne descends by the law of primogeniture; in Russia by the law of regicide. Russian history is pockmarked with "times of trouble," "false Czars," murders of the sovereign by his son and murders of the heir apparent by the sovereign.

Peter the Great, aware of the problem (and himself the murderer of his own heir apparent, his eldest son) sought to remedy the situation by giving each sovereign, in effect, the right to designate his successor. This reform, like so many Russian reforms, had little merit. Sovereigns died suddenly— by poison, by the dagger or even of natural causes—and had no time, in most cases, to name their successors. Inheriting this tradition of tyranny and violent power transfers, the Communists tended to succumb to the mores of the country rather than to create a new tradition of their own.

Lenin himself, before he died in 1924, was probably the first to realize that the rule which the Bolshevik party was imposing on Russia did not constitute a genuine system of government. The Communist party which he had created as an underground, fighting organization with a single purpose —the overthrow of the Czar and the carrying out of the Revolution—was now, after the November *coup d'état,* civil war and foreign intervention, settling down to the tasks of civil reorganization and the reconstruction of a very backward country.

The Communist party was still a lean fighting élite with military rules and spartan discipline. To try to use this small vanguard to rule a vast country was something like putting a commando unit in charge of General Motors.

Alongside the party stood the hollow shell of conventional government apparatus—a council of ministers (then called "commissars"), the usual departments and offices and a flowering bureaucracy. This apparatus had been inherited, by and large, complete with civil servants, from the Czarist regime. It continued to do business very much as it had under the Czars. Given the necessary powers, it could, after a fashion, have administered the affairs of the Soviet Union.

Lenin had no illusions about the "government." He described it as "the same Russian apparatus * * * taken over from Czarism and only thinly anointed with Soviet holy oil." As he watched its workings in Moscow he asked, a little plaintively, "If we take that huge bureaucratic machine, that huge pile, we must ask: Who is directing whom?" He made no secret of his fear that, because of their low level of "culture," the Bolshevik cadres would be swamped by the traditional Russian bureaucracy, just as the Mongol invaders were swamped by the superior culture of the Chinese kingdom they conquered.

Mainly for this reason the Communists have always tried to keep real power concentrated inside the party. The real decisions of state have been made not in the Council of Commissars or Ministers—the Government— but in the Politburo or the Central Committee of the party.

This division and confusion of authority prevented the establishment of a traditional line through which power might be conveyed. It tended to make the Government little more than a facade. "Everything that comes up in the Council of People's Commissars is dragged before the Politburo," Lenin said in despair. This meant that even the smallest questions had to go to the very pinnacle of power before being decided. Lenin blamed himself because, as both Chairman of the Council and Chairman of the Politburo, he formed a personal bridge between the shell of Government and the power of the party.

"The leading comrades take shelter behind commissions," he wrote. "The devil himself would lose his way in this maze of commissions. Nobody knows what is going on, who is responsible; everything is mixed up and finally a decision is passed to the effect that everybody is responsible."

Lenin saw that to a great extent these ills stemmed from the fact that "there is only one Government party at the head of affairs in our country." But he was not able to invent a solution because he was not willing to permit any transfer of power out of the hands of the dynamic élite which he had created in the name of the Communist party.

One of the devices which Lenin invented to give his revolutionary corps a greater cohesion and discipline was a procedure called "democratic centralism." Democratic centralism meant, in essence, that free discussion was permitted within a party group until a question was decided. But once the decision was taken each member was pledged to support it with all his power regardless of his previous attitude. This was a rigid military rule and it gave the small revolutionary corps a power far beyond its numbers.

But, although the party did not appreciate the importance of this, democratic centralism, combined with the monopolistic role of the Communist party, established an impenetrable barrier against the evolution of any system of checks and balances. It was made to order for the evolution and persistence of personal dictatorship.

Lenin did not see or did not wish to see the fatal consequences of the rule of democratic centralism. But he did see that conditions within the party were leading directly toward a split and a bitter personal fight for power. He saw the intrigues of Stalin, analyzed the weaknesses of Trotsky, dispassionately evaluated the other Communist party leaders and sought to warn his followers against the inevitable struggle. But the corrective measures which he proposed (such as doubling the size of the Central Committee) were unrealistic, his warnings were ignored or minimized, and Stalin ruthlessly utilized the mechanism of the party and the ritual of its combat discipline to rout his opponents and establish as tyrannical a dictatorship as any of his Czarist predecessors.

In many ways the enervating dichotomy of the party and Government grew worse under Stalin, who demonstrated complete disinterest in any theory of government. For years he ruled the country while nominally holding only the general secretaryship of the Communist party. His cabinet ministers had no more real power than tailors' dummies. Stalin gave Russia a constitution (written by Bukharin just before Stalin had him arrested, tried and executed), but even though he attached his own name to it Stalin paid no heed to its provisions. He often announced changes in government statutes over the signature of the Central Committee of the Communist party. Sometimes, he used both party and Government signatures. There was no rhyme or reason about this. It seemed to depend on which rubber stamp his hand first touched.

Nor is there any indication that Stalin ever gave serious thought to the problem of the transfer of power after his death. Like many a tyrant before him, Stalin found the thought of his death abhorrent. He did not think about it nor did he make any move to prepare the Soviet state for this event. Thus, Stalin's death in 1953 confronted Russia with the precise dangers which had preoccupied Lenin's thoughts in his last months, a generation before. There was still no system for selecting a successor.

Personally aware of the enormously evil consequences of the power struggle which Stalin had waged, the new post-Stalin leaders embarked on a policy which they called "collective leadership." Their watchword was "*kollektivnost*," and they cited many quotations from Lenin in support of the virtues of rule by the party's Central Committee.

But behind these verbal trappings began almost immediately a time of test and challenge to determine which of the leaders had actually inherited substantial elements of the great power which Stalin had gathered. The principal elements of this power were vested in the Communist party organization, the Government bureaucracy, the secret police and the army.

The first test of strength may have come over power in the party. Just eight days after becoming Premier of the Soviet Government, Georgi M. Malenkov resigned as party secretary. This opened the way for Nikita S. Khrushchev to gain control of the party secretariat and, like Stalin, to use the secretariat to capture the party organization.

A second show of strength occurred late in June, 1953, when Police Chief Lavrenti P. Beria defied a demand to submit his police to the direction of the "collective leadership." He paid for his defiance with his arrest and eventual execution along with a group of his top aides.

The army, led by Marshal Georgi K. Zhukov, provided the force which enabled the "collective leadership" to cope with Beria. Part of its price for this aid was liquidation of the secret police as a basis of political power.

Having lost his party base Malenkov then sought to build up the power and prestige of the Government; but this effort was doomed to failure because of the built-in Soviet bias which vests all real authority in the party.

It was only by this series of tests that the Soviet leaders were able to judge their own respective strengths. After Malenkov peacefully stepped down as Premier in February, 1955, the dominance of Premier Nikolai A. Bulganin and Party Secretary Khrushchev became more pronounced, although it still appeared that the Soviet group might actually be evolving a new kind of rule, a sort of Communist board of governors. Precedent was against them, but the idea was not completely impossible. Venice was ruled for some 200 years by a similar system.

Without the handicap of a "democratic centralism," without the tradition of a single party, without the long history—both Czarist and Communist —which equated opposition with conspiracy against the state, the experiment might have worked. But the odds were against it. Under Soviet conditions a high-level power contest is not like a friendly game of penny ante in which there is one good-sized winner, several who come out a few dollars ahead, one man who winds up even and two or three moderate losers. The Soviet version is cutthroat—one man after another is eliminated until a final showdown in which the winner takes all.

One day right in the midst of his June struggle with Malenkov, Molotov, Kaganovich and Shepilov, Khrushchev took a couple of hours out to give an interview to a Japanese newspaper man. What Khrushchev called the "law of the jungle" was very much on his mind. He was talking, ostensibly, about the world situation. But, in the light of the struggle he was going through, events much closer to home may have colored his remarks.

"Here is the real law of the jungle," Khrushchev said. "I am **strong** and you are weak—therefore you must bow to me. We do not want to be like lambs who are defenseless against wolves. But lambs and wolves live in the same world. And wolves by right of strength devour lambs. We do not want to be in the position of lambs. We must have teeth so that the wolves will know that they will not get away with an attack * * * without a mark. The wolves may lose their skins and, perhaps, even their heads * * *."

Such a life, Khrushchev said two or three times, is intolerable. "It is impossible to be guided by the law of the jungle that right is strength, and to dictate one's will to others * * * people want peace and quiet * * * The chief thing is to listen attentively to the voice of the people and not to permit mistakes which damage mutual relations between the leaders and the people. We are confident that it is impossible to rule the people only by force, to hold the population in terror."

The battle in which Khrushchev was then engaged was one in which only the law of the jungle applied. He came out on top—with the aid of Marshal Zhukov. Thus, by the very act of victory the stage is set for another eventual test of power—between Khrushchev and Zhukov.

This may not come. The two men may exercise restraint. Their policies may be identical and their personalities complementary. But the rule of democratic centralism will tend to make sharper differences which arise. And the inadmissibility of opposition groups or opposition opinions will constantly tend to split leader from leader until only one remains.

In the end, of course, Khrushchev or Zhukov will be replaced by a newer, younger man, succeeding to the scepter of power either through the intervention of death or through the gradual weakening of the dictator with the onset of age.

There is, however, another alternative. It may be that over the long period of years the Russian people are gradually beginning to tire of a method of rule which is so arbitrary and inflexible. There is a great weariness with the "law of the jungle" reflected in Khrushchev's statement to the Japanese newspaper man. And this weariness may be shared by many of his countrymen.

The Russian dictatorship, contrary to popular supposition, is not immune to the trends of public opinion. In fact, since the death of Stalin it has been assiduous in courting Soviet opinion. No one has gone to greater efforts in this direction than Khrushchev himself. He has tried to link his fortunes with all of the things which he thinks the Soviet people want—peace, a better and easier life, relaxation of police rule, more personal liberty, more money for the farmer and more meat for the factory worker.

The time may be at hand when Soviet citizens can and will insist that their rulers begin to observe the rules and procedures laid down in the Soviet Constitution. The Constitution is not the most democratic in the world, but it does provide a system of government which should function fairly well and even fairly representatively—if the Soviet leaders ever permitted it to be tried out.

The Communist party structure, with its tight leadership control, proved itself an excellent instrument for revolution and for conducting a war (its pyramid of power resembles that of an army and general staff). But as a peacetime organ it is subject to the same conflicts and uncertainties as a military junta. It is made to order for internecine strife and intrigue.

Today the question is being posed in ever stronger terms to the Soviet public and to their leaders: Can a modern technological state afford the fantastic price of a murderous struggle for power each time a transition in leadership is required? Whether Russia can survive many more such contests becomes increasingly doubtful.

EDITOR'S NOTE: Pravda *reported on July 15, 1957, that Marshal of the Soviet Union, Georgi K. Zhukov, in a speech delivered in Leningrad had supported the ouster of Malenkov, Kaganovich, and Molotov from high office and had stated: "As you know, this anti-Party group resisted the measures for a decisive rise in agriculture. Its members objected especially to the slogan 'catch up with the United States of America in the near future in the per capita production of meat, milk and butter,' put forward by the Central Committee on the initiative of Nikita Sergeyevich Khrushchev, a slogan which was unanimously approved by all the Soviet people. The anti-Party group opposed expanding the political, economic and legislative powers of the Union republics, apparently not wanting to give up the powers it had held for nearly 30 years . . . and stubbornly resisted the measures pursued by the Party for eliminating the consequences of the cult of the individual leader, particularly the disclosure and calling to account of those mainly responsible for violation of legality in the past."*

Subsequently, on November 2, 1957, the Central Committee of the Communist Party of the Soviet Union announced that its plenary meeting late in October had adopted a resolution which "has excluded Georgi K.

Zhukov from membership of the Presidium of the Central Committee and from the Central Committee of the Communist party." It further noted that "of late former Defense Minister Comrade Zhukov has violated the Leninist party principles of guiding the armed forces, pursued a policy of curtailing the work of party organizations, political organs, and military councils, of abolishing the leadership and control of the party, its Central Committee and Government over the Army and Navy."

The announcement continued: "The plenary meeting . . . has established that the cult of Comrade Zhukov's personality was cultivated in the Soviet Army with his personal participation. With the help of sycophants and flatterers, he was praised to the sky in lectures and reports, in articles, films and pamphlets, and his person and role in the Great Patriotic War were over-glorified." He was charged with lack of "modesty," with imagining "that he was the sole hero of all the victories achieved by our people and their armed forces under the Communist party's leadership," and with being "a politically unsound person, inclining to adventurism. . . ." It was stated that "the decision was adopted unanimously by all the members and alternate members of the Central Committee and the members of the Central Auditing Commission. It was approved by all the military men, Communist party and Government executives present at the meeting."

The following day Marshal Ivan S. Konev wrote in Pravda: *"One should not forget that Comrade Zhukov occupied the high position of Chief of General Staff during the period immediately preceding the war, and bore a considerable share of the responsibility for the condition of the Soviet armed forces and their ability to meet Fascist aggression." While Stalin's "incorrect assessment . . . lay at the bottom of the serious miscalculations," "serious responsibility for the fact that the troops of our military frontier areas were taken unaware by the sudden attack of the Fascist army also falls upon the Chief of General Staff, Comrade Zhukov. . . ."*

On September 6, 1958, Radio Moscow briefly announced that the Central Committee of the Communist Party had "relieved Nikolai A. Bulganin of his duties as a member of the Presidium of the Central Committee of the Communist Party of the Soviet Union." Earlier, Marshal Bulganin, who for a time appeared to enjoy almost coordinate power with Khrushchev, had been ousted from his chairmanship of the State Bank and given an economic post in Stavropol in the North Caucasus. His decline was generally regarded as dating from June 1957 when he apparently stood with Malenkov, Molotov, and Kaganovich in their unsuccessful challenge to Khrushchev. This was confirmed when, on November 14, 1958, Khrushchev for the first time openly and publicly linked Bulganin with the "anti-Party group."

VII

THE SOVIET ECONOMIC SYSTEM

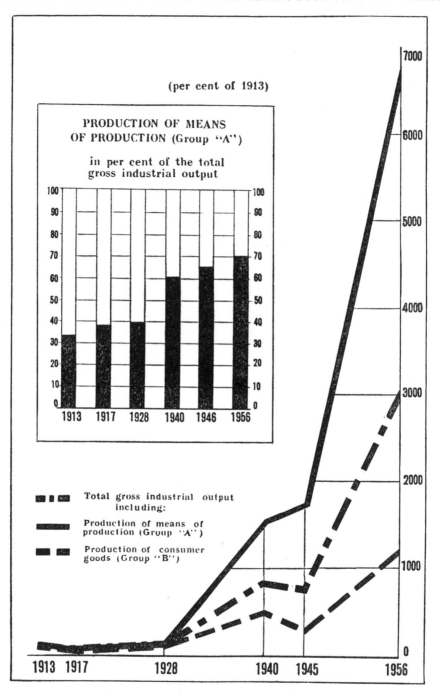

(per cent of 1913)

PRODUCTION OF MEANS
OF PRODUCTION (Group "A")

in per cent of the total
gross industrial output

Total gross industrial output
including:

Production of means of
production (Group "A")

Production of consumer
goods (Group "B")

Source: Central Statistical Board of the U.S.S.R. Council of Ministers, Moscow,
1958. (These are *official* estimates of the U.S.S.R.)
For target goals of Seven-Year plan for 1959-1965, see pp. 473-475.

EDITOR'S NOTE: *By way of introduction to the several sections concerned with the Soviet Economic System, it must be emphasized that there is in the U.S.S.R. a close interdependence and interrelationship, both in theory and practice, between economics and politics—beyond anything known to the capitalist world. It must be said, too, that the belief of Russian leaders (and of many Russian people) in the ultimate triumph of socialism throughout the world is predicated, in major part, upon what they regard as the demonstrated superiority—and, hence, the ultimate irresistible appeal— of the socialist economic system over capitalism. Typical, for example, were the statements made by Khrushchev in a recent interview with the correspondent of* Figaro:

We, Communists, are convinced that mankind's only right path is the path of socialist development. Socialism expresses the vital interests of the people, of all men and women who live not by exploiting working people, but by their own labor. It brings the peoples deliverance from social and national oppression, from the horrors of unemployment and the arbitrary rule of a handful of monopolists who usurped all the wealth of a country. We are convinced that the peoples of all countries will come to socialism, to Communism, but when and how—this is the internal affair of each people.

M. A. Suslov stated at the 20th Congress: "The urge of the peoples to socialism is irresistible, the attractive power of the socialist ideas increases from day to day, and the process will be accelerated by the continued achievements of socialism in our country, China and all the People's Democracies."

Obviously these claims deserve the most careful analysis even though the merits of a system rest on bases which transcend the purely economic.

Chapter 15

ON THE RELIABILITY OF SOVIET STATISTICS

There is no intention to suggest that the question of the reliability of Soviet statistics—an extremely difficult and complex problem—can be resolved by reference to the two brief excerpts that appear in the following pages. It was simply considered desirable to give some indication—from opposing vantage points—of the complexities of the problem and the dangers of easy and shallow judgments. The interested reader will find some suggestions for further reading in the bibliography.

COMMENT ON SOVIET ECONOMIC STATISTICS

Maurice Dobb*

The view that all Soviet figures are naturally suspect, designed as propaganda-instruments to deceive the unwary, is no longer seriously held, and scarcely merits attention here. Though commonly met with in uninformed circles before the war, it was seldom if ever accepted, at any rate in its crude form, by anyone with much experience of handling Soviet statistics and submitting them to normal tests of consistency.[1] Gaps there were, of course (which grew larger towards the end of the 'thirties for security reasons), and continuous series were difficult to construct in many cases owing to changes of base and of definition. A notable post-war gap

---

* Lecturer and Fellow of Trinity College, Cambridge. The selection is from *Soviet Studies*, Vol. 1 (1950), pp. 18-19, by permission, and from *Soviet Economic Development Since 1917* (London: Routledge & Kegan Paul Ltd., 4th ed., 1957), pp. 330-332, by permission of the publisher and of International Publishers, New York.

[1] Cf. Dr. A. BAYKOV: "I do not share the view that Soviet statistical and other sources are less reliable than those published in other countries. On the contrary, systematic study over a number of years has convinced me that they can be used to analyse the economic process . . . of the U.S.S.R. with the same degree of confidence as similar sources published in other countries." (*The Development of the Soviet Economic System* xiv.)

has been the absence of regular annual output figures of particular industries (although these can to some extent be deduced from the published index-figures which have 1945 as a base, and from information as to the relationship of post-war output to 1940 output). But such difficulties are met with in varying degrees in the handling and interpretation of the published data of all nations. And although in some respects Soviet published data before the war were deficient by comparison with this country [England], in other directions they were more plentiful.[2]

One deficiency that aroused much comment in the West during the 'thirties and was often cited as a reason for suspicion, was the absence of any index number of general prices; the publication of such indices having been discontinued in the early years of the first Five-Year Plan. This deficiency is qualified, however, by two considerations. Firstly, we have now learnt from our own experience of recent years that price-indices have very restricted meaning and limited use in conditions of rationing and controlled prices and wide dispersion of price-movements,[3] and that they may be positively misleading at a time when consumption-habits are subject to considerable change. Secondly, value-data concerning production were generally given in "constant prices of 1926-27," and accordingly did not depend on the use of a price-index for conversion from money into real terms when comparing the value-data for different years. What this meant was that the constituent items of the total in question (e.g. for some branch of industry) for any year were valued at the prices ruling in the base year; 1926-27 being chosen as this base year on the ground that it was the first "normal" year after the reconstruction-period following the war and civil war, when prices had been restored to some kind of normal relationship with one another. This practice of valuing output in different years in the prices of a single year is now familiar to us in this country; seeing that it has become the practice since the war in our own official statistics to express the gross value of consumer goods and services (i.e. consumers' expenditure) "in 1938 prices." . . .

In conclusion one should perhaps mention that criticism during recent years among Western economists in relation to Soviet economy has largely been directed towards the valuation of gross industrial output in terms

[2] The fullest collection of quantitative data is the 500-page *Socialist Construction: a Statistical Abstract* (in both Russian and English) of 1936. For the years subsequent to 1936 nothing of the kind was published; and one had to rely on particular sets of published figures (e.g. of output of selected industries).

[3] In U.S.S.R. between 1929 and 1934, there was not only a spread between the price-movements of rationed and unrationed commodities, but multiple prices for the *same* commodity according to whether it was bought "on the ration" or "off the ration" (the Soviet ration-system taking the form of a minimum quota to which one was entitled at a fixed "ration price"; additional amounts being purchasable, if available, at a much higher price), and in the case of the latter according to the market in which it was purchased (e.g. in the "closed co-operative," the State "commercial stores" or on the free market).

of which official calculations of growth-rates have been expressed. The practice of valuing industrial output in "constant prices of 1926-7" has been criticised on the ground that it gives an "upward bias" to the valuation of the increase since, according to the price-structure prevailing in 1926-7, products like tractors, motor-cars and machine-tools that were destined to show the highest rates of increase, were highly-priced relatively to other things and hence highly-weighted in the resulting index. To this has been added the charge that new products, introduced into production after the base year (1926-7), were valued at the *current* price-level of the year of their introduction, and that since there was price-inflation after 1929 this meant that these new products were given an exaggerated weight in the index compared with older products. The author has made his own comments elsewhere[4] on this controversy. It is undeniable, of course, that measurement of the change in an output-total will be very different when conducted in the different price-structures of various years (the problem is well-known to statisticians under the name of the Paasche-Laspeyres discrepancy —the discrepancy between valuing a change according to the prices of the end-year or the beginning-year of the period in question—and is by no means confined to the statistics of industrial production in the U.S.S.R.).[5] It is also probably true that valuation at the prices of an early year yields a higher rate of increase than valuation at the prices of a later year in a period of rapid industrial development.

What this Western controversy has tended to conceal is that, even when allowance has been made for such discrepancy and for such criticisms, the magnitude of the qualification involved is not very great compared with the rate of growth that is in question—it does not go beyond 25 or 30 per cent. for the period of the First and Second Five Year Plans (to which criticisms chiefly apply). An American economist has recently attempted to construct an index of his own of Soviet industrial output, using for this purpose wages and salaries prevailing in the year 1934 as weights instead of selling-prices seven years before. The result is to show an annual rate of growth of industrial output from 1928-1937 of about 14 per cent., or for the decade as a whole slightly less than a fourfold increase, compared with an increase of five-and-a-half times shown by the official index.[6] Such a rate of increase represents almost a doubling of output

---

[4] In *The Review of Economics and Statistics,* Feb., 1948, and in his *On Economic Theory and Socialism* (London, 1955), 247-53.

[5] An American calculation of the output of items of machinery in U.S.A. has shown that a valuation in prices of 1899 yields a *fifteen*-fold increase between 1899 and 1939 and no more than a *two*-fold increase when valued in prices of 1939. (A. Gerschenkron, *A Dollar Index of Soviet Machinery Output, 1927-8 to 1937,* California, 1951, 52).

[6] D. R. Hodgman, *Soviet Industrial Production 1928-1951* (Cambridge, Mass., 1954). This rate of increase comes remarkably close to the results of a calculation of the unweighted average of quantity-increases of basic metal-fuel-power output made by the present writer (*op. cit.,* 119-23). For the period between 1937 and 1951 Prof. Hodgman's index shows a somewhat larger discrepancy from the official index than for 1928-37 (but

every quinquennium and is something very much larger than has previously been attained by other countries.

This controversy, however, is to-day only of historical interest, since the method of valuation in 1926-7 prices was terminated with the Fourth Plan. Since 1950 industrial output has been calculated in terms of the prices of a particular month or year of the quinquennium in question:[7] throughout the Period of the Fifth Plan in terms of the prices of January 1, 1952 (new products of subsequent years and "that part of production which is not reckoned in natural units" being reduced to the basis of January 1, 1952 by an index of the average price-changes of the remaining output of the enterprise or industry in question);[8] and for the Sixth Plan in terms of the prices prevailing on July 1, 1955.[9] The method of valuing output, in up-to-date (but "constant") prices, has accordingly been assimilated to the method previously adopted for valuing investment at the prices prevailing in a given year of the quinquennium in question.

PROBLEMS OF ANALYZING AND PREDICTING SOVIET BEHAVIOR

JOHN S. RESHETAR*

SOVIET STATISTICS

The amount of available statistical data regarding the Soviet economy and what it can produce has dwindled to a small fraction of what it was. The statement of the First Five Year Plan comprised more than 1700

---

then his data for this period are much more scanty): his index shows a doubling of output between 1937 and 1951 as against an increase of three times according to the official index. Another American, G. Grossman, has made an estimate for national income as a whole (including, e.g., agriculture), and reaches a figure of 6.5-7 per cent. as the annual rate of increase between 1928 and 1937. This compares with 3 per cent. for U.S.A. between 1929 and 1950 (*Soviet Economic Growth*, ed. A. Bergson, Evanston and New York, 1953, 9). In this case the discrepancy from the official estimate was much greater, the latter being more than double the former.

[7] I.e. of wholesale (*optovie*) prices, *without* turnover tax.

[8] *Planovoe Khoziaistvo*, 1952, No. 1, 77-9; cf. also G. I. Baklanov, *Promishlennaia Statistika* (Moscow, 1953), 123, where the defects of measurement in 1926-7 prices are explicitly mentioned, including the difficulty of valuing new products, but without any indication of the net effect of these defects.

[9] *Voprosi Ekonomiki*, 1955, No. 8, 74-5. Output in 1955 was to be valued both at January 1952 prices and in July 1955 prices so as to link the index-series relating to the past quinquennium with the new one.

* Department of Political Science, University of Washington in Seattle. The selection is from pp. 48-51 of *Problems of Analyzing and Predicting Soviet Behavior* by John S. Reshetar. Copyright 1955 by Random House, Inc. Reprinted by permission of Random House, Inc.

pages, while those of the Fourth and Fifth Plans were published as small pamphlets. A decree of June 9, 1947, increased the amount of economic information which must not be published and made the divulging of such information a serious offense punishable by imprisonment. Not since 1929 has the Soviet regime published a cost-of-living index such as that prepared by the United States Bureau of Labor Statistics. Besides the paucity of data there is a deliberate effort on the part of the regime to exaggerate economic growth by the use of such propaganda devices as the increase in terms of percentages with a period and base year which will give the impression of phenomenal growth. Thus Malenkov, speaking at the Nineteenth Party Congress in October 1952, boasted that Soviet industrial production had increased more than twelvefold between 1929 and 1951 while that of the United States had only doubled during the same period.

One can also question the value of some Soviet statistics in view of the known falsification of production reports by the administrators of economic enterprises in order to make it appear that production goals have been fulfilled or overfulfilled. Indeed, the constant preoccupation of the Soviet leadership with production goals and the use of figures referring to goals as well as to actual achievements of the economy serve to confuse the picture. While the falsification of production data is discouraged by the central statistic-gathering authorities (since it compounds the difficulties of the forecasting which a fully planned economy requires) they are not in a position to prevent it because the system of incentives and sanctions in the Soviet Union is such as to encourage this practice. Another difficulty is that Soviet statistics, to the extent that they are accurate, reflect production in quantitative terms but tell little or nothing about the quality of the commodities being produced.

Soviet statistics can also be misleading when the particular concept upon which the statistical formulation is based has doubtful validity. Thus statistics regarding Soviet grain production have been based on the concept of "biological yield" rather than "barn yield"—although the regime is presumably attempting to rectify this. This has importance because the concept of "biological yield" represents unharvested grain in the field, while that of "barn yield" represents the actual amount of grain harvested. The use of the former concept after 1933, first with a deduction for losses during harvesting and later without any such deduction, has given to Soviet grain statistics an inflated character, since there has frequently been a great difference in the Soviet Union between the amount of grain on the sheaf and the amount actually harvested. Another Soviet statistical concept which is unique is that of national income. In the Soviet Union this includes only the production and distribution of goods and omits all services, whether rendered by the government or by individuals, such as are an integral part of the American concept of national income.

A related problem is that of the price indices used for determining gross industrial production in the Soviet Union. The value of the industrial output was determined for more than two decades in terms of "constant" 1926-1927 ruble prices. Serious difficulties arose, however, when new products were added to the Soviet industrial output and could not be given prices in terms of 1926-1927 rubles because they were not being produced at that time. Instead, these new commodities were given arbitrary prices at the time they were first produced on a large scale during the Five Year Plans. (Such commodities were often produced at a very high cost in the beginning because of inefficiencies in production methods.) This practice led to the introduction of an inflationary bias into the indices and to the exaggeration of Soviet statements regarding increases in individual output. Thus the value of Soviet industrial production was inflated to make it appear that the system had produced more goods than it had in fact. Another factor which "increased" industrial production was the transfer of such activities as fishing and forestry from agriculture to industry.

Use of this index of industrial production by Soviet economists and planners involved many difficulties, since it was not a homogeneous index: goods which were being produced in 1926-1927 (as contrasted with products introduced in later years) were included in the index at their prices during that base period. Thus there was lack of comparability within the index. In an effort to remedy this the Soviet regime in 1949 abandoned the index based on 1926-1927 ruble prices and shifted to the use of current wholesale prices. In 1952 the new index was regularized in terms of wholesale prices prevailing on January 1 of that year, and it was decreed that new goods produced by the economy after 1952 were to be given "comparable 1952 prices" in terms of the prices which have been assigned in the 1952 index to similar goods. However, the inflationary nature of the earlier index, which exaggerated Soviet economic development, was retained, since Soviet economists were told that in comparing production of years following 1952 with that of the years prior to 1950, they must accept the production data of the pre-1950 period as reflected in the old index.

The propaganda aspect of certain Soviet economic and statistical practices is also well illustrated in the case of the valuation of the ruble. The Soviet regime carried out a currency reform in December 1947, issuing one new ruble for ten old rubles in circulation. Deposits remained unchanged up to the amount of 3000 rubles; larger sums on deposit in banks were revalued at lower rates. This measure was designed to wipe out the accumulated cash reserves held by peasants and tradesmen of the more conventional and black-market variety. At that time the ruble was declared to be worth 19 cents (5.3 rubles to the dollar) at the official rate of exchange. However, since foreign trade is a monopoly of the state in the Soviet Union, this figure was meaningless. The rate of exchange for diplomats was reduced from 12 to 8 rubles to the dollar. Actually the ruble has been worth little more than three cents or, at the most five cents. A subsequent "revaluation" of the ruble was decreed in March 1950, when it was given an arbitrary value of 25 cents. The special diplomatic rate of exchange was abolished, thus adding greatly to the maintenance costs of foreign embassies in Moscow. The ruble was also declared at that time to be based on gold instead of on the dollar, but it was not made convertible into gold internally. This action was accompanied by a propaganda claim that the value of the ruble had "increased" while other currencies—such as the British pound and the French franc—had suffered a decline through devaluation.

The difficulty in determining the real value of the ruble has been increased by the Soviet regime's refusal to allow any free exchange of currencies and its insistence upon an artificial and ridiculously high rate of exchange. This has led to numerous comparisons between American and Soviet prices—which have appeared in the American press—based on the simple conversion of Soviet prices into dollars at the official rate of exchange of four rubles to the dollar. A more meaningful approach involves a very complex analysis aimed at determining the real value of the ruble in terms of what can be purchased with it. This, of course, entails a close study of price levels as related to wage and salary scales and market supplies. Prices have fluctuated widely in the Soviet Union, and for some commodities, such as rye bread, have increased by as much as 3500% over a period of twenty-two years, with increases in the money wage lagging far behind. Price cuts since December 1947, when rationing was abolished, have reduced this percentage increase substantially. Prices of other commodities increased tremendously in the 1930s and during World War II, but less than for rye bread.

Although we know the price which Soviet subjects pay for rye bread today as compared with that of 1928 or 1946, as well as for other commodities, we do not know the price of a Soviet tank or jet airplane. This lack of data regarding the whole price structure of the Soviet economy is one of the difficulties encountered in attempting to estimate the meaning of the Soviet military budget. We know the size of the expenditure for the Soviet military establishment in billions of rubles, but we encounter serious difficulties in estimating its significance and all of its implications, or in making comparisons between the Soviet military budget and the budgets of other states. Since we do not know enough about the cost factor, it makes little sense to convert the ruble sum into dollars at the official rate of exchange or at an arbitrary rate and make a comparison on a strictly monetary basis. Indeed, it is likely that one ruble is worth more than another in the Soviet economy, and the ruble used to purchase a tank or artillery piece may be worth much more than that used to purchase a home appliance. Thus a reduction in the military budget in monetary terms may not mean a reduction in armaments if the cost of heavy industrial goods has been substantially reduced at the same time.

Another problem is encountered if the amount appropriated for the Soviet military budget is taken as a percentage of the total state budget and then compared with the military expenditures in the budgets of non-Soviet states. The difficulty stems from the fact that the Soviet state budget includes many forms of capital investment not to be found in the budgets of non-Soviet governments and embraces a far greater percentage of the national income. This tends to minimize the military budget and makes it possible for Soviet statisticians to "prove" that other states are spending "more" for armaments percentagewise than the Soviet Union, in terms of the total state budget. An additional factor which prevents exact comparisons is the unusually low pay of Soviet rank-and-file military personnel as contrasted with that of the armies of other states. There is also the very real possibility of hidden appropriations in the Soviet state budget which are actually military in character but are included under capital investment (as, for example, the construction of munitions plants) or under "education" as part of the military training program.

Soviet demographic statistics also have their lacunae. There are few data available between the censuses of 1926 and 1939, and Soviet writers hesitate to use what there are because of the deficit caused by famine during the collectivization in 1932-1933. The census of 1937 was declared to be the work of "wreckers" and was suppressed, probably because it revealed the high mortality rate during the famine to a greater extent than did the census of 1939. The fact that important data of this kind can be suppressed by the regime makes it necessary for the scholar to extrapolate and interpolate on the basis of the meager data which are available.

Economists who study the Soviet system have attempted to fill the gaps in their data by developing estimates based on a variety of assumptions as well as upon rule of thumb guesses. Some economists, notably Colin Clark and Naum Jasny, have been critical of some of the assumptions which other economists have employed in utilizing Soviet statistics. Yet the obvious as well as the concealed pitfalls in work with Soviet statistics should not be regarded as precluding their use if adequate attention is given to the biases inherent in them.

Chapter 16

ON THE TEMPO OF INDUSTRIALIZATION

The tremendous advances which have made the U.S.S.R. the second mightiest industrial nation in the world were achieved in an incredibly short period of time and with the imposition of tremendous hardships and sacrifices. Stalin offers his explanation and justification of the methods and tempo involved, and Bertrand de Jouvenel raises some questions about the necessity for the sacrifices imposed.

ON SOVIET INDUSTRIALIZATION

Joseph V. Stalin*

PREPARATION FOR DEFENSE

What material potentialities did our country command before the Second World War? To help you examine this point, I shall have to report briefly on the work of the Communist Party in preparing our country for active defense.

If we take the figures for 1940, the eve of the Second World War, and compare them with the figures for 1913—the eve of the First World War— we get the following picture. In 1913 our country produced 4,220,000 tons of pig iron, 4,230,000 tons of steel, 29 million tons of coal, nine million tons of oil, 21,600,000 tons of marketable grain and 740,000 tons of raw cotton. Those were the material potentialities with which our country entered the First World War. Such was the economic base of old Russia which could be drawn upon for prosecution of the war.

Now as regards 1940. In the course of that year our country produced 15 million tons of pig iron, or nearly four times as much as in 1913; 18,300,000 tons of steel, or nearly four and one-half as much as in 1913;

* From a speech delivered in Moscow on February 9, 1946.

446

166 million tons of coal, or more than five and one-half times as much as in 1931; 31 million tons of oil, or nearly three and one-half times as much as in 1913; 38,300,000 tons of marketable grain, or nearly 17 million tons more than in 1913; 2,700,000 tons of raw cotton, or more than three and one-half times as much as in 1913. Those were the material potentialities with which our country entered the Second World War. Such was the economic base of the Soviet Union which could be drawn upon for prosecution of the war. The difference as you see is tremendous.

Such an unprecedented increase in production cannot be regarded as the simple and usual development of a country from backwardness to progress. It was a leap by which our Motherland was transformed from a backward into an advanced country, from an agrarian into an industrial country.

FIVE-YEAR PLANS

This historic transformation was accomplished in the course of three Five-Year Plan periods, beginning with 1928, the first year of the First Five-Year Plan. Up to that time we had to concern ourselves with re-habilitating our ravaged industry and healing the wounds received in the First World War and the Civil War. Moreover, if we bear in mind that the First Five-Year Plan was fulfilled in four years, and that the fulfillment of the Third Five-Year Plan was interrupted by war in its fourth year, we find that it took only about 13 years to transform our country from an agrarian into an industrial one. It cannot but be admitted that 13 years is an incredibly short period for the accomplishment of such an immense task. . . .

METHODS OF INDUSTRIALIZATION

By what policy did the Communist Party succeed in providing these material potentialities in the country in such a short time? First of all, by the Soviet policy of industrializing the country.

The Soviet method of industrializing the country differs radically from the capitalist method of industrialization. In capitalist countries industrialization usually begins with light industry. Since in light industry smaller investments are required and there is more rapid turnover of capital and since, furthermore, it is easier to make a profit there than in heavy industry, light industry serves as the first object of industrialization in these countries.

Only after a lapse of much time, in the course of which light industry accumulates profits and concentrates them in banks, does the turn of heavy industry arrive and accumulated capital begin to be transferred gradually to heavy industry in order to create conditions for its development.

But that is a lengthy process requiring an extensive period of several decades, in the course of which these countries have to wait until light industry has developed and must make shift without heavy industry. Naturally, the Communist Party could not take this course. The Party knew that a war was looming, that the country could not be defended without heavy industry, that the development of heavy industry must be undertaken as soon as possible, that to be behind with this would mean to lose out. The Party remembered Lenin's words to the effect that without heavy industry it would be impossible to uphold the country's independence, that without it the Soviet order might perish.

Accordingly, the Communist Party of our country rejected the "usual" course of industrialization and began the work of industrializing the country by developing heavy industry. It was very difficult, but not impossible. A valuable aid in this work was the nationalization of industry, and banking, which made possible the rapid accumulation and transfer of funds to heavy industry. There can be no doubt that without this it would have been impossible to secure our country's transformation into an industrial country in such a short time.

AGRICULTURAL POLICY

Second, by a policy of collectivization of agriculture.

In order to do away with our backwardness in agriculture and to provide the country with greater quantities of marketable grain, cotton, and so forth, it was essential to pass from small-scale peasant farming to large-scale farming, for only large-scale farming can make use of new machinery, apply all the achievements of agronomical science and yield greater quantities of marketable produce.

There are, however, two kinds of large farms—capitalist and collective. The Communist Party could not adopt the capitalist path of development of agriculture, and not as a matter of principle alone but also because it implies too prolonged a development and involves preliminary ruination of the peasants and their transformation into farm hands. Therefore, the Communist Party took the path of the collectivization of agriculture, the path of creating large-scale farming by uniting peasant farms into collective farms.

The method of collectivization proved a highly progressive method not only because it did not involve the ruination of the peasants but especially because it permitted, within a few years, the covering of the entire country with large collective farms which are able to use new machinery, take advantage of all the achievements of agronomic science and give the country greater quantities of marketable produce. There is no doubt that without a collectivization policy we could not in such a short time have done away with the age-old backwardness of our agriculture.

ON THE CHARACTER OF THE SOVIET ECONOMY

BERTRAND DE JOUVENEL*

Man is free to choose his purpose: but once wedded to a purpose, he is bound to the conditions of its fulfillment. The avowed purpose of the Soviet government is to bring Russian industrial power, in the shortest possible time, to parity with that of the United States. There is nothing specifically "communist" in this purpose. Indeed it stands in stark contradiction to the Marx-Engels picture of a communist economy which would not be concerned with building-up of capacities but with their full employment for the consumer satisfaction of the workers. The purpose of the Soviet government might just as well be that of a modern Colbert whom we can imagine presiding over the eventually blended destinies of the six European nations which have begun to associate in the Coal-Steel Community.[1]

It is worth stressing that the Soviet program is the conscious and systematic imitation of something which exists, but which was not brought about either consciously or systematically. Take, for instance, steel: steel capacity did not, in the U.S., reach its successive levels because someone enjoying supreme power had decreed that steel capacity should reach such a level by such a date, but additions to capacity occurred in response to demands made upon it by steel-consuming industries, which, in turn, attuned their capacities to rising demand, ultimately consumer demand. There is no question in Russia of steel capacity growing under the prodding of demand: it must grow, period. Evidently if the growth of steel capacity is regarded as an end in itself, it can be best served by reserving all the steel presently produced for the building of more steel capacity.

This is, of course, driving things to the extreme; but it can serve at least to stress the orientation of Russian industry. Russian industry is, to a considerable degree, employed in producing industrial capacity. Of course every industrial nation has some part of its industrial plant engaged in producing plant and equipment. This is necessary in order that plant and equipment which wears down or becomes outdated can be replaced,

* French political philosopher and economist. Author of *Power* and of *Sovereignty*. The selection is excerpted from the *Bulletin of the Atomic Scientists*, Vol. 13 (November 1957), pp. 327-330. By permission of the publication and the author.
[1] These nations, France, Western Germany, Italy, Belgium, the Netherlands, Luxembourg, muster together 160 million inhabitants. They are however far poorer in natural resources than either the U.S. or the U.S.S.R.

and so that in every field the productive apparatus can be enlarged and improved.

But in Russia the production of plant and equipment has absolute priority, which is understandable enough, given the aim, which is to reach a stated level of productive capacity. According to the statistical publication which the Soviet government has recently brought out, industrial production in Russia consisted of consumer goods in the proportion of 66.7% in 1913, of 60.5% in 1928 (when total industrial production was no greater than in 1913, as far as one can tell on other authorities), and the proportion of consumer goods in total industrial production fell successively to 29.4% in 1955, the last figure given, producers' goods having risen to 70.6% of total industrial production. The Russian publication also gives indexes of growth of the two sectors of industry: all outside experts agree that these indexes are fantastically exaggerated, but the relation between the two indexes may presumably be trusted. From 1928 to 1955 it is claimed that the sector producing means of production multiplied its output almost 39 times, while the sector producing consumer goods multiplied its own output only 9 times.

The much faster expansion of the sector producing means of production has been obtained by a priority which is perhaps the decisive feature of the Russian economy. That sector, which bears the A label in Russian economic vocabulary (as against the B label for consumer goods industries) is bidden to produce means of production for itself instead of producing them for the consumer goods industries. The Soviet reasoning is that providing plant and equipment to consumer goods industries competes with providing the same to producer goods industries, and that the faster the A sector grows, the easier it will be for it then to fill out the voids existing in the plant and equipment of the consumer goods industries.

The logic of this reasoning cannot be attacked. It is quite true that the more steel that goes into not only motorcars but also the motorcar industries, the less there is available for building steel furnaces and hydraulic presses; and that the sooner you have a great deal of the latter, the easier you will find it to equip the motorcar industry.

Russian economic history from 1928 to date can be contrasted with American economic history up to 1914 as a thing different in kind: building as against growing. In the process of growth, the bones and the flesh develop together. In building, you first construct the skeleton, then you put on the flesh: that is the Russian formula—which is incidentally convenient for purposes of world power since it gives you means of war far in advance of your means of comfort.

INVESTMENT, SAVING, AND POLITICAL STRUCTURE

An economy is most easily understood if you analyze it in terms of concrete goods. The manpower of Russian industry has risen from less than 4 million in 1928 to approximately 18 million in 1956: this is about the same manpower as that of American industry. Russian industry however produces less of everything, and the difference in amounts produced is far more pronounced in consumer goods than it is in investment goods. There are indeed some investment goods which are produced in greater quantities in the U.S.S.R. than in the U.S. In other terms, the percentage of resources going into investment activities is much higher in Russia than in America. If this fact is formulated in the language of national financial accounting, we have to say that the rate of investment within the industrial product is very much higher in Russia than in the U.S. . . .

Marx's critique of the capitalist system was based upon his postulate that the whole of added value belonged by right to the workers: and therefore the distribution of profits was an expropriation of the workers. It was an injustice, but at the same time it was necessary. Only through profits, as he clearly saw, could there be reinvestment, building up of the productive apparatus. Therefore this injustice would have to endure until the productive apparatus had been sufficiently built up. When no further capital investment was necessary, then the capitalist would become unnecessary. But he would not readily perceive his redundance; therefore he would have to be forcibly done away with. His redundance would be revealed by the fact that he would be able to find no productive employment for the capital arising out of profits: opportunities to invest would have withered away, and therefore his levy upon added value would be useless and nefarious, depriving the working consumers of the buying power needed to absorb rising production.

The historical necessity of the capitalist's disappearance was based primarily upon the postulate, widely prevalent in Marx's day, of the dwindling opportunities for productive investment: this is to be found in Ricardo. It was based also on the assumption that capitalists would not allow workers to get directly or indirectly (through government redistribution) a rising share of added value. On the other hand, the capitalist was held necessary for the process of accumulation because Marx could not imagine (and here he was no doubt right) that the workers, if they received the whole of added value, would be willing to save a large part of it for investment.

The class struggle was regarded by Marx as a struggle over "value added," the workers wishing to obtain the whole of it and to apply it to consumption, the capitalists wanting to retain as much of it as possible, and to apply it to investment. The workers were bound to win this fight,

might turn upon the question whether so steep a rise by so arduous a path was a desirable thing.

Let us further assume that Russia persists in its procedure of rapid growth, and therefore catches up with the U.S.[3] in basic capacities by a certain date T, and in production of consumer goods by a certain later date T'. Is anyone ready to argue that the total welfare of the Russian people between the years 1928 and T' will have been maximized by the procedure followed? Is it not far more plausible that the total welfare of the generations concerned would have been greater if a less arduous path had been followed?

It is natural to discount very distant satisfactions as against immediate satisfactions. Tinbergen has produced striking estimates of such discounting.[4] Acting as self-constituted "representatives" of the Russian people, the Soviet leaders seem to have turned things the other way round and to have set future satisfactions at a premium as against the present. But have they really reasoned in this manner? And have they not rather thought in terms of equalization of power?

For over a century, starting with Sismondi if not earlier,[5] there has been a ceaseless critique of capitalism, arguing that its unquestionable achievements in the building up of capacities were not worth the price paid in the uprooting and hustling of men, that in fact men would have been better off, and happier with a more leisurely pace of change than that forced upon them by capitalists and their sales pressure. It is interesting to find the communists enamored of the buildup achieved by the hated and despised capitalism, to the point of thinking that its speedy emulation justifies greater pressure upon men than was ever exerted under capitalism.

[3] As far as one thinks of consumer goods, one should, of course, picture the catching up as involving equalization of consumer goods per capita; if one thinks of power, then the catching up is to be thought of as merely the equality of productive capacities between the two nations, regardless of differences in population.

[4] See Tibergen's remarkable article in the *Economic Journal,* December 1956.

[5] One might say that this critique starts with Rousseau's *Discourse on the Sciences and the Arts.*

Chapter 17

RECENT DEVELOPMENTS: THE SOVIET VIEW

On February 14, 1956, Khrushchev delivered the official Report of the Central Committee to the 20th Congress of the Communist Party. This Report covered a vast range of subjects from which only portions dealing with claimed economic and social advances and problems in the U.S.S.R. are reproduced below.

REPORT OF THE CENTRAL COMMITTEE TO THE 20TH PARTY CONGRESS

NIKITA S. KHRUSHCHEV*

Comrades, the period separating us from the Nineteenth Party Congress is not a very long one—only three years and four months. But the amount of work the Party has done, and the significance of the events that have taken place during this time both at home and abroad make it one of the important periods in the history of the Communist Party of the Soviet Union and its efforts to increase the strength of our country, build a communist society, and ensure world peace. . . .

I. THE STEADY ECONOMIC ADVANCE IN THE U.S.S.R.

. . . The rates at which industrial output has increased in the Soviet Union and in capitalist countries from 1929 to 1955 can be seen from the following table:

* First Secretary of the Communist Party of the Soviet Union and Chairman of the Counsel of Ministers of the U.S.S.R.

455

VOLUME OF INDUSTRIAL OUTPUT IN U.S.S.R. AND CAPITALIST COUNTRIES (1929 = 100)

	1929	1937	1943	1946	1949	1950	1952	1955
U.S.S.R.	100	429	573	466	870	1,082	1,421	2,049
All capitalist countries	100	104	—	107	130	148	164	193
Of which:								
United States	100	103	215	153	164	190	210	234
Great Britain	100	124		118	144	153	153	181
France	100	82	No data published	63	92	92	108	125
Italy	100	99		72	108	124	148	194
Western Germany	100	114		35	93	117	150	213
Japan	100	169	231 *	51	101	115	173	239

* Data for 1944.

These statistics show that in a quarter of a century, or, to be more exact, in 26 years, the Soviet Union increased its industrial output more than 20-fold, despite the tremendous damage done to its national economy by the war. Meanwhile, the United States, which enjoyed exceptionally favourable conditions, was able to do little more than double its production, while industry in the capitalist world as a whole failed to register even that growth. . . .

High rates of development of industrial production are a guarantee of new successes for socialism in its economic competition with capitalism. The U.S.S.R. now holds second place in total volume of industrial output. In the production of pig iron, steel, aluminium, copper, machinery, electricity, cement, and coal, the Soviet Union long ago outstripped France, Western Germany, and Britain and is steadily catching up with the United States.

A feature of the Soviet economy and of that of all the socialist countries is their all-round development and general peaceful trend. The countries of socialism are giving unremitting attention above all to the development of heavy industry, which is the foundation for the continuous expansion of social production as a whole. At the same time they are giving great attention to the growth of agriculture and the light industries. Living standards are steadily rising; culture is flowering.

Still more impressive are the prospects opening up before our peoples. The time is not far distant when in the U.S.S.R. atomic energy and other achievements of modern science and technology will be placed at the service of man on a large scale, when mineral wealth will be utilized still more fully, when mighty rivers will be harnessed and vast tracts of new land developed, which will ensure abundance of food and consumer goods. . . .

II. THE INTERNAL SITUATION OF THE U.S.S.R.

Comrades, the internal situation in the U.S.S.R. during the period under review featured a steady growth of all branches of social production, the further strengthening of the Soviet social and state system, the advancement of the material well-being of the people, and the all-round development of Soviet culture.

Industry and Transport

Guided by the behests of the great Lenin, the Communist Party of the Soviet Union has always worked steadfastly to ensure the priority, development of heavy industry, which is the foundation for the growth of all branches of socialist economy, the raising of our country's defence potential, and the improvement of the well-being of the people.

This is the general line of our Party, a line tried and tested in the course of the entire history of the Soviet state and corresponding to the vital interests of the people. The Communist Party will follow this general line with all firmness and consistency in the future as well.

The Basic Results of the Fifth Five-Year Plan in Industry. During the Fifth Five-Year Plan the Party achieved a further rapid advance in all branches of industry. As we know, the Fifth Five-Year Plan in industry was fulfilled ahead of time, within four years and four months.

The following figures throw light on the increase of industrial production in 1951-55:

	Industrial output in 1955, in percentages of 1950		Average annual rate of increase in 1951-1955 (in percentages)	
	Five-Year Plan Target	Actual Output	Five-Year Plan Target	Actual Increase
Industry as a whole...........	170	185	12	13.1
Production of the means of production (group A)...........	180	191	13	13.8
Production of consumer goods (group B).................	165	176	11	11.9

Production of metal, fuel and electricity, and the output in other key branches of heavy industry increased considerably. Here are the figures:

	Production in 1950	Production in 1955	Per cent increase
Pig iron (in millions of tons)	19	33	174
Steel (in millions of tons)	27	45	166
Rolled metal (in millions of tons)	21	35	169
Coal (in millions of tons)	261	391	150
Oil (in millions of tons)	38	71	187
Electricity (in thousands of millions of kwh)	91	170	187
Cement (in millions of tons)	10	22	221
Tractors (in thousands)	109	163	150
Mineral fertilizers (in millions of tons)	5.5	9.6	175

The engineering industry developed at the most rapid pace during the Fifth Five-Year Plan. The volume of production in the engineering and metal-working industries increased in 1955 to 2.2 times the 1950 figure and 4.7 times the figure for 1940.

Together with the production of the means of production, the output of consumer goods has been mounting from year to year. I shall give some figures to illustrate this:

	Production in 1950	Production in 1955	Per cent increase
Cotton fabrics (in millions of metres)	3,899	5,904	151
Woollen fabrics (in millions of metres)	155	251	162
Footwear (in millions of pairs)	226	299	132
Granulated sugar (in millions of tons)	2.5	3.4	136
Meat—output of industrial packing houses of the Ministry of the Meat and Dairy Products Industry (in millions of tons)	1.3	2.2	168
Butter and other dairy produce in terms of milk (in millions of tons)	8.5	13.5	159
Vegetable oils (in millions of tons)	0.8	1.1	143
Fish (in millions of tons)	1.7	2.7	156
Bicycles (in millions)	0.6	2.9	444
Clocks and watches (in millions)	7.6	19.7	260
Radio and TV receivers (in millions)	1.1	4.0	372

In its economic competition with capitalism, our country, owing to the advantages of the socialist system of economy, is showing immeasurably higher rates of increase in production than the most advanced capitalist countries. For instance, our average annual rates of increase in industrial output during the past five-year period were more than three times as high as that of the U.S.A. and 3.8 times that of Britain.

Per capita output in the U.S.S.R. is steadily increasing. During the Fifth Five-Year Plan per capita output of pig iron increased by 60 per cent, of steel by 52 per cent, coal by 37 per cent, oil by 72 per cent, electric power by 71 per cent, cotton fabrics by 40 per cent, woollen fabrics by 48 per cent, and sugar by 24 per cent. Nevertheless we still lag behind the leading capitalist countries in per capita production. No little effort is still required to fulfil our basic economic task—to catch up and surpass the most advanced capitalist countries in this respect.

During the Fifth Five-Year Plan capital investment in industry increased by 94 per cent compared with the Fourth Five-Year Plan. In construction of electric power stations it went up 3.4 times, in the oil industry, 2.3 times, the iron and steel and non-ferrous metals industries, 1.8 times, the chemical industry, 1.8 times, engineering, 1.7 times, production of building materials, lumber, and paper, 2.2 times, and in the light and food industries, 1.5 times.

In 1955 the productivity of labour in industry was nearly double the pre-war level. Indeed, higher productivity accounted for more than two-thirds of the total increase of industrial output during the Fifth Five-Year Plan. During the same period the cost of production was reduced by 23 per cent. Quality of output improved and the variety and assortment of goods turned out increased.

Comrades, as you can see from the above data, during the period under review our Party and the Soviet people brought about a new upsurge in the national economy, developing heavy industry further and, on this basis, achieved an advance in agriculture and the light and food industries. The Soviet Union took a new major step forward in its gradual transition from socialism to communism. (*Prolonged applause.*)

Soviet industry is beginning the Sixth Five-Year Plan with considerably greater potentialities for growth and improvement in production than ever before. Now we can assign to industry bigger and qualitatively new tasks, whose realization will make it possible further to enhance the country's economic might and improve the well-being of our people.

During the period under review the Central Committee of the Party carried out important measures aimed at further improving the operation of industry, and above all at introducing the latest achievements of science and technology in production. Why did the Central Committee direct the attention of the Party and the people precisely to these questions?

The point is that our industrial successes turned the heads of some of our business executives and Party workers, made them conceited and complacent, and in a number of cases led to underestimation of the need for constant modernization of production by introducing the latest achievements of both our own and foreign science and technology. We still have a good many such hidebound executives who prefer to play safe and tend to steer clear of all that is new and progressive. These hidebound seat-warmers reason thus: "Why should I bother with it? It will just be a lot of trouble and for all I know unpleasantness too. They talk about modernizing production, but is it worth while breaking my head over it?

Let the chiefs up above worry about it. When a directive comes down we'll see about it." Some, even after receiving the directive, just wave it aside and go through the motions. . . .

It was necessary to mobilize the Party to overcome the shortcomings in the work of our industry, to make more effective use of our tremendous latent potentialities, to work for technical progress. With this in view conferences of leading workers in industry were held. The question was thoroughly examined at the July Plenary Meeting of the C.C. of the C.P.S.U. last year. Since the Plenary Meeting much has been done, but we must regard this only as a beginning of bigger and more important things to come.

The Draft Directives for the Sixth Five-Year Plan outline a sweeping programme for the development of all branches of the national economy. The prime tasks of the Sixth Five-Year Plan in industry are further expansion of the iron and steel, non-ferrous metals, fuel, and chemical industries, the steady acceleration of electric power station construction, and the rapid development of the engineering industry.

The Draft Directives were drawn up with a view to raising the level of industrial output in 1960 by approximately 65 per cent compared with that of 1955, with a planned 70 per cent increase in means of production, and 60 per cent in consumer goods. With the fulfilment of the Sixth Five-Year Plan we shall raise the level of industrial output in the U.S.S.R. to more than five times the level of the pre-war year 1940. . . .

While continuing to maintain a high rate of development of heavy industry in the future, we can and must expand the production of consumer goods.

The aim of capitalist production is, as we know, to extract steadily increasing profits. This is achieved by constantly intensifying exploitation of the workers and by the expansion of production. However, the tendency towards expansion of production comes into conflict with the narrow limits of popular consumption, due to the decline—inevitable under capitalism— of the working people's effective demand. Capitalist society features a deep-going contradiction between production and consumption.

Socialism has abolished this contradiction of capitalist production. The aim of socialist production is the maxmum satisfaction of the steadily growing material and cultural requirements of the working people, of society as a whole. As heavy industry expands, the development of industries directly engaged in meeting the growing needs of the population acquires an ever greater scale. Now that we possess a powerful heavy industry developed in every respect, we are in a position to promote rapidly production of both the means of production and consumer goods. Suffice it to mention that in 1960 the output of consumer goods will be almost three times more than in 1950. The Party is doing and will continue to do its utmost to ensure that the requirements of the Soviet people are satisfied more fully and better; it considers this its prime duty to the people. . . .

Agriculture

Comrades, together with a powerful industry our country must have a comprehensively developed agriculture, capable of producing foodstuffs and raw materials in quantities sufficient to satisfy fully the needs of the population and meet all the other requirements of the state.

The development of socialist economy, the growth of labour productivity, and the reductions of retail prices during recent years have substantially raised the real wages of factory, office and other workers and the incomes of collective farmers, increasing the purchasing power of the population.

These conditions confronted the Party with an urgent national task —sharply to increase the output of farm produce. At its Plenary Meetings the Central Committee of the Party has brought to light serious shortcomings and mistakes in the guidance of agriculture, and drawn up an extensive programme for expanding the output of grain and animal products.

Our Party, with the active support of the working class and the whole people, has carried out large-scale measures for the development of agriculture. During 1954 and 1955 alone, capital investment in agriculture totalled 34,400 million rubles, or 38 per cent more than the total capital investment in agriculture during the entire Fourth Five-Year Plan. In these two years collective farms, machine and tractor stations, and state farms received 404,000 tractors (in terms of 15 h. p. units), 228,000 lorries, 83,000 combine-harvesters, and a large number of other machines.

To provide greater material incentives for the collective farms and collective farmers to develop their socially-owned economy and increase output for the market, the procurement prices of grain, animal products, potatoes and other vegetables, flax and hemp were raised considerably. These measures and increased production for the market added 20,000 million rubles to the incomes of the collective farms in 1954 and 1955.

In the MTSs regular operating staffs have been built up, a factor of prime importance in their transformation into model socialist establishments. Many thousand engineers, technicians, Party functionaries, and government officials have gone from cities and industrial centres to work at MTSs, collective and state farms. More than 120,000 agricultural specialists have been sent to collective farms. More than 20,000 Communists, sent from town to country, have been recommended as collective-farm chairmen. The Central Committee of the Party and the Government have introduced a new planning system in agriculture which has given scope to the initiative of the collective farmers. Measures have been taken to improve the work of the state farms, to reinforce existing state farms, and to set up new ones.

The fulfilment of the measures for the further advance of agriculture, drawn up by the Party, has made it possible to take the first big step to increase the output of grain and industrial crops. This is graphically shown by the following table:

TOTAL OUTPUT OF GRAIN AND INDUSTRIAL CROPS IN THE U.S.S.R.
(1950 = 100)

	1950	1951	1952	1953	1954	1955
Grain..................	100	97	113	101	105	129
Sun-flower seed........	100	97	123	146	106	207
Sugar-beet.............	100	114	107	111	95	147
Raw cotton.............	100	105	106	108	118	109
Long-staple flax fibre.....	100	76	83	64	85	149

It should be noted that while during the first 3 or 4 years of the Fifth Five-Year Plan the production of grain and industrial crops hardly rose at all, in 1955 gross harvests increased considerably thanks to the carrying out of a number of measures of which you know. Compared with 1954, grain production last year increased 22 per cent, sunflower seed 95 per cent, sugar beet 54 per cent, and flax fibre 74 per cent. We had no increase in the cotton crop because plants were damaged by early frosts. Potato yields were low in a number of districts, particularly in the non-black-earth zone.

1. Grain Farming—Foundation of All Agriculture. . . . The development of virgin and long-fallow lands in Kazakhstan, Siberia, and other areas, undertaken following a decision by the Party, is of particularly great importance for the continued advance of agriculture. The Central Committee of the C.P.S.U. set the task of bringing no less than 28-30 million hectares of new land under cultivation by 1956. The solution of this problem is of historic significance for our state. What will the virgin lands give the country? Estimates show that we can get on the average no less than 2,000 million poods of grain annually from the new lands. With a big quantity of marketable wheat from the virgin lands, the Government can confidently undertake a big expansion of the area under maize in the Ukraine and the North Caucasus in order that these areas may sharply raise meat and milk production and also the production of industrial crops.

Within a short time over 200,000 tractors (in terms of 15 h.p. units) and thousands of other machines and implements have been sent to the virgin land development areas. . . . In 1954 and 1955 some 30 million hectares were put to the plough in the virgin and long-fallow land areas; over the whole country the total reached 33 million hectares. This is a big victory for the Party and the whole Soviet people. (*Stormy, prolonged applause.*)

The ploughing up of virgin lands has made it possible to substantially expand the area under grain. In 1950 grain was sown on 102.9 million hectares in the U.S.S.R.; in 1955 the figure was 126.4 million hectares— an increase of almost 24 million hectares. . . .

Our main task in farming is to bring up the annual total grain crop to 11,000 million poods by the end of the Sixth Five-Year Plan through raising yields and developing more new lands; to extend the areas and increase considerably the yields of industrial crops—cotton, sugar beet, flax, hemp, and sunflower seed; and also sharply to expand the production of potatoes and other vegetables. In the next two years we can and must accomplish the task of fully supplying the country with potatoes and other vegetables of high quality.

Orchards and areas under vines and berries should be increased. The planting of shelter belts should be developed and our youth urged to take an active part in this work. It is very important to extend the scale of irrigation development and at the same time to improve the use of irrigated and drained lands.

The Central Committee of the Party deems it necessary to increase the production of mineral fertilizers and chemical weed and pest killers. We must continue to raise the efficiency of farming, persistently introduce advanced agrotechnical methods, and proper crop rotations, cutting the time of agricultural jobs and on this basis assure higher yields of grain and industrial crops in all areas.

2. The Tasks of Further Advancing Livestock Farming. Comrades, the further development of animal husbandry and an increase in the output and procurement of animal products is one of the most difficult and at the same time most urgent tasks our Party has faced in the recent period. The Central Committee of the C.P.S.U. and the Government have drawn up and implemented a number of major economic and organizational measures designed to increase herds and to raise livestock productivity.

The Central Committee of the C.P.S.U. and the Soviet Government have found it necessary to give collective farmers greater material incentives to develop livestock farming. An extensive plan for the mechanization of work in animal husbandry and the building of livestock barns has been adopted and is being carried out. Local Party organizations have done considerable work in reinforcing the personnel engaged in key sections of livestock breeding.

All this could not but produce, and did produce, favourable results. Allow me to cite some figures illustrating the state of our animal husbandry.

Our country has immense livestock farming reserves. If persistent organizational work is carried on in the collective and state farms, exceptional results can be achieved in a year or two. . . .

3. For Better Guidance of Agriculture. . . . To seriously improve ag-

HEAD OF PRODUCTIVE LIVESTOCK IN THE U.S.S.R.
(1950 = 100)

	1950	1951	1952	1953	1954	1955
Cows	100	102	100	107	113	120
Total head of cattle	100	103	99	110	114	117
Pigs	100	111	117	195	210	214
Sheep	100	110	114	139	142	151

OUTPUT OF THE MAIN ANIMAL PRODUCTS IN THE U.S.S.R.
(1950 = 100)

	1950	1951	1952	1953	1954	1955
Meat (slaughterhouse weight)	100	96	106	120	129	130
Milk	100	102	101	103	108	119
Wool	100	107	122	130	128	142
Eggs	100	113	123	137	147	154

ricultural management we should call the attention of our leading workers
to problems of economics, to cutting the expenditure of labour in production. Learn to count—Lenin told executives in the first years of Soviet
power. If it was important when our state was born, it is a hundred times
more important today, when we are accomplishing the task of catching up
and surpassing the principal capitalist countries in per capita production.

Available data show that in our country considerably more labour is
spent to produce a ton of milk or meat than in the United States. The
result is that more of the population are engaged in agriculture in the
U.S.S.R. than in the United States. We, of course, cannot blindly follow
the American example. In America one man makes profit by ruining another. Suffice it to recall that from 1940 to 1954, that is, in 14 years, nearly
1,300,000 farmers in the United States were ruined, lost their land and,
together with their families, flocked to the cities in search of work in industry, or became "migrant farmers" who roam from state to state in
search of shelter and a livelihood. In the last four years alone the number
of farms in the United States dropped by 600,000, according to agricultural
census returns. The big farmer, an owner of a capitalist enterprise, looks
upon labour power as a source of profit. If the worker has ruined his
health, if he is unable to produce maximum profit, the capitalist throws
him out.

Things are different in our country. A collective farm is a co-operative
enterprise. All the collective farmers are its owners; they are full-fledged
members, they distribute the work among themselves. And this is fully understandable. In our socialist society everything is designed to satisfy the
growing requirements of man. The collective farmers do not cast out one

of their number who is unable to work at full capacity. Therefore, even when labour outlay per unit of product in our country is lower than in the United States—and we will achieve this—it is possible that the agricultural population in the U.S.S.R. will be somewhat larger than in the United States. Nevertheless, it must be said that we do not as yet employ labour productively enough. So we must assess our work critically and utilize everything that is useful in foreign experience.

The implementation of measures in the field of agriculture, outlined by the Party, has created all the requisites for increasing agricultural production to a level satisfying the country's growing requirements within the shortest possible time. We may be sure that the Soviet people, headed by the Communist Party, will discharge this vitally important task with honour. (*Prolonged applause.*)

The Rise in the Material and Cultural Standards of the Soviet People

Comrades, the Soviet people's standard of living has risen steadily thanks to progress in industry and agriculture. During the Fifth Five-Year Plan the U.S.S.R.'s national income—three-quarters of which, as you know, goes to satisfy the personal requirements of the population—increased by 68 per cent. The real wages of factory, office and other workers increased by 39 per cent, and the real incomes of collective farmers by 50 per cent. The state spent 689,000 million rubles on social insurance benefits, paid holidays for factory, office and other workers, accommodation in holiday homes and health centres provided free of charge or at reduced rates, pensions, medical service, grants for students, and so forth.

Popular consumption has increased from year to year in step with the development of the socialist economy. The state and co-operative trade networks sold 90 per cent more goods to the population in 1955 than they did in 1950.

Here are some figures showing how the sale of goods to the population through the state and co-operative trade systems has increased (1950 = 100):

	1950	1951	1952	1953	1954	1955
Meat and meat products.......	100	120	124	171	206	220
Fish and fish products.........	100	112	128	137	162	185
Butter.....................	100	107	110	150	160	158
Vegetable oils...............	100	135	170	182	222	222
Wearing apparel.............	100	107	115	151	182	198
Footwear...................	100	108	118	150	163	168
Furniture..................	100	142	154	201	272	307

Sales of sugar, silks and cottons, clocks and watches, sewing machines, and other commodities have also grown considerably.

There has been a sharp increase in the sale of radio and television sets, musical instruments, bicycles, and other articles that go to meet cultural requirements and household needs. The Soviet people are now better supplied with food and clothing and are satisfying their cultural requirements more fully.

This improvement in the people's material well-being accounts for the fact that the population of our country increased by 16,300,000 during the Fifth Five-Year Plan.

1. Fuller Satisfaction of the People's Growing Material Requirements. These are substantial achievements. But we must base ourselves not only on a comparison with past years, but mainly on the steadily growing material and cultural needs of the people. When we approach the matter from this point of view, we must say that we do not yet have an adequate quantity of consumer goods, that there is a shortage of housing, and that many important problems connected with raising the people's living standards have not yet been solved.

The fact that our country was economically backward before the October Revolution, when its industries were underdeveloped and its agriculture primitive, must of course, be taken into account. In the 38 years since its establishment the Soviet state had to go through two wars which caused incalculable damage to the national economy and cost millions of lives.

That is why, notwithstanding the considerable rise in the living standards of our people, the Communist Party and the Soviet Government have a lot to do to raise it to a level corresponding to the potentialities of the socialist system and the Soviet people's constantly growing requirements.

In the past few years the Central Committee has adopted a number of measures to raise the people's living standards still higher. Nevertheless, production of many important foodstuffs and manufactured goods still lags behind the growing demand. Some towns and communities are still insufficiently supplied with such items as meat, milk, butter, and fruit; there are even cases where supplies of potatoes and other vegetables are irregular. There are also difficulties in supplying the population with certain high-grade manufactured goods. Inefficient work by our trade organizations is partly to blame for this, but the main reason is insufficient production. The task is to achieve a sharp rise in agriculture and more rapid expansion of the light and food industries, on the basis of the priority development of heavy industry.

Comrades, the Draft Directives for the Sixth Five-Year Plan set the task of raising the real wages of factory, office and other workers by about 30 per cent and the collective farmers' incomes by not less than 40 per cent.

A number of measures which the Central Committee of the Party has recently outlined will contribute to the fulfilment of the task of further raising the material standards of the people.

Instructions to draft a decision raising the wages of low-income categories of workers were issued not long ago by the Central Committee of the Party and the Council of Ministers of the U.S.S.R. This wage increase is to be carried out side by side with general measures to introduce order into the system of wages and salaries of factory, office and other workers in various branches of the economy. A correct ratio should be established between the wage level of different categories of workers, depending on their qualifications and the burden of their work.

It must be pointed out that there is a great deal of disorder and confusion in the system of wages and rate-fixing. Ministries and other bodies and the trade unions have not taken up these matters in the way they should; they have neglected them. Cases of wage levelling are not uncommon. On the other hand, payment for the same kind of work, sometimes differs between various bodies, and even within a single body. Alongside the low-income workers there exists a category of workers—a small one, it is true—in whose wages unjustified excesses are tolerated.

We are faced with the important political and economic task of introducing proper order into the payment of labour. We must consistently apply the principle of giving workers a personal material incentive, bearing in mind that application of this principle is a prime condition for the uninterrupted growth of production. Lenin taught us that "every major branch of the national economy should be based on personal incentive." (*Works*, Vol. 33, p. 47.)

We must work persistently to improve and perfect the wage system in all branches of the economy, make wages directly dependent on the quality and quantity of the work done by each worker, and fully utilize the powerful lever of material incentive in order to raise labour productivity. Part of the salaries of engineers, technicians, and managerial personnel should also depend strictly on the basic work indices of the given shop, establishment, industry, collective farm, MTS or state farm. This will be in line with the socialist principle of payment according to the work performed. The correct solution of this problem will help to bring about a further rise in production and in the well-being of our people.

Comrades, the Central Committee of the Party considers that conditions now exist in which we can return to that question of primary importance, reduction of the working day. (*Prolonged applause.*)

. . . The Central Committee reports to this Congress that it has adopted a decision on going over, during the Sixth Five-Year Plan, to a seven-hour day for all factory, office and other workers (*prolonged applause*), and a six-hour day for workers of the leading trades in the coal and ore-mining industries employed underground; also to reestablish the six-hour day for young people between the ages of 16 and 18. (*Applause.*) It has also decided soon to establish a six-hour day for factory, office and other workers on Saturdays and the eve of holidays. (*Prolonged applause.*)

Beginning with 1957 the Party and the Government will gradually transfer one branch of the national economy after another to a seven-hour day, or, where it is expedient in the light of conditions of production, to a five-day working week (with an eight-hour day and two free days), with the aim of completing all this work by the end of the Sixth Five-Year Plan. (*Applause.*)

The switch to a shorter working day will not be accompanied by any reduction in the wages of factory, office and other workers. (*Applause.*)

The Central Committee's decision on reducing the working day has great national-economic and political significance. There is no doubt that the Twentieth Party Congress and the entire Soviet people will unanimously welcome this decision. These measures will call forth a new surge in the Soviet people's efforts to fulfil and exceed the national-economic programmes. (*Stormy, prolonged applause.*)

It should be brought to the particular attention of heads of enterprises and of Party and trade-union bodies that they will have to do considerable organizational work to ensure the successful fulfilment of the five-year plan targets under the shorter working day.

Another urgent need, besides introducing order into the wage system and reducing the working day, is that of improving the pension system. (*Applause.*) The pension system in the U.S.S.R. is financed by state and public funds, which are growing from year to year. This is a great achievement. But there are serious shortcomings in the pension system. For one thing, there are impermissible disparities in pensions. Low pensions have been established for a number of categories of pensioners, while some citizens, including people who are able to work and are not yet old, receive high pensions. . . .

The Central Committee of the Party and the U.S.S.R. Council of Ministers are taking steps to introduce order into the pension system, with a view to considerably increasing the lower categories of pensions and somewhat reducing the size of the unjustifiably high ones. (*Applause.*) A bill providing for a unified pension system for the U.S.S.R. making a fundamental improvement in this matter will soon be submitted to the U.S.S.R. Supreme Soviet for approval. (*Prolonged applause.*)

. . . All these measures will require considerable funds, of course. Where will they come from? First of all, we shall have to use part of the funds accumulating in the national economy as a result of increasing labour productivity, strict economy, elimination of excesses, and further pruning of the administrative and managerial apparatus. It may also be expedient to use for this purpose some of the funds earlier allocated to cover government expenditure in connection with retail price cuts. During the next few years price cuts should therefore be smaller than before so that part of the funds earmarked for them may be diverted to carrying out these measures. (*Applause.*)

The Party regards a fundamental improvement in the people's housing conditions as one of its important tasks. You know, Comrades, what tremendous damage was done to our country by the war. The Government had to spend huge sums to restore the housing that was destroyed. Housing appropriations are increasing from year to year. In the last five-year period, for instance, government capital investment in housing construction totalled about 100,000 million rubles, or 120 per cent more than under the Fourth Five-Year Plan.

A lot has been done, yet the speed of house building seriously lags behind the development of our national economy and the growth of towns and industrial centres. Besides, many ministries and other bodies regularly fail to carry out their housing programmes. We cannot tolerate such a disgraceful state of affairs any longer.

The volume of urban housing construction under the Sixth Five-Year Plan is to be nearly double that of the Fifth Five-Year Plan. Dwellings with a total floor space of about 205 million square metres are to be built with government funds allocated under the plan. In 1956 alone the government will build about 29 million square metres. The rates of housing construction will increase from year to year. . . .

Improvement of housing conditions in such big cities as Moscow, Leningrad, and Kiev is closely connected with the growth of population because of people arriving from other parts of the country. How great this increase is can be seen from the example of Moscow, whose population grew by nearly 300,000 because of arrivals alone during the Fifth Five-Year Plan. In that time 4,305,000 square metres of housing was built in Moscow. The result is that, although house building is going ahead on a large scale, the need for housing has hardly dropped.

Since the natural increase in our urban population is quite large, we can stop drawing in labour to the cities from other places and meet any labour needs that may arise by employing members of the city population themselves. (*Applause.*) This does not present any difficulty, because new industrial construction is not being carried out in the major cities, while in the existing enterprises the technical level is rapidly advancing, the technology of production is being improved, and productivity steadily rising. If we can stop the influx into the major cities from other districts we shall create conditions for satisfying urban housing needs more quickly. . . .

Individual house building should be developed on a larger scale side by side with government construction; more extensive assistance should be given to factory, office and other workers in building their own homes with their personal savings; the manufacture and sale to the public of building materials and sets of parts for standard houses should be expanded.

Not enough attention is being paid to the daily needs of the population. To improve the life of the Soviet family we must manufacture more labour-saving household machines and articles—electric appliances, washing machines, sewing machines, improved kitchen utensils; besides, they must be made cheaper. We must open more public service establishments, laundries, tailoring establishments, and clothing and boot and shoe repair shops. . . .

Further improvement of the public health services is an important task. Our achievements in this field are universally known, but here, too, there are serious shortcomings, particularly in the rural areas. In the next few years we must set up many more medical establishments and improve their work.

There is not a single aspect of improving the people's well-being in which a great deal of urgent work does not lie before us. The exceptional importance of this work does not have to be demonstrated, for it is the people's vital interests that are in question. And concern for the welfare of the people always has held and will hold the centre of attention in the work of our Party and the Soviet Government. (*Stormy, prolonged applause.*)

In the sphere of home policy the paramount tasks for the next few years are:

1. Persistently and energetically to widen the material and production base of socialist society, to introduce into all branches of the national economy higher techniques, the latest achievements of home and foreign science and engineering, and the production methods of the foremost workers.

2. To ensure a steady rise in labour productivity, on the basis of technical progress and above all of extensive electrification of the country, decisive improvement in the organization of work and production, and undeviating observance of the Leninist principle of the material interest of workers in the results of their labour.

3. Tirelessly to reduce the cost of industrial and agricultural production, to apply the cost-accountancy principle more widely in industrial enterprises, state farms, and MTSs, to exercise the strictest economy, cut down expenditure of labour and material values per unit of output, and constantly improve the quality of the goods produced.

4. Along with a decisive improvement in capital construction, to utilize existing production capacities efficiently, to seek for and increasingly utilize potentials existing in all branches of the natonal economy, at every enterprise and construction scheme and every collective and state farm.

5. To continue to ensure in future priority in the rate of development of heavy industry—the foundation of the entire socialist economy— to expand considerably the production of consumer goods, and untiringly to push the development of the light and food industries.

6. Using the experience of the foremost collective farms, state farms,

and MTSs, to bring the annual production of cereals up to 11,000 million poods and considerably to increase production of cotton, sugar beet, flax, potatoes and other vegetables, and other farm produce by the end of the Sixth Five-Year Plan. Production of meat is to be doubled, of milk nearly doubled, and production of wool is to be increased by 82 per cent.

7. Steadily to raise the material welfare and cultural standards of the working people, to implement the decisions of the Party on a shorter working day in an organized manner, and to carry out a wide programme of housing construction for the working people.

8. Persistently to improve the work of the Soviet state apparatus, to reduce it and make it less expensive, energetically to eradicate bureaucracy and red tape, improve the guidance given to all sectors of the national economy, work to make the guidance as concrete as possible so that it may provide practical help to lagging enterprises, collective farms, MTSs, and state farms in order that they may reach the level of the most advanced.

9. Widely to develop the initiative and creative effort of the millions of workers, collective farmers, and intellectuals, militantly to organize and lead the country-wide socialist emulation for the fulfilment and overfulfilment of the Sixth Five-Year Plan.

10. Tirelessly to strengthen the great alliance of the working class and collective-farm peasantry, the indestructible friendship of the peoples of the U.S.S.R., the moral and political unity of the whole of Soviet society, to educate the working millions in the spirit of Soviet patriotism and proletarian internationalism, and to rally them still more closely around our glorious Communist Party and around the invincible banner of Marxism-Leninism. (*Stormy, prolonged applause.*)

EDITOR'S NOTE: *Subsequent to Khrushchev's Report, there were several important economic developments in the U.S.S.R. to which reference must be made—although it is not yet possible to evaluate fully their effects.*

Early in 1957, it became clear that a downward revision had been made in the tempo of industrial growth envisaged in the Sixth Five-Year Plan—to a 7.1 per cent overall rate of industrial increase for 1957, as against possibly 11 to 12 per cent realized in previous years. In September, the government officially scrapped its Five-Year Plan and announced that it was substituting a Seven-Year Plan to begin in 1959. However, at the end of 1957, it was claimed that the "assignment of the state plan has been considerably exceeded" and that the rate of growth had come close to that of previous years. For the first six months of 1958, the Central Statistical Administration of the Council of Ministers announced that gross industrial output rose 10.5 per cent compared with the first six months of 1957 and that substantial advances had been made on other fronts.

In July 1957, after some months of discussion and preparation, a major reorganization and decentralization of the economy was launched. Twenty-

five of the thirty-two centralized industrial ministries were abolished. Their industrial and building enterprises were transferred to approximately 100 newly formed Regional *Economic Councils. Of the seven ministries retained, only one—atomic energy—remained* entirely *under central control. A typical Soviet enterprise will now take direction from a Regional Council, accountable to the Council of Ministers of its particular Republic. Party spokesmen said that the plan is designed to eliminate waste and overlapping, improve coordination, initiative, and cooperation at the local level and reduce unproductive bureaucratic staffing at the center. One American observer, Philip Mosely, writing for* Foreign Affairs *in July 1958, commented that " 'Decentralization' is a misnomer. There has been a devolution of decision-making functions to strong regional agencies, but all important decisions are still made in the center and are now coordinated through an expanded super-ministry,* Gosplan."

In April 1958, the Central Committee of the Communist Party and the Council of Ministers jointly put into operation a far-reaching scheme proposed by Khrushchev which will permit and encourage those collective farms, which are able and willing, to purchase and maintain their own tractors, combines, and other machinery. The machine and tractor stations—which exercised such vast political as well as economic power—will be reorganized and reduced to repair and technical service stations. On March 1, Pravda *had editorially described the proposal as part of "a broad movement to overtake the United States in the next few years in the per capita production of meat, milk and butter." It had further explained that,*

Under the present conditions—when the collective farms have matured and become strong, when the fundamental issue of the Party's domestic policy is the drive for higher productivity of labor—the technical servicing of the collective farms by the machine-and-tractor stations can no longer satisfy the requirements resulting from the growing collective-farm production and is beginning to hinder the progress of the productive forces in agriculture. The fact that there are two masters over one plot of land, to wit, the collective farm and the machine-and-tractor station, does away with personal responsibility, interferes with the more efficient and rational employment of tractors and other machinery, and also the punctual observance of the time-table of farming jobs.

In June of 1958, it was announced that an end had been put to the system under which collective farms had disposed of their produce principally through "compulsory" deliveries to the state of certain amounts at relatively low, fixed prices and through "surplus" sales at somewhat higher prices. Compulsory deliveries have now been abolished and all farm produce will be obtained as purchases. Prices will continue to be set by the government but at levels which will reflect actual costs of production more realistically and encourage efficiency. The new system, however, "must guarantee" the delivery of necessary supplies—which implies the continuance of quotas. Commenting on this program, Harry Schwartz stated in the New York Times *that it apparently reflects the realization "that the market forces of supply and demand, price and cost, profit and loss are more efficient stimuli for an efficient agriculture" than exhortations and orders.*

Radio Moscow announced on September 6, 1958, that the 21st Communist Party Congress would be convened on January 27, 1959 (less than three years after the 20th Congress of February 1956). The Congress will be concerned with "target figures for the development of the national economy" for the seven years, 1959 through 1965.

It is clear that, under the leadership of Khrushchev, the U.S.S.R. is using the viability of a planned economy and a political dictatorship to embark upon large-scale programs to increase both industrial and agricultural productivity—with potential economic benefits and political risks that are—as of now—incalculable.

SUMMARY OF PROJECTED SEVEN-YEAR PLAN FOR 1959-1965

The New York Times

On November 14, 1958, the Central Committee of the Communist Party of the U.S.S.R. proposed a new economic Seven-Year Plan for nation-wide discussion prior to submission to the 21st Party Congress convening early in 1959. This summary of the basic objectives of the Plan appeared in the New York Times *on November 15, 1958, and is presented here with its permission.*

(The Plan envisages an 80 per cent increase in gross industrial production, a 65 per cent increase in consumer goods, and a 70 per cent increase in agricultural output. An average of at least 40 per cent increase in real income is promised and a vast housing program to ease the critical shortage.)

An evaluation of this Plan by Harry Schwartz, New York Times *Soviet specialist, will be found in Chapter 18.*

HEAVY INDUSTRY

Heavy industrial output by 1965 will increase 85 to 88 per cent. Production of steel will reach 86 to 91 million metric tons, an increase of 56 to 65 per cent over 1958. Pig iron will reach 65 to 70 million tons, increasing 65 to 77 per cent. Rolled steel will reach 65 to 70 million tons, an increase of 52 to 64 per cent. Raw iron ore will reach 230 to 245 million tons to yield 150 to 160 million tons of marketable ore.

Aluminum production is to increase 180 per cent over 1958, refined copper 90 per cent and other nonferrous metals "considerably,"

At least 140 large chemical enterprises are to be completed and 130 others will be modernized to meet previously announced goals for considerable increases in chemical and synthetic fiber production.

Oil and gas will become the dominant fuels.

Electric power production is to increase 100 to 120 per cent for a 1965 output of 500 to 520 billion kilowatt-hours.

LIGHT INDUSTRY

Light industry's gross output is to increase about 50 per cent.

Production of cotton fabrics is to increase from 5.8 billion meters in 1958 to 7.7 or 8 billion in 1965. Woolen fabric output is to rise from 300 million to 500 million meters. (One meter equals 39.37 inches.)

One hundred fifty-six "major light-industry factories" are to be built and 114 that already have been begun will be completed. Output of household goods is to be doubled.

FOOD INDUSTRY

State food enterprises are to turn out 6,130,000 metric tons of meat by 1965, an increase of 117 per cent over 1958; 1,006,000 tons of butter, a 60 per cent increase; 13,546,000 tons of milk products, up 125 per cent; up to ten million tons of ground beet sugar, an increase of up to 94 per cent; 1,975,000 tons of margarine, up 62 per cent, and 4,626,000 tons of fish, up 62 per cent.

AGRICULTURE

The total volume of agricultural production will increase by 70 per cent.

The yields per acre of major farm products in 1965, the Government said, will exceed the 1957 yields per acre in the United States.

CAPITAL INVESTMENT

Capital investments in 1959-65 are scheduled to increase by 80 per cent over 1951–1958. Investments in rubles planned for some sectors of the economy were listed as follows (4 rubles to $1 at the official exchange rate):

Ferrous metals industry, 100 billion; chemical industry, 100 to 105 billion; oil and gas industries, 170 to 173 billion; coal industry, 75 to 78 billion; power industry, 125 to 129 billion; wood and paper industry, 58 to 60 billion; light and food industries, 80 to 85 billion; housing and municipal construction, 375 to 380 billion; agriculture 150 billion, and railroads, 110 to 115 billion.

TRADE

Retail trade is to increase 57 to 62 per cent. Trade with other Communist countries is to increase more than 50 per cent.

WELFARE

The national income is to increase 62 to 65 per cent. Real wages are to increase at least 40 per cent and pensions are to be improved. A thirty-five-hour work week of five or six days "is to be introduced" apparently in some industries.

EDUCATION

A compulsory eight-year school program will replace the current seven-year schools in the countryside and the ten-year schools in the cities. All basic schooling is to combine vocational and academic training.

SCIENCE

Large-scale research programs are to be undertaken, especially in areas of immediate practical value. Physicists are to concentrate on problems of cosmic rays, nuclear reactions and semi-conductors. Mathematicians are to work on computing machines and chemists on the theory and practice of creating new synthetic materials.

Chapter 18

RECENT DEVELOPMENTS: SOME OTHER APPRAISALS

This section presents the viewpoints of two specialists and those of the head of America's Central Intelligence Agency on recent economic developments in the U.S.S.R. The first, by Maurice Dobb, an acknowledged Marxist, is largely an historical account. The contribution of Mr. Allen W. Dulles should be read along with his "The Communists Also Have Their Problems," which deals with Soviet economic—as well as other—problems. It appears in Chapter 19 in this volume.

It is not suggested, of course, that the positions represented in this and earlier sections exhaust the range of views on the Soviet economic system. But they do at least have the merit of presenting some varying positions on a subject of great intricacy and controversy.

FROM THE FOURTH FIVE-YEAR PLAN
TO THE SIXTH

MAURICE DOBB*

I

The reconstruction years, following the ravages of war and military occupation, were neither easy nor untroubled; and the first two years, in particular, of the Fourth Plan were ones of acute difficulties and of intense hardship. 1946 was overshadowed by a crop-failure due to what was officially described as "the worst drought in our country for the last fifty years"; and it was also a year of reconversion of industry from a war-time to a peace-time basis, as a result of which industrial production fell below the pre-war level by about a quarter (and consumer goods production by considerably more than this—probably by as much as a third or even two-

* Lecturer and Fellow at Trinity College, Cambridge. Author of _Political Economy and Capitalism; Studies in the Development of Capitalism;_ and _On Economic Theory and Socialism._ The selection is from chapter 13 of _Soviet Economic Development Since 1917_ (London: Routledge & Kegan Paul Ltd., 4th ed., 1957), by permission of the publisher and of International Publishers, New York.

fifths).[1] It seems likely that the grain harvest in 1946 was only about a half of the pre-war level; and since fodder-grains were particularly affected, there was a serious setback to the recovery of livestock (and especially pigs) from devastating war-time losses.[2] In reporting six years later to the 19th Party Congress Malenkov was to state that "the war retarded our industrial development for eight or nine years, that is, approximately two five-year plans." [3]

The following year 1947, however, witnessed considerable improvement. Firstly there was a large improvement in the harvest: grain-yields per hectare were said to have been restored to their pre-war level and the grain crop to be larger than the year before by as much as 58 per cent. (the sugar-beet crop was nearly three times that of 1946). Industry had surmounted most of the dislocations attendant upon reconversion and re-tooling; and industrial production as a whole had recovered to more than 90 per cent. of the pre-war level (heavy industry to just above it; but consumer goods production was still some 20 per cent. below it). In 1948 it was announced that for the first time industrial production had passed the pre-war level in the course of that year, although it was not until the end of 1949 that industrial output in the devastated western areas (where the bulk of consumer goods industries were located) was restored to pre-war.

In view of the improvement in the situation in 1947, derationing of foodstuffs was undertaken in December of that year, and coupled with it a monetary reform designed to reduce the amount of money in circulation (expanded by some two and a half times during the war),[4] by the issue of new money to replace the depreciated war-time rouble. The official decree of December 11 announcing the change contained this explanation: "During the years of the Patriotic War the expenditure of the Soviet State on maintenance of the Army and on the development of the war industry rose sharply. The enormous war expenditure demanded the issue for circulation of large amounts of money . . . At present, when the transfer to open trade at unified prices has become the task of the day, the great amount of money issued during the war hampers the abolition of the rationing system, since the surplus money in circulation inflates market prices, creates an exaggerated demand for goods, and increases the opportunities for speculation."

A leading object of the change was, no doubt, to tax hoarded stocks

[1] Cf. G. Malenkov, *Report to the Nineteenth Party Congress* (Moscow, 1952), 53. The production indices (1940 = 100) for 1945 and 1946 were here given as 92 and 77 respectively for "All Industry," and 112 and 82 respectively for "Production of Means of Production." Also cf. A. Bergson, J. H. Blackman and A. Erlich, "Post-war Economic Reconstruction and Development in the U.S.S.R." in *Annals of the American Academy of Political and Social Science*, May 1949, 59, 62.

[2] *Ibid.*, 62-3.

[3] G. Malenkov, *op. cit.*, 52.

[4] N. Voznesensky, *War Economy of the U.S.S.R. in the period of the Patriotic War* (Moscow, 1948), 111.

of money accumulated (largely, though not entirely, in the countryside) by war-time sales of scarce foodstuffs at greatly inflated prices (e.g. on the collective farm markets and by private speculation). A central feature of the monetary reform was that the new money was exchangeable for the old at parities that varied according to different categories. *Cash* holdings were exchangeable on the basis of ten old notes to one new; whereas savings bank deposits under 3,000 roubles were exchangeable on a one-one basis (with deposits of over 3,000 at progressively less favourable ratios). State bonds of recent loan issues were exchangeable for a new conversion loan (carrying 2 per cent. interest) at a ratio of one rouble of the new loan for three of the old; the reason for this discrimination as officially given being that "a considerable part of the State Loans were created during the war, when the purchasing power of money fell, whereas after the currency reform the State will redeem that debt with full-value roubles." [5] But while the main burden of the change was borne by hoarders of cash, the level of wage and salary payments remained unaffected (except for a raising of the very lowest wage categories). The new uniform retail prices were fixed at a level intermediate between the former ration prices and the higher "commercial prices" at which off-ration purchases could be made in the State shops. It seems probable that the result was to reduce the urban cost of living by approximately a half compared with what it had been in the years prior to the monetary reform.[6] Thereafter the policy was adopted of making successive price-reductions (while keeping money wages more or less stable) as increased supplies of consumers' goods became available; the result of this series of price-reductions being to bring the retail price-level by the end of 1954 to about 20 per cent. above the immediate pre-war level (i.e. 1940) and the level of real wages (excluding the value of free services) to about 65 per cent. above pre-war (i.e. 1940).[7] It seems probable that the average real income of the collective farm peasantry rose during this period by rather more than that of industrial and other workers.

The progress of reconstruction in the course of 1948 was sufficient to justify the hopes on which the monetary reform was based; and of the agricultural situation at the end of that year the Central Statistical Ad-

[5] Decree of Dec. 11, 1947.

[6] M. C. Kaser, "Soviet Statistics of Wages and Prices," in *Soviet Studies* (University of Glasgow), Vol. VII, No. 1, 39. On the eve of the monetary reform retail prices were about three times the level of 1940; while the average level of money wages was less than double pre-war.

[7] *Ibid.*, 42-3; *Politicheskaia Ekonomia: Uchebnik* (Moscow, 1954), 462. Including the value of free services, the average real income of workers was almost double pre-war and between three and four times the level of 1947. An article in *Planovoe Khoziaistvo*, 1955, No. 4, 8, claimed that by 1955 real wages had reached a level of 90 per cent above 1950. The recently published *Narodnoe Khoziaistvo S.S.S.R.* (Moscow, 1956) gives for 1955 an index number of retail prices in State shops of 138 (1940 = 100) and for prices in Kolkhoz markets of 111 (1940 = 100). It is to be noted that prices in 1940 were appreciably above the level of 1937 and real wages lower. A comparison with 1937 instead of 1940 would therefore yield a rather smaller increase than the above mentioned.

ministration was able to report that "despite unfavourable weather conditions in most of the Volga regions, the gross grain harvest practically reached the pre-war level of 1940, while average grain yields per hectare exceeded the pre-war level." [8] As regards livestock, the number of cattle and of sheep and goats was said to have been restored to the pre-war level by the end of the year, although not yet the number of cows or the number of pigs. Industrial output showed the remarkably large rise of 27 per cent. over the previous year. Altogether during these first three years of the Five Year Plan some 4,000 industrial plants had been put into operation, of which about a half were completed in the course of 1948.

The main targets of the Five Year Plan were actually attained ahead of time, and the overall industrial target set for 1950 was exceeded by 17 per cent. The Report on the Fulfilment of the Fourth Five Year Plan, issued by Gosplan and the Central Statistical Board in April 1951, announced that the plan had indeed been completed in four years and a quarter.[9] Industrial output in 1950, the last year of the plan, stood at 73 per cent. above 1940, with capital goods about double but consumer goods no more than 23 per cent. above pre-war. Ferrous metals exceeded the pre-war level by 45 per cent., coal by 57, oil by 22 and electricity by 87, but textiles, clothing, footwear and other light industries only by 17 per cent. Grain output, although short of the plan-target, was some 5 million tons above 1940. More surprisingly it was announced that the total head of productive livestock, sharply reduced during the war, was restored, and in 1950 increased by 4 per cent. compared with 1940 in all categories of farming.[10] However, while cattle and sheep and goats were above the pre-war level, cows and pigs were still below (horses were also very substantially below), as the following table shows:[11]

LIVESTOCK NUMBERS
(*in millions*)

	1940 (post-war territory)	1950
Cattle.	54.5	57.2
of which:		
Cows.	27.8	24.2
Pigs.	27.5	24.1
Sheep and Goats.	91.6	99.0
Horses.	20.5	13.7

[8] Report on the Fulfilment of the State Plan for 1948.

[9] See *Planovoe Khoziaistvo*, 1951, No. 2, 3-13.

[10] Report of Gosplan and Central Statistical Board on "Results of the Fulfilment of the Fourth Five-Year Plan."

[11] Cf., "Results of the Fulfilment of the State Plan for 1950" (Report of Central Statistical Administration, § IV; United Nations Economic Commission for Europe, *Economic Survey of Europe in 1950* (Geneva, 1951), 40, and *Economic Survey of Europe in 1951* (Geneva, 1952), 134.

As was to transpire in the course of the next few years, the failure of grain crucial limiting factor upon the rise in the standard of life in the course and livestock to recover as rapidly as industrial production was to be the of the 1950's.

II

Details of the Fifth Plan were not publicly announced until just before the 19th Party Congress in October, 1952.[12] Its two main features were: (1) a rate of increase of industrial production of 72 per cent. over the quinquennium, which was lower than that of previous plans (even somewhat lower than in the unfinished Third Plan);[13] (2) a narrowing of the divergence between the rates of growth of the two main departments or sectors of industry producing capital goods and consumer goods: output of the former was to grow by 80 per cent, and of the latter by 65 per cent., whereas, by contrast, between 1928 and 1940 the former grew about double as fast as the latter. The result was accordingly to place more emphasis on raising the level of consumption.

If we take some individual commodities for which quantity figures were given, we find that ferrous metals, fuel and power are listed for increases close to the average for industry in general; the exception to this being coal, the figure for this (43 per cent.) being lower than in previous plans (oil, however, was equivalently higher). Non-ferrous metals, on the other hand, such as copper, lead, zinc, tin and aluminium were scheduled for considerably higher rates of increase. For grain an ambitious target of a 40-50 per cent. increase was set, and a similar figure for gross agricultural output; the intention being that this increase should come mainly from higher yields rather than from extended acreage (the "Directives on the Plan" stating that "the main task in the sphere of agriculture still remains the raising of the yields of all agricultural crops"). Similarly in industry prime emphasis was placed on a rise in labour productivity (of approximately 50 per cent.), while the rise in the number of "factory and office workers" over the quinquennium was set at 15 per cent. In this connection Mr. Malenkov in his report to the 19th Party Congress claimed that "labour productivity in industry increased 50 per cent. between 1940 and 1951" and that this accounted for two-thirds of the rise of industrial output over that period.

Investment in house-building was to be raised, and urban housing financed by the State was to be higher by about a fifth (measured in floorspace provided) than in the previous quinquennium of reconstruction. During the period of the Fourth Plan about 100 million square metres of

[12] See "Directives of the Plan" in *Planovoe Khoziaistvo,* 1952, No. 4, 4-25.

[13] A quinquennial increase of 72 per cent. represents an annual (compound) rate of 12 per cent., which is to be compared with 18.3 per cent. between 1928 and 1940 according to the official index (on which see below, 330-2) and 20 per cent. in the concluding three years of the Fourth Plan.

floor-space were built by "State enterprises, institutions and local Soviets, and also by the population of towns and workers' settlements with the aid of State credits." [14] This was equivalent to about 2½ million small flat-dwellings of 2 rooms *plus* kitchen and bathroom. In addition, about 2,700,-000 rural houses were built. The new Plan mentioned a figure of 105 million square metres for urban building by State organisations alone (i.e. excluding building "by the population of towns and workers' settlements with the aid of State credits," which had previously accounted for some 12 per cent. of the whole); but it was silent about the volume of rural building.[15]

The successive price-cuts and the rise in the standard of life from 1949 onwards has been mentioned in the previous section. In the course of 1953 a new emphasis on raising living-standards came into official pronouncements and policy. The price-reductions announced in the spring of that year were larger than usual, and had the effect of increasing consumers' purchasing power probably by a sixth. Retail turnover, measured in constant prices, was at any rate greater by 15 per cent. in the first half of the year compared with the corresponding period of the previous year, and State Loan issues during the year were reduced by more than a half. In the autumn a series of Ministerial Decrees were issued to improve incentives to agricultural production (by tax revisions and price-adjustments), to increase the supply of foodstuffs to the urban population and to raise the targets for the output of consumer goods in the two concluding years of the Fifth Plan. This was the first occasion on which revision of a Plan in the middle of a quinquennium had been in favour of consumer goods industries (in the pre-war period such a revision had invariably been at the expense of this sector of industry and in favour of heavy industry under the pressure of rearmament). In the second half of 1953 the output of consumers' goods increased by 14 per cent. over the same period of the previous year, or by more than the increase of industrial output in general.[16] There was talk of giving priority to light industries in the supply of personnel, of materials, of power and of equipment and repairs; and in the course of the year about 300 new industrial enterprises producing consumer goods were brought into operation and some 6,000 new shops were opened; while a decree of October 23 outlined a programme for building 40,000 new shops and 11,000 new restaurants in the course of the next three years. At the same time there were adjustments in the import-programme to provide more room for the import of consumer goods.

It was to transpire, however, that the position in agirculture during

[14] *Planovoe Khoziaistvo*, 1951, No. 2, 13.

[15] *Planovoe Khoziaistvo*, 1952, No. 4, 21; U.N. Economic Commission for Europe, *Economic Survey of Europe since the War* (Geneva, 1953), 49.

[16] Indeed from 1951 to 1954 the growth-rates of capital-goods and consumer-goods industries were identical. 1937 was the only year previously when consumer goods had increased faster than capital goods.

the early years of the '50's had in crucial respects actually deteriorated. The head of cattle declined between 1950 and 1953 (the fall being among those privately owned, which was not compensated by the increased number in the ownership of State and collective farms), and the number of cows remained below, not only the 1928 level, but also the (lower) 1940 level. Supplies of meat and milk to the towns remained practically stationary over the years 1950, 1951 and 1952. Sheep and goats (which are mainly owned by State or collective farms) increased by only 10 per cent. over the three years and even pigs by no more than 18 per cent. A leading reason was shortage of fodder. Grain output in these years showed no improvement, being on the average of 1951-53 only 3 to 4 per cent. above 1950, which as we have seen was very little above the pre-war level. Sugar-beet and raw cotton did only a little better, and the output of flax declined drastically. This was the reason for renewed attention to agriculture, to overcome this grave "agricultural lag"; which took the form, not only of increased investments in agriculture in the next two years and improved procurement-prices to farmers for grain, vegetables and livestock, but a campaign to encourage the extension of maize cultivation and the "virgin lands campaign" to bring under the plough over the next three years some 70 million acres (30 million hectares) of steppeland in Siberia and Kazakhstan, thereby increasing the sown area of the country by about a sixth (of which by the end of 1954 rather more than a half had already been ploughed-up).

In the last year of the quinquennium these measures were to bear fruit in an increase of grain production to 29 per cent above 1950, and in quite remarkable recoveries in sugar-beet and flax (although not in cotton or potatoes which suffered in 1950 from weather conditions). By 1955 the number of cows had recovered to above the pre-war level, and of all cattle to above even the 1928 level; while the number of pigs had doubled over the quinquennium and the number of sheep had grown by 50 per cent. The data on livestock are summarised in the following table:[17]

As regards industrial output, the quinquennium showed a rather greater increase both in total output and in industrial consumer goods than had been set in the plan-targets. The total increase from 1950 to 1955 was 85 per cent. as against a planned increase of 72; while the increase in the consumer goods sector was 76 per cent., compared with a planned increase of 65. The capital goods industries still held the lead (although a comparatively small one) with a 91 per cent. increase, compared with a plan-target of 80. The result was to raise the level of industrial output to more than double the pre-war level, and even industrial consumer goods

[17] Report of N. S. Khrushchev to the 20th Party Congress, Feb. 14, 1956; Results of the Fulfilment of the Fifth Five-Year Plan; U.N. Economic Commission for Europe, *Economic Survey of Europe in 1953* (Geneva, 1954), 52, and *Economic Survey of Europe in 1955* (Geneva, 1956), 170.

LIVESTOCK NUMBERS
(*million head, on present territory*)

	1928 end of	1940 end of	1945 end of	1950 end of	1951 end of	1952 end of	1953 Oct. 1st	1954 Oct. 1st	1955 Oct. 1st
Cattle	66.8	54.5	45.3	57.2	58.8	56.6	63.0	64.9	67.1
of which:									
Cows	33.2	27.8	—	24.2	24.8	24.3	26.0	27.5	29.2
Pigs	27.4	27.5	3.4	24.1	26.7	28.5	47.6[2]	51.1	52.1
Sheep and Goats . . .	114.6	91.6	56.0	99.0	107.5	109.9	114.9[3]	117.5[3]	124.9[3]
Horses	36.1	20.5	9.1	13.7	14.6	15.3	—	—	—

[2] Nearly the whole of this very surprising increase came from those privately owned, which almost trebled in number within less than a year.

[3] Sheep only. Mr. Khrushchev in his report gave 50 per cent. as the increase of sheep between 1950 and 1955; and it seems probable that the inclusion of goats in the later years would raise the figures as stated by about one-sixth.

to double the pre-war level. The rise of the national income over 1940 was officially stated as being 80 per cent., and "the turnover in State and Co-operative retail trade during the same period more than doubled." [18] House-building in towns (including building on private account with the aid of State credits) amounted to about 154 million square metres of floor-space, or some 50 per cent. more than in the previous quinquennium; while rural house building, at 2.3 million houses, was smaller by about half a million than it had been during the period of the 4th Plan.[19]

Detailed increases for particular products can be seen from the output table that is given below. It may serve to put them in historical perspective if one points out that the general growth-rate of industrial output over this quinquennium, although lower than in the pre-war decade, represents a rate of growth some 50 per cent. above that attained by capitalist economies in the past during exceptional boom periods (e.g. Japan between 1907 and 1913, U.S.A. between 1885 and 1889 and the United Kingdom in the immediate post-war years). It is more than three times the average rate of industrial growth in U.S.A. between 1899 and 1937, three times the rate of growth of industrial production in the countries of Western Europe between 1950 and 1955, and double that in U.S.A. during the same period.

It should, perhaps, be mentioned that in the concluding years of this quinquennium some important changes were introduced into the machinery and methods of planning, especially in relation to agriculture. These changes were in the direction of decentralisation, with less detail specified

[18] Report on the Results of the Fulfilment of the Fifth Five Year Plan.
[19] *Planovoe Khoziaistvo*, 1956, No. 2, 7.

in the central plan, greater discretion to lower levels likely to be more in touch with the actual situation in their regions or their special branches of industry, and more reliance on economic incentives as a way of getting things done, with less reliance on "administrative" methods and compulsion. In 1953 a start was made by introducing simplified planning methods in agriculture (previously there had been 200 or more targets for each collective farm in the annual plan), with a decentralisation to the provincial administration (where in future detailed plans for individual farms are to be worked out) and greater discretion to the farm management to decide questions about production on the basis of appropriate financial incentives. In 1954 the functions of Gosplan were narrowed somewhat in order to concentrate attention "on the cardinal questions of the national economy —the establishment of proper proportions in the development of individual branches, the elimination of bottlenecks, the maximum utilisation of the reserves available in the national economy"; and measures were taken "to cut the list of targets approved in the annual plan, both in industrial and agricultural production." [20] This was done under the slogan of "encouraging creative initiative and a struggle against bureaucracy in all its forms and manifestations." [21] Later, some economic Ministries were transferred from the All-Union to the Republican level, and Gosplan itself was divided into two (in May, 1955), the one body to be responsible for the preparation and operation of the annual plans (*Gosekonomkomissia*) and the other to confine itself to long-term planning (*Gosplan*).

III

Announcement of the Sixth Plan came close on the heels of the report on the carrying-out of the Fifth—namely, at the famous 20th Party Congress in February, 1956. In the overall rates of growth for which it provided, as well as the balance between the two main departments of industry, it was fairly similar to its predecessor. The Fifth Plan, as we have seen, provided for an overall rate of industrial growth of 72 per cent (or 12 per cent annually) and achieved an increase of 85; the new Plan set its sights somewhat lower and provided for an increase of 65 per cent., with an increase for capital goods of 70 per cent. and for consumer goods of 60 per cent.

In the course of 1954 a controversy had developed round the question of the traditional priority of heavy industry (Marx's Department I, producing means of production) in investment-policy and in *tempo* of development. In his *Economic Problems of Socialism in the U.S.S.R.* of 1952, Stalin had laid down as an essential principle of development ("in order to pave the way for a real, and not declaratory, transition to communism") "a continuous expansion of all social production, with a relatively higher rate

[20] G. M. Malenkov in speech to the Soviet of Nationalities, April 26, 1954.
[21] *Ibid.*

of expansion of the production of means of production." At the same time he defined the "basic economic law of socialism" as being: "to secure the maximum satisfaction of the constantly rising material and cultural requirements of the whole of society." In the course of 1953 to 1954 a number of economists advanced the thesis that past achievements in building heavy industry had laid the basis for a reversal of the traditional priority, and that in the period ahead expansion of consumer goods production should take the lead.[22] Against them it was argued that an expansion of the industries producing means of production was the essential pre-requisite for the expansion of the economy as a whole, and that if the consumer goods industries were expanded at a faster rate over a period, their further progress would very soon be halted by insufficient productive capacity in the capital goods industries to provide the means (in the shape of machinery and equipment etc.) for both capital-replacement and new investment in the expanded consumer goods industries. The official view expressed at the end of this discussion came down in favour of maintaining the traditional priority for heavy industry, and this priority is maintained in the Sixth Plan. At the same time the growth-rates of the two sectors are fairly close together, so that the views of what one could call the "consumer goods school" were by no means ignored. Indeed the preamble to the Directives on the Plan, as presented to the Party Congress, put the matter in this form:

The present level of social production makes it possible for the Soviet State to develop rapidly not only the production of means of production—which has been and remains the immutable foundation of the entire national economy—but also the production of consumer goods, to increase social wealth considerably, and thus advance further towards the establishment of a communist society in our country.

And in his report to the Congress Mr. Khrushchev expressed the matter thus:

Now that we possess a powerful heavy industry developed in every respect, we are in a position to promote rapidly the production of both the means of production and consumer goods . . . The Party is doing, and will continue to do, its utmost to ensure that the requirements of the Soviet people will be satisfied more fully and better; it considers this its prime duty to the people.

An idea of what the increases envisaged by the Plan amount to can be gauged by some rough international comparisons of the output-levels reached to-day and stipulated for 1960. In 1955 the U.S.S.R. produced more coal, steel and electricity than Britain and Western Germany combined; and Mr. Malenkov, in his speech at the Party Congress, claimed

[22] E.g. P. Mstislavsky in *Novy Mir*, 1953, No. 11, I. Vekua in *Voprosi Ekonomiki*, 1954, No. 9 and E. Kazimovsky cited in *Voprosi Ekonomiki*, 1955, No. 1, 20. For the contrary opinion, S. G. Strumilin in *Voprosi Ekonomiki*, 1954, No. 11, 22-39, and K. V. Ostrovitianov in *Pravda*, March 27, 1955.

that in output of electricity his country "firmly holds second place in the world." In 1960 (according to Mr. Bulganin's claim in introducing the Plan at the Congress) she will produce "more steel, power, cement and fuel than is now produced by Britain, France and Western Germany combined." She is likely before 1960 to lead the world as a coal producer, and by 1960 to be producing about half as much electricity and two-thirds as much steel as the present U.S.A. figures. A commentator on the Plan in *The Times* (London) estimated that Soviet engineering output by that date might "not be smaller than the present American volume";[23] and regarding total output a writer in one of the London bank reviews estimates that "the U.S.S.R. may have reached America's *present* industrial output by about 1963." [24]

The population of the U.S.S.R., however, is larger than that of U.S.A. and about double that of Britain and Western Germany combined. The task of "catching up and overtaking" the capitalist world in production *per capita* is, therefore, further from being achieved than this comparison of absolute output-levels would suggest. About this Mr. Khrushchev in his Congress speech was quite frank. "We are still lagging behind the leading capitalist countries in *per capita* production," he said. "No little effort is still required to fulfil our basic economic task—to catch up with and surpass the most advanced capitalist countries in this respect." However, one may, perhaps, again quote the commentator in *The Times* in this connection: "The Plan aims at bringing consumption of the main articles of food and clothing near Western European standards. There is to be 1½ lb. of meat a person a week (in towns); about 32 yards of cotton fabrics a person a year; less than two yards of woollen fabrics; and what is quite remarkable for a traditionally barefoot nation, more than two pairs of shoes a person a year." [25] To which one should add that State-financed housing is to amount over the five years to some 205 million square metres (the equivalent of about 5 million small flat-dwellings of 2 rooms *plus* kitchen and bathroom), or "nearly double the figure for the Fifth Five-Year Plan." [26]

In view of the grave lag of agriculture during the previous Plan, it was to be expected that special emphasis would be laid on agricultural development in the new plan. For grain an ambitious target-increase of 38 per cent. is laid down, largely on the basis of the expected results of the

[23] Isaac Deutscher, *The Times*, Feb. 3, 1956, 9. Already in 1950 it seems likely that the *stock* of machine-tools in Soviet industry (at about 1.3 million) exceeded the *pre*-war American figure, but it still fell some way behind the American *post*-war figure (U.N. Economic Commission for Europe, *General Survey of the European Engineering Industry* (Geneva, 1951), Table 36, and *Survey of the Econ. Situation and Prospects of Europe* (Geneva, 1948), 149).

[24] A. Nove in *Lloyds Bank Review*, April, 1956, 21.

[25] Isaac Deutscher, *loc. cit.* For shoes the British *per capita* figure is under three and the American about three and a half.

[26] Directive of the 20th Party Congress on the Sixth Plan, §VIII, para. 8.

"virgin soil campaign," combined with the extension of maize cultivation to cover some 28 million hectares. Special emphasis is laid on reducing harvest losses (by shortening the harvesting period and the so-called "two-stage harvesting" of grain); the production of combine-harvesters is to be sharply increased and agriculture supplied with more than half-a-million of them over the quinquennium (two-and-a-half times the number supplied over 1951-55), together with over a million and a half tractors (in terms of 15 horse-power units), or more than was supplied in agriculture during the first four Five Year Plans. The increases set for meat and milk and vegetables are much higher than for grain: a doubling of supplies of meat[27] and milk, an increase of 85 per cent. for potatoes and more than a doubling for "other vegetables."

In his speech of February 17, 1956, Mr. Malenkov claimed that in labour productivity in industry "we have now outstripped Britain and France, but as yet lag behind the United States." A feature of the Sixth Plan is the emphasis laid on technical innovation to raise labour productivity and on the automation of industrial processes. In the early days of the Five-Year Plans increased production came as much, if not more, from an expansion of the labour force in industrial employment as from increase in productivity per worker, and the provisions for the latter were seldom fulfilled. Although this led to a larger increase in the wage-bill (and hence in consumers' demand) than had been budgeted for (since increased production had to come from more employment in place of more productivity), this exceptional increase in industrial employment did not seriously matter so long as there was still a substantial labour reserve in the countryside. But despite increased mechanisation of agriculture and a high natural increase of population, this labour reserve cannot be regarded as inexhaustible, especially in face of ambitious plans for extending the sown area and drafting urban volunteers to assist the development of the new lands. During the Fifth Plan the target for increased productivity in industry was nearly, but not quite, fulfilled: an increase of 44 per cent. against a plan-figure of 50. The total labour force in the economy as a whole grew from 39 million to 48.4 million, and in industry from 14 million to 17.4 million —an increase of about 23 or 24 per cent. in each case.[28] Under the Sixth Plan total employment is to grow to 55 million, or by no more than 15 per cent., and in industry alone by only 10 per cent., while labour productivity in industry and building is to be raised by 50 per cent. Compared

[27] This high figure for meat is to be attained largely by emphasis on pig-breeding ("as the branch of animal husbandry that gives the quickest results,") "the proportion of pork to the country's total output of meat" being "raised to 50 per cent." by 1960. In increasing meat supplies, as well as with milk and wool, as much emphasis is laid on increased animal-yield (e.g. by pig-fattening) as on increased numbers; but this is of course itself limited by the supply of fodder.

[28] *Narodnoe Khoziaistvo S.S.S.R.* (Moscow, 1956). Total employment in 1940 was 31.2 million and in industry alone 11 million.

COMPARATIVE OUTPUTS OF MAIN PRODUCTS

Product	Unit	1940	1950	1955	1960 planned
Coal	million tons	166	261	391	593
Oil	million tons	31	38	71	135
Electricity	milliard kWh.	48	91	170	320
Steel	million tons	18	27	45	68
Rolled Steel	million tons	13	21	35	53
Pig Iron	million tons	15	19	33	53
Copper	thousand tons	161	255	390[1]	624[1]
Cement	million tons	6	10	22	55
Bricks	milliards	7.5	10.2	21.0	not available
Mineral Fertilisers	million tons	3.0	5.5	9.6	19.6
Caustic Soda	thousand tons	190	325	563	1000
Artificial Fibres	thousand tons	11	24	110	330
Steam Locomotives	units	914	985	654	—
Diesel and Electric Locomotives	units	14	227	328	2180
Goods Wagons	thousands	31	51	34	52
Tractors	thousands (natural units)	32	109	163	322
Motor Vehicles	thousands	145	363	445	650
Motor Cycles	thousands (natural units)	7	123	244	395
Bicycles	millions	.3	.6	2.8	4.2
Paper	million tons	.8	1.2	1.8	2.7
Cotton Fabrics	million metres	3954	3900	5904	7270
Linen Fabrics	million metres	285	282	305	556
Woollen Fabrics	million metres	120	155	251	363
Silk Fabrics	million metres	77	130	526	1074
Leather Footwear	million pairs	211	203	274	455
Rubber Footwear	million pairs	68	105	112	not available
Clocks and Watches	million	2.8	7.6	19.7	33.6
Radio and Television Sets	million	.2	1.1	4.0	10.2
Knitted-wear	million garments	183	198	430	580
Soap	million tons	.6	.8	1.0	not available
Granulated Sugar	million tons	2.15	2.52	3.42	6.53
Tinned Foodstuffs	milliard tins	1.1	1.5	3.2	5.6
Vegetable Oil	million tons	.71	.78	1.12	1.84
Meat (State Slaughter House Production)	million tons	1.1	1.3	2.2	3.9
Fish	million tons	1.4	1.7	2.7	4.2
Butter	thousand tons	206	319	436	680
Grain	million tons	119	125[2]	129[2]	180[2]

[1] Estimated from percentage-increases as stated.

[2] The figures for grain in 1955 and 1960 are in terms of so-called "barn yield" (i.e. allowing for harvest losses) whereas earlier figures are apparently of "biological" yield. The E.C.E. Report (mentioned under SOURCES) estimates the 1950 crop in *barn* yield to have been 100 million instead of 125.

SOURCES: *Results of the Fulfilment of the State Plan for 1955; Directives of the Twentieth Party Congress on the Sixth Five-Year Plan; Report of N. S. Khrushchev to Twentieth Party Congress;* U.N. Economic Commission for Europe, *Economic Survey of Europe in 1955*, Table XXX; *Narodnoe Khoziaistvo S.S.S.R.*, 1956.

with this the real wages of "factory, office and other workers" are to rise by some 30 per cent., and the incomes of collective farmers "in cash and in kind" by 40 per cent.

Certain social changes that fall within this period are indicative of recent trends in policy. Mr. Bulganin announced to the 20th Congress the intention during the period of the 6th Plan to effect a reduction in working hours from eight to seven per day (with six hours in mining and dangerous occupations and for young persons between 16 and 18 years of age), "or in some branches to a five-day week with an eight-hour working day, and two days off"; and in addition to reduce Saturday working by two hours, commencing with 1956.[29] Measures were also announced to raise the wages of the lowest-income categories and to remove some of the existing disparities in wages. In May 1956 there was promulgated the draft of a new law on State pensions, under which old age and disablement pensions were substantially raised (the minimum old-age pension being fixed at 300 roubles a month); and this was duly adopted by the Supreme Soviet in July. About the same time[30] there was a final repeal of the 1940 Labour Decrees (already considerably modified by a previous amending Decree of July 14, 1951) which restricted a worker's right to leave his job and imposed penalties for lateness and absenteeism and infringements of factory discipline. All previous convictions for quitting employment without leave or for absenteeism were to be cancelled; and in future any "factory, office or other worker" was declared free to leave his employment with a fortnight's notice.

RECENT TRENDS IN THE SOVIET ECONOMY

Joseph A. Kershaw*

It is now a decade since World War II came to a conclusion. That conflict inflicted great punishment on the Soviet economy. The valuable industrial and agricultural areas of the west and southwest were laid waste once by the Soviet armies retreating eastward, and again by the German armies retreating westward. This destruction, coupled with the intensive use of capital during the war and the failure to replace a good deal of it, could not help weakening the economy seriously.

---

[29] The six-hour day for young persons was also introduced in 1956 (by a decree of May 26 of the Presidium of the Supreme Soviet), to operate from July 1.

[30] Decree of Presidium of the Supreme Soviet dated April 25, 1956.

* Economist, Rand Corporation, where he has supervised research on the Soviet economy. The selection originally appeared in the *Annals of the American Academy of Political and Social Science*, Vol. 303 (January 1956), pp. 37-49. By permission.

It is true that by the end of the war reconstruction had already begun in a serious way. Nonetheless, the economy in 1945 was considerably smaller by almost any measure than it had been five years earlier. Casualties had been high, the people were tired, farms were depleted of their best manpower, and the nonagricultural labor force had been reduced by the operation of the draft. With the possible exception of Germany and Poland, the Soviet economy enjoyed the dubious distinction of having suffered more than any other as a result of the war.

The details of economic development following the conclusion of the war are not well known to Western scholars. The broad outlines, however, are unmistakable, and there is rather general agreement that the recovery has been little short of remarkable. The Soviet economy is now the world's second mightiest, and the scars of the war that ended just one short decade ago have all but disappeared.

The main purpose of this paper is to examine some recent trends in the Soviet economy, especially from the viewpoint of their influence on Soviet rates of growth. To do this, we shall have to look at the growth rates in effect before Stalin's death in order to evaluate the influence of the post-Stalin changes. We shall also want to speculate on future developments in the economy with particular emphasis on the probabilities that rates of growth in the future will or will not vary significantly from those that have characterized the past.

DIMENSIONS OF SOVIET GROWTH

While there is general agreement that Soviet growth since the end of the war has been rapid, there is some disagreement as to just how rapid it has been. This disagreement stems in part from the fact that there are serious conceptual difficulties in describing the growth of an economy; in the case of the Soviet Union there is the added difficulty that the Soviet authorities have restricted the amount of data made available to Western and, perhaps, Soviet scholars. The Iron Curtain has not been able to impose a blackout, since a centrally directed economy requires the existence of considerable amounts of data for the implementation of its own instructions; many of these data cannot be kept from the eyes of the West, but quantitatively and qualitatively the statistical dim-out has been impressive.

The Russians have published data on Soviet national income for some time, but those who have studied the data and the concepts and practices of Soviet national income statistics find it impossible to accept the rates of increase implied by these data.[1] There has been as yet no definitive Western study indicating the rate of growth of the Soviet economy as a

---

[1] Paul Studenski and Julius Wyler, "National Income Estimates of Soviet Russia— Their Distinguishing Characteristics and Problems," *American Economic Review*, Vol. 37, No. 2 (May 1947), pp. 595-610.

whole. We are not able, therefore, to describe the dimensions of Soviet growth with either exactness or confidence. But we do have estimates that are plausible.

Several years ago, at a conference of economists who are students of the U.S.S.R., Professor Gregory Grossman set forth an estimate of the growth of the Soviet economy which may be taken as of the right order of magnitude, at least pending the completion of more definitive studies. Professor Grossman found that the annual rate of growth of the Soviet economy before World War II was 6.5 to 7 per cent.[2] In the postwar period, but with the exception of the immediate postwar years when reconstruction obviously meant a rapid rate of growth, the annual rate of growth of national income seems to have been about the same. There is some discernible tendency for this rate to slacken off, but more will be said on the subject on a later page.

To some, this sort of percentage rate of increase sounds fairly modest. It is, however, large by any standards of Western experience. It may be well to keep in mind that such a rate implies a doubling in size every eleven years. Perhaps more germane is a comparison of rates of increase of the United States economy. Most American economists, when they think about the future of the United States economy, think in terms of growth rates on the order of 2.5 to 3 per cent a year. This, for example, is the range used by President Truman's Materials Policy Commission and by Gerhard Colm in a recent publication of the National Planning Association.[3] There have been occasions when the United States growth rate has been higher than 3 per cent, but there have seldom if ever been occasions when, over a prolonged period of time, the growth rate in this country has approximated that which has apparently been maintained in the Soviet Union since 1928, with the exception, of course, of the war years.[4]

But there is a real question as to whether a growth rate for the Soviet economy as a whole is the significant figure to look for. For one thing, the total economy is made up of many sectors which grow at very disparate rates. This creates serious statistical problems, and casts real doubt on the significance of a single growth rate. Moreover, when comparisons are made between two economies with rather different structures, there is a serious question as to the meaning of over-all rates of increase.

Significance of industry and agriculture in total economy

This leads to the desirability of examining separate sectors of the economy separately. Among those which might be examined, two sectors—

---

[2] A. Bergson (Editor), *Soviet Economic Growth* (Evanston, Ill.: Row, Peterson and Company, 1953), p. 9.

[3] G. Colm, *The American Economy in 1960* (National Planning Association, 1952), p. 19.

[4] See, for example, Simon Kuznets, *National Product Since 1869* (New York: National Bureau of Economic Research, Inc., 1946), p. 119; also see the Grossman chapter in A. Bergson (Editor), *op. cit.* (note 2 *supra*), p. 12.

industry and agriculture—are of particular interest in themselves, because of their importance in the total economy, and because of economic relationships between them. The output of industry, or rather its relative size and rate of increase, is the magnitude of greatest interest to us when we attempt to assess the degree and rate of industrialization. Furthermore, industrial strength determines economic strength, at least in the short run when capability to make war (cold or hot) is the central issue. It is the output of the basic industries like coal, machinery, electric power, steel, and petroleum that we are really interested in when we are thinking of the comparative size of the Soviet economy and economies of the West.

On the other hand, the ability of an economy to satisfy its people becomes important in the longer run. And here, though industry too supplies consumer goods, the success of industry in this respect rests, in a virtually closed economy like the U.S.S.R., on success in agriculture. Furthermore, in a developing economy, it is agriculture which supplies an important part of the growing industrial labor force and which, to do so, requires an increasing amount of machinery.

Thus, we are led to examine the industrial and agricultural sectors of the Soviet economy. Perhaps the most important characteristic of these sectors is that they are growing at vastly different rates. To some extent this is a result of deliberate policy, but in a very important sense it is not. In any case, the difficulties of talking about growth of the total economy are perhaps best illustrated by pointing out that the total economy is made up, among other things, of a sector (industrial output) which has grown at a very rapid rate for twenty-five years, and another sector (agriculture) which has grown at a very modest rate.

Industry

Turning first to the industrial sector, we find rates of increase that are consistently and outstandingly high. The most careful study of this sector has been that by Professor Donald Hodgman.[5] He has accumulated indices of physical output for as many industrial commodities as he could find, and has combined these indices with an approximation to value-added weights, to get an over-all index of physical production. His index is a good deal more comprehensive for the years before World War II than for the period since the end of the war. Nonetheless, it shows that industrial production (again with the exception, of course, of the war years) increased during the prewar period at a rate of approximately 15 per cent per year,[6] and for the postwar years, until the death of Stalin, at a rate of

[5] Donald Hodgman, *Soviet Industrial Production 1928-51*. Cambridge, Mass.: Harvard University Press, 1954.

[6] Hodgman's index is for large-scale industry only. Since small-scale industry grew less rapidly, Hodgman's index overstates growth of total industry before the war, perhaps by two or three percentage points. Incidentally, the cited rate applies to the 1928-37 period. In the three years before the war the rate fell rapidly as the economy began to

10 per cent. As in the case of national income, these are rates of increase that are rarely if ever known in Western economies.[7]

For the postwar period the Hodgman index probably understates the annual growth rates. This is because the commodities he is able to include are mostly basic ones; very few of the more fabricated items like machinery appear, and it is these which have grown most. It is not clear, therefore, that Hodgman's postwar 10 per cent is really lower than his prewar 15 per cent.

What *is* clear is that the rates are still high. Six years ago THE ANNALS devoted an issue to the Soviet Union. The article on the Soviet economy contained a table showing physical outputs for a selected list of commodities. When one compares these with the 1954 output, one finds that the increases imply annual growth rates of between 10 and 20 per cent in almost every case.[8] Rapid growth in industry has been and is unmistakable.

Agriculture

The situation in agriculture is quite different. Agriculture has been much in the news of late, and most of the leaders of the U.S.S.R. have been clearly anxious about the general agricultural situation. In brief, the increase in output of most agricultural commodities in the last twenty-five years has scarcely kept pace with the increase in population, so that agricultural output per capita is no greater than it was before the period of the Five Year Plans began.

Two major items of agricultural output are grain and livestock. The Russians have put great emphasis on the need to increase the output of both these items, but with marked lack of success. Grain output for 1954 was less than in 1937, much less on a per capita basis;[9] and in the mid-1950's per capita grain output was below even the 1928 level. The livestock situation was no better. In no year since 1950 has the stock of cattle been as large as it was in 1928 and, while there have been some recent successes in increasing the number of hogs, it is clear that the output of meat and

---

mobilize. One other study may be cited here. Professor Gerschenkron, using 1939 dollar price weights, computed an index of heavy industrial production (more specifically machinery, iron and steel, coal, petroleum products, and electric power) for the period 1928/29 to 1937. His index increases at an annual rate of 17.8 per cent. *Review of Economics and Statistics*, Vol. 37, No. 2 (May 1955), p. 126.

[7] It is possible that Japan, in the latter part of the nineteenth century, may have enjoyed comparable growth rates.

[8] The 1948 data came from Abram Bergson, James Horton Blackman, and Alexander Erlich, "Postwar Economic Reconstruction and Development in the U.S.S.R.," THE ANNALS, Vol. 263 (May 1949), p. 56. The 1954 data were compiled by Nancy Nimitz from scattered Soviet sources.

[9] These developments have to be interpreted with care, since there is less current use of grain in feeding horses now that tractors have replaced so many horses. But even so, more grain is urgently needed, as is indicated by the 1960 planned output, which is a third larger than 1950.

dairy products per capita is not as large as it was in 1928.[10] All in all, the Soviet diet has unquestionably deteriorated.[11] . . .

One should note that the lack of real progress in agriculture has come about not because the sector has been starved by the planners, for in one sense at least agriculture has been favored. There has been a consistent policy of directing appreciable proportions of total Soviet investment into agriculture. There has been a good deal of discussion about the need to mechanize, and a good deal of bragging about the extent of mechanization on the farm. Indeed, the primitive agriculture of the late 1920's has been very substantially transformed through the investment program that has been a central part of all the Five Year Plans.

In one sense, agriculture has made a real contribution. One output of Soviet agriculture is labor. In good part, the investment in agriculture which has looked toward mechanization has had as its main purpose the release of labor from the land. We shall discuss this at a later point, but it may be noted here that the Soviet countryside constituted and perhaps still constitutes a large reservoir of labor for the rapidly expanding Soviet industry. Soviet agriculture in this regard has succeeded in supplying large quantities of labor. Most of the productivity increases have resulted in freeing labor from the land rather than in increasing output on the land. To a certain extent, this is a choice that the planners have made, although it will be pointed out later that they are faced with serious constraints in their exercise of choice.

EXPLANATION OF HIGH RATE OF INDUSTRIAL GROWTH

The consistently high rate of industrial growth in the U.S.S.R. is something which has a quite plausible explanation. Part of this lies in the distinction between the institutions of a centrally planned economy and a market economy. In a market economy such as the United States or the United Kingdom, there is a rather effective way in which the people as consumers, savers, and investors determine the over-all allocation of resources. This mechanism is by no means perfect, and it is of course seriously interrupted in times of war and major depression but, by and large, the people through the marketplace determine the way in which the society allocates its resources. In their performance of this function, the people are guided by their own efforts to derive the greatest possible utility from the fruits of their own labor. In other words, the important thing is the preferences of the people themselves.

[10] Two RAND "RM" studies, one published and one forthcoming, bear on these difficulties. Both are by Nancy Nimitz. "Statistics of Soviet Agriculture," RM-1250, has been published.

[11] The loss in calories has been made up to a considerable extent (perhaps completely) by the rapid growth in output of potatoes and vegetables. But the change in diet has been quite involuntary.

In a centrally directed economy, the situation is very different. The dictator decides how he wants the resources of the economy allocated, and then proceeds to do so by direction. In the case of the U.S.S.R., the planners decide that they are more interested in the production of heavy industrial goods than in the production of consumer goods. They are able to implement this decision by various techniques: by subsidies on industrial goods, for example, or by high taxes on consumer goods. So long as they exercise effective control over the people, they can continue to allocate the resources of the economy in a way at variance with what the people themselves would decide if they had any real choice in the matter.

It is clear from the statements of the Soviet leaders that they consciously set out in 1928, through the device of the Five Year Plans, to build up the heavy industrial sector of the economy at the expense of the consumer. A recent *Pravda* editorial puts it this way: "Heavy industry has always been and continues to be the basis of the constant development of our national economy. The Communist party has always considered rapid development of heavy industry its main task." [12] In other words, the emphasis on heavy industry has been a deliberate policy for a long period of time. The driving force has been an unswerving desire to "catch up with the West." In a perverse sort of way, the basest villain of them all, the United States, has been the ideal.

In pursuing these goals, the U.S.S.R. has had a number of advantages. For one thing, he who starts late can copy. It is clear that the Russians have practiced emulation, either by importing engineering skill and exploiting it, or by the cruder technique of purchasing equipment from abroad and imitating it. Whatever form it took, emulation has made it easier to take initial strides more rapidly than the pioneer, who had to learn as he progressed.

A second important factor has been the vast reservoir of labor on the countryside. The process of industrial growth in any country is accomplished by a rapid shift of labor from agriculture to industry, and the Soviet Union has been no exception. The only peculiar feature of the Soviet experience is that there still exists a very large agricultural labor force in spite of the large industrial advances that have already been made. At the present time the Soviet regime still has around half of its total labor force in agriculture; the corresponding figure in the United States is about 10 per cent. Millions of people have already moved from the farm and, if solutions to the basic agricultural problems are found, the flow of labor from the farm to the city can remain high. This flow is of course in addition to the increase that results from the growth in population.

Much should also be made of the absence of the business cycle in the U.S.S.R. Prolonged periods of depression such as that in the 1930's in the

[12] *Pravda*, March 7, p. 1. Translated by *Current Digest of the Soviet Press*, April 13, 1955, p. 19.

United States can and do interrupt industrial progress. In the Soviet Union, the institutional arrangements are such that periods of this sort have not occurred and will not occur in the future. To be sure, Soviet society has its disadvantages, some of them coming about for the same reason that business cycles do not, but from this one difficulty, at least, it is free.

Soviet Investment Policy

But the most important determinant of the high rate of industrial growth is certainly to be found in Soviet investment policy. There are two things about this investment policy that are deserving of emphasis. Both are the results of conscious decisions of the economic planners.

TYPICAL POSTWAR DISTRIBUTION OF INVESTMENT BY SECTORS, U.S.A. AND U.S.S.R.

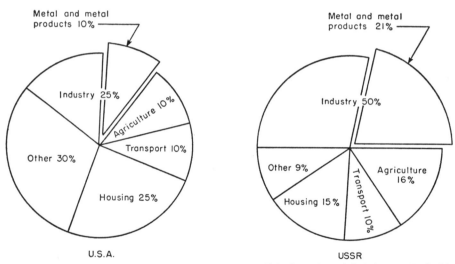

(From *Annals of the American Academy of Political and Social Science.* **Vol. 33,** January, 1956, pp. 37-49)

The first is that the rate of investment (that is, the ratio of gross investment to gross national product) has been consistently high. More specifically, for the last twenty-five years, with the exception of the war years, the Soviet government has, year after year, allocated 20 per cent or more of the economy's total resources to investment. This is a percentage which the United States and other Western countries equal on occasion, when economic activity is at very high levels. The difference is that in the U.S.S.R. it happens every year, and no Western economy has had this experience.

The second feature regarding Soviet investment is equally important. Of the resources that are invested, a far larger proportion than is true in our case goes into heavy industry. For each unit of total investment, therefore, the payoff in terms of continued high rates of increase of industrial output is high. Whereas in the United States a good proportion of investment goes into things like luxury hotels, laundry facilities, and the like, the Russians devote every possible kopeck of their investment to electric power, steel, chemicals, and so forth. The accompanying pie chart contrasts the postwar Soviet and American practices.

The effect of these two peculiar features of Soviet investment is a continuous plowing back of resources into those areas which in turn create more resources which can be plowed back. This reflects itself in the rate of increase of industrial production, and largely accounts for its being high. It may be noted that there is no real reason why both the rate and the direction of investment should not be continued in the future as they have been in the past for an indefinite period. That is to say, there is nothing inherent in what is going on which says that there must be a change at any foreseeable date. It is possible, of course, that the policy which has dictated the nature of investment may be changed.

THE ECONOMY AT STALIN'S DEATH

It may be appropriate to summarize the situation in 1953 which had resulted from the general trends that have been thus far described. Several features stand out.

In the first place, the Russians had managed to build up a very strong industrial base. In most of the important commodities, they were second only to the United States. In spite of the terrible devastation of the war, they had managed by 1948 or so to recover their prewar position, and then had pushed ahead so that by 1953 they had passed England, France, Germany, and all others except the United States.

Secondly, and paradoxically, in spite of all this, the Soviet economy in a very real sense was still an agricultural economy. In many ways, the proportion of an economy's labor force engaged in agriculture is a measure of its stage of development, and it is noteworthy that this proportion in the U.S.S.R. was still around half in 1953.

In 1953 the Soviet people were still experiencing a very low standard of living. The emphasis on heavy industry, which has been discussed, had as a natural result a standard of living which was bound to be very low. Actually, it appeared for many years as though the Five Year Plans regarded consumption as the residual claimant, while the planners determined the rate of investment that they wanted largely in terms of what they could get away with in denying consumption to the people.

In the two or three years before 1953, the standard of living had been permitted to turn rather sharply upward. It is interesting to speculate on why this should have been done, and even more interesting to wonder whether the trend will continue. To be sure, it may be that some of the increase is illusory, since about this time stories of queuing up and bare shelves began to creep into the press.

Real wage comparisons with the West are, of course, extremely difficult. Nonetheless, it may be interesting to point to some research under way at the RAND Corporation, which compares the ruble prices of a substantial number of consumer goods and service items with dollar prices in the United States of the same or comparable items. When this is done, a 1950 ruble-dollar price ratio for consumer goods, including food, services, and manufactured goods, comes out to 20 to 1 when United States weights are used, and 15½ to 1 when Soviet weights are used. In 1950 the average wage in the U.S.S.R. was something like 7,500 rubles, in the United States about $3,000. The Soviet worker's real wage in 1950, then, was some one-sixth to one-eighth that of the American, depending on the weighting system used.[13]

Finally, we may note that the Soviet economy at the time of Stalin's death was supporting a substantial military establishment. Some four million men were reputed to be in uniform, and the Korean experience had indicated a modern military technology to be characteristic of Soviet military equipment. The Russians had exploded their first A-bomb three and a half years previously, and were soon to begin talking about their prowess in the manufacture of H-bombs.

As nearly as we can calculate, the proportion of total resources in the U.S.S.R. going into the military establishment in 1953 was around 15 per cent. It is important to understand the meaning of this, since there has apparently been a good deal of uniformed speculation about it recently. It should be clear that resources spent for the military, unlike those devoted to capital goods, are not productive. A blast furnace can be used to produce something else, a military tank cannot.[14] To this extent, therefore, the Soviet economy like any other is penalized by the resources it allocates to the military. The military is competing for resources with other sectors of the economy. It does not follow, however, that the drain is necessarily serious, so long as the total is rising and the military sector does not rise more than proportionately. Indeed there is no reason to assume that the Soviet leaders could not go on indefinitely devoting a given percentage of their total resources to the military or spending resources equal in amount to those they were spending in 1953. To repeat, what is spent on the military cannot be spent on investment or for consumers, but there is nothing to indicate that the drain represented by the military program at the stated level threatens to bring about economic collapse in any sense.

[13] For trends in real wages, see Janet Chapman, "Real Wages in the Soviet Union, 1928-1952," *Review of Economics and Statistics*, Vol. 36, No. 2 (May 1954), pp. 134-56.

[14] It does produce "national security." There is no intent to imply that military production is necessarily wasteful. The point is that military end items, unlike capital goods, do not produce additional economic goods.

MALENKOV-KHRUSHCHEV CHANGES

The end of an era occurred in March 1953 with the death of Stalin. There followed two years during which Malenkov was at least nominally in charge. Then in February 1955 Malenkov was succeeded by Bulganin or Khrushchev or both. When Malenkov's economic program began to emerge, it appeared to constitute a real break with the immediate past. Its main outlines were as follows. There was to be a sharp shift in the distribution of investment, away from heavy and toward light industry and trade. Much more of the fruits of the economy were to be distributed to the people. In fact, promises to the consumer were lavish and, to some of us, seemed surprisingly specific. Finally, the ever-present problem of agricultural output was given even more emphasis, and price and tax policies were altered to improve the earnings of farmers and to give them incentive to produce more.

It was not apparent in 1953, and still is not, how much of all this was propagandistic and how much was substantive. A great deal was made of the fact that aircraft factories had been instructed to begin turning out aluminum pots and pans. Indeed, extremely large percentage increases in things like television sets and other durables were enthusiastically reported in the press. Large percentage increases in many of these things were in fact achieved, but since the base figures from which these percentage outputs were measured were in most cases extremely small, these "triumphs" are not to be taken very seriously.

It is not easy to determine what really did happen during this period, but the data at hand point toward the tentative conclusion that changes in the structure of the economy were minor and unimportant. The revolution, if it was ever really intended, failed to come off.

If we look at the official Soviet indices of gross industrial output in the 1950's, we find that the ratio of increases in the producers' goods area to those in the consumers' goods area remained practically constant from 1951 through 1954. It is true that the latter half of 1953 indicates that the increase in consumers' goods was a bit higher than it had been earlier; but by 1954, the year in which these changes should have been reflected in the statistics, there is a decline in this rate. It is possible that the time required for true structural shifts was more than Malenkov had at his disposal. Whatever the cause, the shift did not take place, and there was, therefore, no appreciable interruption to the economic trends we have been discussing.

Although there is little evidence of such structural shifts, Malenkov was more successful in keeping his promise to improve the lot of the consumer. This appears to have been done in two ways. In the first place, there was apparently a significant drawing down of state reserves of various sorts. In the second place, there was an increase in the volume of imports that took place, beginning in the middle of 1953, and a simultaneous and substantial increase in the proportion of total imports made up of foods and consumers' goods.[15]

With the ascendancy of Bulganin and Khrushchev in 1955, Malenkov's agricultural reforms were intensified, but other parts of his program were repudiated. Bulganin reproached Malenkov specifically for what he termed errors in policy inherent in using the state reserves for current consumption.[16] The much-publicized charges of having corrupted true party ideology by asserting that the time had come to let light industry expand at a faster rate than heavy industry were explicitly directed at political unknowns, but undoubtedly were aimed at Malenkov, and whoever were his major henchmen in the intended reversal of economic policy. The announcement by Bulganin of the annual 1955 Plan targets for industry left no doubt that heavy industry was to continue to receive favored treatment, and the rate of increase for consumer goods was planned at only about half what had actually been achieved in this field in 1954. We may summarize the experience of the Malenkov interregnum by hazarding the opinion that the changes that took place were much less important, at least in areas other than agriculture, than we thought might be the case, and in fact had a minor impact on the course of economic development.

Change in Economic Policy?

By way of pure speculation, it may be said that a genuine change in economic policy is not completely unlikely in the future. The current soft international policy seems to have a logical counterpart in an economic policy favoring the consumer, and there are some who are expecting the change to take place if the current softness in international dealings continues. It may be interesting to consider briefly what might happen if this consumer goods reorientation should appear. A successful program would certainly have interesting propagandistic effects throughout the world. We may ask, then, what would be the result of a sincere and prolonged attempt on the part of the Soviet economic planners to move their economy away from the heavy industrial economy toward one that emphasized the output of consumer goods. It seems fairly clear that rather startling improvements in the standard of living in the near future could be achieved. Among other reasons, this could be expected because most of the small amount of consumers' goods capital in the U.S.S.R. is obsolete, worn out, and inefficient. As a result, its replacement by new equipment would bring about very substantial increases in the productivity of these industries. In the economist's lingo, the marginal productivity of capital in the consumers' goods industries must be regarded as very high.

[15] Cf. the article by O. Hoeffding in this issue of *The Annals*.
[16] *Pravda,* February 10, 1955, p. 1.

The probability is that the resulting rapid increases in the standard of living could be expected to continue for some years. Following this, however, there would be an inevitable slowdown in the rate of increase. One reason for this is that a great deal of consumer capital is very costly. All of the capital for consumer services in cities, for instance, is costly to install, and has little immediate payoff. Streets, transportation facilities, sewers, and so on are of this sort. The construction of housing in the U.S.S.R. before the war did not keep pace with the growth of the urban population, and yet the improvement of housing facilities is essential to a balanced increase in the standard of living. A housing program designed to obtain accommodations merely approaching the decency level would require a tremendous investment effort in the U.S.S.R.[17]

There is another factor which would tend to bring a slowdown in due course. De-emphasis of heavy industry would mean that a larger proportion of the output of industry would be consumed. When output is consumed it cannot be used to make more output, except of course insofar as it increases the productivity of labor. The output of capital goods industries, on the other hand, is used directly to make more goods. One type of industrial output therefore produces satisfaction for consumers, whereas the other produces measurable outputs for statistical series. Paradoxically, consumers' goods production is analogous to military production. Both are consumed directly and add nothing in direct ways to the future output of the economy. Last but not least, the hypothesized policy would presuppose genuine success in expanding agricultural production, to supply more food and raw materials for consumer goods. Reliance on imports is an unlikely alternative, as we suggest below.

It is difficult, if not impossible, to quantify the course of action just described in general terms. It is also difficult to say what the propagandistic effects of a rather rapidly and continually increasing standard of living would be. It would seem, however, that they should be considerable, particularly in countries like France and Italy, where the standard of living is not high and is not increasing rapidly. And they ought to be very substantial in many of the Asian countries, where freedom means a good deal less than it does in the West and where the competition of the Communistic versus the capitalistic societies is being closely watched. Indeed, it does not appear at all clear that an economic course of this sort, perhaps coupled with a substantial decline in the military claims on the economy, would be less dangerous to the West than the piling up of impressive growth rates in steel, electric power, machinery, and chemicals.

[17] For a summary of the housing situation, see Timothy Sosnovy, *The Housing Problem in the Soviet Union.* New York: Research Program on the U.S.S.R., 1954.

POSSIBILITIES FOR FUTURE GROWTH

We turn now to a look into the future, and an attempt to assess the probability of continued future growth. We assume, of course, that hot war does not break out. We also assume that the Soviet leaders have debated the matters referred to in the immediately preceding paragraphs and have decided to retain the present policy of building up the industrial base as rapidly as is consistent with political stability.

The first thing to say is that at some time in the future, if the time has not already arrived, a modest decline in the *rate* of industrial growth may be expected to take place. The chief reason for this expectation is that there has to be a time when the rate of release of labor from agriculture to industry must decline. This is true if only because there will always have to be some agricultural labor on the farm, and the withdrawal, therefore—and the curve indicating withdrawal—will level out in asymptotic fashion. The flow of labor from agriculture to industry can be expected to continue, therefore, but beyond some point at a diminishing rate.

Actually, the data seem to indicate that a decline in the rate of growth of nonagricultural labor has already set in. Between 1928 and 1937 the annual rate of increase of workers and employees was about 10 per cent. In the 1950's it is only about half that. Much the same changes have been taking place in the number of industrial wage earners, which means workers in manufacturing, mining, and electric power production.

Recent Soviet statements have stressed that the cities cannot in the future count on an influx of peasant labor at the rate which formerly prevailed. The decline has created a considerable campaign in recent years for a more rapid increase in labor productivity, in particular through the introduction of new techniques. The campaign has not been wholly successful; the official statistics indicate that the labor productivity goals will not be met by 1955. This has been partly compensated for by an overfulfillment of the nonagricultural labor force goal. This type of compensation cannot continue indefinitely, of course. As a consequence we can expect to see the beginnings of a reduction in the rate of increase of industrial output.

In spite of this, there is reason to believe that the rate of increase can remain above that in the West almost indefinitely. It may be noted, parenthetically, that this does not mean greater absolute increases, at least not necessarily so for some period of time. But the investment policy, in terms of both rate and direction of investment, should be sufficient to maintain rates of growth in industry which are higher than those that prevail in Western nations. And unless the Soviets run into a genuine bottleneck, this inequality can remain indefinitely.

Bottlenecks

We turn now to the bottleneck possibility. There is a good deal of loose thinking on this matter. At various times we are told that the Soviet economy is in danger of imminent collapse because the military burden is excessive, or because the transportation situation is acutely critical, or because it lacks crude oil—and there are many other culprits. It is important to recognize that in any society which is proceeding at forced draft, there will always be one or more bottlenecks operating somewhere. It is not easy to plan the detailed growth process of a large and complex economy. The planner who seeks to maximize the rate of growth has as his ideal a situation where everything in the economy is equally critical at any given moment. If his plan results in surpluses in any parts of the economy, this is a sign to him that he is not planning well. If everything is in equally short supply, this means that he is using to the fullest everything that is being produced.

Now it is clear that no planner can be efficient enough to maintain a situation of this sort at all times. What actually happens, therefore, is that on occasion the economy seems to be held up by a shortage of freight cars or locomotives. There will be other years when rolling stock cannot move because of lack of petroleum; there will be shortages of skilled labor in certain industries where the needs have not been foreseen sufficiently far in advance; and so on. To a considerable extent, the Russians could overcome some of these difficulties, at modest cost, by maintaining fairly substantial inventories, although there is little evidence of what their practices are. But to become true bottlenecks, these difficulties would have to be more than temporary, and there seems to be almost no difficulty that, given time, cannot be alleviated by a reallocation of effort. One needs, therefore, to place in proper perspective the continual minor crises that are likely to occur and not regard them as evidences of imminent breakdown.

Agriculture a Real Difficulty

There is one sector which is different from others and which, because of this difference, may turn out to constitute a genuine brake on economic development. We refer to agriculture. . . .

The great thing that sets off agriculture from other parts of the economy is its dependence upon natural factors. There is scarcely any limit to the production of most industrial commodities if the planners devote enough effort to it. There is a very real limit to the production of agricultural commodities. Man can, it is true, alter nature to some extent, but it is hard to get around the fact that the endownment by nature of agricultural resources in the U.S.S.R. is very poor. The latitudinal position of the great bulk of Soviet land is such that the growing season is very much shorter than it is, for example, in United States agricultural areas. There are very few agricultural areas in the U.S.S.R. where the average annual rainfall is as high as twenty inches. Also, the quality of the land itself in Soviet Russia is poor. All this means that the best agricultural lands in the U.S.S.R. more nearly resemble North Dakota than Iowa.

This niggardliness of nature goes far to explain the dramatic efforts that have been made in recent years to reclaim vast quantities of land, to institute very large programs of reforestation for wind sheltering, to create the huge irrigation projects of which we have heard so much, and so on. All of these things will certainly help, but they are all expensive and the payoffs are limited. The niggardliness of nature likewise helps explain why the Russians still have half of their labor force in agriculture. One Russian farmer feeds himself and three other Russians. One American farmer feeds himself and twenty other Americans, and he embarrasses his government by insisting on producing "too much." The disposal of agricultural surpluses is a problem with which the Soviet planners would love to be faced.

To an undetermined extent, the organization of Soviet agriculture contributes to its inefficiency. The state and collective farm system is such that it is very difficult for any farmer to relate the income he receives and the effort he puts into the farm. Incentives toward hard work are so indirect as to be virtually nonoperative; the government has not helped by its practice of procuring at very low prices and under compulsion a good proportion of total output. There is no simple solution to this problem.

The population in the U.S.S.R. is increasing at a rate of about 1.5 per cent per year. Soviet agricultural output, therefore, has to increase this much simply to maintain per capita consumption at its current low levels. But this is not enough. If the Soviet economy is to continue to grow, output must increase even more in order to produce surpluses. Furthermore, this must be done with less manpower than is now available, since the growth of industry requires a continuous flow of labor from the countryside. The experience of Soviet agriculture raises serious question as to whether the planners are going to be able to solve the problems that are becoming increasingly critical. If they do not solve these problems, it seems clear that the rate of growth of the economy as a whole, and of the industrial sector, must slow down. . . .

There is, of course, one obvious method of solving agricultural problems. The British pointed the way in 1846 when it had become clear that British farmers were unable to feed the British people. In that year the Corn Laws were repealed; and the British changed their policy from one of self-sufficiency to one of ever increasing reliance on international trade. This avenue is open to the Russians. There is no reason, for example, why they should not import their cotton, and use the land in the U.S.S.R. devoted to raising cotton for raising food. There is no reason why they should not go farther and import their grain or their beef in trade for manufactured goods. The probability of their doing so, of course, is very low, since it is a cardinal sin according to their ideology to make themselves dependent upon outsiders. Nevertheless, the possibility is there, and one cannot but watch with fascination for signs that international trade is increasing on a substantial scale.

DIMENSIONS OF THE SOVIET ECONOMIC CHALLENGE

Allen W. Dulles[*]

The economic challenge [of the U.S.S.R.] is a dual one. They are setting goals for their own domestic production to compete directly with our own and to quote their words, "to get ahead of us in the economic race." The other phase of their challenge is through their foreign economic penetration program. . . .

[Editor's note: That portion of Mr. Dulles' speech which dealt with the Soviet challenge "through their foreign economic penetration program" has been omitted.]

To understand the seriousness of the Soviet economic threat, it is essential to understand the Soviet economic and industrial base on which they are developing their economic penetration program.

Since 1928 the Soviet Union has developed rapidly from a predominantly agricultural and industrially under-developed country to the second largest economy in the world. Forced-draft industrialization, emphasizing heavy industry, was carried out by Stalin to prevent, to quote his words, another beating of backward Russia by the more economically advanced capitalist countries.

Forced-draft industrialization continues in Russia today, and now the emphasis is more positive: namely, to meet Khrushchev's goal of, "catching up and surpassing the United States in per capita production within the shortest possible historical period of time." This theme is being used not only as internal propaganda but also to propagate the Soviet faith abroad.

Comparison of the economies of the United States and the U.S.S.R. in terms of total production of goods and services indicates the U.S.S.R.'s rapid progress.

Whereas Soviet gross national product was about 33 per cent that of the United States in 1950, by 1956 it had increased to about 40 per cent, and by

* Director of the United States Central Intelligence Agency. The excerpt is from a speech delivered by Mr. Dulles before the United States Chamber of Commerce on April 28, 1958.

1962 it may be about 50 per cent of our own. This means that the Soviet economy has been growing, and is expected to continue to grow through 1962, at a rate roughly twice that of the economy of the United States. Annual growth over-all has been running between 6 and 7 per cent, annual growth of industry between 10 and 12 per cent.

These rates of growth are exceedingly high. They have rarely been matched in other states except during limited periods of post-war rebuilding.

DOLLAR COMPARISON MADE

A dollar comparison of U.S.S.R. and United States gross national product in 1956 reveals that consumption—or what the Soviet consumer received—was less than half of total production. It was over two-thirds of the total in the United States. Investment, on the other hand, as a proportion of the gross national product in the U.S.S.R., was significantly higher than in the United States. Furthermore, investment funds in the U.S.S.R. were plowed back primarily into expansion of electric power, the metallurgical base, and into the producer goods industries. In these fields, it was over 80 per cent of actual United States investment in 1956, and in 1958, will probably exceed our own. Defense expenditures, as a proportion of the gross national product in the U.S.S.R., were significantly higher than in the United States; in fact about double.

Soviet industrial production in 1956 was about 40 per cent as large as that of the United States. However, Soviet heavy industry was proportionately larger than this over-all average, and in some instances the output of specific industries already approached that of the United States. The output of coal in the U.S.S.R. was about 70 per cent of that of the United States. The output of machine tools about double our own and steel output about half.

Since 1956, Soviet output has continued its rapid expansion. In the first quarter of 1958, Soviet industrial production was 11 per cent higher than a year ago. In comparison, the Federal Reserve Board index shows a decline of 11 per cent in the United States.

According to available statistics, in the first quarter of 1958, the Sino-Soviet bloc has for the first time surpassed the United States in steel production. The three months figures show that the U.S.S.R. alone turned out over 75 per cent of the steel tonnage of the United States.

A recession is an expensive luxury. Its effects are not confined to our own shores. Soviet propagandists have had a field day in recent months, pounding away at American free enterprise. . . .

In the analysis I have given above, I have stressed their very real achievements, their growing power, and their rapid rate of progress. These factors we must not underestimate. However, the realization of many of the goals they have set depends on resolving some very real obstacles to success.

For example, Khrushchev has repeatedly promised his people startling improvements in the quality of their diet. The realization of these dreams rests on a precarious agricultural base, whose crops over large areas, as we saw in 1957, are vulnerable to serious drought. Further, Khrushchev has brought the antigeneticist Lysenko back into favor, a theorist whose plant and animal breeding ideas are regarded as nonsense by all competent Western scientists.

They are now engaged in a massive reorganization of the control of their industry, and this move toward decentralization has built-in, long-run dangers for any dictatorship such as that of the Kremlin today.

The myth of collective leadership has been abandoned and there are signs today of a reversal to a harsher line with consequences of a far-reaching nature. Khrushchev, despite his gregarious characteristics, as he assumes new positions of power and eliminates his rivals, becomes more and more an isolated and lonely figure. . . .

Possibly today the most acute problem facing Khrushchev is that of meeting the growing demands of the Russian consumer for a greater share in the over-all production of the Soviet Union. With a gross national product of around 40 per cent of our own, they put into the military sector a national effort roughly comparable to our own, leaving only a modest share for consumer goods.

If the Kremlin responds to popular pressures, they will be forced to give more and more to the consumer. This trend has already started. The Russians have somewhat improved living standards and the national output of such consumer goods as TV sets and washing machines has been stepped up. Some former armament plants are now producing civilian goods.

THREAT TO DICTATORS IMPLIED

All this may help to develop a society where people will have more opportunity to satisfy the individual yearning for a fuller life. Economic betterment, added to the massive educational system they have already installed, may help to build up generations of people more and more inclined to question the basic tenets of a totalitarian philosophy and less willing to tolerate the autocratic forms of government under which they are living.

Under Khrushchev there has been, undoubtedly, some relaxations of the old Stalinist policy system, but every two steps in advance seem to be followed by one step backward as they wrestle with the problem of reconciling a measure of freedom with the stern line of the Communist doctrine and discipline.

The fact that the leadership of the U.S.S.R. faces these very real problems is, however, no excuse whatever for complacency on our part. During and since the war, their leadership has faced even more serious problems and has surmounted them.

The economy of the Soviet Union has momentum and versatility and, while I predict that their people will undoubtedly press for an improvement of their lot, some real concessions can be made to them without fundamentally altering the general tempo of their present industrial and military programs.

Certainly here we have the most serious challenge this country has ever faced in time of peace. As this challenge is very largely based on the economic and industrial growth of the Soviet Union, it is one which concerns very directly the business leaders in our country.

RUSSIA'S BOLD NEW PLAN

Harry Schwartz*

The political, propaganda and economic challenge posed by the new Soviet Seven-Year Plan for 1959-65 is the most ambitious such document ever unveiled by the Kremlin.

Premier Nikita S. Khrushchev boasted some time ago that this new plan would "astonish" the world when it was made public. On this score, at least, he proved a prophet. The astonishment was generated, of course, by the boldness of the goals he set.

The full extent of Mr. Khrushchev's audacity can be summed up simply: If the targets outlined by him for 1965 and 1970 are actually attained on schedule, then in the next decade or so the Communist world will clearly have won the economic competition with the West and, quite possibly, the political and propaganda contest for the allegiance of the uncommitted under-developed nations of Asia, Africa and Latin America as well. Conversely, of course, by setting such ambitious goals, Premier Khrushchev created the risk that a gross failure to reach them would have major undesirable consequences for the Soviet regime at home and abroad.

THE MAIN TARGETS

This conclusion emerges from an examination of the main targets he set for 1965 and 1970:

* Economist, specializing on Soviet affairs, *New York Times*. Author *of Russia's Soviet Economy*. The article originally appeared in the *New York Times*, November 16, 1958. Reprinted by permission.

By 1965, Mr. Khrushchev predicted, the Communist bloc as a whole will have greater industrial production than the rest of the world put together, while the Soviet Union will have sharply reduced the substantial economic lead over it held by the United States. During the next seven years, he asserted, the Soviet people can produce and have far more of everything—steel, machine tools, homes, television sets, food—than they have ever produced or had before.

By 1970, he added, the Soviet people will have the highest standard of living in the world, and in addition will be out-producing the United States both in absolute terms and on a per capita basis. Implied in this, of course, is the notion that by 1970 the Communist world as a whole will be so far ahead of the free world in production that the free world will have no chance of ever catching up, at least so long as it stubbornly refuses to enter the Communist "paradise."

Apparently spurred by recent Soviet economic and scientific successes, Premier Khrushchev has obviously decided to gamble in the grand manner, seeking a quick victory for his cause.

THE ASSETS

Let us look initially at the assets which have encouraged this gamble:

(1) There is the enormous mineral wealth of the Soviet Union, far exceeding that of the United States. With respect to iron ore, oil, bauxite, coal, and many other such commodities, the Soviet Union has the raw material base to support a much larger industrial production.

(2) The Soviet Union is today one of the most technologically advanced nations in the world. There can be little doubt that Premier Khrushchev intends to harness the most modern available technology—from automatic factories run by computers to the latest achievements of polymer chemistry and nuclear physics—to raise labor productivity and production rapidly.

(3) The Soviet population is still a tractable labor force which does not indulge in strikes, slowdowns, feather-bedding or other production-restricting activities. Moreover, the Soviet population is today better educated—and therefore potentially more productive—than ever before in Russian history.

(4) The Soviet economy seems not subject to recessions or depressions such as have historically interrupted the production progress of non-Communist countries. Each year since 1946 Soviet industry has produced more than the year before, and there is no present reason to suppose that this steady upward movement will not continue.

(5) Mr. Khrushchev has produced a set of agricultural reforms—higher prices for farmers, the virgin-lands and corn-raising programs, and the like, which have finally ended the post-war stagnation of Soviet agriculture. The

farmers of Russia had never produced so much as they have in recent years, particularly in 1956 and this year.

THE OBSTACLES

These assets, however, must be balanced against the obstacles in Premier Khrushchev's way:

(1) To realize his production targets, the Soviet economy will have to receive enormous capital investments for new factories, mines, railroads, and the like. Yet at the same time Mr. Khrushchev is committed to an enormous housing construction program, to providing a rapidly rising living standard and to permitting reduced hours of work—there is even pressure for a five-day week. Moreover, he presumably plans continued large expenditures on arms production and space exploration. It is far from clear that even the vast Soviet resources are adequate to do all these things simultaneously. Shortage of capital forced the abandonment in September, 1957, of the original sixth Five-Year Plan for 1956-60. The same problem may recur.

(2) Many of the richest raw material sources found by Soviet geologists in recent years are in the thinly populated areas of the Urals. To realize the plans for exploiting these resources by creating giant new production complexes in Siberia will require the movement of large numbers of workers there from European Russia. Short of using compulsion on a Stalinist scale, can the required number of workers be induced to migrate?

(3) In the years immediately ahead, the number of new entrants to the Soviet labor forces will be cut sharply from past years because of the greatly reduced birth rate in the period of World War II. Thus the question of the overall adequacy of the labor supply arises. It is already likely that Moscow's educational reform that will send youngsters to work after they have finished only elementary school is a move prompted by the seriousness of this problem.

(4) Premier Khrushchev is counting on getting some of the capital he needs and on being able to reduce prices to consumers in the belief that the efficiency of Soviet farming will soon improve sharply. He expects this will reduce production costs and permit him to lower the prices farmers are paid for the produce they grow. But will the Soviet farmers accept such price cuts?

(5) At a minimum Mr. Khrushchev's ambitious plans presuppose some important political conditions that cannot be taken for certain. They assume there will be no very heightened international tension that will require sharply stepped up military preparedness. They assume there will be no more catastrophes like the Polish and Hungarian revolts requiring direct Soviet military intervention and the large scale pouring in of Soviet goods to quiet discontent.

WHAT THE WEST FACES

At the very least, realization of the problems before the Soviet economy should warn against any facile assumption that the Khrushchev goals are certain to be met on schedule. Yet even taking account of these problems, the assets seem substantial enough to suggest that rapid and substantial Soviet economic progress will continue over the next decade or so. On this assumption certain difficult problems seem likely to assume great urgency for the West in the years ahead.

One is the problem of counteracting the impression made on underdeveloped countries if there is anything like the rapid progress in the Soviet Union and the Communist bloc that Premier Khrushchev envisages. That problem might well become insoluble, and Soviet victory assured, if rapid Communist progress were to be accompanied by anything resembling a serious depression or recession in the West.

If realized, a sharply higher Soviet living standard would increase the political attractiveness of the Communist system, not only in the underdeveloped nations but even in the poorer countries of Western Europe such as Italy.

A second problem is likely to be that of meeting the greatly increased Communist military strength that may emerge as the Communist bloc increases its output of steel and other basic materials and equipment.

A third problem is the very much greater competition Western businessmen are likely to face in world markets as the flood of Communist goods mounts. The unhappy experiences this last year of free world producers of aluminum, tin and platinum—who have seen their prices reduced by sudden Soviet sales campaigns—may well be repeated in many key international markets.

VIII

THE SOCIAL IMPACT AND THE PROSPECTS OF SOVIET TOTALITARIAN CONTROLS

"It is not technical and economic innovations but the human aspects of a society that matter."

KARL KAUTSKY

"Without freedom, heavy industry can be perfected but not justice or truth."

ALBERT CAMUS

"Let us not, having criticized the Russian Communists all these years for being too totalitarian, pour scorn and ridicule upon them the moment they show signs of becoming anything else."

GEORGE F. KENNAN

maintaining and substantially strengthening the present structure of Soviet society and toward creating a world predominantly, if not wholly, Communist under Soviet leadership or hegemony. Current policy is, of course, always considerably influenced or determined by the actions of the United States and other nations involved in the total international scene and by practical considerations arising from the resultant balance of forces. In addition, the regime's long-range policy appears subject to the important reservation that every precaution should be taken to avoid immediate and major risks to the security of the home base. Thus, ultimately, the domestic requirements of the system set an absolute limit on the degree of risk undertaken in foreign affairs. Nevertheless, many of the difficulties on the domestic front stem from the regime's ambitious foreign policy goals and the consequent commitments to offensive and defensive preparedness, which strain the resources of the system to the utmost.

3. While the long-range goals of the leadership are highly stable, there have been, from a shorter-term point of view, enough sudden alternations in both domestic and foreign policy, both between rigidity and flexibility and between two drastically contrasting courses of policy and action, to justify naming "cyclical behavior" one of the most distinctive operating characteristics of the Soviet system. This adds an important element of insecurity to the life situations of both the elite and the rank and file, which the regime may exploit to its advantage, but which also makes it more difficult for the Soviet citizen to regard the system with equanimity.

4. In large measure, the internal problems of the regime stem from the leaders' persistent tendency to overcommit the system's resources. The system involves, in effect, permanent rationing and perpetual mobilization. Goals are invariably set too close to the theoretical capacity of the available resources in the effort to stimulate each unit to maximum output. Furthermore, effective expenditures of energy are usually characterized by mass assault on a single objective or a relatively narrow range of objectives, while other considerations are ignored until their sheer neglect causes sufficient problems so that they, in turn, rise to a high position on the scale of priorities and become the focus of mass assault. As a result, despite the extensive machinery of allocation, there are always localized scarcities of resources, resulting in hoarding and inevitable costs in the form of malcoördination of effort. Overcontrol and overcentralization are therefore chronic features of the system.

5. Both because of their addiction to rational planning and because of their conviction that "everyone who is not completely for us is against us," the ruling elite have made tremendous efforts to stamp out growing centers of independent power and communication. Their success, however, is not complete, particularly with regard to the military, who retain continuing capabilities for independent action and are possessed of notably increased relative power and prestige.

6. The needs of the citizen are relatively low in the priority scheme of the leaders. Nevertheless, the individual is recognized as the most flexible resource in the system. The regime is therefore necessarily concerned with the morale of the population—not as an objective in itself but as an unavoidable prerequisite to effective economic production and military preparedness. The regime's objective is to extract from the citizen a maximum of effort with a minimum of reward. The purge and the terror are the standard instruments for insuring unhesitating obedience to central command. But to maximize incentive the regime also relies heavily on sharply differentiated material and social rewards. Further, it may periodically relax the pressure and make a show of concern for popular welfare when the results of increased pressure appear to have passed the point of diminishing returns.

7. Certain features of Soviet society win strong, widespread support and approval. These are notably the welfare-state aspects of the system, such as the health services, government support of the arts, and public educational facilities. In addition, the regime is credited with major achievements in the technological development of the country, in which Soviet citizens take obvious pride. The armed might and international prominence of the regime are recognized and held somewhat in awe. The depth of loyalty to "the motherland" is an outstanding sentiment in all classes of the population, irrespective of religion, political attitudes, and personality structure. This is coupled with a genuine fear of foreign aggression. These sentiments are strongest in the heartland of Great Russia, but they prevail generally.

8. Our data show that ignorance and distorted views of the outside world are deeper and more widespread—even among the intelligentsia—than heretofore had been realized by most students of the U.S.S.R. It is almost impossible to exaggerate the ignorance of the outside world prevalent among Soviet citizens. And, while feelings toward the American people and toward certain American achievements have distinctly positive elements, there is a general distrust of American intentions and a fear of "capitalist aggression." Most attitudes toward the West change after emigration, but not in a uniformly favorable direction.

9. The general features of Soviet life and the Soviet system that are most intensely resented are the low standard of living, the excessive pace of everyday life, the invasion of personal privacy, and the "terror," i.e., the threat of arbitrary political repression. We found little concern with "civil liberties" per se, and little pressure toward a democratic form of government. The specific institution most resented was the collective farm, which all groups, virtually without distinction and nearly unanimously, want eliminated. There was strikingly little complaint about the factory system other than dislike of harsh labor-discipline laws, which now are no longer being stringently enforced.

10. Hostility is directed mainly toward the regime—the actual people in power—rather than toward the idea of a welfare state with high concentration of economic and social as well as political power in the hands of a few men. There is a strong tendency for the rank-and-file citizen to establish a "we-they" dichotomy, in which "they" are the people, regardless of rank, who are closely identified with the regime. In general, but not exclusively, this distinction tends to correspond to that between Party and non-Party personnel, although some members of the Party are accepted in the "we" category. In any event, wherever the line is drawn, "we" see "them" as having no regard for "our" feelings, depriving "us" of just rewards, terrorizing "us" without cause, and generally failing to show proper trust and respect for the citizenry. All classes appear to channel much of their hostility and aggression in this way. Indeed, many of the routine daily frustrations of life are charged to the regime because the immediate source of those frustrations is defined as a representative of "them."

11. The conflict over straightforward matters of policy, which creates a gulf between the leaders and the rank and file, is aggravated by the important psychological differences which separate the elite and the masses. The masses remain rather close to the traditional picture of Russian character. They are warm-hearted, impulsive, given to mood swings, and contradictory in behavior. The goal of the elite is the rather puritanical "new Soviet man": disciplined, working steadily and consistently, subordinating personal conduct and motivation to the requirements of Party discipline. It appears that the Soviet leaders have succeeded to a certain degree in developing among the elite a considerable proportion of people of an externally disciplined and driving character, and their patterns of behavior add to the sense of alienation felt by many of the rank and file toward the leaders.

12. Despite the high level of dissatisfaction and discontent, there seems to be only a relatively small amount of disaffection and disloyalty. The life histories of our respondents left little doubt of the extent to which most of them were unhappy about many aspects of their life situations. But these same life histories indicated that most of the citizens of the U.S.S.R. feel helpless in the face of the power of the state and desire only to live peacefully. There is scant evidence for the view that more than a very tiny part of the population would, except under conditions of extreme crisis, take appreciable risks to sabotage the regime or to aid Western democracy.

13. Certain traumatic experiences, such as being arrested, had less effect than we had anticipated. Being arrested has virtually no impact on a person's general social and political attitudes and values. The individual does not generalize his experience to the point of revising his judgment concerning the kind of society in which he lives or would want to live. Arrest, however, does increase the *intensity* of his hostility *to the regime*. Further-

more, arrest—whether his own, or that of a family member—makes him anxious about his own future, and thereby increases the probability of his leaving the Soviet Union voluntarily if the opportunity arises.

14. Degree of dissatisfaction with, or even disaffection from, the system does not necessarily detract from the energy with which a person does the job assigned to him by "the system." The disaffected person often does his job well and may work with a little extra energy, either because he feels he has to prove himself or because he finds comfort in his work. Thus, the fact that the Soviet system tends to produce dissatisfaction in its citizens does not in itself mean that it gets less effective work from them. This applies, however, mainly in the professional and white-collar classes. In the working class and the peasantry there appears to be a fairly direct relation between the individual's level of satisfaction and the quality and quantity of his work.

15. The Soviet elite, a markedly privileged social class, inevitably has a vested interest in maintaining and perpetuating the system. This tendency, however, varies with different individuals and under various combinations of circumstances and is partly counterbalanced by one or more of the following factors: (a) the conviction that the ruling clique is acting contrary to the interests of the nation-state; (b) the conviction that the regime has betrayed the humane goals of Marxism; and (c) personal insecurity. On the other hand, even when these factors are operative, the conflicted members of the elite often fall into line of their own choice because of deep-rooted attitudes, such as suspicion of foreigners and their motives; belief that, after all, national patriotism and loyalty to the regime are inextricably linked; acceptance of Communist ideology; a conspiratorial mentality; and the habit of disciplined obedience.

16. A Soviet citizen's social class and his occupation largely determine both his opportunities for advancement and his attitudes toward the Soviet system, as well as his general social and political values. The individual's social position is more important than such factors as nationality or arrest history in affecting his hostility toward, passive acceptance of, or positive identification with the regime. Members of the intelligentsia, being the more favored beneficiaries of the system, understandably show substantial satisfaction with the conditions of daily life and with opportunities for development and advancement. They are generally the persons most accepting of the broad outlines of Soviet society, with the exception of its political patterns which hit them especially hard owing to the greater surveillance to which the regime subjects them and their work. At the other pole, the peasant emerges as the "angry man" of the system, strongly rejecting most of its features, convinced of his exploitation, resentful of his deprivation of goods and opportunities, and outraged by the loss of his autonomy. The workers shared many attitudes and life experiences with the peasants, thus forming a broad manual group which can regularly be distinguished from the non-

manual. The workers are, on the whole, less intense and resentful than the peasants and generally accept the sociopolitical structure of the Soviet factory as natural and proper.

17. It has been asserted that the Soviet youth, although showing a strong early allegiance to the regime, have a high probability of becoming disaffected as they mature and experience the full dimensions of the regime. Our materials indicate that there is a period of crisis in the relation of youth to the regime as the individual reaches maturity, but that only a small minority actually turn against the system because of disillusionment. In most instances, they are able to reconcile their conflicts. Furthermore, the younger generation is coming to accept as natural many aspects of Soviet life and the Soviet system against which the older generation rebelled. The youth is relatively unlikely to turn against the regime, in spite of experiences that Americans would think would lead to disaffection.

18. The individual's nationality appears to play a lesser role in determining his attitudes toward the regime than has often been supposed. Indeed, people in the same occupation or social group hold essentially the same attitudes and values regardless of nationality, and those in the national minorities feel the same resentments toward the regime and experience the same dissatisfactions with the system as do all other citizens of the U.S.S.R. Generally, therefore, nationality is only a secondary, contributing cause for disaffection. There is a distinctive nationality feeling in sections of many national groups, however, and this national identification is supported by a sense of oppression and resentment of Great Russians.

19. Certain scholars had advanced the plausible and provocative thesis that political domination within the Soviet system was threatened by a "managerial revolution." Our data, however, indicate that technical and managerial personnel, having a stake in the existing system, have developed an interest in maintaining it in predominantly its present form. They are concerned mainly with reducing interference and extreme pressure from the center and in improving the system and making it work more smoothly. They feel that they can obtain the rewards they deserve without the risks involved in ownership.

20. The Project findings yield strong evidence as to the importance of informal mechanisms in the operation of a society that, on the surface, appears and pretends to be highly centralized, controlled, and rationalized. The rank-and-file citizen learns to apply complicated techniques of accommodation and evasion in order to carry on his day-to-day affairs and to maintain himself in reasonably successful, or at least untroubled, adaptation to the regime. In this he is often aided by others—doctors, for example— who serve as buffers between him and the pressures of the system. In addition, "localism" or "familism," the tendency for local loyalties and informal mutual protective associations to develop on the local level as defense against the pressures of the center, plays a major role. In fact,

Soviet society works as well as it does only because of the existence of a series of informal, extralegal practices which are tolerated, up to a point, by the regime, even though officially disapproved. Nevertheless, these informal adjustive mechanisms create problems for the leadership as well as facilitating the functioning of the society in significant respects.

21. The life histories of our respondents indicate that the stability of the Soviet system involves a nice balance between the powers of coercion and the adjustive habits of the Soviet citizenry. The stability of the system and of the citizen's loyalty depend to a high degree on the citizen's own belief in the stability of that system and on his having no alternative but to adjust to the system. For the average citizen, political loyalty to the regime is a strange compound of apathy, passive acceptance, and cynicism. Among the elite groups, some individuals are conforming loyalists to the system; some, the "careerists," are really loyal only to themselves; more than a few are loyal to Communist "ideals." Our pessimistic finding is that the new regime can gain much more solid popular support if it supplies more consumer goods and better housing, eases up on the terror, makes some concessions to the peasants, and relieves somewhat the frantic pace at which all the population has been driven. Such a change of policy would not only alleviate many of the day-to-day grievances of the citizen, but also change his basic image of the regime as a harsh and depriving force. These may be precisely the lines along which the current regime is proceeding.

THE NEW SOVIET MAN

"L" *

It might be supposed that as a result of so many years of Stalinist conditioning the new Soviet man would be a new creature, as different from his Western counterpart as the Soviet system differs from Western forms of government. But this has not, in fact, turned out to be so. In so far as recent conversations of mine with students, clerks in shops, taxi-drivers and stray acquaintances of all sorts can convey a just impression, the result is a kind of arrested infantile development, not a different kind of maturity.

In the Soviet Union today one finds the conditions that are often found to prevail in organizations in which degrees and types of responsibility are very sharply defined—strictly disciplined schools, armies or other rigid hierarchies in which the differences between the governors and the governed

---

* Anonymous. The article originally appeared under the title "The Soviet Intelligentsia" in *Foreign Affairs,* Vol. 36 (October 1957), pp. 122-130. Copyright held by Council on Foreign Relations, New York. By permission.

are extremely precise. Indeed, the chasm between the governors and the governed is the deepest single division noticeable in Soviet society; and when one speaks to Soviet citizens it soon becomes quite clear to which of the two groups they belong. Honest public discussion, either of the ends for the sake of which the new society supposedly exists, or of the more important means supposedly adopted for the forwarding of those ends, is equally discouraged on both sides of this great dividing line. The work of the ant-hill must be done, and anything that wastes time or creates doubts cannot be permitted. But the consequences in one case are somewhat different from those in the other.

Let me begin with the governed. Those who have no ambition themselves to become governors, and have more or less accepted their position in the lower ranks of the Soviet hierarchy, do not seem to be deeply troubled about public issues. They know they cannot affect those issues in any case, and discussion of them is, moreover, liable to be dangerous. Hence when they touch upon them at all they speak with the gaiety, curiosity and irresponsibility of schoolboys discussing serious public issues outside their ken, more or less for fun, not expecting to be taken too seriously, and with a pleasing sense of saying something daring, near the edge of forbidden territory. Such people cultivate the private virtues, and retain those characteristics that were so often noted as typically Russian by foreigners before. They tend to be amiable, spontaneous, inquisitive, childlike, fond of pleasure, highly responsive to new impressions, not at all blasé, and, having been kept from contact with the outside world for so long, essentially Victorian and prudishly conventional in their outlook and tastes. They are not as terrified as they were in Stalin's day, when no one knew what might not happen to him, and no effective appeal to any institutions of justice was possible. The tyrant is dead, and a set of rules and regulations rule in his place.

The rules are exceedingly harsh, but they are explicit, and you know that if you transgress them you will be punished, but that if you are innocent—if you live a very careful and circumspect life, take no risks, see no foreigners, express no dangerous thoughts—you can reasonably count on being safe and, if arrested, on a reasonable chance of clearing up the misunderstanding and regaining freedom. The justice of the rules themselves is not, one finds, much discussed. The question is not asked whether they are good or bad. They appear to be taken for granted, like something from on high, on the whole disagreeable, and certainly not believed in with the kind of religious devotion expected of good Communists, but, since they are clearly not alterable by the governed, accepted by them almost like the laws of nature.

Taste remains simple, fresh and uncontaminated. Soviet citizens are brought up on a diet of classical literature—both Russian (which is almost unrestricted now) and foreign—mainly of authors held to be of "social significance": Schiller, Dickens, Balzac, Stendhal, Flaubert, Zola, Jack London, plus "boy scout" novels celebrating the social virtues and showing how vice is always punished in the end. And since no trash or pornography or "problem" literature is allowed to distract them, the outlook of the pupils in this educational establishment remains eager and unsophisticated, the outlook of adolescents, sometimes very attractive and gifted ones. At the marvellous exhibition of French art in the Hermitage in Leningrad, Russian visitors (according to at least one foreigner who spoke to several among them) admired few pictures after the eighteen-fifties, found the Impressionists, particularly Monet and Renoir, difficult to like, and quite openly detested the paintings of Gauguin, Cézanne and Picasso of which there were many magnificent examples. There are, of course, Soviet citizens with more sophisticated tastes, but few and far between, and they do not advertise their tastes too widely.

Students are encouraged to take interest in scientific and technological studies more than in the humane ones, and the closer to politics their fields of study are, the less well they are taught. The worst off are, therefore, the economists, modern historians, philosophers and students of law. A foreign student working in the Lenin Library in Moscow found that the majority of his neighbors were graduate students, preparing theses which consisted largely of copying passages from other theses that had already obtained doctorates and, in particular, embodying approved quotations from the classics—mainly the works of Lenin and Stalin (still Stalin in 1956)—which, since they stood the test of many examinations, represented the survival of the fittest. It was explained to this foreign student that without these no theses could hope to pass. Evidently both examinees and examiners were engaged in an unspoken understanding about the type of quotations required, a quota of these being a sine qua non for obtaining a degree. The number of students reading books was very small in comparison with those reading theses, plus certain selected copies of *Pravda* and other Communist publications containing quotable official statements of various kinds.

In philosophy the situation is particularly depressed. Philosophy—that is, dialectical materialism and its predecessors—is a compulsory subject in all university faculties, but it is difficult to get any teacher of the subject to discuss it with any semblance of interest. One of these, perhaps in an unguarded moment, went so far as to explain to a puzzled foreign amateur of the subject that under the Tsarist régime a clergyman was expected to visit every form in the school, say, once a week, and drone through his scripture lesson, while the boys were expected to sit quiet. They were scarcely ever asked to answer questions; and, provided they gave no trouble, did not interrupt or give vent to aggressively anti-religious or subversive thoughts, they were by tacit consent permitted to sleep through the hour

—neither side expecting to take the other seriously. The official philosophers were the cynical clergy of today. Lecturers on dialectical materialism simply delivered their stock lectures, which had not altered during the last 20 years—ever since debates between philosophers had been forbidden even within the dialectical materialist fold. Since then the entire subject had turned into a mechanical reiteration of texts, whose meaning had gradually evaporated because they were too sacred to be discussed, still less to be considered in the light of the possibility of applying them—except as a form of lip service—to other disciplines, say, economics or history.

Both the practitioners of the official metaphysics and their audiences seem equally aware of its futility. So much could, indeed, be admitted with impunity, but only by persons of sufficient importance to get away with it: for example, by nuclear physicists whose salaries are now probably the highest of all, and who apparently are allowed to say, almost in public, that dialectical—and indeed all—philosophy seems to them meaningless gibberish upon which they cannot be expected to waste their time. Most of those who have spoken to teachers of philosophy in Moscow (and a good many Western visitors have done so by now) agree that they are one and all passionately interested to know what has been going on in the West, ask endless questions about "Neo-Positivism," Existentialism and so on, and listen like boys unexpectedly given legal access to forbidden fruit. When asked about progress in their own subject, the look of guilty eagerness tends to disappear, and they show conspicuous boredom. Reluctance to discuss what they know all too well is a dead and largely meaningless topic before foreigners who are not expected to realize this is almost universal. The students make it all too clear that their philosophical studies are a kind of farce, and known to be such, that they long to be allowed to interpret and discuss even such old-fashioned thinkers as Feuerbach or Comte, but that this is not likely to be found in order by those in authority. Clearly "the governed" do not seem to be taken in by what they are told. The philosophy students know that the philosophy dispensed to them is petrified nonsense. The professors of economics, for the most part, know that the terminology they are forced to use is, at best, obsolete.

At a wider level, it is difficult to find anyone with much belief in the information that comes from either their own newspapers or radio, or from abroad. They tend to think of it as largely propaganda, some of it Soviet, some of it anti-Soviet, and so to be equally discounted; and they avert their thoughts to other fields in which freer discussion is possible, mainly about issues of personal life, plays, novels, films, their personal tastes and ambitions and the like. On all these subjects they are fresh, amusing and informative. They suffer from no noticeable xenophobia. Whatever they might be told by the authorities, they hate no foreigners. They do not even hate the Germans, against whom there really was strong feeling of a personal kind in 1945-46, and certainly not the Americans, even though they fear that because of the quarrels of governments, the Americans may make war upon them; but even this is viewed more like the possibility of an earthquake or some other natural cataclysm than something to which blame attaches. Those who ask questions about current politics usually show little bias, only the curiosity of bright, elderly children. Thus the taxi-driver who asked his passenger if it was true that there were two million unemployed in England, and upon learning that this was not so, replied philosophically, "So they have lied about this too," said so without the slightest indignation, not even with noticeable irony, very much like someone stating a fairly obvious fact. It was the Government's business to dispense these lies, he seemed to say (like that of any Ministry of Propaganda in wartime), but intelligent persons did not need to believe them. The amount of deception or illusion about the external world in large Soviet cities is not as high as is sometimes supposed in the West—information is scanty, but extravagant inventions are seldom believed. It seems to me that if by some stroke of fate or history Communist control were lifted from Russia, what its people would need would be not reëducation—for their systems have not deeply absorbed the doctrines dispensed—but mere ordinary education. In this respect they resemble Italians undeluded by Fascism, rather than Germans genuinely penetrated by Nazism.

In fact, the relative absence of what might be called Communist *mystique* is perhaps the most striking fact about the ersatz intelligentsia of the Soviet Union. No doubt many convinced Marxists exist in Poland and Jugoslavia and elsewhere; but I cannot believe that there are many such in the Soviet Union—there it has become a form of accepted, and unresisted, but infinitely tedious, official patter. What writers and intellectuals desire—and those who have made their protests at recent meetings of writers' unions and the like are symptomatic of this—is not so much to be free to attack the prevailing orthodoxy, or even to discuss ideological issues, but simply to describe life as they see it without constant reference to ideology. Novelists are bored, or disgusted, with having to put wooden, idealized figures of Soviet heroes and villains into their stories and upon their stages; they would passionately like to compose with greater—if still very naïve—realism, wider variety, more psychological freedom. They look back with nostalgia to what seems to them the golden age of the Leninist twenties, but not beyond, which is different from seething with political revolt. The writers—or, at any rate, some of them—wish to discuss or denounce bureaucracy, hypocrisy, lies, oppression, the triumphs of the bad over the good, in the moral terms to which even the régime ostensibly adheres. These moral feelings, common to all mankind, and not heterodox or openly anti-Marxist attitudes, are the form in which the Hungarian revolt seems to have been acclaimed or condemned, and in which the new novel (almost worthless as literature, but

most important as a social symptom) that has stirred everyone so deeply—
"Not by Bread Alone," by Dudintsev—is written and discussed.[1]

The governed—the subject population—are for the most part neither
Communist believers nor important heretics. Some, perhaps the majority,
are discontented; and discontent in totalitarian states is ipso facto political
and subversive. But at present they accept or at any rate passively tolerate
their Government—and think about other things. They are proud of Russian economic and military achievements. They have the charm of a sheltered, strictly brought up, mildly romantic and imaginative, somewhat
boyish, deeply unpolitical group of simple and normal human beings who
are members of some ruthlessly ruled corporation.

As for the governors, that is a different story. Individually ruthless and
anxious to get on, they seem agreed that Communist language and a certain
minimum of Communist doctrine are the only cement that can bind the
constituent parts of the Soviet Union, and that to modify these too greatly
would endanger the stability of the system and make their own position
excessively precarious. Consequently they have managed to translate the
thoughts in their heads into a reasonable imitation of Communist terminology, and seem to use it in their communication with each other as well
as foreigners. When you ask them questions (and it is always clear whether
or not one is talking to a member of the upper tiers of the hierarchy or
someone who is aspiring to get there, if only from his looks and the tone
of his voice and the clothes he wears and other less palpable things) they
launch into something which at first seems a mere propagandist turn; then
gradually one realizes that they believe in what they are saying in much
the same way as a politician in any country can be said to believe in a
performance which he knows that he manages well, which he has adjusted
to his audience, upon which his success and career depend, which has
patently become bound up with his whole mode of self-expression, possibly
even to himself, and certainly to his friends and colleagues.

I do not believe that a double morality prevails in the Soviet Union:
that the Party leaders or bureaucrats talk in the consecrated mumbo jumbo
to their subjects, and then drop all pretense and talk cynical common
sense to each other. Their language, concepts, outlook are an amalgam
of both. On the other hand, again perhaps like that of the Russian bureaucrats of old, and of certain types of political manipulators and power-
holders everywhere, their attitude toward their own official doctrine, but
still more toward the beliefs of the outside world, is often skeptical and,
indeed, cynical. Certain very simplified Marxist propositions they certainly
do hold. I think they genuinely believe that the capitalist world is doomed
to destruction by its own inner contradictions; that the proper method of

[1] Nor does the "oppositionist" literary almanac *Literaturnaya Moskva* do more than
this: it is neither for "pure" art nor for some alternative political policy, however covertly.
Its "suspect" articles cry out for human values.

assessing the power, the direction and the survival value of a society is by asking a certain type of "materialistic" economic or sociological questions (taught to them by Lenin), so that the answers to these questions play a decisive part in the conception and formulation of their own most crucial political and economic policies. They believe that the world is marching inexorably towards collectivism, that attempts to arrest or even modify this process are evidence of childishness or blindness, that their own system, if only it holds out long enough against capitalist fury, will triumph in the end, and that to change it now, or to retreat too far simply in order to make their subjects happier or better, might mean their own doom and destruction, and—who knows?—perhaps that of their subjects too. In other words, they think in terms of Marxist concepts and categories, but not in terms of the original Marxist purposes or values: freedom from exploitation, or coercion, or even the particular interests of groups or classes or nations, still less in terms of the ultimate ideals: individual freedom, the release of creative energy, universal contentment and the like. They are too tough and morally indifferent for that. They are not religious; but neither are they believers in some specifically proletarian morality or logic or historical pattern.

Their attitude towards intellectuals can be compared in some degree to that of political bosses everywhere: it is, of course, largely conditioned by the tone set by the leaders—the members of the Central Committee of the Communist Party. The majority of these, in addition to their suspicion of those who are concerned with ideas in any form as a perpetual source of potential danger, feel personally uncomfortable with them, and dislike them for what can only be called social reasons. These are the kind of reasons for which trade unionists in all countries sometimes feel a combined attitude of superiority and inferiority to intellectuals—superiority because they think themselves more effective, experienced and with a deeper understanding of the world gained in a harder school, and inferior socially, intellectually and because they feel ill at ease with them. The group of roughnecks who preside over Russia's fortunes—and one glance at the Politbureau (now called the Presidium) makes it clear that they are men happier at street corner meetings or on the public platform than in the study—look upon intellectuals with the same uneasy feeling as they look on the better-dressed, better-bred members of the foreign colony—diplomats and journalists—whom they treat with exaggerated and artificial politeness, envy, contempt, dislike, intermittent affability and immense suspicion. At the same time they feel that great nations must have important professors, celebrated artists, cultural trappings of an adequate kind. Consequently they pay the topmost practitioners of these crafts high salaries, but cannot resist, from sheer resentment, an irresistible desire to bully and, from a deep, jealous sense of inferiority, the temptation to knock them about, kick them, humiliate them in public, remind them forcibly of the chains by which they are led whenever they show the least sign of independence or a wish to protect their own dignity.

Some intellectuals do, of course, themselves belong to the upper rungs of the hierarchy; but these are looked on by the bulk of other intellectuals either as semi-renegades and creatures of the Government, or else as blatant political operators or agitators, required to pose as men of learning or creative artists. The difference between genuine writers who can talk to other writers in normal human voices, and the literary bureaucrats—a difference, once again, between the governors and the governed—is the deepest single frontier in Soviet intellectual life. It was one of the former—the governors —who, talking not ostensibly about himself but about intellectuals in general, told a visiting American journalist not to think that Soviet intellectuals as a class were particularly keen about the granting of greater personal freedom to the workers and peasants in the Soviet Union. He said, in effect, that if they began giving liberties too fast, there might be too much unruliness—strikes, disorder—in the factories and the villages; and the intelligentsia, a most respected class in Soviet society, would not wish the order from which they very rightly get so much—above all, prestige and prosperity—to be jeopardized. "Surely you understand that?" he asked.

So far, then, have we travelled from the nineteenth century, when the whole of Russian literature was one vast, indignant indictment of Russian life; and from the agonies and enthusiasms and the bitter, often desperate, controversies and deadly duels of the twenties and early thirties. A few pre-Stalin men of letters survive, great names, but few and far between; they are half admired, half gaped at as semi-mythical figures from a fabulous but dead past. Bullying and half-cynical semi-Marxist philistines at the top; a thin line of genuinely civilized, perceptive, morally alive and often gifted, but deeply intimidated and politically passive, "specialists" in the middle; honest, impressionable, touchingly naïve, pure-hearted, intellectually starved, non-Marxist semi-literates, consumed with unquenchable curiosity, below. Such is Soviet culture, by and large, today.

THE COMMUNISTS ALSO HAVE THEIR PROBLEMS

Allen W. Dulles*

Tonight I propose to give you the results of an analysis of the recent happenings within the Soviet Communist world and I shall be bold

* Director of the United States Central Intelligence Agency. The selection is from a speech delivered by Mr. Dulles on September 19, 1957.

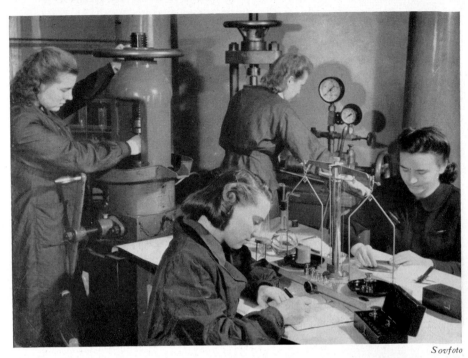

Geology students at work in a laboratory of a Soviet university.

Magnitorsk, Urals. Workers on their way home after their work shift.

A Kazakh child reading from the book of Jambul, a celebrated folk bard, to an aged collective farmer.

Turkmenian farmers in native garb.

Sovfoto

At a picnic party in Moscow are N. S. Khrushchev, G. Malenkov and N. Bulganin, with foreign press correspondents.

Sovfoto

A candid shot of N. S. Khrushchev talking to the Seventh Congress of the Bulgarian Communist Party in June 1958.

but yet maintaining complete authority, of doing away with the Stalinist type of secret police repression and yet keeping the people under iron discipline, of maintaining a tight rein but still creating the impression, and giving some of the substance, of a new measure of freedom.

Beria found it hard to fit into this picture. He did not want to relinquish his personal control of the secret police through which he hoped to gain the top position. His plot was discovered and he was liquidated. Since then the military seems to have become the decisive element where force or the threat of force was required to support a political decision.

After the Beria crisis we were told that the dictatorship of the proletariat had become a collective leadership—more properly described as a collective dictatorship. True enough, the crisis of readjustment to the post-Stalin era brought together in uneasy harmony the surviving members of the governing body known as the Presidium of the Party. Many here at home and abroad wrongly estimated that this might be an enduring form of government. Actually bitter personal rivalries and basic differences of philosophies and outlook remain unreconciled.

The ultimate authority to make crucial decisions must rest firmly somewhere and that "somewhere" is unlikely for long to be in a collective. Majority rule is appropriate for legislative and judicial bodies, but it does not function satisfactorily in the executive field, where decisiveness of action is essential.

For a time after Stalin's disappearance from the scene, Malenkov tried to lead the collective team, seemingly down a course which promised a better break for the people than they had ever had before. In 1955 he was forced to confess his incapacity and Khrushchev took over, committing himself, like his predecessor, to the collective rule formula.

Then, last June [1957], the inevitable irreconcilable conflict of opinions emerged, the collective broke down and, with the approval of the military, in particular Zhukov, Khrushchev eliminated his rivals—Molotov and Kaganovich, who really felt that the old Stalinist and foreign policies were preferable, and Malenkov, who due to his relative youth, political experience, and apparent popularity, was a dangerous potential rival. At the moment, Khrushchev is busily engaged in implicating Malenkov in the crimes of Stalin's later days, classing him as "shadow and tool" of Beria. Since Beria was shot for treason, the threat to Malenkov is naked enough for all to see.

So the history of Soviet governmental changes repeats itself, although in a slightly different pattern from that of the two previous decades. Those recently purged have not yet been liquidated like Beria or eliminated by mock trials such as those of the late 1930's. With a touch of almost sardonic humor, the miscreants have been assigned to the oblivion of Siberia or the darkness of Outer Mongolia.

It was the hand-picked Central Committee of the Communist Party, to the charge of having opened the flood gates to revolt by stimulating support for the doctrine of "differing roads to Socialism," a heresy that is now threatening the monolithic structure of the Soviet empire.

For a time during the Hungarian Revolution, the ranks in the Soviet leadership had closed and Khrushchev personally as well as his opponents must bear the responsibility for the ruthless intervention in November 1956. The scars of dissent remained, however, and in the indictment of Molotov by the Central Committee, his Yugoslav and Austrian policies are the subject of particular criticism. Hungary goes unmentioned.

Moscow's future policy toward the European Satellites remains unresolved. Though Molotov was vigorously attacked for his mistaken attitude, Khrushchev, since the Polish and Hungarian revolts, has feared the contagious influence of granting more freedom anywhere. Certainly none of the Soviet leaders cares to remember the precepts of Lenin, who had this to say in 1917:

If Finland, if Poland, if the Ukraine break away from Russia there is nothing bad about that. . . . No nation can be free if it oppresses other nations.

These were the major issues on which Khrushchev fought for, and by an eyelash won, the leadership of the Soviet Union.

There are many other burning problems facing the new group ruling the Soviet Union. First of all, they have the problem of East-West contacts, which for propaganda purposes at least they strongly claim to favor. Can the leaders really permit the people of the U.S.S.R. to have knowledge of the facts of life? Do they dare open up to the press, to radio, to television?

Except for certain supervised and guided tours, the answer to this so far seems to be "no." We can guess how frightened they are from their panicky warnings to Soviet youth about being deceived by the words of the American boys and girls who went to Moscow recently for the big Soviet Youth Festival.

Similarly, they do not dare publish such documents as the Khrushchev secret speech, the U.N. report on Hungary, nor the basic attack on Communist doctrine by the Yugoslav, Djilas, in his recently published book, "The New Class." Instead of dealing with such criticisms openly, Soviet leaders try to sweep them under the rug and keep their own people in the dark.

There was recently published in Moscow a highly realistic novel, with the eloquent title *Not By Bread Alone*. It evoked great popular interest in the U.S.S.R. because it showed some of the seamier side of political life and bureaucracy in the Soviet Union today. All the big guns of the Soviet regime began to fire at the author, Dudintsev, and Khrushchev himself recently lambasted the book as misguided and dangerous. It is significant that they have not yet banned it. Probably they were too late in realizing its subtle attack on the foundations of the Communist system.

By and large the bulk of the Russian people still live in a dream world about everything outside the U.S.S.R., and the most tragic part about this is the distorted facts and fancies the Soviet leaders give their own people about the allegedly hostile attitudes of Americans toward them. The exchange of a few controlled travelling delegations is not enough. The barriers to information and knowledge must be torn down.

The Soviet leaders also have to deal with the problems created by their own educational system and by the development of an industrial and technical elite. Under the lash of its pell-mell industrialization program, the U.S.S.R. in the past decade has enormously speeded up the education of the Russian people, particularly in the scientific and technical field. As a result, the U.S.S.R. is turning out hundreds of thousands of graduates of schools corresponding to our high schools and colleges.

It is true that in their educational system they emphasize scientific and technical fields much more than social sciences and the humanities. But knowledge is not an inert substance. It has a way of seeping across lines and into adjacent compartments of learning. The Soviet leaders, I firmly believe, cannot illuminate their scientific lecture halls and laboratories without also letting the light of truth into their history and economics classrooms. Students cannot be conditioned to turning off their analytical processes when the instructor changes a topic.

Student and intellectual unrest is a troublesome challenge to a dictatorship. The Chinese Communists experimented briefly with placating critics by liberalizing their thought-control system—enunciating the doctrine known as "let a hundred flowers bloom, let a hundred schools of thought contend." In the face of the far-reaching criticisms promptly voiced by Chinese intellectuals, the Peiping regime quickly reversed itself and has only a few weeks ago resumed the practice of publicly executing students who dared to suggest that China's ills result in part from flaws in the Communist system itself.

The education which Soviet and Chinese Communist leaders give their people is a dangerous commodity for a dictatorship. Men and women who have their critical faculties sharpened are beginning to question why the Russian people cannot be freed from rigid Communist Party and police-state discipline, given a greater economic share of the fruit of their labors, and allowed to participate—at least by an effective expression of consent—in their own governing.

In the past the Soviets counted particularly upon their ability to appeal with success to the youth and the students. In 1905 Lenin wrote, "We are the party of the future but the future belongs to the young. We are the party of innovation, and it is to the innovators that youth always as to whether this last phase of the French Revolution will be repeated in the case of Soviet Communism. I have no crystal ball answer, but certainly military dictatorship is one of the possible lines of evolution in the Soviet Union.

From this analysis of developments in the Soviet Union, it is fair to conclude that I believe that the old Communist dialectic of Marx, Lenin and even Stalin does not answer the problems of the Soviet Union today— either those of its industrial growth or of its lasting control over the great peoples living within the Soviet Union. It would flow from this that Khrushchev and whoever he may associate with himself in the leadership, assuming he keeps his control for a time, will have to determine how they are going to accomplish this dual task. Will they meet it by further relaxation, thereby increasing the moral and industrial potential of the Soviet Union itself, and the prospects of peace, but risking the loss of the Satellite countries? Will they attempt a reversion to something like Stalinism under another name as some of the tough, uncompromising language and actions from Moscow of recent days would suggest? Or will they be tempted to risk foreign venture with a view to uniting their people and their energies to meet alleged enemies they claim are encircling them?

These are the issues. I would not wish to suggest that what I have referred to as the decline of Marxist Communism has left the Soviet Union materially weak in facing them. The Soviet may be ideologically less menacing, technologically its power is still increasing.

Throughout the entire revolution, once the Communist regime was firmly established in Russia, the emphasis was placed on heavy industry, and on building up the war machine. This has been a constant policy and has been one phase of Soviet life that has not been affected by changing leaders or interpretations of Communist ideology. After all, the men who are at the helm in the Soviet Union are not the original revolutionary heroes. Khrushchev and Mikoyan and their henchmen belong to the ever-present class of political careerists who see in a revolutionary movement the path to power and privilege. They did not make the revolution, like Lenin. It made them, and they want above all else to preserve their positions.

While Marxism at one time or another has invaded most segments of Soviet life, including the army with its political commissar and indoctrination agents, those who have planned the Soviet military buildup have been little hampered by it. In their concentration on the fields of nuclear energy, aircraft design and construction, and the development of guided missiles, they experienced little ideological interference except during brief periods of Stalin's last hectic days.

Take, for example, the case of guided missiles. Here they never ceased work from the days of 1945 when they took over the German missile installation at Peenemunde with its rockets of a range between 150 to 200 miles. Now we know they have developed modern missiles of many times the power and efficiency of the German wartime models.

The Soviet Union which we face today presents a series of contradictions. Its leader has practically unrestrained power except for such control as the military may exercise, backed by a formidable war machine—a leader committed by his express policies to improve the lot of his people, and presumably committed also to relax the harsh controls of Stalin which he has described so vividly himself and which he purports to abhor.

At the same time, this leader, Khrushchev, faces the dilemma that any substantial relaxation at home or abroad, given the nature of the Communist dictatorship as it has evolved, may spell his own downfall. For he faces, and he knows it, a people who are questioning the basic tenets of Marxist Communism, and in particular a student body that is becoming more and more vocal in demanding the truth and may not be satisfied with half measures.

The Communist leaders are also facing a growing body of highly educated, technologically competent men and women in the field of industrial management and production. It may prove impossible for them to stop the growing wave of intellectual unrest in the Soviet Union. Khrushchev cannot turn back education or stop technological development and keep the U.S.S.R. a great power.

Yet Khrushchev seems to be in a hurry to solve a whole series of such problems as I have described and gain the personal success necessary to maintain his own position. In addition to all this, he has deeply committed himself in certain foreign adventures, particularly in the Middle East—partly, it may be assumed, to distract attention from problems at home and in the Satellites. All this rightfully makes us cautious in our judgments and does not suggest that there are any quick or easy ways out in our relations with the U.S.S.R.

But over the longer range, we can rest assured that revolutionary Communist tyranny cannot provide a final answer or a satisfactory answer to the needs of a civilized community. No power on earth can restore the myth that Communism is the wave of the future after 10 million Hungarians, after a decade of experience with it, and at the risk of their lives, gave it such a resounding vote of no confidence. The people of Russia, if given the time to continue their evolution to freedom out of the narrow bounds of Communist dictatorship, will themselves help to find a peaceful answer.

Chapter 20

Twilight of Totalitarianism?

A *seriously controverted question today—and one that is pregnant with consequences for much of the world—is whether we are witnessing, since the death of Stalin, the twilight of totalitarianism in the U.S.S.R. or simply a form of relaxation which will leave the basic foundations of Soviet despotism undisturbed.*

This is not simply a matter of idle speculation, since our policies must necessarily be affected by our evaluation of the nature, scope, future course, and durability of Soviet totalitarian controls.

The three contributors to this discussion present variant and, to some extent, conflicting positions.

RUSSIA IN TRANSITION

Isaac Deutscher*

1

Who would still maintain nowadays that Soviet society has emerged from the Stalin era in a state of petrified immobility, decayed and incapable of inner movement and change? Yet, only a short time ago this was the opinion commonly accepted; and a writer who defied it and claimed that, despite all appearances to the contrary, the Soviet universe did move seemed to argue from mere faith or wishfulness. Yes, the Soviet universe does move. At times it even looks as if it were still a nebula unsteadily

* Author of *Stalin: A Political Biography,* and *The Prophet Armed.* Reprinted by permission of Coward-McCann, Inc., from chapter 1 of *Russia in Transition* by Isaac Deutscher. Copyright 1957 by Hamish Hamilton, Ltd. This essay was written January 1, 1957.

540

revolving around a shifting axis—a world in the making, rumbling with the tremor of inner dislocation and searching for balance and shape.

It is the twilight of totalitarianism that the U.S.S.R. is living through. Again, how many times have not "political scientists" told us that a society which has succumbed to totalitarian rule cannot disenthrall itself by its own efforts, and that such is "the structure of Soviet totalitarian power" (the like of which, it was said, history has never seen before!) that it can be overthrown only from the outside by mighty blows delivered in war. Yet, it is as a result of developments within the Soviet society that Stalinism is breaking down and dissolving; and it is the Stalinists themselves who are the subverters of their own orthodoxy.

It is nearly four years now since the U.S.S.R. has ceased to be ruled by an autocrat. None of Stalin's successors has "stepped into Stalin's shoes." Government by committee has taken the place of government by a single dictator. A French writer, still somewhat incredulous of the change, recalls that in Rome, when a Caesar died or was assassinated, his head was struck off the public monuments but "Caesar's body" was left intact until another head was put on it. Yet, in Moscow not one but many heads have been put on Caesar's body; and perhaps even the "body" is no longer the same. It is pointless to argue that it makes no difference for a nation whether it lives under the tyranny of an autocrat or under that of a "collective leadership." The essence of collective leadership is dispersal, diffusion, and therefore limitation of power. When government passes from one hand into many hands it can no longer be exercised in the same ruthless and unscrupulous manner in which it was exercised before. It becomes subject to checks and balances.

It is not only Caesar's head that has vanished. What used to be his strong arm, the power of the political police, is broken. The people are no longer paralyzed by fear of it. The stupendous machine of terror which overwhelmed so many people with so many false accusations and extorted so many false confessions of guilt, the machine which looked like an infernal *perpetuum mobile* at last invented by Stalin, has been brought to a standstill. Stalin's successors themselves have stopped it, afraid that even they would be caught by it; and they can hardly bring it back into motion, even if they wished to do so—the rust of moral opprobrium has eaten too deep into its cogs and wheels.

Nearly dissolved is also the Stalinist *univers concentrationnaire,* that grim world of slave labor camps which in the course of several decades sucked in, absorbed, and destroyed Russia's rebellious spirits and minds, leaving the nation intellectually impoverished and morally benumbed. Rehabilitated survivors of the Great Purges of the 1930's have returned from places of exile. There are, unfortunately, few, all too few, of them; and some may be broken and exhausted men. Yet, few as they are and such as they are, they are a leaven in the mind of post-Stalinist society—a reproach and a challenge to its disturbed conscience. Multitudes of other deportees have been allowed to leave concentration camps and to settle as "free workers" in the remote provinces of the north and the east. Temporarily or finally, the nightmare of mass deportations has ceased to haunt Russia.

The mind of the nation has stirred to new activity. Gone are the days when the whole of the Soviet Union was on its knees before the Leader and had to intone the same magic incantations, to believe in the same bizarre myths, and to keep its thoughts tightly closed to any impulse of doubt and criticism. To be sure, it is only slowly and painfully that people recover in their minds from monolithic uniformity and relearn to think for themselves and express their thoughts. Yet, a diversity of opinion, unknown for decades, has begun to show itself unmistakably and in many fields. A fresh gust of wind is blowing through the lecture halls and seminars of universities. Teachers and students are at last discussing their problems in relative freedom from inquisitorial control and dogmatic inhibition. The Stalinist tutelage over science was so barbarous and wasteful, even from the State's viewpoint, that it could no longer be maintained; and so it is perhaps not surprising that scientists should have regained freedom. What is more startling and politically important is the freedom for people to delve into the Soviet Union's recent history—a freedom still limited yet real. In Stalin's days this was the most closely guarded taboo, because the Stalin legend could survive only as long as the annals of the revolution and of the Bolshevik Party remained sealed and hidden away, especially from the young, who could find in their own memories no antidote to it.

Even now the annals have not been thrown open indiscriminately. They are being unsealed guardedly, one by one. The historians reveal their contents only gradually and in small doses. (The history of the October Revolution is still told in such a way that the giant figure of Trotsky is kept out of it—only his shadow is allowed to be shown casually, on the fringe of the revolutionary scene. But if Hamlet is still acted without the Prince of Denmark, the text of the play is becoming more and more authentic, while in Stalin's days the whole play, with the Prince cast as the villain, was apocryphal.) Every tiny particle of historical truth, wrested from the archives, is political dynamite, destructive not only of the Stalin myth proper, but also of those elements of orthodoxy which Stalin's epigoni are anxious to conserve. The old-Bolshevik heresies, of which even the middle-aged Russian of our days has known next to nothing, and the authors of those heresies, the ghostly apostates and traitors of the Stalin era, are suddenly revealed in a new light: the heresies can be seen as currents of legitimate Bolshevik thought and as part and parcel of Russia's revolutionary heritage; and the traitors—as great, perhaps tragic, figures of the revolution.

The rehabilitation, even partial, of past heresy militates against wholesale condemnation of present and future heresy. It corrodes the very core of orthodoxy to such an extent that the ruling group shrinks from the consequences. But the ruling group is no longer in a position to stop the process of Russia's historical education which forms now the quintessence of her political education.[1]

This is not the place to discuss further the intellectual ferment of the post-Stalin era, described elsewhere in this volume.[2] Suffice it to say, that in its initial phases de-Stalinization has been or was primarily the work of the intelligentsia. Writers, artists, scientists, and historians have been its pioneers. Their demands have coincided, at least in part, with the needs and wishes of the managerial groups and of influential circles in the party leadership. This accounts for the peculiarly limited, administrative-ideological character of the reforms carried out. Yet, as at the turn of the century, the intelligentsia has acted once again as the *burevestnik,* the storm finch. Its restlessness augurs the approach of an upheaval in which much wider social forces are likely to come into play.

2

The new working class which has emerged from the melting-pot of forced industrialization is potentially a political power of a magnitude hitherto unknown in Russian history. There are now in the U.S.S.R. four to five times as many industrial workers as there were before the revolution and even in the late 1920's. Large scale industry then employed not much more than three million wage laborers. It now employs at least fifteen million (not counting transport workers, state farm laborers, the medium and higher technical personnel, etc.). The working class has not only grown in size; its structure and outlook, too, have changed. These are not the old Russian workers who combined exceptional political *élan* with technological backwardness and semi-illiteracy. This, in its main sections, is a highly advanced working class which avidly assimilates skills and absorbs genreal knowledge. Among the young who now enter industry many have gone through secondary education. The change may be illustrated by the following comparison: about a quarter of a century ago as many as 75 per cent of the workers employed in engineering were classed as unskilled and only 25 per cent as skilled. In 1955 the proportion was exactly reversed: 75 per cent were skilled men and only 25 per cent re-

---

[1] It is difficult to find an analogy in any other nation at any time for so close an interdependence of history and politics as that which exists in the U.S.S.R. at present. The controversies of Soviet historians which preceded the 20th Congress foreshadowed Khrushchev's and Mikoyan's revelations at the Congress; and it was no matter of chance that even before Khrushchev, at the Congress itself, Professor Pankratova, an historian, made one of the most startling pronouncements. Since then the historians' disputes have gone on almost uninterruptedly.

[2] See the essay "Post-Stalinist Ferment of Ideas," p. 52 [of *Russia in Transition*].

mained unskilled. The relation is certainly not the same in other industries: engineering represents the most progressive sector of the economy.
But the situation in this sector is highly significant, if only because engineering employs about one-third of the industrial manpower and accounts
for about one-half of the total gross industrial output of the U.S.S.R.

The power of the Soviet bureaucracy was originally rooted in the
weakness of the working class. The Russian proletariat was strong enough
to carry out a social revolution in 1917, to overthrow the bourgeois regime,
to lift the Bolsheviks to power, and to fight the civil wars to a victorious
conclusion. But it was not strong enough to exercise actual proletarian
dictatorship, to control those whom it had lifted to power, and to defend
its own freedom against them. Here is indeed the key to the subsequent
evolution or "degeneration" of the Soviet regime. By 1920-1921 the small
working class which had made the revolution shrank to nearly half its size.
(Not more than 1½ to 2 million men remained then in industrial employment.) Of the rest many had perished in the civil wars; others had become
commissars or civil servants; and still others had been driven by famine
from town to country and never returned. Most factories were idle. Their
workers, unable to earn a living by productive work, traded in black markets, stole goods from the factories, and became *déclassés*. As the old landlord class and the bourgeoisie had been crushed, as the peasantry was inherently incapable of assuming national leadership, and as the industrial
working class was half dispersed and half demoralized, a social vacuum
arose in which the new bureaucracy was the only active, organized, and
organizing element. It filled the political vacuum and established its own
preponderance.

Then, in the course of the 1920's, the working class was reassembled
and reconstituted; and in the 1930's, the years of forced industrialization,
its numbers grew rapidly. By now, however, the workers were powerless
against the new Leviathan state. The bureaucracy was firmly entrenched
in its positions, it accumulated power and privileges and held the nation
by the throat. The working class could not at first derive strength from
its own growth in numbers. That growth became, on the contrary, a new
source of weakness. Most of the new workers were peasants, forcibly uprooted from the country, bewildered, lacking habits of industrial life, capacity for organization, political tradition, and self-confidence. In the
turmoil of the Second World War and of its aftermath, society was once
again thrown out of balance. It is only in this decade, in the 1950's, that
the vastly expanded working class has been taking shape and consolidating
as a modern social force, acquiring an urban industrial tradition, becoming aware of itself, and gaining confidence.

This new working class has so far lagged behind the intelligentsia in
the political drive against Stalinism, although it has certainly had every
sympathy with the intelligentsia's demand for freedom. However, the

workers cannot possibly remain content with the administrative-ideological limitations of the post-Stalinist reform. They are certain to go eventually beyond the intelligentsia's demands and to give a distinctive proletarian meaning and content to the current ideas and slogans of democratization. Their thoughts and political passions are concentrating increasingly on the contradiction between their nominal and their actual position in society. Nominally, the workers are the ruling power in the nation. In the course of forty years this idea has been ceaselessly and persistently instilled into their minds. They could not help feeling edified, elevated, and even flattered by it. They cannot help feeling that they should, that they ought, and that they must be the ruling power. Yet, everyday experience tells them that the ruling power is the bureaucracy, not they. The bureaucracy's strong arm has imposed on them the Stalinist labor discipline. The bureaucracy alone has determined the trend of economic policy, the targets for the Five-Year Plans, the balance between producer and consumer goods, and the distribution of the national income. The bureaucracy alone has fixed the differential wage scales and wage rates creating a gulf between the upper and the lower strata. The bureaucracy has pulled the wires behind the Stakhanovite campaigns and, under the pretext of socialist emulation, set worker against worker and destroyed their solidarity. And, under Stalin's orders, it was the bureaucracy, aided by the labor aristocracy, that conducted a frenzied and relentless crusade against the instinctive egalitarianism of the masses.

Until recently the bureaucracy itself was subject to Stalin's whimsical terror and suffered from it even more than the working class did. This veiled, up to a point, the contrast between the theoretical notion of the proletarian dictatorship and the practice of bureaucratic rule. In their prostration before the Leader, worker and bureaucrat seemed to be equals. All the stronger did the beginning of de-Stalinization expose the contrast in their real positions. De-Stalinization was, at first, an act of the bureaucracy's self-determination. The civil servant and the manager were its first beneficiaries: freed from the Leader's despotic tutelage they began to breathe freely. This made the workers acutely aware of their own inferiority. However, the bureaucracy could not for any length of time reserve the benefits of de-Stalinization exclusively for itself. Having emancipated itself from the old terror, it willy-nilly relieved of it society as a whole. The workers too ceased to be haunted by the fear of the slave labor camp. Since that fear had been an essential ingredient of the Stalinist labor discipline, its disappearance entailed the end of that discipline. Malenkov's government proclaimed the obsolescence of the Stalinist labor code. That Draconic code had played its part in breaking the masses of the proletarianized peasantry to regular habits of industrial work; and only to those masses, bewildered and helpless, could it be applied. Vis-à-vis the new working class it was becoming increasingly useless and ineffective. A freer climate at the factory bench had indeed become the prerequisite for a steady rise in labor productivity and higher industrial efficiency.

Nor could the worker remain content merely with the relaxation of factory discipline. He began to use his freshly won freedom to protest against the pre-eminence of the managerial groups and of the bureaucracy. By far the most important phenomenon of the post-Stalin era is the evident revival of the long-suppressed egalitarian aspirations of the working class.

From this point the workers' approach to de-Stalinization begins to diverge from that of the intelligentsia. The men of the intelligentsia have been intensely interested in the political "liberalization," but socially they are conservative. It is they who have benefited from the inequalities of the Stalin era. Apart from individuals and small groups, who may rise intellectually above their own privileged position and sectional viewpoint, they can hardly wish to put an end to those inequalities and to upset the existing relationship between various groups and classes of Soviet society. They are inclined to preserve the social *status quo*. For the mass of the workers, on the other hand, the break with Stalinism implies in the first instance a break with the inequalities fostered by Stalinism.

It should not be imagined that the renascent egalitarianism of the masses is politically articulate. It has not yet found any clear and definite expression on the national scale. We know of no resolutions adopted by trade unions or by workers' meetings protesting against privilege and calling for equality. The workers have not yet been free enough to voice such demands or to make their voices heard. They may not even have been capable of formulating demands as people accustomed to autonomous trade-union and political acitvity would do. It is more than thirty years since they had ceased to form and formulate opinions, to put them forward at meetings, to stand up for them, to oppose the views of others, to vote, to carry the day, or to find themselves outvoted. It is more than thirty years since as a class they had ceased to have any real political life of their own. They could hardly recreate it overnight, even if those in power had put no obstacles in their way. Consequently the new egalitarianism expresses itself only locally, fitfully, and incoherently. It is only semiarticulate. It works through exercising pressure at the factory level. Its manifestations are fragmentary and scattered. Yet it makes itself felt as the social undertone to de-Stalinization, an undertone growing in volume and power.

Many recent acts of official policy have clearly reflected this egalitarian pressure from below. For the first time since 1931 the government has tackled a basic reform of wages; and although the reform has not yet taken final shape, the reversal of the antiegalitarian trend is already clearly discernible. Hitherto the piece rate has formed the basis of the whole wage system: at least 75 per cent of all industrial wages were, until quite recently, made up of piece rates, because these lend themselves much more easily than time rates to extreme differentiation. Within this system the so-called progressive piece rate was favored most of all, a method of payment under which the Stakhanovite producing 20, 30, and 40 per cent above the norm of output earned not just 20, 30, and 40 per cent more than the basic pay, but 30, 50, 80 per cent or even more. This method of payment, glorified in Stalin's days, as the supreme achievement of socialism, has now been declared as harmful to the interests of industry and workers alike. The grossly overadvertised Stakhanovite "movement" has been given a quiet burial. The time wage has again become the basic form of payment. It would be preposterous to see in this a triumph of socialism. Both the piece wage and the time wage—but the former much more than the latter —are essentially capitalist forms of payment; and it is only a measure of the retrograde character of some aspects of Stalin's labor policy that the return to the time wage should be regarded as progress. Yet progress it marks. It shows that workers no longer respond to the crude Stalinist appeal to their individual acquisitiveness which disrupted their class solidarity and that the government has been obliged to take note of this.

The year 1956 brought two further significant acts of labor policy: a rise by about one third in the lower categories of salaries and wages; and a new pension scheme with rates of pensions drastically revised in favor of workers and employees with low earnings. While in the Stalin era the purpose of almost every government decree in this field was to increase and widen the discrepancies between lower and higher earnings, the purpose of the recent increase has been to reduce such discrepancies.

The reawakening egalitarianism has likewise affected the government's educational policy. Beginning with the school year 1956-1957, all tuition fees have been abolished. It should be recalled that these had first been abolished early in the revolution, when Lenin's government pledged itself to secure free education for all. Poverty, cultural backwardness, and extreme scarcity of educational facilities made universal free education unattainable. The pledge remained nevertheless an important declaration of purpose. Stalin then reintroduced fees for secondary and academic education. Only the bureaucracy and the labor aristocracy could afford paying; and so education was almost defiantly reserved as a privilege for the children of the privileged. The tuition fee extended to the ranks of the young generation the social differences which Stalin's labor policy fostered among their parents. It tended to perpetuate and deepen the new stratification of society. On this ground Stalin's Communist critics, especially Trotsky, charged him with paving the way for a new bourgeoisie. All the more significant is the present abolition of all fees. This renewed pledge of universal free education, given by Stalin's successors, is of far greater practical value than was Lenin's pledge, because it is backed up by a tremendously expanded and still expanding school system. Even so, Soviet society has still a long way to go before it achieves genuine equality in education. Only in the towns are there enough secondary schools to take in all children—in the country there will not be enough of them before 1960 at the earliest. Universal academic education is *Zukunftsmusik*. All the same, the abolition of school fees is the rulers' tribute to the new egalitarianism. . . .

3

Of Stalin it has been said that like Peter the Great he used barbarous means to drive barbarism out of Russia. Of Stalin's successors it may be said that they drive Stalinism out of Russia by Stalinist methods.

The procedures of de-Stalinization are characterized by ambiguity, tortuousness, and prevarication. At first it was allegedly only a matter of doing away with the "cult of the individual," the grotesque adulation of the Leader. When the issue was first posed, in the spring of 1953, even the name of the "individual" who had been the object of the cult was not mentioned; and up to the Twentieth Congress, up to February 1956, the press still extolled the great Apostolic succession of "Marx-Engels-Lenin-Stalin." The cult was abandoned, yet it was kept up. But having made this first step, Stalin's successors could not help making the next one as well. They had to denounce the Leader's "abuses of power." They denounced them piecemeal and shrunk from saying frankly that these were Stalin's abuses. They found a scapegoat for him. As Beria had for fourteen years been Stalin's police chief, the responsibility for many of Stalin's misdeeds could conveniently be placed on him.

For a time this particular scapegoat was constantly held before the eyes of Russia and the world—until it refused to do service. For one thing, Stalin could not be dissociated from the man who had for so long been his police chief. For another, many of the worst "abuses," to mention only the Great Purges of 1936-1938, had occurred before Beria took office in Moscow. The denunciation of Beria implied the denunciation of Stalin himself; and it led directly to it. It was as if the scapegoat had returned from the wilderness to drag the real and the chief sinner down the steep slope. It threatened to drag others as well. Malenkov, Khrushchev, Kaganovich, Molotov, Voroshilov, had all been Beria's close colleagues and associates. The more they revealed of the horrors of the past, the stronger grew their urge to exonerate themselves and to find a new scapegoat—this time for themselves. That new scapegoat was none other than Stalin. "It was all his fault, not ours" was the *leitmotif* of Khrushchev's secret speech at the Twentieth Congress. "It was all his fault," *Pravda* then repeated a hundred times, "but nothing has ever been wrong with our leading cadres and with the working of our political institutions."

It was a most hazardous venture for Stalin's ex-associates to try and acquit themselves at his expense. This scapegoat too—and what a giant of a scapegoat it is!—is returning from the wilderness to drag them down. And so they are driven to try to re-exonerate Stalin, at least in part, in order to exonerate themselves.

Such attempts at "tricking history" and playing blindman's buff with it are all in good Stalinist style. In effect, Stalin's successors avoid telling the truth even when, on the face of it, truth should reflect credit on them. Their first move on their assumption of power was to repudiate the "doctors' plot." Yet, to this day they have not told the real story of that last great scandal of the Stalin era. What was hidden behind it? Who, apart from Stalin, staged it? And—for what purpose? Khrushchev's "secret" speech has not yet been published in the Soviet Union, a year after it was made; [nor by the date of publication of this volume]; and this despite the fact that its contents have in the meantime been shouted from the housetops outside the Soviet Union. Special commissions have been at work to review the many purges and trials and to rehabilitate and set free innocent victims. But their work has remained a secret. Not even a summary account of it has been published to explain officially the background, the motives, the dimensions, and the consequences of the purges. Masses of slave laborers have been released from concentration camps; and many prisoners have regained freedom under a series of amnesties. Yet, not a single announcement has been made to say how many convicts have benefited from the amnesties and how many have left the concentration camps. The present rulers are so afraid of revealing the real magnitude of the wrongs of the Stalin era, that they dare not even claim credit for righting the wrongs. They must behave like that "honest thief" who cannot return stolen goods to their owner otherwise than stealthily and under the cover of night.

How many of the "stolen goods" have in fact been returned?

The break with Stalinism was initiated under the slogan of a return to the "Leninist norms of inner party democracy." The Twentieth Congress was supposed to have brought about the practical restitution of those norms. Yet to anyone familiar with Bolshevik history it is obvious that this was far from being true. The Congress adopted all its resolutions by unanimous vote, in accordance with the best Stalinist custom. No *open* controversy or *direct* clash of opinion disturbed the smooth flow of its monolithic "debates." Not one in a hundred or so speakers dared to criticize Khrushchev or any other leader on any single point. Not a single major issue of national or international policy was in fact placed under discussion.

The change in the inner party regime has so far consisted in this: major decisions of policy are taken not by Khrushchev alone and not even by the eleven members of the Presidium but by the Central Committee which consists of 125 members (or 225 if alternate members are included). Inside that body free debate has apparently been restored; and differences of opinion have been resolved by majority vote. Only to this extent have

"Leninist norms" been re-established. But under Lenin the differences in the Central Committee were, as a rule, not kept secret from the party or even from the nation at large; and the rank and file freely expressed their own views on them. The post-Stalinist Central Committee has never yet aired its differences in the hearing of the whole party. Thus, only the upper hierarchy appears to be managed more or less in the Leninist way. The lower ranks are still ruled in the Stalinist manner, although far less harshly. In the long run the party cannot remain half free and half slave. Eventually the higher ranks will either share their newly won freedom with the lower ranks, or else they themselves must lose it.

4

Within the Soviet Union de-Stalinization has so far been carried out as a reform *from above,* a limited change initiated and controlled at every stage by those in power. This state of affairs has not been accidental. It has reflected the condition of Soviet society both *"above"* and *"below,"* in the first years after Stalin.

Above—powerful interests have obstructed reform, striving to restrict it to the narrowest possible limits, and insisting that the ruling group should in all circumstances hold the initiative firmly and not allow its hands to be forced by popular pressure. The attitude of the bureaucracy is by its very nature contradictory. The need to rationalize the working of the state machine and to free social relations from anachronistic encumbrances has induced the bureaucracy to favor reform. Yet, at the same time the bureaucracy has been increasingly afraid that this may imperil its social and political preponderance. The labor aristocracy has been troubled by a similar dilemma: It has been not less than the rest of the workers interested in doing away with the old terroristic labor discipline; but it cannot help viewing with apprehension the growing force of the egalitarian mood; and it resents the changes in labor policy which benefit the lower-paid workers without bringing compensatory advantages to the higher-paid. The various managerial groups and the military officers' corps are guided by analogous considerations; and they are, above all, anxious to maintain their authority. The attitude of these groups may be summed up thus: Reform from above? Yes, by all means. A revival of spontaneous movements from below? No, a thousand times no!

Below—everything has so far also favored reform from above. Toward the end of the Stalin era the mass of the people craved for a change but could do nothing to achieve it. They were not merely paralyzed by terror. Their political energy was hamstrung. No nation-wide, spontaneous yet articulate movements rose from below to confront the rulers with demands, to wrest concessions, to throw up new programs and new leaders, and to alter the balance of political forces. In 1953-1955 political prisoners and deportees struck in the remoteness of subpolar concentration camps, and these strikes led to the eventual dissolution of the camps. This was a struggle on the submerged fringe of the national life; but whoever has any sense of Russian history must have felt that when political prisoners were in a position to resume, after so long an interval, the struggle for their rights, Russia was on the move. Then the year 1956 brought much agitation to the universities of Leningrad, Moscow, and other cities. However, these and similar stirrings, symptomatic though they were, did not as yet add up to any real revival of the political energies in the depth of society.

It is not only that the working class had lost the habits of independent organization and spontaneous action. Stalinism had left a gap in the nation's political consciousness. It takes time to fill such a gap. It should be added that the gap is only relative. It is not by any means a vacuum. By spreading education, by arousing the people's intellectual curiosity, and by keeping alive the socialist tradition of the revolution, be it in a distorted and ecclesiastically dogmatic version, Stalinism has in fact accumulated many of the elements that should eventually go into the making of an extraordinarily high political consciousness. But Stalinism also forcibly prevented these elements from coalescing and cohering into an active social awareness and positive political thought. It increased enormously the potential political capacities of the people and systematically prevented the potential from becoming actual. Stalinist orthodoxy surrounded the nation's enriched and invigorated mind with the barbed wire of its canons. It inhibited people from observing realities, comparing them, and drawing conclusions. It intercepted inside their brains, as it were, every reflex of critical thought. It made impossible the communication of ideas and genuine political intercourse between individuals and groups. De-Stalinization has given scope to these constrained and arrested reflexes and has opened for them some channels of communication. This does not alter the fact that the people entered the new era in a state of political disability, confusion and inaction; and that any immediate change in the regime, or even in the political climate, could come only through reform from above.

Reform from above could be the work of Stalinists only. Had any of the old-Bolshevik oppositions—Trotskyist, Zinovievist, and Bukharinist—survived till this day, Khrushchev, Bulganin, Voroshilov & Company would surely have long since been removed from power and influence; and anti-Stalinists would have carried out de-Stalinization wholeheartedly and consistently. But the old oppositions had been exterminated; and new ones could not form themselves and grow under Stalinist rule. Yet the break with Stalinism had become a social and political necessity for the Soviet Union; and necessity works through such human material as it finds available. Thus, the job which it should have been the historic right and privilege of authentic anti-Stalinists to tackle has fallen to the Stalinists themselves, who cannot tackle it otherwise than halfheartedly and hypocritically. They have to undo much of their life's work in such a way as not to bring about their own undoing. Paradoxically, circumstances have forced Malenkov and Khrushchev to act, *up to a point,* as the executors of Trotsky's political testament. Their de-Stalinization is like the "dog's walking on his hinder legs." It is not done well; but the wonder is that it is done at all![3] . . . No one, however, can foresee the actual rhythm of historic developments. In moments of great crises spontaneous mass movements *do* run ahead of all political groups, even the most radical ones, and of their programs and methods of action. So it was in Russia in February 1917. The workers then found in the Soviets, the Councils of *their* deputies, the institutions within which they learned to harmonize impulse and thought, to test conflicting programs, and to choose leaders. Of those institutions Stalinist Russia preserved no more than the name and the dead shells. Yet in the memory of the working class the Soviets have survived as *the* instruments of socialist government and self-government, *the* organs of a "workers' state." Even in Hungary, amid all the confusion of revolution and counterrevolution, the insurgent workers hastily formed their Councils. Any political revival in the working class of the U.S.S.R. is almost certain to lead to a revival of the Soviets which will once again become the testing ground of political programs, groups, and leaders, and the meeting place of spontaneous movements and political consciousness.

Whatever the future holds in store, a whole epoch is coming to a close— the epoch in the course of which the stupendous industrial and educational advance of the U.S.S.R. was accompanied by deep political lethargy and torpor in the masses. Stalinism did not and could not create that state of torpor; it spawned on it and sought to perpetuate it but was essentially its product. Basically, the apathy of the masses resulted from the extraordinary expenditure of all their energies in the great battles of the revolution. The aftermath of the French revolution was likewise one of a deadening lassitude in which the people "unlearned freedom," as Babeuf, who was so close to the masses, put it. Christian Rakovsky, recalling in his exile at Astrakhan in 1928, Babeuf's remark, added that it took the French forty years to relearn freedom. It has taken the Soviet people not less time—but there is no doubt that they are at last relearning freedom.

[3] History knows quite a few instances in which necessity worked through the most unsuitable human material when none other was available. Of course, whenever conservative rulers had to carry out progressive reforms, their work was self-contradictory and patchy; and it accumulated difficulties for the future. In my *Russia: What Next?* (1953), analyzing the social circumstances which would drive Stalin's successors to break with Stalinism, I compared their position with that of Czar Alexander II, the First Landlord of All the Russias, who, in conflict with the feudal landlord class and with himself, emancipated Russia's peasants from serfdom. Another example is Bismarck, the leader of the Junker class who transformed and adapted feudal Germany to the needs of bourgeois development. . . .

THE DURABILITY OF SOVIET DESPOTISM

BERTRAM D. WOLFE*

At every turn the historian encounters the unpredictable: contingency; historical accident; biological accident intruding itself into history, as when the death of a history-making person brings a change of direction; changes of mood; emergence of new situations; sudden leaps that seem to turn an accretion of little events into a big one; the complicated interaction of multiple determinants on every event; the unintended consequences of intended actions.

Still, history is not *so* open that any event is just as likely as any other. As in the flux of things we note continuing structures, as in biology we note heredity as well as variation and mutation, so in history there is an inter-relation between continuity and change.

Though all lands go through a history, and all orders and institutions are subject to continuous modification and ultimate transformation, there are some social orders or systems that are more markedly dynamic, more open, more mutable, even self-transforming, while others exhibit marked staying powers, their main outlines continuing to be discernibly the same through the most varied vicissitudes.

It may be difficult to determine except in retrospect just when a system may be said to change in ways so fundamental as to signify its transformation; still, it is possible and necessary to distinguish between self-conserving and self-transforming systems, between relatively open and relatively closed societies, and between changes so clearly of a secondary order that they may be designated within-system changes, and those so clearly fundamental that they involve changes in the system or basic societal structure. That this distinction may in practice be hard to make, that there may be gradations and borderline cases and sudden surprises, does not relieve us of this obligation. Merely to reiterate endlessly that all things change, without attempting to make such distinctions, is to stand helpless before history-in-the-making, helpless to evaluate and helpless to react.

* Author of *Three Who Made a Revolution; Six Keys to the Soviet System;* and *Khrushchev and Stalin's Ghost.* The selection is reprinted from the article by the same title in *Commentary*, Vol. 24 (August 1957), pp. 93-103. By permission of *Commentary* and the author. The article was first presented as a paper to open a Conference on Changes in Soviet Society Since Stalin's Death, held June 24 to 29, 1957, at Oxford University, under the sponsorship of St. Antony's College in association with the Congress for Cultural Freedom.

If we look at the Roman Empire, say from the time of Julius Caesar to the time of Julian the Apostate, or perhaps from Augustus to Romulus Augustulus, we can perceive that for three or four centuries, despite its many vicissitudes and changes, it continued in a meaningful and determinable sense to be the Roman Empire. In similar fashion we can easily select a good half millennium of continuity in the Byzantine Empire. Or if we take one of the most dynamic regions, Western Europe, in one of its more dynamic periods, we can note that monarchical absolutism had a continuity of several centuries. This is the more interesting because monarchical absolutism, though it was one of the more stable and monopolistically exclusive power systems of the modern Western world, was a *multi-centered system* in which the monarch was checked and limited by his need of support from groups, corporations, and interests that were organized independently of the central power: the castled, armed, and propertied nobility; the Church with its spiritual authority; the burghers of the wealthy, fortified towns.

It is the presence of these independent centers of corporate organization that makes Western monarchical absolutism an exception among the centralized, long-lasting power systems. It was these limiting forces that managed to exact the charters and constitutions, the right to determine size and length of service of armed levies, size and purpose of monetary contributions, thus ultimately transforming the absolute monarchy into the limited, constitutional monarchy of modern times. And it is from our own Western history, with its exceptional evolution, that we derive many of our unconscious preconceptions as to the inevitability, sweep, and comparative ease of change. To correct our one-sided view it is necessary to compare the characteristics of multi-centered Western absolutism with other, more "complete" and "perfected" forms of single-centered power and despotism.*

In the *samoderzhavie* of Muscovy we find a more truly single-centered power structure, stronger, more completely centralized, more monopolistic, more despotic, more unyielding in its rigid institutional framework than was the absolutism of Western Europe. The Czar early managed to subvert the independent boyars and substitute for them a state-service nobility. The crown possessed enormous crown lands and state serfs. Bondage, both to the state and to the state-service nobility, was instituted by the central power and adjusted to the purposes of the recruiting sergeant and the tax-gatherer. When the Emancipation came, in the 19th century, it was a state-decreed "revolution from above" (Alexander's own words for it), and

---

* This comparison is a central part of Karl A. Wittfogel's *Oriental Despotism: A Comparative Study of Total Power* (Yale, 1957). His attention is centered on the countries in which "the state became stronger than society" because of the need to undertake vast state irrigation and flood control works by *corvée* organization of the entire population, with the consequent assumption of enormous managerial functions. But his study is full of insights into modern, industry-based totalitarianism highly suggestive for the purposes of our theme.

carried with it state supervision and the decreeing of collective responsibility to the village *mir*.

To this universal state-service and state-bondage, we must add the features of Caesaro-papism: signifying a Czar and a state-dominated church. And the administrative-military nature of the Russian towns checked the rise of an independent burgher class.

Industrialization, too, was undertaken at the initiative of the state. From Peter I to Nicholas II, there were two centuries of state-ordained and -fostered industrialization; the state-owned and -managed basic industry —mining, metallurgy, munitions, railroad construction and operation—and some commercial monopolies, all crowned with a huge state banking and credit system.

The rudiments of a more multi-centered life were just beginning to develop in this powerful, single-center society when World War I added to the managerial state's concerns the total mobilization of men, money, materials, transport, and industry.

The "model" country in this new form of state enterprise was wartime Germany. The system of total management by the state for total war has been variously, but not very intelligibly, termed "state capitalism" and "state socialism." In any case, Lenin was quick to welcome this development as the "final transition form." In it, as in the heritage from the Czarist managerial autocratic state itself, he found much to build on in making his own transition to the new totalitarianism.

From Ivan the Terrible on, for a period of four centuries, "the state had been stronger than society" and had been ruled from a single center as a military, bureaucratic, managerial state. Amidst the most varied vicissitudes, including a time of troubles, wars, conquests, invasions, peasant insurrections, palace revolutions and revolutions from above, the powerful framework endured. Weakenings of the power structure, even breaches in it, were followed by a swift "restoration" of its basic outlines. When the strains of a world war finally caused its collapse, there came a brief interlude of loosening of the bonds. Then Lenin, even as he revolutionized, likewise "restored" much of the four-century-old heritage. Indeed, it was this "socialist restoration of autocracy" which Plekhanov had warned against, as early as the 1880's, as a danger inherent in the longed-for Russian revolution. He admonished the impatient Populists that unless all the bonds were first loosened and a free "Western" or "bourgeois-democratic" order were allowed to develop and mature, the seizure of power by would-be socialists could not but lead to a restoration of Oriental, autocratic despotism on a pseudo-socialist foundation with a pseudo-socialist "ruling caste." Things would be even worse, he warned Lenin in 1907, if this new "Inca ruling caste of Sons of the Sun" should make the fatal mistake of nationalizing the land, thus tightening even more the chains that bound the peasant to the autocratic state.

The term "Oriental despotism" applied to Russia in the course of this controversy among Russian socialists serves to remind us that there are yet more durable social formations with even greater built-in staying powers than those we have so far noted. These reckon their continuity not in centuries alone but even in millennia. As a Chinese historian once observed to me: "Your Renaissance was a fascinating period. We had seven of them." If we substitute restoration for renaissance, both in the sense of restoration of vigor and restoration of basic structure, he was right. For though China suffered upheavals, invasions, conquests, falls of dynasties, rebellions, interregnums, and times of trouble, a Chinese villager or a Chinese official of the 19th century, if transported to the China of two thousand or more years ago, would have found himself in a familiar institutional and ideological environment.

With the exception of Western monarchical absolutism, what all these enduring social structures had in common was a single power center, a managerial state, a lack of independent social orders and forms of property, an absence of checks on the flow of power to the center and the top, and an overwhelmingly powerful, self-perpetuating institutional framework.

Modern totalitarianism, I believe, is one of these comparatively closed and conservative societies, with a powerful and self-perpetuating institutional framework calculated to assimilate the changes which it intends and those which are forced upon it, in such fashion that—barring explosion from within or battering down from without—they tend to remain *within-system* changes in an enduring system.

At first glance the word conservative may seem out of place in speaking of a society that is organized revolution. And indeed there is a striking difference between Communist totalitarianism and all previous systems of absolute, despotic, undivided (and, in that sense, total) power. For whereas despotism, autocracy, and absolutism were bent on preserving the status quo, Communist totalitarianism is dedicated to "the future." This powerful institutional structure which tolerates no rival centers of organization has a vested interest in keeping things in flux. The omnipotence of state and ideology is maintained by carrying on a permanent revolution. Like Alexander's it is a revolution from above. But unlike Alexander's, its aim is nothing less than to keep a society atomized and to create, as rapidly and as completely as the recalcitrant human material and the refractory surrounding world will permit, a new man, a new society, and a new world.

Like the earlier systems referred to, it possesses a state that is stronger than society. Like them it represents a system of total, in the sense of undivided, power. Like them it lacks any organized and institutionalized checks on the flow of power to the top. Like them, it possesses a state-centered, state-dominated, state-managed, and, for the first time, a completely state-owned economy.

But if the other societies are distinguished by the high specific gravity of state ownership, state control, and state managerial function within the total activity of society, under Communist totalitarianism state ownership and state managerialism aspire to be total in a new sense. In the other cases, we have been contemplating total power in the sense of undivided power: power without significant rival centers of organization. But now, to the concept of *undivided power,* we must add that of *all-embracing power.*

No longer does the state limit itself to being "stronger than society." It now strives to be *coextensive* with society. Whereas the earlier power systems recognized certain limitations on their capacity to run everything, leaving room, for example, for pocket-handkerchief farms and the self-feeding of the *corvée* population, for private arts and crafts unconnected with the managerial concerns of the state, for certain types of private trade, and even finding room for village communal democracy under the watchful eye of the state overseer—what Wittfogel has aptly called "beggars' democracy"—the new totalitarianism strives to atomize society completely, to coordinate the dispersed villages into its centralized power system, to eliminate even the small private parcel of the *kolkhoznik,* already reduced from a "pocket handkerchief" to a mere swatch.

For the first time a total-power system in the earlier sense of undivided and unchallenged power aspires to be totalist or totalitarian in the further sense of converting the state-stronger-than-society into the state-coextensive-with-society.

We cannot deduce much from a comparison with other modern totalitarianisms. For historical and physical reasons Italian Fascism was more totalist in aspiration than in realization. And, though Nazism and Stalinist Communism suggestively moved towards each other, Nazism did not last long enough to complete its evolution. But it did live long enough to dispose of certain illusions concerning the supposed incompatibility of totalitarianism with certain aspects of modern life.

Thus it is widely held that the monopoly of total power and the attempt to embrace the totality of social life and activity are incompatible with the complexity of modern industry and advanced technology. But Germany adopted totalitarianism when it was the foremost country of Europe in industry and technology.

Indeed, it is precisely modern technology, with its all-embracing means of communication, its high-speed transmission of commands and reports and armed force to any point in a country, its mass-communication and mass-conditioning techniques and the like, which for the first time makes it possible for total (undivided) power to aspire to be totalist (all-embracing) power. That is what Herzen foreboded when he wrote: "Some day Jenghis Khan will return with the telegraph." If total power tends to arise wherever the state is stronger than society, totalitarian power can aspire to prevail over a great area and in great depth only where the state is both stronger than society and in possession of all the resources of modern technology.

Closely akin to the illusion of the incompatibility of totalitarianism with modern technology is the view that totalitarianism is "in the long run" incompatible with universal literacy, with advanced technological training, and with widespread higher or secondary-school education. Once more it is Germany that serves to remind us that one of the most highly literate and technologically trained peoples in the history of man adopted totalitarianism. Nay more, modern totalitarianism *requires* that everybody be able to read so that all can be made to read the same thing at the same moment. Not the ability to read, but the ability to choose between alternative types of reading, is a potential—and only a potential—liberating influence.

II

When Stalin died in 1953, Bolshevism was fifty years old. Its distinctive views on organization, centralization, and the guardianship or dictatorship of a vanguard or elite date from Lenin's programmatic writings of 1902 (*Where to Begin; What Is to Be Done?*). His separate party machine, which he controlled with an authoritarian hand, dates from the Bolshevik-Menshevik split of 1903 in the Russian Social Democratic party.

During these fifty years Bolshevism had had only two authoritative leaders, each of whom set the stamp of his personality upon it. Lenin, as we have suggested, inherited much from Czarist autocracy, yet his totalitarianism is different in principle from the old Muscovite despotism. He regarded himself as an orthodox Marxist, building upon and enlarging some aspects of Marx's conceptions while ignoring, altering, or misrepresenting others. His Marxism was so different from Marx's that a not unfriendly commentator, Charles Rappoport, called it *Marxisme à la Tartare*. Stalin's Leninism, in turn, differed enough from Lenin's that we might term it *Marxisme à la mode caucasienne*. Yet there is discernibly more continuity between Stalin and Lenin than between Lenin and Marx. The changes Stalin introduced involved the continuation and enlargement of certain elements in Lenin's methods and conceptions, along with the alteration of others. He inherited and used, now in Leninist, now in his own "Stalinist" fashion, an institutional framework involving a party machine, a state machine, a doctrine of infallibility, an ideology, and the determination to extend the totalization of power, to transform the Russian into the "New Communist Man," and win the world for Communism.

With Stalin's death, once more there are new leaders or a new leader. It is impossible to believe that this new personal imprint will not make alterations in Stalinism as Stalin did in Leninism.

But it seems to me useful, after four years of unsystematic talk about changes, that we should remind ourselves that the "new men" are not so new, that they have inherited a going concern, and that actually we are confronting changes within a single-centered, closed, highly centralized society run by a power that is both undivided and all-embracing. And we should remind ourselves, too, that such societies as I have classed it with have tended to exhibit built-in staying powers and a perdurability despite changes like the death of a despot, an oligarchical interregnum, or a struggle for succession.

These "new men" are, of course, Stalin's men. They would not now have any claim to power over a great nation were it not that they managed to be the surviving close lieutenants at the moment of Stalin's death. It is my impression that they are smallish men. There is a principle of selection in personal despotisms which surrounds the despot with courtiers, sycophants, executants, and rules out original and challenging minds. This almost guarantees a crisis of succession where there is no system of legitimacy, until a new dictator emerges. Moreover, the heirs are no longer young (Khrushchev is sixty-three), so that a fresh crisis of succession may well supervene before the present muted and restricted crisis is over.

I would not write these "smallish men" too small, however, for when you have a sixth of the earth, 200,000,000 population, and a total state economy and a great empire to practice on, you learn other trades besides that of courtier or faction lieutenant. Even so, not one of them at present exhibits the originality and the high charge of energy and intellect that characterized Lenin, or the grosser but no less original demonic force of Stalin.

Whenever a despot dies, there is a universal expectation of change. The new men have had to take account of it, and have taken advantage of it to introduce changes which the old tyrant made seem desirable even to his lieutenants: they have taken advantage of the expectation of change to rationalize elements of a system which has no organized, independent forces which might change it from below, and to make limited concessions while they are consolidating their power. But the institutional framework they have inherited is one they intend to maintain.

Some parts of this power machine are now more than a half century old, others date from 1917, others from the consolidation of the Stalinist regime in industry, agriculture, politics, and culture in the 30's. But even these last have been established for more than two decades.

What the epigoni have inherited is no small heritage: a completely atomized society;* a monolithic, monopolistic party; a single-party state; a regime of absolute force supplemented by persuasion or by continuous psychological warfare upon its people; a managerial bureaucracy accustomed to execute orders (with a little elbow room for regularized evasion); a centrally managed, totally state-owned and state-regulated economy including farms, factories, banks, transport and communications, and all trade domestic and foreign; an established dogmatic priority for the branches of

* This does not apply to the Soviet empire but only to the Soviet Union. In general I have omitted any consideration of the empire here.

industry which underlie the power of the state; a bare subsistence economy for the bulk of the producers; a completely statized and "collectivized" agriculture which, though it has never solved the problem of productivity, threatens to reduce even the small parcel to a mere "garden adornment"; a powerful, if one-sided, forced tempo industry centralized even beyond the point of rationality from the standpoint of totalitarianism itself; the techniques and momentum of a succession of Five Year Plans of which the present is the sixth; a completely managed and controlled culture (except for the most secret recesses of the spirit which even modern technology cannot reach); a monopoly of all the means of expression and communication; a state-owned system of "criticism"; an infallible doctrine stemming from infallible authorities, interpreted and applied by an infallible party led by an infallible leader or a clique of infallible leaders, in any case by an infallible "summit"; a method of advance by zigzags toward basically unchanging goals; a system of promotion, demotion, correction of error, modification of strategy and tactics and elimination of difference by fiat from the summit, implemented by purges of varying scope and intensity; a commitment to continuing revolution from above until the Soviet subject has been remade according to the blueprint of the men in the Kremlin and until Communism has won the world.

It is in this heritage that these men were formed. In this they believe. It is the weight and power and internal dynamics of this heritage that in part inhibit, in part shape such changes as these men undertake, and enter as a powerful influence into the changes which they make involuntarily.

It would require a separate study to attempt an inquiry into what is fundamental to totalitarianism, so that a change in it would represent a "change in the system," and what is of a more superficial order, so that a change may readily be recognized as a "within-system" change.* Here we shall have to limit ourselves to a glance at a few post-Stalin political developments. The first change that obtrudes itself is "collective leadership."

The party statutes do not provide for an authoritative leader, a dictator or *vozhd*. Just as this, the most centralized great power, still professes to be federal, a mere union of autonomous republics, so the party statutes have always proclaimed party democracy and collective leadership.

It was not hard to predict that Stalin's orphaned heirs would proclaim a collective leadership at the moment of his death, even as they began the maneuvers that led to the emergence of a still narrower ruling group (triumvirate, duumvirate) and a muted struggle for the succession. Stalin, too, for a half decade found it necessary to proclaim a collective leadership

---

* At the Oxford Conference to which this paper was presented, Leonard Schapiro offered a brief and simple criterion of distinction between within-system changes and changes in the system. He said: "Any changes which leave undisturbed the monopoly of power by the party and its leaders may be regarded as a 'within-system' change. Any firm limitation upon this monopoly of power would represent a 'change-in-the-system.'"

and pose as its faithful wheelhorse, and took a full decade before he killed his first rivals.

Stalin's successors had the same reasons as he for proclaiming the collective leadership of the Politburo, and some additional ones as well. The harrowing and demoralizing experiences of the 30's, the signs of the beginnings of a new mass purge (in the "poison doctors' case") a few months before Stalin's death, the terror that gripped even his closest collaborators, and their justified fears of each other—all combined to make necessary the proclamation of a "collective leadership."

There is nothing inherently incompatible with total, undivided power, nor with totalitarian, all-embracing power, in the rule of an oligarchy, or in an interregnum between dictators or despots. What is noteworthy here is the swiftness with which the first triumvirate (Malenkov, Molotov, Beria) were demoted, compelled to confess unfitness, and, in the case of Beria, killed. It took Stalin ten years to shed the blood of potential rivals or aspirants to power; Beria disappeared in a few months. In less than two years the skeptical were obliged to recognize that Khrushchev was "more equal than the others" and was making all the important programmatic declarations.* Those who follow the Soviet press can perceive that Khrushchev is already the *Khozyain* (Boss), though not yet the *Vozhd* (Führer, Duce, Charismatic Leader).

This is not to say that Khrushchev must necessarily emerge as the undisputed and authoritative leader in the sense that either Stalin or Lenin was. Combinations and counter-forces in the oligarchy and limitations in his own capacity may check or slow or, in view of his age, even nullify the manifest trend. But triumvirates, duumvirates, directories are notoriously transitional in the succession to a despot where there is no legitimacy in providing a successor, and no checks against the flow of power to the top. Moreover, the whole dynamics of dictatorship calls for a personal dictator, authoritarianism for an authority, infallible doctrine for an infallible interpreter, totally militarized life for a supreme commander, and centralized, undivided, all-embracing, and "messianic" power for a "charismatic" symbol and tenant of authority. Unless the "collective leadership" should broaden instead of narrowing as it already has, unless power should flood down into the basic units of the party (which was not the case even in Lenin's day), and then leak out into self-organizing corporate bodies independent of the state, restoring some initiative to society as against the state—in short, unless the whole trend of totalitarianism is not merely slowed (as may be expected during an interregnum) but actually reversed, there is good reason to regard a "directory" or a "duumvirate" as transitory.

---

* For a time Bulganin made the "purely" economic pronouncements, but that period seems to have ended with the Twentieth Congress.

Both purge and terror were instituted by Lenin and "perfected" and "over-perfected" by Stalin. Leaving on one side the purely personal element (paranoia and relish for vengeance), both purge in the party and terror in society as a whole serve many of the "rational" purposes of the totalitarian regime: the establishment of the infallibility of the party, of its summit, and its doctrine; the maintenance of the party in a "state of grace" (zeal, doctrinal purity, fanatical devotion, discipline, subordination, total mobilization); the atomization of society as a whole; the breaking up of all non-state conformations and centers of solidarity; the turn-over in the elite, demotion of deadwood and promotion of new forces; the supplying of scapegoats for every error and for signaling a change of line; the maintenance of the priority of heavy industry, of forced savings for capital investment, of unquestioned command and relative efficiency in production, of "collectivization" in agriculture, of control in culture, and a number of similar objectives of the totalist state.

All of these institutions have been so well established that to a large extent they are now taken for granted. Stalin himself promised in 1939 that there would never again be a mass purge. Except in the case of the army and the Jewish writers, the purge became physically more moderate, until, with increasing marks of paranoia, Stalin gave every sign of opening another era of mass purge a few months before his death. The first thing the heirs did as they gathered round the corpse was to call off the purge, both because it had no "rational" purpose and because it had threatened to involve most of them.

But it would be a mistake to believe that the "moderated" purge can be dispensed with. In the preparation of the 20th Congress the heirs showed how well they had mastered the "Leninist norms," according to which every congress since the 10th had been prepared for by a prior purge of the party organization. All the regional secretaries and leading committees were "renewed," 37 per cent of those who attended the 19th Congress disappeared from public view, 44 per cent of the Central Committee failed to be elected as delegates or to be re-elected to the new Committee. All we can say is that the purge today resembles those of Stalin's "benign" periods or of Lenin's day. Yet the liquidation of Beria and at least twenty-five of his friends shows that the techniques of the blood purge have not been forgotten. That the party ranks breathe easier and are glad of the self-denying ordinance of the leaders in the struggle for position we do not doubt. But there is no evidence that the party ranks ordered this change, or could do so, or would venture to try.

The terror in society as a whole has also diminished. No longer are there such bloody tasks as forced collectivization to carry through. Habitual obedience, the amnesties and concessions of an interregnum, the shortage of manpower for industry, agriculture, and the army because of continued expansion, and the deficit of wartime births that should now have been reaching the labor age—these and many other things account for the fact that artists and writers, workmen and peasants and managers, do not at this moment feel that public reproof (which they are very quick indeed to heed) must necessarily be followed by incarceration in the concentration camp. In a time of manpower shortages, the fact that the concentration camp is the most wasteful and least productive way of exploiting manpower is especially felt. The camps are gentler now, yet they are there. Their size is shrinking, yet no one dares to propose their abolition or even to take public notice of them. Even as this paper is being prepared, at least one new class of young people, the rebellious student youth, is being moved in increasing numbers into the camps.

The police has been downgraded and, in a regime so in need of naked force, the army has been upgraded: i.e. given more internal political functions. The public prosecutors have been given more control of trials and pre-trial inquisitions—like making the fox the guardian of the chicken coop. There are some other minor legal reforms. Above all there has been much fuss made about a promise to codify and regularize the laws.

This new code was begun in Stalin's last months. It was promised "within sixty days" by Lavrentii Beria when his star seemed in the ascendant. It has not been promulgated yet, four years after Stalin's and almost four years after Beria's death. Sight unseen, we can predict that the new code will not touch the foundations of the totalist state: it will not alter the subservience of courts and laws and prosecutors and judges and police to the will and purposes of the oligarchy or the single leader. It is necessary to remember that any total power, and a fortiori any totalist power, may obey its own laws whenever it suits it to do so without giving those laws power over itself or making them into limitations upon its powers. A power center that is both legislator and administrator and judge and enforcer and even self-pronounced infallible "critic" of its own acts, may declare any activity it pleases a crime. In the Soviet Union, even loyalty to the underlying principles on which the state itself was founded has been declared a degrading crime and punished with incredible cruelty. How easily this totalist state may set aside its laws and negate its most solemn and "binding" promises is evidenced anew—after the proclamation of "socialist legality"—by the sudden repudiation by the "workers' state" of the state debt owed to the workers themselves, without so much as the possibility of anybody making a murmur. The owners of the repudiated bonds, in which they had invested their now wiped out compulsory savings, were even obliged to hold meetings and pass resolutions in which to express their delight at being expropriated.

The longer such a regime endures the more it has need of regularization of the duties and expectations of its subjects, even as it keeps up undiminished its powers of sudden reversal and unpredictable and unlimited intervention. The only guarantee against a totally powerful state is the existence of non-state organizations capable of effective control of or effective pressure on the governmental power. Otherwise, to attempt to check, or limit, or even question is to invite the fury of exemplary punishment.

"Betwixt subject and subject [Locke wrote of the defenders of despotism], they will grant, there must be measures, laws and judgments for their mutual peace and security. But as for the ruler, he ought to be absolute, and is above all such circumstances; because he has the power to do more hurt and wrong, it is right when he does it. To ask how you may be guarded from harm or injury on that side . . . is the voice of faction and rebellion. . . . The very question can scarcely be borne. They are ready to tell you it deserves death only to ask after safety. . . ."

It is well for us to remember that the most despotic rulers have on occasion handed down elaborate law codes. The famous and in many ways justly admired Roman Code was compiled and proclaimed only after the emperor himself had become a god, no longer subject to question or limitation, only to worship. Though laws must multiply and be regularized so that the subjects may know what is expected of them and what they can count on in their relations with each other wherever the central power is unaffected, the lack of independent courts, of independent power groups or corporate bodies, of an independent press and public opinion, deprives these laws of any binding force upon the rulers. In Communist totalitarianism, the place of imperial divinity is taken by the infallibility of doctrine, the dogmatic untouchability of the dictatorship, the infallibility of the masters of the infallible doctrine, and by such spiritual demiurges as "revolutionary consciousness," "historical necessity," and "the interests of the revolution and of the people." Those who *know* where History is going surely have the right and duty to see to it that she goes there.

"The scientific concept, dictatorship," Lenin reminds us with beautiful simplicity, "means neither more nor less than unlimited power, resting directly on force, not limited by anything, not restricted by any laws or any absolute rules. Nothing else but that."

And to Commissar of Justice Kursky, when he was elaborating the first legal code, Lenin wrote:

"[My] draft is rough . . . but the basic thought, I hope, is clear: openly to set forth the proposition straightforward in principle and straightforward politically (and not merely in the narrow juridical sense) which motivates the *essence* and *justification* of terror, its necessity, its limits.

"The court should not eliminate the terror: to promise that would be either to deceive oneself or to deceive others, but should give it a foundation and a legalization in principle, clearly, without falsification and without embellishment. It is necessary to formulate it as broadly as possible, for only a revolutionary consciousness of justice and a revolutionary conscience will put conditions upon its application in practice, on a more or a less broad scale."

In these regards the new men do not have to "return to Leninist norms," for they have never been abandoned for a moment.

If we can hope for, even perhaps count on, the diminution of the apocalyptic element in the ideology of a going, long-lasting society, we must remind ourselves that Leninism was peculiar in that its central "ideas" were always ideas about organization, and they have been strengthened rather than weakened in the course of time.

Bolshevism was born in an organizational feud about the definition of a party member, and who should control a paper (*Iskra*) which should act both as guardian of the doctrine and organizational core of the party. "Give me an organization," Lenin wrote at the outset of his career as a Leninist, "and I will turn Russia upside down." The organization he wanted, he explained, must be one in which "bureaucratism" prevailed against "democratism," "centralism" against "autonomy," which "strives to go from the top downward, and defends the enlargement of the rights and plenary powers of the central body against the parts." When at the 1903 Congress an exalter of the Central Committee urged that it should become the "omnipresent and one," the all-pervasive, all-informing and all-uniting "spirit," Lenin cried out from his seat: *"Ne dukh, a kulak!"* ("Not spirit, but fist!"). The idea of the rule of the elite, the idea of a vanguard party, the idea of the hatefulness of all other classes and the untrustworthiness of the working class, the idea that the working class too required a dictator or overseer to compel it to its mission—it is amazing to note that these "ideas" about organization form the very core of Leninism as a special ideology. Far from "eroding" or growing "weak" and merely "decorative," it is just precisely these structural principles which have grown and expanded, and become systematized.

Resentments, discontent, longing for a less oppressive regime and an easier lot exist under despotisms, autocracies, total-power states, and totalist states, even as in other social orders. Indeed, whenever hope or expectation stirs they are apt to become endemic and intense. The problem of "state-craft" in a despotism is that of preventing the discontent and longing from assuming *organized* form. Since the totalist state penetrates all social organizations and uses them as transmission belts (destroying whatever organization it cannot assimilate to its purposes and structure), it is particularly adapted to keeping discontent fragmented and unorganized.

By 1936, Lenin's central idea of an elite, single-centered dictatorship had gotten into the "most democratic constitution in the world" as Article 126, which proclaimed the party to be "the vanguard of the working people and the leading core of all organizations both social and state." And last summer, when Khrushchev and the rest were summing up the discussion over Stalin, they declared in *Pravda:* "As for our country, the Communist Party has been and will be the *only master* of the *minds,* the *thoughts,* the *only spokesman, leader and organizer* of the people" (my italics).

It is foolhardy to believe that they did not mean it, self-deluding to persuade ourselves that the forces pressing for concessions within the country are likely to find the road open to separate and effective corporate organization, which is the condition precedent to the development of a limited, multicentered state and a society which is stronger than it.

Even before Stalin died, we got evidence that the spirit of man is wayward and not as easily subjected as his body—the mass desertions at the war's end; the escape of millions who "voted with their feet" against totalitarianism; the two out of three "Chinese volunteers" in the Korean prison camps who preferred exile under precarious and humiliating "displaced person" conditions to return to their native scenes and homes. Since Stalin's death there have been East Berlin and Pilsen, Poznan and Vorkuta, Warsaw and Budapest, to prove that men will sometimes stand up unarmed to tanks and cannon and machine guns. They have proved too that the armies of the conquered lands have never been the pliant instruments of the Kremlin that faint-hearted men thought they were.

We have seen that forty years of *Gleichschaltung,* corruption, and terror have not rooted out of the artist the ineradicable notion that sincerity to his creative vision is more to be desired than *partiinost* and *ideinost.* We have seen that the youth—although the faint-hearted had thought they would be turned off the conveyer-belt as "little monsters"—are born young still, and therefore plastic, receptive, questioning, capable of illusion and disillusion, of "youthful idealism" and doubt and rebellion. Now the expulsions among the university youth are for the first time providing a pariah elite as a possible leadership to future undergrounds which may form under even this most efficiently regimented of societies.

I have never for a moment ceased to cast about for grounds of hope: that weaker heirs might make less efficient use of the terrible engines of total power; that a struggle or series of struggles for the succession might compel a contender to go outside the inner circles and summon social forces in the lower ranks of the party or outside of it into some sort of independent existence; that the army, disgraced as no other in all history by the charge that it gave birth to traitors by the thousands in its general staff, might develop sufficient independence from the party to make it a rival power center or an organized pressure body; that intellectuals, technicians, students might somehow break through the barriers that hinder the conversion of discontent into an organized, independent force.

But if I put the emphasis on the nature of the Soviet institutional framework and its built-in staying powers, it is by way of bending the stick in order to straighten it out. For the Western world has found it hard (or so it has seemed to me) to gaze straight and steadily at the head of Medusa, even if only in the reflecting shield of theoretical analysis. Brought up in a world of flux and openness, we find it hard to believe in the durability of despotic systems. Our hopes and longings are apt to betray us again and again into a readiness to be deceived by others or to deceive ourselves. And the "journalistic" nature of our culture has made us too ready to inflate the new because that alone is "news," while we neglect to put it into its tiresomely "repetitious" historical and institutional setting.

From the NEP to Socialism in One Country; from the Popular Front and Collective Security to the Grant Alliance and One World; from Peaceful Coexistence to the Geneva Spirit—the occupational hazard of the Western intellectual has been not to read too little but to read too much into planned changes, involuntary changes, and even into mere tactical maneuvers and verbal asseverations.

Each has been hailed in turn as the softening of the war of the totalist state on its own people and the world, as the long awaited "inevitable change" or "fundamental transformation"; "the sobering that comes from the responsibilities of power"; the "response to the pressure of the recognition of reality"; the growing modification of totalist power by "a rationalist technocracy"; the sobering "effect of privilege upon a new privileged class"; the "rise of a limited and traditionalist despotism"; a "feeling of responsibility to Russia as against World Revolution"; the "quiet digestion period of a sated beast of prey" no longer on the prowl; the "diffusion of authority which could lead to a constitutional despotism"; the "mellowing process that sooner or later overtakes all militant movements"; the second thoughts on the struggle for the world which have come at long last "from a recognition of the universal and mutual destructiveness of nuclear war"; the "inevitable work of erosion upon the totalitarian edifice." (Each of these expressions is quoted from some highly respected authority of Soviet affairs in the Anglo-Saxon world.)

Because of the nature of our mental climate and our longings, because too of the injection of "revolutionary methods" into diplomacy in a polarized and antagonistic world, the danger does not lie in a failure on our part to watch for change, nor in a failure to "test"—though generally without sufficient skepticism—the meaning of each verbal declaration. No, "the main danger," as the Communists would say, has not lain in insensitivity to hope, but in too ready self-deception.

SOVIET SOCIETY IN TRANSITION

Raymond Aron*

The future development of Soviet society is manifestly one of the most crucial issues under investigation by social scientists today. Studies in this field are necessarily speculative not only for the obvious reason that they deal with future unknowns but because there has been so little opportunity for outsiders to familiarize themselves with the Soviet-Russian reality. Social scientists face a further difficulty in that there are several possible— and somewhat incompatible—approaches, or bases, for an interpretation of Soviet society.

Studies to date have proceeded along three principal avenues of approach, investigating Soviet society, first, as an industrial civilization; second, as a totalitarian system (dealt with as a unique phenomenon without historical precedent); third, as the successor to Tsarist Russia (with stress laid on aspects of cultural continuity between past and present). Any of these conceptual approaches can lead to confusion in attempts to predict the Soviet future. In the first instance, little is known as yet about the laws of economic development in a system of the Soviet type. Analyses stressing the totalitarian aspect often suffer for lack of a clear definition of totalitarianism itself (*e.g.*, does it date back to Lenin or just to Stalin?). As for the continuity approach, stress on the constant factors in Russian culture as a key to the future can too easily lead to underestimation or disregard of the impact of economic and political changes.

Synthesizing the issues implied by these three approaches, the basic question to be answered may be phrased: To what extent, if any, will the development of industrial civilization bring about an evolution of the Soviet totalitarian regime and of the social forms inherited from the past? What direction will this evolution take? Some observers, in attempting to answer this question, have put forward theses based on one or another of the above schemes of interpretation in virtual disregard of the issues raised by the others.

Two such theses are worth mention as categorical and contradictory extremes of opinion; both, in this writer's view, are invalid. One asserts that the stupendous development of productive forces in the Soviet Union will pave the way to democracy; the other, that the totalitarian regime is invulnerable to economic forces.

* Professor of Sociology at the Sorbonne. Author of *The Opium of the Intellectuals* and *A Century of Total War*. The selection is from *Problems of Communism,* Vol. VI (November-December 1957), pp. 5-9. By permission.

EXTREMIST THEORIES

The first of these has been expounded in particularly crude terms by Mr. Isaac Deutscher. His formation lends itself to numerous objections, raised so often already that they can be dealt with briefly here. The explanation that terrorism and ideological orthodoxy are determined solely by the needs of primary accumulation or of the Five-Year Plans runs up against the incontrovertible fact that the great purge of 1936-38 took place after the first Plan had already been carried out and the collectivization of agriculture completed. The terror that accompanied the latter may, at a stretch, be attributed to economic "necessities," but this explanation cannot apply to the great purge, during which millions of real and imagined opponents, faithful Bolsheviks and even Stalinists were thrown into prison.

The tremendous development of Soviet productive forces, on which neo-Marxists always dwell as a portent of the better life to come, is of course no fiction. By and large, however, it applies only to heavy industry. The lot of the Soviet citizenry has remained relatively unaffected, since the living standard is determined not by *per capita* production but by the value of goods intended for consumption by individuals. Considering additionally the lag in agricultural output, it is unlikely that the Soviet planners can greatly increase the purchasing power of the population in the foreseeable future.

In any thesis on the Soviet future, the meaning of the word "democracy" is crucial. If by democracy is meant the organized competition of parties—as it seems to in Deutscher's formulation—then there is no obvious connection between democracy and economic progress. But it is absurd to insist on rigid and unalterable concepts of democracy in its Western form (characterized by multi-party systems, legislative representation, intellectual liberties, *etc.*) as opposed to totalitarianism (characterized by the single party, ideological terrorism, police controls, *etc.*). Neither Western democracy nor Stalinist totalitarianism can be considered as fixed entities, as "historic atoms" which cannot be transmuted. Thus, if it is illogical to assert that totalitarianism will develop into full-fledged democracy with the development of productive forces, it is just as illogical to exclude dogmatically a softening up of totalitarianism.

This is the weakness of the second theory, opposite to Mr. Deutscher's, which asserts that totalitarianism is invulnerable to outside forces. It is usually posited as part of a political and almost metaphysical interpretation of totalitarianism, conceived of as a disease which is liable to infect any modern society—even though, so far, only Russia and Germany have experienced it in "pure" form. Its proponents argue that although totalitarianism is favored by certain economic and social circumstances, it is essentially something political and ideological. It is supposed to be the outcome of an obsessive drive of a group of people bent on shaping society according to their own ideology. The power of a single party, ideological orthodoxy, police terror, the creation of a world of superimposed conventional meanings, with no reference to the real world and yet forced on the masses as something truer than reality—all these features, we are told, are linked together and constitute the characteristics of a global, or self-contained, phenomenon—a phenomenon which has emerged and will eventually disappear, but which it would be idle to expect to return to normality by gradual stages.

In this definition of totalitarianism, three of the above features are essential: ideological orthodoxy, police terror, and world-wide victory or else apocalyptic collapse. These three elements are said to be closely linked. The will to set up an arbitrary and often absurd ideology as The Truth necessitates the recourse to police inquisition, which is used for hunting not only enemies, but also heretics. The truth of the ideology can triumph only when it is no longer rejected by anybody. So long as there is opposition anywhere, communism will not be entirely true, because its truth will still clash with reality, and its compete truth depends on its universal application. Thus communism is in a constant state of war with unbelievers both inside and outside its borders. The greater the progress, the more it is impelled to struggle, for nothing has been achieved so long as something still remains to be done. This line of analysis affords an explanation for the great purge having descended upon Soviet society after the completion of rural collectivization; the latter is viewed not as an economic and rational—however ruthless—measure, but as the expression of a policy which is *alien* to economic rationalism, and is intelligible only in terms of an ideological and emotional logic.

This kind of interpretation, which Hannah Arendt has developed with great skills, seems to me to be dangerous. It amounts to creating a certain ideal type, a kind of essence of totalitarianism—and to assuming, thereupon, that the regime, both in the present and in the future, must conform to this type or this essence. If the Soviets behaved as "perfect" totalitarians, as Miss Arendt understands the word, then it is quite true that we could expect no normalization or evolution of the Soviet regime. The real question is, however, whether the regime has even been completely totalitarian, whether the "essense" has not simply been created by theorists like Miss Arendt on the strength of certain historically-observed and historically-explicable phenomena. The Soviet regime *became* totalitarian by degrees, under the influence of certain circumstances. Why, then, could it not cease to be totalitarian, or become less totalitarian under the influence of other circumstances?

THE IMPACT OF ECONOMIC DEVELOPMENT

Once the extremes of the neo-Marxist and the totalitarian theory have been rejected, it must be decided what either of them can contribute to a logical assessment of the Soviet future. What transformations, social and economic, are brought about by the development of productive forces? What is the likely effect of these transformations on the political regime? To what extent is totalitarianism (or certain totalitarian elements) inseparable from the regime, regardless of economic progress?

There are at least three important social and economic consequences of the development of productive forces. The first is a rise in the general level of culture and the creation and development of an intelligentsia, whose broad base—in addition to traditional cultural and professional elements—is the swelling ranks of technical and managerial specialists who man the economy. It is as true for the Soviet Union as for the West that modern industry requires a higher proportion of technicians and specialized "cadres" than in the past, and Soviet statistics show a steady increase in the proportion of intelligentsia to the whole working population.

Even outside this intelligentsia with its higher-level specialization, the priority given to production and to productivity is bound to encourage the spread of specialized training and of technical education. More than half the Soviet labor force is at present employed in industry or its auxiliary services, and more than half the population is urban. This urban population can read and write, and it is no longer as cowed—or as malleable—as it was in the early years of Stalin's reign.

The second consequence of industrial development, closely related to the first, is an increase in the economic wants and demands of the population. In the Soviet Union, the development of productive forces has not been accompanied by a corresponding rise in the standard of living of the masses. The concentration of capital investments in heavy industry, the failures in agriculture, and the housing shortage have meant that the average citizen is worse housed, worse fed and less well-dressed than the average citizen of the West, even in some of the less prosperous countries. In recent years, however, there has been some improvement in material conditions, and various pressures have led the regime to pay some limited deference to consumer needs. The indications are that this limited satisfaction of certain wants has whetted the population's appetite for more goods. In particular, the intelligentsia has shown increasing eagerness to acquire commodities typical of the way of life of the Western bourgeois (durable consumer goods, automobiles, refrigerators, etc.).

The third consequence of developing productive forces is a trend toward a more rational economy. Over the last thirty years, the Soviet economy has become not only more powerful but technologically far more complex. To what extent and how long the crude planning methods of the first Five-Year Plans can continue to be applied is a highly complicated and controversial issue. Yet the general direction of evolution seems fairly clear to this writer. As shortages become less severe, the consumers' choice will tend to be of growing importance to the market. Technological complexity will strengthen the managerial class at the expense of the ideologists and the militants, at any rate on the enterprise level, if not on the state level. The decentralization of industrial administration, in reinforcing the managerial elements, should reduce the part played by fear and cocercion in the Soviet management of an industrial society.

STABILIZING FORCES IN SOVIET SOCIETY

While the rate at which any of these social and economic trends will develop is hard to foresee, certain political implications seem clear. Briefly, it is the writer's view that none of these trends—toward a higher cultural level, toward increasing popular demands, or toward a more rational economy—constitutes a threat to the basic organization of the Soviet state or society.

Apart from its peculiarly totalitarian features, Soviet society is essentially bureaucratic and hierarchical, just as was prerevolutionary Russian society. The reliance of an industrial society on a state bureaucracy with vested interests—under a system which prevents the formation of organized opinion or pressure through professional groups, genuine trade unions, or political parties—obviously creates a certain tendency toward stability. A further stabilizing factor is class mobility; since the intelligentsia is expanding with each generation, it can absorb the ablest children of the masses without the regime's having to resort to purge or to demotion of the children of the already privileged.

As noted above, there is bound to be some tension between the economic desires of the masses and the intelligentsia, on one hand, the exigencies of regime policy on the other (requiring the continued priority of heavy industry). There is probably also a latent conflict between the desire for rationality and security on the part of the managerial and technocratic elements, and the desire for power and prestige on the part of the party men. But such conflicts do not imply any explosions or fundamental changes in the society.   .

In short, there is nothing to indicate that economic progress will force the ruling class, composed of party men and higher-level bureaucrats, to authorize the creation of rival forces—in the form of either parties or workers' trade unions. And there is nothing to indicate that such a challenge can come from below; neither the masses nor the intelligentsia have the means of overriding the ban on organized pressure groups. The leadership seems quite capable of maintaining the principle of the single hierarchy, of the single party, and of the legal *status quo* of the ruling bureaucracy. If any basic change is to take place, it will have to occur *within* the ruling elite—*i.e.,* inside the Communist Party.

EVOLUTION AND THE REGIME

What can be said, then, of the effects of progressing industrialization on the Communist regime itself, and specifically on those aspects of the regime which have come to be identified as "totalitarian." The question may be discussed under several heads: 1) Will the internal structure of the party undergo basic changes as a result of the spontaneous evolution of the economy and the society? 2) Will ideology continue, in the long run, to play the same role as it has in the past? 3) Is the movement still inspired by the same boundless ambition, by the same violence, or may it be expected eventually to rest content with what it is—that is, something less than universal?

The most crucial change in the party structure of recent years—the substitution of collective leadership for one-man dictatorship—is attributable to an historical event, to the death of an individual, rather than to the evolution of either the society or the regime. Nevertheless, the change was, in a way, logical. For the very nature of Stalin's power—or his misuse of it—dictated against the rise of a single successor. None of the members of the Presidium could face without anxiety the prospect of a repetition of the process whereby Stalin, little by little, had liquidated virtually all of the men who had once been his allies in the party leadership.

Some observers have held that Khrushchev's increasing domination of the ruling clique has already put an end to collective leadership. But Khrushchev has had to lean heavily on the support of allies to push through his policies, and in this sense group rule certainly continues. Acting as a group of leaders, the Presidium has appeared to be less indifferent to public demands, less able or less determined to carry out programs regardless of cost, than was Stalin with his unlimited personal power.

Whether further fundamental changes will take place in the structure and balance of power within the party is a matter of conjecture at this stage. However, it is worth noting that Khrushchev effected his purge of the so-called "anti-party" leaders last June through appeal to the Central Committee, over the objections of a majority of the Presidium. Before that time the Presidium appeared to be just as independent of the Central Committee as Stalin had been. Since the authority of the proletariat originally passed from the party to the Politburo (*i.e.,* Stalin) *through* the Central Committee, it is interesting to speculate on whether the reverse could take place. So far, there is no sign that any such basic shift in power is in the offing; if it were to occur, however, it would be directly attributable to the struggle for power rather than to broader forces of evolution.

The changeover from personal to collective leadership has been accompanied by the mitigation or abandonment of certain aspects of totalitarian rule. Perhaps the epitome of totalitarianism, certainly the feature most frequently mentioned, is the instrument of the purge, characterized by a combination of arbitrary police action (pragmatically unjustifiable), ideological terrorism and pure fantasy, defined by the inquisitor-theologians as more real than reality itself. The confession trials were the symbolic expression of this aspect of totalitarianism.

The collective leadership has renounced such excesses, and in doing so has revealed that it was never taken in by the mad logic of Stalinist ideological terrorism. At the same time, it may reasonably be objected that Khrushchev has not hesitated, on occasion, to employ it himself, as for instance when he has called Beria an "imperialist agent" or the Hungarian revolution a "counterrevolution." This leads us to perhaps the most crucial issue under consideration in this paper: that is the future role of ideology in the evolving Soviet society.

A TREND TOWARD SKEPTICISM?

Communist ideology is based on a few simple ideas: the party *is* the proletariat; the seizure of power by the party is the *sine qua non* for the establishment of socialism. In places where the party has not taken over power, capitalism reigns and the masses are exploited. The inevitable culmination will be the extension throughout the world of regimes similar to the Soviet regime.

As is frequently pointed out, this orthodoxy has little connection with either Marx *or* reality. A society which has developed a great industrial complex side by side with a relentlessly low standard of living resembles what Marx called capitalism: a welfare state, albeit "capitalist," in which the additional resources accruing from technical progress are used for the benefit of the masses, does not. The dialecticians have been obliged to place an arbitrary interpretation on facts, often at variance with the most obvious reality. The element of fantasy in the great trials is merely the supreme expression of this logic.

It is the writer's belief that Soviet society, with the improvement in its standard of living, its culture and its technology, not only is becoming economically more rational, but must in the long run lose its ideological fervor. As it makes further progress and becomes more stable, as its technical level draws closer to that of industrialized Western societies, so both its militants and the people at large are bound to incline to some degree of skepticism. They will come to admit certain incontestable facts, such as the plurality of methods of industrialization, the raising of the standard of living in the West, *etc.* As soon as Polish writers and educators were able to talk freely, they proceeded to admit these facts and to escape from the absurd logic of Communist ideology.

ORTHODOXY VS. RATIONALITY

Does this mean that the dialecticians and Soviet leaders will cease to profess their belief in the universal mission, in the coming, through socialism, of a classless society? Certainly they have shown no such tendency thus far, leading to still another question: is it possible for Soviet society, under its present organization and ideological restrictions, to go very far in the direction of *either* economic rationalism *or* the return to common sense? In both respects, regime attitudes are the source of basic contradictions in the society, in conflict with evolutionary trends.

In the matter of ideology, the Soviet leadership is faced with a profound dilemma: it is hard to maintain a faith, but it is harder still to do without one. The leadership could, without too much difficulty, abandon the absurd excesses of Stalinist orthodoxy. Stalin had not only made a nightmare farce out of the system of trials and confessions. He had set himself up as the supreme arbiter in matters of biology and linguistics. He had decreed what, in literature, painting or music, conformed or failed to conform to socialist doctrine. But this kind of madness was not inherent in the system. It was simple for his successors to restore to biologists the right to accept the laws of genetics or to grant novelists or composers a greater measure of freedom in their work.

The leaders cannot, however, permit freedom of discussion to extend to the dogma itself, since its premises, as we have seen, are patently absurd and at variance with the facts. They do not want to return to Stalinist excesses, but they cannot permit any challenge of the dogma, which legitimizes their rule and provides the justification for the perpetuation of communism. The compromise is an uneasy one. The leaders are constantly threatening to deprive the intellectuals of some of the freedom they have been granted, while the intellectuals, on their side, are continuously straining to transcend the limits which have been set for them.

In Poland and Hungary, where the desire for intellectual freedom was reinforced by the desire for national freedom, the conflict was resolved by explosion. In Hungary, order has been restored—but it is a foreign order, a police and military order. In Poland, a large measure of intellectual freedom still exists, but the dogma *as such* has vanished. The regime still pursues a socialist path of development, but the people are aware that it is simply one of many systems, that it offers no mystical guarantee of the welfare of the masses.

In the Soviet Union, on the other hand, the dogma is still intact; even though it is no longer as comprehensive or imperative as in the past, it continues to permeate the society. Certainly the leaders, judging by their pronouncements, still believe in the perpetuation of communism. They have not ceased to see themselves as engaged in a relentless struggle with the capitalist camp. Their outlook on the world is a long-term one, dominated by an over-simplified conception of good and evil.

This leads us to the second major contradiction in Soviet society—the obstacles which stand in the way of economic rationalization. From the inception of the Five-Year Plans, the objectives and methods of Soviet economic planning have been keyed to the concept of world struggle and to a desperate effort to catch up and surpass the level of industrialization in the capitalist countries. The system has the characteristics of what, in the West, would be a war economy: a rigid system of priorities has been established to ensure that the goals of heavy industry are achieved at all costs, the rest, if necessary, being sacrified. When these goals have not been reached quickly enough, additional labor has been brought in from the countryside, and out-of-date industrial equipment has remained in operation.

Gradually however, transferable labor reserves have dwindled, with the result that increases have to come, in ever greater measure, from increased productivity. The problems of depreciation, renewal of equipment and economic planning are becoming more and more acute. Light industry and agriculture can no longer be sacrificed indiscriminately. The situation obviously demands an increasingly rational economy; but what kind of rationality is there in a planning system which concentrates not on satisfying demands but on the expansion of heavy industry, which refuses to great enterprises more than a bare minimum of independence, which continues to allocate the country's resources on the basis of decisions taken at the top, and which still aims at authoritarian administration in so large a sector of the system? The recent highly-touted reform of industrial administration, while transferring various executive functions to newly-created regional authorities, does not basically change these governing principles of the Soviet economic system.

As long as the Soviet leaders adhere to Stalinist principles, insist on the priority of heavy industry, and maintain disproportionate ratios between investment as *vs.* consumption and heavy industry as *vs.* agriculture and light industry, the Soviet economy will continue to bear the marks of an authoritarian, police regime. The return to a normal peacetime economy depends, in the final analysis, on the modification of the objectives fixed by the leaders—in short on their outlook.

All of the foregoing suggests two conclusions. It is not true to say that the Soviet regime is becoming increasingly totalitarian as the society comes to need totalitarianism less and less. Many of the worst aberrations of the regime appear to have stemmed from the abnormality of Stalin himself; and they have disappeared with him. But neither is it true to maintain that the main features of the economic system and of the political regime are attributable to Stalin exclusively; they are rooted as firmly in the views and methods of the men who helped build the U.S.S.R. and who now rule it.

These conclusions, however, still do not answer the basic issues of the future; namely, *could* the regime change fundamentally without crumbling? And what freedoms is it capable of tolerating?

THE PROSPECTS FOR A FREER SOCIETY

When making a simplified analysis, a distinction can be drawn between three different kinds of freedom: firstly, what Montesquieu called security; secondly, the freedom the Hungarian intellectuals claimed, namely, the right to tell the truth about everything; and finally, Rousseau's freedom, participation in sovereignty, represented in the twentieth century by free elections and the multiparty political system.

Individual security is, as a rule, most favored by a parliamentary type of government. But many nondemocratic regimes, give a fairly broad measure of security to those who do not engage in politics. The Tsarist regime, during its final period, interfered little with the life and liberty of citizens who minded their own business. In the Soviet Union, the insecurity of the Stalin era appears to have been greatly lessened by Stalin's successors. But as long as the Soviet regime continues to apply political sanctions in order to make the economy work, as long as it demands unquestioning respect for the dogma, the Soviet citizen will not be able to enjoy a true or stable measure of security.

To what extent could intellectuals and ordinary Soviet citizens be allowed to enjoy the second kind of freedom—to tell the truth about things, to exchange ideas, to visit the capitalist West, *etc?* In the writer's view, the regime could, without endangering its own safety, grant musicians, painters and writers, more freedoms than it does at present. But the word "could" here has a double application; the question is whether the leaders of the regime and the party could bring themselves to grant such freedoms. Again, as long as they believe in their dogma, they will not allow it to be discussed, and there will be a harness on truth. Yet even if they themselves become skeptical, would they admit it publicly? For the future this is a matter of speculation; for the present, they certainly would not dare to do so. For even though there may be a tendency in Russia to evolve into a semi-ideological technocracy, the dogma is still a vital factor in less-advanced Communist countries and is crucial in justifying the unity of the socialist camp. To hope that the dogma will fade out in the near future would be over-optimistic.

In the long run, however, this writer holds to his view that increasing ideological skepticism is inevitable among both the leaders and the masses. Already the problems of Soviet planning are completely out of touch with the official economic textbooks, which are simplified versions of *Das Kapital*. Though tribute may still be paid to Marx, the day may come when an industrial society, concerned more with efficiency than with orthodoxy, will cease to follow the Lenin-Stalin ideology. Revolutionary fervor—though revived by the successes of communism in Asia and the Middle East—is nevertheless bound, in the end, to die down, and probably to die out.

Will the Soviet citizen eventually obtain Rousseau's freedom—participation in sovereignty—through either the development of factions within the party, or perhaps even the emergence of a multiparty system? The prospect of any move toward full-fledged political freedom in the Western style is so far beyond the scope of present or even predictable evolutionary trends that speculation would be foolish. Only time and the forces already at work in Soviet society will provide the clues to Russia's political future.

Sources of Readings

(Bracketed numbers refer to pages in *this* volume. Book titles are italicized; pamphlet, article, speech, and report titles are quoted.)

ALEKSANDROV, G. F., "The Pattern of Soviet Democracy" (Speech: December 4, 1946) [333]

ARON, RAYMOND, "Soviet Society in Transition" [568]

BAUER, RAYMOND A., INKELES, ALEX, and KLUCKHOHN, CLYDE, *How the Soviet System Works* [516]

BERMAN, HAROLD J., "The Devil and Soviet Russia" [3]

CARR, E. H., "Who Rules in Soviet Society?" [410]

CENTRAL ELECTION COMMISSION, "Official Returns on 1958 Election to Supreme Soviet" [350]

CHAMBERLIN, WILLIAM HENRY, *The Russian Enigma* [12]

COHEN, MORRIS RAPHAEL, "Why I Am Not a Communist" [181]

CURTISS, JOHN C., *The Russian Revolutions of 1917* [194]

DEUTSCHER, ISAAC, *The Prophet Armed* [229]

———, *Russia in Transition* [540]

———, *Stalin: A Political Biography* [264]

DJILAS, MILOVAN, *The New Class* [413]

DOBB, MAURICE, "Comment on Soviet Economic Statistics" [438]

———, *Soviet Economic Development Since 1917* [439, 476]

DULLES, ALLEN W., "The Communists Also Have Their Problems" (Speech: September 19, 1957) [529]

———, "Dimensions of the Soviet Economic Challenge" (Speech: April 28, 1958) [505]

FAINSOD, MERLE, *How Russia Is Ruled* [114, 354]

———, "The Party in the Post-Stalin Era" [417]

FREUD, SIGMUND, *New Introductory Lectures on Psychoanalysis* [111]

HOOK, SIDNEY, *Reason, Social Myths and Democracy* [298]

HUNT, R. N. CAREW, "The Importance of Doctrine" [52]

———, *The Theory and Practice of Communism* [89]

JOUVENEL, BERTRAND DE, "On the Character of the Soviet Economy" [449]

KERSHAW, JOSEPH A., "Recent Trends in the Soviet Economy" [489]

KHRUSHCHEV, NIKITA S., "Report of the Central Committee to the 20th Party Congress" (Speech: February 14, 1956) [455]

———, "Stalin and the Cult of the Individual" (Unpublished speech to the 20th Party Congress: February 24-25, 1956) [376]

"L," "The Soviet Intelligentsia" [522]

LASKI, HAROLD J., "Karl Marx: An Essay" [187]

LENIN, V. I., "Communist Ethics" (Speech: October 2, 1920) [174]

———, "The Teachings of Karl Marx" [83]

———, "State and Revolution" [142]

579

————, "Testament" [280]

————, "What Is to Be Done?" [130]

MARX, KARL, *A Contribution to the Critique of Political Economy* [73]

MARX, KARL, and ENGELS, FRIEDRICH, "Manifesto of the Communist Party" [59]

NEW YORK TIMES, "Summary of Projected Seven-Year Plan for 1959-1965" [473]

PLAMENATZ, JOHN, *German Marxism and Russian Communism* [166, 296]

PLEKHANOV, GEORGE, "The Materialist Conception of History" [75]

————, "The Role of the Individual in History" [79]

RESHETAR, JOHN S., "Problems of Analyzing and Predicting Soviet Behavior" [441]

ROSTOW, W. W., *The Dynamics of Soviet Society* [48]

SABINE, GEORGE H., *A History of Political Theory* [153]

SALISBURY, HARRISON E., "Fatal Flaw in the Soviet System" [427]

SCHAPIRO, LEONARD, *The Origin of the Communist Autocracy* [245]

SCHWARTZ, HARRY, "Russia's Bold New Plan" [508]

SCHUMAN, FREDERICK L., *Russia Since 1917* [337]

STALIN, JOSEPH V., "On Soviet Industrialization" (Speech: February 9, 1946) [446]

————, "On the New Soviet Constitution" (Speech: November 25, 1936) [328]

TROTSKY, LEON, *The Revolution Betrayed* [283]

————, "Their Morals and Ours" [175]

VERNADSKY, GEORGE, *A History of Russia* [26]

WOLFE, BERTRAM D., "The Durability of Soviet Despotism" [553]

Constitution of the Union of Soviet Socialist Republics [306]

BIBLIOGRAPHY

BALZAK, S. S.; VASYUTIN, V. F.; and FEIGIN, YA. G. eds. *Economic Geography of the U.S.S.R.* The Macmillan Company, New York, 1949.

BARANSKY, N. N. *Economic Geography of the U.S.S.R.* Foreign Languages Publishing House, Moscow, 1956.

BARGHOORN, FREDERICK, C. *The Soviet Image of the United States.* Harcourt, Brace and Company, New York, 1950.

BARGHOORN, FREDERICK C. *Soviet Russian Nationalism.* Oxford University Press, New York, 1956.

BAUER, RAYMOND A. *The New Man in Soviet Psychology.* Harvard University Press, Cambridge, 1952.

BAUER, RAYMOND A.; INKELES, ALEX; KLUCKHOHN, CLYDE. *How the Soviet System Works.* Harvard University Press, Cambridge, 1956.

BAUER, RAYMOND A. and WASIOLEK, EDWARD. *Nine Soviet Portraits.* John Wiley and Sons, New York, 1955.

BAYKOV, ALEXANDER. *The Development of the Soviet Economic System.* Harvard University Press, Cambridge, 1946.

BELOV, FEDOR. *The History of a Soviet Collective Farm.* Frederick A. Praeger, New York, 1955.

BERDYAEV, NICOLAS. *The Origin of Russian Communism.* Geoffrey Bles, London, 1948.

BERGSON, ABRAM, ed. *Soviet Economic Growth.* Row, Peterson and Company, Evanston, 1953.

BERGSON, ABRAM. *The Structure of Soviet Wages.* Harvard University Press, Cambridge, 1944.

BERGSON, ABRAM and HEYMANN, HANS, JR. *Soviet National Income and Product, 1940-1948.* Columbia University Press, New York, 1954.

BERLIN, ISAIAH. *Karl Marx.* Oxford University Press, New York, 1956.

BERLINER, JOSEPH S. *Factory and Manager in the U.S.S.R.* Harvard University Press, Cambridge, 1957.

BERMAN, HAROLD J. *Justice in Russia.* Harvard University Press, Cambridge, 1950.

BERMAN, HAROLD J. *The Russians in Focus.* Little, Brown and Company, Boston, 1953.

BECK, F. and GODIN, W. (pseuds.). *Russian Purge and the Extraction of Confession.* The Viking Press, New York, 1951.

BIENSTOCK, GREGORY; SCHWARTZ, SOLOMON M.; and YUGOW, AARON. *Management in Russian Industry and Agriculture.* Cornell University Press, Ithaca, 1948.

BLACK, CYRIL E., ed. *Rewriting Russian History.* Frederick A. Praeger, New York, 1956.

BOBER, M. M. *Karl Marx's Interpretation of History.* Harvard University Press, Cambridge, 1948.

BRZEZINSKI, ZBIGNIEW K. *The Permanent Purge.* Harvard University Press, Cambridge, 1956.

BRZEZINSKI, ZBIGNIEW K. and FRIEDRICH, CARL J. *Totalitarian Dictatorship and Autocracy.* Harvard University Press, Cambridge, 1956.

BUKHARIN, NIKOLAI I. *Historical Materialism.* International Publishers, New York, 1928.

BUKHARIN, NIKOLAI I. et al. *Marxism and Modern Thought.* Harcourt, Brace and Co., New York, 1935.

BURNS, EMILE, ed. *A Handbook of Marxism.* International Publishers, New York, 1935.

CARR, E. H. *The Bolshevik Revolution,* 4 vols. Macmillan and Co. Ltd., London, 1954.

CARR, E. H. *Studies in Revolution.* Macmillan & Co. Ltd., London, 1950.

CHAMBERLIN, WILLIAM HENRY. *The Russian Enigma.* Charles Scribner's Sons, New York, 1943.

CHAMBERLIN, WILLIAM HENRY. *Russia's Iron Age.* Little, Brown and Company, Boston, 1934.

CHAMBERLIN, WILLIAM HENRY. *The Russian Revolution, 1917-1921.* 2 vols. The Macmillan Company, New York, 1935.

COLE, G. D. H. *What Marx Really Meant.* A. A. Knopf, New York, 1934.

COMMITTEE OF CENTRAL COMM. OF THE C.P.S.U. *History of the Communist Party of the Soviet Union, Short Course.* International Publishers, New York, 1939.

CONDOIDE, MIKHAIL V. *The Soviet Financial System.* Ohio State University, Columbus, 1951.

COUNTS, GEORGE S. *The Challenge of Soviet Education.* McGraw-Hill Book Company, Inc., New York, 1957.

CRANKSHAW, EDWARD. *Russia and the Russians.* The Viking Press, New York, 1948.

CRANKSHAW, EDWARD. *Russia Without Stalin,* Michael Joseph, London, 1956.

CRESSEY, GEORGE B. *The Basis of Soviet Strength.* McGraw-Hill Book Company, Inc., New York, 1945.

CRESSEY, GEORGE B. *How Strong Is Russia? A Geographical Appraisal.* Syracuse University Press, Syracuse, 1954.

CURTISS, JOHN S. *Church and State in Russia, 1900-1917.* Columbia University Press, New York, 1940.

CURTISS, JOHN S. *The Russian Church and the Soviet State, 1917-1950.* Little, Brown and Company, Boston, 1953.

CURTISS, JOHN S. *The Russian Revolutions of 1917.* D. Van Nostrand Company, Inc., Princeton, 1957.

DALLIN, DAVID J. *The Real Soviet Russia.* Yale University Press, New Haven, 1947.

DEUTSCHER, ISAAC. *The Prophet Armed.* Oxford University Press, New York, 1954.

DEUTSCHER, ISAAC. *Russia in Transition, and Other Essays.* Coward-McCann, Inc., New York, 1957.

DEUTSCHER, ISAAC. *Russia: What Next?* Oxford University Press, New York, 1953.

DEUTSCHER, ISAAC. *Soviet Trade Unions.* Royal Institute of International Affairs, New York, 1950.

DEUTSCHER, ISAAC. *Stalin.* Oxford University Press, New York, 1949.

DEWITT, NICHOLAS. *Soviet Professional Manpower.* National Research Council, Washington, 1954.

DJILAS, MILOVAN. *The New Class.* Frederick A. Praeger, New York, 1957.

DOBB, M. *Soviet Economic Development Since 1917.* Routledge and K. Paul, London, 1958.

ENGELS, FREDERICK. *Ludwig Feurbach.* International Publishers, New York, 1941.

ENGELS, FREDERICK. *The Origin of the Family, Private Property and the State.* International Publishers, New York, 1942.

ENGELS, FREDERICK. *Selected Works.* 2 vols. Co-operative Publishing Society of Foreign Workers in the U.S.S.R., Moscow, 1935.

ENGELS, FREDERICK. *Socialism, Utopian and Scientific.* International Publishers, New York, 1935.

FAINSOD, MERLE. *How Russia Is Ruled.* Harvard University Press, Cambridge, 1953.

FISCHER, LOUIS. *Russia Revisited.* Doubleday & Company, New York, 1957.

FLORINSKY, MICHAEL T. *Russia: A History and an Interpretation.* 2 vols. The Macmillan Company, New York, 1953.

FLORINSKY, MICHAEL T. *Towards an Understanding of the U.S.S.R.* The Macmillan Company, New York, 1951.

GALENSON, WALTER. *Labor Productivity in Soviet and American Industry.* Columbia University Press, New York, 1955.

GOLDER, F. A. *Documents of Russian History 1914-1917.* Century Company, New York, 1927.

GORER, GEOFFREY and RICKMAN, JOHN. *The People of Great Russia.* Chanticleer Press, Inc., New York, 1950.

GORKY, M. et al., eds. *The History of the Civil War in the U.S.S.R.* 2 vols. International Publishers, New York, 1938.

GRANICK, DAVID. *Management of the Industrial Firm in the U.S.S.R.* Columbia University Press, New York, 1954.

GREGORY, JAMES S. *Land of the Soviets.* Penguin Books, New York, 1946.

GRIERSON, PHILIP. *Books on Soviet Russia 1917-1942.* Methuen & Co., London, 1943.

GRULIOW, LEO, ed. *Current Soviet Policies: The Documentary Record of the Nineteenth Communist Party Congress and the Reorganization after Stalin's Death.* Frederick A. Praeger, New York, 1953.

GRULIOW, LEO, ed. *Current Soviet Policies: The Documentary Record of the Twentieth Communist Party Congress and Repercussions of De-Stalinization.* Frederick A. Praeger, New York, 1957.

GSOVSKI, VLADIMIR. *Soviet Civil Law.* 2 vols. University of Michigan Law School, Ann Arbor, 1948-1949.

GUINS, GEORGE C. *Communism on the Decline.* Philosophical Library, Inc. New York, 1956.

GUNTHER, JOHN. *Inside Russia Today.* Harper & Brothers, New York, 1958.

GURIAN, WALDEMAR. *Bolshevism: An Introduction to Soviet Communism.* University of Notre Dame Press, Notre Dame, 1952.

HAIMSON, LEOPOLD H. *The Russian Marxists and the Origins of Bolshevism.* Harvard University Press, Cambridge, 1955.

HARPER, SAMUEL N. and THOMPSON, RONALD. *The Government of the Soviet Union.* D. Van Nostrand Company, Inc., New York, 1949.

HAZARD, JOHN N. *Law and Social Change in the U.S.S.R.* Carswell, Toronto, 1953.

HAZARD, JOHN N. *The Soviet System of Government.* University of Chicago Press, Chicago, 1957.

HODGMAN, DONALD R. *Soviet Industrial Production, 1928-1951.* Harvard University Press, Cambridge, 1954.

HOLZMAN, FRANKLYN D. *Soviet Taxation.* Harvard University Press, Cambridge, 1955.

HOOK, SIDNEY. *Marx and the Marxists.* D. Van Nostrand Company, New York, 1955.

HOOK, SIDNEY. *Towards the Understanding of Karl Marx.* The John Day Company, New York, 1933.

HUBBARD, LEONARD. *The Economics of Soviet Agriculture.* Macmillan and Company, Ltd., London, 1939.

HUNT, R. N. CAREW. *Marxism: Past and Present*. The Macmillan Company, New York, 1955.

HUNT, R. N. CAREW. *The Theory and Practice of Communism*. The Macmillan Company, New York, 1957.

INKELES, ALEX. *Public Opinion in Soviet Russia*. Harvard University Press, Cambridge, 1950.

JASNY, NAUM. *The Socialized Agriculture of the U.S.S.R.* Stanford University Press, Stanford, 1949.

JORRE, GEORGES. *The Soviet Union, the Land and its People*. Longmans, Green and Company, London, 1950.

KAMMARI, M. D. *Socialism and the Individual*. Foreign Languages Publishing House, Moscow, 1950.

KARPINSKY, V. *The Social and State Structure of the U.S.S.R.* Foreign Languages Publishing House, Moscow, 1950.

KARPOVICH, MICHAEL. *Imperial Russia 1801-1917*. Henry Holt and Company, New York, 1932.

KELSEN, HANS. *The Political Theory of Bolshevism*. University of California Press, Berkeley, 1949.

KLINE, GEORGE L., ed. *Soviet Education*. Columbia University Press, New York, 1957.

KLUCHEVSKY, V. O. *A History of Russia*. Five vols. E. P. Dutton and Company, New York, 1931.

KOHN, HANS. *Basic History of Modern Russia*. D. Van Nostrand Company, Inc., New York, 1957.

KOLARZ, WALTER. *The Peoples of the Soviet Far East*. Frederick A. Praeger, New York, 1954.

KOLARZ, WALTER. *Russia and Her Colonies*. Frederick A. Praeger, New York, 1952.

KOROL, ALEXANDER G. *Soviet Education for Science and Technology*. Massachusetts Institute of Technology Press, Cambridge, 1957.

KOVALEVSKY, MAXIME. *Russian Political Institutions*. University of Chicago Press, Chicago, 1902.

KROPOTKIN, PETER. *Fields, Factories and Workshops*. G. P. Putnam's Sons, New York, 1907.

KULSKI, WLADYSLAW W. *The Soviet Regime*. Syracuse University Press, Syracuse, 1956.

KURSKY, A. *The Planning of the National Economy of the U.S.S.R.* Foreign Languages Publishing House, Moscow, 1949.

LAMONT, CORLISS. *The Peoples of the U.S.S.R.* Harcourt, Brace and Company, New York, 1946.

LAMONT, CORLISS. *Soviet Civilization*. Philosophical Library, New York, 1952.

LANGE, OSCAR. *The Working Principles of the Soviet Economy*. Research Bureau for Post-War Economics, New York, 1944.

LEITES, NATHAN C. *The Operational Code of the Politburo*. McGraw-Hill Book Company, Inc., New York, 1951.

LEITES, NATHAN C. *A Study of Bolshevism*. Free Press, Glencoe, 1953.

LEITES, NATHAN and BERNAUT, ELSA. *Ritual of Liquidation*. Free Press, Glencoe, 1954.

LENIN, V. I. *Selected Works*. Vols. I-XII. Co-operative Publishing Society of Foreign Workers in the U.S.S.R., Moscow, 1934.

LEROY-BEAULIEU, ANATOLE. *Empire of the Tsars*. 3 vols. G. P. Putnam's Sons, New York, 1896.

MARCUSE, HERBERT. *Soviet Marxism*. Columbia University Press, New York, 1957.

MARX, KARL. *Capital*. 3 vols. Charles H. Kerr and Co., Chicago, 1909.

MARX, KARL. *A Contribution to the Critique of Political Economy.* Charles H. Kerr and Company, Chicago, 1904.

MARX, KARL. *Critique of the Gotha Program.* International Publishers, New York, 1938.

MARX, KARL. *Selected Works.* 2 vols. International Publishers, New York, 1942.

MARX, KARL and ENGELS, FREDERICK. *Selected Correspondence.* International Publishers, New York, 1942.

MASARYK, THOMAS G. *The Spirit of Russia.* 2 vols. The Macmillan Company, New York, 1919.

MAVOR, JAMES. *An Economic History of Russia.* 2 vols. E. P. Dutton & Co., New York, 1925.

MAVOR, JAMES. *The Russian Revolution.* The Macmillan Company, New York, 1929.

MAYNARD, SIR JOHN. *Russia in Flux.* The Macmillan Company, New York, 1948.

MAYNARD, SIR JOHN. *The Russian Peasant and Other Studies.* V. Gollancz Ltd., London, 1942.

MAZOUR, ANATOLE G. *Russia, Past and Present.* D. Van Nostrand and Company, Inc., New York, 1951.

MEAD, MARGARET. *Soviet Attitudes Toward Authority.* Tavistock Publications Limited, London, 1955.

MEDINSKY, Y. N. *Public Education in the U.S.S.R.* Foreign Languages Publishing House, Moscow, 1950.

MEHNERT, KLAUS. *Stalin Versus Marx.* G. Allen and Unwin, London, 1952.

MEISEL, JAMES and KOZERA, EDWARD. *Materials for the Study of the Soviet System.* George Wahr Publishing Co., Ann Arbor, 1953.

MEISSNER, BORIS. *The Communist Party of the Soviet Union.* Edited with a chapter on the Twentieth Party Congress by John S. Reshetar, Jr. Frederick A. Praeger, New York, 1956.

MEYER, ALFRED G. *Leninism.* Harvard University Press, Cambridge, 1957.

MEYER, ALFRED G. *Marxism.* Harvard University Press, Cambridge, 1954.

MILIUKOV, PAUL. *Outlines of Russian Culture.* 3 vols. University of Pennsylvania Press, Philadelphia, 1942.

MOORE, BARRINGTON, JR. *Soviet Politics—the Dilemma of Power.* Harvard University Press, Cambridge, 1950.

MOORE, BARRINGTON, JR. *Terror and Progress, U.S.S.R.* Harvard University Press, Cambridge, 1954.

OLGIN, MOISSAYE J. *The Soul of the Russian Revolution.* Henry Holt and Company, New York, 1917.

PARES, SIR BERNARD. *The Fall of the Russian Monarchy.* Alfred A. Knopf, Inc., New York, 1939.

PARES, SIR BERNARD. *A History of Russia.* Jonathan Cape, London, 1926.

PIPES, RICHARD. *The Formation of the Soviet Union: Communism and Nationalism 1917-1923.* Harvard University Press, Cambridge, 1954.

PLAMENATZ, JOHN. *German Marxism and Russian Communism.* Longmans, Green and Co., Inc., London, 1954.

PLEKHANOV, GEORGE. *Essays in Historical Materialism.* International Publishers, New York, 1940.

POKROVSKII, M. N. *History of Russia from the Earliest Times to the Rise of Commercial Capitalism.* International Publishers, New York, 1931.

REED, JOHN. *Ten Days That Shook the World.* The Modern Library, New York, 1935.

RESHETAR, JOHN S. and NIEMEYER, GERBART. *An Inquiry into Soviet Rationality.* Frederick A. Praeger, New York, 1956.

ROBINSON, GEROID T. *Rural Russia Under the Old Regime.* The Macmillan Company, New York, 1949.

ROSENBERG, ARTHUR. *A History of Bolshevism.* Oxford University Press, New York, 1934.

ROSTOW, W. W. and LEVIN, ALFRED. *The Dynamics of Soviet Society.* W. W. Norton & Company, Inc., New York, 1953.

RÜHLE, OTTO. *Karl Marx.* The Viking Press, New York, 1929.

SCHAPIRO, LEONARD B. *The Origin of the Communist Autocracy.* Harvard University Press, Cambridge, 1955.

SCHUMAN, FREDERICK L. *Russia Since 1917.* Alfred A. Knopf, Inc., New York, 1957.

SCHWARTZ, HARRY. *Russia's Soviet Economy.* Prentice-Hall, Inc., New York, 1954.

SCHWARTZ, HARRY. *The Soviet Economy: A Selected Bibliography of Materials in English.* Syracuse University Press, Syracuse, 1949.

SCHWARZ, SOLOMON. *Labor in the Soviet Union.* Frederick A. Praeger, New York, 1952.

SCOTT, DEREK J. R., *Russian Political Institutions.* Rinehart & Company, Inc., New York, 1958.

SETON-WATSON, HUGH. *The Decline of Imperial Russia.* Frederick A. Praeger, New York, 1956.

SHABAD, THEODORE. *Geography of the U.S.S.R.* Columbia University Press, New York, 1951.

SHUB, DAVID. *Lenin.* Doubleday and Company, New York, 1948.

SIMMONS, ERNEST J., ed. *Continuity and Change in Russian and Soviet Thought,* Harvard University Press, Cambridge, 1955.

SOMERVILLE, JOHN. *Soviet Philosophy.* Philosophical Library, New York, 1946.

SOUVARINE, BORIS. *Stalin.* Longmans, Green and Company, New York, 1939.

STALIN, JOSEPH. *Economic Problems of Socialism in the U.S.S.R.* International Publishers, New York, 1952.

STALIN, JOSEPH. *Problems of Leninism.* Foreign Languages Publishing House, Moscow, 1953.

STEIN, SOL, ed. *Culture in the Soviet Union.* Frederick A. Praeger, New York, 1955.

STEINBERG, ISAAC N. *In the Workshop of the Revolution.* Rinehart & Company, Inc., New York, 1953.

TIMASHEFF, NICHOLAS S. *The Great Retreat.* E. P. Dutton & Company, New York, 1946.

TIMASHEFF, NICHOLAS S. *Religion in Soviet Russia: 1917-1942.* Sheed and Ward, New York, 1942.

TOWSTER, JULIAN. *Political Power in the U.S.S.R. 1917-1947.* Oxford University Press, New York, 1948.

TROTSKY, LEON. *The History of the Russian Revolution.* The University of Michigan Press, Ann Arbor, 1955.

TROTSKY, LEON. *My Life.* Charles Scribner's Sons, New York, 1930.

TROTSKY, LEON. *The Revolution Betrayed.* Doubleday, Doran and Company, Inc., New York, 1937.

TROTSKY, LEON. *Stalin.* Harper and Brothers, New York, 1941.

TURGEON, LYNN, and BERGSON, ABRAM. *Prices of Basic Industrial Goods in the U.S.S.R.* The Rand Corporation, Santa Monica, 1957.

U. S. DEPARTMENT of HEALTH, EDUCATION and WELFARE, OFFICE of EDUCATION. *Education in the U.S.S.R.* U. S. Government Printing Office, Washington, 1952.

VERNADSKY, GEORGE. *A History of Russia.* Yale University Press, New Haven, 1951.

VERNADSKY, GEORGE and KARPOVICH, MICHAEL. *A History of Russia.* 3 vols. Yale University Press, New Haven, 1953.

VOLIN, LAZAR. *A Survey of Soviet Russian Agriculture.* United States Department of Agriculture, Washington, 1951.

VUCINICH, ALEXANDER. *Soviet Economic Institutions.* Stanford University Press, Stanford, 1952.

VYSHINSKY, ANDREI Y. *The Law of the Soviet State.* The Macmillan Company, New York, 1948.

WALSH, WARREN B. *Readings in Russian History.* Syracuse University Press, Syracuse, 1950.

WEBB, SIDNEY and BEATRICE. *Soviet Communism: A New Civilization?* 2 vols. Charles Scribner's Sons, New York, 1936.

WILSON, EDMUND. *To the Finland Station.* Doubleday and Company, Garden City, 1955.

WOLFE, BERTRAM D. *Khrushchev and Stalin's Ghost.* Frederick A. Praeger, New York, 1957.

WOLFE, BERTRAM D. *Three Who Made a Revolution.* Beacon Press, Boston, 1948.

WOLIN, SIMON and SLUSSER, ROBERT M., eds. *The Soviet Secret Police.* Frederick A. Praeger, New York, 1957.

YUGOW, AARON. *Russia's Economic Front for War and Peace.* Harper & Brothers, New York, 1942.

An Index to Persons

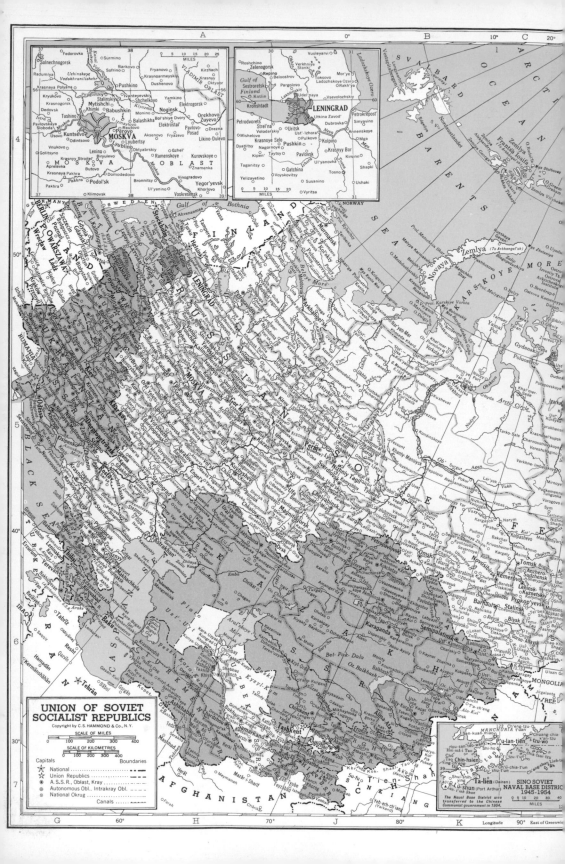